BEST SERVED FROZEN
GERALD HANSEN

BEST SERVED FROZEN

Gerald Hansen

To Mom and Dad, Lorna and Colin; what would I do without you all?

"Revenge is a dish best served cold," Eugène Sue, *Memoirs of Matilda*

ACKNOWLEDGMENTS

Many thanks again to everyone who has been so supportive to me! I couldn't have written this book without you. You have truly helped me during those dark, lonely hours when I'm hunched over the computer, a hermit, making these characters and their story come alive. Thanks, first of all, to all the many, many fans I've received over the past few years. You're the reason I wrote this book. I'm grateful what I've written has sparked your interest, and that you've allowed the Floods and Barnetts into your lives. I know there are millions of authors to choose from out there, and I'm delighted you decided to choose me. I'm relieved, actually, when anyone reads my books and enjoys them, so, truly, my deepest thanks to each of you. Special thanks to Dawna Bate, Marla Brugger and Deja Allen Cheek. Also to Gina Moye, Lana Lynch, Julie Fuchs, actually, *all* the Words and Wine Book Club in Camarillo, CA, and also the Fanwood Book Club, including especially Alice Ritchie Ballan and Barbara Singer Kitchen. And Anita Orlovich Fleming, one of the first fans! Thanks so much everyone!

Specific thanks must go to my mentor Lorna Matcham. It was truly a special day when we met. I can't imagine my life without you now, even outside the writing arena. You have given me so much strength, brightened my days with your insight, your humor and your advice, which is always spot on. The reaction of the readers proves that. And a shout out to all the amazing writers I met through Authonomy, especially the wonderful Kate Rigby, Katherine L Holmes and Cynthia Cordell. Also, special thanks to Erin Lynch for her help, as usual, and to Gosia Kurek. You both help make sure what I write is readable! Aldercy Flores, once again, you have been a treasure-trove of inspiration! So many parts of this book are down to you, and I thank you! Colleen Reeves Taylor, who would've ever believed when we were riding that bus around the base at A T Mahan that you would years late become almost my personal publicist? Thanks so very much for all your hard work spreading the word! And for this I also simply must thank Maciej Rumprecht. We're a great duo together on Fridays and Satudays, aren't we? And Chingiz Akchurin, thanks for everything. Thanks as well to Zenya Prowell and Antonella Iannarino. You both made me realize my worth as a writer. Thanks for gems of inspiration to Ben Dimond, Estee Adoram, John Kelly and Carl Holder. And to Mark Gondelman for all his help. Ricky Lee, your finance/math skills were essential to the 'Killer Investors' part of this book, and for that I truly thank you! Anna Chernysheva, it was fun going on this journey with you. Jeana Barenboim, thanks for arriving early, Alysha Pilkey, thanks for getting me out quickly, Brandon Piazza, thanks for waiting patiently, and Rodney Hanna, thanks for taking my Saturday 5 to 9. Lawrence Martinetian, what would my life be without you? Thanks for showing me the world! Truly! You are a great friend. And to Kate Flood, thanks so much for enduring with great humor my constant maligning of your family name. I want it known that the Floods in this book are in no way based on actual Floods in Kells, Co. Meath!

Also, the book wouldn't exist without the amazing skills of my photographer Marcin Kaliski, and the brilliant cover of Marco Maldera, and my website courtesy of Fabrizio Caso. Thanks for your talent, and for being friends.

And of course, thanks so much to all my students and the marvelous people at both Manhattan Language and the Olive Tree/Comedy Cellar, NYC, especially Bonita Vander and Noam Dworman.

BEST SERVED FROZEN
GERALD HANSEN

HOW TO PRONOUNCE THE NAMES:

Fionnuala: Fin-**noo**-lah
Dymphna: **Dimf**-nah
Siofra: **Shee**-frah
Eoin: Owen
Padraig: **Paw**-drig
Seamus: **Shay**-mus
Ursula: **Uhr**-suh-lah
Sorca: **Sor**-kah
Maire: **My**-ra
Ailish: **Eye**-lish
Maeve: Mayve

PROLOGUE—DERRY, NORTHERN IRELAND

Fighting back the tears, Dymphna Flood crouched over the plush carpeting with the fifth match. The black silk and white lace trim of the La Perla camisole strained against the heft of her breasts. The matching tap panties were taught against her thighs as she lit one Jo Malone scented candle after the next.

She had found the candles on a shelf of her future mother-in-law's walk-in closet. They seemed expensive, and were just sitting there in a box doing nothing, so Dymphna had appropriated them for the evening's mission. Costly or not, Dymphna thought, Zoë Riddell could well afford them, minted Derry Businesswoman Of The Year as she was. Well, runner-up, anyway. And...future mother-in-law? *Please, please, please, merciful Father, and the Virgin Mary and all, let it be!*

Sniffling, Dymphna crab-walked on her haunches, flames flickering anew in the wicks of the wild fig and cassis, the lime basil and mandarin, the vanilla and anise, the English pear and freesia. The candles formed a path of two rows from the bathtub, out the bathroom and wound down the hall, through her bedroom door and on towards the foot of her bed. The match went out, and she reached for another.

Dymphna knew lads weren't into candles and romantic things like that, but she prayed Rory would find the journey through them towards the bed enticing. If he didn't—

But, no. She bit a knuckle and new tears welled in her eyes. A little moan escaped. She couldn't think like that. This plan *had* to work. For the sake of the new little being forming itself inside her womb. Her third. But, sadly, not *their* third.

Calming herself, she flicked the match and lit a pomegranate noir, hoping against all hopes Rory would never find out he probably wasn't the father of this new child either. And if the candles, the bubble bath, the massage with the loofah sponge, the rose petals on the bedspread didn't work their magic, she always had the allure of her firm 22-year-old body offered up to him, gift-wrapped in the scalloped leg openings that made her look like a sex-rabid French maid. Saucy! Lads went mad for that look, didn't they? She could almost hear the *'Pwoar!'* from Rory as she lit a wild fig wick. A breast threatened to spill from the scanty camisole. Dymphna shoved it back where it belonged. Maybe Zoë was a size smaller than her after all.

Dymphna had found the La Perla in Zoë's closet as well. It had been next to

1

the candles, folded, the tags still on. Unworn. Dymphna's eyes had saucered at the price. And it was much more enticing than her own tired, frayed bed clothing. She would tie the tags on again and slip it back when she was done this evening. She wouldn't be wearing it long, God willing. Rory should rip it from her, so there'd be no need to wash it. One part of her brain wondered why Zoë didn't make use of it. It seemed made only to nab a man. But then another part of her brain answered: Zoë didn't need to.

Mrs. Riddell already had everything a woman could possibly want—a child, and a son at that!, one 'real' grandchild, thanks to Dymphna, a fully-paid house, a posh one with heated kitchen tiles, seven heads on the shower, a DeLonghi steam espresso and cappuccino maker, a bulging bank account, Chanel No. 5 on her vanity table, a gym membership that she actually used to good effect, and glasses with frames from Burberry. And no man, no husband to complicate things (Mr. Riddell, Dymphna didn't know his first name, had been killed by the IRA decades before).

What Zoë had was freedom. And speaking of freedom, though lack of it, Zoë also had a skivvy, a sort of indentured servant—Dymphna herself—to toil away at one of the family businesses for a pittance. After Rory had proposed and Dymphna had moved in, it had been at the Pence-A-Day storage units, and now at the fish and chip van. To teach her, Zoë had said, 'the value of money,' but that was flimmin stupid. Dymphna already knew there were 100 pence in a pound, five pounds in a fiver, ten pounds in a tenner and so on. Did the woman think she was a simpleton?

The flame flickered in her unsteady fingers, and as Dymphna wondered suddenly what the bleeding hell wild fig, anise and freesia were and why the pear was 'English,' the blood pounded in the veins of a brain still struggling to overcome the hangover from the night before...and it was now—she peered through the frame of her bedroom door at the alarm clock on the nightstand—a quarter to six in the evening!

Rory would be back from his soccer game soon—the blue and white stripes of his kit covered with muck, stinking of male sweat, a pint of lager or two on his breath and ready for the shower she had revamped into a seductive bath would include a stint with the massaging nozzle. She still had to prepare the bed. She lit the last candle, blew out the match, and padded down the stairs to collect the roses she had tugged from the back garden.

She would remain true to Rory Riddell, her betrothed. She loved him. *Loved* him. She couldn't cheat on him. At least, that was the thought that consumed her as she had scrawled the lipstick on her mouth the night before. The lipstick was Sephora's Red Seductress and not Zoë's. Dymphna had nicked it from the makeup counter at the Top-Yer-Trolly superstore downtown. The expensive lipsticks were kept under lock and key; you had to ask a sales assistant to unlock the cabinet if you wanted one, and then they carried the tube over to the till for you, hawk-eyed as it sat on the conveyor belt before it was finally rung up. But Dymphna knew from her time working there they had the samples just laying there on the streaked glass, having touched who knew how many scabby lips, but just begging to be stolen.

But the night before she had ended up shagging the guy who worked as a shelf stacker at the Top-Yer-Trolly in the loo of the pub. She had woken up in the morning with strange pains and a head burning with the shame of a slapper.

While Rory and his mother nattered over toast in the kitchen, Dymphna had thrown Keanu and Beeyonsay into their stroller, sneaked out of the house and caught the mini-bus to the Moorside. She had inched herself into the church and crept into a confessional as a matter of course. The stroller wouldn't fit, so she had to leave it outside (the confessional, not the church). But the Hail Marys she had rattled off as penance, and all the stations of the cross with a rosary, hadn't done much to assuage her guilt. It had made it worse it, with the eyes of Peter and Paul and Luke and all the other saints staring down at her accusingly like that. And the eyes of the children staring up. The wanes. Beeyonsay was Rory's, but Keanu was Henry O'Toole's. And this new wane? Whose was it, exactly?

Rory's? Fabrizio's? Dymphna hadn't been able to control herself when she met the hot Italian on the cruise a few weeks back. She knew what his sexual equipment looked like, knew what his arse looked like, but struggled to remember his face and didn't even know his last name, his job, how many brothers or sisters he had or if he had none, where in Italy he came from (indeed, if it weren't for the fact that it was shaped like a boot and easily discernible on every map, she might have also struggled to know where the country actually was) or where he might be right now. *Why* hadn't she thought to friend him on Facebook?

Dymphna tossed rose petals around the foot of the bed, removing little clumps of dirt as she went, then sprinkled some petals on the bedspread. It was flung open invitingly on one side. And for the finishing touch...she placed petals in the middle of duvet so that they spelled out M-A-R-C-H 4-T-H. She had wanted to spell out the second word, but couldn't decide if it was spelled 'forth' or 'forthe.' March 4th, in any event. The date she would demand, that evening, Rory finally marry her. Maybe it was hopeless. Was it really possible to coerce a wedding date out of someone with some posh candles and a few strokes of a loofah sponge?

After the cruise, she had thrust down Rory's y-fronts and demand he take her the moment she got home, in case Fabrizio's Italian spermatozoa was particularly abundant. For a week, she had had Rory every place she could, a marathon of sweaty, lager-infused copulation on any flat surface they could find, and a few vertical as well. She hoped somehow, if Fabrizio had impregnated her, Rory's Irish Proddy sperm would force its way into her already fertilized egg, Isn't that was the Orange Proddy bastards were good at? Invading others and disrupting their ways of life? It was the history of British world-wide imperialism; she wanted Rory to invade her womb just as his ancestors had invaded her country. Rory couldn't believe his good luck, and Dymphna was thankful for their sex-a-thon, because her instincts had been right. First her period was late, and then it never came. Or was that because Rory had made her pregnant?

She might never know. If the child inside her were Fabrizio's, it would probably have black hair, but then again, so did Rory. Though if it was curly...? Rory's hair was matted, but maybe it was the grease that kept it from curling. If the baby popped of out her without olive skin, then perhaps she could relax. Though, on second thoughts, even then she wouldn't be able to be sure. And only later, when it couldn't speak English correctly, would she know it was the Italian's. And Rory would know too.

Somewhere downstairs a clock struck six. Rory usually came home at the same time, knackered from the soccer. Dymphna spritzed some scent under her arms, then daubed some of the holy water her Aunt Ursula had brought her back from Lourdes years ago behind her earlobes for good luck. She was half-surprised it didn't sting her flesh. She was a shameless slapper. A tart. A harlot. A slag. A *sinner.* She looked in disappointment at her face in the mirror and imagined, instead of this dark halo of shame that hung over her everywhere she trudged around town, her head bowed and more often than not staring down at two shrieking infants in a stroller before her, the results of her fecund love pot, she imagined that her head was instead held high and adorned with that accessory dreaded by some but pined after by most girls worldwide, a wedding veil... She hoped the Blessed Virgin wasn't busy elsewhere that evening and would see fit to redeem her.

The front door clattered open. Dymphna tensed. She hoped she would soon be hearing a 'Pwoar!' and she hoped, hoped with all her might that her dream was finally going to come true. On March 4th. She heard the door close and his heavy steps up the stairs.

4

CHAPTER ONE

Fionnuala Flood dreaded what the neighbors might think if they caught wind of her trip to the Waterside. She had shot her head from side to side, thankful for the cover of pelting rain, to make sure nobody was watching her heave herself up the steps of the bus. It displayed its destination far too plainly on the front, the neighborhood of the minted Orange Proddy bastards. Fionnuala had lived her entire life in Derry; indeed, she had rarely stepped outside it, and had never had the need, and certainly not the desire, to cross the River Foyle. Every curb the bus passed, she had cursed her daughter Dymphna for pairing up with a Protestant.

Now the springs of Zoë Riddell's settee, her sofa, groaned under Fionnaula's bulk, and the dainty teacup was dwarfed by her meaty fingers, nicotine-stained and nail-chipped. Bleached ponytails swinging, she lowered her head towards the rim of the Wedgwood as if it were a trough and she a sow. She guzzled down a mouthful—milky with three sugars, just as she had asked for—then reached forward for a biscuit she had never seen the likes of in her life before. She longed to scoff it down, but daintily nibbled a corner, horsey teeth chipmunk-like. She felt a breeze on the nape of her neck and realized it was her daughter's excited breath, the usual scent of stale alcohol on it.

And, though she thought surely it must be her imagination, she felt behind her the little bump in Dymphna's stomach pressing against her back, radiating all the shame and sinfulness of the secret carried within the girl's womb, in a few months a secret to wagging tongues in Derry and the world no longer. Already two children born out of wedlock! Well, this third wouldn't be a bastard, as least. What was she to do with the shameless slapper?

Zoë's eyes inspected Fionnuala across the coffee table through her Burberry frames, and the businesswoman leaned forward with nails manicured like scissors. She had an air of confidence that matched her furniture. But to Fionnuala, the sea of chrome and glass in which she was marooned was one of swanky brands she had never heard of, all style and no substance. The settee was hard on her arse. And, most peculiar of all, this snooty house smelled of...nothing. A sitting room that smelled of air. How was that possible?

Fionnuala had seen the woman's scullery, her modern kitchen, with taps that didn't drip, window panes you could see through, and in here, the carpeting looked as fresh as the day it was bought. No dust, so that the things she saw were the actual colors she was seeing. What a peculiar, inhuman house!

"Mmm, lovely tea," Fionnuala murmured, though she could detect no difference from the jumbo packs of 100 she bought at the Top-Yer-Trolly superstore in the city center for £1.99. She was only paying lip service, making conversation. She had recently read in Chapter Two, Conversation Etiquette, it was the done thing in polite circles. Two weeks before, she had chanced upon a book under a pile of used beer mats at the market stall. Normally she recoiled from the printed word if it wasn't a hymnal; those at least had little drawings of the music that were interesting to look at. But as she stood there, shoppers' elbows poking her from all sides and the coasters in her hand, her brains cells had started to trundle. *How To Be A Lady*'s cover had a cigarette burn, its pages were tattered, and it was a book, but it was only 50 pence. And there were drawings!

She always knew she would have to go through this grand introduction to Dymphna's future mother-in-law at some stage and was dreading it; she didn't want to show herself up. She had had a lifetime of Proddy bastards staring down their noses at her. It came to her suddenly as she stood there in the market that the Heavenly Father himself must have placed the book on the stall for her benefit. Or for a minor task like that, He had probably just sent down some unimportant angel. She still offered up a quick prayer of thanks to Him as she handed over the 50 pee. She ignored the smirk of the drug addict behind the stall, and had a furtive flick through it on the mini-bus on the way home. She had roared abuse at the two Goth-type girls across the aisle who sniggered at her for having her nose in a book, and lately had been secretly reading it in the loo when Paddy was sleeping off the drink, a page a night. If they were being forced to include this horrid woman, this Zoë Riddell, in their lives, there would be years of fixed grins and thumbed pages stretching before her. She wanted to start as she hoped to go on. If she could stomach it. "Is it some special brand, this tea?"

"Oh, yes, Panda Tea," Zoë said, nodding enthusiastically. "The world's most exclusive, shipped in from China."

Fionnuala tasted sudden bitterness. *The land of chinky Communist bastards!* And she knew 'most exclusive' really meant most expensive. She placed the teacup down with sudden force, but still managed her smile and her comportment: sitting with a straight back as the book instructed in Chapter One, legs slightly folded and tilted to the left, ankles crossed, heels a bit under the sofa frame. It was a dainty, totally uncharacteristic pose, and difficult with her big bones. She had practiced this pose and more in the mirror of her bedroom before she had caught the bus. She didn't know if she had been disappointed or relieved to see there was no sugar bowl with cubes inside it and little tongs to serve them with. Zoë had offered her a selection of sugar and sweeteners in a sterling silver caddy instead, efficiency usurping tradition (though Fionnuala didn't put it like that in her mind). She cursed the 20 minutes she had spent training herself how to move the cubes from a bowl to a cup. She had she read the chapter instead of following the drawings, she would've learned it was the hostess' responsibility to serve out the sugar in any event. "Does this tea be special in some way? To make it so exclusive, I mean?"

"Oh, my, yes. It's very environmentally friendly, and competitively-paid workers grow it in fertilizer made from panda, er, leavings in the Szechuan province. That's what gives it its distinctive—"

"Ye mean...*shite?*" Fionnuala fought the urge to boke.

"Dung, yes. But, darling, I think many fertilizers—"

"Look, Mammy!" Dymphna brayed from behind her back. Fionnuala jumped. She had forgotten the girl was there. Why the bloody feck was the daft bitch lurking behind her head? It wasn't for lack of space; Zoë's sitting room could have hosted a soccer match, locker rooms, concession stands and all. "Here's the guest list for the wedding."

"Ahh! The wedding list!" Zoë's hands made little claps of joy. "Very special, I'm sure you agree. You must be enthralled. I know I was. How do you feel, Mrs. Flood?" Zoë asked it with genuine interest, her eyes shooting back and forth behind the lenses.

Truth be told, Fionnuala felt ill at ease, sat in her threadbare cardigan surrounded by the alien knickknacks, cold and godless, that lined the glass shelves, even aware of the rattiness of her knickers, the saggy elasticated band on them, as though the lenses of Zoë's Burberry's were x-ray. Worse, she felt a traitor, lounging in an Orange Proddy bastard's house in their encampment across the river.

But her unease at where she found herself, and even the disgust in the back of her throat from her tea, couldn't mask the excitement she felt as she prepared to read the wedding list on the paper before her, a swanky type, heavy in the hand and silky to the touch.

It was the list every mother counted down the days to in her mind: the guest list for the first of her children to take the plunge up the aisle towards holy matrimony, exchanging vows with her loved one, her soul mate, her lifetime partner, there at the altar in the sight of the Lord and ridding Fionnuala's house of another mouth stretching itself open to be fed. Though, really, Dymphna had already moved across the river yonks ago and shacked up with her Proddy fancy man. Fancy boy.

Fionnuala struggled to make her way through the names and match them to people she knew in real life. It had less to do with Dymphna's poor penmanship and creative spelling and more to do with the names written there.

"Who in the name of God Almighty *are* all these flimmin people? I don't know em from Adam, sure!"

"Sorry, Mammy, I've given ye the wrong list. Themmuns was the Riddells."

As another piece of posh paper was pushed into her fingers, Fionnuala was taken aback. Somehow, all those times she had made such a list in her mind, it had never occurred to her the groom would have friends and relatives there. The son-in-law had always been some shadowy, slightly malevolent presence lurking in a corner just out of sight. She struggled to rearrange some brain cells, as it was now obvious that these strangers would be gatecrashing her daughter's wedding.

"There's all the Flood guests," Dymphna said from behind the sofa, nodding down at the paper. Fionnuala had to crane her neck to see her, and this was especially difficult given the configuration of her legs. Then it hit her. Dymphna was hiding the bulge of the new baby in her belly behind the sofa! Since Fionnuala had walked in, her daughter had been engaged in a variety of slouches, and there had been strategically placed cushions and magazines, a teacup that had never left her navel, and now there was a whole sofa to shroud her. Had she not told Zoë? Or Rory? "And yer lot and all."

Fionnuala filed that alarmed thought away for inspection later on, looked down and immediately felt comforted. There, on this sheet, was the entire Heggarty clan: her mother, Maureen, her brothers (she had no sisters), her nieces and nephews, with many cousins and second cousins thrown in for good measure to make up the numbers and ensure the pews would be heaving, as Fionnuala's brothers had all left Derry and probably wouldn't come. Then she flipped the paper and saw all the Floods, her husband's family. They were all written down there as well, his brothers and sisters, Cait, Roisin...

"I've still to add all the bridesmaids and pallbearers and what have you," Dymphna said.

"I think you'll find, darling, that pallbearers are more for funerals," Fionnuala heard Zoë say, but it was if the voice came from many miles away. She was too busy staring in horror at a name on the list. She jerked, and one of her painfully arranged knees hit the table. Her teacup clattered to the carpet. Zoë screamed as if a rusty screwdriver had been plunged into her breastplate. She fell to her knees, clutching at the shag of the cream carpet, where blotches materialized and began to spread.

"My Fendi carpet!" she shrieked in horror. "Have you any idea how much —?! Dymphna! Damp rag!"

Dymphna and a cushion raced off toward the kitchen. She quickly came back with a pristine rag and a can of something and knelt between her mother's knees and the coffee table, scrubbing away as Zoë heaved pants and gasps. Fionnuala couldn't help but snipe, "If ye didn't want shite on yer carpet, ye shouldn't've served it in yer tea."

8

"Gently!" Zoë barked. "Gentle strokes, girl." Fionnuala had dismissed the stain as quickly as she did those in her own home, and was back to the list.

"What," she sputtered, a shuddering finger jabbing at the paper, "is that tight-fisted toerag yer auntie Ursula doing on this list?"

Still scrubbing away, Dymphna looked up at her mother in disappointment. "Och, Mammy! I thought surely youse two had made up! If ye mind, she saved us all from being blown to bits from that bomb in the Top Yer Trolly the other year, and she give me that check for wee Keanu." Long since poured down Dymphna's throat, Fionnuala had no doubt. "Ye know she's me favorite aunt, and Jed's me favorite uncle—"

"When ye've loads of me own brothers to choose from?"

"Ye've nothing against me uncle Jed anyroad. And he's daddy's best mate and all."

"Was! Yer auntie Ursula be's worse than yer woman here," Fionnuala said, a wave in Zoë's direction, "staring down her nose at me like a pile of shite on the heel of her shoe." Even in her anger, she remembered her new Manners. "No offense, like," she said with a quick nod to Zoë, who by this stage was back to an ice maiden. Then she barked down at Dymphna's shoulder blades, "Winning the lotto, keeping all the money for herself, snatching yer Granny Flood's caretakers allowance for herself, buying the family home, though that burned down, and..." she sputtered her anger. Long was the list of offenses she blamed her husband's sister for.

"And ye must admit ye were relieved when she didn't die in that hurricane in Puerto Rico last year. Ye told me so yerself."

"Aye, that but," Fionnuala snapped, her face not knowing whether to drain with color or turn beet red, "was only as..." Here she turned apologetically to Zoë, "I'm wile sorry, I know I'm not meant to whisper in front of ye, it's not the right thing to do; like, what I've to tell me daughter, but, ye're better off not hearing. It's for yer own good, like." She hissed into Dymphna's ear, "That was only as I don't want any more dead Catholics, and yer auntie be's a Catholic same as us. I only want more dead Proddy bastards in this world. One more living Catholic makes wer percentage higher...even if it's the misfortune to be that flimmin awful Ursula."

"Might I suggest," Zoë broke in, eying a tiny watch that clung to her skinny wrist and sparkled, "the two of you discuss this matter on your own time? Mine is not only expensive, it is also limited. I have meetings, you understand. Important ones. I've given you a window of opportunity in my busy day to plan this wedding. I suggest we get down to it now."

Fionnuala jerked back in surprise as the woman revealed from somewhere a pile of thick, glossy magazines and one of those slim, silver contraptions that was an entire computer shoved into a quarter-inch thick piece of metal—she didn't know how it was possible, but they existed, the ones with the apple with the chunk bitten out of it. She had seen ads for them on the telly. Zoë flicked it open and turned it towards her. To add to all the other luxuries, this house was one of the blessed few to have the Internet humming around *inside* it. But of course it did. The minted bitch probably had one of those phones that connected up as well, Fionnuala thought, so she could waltz around the streets of Derry taking the Internet with her everywhere she went, hogging it up for her own personal use.

"We can go through the magazines later, they are marvelous sources of inspiration, but right now I want to show you something I drummed up the other day. So that we can begin planning the wedding on a theoretical, meta-level."

She thrust the computer under Fionnuala's nose and her fingernails clacked lightning-speed over the keys. The screen burst into life. How did this woman know all about technology? Fionnuala wondered. Surely they were the same age, as their wanes were a similar age. Why did Fionnuala feel so much older? And Fionnuala knew she certainly looked it, as the smarmy creature had bags of money to cheat time.

"This," Zoë said, "is a virtual mood board. You see, it allows us to take items from all different aspects of the wedding, and, indeed, from every source available to us on the Internet, drag them in, and arrange them together so that we can *bla bla bla...*"

Fionnuala was paying the woman's high-minded babbling no mind. She was thinking of something else. As she gazed down upon things on the screen her eyes couldn't make sense of, she was resolving to make a plan. There was no way on God's green earth that invitation would ever reach Ursula and Jed's mailbox in what Fionnuala was sure was their luxury lotto mansion in Wisconsin. *Never!*

The planning began in earnest.

CHAPTER TWO

From somewhere above the Artemede Mercury suspension light fixture (which resembled mini UFOs to Fionnuala), they heard sounds of small forest animals in pain.

Fionnuala looked up in alarm. The corner of a biscuit fell to her lap. Zoë and Dymphna seemed merely resigned; they had apparently heard this caterwauling before. Was it some fancy new wildlife-type alarm system in this strange house?

"Och, Keanu and Beeyonsay wants changing. Or feeding," Dymphna said.

Zoë nodded, and the girl slipped upstairs. That left Fionnuala with the Proddy bitch and the peculiar things on her computer. Alone together amongst the modernity that was hurting her eyes. Fionnuala wondered where her grandchildren were being kept, what posh wonderland they were being brought up in on the second floor. And, with only the two of them in the sitting room, she realized now that Zoë wasn't sitting properly, not following the drawings in *How To Be A Lady,* and that she hadn't been since Fionnuala had entered. Far be it from Fionnuala to suggest that Zoë was a fake, a fraud of her income bracket, but she smiled a secret smile of superiority. Then she tried to focus on what the woman was showing her. She still couldn't make sense of it.

"And the mood board...special internet sites...and magazines, one for cakes, one for hair, one for accessories, one for..."

Fionnuala thought back to her own wedding with a feeling of sadness, the notion that something had been missed out on. It had been a rushed affair at St. Moluag's, every expense spared. Her head banging from the hen party the night before, which had turned into a boozy pub crawl filled with slurred insults and violence, she had tugged on her favorite velor hot pants, adjusted her camel toe, then slipped into her knee high boots, shoved a floppy hat on her head, and that had been that. She had taken the mini bus down to the church. With a fistful of dandelions she had plucked from the neighbor's front garden in case Paddy forgot to get flowers, which of course he had. How different from Dymphna being coddled over by her future mother-in-law, a magazine, a website for each of all the matrimonial minutia.

But then, Fionnuala considered, this woman had only one child, and a lad at that. Zoë Riddell could bestow all her maternal feeling on one being. Whereas Fionnuala had seven at last count. She didn't have unlimited love to spread around, nor the funds, and so had to parcel both out piecemeal, carefully, and many times not at all.

Zoë's lips continued flapping: "We can drag these images onto the board and see how it makes us feel. You understand, the point is that the color will dictate the atmosphere of the wedding. I wonder if you've given it any thought. Rory doesn't care, men wouldn't, and I've asked Dymphna, and she said to leave it up to you. Have you, Mrs. Flood, any suggestions about the color of the wedding? What color would you like it to be?"

Fionnuala stared at the woman as if she'd taken leave of her senses.

"Not yer Proddy Orange, I can tell ye that straight off. Green!" Fionnuala barked the color.

In Ireland, the religious factions had appropriated colors of the national flag for themselves. Green was Catholic, and Orange was Protestant. Neither side seemed interested in claiming the white.

"Leaving religion to the side for the moment, there needs to be a color scheme. It can be green if you want, of course, but we have a wide array of colors available to us. All the colors of the rainbow, if you will. For the flowers, the cake, the stationary—"

"Stationary?!" Fionnuala looked stricken. "What sort of writing will we have to be doing?"

"By stationary, I'm talking about the invitations to be sent out. And there are many other things to consider. There's the reception décor, the clothing of the wedding party, the—"

Fionnuala's brow wrinkled with incomprehension. "Doesn't the reception be the party, but?"

"No, by 'party' I mean, the bridesmaids, the maid of honor, the best man and what have you. Those closest to the bride. The bridal party. The clothing of the party should be coordinated so that—"

"Would ye stop calling people parties? A party doesn't be a person. It be's an occasion where ye drink and dance and maybe unwrap a gift or two. Ye're doing me head in."

"If I may continue. The color scheme can even be incorporated into the bride's hairstyle, perhaps woven in. Might I suggest this selection of spring flowers?" Fionnuala jumped as Zoë tugged out a magazine from the pile and jabbed her finger at a page she had marked with a little pink piece of sticky paper. "Artfully arranged on the left side of the head, and with a matching echo here on the corresponding shoulder. You see? And depending on the flowers we choose, they can echo the color of the wedding."

"God bless us and save us! Some of them roses still has the leaves on. It looks like a garden exploded on top of yer woman's skull!"

Zoë ploughed on. "And also, the wedding car, the rings—"

"The...wedding car?"

"Yes, the car that will deliver them to the cathedral, then take them off to their honeymoon."

"I never said anything about a cathedral."

"Ah, yes, we've also to discuss," Zoë took a deep breath. It seemed she knew this would be a point of contention. To say the least. "...the venue."

"Eh? What are ye on about? Speak the Lord's English, for the love of Christ."

"The place. Where."

Fionnuala tensed. Catholic or Protestant church?

"Not to fear, Mrs. Flood, I'm willing to concede defeat even before the battle and allow you to choose. It's immaterial to me, and, if I'm not mistaken, I think it matters quite a bit to you."

Fionnuala deflated with relief. Now that this hurdle had been passed, this battle swiftly won, everything seemed to click in her mind. She was surprised to feel sweat trickle from her armpits. She took a victorious sip of tea and arranged her lips into a smile.

"You'd think me local, St. Moluag's would be the obvious choice. I was wed there, but, and I think someplace else might be more exciting. I was thinking of St. Fintan's, smack dab in the middle of the city center, so's it's easier for everyone to find. Ye know the one, between the betting office and that new homeless shelter they just put up? One of me husband's fishing mates works there, the caretaker, like, and it's wile easy for him to make the reservation. I'll arrange for the priest. Me own priest be's Father Hogan, but I don't want him. Not flash enough. Me cousin Charlotte told me about their new priest, Father Steele. Dreamy, even sexy, like Johnny Depp, so he is. I'll see what strings I can pull to make sure he's available for the day. And I think...we should have a different color for each thing. Pink for the flowers, red for the cake, purple for them invite thingies, yellow for the bride, blue for the party, the only color I don't want to see on the day be's orange." She stared pointedly at Zoë, daring the Protestant woman to confront her.

Zoë rolled her eyes up at the ceiling, to her alien Protestant God, no doubt.

"There needs to be one main color so the senses aren't attacked the moment the guests walk into the reception hall. I think perhaps you've missed the point."

Fionnuala fought to urge to slap her. Gone was the restraint taught by *How To Be A Lady.*

"And I think ye're a jumped-up intellectual twat with more money than sense. I've told ye want I want. All the colors of the rainbow, like ye've said. And...do ye know ye're not sitting the right way? C'mere, how much is all this gonny set us back?"

It was as if Zoë had expected an insult or two to fly from Fionnuala's mouth. She ignored what she said, though seemed perplexed about the sitting comment, and, looking kind and concerned, she bent forward. She placed a hand, silky and smooth, on Fionnuala's bloated claw.

"I know that traditionally the bride's family pays for the wedding, but considering our differing economic circumstances, I'm happy to foot the bill. More than happy, actually. One could say delighted." She didn't seem too delighted as she said it.

"Are ye saying we kyanny afford it?!"

"No, I'm sure you could. But I only have the one son, and I don't mind. I'm looking forward to paying whatever needs to be paid. Though...your daughter has told me you've been recently...let go...from your place of employment. And this brings up something totally unrelated I wanted to discuss with you. Only accept if you truly, truly want to, but I think, Mrs. Flood, now that we are going to be related, part of the same family, so to speak, I want to help you any way I can. If you'd like..."

She reached behind again and pulled out a brochure. She seemed to know exactly where everything she wanted was. Exactly when she wanted it. Fionnuala couldn't imagine such a thing. She looked down, startled, at a black and white photo of a female aviator posing before the propeller of an old-fashioned plane, goggles on her head, smiling out at her with high cheekbones and freckles. She couldn't have been more surprised if Zoë had shown her a pamphlet on intrauterine devices.

"What the bleedin hell is this?"

"I don't know if you realize, but I recently opened up that new Amelia Earhart interactive center on Shipquay Street. Amelia's Exploreworld."

"Ye mean...that place run by the Historical Society? I thought that closed down...?"

Fionnuala knew well what she meant, but she didn't want to give Zoë the satisfaction of knowing the woman had been involved in something all Derry had talked about, and all tourists raced to see.

"No, that's a smaller one located elsewhere. I'm not sure if it's still open or not. But I've opened a different one. And I've been having some staffing issues."

"Plain English, woman."

"Problems with the people who work there. I wondered if you would like to work there? You'd be helping me out greatly. I'll give you a competitively-priced wage, of course, and the hours aren't too long."

"As if I was a chink planting tea in shite, ye mean?"

"Then you'll have some disposable income, wedding or not, and I'm sure there are things you'd like to buy to pamper yourself. Now you'll have the chance."

Fionnaula's eyes glinted with suspicion. "What would I be doing, like?"

"No hard graft, I can assure you. All you have to do is open up and sell tickets. Perhaps some light dusting now and again, when the mood hits you. There's one girl I trust and who I'd quite like to keep on, Una, and you two can arrange between yourselves your days off and so on."

"Sundays?"

"Are a day of rest."

There was silence. Paddy had warned her about this: Derry's runner-up for Businesswoman of the Year snatching them all up, slave labor for her various enterprises, Dymphna already ensconced in the fish and chip van she owned. He and Lorcan would never, ever give up their jobs at the fish packing plant, he had vowed.

"It's your decision, Mrs. Flood. I asked your daughter if you might like it, and she said she thought so."

"Talking about me behind me back, were youse?"

"No, I can assure you bla bla bla..."

Steamrolling over us all, Thy will be done, ye smarmy, hateful Proddy geebag, Fionnuala thought even as she gave the woman a halting nod.

Zoë clapped her little claps again.

"Marvelous! That's that sorted. We can sign the contract later. You can start next week." Seeing Fionnaula's look, she added, "Or whenever you feel fit. And now back to the wedding. With this additional income, perhaps you can choose a wedding item and pitch in. The last thing I want is for you to feel that I'm steamrolling over you all as far as the wedding is concerned." Fionnuala froze. X-ray vision and telepathy? How she hated this woman! "But it is the coming together of our two families, so as much as I'd like to foot the bill, I'd also like you to feel comfortable. So, perhaps an item of some importance, then you might feel more in control of things. Shall I suggest...hmm...the cake?"

"Aye," Fionnuala was warming to the idea. She loved cake.

"Here's a magazine."

Fionnuala eyed the pound signs and the alarming numbers that followed them. She blanched.

"Or perhaps I can take care of that as well. Even with your new employment opportunity?"

The look she gave Fionnuala implied there was no choice.

"I don't want yer charity!" Fionnuala seethed, quoting from many movies and telly programs she had seen. "I'll buy the flimmin cake on me own!"

"As you wish. Shall we move on to the...?"

Fionnuala still sat on the settee with the practiced look of offense plastered on her face, but inwardly she reeled. The chrome and glass she was surrounded by, Zoë too, seemed to recede. She hadn't realized Zoë would withdraw the offer of money from one sentence to the next. It was as if the bank had told her she had to pay a £5000 debt before the end of closing that day. Her heart plummeted.

"That tea's gone straight through me. I'm bursting for a wee. Where's the loo in this palace of yers?"

Zoë gave her directions, and, unraveling her legs and walking as she had been instructed, Fionnuala grabbed her satchel, "I've to powder me nose," she said, per the book. She made her way out of the room and up the stairs. Her heart pounded in her breastplate, and her head spun. Why had she said it? Why had she agreed to pay for something as daft, silly, *stupid* as Dymphna's wedding cake? The daughter she couldn't stomach! She had a surprise new source of income, certainly, but now it seemed precious little would be put towards 'pampering' herself, all the household bills pressing down upon the family taken into account. She was especially troubled by Zoë's comment about light dusting. What did that really mean? As she hauled her poundage up the plushly-carpeted stairs, she envisioned hours and hours, *weeks!* of her life wasted, toiling away like a slave just so she could unveil some wondrous creation, an upmarket, money-bleeding slab of dough and icing that people she didn't like and didn't know—half of them Protestant!—would shovel down their throats and make disappear. There had to be a better way. If she—

She yelped as she rammed into Dymphna on the landing, the stench of stewed plums and infant detritus wafting up from her.

"Ye daft geebag!" Fionnuala hissed with all the force of anger she could muster in a whisper. "Why did ye tell that smarmy bitch about me being made redundant?"

"Mammy, I—"

"It's no odds, but. I'll take her flimmin job. And as for yer wedding, Mrs. Moneybags is gonny be footing the bill. I'm to pay for yer wedding cake, but."

Fionnuala was enraged at the flicker of disappointment in Dymphna's eyes.

"Mammy, why—?"

"Ye're a selfish bitch, so ye are, Dymphna! Always have been! Only thinking of yerself! Ye think a wedding cake from me's gonny be any less spectacular than from yer woman down there? I volunteered so that it won't be making me...*beholden* to that Orange creature!"

And off she raced down the hall. The bathroom door slammed. Once she was done, she looked down with marvel at the loo roll the woman had. *Grand and fancy,* she thought, *them little flowers pressed into the paper like that. Two ply, it be's and all.*

She tried to make a show of using the sink; just in case Zoë had wandered upstairs for some reason and might be listening in, but she couldn't figure out how to turn on the space age taps. She pried open the door to the cabinet underneath and peered inside. She took six rolls of toilet paper—there was a month's supply in there—and shoved them into her satchel. That at least would be the wages from a few minutes' work she wouldn't be wasting on loo roll.

Nobody but over-privileged gits with more money than sense, Protestants, she thought, wasted good money on toilet paper when it was available everywhere for free. It was easy to pry from the dispensers of public lavatory stalls in pubs and fast food restaurants and health clinic waiting rooms. Her trusty Celine Dion/Titanic satchel never left one empty. And this luxurious toilet tissue was the best she had come across so far.

She opened the door, thinking how exciting it was going to be to make use of the posh paper in her own drab home. Perhaps this wedding would move her up in the world after all.

CHAPTER THREE—THREE MONTHS LATER
FOUR DAYS BEFORE THE WEDDING

The doorbell was broken, but Fionnuala wouldn't have pressed it in any event. Bells were rung only by the Filth when they came to haul someone off to the cop shop. And bill collectors. She stooped and clanked the letter box to announce their arrival.

Under the Jackie-O-type pillbox mourning hat with veil, her hardened features were stretched with misery, and it had little to do with the strain of configuring her middle-aged spread to bang the letter box. Her meaty, dishwater-worn fingers reached under the latticework, and she daubed at her eyes with the strand of 2-ply toilet paper she was using as a tissue.

Nobody was racing to the door, so before she banged the letter box again, Fionnuala took a quick look around to see if everyone looked suitably distressed. Below her left elbow, tears carved tracks through the usual filth on 9-year-old Siofra's face. Her matted black hair with the purple butterfly barrette was splatting against her neck like a wet mop from the force of her sobs. Fionnuala nodded in her mind, though she was alarmed the little girl was so traumatized. But this might not be because of the family tragedy, more the black corduroy dress with white lace at the neck and arms, a size too small, and the white tights with ladders she had forced the girl, screaming, into that morning.

At Fionnuala's right, 13-year-old Padraig, though he looked 8, squirmed stroppily in his bargain bin trainers, track suit bottoms and the tattered soccer jersey that hadn't seen the inside of the washing machine since the night before his birthday, and that had been seven weeks ago. At least it was black. What sounded like rap music was streaming from his headphones, and he seemed more interested in the cat pawing through the innards of the burnt-out refrigerator dumped in the overgrown weeds of the McDaid's front garden. He eyed the charred pipes and whatnot inside, and seemed to be debating when to close the door and lock the cat inside. There was not a trace of grief to be seen on his face, only evil malice. That wouldn't do.

Fionnuala trailed off his headphones. Her hand hand shot out and slapped the mania off his face. Siofra started, the hand print throbbed on Padraig's cheek, but he was unmoved. The wee devil was imperious to her smacks as of late. So, just because Fionnuala couldn't stomach the sight of the rage he glared up at her with, nor the orange hair and invisible eyelashes behind those urine-colored specs of his, her hand shot out and cracked against his cheekbone again.

"Ow! What the flimmin hell's that for, Mammy?"

"We're after having a death in the family, ye mindless eejit! Don't forget that! The tears are meant to be streaming outta yer eyes and cascading down yer face, and the good Lord alone knows when I have the misfortune to glance at that awful thing propped atop yer neck, crying be's what me eyes want to do, pig-ugly as it is. I know ye're of the age where ye think ye're meant to be a right hard man, that boys kyanny cry. That only be's in front of yer mates, but. And do ye see any of yer mates round here? Can ye not shed a tear, can ye not grieve for yer poor dead sister?" Her fists of fury rained down on his little skull. It shot from side to side. "Cry! Cry, ye daft cunt, ye! Cry for yer beloved sister's cold, dead body!"

"Mammy! Naw!" Siofra squealed, her twiglet arms trying in vain to grab at her mother's flailing wrists, her sobs more wrenching. "Leave him be!"

"Ye want a taste of yer brother's medicine yerself, wee girl?" Fionnuala's elbow knocked her aside, and her fists flew until Padraig howled like the beast Fionnuala thought he was, and his eyes brimmed with tears. Of pain rather than sorrow, but the McDaid family wouldn't know the difference.

"About time!" Fionnuala muttered. She glanced down at the stroller before her. "What's up with them wanes? Slumbering as if they'd not a care in the world while their dear mammy's body is meant to be spread out on a slab in the morgue!" How Dymphna's babies could sleep peacefully, Fionnuala couldn't imagine, crammed together like that as the stroller should only fit one. "...and this when every hour God sends they usually be's shrieking bloody murder! Bleedin piggin typical!"

She gave the wheels a swift kick. Screams erupted from both infants, little limbs flailed. A pacifier popped onto the cracks of the front path. Fionnuala smiled. Their shrieks would pull the heartstrings of even a cold-hearted cow, and that's what Mrs. McDaid was. The woman had reared her hooligan sons, Caoilte, Fergal and Eamonn, and lorded over their drug dealing empire, a modern Ma Barker.

With Siofra sobbing to her left, Padraig crying to her right, the infants squealing at her knees, all were now an appropriate tableau of grief, a nativity scene of darkness on the doorstep. Fionnuala snickered under the veil and turned to herself. Inside the cavern of her mouth, she chomped down on her tongue; it was difficult with the outward configuration of her front teeth, but real tears were summoned to her eyes. She banged the letter box again.

She clacked her teeth impatiently and tried to peer through the window on the door for some movement down the hallway towards them, but not only was the glass beveled, it was also thick with grime.

"Och, for the love of God, woman! What's keeping ye?"

Fionnuala hoped the door would be answered before the tears dried. Or she'd have to beat them out of the children again. She froze as there was a rattling at the knob, and the clink of chains being drawn. Fionnuala pressed the toilet paper to the corner of her eye, squeezed out another tear, pried open her maw, and the moan of a tortured forest animal rose through the air. With the scrape of wood against linoleum, the door to the druggie lair was pried open.

CHAPTER FOUR

"Fight! Fight! Fight!" they chanted.

"Knock the bastard's head offa his neck, Brian!" roared one.

"Rip that fecking Flood to shreds, boyo!" yelled another.

They jeered and catcalled, their whistles and raucous laughter piercing the frigid packing plant air. Their oversized gloves clapped as they chanted in a semi-circle, bawdy taunts ringing out, necks craned towards the catwalk. They urged Brian Sheeney on, goggling in rapture at the flying fists above. On the sidelines, some of the men joined in too, urging Sheeney on to beat the crap out of Lorcan Flood.

The women had been working on the conveyor belt of the mixing and grinding machines when the scuffle broke out two stories above them. Now it was a bloody brawl, and their conveyor belt trundled on unattended. Cigarettes had been lit, and they bellowed away, happy spectators of any bloodsport.

"Fight! Fight! Fight!"

Brian wrenched Lorcan's cap from his head. A roar erupted as it fell to the floor at their feet. A bloody hairnet fluttered after it.

A few machines away, Paddy Flood was slicing through the innards of a haddock on the fish cakes production line when he heard the noise over the churning and clanking of the machines and the Ella Henderson—"Ghost"—blaring from the factory-wide speakers. It seemed Ella had been telling them for months now she kept 'going to the river to pray.' The woman on the conveyor belt to his left, pouring the cut fish into the potatoes and seasonings, nudged him.

"What daft eejit has gone and got himself into a fight, and on that catwalk way up there and all? Eejit!"

Paddy tugged the innards out of the fish and had a sinking feeling. Where violence was concerned, there was someone who was probably involved and, as he looked up at the catwalk, yes. It was Lorcan. His daft eejit of a son.

"Och, for the love of...!" Paddy moaned, flinging the knife down and charging across the factory floor. "Stop! Stop this foolishness now, youse!"

The morning at the Fillets-O-Joy packing plant had begun badly enough for him. And now as he pushed through the cheering throngs to save his son, the afternoon was worse.

Paddy had clocked in with Lorcan at 7:34 AM, and been tapped on the shoulder by one of the sharp-suited nancy boys from the offices, a clipboard pressed to his chest. Management wanted to see him. Immediately after he had changed into his gear. And he had better change into his gear sharpish. Then the nancy boy had minced off. Paddy's first panicked thought was that there had been more trouble with Lorcan.

"What have ye gone and done now?" he had asked, shoving his time card into its slot with a sigh of resignation. "I told ye to give that Sinead Sheeney a wide berth."

"Nothing, Da!" Lorcan insisted. "I haven't given yer woman so much as a glance! Not after all that bother last week. Do ye think I'm demented?"

Paddy did.

"Ye know I put me own job on the line begging them to take ye on here. The strings I had to pull. Me years of service on the line, fresh outta prison with a reputation for violence as ye have, like. Pulling strings, naw. More like pulling teeth, it was."

"I've done nothing, but! I swear to the heavenly Father!"

Paddy knew only too well that saucer-eyed look of innocence and, made as it was by those piercing blue eyes and framed by that handsome face, knew it was usually effective, especially where the ladies were concerned. Ladies like their co-worker Sinead Sheeney, who was a newlywed and should have been immune for at least a few months after the wedding bells had stopped ringing. But Paddy had noticed her tittering with Lorcan amongst the pistons and grinders at his every lame joke, the batting of her eyelashes, the glances too long at Lorcan's backside, even though, as far as Paddy could tell, it was basically shapeless in the padded overalls, and then he felt queasy for having dared look at his son's backside.

Paddy saw the look for what it was, a peacock showing off its feathers. He wondered if Lorcan practiced that look in a mirror at night, wondered if he had practiced it for the year and a half he had been locked up for grievous bodily harm, but he didn't know if Magilligan Prison had mirrors in the cells, or even something with a shiny surface that could serve as one.

Though his wife chose to believe the sun shone out of that backside of Lorcan's, Paddy realized what a chancer he was, and he feared for him. Fionnuala had forced Paddy to get him a job at the plant, and Paddy wasn't fool enough to cross her path. For 24 years, the boy had been unemployable, a young life spent doing little but being charming and throwing the drink down his gullet, with a quick temper and fists to match. And in the five weeks he had been working at Fillets-O-Joy, Lorcan had put those fists into action again and again. Always outside the plant itself, usually in the Rocking Seamaid, the pub all the workers ran to once they had clocked out. With this summons to management, Paddy wondered if Lorcan's temper had somehow spilled onto the factory floor.

But when Paddy saw the nancy boy circulating through the other workers and pausing before he tapped one or another of them on the shoulder without even consulting some list on his clipboard, Paddy realized they were being chosen, *he* had been chosen at random. Similar to how the SS had, with the point of a finger, sealed the death of many an Auschwitz victim. He wondered if the nancy boy even knew his name. He chose to give Lorcan the benefit of the doubt, but then he wondered why he had been called into the office. Unease filled him. Fewer cigarette breaks? A pay cut? Redundancy?

He and his son changed tensely in the locker room, excluded from all the guffawing, good-natured sniping and and back slaps around them.

Since his sister Ursula had given him an extra house after the lottery win a few years earlier, Paddy was the outcast of the plant, the social pariah. He was, in their eyes, slumming it. He tried to remain invisible to quench abuse verbal or physical.

It didn't help that Paddy was quite a looker himself, and that had caused resentment and hatred, and it was now worse that Lorcan had been added to the mix, he being a younger, more fit, charming version of his father, without the paunch and the gray bits in his shiny black hair.

"Och, hi ho," Paddy sighed behind his locker door. "I wonder what yer man wants with me in the office. Well, I'll find out soon enough anyroad. Are ye on them mixing and grinding machines again today?"

Their tasks changed suddenly according to some mysterious roster. Paddy himself was on fish chilling with slurry ice. The day before he had been on liquid wastes.

"Aye. It's not doing me vertigo good, so it isn't."

Being on the mixing and grinding machines meant workers had to perch themselves on a catwalk above the packing plant floor and dump tubs of fish waste—skin, internal organs, heads and carcasses—down a chute that led to the machine. This would transform the waste into a brownish powder that was fish feed, and spit it out onto a conveyor belt where other unfortunates would package it to send to pet food and fertilizer factories.

"I feel for ye, son. The weeks I'm on it I wake up with terrible nightmares of falling through space and clawing at fish scales as they whizz by. Not to worry, but. Next week ye might be moved to liquid wastes. The stench be's something terrible, and the acids be's wile caustic, but at least ye've not much effort to put into the job."

"Liquid wastes? I don't much like the sound of them. What are they, anyroad?"

"They're the blood water and brine from the storage tanks, together with the discharges from the washing and cleaning. They pour into them grand big tubs ye see the others hauling around through the factory floor, and ye've to sift out the solids from the organic doodahs, the nitrogen from the phosphates and what have ye, the oil from the grease, and dispose of em all as the plant sees fit. It depends, so I've heard, on the acidity level, the temperature, the general odor and—"

"And here was me thinking nothing could be worse than the fish wastes! I'll be phoning in sick."

"Don't ye dare!"

Lorcan took his flask out of the locker and guzzled down. He passed it to his father.

"About this job, Da, I don't know if it be's a right fit for me... I've been speaking to me mate Eddie, and ye know he got one of them passports like wer Eoin did, with the working visa attached, and—"

Paddy took a swig, wiped the whiskey from his chin, and passed the flask back to his son.

"I don't want to hear it!" He shuddered as the drink entered his system and goodwill coursed through his veins. "It's decent, honest work."

From the look Lorcan gave him, decent, honest work was the last thing his son wanted.

"I'm away off to the office. Mind ye stay clear of that Sinead Sheeney," Paddy warned as he headed to whatever fate awaited him.

In padded overalls, hairnet, peaked cap, clunky boots with steel toes to avoid them being chopped off by the many machines in the plant that could, oversized gloves swinging at his side, Paddy plodded upstairs to the office, each step seeming like he was heading for the gallows.

But when he entered, the snide bastard behind the desk told him that Paddy had merely been moved from liquid wastes to fish cakes.

The fish cakes machine had broken down, he explained, looking down at a stapler, and as there were quotas to meet, management had chosen ten workers. They now had to perform the tasks the machine usually did. Two to eviscerate the fish, two to mix them with potatoes and seasonings, two to shape them into cakes, one to coat half of the cakes in batter, one to bread the other half, and two to package them, put them on pallets and wheel them to the freezer. Paddy would receive his task when he got to the floor.

"Where on the floor do I go, hi? And...I've never made fish cakes before. The machine always did it, sure. I haven't a clue what be's involved. Will there be training of some sort...?"

"Ye'll see where they've set everything up. Next to the canteen door. And no training is necessary. I'm sure youse can all figure it out, big man."

This did not comfort Paddy. Confused about what he was meant to do, he approached the production line on a hastily-cobbled together conveyor belt that had a 'will this do?' look about it. It didn't look like it even moved, for which Paddy was grateful. A stationary conveyor belt. The same nancy boy stood before the bewildered workers, consulting his clipboard. He told Paddy he would be on packaging. Paddy was relieved. He could pack. But when all the jobs had been allocated, it was clear the list had been mixed up, so that there were somehow five on battering and breading, none on shaping, mixing, or eviscerating, three on packing and one on breading.

The nancy boy made some changes, and Paddy was handed a knife and told to eviscerate. And he had. For five hours. Through Simply Red, Lady Gaga, Swing Out Sister, Wham!, Britney Spears, A Flock of Seagulls, Adele, and the Charlie Daniels Band.

"Are ye outta yer mind, Lorcan?" Paddy now roared up at the catwalk, racing around the vat of liquid waste in his path. The two rolling it toward the exit stopped to stare upwards, eyes dancing with delight. They pulled out cigarettes. Paddy gripped the sides of the ladder and hauled himself up the first few rungs. He saw them tussling, heard the thud of flesh on flesh, and, just as he was about to reach the catwalk, he froze as a body sailed through the air behind his straining limbs. He turned. Lorcan landed with a splat in the vat of liquid waste.

"Whooo-haaay!!" Like a goal had been scored against England.

Paddy stared down in horror, a crick in his neck. He descended. Applause rang out as Lorcan's head popped out of the liquid waste, panting for air, hair slick with brine and fetid glop, face slick with blood from his lip and the carcasses of fish. Paddy reached him as he was hauling himself over the edge of the tub, his overalls dripping industrial toxins and offal. Paddy stepped forward, then quickly stepped back, the stench gagging him.

"I'll fecking murder ye, Brian Sheeney!" Lorcan roared up at the catwalk, shaking a discolored fist upwards.

"Naw, ye won't," said the nancy boy, who had materialized at their side. "Ye're coming with me. To the office."

CHAPTER FIVE

"Jesus, Mary and Joseph! Who the bleedin feck—?!" Mrs. McDaid wasn't a pleasant woman even at the best of times—for instance the January sales—but now she was positively spitting. She brandished the mop as if it were an assault weapon. "Fionnuala Flood?! What on God's green Earth are ye blackening me doorstep for?"

She made to slam the door. Fionnuala charged forward, the stroller a battering ram. The babies shrieked as they were caught in the jaws of the door. It bounced open, and Fionnuala forced herself and the infants past a startled and fuming Mrs. McDaid.

Fionnuala reached around and shoved Padraig and Siofra into the front hall before her. The Floods' own smells mingled with the stench of stale drink, cabbage and sweaty socks within. And a chemical-like fug that hung in the air from the hundreds of thousands of pharmaceuticals that had passed through. She pushed the children toward Mrs. McDaid so that, even with her short-sightedness, the woman could see the grief on their faces plain as day.

"Dear God in Heaven!" Mrs. McDaid spat. "Have ye taken leave of yer senses?" As alarming as the invasion seemed to be to her, she still had time to notice: "And what's up with yer hair, woman?"

Fionnuala had hidden her usual bleached ponytails with a temporary rinse, blue-black, to accentuate her bereavement.

"Ye may well ask!" Fionnuala wailed, trembling her lower lip and forcing the tears from their ducts. She threw back her dyed head and bayed coyote-like. Mrs. McDaid took a step back, a hand on her breast. The anger in her eyes had dissolved into alarm. Padraig and Siofra apparently felt their mother's laser eyes boring into the backs of their heads, for their hands suddenly wrung in unison, and their sobs and moans rose into the air to join their mother's. Mrs. McDaid didn't know where to look. Her alarm turned to concern. She wiped her hands on her housekeeping smock.

"I'm in mourning!" Fionnuala blubbered. "We...we're all in mourning. We're after coming from the undertaker's, so we are. The one down Shipquay Street. Tommy Murphy's place."

"Terrible tragedy and all that. But...but..." Mrs. McDaid sputtered and harrumphed and glanced down in all manner of ways at her wrist which didn't even have a watch. "What's all this to do with me? I've me appointment at Xpressions —"

"Och, that I know, sure." Tuesdays at 2, wash and set. All the Moorside knew.

"And I've the movers coming over tomorrow. As ye can see." Her chins indicated the boxes piled everywhere. The house was indeed empty except for the mop, the bucket, her body, the Floods, the boxes, two suitcases, the light bulb above them, and the dirt. She must have sold all the fittings. "And then I've to make me way to Belfast. I've me flight to make tomorrow night. We're on wer way to," she sneered triumphantly, *"Florida!"*

Fionnuala stiffened. Everyone in the Moorside knew a visa to the USA was difficult to come by; if you could get to the States, you had made it. Commissioned by the Police Service of Northern Ireland, the PSNI, there were advertising posters on the minibuses, next to the ones for HobNobs and the latest Rhianna release, warning that a criminal prosecution would ban you from getting a US visa. Although there were fifty states, everyone seemed to choose the same one. Florida. And nothing save the funeral of a much beloved made them fly back to Derry again. And by way of funerals, Fionnuala's veil bobbed up and down.

"That I know and all, aye. That's why I'm here. To catch ye before ye leave the misery of life here behind ye and start yer new life basking in the Florida sunshine. And...wourwugh!" She let loose another theatrical moan, and daubed her face here and there with the toilet paper, smearing the mascara which trickled down her face so that she looked like Alice Cooper caught in a sudden summer rainstorm. She then reached forward with the sopping, blackened shred to touch Mrs. McDaid's right shoulder. Mrs. McDaid fought the urge to recoil. "Och, I know there's been a history between wer families, sure. Yer youngest, Declan, was me Padraig here's best mate." She dug her nails into Padraig's shoulder blades in case Mrs. McDaid had forgotten who Padraig was. Padraig pointed to himself. "And, aye, right enough, wee Padraig introduced yer lad to flinging rocks at pensioners and torching phone boxes with petrol bombs, so I understood enough, forgave yer wee dote Declan enough, and, not to come banging on yer door when he attacked me in me own back garden with a rusty aul poker a few years back. Ye mind?" Fionnuala nudged Padraig.

"I'm terrible sorry for being a bad in— influench on Declan, hi," Padraig recited, automaton-like.

"Me hair—"

"Calm you down," Fionnuala cooed. "Sure, if ye're a few minutes late ye woman Molly won't mind. I've just told ye I've forgiven yer Declan, aye? And, come to that, do I have to remind ye of the time them older sons of yers, that Caoilte, Fergal and...?"

"Eamonn?"

"Aye, that's the one. Eamonn. Anyroad, ye mind when they was but teens and hadn't started pushing their drugs all round town yet and they broke into me granny's graveyard and lifted her leg bones, her femurs or somesuch as the Filth called em at the time, from her holy resting place and gave em to the drummer of their goth band what used em as drumsticks? Months of going to gigs down the town, it took me, for to retrieve em and place em back in the aul woman's coffin so's she could rest in peace in one piece. And did I come banging on yer door then, shouting the odds? Did I feck! Did I give yer lads up to the Filth? Did I me arse! I let ye be, as I know ye're a kind-hearted, church-going member of the parish, sure, who works all the hours Gods sends at that packing plant, for which I've no doubt ye was paid a thankless pittance. And I understand the parents doesn't be responsible for the actions of the wanes. And I know yer fella, what was it they called him...?"

"Sean."

"Aye, yer Sean was struck down by a paratrooper's rubber bullet during the Troubles years back and popped his clogs on the operating table, and it must be a terrible wile strain raising them four lads on yer own, like, so I hadn't the heart to add more grief to yer life back then. And, aye, some round town says ye and yer lot's single-handedly responsible for the denigration of wer youth here in the Moorside, what with them supplying all and sundry them Es and amphetamines and I know not what. And I know me other lad Eoin was even one of their pushers for a wee while, and, aye, he was banged up for his transgressions, as was yer lads and all. Though, of course, wer Eoin has since been released, and be's living in the States now. And all over town, and the telly and all, I've heard yer lads broke outta the prison the other week."

Mrs. McDaid's listening ears were beginning to wilt. Fionnuala saw the twitching of impatience at the corners of her lips, the anger seeping into her eyes again. Perhaps that was enough guilt-tripping. She held up her hand. "Hear me out, love. I'm almost at the end, so am are. I know yer family's dead kind and generous and, if I may be candid here, them lads of yers be's terrible good-looking to boot. Lovely, strapping young lads ye've raised there."

Unable to help herself, Mrs. McDaid beamed with pride, and she touched the gray fuzzlets of hair that poked out of her scarf, and now the mop was held like a scepter. She was queen of her kingdom, listening to the words from Fionnuala's chapped lips, and what a fine kingdom it was. The chapped lips continued flapping. "I've brought me Siofra here along with me as proof of yer lads' kindness and generosity, like."

Fionnuala looked down at Siofra's still-bobbing, still-sobbing head. She paused, having given the girl her cue. Siofra was like a wind-up toy whose only function was to shuffle there on the floor you wouldn't dare eat off of, wring her hands, sprout tears and mew miserably. Fionnuala smacked the back of her head to prompt her into action.

"Aye," Siofra managed through her tears. She took a breath, tugged her tights a bit, then the words poured out: "I was desperate for a wile dear communion frock, the Maria Theresa, for me first holy communion that me mammy didn't have the funds to afford, so I was. She wanted me to have it, but. I heard her crying about it late one night sitting at the table in the scullery when she hadn't a clue I was listening in. And I came here with me hand out, and Caoilte, Fergal and Eamonn give me the money. They was effin magic! I got the parasol, the tights, the Andromeda veil, and me mammy scrabbled together enough for to get me the flashing tiara and all!"

Under the veil, Fionnuala stifled her smile. Word perfect! Siofra's amateur dramatic skills were miles better than Padraig's. She would be a natural on the stage, if the delivery of the soliloquy she had demanded the girl memorize was anything to go by. Wondering if she should sign Siofra up for those acting classes down at the youth center on a Wednesday night and how much they might cost, she moved on to the next stage of her scam: their shared religious upbringing and all it taught, appealing to Mrs. McDaid's sense of Catholic benevolence. And she had been lucky enough to notice poking from the tattered housekeeping smock, as if the Lord's holy hands had draped it across the woman's bosoms for Fionnuala's benefit—

"Och, ye've the same wee cross on as I've got, so ye do! Would ye credit it?" She fiddled with her gold-plated crucifix as Mrs. McDaid looked down in surprise at her own. "I wear me wee cross with pride, as I'm sure you do. As I think every good Catholic should. The female ones at least. Lovely, doesn't they be? Did ye get yers down at Knock and all? From that Marian Shrine gift shop?"

"Aye, surely, on that bus run last year. Mines's bigger than yers, but," Mrs. McDaid said, as if that somehow made her holier than Fionnuala, closer to the Pearly Gates. Fionnuala didn't rise to the bait.

"C'mere," she said with a strained lightness, "they was terrible dear, but. Do ye not agree?"

Mrs. McDaid stifled a chortle, "Och, catch yerself on! I lifted it from the gift shop when yer woman behind the counter's head was turned, sure! As I'm sure ye did and all."

Fionnuala's veil bobbed up and down. Mrs. McDaid had caught her out. But not, she thought, about the most important thing: the reason they were there.

"Entertaining as this stroll down memory lane be's," Mrs. McDaid's tone said it was anything but, "Would ye kindly get to the point, woman? What's all this palaver about mourning? There'll be no need for me to mop the front hall with them wanes flooding the floor with tears. What are ye mourning? Or, more to the point, *who?* And what's it to do with me? Somebody I know?"

There was a silence marred only by the squealing of the infants bunched together as one in the stroller. Then Fionnuala, Siofra and Padraig, as they had rehearsed earlier that morning before the mirror on the door of Fionnuala's wardrobe, wailed in unison:

"Wer Dymphna!"

"I loved me sister," Siofra wailed.

"And I miss her," Padraig grumbled.

Fionnuala continued, voice hoarse with the tragedy of it all: "Pride of the family, a ray of sunshine in wer lives of gray, the wee girl was, a young mother with all her life ahead of her, and yesterday...yesterday... They found her lifeless in the fish and chip van, ye know she worked there, aye? And now there be's a broken-hearted fiancé with nobody now to take to the altar in holy matrimony. Aye, I know her promised be's an Orange Proddy bastard, but he be's a human with feelings nevertheless, and we've laid down a deposit for a reception at the Rocking Seamaid which we're never gonny see the light of no matter how we try. And them two wee poor, innocent, precious even, infants in the pram over there, now left orphans. Ye might think they be's screaming bloody murder as their nappies need changing, but it be's the absence of their loving mammy they feel. Infants know when their mammy has been taken away from them, ye know. And perhaps word hadn't gotten out, but wer precious Dymphna was up the scoot again. Aye! She had a third on the way. A wee young one growing within her womb. So that be's two lives snuffed out in one fell swoop! *Oh, the humanity!"*

She buried her head in her hands. Her shoulders heaved, wracked with anguish. She reached out to her children's frail shoulders and clutched them for support. She didn't know what that last bit of her speech meant, but she had caught the tail end of a documentary about the *Hindenburg* on the telly the night before, and threw it in for good measure. It sounded dramatic.

"And all this," Fionnuala sobbed, "at the tender age of..." her lips could barely form the word, "...eighteen." It was a strangled whisper.

Fionnuala knew damn well Dymphna was almost twenty-three—she had counted off each birthday around the cake in a pointy paper hat with a sense of disgust, every year the girl got older, so did Fionnuala—but a mother of two with another on the way at 'the tender age of eighteen' somehow seemed more tragic. She would've said sixteen, but that would bring her parenting skills into question. Mrs. McDaid seemed unmoved in any event. She was staring at her in incomprehension. Fionnuala sidled over to her, using the children's shoulders as a handrail, and pressed her fingers against a forearm that felt like what she imagined a dead rhino's carcass might feel like.

"I know I can rely on ye, love," Fionnuala whispered to Mrs. McDaid, eying her cross meaningfully, "for to do the right thing."

Mrs. McDaid struggled to understand.

"Like...attend the funeral, ye mean? Send a flower or two? I've never met yer wee girl, like! Laid eyes on her, aye, staggering outta the pubs at closing time with her arms draped around a fella more times than not, and last June I passed her as she was vomiting into her handbag outside Austin's on the Diamond once. Aiming for her handbag, anyroad. The blootered bitch missed, and I almost trod in it and all. Spewed up and down the length of the cobblestones, so she did. And roared drunken abuse at me as I passed. Och, and I mind now. She always serves me a curry chips from that van in the city center where she worked. Always used to serve me, anyroad, now she's gone, like."

She shortchanged me on a twenty pound note once and wouldn't give me back what was due me after I pointed it out. Said it was me own fault for not counting me change before I left the van, but how could I do that with me hands full of chips and all me shopping? They've new signs posted everywhere saying the chips now be's made with that swanky new goose fat. Kyanny detect no difference in the taste, but, and fifty pee a portion more they be's charging. Never felt so fleeced. And she always under weighed me cheddar when she was working behind the meat and cheese counter at the Top-Yer-Trolly a few years back and all. It's a terrible tragedy she's gone but, aye, I'll grant ye that, and I feel for ye. No parent should lose a child. But...for the third time, I think it must be now, what's this to do with me? I've the patience of a saint, so I do, everyone tells me so; me patience won't be long in fleeing, but, I can tell ye."

"It was the drugs," Fionnuala revealed with another sob. "The drugs has gone and killed her. An overdose, she took, and the light was snuffed outta a young girl's, a young *mother's* life. *Yer sons' filthy drugs!"*

She paused to let it sink in. Her eyes twinkled their accusation. Mrs. McDaid blinked. She thrust off Fionnuala's hand. She bristled with anger. She brandished the mop menacingly.

"Och, I kyanny be dealing with this foolishness now. I haven't the time nor the disposition. How can ye possibly know it was me sons' drugs to blame? Let alone, it be's more like yer Dymphinia's simple mindedness for shoveling em down her throat. What was she doing...an overdose, ye say? Scoffing em down like sweeties? Flimmin daft cow!"

"Dodgy E's it was. It's all over town, sure. Since yer three lads broke outta prison, ye've had em holed up somewheres, fugitives of the law. Some says down yer auntie Lily's in Creggan Heights, others across the border at yer second cousin Susie's in Muff, some says right here in the loft upstairs. And right back to their filthy drug pushing they went, poisoning the wanes of wer town with their disgusting, godless wares. And I'll remind ye her name be's Dymphna, not Dymphinia."

"Why are youse here, for the love of God?" Mrs. McDaid implored more to the heavens than the Floods.

"Compensation!" Fionnuala barked. All jumped at the sudden rage. "I'm here as ye're gonny pay for yer lads' mistakes, and I do mean *pay.* After the litany of bother yer family's put us through, and now with wer Dymphna lying cold on a slab, the least ye can do is brush off them cobwebs from that handbag of yers, reach inside and give us what we be's due. Don't ye think?"

She stared at the woman expectantly.

"Yer story be's pure tugging me heartstrings," Mrs. McDaid said, "I *don't* think. Ye've not an ounce of proof me lads was involved. Sure, there are drug pushers on every corner down the town. Sometimes it's terrible difficult for me to make me way through the doors of the Top-Yer-Trolly to do me weekly messages," *shopping* "from pushing them to the side. Ye said yerself yer Eoin was involved in it and all. Maybe he give em to that slapper of a daughter of yers. And that Dymphna of yers was always mindless even without the help of me sons drugs deranging her brains further, if I recall. That randy cow of a slag of yers seems to have been born doing the splits. Tell me now, have youse special ordered a Y-shaped coffin for her?"

"Ye spiteful cunt!"

"Pay youse off, but? Pay ye for yer grief? Aye, surely I will..." She placed the mop against the wall, made a quick trip to the kitchen, materialized, handbag in fist, and made to reach inside. Fionnuala deflated with relief. The Floods, except the infants, leaned forward, their heads craning forward, their eyes following Mrs. McDaid's hands as they reached for her wallet. Gone was the grief. Replaced with greed.   "...in me *arse!* Not a rusty ha'penny piece are youse getting from me! Now, clear on off outta here, the lot of youse or I'll spray youse to Altnagelvin Hospital!" Mrs. McDaid roared. "The stench from that pram has the sick shooting up me throat. I'm about to boke."

"Where are they? Where's them murdering bastard sons of yers? Where've ye got em holed up? Lemme up at that loft of yers! Holed up there, themmuns must be! Yer auntie Lily's only got the one bedroom, after all! Lemme at em! I'm a grieving mother, and I kyanny be held responsible for me actions. *Lemme at em!"*

Fionnuala thrust the stroller aside and barreled towards the stairs to get at the attic. Mrs. McDaid grabbed the mop and tossed it like a javelin. Fionnuala's right foot reached for the first step, but found the mop handle. She crumpled against the wallpaper and landed on her arse. The children hid their sniggers behind their hands, fearful their mother would see them and the retribution that would ensue.

"Outta me house!" Mrs. McDaid roared. "All of youse! Money-grabbing arseholes, the lot of youse! Out of me house now!"

She grabbed the stroller and, as Fionnuala struggled to haul herself upright, flung open the door and shoved it outside.

"Bleedin deadly!" Padraig chortled, jumping up and down and clapping his hands with glee at the sight of the stroller stuffed full of shrieking infants bouncing down the steps. It crashed against the front gate. A baby bottle filled with fizzy lemonade popped out and rolled in the weeds.

"Piggin child abuse!" Fionnuala yelled, fixing the lattice of her veil, the spittle spraying from her lips. She staggered on a broken heel towards the door with as much dignity as she could muster, which wasn't much. "C'mere, youse wanes. Let's clear on off outta this house of sin. It's not a suitable location for any of us. And you, ye heartless bitch..." She singled out Mrs. McDaid with a shuddering finger as she tripped over the doorstep. "I'll be down to the Filth shop to tell them all about it! And all about yer sons and all!"

"Och, tell me *hole!*" Mrs. McDaid snorted as Fionnuala shepherded Padraig and Siofra into the pelting rain outside. "As if ye'd grass us up to the peelers! Ye know you and yours would be stoned the next day! Or tarred and feathered!"

She had her there. Fionnuala knew well that, in the Moorside, snitching to the police was a social crime on par with pedophilia, maybe even worse.

"Ye cunt ye!" Fionnuala called towards the slamming door. "Ye'd do well to clear on off outta town, the misery ye've caused not only me but other good, God-fearing mothers, the palaver they've had to put up with with their wanes turned to mindless druggies and alkies thanks to them fecking bastard sons of yers! Florida's misery is Derry's celebration. I'm happy to see the back of youse all! And ye've a fat, shapeless arse and all! And ye'd do well to have that Molly add a bit of color to yer hair and all!"

But the door had long since closed. There wasn't even a flickering of the net curtains.

Fionnuala smiled at a passing stranger. And when he rounded the corner, something she now realized was on his forehead made her clutch her chest in shock.

"Och, for the love of—! It's bloody Ash fecking Wednesday! We've to get to church to get blessed with them ashes, wanes."

As Siofra and Padraig whined their protest, Fionnuala's mind ran through the Rolodex of Derry's churches she had in a special corner of her brain. "We can cut through the industrial estate and make it over to St. Columb's in ten minutes. C'mon, wanes. Padraig, you wheel that pram."

They moaned, but followed their mother, steps dragging.

"The frost be's barely gone from the ground!" Fionnuala snarled. "It comes effin earlier every year, for Christ's sake!"

When they got to the abandoned estate, dilapidated warehouses surrounding them, rusty barbed wire all around, Padraig handed off the pram to Siofra, ran up and rugged on his mother's elbow.

"Leave me in head peace, wane," Fionnuala spat.

"We've done what ye asked at the McDaid's," Padraig said, staring at her expectantly through the greasy lenses of his yellow specs, "And ye promised me Grand Theft Auto for me part in it. After the ashes, are we off to the Top Yer Trolly for to get it?"

Siofra whined from behind, "And I want me Little Princess Wets Her Pants dolly and all."

Fionnuala whipped the veil from her head and snarled down at them. So much mascara had fled from her eyes, she looked like she was auditioning for the *Black and White Minstrels.*

"Youse was useless in there! Did ye see me get me mitts on some money? Selfish wee cunts!"

The children raised their hands and wailed as Fionnuala's palm sliced through the rain towards them. It halted, to their shock, then started to tremble, then shake. Siofra and Padraig gasped as a unit as their mother's body shuddered before them, twitched and shook as if she had thrown a radio into the bathtub with her. Then it collapsed at their feet.

CHAPTER SIX

Rain clattered down on the roof of the fish and chip van. Rory Riddell passed the portion of curry chips through the slot of the serving hatch. His fingers trembled. His eyes, speckled with bloody veins from endless pints of lager the night before, were now swollen with tears.

"Ta," he said, scooping up the coins and tossing them in the open drawer of the register. He turned and picked up the knife to continue chopping. Fresh tears would soon be rolling down his cheeks. Rory heard the old woman's exaggerated sigh of discontent, the clicking of her dentures even over the rain and the blare of Rhianna from the grease-spattered radio in the corner next to the slightly stale burger buns—she had been insisting for what seemed like years now that 'we found love in a hopeless place' (Rhianna, not the customer). He turned back around, wiping his eyes, knife clutched in his bony fist.

"C'mere a wee moment there, boyo," she said. Over the shelf poked haggard eyes, a row of too-perfect teeth and the daisies of her plastic rain cap, scanty wisps of pinkish hair splayed underneath. And the styrofoam container. She had pried it open and peered within. She eyed Rory, eyes glinting with irritation. "I think ye forgot to scoop the rest in, like. I didn't ask for a half portion."

"Them be's the size of the portions."

"And here was me thinking that with the rise in prices, ye'd increase the size of the portions, not make em smaller. I'd need larger eyes or a smaller stomach for this to make sense."

"The rise in prices be's down to the new goose fat, sure. Dead dear, so it is."

She peered at him with suspicion. The container wafting curry steam through the raindrops remained an accusation on the shelf.

"Where's the wee girl what normally be's serving here?" the woman asked. "A lovely full portion of curry chips she always gives me, so's the container can barely shut and the curry be's seeping out the sides." To make her point, she rattled the container, and the few chips within tumbled sadly through the gooey brownish curry sauce. "And two serviettes. And a wee fork to eat with."

"That might be the reason me mammy keeps blathering on that this van hasn't been turning a profit, hi."

He handed over another napkin and a plastic fork.

"Sometimes the wee girl throws in a free sausage roll as a bonus, what with —"

"And that and all."

"—me being an old aged pensioner on a fixed income, like, struggling to make ends meet. And a smile when I'm ordering, she's be's happy to give, which is more than can be said for you. Though how she can be smiling, what with them two infants of hers howling in the pram next to that vat what be's spitting what ye're calling that new goose fat of yers, I kyanny fathom. And looks like she's another on the way and all, another wane, I'm talking about, the size of her stomach lately. Unless she be's scoffing down chips in the van all day long. I wouldn't know what it be's like to have a stomach full of chips, but, as..." She rattled the container again.

Mrs. Mulholland looked up—in the van, he was taller than her—and ran her eyes over the spotty-faced youth in the dingy smock. Was he a teen who too many nights on the lash down the town had made look older, or an adult whose small bones made him look younger than his years? Were the greasy black bangs plastered over the pimply forehead due to the fetid air inside the van or a lack of shampoo and soap? She couldn't tell. He had the face of a small animal, something feral and cunning with tiny, sharp teeth, one of those creatures that didn't instill trust, perhaps a weasel or ferret? She wasn't one to prop her feet up before a nature show on the telly, so she didn't know which was which, but he gave the impression of something undomesticated, in any event. But now his white face with the red splotches was just looking at her with those teary, boozy eyes it had.

"Why are ye stood there gawping at me like a spastic with an algebra problem in front of him? Gimme me me full portion of chips!"

Rory looked down, and his face softened. "Och, that portion does seem a bit...scanty, aye, I'm terrible sorry. I've me mind on other things."

Rory took the one step to the vat, grabbed the scoop and shoved it into the chips languishing there, filled it to the brim and took the one step back. He towered over the woman, and she half feared he would grab her jaw and force the chips down her throat. But he didn't. She nodded as the chips clattered into the container.

"Ta. And a wee spoonful more curry sauce on top, if ye would. Love."

He grabbled a ladle from a pot and splat curry on her chips. Mrs. Mulholland fastened the container with newly-squared shoulders and a smile of personal satisfaction, a small battle won in her day of many such battles waged in her mind. She asked with a lightness in her voice, as if said in passing, only making conversation, "And when do ye think the wee girl will be back here serving in the van? What was it ye call her?" Her face demanded the information.

"Not that it's any of yer business, they call her Dymphna, but."

If it wasn't her business, Mrs. Mulholland soon made it so. She had spent a lifetime doing it.

"And she'll be back...?"

His eyes shot around wildly. His fingers gripped the counter top. His nails were bitten. "I...She..."

"I'd think it's a bit too early for her maternity leave, like."

"I'd rather not discuss it, if ye don't mind. All I know is me mammy has me working here, filling in Dymphna's shifts, like."

"The poor wee soul. Two wee newborn critters, up the duff with another, slaving away here for what I'm sure is a pittance, and not a man in sight."

He leaned toward her and managed: "I'll have ye know, I'm the father of them wanes of hers."

She took a step back, hand on her breast and a gasp in her mouth, but the rain beat down on her back, so she took the step forward again. Her eyes were little pebbles of anger. So he was the filthy culprit! And he had the gall to seem *proud* of his transgressions!

Mrs. Mulholland had, of course, zeroed in on the ring finger of the girl, that hard-working wench she now knew was called Dymphna, and knew the two infants shrieking in the stroller were bastards conceived out of wedlock. Half her brain had always thanked the girl for being kind and generous and cheery, while the other half shuddered at the thought of being served by a shameless, spread-her-legs-like-a-switchblade slapper. She had always longed to know the full story. She was an old aged pensioner with nothing to do all day long but fill time, and gossip, even sinful, repugnant gossip that made her brain bemoan the sorry state of the modern world—she blamed the 60s and Yank telly and films—caused a tingle of excitement in her. In fact, perhaps that gossip was the most exciting kind. And here she had the impetus, the push down the sloping road to eternal damnation the poor misguided girl was on. Her dentures clinked in disgust.

"And ye've not seen fit to make yer way to the altar to—"

But most Lotharios spilled their seed and ran. They didn't pick up their victims' shifts at the fish and chip van. Her brain cells trundled. Her eyes searched him, struggling to comprehend.

"Yer mammy, did ye say? What does she make of this, this *unseemly* state of affairs? She owns this van, does she?"

"Aye. Zoë Riddell."

Mrs. Mulholland was lost for words. It seemed a first for her. Finally she managed to get out: "D-doesn't she be, if I've heard tell rightly, the same woman what owns the Pence-A-Day storage units? The woman that be's after opening that Amelia Earhart museum around the corner on Bishop Street? Derry businesswoman of the last three years?"

"Runner up, aye. And it's an interactive center. Ye can sit in a mock-up of her plane and imagine ye're making the flight across the Atlantic along with her."

Something strange was happening to Mrs. Mulholland's face, and it had nothing to do with the mock-up of Amelia Earhart's single engine Lockheed Vega. She had been moaning and complaining and shouting the odds, yes, but her face had been open, as if haggling over the portion of chips were only sport and they were both enjoying it, though on second thoughts the lad hadn't appear to be enjoying it one bit, so less of the 'they' and more of the 'she.' Now, however, it was as if a steel barrier had slammed down, or perhaps a portcullis of iron spikes had suddenly risen up between them.

"The lockups, aye, and the museum, I knew about and all. And the butcher's. And that swanky café down Shipquay Street. Never step foot in it, and I never will. I hadn't a clue, but, that that Proddy...*woman!* owns this chip van!"

And...Dreams and Wishes! Zoë Riddell owned *that card shop!* Mrs. Mulholland still raged about it, though it was three years on. She gave Rory a look that said she felt like spewing up right there before him all the portions of curry chips she had consumed from the van since its inception. It was a sly trick. A sleekit, dishonest trick. A typically Protestant trick. The café and the lockups and the museum she could understand. They were either large or upmarket enterprises, requiring funds to get off the ground that Protestants could supply with ease. The chip van, but! One would approach it safe in the knowledge that one would be supporting a family enterprise, a struggling *Catholic* family enterprise. That's why she hadn't asked the girl Dymphna about her predicament herself; she hadn't wanted to embarrass a fellow Catholic. And why she paid the extra fifty pence, though she doubted it was really goose fat they were frying the chips in. Now, however...

Mrs. Mulholland knew that, in this town divided by religion, sometimes with barbed wire and barricades of burned out cars, as it had been years before, if Catholics didn't frequent Protestant-run enterprises out of principle, they'd soon die of hunger, thirst and overexposure to the elements, considering who owned the clothing stores. The downtrodden majority was paid Protestant pounds in their pay packets at the end of every week, the pounds of the oppressors were in their hard-working hands and their handbags and wallets and pockets but briefly, and were handed over to fill equally Protestant tills. That seemed to be the way of their world. They did it, but that didn't mean they had to like it.

But Mrs. Mulholland would never have suspected the three pounds—now three pounds fifty!—she handed over the counter of the chip van on a weekly basis went towards remodeling Protestant homes and paying for Protestant flights around the world and flash overpriced gear from the likes of Next and Harvey Nichols. For none other than Mrs. Zoë Riddell, her arch-nemesis. In fact, the Kebabalicious fast food restaurant around the corner had a special of a small chips for 99 pence, and curry sauce for 50 pee, it said so on a poster on the window, but she had wanted to support struggling Catholic businesses.

Did her neighbors and bingo partners, Mrs. Stokes and Mrs. O'Bryan and Mrs. Leech, all know the van's secret? Had their hunger for a fish fillet and a battered sausage made them overcome their sectarian dislike and buy from the van? She knew they visited the van—it appeared to have no name—after a day's shopping in the city center every Thursday; they had all gossiped about Dymphna, wondering who the father was. It didn't seem likely they knew. Mrs. Mulholland hid a smile even as she sputtered with moral outrage. She realized she had hot gossip that would soon be spreading through her neighborhood of the Moorside like Protestant sperm through that Dymphna's womb; she would take great pleasure and that sense of moral outrage from 'outing' the van. She seemed to undress the youth before her with her eyes, or at least to disrobe his smock in her mind.

"And does that be a shirt from the Northern Ireland football team ye've on ye there?" she asked. "I can see the green and red colors poking out from under the collar of yer smock, so I can."

Mrs. Mulholland knew all the NIFC players were Protestant, or the majority of them anyway. And 97% of their supporters. Wearing such a shirt in public was like a red flag to a bull for Catholics. Just like the red and white of a Derry City soccer team shirt was a red flag for Protestants. And not just shirts. Many a drunken Catholic versus Protestant brawl on the cobblestones had started with the sighting of a Northern Ireland soccer scarf fluttering in the wind from around the neck of a Protestant bastard, shoving his Protestantness in their faces with his scarf. Wearing such things with pride! The bold-faced cheek of it!

"And what if it is?" Rory asked, his cheeks burning, and it seemed to have little to do with the swelter of the inside of the van.

"Ye know flimmin well what that means," she seethed, as if he had suddenly revealed to her he harbored some horrific perversion—incestuous child molestation or transsexualism or the like. "You and yer mammy be's *Proddies! Orange bastards!* Pulling the wool over wer eyes with this van of yers and snatching the money outta wer hands! And...*you!*" She singled him out with a finger stained at the tip with curry juice. "That poor innocent wee girl ye've ruined the life of! Not only has yer mammy got her toiling away here—I've not noticed yer mammy hasn't been forcing *you* to work here—"

"I'm a student! I haven't the time—"

"—ye kyanny keep yer vulgar wrinkly thing safely locked up in them baggy jeans of yers! It's disgusting, so it is, I'm affronted, so am are, at the thought of it! Populating the world with alien, half-Green, half-Orange creatures what'll have no place in the future, no place and no one to call their own. A disgrace to all that's sacred in the world, so ye are! A flimmin bloody disgrace, I tell ye!"

If she were younger, she would've scooped a rock from the ground and flung it at the van while the sinner gasped and sputtered above her. But she didn't need to, as behind her, three youths under ten, good Catholic ones, zoomed up through the pelting rain. Gravel scattered as their bikes screeched to a halt. "Where's that ginger-haired Orange-loving slag with the big tits?" one screamed. Their hands were full, and they launched their ammo through the air towards the van and the cowering Protestant in the van. Though from the splat of it and the smell of it, Mrs. Mulholland gathered it was not rocks but dog droppings they were flinging. She wiped a speckle from her collar, grabbed her curry chips, and waddled over the cobblestones through the sheets of rain towards the video store, beaming a smile to the hooligans clutching each other with hoots of laughter on their bikes.

Rory roared out: "Clear on outta hear, youse flimmin fecking hooligans!"

Mrs. Mulholland couldn't hear him through the laughter, the clanking of the raindrops on her plastic cap, and the sudden wailing of sirens off to a different crime. Behind her, Rory slammed down the hatch, and, because her back was to it and she was inspecting her crucifix in any event, Mrs. Mulholland didn't see the graffiti over the CLOSED sign. Someone privy to Dymphna Flood's plight had spray painted "CHIPS FROM ORANGE LOVING BICTH!" It seemed the older generation of the town was out of the loop on some things the youngsters of the day knew as gospel.

CHAPTER SEVEN

"Padraig!" Siofra squealed. "What's gone and happened to Mammy? Do we need to do something like...like...check her pulses?"

The infants, limbs a tangled mass in the one stroller, screamed bloody murder. Siofra's lower lip trembled at the sight of her mother's portly, veiny thighs splayed on the sopping concrete for all the world to see. Her dress had hiked up. Siofra was embarrassed for her. Fionnuala's puffy, pink face, framed either side by the black-rinse ponytails and stretched in anguish, stared up at the dark clouds with sightless eyes. Her Jackie O hat had rolled against a corroded pipe. The beaded black veil danced in the wind. The chimneys which

37

towered over them spewed horizontal black smoke. Soot fluttered down on their little heads.

Siofra turned to her brother, she didn't know if for verification of her mother's death or help. Padraig's eyes glistened behind his specs, but it seemed to Siofra not with the tears of a mother lost, but the excitement of all his Christmases having come at once. He often talked to Siofra in barely contained tones about how thrilling--'magic,' he termed it, it would be to come across a corpse one day; they always seemed to be doing it on the telly and in the movies. Siofra had agreed with him a few times it would be exciting, but she had never imagined that the corpse would belong to someone she knew, let alone her mother.

Padraig grabbed a mangled windshield wiper that was at his feet and poked Fionnuala's lifeless left arm with the tip of it. The tip disappeared into the fleshiness of the upper arm. He moved it to other parts of her body, prodding in wonder. But for all his death-obsessed nascent-adolescent bravado, he was keeping a distance, and Siofra suspected it was out of fear rather than respect. He squatted down and hovered over the body as close as he dared, inspecting Fionnaula's emotionless face with wonder. She couldn't yell at them now. The wiper inched towards her face.

"Deadly, aye?" he said.

This was the wrong choice of words for little Siofra, who burst into tears, her wails joining those erupting from the jowls in the stroller.

"We've to get Mammy to Altlnagelvin!" she sobbed, wrenching the wiper from her brother's grip and imploring him with all the force her little eyes could muster. She threw the wiper to the ground. "We've to call the amulance!"

"The amulance won't be much help to her if she's dead. They can only dump her body in the back of it. They won't even turn on the lights and sirens."

"Don't ye be calling it her body! It doesn't be a thing! It's a mammy! It's still Mammy! *Wer* mammy!"

"If she be's dead, but——"

"Naaaaw!"

"——we should ring that funeral place, like where Mammy told Mrs. McDaid we've just come from to see wer Dymphna at. Serves Mammy right. Spreading them lies about wer Dymphna dying, then she goes and snuffs it herself. I think God did it to teach her a lesson, like."

Siofra didn't know if God had done it or not. She didn't even know if her mother was dead or not. Even though, in a corner of her mind, she remembered that not a long time back Fionnuala had left her for dead in the hull of the creaking cruise ship they had been working on, she still hoped her mother wasn't knocking on the Pearly Gates even as they stood there around her body. She couldn't understand what Padraig was saying or why. But she knew he wasn't helping. Her little heart raced and her thoughts spun.

"We've to take her somewhere, anywhere. Outta here. To get her help. There's no help round here. Only buildings. And dog shite." She indicated the latter with a halting nod. She twirled her black locks with trembling fingers, stuck some in her mouth and began to gnaw frantically.

"We've no phone, but. That'll serve Mammy right for not getting me one."

"Mammy's got her own mobile, but!"

Siofra sobbed as she bent down and gingerly slipped her hand into the pocket of Fionnuala's jacket. She avoided touching the squelchy places underneath the polyester which were her mother. Padraig picked up a stick and resumed poking. Siofra tugged the phone out and punched numbers at random, Something popped up on the screen. The mobile was a pay-as-you-go, and Fionnuala hadn't topped it up, according to the message. It had run out of minutes. The phone sat in the palm of Siofra's hand, a useless, dead thing. Just like...

No! She wouldn't believe it, wouldn't accept her mother was dead! As she stood there and inspected from afar the monstrous form before her for signs of life—a breath, a twitch, a throbbing vein—she frantically searched the compartments of her brain for all the fun moments they had shared, mother and daughter smiling and laughing as one. She drew a blank. There was nothing but an endless stream of outstretched palms zooming towards her naked face, insults spewing from her mother's mouth. Desperate, she thought instead of some times she herself had been happy and her mother had just happened to be in the vicinity. She was pleased her brain could conjure up a few of these. They flashed on the backs of her eyelids like trailers in the cinema that were more exciting than the main feature: shimmying before the mirror in the flashing tiara her mother had broken down and bought her for her First Holy Communion, the family holiday to the beach at Buncrana, across the border, where there was no sand, only pebbles, and it had been drizzling, but there was a donkey and you could ride it if you paid, though they claimed it was a Shetland pony, but Siofra knew a donkey when she saw one, and she had begged her daddy for the five pounds so she could ride it, and her mother had snapped a photo of her on the beast, waving (Siofra, not the donkey). All this took seconds to recollect.

"If we're gonny help her," Padraig reasoned, "we've to make it up to the motorway over there and wave for a car or a lorry. A lorry, most likely."

He pointed up the hill. They could see the tops of trucks zooming by.

"We kyanny leave her here alone, but, exposed to all the elements, and ye know flimmin well there be's packs of homeless dogs roaming Derry, and ye heard about them wild foxes what've been seen on the outskirts of town, haven't ye? Magella's brother caught one in their back garden and made it a pet. Charges fifty pee for a look at it in the cage. Made that cage himself, so he did, and painted it purple and black. I'm afeared some wild creatures are sure to come upon Mammy and feast upon her if we leave her here all on her lonesome!"

"One of us should go, then. And the other stay here. With the bo—," he didn't want to torture Siofra any longer, apparently, "Mammy and the wanes."

Siofra considered this, but a queasiness was spreading. She knew Fionnuala was her mother and she didn't mind being left alone with her mother too much, but being left alone with a maybe dead mother was another matter. And she couldn't be the one who trawled to the motorway, because, from the poking and prodding Padraig was putting their mother's body through, she didn't trust him alone with her body. Once she came back with help, her mother might be stripped of her dangly earrings and wedding band, and who knew how many holes Padraig might have poked into her body, what state it might be in.

"Will she fit in the pram, do ye think?"

She dismissed her own idea even before Padraig's snort. A glance at the size of her mother and another at the stroller sufficed to let her know the idea was madness.

While Padraig continued to prod the body with manic glee, his sister's eyes wildly searched the area that had once been the shirt factory. She was looking for a shopping cart, a trolley from the Top Yer Trolley probably, they were always scattered throughout the town in the most peculiar locations, always getting in the way of Zimmer frames and speeding mopeds. But there wasn't one to be found where they were now. Bloody typical!

In an industrial area like this, there should be one of those flat things with a handle and wheels they always carried things on. A dolly, was it called? Something for moving bulky, oversized cargo. That's what her mother's body now was. She scampered towards a rusty skip brimming with wilting and decayed foliage and looked behind it. She reappeared, dragging a sheet of corrugated tin behind her. She grinned triumphantly.

"This is perfect! Now we're in need some wheels. And if not wheels, something round."

"Could we not prize the wheels off the pram?"

"And how would we get the wanes up the hill to the motorway? Ye know they kyanny walk of their own accord!"

"When we carry her, themmuns'll be have to stay here anyroad, at the mercy of all them animals ye was going on about."

She hadn't thought about this, but threw her brother a look which said, 'eejit,' then scrabbled through her mother's satchel. She gasped as she unearthed some toilet paper. "Loo roll! It's round, just like mini wheels!"

She danced with delight, brandishing the rolls aloft as if they were the cure for a horrible disease. Which maybe her mother had. She sobered, then placed four rolls of double ply toilet tissue on the ground in a square, then hauled the tin on top. She gave the metal a little push. The sheet did trundle an inch or so.

"Effin brilliant! This was how themmuns in Egypt built the pyramids! We'll push her until the two rolls in the back come free, then put them in the front and push some more. I learned it in Mrs. O'Donnell's class in primary three! Wile easy to carry heavy weights long distances, it made it, they said. And Mammy's a heavy weight. We've just to heave her onto this doodah here and roll her up to the motorway."

Padraig stared at her

"Don't be a bloody eejit! The weight will squash the loo rolls, and they'll be useless. And that hill be's steep. Her body's sure to roll off...and roll back down the hill."

"Ye're the bloody eejit! Have ye a better plan, then?" She stuck her tongue out at him. "Hurry! The more we dally, that closer Mammy's getting to death."

"If she doesn't already be dead."

As Padraig looked doubtfully at the corrugated tin, Siofra's conviction faltered. To get their mother on it, they would have to lift it only five or six inches above the ground, but she didn't know how they would have the strength to lift her even that short distance. Padraig must have been thinking the same thing.

"Do ye think we've the strength to haul her on top of that, hi?" he asked. "She's sure to weigh a ton. Dead weight, haven't ye heard about?"

Siofra put her hands over her ears, shaking her head furiously. "Don't ye say the D word again!"

She glanced over at the shrieking stroller, wondering how Keanu and Beeyonsay might help, but dismissed the thought as soon as it came. They were too small. And then the heavens opened and rain clattered down from the sky. Huge, hail-like boulders that bounced up from the cement at their feet and splatted into their faces and eyes. Siofra squealed, the infants roared more, which she hadn't thought was possible, but clearly it was. Padraig bellowed up at the sky: "Christ almighty!"

"Now!" Siofra barked through the curtain of rain. She flung the infant's blanket over their heads, then rushed to her mother. "We've to move now! Go ahead you and grab a hold of Mammy's head. I'll take her feet."

He inched towards Fionnaula's head and looked down. The thought of clutching his mother's dead head in his hands was making Padraig queasy, if the look on his face under the red hair plastered to his skull was anything to go by. Siofra was surprised.

She reached through the stinging rain and grabbed her mother's shoes, awkward, clunky things like clogs, but with strappy bits for the ankles and in a crocodile pattern. Now slick, they slipped from the feet and clattered to the ground. She threw them into the stroller under the blanket. The infants gnawed on the straps.

Siofra grappled her mother's stockinged feet and hunched over for leverage. Her mother's lumpen, misshapen toes were inches from Siofra's face.

"Ready, steady..." Siofra said. Padraig avoided his mother's head and grabbed her shoulders instead.

"Go!" they said as a unit.

They grunted. They tugged. Their little faces scrunched with effort. But Fionnaula's body didn't budge.

"I'm gonny haveta slide me body under her back to be able to budge her an inch even," Padraig decided.

"Do what ye have to." Panic rose within Siofra's breast. If they couldn't get help for their mother, if she died here in the middle of nowhere... It would serve her right, a not insignificant part of Siofra's mind thought, but then another part was consumed with guilt at the thought. She gripped the heels with all her little might and tried to shove all thoughts out of her mind.

Padraig got into position on the concrete, the rain clattering down, dragging up his mother's shoulders and shoehorning his spindly legs under her back.

"Go on," he said. "You tug her towards the metal now. I'll follow."

"Ungh!" Siofra heaved. "Ungh! Ungh!"

She saw Padraig's face melt into anguish, bright red and drenched, heard his grunts and moans, as he clamped his fingers into his mother's shoulders, used his knees to lift her chest from the ground, and twisted his whole body to thrust her up the six inches and onto the corrugated tin. He roared with delight, and Siofra's heart danced as the top part of their mother's body thudded onto the tin. Her lolling head banged atop two curves.

"Now move you her bloody feet!" Padraig moaned.

Siofra bit her lower lip and grappled the feet. She heaved and—

wailed as her fingers slipped through the wet heels. Her little body flew backwards through the air. Her head cracked against the stroller. It toppled, stood diagonally on the concrete for a second. Wobbled. Then plunged to the concrete. The infants shrieked as they spilled out into the rain. Keanu's diaper popped open and brown juices sprayed into the air. A baby bottle sprinkled with brown droplets rolled between Siofra's legs. A clog/shoe hit her head.

As Siofra straightened the stroller and reached for one of the infants (she didn't know which), Padraig jumped backwards, roaring with a shock greater than that of the infants. He scrabbled backwards from his mother half on the tin and half off.

"Bejesus! Her foot's after moving! And one of her eyes rolled and all!"

Siofra wiped dirt off a cheek and placed flailing limbs into the darkness of the stroller.

"Mammy doesn't be dead after all!" Siofra marveled She clapped her hands with glee. Padraig looked too shocked to be disappointed. They hovered over Fionnuala's prone body. Then they heard a noise like a malfunctioning garbage disposal come from her cracked lips.

"Dial the fecking ambulance, ye bleedin eejits!" their mother croaked. "999 calls be's free! Flimmin bloody useless, so youse wanes are!"

How could Siofra have known? She was only nine, after all, and didn't have a mobile phone. She wasn't American. She dialed as her mother, drenched but alive, thrashed and moaned on the tin and concrete. Siofra was relieved.

CHAPTER EIGHT

The building that housed Xpressions beauty parlor had been built during the dark days of the Troubles, when the streets outside were a battle zone of barbed wire and tear gas, and construction materials limited to unsightly cinder blocks. Back then, it was the lone outpost for hair care in the middle of the Moorside ghetto, scene of the worst sectarian violence in Derry and home to at least seven barricades of burnt-out cars.

Many women want to look their best, even during a civil war, and in the Derry of the 70s, this probably meant getting a shag, bowl, wedge or pixie cut, and, as the fighting dragged on into the 80s, feathered wings, teased poufs, and those styles that seemed to come from a crimping iron in the hands of a madwoman. For these transformations to occur, they had to venture through the reinforced door next to the butcher's and haul themselves up a steep staircase with concrete steps and no hand railing that stunk of relaxing agent, black sausage and urine. And sometimes, during periods of particular unrest, hearty souls raced on their haunches through tear gas, past singed picket fences, alcohol-soaked handkerchiefs pressed to their faces to quench their coughing and crying, to get their hair done. There was nothing heroic or desperate about this to the women who did it, and there were many, even pensioners in need of a rinse and set, who never missed an appointment. It was just the way life was.

The junior stylists of Xpressions today knew little of this. The British occupation of their city had happened in another time, and, it seemed to them, another place. But they saw the colorful murals that had been painted on the Moorside walls as they trudged through the cracked pavements to their shifts, monuments to those bloody, grim days—and they had heard plenty about it from their mammies and daddies, and even more from their grandas and grannies.

Decades later, the walls of the salon still hadn't been plastered over, let alone painted, but glossy posters showing off the latest styles of the 2010s had been taped to the unsightly cinder blocks, the only remainder of that harder, harsher era, though the butcher's was still next door and the stairwell still stunk. Now that stairwell was littered with graffiti, broken cider bottles and hypodermic needles. Derry might now be a showcase of Irish charm, indeed, the European City of Culture for 2013, but the forgotten neighborhood of the Moorside, once a military no-go zone, was still, the Tourist Board suggested, a no-tourist zone.

44

The owner of the salon, Molly Harris, had been a toddler during the Troubles, and knew danger still lurked around every corner of the area. Broken lamp posts gave off no light and the panorama was more distressed industrial than Celtic charm. The danger now was homegrown rather than shipped in from Britain, different battles fought on the same front, danger now not from paratroopers but from druggies searching for handbags and hooded teens searching for mindless violence.

Molly had tried to spruce the salon up to make it inviting, not only hiding the cinder blocks with the posters, but also buying a plant for the windowsill. She had added a touch of class, a neon sign over the cashier's head that spelled Xpressions and blinked, one letter lighting up at a time, each a different color, then the entire word blinked three times. The 'p' and the 'i' had burned out years ago. Under the sign and to the left of the cash register, there was a sad selection of salon products on a shelf hanging from the wall, their boxes covered in dust as they were twice as expensive as the same things down at the Top-Yer-Trolly. But Molly served free tea and, for those who wanted to put on American airs, coffee, and even had a plate of biscuits on the table between the chairs of the waiting area between the chairs.

Now, a plate of HobNobs in one hand, a curling iron in the other, phone clamped between her neck and shoulder, she read a client back the details of an appointment and fought the urge to shriek. Two junior stylists had called in 'sick.' She suspected that meant they had too much drink the night before and couldn't be bothered to drag themselves out of bed. And she was fully-booked! Every ten minutes the door flew open, and Molly tensed as another old one staggered in. The biscuit plate was empty, she was out of teabags, she was even out of coffee, and they were almost sitting atop one another in the waiting area, cackling in a circle.

The trainee was close to useless. Molly had told her to drag the shampoos out as long as possible to give her and the other stylist, Magella, time to stagger the appointments. She suggested the trainee make them quasi-massages, and now Mrs. Devlin had been under the water so long she was casting the trainee glances like she suspected lesbianism in those playful fingers. Molly hung up, noting the dryer next to the window had gone off. She sputtered in exasperation. Mrs. Heggarty seemed to have dozed off, so Molly decided she could rest there under the helmet while she finished off Mrs. Breeney's highlights. From what Mrs. McDaid had said when she came in, Mrs. Heggarty would need her sleep. A terrible shame what had happened to the old woman's granddaughter, Dymphna. Molly rushed over to the tinfoil strips atop Mrs. Breeney's skull.

The dryer had gone off a few moments earlier, but Maureen didn't mind sitting there on the plush chair breathing the oxygen in and out. It gave her a break from her six-year old Seamus. He was jumping up and down and shrieking like a spastic next to the relaxers and surrounded by strollers and screaming infants in what was called the 'wanes' corner.' Crayon scrawled up the length of the corner's wall. He banged his sippy cup, filled with fizzy lemonade, on the wall. Maureen continued to breathe in and out. The radio was blaring some mindless pop hit of the day (it sounded like Africa Gone Mad to her), but her ears strained, on the hunt for juicy gossip from the crowded waiting area.

"And there was them expecting me to put me bladder's needs before them of me daughter's! When Hell freezes over!"

Maureen smiled and discreetly reached to her lap for the celebrity magazine whose pages had long since lost their glossy sheen and feigned interest in the old gossip before her—Britney Spears dropping her child but not a drop of her drink.

"I found them down the market stall for fifty pence cheaper..."

"...A face like a busted cabbage, so he had, when he found out yer woman had a fancy man of her own..."

"...She told the inspectors, why should she pay for a telly license for a telly she stole?..."

"...When they came knocking on my door, I told them I was barred from the corner shop to make the payment because they had caught me shoplifting there..."

"...I told them I just used the glow of the telly to read by. Didn't work, but..."

Far from juicy. Maureen flicked a page and drifted off, thinking back to her trip to the lavatory in the salon and the note written on a scrap of paper and taped to the wall over the toilet roll dispenser: Please Use Sparingly. Now she knew where her daughter Fionnuala had gotten the idea from, as a similar note had appeared in the lavatory of their house a while back, though without the 'Please' (and Fionnuala had spelled it Spraingly, and Maureen hadn't had a clue what the note was supposed to mean. Now she understood).

Then she thought about her grandson Eoin, once an altar boy and a source of pride for the family. He had grown up and turned into one of those drugs dealers, getting himself locked up in Magilligan Prison and making the family more proud. He had been two cells down from his older brother Lorcan, in for Grievous Bodily Harm. A few months ago, they had both been released.

Fionnuala had secretly fumed to her mother; she was happy to have her sons back, what mother wouldn't be, but wished the prison service had seen fit to stagger their releases. Two mouths demanding to be fed had suddenly shown back up in the household. And Fionnuala had gotten used to the extra space in the house.

But during the drunken tail end of the hastily-thrown together celebration for their homecoming—a banner on the fireplace mantel that read "TWO FINGERS TO THE FILTH," a carton of bootleg cigarettes, cans of lager, a gin and tonic for Maureen, a hot and spicy pizza, a sweet and sour chicken (but with chips instead of rice) and a few packets of potato chips, assorted flavors— Eoin revealed he was off to the States. As they gawped, he explained he had bought one of those knockoff passports from the Mountains of Mourne stall...with a working visa attached. They didn't want to ask where he had gotten the money from, fresh from prison as he was. Those passports with the visas were very expensive.

Maureen was surprised at Eoin's decision. There had been an economic upturn in Ireland recently, it had to do with something called software, if she had heard it correctly, and though most of this software stuff had happened down South, the feeling had trickled up across the border to the North as well, instilling in the young ones of the day a feeling of confidence and pride in their country, no need to rush to the airport for greener pastures abroad, Ireland had all the green pastures, forty shades of green, folklore had it, but... Well, the planes from Belfast to the States were bulging...

Three weeks earlier, the family had walked Eoin down to the bus depot to wave him off for his ride to Belfast International Airport, his flight from the country for Yank dollars. Fionnuala had sobbed as the doors hissed shut, but Maureen saw the relief dancing in her eyes through the crocodile tears. One bottomless pit gone. This Maureen could understand, as Fionnuala had to supply the food for them all, while Maureen just ate whatever materialized in the fridge and larder shelves.

It had happened to all of Maureen's sons as well, it was history repeating, she had watched them leave one after the other, until only Fionnuala was left at home in Derry, their hometown on the River Foyle. It was sad, but although all Maureen's sons had gone and her grandchildren seemed to be following suit, ah, at least they still had Lorcan... Maureen flipped another page. A Paris Hilton DUI. Her eyelids drooped and she nodded off.

"...ye mean the Proddy-loving slapper shacked up in the Waterside with her Orange fancy man? That Dymphna one?"

Maureen stirred.

"Would ye shut yer bake, you!" hissed someone else. "Her granny be's sitting right there!"

"Och, she's nodded off, and the aul one kyanny hear a thing anyroad. She's a problem with her ears, always needing em to be syringed down the Health Center. And with that dryer on her head and all, she kyanny make out a word we say, so she kyanny."

Maureen let a fake snore exit her lips, fleshly-syringed ears atwitter.

47

"C'mere, wasn't they meant to be tying the knot? The Proddy bastard and the tart?"

"Aye, Saturday next, so I've heard."

"Terrible shame what's happened, don't youse think?"

"Aye, young love dashed and all that. And I've heard..." this one lowered her voice, but Maureen still heard, "she was *up the duff. Again.* And the good Lord alone knows who the father of them other two wanes might be. *"*

"Disgraceful!"

"Shocking!"

"Molly said Mrs. McDaid told her the lass's mother, that Fionnuala one, paid her a visit and told her, that's Mrs. McDaid, they'd taken the wane's body to be done up at the undertaker's. Tommy Murphy's wee brother's place."

"A hard-faced bitch, that Fionnuala. A drop of her piss would burn through metal. Chased her sister-in-law Ursula off to the States after her lotto win. Wanted it all for herself."

"Ye mean that undertaker's down Shipquay Street?"

"That's the one, aye."

"We took wer Jacintha there last fall when she succumbed to the AIDS. A lovely job they do, make them what's passed on look like they was still living. We weren't gonny have an open casket, but when we seen the lovely job they did on her, the mascara and rouge and even some glitter, well...if yer woman had looked like that when she was living, she would've maybe nabbed herself a fella. And put an end to them stories about her being a lesbo perv, one of them beanflickers. Shoulda sent her there earlier, like. All the family said so. And their rates be's wile reasonable. But, c'mere, how did that Dymphna one pass on? It was terrible sudden, was it not? She couldn't have been more than twenty! And her popping out the wanes like that like having wanes was going out of style. With her gone, the birthrate in Derry's sure to plummet."

"Are youse sure about this? Where've youse heard it from, I'd like to know."

"Well, Mrs. McDaid was sitting next to me, so she was, in for her wash and set, and for a new rinse and all, if I'm not mistaken, and she said that Fionnuala one was spreading it all about town that it was her boys that caused that Dymphna one's death. And did ye know that Mrs. McDaid's off to Florida? She said so. The day after tomorrow. With her lads in tow and all."

"A drugs overdose, it musta been, then. Ye know what Mrs. McDaid's lads be's up to. Pushing them filthy E's to all and sundry. Me niece was always a regular client. Tried to beat the desire outta her, it was useless, but. Been in and out of rehab more often than I've had hot dinners."

"Why does Mrs. Heggarty be sitting there like that, but? She swanned in here, well, not exactly brimming with the joys of spring, ye know the likes of that sour look always plastered on her face, but she came in like she's not a care in the world!"

"Getting her hair done for the funeral, do ye think?"

Maureen came to sudden life under the dryer. They screamed as one. She ripped the helmet from her fluffy locks. She hauled herself forward on her cane and towered over them. Her pink plastic cape fluttered. She waved her cane. They cringed over the empty teacups.

"What's this youse are saying? Me granddaughter's gone and died of a drugs overdose?"

"Did ye not know?"

Molly hurried over, nibbling her lower lip. She placed a hand on Maureen's shoulder.

"Mrs. Heggarty—"

Maureen shoved the hand away.

"Don't ye Mrs. Heggarty me! Just tell me what youse've heard!"

Seamus looked up, alarmed, and wobbled over on his baby giraffe six-year-old legs. Now Maureen understood the looks they had given her when she had walked in, Molly and the trainee and the stylists and those clients who were in the know unable to meet her eye, weird ear-to-ear grins stretching their faces.

"Granny! Granny!" Seamus whimpered, grabbing hold of her cane for support as he usually did. Maureen almost toppled into their tin foiled heads.

"Get offa me cane, wane!" she snapped. She steadied herself, thrust him off and pointed a knobby finger at the faces trembling around her.

"Shame on youse for not letting me know! Or at least for not offering yer condolences! Ye could've had the decency to!"

"But it's wile terrible—" Molly began.

"Shocking!"

"Disgraceful!"

"We wouldn't have known what to say."

Maureen sputtered and gasped her rage, grief and shock.

"If it's any consolation," Molly continued, "I was gonny give ye yer wash and set on the house. Ye would've realized then me thoughts are with ye and yers."

"Och, go on away and shite, you!" Maureen barked. She grabbed Seamus and dragged him through the trail of hair clippings toward the door. She paused to snatch her handbag and duffel coat from the hooks on the wall. She fought back a torrent of tears. "Heartless, youse are! Using me poor wee granddaughter as fodder for yer mindless gossip!"

"What's wrong, Granny?" Seamus whimpered behind her as she struggled to make her way down the steep concrete staircase.

"Nothing!" Maureen wailed, the neurons of her brain aflame. It was Fionnuala's job to explain death to her children.

Seamus cried in fear, Maureen cried in grief. Her left claw clutched the wall for support, each thrust of her cane down the steps a danger that might send her tumbling down the stairs to join her granddaughter in the cemetery.

She turned when she reached the bottom. Seamus was crawling down the stairs backwards.

"Och, for the love of God, wane. Hurry yerself up." She tapped her cane impatiently. "Ye're six years of age, so ye are. Can ye not walk like a normal wane?"

Fionnuala thought Seamus suffered from developmental issues both mental and physical, "a flimmin spastic of the mind and body," were her exact words, and Maureen had always chided her for that. Maureen had always given Seamus the patience he needed. Now, but...

The moment he reached the bottom, Maureen flung him out onto the street and the rain.

"We've to find a phone, wane."

Her mind raced. Paddy was at work, Fionnuala was...where? She had heard one of the women say Fionnuala had taken Dymphna's body to the undertakers. How could that be? Why wouldn't they have told Maureen? She needed to know.

Fionnuala had one of those mobile phones, but Maureen had never seen the sense of them. She saw the sense of them now. There was a payphone booth next to the butcher's, but through her tears she saw wires hanging where a receiver should have been. A teen passed her, ashes on his forehead under the hoodie.

"Could ye give me a lend of yer phone?" Maureen begged. Teens always had them.

"Feck off, gran."

Seamus wailed as Maureen roared abuse at the teen's back. She hobbled over the cobblestones in the pelting rain, Seamus teetering behind, past the Top-Yer-Trolly, past the Kebabalicious where Dymphna used to work..and then it hit Maureen. The chip van! Dymphna should be working there. Dymphna was the lone employee, as far as Maureen knew. If she were dead, it would be closed. Maureen rounded the corner. Her cane clacked down the alley between the Guildhall and the post office towards where the van was usually parked.

A sense of loss gripped her. She thought back to her granddaughter, knew Dymphna was supposed to be a town disgrace and scandal, the infants popping out of her with murderous regularity, and an impending wedding to a Protestant, of all things! Maureen knew Fionnuala hated Dymphna, but Maureen loved the girl's spunk, her kindness, her red curls... Maureen grieved with every tortured step, her heart racing.

When she saw the hatch of the chip van open, Mrs. Mulholland at the counter—Maureen knew her rain cap—her heart was gripped with hope. It was only malicious gossip after all. She quickened the thrusts of her cane over the cobbles. But when she saw the wee boy Rory, Dymphna's beau, behind the counter, the tears streaming down his face, a high pitched wail of grief escaped her. It must be true. Not one for speaking to Protestants if it could be avoided, though she really didn't mind them as such, she turned. Seamus banged into her knees.

"C'mon, wane, we've to get the mini-bus home," she said through her sobs. She hobbled back the way she had come to the bus stop, Seamus wobbling behind. She paused at the mail box to click open her handbag, She rummaged through it, first to ensure nobody had stolen anything while it had been hanging on the hook at the salon, then to find her heart pills. The trauma was causing it to beat in strange ways. She gulped down a few, then continued on her way. She realized when she passed the public toilets she was still wearing the pink cape under her coat.

"What's them tablets for, Granny?" Seamus asked.

"Them tablets is for to keep me alive, wane. Leave me cane be!"

"Wh—why've I not got tablets to keep me alive and all? Doesn't ye and me mammy want to keep me alive?" His lower lip trembled.

"Ye've got yer food for to keep ye alive. Calm yerself down. I've other troubles at the moment. And leave me handbag be and all. Walk on yer own two feet!"

"Food?"

"Aye. And drink."

"Food and drink keeps me alive?"

"Aye. And oxygen and all. Breathing it in, like. Quit questioning me, wane!"

"Do ye not eat and drink, then, granny? But I've seen ye, like."

"Aye, I do. Leave me cane be, I've told ye!"

"But—"

"Och, give me head peace, wane!" Maureen finally snapped as they reached the bus stop. "I haven't the time to explain it to ye now. And I've told ye to leave me cane and handbag in peace! Ye want me toppling onto the cobblestones? Ye mind it happened last month, and I had to walk around town with plasters on me forehead for a week!"

A week of people everywhere she went—at the bingo, the health clinic, Xpressions, staring at the Band-Aids instead of her eyes. The bus pulled up. There was a pneumatic whoosh, and they boarded.

When they got home, the house was draped in silence. And with the amount of beings trapped in life under that roof, silence was almost unheard of. But

51

Maureen tried to think rationally. She knew Paddy and Lorcan were at the fish packing plant, Siofra and Padraig would maybe be at some after-school activity, Eoin was in Florida, and Moira was in Malta. And Dymphna was dead. Only Fionnuala was unaccounted for. The house was empty, as it should be at this time, but a feeling of disquiet crept up the spine of Maureen's velor tracksuit. She shivered. It was as if someone were walking over her grave. Perhaps Dymphna.

Seamus ran upstairs to cry. Maybe she had been too harsh on the poor demented thing, but she was under a lot of strain. The pills were helping, though. She'd give him some sweeties later for losing her temper with him. Some Jelly Babies. They were his favorites. She clacked her cane into the empty sitting room. She tensed. Could she *smell* Dymphna?

Was there the scent of her in the dusty air of the room? There was a perfume she always wore, something cheap and brash, sweet and sickly, with a hint of citrus and strawberries. Maureen sniffed like a bloodhound on a hunt, then shook her head. She was going insane. The trauma of her granddaughter's untimely death was affecting her.

She padded out of the sitting room, into the hall and onto the linoleum of the kitchen. She hobbled past the kitchen table with its rocks and paints for Fionnuala's latest 'project' for the Amelia Earhart Interactive Center. Then, through the grease streaks and hand prints of the window, the part that wasn't taped over with cardboard, her eyes clamped upon a sight that caused her to clutch her brittle breast in fear. Tentacles of terror coursed through her veins. Cold sweat trickled down the wrinkles of her forehead. She removed her red-framed glasses with a trembling finger and wiped the lenses with a dirty dishtowel. She peered through the window again. Her eyes saucered behind the lenses. She gasped, her breath short. She fought to shove it into her lungs as she struggled to comprehend what she was seeing.

A being, an *otherworldly creature* was leaping through the rain in the back garden. It was draped in a flowing white robe, half forest-nymph, half heavenly angel, face eerily pale, sunken eyes, like sucked gobstoppers, red curls bouncing through the air. Maureen made the sign of the cross, her head spinning. The dizziness had her head on the verge of toppling into the sink. One part of her brain bemoaned the fact the last thing she would gaze upon before the heart failure killed her was a mountain of fish sauce-encrusted plates and a serving spoon with mushy peas clinging to it.

"Heavenly Father, protect me," she moaned, lips trembling, fear and wonder coursing through her veins, heart pounding against her breastbone. Was the creature wicked or benign? She clutched her crucifix, then grappled her chest as a ton of invisible weight seemed to crush it.

She bit her trembling fist as the weight shoved down on her chest. She was vaguely aware of thinking she detected the flutter of wings from the creature's shoulder blades as pranced in the ether of this mortal coil, not a care in the world. Maureen wondered if she was about to join it, if she should wave her crucifix at the, the...she had to say it to her brain—

The ghost of Dymphna! Descending straight from the pearly gates, or sideways from limbo?, to haunt them all! She clutched her undulating chest, labored pants escaping her mouth as she understood it all now. This was how her life would end. Her granddaughter's ghost had come to take Maureen Heggarty to meet her heavenly maker.

CHAPTER NINE

Father and son sat in a darkened corner of the Rocking Seamaid. Lorcan had been hauled into the industrial showers for a thorough sanitizing before his trip to the office, but even so, Paddy had difficulty keeping the lager down his throat, so overpowering was the stench still. He sat as far as he could from his son, but as close as possible so that they could talk.

"They've docked me wages, Da," Lorcan moaned, running fingers through hair that seemed strangely stiff and had a greenish sheen, "and I've to work overtime, and they're not paying me a penny for all the extra work. And they've given me a written warning about drinking on the job and all. I've heard that skegrat git Brian's threatening to press charges. He threw the first punch, but. I swear to the Holy Father. I did nothing but defend meself after he accused me of wanting to shag the knickers offa that Sinead one. What if he does go to the Filth? They'll bang me up again, me being out on probation as I am. It's his own fault he had to get hauled off to Altnegalvin to get his jaw wired. Would've done worse to him, but, if I hadn't slipped and fallen over the edge of the catwalk."

A second of pride was replaced with despair.

"Och, Da, I kyanny take this no more .Even before this, ye heard me this morning, I've been thinking of fecking away off from Derry. From the whole country."

"Catch yerself on, son. Ye know as well as I do that that Brian'll never go the Filth. A grass, he'd be branded, and hated more than we are round the neighborhood."

"That be's but faint comfort to me Da. I'm away off outta here. There's no life for me in this godforsaken city no more. "

Paddy guzzled from his pint, his eyes stricken over the rim of the pint glass.

"But yer brother Eoin's just gone and left. Ye heard yer mammy's sobs when he fecked off to the States. And this after yer sister Moira ran off to Malta. Even wer Dymphna has fled the family home...into the house of Proddy bastards!"

"I know. Ye know yerself, but, that wanes the day don't stay long in this town. Aye, a few years ago we was rolling in the dosh and it made sense to stay. Now, but..." He stared at a coaster. "I know them passports with the Yank visas be's terrible dear, but maybe I can gather the funds together for to get one."

"Ye'll break yer mammy's heart, but." Paddy was alarmed. "Surely ye must know ye're her favorite, son."

Paddy had seen the lists. Fionnuala sat on the sofa in the front room every third Sunday of the month when she got home from mass, and, a cup of tea at one side, a bar of chocolate on the other, Songs of Praise playing on the telly before her, and comprised a list in a little notebook with a pencil of who her favorite children were. Similar to the pop charts, some of the seven children climbed up the charts, and some moved down. It had been years, and Paddy was thankful for it, since there had been a new entry on Fionnuala's charts. Six years, to be precise (that's how old the youngest, Seamus was, and he had debuted at number one). But the all-time bestseller was golden boy Lorcan. Paddy knew how Fionnuala saw him: her handsome, charming, strapping lad with shiny-black locks and piercing blue eyes and a heart of gold, virile and able to sire a litter of grandchildren, hopefully grandsons, if not for her pleasure—she didn't seem to like children much—at least for her pride..

Paddy's brain cells trundled to think of something that might coerce Lorcan to stay.

"You know it's true...everything I do..." warbled Bryan Adams from the jukebox.

Like one of Pavlov's dogs salivating to the sound of a bell, the song instinctively made Paddy tense. He felt sudden revulsion, and this time it wasn't Lorcan's smell.

His brain couldn't erase the dark days of radio broadcasts in the early 90's, when "(Everything I Do) I Do It For You" blared non-stop in the background of his life, in the factory, during the pub quizzes, dart tournaments, at the bookies and the off-licenses, in the supermarket, though he rarely ventured there; shopping was left to the women, and it wasn't because Paddy had no desire to be a New Man, but because that was the way it was.

Paddy recalled reading in a newspaper at the time, as he had been flipping through for the soccer results, that the song had spent 16 weeks at number one on the UK charts. (In Northern Ireland, they listened to the UK charts more than the Irish ones.) And then, a few years later, Wet Wet Wet's "Love Is All Around" spent 15 weeks at the summit. Paddy had wanted to plunge screwdrivers into his ear canals on both occasions.

Back to Fionnuala's lists. Moira used to regularly feature at number one, but when she shamed the family by revealing she was a sinful lesbian, she never got higher than number five, and that was only because Dymphna was always taking up one of the bottom two positions. The only time Dymphna had come close to the top was six years earlier, when she saved up her pocket money and bought Fionnuala a hand-held electronic massager sent specially from Sweden for her 40th birthday, and even then she could only manage number two. By the time the next charts were compiled, Dymphna had plummeted. But Lorcan was Fionnuala's Bryan Adams, her Wet Wet Wet. Always at number one.

"Can ye imagine yer mammy's grief if ye was to leave? Ye know she looked forward to them prison visits when ye were first banged up. Counted down the days to see ye, so she did. Until they barred her from the visits when she smuggled ye in that Vicodin. "

Lorcan inspected his father with his eyes. He leaned closer.

"I kyanny live me life to please me mammy, hi. Ye know I love her. Surely ye can understand me way of thinking, but. It's the same way of thinking as wer Moira and Eoin and Dymphna."

They had left left the family, abandoning the home one by one. Paddy felt a lump in his throat, a welling of tears in his ducts, due to Lorcan's impending departure or the smell of him or the ensuing abuse Fionnuala would unleash upon him and the remaining family members once Lorcan told her the news of his departure Paddy didn't know.

The only thing that might save them would be if his wife had gotten the money she wanted from the drug dealers' mother. Fionnuala had told him in detail about her plan to visit Mrs. McDaid. With a handbag freshly bulging from someone else's money, she would be tolerable before she heard the news; she might even be smiling. They downed their pints, smacked the glasses down and set off first to the church to get their ashes, and then home. While Father Hogan ground them into his forehead with his fat thumb, Paddy hoped Mrs. McDaid had been generous...

CHAPTER 10

Maureen heaved huge breaths over the dirty dishes. *That was wile speedy,* she had the presence of mind to think. *The holy spirit of wer Dymphna descending from Heaven like that even before she be's laid in the earth... or is it up from Hell she's crawled?* What she thought was a heart attack passed. The weight seem to lift from her sopping, heaving bosom. She twittered in fear still, but the cold sweat was evaporating, her heartbeat decelerating.

Although Dymphna had been shacked up across the river in the posh Proddy Waterside, her spirit had chosen to come back across the Craigavon Bridge to haunt them in the family home on the Moorside. The old woman struggled to comprehend what mixture of supernatural being Dymphna had come back as. The creature leaping in the back garden seemed a mixture of myth and scripture, a being half-Biblical, half-pagan. What sort of ritual dance was it doing? It seemed familiar. Had she seen a documentary on it?

Then Maureen realized: it reminded her of that old Kate Bush video, what was the song called? Some famous book she'd never read...? Yes, that "Wuthering Heights" one. Maureen wasn't one for pop songs, or for reading classics for that matter, but she remembered a young Fionnuala in the late 70's, sitting before *Top Of The Pops* on the telly, enraptured, forcing her mother to watch the video of the new number one, where a singer—who, now that Maureen thought about it, didn't look miles off from Dymphna—sang in a high-pitched voice Maureen thought strange about being the ghost of someone called Cathy come back to haunt some fella called Heathcliff.

The video had impressed Maureen, voice notwithstanding, and she remembered it still all these years later, not least because Fionnuala had forced her to watch it for the next three weeks on the show when it was at the top spot on the charts, her daughter warbling along like nails down a blackboard. The singer had been wearing the same type of white gown as the ghost of Dymphna now was, but instead of reaching toward the screen as if she wanted to snatch the souls of the viewers with her long ghost-nails, this version had directed her talons towards the sky and was clawing...was that a pair of knickers?

Maureen wondered when the being in the back garden might, like in the video, break into an impromptu cartwheel or two. With a sense of wonder, she pressed her face closer to the grimy glass of the window.

The spirit dropped its jaw and, even through the window, Maureen heard the burp. A rude, manly one that the physical, living Dymphna was apt to let rip.

Maureen was taken aback. *Did ghosts have the vocal chords to...?* She wondered. Then, *Do you even burp with vocal chords...?*

On closer inspection, the heavenly robe was a dressing gown, a tattered dressing gown at that, she now saw, more gray with age than white, and speckled with little primroses and the sick of an infant sick up one lapel and down one shoulder, the 'wings' the ends of a towel that had been twisted up (now falling off her head) over what Maureen supposed was wet hair. And the leaping dance was a mad attack to tug the washing off the line. Fionnuala had hiked up the washing line a few months ago when one of the homeless dogs or a fox had tugged the sheets off; she had a step ladder she had to stand on to get the washing, but it was hidden behind the rhubarb patch to stop thieving neighborhood children from getting their mitts on it, but Dymphna wouldn't know about that. Dymphna was clutching a clothing basket in her right hand and shoving the clothing in. How had Maureen not spotted that before? The clothing line was now just pegs, and Dymphna picked up the towel, which had fallen in the muck, and hurried towards the back door.

Maureen muttered curses under her breath, hobbled on her cane to the door and poked her head into the pelting rain, thinking she'd have to get her eyeglass prescription seen to. And quit reading those horror stories before she put the light out on her bedside table at night. Still, she was frail from the shock her heart and brain had been put through.

"Is that you, love?" Maureen asked, her voice reedy.

What she had thought was a spirit blinked as it approached, basket overflowing with knickers and bras. The girl seemed confused at the look on Maureen's face, the wrinkled hand that shuddered as it reached out to confirm her elbow was actually bones and flesh.

"Who else would it be, Grannie?" Dymphna dropped the basket on the linoleum and shook her head like a Saint Bernard. "I was just after coming outta the bath, fiddling around in the bathroom, like, when I heard the rain beating down on the roof. and knew I had just put me washing out on the line. Soaked even more, me smalls now are. Never fails to happen. C'mere, what's wrong with the telly here? I kyanny get any programs on it!"

"Kyanny pay the bill. Wh-what are ye doing here, but, and with yer clothes with ye?" Maureen ran her hands over the rim of the basket and a bra strap to confirm they, too, were real. "Put the fear of the Lord into me, so ye did. On the brink of heart failure, so I was."

"Och, did Mammy not fill ye in? I'm to be holed up here with youse for the next three days or so. Hiding out, more like, I should say."

"Naw, I mean, are ye not meant to be dead?"

...."Ye look wile pale, so ye do. Let me sit ye down, hi, and let's get some whiskey down yer throat."

She guided Maureen to a chair at the kitchen table and shoved aside the paints and rocks and little plastic boxes.

"I need some of me tablets and all. Where's me handbag?"

It was hanging from her elbow. As Maureen scrabbled into the depths for her heart pills, Dymphna grabbed the generic whiskey from the shelf and filled a One Direction tea mug (Siofra's) to the brim. She wrapped Maureen's fingers around it and guided it to her lips. Lips pinched with anger. Dymphna sat beside her grandmother. Wet drops fell from her curls.

"Get that down yer neck, Grannie."

Maureen had the teacup emptied before the sentence was finished. The old woman wiped her lips, then gulped down two tablets. She inspected the rain-streaked gloop oozing down Dymphna's face, which gave her the ghostly sheen. "And what's that shite plastered all over yer bake?"

"Och, this do ye mean?" Dymphna touched her face with a bit of embarrassment. "It's me home made face pack of milk, carrots and egg whites. I saw on the telly it's grand to clear up the spots. Ye've seen the state of me face since I started working at the chip van, like."

"Them black eyes in the middle of yer white face...!"

"Me mascara from last night."

"Such a fright ye've given me. And speaking of the chip van, I'm after seeing yer fancy man working there, the tears streaming down his face. I was of the mind he was crying cause of yer death."

"Rory? Chopping onions, probably. There's loads of onions to chop every day."

"And them women at Xpressions had nothing on their lips but some foolish, goofy story about how ye'd gone and kicked the bucket. About how the McDaid brothers had sold ye some dodgy E's or smack or I don't know what, and were fleeing the jurisdiction, and their mammy and all, the whole family clearing out to Florida as their drugs give ye an overdose. I heard tell, yer mammy went to visit the McDaid's after visiting yer dead body at Tommy Murphy's wee brother's undertaker, the one down Shipquay Street. Can ye imagine me shock? Here ye be, but, living and breathing before me."

"I haven't a clue what ye're on about, Grannie. A drugs overdose? Me?" Dymphna said, but she could never lie convincingly. Her eyes looked everywhere but at Maureen's. Maureen grew angry.

"I wasn't always this age, ye know! I'm still not in me dotage, not yet, and I won't be patronized. I know flippin well ye're lying through yer teeth at me, wee girl. Don't take me for a simpleton! Ye kyanny look me in the eyes, sure. Ye know flimmin well what all these rumors about yer death be's about! I'll clatter the shite outta ye with me cane, though it would pain me to do so, as I love ye, love, but I won't be make a fool of. What's all this palaver about the drugs overdose? Out with it, wee girl!"

"If ye must know..." She took a deep breath. "I didn't want to let ye in on it, as it be's a wee bit embarrassing to me. But if ye insist...Och, does that be the time? I've to get the tea ready. I promised Mammy. And ye know what she's like when the hunger be's gnawing a hole in her stomach." Dymphna hauled the potatoes out of the bag in the cabinet next to the garbage pail under the sink. "Me mammy said I've to make the tea for the entire family tonight. Fadge, spuds and white sauce, we're to be having."

Dymphna seemed proud of her domestic chore, cooking for the family, but Maureen set her lips. The way Dymphna said the menu, it sounded like three different things, but fadge was butter-fried potato bread, a staple in Northern

Ireland, spuds were spuds, and white sauce was butter and flour and milk, though the Floods generally used water as it was cheaper than milk. It didn't escape Maureen, even with the drink and the medication dulling her brain, they were to dine that night on buttered potatoes with potatoes and butter. She'd be reaching frantically across the table for the pepper and HP sauce to add some flavor. Again. She poured more whiskey and gulped down. The bottle was almost empty.

Dymphna peeled fast and furious, back arched.

"What are ye doing here?" Maureen demanded to know. "Is it some newfangled thing to do with the wedding, the bride must be separated from the groom for a week beforehand?"

"If only it were something nice like that," Dymphna said, peeler flying. She sighed. "Naw. Mammy knew the McDaid lads had broke outta prison, and they was all planning on fleeing the city, would be leaving Derry, like, and never coming back. If she told their mammy I was dead, killed by an overdose of their sons' drugs, Mrs. McDaid wouldn't be in the city ever again to see me walking around town, and wouldn't know it was a lie. Ye, see, granny, she knew they was bulging with dosh, and wanted to make yer woman feel guilty and hand some over."

"Why, but? To what end?"

"For to afford to buy me wedding cake, she said. Ye know that Zoë Riddell's to be paying for everything but that. The wedding be's days away, and Mammy still hasn't got the funds together for the cake. Me mammy insisted on paying for it. Why, but, I haven't a clue."

"Och, of all the foolish, goofy...!" Maureen guzzled down more whiskey. "Some misguided sense of pride, I suppose. I kyanny comprehend why it's surfaced this time, but. Yer mammy's never backwards in coming forwards when it be's a question of snatching the funds outta other people's hands. Why would ye agree for such a daft plan, but? For yer mammy to do that to ye? It's all over town ye've gone and snuffed it. With a drugs overdose, of all shameful things! Mortified, so I was, at the salon, me face pure red. What must they think of wer family, a druggie in the ranks. I kyanny step foot in Xpressions again, and ye know I've had a standing appointment Wednesday at four since I don't know when! Another salon I'm gonny haveta find, and yer mammy's to blame! All the other salons be's terrible dear, so yer mammy's shenanigans is to be causing trauma to me handbag...again! Have ye no sense of self-respect yerself, but, hi? It's yer good name ye're allowing her to sully. And with all them wanes popping outta ye, and an Orangeman as yer future husband, that reputation already be's in tatters. All that ye're willing to let yer mammy ruin, and in the name of a flimmin wedding cake."

Maureen stopped, realizing her anger should be directed at Fionnuala, not at

Dymphna.

Peeler aloft, Dymphna faced her with a look of surprise. "Am I not meant to listen to me elders and betters?"

Maybe it was the tea mugs of whiskey on her empty stomach that did it, but Maureen forged ahead, her voice tinged with anger.

"Yer mammy's certainly yer elder. That don't automatically make her yer better, but. Ye're trying to please a woman what kyanny be pleased. Shall we sit down and the two of us compile a list of all the terrible things yer mammy's done? Just like the lists she compiles of which of her wanes she loves the most? Ye've not a clue? Aye, I've seen em. And you, Dymphna, have never been at the top. Never. And this is the woman ye're prepared to allow to spread all around town that ye've died of a drugs overdose? Disgraceful!"

Tears welled in Dymphna eyes. Her peeling faltered.

"Och," Maureen said, "ye're a lovely lass, you, with all them red curls and all. So young, yer fresh face. Ye've so much to live for, them two wanes, and the new one on the way, the wedding coming up... Don't let yer mammy bully ye."

"Ta, Grannie," Dymphna sniffled into the potato peels. "Them be's some of the nicest words anyone's ever said to me. Och, I kyanny see the spuds to peel em correctly." Then she looked around the kitchen as if she suddenly remembered something. "Shite! I used the last of the milk for me face pack. I'll have to use water for the white sauce."

Maureen was growing less hungry the more teatime approached.

"We've not nearly enough spuds for the throngs that's to be eating, anyroad. Put you that peeler down, love. Have ye seen that takeout menu for Pasta-U-Like? I won a voucher for them at bingo Wednesday last. Fifty percent off. I'll ring for a pizza for us all. Two pizzas, it's gonny haveta be. Ye can give me me handbag in a moment. Sit you here beside me a wee moment, now, but."

Dymphna sat. Maureen gripped her hand.

"I love yer mammy as one of me own. Och, she is one of me own, much as it pains me to say it, but ye know what I mean. She's been the cause of all manner of drama the past few years, but. It's gotten worse ever since that Ursula won the lotto, she's unhinged. She's deranged. She's due some comeuppance. It might be the whiskey letting ye in on all this. It has to be said, but. She's long due some retribution. How she enters that confessional at St. Moluag's every Wednesday and can hold her head high as she does it be's a mystery to me. Och, that drink's gone straight to me head, so it has. Drink on an empty stomach's never been me thing."

Dymphna stared at her granny with a sense of betrayal. Maureen knew the girl was probably too dim to realize what she was talking about.

"This wedding will be the making of ye, dear. Living there across the river will do ye good. It's all yer dreams coming true that about to happen to ye now."

"Ye know what I want most in the world, Granny?"

"To finally get that ring round yer finger and make them bastards of yers legal?"

"For Auntie Ursula and Uncle Jed to make it here for me wedding."

"Well, make that happen if that's what ye want. Don't let yer mammy's hatred for em stop ye from making it happen."

"Och! I clear forgot!"

Dymphna jumped from the table, went the oven and took a peek inside. Maureen jumped at her shriek.

"Blessed Virgin! Just as I suspected. When did Mammy last scrub out the oven? It looks like a cave in there, what with them things hanging from the top and them other things rising up from the bottom."

"Stalagmites and stalactites. To think of all the roasts I've had down me throat that've come outta that...place." Maureen's face had taken on a greenish tinge. "Have ye a chisel handy? Or some other tool?"

"I've something better!" She went to her handbag and pulled out a can. "I brought Mammy along some stuff that Zoë's housekeeper uses on her stove, though, of course, Zoë's is self-cleaning, but she says ye can never be too careful where cleanliness is concerned. That I don't understand that, but. But this be's one of them tins of oven cleaners. I've seen Zoë's housekeeper spray it in, let it sit for a few wee moments—ye can put yer feet up and do I don't know what, whatever ye feel like, and it'll do the work itself for ye while ye've them feet up, and then all the filth wipes off with a damp rag. Like magic, so it is."

"Never heard of it!" Maureen said. "Is it some Yank invention?"

"That I don't know. But it's a wee present for Mammy."

Maureen shook her head. "Ye see what I'm talking about, wee girl? Showering gifts on her, while she expects ye to hole up here with that rumor spreading around town about ye on yer wedding week!"

While Dymphna pondered that, Maureen rifled through her handbag for the pizza coupons. The phone call from the hospital came a few minutes later.

CHAPTER 11—WISCONSIN

Why wasn't St. Christopher helping her? Ursula Barnett clucked in dismay at the little plastic statue on the dashboard as she passed the Qwik Pik convenience store for the third time. In addition to epilepsy, toothache and bachelors, Christopher was meant to be the patron saint of driving and traveling, helping travelers find their way. She had glued the statue there after she couldn't find her way home from the shopping mall one day and all the frozen food she bought thawed. With St. Christopher guiding her, she always got home with the peas still frozen, but today she was lost.

...though of course, she considered, St. Christopher hadn't even been alive when the Golden Sunsets Trailer Park was built; nobody knew when he was born, but he had died in 251 AD—she had looked it up on the Internet—and he had never visited the United States. So how could he help her find a place that hadn't existed when he was roaming the Earth? She was more kindly disposed towards St. Christopher now. But she was still lost. In an undesirable location on the periphery of town.

How she regretted the day she decided to volunteer for Our Lady Help of Christian's weekly soup kitchen, the day she served Randaleen Jagger lasagne there, the day she hired her to clean her house, and how she now regretted not having brought Jed along for protection. Randaleen was menacing: big-boned and tall, tall enough, she told Ursula once, that people in supermarkets asked her to reach top shelf items, men too, and Ursula wondered if the woman might turn violent when she confronted her. She could've used Jed for backup.

But her husband was with his brother Slim; Slim had called an emergency meeting for the store they co-owned, *Shooters, Sinkers and Scorchers (and Beef Jerky).* They sold firearms, fish tackle and hot sauce. And now they were selling their own brand of beef jerky, Slim Jed Jerky. Apparently Slim was 'teed off,' his words, with Jed for something to do with the finances. Again. Ursula preferred not to know the details.

It caused her unease enough as it was to know the store was on the verge of failure. It was getting so bad that a few weeks earlier, Jed had forced her, Slim and Louella to film an audition video to see if they could nab a spot on the reality show *Attack of the Killer Investors!* to get a millionaire to invest in them. They had rejected them, but she didn't much care anymore. Ursula had been poor, then she had married Jed and been a bit rich then they had won the lotto a few years before and then they had been mega-rich, and then they had frittered the money away, and were about to be poor again. It was the way of life.

She passed the condemned roadhouse again, and the CD player clicked. Even in her distress, Ursula smiled at the trumpets of the Triumphal March. She had the *Condensed Aida,* her favorite opera, on shuffle, and the march was the only upbeat song on it.

"Gloria!" she warbled, momentarily uplifted, tapping her hands, at 10 and 2 PM, on the steering wheel. *"Gloria! Gloria!"*

She couldn't sing anything else; the rest of the words were strange foreign ones, not only in this song, but in the entire opera, and, in fact, it seemed, all operas, so she just hummed along, though glorious was far from how she felt. Although...she knew she had things to be thankful for. The heat was blazing inside the car for one and, also, a few months earlier, she had thought she was a fugitive for defrauding the churches of her parish out of $100,000. But she was here, now, free, on the right side of a prison wall. Unlike, she thought with a nervous glance out the window, where many of the people slouching through the sleet in this neighborhood were likely to find themselves in the future.

She had never gone back to her old church, such was her shame, and had started to attend Our Lady Help of Christians, 20 miles from her house, instead. And in her renewed vigor to be a better Catholic, she introduced herself to Father Bishop after the first Sunday Mass and explained she wanted to help the community. It was partly for this, and also because of the housekeeping she had let slide, that she had invited Randaleen into her home to clean it once a week. Randaleen had been cleaning for a month now. Ursula paid her of course.

When Jed couldn't find his binoculars one day—he enjoyed the occasional spat of bird watching—she thought he had just misplaced them. And his sunglasses. Then she couldn't locate her Elizabeth Taylor White Diamonds perfume. Or her Chanel No. 5, but that she didn't care about as much because it always made her break out in a rash. And then her jewelry started disappearing, first her smoky topaz ring, then her charm bracelet, then her pearl drop earrings. Then her rosary beads from Lourdes, which she always kept on her nightstand table, vanished as well. And once Ursula had come home from choir practice, and Randaleen claimed one of the ceramic heads from Ursula's beloved collection of people from around the world—the Azerbaijani nomad— had jumped off the wall and shattered into so many pieces that he couldn't be glued together. When Randaleen had gone for the day, Ursula had inspected the garbage cans for the shards, but, of course, Randaleen had emptied them all.

It was only the day before, when Randaleen was taking a break from the vacuuming and sharing a tea and some carrot cake with Ursula at the kitchen table, their conversation stilted as usual, as Ursula was always at a loss as to what to chat with her about, having nothing in common except for their sex, as far as Ursula could tell, and even that was debatable, and Randaleen has asked her if she could smoke right there in the kitchen and Ursula told her no but she could have one on out on the patio later, that Ursula had seen to her shock and disbelief her pearl drop earrings dangling next to the grease of Randaleen's grimy-curtains-type hair. *The brass-necked cheek! Taunting her like that!*

Ursula had claimed a sudden migraine and shuffled her out of the house, shoving a full day's pay into her hand.

She didn't want Randaleen in the house again. She had talked it over with Jed, then tried to call Randaleen, to say what she really wasn't sure. But a recording in a mechanical voice told her the number was disconnected. How, Ursula couldn't understand, as the jewelry Randaleen had stolen should've earned her a pretty penny at the pawn shop, and she could've paid her phone bill with the ill-gotten gains. That Randaleen had keys to their house weighed heavily on Ursula's mind.

The obvious solution—changing the locks—was out of the questions. If Ursula changed the locks, and Randaleen tried to get in, then she would know Ursula suspected something. And Randaleen would attack her some time in the future.

She had raced to the church and spoken to Father Bishop. She didn't know what she should do. Perhaps the earrings really were Randaleen's, but if not, the woman was either mental or an imbecile to wear them in front of Ursula like that. Should Ursula confront her? She knew only too well the fury that could erupt from people accused of stealing, even the put-upon rage from those who were guilty. She had seen it often enough on *Judge Judy.*

Father Bishop asked her if she could just let it slide. He placed a hand on hers and told her he was concerned about what might happen if she hurled accusations at Randaleen without a shred of proof. He told her she had to weigh the importance of the missing items against the trials and danger to mind and body that might come into play by calling someone a thief, even a petty one. It was more grand theft, Ursula told him, the price of the ceramic head and the pearl earrings. But she couldn't let it slide, she had told him. She wouldn't go to the police. She had enough sense for that. If she did, there would certainly be some sort of retribution. But she had to confront Randaleen.

Not in Ursula's home, Father Bishop warned her. In some neutral area, or, better, on Randaleen's home turf, so Randaleen didn't feel so threatened and her reaction would therefore be less...violent? But Ursula didn't know where she lived. She asked him if he would give her Randaleen's address. Didn't he have it in some list of parishioners somewhere? A mailing list of some sort? He told her he couldn't.

But when he was called out of the rectory for some parochial matter, Ursula flipped through the Rolodex on his desk—yes, he had a Rolodex still—and found Randaleen Jagger's address and phone number. She had scribbled it down. And now she was searching for her trailer park. To say what, she still wasn't sure. But she wanted her things back. And Jed's as well.

There was a young man standing at a bus stop next to an elementary school with paint peeling from its walls. He was facing away from her. A parka was slung around his skinny shoulders and worn across his back like a stole. A stole of polyester blend. The waist of his jeans clung to the bottom of his pelvic bone, defying gravity somehow, and his tatty underwear and the outline of his repugnant young buttocks was all too evident.

She pulled up to ask for directions; she wasn't a man, after all. They never wanted to ask for directions. The window whirred down. Ursula stuck her head into the stinging sleet and yelled over the opera, "Young fella! Young fella!"

He turned to face her.

"C'mere, could ye tell me where's that trailer park round here?"

The toothpick in his mouth twirled like a baton.

"Smoke?"

God bless us and save us! Inwardly, Ursula's eyes rolled, but her face beamed out a smile. *A fag in exchange for directions? Cheeky wee upstart!*

"Och, I'm terrible sorry. I gave em up, but."

"Weed?"

Ursula, perplexed but intrigued, continued to smile upward through the pelting icy bits into what she was now realizing were blood-speckled eyes.

"...we'd *what?*"

"X?"

"...Y?" Ursula countered.

And then it dawned on her. Her face suddenly tight, her lips disappearing as if attached to a string, she pressed the button and the electronic window slowly whirred up. *One of them vile drug pushers!* She had seen them on *Law and Order! Trolling for victims of his sordid trade! Why would yer man ever think I...?*

Wondering what she looked like, she sped off. She stared at her eyes in the rear view mirror, and couldn't believe what she was seeing. She reached forward and tugged down the little vanity mirror above her, the leather of the seat squelching under the fullness of her bottom. The light above it flickered to life as her flowered skirt hiked up and the fleshiness of her thighs strained the hem. She saw the haggard look in her eyes, the rattiness of her usually impeccable eggplant-colored bob. One of her eyes had mascara. She was a woman on the wrong side of both fifty and this godforsaken town of malice, and it showed.

She almost missed the sign to the trailer park a fourth time. She flipped up the mirror, shuddering, and turned off the tarmac. The wheels bounced over clumps of dirt and small rocks. And finally the trailer park was in her vision through the sleet. When she saw the state of it, her arteries clenched with fear.

Welcome to Golden Sunsets RV Community! A Happy Home! said the sign, but Ursula wasn't fooled. Shit Dick Balls someone had spray-painted in a happy yellow underneath; to her, that seemed a more apt greeting. She peered through the windshield at the concrete walls which surrounded each side of the gates. Cemented at the top, shards of broken brown and green glass glinted upwards, but whether they were to keep people out or in Ursula wasn't certain. She realized now St. Christopher had been trying to spare her.

Making a quick sign of the cross, Ursula wondered how to inch the front wheels of the car past what looked like the remains of a corpse at the gate. Alarm, fear, and despair vied for attention in her mind and on her face. The car slid forward through the rusty gates, Ursula's palms damp against the steering wheel.

Certainly there were trailer parks around the nation where people led happy, constructive lives, but—and maybe this was nothing more than her feverish imagination unable to stifle itself—these dilapidated, graffiti-defaced homes with the occasional windows boarded with cardboard, and riddled with what she feared were bullet holes, seemed a hive of not only casual violence of all types, including, from the skeletons of burnt trees, teen pyromania, but also wife-beating, and, her mind racing, she added, if the broken beer and gin bottles that lined the path were anything to go by, alcoholism. She also added rampant tooth loss, animal abuse and the occasional child molestation.

She braked hard as a toddler with a filthy face and saggy diaper materialized in the dirt inches from her bumper. He flipped her off, then wobbled into one of the homes. She added incontinence to the list of ails. The park was supposed to be a Happy Home, but it looked like these people were teetering on homelessness.

She tried to conjure up some shred of Christian compassion for these unfortunates and the inhumanity of their pitiful existence, tried to remind herself that they needed kindness, benevolence and help—wasn't that why she had volunteered for the soup kitchen in the first place? why she had hired Randaleen, in fact?—but her fear and sense of self-preservation were too strong. It seemed as if the only reference needed to join this particular community was a police record, and the longer and more salubrious the better. Temperance, virtue and, if Randaleen was anything to go by when she stood next to her, hair conditioner and deodorant seemed to have never paid Golden Sunsets a visit.

She looked, the memory of the bus stop man still fresh, for evidence of illicit drug use. A skeletal man in a faded Ozzy Osbourne t-shirt sprawled on a milk crate on what looked like a homemade porch outside his trailer. He seemed to be wearing only underpants, and in this weather!, but perhaps they were old Speedos. What was that in his hand? Was he injecting illegal drugs into a vein of his left arm even as she looked...?

Och, catch yerself on, Ursula! She had a musical lilt to her voice that most people warmed to, thanks to her Derry accent, even if they struggled to comprehend what she was trying to say. But the charm of her accent hid the steeliness of character that a youth of dodging rubber bullets and crying from tear gas had instilled in her. She was hardened as a matter of course, by an upbringing in the Moorside, Northern Ireland's most notorious Catholic slum, and half of that upbringing had been during a civil war! But after she married Jed, a Yank, she had spent the decades in the abundance and comfort of American life. She had grown as soft as her voice. She tried to will that hardened youth from some forgotten reserve of her character into the present.

Ye're to be confident, so ye are, she told herself. *Ye've to walk briskly and with an air of confidence to yer woman's home, Ursula.*

But she didn't know in which of the sad trailers Randaleen lived. The address she had taken from Father Bishop was a confusing smattering of numbers and dashes, lot this, route that. She would have to ask for directions. And other than the group of terrifying teens cackling and smoking something next to what looked like a water pump, the man on the porch was the only person in sight. She grabbed her handbag and opened the door. *Yer man there doesn't be doing drugs, ye simpleton,* she tried to convince herself. *Walk with confidence. And a wee bit of grace and all.*

She got out of the car, slammed shut the door, and thrust her right foot forward to do just that. Her coat was caught in the door, and she almost splat face down on the gravel. She freed herself, and took that confident and graceful step onto the edge of a discarded toilet seat. It flipped up and smacked her knee. The youths roared with laughter.

Wincing and limping, she staggered forth through the sleet towards the man on the porch. She arranged her lips into a smile.

She didn't see the mother of his three urchins staggering along behind her, one hand clawing at charred twigs for support, the other clutching a bottle of generic vodka that was almost empty.

"Ya goddamn whore!" the man roared. Ursula's smile faltered. She pointed to herself. Me? she mouthed in confusion and fear. Was there something about her that made her seem like a— "Whore! Take another step closer and I'm gonna kill ya!"

She scuttled back to the car as he kept yelling things she didn't understand. "Don't know why you're dragging yourself home again after a night out on your back! There ain't no stash left nohow!"

And as Ursula sat scrabbling the key in the ignition, heaving huge pants of terror on the leather, as she revved up and reversed out like a madwoman, she realized she'd have to confront Randaleen in her own home. With Jed a few feet away in the same room. She would arrange it, she thought as she sped out of the gates into the safety of the rest of the world, so that when she pointed the finger at the thief, her husband was serendipitously cleaning some of the shotguns from the store at the same time, some of the more threatening-looking ones.

From the speakers in the warmth of the car, a voice was belting out a heart-wrenching tune from the Judgment scene of *Aida,* where, as far as Ursula could tell, Ramadès was being sentenced to death for something he did.

Ahime...morir mi sento...!

Had she known the translation, Ursula would've realized she felt the same way.

Alas...I feel death...!

The car roared past the Qwik Pik.

CHAPTER 12

"So wake me up when it's all over...!"

Dymphna wore a sparkly pink and white top with spaghetti straps, a light green mini-skirt and mulch-colored leg-warmers. Silver open-toed stilettos adorned her feet. The battered pub door before her shook with the bass beat of Avicci's country-dance blasting from the pub within. The Swedish DJ had been inviting them all to Wake Him Up since Christmas.

Dymphna blot her lips on a Kebablicious napkin she found in her handbag and plumped up her red curls, she offered up a small prayer up to the Lord that her mother would be well, but then forgot all about her mother and the Lord as she entered the dome of sin that was the Craiglooner. She had left Keanu and Beeyonsay at the house and was gagging for a laugh, some gossip, a dance around her handbag, a string of cigarettes in her mouth and copious amounts of alcohol down her throat. Even if it was with girls who belonged to her life before. Before Rory, before her move to the Waterside.

When, out of desperation, she had chosen Maire, Ailish and Maeve to be her bridesmaids, she had had to call them out of the blue. Each had seemed startled at the invitation—Dymphna hadn't laid eyes on them since her move to the Waterside months before—but all had accepted.

Dymphna scanned the masses, slipped on a bottle on the floor, and elbowed through the heaving male chests in soccer jerseys and the barely-concealed female breasts. Drunken roars and acne greeted her from every angle. She spied her former friends in a nook in the corner. Maire, Ailish and Maeve had already been at the drink for some time, if their eyes under the alarming hues of eyeshadow and the empties on the table were anything to go by. They jumped up at the sight of her, and squealed and hugged and laughed as if they had last seen her the previous night.

"Yer round, ye jammy cunt!" one brayed. The other two stared eagerly at her handbag.

Not offered the chance to sit down, Dymphna fought her way to the bar, bought the round, four pints of lager and four shots of tequila, scuttled over with the drink sloshing on a little round tray she had asked for, then settled down betwixt them in the nook. The table was sticky and peppered with ancient cigarette burns. They snatched the glasses from the tray and poured the liquor down their throats.

"Right, Dymphna!" one said.

"So ye're still alive after all!" another said.

"We hadn't a clue whether to show up or not."

"C'mere, do ye know it's all over town ye've kicked the bucket? What are ye doing alive?"

Dymphna took a little sip of lager and scrunched her face in embarrassment.

"Aye, that was me mammy. A misunderstanding, so it was. Sure, ye see me sitting here before youse and youse is not in Hell yet, are youse?"

"Dymphna, now that I see ye're indeed alive and kicking, I don't mind telling ye that when I'd heard ye'd died, I thought the wedding might be canceled, and pure spitting I was. Have ye any clue how dear them bridesmaids frocks is?"

"Aye, here was me wondering how to return mines, as the smarmy prick in the shop said there was to be no refunds."

"Scrimped and saved for weeks for to be able to afford mines, so I had to! Me mammy had to pitch in forty quid, and ye didn't even invite her, like."

Then it cost ye but 70 pee. The bold-faced cheek! Dymphna thought, but continued to smile as she drank; she well understood the financial strain she had subjected her former schoolmates to.

The gowns had each cost £80.70, which verged on a week's wages for Marie at the bookies down the Strand, and a week and half's for Ailish at the Sav-U-Mor (she had been let go from Pricecutters for 'discrepancies of stock'), and Maeve from the swanky café on Shipquay Street that had once been new but was now no longer, so Dymphna had given them each £40 out of her paycheck to offset the cost of the gowns, even though Zoë didn't pay Dymphna herself much for her hours in the fish and chip van. Dymphna knew if she told them how much it had hurt her financially to subsidize their dresses they wouldn't believe her. She saw the meaningful looks in people's eyes when they heard she was marrying somebody from the Waterside, saw how they folded their arm around their chests and took a little step back. Dymphna herself barely believed how little she earned, and her own eyes saw the paycheck every second Friday of the month. Marrying into a Protestant family hadn't made her rich herself. Maybe the money would come later. Maybe there were things that were obvious to others that weren't obvious to her. Maybe it was a well-documented fact that Catholics who married Protestants never got to see any of the money. She just didn't know. All she knew about marrying Rory Riddell was that she wanted a father for her three children. One father.

"C'mere, what's up with yer arm, hi?" Dymphna asked Maeve, to change the subject.

Maeve rolled her eyes as she nodded down at the cast on her right wrist.

"Och, I fractured me wrist, so I did."

"Blootered, was ye?"

"Aye, I was, so ye know I haven't a clue how the bloody feck it happened. I woke up to me shock under one of them cannons on the city walls Wednesday last after the karaoke, and there was terrible pains shooting from me bones, like, and swollen like a beaten backside, me wrist was, all purple and all, and me hand sticking out at the end of it like a useless thing. Ye shoulda seen me trying to hail a mini-cab. A right gack, I musta looked. Pure red, I was and all. And then when we pulled up to the A & E at Altnegalvin, I was searching through me handbag for the money for to pay yer man with, and it be's wile difficult to scrabble in yer handbag with only one hand, when I saw hadn't a hi'penny to rub together. I had to crawl into the front seat and pleasure yer man with me good hand then and there in the parking lot for to pay for the journey, and that with the pains shooting up and down me wrist and the stench from yer man's sweaty bollocks making me wanny gag. Have youse ever wanked a lad off with yer left hand? Unnatural, it be's, just like ye kyanny write correctly with that hand either. Thank Christ, but, yer man in the mini-cab wasn't one of them poofs, for he was well up for it. An arse bandit woulda knocked me back. Didn't take yer man long to reach satisfaction as he was a sad fat bastard and probably couldn't believe his good luck in nabbing a looker like meself. He made a wee noise and it was all over, and for that I'm grateful. I did have to ask him to wipe me fingers off after as I couldn't do it meself, like. And it was only after they did the x-rays and I was getting this God-awful cast wound round me wrist that I remembered I had me emergency twenty next to me tampon in me secret compartment all along, and so there was no need for me to have compromised meself in that manner. The twenty got me back home, but, so..."

"Was yer Morris raging?" Dymphna asked. That was Maeve's husband.

"Aye, pure spitting with anger, he was, near beat the shite outta me, as now he has to change the wanes' nappies, me being an invalid with the one functioning hand for the next six weeks."

"Naw, I meant about ye being on yer knees flinging yer fingers over yer man the mini-cab driver's kno—"

"Sure, how would Morris know about that, hi?"

It was a shot of whiskey later and halfway into another conversation that Dymphna realized how stupid her question had been.

Struggling to hear under the pounding of the British drum and bass and American rap, between pouring more beer down her gullet, she asked them what they thought about her fiancé, about Rory. Their eager answers reminded her they had been all for it when she revealed many moons ago he had proposed.

"Och, Rory's lovely, so he is."

"Fit."

"Fine arse, hi. Ye kyanny see it in them baggy track suit bottoms he wears. I reached out and grabbed it once, but, when he was before me in the queue of the Kebabalicious one night. Before youse was together, like."

"And that lovely black hair of his!"

"Them dark eyes! Gorgeous!"

"Rory's eyes is a wee bit squinty, but."

"Like a young Colin Farrell, so he is."

"Aye, a dead ringer for him, so Rory is, if yer man Colin were playing a role in a film about a hunger striker, ye know what I mean, like at the end of the film where he hasn't had anything to eat for weeks and weeks or even months. And if at the end of the film he got caught in a rainstorm, like, or maybe the sprinklers went off in the prison I guess, and the hair was plastered to his skull."

"I've noticed his lack of beauty products and all."

"And maybe if he had that nose of his seen to. And them teeth whitened a bit. Not that I'm for teeth whitening, dead Yank, so it is, but I don't think the shade of a banana be's normal, like."

"And not a bad word to say against anyone, Catholic or Protestant. Since he stopped hanging around them hard-cased hooligan thug mates of his, anyroad."

"That's all grand and lovely to be saying. If youse don't mind *me* saying, but, though it turns me stomach, it's well overdue, this wedding."

They all turned to look at Ailish. There was a sanctimonious air in her voice. She was staring at Dymphna as if down from on high. Maire and Maeve shifted uncomfortably. Dymphna's eyes shot from side to side, seeking an escape. Ailish was the most traditional of them; she even went to church on holy days. It was the dangerous time of the drink, when tongues geared up to spill home truths, threatening to turn any celebration black.

"Youse know what I mean. Having them wanes outta wedlock and all... And I'm not quite sure this mixing of the religions is the way to the future. More down the road to eternal damnation."

As they stared at her, Ailish's face turned bright red, but then she forced her head up, a flicker in her boozy eyes, her bright pink lips taut.

"Well. It does be a sin, don't youse agree in yer heart of hearts?" she slurred. "It's unnatural, like."

"Och, catch yerself on," Maire said. "It's the new century, so it is. Sure, even popes be's changing like songs at the top of the hit parade, a new one every week, it seems."

"Aye, but the Catholic church looks down on them what...what..." Either it was the liquor or the complexity of what she wanted to say that was flustering Ailish. Finally, she forged ahead, voice ringing with righteousness: "Me mammy wasn't best pleased at me taking part. Blasphemy, she called it. Part of me mind agreed. It be's like chips. Ye want em with vinegar or ye want em with tomato sauce. They tastes grand with one or grand with the other, but like shite if ye put both together. And the way ye rang me up outta the blue like that for to ask me to be yer bridesmaid. Sure, none of us knows what ye've been up to since ye moved to the Waterside. We don't know what's been going on in yer mind. Me only consolation was yer mammy, Dymphna. A staunch churchgoer, so she be's. So I trust her. And if she's given this unseemly, sinful pairing her blessing, who am I to disagree? And also, me gown had already been bought, and we've all since discovered there be's no returns. Something to do with the alternations. I'll be proud to stand by yer side, but, as ye're a good laugh, Dymphna, and ye was one of me first mates in primary school. I only wish ye had chosen a lad what was more appropriate. Not an Orange bastard. Have ye not seen the graffiti what's been sprayed over the awning or whatever ye call it of the chip van where ye work that ye pull down when it be's closed? I must say I quite agree. A life of misery, I think ye're setting yerself up for. If ye want to know what I think." She burped. She wiped the drool from her chin.

The other girls' eyes stared at beermats, jukebox buttons, the arses of the barmen. Anywhere but at Dymphna. She was noticing that all three girls sported bruises in a wide array of sizes, colors and locations, from small to large, purple to yellow, on elbows and forearms and cheeks. She didn't know if they were from their wanes—they all had as many as she did, if not more, though legal ones—from their wanes slapping them too hard accidentally or their husbands slapping them too hard deliberately.

Maeve cleared her throat and wondered where the diamond engagement ring that used to dangle from her finger was. Dymphna explained that, a while back, Zoë had forced it off her finger and locked it up in her jewelry box so that Dymphna wouldn't be able to pawn it if she decided to. This was met with an awkward silence. Dymphna handed over another twenty. The girls jumped up, shoved through the press of bodies at the bar, and Dymphna could hear their roars for tequila over Daft Punk.

She sat in the nook alone and fiddled with an empty crisp packet. Tomato and sausage.

"We're up all night to get lucky...!"

CHAPTER 13

"In the hospital room, they was ready to read me me Last Rites, so they was," Fionnuala croaked in a voice of well-rehearsed agony. "All staring down at me in the bed, their eyes peering over them creepy wee masks, and gearing up to drag me body to the knacker's yard. I sent the priest away, but, and not because it was that aul Father Grogan whose sermons always bored me senseless, but because I was ready to *live.* I've to see me daughter wed, after all. If I make it to the end of the week." She gave a little moan.

Fionnuala had claimed she was too frail to climb the stairs. Swaddled in a frayed bathrobe, wreathed in hot water bottles, her face glowing orange from the space heater propped on the floor before her, her time-ravaged body languished on the lumpy settee in the front room, as if, it seemed to Maureen, she were the model for Jesus in Michaelangelo's *Pietà*. Padraig, Siofra and Seamus knelt before their ailing mother on the threadbare carpeting and fed her leftover cold pizza they had torn into little bits to fit into her barely-parting lips. The pizza had arrived hours before Fionnuala, Padraig and Siofra, so first Maureen and Dymphna had dug in, then Paddy and Lorcan when they arrived from the pub. All the exciting flavors had been devoured, so Fionnuala was left with cheese.

Straddling the arm of the settee, Paddy pressed a cold rag to her forehead and muttered consoling noises. Lorcan was perched at her feet like a loyal dog, his puppy eyes taking her in with concern, his hands touching a leg here and knee there, trying for a show of comfort.

Maureen sat in a chair beyond the china cabinet, far removed from the display. She gripped her cane, knuckles white as she fought to restrain herself. She wasn't about to be taken in; her role was definitely not going to be Mary to Fionnuala's Jesus. Maureen inspected the body on the settee. Fionnuala did look sick. Older. The whites of her eyes were grays, her crow's feet claws, her wrinkles now crevices. And her hands, especially, seem to have been affected by the health being siphoned from her body; the fingers dangled like wrinkled sausages left too long in the microwave. Maureen thought Fionnuala looked more like one of the people in Picasso's *Guernica,* her face all twisted and contorted.

Still... Her daughter had passed out, certainly, and had something wrong with her, but now she was milking it for all it was worth, that's what Maureen thought. If Fionnuala demanded one of the children massage her feet, Maureen'd have her up for child abuse.

73

Fionnuala reached up and caressed Paddy's hand with five of her wrinkled sausages.

"Light me a fag, would ye Paddy, love, and place it in me mouth."

Leaving the rag resting on her forehead, Paddy hastened to comply.

"Right man ye are. And, youse, wanes, could youse do yer mammy a favor and pick out all them wee little green grassy bits outta the pizza before ye feed it to me? Yer fingernails be's small enough. I'm afeared they be's interfering with me medication, like. Good wee dotes."

Seamus' little face crinkled with concentration as he set about doing just that, but Padraig and Siofra were having none of it. And the little girl was lucky her mother's head, fluttering her eyes dramatically and moaning with satisfaction as the nicotine filled her lungs, was lost behind a cloud of cigarette smoke. Fionnuala missed the rolling of her daughter's eyes.

Paddy sneaked looks a the telly, but it was broken. There was nothing else to look at. And Lorcan kept glancing at his mobile every time his mother closed her eyes and burrowed her head in the cushions with a moan. He was the only one in the family that had a phone hooked up to the internet always so that he could see Facebook and Twitter and who knew what else.

After the initial fuss and concern of Fionnuala's arrival from the hospital, the rest of the family was starting to get antsy. It seemed any immediate danger had passed, and they didn't much relish the thought of hours checking to see if she was still breathing in and out.

"And just where is me soon-to-be wed daughter? Wer Dymphna? Has she no interest in her mammy's well-being?" There was accusation in Fionnuala's voice.

"She's out with her bridesmaids," Maureen explained. "Making sure the wedding plans is all in order. Once she heard ye didn't get the funds from that McDaid article and that there was no need for her to stay holed up in the house for three days, presumed dead by the entire town, like, out the door she raced, and good on her, I say. She was all up for making the tea, but I—"

"Selfish cunt!" Fionnuala croaked. "I should've realized that one would be more interested in herself than her poor aul mammy. Bleedin fecking typical. As I lay there in the hospital, I half-expected the slag, wer Dymphna, to wheel them half-Orange bastards of hers into the ward for me to look after." She moaned and passed her cigarette to Paddy so he could flick the ash for her; the ashtray was perched behind her head and she couldn't reach it.

Maureen could hold her tongue no longer.

"Did they really call for the priest?" she asked. "And just what ailment did them doctors and the team of specialists they had called in say ye was suffering from?"

Fionnuala detected the tone in her mother's voice, and her head whipped from the cushions at a speed remarkable given the supposed state of her weakness.

"Do ye doubt I'm knocking at death's door? I was poked and prodded with that many tools and hooked up to gadgets like things they seemed to have wheeled in from a time machine. And they drained that much flimmin blood from me arms that I almost passed out again. Tube after wee tube yer woman kept attaching to the needle jammed in me arm. Torturing me body for to give up its secrets, so they were."

Maureen greeted her daughter's whines with flinty eyes.

"What's yer illness?"

"If ye must know the specifics, I've none for ye. And that's what sets the fear racing through me veins. Me disease-riddled veins. They be's still waiting for the test results, like, and there are more tests left for them to do. I've to go back next Monday. And tomorrow I've to, I've to..." She pressed her lips shut, then carried on. Maureen wondered what she wasn't revealing. "From what I could make out from their medical blabber, and yer man the doctor's bloody Paki accent, c'mere, why kyanny they speak like normal?, they seem to think there be's more than one thing wrong with me body, that I've a variety of illnesses that be's working at odds against one another and giving em results they think maybe they've never seen before. They said they've to check some medical journals. Could ye imagine if I get written up in one of em as some sort of medical oddity? Mortified, I'd be!"

Her mother could never know what Fionnuala kept secret in the Celine Dion/Titanic satchel she had dumped in the hallway as they had carried her into the house, the evidence of the shameful procedure she was meant to follow the next day under her GP's orders. Even Paddy, who she shared everything with, would never know. She would take it to the grave with her, what the doctor expected her to do. Everything told her it was an inhumane thing to expect a human to do. But, fearful of her health and looking to extend the years she had on the Earth, she would have to comply with his orders. Only she and Dr. Chandrapore would know. When the curtain was pulled and she set eyes on him, it was the one time outside a curry house she had been happy to see a Pakistani face—she had seen on the telly they were good doctors—and *this* was how he had repaid her touchy-feely moment of madness: forcing her to do this *disgusting thing!*

Fionnuala tried flicking on the telly, but remembered it was on the blink.

"How am I meant to recuperate with no telly, hi?" she, remote dangling in her fingers, demanded of all around her. "Languishing here on the settee as I must, with no end to me illness in sight, and with no entertainment to keep me company."

"How about a wee singsong?" Maureen suggested. She didn't notice them all recoiling slightly in horror. Nor the alarm as she opened her lips wide and belted out, hand slapping her knee in rhythm: *"Armored cars and tanks and guns, came to take away our sons...!"*

"Naw, *naw*, Mammy!" Fionnuala spat derisively. "Christ almighty, ye'll put me back in Altlnagelvin with that racket! Naw, I've a better idea." She singled Siofra out with a finger. The girl looked like she wished the crust of pizza was as big as her face so she could hide behind it. But there was nowhere in the sitting room to hide from her mammy. "Go on and be a dote, love, and take off yer mammy's socks."

"Not a massage!" This from Maureen.

Fionnuala snarled contemptuously at her mother. "As if I would, Mammy! What sorta self-centered geebag do ye take me for? Come on, wee girl! Hop to it! Don't sit there with that look of a spastic on yer face! Get me socks off!"

She wriggled her toes inside the monstrous red wool-type things she was fond of. Paddy, Lorcan, Padraig and Maureen looked away, kindly, as Siofra shuffled on her knees over to her mother's feet and, breathing through her tiny nostrils, peeled off the socks. Seamus watched in awe.

"Now what, Mammy?" Siofra asked, fear of the unknown in her eyes.

"Now I want ye to place em on yer hands, one on each, and give yer mammy a wee puppet show. Ye can use the coffee table there as yer stage. Them pizza crusts and them mugs and bottles and whatnot can be yer props. Use yer imagination, love. Lord knows ye're the only one in the family with one."

A younger Siofra might have blindly followed her mother's bizarre instructions. She had certainly been happy to do most everything her mother demanded in the past, no matter how deranged or immoral. She had been the most sterling of all Fionnuala's children, who she had tried to mold into her own little stormtroopers of hatred. But Fionnuala seemed not to have noticed that the girl was getting older. More independent, with thoughts of her own clicking her brain. She was staring at her mother now with a look she would have never dared give Fionnuala in the past: her mouth creased in disgust, her eyes bright with the threat of insubordination.

"Naw, Mammy! I'm not showing meself up like that in front of the whole family, like."

There was silence. Fionnuala threw Siofra a thunderous look, and Maureen had half-risen from her chair, Paddy taken a step forward, when she simply shrugged and said, "Just as I expected from ye. Traitor. *Seamus!*"

Little six-year-old Seamus jumped in shock. Padraig stared in disbelief through his urine-colored specs.

"A-aye, Mammy?" he asked in a voice that was set to bawl.

"Ye're gonny take the place of that selfish wee cunt of a sister of yers. Get them socks on yer hands."

They were too big for Seamus, but Padraig, either pitying his poor little brother or excited to see the show, shuffled over on his knees across the carpet to help him. The red socks dwarfed Seamus's hands.

"C'mon now, me wee dote," Fionnuala cooed, "let the action begin! Curtain up!"

Seamus's face, his little eyes and nose and mouth, screwed up as if he were about to cry. He placed his sock-covered hands on the table before him, elbows between the pizza detritus.

"I don't know what to make yer socks say, Mammy. What do socks say?"

"Och, for the love of Christ, ye daft bastard! C'mere, have ye no clue that I'm of the mind ye're soft in the head? I don't mean an eejit like we call everyone eejits, but a real eejit, one, like, that be's separated from all the other wanes in school and forced to do lessons they call special, but really be's for them demented ones with only half a thinking brain in their heads. I'll help ye, spastic that ye are. Here's the first thing yer auntie Ursula says, that be's the sock that's yer right hand. Yer right be's the hand closest to that bottle of lager. I'm sure ye didn't know. Here's what she says: Ohhh, they call me Ursula Barnett," the cringing audience didn't know why Fionnuala was giving Auntie Ursula a weedy falsetto voice, or a British accent, but she was, and not only that, Paddy's face was hard, his left eye twitching as he fought to contain himself, Lorcan's hands were fists, Padraig was staring at his mother in disgusted awe, Siofra eyed her little brother with pity, and Maureen had retired upstairs to the loo, "Move yer fingers, ye daft cunt!" Fionnuala barked at Seamus. "Jesus, Mary and Joseph! Do I have to do all the work for ye? Move yer fingers when I be's saying what yer auntie Ursula says so it looks like the puppet be's talking!" Paddy wanted to step in when he saw tears welling in Seamus's eyes, but a look from Fionnuala made him step back towards the fireplace again. "I'm gonny begin again, ye daft git, and I want ye to move yer fingers like they was her lips. And wave the puppet about and all."

"Where's the puppet, but?" Seamus whimpered.

"It be's the sock, Seamus," Siofra whispered.

"Don't ye dare help him, ye hateful bitch!" Fionnuala barked. "And I'm never asking ye to do anything for me ever again, wee girl! Ye're dead to me! *Dead!* Do ye hear that?" Paddy feared for his little daughter's safety as she flashed her mother a look that said, "As if I give a flimmin feck," but Fionnuala was back to staring at the 'stage' and the teary eyed puppet master knelt behind it. "I'll begin again, Seamus. Ye'll burn in Hell if ye don't follow yer mammy's instructions." All were concerned as Seamus's lower lip trembled and the tears welled in his eyes. "Move yer fingers, now, of yer right hand." Again the high pitched British accent, and Seamus did as demanded, while Fionnuala warbled out, "I'm a tight-fisted old cow. Me handbag be's bulging with cash, but I'm keeping it all to meself. I've a minted Yank husband, but that doesn't be enough for me. I've won the lottery, but that doesn't be enough for me and all. I moved off to the States as nobody in Ireland can stomach the sight of me. But I travel back to Derry time and again just to flash me millions around so nobody forgets how rich I am. And I want more money. More pounds. Loads and loads of pounds so that I'm the richest woman in Derry. Even though I cleared out ages ago and I don't live here no more. And I'm giving me wads of cash to nobody. I'm eating in the swankiest restaurants and ordering all the food I can shovel down me big fat throat. And would ye look at the state of me! Pig-ugly, so am are! And me hair! Like a purple, what do ye call it? Them things that floated around Nazi Germany I seen on the telly. Back when we had a functioning one."

"Zeppelin," Lorcan said.

"Ta, love," then Fionnuala was back to the British falsetto. Seamus's fingers twiddled inside the sock, his eyes looking up at her, imploring her for a sign, a slight twitch, of approval. "Oh, here's some pizza. Let me grab it and ram it down me throat. *Pick up that crust, Seamus!"* Fionnuala barked. *"It's there in front of ye on the table, sure! Pick it up with the sock and make like she's eating it!"* He did. "And, oh, my, who's that nice younger woman I see peering through the window of the restaurant at me? Och, she's coming inside now, but I don't think they let her type in here. She doesn't look like a nose in the air, me shite doesn't stink bitch like me. She wants to say something to me." She broke off, chortling with glee. "Now, Seamus, use yer other hand. Now it's yer mammy's turn."

Seamus struggled to comprehend.

"The other sock be's Mammy," Siofra whispered, gaining her another glare from her mother. But Siofra seemed made of titanium now.

The others looked on, helpless. None in the prison that was her family dared cross her. They had tried in the past, and the retribution had been relentless. For their own mental and physical health, it was best just to let her get on with it, spewing out her hatred and fear at every turn, every opportunity.

Fionnuala used a husky, but pleading, kindly, voice for herself. "Hello, there, Ma'am. I wonder if ye could help m— *Move me! Move yer other hand, ye useless geebag!"* Seamus understood now. The socks, one with a crust of pizza sticking out of the 'mouth,' danced atop the table beside the overflowing ashtray. "I wonder if ye could possibly help me, kind woman? I'm a working mother, and yer sister-in-law, and me and yer brother and all his wanes are wile hungry. Starving, so we are, desperate for a morsel from all the food that be's piled high on this table ye're sat at, with that silk tablecloth and heaving with all them wile fancy and wile dear hamburgers and pizzas and vegetables and other food I've never seen in me life before, French or Continental, it must be, dead posh, and I wonder if ye might be so kind as to give us a tiny morsel to eat? Maybe a crumb of that bread stick over there—*that fag end be's the bread stick!*—if it wouldn't be too much to ask? Now, Seamus, yer Auntie's gonny speak." The right sock sprang to life. "Naw! Get the feck outta here, ye hateful bitch! What are ye doing in here, anyroad? This restaurant be's reserved for posh arseholes like me. I'm not giving up any of me food. It's for me own massive, hateful, ugly, manky, mingin body! Clear on off outta here before I call the Filth on ye. Ye know I love the Filth. As much as I hate ye and me brother and all them hateful nieces and nephews of mines...."

Fionnuala rolled her prone body on the sofa with glee, laughter spilling from her mouth. The others were speechless. And so the theater of hate continued, to their dismay, line after excruciating line. Thankfully, the 'play' was only one act long. They stood, sat or knelt there, transfixed, until it had reached its surprising climax and was over. "Mammy" had "eaten" "Auntie Ursula," and Fionnuala had clapped rapturously, "Bravo! Bravo, me lad! Och, ye're a blessing, so ye are!" and had wrenched her massive form off the settee and was all set to wrap the terrified and confused little boy in her arms and hug him tight as Maureen resurfaced and Lorcan mouthed at his father, "Christ, that was brutal," but then Seamus, giggling happily, had sock "Mammy" erupting with a coarse burp, for which he received a violent smack on the face and a move a notch down her List instead.

Fionnuala settled back on the sofa, eyes shining.

Lorcan cleared his throat. He gently touched her foot. "I've-I've to leave yer side now, Mammy. I've to ring some lads as I've some plans to put in motion."

Fionnuala's eyes rounded with genuine surprise. Her face crumpled into an exaggerated grimace of agony as she fought to prop herself up on an elbow.

"What've ye got going on, son, that be's more important than tending to yer aul invalid mother? I would expect it from Dymphna and the likes of them," Fionnuala nodded her head at Padraig and Siofra,

Padraig and Siofra were shocked.

"But, Mammy!" Padraig protested.

"We saved ye from death out in that parking lot, so we did!" Siofra said.

Fionnuala appeared not to hear. "...and from that shameless twat-slurper Moira in Malta and traitor Eoin. Not from *ye*, Lorcan, but, the strapping young lad first outta me hole as ye were."

Her eyes were saucered with incredulity.

Lorcan stammered, head bowed in shame. He shot a glance at his father. Paddy looked as if he had just been prodded with a cattle prong. Fionnuala's eyes weren't weak enough with illness to miss the look between father and son. She struggled up on her elbows, face thunderous. A hot water bottle fell to the floor.

"What have youse two been up to behind me back? I seen the look ye give one another. Youse are in cahoots. Ganging up with plans ye've not included me in. Traitors! Bleedin fecking flimmin traitors! And all this while I be's lying on me death bed!"

The three younger children scattered, Seamus bursting into tears. Maureen heard their feet clattering up the stairs, but nothing, not even a chair lift, would make her join them. She had a front row seat to the drama unfolding before her rheumy eyes. She almost clapped her hands with glee.

Paddy cleared his throat. He wiped her head, but she smacked the rag. It splat on the hot water bottle.

"I see the guilt in yer eyes, son! Tell me what ye're up to! Tell me know!"

Paddy put himself in the firing line for his son's sake.

"No use beating about the bush, love," he said quickly. His mouth twitched with a smile, and maybe this was his little revenge for the shameless 'entertainment' about his sister they had been forced to sit through. "Ye're gonny find out soon enough, anyroad. Lorcan's off to the States. Aye, joining Eoin and Moira before him, going to make a life for himself abroad."

"I'm sorry, Mam, but I was suspended from the plant today for a punch up, and I kyanny see any point in—"

As Maureen's ears cringed at the shriek erupting from Fionnuala's mouth, she thought her daughter now a dead ringer for Munch's *The Scream,* and that she herself had seen one too many episodes of *Art Treasures of Europe:The Ones The Nazis Didn't Get* on the telly of late.

The shriek kept spewing from Fionnaula's withered lips, as if the thought of Lorcan deserting her terrified and enraged her more than any sudden mystery illness could.

Lorcan looked pained. He inched towards the door.

"Sorry, Mammy, but—"

Fionnuala wrenched her limbs from the settee, robe trawling open, and lurched after him. Paddy was knocked to the floor in a pile of pizza shreds and cheese bits. Maureen giggled into her hand.

"Over me dead body!" Fionnuala screamed, shaking her fist at Lorcan's quickly retreating back. He leaped up the stairs to safety. "Ye're not leaving me here alone in this shitehole! Over me dead body, I'm warning ye, son! Aurgh!" She gripped her heart at a sudden strange pain, tried to clutch at the door jamb, missed, and slid down the peeling wallpaper between the settee arm and the ironing board. Tears welled in her eyes. Paddy hurried over to her side, but she clawed his hands away and roared like a mental patient.

"Over me dead body!" were, again, Fionnuala's last words moaned up the stairs as Lorcan finally reached the landing. But with the sudden new plans that were shooting through her brain even as she fought off Paddy's hands of comfort, perhaps 'over yer dead body' would be more apt. If she couldn't keep her beloved son, her most loved, her gorgeous, charming, fit golden boy, in Derry on his own accord, she would fix it somehow so he wouldn't be able to leave.

CHAPTER 14

Plastered, Dymphna was again alone in the nook, £100 lighter, and fighting the urge to check out the arses around her, when her goggly eyes zoomed in on the last person in the world she wanted to see. Bridie McFee!

The splintered walls of the nook receded. Dymphna's heart froze, at odds with the bass beat from Pitbull and Ke$ha on the jukebox that shook the rest of her body. *It's goin down, I'm yellin timber!*

Once her best mate in the whole wide world. Now her mortal enemy. Propped up between the fruit machine and the dartboard, next to the entrance to the loos, in bulging leggings and mud-spattered Doc Martens. And glaring across the bobbing throngs of the pub, shooting daggers at her with a menace that would strike fear into any of the McDaid lads.

The drunken synapses of Dymphna's brain flew. Chilled in the sweaty depths, she wrapped her arms around her and searched wildly for her girlfriends, safety in numbers. But a rap song earlier, they had staggered to the smoking area (the street outside); Dymphna had stayed behind, not because she wasn't smoking, of course she was, pregnant or not, and not because she loved Tinie Tempah's rapping, she didn't, but to keep the nook theirs. Her bridesmaids were nowhere to be seen. Dymphna's only comfort was the silver open-toed stilettos she was wearing; their heels always made her feel equipped with two deadly weapons for whatever a night on the town might bring, and she had put them to use twice before.

She was terrified because Bridie seemed many pints past reason. Under hair of no color or discernible style, the glare on her face dissolved into a sneer that shot through the masses towards Dymphna. The bloody lipstick jumped out across the room. The sneer turned to a smile, which was somehow more terrifying because Dymphna didn't know if Bridie was smiling at something in real life or in some fantasy of her mind. She remembered a night the two of them had hallucinated on absinthe, and feared suddenly Bridie might have grown fond of hallucinations and had begun popping strange pills from the 60s. Bridie struggled to remove her shoulders from the fruit machine and take a step in Dymphna's direction.

Dymphna whimpered even as her drunken stupor sought to lull her. She took in Bridie's purple hoodie with LET ME ENTERTAIN YOU emblazoned on it. Her brain thought it a shame nobody was taking Bridie up on the offer right now—only a lad sniffing around her crotch could distract Bridie from her hatred for Dymphna. But it wasn't difficult to see why there were no offers. Few were the faces that lit up at the sight of Bridie approaching them. Her body was like an aging sofa you'd want to dump in a skip, shapeless and uncomfortable, with lumpy bits you couldn't comprehend what they might be sticking out in the most alarming spots. Pimples, early wrinkles from misspent teen years and cold sores that never seemed to heal despite the passage of time vied for attention on her bitter mug. And then there was her personality.

Bridie's Doc Martens stomped a step from the fruit machine. Under the table, Dymphna slipped her right foot out of the stiletto and reached under to take hold.

"Right! Who's got this round? Dymphna? Surely it's yers?"

It was Maire, with Ailish and Maeve in tow, hovering over her. Even as Dymphna stared up at the eyes that orbited around her red curls, several cells of her brain registered the bloody cheek—she had bought all six of the rounds! —but then she softened. It was her wedding and Zoë's twenty pound notes after all that were keeping them on board. The girls' flesh was cold and their skimpy clothes were in a state of disarray; they all seemed to have been groped by passersby as they had stood outside gulping down the carcinogens.

"C'mere, youse," Dymphna hissed. "That Bridie McFee one over there has been casting me filthy looks. I'm heart-scared she's gonny do me bodily harm."

They looked over, and when they looked back, Dymphna could see whose side they were on. She could almost hear them weighing the two up in their plastered minds, and Bridie had never bought them free drinks, nor was she marrying up, so there was no chance she might give them a loan if they needed it in the future, which was conceivable.

"I'll claw the face offa her for ye!" Maeve promised. "I could never stick that face of a busted cabbage of hers!"

She lurched away from the table where Dymphna was sat, but Dymphna pulled her back by a belt loop of her sequined Daisy Dukes.

"I've me screwdriver along with me." Maire reached into her handbag, but she had spewed up in it earlier and her fingers struggled to find the weapon in the mire.

"Sit youse here and protect me," Dymphna said. "Ailish, go you to the bar, here's a twenty, and get us another round in. It's me wedding week, and I'm not gonny let that aul skegrat spoil it for me, sure. Laugh, youse! Laugh like we're having the time of wer lives!"

As Ailish raced off to the bar, Maire and Maeve slipped into the nook on either side of Dymphna and roared bawdily. Their lipstick was smeared over their lips, Maeve especially looked as if she were suffering from some tropical disease of the mouth, and Dymphna could smell the stench of man rising from them.

"Take this serviette and clean them hands of yers," Dymphna instructed Maire. "What were youse up to outside? Wile long fags, ye must've been smoking..."

"Och, ye'll never believe it, but yer man from the Indian takeout and his cousin—"

Dymphna yelped as a coaster cracked against her forehead. Flung across the bobbing heads by Bridie. She had always been suspiciously good at volleyball in school; some suspected lesbianism.

"Yer woman hit me!" Dymphna cried, shocked, and mortified. Even as bladdered as she was, some sane part of her brain insisted she just wanted a night out with her bridal party, not to make a scene. Those days of reveling in the drama of drunken kicks and scratches and tugs of the hair and roaring foul abuse with the public urging her on, chanting and clapping and shouting, were gone. She was soon to be a respectable bride. A younger Dymphna would have called Bridie a 'mad bitch,' not 'yer woman.'

Still, Bridie hadn't flung a dart into her forehead, and those were within easy reach. Though maybe she was too drunk to realize. She didn't seem to know where she was.

Maire reached again for her handbag, but Dymphna gave her hand a little slap.

"Sure, let's not lower werselves to her level," she said. Maire and Maeve looked at her as if she were the mad bitch.

Thankfully, Ailish then arrived, and Maire and Maeve forgot about Bridie and her coaster and her glares. They held their glasses up.

"Slainte!" they roared, then guzzled down.

"Laugh, youse!" Dymphna instructed. "Sing!"

"Timber! Woah-ohh-oh-oh, woah woah-oh-oh-oh, woah, oh-oh!"

Then the song ended. Bridie pushed aside shop assistants and shelf stackers alike as Daft Punk started up again and she staggered across the floor like Frankenstein's monster taking his first steps. She gripped surfaces vertical and horizontal to aid her journey through the protesting throngs, table tops, arms and the hoop earrings of one poor lass. Her hoodie hung at a *Flashdance* angle but wasn't meant to, her sneer grew more menacing, and her deranged eyes bored deep into Dymphna...or, to the right of her, no, the left, no deep into her. Bridie seemed to be seeing double, and didn't quite know exactly where in the space time continuum Dymphna actually sat.

Panting with fear, Dymphna looked to her backup. Three heads lolled on the table, dead to the world. They had passed out. Timber. She sprinted as best she could in her heels to the loo. Bridie lumbered behind. Dymphna whimpered in terror as she tore open the door of the ladies. But she hadn't been to the Craiglooner in so long she didn't know management had broken the locks of the stalls as too much had gone on in them. She cursed as she slammed the door to the closest one, and tears welled in her eyes from fear and the stench. She pressed against the door as the music suddenly spewed into the room. Bridie had wrenched open the door to the bathroom. It slammed shut, and the only sounds were the thumping of "Get Lucky" bass and Bridie's steel-toed boots stomping across the filthy tiles.

Whimpering, one hand pressed against the door, Dymphna reached down and tried to undo the strap to her left stiletto. But her fingers shuddered with alcohol and terror. She struggled to kick it off with her right foot. It clattered to the floor just as the door burst towards her.

"I fffounnd yyyee," Bridie slur-growled.

Dymphna cringed under her at the edge of the toilet bowl, arms raised in defense. She peeked under her right elbow at the deranged eyes inching towards her.

"Bridie, why don't we—"

"Ye cunnttt!"

"Och, c'mere, now—"

"Ye whorrre!"

"Ye don't—"

"Ye bidschtch!"

"Have ye—

"Ye slaaggg!"

"Do ye—"

"Miinggger!"

"Me ma—"

"Slaaapper!"

"I—"

"Flimmmmmin tarrttttt!"

Her insults slurred, her steps into the stall staggers, Bridie lunged a fist to Dymphna's right, she lunged a fist to her left. Dymphna wondered briefly if she was now seeing triple.

"I'm with child! Preggers!" Dymphna begged. "Leave me in peace!"

This revelation seemed to make Bridie more determined to inflict pain. She roared like a tortured animal.

"Rry's gvn ye anthr ne?!" Spittle sprayed from her lips. Her head wavered from right to left, heavy on her neck, and she smirked as she clamped eyes on something on the floor behind Dymphna amongst the toilet rolls and empty glasses.

Trembling atop the porcelain circle (the seat had long since disappeared), sensing the freezing water below her shuddering thighs, Dymphna peeked through her arms to see what Bridie was taking hold of.

The plunger inched towards her face. Dymphna screamed. She dreaded to think of what horrors that suction cup had squelched up against. She knew what type of pub it was.

"Bridie! Naw! It's mingin!" Dymphna wailed through the cross of her arms.

"Thsss bse whattyederserved. Frrr allyedone to mee. Ye bidschtch!"

Dymphna jumped from the toilet. The plunger whizzed past her ear. Bridie grunted she flew forward with it. It plopped against the wall and stuck to the broken tiles. Bridie huffed and panted, trying to free it, roars pouring from her mouth.

Dymphna threw back her head. Teetering in one stiletto, she braced herself on the walls of the stall with her hands. She took a deep breath. Her skull sailed forward. Her red curls flew through the air, *crack!* She yelped as her forehead smacked against Bridie's.

"Arrghh...!"

There was a strange moan. Bridie wavered, the whites of her eyes fluttering *Exorcist*-like. Her head lolled as if attached to a spring. Then she crumpled to the floor to the left of the bowl.

Dymphna was shocked at what she had done. She had told herself she would never headbutt again. It hurt her own head too much. She knelt before Bridie and, as she had seen on the telly, felt for a pulse. There was one. She heaved a sigh of relief. She wiped her hands on a piece of loo roll hanging before her nose, Bridie's skin had been slick and sticky to the touch. Then Dymphna stood up, slipped her shoe back on, and stepped over the body.

As she opened the door and Daft Punk enveloped her, and the laughter and the stench of drink and sweat beyond, she muttered, though it pained her to admit it, "Mad bitch."

CHAPTER 15

A surge of sick threatened to shoot up Bridie's throat, but, eyes watering, fingers grasping what she thought was a bedspread, she forced it back down. She didn't know if the nausea was due to her hangover, the rancid stench that hung in the air or some miraculous pregnancy.

Her right eyelid wrenched itself upwards over a congealed eyeball, her left followed suit, and as the haze of drunken torpor slowly lifted, she found that no matter how many times she blinked, she could see nothing. Except black. It didn't smell like her bedroom. It couldn't be her bedroom. The bed was too hard, and it wasn't even a bed. It felt like a floor. Concrete. It wasn't even her house. She sensed she was captive in a cold, damp, windowless prison, and for a thrilling second she wondered if she had been abducted. But her leggings hadn't been interfered with, her hands weren't tethered, and her mouth was free to scream. Where was she? After a night of drunken abuse, she could be waking up anywhere, if her past was anything to go by.

She had heard stories of people on the Continent waking up in a neighboring country after a night on the town, but she didn't have the funds to travel and, besides, those countries, Belgium, France, Holland and whatnot, were all close together, whereas Ireland was by itself and surrounded by sea. The farthest she had woken up was across the border in Buncrana, in the bed of an old sheep farmer with a sweaty arse. It had taken her three hours in pelting rain to hitchhike home.

She dragged her head from what she now suspected wasn't a pillow, and the synapses of her brain were like the graph of an atom splitting, horrified memories of the night before pinging like trails of particles flying this way and that. She didn't really know the details, just saw images of the fag end of the night before, like slides of shame popping up in her brain from all angles: she herself splayed on one of those half-seats at a bus stop down the town, florescent light pounding on her head, rain bucketing down, a checkered shirt, feet entwined atop mounds of rubbish that overflowed from a bin nearby, Kebablicious styrofoam containers, burger wrappers, half-eaten and half-regurgitated chips and pizza and battered sausages, broken beer bottles and plastic containers that once held cider, his filthy trainers, her stockinged foot – she had lost a Doc Marten somewhere—sliding in a pool of curry, his hands thrusting down her top, her cries of delight, the pounding of his limbs against hers, arms too muscular to belong to her one true love, Rory, hair too blonde, too short, the flash of a nose ring, the thrust of a zipper, her head bobbing up and down in his lap, his roars of rapture, the tug of his hands on her hair, the barks of laughter and slurred taunts from strangers staggering by, her flipping them off and diving down for more, the bra being torn from her, her begging for more. And now her lips were chapped, and there were several peculiar pains in her neck.

She was furious and embarrassed at herself. Not because she had made a show of herself in public—that was fine—but because she had given up men for Lent, and it had only begun the day before. The ashes were surely still smeared on her forehead.

"Not again another fecking year!" she muttered. She usually gave up chocolate, but it was torture surviving the 46 days without it, whereas men, well, they were hardly queuing up to sample her maidenly delights. It was a no brainer, she had thought. This year she would gobble down all the Crunchies and Mars and Lions and Fruit and Nut she wanted without an ounce of guilt and arrive at the church on Easter Sunday a few pounds overweight but with the satisfaction of her penance, her suffering for the sake of the Lord her Jesus Christ, done. But, no. She had already failed again in His eyes. Would He forgive her her trespasses?

Bridie moaned and pulled back sheets that crinkled like huge swathes of thick plastic. Then, as she scrabbled around in the darkness, her hand sweeping around to touch something, anything, to anchor herself, she remembered with a sudden spark of hope. She had also thrown in chips for good measure at the last moment, given them up for Lent as well, as it seemed to be cheating to give up something that never came her way. So she could still be redeemed.

Bridie's teeth chattered as she ran her hands up and down both sides of the darkness. She seemed to be hemmed into the tiny space by cardboard boxes. Some were large, some small. She smacked her hands on the concrete, looking for her handbag. No matter how drunk she got, it was always clamped to her side. She found the familiar frayed straps and, relieved, dragged the handbag onto her lap. She rummaged inside and pulled out her phone, clicked it on, and shone the light on the nearest box. This Side Up ↑, she read, disappointed it was in English. So she was probably still in Derry, and in Northern Ireland, after all.

She shone the light further up the box. Spray-No-Mor Urinal Splash Guards. *That's wile odd,* thought Bridie. Then another box appeared: Scrub-Eaze Jumbo Scouring Pads, then Stench Away Air Purifier and Klassy Kaps, Friendly Fingers Fry Vat Gloves and Giganta Wrapped Straws. When she got to Jiffi-Jet Liquid Descaler, pieces of her brain started to click together jigsaw-like, and when she saw Rat-U-Kill and a bucket marked Soiled Towels, she felt like a daft cow. *Och, Bridie, ye're a right eejit, so ye are!* It was the hangover making her thick. How many times had she done the weekly inventory for Kebabalicious, the fast food restaurant she worked at, counting up the splash guards and scouring pads and purifiers and yellow and purple caps...

How had she not recognized the store room? Admittedly, she had never seen it from this angle, and from the triangle of light from her mobile phone before, but, still. *How the flimmin feck did I end up here...?*

She stood up, wavered for a second, hand resting on a tub of plastic forks as her head spun, then stormed through the boxes in one boot and one stockinged foot. She flipped on the light. The pillow was her folded coat, the blankets industrial strength trash bags.

And it all came back from the night before: the queue to the mini-cabs, miles long, peopled by legless, chattering, slobbering, laughing wee girls and lads she knew to see but couldn't stomach. She had staggered up to the end of the line, but the four in front of her were scoffing down battered sausages and chips and snogging the faces off of each other (it was two lads and their girlfriends) and she shrieked at them about filthy, disgusting, shameless public displays of affection, and two handbags materialized as if from the heavens and clattered down on her head time and again and as she crawled backwards away from them (she had fallen by this stage) and as she scrabbled up from the pavement and teetered on two wobbly legs, still roaring abuse at them, the lads launched sausage bits at her like missiles and bellowed with raucous, taunting laughter, and she hugged a lamppost so she didn't topple over again, and she kept hugging it and and staring at the metal of it as the sausage bits rained down on her, and it came to her somehow as she shrieked at them to leave her be that she didn't know where she lived in any event and had no place to tell a cab driver to take her to, and then she was drooling and crying against the coldness of the lamppost and she staggered off sniveling across the cobblestones with one boot and one curry-covered legging onto unknown streets she had grown up in but somehow couldn't now recognize, battering anyone who approached with her handbag and shrieking general insults and sexual slurs into their equally drunken, startled faces. And reaching down and digging the sausage bits out of her cleavage and gobbling them down as tears coursed down her cheeks. She was mortified now as she remembered it. And then she had come across the Kebabalicious door, and it was miraculous, as if she had teleported across time and space to the most marvelous place in the world, the sudden appearance of its battered yellow and purple facade before her as wondrous to her as if it were the Taj Mahal. And somehow in the depths of her drunken brain she knew she held the key to its magical door.

The night classes she had taken at the community college all those years ago had come to nothing. She was now junior assistant manager of Kebabalicious. It was her lot in life. Seven years before, she had taken a part-time job behind the counter of the ChipKebab as a stop-gap, something after school to pay for her pints in the pub until she got a degree in something impressive so she could nab a man with her mind. She knew she couldn't do it with her body or her face. Maybe art history or design, perhaps architecture or forensics. A few years before, the ChipKebab had been bought out by the multinational Kebabalicious chain, and Bridie was suddenly a cog in its relentless wheel, and one day she had woken up and realized her McJob had become her career. And that she was still single. And destined to remain so.

It was her big bones and the cold sores that refused to clear up, she told herself. Not the way she threw herself at every male with a pulse. She occasionally wondered if she suffered from low self-esteem, but then she realized—

She wailed. Pain stabbed her stomach, sweat popped on her brow and weakness attacked her arms and legs. Whimpering, she struggled to wrench open the stockroom door with trembling fingers and raced on rubbery legs to the loos. She made it just in time. And when she was done, she still had the sense of mind to notice the bathrooms hadn't been mopped by the closing shift. She would have to check the staff roster. There would be hell to pay. She hadn't been made junior assistant manager for her charm.

Now that her stomach and intestines were empty, she was consumed with a ravenous, feral hunger. She looked at her watch. Ten fifteen. The first shift wouldn't be in for another hour or so. (The Kebabalicious didn't yet have a breakfast menu, though upper management was considering it). She just might have time to whip up a batch of chips. *Feck Lent.*

She angrily tugged off her one Doc Marten. Hobbling along was driving her mental. She made a beeline for the chip fryer, but even as she did so, her assistant manager eyes noted the night shift's infractions of the closing procedures. The ketchups hadn't been married, the soda dispenser hadn't been wiped down, the trays were in an untidy mound. She'd be passing out quite a few written warnings.

She stared down at the chip fry vat. Flimmin *lazy eejits!* They hadn't siphoned out the lard from the night before. Most other chains had switched over to what their lawyers claimed were a healthier method of frying chips, vegetable oil, but an executive decision had been made at Kebabalicious. Switching over would lose them not only a tradition, but also taste and therefore customers. Lard was natural and had no trans fats. Their lawyers had been nervous, especially when one of the executives (Bridie had heard he had had a few too many pints before the meeting; it was Kebablicious lore) had bleated something about the banning of pig fat being due to the Jewish influence in the US, but a line had been drawn. There was no smoking in pubs, hip hop blared from the radios, but Ireland wasn't quite all America yet, and the chain's chips continued to bubble proudly in pig fat across all 17 stores nationwide.

So Bridie stared down at the handle of the fry basket that was submerged in old, brown lard that had congealed around the fry basket. She turned on the fryer to 360°. The lard would take a few minutes to melt.

And then! As she was inspecting her cold sores in the metallic sheen of the fryer, there was a little explosion in her brain and...Dymphna! In the loos of the Craiglooner! How had she forgotten? Maybe it was the last memory to surface because it was the most troubling. Dymphna had been her best mate since she could remember. She cringed at the memory of attacking her with the plunger. Her face burned with shame. Had it happened before or after the man in the bus stop? Before. No, after. No, before. She had had two boots on then.

As she jiggled the handle of the fry basket a bit (it was still stuck in the slowly-melting lard), hating herself, she saw lodged on her right hand the Claddagh ring, the love, loyalty and friendship ring Dymphna had given her all those years ago. It was a heart with a little crown on top held by two hands. It was made of gold plastic. How many years had Bridie worn it? The shame continued to fill her heart. It was around the same time that Dymphna had been knitting those jumpers and giving them out to everybody she knew. So Dymphna must have been about 12, and Bridie 14. Ten years ago. Bridie had long ago grown out of the jumper, and, indeed, from the fatty flesh the ring was embedded in, she had also outgrown the ring, but she still wore it. It was the only ring she had ever been given, by any gender.

But then Bridie noticed she wore the ring with the point of the heart facing her fingertips. That meant she was single and looking for love. At a glance, everyone knew she was available, and how! The ring would remain steadfastly on her right hand with the heart pointing out, saying...Look at me, Derry City! Lad wanted! Sad old twat in need of love! Available! Forever! And Dymphna's wedding to the man Bridie loved was three days away. She seethed with sudden resentment as her knuckles grew white around the handle of the fry basket and her face, contorted with rage, was basked with heat from the fryer. Dymphna had given it to her only to mock her!

That jammy cunt! She thought. *She deserved all the abuse I gave her. And will this lard never melt? Me stomach thinks me throat's been cut! Hurry on up, ye bastard! I need me fecking chips!*

She looked down. And her eyes couldn't believe what they saw. She blinked, then blinked again. It was impossible! Was her brain so soaked in spent liquor it couldn't process the images her optical nerves were sending? Was that really...?

Her hand recoiled from the handle as if it had been Tasered. The darkened kitchen of the restaurant, the oven and the warning posters and hanging ladles and spatulas, receded from her line of vision. She heaved huge breaths as fear and wonder coursed through her veins in equal measures.

"Dear Lord in Heaven above!" she gasped. "God bless us and save us! I kyanny believe it!"

She backed away from the fryer and cracked her hip on a counter edge. She didn't register the pain. She whimpered and moaned, her eyes drinking in what they were seeing, trying to commit everything to memory for the rest of her life. She gibbered animal-like as she fiddled in her pocket for her phone. She didn't know if she should bless herself, flee or scream. Or all three.

She tugged on her phone, brandished it like a weapon, and fearfully tiptoed to the fryer, dreading and hoping things would still be the same. She cowered and wailed. And snapped as many photos as she could. But her hands were shaking with wonder and fear and excitement. The one photo she actually took would prove to be blurry and useless as evidence later on. But Bridie couldn't know that as she, gasping in terror and awe, she stabbed the button on her phone again and again.

And then she ran shoeless across the tiles, past the counter and out the door, shrieking on the cobblestones like a lamb being slaughtered. Early morning shoppers flinched and stared. And listened to what she was shrieking. Mrs. O'Dowd dropped her shopping bags in alarm. Three cups of apricot yogurt rolled across the cobbles. And Bridie McFee was changed forever.

CHAPTER 16

The *Killer Investors* would save them! When Jed Barnett had hung up the phone, he was shaking. He couldn't believe his good luck. An hour later, he still couldn't. The amazement hadn't worn off. It was like when he had won the lottery all those years ago. That same feeling that one moment in time had transformed his life, everything had changed so that the minute after was a different life to the minute before.

Humming giddily, a new person in a new life, he placed the tray of London Broil beef strips onto the top rack of the oven and flipped the door shut. The middle and bottom shelves were already full. He whipped the flowered mitts off his hands and set the timer, his salt and pepper goatee crinkled into a smile. Two hours. Then he had to flip the strips over and bake them for another two hours. Fifteen strips per tray, times three, was 45. Enough for half a crate. He'd be able to tell the Killer Investors they had loads of inventory.

He sipped Baileys from the wine glass on the counter—there was plenty to celebrate, after all, then stuck the spoon into the jumbo bowl on the counter and stirred in a frenzy. Johnny Cash was singing "Ring Of Fire" on the radio next to the toaster oven. Jed did a little dance as he swirled the beef strips in the marinade. Though there was music and he was humming, he thought he heard a noise upstairs, a clank. It couldn't be Muffins, as the black poodle was nipping at his heels. Then she dug her claws into the checkered polyester of his slacks, wanting to sink her fangs into some uncooked jerky, or, barring that, Jed's thigh. There was another clank. Probably a raccoon, Jed thought, giving Muffins a sliver of jerky from an earlier batch. Those damn creatures were always climbing on the roof. He went back to stirring.

The plastic bowl was big enough for a salad for ten. Jed had thought Ursula looney for buying it; when did they ever eat salad, let alone have eight guests? In fact, considering where they lived in the middle of nowhere, when did they ever have anyone over besides his brother Slim and his wife Louella? And they didn't count as guests because they were family.

But the bowl was perfect for the beef jerky production line in the kitchen. The marinade was soy sauce, Worcestershire sauce, teriyaki and Cajun seasonings, liberal dashes of liquid smoke (which made the beef smell and taste like it had been cooked on a grill in the back yard), and Jed had ground in loads of black pepper. Jed and Slim didn't like the fine, powdery pepper for their beef jerky. That was for wimps. They liked the coarse, freshly-ground grains that were almost chunks. They gave their beef jerky—called Slim Jed's Jerky—an extra kick. And, finally he had added Ursula's secret ingredient.

She had been helping him in the kitchen a year before and accidentally grabbed the wrong shaker for the marinade and added into the mix a generous helping of something that nobody in their right mind would expect to be in beef jerky. But the taste was amazing. This secret ingredient, Ursula's mistake, is what set Slim Jed Jerky apart from all the others on the market, if the lip-smacking and groans of content from their customers were anything to go by. And the reorders! They were pouring in from all the stores in the area! Now he was envisioning Slim Jed Jerky, his fourth child, on the shelves of convenience stores and gas stations and supermarkets from coast to shining coast. Once the Killer Investors invested in him, Slim, Ursula and Louella. He wondered if all five Knights might decide to invest together. It had happened before, back in season three; he had watched all the old episodes on YouTube for pointers. Now all the Barnetts would be on YouTube in the future. How many hits would their episode get?

"Wa-hooo!"

He dragged another handful of dripping beef strands onto yet another baking tray (they would have to dry there for an hour) and shook his head in wonder. Jed would've never believed that he, a former naval petty officer who had spent a lifetime surrounded by communist aggressors, would now be surrounded by marinated beef, on the verge of overtaking the world with a secret spice.

He reached down to give Muffins another strip, but the dog had disappeared, maybe to inspect the clanks upstairs. She didn't like raccoons. Jed lined up all the strips, then wiped the sweat from his brow with a dirty dishrag and looked at his watch. He wiped up a bit; that would give Randaleen less to clean when she came. Truth be told, she scared Jed a bit. He went outside for a smoke, taking the wine glass with him. He couldn't wait for Ursula to arrive to tell her the good, no, the fantastic, news. It would give her something to talk about besides that damn Randaleen. He had tried his wife's cell phone, but it was switched off. It always was when she was at bingo.

Ursula never spent a Thursday at home, and even though their cleaner with her alleged light fingers was making his wife a frazzled mess, she hadn't changed her schedule . She had the morning bingo with Louella, then the soup kitchen (she would still volunteer, she had told Jed, because she didn't think Randaleen would have the brass neck to show up, hand outstretched while Ursula's earrings jangled on either side of her head, and even if she did, Ursula was supposed to be behaving as if she didn't know she was a thief, and, besides, why should the other unfortunates who went there for a hot meal suffer because of one rotten apple?), then choir practice. Jed called it in his mind Ursula's Trifecta, which maybe showed he had been betting a bit too much. And gambling was what had gotten them into such a mess the month before in the first place. But after that phone call from the show's production office, it was a mess that would take them to a better place. He was sure.

He didn't understand why Ursula didn't just call the police and get the scuzzy creature locked up. He didn't mind the sunglasses, they had only cost $10. He missed his binoculars. But he had been at his wife's side for decades, and knew the circular logic of Ursula's mind. Circular? Maybe labyrinth-like was more apt. Others might not fare so well running to the police with such scant or even total lack of evidence, but Ursula had a special relationship with a detective on the local police force, Inspector Scarrey. But, whatever. Jed gulped down more Baileys—he was feeling quite giddy now—and lit up another cigarette. Randaleen was a minor irritation now that the world had suddenly opened its arms to him and his beefy jerky. He tried to think back to how he had arrived at this point. He was surprised and a bit mortified to realize it had been his gambling.

Besides giving Ursula support, affection and a listening ear (when the TV was turned down), and between running the store with Slim, taking out the garbage, his occasional bird watching, and fishing in the nearby creek, Jed's life revolved around trips to casinos on Indian reservations, and there was a wide array of them in Wisconsin. He had dabbled in online gambling for a while, as well, but the US government had started to crack down on it. When Jed was on the verge of asking one of the whizz kids who did the website for their store to reroute his IP address to Tajikistan, he realized he was being silly, and that online gambling was boring in any event. He liked the feel of the slot machine buttons, the bells and whistles that rang out around, the thick fug of cigarette smoke that hung in the air, and the waitresses that plied him with free alcohol. No. That wasn't it at all. He knew the *real* reason he didn't gamble online anymore:

That night a month earlier unfolded in his mind like a moment of madness. As he crushed the cigarette butt under his shoe and made his way back into the house, he was barely able to understand now how he had done what he had done. He felt ashamed. He remembered being caught up in the excitement, adrenaline heaving through his veins as he hovered over the computer keyboard, having wittered away $5000 of the business account on the online poker championship, and then transferring $10,000 more, then $5000. He kept losing and losing. And losing. He couldn't understand it. Where had his luck gone? Finally he had crawled into bed beside a sleeping Ursula, and as he kissed her on the cheek and she mumbled something, the shock of it reached his brain. He had gambled away $20,000 of the business' money. How could he tell Slim?

He didn't. For a week, he prayed Slim wouldn't check the business account, and every time he shopped for supplies at the wholesalers for the beef jerky, every time he had to pay for a purchase order for the hot sauce or guns or bait for the store, he had mental mathematics racing through his brain with each swipe of the card, each swipe causing him to steel himself for that dreaded word, declined.

It was a far cry from the heady days after the lotto win in Ireland, even after they had bought the two cars and the house and there wasn't much money left and they had Ursula's family attacking them from all angles, hands outstretched, demanding more of what no longer existed. Now he was in a worse position than he had been in before the lotto win. Jed was always hoping lightning would strike twice, but he felt only that lightning had struck once...and the bolt of electricity had deranged his brain. The future looked glum. And one day at the bait wholesalers—he had a shopping cart brimming with grub worms, locusts and minnows—the teenager behind the counter had swiped Jed's card, looked down at the machine, then looked up at Jed. And smirked. Jed's heart fell. He knew what that knowing smirk meant. Declined!

He remembered the meeting at the store with his brother the next day. "Tough love," Slim had called it. Well, Slim could take his 'tough love' and shove it. That's what Jed thought at the time.

"Don't sweat the small stuff," Jed had tried.

"Small stuff?! Are you outta your goddamn mind? We ain't got no cash flow no more! How are we gonna get by?"

And—Jed was still startled at the memory—Slim, who tipped the scales at 350, had lunged towards him, knocked his younger brother into the counter, sending Hot Trout Lure kits and bottles of hot sauce flying, and wrestled him to the ground. Jed's cowboy hat rolled on the floor as he tried to fight back, but his brother's tonnage atop him made all attempts in vain. Slim wrenched the wallet out of Jed's back pocket as Jed wriggled and panted and puffed on the floor beneath him. He flipped it open, found the business credit card, brandished it in the air like bowling trophy, then snapped it in two.

As they sat on opposite ends of the store, nostrils flaring and beads of sweat on their brow, Slim had finally said, "I'm sorry, Jed, but I had to do it. We gotta save the business."

"Aw, come on, Slim. You should've let me keep it for one more week. I feel a big win coming in my bones."

The look Slim had given him!

"Your bones have always been wrong, bud. Well, except that time you won the lotto. But that's ancient history now. Maybe you wanna look into this."

He got up, riffled behind the counter for a while, then wheezed as he made his way across the wooden floor towards Jed. He handed Jed a pamphlet. Are You In Control, Or Are The Horses? Twenty Questions To Help You Find The Answer. It was from a group in the Gamblers Anonymous vein.

"I haven't gone to a racetrack in years," Jed said, somewhat miffed.

"Change 'the horses' for 'online roulette wheel', or 'the ping of a slot machine in a casino on an Indian reservation,' I don't care. Whatever excites you most. But I think you need help. You're running this business—*our* business—into the ground. Think of your kids, your grandkids. How many you got now?"

Jed counted.

"Four."

"Think of those little kids with no inheritance. Whittled away. Think of them having to pay off your debt when you bite the dust, kick the bucket, or should I say cash in your chips?"

Jed thought.

"Aw, come on, Slim. Just one more week. There's a big online poker championship Wednesday night. I already signed up for it."

Slim looked down at his brother in dismay. He shook his head, his cheeks wobbling.

"We...could go on *Attack of the Killer Investors!*" Jed suggested. He looked up hopefully.

Slim crossed his arms across his heft.

"What the heck is that?"

"You ever seen *Shark Tank?* Or even *Dragons Den?* That's the English version. I think Canadian, too. And maybe Australian. It's a reality TV show."

"I don't care what it is. All I know is we got bills we need to pay. And a snowball's chance in Hell of paying them! You wanna end up in the gutter? With Ursula sitting next to you?"

"There are five millionaires, well, four millionaires and a billionaire, at least on *Attack,* and they're all investors. They want to help fledgling or floundering businesses. But at a price. We gotta give them a percentage of the company. We get twenty minutes to pitch to them, though I think they cut that down to ten on the show. And then they give us the money we need. We're one of the floundering businesses. They don't usually get picked, but with the reorders on the jerky... I think you can apply online, and just send them a video or something. We've got that camcorder. Really, Slim, with Slim Jed Jerky, I think we got a chance. They just might back us."

Slim seemed on the verge of telling him to get the hell out and never come back, but then a look came over his face.

"We gotta make a video, you say?"

"I...I think so...?"

"We can have Ursula sing the jingle I wrote."

Jed cringed. "Yeah, I guess so..."

"Hmm! I was gonna yell at you some more, but now I don't know what to do. That might be a good idea. I don't know. Lemme ask Louella what she thinks. She and Ursula would have to go on TV with us. And you know how Lou always wanted to be a movie star."

So the next day they made the video and sent it off. A week later they were told they had been rejected. Jed had cried as he deleted the email.

But now...! It was true, the show would be difficult. They regularly ridiculed businesses. It was a much harsher version of *Shark Tank* and *Dragon's Den,* more like the *Gong Show.* Instead of, "I'm out!" the catchphrase to entrepreneurs they didn't want to back, the Killer Investors yelled, "Get lost!" The female one always said, "Get lost!" apologetically, but the others weren't so nice.

Jed lit a second cigarette, then a third. Then he went back into the kitchen. The house seemed strange, different. As if another presence were there. Muffins yelped from upstairs. Alarmed, Jed tried to make his way through the kitchen, but the Baileys was working its magic and it seemed a chore to maneuver through the stools and the chairs and around the island. And then Muffins came bounding down and raced towards Jed. She was skittish and jumpy and seemed as if she were eager to tell Jed something. But Jed, of course, couldn't understand what the dog was trying to say, though he had once seen *Dr. Doolittle,* the original with Rex Harrison, not the Eddie Murphy one, with Ursula and the kids at a drive in back in the days when they had them and had quite enjoyed it. Then the front door rattled, and Ursula came flouncing in.

"Jeddd!" she squealed with glee, racing towards him. She flung her purse to the counter and raced to him, arms wide. Jed took a step back in alarm. She smothered him as she jumped up and down. Jed almost toppled over. "Ye'll never credit it, Jed! I've just won $1000 at the bingo! I kyanny believe it!"

She let him go and beamed at him, eyes shining with delight.

"On a Stamp and Four Corners, it was!" She flipped open her purse and tugged out wads of money. She threw them in the air.

"Wow!" Jed said, watching the bills flutter onto table, the floor and the drying beef strips. "That's fantastic! And, double wow! You know what else happened, honey? Someone pulled out of *Attack of the Killer Investors*! They asked us to take their place. Tomorrow!"

"Ye're joking!" Ursula squealed with glee."Och, Jed! Marvelous, so it is!"

She wailed and grabbed his hands, just as the twanging opening bars of Anne Murray's "Could I Have This Dance"came from the radio.

"And Jed! It's wer song!"

Jed was shocked. It *was* their song! They sang it on stage at karaoke together every second Friday at the roadhouse down the rural route. Lightning was striking right, left and center. But this was good lightning. Anne Murray began to sing.

"Och, it's perfect," Ursula whispered, her lips close to his right earlobe. "It's a sign from the Lord, Jed. Things are gonny be alright."

Jed looked down at her and smiled. Ursula wrapped her arms around his bulk. He slid his right arm around her waist, took her left hand in his right and held it up. And they slowly waltzed there on the kitchen floor atop the tens and twenties. It there had been more lighting in the kitchen and if the angles had been just right their wedding bands might have sparkled.

Jed sang the chorus when it came. *"Could I have this dance...for the rest of my life?"* He sang baritone. Tears welled in Ursula's eyes. Her heart flooded with love. Her heels scraped against the tiles. Muffins scratched at their feet. Ursula gave the dog little kicks. Could she have that dance for the rest of the song at least? But the dog kept scratching. And then she barked. And kept barking. And then she ran away.

The song ended. An ad for panty liners began. Jed and Ursula parted. They smiled. They knew a memory had been made, filed away to be taken out again and again, forever. He would have told her he loved her, but she already knew. She didn't need to hear it. Jed turned to the beef jerky. Ursula stooped to pick up her winnings.

"Och, Jed! I'm trembling with that much excitement about that program! What am I gonny wear for the telly? And Slim and Louella are to be coming with us, aye?"

"Yeah."

"I should ring her so we can coordinate wer outfits."

"They should be here soon. I called them to let them know the good news. We have to practice our pitch."

"Why didn't ye tell me? The state of me hair! And I've to run meself a bath."

"You know you have to sing the jingle before the millionaires, right?"

"Aye, I'm well aware. I'm heartscared, but, and only because I feel like a daft eejit singing it. All them cameras! Still, there be's piles more people jammed into that church on Christmas Eve when I be's singing in the choir. And what's all this palaver about a pitch? Doesn't that be about baseball?"

"Me and Slim have to make sure our numbers are in order. We need to offer the Knights a percentage of the business that makes sense based on our projected earnings for the next three years, taking into account that the money we ask for will cover all the extra expenses we need to pay for what we plan to make the business more successful. To branch out, future lines and all that. It needs to be enough of a percentage for them to be interested, but not enough so that we'll lose the desire to wake up each morning to run the business."

Ursula's jaw was slack.

"I'm sorry, Jed, but I haven't a clue what ye're on about. Anyroad, it's gonny be ye and Slim what does all the talking. Sure, nobody understands a word I say here in the States, and I haven't a head for numbers in any event. After I sing, Louella and me's just to stand there and smile, aye? Can I help ye in some manner, way or form right now?"

"No. I've just got to wait for the timer to go to turn the jerky around."

"Right. I'm away off to run me bath, love. I think I'll use them special bath salts from the Dead Sea ye got me for me last birthday. Today be's a special day!"

She smiled. She reached forward and pinched Jed on the behind. He yelped, but he was happy. And then she left the kitchen.

The ads segued into "Elvira," but Ursula was still humming Anne Murray as she made her way through the living room.

She loved Slim, but didn't know about this jingle of his. It seemed silly, but maybe that was she was used to singing hymns. But maybe Americans liked this type of thing. Who could say? She didn't know what Americans might like. She had lived amongst them now for almost more than half her life, and along the way she had bits of American culture she had embraced, ice cubes, for instance, and hot summers. With air conditioning attached. But this strange jingle? Would the investors like it? She'd soon find out!

Ursula frowned at some noise from upstairs. It sounded like a clanking with some panting and grunting. She shrieked as she stepped on what she thought was a human hand, but it was only Muffins' rubber bone. And then Ursula wondered what was wrong with the dog, and where she had gone. She stood and listened. She could hear nothing. Maybe it had been one of the raccoons. She passed the coffee table, then headed down the corridor. She placed her hand on the post, then climbed the stairs.

—and shrieked at the sight of Randaleen, halfway up the stairs, hands stretched up the wall, reaching for another ceramic head, a gym bag bursting with loot at her side.

"Jedddd! She's here!"

Randaleen pushed Ursula to the side and raced through the living room. All Ursula could think as she panted there on the stairs was that Randaleen's greasy hair didn't move an inch no matter how fast she was running.

In the kitchen, Jed shrieked at Randaleen as she shrieked at him, both just as scared of each other. Jed grabbed the bowl and threw it at her. The marinade sailed through the air and spattered on her back. She flung herself out the door and down the lawn. Ursula was at Jed's side as he roared at Randaleen through the door. Randaleen reached the gate, jumped on her motorcycle, revved up, sped off down the road, and Ursula still marveled at her stiff hair—

and then there was a squeal of rubber and a scream from Ursula and a gasp from Jed as Randaleen crashed into Slim's Ford pick up as it rounded the corner.

CHAPTER 17

When Fionnuala had dragged her matted bleached locks from the greasy pillowcase, Paddy's side of the bed was empty, a tangle of slightly soiled bedsheets. He had risen two hours before to get to the plant. Her throbbing head was aware that she was facing the new gray dawn alone. She had two unexpected traitors to tackle: Lorcan and her body.

All these years, she had trusted them both to behave as they should. She had long ago given up expecting her body to defy the passage of time—a glance in the mirror, however scuffed, sufficed to let her know this had not happened—and decades of heavy drinking and sucking down the carcinogens and shoveling down carbohydrates, fats, both trans and saturated, preservatives and additives galore had slowly taken their toll. But, until yesterday, her body had always been able to function properly, just as Lorcan had always jumped at her every command. How things changed from one day to the next! Now Lorcan was abandoning her, and there was a horrid mystery illness attacking her from within. Her body was betraying her just as much as her beloved son. Both had to be dealt with. Lacking seven years of medical training, she would have difficulty tackling her body. Lorcan would be easier. But how? Her brain cells trundled.

She had slurped two cups of sweet and milky tea alone in the cold, damp kitchen, practiced a croaky, frail voice from the top of her throat for a few moments, then dialed Zoë Riddell's number to call in sick. No amount of pitiful theatrics down the line about a head hitting the concrete, children, infants and a toddler left defenseless in a deadly area of town, or a barrage of tests and blood samples could chip at Zoë's granite heart, so went Fionnuala's thinking.

"Mrs. Flood, Mrs. Flood, Mrs. Flood," Zoë sighed down the line in an I've-got-the-patience-of a-saint manner. "Your daughter called in with a similar mystery illness just yesterday." Each clearly articulated 't' of the woman's West Brit accent was like an awl in Fionnuala's ear. "You know your colleague Una's on holiday, and Rory is unable to cover your shift. He has a special seminar on in Belfast, something to do with database development. And if you recall, my dear, you yourself phoned in with a similar excuse the week before last. In much the same voice." Fionnuala growled inwardly. She had forgotten her and Paddy's anniversary two Thursdays ago, and they had overindulged in the whiskey. She still couldn't find her belt. "Don't forget, Una will be back tomorrow, and then you will have three free days. Which coincide with the wedding, Do please have a sense of responsibility, dear. And speaking of responsibility, how is the wedding cake coming along? You haven't shown me anything yet, and, as I'm sure you know, everything else has been ordered and has arrived and been inspected and is ready to go. In my mind, though, there's only an outline, somewhat vague and perplexing, about what this cake should be, rather like a black hole, if you will. I must remind you there are only two days left to the big day. I'll feel more secure if I know at least what flavor the cake is meant to be. And I'm quite concerned about the wedding gown you insisted on taking for these mysterious alterations. You have me so scared about it. Please, *please,* Mrs. Flood, handle it with extreme care. It's a Vera Wang, as I've told you many times, very delicate and you've no idea how exclusive. As I've said all along, I'm quite willing to pitch in if you find yourself struggling. But if you *are* struggling, and do please listen to me, darling, I don't think shirking your job, the one reliable source of income you possess, is helping the matter any. Now, I'm afraid I have to be at a meeting, so I must dash. But I think perhaps we should meet up. I'll take you out to lunch and we can discuss everything. Please, though, do go to your work."

"I'll be there," Fionnuala barked into the little holes of the receiver.

And here she was indeed, behind the counter of Amelia Earhart's Exploreworld Interactive Centre, with nothing to smile about, though her lips were stretched into an upward configuration she hoped was welcoming. From the bottles of water clutched in the hands of the family of four walking through the door, and the peculiar cut of their flash clothes, she knew they were American tourists. Fionnuala had experienced a moment of confusion because they weren't staring down, captive, at expensive iPhones, as they all seemed to do nowadays. But now they were smiling back at her, the parents at least, and from the look of those teeth Fionnuala knew they could only be Yanks.

She had slammed down the phone on Zoë, taken a whore shower (a quick swipe of the armpits and private areas with a damp rag), used the loo—because a quick look at the instructions told her she could—guzzled a third tea, then arranged her ponytails. Worried about that third tea, she had twisted the mammoth red plastic jug, along with Dr. Chandrapore's harrowing instructions, into her Celine Dion/Titanic satchel and trudged, scowling, down the town to work, mortified at the way the top of the jug poked out of the top of the satchel and pressed against her upper arm and a rib. That's how big the flimmin jug was! Exposed for all the world to see! She was mortified.

She now turned to what she supposed was the mother. Probably the step-mother, she thought, as all Yanks seemed to be divorced. *Heathens!* But rich heathens ripe for the fleecing. And now that her elaborate scheme of faking Dymphna's death to pry funds from Mrs. McDaid had failed, Fionnuala needed money. As Zoë had pointed out, another day at the interactive center was another day to earn money. But she would earn more than her paycheck. Much, much more, if the family's teeth were anything to go by. She had seen a program on the telly about how expensive dental work was in the States. Now Fionnaula's returning smile was genuine. If wily.

"Welcome, all, to Amelia's Exploreworld!" she said over the swing music that always blared in the center. She knew the charm of her accent would endear her to them, it would be like shamrocks and pots of gold spilling out of her mouth to them, no matter what lurked in her brain. "Are youse a wee bit hot there? We've a cloakroom here," she suggested, motioning behind her and hoping they wouldn't see it was only the office. "A coat check, I believe youse all call it in yer land. Youse can make use of it if need be."

"Oh, that's great," said the father, wriggling out of his jacket. "It *is* a bit...stuffy in here."

The mother and teenage boy and girl did likewise, gratefully, and Fionnuala kept smiling as she snatched up the belongings and clutched them, captive, in her hands.

"That's £5 per item." She said it with the same smile.

As they exchanged looks, taken aback, the husband reached reluctantly for his wallet. Fionnuala turned and entered the office, tossed the jackets and coats onto the floor, then came back out, hand outstretched for the twenty pound note.

Though the day was turning out to be unseasonably warm, very un-Derry-like, the first thing she had done when she opened up the center was turn up the heat. Full blast. And it wasn't to increase Zoë's heating bill, though that was an extra perk.

"And I must take yer handbag and all," she said apologetically to the mother, having grabbed the twenty. And then the first sudden urge hit her in her bladder. She faltered slightly, and fought to ignore it. "A-and them backpacks of the wanes, the, erm, the children, no, the teens."

"Do you want us to pay for them too?" asked the father, a vein throbbing on his forehead.

"Och, naw. Free of charge, it is. Youse looks wile respectable, so youse do, but we've hordes of thieving gits in and out that door since the very day we opened, so it be's now company policy not to let in bags of any sort. Ye've not a clue what them knackers has had the bold face cheek to lift from wer museum!

A display of Amelia's favorite breath mints, gone. Them X-rays of her broken ankle from when she was nine, ripped from the wall. Disgraceful, so it was. But that's filthy knackers for you. The town be's heaving with em. And, of course, youse must know wer town's history, and ye never know who might be lugging around a bomb with them. There still be's bomb scares, ye know, even after all these years."

The woman looked suddenly fearful as she handed over her bag.

"Are we in any danger in this part of town?" she asked.

Fionnuala snatched the bags and backpacks and hid them behind the counter. She'd root through them later. The urge to urinate was getting stronger. She cursed herself for having drunk all that tea. She knew what the doctor's orders were, what she had to do today. And that now, thanks to Zoë, she had to do it away from the privacy of her own home. But she couldn't live without tea. She focused on the woman's plucked eyebrows.

"Only after dark, when the pubs let out. Like the Troubles never ended, them streets be's at that time, a no-man's land of wild packs of lads up to their eyeballs on E and armed with bricks and ready fists and I dunno quite what, rocks flying through the air for no reason that I can fathom, and right bladdered gangs of scantily-clad tarts roaring abuse at all and sundry and spewing up loads of sick whichever way their necks are turned. Now, the entrance fee be's £15 each—"

"But the online guide said—"

"Cash only, like, and an additional £10 if youse want to take some photos. We've marvelous things inside, so we do, so youse'll probably want to snap away as if there was no tomorrow. Ye'll find not only a three-quarter scale mock up of yer woman's plane, the Friendship, a Lockheed Vega 5B, so they say it is, but half a real propeller from the same type of plane and all, and then ye've got her lavatory, sections of the fuselage, several cartons of her type of fags, Lucky Strikes, real ones from the 1930's, I don't mind pointing out, and piles of scarves and goggles what was worn by similar female fliers from the same time, aviators, they was called, what few there was, ye understand, females ones, I mean. And for the two of youse," she nodded at the horrible teens, "There be's video games where youse can sit on a seat similar to the ones on yer woman's plane and make like youse are flying across the Atlantic back in 1932. Which of youse what hits the fewest birds and clouds goes and wins. And, best of all, there be's a life-sized cutout of the famous woman herself ye can pose with. Wonderful for the Christmas cards, so it is. Ye can actually wrap yer arms round her shoulders like she was yer mate. I could take one of all of youse surrounding her if youse'd like? "

"Would I have to pay you for that too?" the father asked, an edge to his voice.

Fionnuala kept smiling, though under the counter her upper thighs twisted inwards towards each other.

"That I'd be happy to do free of charge, like."

"Don't bother, Dad. Let's just get our stuff back and clear outta here," said the son, and the mother seemed relieved her boy had spoken up and turned to her husband as if to say she agreed, but Fionnuala had already snatched the money from his hand and locked it in the till. She was happy to see he had included the the photo-taking fee, or maybe he hadn't but she wasn't about to give him any change. The man was looking down at his yawning wallet, and he seemed to be wondering how and when the money had been taken from it. One moment it was there, the next it was in the till. The boy continued, "This place looks crappy. Lame. And I don't know what that thing about fags was, but I wanna steer clear."

Cheeky wee bastard, Fionnuala thought as she pressed the tickets into the father's hand.

"Fags be's cigarettes."

"I don't wanna go in there either, Daddy, it smells strange," whined the girl.

Cheeky wee cunt.

"Maybe it's better if we just leave, Richard," whispered the mother.

"Youse've already paid, but. And there be's no returns."

That's why Fionnuala always turned on the heat first thing. After already paying £20 for a service they assumed was free, very few fathers demanded their coats back and shepherded their families out. They were going to enjoy the center if it killed them. The look on the father's face said just that.

"Oh, it's not so bad. Now that we know homosexuals aren't involved, ho ho! It'll be fun. We get to climb inside her plane. It's the chance of a lifetime! Where else can you do it but here? Come on, guys, lets go in."

The girl was staring at the corridor which led to the center—there was a flashing neon sign that said This Way to Exploreworld!—with the same contempt she would give an old person. She flipped her hair and folded her arms.

"Amelia Earhart sucks," she said. "This music sucks."

"This whole town sucks," said the boy. "And the people are freaks."

The lone eye visible through the mess of gelled hair glared at Fionnuala defiantly, and her hand twitched uncontrollably beside the till. She forgot all about her frequent, sudden urge. Here she almost did the mother/step-mother's job for her; she had read on the Internet somewhere that Yanks were forbidden by Yank law from touching their children. She didn't know if it were true, but she would be happy to smack the entitlement off their whinging, whiny faces. How dare this ugly, over-nourished, entitled bag of shite insult her beloved hometown! And the wee slag-in-the-making with the pout she wanted to kick off her face Amelia Earhart and the Andrews Sisters!

"They're still suffering from jet lag," the mother said by way of explanation, and a weak one it was, but it was no excuse, and Fionnuala couldn't stomach the affectionate way she took her daughter's shoulder and shoved her towards the entrance. She wondered if that counted as touching and she could get the woman arrested by the Yank authorities. There was a consulate over in Belfast. The boy loped after them, and the father took up the protective stance in the rear. He turned around and gave Fionnuala a thunderous look, then followed them in.

She leaned across the counter and, she knew she was pressing it but there was no harm in trying, who dares wins and all that, she called out in a singsong voice over *Chattanooga Choo Choo,* "We've personal guided tours and all if youse are interested. Twenty-five quid. Quite a bargain, so it is." She nodded and smiled and gave half a wink but it was all to the father's back.

"We'll pass on the tour," he said in a clipped tone, not even turning around. Fionnuala was taken aback as he flipped her off, and not the two-fingered V she was used to, and used often, but the horrible American one she had seen in films with the middle finger pointing up. What a shocking way for a father to behave! But Fionnuala wasn't bothered. She'd be out £25, but would have more time to go through their things if she weren't conducting the tour. And that would be worth far more than £25, if the past few weeks while Una was on holiday were anything to go by. As excited as she was, she was still angered by the teens' terrible remarks. Taking this family for all they were worth would give her a great and special pleasure.

The city and Amelia's record-breaking solo flight across the Atlantic in 1932 were inextricably linked. There was a special affinity, a bond between her and many of the people of Derry, especially the older ones. The aviation heroine held a special place in their hearts. Although Amelia had planned to land in Paris as the first woman to fly transatlantic, she had somehow ended up in a pasture in Culmore, a few miles north of Derry. Fionnuala still didn't understand it. There must have been something wrong with their maps back then, she always thought. Paris and Derry couldn't be more different.

Paddy's father or his grandfather, or maybe a great uncle, Fionnuala hadn't been told exactly who, but one of the many Patrick Floods, had been there in Culmore as she touched down, a teenager guzzling down the drink in an adjacent pub, but in the vicinity nevertheless. There was a photo of him leaning against the plane for support as proof. The photo still had pride of place on the mantelpiece of their home, though it was difficult to make out, not because it was black and white and blurry or almost a century old, though it was all three, but because Fionnuala had never gotten around to dusting its frame.

The Floods had taken a bus to see the famous site a few years before. A bus with no shock absorbers and blaring rave music carted them over the moors, through marauding packs of pigs and sheep, and onto the clearing where, a century before, Amelia Earhart and her plane had landed.

The field used to house an Amelia Earhart museum, but it had closed due to lack of funding during some economic downturn. And, indeed, the paltry number of visitors its remote location afforded it. The Floods themselves, when they had gone, had spent more time in the neighboring penny arcade and the pub than in the actual field itself. They had lasted three minutes in the museum, and had only entered anyway because it was free. They weren't ones for museums.

In a move that had made her a shoe-in for the short list of Derry Businesswoman of the Year, Zoë Riddell had decided to expand her portfolio and open a new, more interactive shrine to the great lady—she apparently admired Amelia Earhart dearly—but this time in Derry itself, where it would have a higher profile and attract more visitors. It had opened to great fanfare the year before, when Derry had been the UK's City of Culture, and many marveled at its sleek, modern design. The clean lines of the design were still there a year on, marred only by the inch of dust that clung to every surface except the buttons of the till.

As Fionnaula carried the bags into the office, she knew time was of the essence. There wasn't much in the center to keep the horrid little family entertained, and though she still had to wee, she couldn't without rereading the instructions Dr. Chandrapore had given her. They were very confusing. And the act itself seemed like it would be a production of sorts. She had to go through their belongings while she knew she had the time. She pressed the sudden urge to the back of her mind as, with hands shuddering both with excitement and the urge to relieve herself, she perched herself delicately on the revolving chair at the desk and pawed through the teens' backpacks.

There was nothing of use nor ornament to her. More bottles of water in both —*why* did they always cart them around?—in the girl's, strawberry and kiwi lip glosses, a tampon and hair accessories, in the boy's, a violent fantasy graphic novel, an iPod, an iPad, strange American gum and what seemed like crusty socks. Her fingers twitched as they wound first round the iPod and then his iPad, but she had to let them go. She knew she would be a fool to take both, or even one. He would notice immediately.

It was only when she sprung open the mother's purse that she offered up a quick prayer of thanks to the Lord. She pawed through the packs of tissues and bottles of hand sanitizer—another clue to a Yank—and finally rested her claws on the wallet. It looked like crocodile leather, purple yet real. She pried it open, and her eyes drank in the seven credit cards lined up in their neat little slots. Only an amateur would take them all. But it would take the mother a while to realize one small card was missing. So not the Black Amex. She faltered a second, then chose a lowly-looking Visa. She pinched it with eager fingernails and eased it out of its slot, then slipped it into her satchel, which was propped against the desk. She didn't want it on her person until she reached a ready till. Who knew what body searches the PSNI might subject her to on a whim; she was Catholic, after all.

As she slipped the wallet back in, she noticed she was nestling it next to some Kleenex Moist Wipes, and these reminded her of the harsh barks for service from her bladder. She realized suddenly sweat was trickling down her face, and it had nothing to do with the unbearable heat. Her hands and legs shuddered. The feelings of accomplishment and excitement were now tempered by the pain in her nether regions. She'd have to forgo their pockets.

Grieving, she picked up her satchel and made her way to the counter on weak legs twisted at the knees. She tiptoed toward the entrance of the center, and over the strains of *Boogie Woogie Bugle Boy,* she heard the beeps and blings of the video game, the boy's unhinged laughter, and the splat! splat! splat! of one bird after another being murdered by the plane. The deranged creature was losing on purpose. He reminded Fionnuala of her Padraig, except she could always see both of Padraig's eyes. She heard the father's laughter, the girl's squeals of delight, and the mother's coos. They seemed to be amused. She should have time for that bathroom break after all.

There was no staff loo, so she'd have to use the customers" opposite the entrance. She opened the bathroom door and realized with a sinking heart the lock was always broken. Zoë had never gotten around to sending someone in to fix it. If that Yank girl or her mother came in and saw her while she was in the middle of... Fionnuala shuddered at the thought.

She looked around the little cubicle, but found nothing to prop the door shut with. She would have to use her hand. She pulled the jug out of the satchel, placed it between the door and the toilet, and took out the instructions.

No, there had not been a team of experts specially called in for her at Altnagalvin. She had only said that to cause her family alarm. The first test to come back while she was still in with Dr. Chandrapore had shown there was, he said, a extremely large amount of protein leaking from her kidneys into her bloodstream. He seemed alarmed, so so was she. And she had asked what might cause that. There were various likely causes, he had said. She had asked and asked again, but the doctor wouldn't commit to what these 'various causes,' nor their eventual outcome for her health and life expectancy, might be. They would have to wait for more test results. And anyway, this was a surprise new find. It couldn't have anything to do with her fainting spell.

What was protein, anyroad? Fionnuala asked herself. It sounded like it should be good, so one would think extra protein in her system should be making her healthier. But Dr. Chandrapore seemed to disagree, and he was the expert so he ought to know. Maybe, thought Fionnuala, the problem was that is was leaking from her kidneys. Anyway, she would have to collect a 24-hour urine sample and deliver it to the hospital within two days.

The instructions were written in large capital letters, as if problems with her kidneys somehow affected her eyesight. She read:

FIRST, EMPTY YOUR BLADDER UPON RISING IN THE MORNING AND DISCARD THE URINE. When she had first read that the day before, she had almost rung the hospital to tell them they hadn't given her a bladder with her kit, but then she realized they must mean a bladder inside her own body, and that it meant doing a wee. She had already risen and already emptied her bladder, but then this morning she had faltered, as 'discarding the urine' sounded like she had to throw it in the garbage. But then she realized if she just flushed, that was discarding.

SECOND, FROM THAT TIME FORWARD, COLLECT ALL URINE DURING THE DAY AND NIGHT, AND ADD IT TO THE COLLECTION CONTAINER. She had been confused about this step as well, because she couldn't understand why, where or how she could 'collect' her urine and then, at some later stage, add it to the container (which she guessed was the jug). But now she realized she'd have to forgo the 'collection' step and just move on to going to the bathroom in it, regardless of the complicated instructions. That was where her wee was supposed to wind up, after all.

FROM THAT TIME FORWARD, COLLECT ALL URINE DURING THE DAY AND NIGHT, AND ADD IT TO THE CONTAINER. So she would have to do it for 24 hours. Regardless of where she was. Which meant the jug would have to stay at her side, ready for action.

THE FINAL COLLECTION WILL BE THE NEXT MORNING SPECIMEN. EMPTY YOUR BLADDER AND ADD TO THE COLLECTION CONTAINER.

FINALLY, KEEP THE COLLECTED URINE REFRIGERATED AND RETURN TO THE LABORATORY AS SOON AS POSSIBLE.

She couldn't even think of that step until it was necessary. The amount of times Paddy, Lorcan, Padraig, Siofra and even her mother pried open the fridge door and stared at the items on the shelves as if they might break into song or maybe a wee dance didn't bear thinking about. And sometimes wee Seamus, when he expended all his effort, could tug open the door and have a look inside as well. What would they make of her special jug next to the milk and Lucozade? It didn't bear thinking about.

She faced away from the door and hiked up her skirt. She tugged down her panties. Then, with as much dignity as she could muster, one hand keeping the door shut behind her, she hovered, wavered on the clunky heels of her clog-like shoes a bit, then squat over the jug. She looked down and aimed at the hole and fired away. Three full teacups, and then a lot more, if the streams spewing from her were anything to go by. Fionnuala felt relief ooze into her as the waste spilled out. Her ponytails swayed. She thought of all the proteins that must be swimming around in her urine and wondered what they might look like and where they might come from. And then it was over. She stood up, twisted on the top, and shoved the jug back into her satchel. She would inspect it later. Doctor Chandrapore had said something about foam. She draped a scarf across the top so it wouldn't be seen.

That wasn't so bad after all! It was certainly a peculiar thing to have to do, but now she'd done it once she was sure she'd be able to repeat the process all day long. Most loos would have locks.

Just as she was pulling the door shut behind her, the family trooped down the corridor and into the lobby. There must have been some argument at the video machine, because they didn't look how they had sounded before.

"Where's our stuff?" barked the father.

Fionnuala knew well enough not to push them any more. She wouldn't offer them any of the 'souvenirs' she had on sale, stones she had plucked from her back garden, next to the rhubarb patch, placed in little plastic cases, tied in a bow, and painted May 21, 1932 on them with her own hand at the kitchen table back home, which she claimed were stones from the original pasture Amelia and the Friendship had landed in on that very date. £50 each. She had fleeced them enough, when she took into account the cloakroom fees and the fact that admission was really only £5. And she had the credit card. She hurried into the office and came back with their gear.

"Here youse go," she said, the smile on her face and a dance in her fingertips as she handed over their things. "I hope youse have enjoyed yer stay here at Amelia's Exploreworld."

The girl rolled her eyes, the mother looked away, the father glared still and the boy muttered 'bucktoothed old bitch.'

Fionnuala didn't care. She didn't want an international incident, and life seemed brighter and happier now that she had 'collected' both urine and easy cash.

It was only when they were outside, after the boy had kicked the trash can next to the door, that Fionnuala noticed through the window—the front was all glass—the look in the mother's eyes. Fionnuala knew that look; it glinted often enough in her own eyes: suspicion. She couldn't hear what the woman was saying, but her lips were flapping and flapping and flapping at the family, her face was flush, and her finger was jabbing in Fionnuala's direction again and again. And—Fionnuala froze. The father cast her a furtive look through the glass, the teens nodded, and then the boy and girl took off their backpacks and the mother opened her purse. Their hands reached into them and rooted around. The father was turning all the pockets of his jacket inside out.

She knew! The fat Yank bitch somehow *knew!* It was only a matter of time before the mother discovered a credit card was missing. Oh, they had no proof, Fionnuala knew that. And the PSNI, as horrible as they were, would be on her side rather than some alien heathen tourists from the land of everything. She had seen it happen time and again: tourists being robbed and the circling of the Derry wagons, including the police. But...

She grabbed her satchel and flung it over her shoulder. She strode to the entrance, flipped over the sign so that it read CLOSED FOR LUNCH, it was only 10 AM, and wrenched open the door. As she was stabbing the key at the lock the husband called out, "Hey, wait a minute, did you—"

Fionnaula elbowed him in the stomach. "Och, sorry, love, it's me poor wee Dymphna. A car crash, ye understand. The hospital's just after ringing."

Off she raced.

"Hey! *Hey!*" he called after her.

"Cheerio!" she trilled.

The slosh from the jug was an unexpected sound in her ears as she sped on her clogs down the steep slope of Shipquay Street toward the city center. She was going to have to run, *run* to some retail establishment to max out that card. Before the woman dialed an international number and turned it into a useless piece of plastic. She was so concentrated on the slosh and the clack of her clogs she didn't hear their footsteps fast behind her.

CHAPTER 18

The chip van rattled and the infants roared bloody murder. Fuming, still nursing a hangover, Dymphna flung the mushy pea fritters back into the freezer and grabbed the hurling stick she kept for emergencies. She shoved past the stroller, almost slipping on a pickled egg in a pool of rancid grease, undid the lock and kicked open the side door.

"Let's have at ye, ye flimmin—!"

But it wasn't a pack of feral children ready to fling abuse and rocks her way. The hurling stick fell to her side, and the anger on her bonny-ish face dissolved into affection. With a bit of confusion.

"Rory! Are ye not meant to be in Belfast? That seminar on...?" She, like most, hadn't a clue what he was studying.

He nodded haltingly. She saw the state of his eyes. Two raisins stuck in bloody snow.

"Och, me poor wee Rory. Ye look shattered, love. C'mon inside, you."

She waved towards the dank, dingy innards of the van that stank of rotting fish and pickled onions and burnt curry. Rory had just left it the day before, and seemed reluctant to step foot inside again so soon. The shrieking of tortured infants reverberating in the cramped space, and Dymphna's cloud of cigarette smoke didn't help. But climb inside he did.

Dymphna wrapped her arms around him. Her fetid apron, almost stiff, crinkled as her voluminous breasts pressed against his non-chest.

"Aye, knackered, so I'm are," Rory said. "What are ye doing here, but? After standing in for ye here yesterday, I went to the pub with Georgie, as I thought I was meant to work for ye again today, that's what ye told me, like, and I knew I couldn't be here, so I was all set for Georgie to take over. But I had to ask him first, and I knew the only way he'd agree was if I got him bladdered. I thought a pint might do the trick, but that one pint—"

Tears had welled in Dymphna's eyes at first, but now she was getting used to the fumes of stale alcohol that spewed like little monsters from his lips.

"Aye, I can smell right enough that one pint turned into seven, with some Es thrown in and a few mad thrashes on the dance floor at Starzz and all. Youse was there til closing time, if I'm not mistaken."

She knew him too well.

"Ye know me too well. Offa wer heads, so we was. Woke up an hour since on Georgie's bedroom floor. I knew I had missed the bus to Belfast, so I let him sleep on and made me mind up to work the shift meself. Sure, I know I kyanny go back to the house, as Mammy might drop by, and she'll see I've not attended that seminar. She's sure to claw the face offa me. So here I'm are. An hour late, aye, but—"

"Ye're wile civil, so ye are. Ta for this, and for taking over me shift yesterday, like."

"What are ye doing here, but? I thought ye told me ye had to lie low for three or four days, that nobody in Derry could clamp eyes on ye. What's that all about anyroad?"

Dymphna wasn't about the reveal the mad scheme her mother had drummed up to entice money out of the local drug dealers for the wedding cake. Some secrets are best left between blood relatives. She didn't want Rory backing out, now that the wedding was so close.

"Never you mind. All ye need to know be's that I've no need to hide away nomore. So I'll be back at yer mammy's tonight after I've finished up here. Och, ta once again for all ye've done. I've to thank ye the best way I know how..."

She puckered her lips, as voluptuous as her breasts, and inched them towards the two thin lines that were his lips, ran her fingers over his rake-like limbs, and clutched at the skeletal shoulder blades that poked out of his back, oh, she made him sound so unsightly if she put it like that, but really he was handsome and charming and seemed to have a heart of gold. What other Protestant lad would be willing to face the taunts, jeers and social exclusion of the mates he had grown up with to take the plunge and marry a Fenian from across the river?

Their lips pressed together. Tongues wriggled. Fingers roamed under unwashed clothes.

A filthy Green slag, that was what the rest of Rory's soccer team always called Dymphna (everyone on the team was a fellow Protestant as a matter of course), even after he revealed he was going to marry her. Rory had defended his decision—he could hardly defend her honor!—with fists and headbutts and strange martial art kicks he had learned from repeated viewings of the *Matrix*. All were remarkable, given his emaciated look.

Dymphna was still a looker, even after two children, and even with the slick sheen and reddish blotches that had been marring her face lately from too many hours hovering over the fryer, and the slight pustule-like lesions that seemed to take forever to heal from where grease had spattered up.

Fingers roamed some more. Dymphna moaned and thrust herself against him. Even as her tongue rolled around the cavern of his mouth with its unbrushed teeth, she wasn't sure if she loved Rory or just loved the idea of him. Dymphna could tell from the way his eyes went all big and shiny when he saw her that he was in love with her. Or maybe it was just her body, but, no, that was what Bridie had said, back when they were best mates, Bridie's voice popping up into her head, planting nasty thoughts in her mind and words on her tongue.

Aye, Dymphna decided as he twiddled her nipples, she did love Rory. Perhaps not as much as he loved her, but lads were always more sentimental when it came to pairing up for life. They could afford to be. For the fairer sex, romance and marriage were a matter of life in life or death on spinster row. At least that was another thing Bridie had said.

He ground his hips against her. They toppled against the jars of gherkins. She resisted.

"Och, Rory, ye know I'm up for it. Ye've got me so randy I feel me juices spitting! Not here, but. Not now."

Dymphna wasn't averse to having sex in strange places—indeed, so used to it was she that a bed would be a strange place—but there were sausages to batter, and mushrooms too, gravy and curry sauce to heat, the meat pies to sort out, and the infants were eying them even as the little dears coughed and sputtered in the smoky fug. Plus, the hatch to the van was open, so any passing stranger could glance in.

Many others, especially on his soccer team, might have called her a cock-tease, but he and Dymphna were usually at it like rats, so Rory just shrugged. "In that case, I'm ravenous! What've ye got for me to scoff down?"

"I was fancying a mushy pea fritter when ye came. Ye fancy one and all?"

"Aye, surely. Two, ta."

Dymphna pulled three back out of the freezer and dropped them into the oil. It fizzled and spat.

"And then, Rory, ye've to help me with the meat pies. Och, what a state they're in! The labels've gone and fell off, and I haven't a clue which be's what." She prodded the fritters with a stick.

He stopped in the corner to say hello to his children. He was still uncomfortable, out of his depth, when confronted with them. How were infants meant to be touched? Spoken to? He tried to lift one up, but Keanu and Beeyonsay were wedged too tightly together. He settled for touching their arms and fiddling with their kicking legs with motions he hoped resembled fatherly love.

"Are youse right, there, wanes? Hellooo, helloooo," he cooed. "C'mere, Dymphna. Ye know I love em, but themmuns isn't wile interesting. They just sit there and shite. I've been thinking...could we not train themmuns to do things? Tricks, like? Maybe roll over? Or fetch? It would be magic, so it would! And I struggle to tell em apart." He pointed at one. "Which one be's this, hi?"

Men! Dymphna thought as she pulled out the fritters. Though Keanu was a year older, they were both as small and undernourished as each other and therefore indistinguishable. And with their matching blue bonnets, you couldn't see Keanu's orange hair. But Dymphna had clearly taped three pink bows atop Beeyonsay's bonnet. She plopped two fritters on a paper plate and handed it to Rory.

"That be's wer Beeyonsay," she said through a mouth of green mush that was meant to be peas. "And, about the training, naw, apparently not. I tried to get Keanu to do a simple thing like feed his sister, to save me the trouble, like, and the daft beast kept tossing the spoon at me. Why don't ye make yerself useful and change them wanes' nappies?" She licked her fingers and wiped dark green slime from her chin.

"I'll sort out the pies." He swallowed the last of his fritter as Dymphna turned the heat on the two pots, one with curry, the other with gravy. Soon their smells invaded the van along with Dymphna's smoke, the grease, the infants, Rory's sweat and drink and a few days of rubbish that had yet to be thrown out.

"Grand. Their nappies can wait, I suppose, but the pies kyanny. I kyanny sell em without knowing what be's inside. I took em outta the freezer the moment I got here so's they could thaw out a wee bit. I want ye to stick this knife into em one by one, and have a wee look inside so's you can tell what flavor it is, and then label it and put it back in the freezer. If ye kyanny tell from sight, I dunno when what ye should do. Smell em or something."

"What flavors are there meant to be? Steak and kidney, and...?"

She had worked there for months, but still couldn't remember the flavors. There were many, and they weren't all great sellers; some she hadn't laid eyes on in months. She consulted a list.

"Chicken and mushroom, minced beef and onion, meat and potato, beer and veal."

She handed him a knife, and he set to work next to her at the tiny corner of a counter next to the vat and the grill. Their elbows brushed against each other as they worked. Just like their children.

Some might be alarmed at how small their children were, but it was a godsend to Dymphna. That's how she could make them both fit into a stroller made for one; it had saved her the unnecessary expense of a second stroller. She wondered, when their little brother or sister came, if that stroller might fit three... Rory had tried to shove them in once, but, grand and lovely father though he might be, even taking into account the drink, drugs, flying fists and Zoë, he didn't have their mother's special touch.

"I'm wondering..." Dymphna said, dipping a sausage into a bowl of batter, "when the new wane comes, do ye think we'll have room to shove that one in and all, or should we buy a new pram? Thank God ye still kyanny see it on me body. After I've had it, after the wedding, like, we'll just tell everyone it was premature, four months premature. I've me dignity to think of, ye know."

"I kyanny make out what's meant to be in these pies," Rory said. He had already prodded five with a knife and peered inside. "All of em looks like there be's shite inside."

"Just do yer best. The chicken'll be a bit more yellow with some little gray bits what be's the mushrooms, the meat and onion ye should see the onion, and, I dunno, smell for the beer of the beer ones. That should be simple enough."

"Aye, there's a yellow one, and I see the minced beef now in that one now." He dug into a few pie crusts, then he said. "I hope when this new wane comes outta ye, it'll finally be one that resembles me a bit, hi."

"I hope to God and all." Thinking of Fabrizio, she really meant it. She popped another sausage into the batter.

There was a greater noise in the corner. Rory put down the knife and went to the children they now had. He looked down in slight alarm.

"Could we not turn on that vent, hi? Themmuns can hardly take a breath."

"I'm afeared it'll give em a chill."

From the hacking of the two purple heads in the stroller, a chill seemed to be the least of the infants' problems.

"Go on and turn on that vent. It's the wanes breathing in all the smoke from the, er, the grill I'm thinking of."

"Och, ye're a grand father, so ye are. So thoughtful," Dymphna flicked on the vent, lit another cigarette, and went back to the sausages. "And ye'll make a grand and lovely husband and all."

"Speaking of which, how are plans going for the wedding?"

"Ah, Rory, how far we've come! Ye mind when we hooked up it was but a one night stand, and I was repulsed at the sight of ye after that! When ye found out I was up the duff with wer wee Keanu, but... Ye mind when ye give me that engagement ring when I was working behind the counter of the Chipkebab? Before it was turned into Kebabalicious? Dead romantic, so it was. Ye said there was a problem with yer purchase, ye'd found a foreign object in it, and ye wanted to return it, I think it was a TakkoKebab, and ye told me to have a look inside and see how mingin it was. Instead, but, the foreign object was me lovely engagement ring. I wonder if yer mammy will see fit to let me wear it again after the wedding? I'd hardly pawn it then, like."

"I thought it was a ChipKebab I bought."

"It wile seems so long ago. Look at us now, but."

There wasn't much to see, except her with a battered sausage in her hand and a fag in her mouth, him with a knife stuck in a beer and veal pie, and two undernourished infants shoved into one stroller.

"It *was* long ago! Two wanes ago!" He looked again at the stroller. The curry bubbled. The gravy simmered. She saw what looked like fatherly pride on his face. If he only knew...

Dymphna stabbed out her cigarette in a tea mug and said with a sigh, "Two days to the big day, and still no sign of a wedding cake. I wonder what me mammy's up to. The flippin cake I don't care much about, though. If need be, at the last minute we can get one from the Top Yer Trolly and stick two wee dolls on the top. Of more concern to me, but, be's that there's no sign of me auntie Ursula. I kyanny understand why she didn't respond to the invite, like. I wish I had her email address. I've her number written on a scrap of paper, I think, somewhere, but I've no international on me phone. I've heard about that Skype thingy, but me auntie be's old, so I doubt she's on it."

"Why didn't ye mention it? I've international on me phone."

"Och, sure, I forgot about that." But she hadn't; Dymphna had phone envy. Maybe when she was Mrs. Dymphna Riddell, she would get one. And get her engagement ring back. "But it's too late now. There's only a few days left, and she kyanny make it here in time. Maybe...I wonder if me mammy was right about her all along. Naw, that kyanny be, but. Ye know how me mammy likes to spread her poison. I can only hope Auntie Ursula shows up on the day. Like maybe for a surprise. It's something to dream about. Now, but—"

"C'mere, is that not yer mammy I just seen running past?"

Dymphna poked her head out of the hatch. It was indeed Fionnuala, making a bee-line for the Top-Yer-Trolly across the square. Even without the flying ponytails, Dymphna could recognize that look of determined intensity from a mile off.

"Aye, so it is. C'mere, what's she got in that satchel of hers? It looks like it be's bulging to explode! And who's themmuns running after her? Looks like some Yank tourists."

And then they forgot about Fionnuala as the first customer's head blocked the view from the hatch. It was the lad that worked at the butcher's down the Strand. He reeled slightly as he looked up at Dymphna.

She touched her hairnet and scowled, wondering what he was staring at. What did she look like? Her fingers moved to her cheeks. Was it the pustules?

"What are ye looking at?" she snapped.

"Have I not heard...I mean...are ye not meant to be dead?! Of a drugs overdose?"

"Eejit! Do I look dead to ye?"

He seemed unable to answer this.

Dymphna roared down into his face: "I've two wanes keeping me up all hours of the night, another on the way, and this mingin job here! Is it any wonder I look like a fecking corpse?! What's yer fecking order or away off with ye!"

"A portion of curry and chips and a pickled egg."

"Right ye are."

Dymphna turned to the pot.

CHAPTER 19

"Well, honey, what do you think? Are we gonna strike it rich or strike out?"

What Ursula thought, endless fields of corn—or oats?—whizzing by the window to her right, was that she was leaving behind the guilt of the hospital and heading towards the anxiety of the studio, sitting in a murky no-woman's land which wasn't helped by the schizophrenia of a CD Jed had somehow burned on the computer. It jumped from country classics to big band marches to Irish drinking songs to national anthems from around the world. A map of Wisconsin was spread on her lap like a quilt. Satnav was not for them; inside the car it was like the 80s never ended, Jed's cigarette butts spilling out of an ashtray to her left knee.

She rattled the ice cubes that were now pebbles in the A&W cup as she considered her answer. *"Oh, Mary, this London's a wonderful sight..."* It was

"The Mountains of Mourne" on the CD, and Ursula felt a stabbing in her heart. She always did when she heard Irish music in the States. She bent forward, the map crackling and the little things she had placed on it to gauge the distance they had to go falling to the floor, and she pressed Forward. *"Oh, the crystal chandeliers light up the paintings on your wall..."* Charlie Pride, country and western. Wondering how many songs began with "oh," Ursula took a sip of what had been diet root beer a few hours earlier. Burger wrappers and fry cartons clustered around her ankles, along with the barrette, two nickles and a Listerine strip that had been on the map.

"I haven't a clue. You and Slim knows all the numbers, sure. Och, Jed, I'm wile afeared of stepping foot in that studio. AARGH!!"

Jed swerved to avoid a coyote. Seats belts bit into flesh. A pack of Marlboros, a lighter and a box of tissues slid across the top of the dashboard.

"Phew! That was close! Don't worry, honey. All you have to do is sing the song, then introduce yourself. You won't have to do much talking. Just smile at them. They're usually nice if you know what your numbers are. Well, except for the mean one."

"Aye, Jed, but I don't have a clue about them numbers ye keep banging on about. Margins and percentages and whatnot."

"I'll take care of everything. As I told you, they want to know we have sales and business savvy. Solid numbers and a savvy business plan. The first 90 seconds, like I said—"

"Ye've terrified me with them first 90 seconds. I've been thinking about it, but. Doesn't that be when I'm singing? Is that not the first 90 seconds?"

"No, the first 90 seconds after that I mean. That's the deal breaker. We'll lose if we—if *I*— can't say what our product is and how *they* can make money from it. Quickly. We need to make a great first impression, to captivate, show passion, let them see it's an opportunity they can't pass up. We need to, uh, crystallize the opportunity. Oh, and they hate the words 'uh' and 'um,' so don't say them. But don't worry, you won't say much."

"Left! Turn left, Jed!"

He turned left. "They want a big sell. They don't want us asking too much too soon for too little. Most people lose because of bad math. We need to know our numbers, know what we're talking about, let them see our business has potential, and make it obvious how they can make money from it. In the first 90 seconds."

"If *that's* all then...!" Ursula's head spun even as she rolled her eyes. She sighed. "If only Slim and Louella was here with us. I'd feel better with more of us on the stage, like."

Jed's face, peering down the highway, grew grim.

"Well. They can't be here. Oh, and I saw that Randaleen in the room next to them. At the hospital, I mean."

This was news to Ursula. "Why didn't ye tell me?"

"I didn't want to upset you. But I thought maybe you saw her too. You mean you didn't see her?"

"How did she look? Worse than Slim?"

"Just about as bad."

Ursula didn't know if that made her feel better or worse.

The taping of that night's episode of *Attack of The Killer Investors!*, of course, was what was making her anxious. She hadn't known it was recorded live. They had been on the highway for four hours now, heading to the TV studio in Milwaukee.

They had dragged themselves out of bed at dawn, both to make it for the hospital's bizarre visiting hours, and then to make it to the studio on time. Taping began at 7:00 PM. They had bought flowers and Get Well Soon balloons, and Ursula hoped she could hide the shame she felt burning on her face behind them. She felt responsible for the crash. But they had been told at the entrance to the ward that they were both banned from the hospital. At first, they thought the guard meant themselves, but it dawned on them he meant the flowers and the balloons. Some patients might be allergic to the flowers the guard said, though they were snapdragons which produce no offending pollen and had no history of causing allergic reactions, and the balloons might contain latex. Ursula's eyes told her they were that modern kind made of foil.

"What the hell is going on in this country?" Jed had asked in disbelief as he tossed the flowers in the trash. "Why is everybody allergic to everything all of the sudden? Nuts, eggs, tomatoes, wheat, crabs! They weren't in my day! It's the smoking ban. It's turning people into wimps. Their bodies can't handle real life any more."

He couldn't put the balloons in the garbage because they were floating and they wouldn't stay put. He let them fly away.

"We shoulda bought them those grapes after all," Ursula observed.

They had had to enter the room barehanded. Jed expressed surprised that they weren't asked to wear masks and SOCO uniforms. They looked down in sorrow. Slim had borne the brunt of the accident. Louella, a halo of scouring pads atop a Lutheran rake, sat in the plastic orange chair beside the bed, moaning and rocking back and forth and squeezing Slim's walrus-hand. Tears had welled in Ursula's eyes as she gazed upon his massive form, close to lifeless in that hospital bed. Slim, an older version of Jed plus two hundred pounds and minus a cowboy hat, strained the mattress. A bandage was wound around his head, his neck was in a brace, his right arm in a cast, and a pulley held his left leg, also in a cast, hovering above him like a zeppelin. He had sustained a mild concussion, three bruised ribs, moderate whiplash, a fractured

117

ulna (that's what the doctor had told them on the phone; the Lord alone only knew where or what that actually was), and a broken fibula. Louella had a toe sprain and a headache. The doctor had raved about how Slim was like a massive human air bag, and his poundage, although bad for his heart, had saved Louella from bodily harm. Louella was fine, but—

"I'm not going with you," she snapped the moment they walked in. "I want to look after Slim." She glared accusingly at Ursula.

Ursula fiddled with the cross around her neck as she stared down at the distressing sight of her brother-in-law on the hospital bed. It was distressing in many ways, as were Louella's eyes boring into her. Ursula was riddled with guilt, consumed with unease. She had taken Randaleen on to give the useless article a chance, but her compassion had put them all in harm's way. Why hadn't she gone to Inspector Scarrey? Or why hadn't she confronted Randaleen directly? Or gotten the locks changed? She reached out and gently touched one of Slim's toes (not a zeppelin one). "I'm wile sorry."

He grunted a reply. She removed her fingers and discreetly wiped them on a rails of the bed.

"I'm sorry to be so angry, Ursula," Louella said, clenching and unclenching a tissue. She didn't sound sorry in the least. "I know it's not the Christian way to behave. But I can't help it. And about the show, it's not because I'm angry at you that I can't leave my chipmunk's side. It's because I don't know what to do in front of those dang cameras."

Louella admitted that after Jed had called and told them they'd been accepted, she and Slim had clutched each other by the shoulders, screamed and jumped up and down—most at odds with their years—but other than clutching, screaming and jumping, they didn't know what to do. They didn't understand the show, they had never seen it, and thought that sending in the video was enough. Jed hadn't explained clearly. Louella wouldn't move and Slim couldn't. Jed and Ursula had understood that.

They had lingered as long as was polite; not that they didn't care, they did, but the clock was ticking, they had five hours to travel, and Jed still didn't have the pitch complete.

"How far do we have to go now?" Jed asked.

"We're close," Ursula consulted the map. "Only a fingernail away."

"We're making good time. An hour ago we were, what did you say? Two nickels and a Listerine strip away?"

Ursula couldn't understand the scale of the map. But now they were finally passing signs, and one at that moment clearly told them Milwaukee was only 25 miles away. And then, all too soon, before Ursula felt fully prepared, they were off the highway and following signs to Biggbee Studios. Then they were pulling up in the parking lot and Ursula was getting out of the car and adjusting the hem of her flowered skirt and fixing her hair and closing the door and walking past the bumpers of unknown cars towards the studios, straining under the weight of the carton of Slim Jed Jerky samples and promotional materials she was lugging, but she was seeing it all as if it were someone else doing all the movements and she were floating above and looking down and pitying the woman below.

Then she was startled to see she was perched on a lumpy sofa in an unloved and uncared-for Green Room. She was drinking coffee from a stryrofoam cup. The boxes of jerky were at her feet. She was apparently guarding them. Ursula couldn't remember how she had gotten to this room or where the cup had come from, though she did see a coffee and soup vending machine in the corner, chicken and tomato soup, it said. She longed to reach out to Louella for support, clasp her hand, and maybe have her tease her hair a bit, but the chair of cracked purple pleather beside her was empty.

Jed was walking around, playing the social aspect of the show, she supposed, handing out jerky samples and shaking hands with the other wannabe entrepreneurs. The rules of the show (Jed had forced her to read them aloud as he drove) forbade the contestants from mingling with the investors before they met on the air, so Ursula guessed the rich people had dressing rooms and makeup artists and functioning air conditioning on the other side of the studio. A rusty fan beside her gave off more noise than air. She fanned herself with a sweaty hand and vaguely recalled at some stage in the past being pointed to a room where there was community makeup available for the contestants to use. She now remembered looking down at the meager selection and the state of it, and being disappointed the makeover she had been looking forward to wasn't included. She had tried to apply some rouge, but it was caked and crumpled on her cheek.

Ursula drank the muddy coffee, ignored the sweat trickling down some fold of flesh and tried to listen to what the others around her were saying. From what she could gather at this distance, there was a youth with baggy jeans and a computer game where dragons fought elves on a distant planet in the future, a pair of housewives with hoodies for infants with edible drawstrings, two badly-aged former frat brothers with plans to franchise their stall which sold meat-flavored milkshakes, a woman with purple hair and a nose ring who, surprisingly, came with both a book of poems about ferns and a board game about quantum mechanics (The Properties of Spin), a transgender circus troupe that wanted to put their show on the road, and an older man with a prototype of a device that allowed cats to self-clean their litter boxes. He needed money to make the real things in China. Ursula couldn't tell if Jed and Slim's beef jerky was better or worse than these products, except perhaps the circus troupe.

Ursula still wasn't sure what exactly this show was like, but she thought

maybe *American Idol* or *Hell's Kitchen* or maybe even *Survivor,* and that she
and Jed would be pitted against these others. She didn't want to be friendly
with them if they had to beat them. It seemed disingenuous.

   C'mon, Ursula, she thought. *Get yerself up there, ye eejit, and be friendly to
the people. Help Jed out. He's being so lovely. Put yer terror of being on air
live talking about something ye don't know nothing about to the side, and all
them horrid thoughts of Randaleen almost killing the only two people in this
land ye can call yer friends to the side. Smile! Smile and be friendly to all
themmuns! Themmuns is probably just as heartscared as ye are. Maybe not
them half-man, half-woman, people, but, as they're in a circus and be's used to
performing before others, like. But all the others besides them. Ye're like a
flimmin Queen perched on her throne here, high and mighty, afeared of mixing
with the peons. Get up! Aye, that's it!*

   Jed had pulled her toward the coffee and soup machine before she could
speak.

   "What's up?" he asked. "They seem to like the jerky."

   "Jed, but, isn't themmuns wer competition?"

   He smiled apologetically. "I'm sorry, Ursula. It's my fault. I was so busy with
the pitch, I didn't explain it to you." She listened, pressing the buttons of the
machine dejectedly, as he explained that the investors might choose to invest in
all of them all. Or none of them. He had seen shows that went both ways. So
there was no competition.

   That wasn't so bad, then. Ursula finally smiled real smiles, walked up to the
older man and told him she liked his device. She took a sip of a Rib Eye
milkshake, read one of the poems (*Ode To The Friendly Fiddleheads),* but
reading them was not like eating potato chips and she could indeed stop after
just one. She couldn't bring herself to try *Mosses Beware, Sweetfern Is Not A
Fern,* or, most disturbingly, *O! Leptosporangiate!,* though she feigned interest,
flipping through them with a look of marvel on her face. She also nibbled on a
strawberry drawstring, but was scared to approach the circus troupe, though
she had to admit they seemed friendly enough. She smiled warmly at the youth.

   And then a girl with Buddy Holly glasses, a clipboard and the smugness of
her age poked her head into the room and told them the taping had started. "Ed
and Norm?" It was the milkshake guys. "You're on!"

   Ursula and a few others wished them good luck as they gathered up the
sample shakes and the machine and their posters, and then they were gone.
They talked about Ed and Norm. They drank bad coffee. The teen drank worse
chicken soup. And after twenty minutes the frat men were back. They were
different people. Older. Stunned. Even shell-shocked. The contestants all
gathered round the two, except for the older man, as Ms. Clipboard had barked
"Nestor!," and he had disappeared through the door.

"It was horrible!" Ed said, fighting back tears.

"What happened?" someone asked.

"What do you think happened?" Norm yelled. They jerked back in alarm. Twenty minutes ealier, he had been so nice. "They yelled 'Get Lost!' at us. All of them."

"We were so sure..." Ed sobbed.

"Did you know your numbers?" Jed asked gently.

Norm threw off his hand. "They were perfect!"

"But if you knew your numbers—"

"Leave us alone! Leave us alone all of you!" barked Norm.

"B-but..." Fern Woman chanced. "We can't. We're stuck here."

"Then *we're* getting the hell out of here."

"And never coming back."

They looked on, unable to help, as Ed and Norm threw together their things and stormed out of the room. The door slammed behind them.

And Nestor came back in. Crying.

"Circus Troupe!" called Clipboard.

Over and over it happened, out they strut, confident, excited, proudly brandishing their wares, and then they disappeared down the hall. Twenty minutes passed. And back they stormed, tearful, angry, their hair mussed, buttons awry, confused, flinging their products and related promotional materials to the floor. How could their dead cert be a dead horse? Were the investors insane? Idiots? Assholes?

With each new rejection, Ursula's heart pounded even more. Her fingers shook. She gripped Jed's elbow with those shaking fingers.

"We'll be fine, sweetheart," Jed said. "Don't worry about a thing. I'll do all the work. All you have to do is sing. Don't worry."

"Och, Jed, all I can do is worry. I'm so afeared. Them first 90 seconds...!"

And then it was their turn.

"Jed and...uh, Jed and..." Clipboard glared accusingly. How dare someone have a name she couldn't pronounce! She had prided herself on having chosen a racially diverse group of friends at her expensive college and knew all the common Indian, Pakistani, Mid-Eastern and Chinese first names.

"Ursula," Ursula said weakly. She wanted to wind her arm around Jed's, but she had to carry the box of jerky so she couldn't. Jed picked up his box, and the teen (the only one left) wished them good luck. Ursula heaved deep breaths. They walked out the door and down the hallway of doom. "Quickly! Quickly! It's live, you know!" Clipboard barked. Ursula wanted to trip her.

Feeling like she and Jed were Christians being led into the Colosseum, though the walls there were stone and crumbly and curved, and these were sheet rock and smooth and straight, Ursula blessed herself in her mind, right shoulder, left shoulder forehead, breast. She couldn't do it with her hands because they were full of jerky. They turned a corner and saw the piercing massive lights before them just as they felt the temperature from them blast upon their skulls.

"Get out there!" Clipboard hissed with a little push on their backs with her namesake. "And smile!"

Ursula followed Jed onto the sound stage.

CHAPTER 20

Slosh, slosh! Clunk, clunk!
Fionnuala hightailed it, a bizarre hybrid of power walking and that of an obese person trailing behind a speedy dog on a leash; she had seen it on the telly, never in Derry, as nobody ever seemed to lead dogs on leashes in that town. She struggled to propel her poundage down the steep slope of Shipquay Street without toppling over and rolling headfirst down the pavement.

At the Crafts Village (a Derry must-see), a sudden throng of tourists streamed out of its gate, babbling in tongues. Fionnuala scowled, cursing 2013. It was the year Derry had been voted the UK's City of Culture. And aliens had been invading her town every since. She used her elbows as battering rams to carve her way through the Asian shoulder blades and French backsides, the throngs of the unbathed and unbaptized. The acid of her tongue and what it unleashed on them as she passed they would find in no guidebook, no translation app. *"Mingin slitty-eyed toerag! Flimmin flash eejit! Froggy flimmin arse bandit!"*

The jug sloshing on her right and banging into her ribs, Fionnuala was all set to run to that swanky new baker's on Rossville Street next to the Bloody Sunday memorial and use the card to finally get that flimmin wedding cake—the bane of her existence. Not the cake itself, more her slapper half-bastard offspring Dymphna. But somehow, as she clutched a lamp post and heaved breaths into her aching lungs, her brain cells realized that the baker or whoever was at the till wouldn't just hand her a cake then and there over the counter, with the names spelled correctly and the color of the icing matching the mood of the wedding—green had finally been decided on, an avocado-type one, which Fionnuala thought quite sophisticated—and two dolls on top bearing the correct resemblance to the happy couple (curly red hair on the female doll, black hair on the male).

She hazarded a glance behind her. The Yank family was still hot on her heels, pushing through the phalanx of tourists still glued to the Craft Village.

Their faces were pink, their mouths stretched with some strange American emotion Fionnuala couldn't make sense of, the mother continuing to dig through her purse. The woman still had no proof. Perhaps she had so many credit cards she'd never realize? Fionnuala smirked, adjusted the satchel handles that bit into her fleshy shoulder, then flung herself further down the street, brain cells pinging like sparklers.

It would take the bakers a few days to personalize the cake, and they'd need her information, her name, address, phone number, maybe even her email. Even if she didn't give her information, whoever was working at the counter probably knew her to see, and even if they didn't, which was unlikely, they'd still have the names Rory and Dymphna to go on, and when the credit card company flew someone over to Ireland investigate, the fraud investigator could go through all the wedding registries and church records in the city for a Rory and a Dymphna wed on such and such a day, or around such and such a day, and Fionnuala would eventually find herself shackled in a cell with bastard Proddy peelers staring down their noses at her through the little slot like a mailbox in the door. So, no.

How she thought all this in a minute or two while she was puffing and panting—the only day Derry had seen sun in a month, bloody typical!—down the steepest slope in Derry she didn't know, didn't know from which hidden cranny she was mining these gems of inspiration, but she was proud of herself. Delighted.

She reach the bottom of the street and paused at Magazine Gate for breath, resting her hand on whatever ancient stones the gate was made of. The 17th century city walls that surrounded the city towered above her and stretched down as far as she could see. She thanked Jesus and Mary for the shade. On this side were tiny, cramped streets. On the other side of the gate, the wide expanse of the city center. She wiped the sweat from her forehead and flung herself into the blessed darkness and damp inside. Smiling and nodding hello to old Mrs. Dinh, next door but three, who passed her under the gate, trailing an apparent granddaughter behind her, Fionnuala and her feverish brain raced on.

If that Yank tourist geebag finally found her card missing and tried to phone her credit card company, she wouldn't be able to get through. Fionnuala had heard group after group of tourists at the interactive center complaining about spotty international coverage—they kept moaning on and on about lack of bars or something as they tried to do their relentless texting and facebooking and twitting or whatever the flimmin feck it was when they were supposed to be concentrating all their efforts on viewing Amelia's wonders, but they were thick, Fionnuala thought, for there were bars aplenty in Derry, on every street corner practically and sometimes two a block, and didn't the daft eejits know they were called pubs here?!

So she knew she had time, some time, anyway. She came out into the city center, just as she was thinking that that Mrs. Dinh hadn't given her a proper hello and that that grandchild of hers looked like a right spastic. She'd blank the sarky, crabbit aul bitch the next time she saw her, and heaven help Siofra if she ever brought the wee girl round their house, touched in the head, a Mongoloid or worse, she looked, and Fionnuala had heard it could be contagious; she didn't want her infecting their home.

The Guildhall was before her, the green of the ancient bronze top of the Big Ben-type clock tower gleaming, and to its left, the city center. Fionnuala raced over the slick slabs of rock, glittering in the sunshine. In this area of the city center, the cobblestones of yore had been replaced. All of Derry had been delighted by the modern makeover, until the first rain, when the slabs proved to be extra slippery. And it always rained. She passed the Guildhall and the chip van where Dymphna worked, then she was in the city center, home to the main attractions of the Top Yer Trolly and the public loos, and as she looked around, frenzied, it struck her that this hideaway was like the wide expanse of that plaza in the Vatican City where the Pope always said Easter mass, or his speech to the masses after the mass, in any event. She had seen it twice on the telly, once with John Paul II and once with Benedict. She felt exposed.

Where were the usual shoppers? The mothers pushing prams and trailing hordes of shrieking wanes behind them? The gangs of hooded, slouching teens with fags hanging out of their mouths and sneers on their faces that always yelled out insults as she passed? Not here. There was nowhere to hide. Where should she go? Behind the Guildhall? To the quays? The bus station?

The sight of the public loos made her aware of a new urge in her lady's arena. Cursing the tea yet again, vowing never to take another sip (at least until the 24 hours were up), she wondered...did she have time for a quick slash? Maybe the public loos were perfect as a hiding place. As long as they didn't see her going in. She looked back. She froze. The family was just exiting Magazine Gate, yapping and waving their arms to a member of Derry's worst, a member of the hated Police Service of Northern Ireland, the PSNI. Fionnuala blessed the Lord for placing a mail box right beside her. She slipped behind it and clung to it, her head lolling against the ROYAL MAIL embossed on it, and the BRIT BASTARDS graffiti underneath. She pressed her left ponytail to her neck so it wouldn't swing out and peered around the curvature. The family was pointing in her general area. The peeler was looking around. Fionnuala percolated with anger. Not only was the copper probably Proddy, but it also grated on her nerves that he was so young. A bus trundled past, blocking them from her view. Did she have time? Could she sprint to the restroom? And then she realized, she was leading them to where they could use their phone. If they got the public loos, reception would be fine, or so she had heard a Kraut tourist tell a Kiwi one the week before.

Pressing the urge to the back of her mind, she stared around the square. And, of course! There was the Mountains of Mourne Gate to the city walls! How had she not thought of it before? Whereas the city walls and most of its gates were wonders of historical Derry fit for any tourist's iPhone camera, the section near the Mountains of Mourne Gate was...something else.

Fionnuala took a deep breath, braced herself, and hoofed it across the square. Her clogs clacked and seemed to echo in the vacant expanse. Before the gate, and it was no surprise, she almost collapsed against a wall of stench. There, as usual, huddled a collection of the unwashed, the unwanted, the unconscious: Derry's detritus of drunks and druggies. Alternatively charming and menacing, genius and looney, they had chosen the gate as their pied à tierre. In this area, raucous laughter vied with roars of anger and moans of hopelessness. Sometimes it reminded Fionnuala of her house. And beyond the gate...Brilliant!

Brain cells trundling, eyes flickering over the limbs, Fionnuala chose the drunk closest to her, who seemed diseased yet alive and cogent.

"Here, lad, do ye want to earn 50 pence?"

He jerked as if someone had poked his eye with a stick, and rose like an underwater creature, hair like seaweed, drool on his chin, gravy and brown sauce on his shirt with no buttons, delight in his ravaged eyes. A bottle holding a dribble of some brown liquor fell to the ground. He wavered back and forth before her on the sidewalk. To avoid the unseemly sight of his pink chest, she looked around. The family and the copper were milling in front of the Top Yer Trolly, clueless. The girl was peering through the window of the superstore. Fionnuala relaxed, but only a smidgen.

"Ye see them Yanks over there? With the copper bastard? At the Top Yer Trolly?"

"Aye."

"I'm gonny go into the market here, and if themmuns tries to follow me, I want ye to keep em at bay. Any way ye can. Are ye up for it?"

"Yanks and the Filth? Aye, surely!"

They smiled their hatred together. She dug around in the satchel for her coin purse. The drunk eyed the jug.

"What've ye got in there, dear?" he asked as she pressed a shiny 50 pence piece into his filthy palm. "Something for me to drink? Give me some of that and all. Is it fit to drink? What's in it? Looks like I might enjoy it. C'mon, just a wee tipple. Be a dear."

"It's me own piss!" Fionnuala spat, then slipped through the gate.

She hoped he didn't suspect sarcasm, as then he might not help her. But as she came out the other side of the gate, Fionnuala felt liberated, revealing her sordid secret to at least one pair of ears in the world, no matter how deranged with decades of drink and, she suspected, bargain bin recreational drugs the head attached to those ears might be and no matter that they would forget what had been said to them and never remember again. And why wasn't that daft grandchild of Mrs. Dinh in school at this hour of the day, anyway? Fionnuala suddenly wondered. As demented as the girl was, she needed all the schooling she could get!

Fionnuala slunk into the dank, shadowy melee that was the Mountains of Mourne Gate makeshift market (a Derry must-not see). It was an alley sandwiched on one side by the city walls, on the other by boarded up shop windows. There was the stall where she had bought *How To Be A Lady* and the beer mats. Few tourists dared tread in this area, lurking in the cover of damp and the stench of beer and armpits as the market did. But, though she didn't know why, Fionnuala felt at home. She stepped over a body. Drum and bass blasted from the speakers market-wide, prams piled high with screaming children rolled by, drunks were passed out this side of the gate as well, along with a smattering of drug addicts, and most of the customers seemed unsteady on their feet as well. The sellers were also living an edgy life, hands shuddering from some chemical stimulants, eyes drooping from downers and drink.

Most stalls were illegal, but, to gain favor with a public that detested and distrusted them, the PSNI turned a blind eye to all the infractions of laws that were going on...the smuggling, the former Eastern Bloc cigarettes, the knock off handbags and perfumes, the beer in cans with strange symbols that were someone else's language, the auto parts and whole engines at times, homemade designer shirts and soccer scarves that unraveled the moment you got them home, the DVDs and CDs, still!, the arts and crafts in one misguided stall, and the one that sold, as if it were 20 years earlier, peat and coal and firelighters and advertised New Potatoes.

A quick look behind let Fionnuala know the family hadn't found her yet. She scanned the stalls. Lately she had seen things begin popping up in the market that had once only accepted cold hard cash: hand held machines that could process plastic. A wonderment of technology, she realized now.

But what should she buy? She had all the Yank's money at her avail. Most top shelf items were electronics that came from some chinky land, but not, thankfully, that Communist China. Above the bobbing heads of shoppers, over the scarves and hoods of hoodies, she saw a Soni TV, an iPed, a selection of Sansumg phones. She pushed through the throngs at the front of the electronics stall and pointed at a shelf.

"C'mere, gimme a me look at that stereo thingy." It might be a wedding gift at the very least, she mused, or perhaps she could use it to entice Lorcan to stay. How could she know he had moved on to mp3 players? As the man handed over the ghetto blaster, Fionnuala placed her satchel on the ground.

She made a show of pressing a few buttons and turning a few dials. Out of the corner of her eye, she saw the three to her right, who had been digging through little plastic cases with flags and Britney Spears and soccer teams and she didn't know what on them, turn their heads at the same time.

"What's up there, hi?" one asked.

Fionnuala felt dread as she slowly looked to the right. She gave a sharp intake of breath. At the gate, their silhouettes seeming to rise up before her, as large as them yokes on Easter Island and as peculiar, was the family. The drunk was yelling and gesticulating wildly before them, waving his arms ineffectually, but the woman was clutching her daughter tight and the father and son were stepping back in alarm. Fionnuala flung the stereo on the stall counter. She hunched over and crept to the next stall. Then the one after. And the one after that, further and further away from the gate. She crouched behind a sack of potatoes, dust billowing around her head. She peeked over the burlap. The drunk was certainly doing the best he could for the 50 pence, Fionnuala thought with pride.

More than the stench, the fear, the drunk, it seemed to be the crowd that was gathering, pointing at them and laughing, that made the family finally inch back the way they came and stomp through the gate and out of sight. Fionnuala heaved a sigh of relief. But she still had to act quickly. And where was that Filth bastard who was with them? As she struggled to haul herself upright, she was struck by the lightness of her right shoulder. Panic gripped her. Her satchel! Where was it?

And just as she remembered...leaning up against the electronics stall, she saw it all unfold before her as if in slow motion.

The copper appeared out of nowhere, but that didn't bother her. The family had fled. But one of the women who had been pawing at the little plastic cover thingies looked down at the satchel and, concern and sudden fear on her face, barked something to the seller. His face shot up, alarmed. The crowd around the stall parted as if a blood-spurting corpse had just plummeted from a plane above and splatted at their feet. They screamed and jabbed their fingers. The PC marched forward supposedly purposefully, but Fionnuala could tell he was an amateur and was secretly bricking it. He tried to mask the fear on his pimples as he took charge, pushed through the crowed and pointed down at the satchel. Her satchel.

"Whose bag is this?"

The stall owner jabbed an accusing finger at her. Three stalls away, beside a case of firelighters, Fionnuala didn't know where to look.

The PC pushed past a few shoulders and demanded, "Is that bag yours, madam?" He said it accusingly, his Protestant eyes glaring at her with hatred or excitement or the love of power, she didn't know which.

"Naw!" Fionnuala barked. "Never set eyes on it before in me life!"

The moment the words were out and she made a show of recoiling from the satchel, her beloved My Heart Will Go On Tour satchel, Paddy's present for their 15th Anniversary, her second most loved possession after her Kenny Roger's The Gambler tea set, the satchel she had even retrieved from the rubbish bin and spent many hours delousing after it had been infested, she was shocked she had said it. She couldn't understand why. She was ashamed. It was if she had turned her back on a beloved relative. But—and where in the name of God had this totally inappropriate thought sprung from, was it her illness?—hadn't she done that? To Ursula Barnett?

Was it a knee-jerk reaction to the barked question of a hated PSNI officer in his cap that screamed 'I am your superior?' She had always sat her children down on the settee at home at one stage in their youth and taught them to never, ever tell the Filth the truth. Was that why? Or was it the embarrassment of the horrid contents inside? Her diseased, protein-infected urine festering, toxic, in the massive red plastic jug? What if the copper demanded to search the bag and dragged it out? With the masses looking on. The mortification! They all knew her. At least to see. Or was it that inside the satchel there was—flimmin feck!—the Yank woman's credit card?! If he found that, she was a goner.

She yelped at a bony finger poking into her back.

"Aye, surely, it's yers, Mrs. Flood!" said a voice behind her.

Fionnuala turned and gawped at Mrs. Dinh and her horrid, stupid face. The spastic grandchild grinned up at her like the loon she was.

"N-naw," Fionnuala said, inching back into the case of firelighters.

"Aye it is! That Celine Dion bag! Ye ranted on about it for hours at the hair salon, sure! I had the misfortune to be sat next to ye, like, at the dryers. With that Titanic ship and the wee mechanism that allows the ship to sink the more ye fill it, ye said."

"Naw! It doesn't be mines!" Fionnuala roared. Many emotions were passing the PC's face; Fionnuala couldn't take them all in. And suspicion had seeped through the crowd. They were all in a semi-circle around her now, though they seemed fearful their backs were to the mystery item, and were glaring at her as if she had suddenly announced her daughter was marrying a Protestant.

And then, to her shock, though she should've realized it...her brain crannies and their gems were deserting her now...while the crowd inched away from the stall and the murmuring and noises of fear and a scream here and there rang out, the smarmy Proddy bastard in the uniform thrust her to the ground with some leg movement she didn't see. Her nose pressed against an empty crisp packet, pickled onion, and her ear clamped on an empty gin bottle, generic, and she felt plastic handcuffs digging into her wrists. She heard him press a button on his walkie talkie, and she heard him hiss into it, "Alert! Possible bomb at the Mountains of Mourne Gate market! Suspect apprehended! Send the bomb squad as soon as! And back up! Alert! Alert!"

CHAPTER 21

Lorcan cracked his knicker-wetting smile.
Flash!
And again. His eyes *yearned.*
Flash!
Then he made a silly face, just for the craic of it, his hands in some gangsta pose.
Flash!
And then he was all menace, a hard man boxer, jabbing a right hook at where he thought on the wall opposite the camera must be.
Flash!
He pulled aside the curtain of the photo booth at the Top Yer Trolly, all swagger, and slouched against the machine, waiting for the pictures to drop out into the little slot. He couldn't know it, but the four photos were Lorcan Flood in a nutshell: sexy and silly, with a dash of assault. He wriggled his eyebrows suggestively at Ciara Malloy as she passed with a cart of tinned prunes she was about to shelve. She blushed and grinned back, and her eyes said, if only I hadn't married that Conor Malloy. And if only I hadn't had two wanes me mammy has to look after for me during me shifts here. Thick blue-black hair gelled into a fauxhawk, red Umbro soccer jersey clean for once, and that his mother had ironed (!) the week before, jeans that showed off what they were supposed to, and a generous helping of Lynx body spray, Oriental scent, in his gentleman's area. Lorcan was usually a ride, but he knew he looked more drop dead gorgeous than usual, and that was by choice. He was on a mission.

Passport? Check. Work visa? Check. He had called in a favor from a mate; everyone knew you could buy fake passports from the man with the tartan scarf and the limp at the Mountains of Mourne Gate market, but they cost more than his last pay check from Fillet-O-Fish would be. There was a click and a whirr, and the photos dropped into the tray. Passport photo? Check. All he needed was the plane ticket to Tampa, Florida, the USA. That's where the gel and the body spray came in.

He circled down the aisles of the superstore, and every shiny surface, the side of a toaster here, the blade of a hoe there, was an opportunity to check himself out. Not that he fancied himself, thought songs were about him, he didn't, but this was a time-based operation, and things had to unfold just right. When he was past the registers, he caught the eye of a girl peering through the streaky windows between two promotional posters: Everything! Every Day! Five For The Price of Four! and Manager's Specials: Xmas Puddings, 50 p Off! Dented Brussels Sprouts Only 99 p! "Macarena" CDs £1.99! A Yank tourist, by the look of her teeth. He flashed his smile. She wilted against the window. He waved. She waved back. A woman's hand pulled her out of sight. Lorcan shrugged. It was Sorcha O'Shaunessy he was after, anyway.

Right! Down to business! He pushed through the revolving doors and thought where she might be. Across the slick slabs, past the public loos, he saw the Yank family approaching Magazine Gate with a copper. What was going on? Not his concern. Focus. Time was ticking. The Craiglooner first, and if Sorcha wasn't there, the Rocking Seamaid, then the Idle Fiddle, then the Hairy Lime, and if he still hadn't found her... And what if she had found a boyfriend? It could happen. But he couldn't think like that. His freedom was at stake. And in his life, his 25 years, he had had precious little of that.

Lorcan had spent three years in Magilligan Prison, banged up for grievous bodily harm. He had beaten Sean O'Gallagher senseless after he had spilled his pint of lager in the Craiglooner one night years ago. Sean had paid dearly for that pint, but Lorcan even more. Nobody was quite sure how the Filth had shown up; perhaps they had just been passing. No one in their right mind would get the hated coppers involved, just as nobody would call an ambulance, both symbols of authority from a hated Empire who tried to keep them under their control. Justice on the streets of Derry was usually dished out just there: on the streets.

But on that night, while Lorcan was yelping in pain as he washed the blood off his fists in the loo, and the victim's mates were outside trying to fold his limbs to fit them into a mini-cab bound for intensive care, shown up the coppers had, in their daft blinding yellow vests, and Lorcan found himself down the cop shop, and then in the holding cell, the blood congealing on his shirt and the drink and the E draining from his system and wondering how he had ended up there and who his one phone call would be to.

Lorcan wasn't quite a violent maniac. It hadn't been just the wasted beer, though there was that. Drink was expensive. There had been history between Sean and him. Lorcan suspected that back in primary school, when he was seven or eight, Liam had been the one who stole the pencil and eraser set he had gotten from his granny at Christmas, and he was sure Sean had tried to steal Charlotte Teague from him when he was sixteen. And, strangely, considering Sean had tried to steal Charlotte away years earlier, Lorcan had seen him staring at his arse that night and suspected he was a nancy boy. The drink must had been exposing Sean's true, sinful, sordid nature.

But, still, all were surprised when charges were actually pressed. Rumors spread there must be a Protestant in Sean's family tree; that was the only reason a Catholic might press charges against another Catholic. Sean O'Gallagher had won the case, the battle, but lost the war. After Lorcan was sent down, for months backs turned in pubs all over Derry when Sean walked into a pub (so Lorcan had heard), and once he was spat on, but the jury was still out on if this was due to suspected Protestantism, getting Lorcan locked up, or being a secret shirt lifter. Sean had left Derry two years ago. For Florida.

Lorcan's initial sentence hadn't been that long—six months—and frequent visits from his mammy and the Vicodin Fionnaula smuggled in her mouth and passed to him as they kissed in greeting had made the stay at her Majesty's pleasure tolerable. But when Fionnuala had been found out and barred from visiting hours, Lorcan had gone off the deep end. A model prisoner he was not, and any excuse had his fists flying. The prison doctors were kept busy. No amount of pleading that cellmates were poofters, arse bandits, after a go at his bum, could make the prison governor melt. Lorcan's eyes and his charm had no power in that office. Month after month was tacked on to his sentence until he finally realized his fists of fury were not his friends, and a complimentary course on anger management offered by the staff helped him. He was finally released and free.

But then his father guilt tripped him into taking the job at the fish packing plant, and Lorcan had felt in prison again. And now he was counting down the days. Again. Realizing that he was finally leaving Derry, he felt freedom approaching again, but this time it was more exciting. Yes, he loved Derry. How could he not? He had spent his entire life there and knew nothing else. Well, except for Magilligan Prison, which was outside the city limits in the middle of a moor, and there had been the trip to Giant's Causeway with that primary school class with Sean and the stolen pencil. But now Lorcan was finally going to begin really living, just like he saw people doing on the telly. He was set to see the world. Or Florida, at least.

Passing the chip van, he waved hello to Dymphna and her fancy man. Then he entered the Craiglooner. Nothing was on the jukebox. The five shaved heads of the lads on the bar stools whipped around, eager for the sighting of a stranger in their midst and the menace that would follow. Seeing Lorcan, they relaxed and turned back to their pints, disappointed. Lorcan walked up to the barmaid, bleached Amy-Winehouse-style do and dangly turquoise earrings, mutton dressed as lamb, "Right ye are," "Aye, right ye are, son," and ordered a pint. Nobody else was there. This time of the day, not even gone noon, there wouldn't be. But Georgie had said Sorcha liked to drink early.

Lorcan handed over the twenty pound note, and felt a bit of guilt as the barmaid pulled it from his fingers and handed him his change. He stood at the bar (there were no more stools) and sipped his beer, thinking about the night before. He had felt bad about his mother's reaction to his plans to emigrate. He had gone back downstairs after making a few phone calls, including the one to Georgie who had filled him in on Sorcha O'Shaunessy. Fionnuala had moved back to the settee, damp rag on her head, but seemed to be feeling better. She was eating a Turkish Delight. He kissed her on the cheek.

"Sorry about the grief I gave ye before, Mammy," he said. "Ye know I love ye and I don't want to leave ye. Don't ye worry, Mam, but. I'll leave for a wee bit, but then I'll come back.

But they never do, said her eyes, and Lorcan realized now it was true. Even his auntie Ursula, who had tried to buck the trend and, after years of following her Yank military husband to bases around the world, had come back to Derry when he retired to live forever, had been terrorized after she won the lotto until she was chased away, and here he felt more guilt, because his mother had roped him in to play a part in the reign of terror, demanding he use some of his released ex-con mates to scare the bejesus out of Ursula until she had escaped to the States, though not Florida. But Ursula was with her Yank husband, Jed, who could have lived in Derry for thirty years and would still be seen as the outsider, the alien, not of this world, some vaguely half-human creature, like a missionary in darkest Africa in the 1880s must have been regarded by the indigenous population, and vice versa. Whereas Derry was Lorcan's hometown. "I swear I'll be back, Mammy. Just let me make me fortune, and back I'll come. With new gear and gifts for youse all, like. Haven't ye always wanted a self-cleaning oven and another Burberry scarf? And I'll send money to youse all here every month. I promise."

She had moaned and grabbed his strong, young hands and clasped them tightly to her sagging breasts. "I'm afeared I'll never see ye again, but! Ye know ye're the only one of me wanes I have any real love for. Ye know ye're always number one on me lists. Even when ye was banged up. How can I live without ye? I'm not long on this Earth ye know, son. Wait till them tests come back, and then ye'll see. Yer mammy's body be's but a living carcass on its last legs." Here she squeezed out a tear. "The least ye can do is stay here and be at me side when the Lord comes to take me. So that the last thing I see on this Earth be's them lovely blue eyes of yers staring down at me with all the love I know ye have for me as I slip away. Only *you* have the power to make me death a happy one, so ye do, son."

Lorcan's hands were still prisoners within her clammy claws.

"Don't worry, Mammy. I'll speak to the neighbors and see if I can't get one of their passwords for wi-fi so'se ye can watch things on the computer instead of the telly. We can take the computer from the scullery and prop it in front of the telly there. Then yer illness won't be so bad, and ye won't have to resort to DIY entertainment. Ye might even be able to see reruns of that program ye love so much, the one with the briefcases with the different money in em."

She was staring at him as if she didn't understand. But he went on. "And let's wait till them tests come back. I won't leave before then. If them doctors give ye a clean bill of health, then I know ye've decades in ye left. Sure, ye're a spring chicken, so ye are, when ye look at me granny Heggarty for comparison."

"Aye, that's as may be. She does be older than me, but, ye know. Being me mammy, like."

"Ye've me word, Mammy. I won't leave if ye've medical problems that haven't been resolved. A year, I'll stay. That's all. Do ye trust me?"

She stared up at him for quite a while. And finally, slowly, haltingly, she nodded her head. And Lorcan had been happy. Her eyes fluttered shut, so he had had to clear his throat.

"And, er, Mammy?"

"Aye, son? What is it?" she had asked.

"Could I, er, have a lend of twenty quid?"

There was silence. Then, croaking, she had said, "Hand me me handbag, love."

Number two on her list could never have gotten away with that!

"C'mere," he asked those at the bar. "Have youse seen Sorcha O'Shaunessy around today?"

"That slag?!"

"Her with the face of a bulldog licking piss offa a nettle?"

"A fire-damaged Lego, more like!"

"And an arse like two exploded airbags?"

"Naw, more like a bag of washing."

"What do ye want with that one? I wouldn't ride her into battle."

"Aye, yer woman's seen more cockends than weekends."

"More helmets than Hitler."

"A quim like a ripped out fireplace, she must have. Poor dear."

"A burst settee, ye mean."

"A stab wound in a gorilla's back."

"Flaps like John Wayne's saddle bags." Even the barmaid was joining in now!

"Right," Lorcan said. "I'm taking that as a no?"

"Seriously, mucker! What do ye want with the likes of her? A trip to the clinic?"

He couldn't say she owed him money; word would spread like the diseases they thought she would give him. He shrugged.

"Just wondering, like. Ta, muckers."

He downed his pint, then headed off to the next pub.

He found her three pubs and three pints later, in the Poked Pig. Georgie had been right. He had told Lorcan she was in town, would be for three days until she took off again. The Poked Pig was gearing up for karaoke later that day, and she of the Lego face and laundry behind—hair like that stabbed gorilla had been electrocuted during a monsoon, they could have added—was flipping through a book of song selections. Alone. There were twenty or so others in the pub, but she seemed to be with none of them. Her wine glass was almost empty. Lorcan saw red dribbles in the bottom. Perfect. He bought a pint and stood at the bar, putting himself in her sight. He revved up his eyes a gear.

She looked up, then quickly back down at the book, then shyly back up. Then back down. She gulped the rest of her wine. Lorcan bought a glass of red.

He loped over, and she seemed to be thrilled and frightened in equal measures. She ran a finger through her hair, her hand down the back of her tights, and coyly batted her eyelashes at him. He knew her to see, who didn't?, but they had never met. Why would he have wanted to?

"Did it hurt?" he asked, handing her the wine.

She tinkled with laughter. "When I fell from heaven, ye mean?"

She seemed legless already. She certainly made use of every waking hour she was in town, the few of them she was there.

"Aye," Lorcan said. "I've been noticing ye for years now. Took me all this time to get the nerve to tell ye what I think. A ride and a half, so ye are." This was a compliment. "I'm called—"

"Aye, ye're called Lorcan Flood, aren't ye?"

"Aye, and aren't ye one of them O'Shaunessy's from Creggan Heights?"

"Aye, Sorcha, I'm called."

And ten minutes later they were headed to her place.

After much moaning and touching and thrusting, some pumping and groaning, and a sudden squawk of "Wrong hole, ye eejit! Ye've got the wrong hole!" there were suddenly many roars of "Ye filthy, dirty bastard, ye! Ye filthy bastard, ye!" in rapture and excitement and pain and a bit of all three, then Lorcan deflated on the sopping sheets, feeling soiled. Sorcha looked like she felt the same. He knew most of the men who had been in the queue, and feared for the health of his knob.

"That was magic, so it was," Sorcha said.

She barely had time to reach for a fag before he had propped himself up on an elbow on the pillow and stared down at her, doing his magic with his eyes.

And the magic he could do with his body was nothing compared to the magic he could do with those eyes.

"So what's all this I hear about ye working for the airlines?"

CHAPTER 22

Ursula had dabbled in amateur dramatics as a teen. She had even been chosen to play the lead in Agatha Christie's *And Then There Were None*, well, the female lead, as the two leads were male. She had worn a blonde wig and was Vera Claythorne, the aloof governess who had merely looked on as the young boy in her charge drowned himself, the boy whose death was being avenged decades later. Revenge a dish best served cold? In *And Then There Were None*, it was practically frozen! Ursula 'was killed' toward the end of the third act; she was 'coerced' into hanging herself (yes, that's what Agatha Christie had written). When the murderer was revealed and the curtain came down and the play was over, there hadn't been a standing ovation, but Ursula had gotten a date out of it, and at least before the play someone had done her makeup backstage, which was more than could be said for Biggbee studios. So she was no stranger to the stage. Nevertheless, she was sopping with sweat yet frigid with fear.

She felt Jed's hand clutching hers, fingernails digging in, as they took step after step into the blinding lights. There sat the investors before them on a slightly raised platform, hair perfect, teeth gleaming, the cut of their clothing telling. The platform was only two inches high, but there was a world of difference in those two inches.

There was the female one, the dashing playboy one, the old one, the foreign-accented one and the mean bearded scary one, an internet baroness, an energy mogul, a marketing giant, an investment guru, and a food franchise king. The billionaire (the old one) sat in the middle on a grand throne-like chair, the others on either side in less grand but nevertheless luxurious leather. Ursula and Jed had to stand before them on the spot marked with an X.

Jed seemed like he couldn't locate the X, so Ursula guided him over to it and stood beside him. Smiling. She smiled ahead into the ten eyes that bored into hers with a mixture of disdain, mistrust and pity. Her best flowered skirt felt like a tattered dish rag, her waistline massive, her flesh like the Dead Sea scrolls and her breasts grotesque. Her aubergine bob, which she had made a special trip to the salon to spruce up, seemed like a laughable purple helmet. Her heart pounded in her throat. She feared the streams of sweat lashing down her forehead would muss her eyeshadow.

There was a camera to her right, one to her left, another by her feet, and behind them all she saw were the limbs and the tufts of hair of the men working them. She sensed one behind her as well. They kept moving around, and red lights kept blinking on and off, so she didn't know which one was on or not, or if she should be looking—no *smiling*—at them or not.

Ursula cleared her throat. She hoped Jed would clear his. And begin *speaking!*

A second crawled by.

Then another.

And another. Ursula was scared because *these were the first 90 seconds! Eighty four, eighty three, eighty two...*

"Hello?!" It was Mean. He waved fatuously at her and Jed. An edge crept into Ursula's smile. Obviously she could see him and he could see her. He didn't need to wave.

"I said *hel-looo?*" He trilled.

Ursula, lips arched upwards, teeth bared to them all, trundled her neck half an inch to the left and tried to catch the eye of Female. She was supposed to be the friendly one. But Female was scribbling something down in the little notebook each of them made their computations or whatever it was in. Her pen was a Montblanc Meisterstück, platinum. Ursula inched her neck back. She nudged Jed. *Seventy six, seventy five...* To their right on the stage, she saw someone had set up a stand with a poster, SLIM JED JERKY in big letters. Spread out was a selection of their wares. The sight of it was comforting and gave her strength. *Seventy two, seventy one...*

"Who aaarre youuu?" Mean warbled. *"We're waaaiting!"*

Playboy and Foreign snorted with laughter, and Billionaire tsked as he snapped a look at his watch. "Come on, people! I've got other things to do, places to be, people to meet." Female looked up from her notebook. She nodded secret encouragement at Ursula. *Fifty nine, fifty eight...*

Och, for the love of God, Jed! Ursula was peeved, didn't know what was worse, the taunting, the sniggers, the fifty three seconds left, or Jed, the statue of silence. She nudged him again so that Female would know it wasn't her messing up, then chanced a glance at him, and shirked at the sight she saw: jaw slack, frigid with fear. His glasses had fogged up. Her heart fell, but somewhere deep inside her something rose up, she didn't know what it was, it felt like a geyser, and it enveloped her. *Forty six, forty five...* She revved up her tongue.

"Hello, Killer Investors." Her voice crackled with the breathlessness of nerves.

"Fiiin-ally!"

"This is me husband, Jed Barnett, and I'm his wife Ursula." She heard her name as if it belonged to someone else. She curtsied. "We're, erm, we're here to ask youse for the lend of $150,000 for 40 percent of wer company, if ye'd be so kind"

She was startled at the roar of laughter that washed over her from their parted mouths.

"You gotta be joking!"

"You better have excellent sales."

"You mean you're valuing your company at...$375,000?"

Ursula didn't know if they were or not. So she just continued.

"Wer company be's called Slim Jed Jerky, and we sell beef jerky," she waved a hand, robot-like, at the stand, " as if ye couldn't tell."

She was putting on the accent she used so that Americans could understand her, something vaguely transatlantic, slurring words in that American way with her thick Derry accent, halfway between Ireland and Tennessee. It was the voice she had used for Vera Claythorne.

"Now I'm gonny sing ye a wee song someone wrote about wer wile tasty beef jerky. I hope ye enjoy it."

I surely don't. She took a deep breath. From somewhere up above, the music from the jingle rained down into the studio. As the investors jumped, startled, Ursula realized she was scared, or was it embarrassed, to sing the jingle, just like she had been in the studio when they recorded it for the radio. But she imagined she was in the choir at church and it was really *Ave Maria* she was belting out. In a voice more suited to praising good than selling goods, her voice rang out:

> *It's jerky! It's jerky!*
> *It's Slim Jed Jerky!*
> *It's brown and flat,*
> *Yeah, brown and flat,*
> *And believe you me, it won't make you fat!*
> *They're chewing, chewing, chewing it*
> *From Milwaukee To Albuquerque!*
> *Get yours today, and chew those blues away!*
> *It's brown, yeah, I know it's brown,*
> *but it'll chew the blues away!*
> *It's jerky! It's jerky!*
> *It's Slim Jed Jerky!*
> *Yee-hay!*

A silence, stunned. All on the platform exchanged glances. Then,

"Horrible presentation!" bellowed Billionaire. "Horrible packaging! Horrible clothing! Horrible jingle! Horrible people! Get lost!" He sat in his chair sideways, as if the sight of them made him sick. He looked down and fiddled with his iPhone.

"I'm agree," sneered Foreign. "Do not like 'is brown and flat.' And no understand this...bif jeeky. Dreadful. Get lost!"

Ursula jerked under the lights. She hadn't expected applause, but two immediate eliminations? She was still smiling, but her voice was sharp, and she was shocked as she heard herself yell back, "How the flimmin hell can ye say that?!" She was fuming. It was as if they had attacked one of her children, no, all three. "What sort of investors do ye think youse are? Ye've not even tasted wer flimmin beef jerky! And ye've not heard Jed speak yet. Jed? JED?!"

Ursula marched to the stand, and it was here she realized she should have left her handbag in the Green Room. But she didn't know who might chose to rummage through it while it lie there unattended. She didn't want to put it on the studio floor, as it looked dirty and the circus troupe had stood there before them. She slipped it from her shoulder and let it dangle from her elbow. She grabbed the tray. There were little plates with pieces of jerky wrapped, so they could see the packaging (Louella had designed it), and unwrapped, so they could try it. There were also napkins.

"Ye're gonny sample wer jerky if I have to shovel it down yer throats meself!"

"Ooohh! Feisty!" Mean trilled as she strode towards the platform. If he wasn't warbling, he was trilling. But he took a plate. Ursula was relieved to see they all did, though they nibbled tentatively, a bit fearfully, as if she and Jed were selling dog food.

Billionaire spat his nibble out and said,"Leathery. Salty. Disgusting."

"I break my tooth." Foreign.

"Youse're already out, so I don't know why ye even bothered snatching the plates outta me hand like that. Do they not feed ye round here? And I'll have ye know, most of wer customers love em and come back for more. Again and again and again. Repeat business, it's called."

Female, Playboy and Mean's faces were lighting up with surprise as they chewed.

"Remarkable flavor!" Playboy said.

"Delicious!" From Mean. Ursula almost choked.

"I'm usually vegan," Female said, wiping the corner of her lip with one of the napkins and taking another bite, "but this is delightful! There's something...some taste...I can't quite place it...that makes..."

"Yer tongue dance? Aye, that's me special ingredient. A secret, so it is. Ye've not heard about wer business yet! Don't ye wanny hear the numbers? Doesn't that be what ye're interested in? Wer *numbers?'*"

Playboy, Mean and Female leaned forward, their notebooks clutched in their hands, their mouths still chewing. The tide had turned, even though the 90 seconds were long gone. Even Foreign seemed to be reconsidering.

"I not really break tooth." He ate another strip.

"And here was me thinking ye told us to Get Lost." She arched her eyebrows pointedly.

"Okay, you can cook," Mean admitted. "But, yes, let's get down to the numbers. What's the cost of customer acquisition? What percentage of the market does your biggest competitor have? What does it cost to make a package? How much do you sell it for? Wholesale? Retail? What are your sales for the past three years? What were your profits, gross and net? Before and after taxes? Your total revenues? Do you pay yourself a salary? If so, how much? What are your projections for the next three years? Gross and net? Do you have other shareholders? What percentage do they own? What's your EBITA?"

"Me *what?*"

Mean rolled his eyes. "Earnings before interest, tax and amortization expenses. Come on, now!"

"Amorti...?"

"That's too many questions for the poor woman at one time!" Female said.

"Ye think I'm *poor?*"

"No, I meant—"

Playboy jumped in. "Are they made offshore?"

"On an island, ye mean?"

"No, in a different country."

"Are ye asking because of me accent?"

"No, I'm asking because I want to know."

"Made in wer scullery."

"Your where?"

"Wer kitchen."

"What's 'wer?'"

"Our."

"Who makes them?"

"Me husband does all the work, slaving over the oven and all that."

"And your husband...?"

"This is him, standing here."

"And you?"

"I clean that oven every month, so in a way I help make em too."

"Where do you sell them?"

"All over."

"All over where?"

"The area."

"How big is the area?"

"Very big."

"What's your target demographic?"

"Eh?"

"Who do you think buys them?"

"People who eat."

"When did you start making them?"

"Two years since."

"How many employees do you have?"

"Me, Jed, Jed's brother and his wife."

"Do they own it with you?"

"Aye."

"What?"

"Yes."

"Why aren't they here?"

"They're couldn't come."

"Where are they?"

"In the hospital."

"How come?"

"Car crash."

Ursula was breathless. It was as if she and Playboy were volleying back and forth on the central court at Wimbledon and it wasn't raining! These were questions she could easily answer. Oh, his eyes were so lovely, the types that turned down at the corners, making him seem like they were always smiling. How she loved eyes like that— And...was that something in that left eye of his, or was he winking at her?! She felt her waistline shrinking, she was suddenly Slenderella, breasts marvelous, hair Vidal Sasoon chic. She touched it in the back and—

"What are your margins?" Playboy asked.

Ursula's ball slammed against the net.

"I—" The ball bounced on the grass. She had always thought margins had something to do with typing. Jed had told her they meant something else. Exactly what, she couldn't remember. A ball boy scooped it up.

"He...he..."

She pointed at Jed.

"About timmme!" Mean thrust himself into the exchange. "Just who is this he he? Tell me, Ursula, *dear,* does the cowboy speak?"

"Er, I..."

"We really haven't heard much about the numbers, I'm afraid," Female said. "And if we don't..."

Their attention shifted from Ursula and they all stared at Jed. Even Billionaire. Jed's voice was apparently more interesting to him than his iPhone. Ursula turned and stared at Jed too. Pleading with her eyes. She wrung her hands.

Mean snorted. "I think we've given you *amateurs* enough airtime. Time to bring on the real entrepreneurs."

"If there are any," Billionaire said. He had turned again in his seat and inspected his watch. "After the load of crap that's been wheeled on stage tonight, I've lost all hope. Where do they get these idiots from? I think we need to fire the casting director. I'd yell Get Lost at you two losers again, but it doesn't work twice."

"Jed's loads to tell youse! Come on, Jed! Wake up! *Wake up!*"

And Billionaire appealed to his fellow investors. "Come on, guys. Put these pitiful wannabes out of their misery. Tell them to Get Lost!" He leaned over Foreign and addressed Mean. "I thought you were supposed to be the mean one. You're making me look bad. Why haven't you ripped them a new..."

"She looks like my mom. I can't help it." Mean sighed. "Entertaining. Delicious. *Buut,* yeah." He seemed resigned, and Female and Playboy were nodding their heads in sad agreement. Female put down her notebook. Mean shook his head in sorrow as he said, "Ge—"

CHAPTER 23

"Million pound girl, you a boss, I like the way—"

The music was wrenched off the market-wide speakers. There came a clearing of a throat, then "Attention shoppers! Just a wee reminder, we've a big sale coming up next weekend! There'll be 70 pee off some of yer favorites here at the market. Make sure youse mark it on yer calendars! And another thing. If youse could all evacuate the area; there's been another bomb scare. The Filth's on their way to the scene, so if youse know what's good for ye, ye'll be running, not walking, to them gates. Ready, steady, *go,* muckers!"

Many in the world might think the Troubles were a thing of the past, the tear gas long since evaporated, but still the fear of terrorist activities lingered in Derry. And some bombs did occasionally surface to interrupt the daily shopping and the soccer games, hiccups, a terrible, violent past reinserting itself even as time marched forward and Derry struggled to look toward a future. There had been bomb scares in the postal sorting office, the chemist's and the bus depot so far that year, and though they had only been scares and this market wasn't a postal sorting office or a chemist's or a bus depot, anything was possible. In fact, did Unattended Item + Derry's Past = Probable Bomb? Definitely maybe.

"Get me up offa the ground, ye eejit! Themmuns is gonny trample me!"

The gin bottle skidded away, the crisp packet disappeared under a rampage of soles. Fionnuala's face was crushed against the pebbles and detritus on the ground. The handcuffs bit into her wrists. She flinched in fear again and again. Filthy trainers and boots clomped inches past her earlobes, shrieks filled the air above her. As the shoppers fled, it was maybe more the threat of the coppers than an explosion of Semtex that had them screaming and scrabbling over one another, the cause of the gridlock of screaming human bodies at the gate. If the past was anything to go by, Fionnuala suspected the drunks and druggies outside, magnets for any type of excitement, were rising en masse and pushing past the throngs clambering out so they could get into the market for a look see.

Maybe she passed out for a moment, another attack of her mystery illness. But then Fionnuala jerked awake in shock. From beyond the city walls, she heard the sirens winding down. There was a sudden grunting and whining from behind her, a strange, inhuman smell. A slab of dripping leather, hot to the touch, rolled against the knuckles of her bound fists. Fionnuala yelped. The bomb sniffing dog! Government cutbacks had reduced their numbers to one. She wriggled in the rubble, unraveled her fingers and tried to claw its nose.

"Get that manky creature away from me! Fecking mingin, so it is! I'm gonny sue if it takes a chunk outta me with them fangs!"

She struggled to move her body out of its reach. It was impossible. Fionnuala had seen the dog many times before; it was always being trotted out, the postal sorting office, the chemist's, the bus depot. It got older and older. She didn't know what breed it was, something smelly, black and menacing. Craning her neck, she caught through her tears of anger and fear flickers of the green cape-type outfit it wore on its back, not avocado like the wedding, more a fluorescent lime. It scampered around her torso, its claws digging playfully into her back. Then she felt it snuffling at the nape of her neck. Its cold wet nose tickled her skin.

"Offa me! Get offa me ye, flimmin beast!"

She knew it had an owner; she had stood behind him in the line at the Top Yer Trolly once and glanced with curiosity into his basket (three yogurts, a frozen chicken tikka pizza, a toenail clipper, Excite body spray and four 60-watt light bulbs). She saw his boots a foot away now, felt his presence staring down at her. And then there were more.

"For the love of God!" she spat as ten or more other pairs of shiny black boots clunked towards her, moving in and circling her head. The bomb squad arseholes! "Youse've got it all wrong!" She struggled to free herself. She yelled as the dog snorted on her ponytails, which were splayed on the rubble, sniffed her forehead, licked the insides of her nostrils.

"It's not me bag! I tell youse, it's not me bag! And as if I'd cart a bomb around in me satchel! Politics bore the shite outta me, sure! Youse'll see!"

The dog turned around, wagged its tail into her face as if to taunt her, then scampered away. It bounded through two black boots, and tried to make its way towards her satchel. She could just see her bag if she arranged her neck and her eyelids a certain way, there on the ground, ten feet from her face.

A stern voice above her barked, "Who've we got there, then? What traitor?"

She roared and buckled her body as hands grabbed her under her armpits and hauled her upright. She kicked and screamed as she was pressed against the city wall, her hands captive between the stone and her bottom. She gasped. She would have backed into the wall, but she was already there. There were that many people—men!—surrounding her, she couldn't make sense of who might do what job, what branch of the hated PSNI they could belong to, glaring at her, hands poised for action, knuckles ready, filled with hate under the visors of their helmets and caps and in their blinding yellow vests and dark uniforms and even one in army fatigues, bristling with guns and ammo, crossed with straps that bulged with clunky, heavy hardware Fionnuala could only fear. She didn't know who they were, but she could guess their religion and it wasn't Holy Roman Catholic. The leader—she could see it in his hideous face—inspected her with suspicion and disgust as his fingers like bananas held her captive against the wall.

"What've you got in the bag? What's in the bag?" His spittle sprayed against her face.

Tikka Pizza was outside the group, holding the dog back as caution tape was being wound round the electronics stall, festooning it, with her satchel in the middle. As if her satchel, with Celine Dion's face smiling into a microphone (the Titanic side was leaning against wall; nobody could see that), as if Paddy's gift to commemorate their love were a harbinger of evil and destruction. More officers poured through the gates. Their outfits were bigger, their faces harsher. Uglier.

Fionnuala began to plead to the leader and the minions who flanked him, "I'm trying to tell, ye, *sir,* I'm trying to tell youse all—" but her voice was drowned by an outburst of inhuman sounds from the opposite end of the alley, a gnarling and a howling that chilled her. She shot her head towards the soccer scarf stall. And screamed. A pack of feral mongrels burst out from underneath the stall and assailed the alley, spitting, barking, biting the air, clawing what they could, a few foaming. Roars from the uniforms joined Fionnuala's screams. Truncheons sprang open and whipped through the air as the deranged, flea-bitten dogs, patches of hair spouting from their skeletal forms, sped towards the bomb sniffing mutt. It whimpered and cowered behind Tikka Pizza's legs. He held his hands up in alarm as the dogs circled him like ravenous wolves, but—

Thunk! Thunk! Thunk! The batons pounded down on their bodies.

"Outta here!" "Clear off, ye bloody mutts!"

Yelping and squealing, the mongrels skittered out of the gate and were gone.

The leader roared into her face: "Do you see what happens when you play silly beggers? *Do you?*"

Fionnuala would have crossed her arms if she could have. She gave him a look which she hoped said, "How the bloody feck can ye hold me responsible for all the packs of stray dogs in Derry?"

Though he still held her pressed against the wall, he was looking to his left. Beyond the crime scene tape. The bomb sniffer was approaching Fionnuala's satchel. Tikka Pizza was encouraging him with little noises. The dog poked its head into Fionnuala's satchel. All were forming a circle around it, faces shining with fear and excitement. Breaths caught in throats. *Sniff! Sniff!* Fionnuala realized she herself was bracing for the worst, though she was the only one in Derry who knew there was no Semtex, no plastic explosives, no wires or timers or whatever the feck else was in bombs in that satchel. Only...she cringed at what the dog would find. This would be a story, she bemoaned, told and retold in Proddy pubs for decades, passed down through the generations, rolled out at cop shop Christmas dos and whatever Proddy holy days they might observe and celebrate and hooted with drunken, bawdy laughter about. The Catholic Moorside housewife and her secret stash of Titanic urine.

And then, as Fionnuala burned with humiliation and shame, the dog excitedly poked its snout under one of the frayed handles and pushed it to the side. The top of the jug was bared for all the coppers and bomb squaddies to see. And the cover of *How To Be A Lady,* a white-gloved hand holding a teacup in the correct manner. Fionnuala cringed, mortified, against the stones as the dog pressed its nose to the red plastic, excitement in its whines, its paws dancing. And then it turned, lifted its left hind leg and...

"Me satchel!" Fionnuala squealed. She was shocked at herself. She never squealed. Roared, barked, shouted abuse and spewed filthy venom, yes. Squealed, never. Her heart fell as she watched her beloved bag being...*soiled* by that hateful Protestant cunt of a dog. "Oh, the humanity!" she moaned. It was becoming quite a useful phrase.

The bastard in charge, the one pressing her against the wall, narrowed his eyes to slits. "I thought it wasn't your satchel?"

And then, just to torment her further, roars of laughter rang out as the dog, whining excitedly, began to hump her satchel. Each thrust of its body, electrified with rapture, was like the stab of a rusty screwdriver into Fionnuala's heart. And after it finished its business, it scampered happily away, looking up at its owner and demanding a treat. But it still hadn't barked. No sign of any explosives.

Now she saw a man approaching her bag with caution even as the laughter trickled to a stop. He was wearing a helmet and holding a pole with a mirror. She rolled her eyes. It was one of those yokes they used to detect bombs under cars. He twiddled it around inside the bag and inspected the interior.

"All clear!" he called.

The leader's hand finally left Fionnuala's chest as the uniformed masses deflated with relief, or was it disappointment? She would've smoothed down her blouse and arranged her breasts, but she couldn't.

"I'll have ye for sexual harassment!" Fionnuala barked.

"I've a laundry list of things I could have you for, dear."

Five of the more bulkily dressed lumbered over to the bag.

"Shall we open it? See what's inside?"

"Naw! Naw!" Fionnuala wailed, *begged.* She made to lunge forward, but found suddenly she was being tightly gripped and pressed against the wall again, this time by five pairs of hands,

Fionnuala had had many bad moments in her life: Her first shag against the cannon on the city walls that were now above her, the night she had walked home from the New Year's Eve party Buncrana in a snowstorm when she had roared drunken abuse at everyone there and nobody would give her a lift back to Derry, Siofra walking in on her and Paddy's ill-conceived conjugal romp atop the washer after one bottle of cheap wine too many (the washer had never worked properly after that, and the dent was still there, eyed pointedly by Siofra when Fionnuala told her she couldn't have any sweeties and they happened to be standing in the scullery), the Christmas, also after a Liebfraumilch too many, when she had kissed Ursula Barnett under the mistletoe—with her tongue!—all sprang easily to mind. But this was the worst.

One of them, tense, unscrewed the lid of the jug. Fionnuala grit her teeth at the sound of plastic against plastic which rang out in the alleyway. The five men bent over and peered in.

"Eeuugh!" the Proddies chorused like the hateful bastards they were.

"What's that mad thing doing, carting that...*filth*...around with her in her bag?"

"Perv!"

Fionnuala wanted the Lord to strike her down dead with a bolt of lightning that very moment. But He didn't, and He was a right hateful Bastard and all, she thought. Even the leader and his squad were moving towards the jug now for a look, and Fionnuala grabbed the moment. With her hands still captive behind her back, she inched down the alleyway and surely, she thought, this was a pose she had seen in *How To Be A Lady,* the stance a wallflower was supposed to make as she waited on the sidelines at the cotillion for an eligible bachelor to ask her to dance. She tiptoed in that correct manner further and further down the alley until she was free.

CHAPTER 24

Sorcha was running a bath. She had to freshen up, she'd said. This was true,
Lorcan knew. He also knew how slowly a bath filled, and that he'd be there on
the bed, sheets alternately damp and crusty, for the long haul. He cringed as he
heard Sorcha start singing Fern Kinney's romantic "Together We Are
Beautiful" from the bathroom down the hallway, *"I am the rain, he is the sun,"*
and with any other girl he would've grabbed his gear and fled for the hills,
"And now we've made a rainbow," but he still hadn't gotten what he had come
for.

He spied Sorcha's cell phone on the nightstand next to the mug she had
thrown up in. His eyes lit up. She was sure to have international on her phone,
flying for the airlines as she did. He rummaged around the many things on the
floor until he found his track suit bottoms. First he checked to see if Sorcha had
lifted the cash from his pocket when he had passed out, post-coital. Lorcan
admitted to himself it was unlikely, but you couldn't be too sure. The leftovers
of his mammy's twenty pound note, all three pounds fifty pee of it, was still
there. He had a bit of respect for Sorcha. Then he found his own useless phone
and looked up Eoin's new Yank number in Florida. He didn't know what time it
might be over there; he had heard the States had their own strange hours (it was
6 AM). But he pressed in the number and heard the phone ringing across the
Atlantic. Lorcan was excited. He had never made an international call before.

"Aye?"

"Eoin? Lorcan."

"Och, what about ye, mucker!"

"Are ye right?"

"Aye, ye and all?"

Eoin's slurred voice was barely recognizable, more suited to the wretched
ones outside the city walls, the voice of a youth prematurely aged, setting
himself up for a life of OTB betting shops and sleeping on park benches with
an empty bottle of generic booze at his side. And he had once been an altar
boy! Beyond Eoin's croak through the phone, in Florida it sounded like a
Friday night at the Craiglooner during a soccer match, young male Derry
voices yelling and slurring, and Lorcan was surprised to hear that they were
playing "Timber" there in Florida as well, but then he wasn't surprised, as he
figured Pitbull and Ke$ha were probably Yanks and so it was a Yank song and
they would play it in the States.

"Aye, so what's the craic?" Lorcan asked. "What've ye been up to over there in Yank land?"

"Och, ye'd never believe it! I was meant to be staying with Eric O'Toole, as a stop gap until I found me own place and a job. Who did I run into at the baggage carousel at the airport, but, but Tommy Flint. Ye know he served mass with me at St. Moluag's. And he was with Nigel O'Malley. They already had jobs lined up, and a house and all, that they was sharing with some lads from Creggan Heights. I think ye know most of them, Mickey Tennet and Jaz O'Rourke and Jerry Feeney."

"Merciful Jesus! Does all Derry be there, like?"

"Near as dammit."

"No wonder the streets round here seems empty. What job've ye got, then?"

"It's an Irish pub. Me and Tommy and Nigel be's working behind the bar there. Bartenders, as the Yanks says. Pots O' Gold & Leprechauns, the pub be's called."

"Jesus, them daft Yanks!"

"Aye, but the money's magic! Ye wouldn't believe it! That much money be's thrown at me nightly, I'm on the verge of begging the punters to stop! Bulging, me pockets be's at the end of a night. And ye should see the digs we're living in, massive, so the house is, and the size of the telly in it! Like at the pictures! And in the back garden, I couldn't believe me eyes, they've a pool! And they've even a machine that dries clothes! And there be's a party every night, like an endless New Year's Eve. Ye know what it's like, waking up every afternoon with lads passed out in the front room I've no idea who they were. But it's a wile craic."

"Have ye been to the beach? Doesn't there be one out there, it being Florida, like?"

"Aye, but the one time we all went, with crates of beer, like, me flesh was near scorched from me bones. Worse than a lobster, I was, and up came the blisters and bedridden for three days, so I was. Ye know what me skin's like, hi." Lorcan did. And his orange hair. "Never again. And ye might think, this being Florida, the sweat be's lashing down me all hours God sends. But these Yanks have air conditioning everywhere, AC, themmuns call it. We spend the day jumping from one air conditioned unit to another. I'm freezing me bollocks off over here, though every day the sun be's blazing down from the heavens. Wrapped up like deepest winter, we've got to be."

"Have ye met any Yanks, then?"

There was a startled silence, as if Eoin had never considered this, as if Lorcan had asked him if he had chanced upon a nine-eyed extraterrestrial who had materialized from behind a palm tree to extend the hand of friendship.

"Naw, I only know em to see, the lasses, anyroad, and to get me leg over.

I've ridden more than me fair share. Which, I'm proud to tell ye, be's more than what yer fair share would be, if ye catch me drift. I open me mouth, they hear me accent, and they fling themselves at me."

"At *you?!"*

"I get me kecks off so often me bollocks is pure aching. Sure, there's no need to be mates with em, as I kyanny understand what they be's blathering on about half the time, what with the accent and them slurring from being legless. Ye'd never believe what them Yanks has here: Happy Hour, they call it. Two for one drinks. And hours it goes on for. And not just in wer pub, but in all the pubs and bars, as they're called here. Ye might think we get bladdered in Derry; that's nothing, but, to what we can afford to get up to over here."

Lorcan was shocked. There was never a discount on drink in Derry pubs. The Rocking Seamaid had once had a Smithwicks promotion and offered 50 pee off a pint, back before Lorcan was incarcerated, and folks were still talking about it nostalgically.

"And there's that many drugs to be smoked and snorted and swallowed, I kyanny keep track of what it is I'm taking, nor what time of day it's meant to be, nor the date. To tell ye the truth, I've no clue how long I've been over here now. How long have I been here, hi, Lorcan?"

"A few months, I think. With all them drugs, but, doesn't the streets be crawling with coppers?" Lorcan had seen all the shows, *CSI, NCIS, 24, Law and Order, America's Most Wanted, Criminal Minds, Hawaii Five-O, The Mentalist, White Collar,* even *Rizzoli and Isles* and *Starsky and Hutch,* and America seemed to be a land of nothing but people committing crimes, being chased by the police and being caught. "Are ye not afeared of being hauled in and spending the rest of yer days banged up again?"

"I understand how ye think I might be scared, just being let out of Magilligan as we was, and, aye, I was afeared at first, but that's another thing that's brilliant about Florida! Sure, the coppers all has names like O'Malley and O'Leary and O'Connelly, all Irish-American, and, indeed, I was caught with a wee bit of hash on me the other week, and for a few E's the week before that, X, they call it here...daft!...but when the Yank Filth hear me accent, they're more interested in knowing if I knew their second great grandmammy once removed who used to live in a thatched cottage with a flock of sheep in Limerick than the drugs they've caught me with! Free reign, we lads here is given, and on the forces there doesn't seem to be a Proddy bastard in sight. The Yanks have told me that a town of only Irish coppers be's somewhat out of style, nowadays they're paired mostly with a Mexican or a lass, but I've been lucky so far. *The Luck of the Oirish! The life of Riley!"* he said it with a fake Yank accent. "And thank feck for that, as they've the strangest laws in this country. I kyanny comprehend em. Normal activities what people does all the time be's considered crimes here. Having a fag in public or taking a slash in public, public urination, they call it, being legless on the streets, public intoxication, they call it, brawling in the streets, disorderly conduct, they call it. All outlawed. Daft. Enough of that, but. Do ye know, Lorcan, och, I can barely believe it, but I'm saving up to buy meself an auto."

"A...*car?!*" The shocks kept coming. So Eoin would be the first of the Floods to own, let alone drive one of those most sacred of indicators of wealth that were so difficult to come by. Being the first in the family to drive a car was like the first to attend university. And here the urgency to leave Derry welled in Lorcan for real. "Can ye drive, but?"

"Sure, ye just stick a key in a wee slot and press on a yoke on the floor with yer foot. And steer like a PlayStation."

"C'mere, why I'm ringing ye for is for to tell ye I'm on me way out there to join ye. I kyanny stick it here no more. I should be there, well...I thought in a few weeks. Might be sooner, but. Tomorrow, like." Lorcan knew he didn't have to ask if he could stay with his brother. If there was someone from the family abroad, it was a free room and board for life, no questions asked.

"Effin brilliant! There be's ten Derry lads jammed into the one house, but it be's massive, as I've said. One more, five more, bring along some of yer former cell mates, the more the merrier. And we watch the footie all the time, take over the pubs when a match be's on, as no Yanks are interested in footie."

Then they chatted for a minute or so about Dymphna's wedding and the price of iPhones and iPads and Calvin Klein boxers over there, and then Eoin had to go as someone had fallen into the pool and seemed to be drowning.

Lorcan had loads to think about as he hung up. He picked at the scabs on his knuckles as he lay there on the crumpled sheets, damp, cold, waiting for Sorcha's perhaps diseased limbs to crawl back beside him, mattress lumpy and springs popping out. He was shocked at Eoin getting his leg over so often, not that casual sex was shocking, but from Eoin it was, with his orange hair and mild, former altar boy manner. Florida, the Yank sunshine, easy money, cheap beer and copious drugs were all turning his younger brother into an amoral party animal. Eoin wasn't living some peculiar foreign life in the States, but the same life he had lived in Derry, though louder, faster, stronger, bigger, better. With more fanny. And more mates; Eoin hadn't had many, on account of his hair and the altar boy thing, and him being suspected of being a police informer, but in that alien land, Lorcan supposed, all Irish expats had to band together against the indigenous population. And a car! And money!

The Lord, and Lorcan, knew a glance around at the boarded up shop windows of the Moorside, at the TO LET signs defaced with anti-Brit graffiti, the misery of the Jobs Office, the drunks and druggies and hooded youths on every street corner with nothing but time and the occasional stray dog to kill that there was none of that in Derry. Or there was, there had to be, but for Lorcan and his non-skilled ilk, it was impossible to come by.

Lorcan moved to the scabs on his other hand. He knew he had to leave. Immediately. With a Mammy diseased or not diseased, Dymphna wed or not wed. Staying for the wedding made no sense to him. It was just an extra day in Derry. He loved his sister, but the suit he'd be wearing reminded him of prison, he had no gift to give her, nor the means to get one, and weddings were for lasses, anyroad. Except for the groom and the best man, and he was neither of them. After three years of the delayed gratification of prison, he wanted what he wanted *now!* And that was to escape Derry.

Sorcha appeared in the doorway, towel on her head and lust in her eyes. Her tatty bathrobe clunked to the floor. "Are ye up for another round?" she asked. She peered at the sheets and gave a filthy, delighted bark of laughter. "Aye, I see ye are!"

"Aye, am are." Sorcha hopped in beside him and wrapped herself around his neck. She smelled like lemons. He stank of sweat. "Before we go at it, but, mind ye were telling me earlier about them free flight yokes yer airline gives ye?"

She couldn't remember it at all and, thinking it was the drink and not Lorcan's lie, the blood seeped into her cheeks.

"Did I?"

"Aye, ye did. And while ye was in the bath, I've just had me brother in Florida ring me. He's laid up in hospital with some strange Yank disease. All on his lonesome, he is, and afeared he's gonny meet his maker without a friendly face at his bedside. I wonder if ye might...?"

He wrapped his arm around her shoulders. Sorcha nibbled on her lower lip, the lip that had been unmentionable places an hour earlier.

"I only get the one, but. One a year. A Free Flight For A Friend, it be's called. They can call it that all they like, but there be's taxes. Though I suppose they're only a few pounds. I'd love to help ye out, Lorcan. Really, I would." She ran her finger down his bicep. "I know how wile dear a flight to the States be's. There's me granny, but. She's always wanted to visit Lourdes, ye know, the Marian shrine over in France, and after that angina attack of hers last week, I think she be's on her last legs. I was thinking of giving it to her, like. She's always been wile kind to me. Bought me one of them heads you can practice all sorts of hairdos on for me eighteenth birthday. I wanted to be a hair stylist, ye see."

"Och, sure, to get to France, but, can she not take the bus to Belfast, the ferry to Liverpool, the train to Dover and then the ferry over to France? Or even that Chunnel. I don't know how ye cross that, in a train or bus or if ye have to walk. Florida, but..."

"Aye, but an aul woman like that, taking all them different forms of transport..."

She seemed uncertain.

"Never mind that now," Lorcan said, running his fingers through her sopping strings of hair. "Ye can have a wee think about it and let me know later. Now, but, let's get wer oats."

And they did. While they were at it, Sorcha squealing in rapture, Lorcan was thinking he would give her what she craved over and over, shag her until she saw sense and forgot her granny and relented and handed the pass over to him. He wouldn't leave that dank bedroom until it was in his hand. He was sure it would happen. He thrust his hips forward. That's how he had gotten the Internet password from Sally Murphy, next door but one. And when he had satisfied Sorcha, he would use her Free Flight For A Friend to Florida and turn his back on Derry, on his hometown, for good.

"Ayyyeee! Ayyeee!" Sorcha gleefully wailed.

CHAPTER 25

Something clicked in Jed's brain.

"She looks like my mom," he heard Mean say. Jed had been trained to fight, to attack the enemy, though it was many years ago, "I can't help it," Deep inside he realized that, compared to the threat of Communist aggressors and the food and latrines of the mess hall in DaNang, "Entertaining," he had nothing to fear from bright lights sizzling above him and millionaires sitting in chairs before him, "Delicious." He remembered his gung-ho spirit, the have-a-go hero of his youth, "*Buut,* yeah." What kind of man was he, letting his wife, a woman, do the fighting for him?!! "Ge—"

"Don't tell us to Get Lost!" Jed barked. The investors jumped as a unit. A notebook fell to the platform. The cameras clamored around Jed and the sweat that poured from the brim of his cowboy hat.

"Aaahh!" Mean trilled, clapping his hands with sarcastic glee. "It *rises from the deaad!*"

Ursula deflated with relief, freed a tissue from her handbag and wiped the sweat as Jed said: "We got great numbers, guys. No, forget that, we got fantastic numbers! It costs us $1.50 to make five jerkies. We sell them for $3.99, so our gross profit margin is a whopping 62.41%! 62.41! That's a markup of 166%, and our customers think that's cheap. Because it is! We don't want to rip anybody off."

"Oh!" Mean was startled. So were the others. They clucked their disappointment to one another. "That's bad business."

"Compared to other jerky, we're 150% cheaper. But more delicious. As I heard you say." For Jed might have had a sudden catatonic fit, but he had been listening. And he had all the answers, the beloved numbers they kept demanding, at hand. From the corner of his eye, he saw Ursula under the super troupers, fixing a stray lock of hair and eying him with marvel. She clutched his elbow now and smiled gaily at the investors, vindicated, as he went on. Her handbag pressed against his hip. Jed added, maybe to really praise Ursula or maybe to add a bit of color or maybe to protect him when she finally got him off the stage, "We toyed with calling it Ursul-urky for a while. That's how important my wife's secret ingredient has been to our success!" He saw their faces, and quickly held his hands up. "Ok! The numbers! The numbers! Last year we made $19,950, with a gross profit of $12,450, and a net profit, taking overhead costs into account, but there aren't many, because I work for free, Slim works for free, Ursula works for free, Louella works for free, really there's only the cost of the electricity to heat the oven, the packaging, the gas to take them to the stores, so our net profit was $11,000."

They roared with laughter.

"Are you insane?" Billionaire asked. "No, let me rephrase that. You *are* insane."

"I wouldn't say so," said Mean. Jed and Ursula looked at him with hope. "I'd say *loooney!*"

Female's brow was creased. "You've made $11,000, and you're valuing your company at almost $300,000?"

"Yeah, but when you invest," Jed saw the looks, "*if* you invest—"

Mean broke in: "You don't even take a salary? How do you *eat?* And from the looks of you two, you *do* eat!"

"Jed's got his navy pension," Ursula said. That as one thing she knew. And Jed had told her to not mention the store; they might want to invest in that as well, and that would muddy the waters.

Jed forged onward: "Our projections for the next three years are, taking into account your investment, and your help, of course," And onward "added exposure, bla bla gross, bla bla net," and on, "get costs down, quadruple sales and more," and on "millions." and on "low cost of customer acquisition," and on "distributors" and on "EBITA" until Playboy finally held up his hands.

"Hold on! Just hold on! It all sounds great, but—"

"Yes, but then why are you—" Mean said.

"Why are you here?" Billionaire asked.

"Tell us why you need the money," Female said. "Tell *me,* Jed." She said it as if his head were resting on the pillow next to her. He cast Ursula a nervous look. But maybe it was the bright lights or the stress of the first ten minutes alone or the difficult math she had just heard or the desperation of their situation or Playboy looking at her with those sexy, down-at-the-corner eyes of his but Ursula didn't seem to care.

"Yes," Foreign said. "Why you here?"

Billionaire jumped in, "You can't keep up with demand? You need to buy machinery and move the factory out of your kitchen and into a real factory?"

There was a squelch of leather on the platform as all leaned forward, even those who were out. Pens posed over notebooks. Jed realized they'd find out during due diligence, anyway. He may as well tell them the sad truth.

"I...I..." he said.

Ursula, perhaps fearing another catatonic shock, gripped his hand and urged him on.

"I'm embarrassed to say this, but I gambled all the profits away. Every last red cent."

All recoiled with a collective gasp of pity and revulsion.

"Red, yes," said Billionaire.

"Ack!" Foreign contorted his hands into some non-American expression of disgust. "Tell no more! I know! Before I rich, I spend year in Gambler Anonymous. We sit in room and they tell we diseased. Diseased people. I diseased. He diseased. She diseased. Now I no more diseased, well, yes, still, never stop, but hidden. You still diseased, but not hidden. I say already Get Lost, but now I tell again...Get Lost!"

There was silence. The power cords on the floor, the behinds of the cameramen, the lines of the empty notepad pages, all seemed suddenly more important to look at than Jed and Ursula on the stage. Female nibbled on the top of her pen. Then she cleared her throat.

"Sometimes it's about investing in the people. I disagree with Mark here. And Per. And Eric. And Mitchell. Don't take what they say to heart. I don't think you're horrible people. I like you," she looked down at her notebook, "Ursula. And Jed, I think you're cuddly. As people, I *adore* you. And we've all made mistakes. Jed, you are to be applauded for trying anything to make amends for the past. It's commendable, so kudos to you!" She smiled brilliantly. "And I really do love your jerky. I'd love to know that special secret ingredient, Ursula. But I'm looking at the numbers, and as much as it pains me to say it, for all the rebuilding that has to be done, and all the work I'd have to do to get you back where you were, and the fact that you haven't gotten around to giving yourselves salaries, I'd have to take 90% of your company. And I don't want to do that to you nice people. Well, I don't think you'd even accept anyway. So, and it pains me to say it, I think I have to say..." Jed cringed at what Female would say, but at least she had the grace to say it apologetically, "Get Lost, please."

And then there were two. As hope seeped from his heart, Jed imagined
Female even blushed, or maybe it was her makeup. He saw Ursula give him a
'what do we say now?' look, and he was looking at her the same way. Tears
welling, she crossed herself, clutched the little cross that sat in the sweat of her
bosom, and she appealed to the lights blazing into her skull and now onto her
forehead, "Please, dear Lord, help us in wer hour of need! Please help us!
Please!"

Billionaire snorted. "Do you know how desperate you sound? Let me tell
you what I think. I think—"

"NAW!" Ursula roared out. The camera before her jerked in surprise. "Shall
I tell *youse* what *I* think?" All heads turned, shocked, to Ursula. Including
Jed's. He froze. Again. He knew all too well those tightened lips, that vein on
her forehead, the purplish tint to her cheeks that vied with her hair for
attention. Ursula was fit to burst with rage. Derry rage. To his horror, Jed saw
her part her lips and open her mouth wide, gearing up to spew out whatever
madness was in her head.

"No, Ursula! Don't!" Jed pleaded.

"Damn right, Jed." Mean raised his hands in mock horror. "No, Ursula!
Don't! I shall tell you what *I* think." He warbled, "Just *Gettt Losssst!"* and he
was laughing. At them. Foreign and Billionaire joined in. Female buried her
head, Jed hoped in shame and not to hide giggles.

And Ursula stared roaring that Derry rage, barbed tongue skewing the air:
"A disgrace to the human race, so youse all are! Would youse all wise up, for
the love of God? Such a pile of flimmin childish, hateful people I've never seen
in me life before! What was the slurs ye hurled our way a few moments since?"
She counted off on her fingers, "Eejits! Losers! Wannabes! It's like a flippin
playground for wanes in here, the amount of name calling going on, as if youse
was bullies just outta yer nappies. And the shame of it all be's that yer bank
accounts be's bulging with millions! What use is them millions if ye've got the
mental age of a flimmin juvenile? Youse should be ashamed of yerselves, as
the Lord knows I'm mortified for youse meself!" She singled Mean out with a
trembling finger, and Jed saw Clipboard on the sidelines of the stage, looking
thrilled at the outburst and edging closer, but with security guards behind her,
ready for action. "So ye're finally out, are ye, ye sarky toerag? Sarcasm be's the
lowest form of wit, don't ye know, and I wouldn't want to work together with
the likes of ye anyroad, let alone let ye make away with part of wer company.
Drive me mental, so it would, so that I don't know what would give me greater
pleasure, to end me misery by shoving a fistful of tablets down me throat or
crushing em up in yer martini to serve em to ye meself. Making the choice to
give up the wee-est smidgen of wer company, the company we grafted hard to
build up from the ground, has been one of the most wile difficult decisions me

and Jed has ever had to make. Days of agonizing, it took us, to make up wer minds to appear here—" Jed knew this was far from the truth, but the Irish were great at guilt-trips. He'd been on the receiving end in Derry loads of times. "And to come out here on this stage, without the dignity of a bit of rouge or a crimping iron at our disposal in that farce of a dressing room ye've set aside for us, while I'm sure teams of stylists was buzzing around youse like flies around a grand big pile of—"

"And why not?" Mean broke in. Jed saw the man was struggling to control his own rage, and. "We are the haves. You are the have nots."

"Smarmy, filthy git! Even to look at ye makes me skin crawl! I wanny fling meself head first into a bucket of bleach, so I do. Have youse no compassion? An ounce of Christian charity in yer bodies? Aye, youse have worked hard and all, I gather that, to be sitting up there now, but if ye had seen them others ye sent packing back into the Green Room, tears streaming down their faces, babbling and bawling like wanes without a mammy, so they was, their hopes for a new life dashed, going back to their desperate, miserable, *poor* lives—"

"They knew what they signed up for. Haven't you seen the show before?" Billionaire said with a world-weary sigh.

"And just who the flimmin hell do you think you are? Pontius Pilate?" Billionaire pointed at himself in shock. "Aye, you, I'm talking to, laying down the law from on high, sat there in yer chair like a throne, staring down yer nose at the likes of us. And you! Aye, you!" she said as very startled Female pointed at herself. "Ye were nice enough to us at first, but then I saw ye making eyes at me husband! I was all for it when ye called me husband cuddly, could put up with it. But then ye...then ye turned us down anyroad. Can ye not find some man on yer own, with yer unlimited millions and them fancy togs of yers?"

Female looked down at her breasts, fearful as to what togs might be, but they were only clothes. "I thought I was being kind."

"Find yer own fancy man!" And to Jed's further horror, Ursula now erupted into tears, and brought the tissue up to her nose and honked into it, then brought it up to her eyes and gave them a little wipe as she wailed, "Jed be's mines! Mines, I tell ye! All mines! I thought the next number ye were set to prize from him was how many years we've been wed!" The tears were but momentary, and then her anger flared again as the pointed at Foreign. Mascara ran down her face. "And you! The foreign one! A trip to the ESL center in town wouldn't go amiss. Ye've got cash enough to pay for the lessons, like. Ye need to learn to speak God's English as the rest of us does. And me husband doesn't be diseased! I sleep next to him every night, and I'm right as rain, sure! Not a rash to be seen nor a fever to be felt."

Mean turned in his chair to Billionaire. "*I* want to know what 'nappies' and 'togs' are. They sound *faaascinating!*"

155

"Enough!" They all turned to Playboy. He had been making little notes in his notebook. "Thank you for your insight, Ursula. Now I'll have my say. I agree with Elaine. It's about people. And I like you both too. In particular, I'm impressed by your fighting spirit, Ursula, and your obvious passion. You remind me of *my* mother, too. And I like your numbers, Jed. The pre-gambling ones, of course. And I enjoy taking risks. High risk, high payback sometimes. So I'm going to make you an offer. It will be contingent, of course, on Jed joining Gamblers Anonymous. Even if you agree to that, you still might not like my offer. In fact you probably won't. But I'm going to make it anyway."

He looked back down at his notebook and made a few more computations. Ursula and Jed stood in the lights, transfixed. Mean and Billionaire looked away from Playboy in disgust. Foreign looked confused. Female had left the stage. Jed reached out and grabbed Ursula's hand. The tissue poked through her fingers and pressed against his palm. He squeezed her hand so tightly, his wedding band bit into the flesh of the fingers to either side.

"Um, yes?" Jed asked Playboy.

"What's yer offer?" Ursula asked.

Playboy finished scribbling, then looked up. He adjusted a cufflink as he said, "Here it is."

"Don't do it!" Billionaire wailed. Jed didn't know if it was directed at them or Playboy, their only chance for survival.

"You'll be *soorrryy!*" Mean warbled. Again, who was he speaking to?

"The suspense be's driving me mental!" Ursula said.

"Already mental," Foreign said.

Ursula's hand curled into a fist, but Jed held it fast in his own.

Playboy finally spoke.

"$150,000," he said. "For...85 percent of the company."

Jed knew the look on his face now was probably the same one he had when he glanced at their bank account that morning. Ursula turned to him, her eyes searching.

"Jed? Does that be good or bad?"

Billionaire, Mean and Foreign were laughing, but that didn't mean anything; it seemed like they had been doing that since Jed and Ursula stepped into the sound studio.

"That's...a lot," Jed said.

"And you've got a lot of problems,: Playboy said. "A *lot*. Would you like to go in the room in the back and discuss it? We've got a room there for that."

Jed nodded haltingly. Ursula turned around, kicked a cord aside, and walked toward the back.

"No, the other way," Playboy said.

She turned and walked the right way. Jed followed her. Behind him, he could hear hoots of laughter and the rumble of a camera as it followed them.

There was indeed a room in the back, with a door Jed had to open. He was startled when the camera rolled inside with them.

"What do ye think, Jed? Does that be a good offer?"

Jed didn't want to reply with the camera there and rolling, and the cameraman behind it, but there was nowhere in the tiny room to hide.

"I don't know," he whispered. The boom mic hovered closer over their heads, almost touching Jed's hat. "It seems like we'll be giving up a lot. But they always say, 100% of something small is worse than 40% of something big. Or something like that."

"Eh?"

"The thing is...With one of the investors on board, honey, Slim Jed Jerky could be *huge!* That guy has all the contacts. A few phone calls, and he could get us into...I don't know, Wal-Mart, K-Mart, Sam's Club..."

Ursula squealed. The mic jerked away. "And the Top-Yer-Trolly?!" she asked, breathless.

"Hmm, international? Maybe there as well!"

Ursula shrieked with delight. "Could ye imagine...all of Derry doing their weekly messages down the town, and they sees wer jerky on the shelves...even Fionnuala?" Her eyes were bright.

"We have to ring Slim and talk it over with him," Jed decided. "I guess that's what this phone is here for."

There was a land line phone on a battered table. Jed picked it up and began to dial. But then he realized... "Slim isn't home. He's at the hospital. We have to call him there. Do you know the number?"

Ursula gave him a look. "And here was me thinking *ye* were the one who knew all the numbers!" Jed opened his mouth to explain, but Ursula shook her head. "Only joking, dear. Naw, I don't have a clue what the hospital number might be. I'm struggling to remember the name. Veteran, something. And, anyroad," she looked down at her watch. "Wasn't he meant to go in for another round of surgery about now? Either that, or he's already been, and they've got him knocked out on who knows how many tranquilizers and whatnot. How about Louella?"

"What could Louella tell us?"

Ursula nibbled on a fingernail. "Och, sure, they won't even let her use her phone. They're forbidden in hospitals. That's another reason we can't call Slim. And she's sure to be at his side still."

"I guess we've got to make the decision ourselves. What do you think, Ursula?"

She regarded him with confusion and fear.

"Why are ye asking me? It's you that's got the business mind. I'm afeared to say one way or the other, for fear that—"

"Hurry *uuupppp!*" They heard Mean all the way across the stage and through the door of the room. "Mitchell's going to change his *miiinnnddd!* If he knows what's *gooood* for him!"

"Och!" Ursula spat, irritated. "That man...!"

Jed was startled to see her rummaging through her handbag. He hoped she wasn't searching for a pistol.

"What on earth...?"

"Heads or tails," Ursula said, pulling out her change purse. She clicked it open. "Heads, we accept, tails, we turn him down. How does that sound, Jed? Like one of yer bets on the roulette table, aye? Red or black. Let's just see where the luck of the draw, or the flip, I guess it must be called, takes us. Aye?"

Jed thought for a second, then nodded his head haltingly. Mitchell had told him no more gambling, but...

The camera moved in on Ursula's hand as she pressed the quarter between her fingers and thumb and flicked. It flew through the air, spinning, bounced off the palm of her outstretched hand, twirled a few times on the dust, then clattered to the floor. They eyed each other, breathless. Then Jed bent down, took at look at it and picked it up. He showed it to Ursula. She saw which side it had landed on, paused, looked him in they eyes and nodded.

The camera rolled towards the door. Jed opened it. They walked back out into the lights. The camera followed behind.

CHAPTER 26

Bridie McFee stared at herself in the mirror. She looked at her eyes and her eyes looked back at her. They were somehow special now, she felt. A fresh wave of wonderment spread through her, veins percolating in that strange way they had ever since the Happening the day before. She gently pressed fingers to her lips, now chaste. The cold sores that had festered and wept there, long the bane of her existence, were gone. There weren't even reddish spots where they had once been. They had magically disappeared. But it wasn't magic. It was divine intervention. She flushed the toilet, flicked off the light, entered the landing and walked down the stairs of her auntie Bernadette's house.

The wallpaper was a barrage of orange and yellow flowers that assaulted the eyes, but Bridie's eyes were now special; the horrid wallpaper didn't affect them. They were super eyes. Her nose, however, wasn't so blessed. The house's fragrance opened with notes of spoiled milk, the heart was sickly sweet bargain bin perfume, and the base secreted sweat. The main accord was old aged pensioner. Bridie didn't care. Her heart sang and, indeed, she began to hum "You Light Up My Life" as she walked to the front hall.

Once she had been filled with an eternal emptiness, lumbering despondently through the rain-soaked streets of Derry, but now she was filled to bursting, brimming with life and all the marvelous possibilities the Lord had arranged for all His creatures, big and small (she was one of the big ones). She tugged open the door to her aunt's overheated front room, and Bernadette Mulholland, she of the daisy-speckled rain cap, flicked off the game show on the telly and turned to her expectantly. The old woman's face, lines of the ages somehow amplified by the brownish foundation troweled on them, the pinkish rinse in her wisps of hair doing her no favors, was filled with a mixture of caution and excitement.

"Have you a wee seat next to me here," Mrs. Mulholland said, pouring Bridie a cup of tea and adding the five sugars.

She patted the lumpy settee, perhaps thinking 'wee' was a poor choice of words. The sofa protested, creaking, under Bridie's weight as she sat, took a guzzle of tea, then grabbed the old woman's hands. Bridie's mother had called her much older sister Bernadette the moment Bridie had told her what had happened at Kebablicious, as Mrs. Mulholland was the one in the family best positioned to deal with it. Indeed, Mrs. Mulholland had been waiting for it all her life.

"I still kyanny believe it, Auntie!" Bridie breathed. "Can ye credit it? Och, the way me eyes feel now! They've seen the blessed Virgin!! There she was, Holy Mary, the Mother of God, looking up at me from the lard and mouthing secrets to me!"

Mrs. Mulholland knew everything about Virgin Mary sightings and how to go about getting them verified. "Song of Bernadette" was her favorite movie, of course, and perhaps one of the reasons she felt a sighting would happen to her was because of the Christian name her parents had given her. But as the years passed and she grew up and got married and grew old, then older, Mary never appeared to her (and she looked for Her everywhere), and she despaired it would never happen. When her sister had called, frantic, ecstatic and fearful in equal measures, and told her that Bridie kept insisting she saw the Virgin Mary no matter how many times she slapped and thumped the girl, Mrs. Mulholland realized this was the moment she had been waiting all these decades for. She hadn't been the lucky one, but for Her to appear to a niece was better than the family slipping away into obscurity. Infamy! She knew what had happened to Mary Beirne and Margaret O'Loughlan when the Virgin Mary had appeared to them in Knock in 1879. They were being talked about still; that Bernadette Mulholland knew their names was proof of that.

And Mrs. Mulholland had been on that bus to the Marian shrine in Knock, across the border in county Mayo, so often, she knew most of the trees and the hedges and which parts of the roads were more bumpy (there were many) and could brace herself before they went over them, while others seated around her spilled their teas and toppled into the aisle. And the woman in the gift shop knew her to see, and she nodded and smiled at Mrs. Mulholland as she entered and pointed out the new stock that had arrived since her last visit and even offered her 10% off on occasion. For which Christian kindness Mrs. Mulholland, scrimping and saving on her pension, which was scant even though it included a special compensation from the British government for her husband, who had been killed by a British paratrooper's bullet in 1973, was most grateful.

Mrs. Mulholland was all set to phone the special contacts in the church she had spent years building up to get the verification process started as quickly as she could. She wasn't long for this earth, and wanted it completed before she was too dead to see it happen. But she knew it was a difficult process, higher and higher up the ranks of the church it had to go, all the way to the Vatican City and the Pope, and she also knew that young people lied all the time. And she knew her niece Bridie McFee only too well. She had to be sure the feckless girl wasn't making an eejit out of herself. She had some questions and tests for the girl. She unraveled Bridie's hand from her own, gulped a mouthful of tea, and stared firmly at the girl in the grubby t-shirt of some rock band the woman had never heard of (Oasis) and muddy boots not befitting a young lady.

"First and foremost, wee girl, Marian apparitions, they're called. Not Virgin Mary sightings. And yer mammy tells me ye're of the mind ye're after having a Marian apparition, are ye?"

"Aye—"

Mrs. Mulholland held up a hand. She knew the girl could talk about it for hours.

"I've a few questions for ye before I take ye to them what matters in the church. I don't want them looking at me as if I'm a mental case."

"I understand, Auntie Bernadette. Ask away."

"Now, Mary only appears to the pure of heart," *Not the black of heart,* she longed to add, as that would have been quite fun to say, but she didn't want to give the girl a complex, and it really wasn't true in any event. Bridie didn't have a black heart, she was only misguided. "And, much as I love ye, dear..."

Bridie bowed her head in shame. As well she should! Her aunt was like most of Derry. They knew exactly what type of person Bridie was. She was especially guilty of the three sins of lust, sloth and gluttony. And a large dose of covetousness. A pint in her path never went un-drunk, an E never un-swallowed, a lad un-shagged. And a steak and kidney pie, a hot cross bun, a chicken vindaloo, an extra helping of apple tart and custard, a shoplifted

Crunchie or Jelly Baby never went uneaten.

"I've to give ye a few pointers about the Catechism of the church. Them priests, then bishops, then archbishops, then cardinals will be wanting to know where the Christian—Holy Roman Catholic!—virtues are in ye. Where's the prudence, justice, fortitude, *temperance* and so forth in ye?"

"Och, auntie, I know they talk about them things at mass all the time, but they be's old fashioned words and I don't really know what the priest be's blathering on about most of the time. Prudence, to name one. The only thing I know about it is that "Dear Prudence" be's an old Siouxsie and the Banshees' song I heard on the radio once, and I liked it and downloaded it." She grimaced, for now she was the new Bridie McFee. "Illegally, I must admit."

Mrs. Mulholland didn't quite know what this illegal downloading meant or how one might go about it, but it seemed suspiciously like the shoplifting of yore. And that was Thievery. *Another* sin!

"Prudence means being sane and *sober* for yer prayers for the Lord, acting the right way."

"Only when I'm saying me prayers?" Bridie looked hopefully at her aunt.

So there were no drunken visits to the church in the girl's recent past then, Mrs. Mulholland thought, and for that Bridie should at least be commended. Mrs. Mulholland sipped her tea and thought about faith, hope and charity. Maybe the girl had faith, but she was hopeless and...charity? Mrs. Mulholland remembered Bridie's gift to her last Christmas, a coupon for half off a portion of chips at the Kebabalicious.

And a *stable disposition* the church would be inspecting Bridie for. And then there were the gifts and fruits of the Holy Ghost, seven gifts and twelve fruits, and Mrs. Mulholland didn't have time to rattle them all off and explain them to her niece, so she plucked a few out of the air at random: "Wisdom, they'll want to see in ye, wee girl! And piety! Patience! Kindness! Gentleness! *Modesty! Self-Control! Chastity!*"

As the last three rang from her withered lips with an air of righteousness, Bridie began to whimper.

"I just want ye to be aware what the process involves. Ye need to be sure ye want to go through with it all. They'll be putting ye through tests of all sorts, Bridie, barraging ye with questions, like an episode of *Law and Order,* so it will be, with ye sitting in a chair and a good priest and a bad priest paired together, the bad one barking the questions at ye, the good one bringing ye a cup of tepid tea, though I imagine it'll be bishops or cardinals instead of priests. It's gonny be a cross between a police interrogation and one of them medical evaluations for them what be's off their rockers, a psychiatric one. Are ye sure ye want to go through with it all?"

The settee groaned and creaked as Bridie squirmed on it uncomfortably. She seemed to have no answer. The warning dealt with, Mrs. Mulholland continued with the investigation of her own.

"Yer mammy said ye took photos? Of whatever ye saw in the chip vat? Let's have a look at them photos of yers."

She seemed to looking around the general area of Bridie for an album. Bridie tugged the phone out of her jeans pocket, pressed a few buttons and handed it, reverently, to her aunt.

"Only the one came out, like," Bridie said sadly.

The girl held her breath, her eyes blazing as if with an excitement she hoped her aunt would share. Mrs. Mulholland looked down at the greasy screen of the phone, flicked away something sticky, and then her eyes struggled to comprehend what they were looking at. She could make out, just, the latticework of the frying basket that framed the photo, but it was blurry and perhaps she knew what it was only because she knew what it was supposed to be. Inside the basket, though, there was only a murky, brownish mass that looked exactly like what it was: a blurred photo of melting lard.

"Pah! That's useless, so it is!"

"Me hand was shaking that much, auntie, I couldn't take the photo correctly." Bridie bent over the phone and a chubby finger tried to point out, "If ye stare enough there, ye can maybe make out Her lips, parted, ye see, and Her eyes be's here, and then Her lovely long flowing hair, here on this side of Her face, and there on the other."

There was a long, uncomfortable silence. Mrs. Mulholland stared down at the phone, alternating with and without glasses, then finally handed it back.

"I kyanny see a thing. Ye said She had a mouth and eyes and hair. Did ye see a nose?"

Bridie looked startled at the question.

"I...I..."

"Look at that portrait over there, love." Mrs. Mulholland nodded in some direction, but her head was so shaky, it seemed Bridie didn't know quite where on the wall and its shocking wallpaper her special eyes were meant to look. She saw a dusty frame and a portrait next to the three flying ducks on the wall and studied it, but it was of three men.

"I don't see the Virgin Mary there, auntie. Does this be a test of me eyesight of some sort?"

"Daft cow! Though, now ye mention it, ye'll be subjected to a barrage of tests mental and physical, so the church might give ye one of them and all. The Vatican has loads of dosh at its beck and call, do ye not know? But, naw, not that picture, that's me granny's portrait of My Beloved Johns, Pope John XXIII, now a saint, by the by, John the Baptist and John F. Kennedy." They all had halos. "Naw, the one over the settee, I'm talking about."

Bridie craned her neck, and there the Bleeding Heart of Jesus portrait indeed was, given pride of place over the sofa. Withered palm leaves from last year's Palm Sunday poked out from the back of it.

"Do ye see the Virgin Mary there, wee girl?"

"Aye. Behind Jesus, so She is, looking on in grief as He shows us His bleeding heart."

"And now I want ye to have a wee juke at these."

Bridie jumped back as her aunt tugged a battered old Quality Street tin, purple, that had once held chocolates when Mrs. Mulholland had received it from her second oldest son back on Christmas Day, 1987.

"Inside here be's me collection of Virgin Mary nicknacks and what have you I've collected over the years."

She pried open the lid with a squeak and rummaged inside.

"Dear God!" she said, and Bridie tensed. But the old woman only pulled out a mound in golden wrapping. She put on her glasses to inspect it. "It's a Caramel Swirl! Isn't that always yer favorite on a Christmas morning, Bridie?"

Bridie nodded glumly. "Used to be."

"How long has it lain there, I wonder? And do ye think it be's edible still? No mind. That doesn't be what we're here for."

She placed it carefully on the coffee table next to Bridie's teacup, then delved back into the tin.

"I'll only show ye a few, like."

One by one the artifacts appeared on the table. A porcelain statue from Lourdes, a plastic one from Knock (10% off), a selection of medals, bronze, silver and gold in color, one with a drop of holy water inside, three prayer cards, a candle her granddaughter had sent her from Ibiza, and a snow globe. Mrs. Mulholland beamed with pride at her collection.

"Now ye have before ye twelve different images of the Blessed Virgin. When ye seen Her in the chip vat, which one did She look most like, hi? Have a look, wee girl. I spent many a nights wondering about this meself. All the Blessed Virgins on all these items be's different. I'm asking this now not only to help ye in the process later on, but for me own piece of mind. Did She look like this one here, with the wee crown on her head, or this one here, with the more showy crown with them hearts on the points as gems, or was she like these here, with a halo, but there's two different types of halos, if ye can see, one with stars sprinkled throughout it, the other just a round ring, or did she look like yer woman over there, with nothing but the blue shawl wrapped around her head?"

Bridie had to make the right choice. Mrs. Mulholland saw in the girl's face Bridie felt like a contestant on a quiz show whose prize was eternal life. Bridie's finger hovered uncertainly until she pointed at the golden medal in the

163

middle. "That one," she nodded her head with sudden conviction. "Aye, that one!"

Mrs. Mulholland's face crumpled with disappointment. It was as if Bridie had chosen the briefcase with £2 in it when the £50,000 one was still in play.

"That, wee girl, be's the Archangel Gabriel I threw in just for to test ye."

Bridie flashed with anger and Mrs. Mulholland jumped as the girl spat out, "Och, they're all wearing flowing robes, and why did men wear their hair so long back then anyroad?"

"*Self control,* girl! Ye see there? That flash of anger? That's what the committee'll be looking for! Them types of emotions is not befitting a messenger of the Holy Father! Or the Blessed Virgin!"

As much as Mrs. Mulholland wanted to believe Bridie's sighting was true, she was still very unconvinced. She sighed.

"Why don't we focus on what ye think has happened since ye saw Her yesterday. What have ye told me about them welts on yer face?"

"Aye, me cold sores, auntie. They've all gone. It must have been Mary what made them disappear. And, this was the most important thing. I'd given up chips for Lent, ye see."

From the size of her niece, Mrs. Mulholland thought, that would indeed show temperance, and bucket loads of it.

"I went to the Kebabalicious to sleep in the store room. Aye, strange, I know, please don't ask why. Anyroad, I wanted to sleep, as I've said, but ravenous with hunger, so I was. I wanted chips. I needed chips. I didn't care that Lent has just begun. The temptation was gnawing at me stomach. I went to that fry vat to make meself some. And it was just as the lard was heating up that She appeared to me."

Mrs. Mulholland stared at Bridie for a long time. She ran her hand over the Mary snow globe, dusting it with the tips of her fingers. She fiddled with a prayer card. She finally looked up.

"Are ye telling me it was the...temptation of the chips? Ye seriously expect me to believe the Blessed Virgin came down from Heaven to stop ye from filling yer fat bake with chips?" The incredulity was thick in her voice.

Bridie either didn't notice or didn't care, such was her conviction. Her face sans cold sores bobbed firmly.

"Aye, aye, that's right! She wanted to keep me on the right road. The road without sin. A life of all them things ye was telling me about, piety, patience, fortitude. Och, and chastity! Och, it's just coming to me now, auntie! Chastity be's one of them virtues I do know the meaning of. And I know I haven't been...chastetic...in the past. But...now I mind, after I saw Her in the lard, I ran out of the Kebabalicious, and when I was wailing in the streets, like, I caught a glance of...oh, I don't wanny reveal this to ye, auntie, I'm mortified, so am are, but ye know Eamonn McGreenly, the one who works as the trainer at the sports complex? The one who be's going out with Charlotte Bleeny?"

"From Rosemount Gardens?"

"Aye, that's the one. Anyroad, Eamonn was just passing, and on normal days I always have a quick peek at his ar—his bum. I don't know what it is, the cut of his jeans or something. Maybe they're ones he bought from some Yank website and had delivered specially."

"And the point of this is?" Mrs. Mulholland didn't know where to look.

"I had not the slightest desire to look at his bum! None! I'm cured!"

Mrs. Mulholland was unimpressed. But Bridie talking about wailing on the street brought up another point.

"That's another thing, wee girl. I know ye blabbed it to everyone right after it happened. Hopefully they've not told anyone else. Seems unlikely, but ye never know. From now on, but, ye kyanny tell a soul. Otherwise, the committee'll think ye're doing it for gain. Or for the fame."

"But it's the most wonderful thing to happen in me life!"

"Aye, I know ye believe that, but them on the committee won't take kindly to ye having spread it around to all and sundry. It won't work in yer favor. Now!" She clapped her hands together and stared Bridie in the eyes. "I'm still of two minds as to whether yer case be's strong enough. Tell me, does yer thoughts revolve only around the Blessed Virgin now, like, dear?"

"Aye, auntie! It be's all I think about. I feel different. New. Me eyes, me fingers, me toes and all. Like they belongs to someone else. Someone holier. I've been blessed, auntie! I don't know why, but yer woman Mary singled me out! Ye've got to believe me!" She burst into tears that were a mixture of joy and excitement and frustration and fear.

Mrs. Mulholland watched the performance for a few moments. Then she spoke.

"The only thing that makes me think..." She paused, and she looked to the left of Bridie's teacup. "I seen ye haven't so much as glanced down at that Caramel Swirl. That was another test I prepared for ye and all. Yer mammy told me it was the temptation of the chips that made Her appear to ye. To keep yer gluttony at bay for Lent. I think the priests and bishops will find that interesting. As if I would leave a Caramel Swirl in that tin since 1987! Naw, I placed it in there just before ye arrived. I needed to see if what ye said was true. Perhaps ye're right and the Virgin Mary has cured ye of yer gluttony. The lust and the sloth I'm not so sure of. Time will tell, but."

She nodded suddenly, satisfied and proud.

"I knew one of me lot would have a vision soon enough. I just had to give it the time it deserved. I'm thankful to the Lord He spared me from that angina attack the year before last, so am are, or I would've never lived to see this day.

This be's what the Lord was saving me for. I've all the right contacts and their phone numbers, the movers and shakers of the Derry Catholic world, written down in me address book. Normally it takes months to set up an appointment. I'm sure the ones I know will zoom ye straight through, though, like that express till at the Top Yer Trolly. I'm warning ye, but, wee girl. I dearly hope ye're in it for the right reasons, and that ye're in it for the long haul, as it could take them years, and I mean decades, to make up their minds. Are ye sure ye wanny go through with it? There are easier ways to get yerself some respect in this town, if that's really what ye're after."

"Does that mean..." Bridie gave her a look as if she could barely believe her ears. "So...so...ye *believe* me, auntie?" She squealed with joy, and the woman flinched as Bridie's massive arms wrapped around her frail chest. Mrs. Mulholland's shoulders ached. Then Bridie wiped the tears from her eyes, and her voice rang out excitedly, "I don't care who thinks I'm a headcase. I know what I saw. Sure, if any of me mates had told me, I wouldn't believe em. Now it's happened to me, but...All I can say is that it happened, and I don't know why I was chosen to spread the Good Word. But I was."

Mrs. Mulholland tried to get up from the settee. Bridie helped her off it.

"Let me get me address book and start making a few calls. Don't ye worry. I'll be with ye every step of the way. Every step of the very long way. I'll see ye right, girl."

"Och, auntie, I kyanny thank ye enough!" Mrs. Mulholland saw tears well in the girl's eyes again.

"Aye, ye can," Mrs. Mulholland said. "I want a free Cow-A-Licious-On-A-Bun every time I go into the Kebabalicious from now on."

"Ye've got it, auntie!" Bridie promised. And this was a promise the new pious Bridie was determined to keep.

Mrs. Mulholland shuffled to the hall, found her phone book in the little drawer of the phone stand, opened to a well-worn page she had decorated with Blessed Virgin stickers from the Knock gift shop, and dialed.

CHAPTER 27

"Yee-haah! We struck it lucky! Again!"

Usually there was fear on Jed's face on the rare occasions he was the passenger and Ursula the driver. He tried to hide it, but Ursula always saw the terror in his eyes. Now, however, her husband's eyes were glassy from excitement and the three Mai Tais he had downed. He pounded the dashboard in tune to "Deşteaptă tu, Român," the Romanian national anthem (one of the few that were upbeat) and took another swig from the bottle of Bailey's he had moved on to. Ursula reached over the shift knob, found his hand and rubbed it affectionately. There was nothing but an endless empty highway before her, pylons to her left, fields and the setting sun to her right, a silo in the distance, so she took her eyes off the road and smiled at him. He had a cocktail umbrella behind his left ear.

The moment they had left the studio, they raced to the nearest bar, desperate for drink. *Attack of the Killer Investors!* had been a harrowing experience. A bar was conveniently located kitty-corner from the studio, but convenience, they soon discovered, didn't equal comfort. Or safety. A scrawny tiki dive whose décor must have been tropical splendor back in the 50s, the bar was now a shambles of woven fish traps that sagged from the ceiling, heavy with years of grime and the carcasses of mosquitoes and flies, torches on the wall whose orange and red light bulbs (meant to be flames of fire) buzzed and flickered maddeningly, cracked lava stones stained with unmentionables, splintering bamboo shoots, and walls painted with hula girls that throughout the terms of the last ten US presidents had been defaced and never scrubbed clean, a wide array of breasts in all cup sizes scrawled on their chests and, further down, reproductive organs that were either scribbled on the girls themselves or entering them at various angles. The bar was called Paradise. It was inhabited by creatures in differing stages of intoxication and medication.

"Contestants on the show across the road?" asked the bartender whose face was covered in so many tattoos that Ursula struggled to know what race he'd been born.

"Yep!" Jed wailed. "And we got a deal! You wouldn't believe—"

He yelped as Ursula kicked him in the shin, and he gave her a questioning look.

"Let's just celebrate," she ordered.

Ursula had learned her lesson. This time they would do better. This time they would keep their mouths shut about the money. She would sit Jed down and instruct him not to breathe a word of this money to anyone they knew or didn't know. And certainly not to her family.

There was a momentary blip in the celebrations as, first, Jed realized he had no cash to pay for the drinks—he had used it to fill the tank with gas for the long journey up—and Ursula's credit card had to be brought into play, and then, after they carried her white zinfandel and his Mai Tai to a booth, fashioned like a Polynesian hut, Ursula tried to insert herself into the seat, but she screamed as the toothless man passed out underneath jerked awake and grabbed her ankle and the bartender had to drag him out and eject him onto the sidewalk. But celebrate they did. Ursula was all set to let her hair down, figuratively of course as her eggplant-colored bob was down as far as it could go, and she had already swallowed half her white zinfandel when she realized they would somehow have to drive the four hours back home. She told Jed he could indulge, she would drive, and he did (indulge, not drive).

"It's almost like winning the lotto again, honey!" Jed had said.

"Aye," Ursula had responded. But it wasn't. A hundred and fifty thousand dollars was barely a fraction of what they had won a few years ago, and in Derry they hadn't been at the beck and call of some playboy millionaire investor. If they had, though, Ursula thought as she smiled at Jed over the rim of her greasy wine glass, or if they had had some investment advice back then, perhaps they wouldn't have blown through the hundreds of thousands they had won and wouldn't have had to beg before an audience of millions, or tens of thousands anyway, for a measly amount that wasn't really all theirs. And they didn't have the check yet. And they didn't own Slim Jed Jerky any more, not fully. But...from rags to riches, to rags and back to riches again...she was as content as she could be. It seemed money, like time, was relative. And the investment was a safety net. Lately she had been tense every time she swiped her card at the supermarket, the drugstore and even the 99 cent stores she loved to visit.

Years had gone by since the lottery win, and it had been the money that gave her the life she now had. She and Jed had been forced into leaving the hometown she loved (Jed not so much), and still the animosity stretched across the miles. Ursula knew only too well Irish Alzheimer's, forget everything but a grudge. And the Floods, well, really only Fionnuala, had a grudge against her. But the family were prisoners under her steely grip. "What was that kick all about?" Jed asked.

"I'll tell ye later," Ursula said. "Now, but...*sláinte!*"

"Yeah, cheers!"

They clinked glasses and laughed. Jed guzzled his Mai Tai. Ursula sipped her wine. She held her handbag close to her.

"When are we to be getting the check, though, Jed? And what's all this about due diligence?"

"Hmmm...they need to check our accounts and files and see that we weren't lying on stage."

"The only time I lied was when I told them horrid creatures at the end it was a pleasure to meet em," Ursula said.

Clipboard had led them through a maze of corridors until they were ensconced in some office-type room where reams of documents of intelligible legalese were pressed into their hands. They didn't know how to pore over them. And Slim was not there to help. Clipboard demanded they sign them. "Here, and here. And here, and here, and here. And here. Oh, and here." She told them there would be an appointment for due diligence in two weeks or so, and if that went well, they would get the check four weeks later. It was apparently all up to the legal and accounting teams of Mitchell Haverton (that was his name, they finally learned) and his advisory committee if the investment would definitely go through. But, seeing their looks of shock, Clipboard told them not to worry. Mitchell had a heart of gold, she said, more so than the other investors, and sometimes he had even gone against the advice of his teams and gone through with the investment anyway. "So I'm 95% sure you'll get the money," Clipboard had said, and Ursula had wanted to scream at the utterance of yet another percentage.

She now passed the same cow she remembered from the trip up. They wouldn't be long for the hospital now. She was scared as to what Slim might make of the deal they had struck. Jed seemed so relieved to have any money, he didn't care about the percentage of his and Slim's blood, sweat and tears they had handed over with fourteen signatures.

The Romanian national anthem ended. The guitar twang of the Kendall's "Heaven's Just A Sin Away" rang out, and Ursula was shocked to realize she been bracing, tense, for what song came on next. In Jed's car at that moment, she would gladly endure the national anthem of Uganda, Communist Vietnam, or even, heaven forbid, Great Britain, or any of the numerous country & western songs she couldn't stand. Just as long as one of the Irish songs on his mix didn't come on. It would put her out of her good mood. Suddenly flush with money once again, or at least the 95% promise of it, she couldn't bear to hear any of them at the moment, they would make her think of home. A country that, because suddenly she hadn't been scrabbling in the gutter, destitute, like the rest of her family, had turned its back on her. If she were stepping off the plane at Tân So'n Nhất International Airport in Ho Chi Minh City, the people of Communist Vietnam would welcome her with wider arms and warmer smiles.

The Kendalls were still fearing and hoping heaven was just a sin away. Jed turned it up and began to sing along. Ursula longed to wrap her arms around him and sing along, their bodies waving back and forth as one, but it was impossible with the bucket seats of the car, and she had the odometer to check, the accelerator to press, the wheel to steer, and the signs to look out for.

As Ursula giggled girlishly and tapped her fingers on the steering wheel, she reflected that Jed looked happier than he had in weeks, no months. Less stressed. Even younger. Cuddly, Female had called him. Ursula agreed, especially now with that drunken smile on his face and his hat tilted at that angle. Ursula wanted to cuddle him. She would. Later. After the hospital. The celebration would continue.

She saw the first sign to the hospital. Wisconsin Veteran's Hospital, she realized it was called. How could that have escaped her? It was 25 miles away.

"Oh, wooh, wooh, Be with you tonight..." The Kendalls faded out, and Ursula tensed again. But... *"Land der Berge, Land am Strome..."* Ursula thanked the Lord. She was being spared the pan pipes and fiddles.

"What country does this be from, Jed?" she asked, just to make conversation.

"Austria."

"Australia?"

"Austria, you know it. We went there."

"Och, aye, when we was stationed in Germany. I mind now. The next country over, to the right. Mind we went with the wanes to that town where they filmed the *Sound of Music?* Lovely weather, it was, the sun was beating down. And we went to them salt mines and all. Was they in the town or outside the town? I kyanny mind now. But we went on that tour and saw all them places they filmed that film in, anyroad. Them palaces and whatnot. And the fountain where Julie Andrews and them wanes sang 'Do Re Mi.'"

She smiled at the memory. She steered into the slow lane to make the turnoff to hospital. And then, to her shock, Jed opened his mouth and began...to yodel! Like in the puppet show from the movie, *"Odl lay ee, old lay ee, Odl lay hee hee. Odl lay ee!"*

Laughter burst from Ursula mouth as she gripped the wheel tight. She knew it was the drink, and the money, and the memory of a good life spent together, but Jed had never yodeled in his life. She couldn't have been more surprised if he had just addressed her in Urdu.

"Odl lay odl lay, odl lay odl lee, odl lay odl lee!" The laughter roared from Ursula.

"Stop, ye daft eejit!" She was bent over the steering wheel, her body shuddering, the tears welling in her eyes, *"Odl lay odl lay odl lay Hoo!"* "I'm gonny crash the car, Jed! Stop it now! I'm warning ye! Och, ye've got me stomach hurting that much! Ha, ha, ha!" *"Lay ee odl lay ee odl-oo!"* "Och, the tears be's streaming down me face! It must be them Mai Tais, making ye a Broadway star! I'm gonny make ye drink em all the time! Ha, ha, ha!" *"Lay ee odl lay ee odl-oo!"* "Ha, ha, ha! And, Jed...Jed..." she laughed into the windshield, "sure, I never knew ye'd even seen the *Sound of Music!* How do ye know the words?"

"Words?! You call those words?"

"Oh, ha, ha, ha. Hee hee! Grab me a tissue from me bag, would ye, love? I've to wipe the tears from me face!"

Her purse was between his feet. Jed rummaged around and found some Kleenex. He handed her a few. Ursula wiped her eyes, groaning at the pains in her stomach, then blew her nose. Then her cell phone, also in her bag, rang.

"Och, as ye're there anyroad, go ahead and get that, love," Ursula said.

170

"Hello? Mrs. Barnett's phone," Jed said in an exaggeratedly polite voice. From lonely goatherd to butler! Was there no end to her husband's talents? "Mrs. Barnett's driving her Bentley. I'm her personal assistant, Mr. Jed. Can I help you in any way?"

Ursula was giggling a little still, until she glanced away from the windshield and at Jed, heard the high pitched wail from the depths of her cell phone, and saw Jed's falling face. Quickly sobering face.

"Wait a second," he said. He put the phone up to Ursula's ear. "It's Francine. She wants to speak to you directly."

"Francine? But...oh, dear God! What's gone and happened?"

Francine O'Dowd, Ursula's dearest—and now only—friend in Derry. She never called; Ursula knew she didn't have international on her phone. It must be a matter of life or death.

Ursula jerked the wheel and the car jerked onto the shoulder of the road. A raccoon skittered in the brush, gravel sprayed against the wind shield, and the driver of the SUV that had been behind them pounded his horn and flipped them off as he zoomed past. Jed turned off the music.

Ursula stopped the car and took the phone he was offering her.

"Francine? Why are ye ringing? Has something happened? Is yer mammy —"

She was aware of Jed at her side, and the dashboard and windshield wipers before her and the sun dropping behind the fields of wheat in the distance, and then she was aware of nothing. Nothing but the terrible things her dear old friend was telling her. Ursula strained to comprehend.

"But...what are ye saying? Ye mean—"

"How, but?" Her voice wavered.

"Och," she began to sniffle, "I kyanny believe it! I kyanny believe what ye're telling me! Och, sure, it's a terrible tragedy, so it is! Do you know when —"

"At Xpressions, ye heard it?"

"A perm?! Why—?"

"Aye, aye, aye. That I understand. That's fine, love. Thanks for filling me in. At least someone had the decency to do it."

"Aye, right ye are."

"Aye, I'll see what I can do. We've...we've two days, still."

"Aye, Cheerio."

Ursula clicked the phone off and burst into tears.

"What, honey?" Jed asked, his hands on her shuddering shoulders. "What happened?"

"Wer Dymphna's gone and died!" Ursula sobbed. "Of a drugs overdose!"

She scrabbled for the tissues she had just discarded and put them to use again, honking into them and wiping at her eyes and cheeks as her head spun.

"Och, Jed! It's hit me like a ton of bricks to me heart. Ye know I loved that wee girl so much. Maybe me favorite niece, I don't know. Her funeral be's in two days. Jed, I know ye don't wanny do it, I know ye don't, and I know we haven't much time, nor money, but we've to make wer way to Derry for the funeral. It's in two days. We have to be there!"

Jed wrapped his arms around her as best he could with his seat belt still on.

"Of course we will, dear. Of course we will."

A fresh wave of grief hit Ursula as she wailed, tears anew, "And, imagine! Me own brother Paddy hadn't the decency to ring me and tell me himself! Do they still hate me so much, Jed, that even death kyanny bring us together? Fionnuala I might understand, aye. But even she kyanny stop me own brother from making a secret phone call to me! Oh, Jed, Jed, *Jed!!!*"

He made comforting, cooing noises. And finally Ursula's tears dried somewhat. Jed drove the rest of the way to the hospital.

Ursula sat outside Slim's hospital room on an uncomfortable yellow plastic chair. She had placed her handbag on the little table beside her, on top of a wrinkled copy of *People* magazine that had coffee rings around...she looked at the caption, Orlando Bloom's smiling young face. She didn't who he was or what he did. She felt drained. Her eyes ached, her heart more so. She was glad she was spared more of Louella's glares of accusation. Her sister-in-law had gone home to feed some animal. Ursula had decided to let Jed and Slim battle it out amongst themselves. She had other things on her mind. Inside, she heard Slim roaring away at her husband:

"Are you an idiot, Jed? Tell me again! You gave away *how much* of our company?"

"I got him down from 85%. That's what he wanted first. I countered with 70, and he agreed at 82.5."

"What? Eighty-two point five percent of our company? You valued our company at, at, at...at *$181,818!* All the work we did! Gone! Just like that!" She heard the snapping of fingers as she tugged another tissue out of her handbag. Tears were welling again. "For a measly $150,000!"

"I tried to call you, but—"

"This is all *your fault,* Jed! You and your damn gambling!"

"You'll see, Slim. I was disgusted with the offer at first, but the more I thought about it, the more I think it's going to take us into the big time. Come on. How far do you think we really would've gotten with the one radio commercial we recorded? I know it's a shock, but you gotta agree, with Haverton on board, we'll sell millions more. Do you know the contacts he has? He can get us on shelves *everywhere!* And we were struggling just to get the jerky in the mom and pop stores around here. He can get us into the *chains!"*

"I never even heard of the dang guy!"

"He owns Blanely's Bagels, and Eat-So-Yum, and Scanty Secrets."

"When me and Lou have to sell our house, when our kids wonder why they can't come home for Christmas no more, and I tell them they can't because their mom and pop live in a trailer down at Golden Sunsets with all the druggies like that *Randaleen*...who's responsible for putting me in here, if I can remind you, and I certainly didn't invite that junkie into my life, and by the way, do you know how much my insurance deductible is gonna go up because of all this?"

"I'm sorry about that, but—"

"Anyway! Off the damn point! The point is, can we get this guy, this Halveringston or whoever he is, to give us back some of our company? Or to give us more money?"

Family and money. Money and family. The curse.

It was turning Ursula's stomach. Literally. She was feeling as queasy as she was mentally drained from the shocking news of young Dymphna's death. She couldn't listen to any more. And she had to make reservations for a flight to Belfast. It was a shortish bus ride from there to Derry. It was sure to be expensive, both the flight and the bus ride, if she remembered UK prices well. She wondered if they would be able to afford it. Probably not. She tried to dismiss from her mind the thought that she wished Dymphna had waited until they had the $150,000 in their bank account before she had taken the overdose. She wondered what type of drugs it had been. Marijuana? Could you overdose on that? Ecstasy? Crystal meth? She had seen enough of the damage that did here in Wisconsin. Were they selling it in Derry now? The way she hoped they'd be selling Slim Jed Jerky at the Top Yer Trolly?

She wrenched herself up from the seat and wandered down the antiseptic corridor. She saw a young woman in an outfit of some sort.

"Excuse me, wee girl. Does there be anywheres here I can access the Internet?"

"What?"

"The Internet. It's like...like, the entire world, but on a computer."

The girl rolled her eyes. "I know what the Internet is."

"Then why did ye—?"

"You speak strange. I couldn't tell what the hell you were saying. On the ground floor there's a visitor's center. Maybe you can use it there. But you gotta pay."

Money. Again.

Ursula did her best to smile. "I'm well aware..."

But she was speaking to a retreating back. She went to the elevator.

Ursula had tried to find a flight for under $1000, but at such short notice, it was proving difficult. Head banging, she surfed a few funeral websites, clicked a few buttons, and then finally went to her email. She wanted to write to Paddy, demanding to know why he—her own brother!—hadn't felt it necessary to inform her—his own sister!—that his daughter—her own niece!—had died. Though Ursula was softening a bit towards Paddy. Maybe he was stricken with embarrassment. If her daughter, her own daughter, had died of an overdose, Ursula wasn't sure she'd be contacting all the branches of the family tree and spreading the news.

She had just signed into her email, and was wondering what she would write when she jumped at the sight of the newest email in her inbox. It was from Moira, Dymphna's older sister, and the family outcast, chased away from Derry to Malta, just as Ursula had been chased away to Wisconsin. Whereas Ursula's sin seemed to be not sharing the lottery money equally to all the the many throngs of her family who thought they were entitled to it by virtue of their birth, Moira's sin was lesbianism. And writing a fictional account of Ursula's struggle with the family, *Lotto Balls of Shame*. It hadn't sold many copies, but Ursula was hoping for a sequel.

Not only was it shocking to get an email from Moira right after Ursula had heard Dymphna's news, just as shocking was the email subject: DYMPHNA!

It must be about the death. Ursula quickly clicked it open, heart racing, finger trembling. She read:

Dear Auntie Ursula,

Have you heard about Dymphna? I think it's absolutely brilliant! About bloody time, I say! She deserves it.

Ursula reeled. Moira and Dymphna had always been close. At least that's what Ursula had thought...? She read on in growing confusion, then horror:

I know it's been ages since we've been in touch, and I'm sorry about that, but after hearing about our Dymphna I just had to write. I don't know how the family feels about it, they're probably not turning cartwheels, but there's one thing I'm sure of: <u>you</u> must be soooo delighted! She told me once what you said you thought about her and her prospects for the future, and I think it's that conversation that eventually led her to go through with it. You should feel so proud! You should pour yourself a glass of wine and have a special wee celebration for yourself! :)

Ursula had never been slapped in the face by an email before. Tears welled in her eyes as she struggled to force herself to read further. Was this sarcasm gone mad? She wondered briefly if Fionnuala could have somehow hacked into Moira's email account and written the message. But Fionnuala having such finesse seemed...unlikely. What, though, had Ursula ever done to Moira to deserve such contempt? She hoped there wasn't worse to come in the email. But:

I'll take you into confidence here, Auntie Ursula, and reveal my true thoughts to you. I'm so envious of our Dymphna. I wish I had been the lucky one, the first of us to take the plunge. I'm the oldest, after all, so you'd think that would be the most natural. But, no. I've no need to spell it out for you, Auntie Ursula; you know my sexuality, and so I'm going to let you in on a wee secret now that not many non-lesbians know: it rarely happens to us. Or if it does, it's horribly short-lived.

Tendrils of cold fear crept through Ursula's fingers and spread throughout her body. The room seemed to reel. She had sudden visions of lesbians cursed with eternal life, never dying, quasi-vampire and zombie-ish members of the Third Sex trolling the Earth. This was taking the entitlement of minorities to a deranged extreme, lesbians thinking they were spared the grief of dying. As much as Ursula now wanted to hate her niece, she was more filled with unease. She feared for Moira's sanity. Had Malta made her deranged? She forced her eyes to focus through the tears and read on:

And, in fact, as you probably know, for years it was actually illegal for us. But thanks to the liberal laws of the EU, we've finally now joined the rest of the human race. Yay! Not many of my friends seem to want to go through with it, though. But two of my friends did, two of the lucky few! And one of them did it twice in as many years! But as far as I'm concerned, I'm almost certain it will never happen to me. I appear to be cursed. I pray, yes I do, but, and maybe it's my upbringing, I have a feeling God thinks I'm a sinner and so he won't allow it to happen. Though if it ever happened to me, however unlikely that may be, there's one thing I do know: nobody in the family would be happy. Except maybe you.

Where did all this hatred, this passive aggressive vileness, come from? The last time she had seen Moira in Derry, the girl had kissed her on the cheek. Now Ursula rubbed that cheek where Moira's lips had touched it; the flesh felt soiled. She knew Moira was a good writer, but she never thought one day her pen would be a dagger aimed at her own heart. It felt like it was bleeding.

I'm on a deadline, so I'll love you and leave you. Are you going to Derry? I can't make it (and I don't know what type of reception I'd get, and you might feel the same; we're neither of us in with the family any more, you because of the money and me because of my book about it), but I think this is the time for everyone to put their differences aside and join together in what should be the biggest celebration our family's had in years!

Ursula could only gawp at the *XOXOXO Love, your niece Moira* at the bottom of the email. Why send such a hateful thing and have the cheek to add kisses and hugs? What sort of drugs was Moira taking over there in Malta? For all her banging on about lesbians being immortal, Ursula was sure the girl wasn't long for a drug overdose—or a least a mental breakdown!—herself!

Confused, angry, grief-stricken, unable to find a cheap flight, her own head deranged, Ursula didn't know where in her cluttered mind the sudden idea sprang from. She dried her eyes, honked her nose, rose and with slow, heavy steps of determination, or like those zombie lesbians Moira was going on about, approached the elevator. She pressed a button and got out on the correct floor. She walked down the hallway until she found the right room.

Ursula looked up and down the hallway. Deathly deserted at this time of the night. She wrapped her fingers around the handle of the door and prayed it wasn't locked. She pressed down. She heard the lock click in the tumblers. The door creaked open. She peered into the darkness. There was only the soft, rhythmic beep from some machine the patient was hooked up to. Ursula crept over to the only closet in the room. A Degas print, three ballerinas in pink tutus, hung crooked on the wall. The glass had a crack in it. Ursula held her breath as she slid open the door. She was surprised. It seemed well-oiled. There was not a sound. A pair of panties and some smelly stockings were folded on the top shelf—there didn't seem to be a bra—a pair of jeans and a grubby t-shirt were on the second. On the third, there was a battered purse. It looked like a fake YSL. The straps were frayed. Beside it was a scant pile of jewelry. A purple Swatch with a deformed band, a garish ring. And...*Aye! There ye are! C'mon back to me!*

Ursula rolled her eyes towards Heaven in thanks. She silently scooped her pearl drop earrings into her palm, then slipped them her into her pocket. She tiptoed back out of the hospital room as Randaleen heaved her peculiar grunt-like snores, and Ursula pressed the door shut. She smiled.

CHAPTER 28

Fionnuala stormed through the field of weeds that was her front garden and threw open the door. She made to shrug her satchel off her shoulder and fling it in the corner of the hallway, but of course she couldn't. It was in police custody.

Her heart was racing still, her temples throbbed, but she was relieved at the silence of the house, comforted by the familiar filth of it, the smell. The wanes were still in school, her mammy was probably at the bingo, Paddy at work, and Lorcan, who knew? The blood pounded through the veins in her temples. She needed a cup of tea. She marched to the kitchen, grabbed the kettle with a shaky hand and shoved it into the mound of tomato sauce encrusted plates and bowls in the sink, secured an abyss for it under the tap and filled it up. Waiting for it to boil, she went to the larder, flung open the door and grabbed Paddy's bottle of whiskey. She guzzled down what little was left, then tossed the empty bottle in the bin overflowing with carrot detritus and potato peels. She wanted more, needed it, but didn't have the time, the energy, or the funds to drag herself to the off license for another bottle. The few drops that were now trickling down her intestines, making their way to her stomach lining, would have to do. Until one of the wanes came home and she could send them to the corner to get 'their daddy' another bottle.

She stood there on the tatty linoleum next to the overflowing sink, her hand palms down on the sticky counter-top. She stared at the boarded up window before her as if seeking redemption or a sign from the Lord that her life wasn't in vain. She got none. She thought about the harrowing ordeal she had just been through. She wondered if the police would link the satchel and the credit card inside to her. Thankfully, they probably wouldn't. It was strange how in Derry it seemed everyone knew everyone else, except the Filth, who needed to know everyone but didn't. It was like they shipped the coppers in from some foreign country. Just like the doctors.

All Fionnuala wanted was a rest, but she had so much to do, and just thinking of it made her exhausted. She was too old for all this. She stood like that for a long time. She heaved deep, labor-like sighs in an effort to calm herself. Finally she felt the whiskey working its magic on her. She wondered why she didn't drink Paddy's whiskey more often. She understood now why he did it every night he came home from work.

She cried out at a sudden piercing sound and braced herself, ready to kick the coppers she imagined were barging through the kitchen door. But it was only the kettle; she had forgotten she had put it on. *Eejit,* she thought to herself, shaking her head in disbelief. She made herself a cup of tea and spooned in the sugar. She looked in the fridge but they were out of milk. Without the whiskey she would have been raging, but now she was just irritated. She took a sip, and cursed as she burnt her lips. And then she knew what she had to do, what she had been putting off for weeks. The whiskey was giving her the strength, the tea a bit less. She turned and strode purposefully into the hallway, her clogs clacking.

She pulled open the door of the cupboard under the stairs and dragged out her sewing machine. She couldn't trust the coppers, couldn't trust her family, the only ones she could put her faith in were the Lord and her Singer 1725. She winced at the pains shooting through her wrists as she hauled the sewing machine into the kitchen. She pushed aside all the rocks and plastic cases and empty packets of cereal and dirty tea mugs and overflowing ashtrays on the table and sat the sewing machine there. She went back to the cupboard and tugged out the big black rubbish bin she had shoved Dymphna's gown into weeks before, and the smaller rubbish bin with all the accoutrements she was going to add to it to beautify it.

Dymphna and Rory had looked down in shock when Fionnuala's head popped up at the hatch of the chip van, her body in a pose more befitting a lady, sweat lashing down her purple face, and she demanding to be cut free. They hustled her inside, protected her hands with old rags, and set to work on the plastic handcuffs with all the implements at their disposal, knives and oven lighters and grease. When she was freed, (they had finally burned them off, and for the recent cutbacks of the PSNI they were grateful, for the handcuffs weren't the impregnable ones of old), they let her use the loo, then Dymphna demanded to know what had happened. But it was a secret Fionnuala would take to the grave. Dymphna kept asking, and Fionnuala kept ignoring her, rubbing her wrists and demanding a meat and potato pie, a battered sausage, a portion of chips and a cup of tea. Rory got the fryer going, and Dymphna made the tea, and then the girl had gone on and on about the gown and the cake, as if they were the most important things in the world. The selfish cow! But she kept repeating something which Fionnuala's brain had been refusing to believe was true: the wedding *was* in two days. Two short days. Where had the time gone? As Fionnuala bit into the pie, which was not beef and potato but beer and veal, she had promised she would get to work on the cake and hand over the gown that evening.

Weeks ago in the sewing section of the Top Yer Trolly, Fionnuala had come across a treasure trove of items to snazz up Dymphna's wedding dress. All at 50% off! She rummaged around in the bag and pulled out the first of these, two yards of purple, pink and green beaded fringe, an inch long, in a zig-zag pattern that reminded her of the wallpaper at the Indian takeaway down the Strand. There had been plastic and glass, but Fionnuala had chosen glass. Only the best for her daughter. Of all people! The perennial flop on her lists! Fionnuala wanted to make it the wedding gown of the season. It wasn't for Dymphna's sake, it was for her own. If she made a disaster out of it, had Dymphna trudging up the aisle in some hideous creation, it would put the family in a bad light. Word would spread throughout the Moorside. Fionnuala would be mortified, no longer able to hold her head high, so, no matter how much it pained her, and it did, she fought to make her least favorite child's gown a thing of beauty and wonder. And considering what Zoë had handed her, the bland gown, it would be an uphill struggle. Fionnuala had been surprised. She thought Zoë Riddell was supposed to have taste.

Fionnuala snipped into the fringe with the scissors and cut it into halves. She would sew these onto the backs of the arms of the gown, so that they would jingle and dance every time Dymphna moved her arms. She was already imagining the spectacular display they would make as Dymphna twirled on the dance floor at the reception to "Mambo No. 5," which the DJ was sure to play. She positioned the fringe and the right arm of the gown under the needle and the sewing machine began to click click clack. Fionnuala knew the gown proper was chiffon—Zoë had said it often enough!— but she didn't know what the material of the arms was, something sheer and see-through, as if Dymphna would be walking down the aisle with her arms draped in white tights. The fringe would look much better.

And then there were another five yards of banding, fringes of alternating 'pearls' and 'diamonds,' two each, hanging down. She would sew these these in four rows on the dress, on the collar, the chest, the thigh and the hem. And the crowning glory, the three-inch pink heart-shaped rhinestone buckle. She would sew it where a buckle should be. She had considered a row of them all around the waist of the dress, but they cost £4.99 each, and she wasn't made of money. One would have to do.

Then there were the iron-on sequin appliqués. After a few hours on the sewing machine, she would move to the ironing board. At the Top Yer Trolly, she had grabbed huge handfuls of two and a half inch sparkly green cloth stars, padded, that she would improve the gown with, a hundred or more, and they had been out of green hearts, so Fionnuala snatched up the turquoise ones, along with two handfuls of sparkly red bows. Her hand had hovered uncertainly over the frogs and the rainbows, but she was determined the gown be restrained and classy. She had scooped up seventy pink pearl-like Apostles' crosses instead. She still remembered from the Catechism of her youth that the bumps at each of the arms represented the Father, the Son and the Holy Ghost. She would have love and religion together in one gown. She had trembled with excitement as she walked to the till with her basket. And then the bag had sat in the cupboard under the stairs for weeks.

Pride filling her now, Fionnuala smiled as the sewing machine whizzed away, her fingers surprisingly nimble considering the size of them and the alcohol in their corpuscles, though when one took into account the speed and the sharpness of the needle shooting up and down between the feed dogs and the bobbin, the nimbleness was perhaps not surprising and only a matter of self-preservation. She couldn't remember what designer name Zoë had yodeled as she ripped the dress from the packaging, someone foreign and strange, but as Zoë had cooed and preened over the gown, and blathered on and on about the simplicity and class and clean straight lines of it, and Dymphna had nodded and smiled and marveled at her side, running her fingers up and down the length of it, Fionnuala had been confused. "An off the shoulder mermaid gown," Zoë had instructed them, but to Fionnuala it looked like a plain white sack. A white sack of purest chiffon, marvelous to the touch, to be sure, but a

179

sack nevertheless.

"Where," Fionnuala had demanded, brow furrowed and feeling a bit betrayed, "does the color of the wedding be in that gown, I'd like to know? Ye kept banging on and on months ago about the color and how it was meant to be in every item! Hours it took us to come up with the green, and not just any green, but the specific color of green, Brookside Moss, I still recall it was called. And then ye present me with this...white shite! Lovely white shite, aye, and dead dear, I've no doubt, but white nevertheless!"

She had glared accusingly across the yards of stark virginal chiffon into the woman's Burberry frames.

Zoë had shrugged.

"Sometimes less is more, Mrs. Flood."

"There's nothing to that frock! Mind ye showed me all them magazines? Yer mood board? Frills and ruffles and I don't know what. That there looks like a sleeping gown!"

"Less is more."

"It needs to be altered. *I* need to alter it."

"There's no need to alter it. The tailors made it to order, they measured every bit of her. They took very precise measurements."

"Aye, Mammy, I can attest to that. Hours, I was there while themmuns went over every inch of me body with a tape measure, like."

"No, not alter. I don't mean alter. I mean I need to *add* to it. Add a wee bit of color to it. For the sake of *yer mood board.*"

"Less is more."

"Would ye stop parroting on about less being more? Gimme that frock here!"

And then, when they seemed to be on the verge of a tug of war, on the verge of treating the fancy café like the January sales at the Top Yer Trolly, something had changed in Zoë's face, and she turned to Dymphna.

"It's your gown, darling. No use us sniping over it. What would you like?"

"I love it, I really do," Dymphna had said. "And I thank ye so much getting me the best of the best. Wile lovely to the touch, so it is. I...I...I must agree with Mammy, but. It's not got anything special about it. No spice or pizzazza or whatever ye call it. It's just white."

But Zoë wouldn't let the veil out of her claws and although Fionnuala's imagination was doing somersaults over how she might improve that, she let the woman keep it. The dress would far outshine the veil.

As Fionnuala sewed away, and then finished, and then as she pulled out the ironing board and began to iron on the stars and the hearts and the bows and the crosses, her mind clicked away. Maybe it was the whiskey, but she was feeling bad, worse, then even worse as her creation grew more and more marvelous.

"Am I that terrible," she thought to herself, "that me own son wants to flee from me as soon as he can?"

Dymphna had also asked if Fionnuala had heard from her auntie Ursula, if she had RSVP'd, and wondered why she wouldn't at least send a card or a note or an email. Fionnuala was feeling bad about Ursula, about the puppet show she had put on the other day, she felt bad demanding to Dymphna two months ago she would take all the invites to the post office and get them stamped and sent off, bad about finding Ursula's invitation in the pile, ripping it up and stomping on the pieces there beside the foreign currency window. She was feeling bad about her own mortality, the mysterious protein flowing in her urine and what it might be doing there, feeling bad about drinking all Paddy's whiskey, and feeling bad there wasn't more to drink. She felt bad that the wedding cake wasn't going to be the marvel she had promised Zoë it would be.

She had tried to raise the money, she really had. All her scams at the Amelia Earhart Center, and her last desperate scam with Mrs. McDaid were proof of that. But as time had gone by and the extra money trickled in, well, she kept realizing she'd need more and more, especially as she had conjured up more things that were needed for the special day.

She was horrified to see she had scorched the gown slightly in two places, but she would cluster some stars in those areas, like mini green milky ways, and nobody would see the brown marks.

She needed thousands of pounds, but had squirrel away barely three hundred. Everyone in the family thought she was saving the money for the cake, but she could have easily placed the £300 as a deposit at the baker's weeks ago. It should've been ordered at least a month ago. But this money, and the money Mrs. McDaid should have given her, was supposed to pay for the things Fionualla had secretly been planning for, things to make her look better for the wedding, and not like her exercise of old with the sofa cushions on the floor, or cutting off her ponytails and dying them brown. She had wanted to lift her head high on the wedding day, literally. She had pored over brochures for a face lift, liposuction and maybe even a vaginal rejuvenation. It would be the best revenge ever, she had thought when she started to scam the money all those weeks ago, to outshine her own daughter on her wedding day, and the Protestant bitch to boot. Marching proudly down the aisle behind her Protestant-loving harlot daughter, her own tight face, trim waist and even tighter lady's arena, the questions at the reception from the unknown Riddell guests if she were Dymphna's sister. But the vaginoplasty alone, including anesthesia and surgical facility fee, cost £9000. It was useless. She'd have to reign in her dreams. There was sale on irregular Spanx at the Top Yer Trolly. And she had her special walking instructions, courtesy of *How To Be A Lady.*

181

That would have to do.

And now there were only two days left to the wedding and there was still no cake. £300 would buy her nothing, and there wasn't enough time anyway. She would just have Padraig and Siofra make it. Seamus could help too. And her mammy. The old woman didn't do much of anything, Fionnuala thought.

The door clattered open, then slammed shut. Fionnuala tensed over the iron. But it was only Lorcan, not the coppers, swinging into the kitchen, a comforting sight with his muscles and youth and handsome face and blue eyes. He made Fionnuala feel more at ease than any amount of whiskey could. He was whistling some pop song of the day.

"Right, Mam?" he asked, wrenching open the door of the fridge and poking his nose in. Disappointed at what he saw there, he closed the door and finally gave her a real look. "What's up with ye? Terrible put out, ye look. Ye've not had another of them attacks of yers, have ye?"

Fionnaula was affronted. Those attacks of hers! As if she had them thrice daily!

"Och, Lorcan," she sighed into the shiny iron-ons as she realized she'd have to make another appointment with Dr. Chandrapore and do the urine sample again. "Naw, not that. Ye wouldn't believe the day I've had, but. I—No, let's just let it lie. I'll start roaring out of me if I try to talk about it."

"Is that wer Dymphna's wedding frock?"

"Aye. Almost done." She tugged it off the ironing board and held it up for him to see. The stars and bows and hearts and crosses sparkled under the strip lighting of the kitchen. The fringes jangled from the arms. The heart buckle shone.

"Looks grand. Effin epic! Ye've got hands of magic at that sewing machine, Mammy, and the iron as well. Ye shoulda been a designer, you."

"Och, the things ye say! Ye've me face pure red, son! In two days, the wedding'll be. I wish I could buy ye a special suit for yerself, but ye know the dosh be's tight. I'm sorry about that, love. Sure, ye've that suit ye wore for yer court appearances to wear, anyroad."

At the mention of the wedding and his being there, he seemed unable to meet her eye. She wondered about that.

"Two days, ye say, aye?"

"I wonder if ye could help me out, give me some of yer advice. That Zoë Riddell kept banging on about the designer of the frock, and I was wondering...I don't see her name anywhere, no label or what have ye. I think maybe it was Vera Wong. Does that sound right?"

"I don't know about designers, Mam."

"Anyroad, I was wondering...what do ye think if I spell out in big letters on the back, V-E-R-A on the left shoulder, W-O-N-G on the right? Would that look nice, do ye think? I haven't the letters bought yet, but I was wondering if I should take a trip down the down to get em. If ye think it be's a good idea?"

"Mm. Aye, ye've loads of marvelous ideas, Mammy. That, but, sounds a bit like a football jersey. And ye don't want anyone at the church thinking wer Dymphna be's called Wong, do ye?"

"Naw, ye're right there, son," Fionnuala agreed. But still, as she stood there holding the gown out like that, her brain cells continued to trundle. D-Y-M-P-H-N-A on one shoulder, F-L-O-O-D on the other? But the girl would be going up the aisle as Dymphna Flood, and coming back down it as Dymphna Riddell, and that confused Fionnuala. She'd have to leave the back be. She placed the gown back on the ironing board.

"Anyroad, Mam, I was—"

They jumped as the door clattered open again and Padraig, Siofra and Seamus stomped in from school. They were surprised to see their mother there. One of them, she didn't know who, wanted to know why she was home early but Fionnuala just scowled and hid behind the steam from the hissing iron.

Padraig asked, "What's for wer tea?" *Tea,* dinner.

"Baked beans on toast."

"Can we not have some meat?" Siofra asked.

"Aye, Mammy, please!" Seamus said, clapping.

"It's been weeks, like!" Padraig complained.

"Naw, youse cannot! Youse ungrateful cunts!" She would've slapped them all but she didn't want to scorch the gown again. And she felt some satisfaction as she intoned like a Lady, "Less is more, have youse wanes not heard?!"

Lorcan spoke up, "Mammy, how about that ham hock? Months, it's been sitting in the freezer."

She softened to make him stay, "For me son, anything," as if a ham hock would make him change his mind. That's how desperate she was.

"I'm warning ye mammy," Lorcan said as the kids jumped up and down around him and clapped and cheered, "it's not gonny make me stay. Ta, but, Mam."

Her head throbbed.

"Take that ham hock outta the freezer for me, Padraig," Fionnuala instructed, though Lorcan was closer to the fridge. "And defrost it in the microwave for yer mammy so's I can boil it. Two hours, it'll take. Can youse wanes keep yer hunger at bay that long? We've to wait for yer daddy and yer granny to get home, anyroad."

"How am I meant to defrost it?" Padraig whined. "I've never done it before."

"Ye see I'm busy so I kyanny do it meself!"

"I'll show ye," Siofra said.

Fionnuala thought...she'd have to watch that one, she was showing intelligence beyond her years.

"And then I want youse to go to the Sav-U-Mor and get me some things for the wedding cake. And some whiskey."

Her brain could only think of so many things at the same time, or one rather. As Padraig and Siofra carried the ham hock over to the microwave and Lorcan swaggered out of the kitchen, Fionnuala propped the iron upright on the board in the special place for it in the sitting room, went back into the kitchen and unearthed an ancient cookbook from the depths of a cupboard behind a tin of asparagus spears and a packet of plain sugar cookies nobody liked that she had forgotten were there. She flipped through, found a black and white photo of an appropriately grand wedding cake, grabbed a pencil from some crevice, licked the tip, then, on a greasy brown bag she found on the counter, she began to write the list of ingredients the children would have to buy. She was relieved she still had the money she had 'earned' from the Yank tourists. Hopefully it would pay for all the ingredients, plus the drink. She thought she heard a strange noise from upstairs, like the loft door being opened, but couldn't pause to consider it. She strained to understand the page before her.

They were odd ingredients, but there were only three. Fionnuala was surprised. She had never baked in her life, but perhaps making a wedding cake was easier than she thought. Maybe making cakes would become a new and interesting hobby for her. She wrote down: 2lbs 4 oz white sugar paste icing, 1lb 2 oz yellow sugar paste, edible glue. Then underneath she read: These are the ingredients for the sugar flowers. *Only the flimmin flowers?* she thought *What about the cake itself?*

She turned the page, the pings from the microwave and the kids' babbling voices unheard. She reeled. *For the 12 inch tier, you will need 1 lb butter, 8 oz brown sugar, 5 oz caster sugar, 12 eggs, lightly beaten, 1 lb flour, 1 lb ground almonds, 2 tbsp cocoa powder, 1 tsp nutmeg, 1 tsp mixed spice, 1 tsp salt, 2 oranges, zest only, 2 lemons, zest only, 2 tsp vanilla essence, 1 lb currants, 1 lb glacé cherries, 12 oz sultanas, 8 oz dried cranberries, 1 lb dried apricots, chopped, 8 oz blanched whole almonds, roughly chopped, 12 fl oz brandy. For the 9 inch tier...*

She passed the other tiers and on the next page she read, her heart sinking, *For this recipe you will need a 15cm/6in, 23cm/9in and 30cm/12in round cake tin, thin cake boards of respective sizes, and 38cm/15in, 35cm/14in and 23cm/9in thick cake boards. You will also need eight doweling rods and eight cake pillars and sugar paste flower molds All of these are available from specialist cake shops. Plus you will need a 3m/9ft 10in x 1.5cm/⅝in white satin ribbon.*

She quickly flipped the pages to a simpler cake and scanned the Ingredients:

Butter, eggs, milk, 2 tsp hot water. *Aye, aye, aye.* She nodded eagerly. She had all that at home already, except the milk, so she moved on to the more exotic items, sugar, it said, but dark muscovado sugar...black treacle...ground ginger...desiccated coconut... Her brain couldn't keep up with what her eyes were reading: pistachios, soft apricots, carrots, peeled and grated, one pineapple, preferably unripe, one sweet potato, sliced thinly, one mango, 2 tbs limoncello, orange blossom water. She would also need cake boards and dowels, a mandolin, a mixer, mini pastry cutters, mini cupcake tin, a sugar thermometer, sugarcraft leaf cutters. She turned the page, then another. There were 33 steps.

Fionnuala's brain was in shock. Regardless of the size of her teeth, she had bitten off more than she could chew. And what the bloody feck would she need a mandolin for? Was she meant to play music as the cake baked? She was about to fling the book the length of the kitchen when her eyes alighted on another recipe: BASIC CAKE. Flour, milk, salt, baking powder, butter, sugar, eggs and...the only exotic thing, vanilla extract. She scribbled down what they needed, added WHISKEY, underlined it, and added three exclamation points.

"Ok, wanes, does that ham hock be defrosted yet?"

"Almost, Mammy," Siofra said.

"Now I want ye to do the messages for me. I've got a list here. All three of youse go. And then we'll have ham hocks. And beans on toast with em."

When they came back laden with plastic carrier bags, she had folded up the ironing board, hung the gown proudly on the back of the kitchen door, and the ham hocks had another half an hour until they were done. Siofra marveled at the gown, tugging it this way and that to hear the fringes jangle and see the appliques sparkle, Padraig and Seamus were uninterested, and Fionnuala emptied out the dregs in her tea mug and filled it with whiskey. She gulped down. And gulped down again. She shuddered with delight as the warmth filled her.

"Youse wanes!"

Padraig, Siofra and Seamus jumped, looking guiltily at her, though they had done nothing wrong they could remember. They had even handed her back the change, and all of it. Though there wasn't much.

"I've got a fun wee activity for youse for tomorrow. A wile craic, it's gonny be."

"Aye? What, Mammy?" Seamus asked, his little face shining with glee. Padraig and Siofra seemed less enthralled.

"Youse're gonny make yer sister's wedding cake. That what ye bought today be's all the ingredients. Plus some butter what we've already got in the fridge, and the salt over there."

"But..." Padraig stared at her through his glasses. "How...?"

Even Siofra looked worried.

"Don't youse worry, wanes. Yer granny'll help youse. Ye'll see, it'll be loads of fun!"

She smiled down at them, and even in her own drink-filled mind she realized the configuration of her teeth was not giving the desired effect of motherly love. She had to use the loo. As their silly questions rang out, she turned and hoofed it up the stairs to the bathroom in the landing.

When she was finished, she heard the wanes in their room, babbling on and on under the dance music that blared, and then she tiptoed up to Lorcan's room and pressed her ear against the splintering wood. She heard some peculiar noises, or imagined she did anyway, her head addled by drink as it was. She wrenched open the door—

And shrieked at what she saw.

"I *knew* it! I bloody well *knew* it!" she roared at Lorcan. "When I told ye about yer suit and the wedding two days away, I saw the look in yer eyes!"

Lorcan stood frozen before the suitcase he had placed on the ripped and stained bedsheets, a handful of socks in his hand. His handsome face was etched with guilt. Betrayal shot through Fionnuala like a sniper's bullet to the skull.

She wailed there at the door, her mouth the only part of her body able to move, "Ye promised me ye wouldn't leave before the doctors had given yer poor aul mammy's body the go-ahead to live a few more years! Ye promised me ye wouldn't leave before the wedding, sure! Ye kyanny wait two extra days? Two flimmin extra days?! Why do ye think ye must up and leave yer mammy's side? *Why?*"

"Och, er, Mammy, I..."

The socks fell into the suitcase. He bowed his head in shame.

"And I'll have ye know," Fionnuala seethed drunkenly, "that's yer granny's suitcase ye've there, and I'll demand she not let ye take it! Ye'll be hauling yer gear down to that airport in a bin bag! *Traitor!* When are ye leaving? *Where* are ye going to? Tell me! Tell me now, ye bloody ungrateful bastard!"

He reached into his pocket and brought out a slip of paper.

"That Sorcha got me a special pass for a flight. I can leave any time I want. There be's a plane for Miami tonight. And I've me passport and all. With one of them working visas attached."

"How did ye get that? Ye've a criminal record, sure! The States won't let ye in!"

But Fionnuala knew she was clutching at straws. For the right price, you could buy anything down at that Mountains of Mourne Gate market. That was where Eoin had gotten his passport as well.

186

"Eoin's waiting for me to come, so. He's got me a job all set up. I'll send ye money, Mammy."

Fionnuala roared out: "So there's the two of ye all set to betray yer mammy, is there? Him I don't mind. You, but Lorcan! *You!* Me lovely, lovely boy! All the sacrifices yer mammy's made for ye over the years! Always putting meself last for ye, all them visits to the prison when I had to smuggle ye in them drugs! All I did for ye, Lorcan, and this is how ye repay me? By fecking off to the States without so much as a by yer leave?"

She raced towards him, arm raised to strike. He flinched. But then she turned and stomped out of the room. The door slammed behind her. And she marched to the bathroom, having made her plan to force him to stay that night of the puppet play on the sofa. It was time to put that plan into action.

She wrenched open the cupboard under the sink and rummaged around until she wrapped her fingers around what she was looking for. The big purple can of hairspray. Extra Super Hold Aquanet, it was called, some strange Yank hairspray Ursula had left years ago. What it was doing in her house, Fionnuala had no clue; the reasoning was lost in the mists of time. But it was Ursula's, nor hers and, her deranged thinking went, if the coppers ever caught wind of what she was about to do, they would blame Ursula and not her.

Fuming, raging, furious, her fingers trembled as she panted huge breaths and brought the can up to her eyes. She read the ingredients crouched there in the bathroom under the sink. These were much different than the ingredients of the cake: *Water, Dimethyl Ether, SD Alcohol 40-B, Vinyl Neodecanoate Copolymer, Acrylates Copolymer, Aminomethyl Propanol, Sodium Benzoate, Cyclohexylamine, Triethyl Citrate, Cyclopentasiloxane, Masking Fragrance.*

She read the warning: *Flammable. Avoid heat, fire, flame and smoking while spraying and until hair is fully dry. Avoid spraying in eyes. Do not ingest. Keep out of reach of children. Contents under pressure. Do not puncture or incinerate. Do not store at temperatures above 120 degrees F. Use only as directed. Intentional misuse by deliberately concentrating and inhaling contents can be harmful or fatal.*

Do Not Ingest. She knew that meant do not eat. But Lorcan would be eating it for tea that night. Sprayed on the slices of ham hocks she would put on a special plate for him. She'd add more salt to his portion to hopefully mask the taste of the Masking Fragrance. She was as fearful as she was sorrowful. And she didn't want him dead. How could she want her favorite son, her perennial number one child dead? But at death's door? That was a different matter. Aye. Just so he couldn't make the bus trip to the airport. And as she nursed him back to health, she would keep spraying his food with the poisons, just enough to keep him weak. Until he realized Derry, at her side, was the only place for him.

She pried open the bathroom door, the can hidden behind her back. There was nobody in the hallway, nobody on the landing. She raced down the stairs, hid the can in the bread box, then went to the front hall and picked up the phone. She dialed Dymphna's number. She wanted all the family to be there. She wanted an audience.

"Dymphna?"

"Aye, er, Mammy? Are ye right? Ye sound wile odd."

"I've just had a wee bit of whiskey. What I'm ringing for to tell ye, but, be's yer gown's ready. Why don't ye come over for yer tea tonight, and ye can see it and maybe even try it on. Bleedin marvelous, it looks, if I say so meself."

Dymphna squealed her delight down the line. "Och, Mammy! I kyanny wait to lay eyes on it! I know yer sewing skills, so I'm sure ye did a grand job of it! Right, me shift here at the chip van be's almost done, and then I'll be over. And, c'mere, dead quick, ye altered that gown, so ye did! Ye *did* say by the end of today ye'd be done, but."

"Ye see? Yer mammy's a woman of her word." She certainly was, Fionnuala thought as she hung up: over her dead body, she had promised Lorcan, or over his dead body. She marched back into the kitchen and went to the ham hocks boiling on the stove, a woman of her word.

CHAPTER 29

Bridie had run home, as much as she *could* run, to freshen up for her visit to whatever inner sanctum of the Church her aunt would be able to gain her entrance to. She had a quick bite to eat, a cucumber sandwich and a tomato dusted with salt, and after she had wolfed it down, she sat there at the kitchen table and wondered if she felt full. She decided she did. But the pressure of her new life was getting to her, so on her way back to her aunt's, she had bought a flagon of hard cider at the Sav-U-Mor and guzzled down, not there on the sidewalk as the Bridie of old, but hunched behind a row of hedges in Mrs. O'Bryan's front garden, cloaked by shadows. Temperance didn't mean abstinence, or so she hoped. There was wine on practically every page of the Bible, with Jesus even in one scene turning water into it! But she only drank half the bottle, to be sure. She put the rest in her handbag in case she needed it.

As she approached Mrs. Mulholland's house, her heart dancing in the sunshine of this fervid new world she was living in—and the cider—she saw the front door was open, but paid it little mind, as sometimes her auntie's mind wandered and she forgot to close it. And so she went in. She caught sight of herself, with her special eyes, in the mirror of the hall stand and was disappointed at the state of her hair. It didn't look presentable, wasn't holy enough. She dug into her purse and found a few bobby pins, and as she was pinning up her hair of no discernible color into something more pious, she heard from behind her aunt's closed sitting room door a clucking and a tutting of elderly voices speaking out in tones of disgust and contempt. Many elderly voices. She strained to hear.

"The day after tomorrow, did ye say?"

"I did indeed, aye. And at St. Fintan's, of all places!"

"God bless us and save us! How can Father Harrigan can have such a display of vulgarity taking place in wer very own house of the Lord? It beggars belief!"

"C'mere, if we're not safe from such revolting, inhuman acts in wer own parish church, where in the name of God *are* we meant to be safe?"

"Tsk, tsk! I ask youse, is nothing sacred in this day and age? I'll be taking me custom elsewhere, and I advise youse all to do the same, good ladies. I'll take up going to that fancy new church down the the Culmore Road instead, if anyone wants to join me. Youse know the one I mean? Lovely stainless steel and marble holy water fonts, they have. Imported from Italy, so I've heard."

Bridie then heard her aunt speaking: "I'd not a clue, but, that that chip van was run by that Proddy creature," and Bridie's hand was on the door handle, ready to press it down, walk in and let herself be known, when her aunt continued, "the one whose son is marrying that Flood tart, that Dymphna. They certainly kept that a secret from us all. Me ears couldn't believe what they were hearing! The chip van, secretly run by Proddies! I'll be taking me custom elsewhere as far as chip eating be's concerned and all!"

"A disgrace, so it is!"

"Aye, shocking!"

"(Unintelligible) kyanny leave well enough alone. All them sermons week after week, Sunday after Sunday, demanding, *insisting* we live together not only side by side, but peacefully at that! I ask ye! After all they've put us through! The bloodshed and the tears and the broken families and broken bay windows and whatnot. And now they are expecting us to...*mingle* together...in such an *unseemly* manner!" The woman here spat her disgust. There were murmurs of agreement that seemed to come from all corners of the room beyond the door.

"There's only so much Christian tolerance we can be expected to tolerate! The whole world's gone demented!"

"It makes me skin crawl!"

"And me stomach turn."

"There's something obscene, something *vulgar* about it! Like the mixing of one species of animal with another, like, I dunno, a sparrow and a gazelle, to name but two. What would their offspring be? It's *unnatural,* so it is!. It's not what the Lord intended."

"Just like" here a woman, whoever she was, whispered fearfully, "*that homosexuality*," there was a collective gasp, scandalized, "though that be's two like creatures mingling together, so it's like the opposite, but youse get me drift, aye?"

"Nothing good will come of that marriage made in Hell! Mark me words! The slippery slope...!"

"And here was me thinking that wee Flood girl had just gone and overdosed on some of them filthy drugs."

"Aye, I heard that and all."

"And me."

"C'mere, did youse hear that that shameful Mrs. McDaid cleared off outta town? To Florida, she's gone. Some says it was that wee girl's overdose what made her flee. Good riddance to that horrid woman and her sons, I say, mucking up the streets with them with disgraceful drugs of theirs! An army of sinners, so they was! Soldiers for Satan!"

"They all seem to clear outta Derry and head for that Florida. What battles the churches over there must be fighting against all them sinners, all them what's fallen from grace, I shudder to think."

"Aye, like Australia in the 1800s. When they shipped all them criminals over there."

"Did they really?"

"Do ye not know? Aye, the entire continent, or does it be a country, anyroad, no matter what it be's, the entire place's nothing but the offspring of degenerates!"

"I was planning the long flight over for me holidays next year. Two weeks in Sydney, with the Great Barrier Reef thrown in. Hrmph! Now ye've put me off...."

"Could someone please help me out here, but? I'm struggling to comprehend. How is it that that girl, that Dymphna one, be's dead if she's to be getting wed to the Orangeman the day after tomorrow?"

"Naw, she's not gone and died. That's what we all thought, but. Musta been some rumor that went astray. I heard it in Xpressions, so I did."

"Aye, me and all."

"I heard it from Mrs. Flannigan in the frozen foods section at the Top Yer Trolly. Why's she not here with us, by the by?"

"Poor aul dear had an angina attack the other day. Did ye not hear?"

Unable to listen to any more, Bridie knocked on the door, then threw it open.

"Ah!" Mrs. Mulholland said, "here she is now!"

All heads turned. Bridie gasped.

Although Mrs. Mulholland had told her niece not to breathe a word to anyone about the wonder at the Kebabalicious, that apparently hadn't stopped the woman from ringing every person she herself knew in Derry. Mrs. Mulholland's sitting room heaving with women. Some were old, some older, some older still. Their rinses bobbled in the dust unsettled from so many people shoved into a room that could comfortably hold only four, rinses pink and blue and silver, but also purple and one green. They were perched on every lower vertical surface the front room offered and their frail limbs could reach, sofa and loveseat arms, end tables, and Bridie could see all the chairs from the kitchen had been dragged in as well.

Mrs. Mulholland had been given pride of place on the middle cushion of the sofa. There was Mrs. Leech, there was Mrs. O'Leary, there was Mrs. Stokes. There was Mrs. Dinh. With a squirming little girl of about 8 years of age looking decidedly out of place and clueless sitting on a cardboard box that had once held a coffee machine beside her. Bridie didn't know the others, but she knew them to see. Some clutched rosary beads, some prayer books, some cups of tea or a china plate with a biscuit, a selection of which Mrs. Mulholland had placed on larger china plates on the sideboard. All were looking at her. No, *glaring* at her. Some with suspicion, some with scorn, some with barely concealed hatred, some with a fierce determination, already prepared, to disbelieve any word that came out of her mouth. Bridie was surprised there was no knitting, but, then again, from those she knew, karaoke and bingo were more likely to be up their alley.

"H-have I come at the wrong time?" Bridie timidly asked her aunt.

"Naw, ye're right on time, love," Mrs. Mulholland said. "We've a seat waiting just for ye."

With a wave, she indicated the lone empty chair smack in the middle of the circle of the elderly masses. It faced the settee with the Bleeding Heart of Jesus over it. Trying for a smile but failing, Bridie inched herself through the rows of trainers and sensible flats and slip-ons towards the chair that awaited her. A chair that was conjuring up images from films she had seen, films about the KBG, Nazi Germany, the Spanish Inquisition and Guantanamo Bay. She sat on the chair and placed her handbag in her lap. She looked at them, the ones she could see before her, anyway.

Bridie, like most of her mates—what few she had left—had a special place in her heart for the aged. She loved visiting her grannies and granddas on both sides of the family, treated them with patience and kindness at the Kebablicious till on the rare occasions they chanced to come in, and she saw in the crevices on their faces, the wispiness of their hair and their pink scalps that poked out from underneath, the frailty of their fingers and the shuddering of their twig-like arms and legs, ready to snap at any moment, in all this, she saw not the terror of the passage of time, didn't feel she was peering at some horror house mirror of a dreaded unwanted future of her own, but she saw shining in their eyes a wisdom, a mellowness she longed for, a capacity for introspection and forgiveness and a love of life for its own sake, and the memories of a life well lived, a love of traditional singalongs, macaroons and fadge sorely missing in her peers of the day. Her shrill, nasty, spiteful peers. She always viewed getting old as she had heard many people do once they finish reading *Lost Horizon,* where everyone in Shangri La was ancient, 150 years old or more, full of romance and dignity and mystery and the excitement of finally realizing what person you are and the wonders life held no matter the age, and that was the reason it was Bridie's second favorite book of all time (nothing could beat *Bridget Jones's Diary*). She had always thought, when her career at Kebabalicious had run its course, she would work in a nursing home, or assisted care facility, or a senior citizens' residence or whatever they were calling them that week. All that being said, she looked around her now, sitting on that chair whose cushion wheezed under the weight of her, with a sense of mounting dread. What had her aunt told them? Why were they here? Why were they glaring at her with such hatred? It was the Virgin Mary who had appeared magically to her! Bridie hadn't summoned her, hadn't forced her down from Heaven! And...she thought she was supposed to meet people at the church! She was prepared for *their* interrogation, the bishops and cardinals or whoever. But...no selection of church officials could be more discerning, more penetrating than this group of fervent churchgoers. Maybe that was the point. Bridie gulped.

"First," Mrs. Mulholland said, "Let me put yer mind at rest, Bridie. I've an audience arranged for ye with Bishop MacAuley and some minions of his from the cathedral, so we'll be meeting with them at 7 PM or thereabouts this evening. He's a new branch of the Top Yer Trolly to open before that, and the reception afterwards, but he'll be there. But ye might be wondering what all me mates is doing here."

"Th-that I was wondering, aye."

Mrs. Leech burst out before Bridie's aunt could continue, her teacup rattling with conviction: "We'll not have ye bringing shame and scorn to the good name of Derry throughout the Holy Roman Catholic world, wee girl!"

And Mrs. Stokes roared from the depths of an armchair: "We're not gonny be made fools of! Before ye taint the good name of the Moorside parish to all Catholics everywhere, ye've to convince us ye really saw what ye're claiming ye saw!"

Clucks and brays of agreement rang out. Heads nodded in all corners of the room. All arms were crossed against the wide array of cardigans they wore. The needed to be convinced. It wasn't going to be easy.

"Calm youse down, Claire and Grace!" Bridie's aunt tutted. "Don't put the fear of the Lord into the girl."

"It needs putting in!" someone called out. Bridie couldn't see who, it was someone behind her next to the fireplace.

"Now, Bridie," Mrs. Mulholland said, "By way of explanation, I rang a few of me friends, told em what ye said, and invited em over. We just want to ensure ye really have the necessary what-have-you to appear before the church. We don't want people to think we're daft eejits. We've the reputation of the parish to consider, the good name of the Moorside and St. Fintan's. I know I already put ye through the ringer, but we've a few more questions to put before ye. Do ye mind?"

"Naw, auntie, I don't mind. And youse don't scare me," Bridie said, and now there was an edge to her voice. "I've seen the Virgin Mary, and none of yer questions can make me say I didn't!"

She looked defiantly all around her. The little girl's lower lip was trembling. Mrs. Dinh put her hands over the girl's ears, her great granddaughter, or second niece, or whoever she was.

"Perhaps ye should remove that wane," Mrs. Mulholland suggested. "We don't know what might be said in her presence here."

The little girl was removed, told to go to the back garden and play, there was a rocking horse next to the rhubarb patch. There was a pause as the girl fled the room and some commotion as seating arrangements were reorganized, what with the extra seat opening up, and finally all eyes were back to peering at Bridie with distaste and mistrust.

"Ye understand the sensitivity of the issue, don't ye?" Mrs. Mulholland asked. "We none of us wants to be the laughing stock of dioceses around the world. It's happened before, ye know. Ones desperate for their parishes to be known world wide, and there always some hoax, and always the Blessed Virgin appearing in a field to a group of children, and then it goes all the way up to the Vatican, and finally the Pope declares it was a hoax all along, what do they call it again, Magella? When a Marian apparition is thought by the Pope to be a fake?"

"Constat de non supernaturalitate!" It was intoned, not said. Some looked at Mrs. Leech with new-found respect.

"Aye, that. We none of us want none of that."

And here Bridie felt the weight of their years and their experience and the march of history and the stories that had gone before—they had been around all of them when mass was said in Latin!—and she understood now, realized the importance of getting the congregation before her on her side, getting them to believe her.

"Pareidoila!!" barked out Mrs. Stokes suddenly, slamming her plate on a

table. The biscuit on the plate and the figurines on the table jumped. Rows of dentures clacked in alarm. Alarmed, all heads turned to her. As quickly as the necks would allow. There was an awkward silence. Had she only said this odd word to one-up Mrs. Leech?

Bridie cleared her throat. "Does that be an example of speaking in tongues?" she wanted to know.

"Naw, it's English, ye silly cow! It means seeing faces where there is none! It's a well known psychological trait. People have been doing it for centuries, it's a basic common need, the struggle, the need to find a likeness in everything the eye sees. Like the man in the moon, or a loved one in a cloud. Or ," here she paused, "the Blessed Virgin in the lard of a chip frying vat!"

Now Mrs. Dinh took up the thread, "Have ye any clue how many supposed sightings of the Virgin Mary there have been, wee girl? Let's count em off, shall we?"

"There was the pretzel,"

"The cheese sandwich,"

"The lump of melted chocolate,"

"The dental X-ray—"

"I think ye'll find, love, the X-ray was Her Blessed Son, not Mary Herself."

"Are ye sure?"

"I know about these matters."

They plowed on, "The piece of firewood,"

"The second floor window of the hospital,"

"The shadow in the laundrette,"

"The caviar, holding the baby Jesus and all."

"That caviar was not a sighting. It was in a gallery. It was meant to be, someone made it as...art. *Russian* art."

Their flashing eyes said all knew what this meant. *Blasphemy! Sinful Communist heathens!*

Mrs. O'Bryan said, "The point being, wee girl, ye claiming to have seen the Blessed Virgin in the chip fry vat of the Kebabalicious be's nothing special that the Church hasn't heard before. Skeptical, them priest and bishops and archbishops is gonny be. Just like am are."

"Aye, and me."

"And me."

"And me and all."

"Just like we all are."

They were all bobbing their heads in unison, eyes flinty and glinting, and daring her to contradict.

"It's yer job to convince us." Mrs. Mulholland said kindly.

"And that the Holy Mother changed yer life for the better somehow." Mrs.

O'Bryan put in.

Bridie thought as she sat there on the chair. Her bum was terribly sweaty.

"Showing ye the photo I took won't change yer mind. The only thing I can tell youse is the change she did to me life. Like black and white, night and day, it be's. I've changed. I'm sure me auntie told youse all about me cold sores disappearing, and me gluttony and all. Sure, I had a cucumber sandwich before I came here. And me...me...lust. That be's gone and all."

One woman asked, "Speaking of the speaking of tongues, have ye been speaking any? Tongues, I mean."

Bridie shook her head.

"Ye must answer out loud," Mrs. Mulholland said. As if it were one of those police interrogations!

"Naw," Bridie said.

"Has She given ye instructions?" another woman asked.

"To live me life in a clean way. Christian. No gluttony, no lust, like."

"Naw, specific instructions, we're talking." Mrs. Dinh said.

"And," Mrs. Stokes went on, "She woulda given ye some special secrets and all. She always does to them what She appears before. Signs that She's gonny place on the earth for all to know of Her goodness. And the goodness of the rest of Her family and all."

"Naw, She give me none of that. I don't know what youse want me to say. To lie be's a sin, and it seems like youse're urging me to break one of the Ten Holy Commandments to satisfy youse."

"Why would we believe ye? Take a look at the state of ye!" someone behind her said. "I can see yer hair's all pinned up like a librarian and all, but look at the rest of ye!"

"Aye, them boots!"

"That rock t-shirt!"

"The shade of yer lipstick! Like a right wee Jezebel, ye look."

"And if ye're expecting us to think She's cured ye of yer gluttony...!"

"How can we be expected to take ye seriously?"

They were all leaning forward as much as they could without toppling over. Biscuits, tea, rosary beads and prayer books were all forgotten. They wanted to hear her answer.

Bridie took a deep breath. "I'm sure," she said quietly, "you've all heard of Mary Magdalene...?"

There were snorts and nudges and looks of scorn. Mrs. Leech's voice rang out again and all watched her breathlessly as she trembled with righteousness: "Aye, yer woman Mary Magdalene's always being trundled out as an example, and always by people the likes of ye, girls with loose morals and low self esteem, tarts and slappers and I don't know what, to put yer minds at ease about

195

being a tart and always thinking ye'll be allowed to approach the Pearly Gates with a shameless skirt up to yer navel and a pierced I shudder to think what and sail past St. Peter with a wink and a nod and being taking up into the Lord's open arms anyroad. I've something to let ye in on, girl. It be's false advertising, so it is. And ye'll find with these committees ye'll be sat before today, there's none of that going on nowadays. In the Lord's time maybe, aye, though I've me own doubts. I'm of the mind there was some wee typo when the monks was copying the Bible during them Dark Ages. That's what they did back in them days, ye know."

"I do know that, aye," Bridie said stiffly. "I saw it on a history program that was half religion. I do watch em, ye know."

"I'm of the mind Mary Magdalene was a *pro*secutor, or a *pro*jectionist, a *pro*ctologist, or some job what began with a P an R and an O, as they didn't have them exact jobs back then, and whatever this job was, the what-have-you, it was written down and turned into 'prostitute' by mistake. They made their copies of the Bible with candlelight back then, and maybe one of them monks had one foot in the grave and bad eyesight to boot, or maybe his writing was difficult to read, and his version was the one chosen by the next monk a hundred years on to copy from, and so on. So, no, I don't believe Mary Magdalene was a prostitute. And I think ye need to have had a straight moral outlook, a life of chastity, temperance, piety, and all that, for us to believe that the Virgin Mary would choose to appear to you. Don't youse agree, girls?"

There were cheers and chants and the banging of teacups upon tables. Bridie saw Jesus with his Bleeding Heart staring down at her above the sofa. Mary was still looking over his shoulder in the corner. She dropped her head.

"And if we don't believe ye, what makes ye think the holy men of the church will believe ye?" Mrs. Leech demanded to know.

Bridie's head was hung in shame.

"But...I know what I saw," she said, her voice shuddering as the tears began to flow. And that's all she said. They waited for five minutes or more, but the girl said no more.

Mrs. Mulholland prized herself from the sofa and placed a hand on the girl's shoulder. She rubbed it for a minute, then said softly to her, "Go on and step into the hall for a wee moment, Bridie, while we have a natter over it. And then we'll have it up for a vote. I've cut up some squares of paper, it's a secret ballot, ye see, and everyone will mark down an X if they think I shouldn't take ye to the Bishop, and a cross if they think I should. We've got to count up the votes, and then we'll call ye back in once wer decision is known. It might take us some while. Have ye a good book or something with ye to pass the time?"

"I have, aye," Bridie said, rising from the chair. She rattled her handbag to let them know the book was there. The cider sloshed, and she felt shame arise anew. Perhaps they were right.

"The Good Book?" Mrs. Leech wanted to know.

"Naw."

"I thought not." She sniffed. That was one vote not going Bridie's way.

"Lotto Balls of Shame." Bridie said.

Her choice of free time reading seemed telling to some and, especially with the 'balls' in the title, highly suspect to many more.

Sitting on the bottom stair in her auntie's hallway, Bridie had read a chapter of Moira Flood's book, delved into her handbag and finished the bottle for cider, then there was a ping! from her phone. It was a text from Ailish. Sorry u woznt invited 2 Dimpnas wedding tried to speak 2 her, but she wont c sense dont think will be good anyway 2 many Orange bastards will b there u lucked out spent small fortune on frock and not even a hen do! cheap bitch! xoxoxoooo

The first half of the bottle of cider had long since stopped working its magic, but now the second half was kicking in. Her head was banging. How much longer would the conclave of churchgoers spend voting? It was already half six! If they voted yes, she and her aunt would have to hustle to make it to the cathedral. Maybe Auntie Bernadette would splurge on a mini-cab to take them there. Both their legs weren't good at walking.

Bridie ran a finger down the side of the peeling wallpaper, the yellow and orange flowers making her head spin even more. And then she stifled a shriek. Her finger jumped from the wall. The yellow and orange flowers seemed to be...moving! It was that...that...paridoily, or whatever the old woman had called it. The small colored bits in the middle of the flowers, she didn't remember what they were called, but two of them were looking at her like eyes, and the stems formed themselves into a shawl around the eyes. There! A mouth! And there! A nose!

Bridie whimpered with fear even as the glory and marvel filled her once again. It was the Virgin Mary! Again! And this time her mouth was moving and she was saying words to her! Giving her instructions! Now her ears were special as well! She listened. And listened. And nodded her head.

"Aye, surely," she breathed. "Aye, surely I'll do it for Ye!"

And she was enveloped with an excitement that overwhelmed what she had felt a few days before at the Kebabalicious.

"Ye can come in now, love!" Bridie barely heard her aunt say. It seemed like she was calling her from another galaxy, another time and place.

Bridie got up and staggered towards the now-opened door with a sense of adventure. No matter the outcome of their vote, she knew now the new instructions straight from Heaven would get them on her side, all of them, her auntie, Mrs. Dinh, even Mrs. Stokes, Mrs. Leech and Mrs. O'Bryant. Even that wee girl they had sent into the back garden. This time she knew exactly what to tell them. They would have to vote again. And this time it would be a unanimous Aye.

CHAPTER 30

Fionnuala's hands were pressed against Dymphna's eyes as she led her daughter into the scullery. The children were all lined up in front of the cooker for the unveiling. Keanu and Beeyonsay were scrabbling about on the sticky linoleum like rats scavenging for crumbs of scraps. The ham hocks were boiling still (they could boil anywhere from two to four hours), and were now joined by one saucepan of baked beans, simmering, and another bubbling and spitting vindaloo curry.

Fionnuala had sent the three children to the corner shop—again!—with the change from the previous purchase to get tins of beer for Lorcan and their daddy, the big fat Australian ones, she had specified, and a packet of extra spicy vindaloo sauce mix. To quench the kids' babbling protests, she had told them they could buy a packet of Wine Gums and share it between the three of them, but they had to save the red and black ones for her, and she knew how many came in a roll so they better give her all there was.

She had refined her plan. She didn't trust mere salt, however much she spooned on Lorcan's ham hock, to mask the toxins in the Aquanet, the ether whatever and the sodium what have you and the citrate what not, whichever daft names, too many letters to be remembered or pronounced correctly, or even at all, they had given the chemicals. Fionnuala knew from her many visits to the Indian takeaway around the corner that vindaloo was strong enough to cover up the taste of goat and lamb, so it would certainly cover up the active ingredients of hairspray in Lorcan's serving, especially if she also plied him with alcohol. And she knew her son loved nothing better than a spicy vindaloo after a night's drinking.

"Ooooh, Mammy! I kyanny wait!" Dymphna managed through breathless gulps, and, indeed, Fionnuala could feel the girl trembling with excitement under her, the jerky rise and fall of her shoulder blades as she and Dymphna took step after step, mother and daughter together as one, towards the cupboard handle where the wedding gown, on a mangled wire coat hanger, hung in all its glory. The Vera Wang-Fionnuala Flood collaboration. It seemed, even, from a wetness Fionnuala suddenly felt gathering on her palms, that Dymphna's eyes were squeezing out tiny tears. Tiny tears of joy. Fionnuala couldn't know that, yes, it was half the excitement of seeing the gown causing these bodily upheavals and tears, and half the stench of the curry—which Dymphna couldn't stand—making her daughter fight the urge to retch.

Siofra squirmed with delight as she watched them move closer, her little hand clamped atop her mouth to quell the giggles of merriment that threatened to spill out. Beside her, little Seamus clapped and drooled. Padraig was playing a game on his phone, and Lorcan stood clutching a can of beer in his hand and looking at his fingernails. Maureen was sitting at the table, cane at her side, barely able to look on as, hand to her heart, she waited, breathless, and braced herself for the shrieks of horror she was sure would erupt from Dymphna's mouth once Fionnuala's fingers were removed. There were so many violations of taste in the hideous creation, so many fashion sins, that Maureen was sure the poor girl's heart would be broken, the mother-in-law furious, and the wedding put on hold. All down to Fionnuala's 'creativity' at the sewing machine. And what was this freakish meal Fionnuala was planning on dishing them out after the 'unveiling'? Beans on toast with ham hock vindaloo? She feared her daughter was finally losing her grip on reality. She had long suspected this day might come.

Maureen stuck out her cane to guide the little infant girl away from an inedible-looking something on the linoleum. She would have bent down to pick one or the other of them up and out of harm's way, but she would have to configure her bones in so many different and awkward positions, and it would take so long and be so painful, and they both looked like their nappies were jammed full, ready to burst, that she focused on Fionnuala and Dymphna instead.

Siofra clapped and giggled girlishly as they stood directly in front of the gown. "Show it to her, Mammy!"

There was an excited pause. Then,

"Ta *dah!*" Fionnuala said, like a magician. She removed her hands.

There was only the sound of bubbling from the cooker.

And then Dymphna's shriek filled the scullery.

Her shriek of unbridled joy.

"Mammy!!! Jesus, Mary and Joseph! It's bloody effin *marvelous! Flimmin, flippin brilliant!*" Real tears, emotional ones, coursed down her face as she snatched the gown off the hanger and clutched it to her alpine breasts, buried her head in the chiffon sleekness, the glassy sheen of the beads, the sparkly mounds of hearts and crosses and bows. She held the gown up, her discomfort at the stench of the curry fleeing from her senses as they were enveloped by the beauty before her, her eyes shooting over every inch of its marvelousness, the bodice, the jingly arms, the jangly hem, drinking in the magic of it, as Padraig and Lorcan wandered out of the kitchen, disappointed, Siofra jumped up and down with squeals of glee that matched Dymphna's own, Maureen stared, stunned, and Keanu and Beeyonsay burst into tears.

Dymphna turned the gown this way and that, discovering hidden delights with each inch her eyes feasted upon. "Och, the buckle be's amazing, Mammy! The perfect classy touch! Nobody will be able to detect me new wane slumbering behind it, like! And them wee galaxies of stars ye have here and here. And ye see how them crosses there on the back are shaped into a D? And them bows in the private area like an R? For Dymphna and Rory! Och, Mammy, how can I thank ye?! Sure, it's impossible, so it is. I kyanny thank ye enough! All that hard work ye put into it. For me!"

Fionnuala shirked as the girl, still clutching the gown, thrust her arms around her and plunged her cheek with her lips over and over.

"Mind me face, wee girl," Fionnuala said, "Them beads is digging into me chin."

She pulled Dymphna off, uncomfortable at the showering of love from her least loved offspring. But Fionnuala was smiling at the praises that continued to spill out of Dymphna's mouth. And why shouldn't they? She had outdone herself on the sewing machine and iron board this time. All the Moorside, all Derry would be talking about the gown for years to come, she was sure. And she was right about that.

Maureen cleared her throat.

"Now that that's over, can we please fill wer bakes? Surely them ham hocks is done by now. Me stomach thinks me throat's been cut. And them wanes needs their nappies changed and all."

"Right!" Fionnuala said. And here her mind clicked from the bright and sparkly side of the wedding to the dark, flinty, poisoning revenge side of her heart, "Dymphna, stop yer babbling over that gown and get some plates on the table. Siofra, help yer sister. And where did them lads get off to? And is yer daddy still in the sitting room, glued to that telly? What he could possibly be watching on that flimmin thing, the choice of programs we have on them odd channels, be's beyond me thinking. And missing the unveiling of the gown and all! Anyroad, call them lads and him for their tea. I'll be spooning it out as soon as."

And then she realized. There were too many people in the scullery. How was she supposed to 'prepare' Lorcan's special ham hock with her mammy, two of her daughters, her youngest son, her grandson and her granddaughter, looking on? Here she cursed Dymphna, as was her wont. If the girl hadn't been getting married, hadn't needed a gown, and hadn't needed a gown spiced up, the scullery would be as empty as the organic food aisle at the Top Yer Trolly. The weapon, the Aquanet, was in the bread box. She had to think of a reason to get everyone to clear out of the scullery for a few minutes. All she needed was thirty seconds to spray the ham hock she would put on a special plate for Lorcan.

"All youse!" Fionnuala barked. Dymphna and Siofra turned around, plates in hand (the gown had been placed reverently on the counter top next to the sink, but its hem flowed into the garbage). Fionnuala was pulling tins of beer out of the refrigerator. "Take these lagers to yer daddy and Lorcan. Give two to yer brother. And I want youse to all clear outta the scullery for a few moments. This be's a special tea. For yer gown, Dymphna, and also it's to be Lorcan's last meal here and all. I want to set the table up nice. And them wanes does need changing, so I'm gonny do it meself. Shocking, I know, aye, but I want ye to rest, Dymphna, as I'm sure the excitement of seeing yer new gown has ye all worn out. And the sight of what be's putrescing in them nappies is one I'm sure none of youse would want to see. Have ye fresh nappies in their pram there, love?"

"Aye." Dymphna still seemed stunned that her mother would volunteer to change the diapers. But happy.

"Right. Now! Into the sitting room the lot of yous—"

But the scullery was already empty except for the crawling infants. There was a knowing smirk on Fionnuala's face as she closed the door. She wouldn't have been surprised if she had seen skid marks from her mother's cane on the linoleum, such was the speed with which Maureen had fled from the nappy changing.

Fionnuala hauled the infants onto the table, pushing aside the plates which had just been sat there, and set to work. "Heavenly Father!" she moaned, then "Dear Lord!" then "God bless us and save us!" and her fingers shook with disgust and she heaved deep breaths through her lips and Keanu and Beeyonsay kicked and screamed bloody murder up at her. But finally the filthy deed was done. She shoved the infants and their fresh diapers into their stroller, shuddered as she wondered if what she had just put herself through was worse than what she was about to do, then marched to the bread box, flipped it open and grabbed the hairspray.

She prized a few dirty bowls from the sink, piled them atop one another and hid the can behind the pile in case anyone might be fool enough to enter the scullery. She grabbed a plate, Lorcan's plate, from the table. She had gone to the back garden and plucked a weed of some sort that looked enough like parsley to place on his plate as garnish. This was his special meal, his special going-away meal, and the garnish was a special touch.

She felt her heart pounding in her breastplate, felt sweat peppering her brow, saw her fingers shudder as she turned the heat off all three pots, picked up the tongs and dug into the frothy water of the ham hocks. She pulled out the biggest, meatiest chunk of gristly, fatty pork attached to the squattest bone and placed it on Lorcan's plate. She felt as if she had left her body, was floating next to the fluorescent strip lighting on the greasy ceiling with its patches of damp, and looking down at herself as she slipped the aerosol can from its hiding place. She shook it violently. She popped off the cap. She pressed the button. It hissed its toxins onto the pork. She kept spraying, righteousness etched on her brow. She picked up the ham hock, turned it around, and sprayed some more. And now Fionnuala was no longer on the ceiling but standing on the floor before the plate and watching the spray dissolve into the meat, her eyes watering, the acidity of the spray sticking in her throat, her hand shuddering so much it was difficult to continue pressing the button. The smell of the hairspray, shocking in its familiarity, took Fionnuala back to the days, long long ago, when she and Ursula did each other's make up and hair before they and their husbands had a night out on the town. That would never happen again. Finally the ham hock was dripping with poison. Do Not Ingest. She smiled. That would teach Lorcan to abandon her!

She ladled the vindaloo on the ham hock, grabbed a piece of toast, grilled half an hour before, from the plate piled high, threw the toast next to the pork, and spooned beans on top. She arranged the sprigs of 'parsley.' She inspected her creation and nodded, satisfied. Gordon Ramsay couldn't have been prouder. And then she set to work dishing out the other plates. She remembered just at the last moment, ladle poised, that Dymphna hated curry, so she left her ham hock bare. That was fine. Fionnuala didn't want to poison her. Yet?

She was ready to call them in, then thought of something else. She didn't know what immediate reaction the chemicals might have on Lorcan, but she didn't want him spewing up all over her scullery floor. So she pulled the garbage bin out from under the sink and sat it beside his chair at the table. She didn't know how she could explain it away, but hopefully in their hunger, nobody would notice. It wasn't as if the scullery were an epicenter of spartan tidiness, in any event.

She opened the door and called out, "C'mon, youse! The wanes is lovely and clean and tea's ready!"

There were noises of general celebration, the sounds of feet scrambling from the sitting room, and in they trooped. Lorcan was first at the table. She could see the drunkenness in his eyes. Perfect! They all looked strange: panting, shaking slightly, their eyes glinting with some emotion, and Fionnuala couldn't put her finger on what that emotion might be. Were they really all so hungry it was showing itself plainly on their faces? Here Fionnuala was ashamed of her family. Had they no restraint? They were no better than beasts from darkest Africa! And now it was as if they were descending upon the watering hole to devour the dead carcass of the wild boar. She filed that thought away for inspection later; she had a much more important matter on her mind at the moment. She pulled the chair out for Lorcan, patted him on the shoulder as he sat, feeling all the strength, youth and health in him, and flung the plate on the table before him.

"There ye go, son," she said. "Them ham hocks ye wanted. Enjoy."

Twenty minutes earlier, Paddy had been stretched out on the settee in the sitting room before the telly, an Australian lager in one hand, a fag in the other. He drank and he smoked. It had been another draining shift at the packing plant. The fish cakes machine was still broken, and he had spent nine long hours molding the fish, potatoes and seasonings into mounds he hoped resembled cakes. He was on his second beer, and had been taken aback that Fionnuala was catering to his needs. She rarely did any more. She was wrapped up in a prickly, self-absorbed world of her own, had been for years.

Though tonight she seemed more interested in shoving beer after beer into Lorcan's hand the moment he was finished with one. Lorcan had told him about his plans to catch the flight to Florida later that night. The bus to Belfast left in two hours. Paddy wished him well. He wished he had a ticket for the seat next to his son. But Paddy would never leave his hometown on the River Foyle. He was there for life. And besides, though he loved the idea of the sun in theory, his skin couldn't handle it, typical Derry pale as it was.

Paddy assumed Fionnuala was trying to get Lorcan so drunk he would miss the flight. Good luck to her, but it was a desperate plan destined to fail. He had seen Lorcan play soccer and score goals, build a cabinet for the loo, and win three pub quizzes, all under the influence of six beers or more. There was no way his son wouldn't get on that bus. Or so Paddy thought.

The night before, Paddy had suffered the misfortune of hearing Fionnuala sobbing and sobbing and sobbing on her side of the bed. "Am I so horrible?" she kept moaning into her pillow and, *Aye, ye are, ye vile monstrous madwoman, ye* Paddy kept thinking in his head, the one he had shoved under his own pillow to drown out her sobs and moans. He had had to rise at 6 AM to make fish cakes, after all.

He was getting fed up with Fionnuala. Paddy clicked from one unsatisfying channel to another and wondered what was going on with his wife. *Dancing black Yanks.* Paddy clucked with annoyance and clicked again. And again. Ever since Lorcan had hooked the telly up to the neighbors' system, they hadn't been able to see any of the familiar shows they loved, nor even the familiar shows they loathed. The shows all seemed to be public access shows from around the world, with horrible production values, shaky cameras and tinny voices, hideous people and inanity in a wide array of unintelligible languages that put his hackles up. He clicked. *Children on a farm coloring pumpkins with crayons.*

Paddy was faithful to Fionnuala, always had been and always would be, though there were plenty of offers from the ladies of the packing plant floor and from a variety of pubs around town (the Church forbade trespassing on his neighbor's wife, after all), and though that passionate love of youth of his had atrophied, they still had the shared experience of decades of raising all those children, those years, not really loving and tender, but the weight of those shared years to fall back on. *News in some Arabic language.* But now that weight was threatening to stifle him. He was seriously wondering about her. He and Dymphna had spoken about it often. *A Japanese game show, not one of the fun ones with colorful and strange props, but what looked like a spelling bee.* And he longed to bring Fionnuala's mother, Maureen, into the discussion as well, but he knew only too well the thickness of Derry blood. *A Yank evangelist pounding a pulpit with Meatloaf blaring in the background.* Even if Maureen agreed with everything he and Dymphna thought—and many times Paddy was sure he saw the disapproval glinting in Maureen's eyes and the tightening of her lips at some of Fionnuala's antics and histrionics, he couldn't trust the woman not to run to Fionnuala and tell her all. And the fallout, as usual, would be catastrophic. Paddy didn't understand what was going on in the bizarre labyrinth of imagined slights and desperate oneupmanship of his wife's mind. He considered leaving her, but it was too much hassle. And now a mysterious illness was invading her body, so he couldn't. But he shuddered at what the retribution might be if he did.

"Mammy! Jesus, Mary and Joseph!"

Paddy jumped at the sounds of Dymphna's shrieks of joy from the scullery. "It's bloody effin *marvelous! Flimmin, flippin brilliant!"* He wiped the beer from his chest with the closest throw pillow and smirked. It was about time Fionnuala did something to please someone in the family besides herself. And Lorcan. But it was too little too late.

Fionnuala had always been...*opinionated,* even when she had been Fionnuala Heggarty. But when Paddy's sister Ursula won the lottery all those years ago, well, her husband Jed, anyway, it seemed to tip Fionnuala over the edge. Paddy had stood by, shocked, as Fionnuala embarked on a campaign of hatred and penny counting that caused Paddy's sister and his brother-in-law to flee to the States. He had even started believing that hatred towards them that spewed from his wife's lips daily, and nightly as well. He had turned on his own sister, and on Jed, who was a right laugh, his mate, and a good man to boot.

He heard footsteps leaving the scullery and clomping up the stairs. It sounded like Lorcan and Padraig. After the cruise last year, Paddy thought maybe things would be different. But when Fionnuala revealed to him she had ripped up Ursula and Jed's wedding invite, he had shaken his head in disgust, though only in his mind. As she was saying it, Paddy's neck stood stock still, and his face had the usual concerned look plastered on it, and all the while his mind was thinking, *Ursula be's Dymphna's favorite auntie, but! And ye're going to die a lonely old hag, so ye are. Love.* There was always time for reconciliation, maybe there would be with Ursula and Jed, Paddy thought, especially now, as he was getting older, his hair graying, no longer the sexy black sheen of old, and his body finding it more and more difficult to drag itself off to the packing plant every morning. He noticed he was having to drink less every night so that his aging body could handle it. He thought that, for himself, that time for reconciliation might have come.

Dymphna was still squealing in the scullery. That must be the gown of the century, Paddy thought. *A Goth chat show.*

"Och, what the feck are these flimmin shite programs?" he asked himself, suddenly disgusted. Where was the boxing? The football, the *Match of the Day? Deal Or No Deal? Gardeners World? Coronation Street? Doctor Who? Casualty?* He pressed buttons on the remote control he had never tried before, and was sat staring at static, then a blue screen, then a screen of many vertical lines of color, then static again. Irritation growing in direct proportion to the amount of alcohol entering his system, he pulled himself from the settee and went to the back of the TV. He fiddled with the cable, tried to press it further in, then twisted it off and twisted it back in. He jiggled it.

He sat back down, swigged some beer, pressed more buttons, and finally found something that looked vaguely entertaining, well, not quite that, but not deathly boring. It seemed like a Yank quiz show. And as he heard the scullery door open, and steps approaching the sitting room, his eyes were arrested by the television. "Christ almighty!"

More beer spilled, but as Dymphna, Siofra, Seamus and Fionnuala's mother entered and another beer was forced into his hand,

"Och, Daddy! Ye should see the gown me mammy made! Lovely, so it—!"

Paddy couldn't even acknowledge their presence. Feeling like he was caught watching some guilty pleasure or pornography, he tried to flip over to another channel, jabbing frantically at the remote, but such was his shock that his finger kept missing the channel change button.

Lorcan and Padraig came into the room, and Paddy could only point a finger at the screen. He was in shock at what had suddenly appeared there. No, *who* had suddenly appeared there.

All seemed to gasp as a unit, including Lorcan and Padraig, who weren't in the habit of gasping. Paddy understood. He had gasped himself. All eyes were fixed to the screen, unable to make sense of what they were seeing, unable to trust their eyes, their brains struggling to comprehend.

"I-is that...?!" Maureen finally chanced.

"Can it really be..?" Dymphna wondered.

"Aye, it is," Paddy verified. "On wer own telly screen! Of all places!"

Siofra clapped her little hands with glee. Padraig wiped his glasses and placed them back on. He blinked and blinked at the screen, but he still kept seeing what he couldn't believe he was seeing. Seamus gurgled. Siofra ran into the hallway, and Paddy thought it was as if her 10-year-old body just couldn't stand still with all the excitement. But then...a horrible thought came to him.

"Siofra!" he inched. "Back here *now!*"

A few seconds passed, during which all jaws remained slack and all eyes remained saucered towards the screen, then Siofra came back in. "I hope ye didn't leave for to tell yer mammy about this?"

Paddy indicated the TV.

Siofra shook her head.

Paddy appealed to them all. "Breathe not a word of this to yer mammy. Do youse all understand? Youse know what it'll do to her. It'll derange her."

"I'm not for stirring up trouble!" Maureen said, hands spread before her as if in defeat. "Lord knows there be's enough of it around to add *that,*" she nodded to the telly, "to the mix!"

Lorcan, Dymphna, Padraig and Siofra all nodded, still shocked at what they had witnessed, what they were still witnessing. But their father had no reason to fear. A deranged Fionnuala was the last thing any of them wanted to encounter.

And then, when it was all over, perfect timing, the door to the scullery opened and Fionnuala yelled, "C'mon, youse! The wanes is lovely and clean and tea's ready!"

They trooped out of the kitchen, the family secret safe from Fionnuala for the moment. As amazing as what they had seen was, they were ravenous.

The nights were still chilly. The hot water bottle was now a tepid, squelchy mound at her frigid feet. The windup alarm clock with the glowing hands on her nightstand was ticking away the small minutes of the night. No, it was counting down. Bernadette Mulholland wiggled her toes to get some heat into them. She would have been tossing and turning all night long, but she was captive under the many lumpy blankets pinning her down, a prisoner upon the mattress. Heating was expensive, and why waste the money when ten blankets would do? So instead of tossing and turning, she was only able to stare up at the ceiling, watching the occasional car lights that moved across the ceiling from one patch of damp to the other.

She was thinking about Bridie barging into the sitting room that afternoon and what she had told them all. Mrs. Mulholland's instincts told her, no, her *faith* told her there was no way the Blessed Virgin would have appeared to her niece and told her to embark on such a...campaign, such a crusade of intolerance and hatred as the girl claimed. The Virgin Mary stood for compassion and kindness. Really, Bridie must be unhinged, it must be the result of too much drink, too many hours breathing in the toxic grease of the Kebabalicious, too much time on her hands and too much resentment in her heart.

But there was something about the way that smarmy git had given her less than her fair share of chips a few days before, the way he seemed to think her money was worth snatching and shoving into his mother's bank account...at her expense!...that had her nodding her head, taking up the gauntlet, agreeing with Bridie while all her elderly bingo partners and choir mates around her cheered and roared and made plans for the big event. She could see his glinty eyes still, his ferret-like teeth, and they made her stomach churn with disgust.

What they were going to do was necessary, it was important, it was what needed to be done. To stop society on the slippery slope to Hell and she knew not what. But in her heart of hearts she knew Mary hadn't decreed it. The Blessed Virgin wouldn't be that cruel. But Bridie could be.

Mrs. Mulholland felt bad sinning, lying to Bridie, telling her the Bishop had rung and told her the supermarket reception was taking longer than anticipated, and they'd have to reschedule. But the truth was Mrs. Mulholland now had no intention of ushering Bridie before the movers and shakers of Derry's Catholic world. She wasn't daft! She had her reputation to think of!

She groaned as she forced her body through the fields of blankets and was finally able to contort herself to do something that resembled a semi-roll on the mattress. She finally drifted off. The countdown continued. Two days to D-Day.

CHAPTER 31

Fionnuala knocked on Lorcan's door. She didn't know how his beer-tainted sweat could permeate the chipped wood, but the landing stank of his secretions. It didn't disturb her too much; she had smelled worse in her life. She looked across at the tray she had prepared for his breakfast, feeling quite sophisticated at how she was carrying it, just like a waitress of some posh Michelin starred-restaurant (she had seen a reality show filmed in London about just such waitresses in just such a restaurant; one got fired every week, and a girl from Limerick—Limerick!—had won. Fionnuala had been dead proud). Lorcan's breakfast was raisin porridge, but with generous helpings of cinnamon she had found to her surprise under the sink in a spice rack she had been given for Christmas years ago by a former employer from a job she longed to forget, and, from a bottle behind some tins in the larder, the dregs of some blackcurrant syrup she never remembered purchasing. Not to improve the taste, of course, but to mask the 'secret ingredient.' She had even arranged the raisins in a swirl so that it looked like a tornado being viewed from above. Fionnuala marveled a how Making Lorcan Stay (she would never consider it Poisoning Her Son) was making her not only a happier person but also a better cook. She had even folded a serviette and put it on the right side of the plate. Gordon Ramsay had better watch his back, she thought with a wry smile. She knocked again.

"Aye...?" It was a barely perceptible groan. Fionnuala barged in as quickly as she could with the tray. She was shocked at the sight of him, and her heart went out to him and his body, but it was his own fault. Much better he languish here in his own bedroom than sleep off a hangover on some sitting room floor in godless Florida. His head lolled on the pillow in the dankness of the room, ghastly pale. His hair resembled a wet black mop, and that made her think of the all the mopping she had had to do of the scullery floor at tea the night before. She shuddered at the memory, but approached the bed as he struggled to sit himself upright.

"I've yer breakfast for ye, love," she said, one hand clearing off the detritus on the nightstand, the other placing the tray on the stains and grime there. She perched herself on the sopping bedclothes beside his trembling torso and placed a hand on his forehead. Hot sweat prickled on the clammy flesh. "Wile shame ye're not eating it in exciting Florida, but. It grieves me heart that ye had to postpone yer flight outta here."

"B-breakfast?" Lorcan moaned, "I don't think I can stomach it, Mam. Terrible cramps, I'm tortured with. The amount of times I had to race to the loo last night."

"Aye, so I heard. All. Night. Long." She didn't sound best pleased, and realized she'd have to keep her voice softer, more one of motherly concern, but for her that was a struggle. "That flushing kept me awake till all hours. Why did ye think I set up this bucket for ye here beside yer bed? Nightmares of falling over Niagara Falls, I kept having." She kicked the bucket, and said accusingly: "Empty, I see."

"Sorry, Mam, but it was streaming outta both ends of me in force and amount like them Niagara Falls ye was on about. With the bucket I wouldn't have known which way to turn. Thank Christ we've that wee sink next to the toilet, like. Me throat still aches, but me arse got the worst of it. Sure, I haven't a mirror, nor would I want to see particularly, but it must surely resemble the Japanese flag by now, or a blood orange what's been peeled. Or a..."

Fionnualla winced. "Alright, son."

"...a fresh bullet wound, or maybe even a—"

"That's enough. I get yer point." Though each word seemed a struggle, he certainly had plenty to say! "Here. Have a wee sip of tea. And here's some paracetamol for ye and all."

She placed the pills on the withered tongue he managed to wriggle out, then raised the cup to his chapped lips like a chalice. His hands shook as he cupped them around hers and gulped down gratefully.

"And get some porridge down ye, son," she said softly, kindly. She wiped his forehead. "Ye need to keep yer strength up. Here's a beer to wash it down with and all. Perhaps ye'd like a few wee sips of the lager before ye taste yer porridge?"

She popped open the can, put one hand around his neck and guided his lips to the beer. His hair was sopping. He took grateful sips. She gave him more. And more. And then she reached for the spoon, scooped up some porridge, and began to feed him. "Just like when ye was a wane," she sighed, voice wistful.

As they had clattered into the chairs around the table the night before, nobody seemed to want to make eye contact with Fionnuala, and at first she wondered if they somehow suspected her plan. But as Lorcan pierced his vindaloo-drenched ham hock and brought the fork to his lips, nobody made to smack the poisonous gristle away to. So she thought that maybe it was some wedding surprise, a special treat for the mother of the bride, that they had been planning in the sitting room while she was changing the nappies and spraying the toxins on Lorcan's food, that was why they didn't want to look at her. Siofra picked up her ham hock and licked at the vindaloo like it was a lollipop, and the little girl babbled on and on about the wedding cake they'd be making the next day, the girl could certainly talk, and Padraig scowled with each new innovation she thought of. He scooped beans and toast down his throat, anger shining in his eyes.

"I'm not gonny help with that effin cake," he said. "That's not for lads, so it isn't."

"Aye, ye are," Fionnuala warned.

"Naw, I'm not!" he insisted.

Fionnuala was too busy shooting glances at Lorcan and how he was eating, and counting how many mouthfuls of ham hock he was chewing, how his Adam's apple reacted with each swallow, the color of his face, the expression on it, to be bothered with Padraig's insubordination. She waved the boy away, "Och, do what ye want, ye selfish bastard. Ye always do anyroad. I don't give a cold shite in Hell. Sure, Siofra's got Seamus and yer granny to help her. And Siofra, ye can ring round some mates to help ye if ye want. Youse've a lot of cake to make. A lot," and their eyes looked a bit surprised over the mouths that moved as they shoveled toast, beans, fat and gristle into them, and Paddy drank more beer and Maureen drank the wine she always did, and Fionnuala was still knocking back the whiskey and the chewing and gulping and screaming of the infants in the stroller by the cooker continued and Lorcan kept shoveling down mouthful after mouthful of the deadly ham.

"Och, Mam," he said, the vindaloo trickling down his chin, "Ye've outdone yerself tonight, so ye have! A special meal for me going-away, and a better tea I've never eaten in me life! I guess ye do believe me now when I say I'm sorry I'm going and that I'll send ye loads upon loads of Yank dollars. Ye can get that new washer ye've always been banging on about. And that swanky shower hose and all."

"Ye really are lovely, Mammy," Dymphna twittered. "All the work ye did on me marvelous frock."

"Aye, and today she give us Wine Gums and all," Siofra smiled.

"Two each," Padraig sniped.

"I love Mammy!" Seamus gurgled, his face hidden behind a mask of beans and vindaloo sauce.

And Fionnuala saw Paddy and Maureen smiling fondly at her across the plates and forks speared with dripping pork, maybe it was the drink, she didn't know, but she saw the looks, and here she was seeing the love of at least three of her four other children, regardless of which rank they held on that week's chart of her current favorites, and just as she was starting to feel guilty, just as she was wondering if she were being too hasty and starting to feel dread tightening her chest, and just as she was thanking the Lord that Lorcan seemed to have a stomach of steel, and a steel inner mouth and esophagus as well, or maybe it was lead she meant, like those lead lungs they once used to have, and just as she was wondering if she had been temporarily unhinged and if she should abandon her insidious plan, Dymphna, who had been teetering on the verge of nausea since she had stepped into the scullery, suddenly pardoned herself, thrust her head over her plate, and bean-spattered ham chunks erupted from her lips. There were squeals all around the table, forks clattering from fingers.

"I-I'm sorry," Dymphna cried hoarsely, wiping tears from her face and looking down at the mess on her plate, "It's the smell of the curry. Youse all know I kyanny abide it. I've been trying me best, but, but..." Her face turned green and her cheeks ballooned.

"Away from the table!" Paddy roared.

"Here's the bin," Lorcan said, grabbing it and shoving it towards his sister, and maybe it was the stench of the carrot detritus and the festering potato peels rising up from it and attacking her nose, or maybe still the curry, but Dymphna spewed up again, and it set off a chain reaction and Fionnuala looked on in horror, Maureen in disgust, and Paddy in surprise as Siofra, then Seamus, then Padraig ejected streams through the air which splattered on their plates, their shirts, the table, on the glasses and the floor. Lorcan roared with laughter as they jumped up from the table, chairs clattering over, and said, "Christ! I'm gonny miss youse all! What a craic wer family is!" He gulped more beer and kept wolfing down, imperious to the chaos around him.

Fionnuala effed and blinded as she tugged out the mop and the bleach, tossed rags all around, and the cleanup began. Paddy and Maureen were unable to take another forkful, but still Lorcan continued to devour down.

"I'd help youse," he said, "but ye know the size of them portions on the plane. I've to shove as much into me stomach while I can."

It was only after Fionnuala had mopped the floor for the third time and her son got up from the table to finish packing that, on the stairs, he suddenly gripped his stomach, a wail of pain roared from his throat, and the attack began.

Lorcan now pushed the spoon away. He had half-hardheartedly allowed his mother to fit three spoonfuls between his lips.

"I kyanny take no more, Mammy. I think there must be something wrong with me tongue. That porridge be's like the ham hocks last night. It tastes...all chemically-like. I didn't want to bring it up last night, as the vindaloo was magic. But..."

Fionnuala reluctantly placed the spoon in the bowl. She removed a raisin from his chin.

"Perhaps that's enough for this morning."

"Sorry, Mam."

"Och, not at all. I think, son, with the wedding being tomorrow, ye surely can wait until after that for to make yer escape from yer mammy and the town that loves ye. Aye? From what I gather about that Free Flight For A Friend ye told me about, ye can leave any time ye want, like. That be's correct, aye?"

"Aye. Sure, how can I be expected to make it to the airport if I can barely make it to the loo? Me legs be's wobbling like they was made of rubber. I can leave anytime. Mortified, I'd be, if I was locked in that wee toilet themmuns have on the plane, with all them noises rising outta me. I can wait, now, as long as it takes."

Fionnuala nodded, satisfied. She tried her best to contain her smile.

"I've to meet Zoë Riddell at some swank restaurant in a few moments. La-di-dah! Apparently she's some last minute wedding details to discuss. And if ye've not recovered properly by the time I come back, I'll take the wanes, and me mammy and all, up to St. Moluag's for to light a wee candle for ye, and to say a prayer as well, to help ye mend and ensure ye're on yer way to Florida as soon as. Oh, and by the by, the wanes'll be in the scullery making yer sister's wedding cake all afternoon. Ye've yer phone here, and if themmuns makes too much noise, just give me a ring and I'll take care of em. I know ye're probably too weak to go down all them stairs to tell em to keep it down, or too weak to even call out to em, so I can do it for ye. I can do whatever ye want for ye."

Except let ye leave. She picked up the tray.

"I'll be back in time for yer dinner. Do ye want fish and chips? Another of yer faves." *Dinner:* Derry for lunch.

"Let's wait and see, shall we?" he said weakly. He gave a moan, and his eyelids fluttered.

She kissed him on the forehead. She was happy it was still clammy.

"There's a good boy," she said.

Then she went into her bedroom to change out of her tattered robe for something suitable to see the Proddy bitch in.

CHAPTER 32

Lorcan loved a good horror film, especially slashers: the bloodier, the gorier, the scarier, the better. The hours he had sat on the settee, usually with a rapt Padraig at his side, rewinding the most horrific scenes of all the *Saw*s, *Hostel, The Texas Chainsaw Massacre*, the sadistic products of questionable Hollywood minds. And he been locked up in Magilligan Prison for three years. But nothing Hollywood had devised, nothing he had chanced upon in prison during his long stay there, was as scary as that Saturday morning and afternoon he endured on that mattress in that cupboard of a bedroom, with the crunchy sheets, drenched with old, cold sweat, clinging to his trembling body, and the shocking pains like living animals gnawing through his innards, his temperature pitching from arctic to hellish, drifting in and out of sleep or was it consciousness?

During the few brief periods of lucidity, where he knew without struggling the English words for all the objects he saw going in and out of focus in the room around him, there was always some important bit of information missing from his brain, either where he was, or what time of day, what year, or who he was. And all the while there were excited, girlish squeals and laughter, banging crashing and thumping noises coming from the kitchen. He whimpered and moaned and cried out at sudden jabbing pains in an intestine here, a bowel there, and wondered...was he back in prison? Was he in God's waiting room? No, he wasn't, he was in his bedroom. Ah, but yes he was in prison. There was just a new prison guard jangling the keys, an old one, but a new one anyway.

He ran a reptilian tongue over lips like papyrus. He was gasping with thirst.

He had long since finished the beer his mother had brought, and couldn't stomach the look of the porridge, now congealed in the bowl. He needed more alcohol, to lose himself in its charms. But...how many girls were down in that scullery? It sounded like a school-full. He waited, waited until finally he heard scampering like a herd of antelopes through the front hall downstairs, yells of "Cheerio!" and the front door slam.

He winced as he tugged off the sopping sheets and staggered out of the bed. His knees buckled and he grabbed the nightstand for support. The room swam. But then he felt better, stronger. He made his way to the door, then took the stairs slowly, feeling some strength seep back, and his own personality seeping back into his brain. He took a breath.

He heard his granny: "Could we not...cut down them towers, love?" then Siofra wail, "Naw, granny! Naw! *Naw!!*"

"Or reshape em a bit, love? Cut em with a knife to make em more like squares?"

"Towers in a princess castle be's round, but!"

"Maybe we can at least take off the...I don't know what ye'd call them. Them *roofs* ye've added to the tops of the towers."

"Naw! Naw!" Siofra wailed. "Mammy said I was in charge of the cake. It be's *my* wedding cake!"

As Lorcan opened the door to the scullery, Siofra was stamping her tiny feet. Tears were flowing down her face, an alarming pink. She roared huge sobs, bubbles of mucous escaping from her nostrils and then being sucked in again. Maureen stood over her, at a loss for what do to. Seamus was sitting on a chair, his head hidden behind a bowl he was apparently licking. There was no sign of Padraig.

Lorcan pushed the door wider, looked to the side and jerked in shock. Was he hallucinating again? Atop the table, surrounded by egg shells, fields of flour, pans crusted with burnt something and cans that had once held vegetables something monstrous skulked: Dymphna's wedding cake. His eyes begged him to look away, but it was like one of those scenes from any of the *Saws*: he just *had* to look. Three shocking layers of lumpy, misshapen cake were plopped atop each other, and it seemed as if the cake were melting before his startled eyes, like someone had left it out in the rain, bright icing flowing down. Also an alarming pink, like flesh that never saw the sun. His eyes took in further horrors: Two figures teetered on the slope of the highest layer. They had taken one of Seamus's action men, the paratrooper, and screwed its filthy plastic boots into the top, and next to it, left hand posed as if it were clutching one of the action man's, was Siofra's old Barbie, which had lost its head when she was six and been charred when 5 Murphy Crescent had burned down. Something that looked like a ping pong ball had been attached to its neck, and a smiling face scrawled in green crayon. Some fuzz had been taped atop it, which Lorcan took to signify hair. At least it was red.

"Lorcan!" Siofra sobbed. "Tell granny it's me cake and I don't have to change it if I don't wanny!"

"Of course ye don't have to—"

As he was speaking, he suddenly understood Maureen's concern. His eyes focused correctly, then blinked incomprehensibly. Rising proudly from the bottom layer of the 'cake' were the towers, which reached the top layer and had domed tops. They were the width of a can around, and three cans tall. Together, and with the fleshy pink, these three towers had the misfortune to resemble—

He howled with laughter. And yelled out as pain struck his stomach.

"Do ye like it, Lorcan?" Siofra asked, her tear- and icing-covered face beaming.

"Like it? I fecking love it!"

Maureen threw her hands up in defeat.

"Yaaay!!" Siofra squealed, and in the chair Seamus echoed her from behind the bowl.

"Alright, then," Maureen said, "Off ye go, wee girl! It'll stay as it is! Good job."

"Yaaaay!!! Dymphna's sure to love the princess wedding cake and all!"

Siofra squealed with glee again, grabbed Seamus by the hand, and they fled from the scullery.

"Maybe only wer Dymphna, in her younger and wilder days, would want to eat them towers," Lorcan said.

"Shush, you!" said Maureen, but she was laughing.

"Too bad she and Bridie aren't mates no more. Both of what that fat slag loves together in one...three...pieces!" He whispered in his granny's ear, "Cake and cocks!"

Maureen was scandalized. "Hush, Lorcan!" She said, pressing her hand against his arm, her body shaking with silent laughter. "C'mere, ye're terrible sweaty. And warm and all."

"Aye, I still feel like shite warmed over. I'm just down to get meself a drink."

He tugged three beers from the fridge.

"Yer mammy's left ye some special food over there."

Maureen nodded to a plate covered with tinfoil.

Lorcan shook his head in dread.

"I'm gonny boke again if I eat anything."

But Maureen had turned her attention to the horror of the cake again, inspecting it from different angles.

"May the Heavenly Father strike me down! I'm filled with that much guilt,

Lorcan. It's me own fault, ye see," she confessed. "I told them, it was Grainne Siofra had over, and that Catherine McLaughlin, ye know the copper's wee girl, and that Proddy girl Victoria Skivvins, and I told them the cake, when there was only them three layers, and not even straight layers, I says it was a wee bit flat, a wee bit boring. Girls, says I, why don't youse jazz it up a bit. Add some towers and such, like a princess castle. They was all for it, clapping their hands and jumping up and down as they do. And it was me what had the idea to open all them tins of vegetables from the larder, empty em out and use em to bake the shape of the towers, as baking pans like. Sure, nobody in this household likes vegetables anyroad, so there was really no waste, except if ye take them wanes in Africa into account. Each tower be's four cans tall, as ye can see. And we had that cupcake pan, so then they made a cupcake for each of the towers to put on top. Marvelous in theory, it was. As ye can see, but, the reality be's something quite different. Something quite *startling*. I hadn't me glasses on, ye see, when they finally, um..."

"Erected them, did ye want to say?"

"And perhaps that was a poor choice of color for the icing. A bit too much like human flesh. And them blue flowers they've done with the icing. Looks like warts all up and down the sides of em. Can ye imagine what the reaction'll be like on the day? And with all them posh Orange bastards from the groom's side in attendance and all! Och, I'm mortified for wer poor Dymphna, so am are, when ye take the state of her gown into account and all! Aye, Dymphna be's simpleminded enough to love the gown, that's as may be, the rest of us, but, has to look at her stepping down the aisle in that most horrid of creations, and then when we have to step up to the table to receive a slice of *that* on wer plates. And put it up to wer mouths and eat it. Me stomach's shuddering just thinking about it. Though...I suppose if I squint at it long enough without me glasses on, perhaps there's a wee bit of something...*Gaudí* about it. That said, lad, though me heart goes out to ye for yer illness, it fills me heart with joy that ye'll be here in Derry for the big day. Quite a wedding this'll be tomorrow."

"Aye," Lorcan said, drinking down a beer, "Maybe I'm happy to be here for it after all."

"Are ye sure ye don't want what yer mammy's made for ye?"

Lorcan pulled aside the tinfoil and looked at more porridge.

"Naw," he said. "I'll pass. I'm going back up to me room. Me mammy said she's making fish and chips for me dinner. Hopefully me stomach will be able to keep that down when the time comes."

"Aye, I hope so and all."

She wanted to ruffle his hair in a show of affection, but it was so slick with grease and old sweat she had to make do with a tiny pat.

"Go you back upstairs and rest yerself, get yerself stronger for the big day tomorrow, lad."

"Aye, I will."

Ten minutes later, Maureen was standing at the cooker waiting for the kettle to boil for a much needed cup of tea. Her back was turned to the cake so she didn't have to look at the monstrosity. And she thought back to the very odd thing Siofra had done once the towers had been assembled and riveted on. The girl had pulled an aerosol can of furniture polish out of the cupboard, shaken it, popped off the lid and, humming gaily, made to spray it on the cake! Grainne, Catherine and Victoria were shocked as well. Seamus too.

"Are ye bonkers, girl?" Maureen had yelled, grabbing the can from Siofra's hand. "Are ye soft in the head? Why would ye want to spray that poison on the cake?"

"I'm doing it just like Mammy does," the girl had said, her lip trembling, eyes telling Maureen she didn't know what all the fuss was about.

"Och, go on away with that, wane! I never heard such foolish, goofy talk in all me days. Why would yer mammy do that?"

"To make it taste better? To make it shine? I dunno, but I seen mammy spray something on the ham hocks yesterday, like. I ran into the scullery to tell her what we was seeing on the telly, but then Daddy called me back."

"Yer mammy did no such thing! Ye're a bad wee brute, Siofra Flood! I'd smack yer lying face if it weren't for the fact that I can hardly lift me arm over me head!"

"She did! Ask her yerself!"

"I'll do no such thing. It's a blatant lie! It's a sin to lie! Ye'll burn in Hell, Siofra Flood, if ye don't take it back!"

Grainne and Catherine were nodding in agreement, and Seamus as well, but Victoria looked like she was on the fence. They stood in a semi-circle around Siofra, waiting. Reluctantly, Siofra had nodded her head also.

"Alright, Granny. I told a lie."

Maureen shook her head, smiling, as she spooned sugar into her tea. *The wanes of the day! Whatever will they think of next?* Then she went to see what was on the telly...if there was anything!...and plan her outfit for the wedding.

CHAPTER 33

Zoë ordered a Hendrick's and tonic. She needed gin for this meeting. With her only son's wedding to Dymphna Flood the next day, she felt that, though a bright spark of excitement burned in one part of her, another part was dying a slow and torturous death. She clicked away at her iPhone and nibbled on a bread stick, or a granary baton, as she called it. The drink came, she squeezed the cucumber slice into it and gulped it down.

"Another," she said, the ice cubes clinking as she handed the waiter the emptied glass. He hadn't even had the chance to leave the table.

When Dymphna had moved into her house for the second time, Zoë had immediately upped the cleaning woman's visits from two a week to four to rid the house of the odor. She wasn't sure what it was, the fluids of the babies, or the beer-, fag- and whiskey-scented sweat Dymphna seemed to secrete from her armpits. Zoë was alarmed one so young could smell so spent. She had sat Rory down and asked him, babies of questionable heritage aside, why he would want to marry Dymphna. He told her that he loved her. He loved her. Rory loved Dymphna. It was as simple as that. Zoë had let Dymphna's slovenly motherhood slide. But now that things were becoming official...

Zoë grabbed the second drink and took her time with this one. Where was that mother of the bride? It was 12:15, and they should have met at twelve.

Zoë had always felt an affinity with the Catholic community. She was delighted her son was marrying someone from the other side of town, from the other religion. She was less enchanted it was Dymphna, especially as there were hordes of Catholic girls to choose from in that town. But in fact, calling her son Rory had been a political decision, and that had been at a time in the past when the city was more divided, more sectarian than it was today. Her mother had been scandalized, choosing such a Catholic name for a child! But Zoë knew even back then that the only way towards the future was to forget the past. She didn't believe the best predictor of future behavior was past behavior, either in people or in business. And it had been this intuition that had made Riddell Enterprises such a success.

She viewed the marriage as yet another example of a high risk/high gain strategy that had helped build that career. The demographic of her customers for her Pence-A-Day lockups, her swanky café and her various other enterprises, such as the card shop and the butcher's, was 88% Protestant. The chip van was another matter; it did most of its trade after last orders at the pubs, and when drink is involved, people don't care what religion they're getting their chips from. And while a pub quiz question like Was Amelia Earhart Catholic or Protestant might have some populaces racing to Google, all Derry, since the opening of the center, now knew the answer as a matter of course. (Clue: Fionnuala never mentioned it on the tour.)

Zoë Riddell's steely business mind viewed this pairing of the two religions, the coming together of the two families who couldn't have been more different, as a chance to double her business opportunities, like a bisexual doubling his chances for a date on a Saturday night.

She took another sip of Hendrick's. Sacrificing her only son for the sake of future profits might appear cold hearted, and though Zoë hadn't risen up the male-dominated ranks of the Derry business world by giggling and playing croquet, she knew that Rory would eventually take over the business and her many enterprises, so she was actually being a loving mother concerned both for her son and his generations after. Or so she told herself. Though how her empire and estate would be divided to those generations in her will was a complicated matter she would have to think about for a long, long time.

She dealt with percentages often, and she was 97% sure Keanu wasn't her son's—the unsightly child had red hair, for the love of God!—Beeyonsay she was more certain about; she gave the girl a 52% chance of being a Riddell. These percentages went a long way to explaining her ambivalence about their upbringing, for example, why she hadn't bought Dymphna a stroller that could comfortably hold two. But a new stroller would be on the way, and an Aston Martin Silver Cross, at that, as Zoë was 95% sure this third one, whatever it might be called, was Rory's. Surely he had been vigilant with the girl, making sure she didn't stray? There was, of course, the two weeks the Flood family, Dymphna included, had been working on the cruise ship, but according to Dymphna, the hours were so long she barely had time to drink, let alone socialize with strange men. Zoë chose to believe her.

So though she didn't trust Beeyonsay's lineage, and totally doubted Keanu's pedigree—they were mutts!—she was sure this new child would be a thoroughbred, as much as it could be with 50% Flood blood in its veins.

Ah, there she was! Zoë waved the Flood woman over to her table. She was surprised there was no sign of that horrid Celine Dion/Titanic tote she always lugged about. Now she was carrying two plastic bags from the Top Yer Trolly instead. Which Zoë considered worse. At least Mrs. Flood seemed to have given up those peculiar old fashioned etiquette mannerisms Zoë had to endure every time they met.

As Fionnuala sat opposite, her eyes lit up at the sight of the bread basket, which brimmed with a selection of bread sticks, some with sesame seeds, some flour dusted; a variety of rolls, poppy kaiser, wholemeal, sourdough pavés, and plain white crusty; and slices, including banana nut, olive and malted wheat; and focaccia, ciabatta, even a naan.

Fionnuala clapped her hands with glee and leaned conspiratorially towards Zoë. "I had a feeling this posh place would have one of them bread baskets. So I came prepared."

Zoë looked on in horror as the woman reached into her plastic bags and tugged out a jar of strawberry jam, some Nutella, a stick of butter and little cheese triangles.

"No sense letting all this bread go to waste, and, as I understand it, there be's no charge. I just brought these few bits and bobs from home to make it a bit more substantial of a meal, and then all I've to pay for be's me tea!"

She unscrewed a jar and, knife aloft, ran her fingers along the breads, musing.

"Put those things away right now, Mrs. Flood!" Zoë hissed.

And as she fought to tug the knife out of Fionnuala's hand, Zoë was crestfallen, glum, filled with a sense of dread, suddenly feeling the weight of all the years she still had to live with this woman, these people, as part of her family pressing down on her, an endless burden pressing down relentlessly, getting heavier and heavier until the flames of the crematorium freed her and her ashes were scooped into the urn and scattered on some body of water she had yet to choose, buoyant at last. She pressed the knife firmly on the table, helped Fionnuala gather all the condiments into the bag, then cleared her throat.

"I would have thought it understood that I'd be picking up the bill."

"Ah! In that case...!" Fionnuala grabbed the menu before her, opened it up, then snapped it shut. "Just as I suspected. It's all in flimmin Foreign."

"No, it's English, Mrs. Flood. Well, now it's English, in any event. Perhaps you wouldn't mind if I ordered for us?"

"Fill yer boots."

"Fine." Zoë waved to the waiter, who had been hovering near them since the knife. He minced over to the table. "We'll have two of the gazpacho to start, then perhaps the arugula with Gorgonzola to share, the beef teriyaki crisps with wasabi mayonnaise for appetizer, or would you prefer the baked feta with Romesco and olive tapenade, Mrs. Flood? Then there's the eggplant crostini...Or this muhammara with crudités. Which sounds more delicious?"

"Ye're the boss."

"The teriyaki, then, and then I'll take the hangar steak tartare with pickled jalapeños and shiitake mushrooms, and how about a filet mignon with Fettuccine Alfredo and asparagus with hollandaise sauce for my, er, friend here. You'd better make it well done. And tiramisu for dessert. I'll have a sparkling water and you, Mrs. Flood? Tea, I believe you said...?"

"Aye. Extra milky, three sugars."

The waiter left and Fionnuala stared at him go for a moment, disgust on her face, then bent over the table and hissed, afflicted, at Zoë: "I see ye ordered the steak for yerself!"

Zoë breathed deeply and slowly and counted to ten. "They are *both* steak, Mrs. Flood. Mine is served raw. I didn't think you would...? No, I thought not."

Fionnuala cast the waiter another glance. "C'mere, how they've found a poofter here in Derry to be the waiter I can't imagine! Arse bandits don't live in this town! Did they ship him in, do ye think?"

"I wouldn't know. But I do believe they're probably spread somewhat evenly throughout the global population in general. There must be some here in Derry. Though, very well hidden, I'd agree with you there."

"Well, I've never seen one walking down the streets of Derry in me life! Except yer 'man' there...er, here."

She silenced herself and looked at him with distaste as he placed the drinks on the table.

"Anyroad, ye're gonny love the gown," Fionnuala said when he was gone. "I outdid meself, if I do say so. Lovely, so it is. And the cake will be, er, the cake is being *delivered* this evening. Maybe it's already at the house, I dunno, but I have me mammy looking out for the van."

Zoë almost couldn't bring herself to ask, "Have you made many adjustments?" and she awaited the reply with dread.

"Calm yerself down, woman. Naw, just a tug here, a nip there."

"Are you sure, Mrs. Flood?" Zoë's hand was clamped on her gin. Her eyes searched Fionnuala's face for a sign, a hint, of mischief. "A Vera Wang shouldn't be touched. That gown is a one-off. I don't want to bring up cost, but per inch, that chiffon set me back—"

Fionnuala clucked, irritated. "Och, Dymphna saw the altered frock and was in raptures. I know what me daughter likes, so I do. Ye're gonny love it and all."

"And I suppose," Zoë sighed, resigned, "what's done it done. It's too late to change anything now. And...the cake?" She leaned across the table, interest shining in her eyes. "What is that going to look like?"

"Ye'll love it," Fionnuala said. "Ye've no need to worry yerself. I told ye I would take care of it, and I did. Though somehow there was a misunderstanding with the baker's and it's come out pink instead of that Brookside Moss. It's still grand and lovely, but. And there'll be enough to feed an army, I'm sure."

"Fine," Zoë said, though she didn't look exactly that, "Now that's taken care of, we can move on to other things."

The soup arrived.

"I'll show you which utensil to use."

"Which...?"

"That spoon there. And I'll warn you now, Mrs. Flood, this soup's *meant* to be cold."

"Cold soup? Raw meat?" She looked around her. "Sure, there's more cooking going on in me own scullery than in this fancy schmancy place. Are themmuns afeared of having the lekky cut off?"

They sipped the gazpacho.

"Mmm!" Fionnuala said, surprised.

"About the honeymoon. I've booked them two weeks in the Maldives."

"The what?"

"Maldives."

"What does them be when they're at home?"

"They are islands in the Indian Ocean. An island nation of twenty six atolls. They will enjoy sun and sand and of course there is a spa, water polo, surfing, snorkeling, a night fishing excursion and what have you."

By the look on Fionnuala's face, she was considering this a nightmare, not a honeymoon. She scooped up the rest of her soup and slurped it down.

"If ye was looking at islands, couldn't ye have chosen Ibiza? More their style. All them rave clubs, and they can gobble down as many Es as can fit into their mouths. I think Ecstasy still be's legal there, or so I'm told anyroad."

"May I remind you your daughter is pregnant? Almost four months on, from what I've been told. Though why I wasn't told sooner..." This was said with a touch of regret. She shook her head. "Anyway, the point is, I don't think she should be taking recreational drugs. Nor should you be encouraging her to do so. They will be greeted with a bottle of champagne and a box of chocolates when they enter the wedding suite, and I even felt guilty checking the box for the champagne. She really shouldn't be drinking. Or smoking, for that matter. But I understand I am helpless to change her behavior, no matter how reckless and harmful. To my...*our*...grandchild's health. Our grandchild."

The salad arrived. Fionnuala's eyes lit up at the sight of it.

"It's drizzled with balsamic vinaigrette," Zoë said. "I hope that's okay for you? I forgot to ask."

"I hope ye don't mind me saying this," Fionnuala said, heaping salad on her plate with two large spoons. "I know ye're speaking English, but I can't get me head around the fact that, though I know the language ye're speaking, I be's struggling most of the times to comprehend what ye're saying."

"Yes. At times I feel the same. Anyway, I was just telling you what the dressing on the salad is."

Fionnuala looked at her for assistance, and Zoë pointed out the correct fork. They chewed away in silence for a few minutes. Zoë considered ordering another gin and tonic, but feared that would set Fionnuala off on a bender that might end in violence and the police being called. She leaned forward and said what she had called this meeting, really, to say.

"Something's been troubling me, Mrs. Flood."

Fionnuala eyed her over her fork with suspicion.

"I'm sure you remember years ago when we were both invited to the Fingers Across the Foyle talent show parents mixer? And I was talking to a girlfriend and business partner of mine in the lavatory? And we were talking about you? And you happened to be in the stall? Surely you recall?"

221

Fionnuala flung her fork down, her face incandescent.

"Och—"

Zoë held up a hand. "Please listen. I said some very unkind things about you then, and I've never properly apologized for my indiscretion. I suppose I could blame the alcohol, they did have Grey Goose in those Apple-tinis of theirs, and quite a lot of it. And I suppose I could blame my friend for starting the discussion. I've learned in business it's never a good thing to speak about a client, no matter how horrid, behind their back in case just such an occasion arises, news of the nasty things said get back to them, and an unfortunate situation arises. As happened in this instance."

The salad plates were removed and the teriyaki crisps were placed before them.

"Mind the mayonnaise," Zoë said as Fionnuala shoveled the food on her plate. "It's very spicy." Zoë served herself as she continued, Fionnuala all ears and grinding molars. "But I won't blame the alcohol and I won't blame my girlfriend." Fionnuala flinched as Zoë's hand reached across the starched white cotton, over the many forks and spoons and knives and the collection of plates big and small that seemed to confuse the woman opposite, and touched her on the hand. "And I am truly sorry for what I said about you. If you recall, I believe I called you a 'hard faced creature,' that you looked older than your years, that I blamed it on bad genes, the lack of nutrition, and the inability to afford the beauty products of the day. I also said your Burberry scarf was sure to be a knockoff—"

"Naw, ye said I probably shoplifted it,"

"That was my friend."

"Anyroad, why are ye dragging all this up now? I wouldn't except anything less from a minted hateful Orange Proddy bitch like yerself." But Fionnuala didn't say it with anger, just as a statement of fact.

"Perhaps you think we 'Orange Proddy bitches,' to coin your phrase, don't have the guilt you Catholics do. But we do. And so I've prepared a little token of my appreciation, and my apology, for you. Here it is."

She pulled out a shiny little folder and pressed it across the table. Fionnuala threw down her fork and tugged it open. She pulled out the itinerary and the tickets.

"All expenses paid," Zoë said.

Fionnuala's brow wrinkled with incomprehension.

"But...where the bloody feck's this Dubyah? Doesn't that be some old Yank president?"

"It's pronounced Dubai, Mrs. Flood. The stress is on the second syllable. It's the new playground for the world. In the U—"

"—SA?"

"—AE."

"UAE? Are ye making countries up? Where the hell is this UAE?"

"The United Arab Emirates. I'm surprised you haven't heard of it. All common laborers, erm, excuse me, many people are flocking there for holidays."

"Ta very much. I woulda preferred Paris, but. Was tickets to there too dear for ye?"

"I'm sure you'll enjoy it. I even got you tickets to ride the elevator to the top of the Burj Dubai. It's the tallest building in the world. Much taller than the Eiffel Tower."

Fionnuala eyed the tickets with new-found interest.

"You see, Mrs. Flood, I am really quite excited about our families joining together. It's like a mini Fingers Across The Foyle, if I may bring up that unfortunate event once again. And I hope you feel the same way?"

"Och, I'm sorry about me Paris comment before. It's wile civil of ye, indeed. At first, I thought this was a charade, and that wer Dymphna was a daft eejit to pair up with an Oran—with a Protestant. But, aye, I...I... I kyanny believe ye apologized to me. That was so long ago. C'mere, ye've got me all choked up!" Zoë was startled to see the woman wipe a tear from her eye. "Or does it be that spicy mayonnaise ye was going on about?"

"Do you know what, Mrs. Flood? Let's raise a toast to this occasion! What would you like to drink?"

"Double whiskey, Glenfiddich. 18 year, if they have it."

"I'm sure they do. Waiter!"

Fionnuala looked at her in surprise. "Do ye not call them garçons?"

"I'll call them whatever the bloody hell they want to be called. Even Kylie's Friend or Mary or Butch or whatever the current homosexual parlance is. As long as they bring us our drinks!"

Now both were surprised as they cackled with laughter together, and Zoë felt a bit of the bright spark burn brighter still.

CHAPTER 34

When Fionnuala laid eyes on the cake, a bark of laughter escaped her mouth. It quite scared Siofra.

"Fitting," was all her mother said, then turned to inspect the bizarre wedding delivery that had arrived while she and Zoë had been dining at Le Restaurant. Siofra knew from the glassiness in her mother's eyes, from the alien friendly patter, from the eerie smile that didn't sit well on her mother's face, that she was paladic. And although this was more rare of an occurrence than might be expected, past experience had taught Siofra that the best thing to do when her mother mixed liquor with her mind was to clear out. She disappeared up the stairs and left Fionnuala alone with Maureen in the kitchen.

"Some flash git's got dosh to throw down the grating," Fionnuala said, and though there was disapproval in her voice, she was sniffing around the new arrival like a hyena in heat. "What eejit would be daft enough to waste the money on wer Dymphna, wedding or not? C'mere, Mammy, ye don't think it could be from that footballer what Dymphna told us about she had on the city walls yonks ago? Ye know the one I mean, he plays for Man United now? Must be raking it in, the amount of money flung at them footballers. And that's an odd set up, an odd shape for a bouquet, do ye not agree?"

"That I couldn't say, love."

It was a two feet round multicolored floral wreath, dazzling, bursting with roses and carnations and gladioli and other fancy flowers Fionnuala had never set eyes on in her life before but were pleasing to the eye and nose, together with a foliage edging that was a selection of lush ivy and ferns. Fionnuala was puzzled by the stand, like a large artist's easel, that the delivery man had hauled in along with it and which was now leaning against the washer, and she struggled to comprehend how and why it had come with the bouquet, but she thought it lovely as she ran her hand over it, all good varnished wood. Who could have sent it?

Maureen put on her glasses and peered at it.

"Just as I suspected!" she said. "That doesn't be a bouquet. That be's a wreath. For a *funeral,* like! That stand be's to display it at the wake. Read the card, would ye?"

Fionnuala pried the card from between a yellow carnation and a fern.

"But...it's not even addressed to wer Dymphna! It be's addressed to me and Paddy!"

"Ye're joking!"

Maureen was about to snatch the little envelope from Fionnuala herself, but her daughter slid out the card and read aloud, shock and anger filling her voice as she continued:

What a horrible way to lose a daughter! I just heard the news, and I wanted to let you know I'm as saddened as I'm sure you all are. Here's hoping none of your other children face a similar fate. I'm sure they won't. We're trying to make it there for the sad event. I know we can no longer laugh together, but I'm hoping you'll allow us to cry together. XXX Ursula (and Jed sends his regards)

Even Maureen's jaw had dropped. And the old woman jerked back as Fionnuala's clogs thrust though the air, kicking the wreath again and again, petals and leaves and thorns and the easel and she knew not what flying through the air as the spittle flew from her daughter's lips: "Evil, spiteful, bleeding flimmin fecking bloody *sarky cunt!* That aul dragon woman musta heard about the wedding from somewheres, and was raging she wasn't invited, and who would want to invite the tight-fisted bitch anyroad, and this is what she goes and does? Flinging her hatred across the miles, and...like placing a curse on all me other poor wee wanes, when none of em have done her the least bit of harm, hoping none of em finds the happiness of marriage! 'I'm sure they won't,' me arse! And, aye, she does indeed be a daft eejit, the biggest daft eejit, with more money than sense that I know. I shoulda realized! Sarcasm be's the lowest form of wit, does she not know?!"

She was breathless now, her face pink, sweat dribbling down, her fists clawing at the twigs and stems and ivy, knuckles bloody from thorns. From upstairs, they heard Seamus's terrified wails.

Maureen's hand kept shooting out, hoping to touch her daughter in comfort, but the fists kept flying, the feet kept kicking. Fionnuala stomped on the stand again and again. Maureen hovered by the safety of the cooker. And finally the easel was nothing planks and splinters, the wreath bare stems on a circular chicken wire frame, the linoleum strewn with tattered flowers. Fionnuala caught her breath and sat on a chair, sobbing, with the gown twinkling before her, the cake rising behind her.

"And is Ursula really coming to Derry for to wreck the day? I kyanny tell! What do ye think, Mammy?"

"I think..." Maureen's eyes darted back and forth behind her specs as she thought. "Could it not be, love, what ye told that Mrs. McDaid one the other day? About wer Dymphna dying? Could she not have somehow caught wind of it?"

"Och, catch yerself on! Ye know well enough wer Dymphna didn't die of that drugs overdose. That's just what I told Mrs. McDaid. That's not real. But the wedding. The wedding's real. How could that Ursula cunt know about something that didn't happen but not know about something that will? Naw! It's hate, pure and simple!"

"Ye know, love, I was at Xpressions the other day and they was all going on about wer Dymphna dying. Nearly had me in Altnegalvin, so the story did. Do ye not know, bad news travels quick and far and wide, and quicker and farther and wider than good news. Good news dies a sudden death, so it does. Nobody's interested in blathering on about people what be's happy, what be's content, what's had their dreams come true, for the love of God! Makes em feel like shite. Anyroad, it doesn't sound like Ursula in her right state of mind."

Maybe it was the double whiskey, but Fionnuala couldn't see sense. "Aye, it does! Ye don't know her like I do! She knew what she was up to!" Her voice voice rang with righteousness and conviction, certain, "As God's me witness,

I'll get me own back on the smarmy, narky cow! I'll throttle the life outta her with me bare hands! I'll slice her throat with a bread knife, laugh as the blood comes spurting out and cascading down! And then dance with glee on her coffin when they haul it towards her grave with the industrial-type crane it's gonny take to lift it!" She sobbed into the arm of her shirt. "I'll even take them Bollywood dance lessons down the community center I've been going on about to make it a right spectacle of it and all. All of Derry will be laughing and clapping around the grave, and the coppers can drag me away in them flimmin flimsy handcuffs they've nowadays, and I'll be laughing. I won't care. She's gonny get hers! Trust you me! Lord help me, heavenly Father help me, I know it be's a sin, but now I comprehend, aye I do, why them lunatics commits the deadliest sin of all. Murder! Och...the rage I've inside me, begging for release, like!"

Maureen patted her daughter's blanched scalp.

"Calm you down, love. And I do believe that if ye killed Ursula, the Filth wouldn't be long in picking ye up and hauling ye in long before ye'd had the pleasure of dancing at her funeral. Ye'd be doing all them odd Bollywood dance moves in yer cell on the day. Alone. C'mere and let me wipe them tears from yer face."

She took out a tissue from some fold of her tracksuit, but Fionnuala knocked her hand away and stood up.

"I'm right now, Mammy," she said, wiping her face herself. "If that woman steps foot back in Derry, but, let alone into the church tomorrow, she'll rue the day she ever wrote them words down! Mark me words, Mammy."

"Aye. I believe ye love." And Maureen did.

"I've to make the tea. Lorcan must be gagging with hunger, like. I kyanny let it go any longer. Leave me be, would ye, Mammy, while I fry the fish and get them chips in the oil."

And as Fionnuala stamped to fridge and pulled out the fish, and as she pottered around with the the knobs and the pans and the oil on the cooker, Maureen and her cane made their way out of the kitchen.

Fionnuala selected a nice, plump fish for Lorcan. She placed it on a plate by itself. She opened the bread box and grabbed the hairspray. She shook it. The can was empty.

"Och, for the love of...!"

She threw open the cupboard under the sink, rummaged around and unearthed a can of furniture polish. She was surprised she had it. She pulled it out and scanned the ingredients: *Soparaffin, Dimethicon, Octylphosphonic Acid, Nitrogen, Polysorbate 80, Sorbitan Oleate, Polydimethylsiloxane, Methylisothiazoline, 2-Amino-2-Methyl-1-Propanol.* She smiled. If anything, this seemed more effective than the hairspray.

She checked the scullery door was closed, then picked up the fish and sprayed it up and down. She hummed "The Power of Love," one of her Celine Dion favorites, as the polish creamed up over the fish. She rubbed it into the fillet.

While the fish was frying and the chips were boiling, she marched into the hallway and rang Dymphna on her cell phone. Although it was her wedding night, she was working at the chip van. Rory was at his stag party, his bachelor party, and Dymphna hadn't been able to find anyone to work her shift. But, anyway, her bridesmaids were skint. And they had gone out a few nights ago. That would have to count as her hen do, her bachelorette party.

"Aye, Mammy?"

"Have ye been drinking?"

"Aye I have! Can ye hear it in me voice? I've the girls around. It's me wedding night, after all, and we've some drinking to do!"

"There in the van?!"

"Aye, Maire, Ailish and Maeve are all in here with me. Keanu and Beeyonsay and all, but they be's sleeping. Or trying to sleep, anyroad. The girls brought a few flagons of cider, and some tins of lager and all. It's a wile craic! They're even helping me with the punters. Well, the ones they fancy, anyroad."

At least the music in the background sounded happy. And it was. "Happy." And if Fionnuala knew from her own radio listening experience, it wasn't the last time the girls would be hearing "Happy" that evening. How it was legal for a radio station to play the same song every twenty minutes when there were millions of songs in the world to chose from, Fionnuala couldn't fathom.

"Anyroad, I don't mean to spoil yer Happy evening, there, love."

"What's up, Mam?"

"I just wanted to let ye in on what's been happening...Ye know ye kept banging on about yer auntie Ursula not answering yer invite? About how she was yer favorite auntie and how much ye loved her and she loved ye?"

"...Aye?"

Fionnuala detected the caution in the girl's voice, and smiled down the receiver as she spat out the news, "I just wanted to tell ye that yer *favorite auntie* has just gone and sent ye a *funeral wreath,* of all things, with a note to me saying she hopes ye and all yer brothers and sisters die after having lived loveless lives, and that ye all rot in Hell!"

"Mammy! What a terrible thing for ye to say! And on the eve of me wedding and all! It's not on, so it isn't."

"Ye think I'm making it up, do ye? I've the card she sent right here. Ripped into shreds in me anger, aye, but ye can piece it together, tape it up, like, and read for yerself what a spiteful, sarky, hateful cunt the aul toerag is. Just like I've been trying to tell ye all along. Not that ye and yer daddy and Lorcan and

Siofra and me mammy and all pays me any mind. I'm telling ye but, I've the proof of her hatefulness! On her way to Derry to wreck yer big day and all. She thinks she's gonny be welcome at the church tomorrow after sending us a note like that? Flimmin soft in the head, ready for Gransha, so she is!" *Gransha*, the mental hospital up on Clooney Road.

"Mammy! Stop it!" Fionnuala heard Dymphna's tears down the line, "Ye're ruining me night! Ailish, hand me that rag, would ye? Aye, and another cider and all. I still don't believe ye, but! I'm hanging up on ye, Mammy!"

"Ye can see the evidence for yerself when come home tonight. Ye *are* coming back for yer tea the night, aye?"

But the line was dead. And Fionnuala knew Dymphna would be coming back to the house. It was the night before the wedding, after all, and Rory couldn't see her. Though, the amount of drink the lad was probably pouring down his throat on his stag do, he probably wouldn't be able to see her if he were looking straight at her anyway. Fionnuala went back to the kitchen, picked up the card where she had thrown it on the floor, searched around for a pen, then turned the card over. And, in a hand remarkably similar to Ursula's— once the Barnetts had won the lottery, Fionnuala had practiced Ursula's signature hoping to get a hold of her sister-in-law's check book one day and go mad—it was like riding a bicycle, she never forgot, Rot In Hell, All Of You she wrote, then tore up the card into tiny shreds. She placed them in the middle of the table. So she could show Dymphna and Paddy and anybody else who might care to look. Her mother had never seen the back of the card, so, though Maureen might wonder why the ink on the back was blue instead of black like the ink on the front, she'd never be able to say it hadn't been sent without the PS.

Fionnuala went back to the cooker. She grabbed the tongs, tugged out the fish and placed them on a piece of paper towel to drain. Then the tongs reached for Lorcan's piece. It hung over the bubbling oil. She dropped it in. The oil spattered. And then the phone rang again. She went to answer it.

Balloons bobbed in the haze of fat- and fag-smog that was the air of the chip van. The grease was splattering, the heat stifling, the space non-existent, the infants were shrieking, and Avicci blared from the transistor radio atop the toaster.

They could only see Maire's arse, as she was bent out the hatch flirting with a construction worker who had asked for a pickled onion, but Ailish and Maeve, eyes glazed, clutching bottles of drink, were shaking their heads at Dymphna.

"Don't do it."

"It's the drink talking."

"I'm not giving ye back yer phone." Maeve had shoved it down her cleavage.

"Ye'll thank us in the morning."

"I kyanny let it lie!" Dymphna roared. "I need to phone the narky cow and tell her what I think of her! Making up them cruel stories about me auntie Ursula! And making me think about me death, and the deaths of me brothers and sisters and all, and this on the eve of me wedding! Bloody typical of her! Kyanny stick anybody having a good time! Miserable aul geebag! Gimme back me phone now!"

"Ye're gonny regret it when ye wake up in the morning."

"Ye're gonny regret it the moment ye ring off."

"Gimme me phone *now!*"

Dymphna trampled over the chips and buns and pickled onions strewn on the floor—they had been using them as playthings earlier—and reached Maeve's breasts, which didn't take many steps.

Maeve squealed with shock then laughter as Dymphna delved into her sopping valley and grabbed the phone. She pressed her mother's number. Maeve and Ailish shrugged, clinked their bottles together, and drank some more.

"Hello? Mammy?" Dymphna was raging. And slurring.

"What do ye—"

"Right! Home truths! I know ye don't wanny hear it, and I know I should probably keep me trap shut. But I just kyanny. Ye see you, Mammy? I've never been able to stick ye. And that call ye just made to me shows just why. Yer constant badgering, this relentless abuse ye shoot off about me auntie Ursula has to stop *now!* The poor woman won that lottery money years ago, sure! It be's ancient history, but ye keep harping on and on about it as if it just happened the afternoon before! Ye've long since chased her off to America, and doesn't that be enough for ye? Ye won. But, naw, that doesn't be enough, does it? How empty is yer life that ye feel the need to keep going on and on about what a tight-fisted cunt she is? Lorcan told me all about that puppet show ye put on the other day. Vile! Disgusting! Thank Christ I missed out on it, as it woulda turned me stomach, and I wouldna been able to keep me bake shut about it, and God alone only knows what devious retribution ye'd have served up for me. But I'm telling ye know. And, aye, I know it's the drink and, aye, I know there's less of a chance ye're gonny put me in intensive care as ye don't wanny lose face and not have yer daughter show up at the church tomorrow morning. But, Mammy, I've some home truths to tell ye. Ye might be a marvel at the sewing machine, but y*e're* the tight-fisted cunt! I love ye dearly, ye know I do, but ye've severe mental problems if ye think ye're some pleasant, kind person anybody with a brain cell in their head would wanny spend time together with. Ye treats us, and me daddy and all, like yer slaves, like yer slaves what ye kyanny stand the sight of. Except maybe wer Lorcan. Ye know what ye are? Ye're a sad aul, useless piece of shite what's gonny die a lonely aul death on yer deathbed, as more people will be lined up down the pub, desperate to celebrate yer passing and ringing bells of joy and I don't know what instead of sobbing at yer side as the life seeps outta ye. Go on ahead, clatter me about the head all ye want the next time ye see me. I've made a new life for meself, and thank bloody Christ for that! If it weren't for Rory dragging me away from the family, and the poor soul had to drag me away, I'da never seen the light of day, so I wouldn't. I know ye've been seeing them doctors at Altnegalvin, I know ye've got some sorta illness, and I feel for ye, I really do, but the only sign of a medical problem I can detect be's ye're flimmin *sick in the head!* Ye're mental, so ye are, and...Mammy? Mammy?"

Dymphna hadn't heard a peep from her mother as she had started her rant into the little slot of her phone. The line had gone dead. She turned off her phone. When had her mother hung up? How much had she heard? Fear crept into her as her bridesmaids surrounded her (the construction worker had friended Maire on Facebook and left) and covered her with tuts and pats and wee kisses here and there. They poured more cider down her throat. And as Dymphna drank down, she realized they had been right. She was regretting it. And she was still drunk! It would be worse in the morning, her wedding day. She would face it with a hangover. And with dread.

"Happy" played again. Dymphna guzzled down.

CHAPTER 35

The sweater Dymphna had knitted with her little twelve year old fingers was tucked away in a safe corner of Ursula's suitcase, right beside her slippers, and that suitcase was now deep within the belly of the Boeing 757-200 that was taking Ursula and Jed to Northern Ireland. The sweater was misshapen and ghastly, yellow, one arm shorter than the other, and with a green felt elephant with a peanut in its trunk sewed on the front, and its rump and tail on the back. When Dymphna had given it to her that Christmas long ago, Ursula had been mortified wearing it at the dinner table, piling her turkey and mashed potatoes high in the hopes of hiding it behind the food. But she would wear it with pride to the funeral. Let Dymphna's spirit see her in it as she stood at the grave.

Ursula's eyes were sick of tears. She had bawled in the car to the airport, wailed against the window on the flight from Madison to Newark, cried in the loo in the departure lounge, and sniffled into the aisle en route from Newark to

Belfast, until now, finally, half-way across the Atlantic two hundred miles or so south of Iceland, she could cry no more. It was such a tragedy, the death of one so young. And Dymphna was one of the best of Paddy's brood, the understanding looks she had, after the lottery win, flashed Ursula when her mother's back was turned, the hidden touches of affection on her arm, the eyes that said "I'm in prison, she be's the prison guard, and I kyanny be caught consorting with the enemy, but I love ye, Auntie Ursula." Or so Ursula hoped. It was difficult at times to read eyes.

Ursula had picked listlessly at what was supposed to be a slice of chicken and whatever the side dish was meant to be, didn't unwrap the round thing that was the dessert, and didn't even wait for the meal to be cleared or to put her tray up before she slipped on her eye mask and forced herself into a slight, unsatisfying sleep. She kept thinking she was being woken up, feeling Jed standing over her, tugging things out of the overhead bin, and, later, feeling him hunched over his tray at her side, hearing him clacking away on his laptop like a maniac for what seemed like hours, heard the scrunching and squelching noises as he moved in his seat. And then the plane was descending and she pulled off her eye mask and struggled to focus and find the two parts of her seat belt and where her shoes were under the seat before her and Jed asked her how she was feeling. How was she feeling?

Home. The land of a thousand welcomes. And not a single one in sight, nor the hope of one to come. Not for her and Jed.

They touched down at Belfast International Airport and caught the bus to Derry. It took an hour and a half, cost £20 and had free wi-fi that wasn't working and an overflowing toilet that was unsuitable for use. Ursula had wanted to watch the countryside she loved unfurl before her eyes as they rode, the forty shades of green, the flocks of sheep and herds of cows, the occasional crumbling thatched cottage, the roadside branches of the Top Yer Trolly, but the windows were so thick with mud and grime she couldn't tell if it were night or day (it was late morning). A relentless throbbing bass punctuated with the startling squeals of a black woman, Ursula supposed it was the music of the day, pounded out of the speakers and made speaking to Jed at her side quite impossible. So she let him sleep. She stared ahead at the video screen, but the driver had chosen one of the *Fast and Furious* movies, and with each car crash that unfolded on the screen, she held Jed's arm tighter and tried to avert her eyes. But there was nothing else to look at, except the soiled jeans of the passed out drunk in the seat across the aisle.

They were traveling on a budget, they had dined at the airport on a budget, and now they were approaching Golden Rooms, Derry's least exclusive hotel. Thank God for the $150,000 in their future.

The glass of the front windows was cracked, and they were accosted for spare change by a man with three teeth who was standing guard. They rolled their suitcases inside with trepidation. But even in this godforsaken dump there was still, thanks to the young man behind the counter, the smile (with a full set of teeth!) and the sparkling eyes, the charm of the lilt of the voice, and in the tattered poster of Riverdance on the wall behind the desk the promise of Celtic delight. Next to Riverdance was a poster of Giant's Causeway, and one for something called the Amelia Earhart's Exploreworld Interactive Centre, apparently Derry's Hottest New Tourist Attraction!

Ursula supposed this was a welcome home of sorts, though from a stranger, and one predicated on the promise of money soon changing hands. Ursula was all too used to welcomes like that, and the money always seemed to go in the same direction, out of her handbag.

"Welcome to Golden Rooms!"

"Hi," Jed said.

"Och, hello, love," Ursula said, not knowing whether to exaggerate her accent or hide it. She was mortified, *mortified,* at having to spend a night in a hotel in her hometown. She and Jed had had to stay at a hotel the last time they visited, and how her family had hooted with laughter. A few years ago, she would have been laughing along with them at the thought of a Flood having to pay to spend a night in Derry. Hotels and the need for them was something the Floods had been brought up not comprehending. What sad old gits, what Betty and Billy No Mates, would have nobody, *nobody,* whose hospitality couldn't be taken advantage of? How things had changed. Now Ursula understood. But if she let the nice young man behind the desk know with her voice she was from Derry, perhaps they'd get a better rate...?

"Have youse a reservation?" he asked, "or will youse be renting by the hour...?"

Ursula's face fell. She pulled her sweater tighter around her. She tried to hide her accent. Unsuccessfully.

"If ye check yer reservations, ye'll see we've booked for three nights. Barnett. Jed." The three nights they would sleep, though how they would fill the days Ursula hadn't a clue. The wake was probably that evening, but they didn't know where it might be. Maybe at Paddy's house, maybe at a pub, or even over on the Waterside. With the Protestant fiancé, that Riddell boy Ursula had heard about, Dymphna's life had probably changed so much she didn't know where the wake might be. She didn't know anything about her family's lives now, about any of them. But perhaps this funeral was a chance to make amends, hopefully patch up some bridges and find out what had been going on.

"I'm wile sorry I have to ask, but we need payment upfront. Youse look wile respectable, so youse do. But I'm sure youse can appreciate that with some of wer clientele, it's the sensible thing to do."

232

He waved to the lobby as if that would make them understand what the clientele usually was. At the sight of the lobby—Ursula feared she detected a condom under the magazine rack—they did.

"Yeah, that's fine." But Jed's voice sounded strange.

"Och, aye surely, we understand."

What Ursula couldn't understand was Jed's problem at the moment. Ever since they had gotten off the plane, in fact. Perhaps it had been the music on the bus, or the thought of being forced to see her estranged family again. He seemed on edge, gritting his teeth and clutching the edge of the counter as if he expected the Earth would soon be knocked off its axis. He was staring at the credit card she clutched as if she were passing the receptionist a handful of human teeth. He had a look on his face, a look of horror tinged with hope. It was an odd look, but then as the receptionist took her card Ursula realized it was one she had seen. Many times before, in fact. As he hovered over the roulette wheel at Slots-O-Fun in Las Vegas that one night, and at the dollar slots at Boulder Casino two years later, at the Ascot horse races they had attended one year (Ursula in a hat, Jed in a tuxedo), at the craps table at the casino on the Indian reservation, and late at night sometimes when Jed was hunched over the computer on one of the illegal poker sites. It was the simultaneous fear and excitement of a high stakes gamble.

"What's up with ye, Jed?"

"I think...I think..." Then he shut his mouth, but that strange hope was simmering through the horror in his eyes.

"I'm sorry," broke in the receptionist. "Have ye another card on ye there?"

"What are ye on about? Ye mean...?"

"Aye, it's been declined." He said it in a manner as if it happened all too often at the hotel, like the stealing of the towels and the raiding of the mini-bar, and recently, the covert raiding of the mini-bar, where customers carefully unscrewed the tops of the vodka bottles, emptied them down their gullets, filled them with water, and placed them back on the shelves, then closed out their credit cards before they could be charged, but Ursula snorted with laughter. It might happen to their usual sleazy customers, but she and Jed weren't in their sphere. She had the confidence of the upper middle-classes, of a former lottery winner, of a successful applicant on *Attack of the Killer Investors!* Of course they had disposable income. Perhaps not much, but some.

"I think maybe ye slid it in that wee machine the wrong way. Go on a give it another try. Maybe harder, this time. There's no way it's not gonny work."

The receptionist did as instructed; he had nothing else to do, after all. He shook his head with an air of sadness as he handed it back. Ursula, perplexed, scrabbled in her purse and handed him her debit card. She had at least two thousand dollars in her account, one thousand her bingo win of the other day.

233

"Try this one, would ye, love?"

She clacked her fingernails on the counter as unease filled her. Jed was making a show of inspecting brochures for pottery classes. He wouldn't meet her eye, no matter how she tried to configure her head so that their eyes should meet. She beamed at the receptionist as he looked up. Her face fell.

"I'm wile sorry, ma'am, but it says ye've insufficient funds."

"What?!"

His hand was out for another card, but Ursula had none to give him.

"I...we...we'll be right back," she stammered, face scorched with embarrassment.

She grabbed her suitcase and Jed and trundled them both through the lobby. And now the drunk outside seemed to be smirking at them as they walked out the front door. Ursula fought the urge to slap the smirk off his face, his outstretched hand away from her bosom. She trailed Jed to the sidewalk and faced him beside the mail box. She was trembling with confusion and a simmering rage.

"Jed!" she barked. "What's going on? What were ye up to in that plane ride over? Ye know, I had a strange feeling the things in me purse was somehow slightly off, in an odd place. Where's all wer money? Tell me now! *Look* at me now! *Where's all wer money gone?!"*

He forced his eyes to look into hers. There was shame and fear in those eyes.

"I think I did something terrible, honey."

Ursula felt dread seep into her heart. She brought a hand up to her mouth.

"What is it? Ye've got me heart-feared now, Jed."

"It's gonna be alright, dear. All we gotta do is phone Slim. He'll give us some money to tide us over. Until we get back home."

"What did ye do?! Where does all wer money be?!"

Her voice rang out in the empty street.

"There...there was Internet on the plane. I saw a sticker on the back of the seat before me. I didn't know they had Internet on planes now. And, well, you were asleep, and I didn't like any of the movies they were showing, and I'd seen all the episodes of *Law and Order* they had—"

"Tell me now what ye did or I'm gonny clatter ye, Jed! We're standing penniless, without a pence to wer name, here in the middle of nowhere in Derry! And I wanny know *why! How!"*

"I—I knew we were in international air, so I knew there were no restrictions on online gambling—"

"Och, for the love of God!" A sharp pain attacked her breastplate. She heaved huge breaths.

"I was winning and winning on this one slot machine. Something about ancient Egypt. And I kept playing and playing and winning and winning. I was up to $5000! And then I started to lose. And I lost and lost. And then I put more money from my card onto the site. And then a message popped up that my card had no more money. I had to win the money back! I had to get back up to $5000 again! Your purse was at my feet. Remember you put it there so you could stretch your feet out more? So I found your credit card and then—"

"Ye daft eejit! Och, don't waste yer foolish, goofy breath to tell me any more! Sure, I can write the sad, desperate script meself! I know exactly what happened. I'm raging, Jed! Absolutely *raging! What are we meant to do? Where are we meant to stay? What are we meant to eat?!"*

Tears of rage and anger cascaded down her face. She smacked away Jed's comforting hands. The hands that had flown over the keys of the laptop and put them where they were now. Mortified, terrified, hungry.

Jed adjusted his glasses. "Slim—"

"When does yer pension get paid into your account?"

"Not for two weeks."

She would've smacked him with her handbag, but she was too worn out, too grieved, too weak with hunger and, frankly, feeling too old at that moment to summon the violence. She dried her tears as she thought. This was their reality, and she needed to think, not cry. She fondled her crucifix while she thought.

Ursula had brought along three pound coins she still had left over from their last visit to Derry, and this was now all the funds they had.

"We kyanny stand here in the street and argue no more. What's done is done. There be's ways today to get money transferred immediately to wer cards. Let's see who we can get to do it. Let's sit on that...does it be a bench?"

She motioned to a bus stop up the street, with those tiny slivers of plastic that folded up and were meant to be folded down and perched on with half your bottom. Actual sitting was impossible. They rolled their suitcases to the bus stop and perched.

First they used their cellphones and tried to call their children (yes, they had three, Egbert, Vaughn and Gretchen) but all they got was voice mail; it was the middle of the night in the states where the kids lived (Texas, Colorado and Washington), then they tried to call Slim, but he was still in the hospital, then they tried Louella at home, but there was no answer there. And then the batteries of their phones died in tandem. And then they searched for payphones, trailing their suitcases behind them, but of the three they were surprised and grateful to find, one had no receiver, one was out of order, and one accepted only phone cards, but they didn't know where to buy a card, and all the shops seemed closed, except for one Sav-U-Mor that was lowering its metal shutters. Ursula rushed in, but then realized she didn't have the money to buy a phone card in any event. She bought a Crunchie chocolate bar with one of her three pound coins, cracked it in half, and they each ate their share there in the doorway of the shop. Two pounds left.

Then it began to rain, and one of the wheels of Jed's suitcase fell off. They went to Francine's to ask if they could stay there—Ursula couldn't bring herself to ask for money—but Francine had her sister, her brother-in-law, their three children, and the wane of her oldest daughter and the wane's father and the wane's father's sister staying with her for the weekend. It was one of the lot's birthday, Ursula couldn't quite make out whose. There was no place to fit them. Then they had gone to Molly's, but Molly was on holiday, two weeks in Ibiza with a complimentary hour at the hotel spa thrown in, so they were told by her neighbor, she had left two days ago, and the night before squatters had broken into Molly's semi-detached house and set up camp, nine or ten of them it seemed, with black clothes and studs and piercings and unwashed hair and music that blared until all hours, this from the neighbor as well. They went to Mrs. McDonald, who had been under Ursula's care when Ursula was an Osteocare provider, and who had told Ursula she had been so kind and if there was anything she could do for her in the future don't hesitate to ask, and Ursula had thanked her, but secretly laughed at the time, as how could Mrs. McDonald ever be of help to her, a lovely woman, but she could barely move, but when Mrs. McDonald opened the door, it was clear she was suffering from dementia, so she couldn't even remember Ursula, though Ursula tried to jog her memory for half an hour, singing songs the woman had enjoyed back when she was her carer, "All Kinds Of Everything" was one, and retelling her some jokes they had laughed at while watching an episode of *Mr. Bean* all those years ago, "Ye mind when yer man was in the loo and had to dry himself?" But Mrs. McDonald wouldn't let them in. Ursula was now a stranger.

And finally they trudged through the rain, past hooded teens who smirked at them on street corners and clutched bottles of beer in their hands, and landed on the doorstep of the rectory of St. Moluag's, where Ursula had sung in the choir until she had been asked to leave, and she hoped to find home Father Hogan who, after the lottery win, Ursula had handed several checks for the collection plate. Several very large checks.

Ursula heaved up the big brass knocker and pounded on the massive oak door. Again and again, desperate attacks on the wood. The door creaked open. Father Hogan appeared before them. He gasped and took a step back in alarm. Ursula's mascara was running from the tears and the rain, her purple bob a mess, Jed's cowboy hat sagging, sopping, on his head, their suitcases heavy, their hearts heavier, hunger and despair etched on their faces.

"Ursula!"

"Hello, Father. And this is me husband, Jed. I think ye met him?"

"Of course. Jed." Whether he remember meeting Jed or not, he smiled kindly at him. Jed did his best to smile back. "Whatever brings you here? I thought you were in the States?"

"Aye, I am. We're here now in Derry, but, for a funeral. Three nights, we're here for."

"Och, a terrible shame. The funeral, I mean, not yer stay."

"Are ye not doing the funeral tomorrow? Dymphna Flood?"

"Dymphna? But..naw, she must belong to another church now. I haven't seen her in donkey's."

"Anyroad, Father, that doesn't be why we're here. Why we're here be's..."

Ursula faltered. She couldn't remember if gambling was a sin. There was, of course, church bingo, but maybe that was a special type of gambling the Lord allowed. She still thought gambling might be a sin, so she blurted out: "We was attacked by yobs the moment we stepped off the bus from Belfast! A drunken pack of hooligan teens, yelling abuse at us, so they were, as they threatened us with screwdrivers what looked like they'd been sharpened and demanded we empty wer pockets. Everything, they took! Down the pub pouring wer money down their hateful bakes I'm sure they are at the moment."

Father Hogan looked down with some surprise at the handbag that swayed from Ursula's elbow.

"They tossed me handbag back to me after they took everything out. Only me tissues and lipsticks be's left inside, like. And a Tic Tac or two. Penniless, we are, Father! Och, I know it be's like a scene from the nativity, but is there any way we can spend the night with ye? Plus the next two nights, actually?"

He looked as if Ursula had asked him to go pole dancing with her.

"But...I...I..." He placed a comforting hand on her shoulder. "Ursula, dear, the Lord helps those who help themselves."

Ursula felt a pang of anger. "And ye know what, Father? I've never understood that. If that does indeed be true, why the bloody hell does the Lord expect us to fill the collection plate every Sunday? Ye weren't backwards about snatching outta me hand all the money I could throw at once we won the lottery. And then ye went and got me kicked outta the choir."

"You know I had no hand in that, Ursula. I was powerless. And, if you recall, I did go visit you in prison. Remember when you were banged up for running over that wee boy?"

"Allegedly! Me point is, anyroad, how can the Lord help them what helps themselves if the Church kyanny even help itself and relies on the congregation for handouts? Explain that to me, would ye?"

He sighed. "I'd let you stay in the guestroom here, Ursula, really I would, but I'm in the middle of renovations. A gale knocked over the old tree in the yard, you remember the one next to the O'Leary mausoleum over there? And it crashed into the roof. There's nothing up there but tools and wooden planks and sheets of plastic and so on."

"Can't you just let us sleep on the sofa?" Jed asked.

Father Hogan seemed to consider this. Then he snapped his fingers.

"I've an idea. Let me make a call. Come in a wee moment."

While they were waiting the hallway and the priest was in some inner room on the phone, Ursula tiptoed up the stairs. She came back down, shaking her head. "They really are doing renovations up there," she told Jed.

Father Hogan bustled back into the room, beaming and clapping his hands with joy. Ursula's heart swelled with relief.

"I've found beds for you both," he said.

"Marvelous! Ta so much!"

"Oh, wow! Thanks a lot! You're great!"

Ursula threw her arms around the priest, and Jed pumped his hand so that they both winced.

"At the Mountains of Mourne Homeless Shelter. I believe it opened up after you left. It's down the town opposite the Top Yer Trolly. Don't look so horrified. It's new, all mod cons, and it surely can't be that filthy? They've only been open a month now! Calm down. There are special delousing cubicles you can make use of, and there is a safe they can lock your suitcases up in. I do recommend you remove those earrings, though. And you, sir, that watch. You know, you might think about pawning them. Perhaps that would help your, shall we call them, money woes?" He looked at his own watch. "You'd do best to be on your way there now. I guess you'll have to walk as you have no funds, so it will take about half an hour. And there is a curfew, so you must make it there by 10 PM. And that's in half an hour."

"Could ye at least give us a wee something to eat before we set off? Ravenous, so we are."

"There is a kitchen at the shelter. And the clock is ticking."

He ushered them out. Ursula's family had turned its back on her, and now her church was.

As they hightailed it through the sopping streets to make the deadline, Jed said, "I'm so sorry, honey."

"I don't wanny hear it!" Ursula roared out at Jed, "Ye've made me lie to Father Hogan! And I was looking forward to having him hear me confession while I was here! Now, but, I kyanny sit there in that confessional and reveal to him I lied...*to him!*"

"What do you think, Ursula?"

"I think... I think I'll be moving me custom to that new church up on Culmore Road."

It was 9:55 by the time they reached the shelter. It did look new. But the people did not. Ursula could smell the building before they entered it. Some of their future roommates were drinking outside, palms outstretched. A vagrant here, a tramp there, hobos everywhere. Jed shook his head at them, "Sorry." Ursula never wanted to hear him utter that word again. Junkies and alkies greeted from from all sides. And as they skulked towards reception, Ursula had a sudden and startling thought, a thought that filled her with dread. This, she thought, is what it feels like to be Randaleen Jagger.

CHAPTER 36

As the sun rose on Derry that Sunday in March, piercing through the mist, dancing off the branches of the still-skeletal trees, serenaded by the chirp of bullfinches stirring in their nests, the top of the Guildhall glinting, the shutters of the Kebabalicious dappled with light, there was no whistling from a cheery post man as he pushed letters and cards from distant loved ones through the letter boxes; this was because it was Sunday, and also, it was 2014, and he usually just passed out junk mail and bills.

In the three bedrooms of the Flood home, one for Paddy and Fionnuala, one for Lorcan, and one for Dymphna, Padraig, Siofra and Seamus; at Bridie McFee's; at Mrs. Muholland's; in the homeless shelter where Jed and Ursula were imprisoned on shaky cots; and across the churning sparkle of the River Foyle, in the Riddell house of glass and chrome, nobody was stirring, pulling across the curtains and smiling out the windows, opening them, and breathing in the brisk air of the dawning of another Irish early spring day as the sunlight light up the world, making the calcite crystals in the dull gray pavements sparkle, drying the dew that clung to blades of grass and petals of dandelions and the damp that had collected in the pot holes and cracks in the pavement from the rain of the night before, nobody was stretching yet, eager to see the new and exciting day. Of course not, as it was only 6:37 AM, and most had been chucking the drink down their throats for one excuse or another and were in catatonic states in their beds, sleeping off the drink in dull, dreamless slumbers.

There were the flagons of cider and cans of beer for Dymphna and her bridesmaids in the confines of the chip van; the generic whiskey for Fionnuala, Maureen and even Paddy himself as they sat before the blank telly screen, bits of wreath and pieces of the card sitting accusingly on the coffee table like police exhibits, as the three sniped, barked and yelled at each other, unable to decide if the wreath from Ursula were a mistake or a joke in very poor taste; upstairs, Lorcan's fat tins of lager his mother kept creeping up to supply him with and parting his lips to pour into his mouth; he was feeling better, but she was ensuring that, though his illness, confoundedly, was disappearing, she would replace it with a hangover that may as well be an illness; Hendricks and tonics glugged down by Zoë, the half-bottle and cucumber slices on the table before her in her living room of clean straight lines, Adele, then Sade, then Adele again crooning out of the Bang & Olufsen speakers around her, humming along as she waited for Rory to stagger home from his stag do and she contemplated the change that was coming to her well-ordered life, maybe a nightmare she would never wake up from, as divorce might be tolerated by a Protestant, but she could never see the bride's mother with her strident Catholicism agreeing to it; the countless flaming Sambucas and Car Bombs and bottle after bottle of Stella Artois for Rory and his soccer mates, arranged by best man Georgie, and poured by the staff at the posh upmarket bar in the Waterside that would be witness to the evening's ever more disturbing pranks as the drunkenness increased, the male stripper Georgie had arranged, the blue-painted dwarf, a 'Smurf,' he had rented and handcuffed to Rory to the howls of laughter all around, the fake tan that would be sprayed on half of Rory's face the moment he passed out, the eggs, flour and cream they would spread on his naked body and the sparkly thong they would slip him into before they tied him (and the Smurf) up to the lamp post on the Craigavon Bridge as the evening's crowning glory; the green apple and kiwi flavored alchopops for Bridie, several of them, as she sat in the living room, hoping for another sighting of the Virgin Mary and staring with unseeing eyes at a rerun of *Dancing With The Stars,* and a 'medicinal' scotch for her mother, babbling into the phone with her aunt, and, on the other end of the line, a glass of sweet sherry from a beveled crystal glass for Bernadette Mulholland as she sat next to the phone stand in the hallway on a chair she had pulled in from the sitting room, arranging the troops for the next day, scribbling away with a pencil into a little notebook the computations and chants and time tables and lists for the demonstration at the wedding she dearly hoped would turn into a riot; and for Jed and Ursula, a bottle of something with a label in a language without regular English letters, offered to them by the man in the next cot, a liquid they all weren't quite sure which family of liquor it belonged to and was brown and acid-like but made them feel happy, well, not happy, but happier than expected, and they guzzled down although the Barnetts had been warned at reception that the drinking of beer and spirits, and the taking of recreational drugs as well, was expressly forbidden in the shelter, and soon all three were singing Irish songs, but quietly, as they didn't want to be tossed out of the shelter for intoxication and God knew they had nowhere else to go; water for Padraig, Siofra, and Seamus; orange soda for Keanu and Beeyonsay, their little lips slurping at the teats of the bottles Dymphna had shoved in their mouths at the beginning of the impromptu bachelorette party; and hot Horlicks with a

HobNob and a nighttime sleep aid for Mrs. Dinh, as she had sworn off drink since her husband had died of cirrhosis of the liver.

It was half an hour later, 7:07 AM, that Jed and Ursula rose, and by then the sun had hidden behind sinister gray clouds which pressed down as if keeping them captive in that town. The Barnetts were the first to rise, as they had been told, again by reception, that the center would start serving breakfast at 7:30 AM, it was first come, first served, and once the food was gone it was gone; that if they left it too late, it would be like the Berlin airlift and they'd have to be prepared to put their elbows and feet to good use; it would also be in their best interests to get to the community showers before any of the others rose; soap was limited.

Still groggy, cricks in their necks and other body parts, Ursula and Jed made their way silently through the rows of spartan cots and the lumpen, snoring, drooling masses atop them. They tiptoed down a stark hallway that stank of antiseptic and homelessness and followed the signs to Dining.

Ursula tried to smile at the woman in a hairnet who dumped a pile of what Ursula supposed was porridge into a bowl and handed it over to her.

"Ta," Ursula said.

"Thanks," said Jed. "Have you got any toast?"

The woman nodded to a table on which there was a loaf of sliced bread and a sad slab of butter. Knives, they had been told, were also forbidden. If they wanted to butter their bread (there would be no toast), they'd have to be creative with their spoons.

"And if there's any teabags left, youse'll find em next to the kettle over there."

"Coffee?" Jed asked, hope springing eternal.

The woman snorted. She peered over the shelf that divided them as if seeing them for the first time.

"Are youse Yanks?" she asked. "Aye, youse are. I can tell. It's the clothes. What are youse doing here? Aren't all Yanks minted?"

"I...I gamb—"

Ursula nudged Jed to silence, and they trudged without a skip in their steps towards the slice of bread and the vague promise of a teabag that awaited them. The porridge sloshed in their bowls.

"While I appreciate ye wanting to own up about yer foolishness, I don't want ye spreading it all over Derry, like." Ursula said, as they sat at the long wooden table and some back part of her brain wondered, if the building were so new, why they had outfitted it with Dickensian furniture. She dipped the teabag into her cup. "Ye've no idea who that woman knows, who she'll run off to spread the news about us, and before ye know it, I'll have Francine calling me to tell me she heard all about it. Or Molly from Ibiza."

"They can't call us," Jed reminded her. "Our batteries have died. And I forgot my charger."

"Aye, I forgot mine and all. I figured I could just buy one when we got here. More fool me, thinking I'd have money to buy things with. Och, Jed! What are we gonny do?"

She dipped the teabag into his cup and eyed the door in alarm.

"The others are starting to rise. We'd better shovel this down wer bakes and head for them showers before themmuns finishes eating." She shuddered at the thought of a group shower, though, thankfully, there seemed to be very few female patrons, and she assumed the showers weren't unisex. She hoped. "And then we've to suss out where the funeral is. If need be, we'll have to traipse to the Moorside and knock on Paddy's door, and just hope Fionnuala doesn't open it. We really must hurry, Jed. Doesn't funerals normally be held in the morning, like?"

"Yeah," Jed said. He slipped the spoon between his lips, chewed for a moment, struggled to swallow, then dropped the spoon into the bowl. "I'm gonna take my shower now. Quick. Before the soap runs out."

"Ye kyanny leave me here on me own!" But then Ursula took a bite and understood. She wiped her lips and stood up. The room swam. It was that mystery liquor from the night before, still in her veins. "Aye, off we go, then, so's we get a clean towel. First in the queue, and all that."

"And then we'll find out where they're laying Dymphna to rest." Jed sighed as he got up. "Oh, honey, I'm so sorr—"

"Don't say that to me again. Ever," Ursula warned. They approached the showers and what horrors might await them. All mod cons, Father Hogan had said, but who knew. She turned to Jed and hissed, "Ye're lucky I'm not flinging divorce papers under yer nose. I know why ye did it, but. It be's the thought of making wer lives better with piles of dosh. Jed, look what money did to us before, but. All I need to say be's the word 'lottery.'"

Jed walked behind her, his head hidden under his cowboy hat.

An hour and a half later, 8:37 AM, Fionnuala dragged herself out of bed while Paddy snored into his pillow. She crept into the kitchen to make Lorcan his breakfast. porridge with raisins again, with a generous portion of cinnamon and furniture polish. She turned on the oven to 450°, reached into the spud bag, chose a big one, and shoved the potato in the oven. She would bring it along in her handbag and find a way to slip it onto his plate that evening. She knew jacket potatoes were on the menu at the reception, and she didn't want him eating an untainted meal. The polish didn't seem to affect him the way the hairspray had. When she had taken the wanes to the church to light a candle for him the evening before, she felt horrible kneeling there on the pew before the flickering flame as the wanes either side of her prayed to the Lord for Lorcan to get better and she prayed for him to get worse, to keep him by her side. Had Fionnuala bothered to read the warning on the can, she would have realized the furniture polish was actually less effective than the hairspray for her purpose. May Cause Mild Abdominal Discomfort was all it said.

As she carried the bowl of porridge upstairs, and the cans of beer, she wondered if she should experiment, try something else in his food. She'd see how this meal made him feel first.

She knocked on the door.

"Aye, Mam?"

He sounded like health incarnate. She scowled, then plastered a smile on her face as she opened the door.

"Yer breakfast, dote," she said. He looked a bit hungover, his hair in need of a wash, but other than that, he seemed fine to her. Too fine.

"Ta, Mam. There's no need, but. Really. I feel fine."

Just what Fionnuala had been fearing. She sat beside him, felt his forehead, plumped his pillow and placed it behind his head.

"Do ye feel up to going to the wedding, dear? I'll understand if ye have to back out."

"With that cake, I wouldn't miss it for the world!" He sniggered with laughter.

Fionnuala touched him on the arm.

"That's one of the things what I love about ye, son. So selfless. Putting the pleasure of yer sister, no matter how undeserving she may be, before yer own health. Are ye sure ye're well enough to put the spoon up to yer mouth yerself?"

"No need, Mam. I can do it meself."

She rubbed his arm again, then stood up.

"And I've ironed yer suit for ye and all. And added a wee flower from the garden and pinned it on the front, like. And as ye see, I've brought some beers up for ye and all. I won't be long in throwing the drink down me own throat, if truth be told. It's gonny be a long day."

"Och, I love ye, Mam. Ta, like," She stood there clutching the door handle, wondering if she should rush over and smack that spoon out of his hand. But she just smiled and closed the door, then went downstairs and into the kitchen.

She shook the furniture polish, wondered why it wasn't giving her the desired results, and had her mind made up for her when she sprayed it and only a little bit fizzled out of the nozzle. It, too, was empty, though how that was possible Fionnuala didn't understand as she had rarely used it all the time it had sat in the house. She scrabbled under the sink again, in the metal bucket that had decades ago held coal but now held rarely-used cleaning products. Her fingers clutched a can and tugged it out. Heavy Duty Yeuch-B-Gone. The oven cleaner Dymphna had raved about and brought over from Zoë's. Fionnuala had yet to put it to use on the oven. But she had a use for it now. She was tired of reading the cleaning products' nonsensical ingredients, and didn't even bother to read these, or the warnings. But if she had, she would have seen the warnings were screaming out at her from the side of the can, the rows of skulls and crossbones telling her how fatal to the human body its ingredients were, demanding she desist with this madness, not introduce the virulent toxins and noxious acids into the innards of her son, a son she claimed to love.

She opened the oven and prodded the jacket potato with a fork. Still raw. She didn't know how much longer the others would be sleeping; surely they were excited about the wedding, and would be up soon, regardless of their hangovers, those that might have them. She removed the potato with one oven mitt and a dirty dishrag, placed it on the counter, sliced open the potato, shook the can and spayed. She closed up the jacket, and popped it back into the oven for another twenty minutes.

Mrs. Dinh, Mrs. Feeney, Mrs. Gee, Mrs. Ming all arrived at Mrs. Mulholland's. They rolled their tartan shopping carts before and behind them though the hallway and into the kitchen, which was now the operating center of the day's attack. The carts bulged with the ammunition.

Mrs. Leech, Mrs. O'Bryan and Mrs. Stokes were already there, putting the finishing touches on the bedspread banners and affixing the placards on the poles taken from mops and brooms others had brought over, and those others, drinking tea and nibbling biscuits, rosaries clanking, crucifixes swinging, milled around Bridie, who sat next to the washing machine and was trying to channel the Blessed Virgin again. These others seemed to be wearing larger crosses than usual; perhaps they thought the Virgin Mary's eyesight wasn't too good, and wanted to be sure She saw their piety.

"Can ye see Her, Bridie?"

"Can ye hear Her, love?"

"What's She saying to ye?"

But, no, Bridie couldn't see the Virgin Mary, and God knows she had been searching for her everywhere. In the dark clouds on the way over, in the grass of her aunt's front garden, in the pattern of the cheese melted on the unwashed plate in the sink. She hadn't seen Her since the wallpaper incident. Where She had told her the pairing of Dymphna Flood and Rory Riddell, of a Catholic and a Protestant, of an Orange slapper and a Green bastard, was blasphemous, heretical, unchristian, ungodly, *a sin!*

"Bridie...Bridie...!" Bridie was certain she had heard the Virgin Mary say

on that occasion, *"Ye kyanny let this wedding take place! It's an affront to the heavenly Father! I want ye to gather together some troops, some onward Christian soldiers, for to show up at the church the day after tomorrow...and shame them sinners into ceasing and desisting this madness, this affront to the Father, the Son and the Holy Ghost, and Me and all."*

Without pondering why the Blessed Virgin would use a Derry accent to speak to her, nor the remarkable serendipity that Her first instructions, what she demanded Bridie do, were exactly what would make Bridie's world better, allowing Rory Riddell, her one true love, to be a free man so Bridie could pursue him herself, Bridie had burst into her auntie Bernadette's sitting room and told the gathered masses her new instructions. No, She still hadn't given her any signs, Bridie had answered in response to their excited questions, but maybe that would come later on, and if they joined in, if they joined the battle against sin and depravity that was the Riddell-Flood wedding, perhaps Mary would soon appear to one of them also, if not all of them. But, Bridie had hastened to add, this was simply her opinion; the Blessed Virgin hadn't explicitly laid this out.

Now Bridie shrieked and her body jerked atop the chair as if it were one of those electrical ones in Florida. Her arm knocked the washing powder to the floor, and it splattered on the linoleum at her feet like the skirt of a Christmas tree. The women gasped and huddled around, their eyes shining with as much excitement as much as their age would allow.

"Aye," Bridie croaked breathlessly, eyes darting around everywhere to let them know Her presence in the kitchen was everywhere, "I hear her now! She spoke to me just then!"

She did no such thing, Mrs. Mulholland thought; Her niece was no Joan of Arc, she wasn't even Joan Crawford; Mrs. Mulholland now understood well why Bridie had never played anything but a bush in the school's dramatic productions. But the woman gathered around with the others, who were covering Bridie with coos and gnashing their dentures with excitement and almost tearing at her clothes at one point, and Mrs. Mulholland feared they were being revved up into a wave of hysteria. Who was she kidding? She didn't fear that at all. It was what she had been hoping for. Giving that Protestant bitch the shock of her life she deserved.

Three years before, Mrs. Mulholland had applied for a job at Dreams and Wishes, the card store down on Rossville Street, to supplement her meager pension, and the owner herself, Zoë Riddell, had interviewed her. But Mrs. Riddell had turned her down, saying she 'wasn't right' for the position. Mrs. Muholland didn't know if that meant she was too old or too Catholic, and had wandered home in a right state, the bills that needed to be paid pressing down.

Three miserable months dragged by, and they were the winter ones, so she shivered in the cold and damp, caught pneumonia and almost succumbed to a lung infection. But then, summoning the courage to face rejection again, she had applied for a job at as a bagger at the Top Yer Trolly and been immediately hired. So she realized there was nothing wrong with *her.* Zoë, the Orange bitch, was the problem. This revenge would be sweet. So sweet. Mrs. Mulholland felt her lungs thanking her for avenging them.

"What did she say?!" Mrs. Gee asked.

"Tell us, Bridie, tell us!"

"Aye! Tell us!"

"She said..."

You could hear the water drop from the tap.

"She said, off youse go now! For to save Derry! For to save Northern Ireland! Save the country from the clutches of depravity and sin! Off youse go! To St. Fintan's! Onward Christian soldiers! I'll be there with youse and all, leading the way! Look up for me in the sky!"

They roared there in the kitchen under the patches of damp and rattled their rosaries and fiddled with their crosses. Mrs. Mulholland rolled her eyes. They grabbed the poles with the signs attached and tried to wave them in the air, but one of them knocked the kitchen light and sent it flying, fringes sailing through the air, and she had to yell at them to stop.

"Ladies! Ladies! There's time enough for all that to come! Only another half hour, and youse can muster up all the aggro ye can on the streets of Derry so all's the world can see youse! And the Blessed Virgin and all!"

They put down the signs, Bridie asked one of her congregation to sweep up the detergent for her, three fought to reach for the dustpan in the corner, two for the brush, and a smile danced on Mrs. Mulholland's lips.

Dymphna gripped the railing for support. Her head under the sleek white veil was still swimming from the night before, and her eyes were trying to find her mother's somewhere down on the hallway and see what she could read in them. She had no reason to fear, as Fionnuala had hung up on her the moment she had slurred, "Right! Home truths!"

She took a step, then another step, then another down the stairs. The flowers of the bouquet seemed like they were shooting out rays of sunshine. Necks craned upwards in the front hall, Fionnuala clicked away with the disposable camera, enchanted by the pearls and diamonds jangling, the bows and hearts and crosses sparkling, the beauty of her creation as it sailed down the primroses of the carpeted stairs, Seamus and Siofra clapped, Paddy's eyes filled with tears, Lorcan and Padraig smirked at each other, Maureen rolled her eyes and they all jumped as the letterbox behind them clanked. And clanked again.

And kept on clanking. Fionnuala felt the blood drain from her face. Had the Filth finally caught up to her? But she had to keep up her front.

"Of all the times!" Fionnuala said with a practiced snarl. "Who the bloody feck be's that? Ruining the moment I've waited all me life for!" But if this was the bride or the gown nobody knew.

Lorcan opened the door. It was the caterers, coming for the cake. Fionnuala deflated with relief. Lorcan ushered them into the kitchen. Dymphna took another step down the stairs, and froze at the roars of laughter from the kitchen.

"Mammy! Why does they be laughing?" She must have realized somewhere in her still-pickled mind she had yet to see the cake herself. The horror rose in her eyes as she saw what was being carted out the door, what it took three men to carry. One tower for each of them.

"But...Mammy!" she gasped, the color rising to her cheeks. "It be's...obscene!"

"Mammy!" Siofra wailed. "Why was them men laughing at me princess cake? What does 'scene mean?"

"Out, youse wanes! Outside now!" Fionnuala screamed at Padraig, Siofra and Seamus. They rushed outside after the caterers.

Fionnuala reached up the five stairs left and trailed Dymphna down them.

"Self-centered bitch!" The veil flew as Fionnuala smacked her.

"Mam!" "Dear!" "Fionnuala love!" Lorcan, Paddy and Maureen all called out, taking steps forward. "It's her wedding day, sure!" Paddy yelled.

"The hours yer sister and yer wee brother and yer granny toiled away for yer special day, while ye sat in that chip van and poured the drink down yer gullet! And now—"

"I was *working!*"

"And now ye've the brass necked cheek, the flimmin nerve, to hurl insults at all their hard work. Ye've not a clue how—"

"Mammy! Dymphna!" Padraig squealed with glee.

All heads whipped towards the front door, even Dymphna's. Padraig and 'glee' never went together if the body of a small animal wasn't involved.

"C'mon out now! The car's come! Ye're never gonny believe the size of it!"

Paddy looked at his watch even as he raced to the door.

"God bless us and save us!" Maureen said, cane tapping towards the door. "They're wile early! There's an hour to the wedding, still."

Still pressing a hand to her burning cheek, Dymphna picked up the hem of her gown, the fringes jostling through the air, and followed them all out.

There it stood in their shabby street in all its glory, a sleek and shiny black Rolls Royce Phantom stretch limousine. As Paddy, Lorcan and the boys raced towards it and ran their hands over it, Fionnuala shot her head up and down the length of the street, hoping for the sign of twitching curtains. She was not disappointed. She slowed her pace—she had almost forgotten herself there for a moment!—and contorted herself into the pose of Chapter 12, *How to Walk At Ascot*. The peacock feathers of her hat barely moved as she glided through the broken gate with its peeling paint and broken lock and made her way across the pavement towards luxury. Then she ran back, almost knocking Dymphna to the floor, and snatched her handbag. She shoved past her daughter and made her way back towards the limousine like a Lady.

After Dymphna locked the front door, and as she walked through the jungle of a front garden and made her way towards the opened limousine door, a momentary space cleared in the clouds over towards the northeast, and a ray of sunshine burst through. The heart buckle shone. The itsy-bitsy child beyond it slept soundly.

Fairy lights twinkled on the ceiling, music crooned from hidden speakers, Fionnuala, Paddy, Maureen, Dymphna, Lorcan, Padraig, Siofra and Seamus lounged on the hand-stitched leather seats, marveling more at the bar and the flat screen TV within than the exotic fiber optic mood lighting or the plush navy carpeting. As the driver had come so early, Fionnuala had asked him if he could take them on a tour of the city. He had agreed, and Fionnuala had spent the first ten minutes with the window rolled down, waving at the gawping faces they passed with that stiff-palm wave of the Queen.

"We're living the high life, youse!" Fionnuala said, gulping back champagne.

"Aye, I could get used to this," Paddy said, reaching for the drinks bin and running his hands over the craftsmanship of the Rolls.

"I already have," Fionnuala replied, as if with Zoë in the family, limousines would always be in her future.

She knocked on the window separating them from the front. It rolled down and she asked the driver to turn on the air conditioning. Not because it was warm and stuffy (in fact, a chill had arrived with the clouds early that morning), but because she could.

"This air-conditioning makes me feel dead Yank!" Fionnuala said, and made to nod in the direction of the air-conditioning, but couldn't tell where it was coming from. She smiled all around her instead.

"Poncy, nancy boy drinks," Paddy said with a scowl, looking down at his bubbling flute.

"I'm sure ye'll find, Da," Lorcan said, "Champagne works just as good as lager."

"I agree," Maureen said.

They clinked their glasses.

Padraig, Siofra and Seamus seemed happy enough with the wide selection of juices and sodas and the many channels on the TV, which Padraig was flipping through.

Fionnuala kicked off her clogs and lay back on the seat, the mannerisms of *How To Be A Lady* long forgotten; who needed them when sat in a limousine? The windows were tinted and nobody could see.

"Dear God in heaven above!" Maureen suddenly gasped.

"What's up, Mammy?" Fionnuala asked in alarm.

"The wanes! Where's the wanes?!"

Paddy, Dymphna and Lorcan looked at the backs of the wanes' heads before the telly.

"They're right here."

"Ye need to get the prescription of them glasses checked out."

"Naw! Dymphna's wanes!"

Dymphna gasped. She put down her flute.

"They're in the bedroom. How could I have forgotten?"

"Ye're a daft eejit, that's how," Fionnuala scowled.

"Just tell the driver—" Paddy said.

"Chauffeur," Fionnuala corrected.

"Yer man behind the wheel there. Have him roll down his wee window and tell him to go back."

"Aye," said Padraig. "It gives us more time in the car, so it does. More time to watch real telly!"

Fionnuala did just that. Their driver looked so handsome, and she was excited he was wearing a cap. She winked at him as he rolled down the window. He didn't look back. The limousine turned around and headed back to the Moorside.

"Och, what a marvelous day it's gonny be," Fionnuala was forced to admit to Dymphna.

"And it's only gonny get better, Mammy," Dymphna replied. "Once we get the wanes on board, of course."

"Aye, that I'm sure of," Fionnuala said with a nod. "Unless, Paddy, ye forgot to make the reservation at the church for the day!"

She hooted with laughter at her little joke, and the others had to laugh along.

All except Paddy. He sat beside her, champagne flute clutched in his large hand. Stunned. Dread filled him as the limo passed the Free Derry City wall (another tourist must-see).

One thing, Fionnuala had asked him to do. One. And he hadn't done it. If he searched the catacombs of his brain, maybe he could understand why. There were the long hours at work, the calling of the church time and again three months before, his mate at its office on holiday, and being placed on hold over and over, the sound of music down the line, the one time it had been Bryan

Adams' "Everything I Do," hanging up and making his mind up to do it again soon. But a day turned into a week, and a week turned into a month and now... Now it was unbelievable. His beloved daughter looked like a dream in that gown, eager and nervous and excited about the vows she and her fiancé were about to exchange. But now there was nowhere to exchange them.

The limo pulled up outside their house.

"Stay youse there!" Paddy barked, to the surprise of them all. Perhaps champagne didn't really suit him at all. But, no, he was taking the champagne with him. "I'll collect them flimmin wanes!"

He threw open the door, heart pounding, sweat pricking his brow, and ran towards the house.

CHAPTER 37

Zoë's BMW pulled up to St. Fintan's 45 minutes early. She wanted to ensure everything was on course at the church. She had left Rory scrubbing his face, trying to remove as much of the fake tan as he could, the handsome black suit she had bought from Harvey Nichols laid out on his bed. She had told his head in the sink the limo would pick him and Georgie up at 11:30. The best man had dragged Rory up the stairs at 4:30 AM and passed out beside him.

Zoë grappled the iron handle of the ancient door and pried it open. She peered inside the dusty grandeur. Odd. There was another wedding going on. She closed the door and looked at her very expensive watch. St. Fintan's certainly didn't leave much time between ceremonies! she thought. Perhaps Catholic weddings were a bit speedier than Protestant ones. Maybe there was a quick, high turnover, like budget airlines did with their passengers and planes, a kind of rent-a-priest express, shove one group in like cattle, bless them, shove the rings on, get them kissed, toss them out, five minutes for cleanup, then shove another group in their place. Peculiar.

Not that she cared much about the ceremony itself. This gloomy old church with its leaky holy water fonts and crumbling stone facade stuck thanklessly between the betting shop and the homeless shelter, the homeless shelter she had made a few charitable donations to, wasn't where the wheeling and dealing would be taking place. Pews weren't made for that; it would come later. The reception was across the river on the outskirts of the Waterside, at the country club she was a member of and occasionally played a round of golf at. Indeed, she had encouraged her invitees, perhaps even coerced, those movers and shakers of the Derry business world to avoid the ceremony itself and show up for the reception at 2:00 PM.

The reception where Zoë had concentrated her efforts. She was hoping to not only give her son a wife, but nab herself a few business deals. After the first meeting with the Flood woman, she realized, as suspected, she'd have to do the majority of the work herself, and she had. Yes, the wedding was avocado, so the linen tablecloths of the country club event room were that color, and the napkins and plates and well. And the welcome totes, which were filled with milk-and dark-chocolate truffles, red-wine vinegar and olive oil, sea salt and crushed pepper (and, it certainly verged on the tacky, but she had had her office staff slip in some promotional material and special deals for her various enterprises, including two-for-one entrances to the Amelia Earhart center, a complimentary cut of meat from the butchers, a £10 gift card for Dreams and Wishes, and a month's free storage at the Pence-A-Day lockups).

Ping! It was as if the caterer had read her thoughts; she was sending Zoë a photo text, letting her know the reception was ready. The photo was a view of the ivy-draped chandeliers that hung over each dining table, their candles, avocado, casting a warm, romantic glow on the floral and moss centerpieces below. *Ping!* A photo of the long garlands of greenery draped across the linen. *Ping!* The dramatic green string lights with intertwined petals that hung from the ceiling between the chandeliers. *Ping!* On the shelves of the sideboards, rows of crystal wineglasses that had been turned into elegant café lamps with mini vellum shades, green. It certainly was a green reception, Zoë considered. A very green room. Though that's what the Flood woman had wanted.

Ping! Ah! Finally a bit of color, or at least a color other than green, the bouquet of berries and calla lilies that were tied to the back of the bride's chair. *Ping!* And the tall centerpieces, the two foot high vases of hydrangeas and oncidium orchids that seemed to hover above the table. They looked startling, frozen in mid-air like that, but the caterer had explained this was so that they wouldn't interfere with the guests' lines of sight. *Ping!* The lower centerpieces of roses, peonies, hyacinths, and hydrangeas.

Ping! Zoë gasped. She clutched her heart. She blinked. She peered at the latest photo on her phone, unable to trust her eyes. What was this ghastly pink thing, this monstrosity that verged on the, the *pornographic?* Was it really meant to be, actually meant to be the *cake?* Meant to be *eaten?* She blanched, and then the blood poured into her face. Her finger hovered uncertainly over her phone. She wondered if she should tell the caterer to 'accidentally' knock down the phalli. But then she had to smile and finally a little laugh forced itself from her Sephora-ed lips. Marvelous! she texted back.

Her clients, already alerted to what Zoë's son was marrying into, would hopefully find the, well, she supposed she'd have to call it the *cake,* as it was supposed to be the cake, entertaining. Racy, saucy. Maybe even a bit titillating. Perhaps they'd have pity on her and sign bigger deals. There rarely seemed to be a dull moment with this Flood family. She was realizing they, especially that peculiar mother, her soon to be sister-in-law, were adding something to her life that had been sorely lacking in her relentless days of spreadsheets and Power Point presentations and net and gross profits: fun. Perhaps this pairing of Rory and Dymphna was for the best.

The veil pressed against the soft leather of the limousine's plush bucket seating. It fell mid-thigh, with scalloped edges and embroidery in metallic silver thread, embellished with caviar beads and tiny pearls. It was stunning. Under it, Dymphna's face was now glowing, and it had nothing to do with her mother's slap. That had long been dismissed, just the latest in a long line of slaps across the face dealt to her over the years. As Dymphna sat there and sipped champagne, enthralled at the luxury that surrounded her, and the promise of the new life stretching before her, a father for her children, a soul mate for her, she felt her old life, the drudgery and squalor, the spewed insults and hatred from her mother, slipping away. The ring finger of her left hand tingled in anticipation. Soon her fresh, clean life, just like the lines of the furniture in Zoë's living room, would begin. She wondered when her new mother-in-law would allow her maternity leave from the chip van. It shouldn't be long now. And then Dymphna would never step foot inside that van again. And she had just thought of the name for her third child. For her and Rory's child, Fabrizio or not. This was indeed the happiest day of her life.

"Right!" her mother roared. All jumped, their heads twisting towards Fionnuala. "Now that we've impressed the neighbors—I know not a soul round these parts we're going through at the moment—now we've some free time, with nothing left to do but show up and sit in the pews, I think now's the time for the wee something I've been dying for to show ye, Dymphna."

Paddy and Maureen eyed Fionnuala with suspicion. She reached into her purse, rummaged around, and tugged something out. Paddy and Maureen yelled their protests.

"Och, for the love of God, woman!"

"Not on the wane's way to her wedding!"

"Ye kyanny be serious!" Lorcan said.

"It's now or never," Fionnuala insisted, brandishing the pieces of the card, which she had carefully taped together so that it approximated what it had when she first slipped it out of its envelope. Siofra, Padraig and Seamus turned back to the soccer on the telly, Lorcan looked down at his phone, and Keanu and Beeyonsay kept sleeping. For once.

Dymphna looked uncomprehending at the card her mother was making her way across the expanse of the limo to hand her. But she felt a sick feeling in her stomach, and it wasn't her third child stirring.

"Them minted bastards the Barnetts might be on their way to the church, quite possibly in a limo even grander than wer own right now, and Dymphna's a right to know what a sarky, hateful bitch her auntie be's. Ye didn't believe me, Dymphna, when I told ye last night. But she *did* send that funeral wreath to ye for yer special day. I'm sure ye saw the remnants of it in the scullery and the sitting room, did ye not? Doesn't matter, but, as here be's what really matters. I've the proof of her hatefulness right here in me hand."

Fionnuala had finally reached her and plopped herself down beside her. She pressed the card into Dymphna's hand.

Paddy shook his head, lips tight with anger. Maureen was like a mirror image at his side. Lorcan gulped down more champagne. Padraig changed the channel. *Transformers.*

A hysterical wail rose from Dymphna's throat.

"Read the back and all." Fionnuala flipped it over for her and pointed at the words. "Ye can see there, plain as day, Rot In Hell. All Of You, she's added as well, so I don't know why youse are defending the disgraceful bitch!"

Dymphna gnawed on her fist as tears rolled down her face.

"Me makeup!" she sobbed, and then the anger raged in her. Her head reeled. Her brain struggled to comprehend. And it had never been primed for comprehension. Was this what it felt like when the reveal came at the end of the long con? Had Auntie Ursula been deceiving her all these years? Was she really cold, hateful, callous? Or...maybe her auntie Ursula had been drunk when she wrote it; the handwriting on the back looked somehow different from her aunt's familiar script on the front. Or maybe she had taken up drugs over there in the States? Dymphna had seen a show about it on the telly, how most Yanks were addicted to a wide array of prescription drugs because the drug companies wanted large profits, how they wanted to hook the entire nation, how the USA was nothing but a country of medicated, out-of-their-minds addicts, putting on a show of being rational, normal human beings as they went about their daily lives, but secretly shoveling down handfuls of the mind altering pills passed to them over the counter...legally!

Whether that were the case or not, as Dymphna stared at the hateful words scribbled on the card, she felt a chasm opening, a distance growing, pushing her further and further away from the kind, generous Auntie Ursula she had grown up with. Life in the USA must have changed her into a cold-hearted, sarcastic *bitch.*

"I hate her! I hate her!" Dymphna wailed. Fionnuala nodded happily even as she cooed and brought a tissue—a real one from the leather box on the side of the limo!—up to her daughter's eyes.

"Hold on a wee moment, now," Paddy warned.

"We don't know, love, if it was just some terrible misunderstanding,"

253

Maureen said.

"I think it's a joke," Lorcan said. "There be's black humor, ye know."

"Why would me auntie want me in Hell?" Seamus asked, lower lip trembling.

"That's not wer auntie," Siofra said. "I don't believe it. And, anyroad, them flowers she sent looked like they was wile beautiful. Until Mammy stamped on em and made em ugly."

Padraig snorted and went back to the cartoon.

"Ye know what yer mammy's like, love," Paddy ventured finally.

"Ye kyanny argue, but, with cold, hard *facts!*" Fionnuala snatched the card from Dymphna and waved it in the air before them.

Paddy ignored Fionnuala's glare. "We've to wait to hear—"

"I'm shocked, *shocked* she would do such a thing," Dymphna bawled, grabbing the card and tearing it back into tiny pieces. They fluttered to the plush carpeting. "Dreadful mingin sarky cow!"

"I'll help ye stomp on them pieces if ye want me to," her mother said.

"And...and..." Dymphna struggled to get out through the tears, "to do such a hateful thing after they just won all that money and all."

Paddy, Maureen, Lorcan and Siofra froze.

"I thought we wasn't supposed to tell—" Siofra began.

"I don't know about 'just,'" Fionnuala said, still shooting daggers over at Paddy. Was he becoming immune to her as well? "That lottery win was years —"

"Naw! Not that!" Dymphna interrupted, the tears still flowing down. "When they won them bags of dosh on the telly the other night! From them investor yokes."

"Pah! What are ye on about?"

But Fionnuala saw them all staring in disbelief at Dymphna (except Padraig). She knew they knew something she didn't. Traitors!

"What," she roared, "are youse not telling me?!"

"They went on that, oh, I don't know, some Yank show. But like *Shark Tank* or *Dragons Den*, it was. $150,000 they won!"

"$150,000?! And youse didn't tell me?! Traitors! Flimmin fecking backstabbing traitors!"

The driver was winding the partition down in alarm.

"Roll that fecking window back up, ye servant!" Fionnuala roared. It slowly went back up. "Ye all saw them win the dosh? Why did nobody tell me?"

"Er...ye were sleeping, like," Lorcan said.

"And did youse not think to wake me up?"

"Why?" Maureen asked. "Just so's ye could spit at the telly?"

"Aye!"

Dymphna was getting more and more riled. "I don't know why youse is giving Mammy such abuse. Do youse think me auntie Ursula and uncle Jed just *happened* to make their way over here to Derry for me wedding the moment they won?"

"Me *arse* they did!" Fionnuala roared into their faces. "They flew over here to rub wer noses in it yet again! Pockets bulging with dosh while we struggle to rub two pennies together."

"Ye're sitting in a limo, Mammy," Lorcan said.

"And *you* keep yer bake shut, son!" Fionnuala roared. "We'll be dumped on the pavement, toppled out back into the gutter, the grating, the moment the wedding's over, and back to wer lives of misery we'll go, except for *you!* Living the life of Riley in that Florida, ye're gonny be! Or so ye think, anyroad! Have you any clue, do ye not know what I...do ye think that illness..."

She clamped her teeth shut. She had the potato in her purse, slathered in the toxins of the oven cleaner, waiting for his palate and his plate at the reception. And she had slipped in the can of Yeuch-B-Gone as well, in case the spud needed a touch up. Lorcan would never make it Florida. She counted to ten, composed herself into a Lady pose, then smiled.

"I don't know what I was on about there," she said into their confused faces. "Right! If them Barnetts does show their faces, they'll rue the day they decided to book that flight. Loads of abuse, they're gonny get, from me and wer Dymphna. And that's all that matters. This be's Dymphna's day, after all. Let's just enjoy the rest of the ride. Oh, look! Look out the right side, would youse? Ye can see the Derry walls! Not much longer, so we've got!"

The limousine rolled towards the city center.

The massive wooden doors of the church flew open. Zoë smiled politely as the crowds from the wedding flooded out, rice and confetti flying, laughter and applause and the flash of cameras ringing out. At the same time, limos and cars and vans were pulling up before the church. Another wedding party. Zoë checked her watch in surprise. Just how tight was the schedule at this church? At this rate, they must turn the church over every ten minutes. A feeling of dread, of unease, clutched her stomach. Something seemed a bit off. Perhaps she should have taken over this part of the planning as well. She didn't want her son to be married in a ceremony that lasted all of three minutes. They might as well have gone to the registry office. Maybe *their* ceremonies were even lengthier than those here at St. Fintan's were seeming to be!

Across the square from the church, beyond the public lavatories, there was a sudden commotion before the Top Yer Trolly superstore. Zoë's eyes were momentarily distracted by the gathering of hordes of old women that rounded the corner, twenty or more, rolling bulging shopping carts and toting signs and unraveling bedsheets with things scrawled on them in paint. The one ray of sunshine that poured from the heavens was right above them, so it made it difficult for her to see them correctly. But she had other things to think about anyway. She looked away.

The first wedding party had disbanded and cleared out, and now the second was streaming past her into the church, the bride lovely, the groom handsome, suits and high heels and low gowns and floppy hats all around. Zoë looked to the left, then looked to the right for the Flood's limousine. All she saw were two pitiful creatures exiting the homeless shelter. What a pair they looked! Down and out, definitely, the man with a battered cowboy hat, of all things!, on his head, the woman with a disheveled purple bob and a lurid, eye-scorching yellow jumper with an elephant on it. What rubbish bin had the poor soul found it in? And, though Zoë could understand the desperation of the homeless for different if not new clothing, perhaps that was one creation that should have been left in the wheelie bin to die its own death.

They seemed to be walking towards the church, and, what troubled her more, searching her face with looks of hope on their own. Zoë made little crab sideways steps towards her car as if to hide behind it. They were probably on her way over to ask for a handout, it was her posh clothes, and she had given enough to the homeless shelter the responsible way, through charity drives. These two would probably only waste it on drink, if their faces and bodies were anything to go by.

Zoë focused on her phone. She heard the opening strains of "Three Times A Lady" from inside the church. Who should she call? Text? The Flood woman? Had she herself gotten the time wrong? Was she at the wrong church?

She was scrolling through her contacts, disturbed, when she felt the two tramps stop in front of her. She scowled inwardly. She forced herself to look up into their wretched faces.

"I'm sorry, I don't have any spare ch—"

"Are ye here for the funeral?" the woman asked. Zoë was taken aback. She saw the woman's eyes, then the crumpled up loo roll in her hand. She had been crying. Perhaps she had looked in a mirror. Surprisingly, they both seemed freshly-bathed, or, considering where they had probably spent the night, showered.

"Why, no. I'm actually here for quite the opposite, you might say. A wedding."

The two tramps eyed each other in disappointment.

"Maybe there's another entrance?"

The man-creature was American! Wonders never ceased on the streets of Derry! Zoë made a mental note to get out of the office and into the real world more often. Life outside Riddell Enterprises really was surprising. And fun.

"Aye, perhaps there be's a grand entrance for weddings," the alkie woman in the vile yellow jumper said, "and a wee one, discreet, in the back for the funerals. Though...I sang many years here in the choir, so I did, and I don't recall ever seeing..."

"Where was this funeral meant to take place?" Zoë asked. Out of the corner of her eye, she saw clunking across the slick slabs of the square three hungover slappers in avocado dresses, one with a cast dyed green, the bridesmaids, she assumed, by the bright red letters embroidered on the décolletages of their gowns DY on one, MPH on the second, and NA on the third, and other people in bargain bin suits and knock off dresses who might just be Flood guests. And then a rather striking young priest with piercing eyes and jet black hair, clutching the Good Book as he rounded the corner. They were all descending on the church. So it must be the right place. But—

"Here. At St. Fintan's," the American said.

"Do they even do funerals at this church? I would've thought..." Zoë shook her head. Other than the venue, she didn't know what to ask them to help them. The name of the deceased wouldn't help her help them. But it was strange that there seemed to be two weddings and a funeral booked for this church at the same time. "Anyway, I'm sorry, but I don't know what to tell you. Erm, I wonder if I might be so forward as to ask you... How shall I word this? How did you two end up in the state you're in? Homeless, I mean. I'm sorry for being so direct, but it's rather odd to come across an Ame—" She saw her son's limo approach. It was the smaller of the two she had ordered. She saw Georgie get out, him pulling Rory out and trying to get him to stand. "Pardon me, I must go. That's my son there. The groom." She said it proudly, which would have surprised her a few months earlier. "Oh! And that must be the bride!"

The tramps turned around as a black Rolls Royce stretch limousine, a Phantom, pulled up and parked outside the church.

Zoë said, "If you'll excuse me..."

Ursula and Jed watched her hurry off towards the opening doors of the second limo.

"What do we do now?" Jed asked.

"I haven't a clue."

Gnarled hands gripped the broom and mop sticks as tightly as they could. Mrs. Gee, Mrs. Leech, Mrs. Stokes and various others would be brandishing the signs. They were practicing in front of the Top Yer Trolly now, before the window with the ads for washing powder and tinned mushy peas and two for one apricots, making sure their twiglet arms could hold the signs high for an extended length of time. The length of a wedding.

Green + Orange = Vile, read one sign.

It's A Sin! another.
Proddy Bastards Get Out Of Our Churches!
Mary Told Us NO To Interdenominational Marriages!
Mrs. Ming and Mrs. O'Bryan unfurled the largest of the bed sheet banners.
MARY SAYS YOU'RE GOING TO HELL! If She had been looking down
from on high at them that day, She would have been saddened at the hatred
being spread supposedly in Her name. And more than a bit mortified.

Mrs. Mulholland was trying to tame the electric megaphone she had
borrowed from her nephew, who was quite political and had used it for various
anti-Brit demonstrations. Feedback kept squawking from it, and she kept
fiddling with the knobs hoping to make it disappear. Bridie was sat on a
cardboard box that had once held deodorant as if it were a throne. She looked
around at the women gearing up around her, hauling the vegetables and fruit
out of their shopping carts and loading up the plastic bags each of them would
carry. She didn't know if she felt like a queen or a general or a prophet. A bit of
all three, actually. She was glaring across the square at St. Fintan's, searching
for a sighting of Dymphna Flood and her Proddy fancy man. Once they
appeared, the attack would begin.

"C'mere, Bridie," the young girl Mrs. Dinh had brought along again said to
her. "It says behind ye there be's a two for one sale on apricots. Do ye want me
to run in and get some more?"

Bridie surveyed the shopping carts and calculated how much they had
shoved into each one. Mrs. Mulholland had contacted Mrs. Leech's uncle, who
owned the fruit and vegetable stand at the market, and he had given them all
the rotten orange fruit and vegetables he could. There were oranges, of course,
and tangerines, mangoes, parsnips, turnips, butternut squash, yams, peaches,
nectarines, the more rotten the better, Mrs. Mulholland had told the man, but a
few were ripe. They had taken them along as well. Maybe they wouldn't spatter
as much, but they would hurt. The uncle had even dredged up a pumpkin from
somewhere, and a papaya. And, of course, apricots. Bridie had thought her
auntie Bernadette not only resourceful, but also inventive. She herself wouldn't
have been able to think of such a fitting punishment. Orange filth flung at a
filthy Orange bastard. And his Green traitor of a tart.

"Naw," Bridie said. "I think we've enough. Good thinking, but."

Bridie patted her on the head. The little girl beamed as if Bridie had handed
her a ten pound note. Bridie loved the way people were treating her now, in a
manner she had never been treated before. With reverence, with respect.

Their plan of attack was threefold. First there would be the chanting, led by
Mrs. Mulholland on the megaphone, then the signs and banners waving in the
air, and finally, the flinging of the rotten orange fruit and vegetables. Bridie had
told them to aim for Dymphna and Rory. But, of course, *anybody* who was part

of this vulgarity was an appropriate target.

"Look!" called out Mrs. Leech. "There the sinners is now! Getting outta that limo! Well, the Proddy one, anyroad."

Bridie jumped up as a geriatric roar went up from them all. They held their heaving bags tightly, brandished their signs high, those with the bed sheet banners shuffled into rows and clutched them with as much force as their hands could muster. Mrs. Mulholland flicked on the megaphone and was pleased there was no shriek of feedback. She held it to her mouth and parted her lips.

"Wait!" Bridie said.

A sea of purple and blue rinses, row upon row of thick spectacles turned to face her, expectant. Their wrinkles awaited her words of wisdom.

"I know youse are all excited. But let's wait a wee moment, shall we, until we see the bride herself. And...and...I feel the Virgin giving me a special message for youse all!"

Some looked startled; they had forgotten all about the poor Blessed Virgin in all of this. This hatred.

"What does She say, Bridie, me love?" Mrs. Mulholland asked, a smile playing on her withered lips.

"She says...*Good luck, girls!*"

A roar went up as if their number had just been called at the bingo, the special Stamp and Four Corners jackpot. They hadn't felt so alive in years.

CHAPTER 38

Paddy hoped the others in the limo didn't notice how skittish, how tortured he was. And as the car purred like the marvelous machine it was through the city gates and headed towards the church, he felt a shame, a deep, all-encompassing guilt, for the call he had placed the moment he went into the house to retrieve the babies. For once, he was happy the family was reduced to using pay-as-you go mobiles, as he had seen on all the copper dramas on TV that they were untraceable. He hoped the wailing infants hadn't obscured his voice too much as he hissed down the line to the police, "Listen, youse. This doesn't be a hoax. There's a bomb in St. Fintan's church. Set to go off in half an hour, so it is." Then he had hung up and rolled the stroller shamefacedly to the limo.

And now they were here, the flying buttresses before them, the gargoyles glaring down, Dymphna's tears wiped away, the excitement and nervousness beaming from his daughter's face under that gorgeous veil and above the colorful gown. How could he have been such a fool, such an eejit, to forget to book the church? He would never forgive himself. But somehow he figured...they could still go through with the reception today, and have a ceremony at a later date. All who had been invited seemed more interested in the free booze and scran than the vows. He wouldn't be disappointing many of the guests, if any. Dymphna would be gutted, but she could always get married whenever. He downed the last few bubbles of champagne as the limo's engine fell silent. Around him, the family whooped and cheered.

The children clambered out, then Lorcan, then Paddy, and finally Fionnuala decided she had fixed her peacock feathers enough, had struck the appropriate pose, and hoped she would be seen by the gathering masses—she had seen them through the tinted window, Zoë, the bridesmaids, the priest she had arranged, her auntie Julie, her uncle Vernon, a smattering of cousins, some Floods, and others she knew to see but didn't understand exactly who they were —she hoped they, especially Father Steele, saw her as *alighting* from the limousine.

Maureen held Dymphna back.

"Ye want to build up the suspense, love," the woman said. "Sit you here with me a wee moment. I'm sure most of the guests are waiting outside the church for the first glimpse of ye. And we don't know where Rory be's. We've to make sure he's well hidden before ye step out, like."

"I understand, aye," Dymphna said, compact out, redoing the mascara that had coursed down her cheeks. "I've to freshen meself up anyroad. Could ye help me with me eyelashes, hi?"

"Aye, I can. I've something to tell ye, love. I think yer mammy doesn't know what she be's going on about. I know yer head must be all over the place, about to be wed and all, and then there must be the hormones from the wee baby growing inside ye, but I don't think yer auntie Ursula meant ye any harm. And I've a suspicion that be's yer mammy's handwriting on the back of the card, altered a wee bit, aye, but her handwriting nevertheless. Ye know the blind hatred yer mammy has for yer auntie Ursula. I love a bit of drama, me, but yer mammy's unhinged. And I'm a wee bit surprised at ye agreeing with her, going along with her campaign of hatred. It doesn't be a day for hatred. It be's a day for love, so it does. Remember what I'm telling ye now if ye set eyes on yer auntie today."

"Hand me that lippy, would ye?"

Maureen did. Then, "C'mere," she said, peeping through the door. "There's a terrible racket out there! What's all that palaver about I wonder...?

Siofra was the first to see them. They looked different somehow, but she knew who they were the moment she jumped from the limousine.

"Auntie Ursula! Uncle Jed!"

She shrieked with delight as she ran towards them, Seamus on her heels, his gurgles of joy ringing out, and even Padraig had a smile on his face as he hurried across to wrap his arms around them, something he hadn't done to a fellow human in years.

Ursula knelt down there on the concrete as the children covered her with hugs and kisses. Jed reached down and ruffled their hair as their arms wound round his legs and they shouted their glee and asked if they had gifts for them.

"Och, Siofra, Padraig, Seamus," Ursula bubbled through her tears, "it's lovely to see yer smiling faces. There's no need, but, for youse wanes to put on brave faces for me. I know youse must be terrible sad. It's an awful day, so it is. Horrible! Youse can cry along with me, but. Ye see?" She pointed at her wet cheeks. "I'm a grown up, but I kyanny hide me tears. Youse wanes is allow to cry and all."

"Sorry, kids," Jed said, his voice breaking. "Really, I'm so sorry."

He took off his glasses and wiped them as tears trickled towards his goatee.

"But Auntie Ursula," Siofra said, "Uncle Jed, ye've no reason to be sad. It's a grand and happy day, so it is!"

"Aye, Mammy said so," Seamus said.

"She *would,*" Ursula sniped. She gave a fearful little nod towards the limo. "Does yer..." she struggled to get the words out, "does yer sister's...does her *earthly shell* be in there?"

"What are ye on about?" Padraig asked.

"What's that mean?" Siofra asked. Seamus cried, apparently because he thought he should.

"Her...body," Jed said.

Padraig crinkled his nose.

"Do ye really think she's gone and *died?*" He looked at them in disbelief.

"Well, yeah," Jed said.

"We heard it from me mate Francine, from yer Moira and all."

"Naw!" Siofra said. "She's not dead! She's getting wed!"

"What?!" Ursula and Jed chorused.

"To Rory Riddell!" Siofra enthused.

"Aye, it's true," Padraig said. "To a Proddy bastard."

"Proddy bastard," agreed Seamus, head bobbing..

"God's honest truth," said Padraig. "In St. Fintan's there. And there's to be a big party after and all."

"I made the cake!" Siofra said, beaming. "It's pink!"

"I help," Seamus said.

"Aye, ye did," Siofra agreed. She clapped her little hands, suddenly realizing something. "Och, Auntie Ursula and Uncle Jed!! Youse can come help eat the cake as well! Youse can have a slice of the special princess towers

I made! With wee purple flowers on em!"

Ursula and Jed stood, stunned, before the children as Siofra, Padraig and Seamus babbled on and on about this apparent wedding. They tried to make sense of what they were hearing, especially from Seamus.

"But I was told..." Ursula said, "The wreath I sent...the lesbians what're never gonny die..."

Jed eyed her as if a breakdown were eminent.

"C'mon and see for yerselves!" Siofra said. "She's a wile lovely frock on and all! Hearts and bows and stars and crosses and long jangly things! Come on to the big car and see her!"

Ursula and Jed felt their little hands urge them across the square.

Paddy was looking around even as he shook hands with twigs from the family tree, clock ticking. W*here* was the bomb squad? He knew the IRA used to give a special password to let the Filth know a bomb threat wasn't just a scare. Maybe they had sussed it was a hoax because he had no password to give. But, hoax or not, his only hope was that they would *have* to send in the troops, the dogs, the equipment to investigate. If only to stop a liability lawsuit, at the very least.

He looked past his second cousin's shoulder and was startled at the sight of two disheveled beings with their paws all over his children. He threw down his cousin's hand and, fears of pedophiles racing through his mind, raced over. As he was thinking he had seen the yellow elephant jumper somewhere many years ago, and as the children pushed the pedos towards him, the pervs' heads were raised and looking at him. Ursula and Jed! Tears seemed to have been streaming down Ursula's face, Jed was teary also. Now smiles were breaking out on their faces, but tentative ones, unsure.

Though one part of Paddy's heart leaped with joy, another part plunged with contempt. So they *had* raced to Derry the moment their pockets were bulging with fresh new cash, choosing Dymphna's wedding to make their superiority known. He approached cautiously. And from behind him Fionnuala's scornful voice pierced the air: "Och, if it isn't the Lady and the Lord of the Manor! The King and Queen of all they survey! Yet again! Go on and get outta here, youse feckin arseholes! Sure, nobody wants ye or cares about yer money!"

Ursula and Jed shirked, and Seamus also, as Fionnuala galloped towards them with that sinister, knowing smirk on her face, her eyes flicking and flashing, lips twitching as her brain cells trundled, those lips readying themselves, eager, to disgorge the vilest poison her brain could devise.

She reached them and the children looked up, tense. What would happen? Fionnuala whispered into Paddy's ear, then nodded towards the limo. The driver was still standing before the open door, his hand outstretched, waiting for a tip Paddy was damned if he would give him. Zoë should've warned them. This, his wife seemed to be saying, would be a test to how tight-fisted the Barnetts were. Forgotten for the moment was the mortgage the Barnetts had paid off for them, and the extra house they had given them, the tanning bed and the ice cream making machine.

"Tip yer man there," Paddy said.

Fionnuala stood at his side, arms folded, eyes shining, waiting to see how much they gave.

"W-we've no money," Ursula said. "None."

"Yeah, it's true," Jed said. "We just came from the homeless shelter over there. Where we spent the night."

"Sarky bastards!" Paddy hissed. His hands curled into fists.

"I told ye, Paddy!" Fionnuala's smile was triumphant. As if she had just won the gold medal for Intolerance at the Olympics of Hatred.

"No, really!" Jed said. "I gam—"

"Not another word, Jed," Ursula broke in. "Themmuns don't need to know."

"Tip yer man!" Fionnuala barked.

Ursula reached into her handbag. She pulled out her coin purse. She sighed as she rummaged around, then took out the two pound coins. She walked over with them glinting in her fingers. She pressed the last of their money into the driver's hand. He looked down at the two coins, then up at her with scorn. He muttered, "Cheap bastards!" then threw the coins to the ground.

"I knew it!" Fionnuala whooped with glee. Paddy's jaw fell.

"Ye're having us on! We seen ye just won that $150,000 on the telly the other night! On that game show! And all ye can do is give yer man two quid!"

"It wasn't a game show," Jed tried to explain. "We had to give away 82.5 % of our company for that money. And we just taped it the other day. We don't have the check yet. And that was the last two pounds we owned."

"And now," Paddy said, "Ye've shown up on wer patch, at wer daughter's wedding, and ye're making out ye need a handout? What sorta cruel joke does this be?"

"A hundred quid entrance fee! Each!" Fionnuala barked.

Ursula could scream at her sister-in-law the way she had screamed at the Killer Investors. She could do it. All she had to do was open her mouth. Except she couldn't. She could have left the studio in Wisconsin and never think of the nameless millionaires again. But her sister-in-law was her sister-in-law for life, especially as divorce was illegal in Northern Ireland. This was just like the lottery win years before all over again: no matter how many times they might try to explain it to Paddy and, especially, Fionnuala, they wouldn't be able to get it through to them that they didn't have the money. Still, anger was slowly simmering inside Ursula. She parted her lips, but they all jumped at a dreadful, ear-piercing, heart-wrenching shriek of horror coming from behind the limousine.

It was Zoë Riddell. *"The Vera Wanggg! Nooooo!"* she screamed, amputation-sans-anesthetic-like.

Half of what was meant to be the congregation gasped with horror, the other in awe as Dymphna clambered out of the limousine, head held high, bouquet brandished like the World Cup trophy, appliqués glistening, the beaded fringes shimmering in the sunlight that poked from the lone hole in the clouds. There was uncertain clapping.

"Och, but that be's a lovely gown, so it is!" one old woman said. Another nodded.

"Ta, all Derry!" Dymphna roared, "for being here to see me be wed! A flimmin, fecking bride I'm finally gonny be! Unbelievable, like!"

Laughter and clapping and camera flashes rang out. Ailish, Moira and Maeve pushed through the gathering masses to be at her side. They lined up, DY, MPH, NA, and the throngs went mad, soccer-goal mad.

"Where's me Rory?" Dymphna yelled through their FIFA applause, eyes scanning the crowds. "Not here, I hope? He kyanny see me, can he?"

"No fear!" Georgie called out. "He's taking a slash!" He nodded at the public lavatory, and laughter rang out again. And then was cut short. Heads whipped around, smiles and dancing eyes faltering.

"Who spoke to us?!" Mrs. Mulholland's harsh roared from the crackling megaphone.

Around Dymphna, the guests looked at each other for an answer to their confusion. They found none.

"Our Lady Mary!" chanted the masses, the army of angered OAPs marching across the square.

"Where does she want the sinners?!"

"Outta Derry!" They might have been slow, but they were steadily approaching the limo.

Maureen struggled to place her glasses on her nose with shaking hands. She simply had to read the signs. The Mary-Hell bed sheet flapped in the wind.

"Blasphemy!" she shouted, enraged.

"No," Zoë, next to her, said stiffly. She nodded at the gown. *"That's* blasphemy."

"Who spoke to us?!" Closer. ***"Our Lady Mary!"*** And closer. The guests clutched each other for support.

"Where does she want the sinners?!" Arthritic hands rummaged into plastic bags and grabbed ammo. ***"Outta Derry!"***

The pumpkin sailed through the air first, followed by a flock of apricots and turnips. The pumpkin smashed against the roof of the limo, seeds and innards ejecting through the air. Apricots splat and turnips splattered. The crowds shrieked and scattered, bodies fell to the ground, some for protection, some from a push. A volley of mangoes, parsnips and nectarines speared the air, their rancid juices lashing down like acid rain. A squash sent Jed's hat flying, a peach clipped Ursula's arm, a yam smacked into Fionnuala's face. Father Steele marched towards the approaching masses, holding up the Bible.

"Ladies! Ladies!" he appealed. "Let us not—"

The papaya knocked the book out of his hand. A tangerine exploded on his chest.

"Sorry, Father!" called out the woman who had thrown it. "But...Mary said!"

Peaches, squashes, oranges rained down upon the scrabbling, crawling masses. Even as Dymphna flung her arms up to protect her makeup and veil, she gasped as she saw she suddenly had not three bridesmaids, but two. Ailish, MPH, was skipping across the street and joining the chanting masses, grabbing the bed sheet and waving it proudly, her voice one of the loudest: ***"Our Lady Mary!"* *"Outta Derry!"***

"Who's this Mary?" Zoë wondered, shaking seeds from her hair, but Maureen was gone, over shoving Dymphna into the limousine.

"Ye're going straight to Hell!" roared Mrs. Mulholland through the megaphone.

"Rory Riddell!" chorused the masses.

Putrid pulp, wrinkled skins and peels fell from the sky.

"Ye're going straight to Hell!" ***"Rory Riddell!"***

Closer and closer they marched, fruit flying, vegetables soaring.

"We want ye covered in blood!"

"Dymphna Flood!"

Splat! Splat Splat!

"We want ye covered in blood!" ***"Dymphna Flood!"***

"Who spoke to us?" *"Our Lady Mary!"*

"Why," Dymphna sobbed into Maureen's shoulder from the safety of the limousine, the infants squealing in the background, "does themmuns want me covered in blood? It's terrible, so it is! How can them aul ladies be so mean?!"

The car shook as thuds pounded on the roof time and again. The windows were seed-peppered mush.

"Shush, you," Maureen tried to comfort her. "Themmuns is only saying it as it rhymes with Flood."

"They could've chosen *'mud'!* Och, granny, what have I done to deserve this?"

"I dunno, dear. But I think maybe this limo wasn't a good idea. It's make ye...making us both, now, a sitting target. Ye never know, they might try to tip it over. Perhaps it's better if we got out and hoofed it. Well, *ye* can run. I'll attempt to."

Dymphna pried open the door an inch and peered cautiously outside. Rory, covered in orange slime, was racing across the square towards her. He slipped through the door.

"Och, Rory! It's wile horrible!"

He kissed her feverishly. Maureen looked away.

"I'm so sorry, Dymphna. At first I thought it was the mammies of me soccer mates, but all them aul harridans seems to be from yer part of town. All them orange fruits and veg, like."

Understanding dawned in Dymphna's teary eyes. "Och, I understand it now. Orange. Protestant. Who could've...? Could it be...?"

Dymphna clambered over Rory and made to open the door.

"Are ye mad?" he yelled, pulling her back. "Ye kyanny go out there! They'll ravage ye!"

"Me granny says they might tip the car over, but," Dymphna said.

"Aye," Maureen agreed.

"I just wanny see..."

She pried open the door and peered out. She scanned the approaching masses. And then Dymphna saw her, poking her head out from behind two pink perms and to the left of a sign, with a grin that stretched from one horrible ear to the other: Bridie McFee!

She was an eejit! She should've known! Dymphna understood now she had done nothing wrong. Except nab Rory Riddell.

"Bleedin jealous minger!"

Dymphna kicked off her high heels, grappled one in her right hand like a Samurai sword, wailed, banshee-like, and leaped out of the limo. Rory's hands tried to grab her or the veil, but clawed the air. The door slammed shut. Dymphna was gone, thrusting herself across the expanse of the square, jingling and jangling, dodging the fruit that flew towards her, ducking the vegetables, Maire and Maeve, who had been cowering behind the rear wheels, hustling after her, and Dymphna saw out of the corner of her eye her auntie Ursula and her uncle Jed, pulp-covered and gawping at her as if she had just risen from the dead, and even more adrenaline shot through her veins. She flashed them a quick smile, shoving through the bed sheet and knocking old women to the ground. Maire and Maeve egged her on with barks of glee, and knocked a few down for good measure as well.

"Clatter the shite outta that Bridie skegrat!" For they had seen her too.

"Seven shades of shite, boyo!"

"Knock her flimmin teeth down her throat!"

266

"So's she be's eating outta her arsehole, hi!"

"C'mere ye manky cow! Let me at ye!" Dymphna wailed, stiletto shining.

Mrs. Dinh used a sign as a sword and knocked the stiletto out of her hand. Dymphna wailed as it flew through the fruit-filled air. She couldn't find it amongst the carpet of shuddering arms and legs on the ground.

Bridie was grinning before her.

"Ye're going straight to Hell," she hissed. "The Virgin Mary told me so!"

"Mad bitch!" Dymphna growled.

She snatched tufts of Bridie's hair in her hands, dug her fingers in, then thrust her body to the ground. Bridie wailed in pain.

"Get offa me!" she screamed, fingernails whizzing through the air.

Dymphna, gown ballooned, billowing and sparkling, over Bridie's struggling body, banged her head again and again on the concrete. Maybe that would knock some sense into her. And over Bridie's screams, over the rush of blood through her own ears, Dymphna heard the roar of sirens.

Fearing the Filth was coming for her, she let go of Bridie's head and, with Maire and Moira whooping at her heels at the clattering they had given Ailish the turncoat while Dymphna was dealing with Bridie, hightailed it through the throngs, a third of them moaning on the ground, a third exhausted, a third fearing being hauled into the cop shop, and she made her way to her family.

The Floods, together with Ursula, Jed, Zoë, Rory, Georgie and Father Steele, were huddling in the doorway of the betting shop for safety and a smoke break. It was a tight fit. Dymphna supposed Keanu and Beeyonsay were safely in the limo. She, Maire and Maeve tried to shoehorn themselves into the cloud of fag smoke of the doorway as well.

"It was that Bridie McFee, Rory!" Dymphna wailed. "She put them aul hags up to it! And, och, now I've gone and clattered the shite outta her and the Filth be's after me!"

"Naw, love," Paddy said. "Bomb scare."

He nodded at the church, where the guests were streaming, screaming, out of the doors and past the flashing lights of the police cars and the bomb squad vans. Uniforms were winding crime scene tape around the church gates, and ever more bulky paratroopers and coppers and bomb experts and they didn't know who were jumping out of a wide range of monstrous vehicles. And a man with a dog.

To Fionnuala, it was deja vu, there they all were again, Tikka Pizza, the hard-faced bastard who had held her against the walls, the ones who had peered into her satchel and seen—

"Let's clear outta here!" she screamed as if they all weren't huddled inches away from her in the doorway.

Paddy nodded surprisingly quickly at Dymphna and Rory. "Youse kyanny get married there now anyroad. A bomb scare'll tie up the church for hours." He nodded at Father Steele. "We've the priest here with us, but, so all we need be's a large space where all the guests can fit." He checked his watch. "And maybe we can even make it to the reception on time!"

"Let's just start running in any direction," Fionnuala insisted. "Now!"

"Do ye think that's wise?" Ursula asked. "We should stay together. Those women might start attacking again."

"I didn't ask ye," Fionnuala snarled. She turned to Zoë. "Ye're the planning expert," she said. "Where do ye suggest we go? Or do we have to assemble a mood board beforehand, like?"

Zoë looked like she was surveying the situation.

"The church certainly does seem to be out of bounds," she mused. "You know, and I must apologize for this in advance, Mrs. Heggarty...it's apparent most of those women engaged in the demonstration, I suppose you'd call it—"

"Och, hurry up, would ye woman? Spit out yer plan!" Fionnuala was arranging her peacock feathers so that they draped across her face and hid it, in case any of the bomb squad would chance to look over and spy her within the cigarette smoke.

"It's apparent they won't be revisiting 70, or even 80. I challenge any of those elderly women to make it up the slope of Shipquay Street. You all know how steep it is. No matter how strong their conviction in their cause, their bodies will find it a struggle to march up there, quickly or not. In fact, I think it will Never. Happen. We can easily outrun them."

"And what are we gonny do once we get there?" Fionnuala asked.

"Haven't you the keys to the Amelia Earhart Center? It's Sunday, so it's closed. I do believe we can all fit in there. It's 1,450 square meters, after all. We can collect all the guests. They seem to be, erm, scattered all over the square, and we have to pass them on the way there. It will be like a caravan. And, considering the occasion, a caravan of love."

While one part of Fionnuala's cranium wondered if the woman were suggesting it only for free advertising for her enterprise—the story of the wedding in front of the Lockheed Vega would be fodder for next Sunday's supplement, she was sure—another part registered that Tikka Pizza was making his way towards them.

"Let's go!" she barked.

But once Bridie's army realized the Filth hadn't been called on them, they were hot on the sinners' trail again as the Floods et al. gathered together the wedding guests from under the benches where they were cringing, and behind the buses and in the nooks of the city walls and made their way up Shipquay Street towards the Amelia Earhart Center. The fruit and vegetable supply had apparently been depleted, but still their chanting rang out at their backs. Padraig was flinging rocks at them.

"I seen a poster of this Amelia Earhart whatsit in the hotel room," Ursula said to Zoë as she puffed up the hill. She added in response to the look Fionnuala shot her, "Where we couldn't stay as we had problems with wer cards. It looks wile interesting."

"It is," Zoë said, beaming. She looked behind her. "My goodness! Those old women are proving remarkably resilient!"

She nibbled on her lip as they all approached the front door.

Dymphna, crying, called out: "They're still gonny ruin me wedding! How can they be making their way up the street? Och, it's awful, so it is! It's as if the Lord has given them extra strength..."

"I believe it's meant to be the Blessed Virgin," Maureen harrumphed.

"For the love of God!" Fionnuala yelped. She was clutching, unsurprisingly, Father Steele's arm. "Me keys!" They were in her satchel. Locked up in some evidence room.

"What about them?" Zoë asked in alarm. All eyes were on Fionnuala.

"They're in me other bag. We kyanny get in. Should we smash a window?" Zoë thought quickly.

"They're gaining on us anyway," she said. She took a deep breath. "There's only one thing for it, then. Dymphna, dear, if I recall, you're not a vegetarian, are you?"

Everyone looked like they feared Derry's Second Best Businesswoman of the Year had gone mad.

"Ha!" Fionnuala spat. "Her? A vegetarian? As if! Maybe wer Moira, but that one, naw!"

"Are any of you?" Zoë asked the crowd.

"Naw!" "Naw!" "Dabbled with it once," Maire said. "Didn't take to it."

"Then," Zoë said, "Let's go up! *Up!* Farther up the street! To the butcher's on the Diamond! *My* butcher's! Riddell & Son! You'll get married there! We can pull the shutters down if they happen to make it *that* far!"

Padraig cheered as a rock clunked against Mrs. Mulholland's head. And ahead of him, the wedding crowd heaved themselves further up Shipquay Street.

CHAPTER 39

"Me name's Dymphna Riddell!" the bride slurred into the faces of everyone she saw or thought she saw. "Me name's Dymphna bloody Riddell! And I just had a flimmin ace fecking wedding!"

Yes, a flimmin ace fecking wedding it had been, if you overlooked the racks of lamb, loins of pork and ribs of beef hanging behind Father Steele's head, and the clanking of the meat hooks as he recited the blessing, the stained aprons of the butcher staff that Zoe demanded act as ushers and ensure everyone found a place inside to fit, the sniggers of Rory's soccer mates over by the pheasants and Cornish hens, the near hypothermia of those guests relegated to watch the ceremony from the walk-in freezer in the back, the air tinged with freshly-spilled blood. But Dymphna's and Rory's self-written vows of love and dedication (Dymphna's purloined from various Beyoncé ballads she was fond of and cobbled together) brought a tear to Zoe's, to Ursula's, to Maureen's eyes, and when they kissed over the special mince and Doherty's sausages, the roars and applause drowned out the bangs from the shutter from the very few of Bridie's brigade who had finally made it that far up Shipquay Street.

Zoe had arranged a fleet of taxis to shuttle everyone across the Craigavon Bridge to the swanky country club events room, and now here they were. Fionnuala had snatched the bouquet as it sailed through the air straight for Maire's fingers. Then the four courses had been wolfed down, Siofra's cake roared with laughter at, given a standing ovation, and gobbled with glee, and it seemed that after the unveiling of that marvel of a cake, the mood of the party, which had started tentative, over-polite, as the two factions, the Riddells' Protestants, the Floods' Catholics struggled to feel comfortable with each other, shifted slightly. Ties were loosened, high heels slipped off under the table as the drink overflowed glasses and mouths. Now it was in danger of teetering out of control.

"Mambo No. 5" was blaring from the speakers for the second time. Arms flailed, legs kicked, jackets were flung off, dresses hiked up, shoulder straps tugged down, hoots, yelps and roars of delight rang out, accountants frugged with shop assistants, the middle class and the working class becoming one; many would find a surprise on the adjacent pillow when they pried their eyes open the next morning. The smoking section had steadily crept indoors, the bartenders tossed away empty after empty, and everyone was glowing with delight and drink. Almost.

At a table piled with dirty plates and bowls in a corner between the kitchen door and the hallway to the loos sat Ursula. Her handbag was on the table before her. Her handbag with the empty coin purse inside. Useless. Jed appeared out of the clouds of smoke and the field of revolving disco lights which were causing Ursula grief, and he made his way to her through the overturned chairs and table cloths scattered on the floor. He had a glass of something in his hand. He sat down. There were plenty of empty chairs around Ursula to choose from. He took her hand and nuzzled it.

"It's great Dymphna's not dead, honey, isn't it? A cause for celebration!"

Ursula thought through the chorus of the song. He wondered for a moment she hadn't heard him, but then she said, "That be's the problem, but. With all them aul women hauled away by the coppers as they was, and wer Dymphna not only alive, but a bride to boot, now we're surrounded by happiness, and it makes me even the more miserable. And the drink isn't helping me." She looked at her almost empty glass of white zinfandel. She sighed. "So here we sit. Here. And everyone else be's over there."

She nodded in the direction of the dance floor and watched as a roar went up from the crowd at a new song from the DJ's turntable. She watched their joy for a moment, then turned to Jed.

"What's this song called? Tragedy, I suppose, as they keep singing it. 'Tragedy! Tragedy!' Ha!" It was a bitter little laugh. "Tragedy. Now the tragedy's passed, or, more to the point, now we've sussed there wasn't one in the first place, it's odd. When I thought wer Dymphna was gone, when I thought she had taken that drugs overdose and was no longer of this world, I felt a part of me was missing. Now, but, there she is, no, Jed, over there, there, dear, by the punch bowl. Ye see her now ? Laughing and dancing away, not a care in the world, even though her lovely frock be's ripped the whole way up her left thigh and her knickers be's showing on that side and she be's covered with grime and filth and seeds and whatnot from them madwomen. There she is, living and enjoying herself, and with the best part of her life stretching out before her, all the exciting years still to come, though she's saddled already with two wanes nobody's a clue who the father is, and another on the way, and the shame of a Proddy bastard husband to live down. Och, don't look at me like that, Jed. That's not how *I* feel. Rory's a lovely lad. Right civil, he was to me, at the dinner, and giving me his helping of croquettes and all. That's how many in this town will feel about him, but. For all Dymphna's life with him. And even with all that, she's happy." As if on cue, the opening bars of "Happy" rang out from the speakers. "Now Dymphna's alive and happy, aye I can see that, and I'm happy for her. But I feel a part of me's still missing."

Jed didn't know where to look or what to say. Ursula folded and unfolded a napkin. And folded it again.

"All me life, Jed, family was all what mattered. That and singing in the choir, I suppose. And the odd game of bingo. Wer own wanes is gone now, have families of their own, and it was ye and me and them, Paddy and Fionnuala and their wanes, here in Derry after ye retired. Then they chased us away. So now I've you. And Slim and Louella, and Muffins and all, I understand. But really there's only you. Now me's family turned me back on me, ye're all I have. Why, Jed, do ye have to gamble all the time? Is it the excitement? Is life with me so boring? Am I not enough for ye?" It was the

271

white zinfandel, making her maudlin, but these were thoughts rising from deep in her brain, thoughts that had been simmering in her subconscious. "A thousand of those dollars ye frittered away in yer madness on the flight over was from me bingo win of the other day, the special Stamp and Four Corners jackpot, ye mind? And ye mind how happy we was then, dancing on top of em in the scullery with Muffins nipping at wer feet? Doesn't that be enough for ye, Jed? Am I not enough? I don't belong here anymore, and I feel I don't belong with ye anymore. What's left for me?"

"Honey..." Tears welled in Jed's eyes. He took her by the hand. His voice shook as he spoke. "When I'm in front of one of those damn machines, all I see is the numbers. Some of the slots don't even call the money I'm putting in dollars. They call them credits. And that's all I see. Numbers. Credits. I don't think of it as real money."

"I've something to tell ye Jed. It *is* real money. Real money we've now not got. Real money we worked hard for, well, that you worked hard for. Aye, a lot of it's yer pension, but think of all them years ye slogged away in the navy. And the rest be's from the store and the beef jerky. How hard ye've worked. And to just toss it all away like that!"

Jed's eyes were shining, she didn't know if it was from tears welling, as he leaned in towards her and said, "Remember the investor told me I had to go to Gamblers' Anonymous? That it was a condition of the deal? I know they're going to investigate that during due diligence. They'll want to see if I've self-excluded myself from all the casinos in Wisconsin. And I think that's what was going through my mind on the plane. It was my last chance. My last chance to ever strike it rich on a slot machine. Once we get that check for $150,000, I was thinking, I can never go back. I can never gamble again, never strike it big. That's what I was thinking. But I lost. Everything. That chance is over. Let's hope Gambler's Anonymous can help me turn a corner. And...about your family...I hate to hear you talking like that Ursula, like you're so alone. I love you. So you're not alone. And I think a corner has been turned. Paddy seems to be sticking up for you, and Dymphna and Lorcan too. And the kids have always been happy to see you, no matter what was going on between you and their parents. The only one, the only hold out, seems, uh, seems to be..."

As if on cue, they jumped at a ruckus over by the bar.

"C'mon, youse! Sing along with me!" Fionnuala brayed into the air, grabbing whatever arms she could, most of which were trying to race in the opposite direction. *"Groove is in the he...ea...ea...ea..ea...eart!"* She had hitched her skirt up, and her legs were attempting a bizarre, drunken can can, an affront to the eye and common decency. *"**Groove** is in the heart! C'mon youse wankers! Sing along with me! Dance along with me, won't youse?! Groove is in the he...ea..."*

Ursula shuddered. She threw down the napkin. "I thought I could put me anger at ye on hold until we got to the end of the funeral at least, until we made them calls to the States and got us a loan of the money from someone to put some on wer cards. But then the funeral became a wedding. And the more the laughter rings out around me, the more I'm raging at ye Jed. And me anger gets stronger and stronger. I wanny shout abuse at ye, I wanny throttle ye, I wanny, I wanny..." Jed sat before her with his head bowed in shame, ready to take anything she said to him. "How could ye do it?" Ursula wailed in incomprehension. "How?! Now we're stranded here in Derry. Stranded! Like two aul alkies or two aul druggies. Like Randaleen and her man. I scrubbed me skin raw in that shower this morning, and still I feel the filth clinging to me flesh. Where are we gonny rest wer heads tonight? Not that shelter again! How can we get the money together for to pay for the bus to the airport? Hitchhike? At wer age? That flimmin bus, sure, costs 20 quid for each of us. Strange how it seemed like nothing on the way here. Now it seems a fortune."

"But...I asked Paddy! He said we could sleep at their place. Didn't I tell you?"

Ursula looked at Jed for a long time. Again. Her lips were tight.

"With Fionnuala laughing down at me sleeping body stretched out on her settee?"

"But...it's better than the homeless shelter!"

"I don't know about that." She moaned as she placed her hand on her forehead. "Och, me head be's banging! I'm that full of the stress of it all, I've been shoveling the painkillers down me throat like Smarties." She grabbed her handbag, it seemed much lighter now, but that really couldn't be true, and rummaged through it. "And now I'm all outta Tylenol. The Tylenol I bought back when we had the funds to buy things. The Tylenol I kyanny afford no more. Because money was just numbers to ye on the screen of a slot machine."

"I'll ask Paddy for a loan."

"No, ye will not. I'll never live down the mortification. Fionnuala will never let me live it down until me dying day. Wer only hope be's calling wer wanes or yer brother or Louella. Och, I feel me head's gonny split open! I need to find some painkillers! And quick!"

"There's a 24-hour drug store, or whatever you call them here, a chemist's, across the street. I saw it when we were coming in."

He shrank back from Ursula's look.

"And just how am I meant to buy them? Or do ye want me to waltz in and shoplift em? Though, to tell ye the truth, a night banged up in the cop shop might be preferable to the shelter or Fionnuala's settee."

Jed looked on the chair behind his wife.

"There's someone's purse," he said. And now his eyes glinted with a bit of mischief. "I'm sure the paracetamol will only cost a pound, one of those little packs of two. We don't we just...slip our hand in there and take out a pound coin?"

Ursula was scandalized.

"Jed!" she gasped. "So this is how quickly them what doesn't have money turns to a life of crime! Is that what ye're telling me we ought to do now? Now we're Bonnie and Clyde, are we?"

Jed was smiling. "Remember that movie? Warren Beatty and Faye Dunaway? They were sexy!"

Ursula struggled to hide the smile growing on her own face. She turned to face the handbag, then turned back to Jed, and now her eyes were dancing, though she still had a look of affront on her face, and a bit of shock.

"It's Fionnuala's bag," she said.

Jed raised his eyebrows.

"She certainly owes you. Us."

Ursula giggled.

"Och, Jed, I kyanny! Sure, it be's one of the ten commandments! Thou Shalt Not Steal! And me singing every Sunday in the choir, like."

"Yeah, but the Lord helps those..."

Their heads came closer as they shared a laugh. Ursula pressed her hand on Jed's arm.

"It does only be the one pound, for the love of God," she considered.

"I'll do it," Jed said, decided up.

"Naw!" Ursula said. She pushed him down. *"I'll* do it. I can always mail her one pound anonymously when we get that money put on wer cards. Stick a wee envelope through the letter box." She smiled at the thought. "She'll wonder about it for years! The one pound coin addressed to her! With a wee note, Ta For Relieving Me Headache."

Jed laughed. Ursula looked around furtively. The partying masses were paying them no mind. She and Jed had been forgotten on the edge of the dance floor.

"Go on, Bonnie," Jed said.

Ursula laughed. "Right ye are, Clyde."

She leaned over, the cross dangling from her neck, and reached the straps of the purse. She dragged it across the seat and sat it in her lap. She pulled across the zipper. Jed watched her. She slipped her hand inside. She rummaged around.

"Och, the light here be's terrible, so it is! I kyanny see a thing! I've to find her coin purse..."

Her fingers fiddled through the morass that was Fionnuala's handbag. Lipsticks, loo roll, a call-as-you-go-phone, Top Yer Trolly coupons, rosary beads, a clunky can of something...

Ursula shrieked and jerked her hand back.

"Dear God! What was that?"

Jed was taken aback.

"What do you mean?" he asked.

"It felt like...something human. In foil."

She peered into the dark interior, but couldn't see anything. She tugged out the can of Heavy Duty Yeuch-B-Gone and placed it on the table.

"Over cleaner?" Jed said. "What the heck?! Why would she carry...?"

Just as Ursula's fingers delved back in, as they were dreading what horrid thing they might uncover when they unwrapped the foil, if fingers could dread, "Auntie Ursula! Auntie Ursula! C'mon and dance with me, would ye?" the shadows of Siofra, Maureen and Lorcan darkened the table.

Ursula yelped, her hand frozen inside the bag.

"C'mere," Maureen said, "doesn't that be Fionnuala's handbag?"

"Aunt Ursula!" Lorcan barked with a drunken laugh. "Don't tell me yer *that* hard up?"

"N-naw," Ursula said, though she felt her cheeks burn as she looked up at them. "It's just that...that..."

She tugged out the thing wrapped in foil as Paddy staggered up.

"What's going on here?" he asked. "A reunion of some sort?" He sounded happy as he said it.

The foil crinkled in Ursula's fingers as she unwrapped it. Six heads bent down to inspect it. Ursula heaved a sigh of relief. It was only—

"A spud?" Paddy asked. "Where did ye unearth that from?"

"It's from Mammy's purse!" Siofra said.

"And this oven cleaner," Jed said, picking up the can. "Why would your wife...?"

"Och, sure, that's what Mammy does with the scran sometimes," Siofra said. "I was gonny do it to me wedding cake and all. Spray it all over, like. Granny wouldn't let me, but. I had a different tin. I think Mammy thinks it makes the food shiny. That must be why she does it."

Ursula was inspecting the potato.

"I was that heartscared at what it might be, and now it's only a regular spud. It seems, but, like it's been...treated in some manner."

All looked on, squeamish, as Ursula brought it up to her nose.

"Wile chemically, its smells."

She looked up at the faces around her as if they might have the answer. It was Maureen who gasped first. And gripped her cane tightly and plopped down on a chair, heaving and clutching at her chest as if the coronary were moments away.

"I *knew* it!" she said. "Lorcan, sit down, lad. I've something to tell ye! You and all, Paddy. And Siofra, as ye're here, ye may as well be party to it and all."

"What are ye on about, woman?" Paddy asked. But they all sat as instructed and pulled their chairs around Maureen.

"Ye know them mystery illnesses ye've been beset by, Lorcan?"

"Aye, Granny."

"Well, I think, naw, now I *know* them all be's down to yer mammy. Wer Siofra there saw yer mammy spraying something on yer ham hocks that one night of the godawful curry. And that's when all yer pains started."

"Oven cleaner, but!" Paddy roared. He grabbed the can and threw it on the ground. "Is the woman mental?"

Jed nodded. "Sounds like it to me," he said. He was the closest thing they had to an objective observer.

The drunkness was quickly seeping from Lorcan's eyes.

"The bitch! She didn't want me to leave!"

"What's going on?" Siofra asked wide-eyed. "I don't understand."

"Nor should ye," Ursula said, placing her hands over Siofra's ears. "Somethings is best for wanes not to hear." She turned to her brother. "Paddy, I think—"

But he was gone, lost in the tangle of arms and legs on the dance floor.

"*FIONNUALA?!*" they heard him roar over the third playing of "Mambo No. 5." "Where are ye, ye lunatic? Ye flimming fecking madwoman!"

Ursula zipped Fionnuala's handbag back up. Jed picked up the can. They placed the evidence on the table next to the pile of dirty plates.

CHAPTER 40

The TV was off for once. They were all jammed into the front room, Paddy, Maureen, Jed, Seamus, Padraig and Siofra. And the victim, Lorcan. Dymphna and Ursula were standing together. Ursula kept clutching her niece, as if she still doubted her flesh and bones were of this world.

Dymphna had burst into tears when she saw the tattered old jumper her aunt was wearing the day before (this had been when they were making their way up to the Amelia Earhart Center). "Why would ye wear that mingin aul jumper? I'm mortified, so am are, that I ever forced it upon ye!" "I'm wearing it," Ursula had said, "because ye made it with love. With the pure love of a twelve-year old wane." Padraig, flinging rocks behind them, had snorted.

And now there were tears again. From the accused. Fionnuala. Paddy had gone up to the bedroom where she was sleeping off her hangover from the reception the night before. He had dragged her from the mattress and, barely giving her time to fling on her tattered bathrobe, her bleached hair a shambles, her eyes swollen with drink and lack of sleep, the mascara from the night before circling her eyes, one false eyelash still clinging on, her mood anarchic, her barks croaks, he had forced her down the stairs. She had been made to sit on the bench of the bay window, been refused a cup of tea, and they were all in a semi-circle around her.

"Anyone woulda done it!" she implored them through her sobs. "Any mother with a heart! With the love for her son! To stop him ruining his life!"

Lorcan was given pride of place directly before her, his fists curled, his face taut with anger.

"No, Mam," he said. "They wouldn't."

"Do ye not realize, woman, what ye've done?" Paddy said.

"Attempted murder, Mammy! That's what it was!" Dymphna said.

A look of scorn passed Fionnuala's tear-and-mascara stained face.

"Och, catch yerself on, would ye? Daft bitch. As ye usually are. No need to be all dramatic! Attempted murder, me arse! Don't make me laugh! A wee bit of hairspray, was all I sprayed on them ham hocks. And in his porridge. And a few spritzes of furniture polish on his fish. Didn't do him much harm. He's standing there shooting daggers outta his eyes before me now, isn't he? The picture of health, so he is!"

"Ye were gonny poison him with oven cleaner!" Ursula said. "Have ye any clue what that wouldn't done to his insides?"

Fionnuala wrapped her arms around her and glared accusingly at Paddy. She had steadfastly refused to acknowledge Ursula and Jed's presence in the room since she had been hauled into it.

"Why is them Barnetts here? I kyanny stomach it, themmuns standing there with them smarmy looks on their faces the both of them, the minted cow and the flash bastard, *passing judgment* on me!"

"Yet another thing," Maureen said, "ye kyanny stomach. Sure, ye kyanny stomach much of anything, love."

"The list be's endless, so it is," Dymphna added.

Fionnuala snorted. "So ye say. I don't give a shite what ye say. Orange-loving slapper!"

Paddy broke in, "Jed and Ursula, me *sister,* if I might remind ye, they've been missing from this family, *their* family, far too long. And most of that be's down to you and yer spite. They've earned the right to be here, so they have. Just as the wee wanes have earned the right to be here for all the clatterings, the beatings, the slaps ye've dealt them since they was in their nappies."

"And it was Auntie Ursula," Siofra piped up, "what found the spud and the tin in yer handbag."

They all turned to her, and Siofra shrank against the china cabinet filled with bits and pieces of electronics and the Kenny Roger's The Gambler tea set. Perhaps this was one fact that shouldn't have been mentioned. Ursula inched her way behind Dymphna for safety. Jed placed a comforting hand on her shoulder. As happy as he was to be invited into the family, he knew he had to keep silent. He watched the proceedings with fascination.

"Who found it out doesn't matter," Maureen said.

"What matters, but," Lorcan said, fighting to keep his anger in check, "be's what ye tried to do. Ye say ye didn't use that oven cleaner on me. Ye clearly had plans to, but. Spiteful cunt!"

Fionnuala's face crumpled and the moan of a ravaged creature escaped her lips.

"Awwww!! Sure, the abuse from all the others I can stick. From ye, Lorcan, but, son, do ye not realize how a harsh word from yer mouth hurts me more than a thousand from any of the others?"

Padraig looked like he would have gladly smashed a brick into his mother's face if one had been available in that room.

"Ye're not right in the head," Lorcan fumed. "Ye're mental!"

"Deranged!" Maureen added for good measure.

"Naw, naw, naw!" Fionnuala sobbed into her lap. Seamus cried along with her and scurried away behind the ironing board leaning against the wall.

Paddy's voice rose above her tortured sobs, and he addressed her shuddering back.

"Ye know the laws of the land prohibit me from divorcing ye. Much as I'd love to. So, the way I see it—"

"The way *we* see it—" Dymphna corrected.

"We *all* see it," Lorcan confirmed.

"Is something drastic needs to be done," Paddy finished off.

"There's no talking sense to youse?" Fionnuala was wildly clutching at straws, flimsy, cheaply made straws from China that had been water-damaged in the shipping.

"Can ye not get it through yer thick deranged skull, Mammy?" Lorcan said. Fionnuala moaned at the insult. "That be's precisely the problem. There's no talking sense to *you!*"

Paddy cleared his throat with such an air of authority all turned to him. It was as if he were the judge about to pass down the verdict. "Ye've three choices, Fionnuala."

"Think of it, Mam," Lorcan said, "like that program with the briefcases on the telly ye love so much. There only be's three left, and ye can choose only one."

Paddy counted them out on his fingers. His voice rang with importance.

"One, we haul ye down to the Filth and get ye banged up by the coppers for the attempted murder of yer son."

"Filicide," Dymphna put in. "Rory looked it up on the Internet for me this morning."

Fionnuala once would've snorted. A Catholic family taking one of their own to the PSNI? Now, as she looked at their grim faces above her, however...

"Two, we turn ye in to Gransha for tests to be done to yer head. I'm sure they've a rubber room and a straight-jacket with yer name on it."

Fionnuala gasped. It was the mental hospital on the hill. They wouldn't! Would they...?

"Three...ye mind that caravan down in Culmore Ursula and Jed bought with the lottery winnings?"

"Ye mean that ramshackle dump in amongst nothing but flocks of sheep and the nearest pub miles away? The one with no electric and a toilet without a seat that doesn't flush properly?"

"Aye, that's the one. Ye move outta here and live there. All on yer lonesome. For the rest of yer days. Ye're dead to me. Dead to all of us. We don't want any more to do with the likes of ye. Them's yer choices."

The scorn refused to leave Fionnuala face, no matter how many tears fell from her eyes.

"Och, sure, ye kyanny be ser—"

"Enough!" Paddy roared with a force that made them all jump. A wail rose from Seamus behind the ironing board. "I've had, *we've* had years of hearing the contents of yer head. Yadda, yadda yadda..." He moved his thumb and his fingers as if his hand were a talking head. "No more blathering. Ye've done enough of it for one lifetime. To inflict as much damage as ye could."

Lorcan spoke up. "We can put it to a vote. Or ye can decide for yerself. Or, like that telly program, the one with the briefcases, we can write all three choices down, put em under tea mugs, and ye can let chance make the choice for ye. What's yer pleasure?"

"What about...what if..." Fionnuala appealed to them with eyes that tried to seduce them all, tried to make them conjure up all the happy times they had spent with her. She shouldn't have wasted her energy.

"Them's yer three choices." Paddy said.

"Which one are ye gonny chose?" Lorcan asked.

They heard a bird chirp beyond the filthy bay window, the groan of the house settling, the ticking of Jed's watch, the sniffles from the ironing board.

Fionnuala's lips moved, and they all bent in closer. But what she muttered they couldn't catch, even with nine pairs of ears struggling to hear.

"Speak up!" Lorcan yelled.

"Get the tea mugs out," Fionnuala said.

"Padraig, Siofra, get youse into the scullery for three mugs," Maureen said. She reached for the notebook and the pencil she had ready on the coffee table. "I'll write out the slips."

Fionnuala was moved to the settee before the coffee table. Maureen scribbled down COPPERS, MADHOUSE and CARAVAN.

Siofra skipped back in, Padraig behind her.

"I've two for ye to choose from," Siofra said. "I've me own One Direction mug, and then that one from the new pope ye bought off the telly the other month. That one has a wee crack in it, but."

The boy band members smiled out at Fionnuala from one, Francis waved at her from the other.

"I'll take the pope one," Fionnuala said.

Siofra looked disappointed.

Padraig sneered as he placed the other two before her, one with rows of daisies, the other that said World's Best Mum XXX, bought by Dymphna years ago in what her daughter must now think an act of madness.

"Turn yer head, love," Maureen said.

Fionnuala glared at her, but did as she said.

Ursula and Jed gripped each other, and Dymphna, as Maureen placed a slip of paper under each mug, then shuffled them on the coffee table. Lorcan was finally smiling, vindicated.

"Ye can look now, love," Maureen said.

Fionnuala turned around and looked down at the three mugs before her. Maureen turned to the others.

"Does anyone want to give em another wee shuffle? Lorcan? Paddy?"

"Naw," Lorcan said.

"I think," Paddy said, "Ursula can do it."

Ursula pointed at herself in shock. Her brother nodded kindly. Jed beamed behind her as she walked uncertainly towards the coffee table. Fionnuala's nostrils were enraged-bull like as Ursula moved the mugs around, then stood back.

All stared down at Fionnuala.

"Choose," Paddy said.

Fionnaula's hand hovered over the mugs. Her fingers were shaking.

"Can we not—"

"Make yer choice, Mam." Lorcan's voice was hard. It tore at her heart, seeing him look at her that way.

She offered up a fevered prayer to the Lord. And then she chose. She grabbed the Pope Francis mug and picked it up. They all leaned over, breathless, silent, and looked at the slip of paper underneath. There were murmurs and little nods. Fitting, each of them thought. Fionnuala's roars of

protest rang out, her legs kicking, her arms swinging.
"Naw! Naw!"
The mug clunked to the floor.

WHAT HAPPENED NEXT (AND HOW WE MIGHT SEE THEM LATER):

Paddy Flood: Paddy was made foreman of the Fillets-O-Joy packing plant until it closed down two months later. He then trained to become a security guard, and Zoe hired him to protect her storage units, Pence-A-Day. He is enjoying life without Fionnuala, and perhaps there is a new woman in his life.

Moira Flood: Moira met a Maltese woman, a sculptress of tin, while shopping in an outdoor market in Malta. They both reached for the same can of Kinnie, Malta's favorite soft drink, at the same time, had a torrid two year relationship, then finally decided to learn Catalan and move to Barcelona to tie the knot there (because Moira had been mistaken all those years, and Malta only allowed civil partnerships, not full blown gay marriages). Her partner, no, her *wife's* career exploded after an article in the Spanish version of Art In America, and Moira gave up writing to look after their two adopted children (one Ukrainian, the other Senegalese), though she does dabble in poetry about baby food and changing diapers occasionally .

Dymphna Riddell: Zoe allowed Dymphna to keep the wedding ring on her finger. She doesn't know exactly what she's going to do with her life, but at the moment she has her hands full with Keanu, Beeyonsay and, after a few months, her and Rory's new child. It was a boy. After agonizing over Willpat or Patwill, a mixture of the very Protestant name William and the very Catholic name Patrick,, she decided to call their son Greenornge (stress on the second syllable). She was relieved her new son had pale flesh and blue eyes and spoke perfect Hiberno-English. And she is pregnant again. This time, the doctor said, it's a girl. Perhaps she'll call her Greenorngetta. Watch this space.

Padraig Flood: Padraig was arrested for setting a chemist's on fire when he was fifteen, and he followed his two older brothers' footsteps to the Young Offenders Unit, but as we have seen from Eoin and Lorcan, that doesn't necessarily mean Padraig won't have a useless life. He is getting therapy on Tuesday afternoons and Thursday evenings, and there are also handicraft and computer skills classes, so perhaps this incarceration will be the making of him.

Seamus Flood: Seamus finally learned how to talk and made his mammy proud by deciding to became a priest. He will be attending theology school soon, and we'll see if he finally does go all the way. Finally! A priest in the Flood family, and a welcome addition after Fionnuala' second uncle the Bishop.

Lorcan Flood: Lorcan joined Eoin in Florida, and though his brother continued to work at the Irish pub for years, Lorcan saw more opportunity and even more money in becoming a gigolo to Miami's female millionaires. Many mother's days came and went before he ever sent Fionnuala a card.

Maureen Heggarty: The Heggarty matriarch lived on and on and on until her 102nd year; in fact, she's still living (that 102nd birthday hasn't arrived yet).

Rory Riddell: Rory graduated from university with his degree in whatever technical thing he was studying. He, Dymphna and their children moved into a new smart house on the Waterside, two blocks down away from Rory's mother, and Zoë bestowed on him an entry level position at Riddell Enterprises. Rest assured, he will be fast-tracked.

Zoë Riddell: The next year, thanks to the popularity of the wedding in all the Sunday newspaper supplement, Zoë won Derry Businesswoman of the Year. Not runner up. She has even more projects up her sleeve, and with the new Catholic in her family, twice as many people in Derry willing to do business with her (though she would call it Londonderry).

Bridie McFee: The Virgin Mary never appeared to Bridie again. If She had even appeared in the first place. But the experience had changed her. Her cold sores never came back, and she did cut back on chips and other fatty foods. A few years later, a slimmer Bridie got promoted to manager at Kebabalicious, and she met a handsome musician who was complaining about a foreign object in his Cow-A-Licious-On-A-Bun. Their first date is next week, and Bridie can't believe her good luck. She thanked the Blessed Virgin for it.

Mrs. Mulholland: Nothing much of interest happened to Mrs. Mulholland. Indeed, the demonstration on Dymphna's wedding day was the most exciting thing that ever happened to her.

Slim and Louella Barnett: Slim was finally released from hospital, and is now practically the same man he was when he went in, except for the twinge in his left knee when it rains, and the 100 pounds he shed. Louella finds the new Slim very sexy. She helps run the business, and has forgiven Ursula for causing the accident. But she still cheats when they all play cribbage together.

Jed Barnett: He and Ursula survived due diligence, because Jed could show Mitchell, Playboy, he really had joined Gambler's Anonymous. They received the $150,000, and, with Mitchell's contacts and marketing nous, and the rewriting of the jingle, sung by a popular female artist instead of Ursula, Slim Jed Jerky exploded across the mid-west, and is on track to conquer the east and west coasts as well. Profits increased 100% in the first three months, and the only way is up. Jed misses gambling, but his love for Ursula is greater.

Ursula Barnett: Inspector Scarrey keeps calling her and asking her to go to dinner with him, but she keeps telling him she's happily married. Since the trip to Derry for Dymphna's funeral, the part of her life that felt missing is now back. She is now no longer blocked from the Floods' Facebook accounts, and she spends many hours chatting with the members of her family she had been estranged from for far too long. She is happy.

Siofra Flood: We look far, far into the future for wee Siofra. The only child to totally escape from her mother's clutches, Siofra worked at the meat and cheese counter of the Top Yer Trolly until she graduated school, and then she worked there a few years longer. But she then won the green card lottery when she was 21. She moved, not to Florida, but to New York City, where she had a brief, successful career as a model, and she invested the money made doing that to start her own clothing company, showcasing her own designs. She attracted the eye of an entrepreneur who was a dead ringer for Playboy. She startled, then charming him with her accent, and wowed him with her style. They got married, and even after the birth of her twins, a boy and a girl, she continued to run the company to huge critical acclaim and profits the percentage of which Slim Jed Jerky could only dream of.

Fionnuala Flood: Dr. Chandrapore had startling news for Fionnuala: they had mixed her blood and urine samples with those of three other patients, and that was the reason for the peculiar test results. He was still uncertain as to what caused her fainting spells. Perhaps it was the stress of family life. Fionnuala is suing for malpractice. From the caravan in Culmore, the purgatory where she has nothing to do but wipe down surfaces, gaze out the mud-spattered window at the sheep and cows and cry herself to sleep at night. She called Paddy, Lorcan, her mother and Dymphna with the frequency of a stalker, and after three months of voicemail, all four numbers were mysteriously changed.

Randaleen Jagger: Randaleen went to rehab and is now a born-again Christian.

Best Served Frozen

BACKPACK
LITERATURE

BACKPACK

LITERATURE

An Introduction to Fiction, Poetry, Drama, and Writing

FIFTH EDITION

X. J. Kennedy

Dana Gioia
University of Southern California

PEARSON

Boston Columbus Hoboken Indianapolis New York San Francisco Amsterdam
Cape Town Dubai London Madrid Milan Munich Paris Montréal Toronto Delhi
Mexico City São Paulo Sydney Hong Kong Seoul Singapore Taipei Tokyo

Vice President and Editor in Chief: Joe Terry
Program Manager: Katharine Glynn
Senior Development Editor: Marion Castellucci
Field Marketing Manager: Joyce Nilsen
Executive Marketing Manager: Aimee Berger
Project Manager: Savoula Amanatidis
Project Coordination, Text Design, and Electronic Page Makeup: Cenveo® Publisher Services
Program Design Lead: Heather Scott
Cover Designer: Tamara Newnam
Cover Image: *Boulders 1935* by Alice Kent Stoddard (1884–1976), watercolor, David David Gallery,
    Philadelphia, Pennsylvania, USA. Credit: David David Gallery/SuperStock
Photo Research: QBS Learning
Senior Manufacturing Buyer: Roy L. Pickering, Jr.
Printer and Binder: R.R. Donnelley & Sons Company–Owensville
Cover Printer: Lehigh-Phoenix Color Corporation–Hagerstown

Credits and acknowledgments borrowed from other sources and reproduced, with permission, in this textbook appear on pages 1169–1178.

PEARSON, ALWAYS LEARNING, and MyWritingLab are exclusive trademarks in the United States and/or other countries, of Pearson Education, Inc., or its affiliates.

Unless otherwise indicated herein, any third-party trademarks that may appear in this work are the property of their respective owners and any references to third-party trademarks, logos, or other trade dress are for demonstrative or descriptive purposes only. Such references are not intended to imply any sponsorship, endorsement, authorization, or promotion of Pearson's products by the owners of such marks, or any relationship between the owner and Pearson Education, Inc., or its affiliates, authors, licensees, or distributors.

Library of Congress Cataloging-in-Publication Data
Backpack literature : an introduction to fiction, poetry, drama, and writing / [edited by]
X. J. Kennedy, Dana Gioia. -- Fifth edition.
    pages cm
Includes bibliographical references and index.
ISBN 978-0-321-96812-8
1. Literature--Collections. I. Kennedy, X. J., editor. II. Gioia, Dana, editor.
PN6014.B26 2015
808--dc23
                                    2015000020

1   16

www.pearsonhighered.com

Student Edition
ISBN-10: 0-13-458644-1; ISBN-13: 978-0-13-458644-1
Instructor's Resource Copy
ISBN-10: 0-32-196849-2; ISBN-13: 978-0-32-196849-4
A la Carte Edition
ISBN-10: 0-13-458249-7; ISBN-13: 978-0-13-458249-8

CONTENTS

2 POINT OF VIEW 28

3 CHARACTER 61

4   SETTING 101

7 SYMBOL 203

8 STORIES FOR FURTHER READING 246

POETRY 359

9   READING A POEM 363

10 LISTENING TO A VOICE 379

11 WORDS 402

12 SAYING AND SUGGESTING 421

14 FIGURES OF SPEECH 447

17 CLOSED FORM 493

20 MYTH AND NARRATIVE 539

21   WHAT IS POETRY? 558

22   POEMS FOR FURTHER READING 560

DRAMA

TALKING WITH *David Ives* 628

23   READING A PLAY 631

24   TRAGEDY AND COMEDY 654

25 THE THEATER OF SOPHOCLES 683

26 THE THEATER OF SHAKESPEARE 736

28 PLAYS FOR FURTHER READING 1001

WRITING 1087

29 WRITING ABOUT LITERATURE 1089

PREFACE

This is the fifth edition of *Backpack Literature*, a specially condensed version of *Literature: An Introduction to Fiction, Poetry, Drama, and Writing*. The primary aim of the book is to introduce college students to the appreciation and experience of literature in its major forms. The book also seeks to develop students' abilities to think critically and to communicate effectively through writing.

Both editors of this volume are writers. We believe that textbooks should not only be informative and accurate but also lively, accessible, and engaging. Our intent has always been to create a book that students will read with enjoyment and which will inspire them to take their own writing more seriously.

Backpack Literature offers selections and apparatus especially suited for instructors teaching a one-quarter or one-semester introductory class. It includes the core selections of our larger *Literature* books and much of the pedagogical material, particularly in the area of student writing. The book offers an alternative to the more extensive selections and critical coverage in the larger editions of *Literature*. Our purpose is to provide the introductory student a smaller, more portable, less expensive book.

Backpack Literature tries to help readers develop sensitivity to language, culture, and identity to lead them beyond the boundaries of their own selves and see the world through the eyes of others. This book is built on our conviction that great literature can enrich and enlarge the lives it touches. The edition's features are detailed below.

WHAT'S NEW IN THE FIFTH EDITION

- **New stories**—eight new stories, including Tobias Wolff's "Bullet in the Brain," Ha Jin's "Saboteur," Zora Neale Hurston's "Sweat," Eudora Welty's "Why I Live at the P.O.," Guy de Maupassant's "The Necklace," and Juan Rulfo's "Tell Them Not to Kill Me!," as well as new fables by Aesop and Bidpai.
- **New poems**—twenty-eight new poems appear in this edition, ranging from classic selections by Walt Whitman, Christina Rossetti, Claude McKay, William Butler Yeats, Robinson Jeffers, and William Shakespeare to fresh contemporary works by Kay Ryan, Donald Justice, Sherman Alexie, Tami Haaland, and Amy Uyematsu.
- **New plays**—five new plays or dramatic scenes provide greater flexibility in studying diverse contemporary trends in a crowded curriculum. The new works include David Ives's *Soap Opera*, Brighde Mullins's *Click*, David Henry Hwang's *The Sound of a Voice*, Milcha Sanchez-Scott's

The Cuban Swimmer, and a scene from Oscar Wilde's classic comedy *The Importance of Being Earnest*.

- **New argument coverage**—a section on using the rhetorical appeals of *logos*, *ethos*, and *pathos* helps students develop their literary arguments.
- **New writing assignments**—new writing ideas have been introduced in many chapters.
- **Updated coverage of the new 8th edition of the *MLA Handbook***—the Reference Guide for Citations has been expanded and updated to reflect the latest MLA guidelines.

KEY FEATURES OF *BACKPACK LITERATURE*

The new edition contains a wide and varied selection of works that both students and instructors have found appealing and accessible. These include:

- **Diverse and exciting stories—44 stories** from familiar classics to contemporary works from around the globe.
- **Great poems old and new—231 poems**, mixing traditional favorites with exciting contemporary work.
- **A rich array of drama—14 plays and scenes** from classical tragedy to Shakespeare to contemporary work by August Wilson.
- **Exclusive conversations between editor Dana Gioia and celebrated fiction writer Amy Tan, past U.S. Poet Laureate Kay Ryan, and contemporary playwright David Ives**—offer an insider's look into the importance of literature and reading in the lives of three modern masters.
- **Illustrated version of William Shakespeare's *Othello***—includes production photos of key scenes.
- **Audio version of Susan Glaspell's *Trifles***—specially created for this book.
- **Complete writing coverage** (detailed below).
- **"Terms for Review" feature at the end of every major chapter**—provides a simple study guide to go over key concepts and terms in each chapter.

COMPLETE WRITING COVERAGE

- **Writing coverage in every major chapter**—comprehensive introduction to composition and critical thinking, including easy-to-use checklists, exercises, and practical advice.
- **Topics for writing in every major chapter**—provide a rich source of ideas for writing papers.
- **Dedicated chapters on composition process and research process**—concise, step-by-step coverage of the writing and research processes, amply illustrated with student writing examples.
- **Reference Guide for MLA Citations**—handy "how to" guide for works-cited lists reflecting new eighth edition of the *MLA Handbook*.

- **Student writing**—7 papers by students with annotations, plus prewriting exercises and rough drafts, provide credible examples of how to write about literature. Includes
  - Argument Paper
  - Explication Papers
  - Analysis Papers
  - Comparison/Contrast Paper
  - Response Paper

TEXTS AND DATES

Every effort has been made to supply each selection in its most accurate text and (where necessary) in a lively, faithful translation. For the reader who wishes to know when a work was written, at the right of each title appears the date of its first publication in book form. If a work was composed much earlier than its first book publication, parentheses have been added around its date.

RESOURCES FOR STUDENTS AND INSTRUCTORS

For Students

The Literature Collection in *MyLiteratureLab*

The Literature Collection is an enhanced online-only literature anthology in *MyLiteratureLab*. *The Literature Collection* includes more than 700 selections as well as trusted pedagogy, valuable teaching and multimedia resources (including professional performances, biographies of key authors, contextual videos, and interactive student papers), and full access to the other resources of *MyLiteratureLab*. *The Literature Collection* will engage students with high-quality content and thoughtful insights on reading and writing about stories, poems, plays, and essays in a vibrant and flexible online environment.

MyLiteratureLab helps students to improve their results through a personalized learning experience with diagnostic tests, adaptive learning, and individualized feedback. If desired, instructors can administer writing assignments using rubrics of their choice, customizing the preloaded rubrics or creating their own. Students stay focused in the course by taking a macro-level pre-assessment that generates a Learning Path—a personalized module that enables students to better understand fiction, poetry, drama, and writing about literature.

All work is tracked in a powerful gradebook, which also enables instructors to create outcomes-based reports for administrators. These features offer support for student learning while also saving instructors' time—relieving some of the burden of "data crunching," and freeing up time for more meaningful student-centered activities.

Audio Production of *Trifles*

So many students today have limited experience attending live theater that we offer a complete audio version of our opening play, Susan Glaspell's *Trifles*, which we use to teach the elements of drama. The audio version was produced especially for this edition by the celebrated L.A. Theatre Works and is available in *MyLiteratureLab*. It includes an introduction and commentary by Dana Gioia.

Handbook of Literary Terms

Handbook of Literary Terms by X. J. Kennedy, Dana Gioia, and Mark Bauerlein is a user-friendly primer of more than 350 critical terms brought to life with literary examples, pronunciation guides, and scholarly yet accessible explanations. Aimed at undergraduates getting their first taste of serious literary study, the volume will help students engage with the humanities canon and become critical readers and writers ready to experience the insights and joys of great fiction, poetry, and drama.

For Instructors

Instructor's Manual

A separate instructor's manual is available to instructors. If you have never seen our *Instructor's Manual* before, don't prejudge it. We actually write much of the manual ourselves, and we work hard to make it as interesting, lively, and informed as the parent text. It offers commentary and teaching ideas for every selection in the book. It also contains additional commentary, debate, qualifications and information—including scores of classroom ideas—from more than 100 teachers and authors. As you will see, our *Instructor's Manual* is no ordinary supplement.

Penguin Discount Paperback Program

In cooperation with Penguin Group USA, Pearson is proud to offer a variety of Penguin paperbacks, such as Tennessee Williams's *A Streetcar Named Desire*, George Orwell's *Animal Farm*, and Charlotte Brontë's *Jane Eyre*, at a significant discount—almost sixty percent off the retail price—when packaged with any Pearson title. To review the list of titles available, visit the Pearson Penguin Group USA website at www.pearsonhighered.com/penguin.

The Longman Electronic Testbank for Literature

This electronic testbank features various objective questions on major works of fiction, short fiction, poetry, and drama. It's available as a download from the Instructor Resource Center located at www.pearsonhighered.com.

CONTACT US

For examination copies of any of these items, contact your Pearson learning consultant; order online through our catalog at http://www.pearsonhighered .com; or send an e-mail to exam.copies@pearsonhighered.com.

THANKS

The collaboration necessary to create this new edition goes far beyond the partnership of its two editors. *Literature: An Introduction to Fiction, Poetry, Drama, and Writing* has once again been revised, corrected, and shaped by wisdom and advice from instructors who actually put it to the test—and also from a number who, in teaching literature, preferred other textbooks to it, but who generously criticized this book anyway and made suggestions for it. (Some responded to the book in part, focusing their comments on the previous editions of *An Introduction to Poetry* and *An Introduction to Fiction*.) Deep thanks to the following individuals:

John Allen, Milwaukee Area Technical College

Susan Austin, Johnston Community College

David Budinger, Broward College

Hal Daniels, Broward College

Johanna Denzin, Columbia College

Denise Dube, Hill College

Justin Eatmon, Wake Technical Community College

Karen Feldman, Seminole State College of Florida

Steven Fischer, Harper College

Julie Gibson, Greenville Technical College

Sandra Havriluk, Gwinnett Technical College

Kevin Hayes, Essex County College

Sylvia Holladay, Hillsborough Community College

Jacqueline Jones, Francis Marion University

Mark Jordan, Odessa College

Tammy Kearn, Riverside City College

William Kelly, Bristol Community College

Damien Kortum, Laramie County Community College

Patricia Landy, Laramie County Community College

Helen Lewis, Western Iowa Tech Community College

Barbara McGregor, Tarleton State University

Trista Merrill, Finger Lakes Community College

Brett Mertins, Metropolitan Community College

Shawn Miller, Francis Marion University

Alan Mitnick, Passaic County Community College

Carrie Myers, Lehigh Carbon Community College

Jennifer Myskowski, Lehigh Carbon Community College

Diorah Nelson, Hillsborough Community College

Margaret Nelson Rodriguez, El Paso Community College – Valle Verde Campus

James Ortego II, Troy University–Dothan

Paige Paquette, Troy University

Carol Pearson, West Georgia Technical College, Carroll Campus

Sally Polito, Cape Cod Community College

John Prince, North Carolina Central University

Josh Simpson, Sullivan University

Matthew Snyder, Moreno Valley College

Chrishawn Speller, Seminole State College of Florida

Wes Spratlin, Motlow State Community College

Michelle Trim, University of New Haven

Leslie Umschweis, Broward College

Michelle Veenstra, Francis Marion University

Melanie Wagner, Lake-Sumter State College

On the publisher's staff, Joseph Terry, Katharine Glynn, Marion Castellucci, and Joyce Nilsen made many contributions to the development and revision of the new edition. Thanks to Joseph Croscup and Gina Cheselka for handling the very difficult responsibility of securing hundreds of reprint permissions. Cat Abelman supervised the expansion of photographs in the new edition. We are also grateful to Celeste Kmiotek who spent long hours working to update our permissions contracts and provided invaluable support for the new edition. Savoula Amanatidis and Lois Lombardo directed the complex job of managing the production of the book in all of its many versions from the manuscript to the final printed form. And lastly, we would like to thank our excellent copyeditor, Stephanie Magean.

For the new edition we have been immensely fortunate to have Dan Stone as an active partner of the editorial team. A graduate of Colorado College with an MFA from Boston University, Dan has an astonishing number of accomplishments for a young author and editor. For six years he worked at the National Endowment for the Arts, where he helped create Poetry Out Loud, the popular national high school poetry recitation contest. He also worked as part of the Big Read team, where he wrote, recorded, and produced nearly thirty radio shows and CDs on classic American authors. He is now founder and editor-in-chief of *Radio Silence*, a San Francisco–based magazine of literature and rock 'n' roll. He has published poetry and prose. Dan's editorial care and literary judgment have helped improve every chapter of the new edition.

Mary Gioia was involved in every stage of planning, editing, and execution. Not only could the book not have been done without her capable hand and careful eye, but her expert guidance made every chapter better.

Past debts that will never be repaid are outstanding to hundreds of instructors named in prefaces past and to Dorothy M. Kennedy.

X. J. K. AND D. G.

ABOUT THE AUTHORS

X. J. KENNEDY, after graduation from Seton Hall and Columbia, became a journalist second class in the Navy ("Actually, I was pretty eighth class"). His poems, some published in the *New Yorker*, were first collected in *Nude Descending a Staircase* (1961). Since then he has published seven more collections, including a volume of new and selected poems in 2007, several widely adopted literature and writing textbooks, and seventeen books for children, including two novels. He has taught at Michigan, North Carolina (Greensboro), California (Irvine), Wellesley, Tufts, and Leeds. Cited in *Bartlett's Familiar Quotations* and reprinted in some 200 anthologies, his verse has brought him a Guggenheim fellowship, a Lamont Award, a Los Angeles Times Book Prize, an award from the American Academy and Institute of Arts and Letters, an Aiken-Taylor prize, and the Award for Poetry for Children from the National Council of Teachers of English. He now lives in Lexington, Massachusetts, where he and his wife Dorothy have collaborated on five books and five children.

DANA GIOIA is a poet, critic, and teacher. Born in Los Angeles of Italian and Mexican ancestry, he attended Stanford and Harvard before taking a detour into business. ("Not many poets have a Stanford M.B.A., thank goodness!") After years of writing and reading late in the evenings after work, he quit a vice presidency to write and teach. He has published four collections of poetry, *Daily Horoscope* (1986), *The Gods of Winter* (1991), *Interrogations at Noon* (2001), which won the American Book Award, and *Pity the Beautiful* (2012); and three critical volumes, including *Can Poetry Matter?* (1992), an influential study of poetry's place in contemporary America. Gioia has taught at Johns Hopkins, Sarah Lawrence, Wesleyan (Connecticut), Mercer, and Colorado College. From 2003 to 2009 he served as the Chairman of the National Endowment for the Arts. At the NEA he created the largest literary programs in federal history, including Shakespeare in American Communities and Poetry Out Loud, the national high school poetry recitation contest. He also led the campaign to restore active literary reading by creating The Big Read, which helped reverse a quarter century of decline in U.S. reading. He is currently the Judge Widney Professor of Poetry and Public Culture at the University of Southern California.

(The surname Gioia is pronounced JOY-A. As some of you may have already guessed, *gioia* is the Italian word for "joy.")

BACKPACK
LITERATURE

Amy Tan in Chinatown, San Francisco, 1989.

FICTION

TALKING WITH *Amy Tan*

"Life Is Larger Than We Think"
Dana Gioia Interviews Amy Tan

Q: You were born in Oakland in a family where both parents had come from China. Were you raised bilingually?

AMY TAN: Until the age of five, my parents spoke to me in Chinese or a combination of Chinese and English, but they didn't force me to speak Mandarin. In retrospect, this was sad, because they believed that my chance of doing well in America hinged on my fluency in English. Later, as an adult, I wanted to learn Chinese. Now I make an effort when I am with my sisters, who don't speak English well.

Amy Tan with her mother.

Q: What books do you remember reading early in your childhood?

AMY TAN: I read every fairy tale I could lay my hands on at the public library. It was a wonderful world to escape to. I say "escape" deliberately, because I look back and I feel that my childhood was filled with a lot of tensions in the house, and I was able to go to another place. These stories were also filled with their own kinds of dangers and tensions, but they weren't mine. And they were usually solved in the end. This was something satisfying. You could go through these things and then suddenly, you would have some kind of ending. I think that every lonely kid loves to escape through stories. And what kids never thought that they were lonely at some point in their life?

Q: Your mother—to put it mildly—did not approve of your ambition to be a writer.

AMY TAN: My mother and father were immigrants and they were practical people. They wanted us to do well in the new country. They didn't want us to be starving artists. Going into the arts was considered a luxury—that was something you did if you were born to wealth. When my mother found out that I had switched from pre-med to English literature, she imagined that I would lead this life of poverty, that this was a dream that couldn't possibly lead to anything. I didn't know what it would lead to. It just occurred to me I could finally make a choice when I was in college. I didn't have to follow what my parents had set out for me from the age of six—to become a doctor.

Q: What did your mother think of *The Joy Luck Club*?

AMY TAN: Well, by the time I wrote *The Joy Luck Club*, she had changed her opinion. I was making a very good living as a business writer, enough to buy a house for her to live in. When you can do that for your parents they think you're doing fairly well. That was the goal, to become a doctor and be able to make enough money to take care of my mother in her old age. Because I was able to do that as a business writer, she thought it was great. When I decided to write fiction and I said I needed to interview her for stories from her past, she thought that was even better. Then when I got published, and it became a success, she said, "I always knew she was going to be a writer, because she had a wild imagination."

Q: *The Joy Luck Club* is a book of enormous importance, because it brought the complex history of Chinese immigration into the mainstream of American literature. Writing this book, did you have any sense that you were opening up a whole new territory?

AMY TAN: No, I had no idea this was going to be anything but weird stories about a weird family that was unique to us. To think that they would apply to other people who would find similarities to their own families or conflicts was beyond my imagination, and I have a very good imagination.

I wanted to write this book for very personal reasons. One of them, of course, was to learn the craft of writing. The other reason was to understand myself, to figure out who I was. A lot of writers use writing as a way of finding their own personal meaning. I wrote out of total chaos and personal history, which did not seem like something that would ever be used by other people as a way of understanding their lives.

Q: Did you have any literary models in writing your short stories or putting them together as a book? Or did you just do it on intuition?

AMY TAN: I look back, and there were unconscious models—fairy tales, the Bible, especially the cadence of the Bible. There was a book called *Little House in the Big Woods*, by Laura Ingalls Wilder. Wilder wrote this fictional story based on her life as a lonely little girl, moving from place to place. She lived 100 years ago, but that was my life.

The other major influence was my parents. My father wrote sermons and he read them aloud to me, as his test audience. They were not the kind of hell and brimstone sermons. They were stories about himself and his doubts, what he wanted and how he tried to do it.

Then, of course, there was my mother, who told stories as though they were happening right in front of her. She would remember what happened to her in life and act them out in front of me. That's oral storytelling at its best.

Q: Is there anything else that you'd like to say?

AMY TAN: I think reading is really important. It provided for me a refuge, especially during difficult times. It provided me with the notion that I could find an ending that was different from what was happening to me at the time. When you read about the lives of other people, people of different circumstances or similar circumstances, you are part of their lives for that moment. You inhabit their lives and you feel what they're feeling and that is compassion.

Life is larger than we think it is. Certain events can happen that we don't understand. We can take it as faith or as superstition, or as a fairy tale. The possibilities are wide open as to how we look at them.

It's a wonderful part of life to come to a situation and think that it can offer all kinds of possibilities and you get to choose them. I look at what's happened to me as a published writer, and sometimes I think it's a fairy tale.

H ere is a story, one of the shortest ever written and one of the most difficult to forget:

> A woman is sitting in her old, shuttered house. She knows that she is alone in the whole world; every other thing is dead.
>
> The doorbell rings.

In a brief space this small tale of terror, credited to Thomas Bailey Aldrich, makes itself memorable. It sets a promising scene—is this a haunted house?—introduces a character, and places her in a strange and intriguing situation. Although in reading a story that is over so quickly we don't come to know the character well, for a moment we enter her thoughts and begin to share her feelings. Then something amazing happens. The story leaves us to wonder: who or what rang that bell?

Like many richer, longer, more complicated stories, this one, in its few words, engages the imagination. Evidently, how much a story contains and suggests doesn't depend on its size. In the opening chapter of this book, we will look first at other brief stories—examples of three ancient kinds of fiction, a fable, a parable, and a tale—then at a contemporary short story. We will consider the elements of fiction one after another. By seeing a few short stories broken into their parts, you will come to a keener sense of how a story is put together. Not all stories are short, of course; later in the book, you will find a chapter on reading long stories and novels.

Here follows a wide variety of stories—with many traditional favorites along with some surprising contemporary selections. Among them, may you find at least a few you'll enjoy and care to remember.

1 READING A STORY

What You Will Learn in This Chapter

- To define *fiction*
- To identify the major types of short fiction
- To explain the elements of plot and key narrative techniques
- To identify the protagonist and antagonist in a literary work

After the shipwreck that marooned him on his desert island, Robinson Crusoe, in the novel by Daniel Defoe, stood gazing over the water where pieces of cargo from his ship were floating by. Along came "two shoes, not mates." It is the qualification *not mates* that makes the detail memorable. We could well believe that a thing so striking and odd must have been seen, and not invented. But in truth Defoe, like other masters of the art of fiction, had the power to make us believe his imaginings. Borne along by the art of the storyteller, we trust what we are told, even though the story may be sheer fantasy.

THE ART OF FICTION

Fiction (from the Latin *fictio*, "a shaping, a counterfeiting") is a name for stories not entirely factual, but at least partially shaped, made up, imagined. It is true that in some fiction, such as a historical novel, a writer draws on factual information in presenting scenes, events, and characters. But the factual information in a historical novel, unlike that in a history book, is of secondary importance.

Many firsthand accounts of the American Civil War were written by men who had fought in it, but few eyewitnesses give us so keen a sense of actual life on the battlefront as the author of *The Red Badge of Courage*, Stephen Crane, who was born after the war was over. In fiction, the "facts" may or may not be true, and a story is none the worse for their being entirely imaginary. We expect from fiction a sense of how people act, not an authentic chronicle of how, at some past time, a few people acted.

Human beings love stories. We put them everywhere—not only in books, films, and plays, but also in songs, news articles, cartoons, and video games. There seems to be a general human curiosity about how other lives, both real and imaginary, take shape and unfold. Some stories provide simple and predictable pleasures according to a conventional plan. Each episode of *CSI* or *The Simpsons*, for instance, follows a roughly similar structure, so that regular viewers feel comfortably engaged and entertained. But other stories may seek to challenge rather than comfort us, by finding new and exciting ways to tell a tale, or delving deeper into the mysteries of human nature, or both.

Literary Fiction

Literary fiction calls for close attention. Reading a short story by Ernest Hemingway instead of watching an episode of *Grey's Anatomy* is a little like playing chess rather than checkers. It isn't that Hemingway isn't entertaining. Great literature provides deep and genuine pleasures. But it also requires close attention and skilled engagement from the reader. We are not necessarily led on by the promise of thrills; we do not keep reading mainly to find out what happens next. Indeed, a literary story might even disclose in its opening lines everything that happened, and then spend the rest of its length revealing what that happening meant.

Reading literary fiction is not merely a passive activity, but it is one that demands both attention and insight-lending participation. In return, it offers rewards. In some works of literary fiction, such as Charlotte Perkins Gilman's "The Yellow Wallpaper" and Guy de Maupassant's "The Necklace," we see more deeply into the minds and hearts of the characters than we ever see into those of our families, our close friends, our lovers—or even ourselves.

TYPES OF SHORT FICTION

Modern literary fiction in English has been dominated by two forms: the novel and the short story. The two have many elements in common. Perhaps we will be able to define the short story more meaningfully—for it has traits more essential than just a particular length—if first, for comparison, we consider some related varieties of fiction: the fable, the parable, and the tale. Ancient forms whose origins date back to the time of word-of-mouth storytelling, the fable and the tale are relatively simple in structure; in them we can plainly see elements also found in the short story (and in the novel).

Fable

The **fable** is a brief, often humorous narrative told to illustrate a moral. The characters in a fable are often animals who represent specific human qualities. An ant, for example, may represent a hardworking type of person, or a lion nobility. But fables can also present human characters. To begin, here is a celebrated Sufi fable, which has been told and retold by many writers, most notably ninth-century Muslim writer Al-Fudhayl bin 'Iyyadh. (Samarra, by the way, is a city sixty miles from Baghdad.)

Sufi Legend

Death Has an Appointment in Samarra   c. 800

One day in Baghdad a man, a student of Sufi, was sitting in the corner of an inn when he happened to hear two people talking. From their conversation, the man realized that one of the figures was the Angel of Death.

"For the next few weeks," Death told his companion, "I'm gathering people in Baghdad." As he said this, Death looked over at the man in the corner.

Terrified, the man fled from the tavern and tried to plan some way to escape Death. He decided that the best course was to leave Baghdad at once and travel as far away as possible. He hired a fast horse and rode to the town of Samarra.

Meanwhile Death met the man's teacher, who was an old friend. As they talked about various acquaintances, Death asked the Sufi master about his student.

"Where is your disciple?" Death asked.

"He is here in Baghdad, busy with his studies," replied the teacher. "Why do you ask?"

"I was surprised to see him here," Death responded. "I have an appointment to take him next week, but it is over in Samarra."

Elements of Fable

That brief story seems practically all skin and bones; that is, it contains little decoration. For in a fable everything leads directly to the **moral**, or message, sometimes stated at the end (moral: "Haste makes waste"). In "Death Has an Appointment in Samarra" the moral isn't stated outright; it is merely implied. How would you state it in your own words?

You are probably acquainted with some of the fables credited to the Greek slave Aesop (about 620–560 B.C.), whose stories seem designed to teach lessons about human life. Such is the fable of "The Goose That Laid the Golden Eggs," in which the owner of this marvelous creature slaughters her to get at the great treasure that he thinks is inside her, but finds nothing (implied moral: "Be content with what you have"). Another is the fable of "The Tortoise and the Hare" (implied moral: "Slow, steady plodding wins the race"). The characters in a fable may be talking animals (as in many of Aesop's fables), inanimate objects, or people and supernatural beings (as in "Death Has an Appointment in Samarra"). Whoever they may be, these characters are merely sketched, not greatly developed. Evidently, it would not have helped the fable to make its point if it had portrayed the teacher, the student, and Death in fuller detail. A more elaborate description of the tavern would not have improved the story. Probably, such a description would strike us as unnecessary and distracting. By its very bareness and simplicity, a fable fixes itself—and its message—in memory.

Aesop

The North Wind and the Sun   6th century B.C.

Translated by V. S. Vernon Jones

Very little is known with certainty about the man called Aesop, but several accounts and many traditions survive from antiquity. According to the Greek historian Herodotus, Aesop was a slave on the island of Samos. He gained great fame from his fables, but he somehow met his death at the hands of the people of Delphi. According to one tradition, Aesop was an ugly and misshapen man who charmed and amused people with his stories. No one knows if Aesop himself wrote down any of his fables, but they circulated widely in ancient Greece and were praised by Plato, Aristotle, and many other authors. His short and witty tales with their incisive morals have remained constantly popular and influenced innumerable later writers.

A dispute arose between the North Wind and the Sun, each claiming that he was stronger than the other. At last they agreed to try their powers upon a traveler, to see which could soonest strip him of his cloak. The North Wind had the first try; and, gathering up all his force for the attack, he came whirling furiously down upon the man, and caught up his cloak as though he would wrest it from him by one single effort: but the harder he blew, the more closely the man wrapped it round himself. Then came the turn of the Sun. At first he beamed gently upon the traveler, who soon unclasped his cloak and walked on with it hanging loosely about his shoulders: then he shone forth in his full strength, and the man, before he had gone many steps, was glad to throw his cloak right off and complete his journey more lightly clad.

Moral: Persuasion is better than force.

Questions

1. Describe the different personalities of the North Wind and the Sun.
2. What was ineffective about the North Wind's method of attempting to strip the man of his cloak?
3. Why was the Sun successful in his attempts? What did he do differently than the North Wind?
4. What purpose does the human serve in this dispute?
5. Explain the closing moral in terms of the fable.

We are so accustomed to the phrase *Aesop's fables* that we might almost start to think the two words inseparable, but in fact there have been fabulists (creators or writers of fables) in virtually every culture throughout recorded history. Here is another fable from many centuries ago, this time from India.

Bidpai

The Tortoise and the Geese

c. 4th century

Retold in English by Maude Barrows Dutton

The Panchatantra (Pañca-tantra), a collection of beast fables from India, is attributed to its narrator, a sage named Bidpai, who is a legendary figure about whom almost nothing is known for certain. The Panchatantra, which means the "Five Chapters" in Sanskrit, is based on earlier oral folklore. The collection was composed sometime between 100 B.C. and 500 A.D. in a Sanskrit original now lost, and is primarily known through an Arabic version of the eighth century and a twelfth-century Hebrew translation, which is the source of most Western versions of the tales. Other translations spread the fables as far as central Europe, Asia, and Indonesia.

Like many collections of fables, the Panchatantra is a frame tale, with an introduction containing verse and aphorisms spoken by an eighty-year-old Brahmin teacher named Vishnusharman, who tells the stories over a period of six months for the edification of three foolish princes named Rich-Power, Fierce-Power, and Endless-Power. The stories are didactic, teaching niti, *the wise conduct of life, and* artha, *practical wisdom that stresses cleverness and self-reliance above more altruistic virtues.*

A Tortoise and two Geese lived together in a pond for many years. At last there came a drought and dried up the pond. Then the Geese said to one another, "We must seek a new home quickly, for we cannot live without water. Let us say farewell to the Tortoise and start at once."

Illustration for "The Tortoise and the Geese" by E. Boyd Smith (1908).

When the Tortoise heard that they were going, he trembled with fear, and besought them by their friendship not to desert him.

"Alas," the Geese replied, "there is no help for it. If we stay here, we shall all three die, and we cannot take you with us, for you cannot fly."

Still the Tortoise begged so hard not to be left behind that the Geese finally said, "Dear Friend, if you will promise not to speak a word on the journey, we will take you with us. But know beforehand, that if you open your mouth to say one single word, you will be in instant danger of losing your life."

"Have no fear," replied the Tortoise, "but that I will be silent until   5
you give me leave to speak again. I would rather never open my mouth again than be left to die alone here in the dried-up pond."

So the Geese brought a stout stick and bade the Tortoise grasp it firmly in the middle by his mouth. Then they took hold of either end and flew off with him. They had gone several miles in safety, when their course lay over a village. As the country people saw this curious sight of a Tortoise being carried by two Geese, they began to laugh and cry out, "Oh, did you ever see such a funny sight in all your life!" And they laughed loud and long.

The Tortoise grew more and more indignant. At last he could stand their jeering no longer. "You stupid . . ." he snapped, but before he could say more he had fallen to the ground and was dashed to pieces.

Questions

1. Under what condition do the Geese agree to transport the Tortoise?
2. What motivates the Tortoise to break his agreement?
3. How would you summarize the moral of the fable?

Parable

Another traditional form of storytelling is the **parable**. Like a fable, a parable is a brief narrative that delivers a moral, but unlike a fable, its plot is plausibly realistic, and the main characters are human rather than anthropomorphized animals or natural forces. The other key difference is that parables usually possess a more mysterious and suggestive tone. A fable customarily ends by explicitly stating its moral, but parables often present their morals implicitly, and their meanings can be open to several interpretations.

In the Western tradition, the literary conventions of the parable are largely based on the brief stories told by Jesus in his preaching. The forty-three parables recounted in the four Gospels reveal how frequently he used the form to teach. Jesus designed his parables to have two levels of meaning—a literal story that could immediately be understood by the crowds he addressed and a deeper meaning fully comprehended only by his disciples, an inner circle who understood the nature of his ministry. (You can see the richness of interpretations suggested by Jesus's parables by reading and analyzing "The Parable of the Prodigal Son" from St. Luke's Gospel, which appears in Chapter 6.) The parable was also widely used by Eastern philosophers. The Taoist sage Chuang Tzu often portrayed the principles of Tao—which he called the "Way of Nature"—in witty parables such as the following one, traditionally titled "Independence."

Chuang Tzu

Independence

Chou Dynasty (4th century B.C.)

Translated by Herbert Giles

Chuang Chou, usually known as Chuang Tzu (approximately 390–365 B.C.), was one of the great philosophers of the Chou period in China. He was born in the Sung feudal state and received an excellent education. Unlike most educated men, however, Chuang Tzu did not seek public office or political power. Influenced by Taoist philosophy, he believed that individuals should transcend their desire for success and wealth, as well as their fear of failure and poverty. True freedom, he maintained, came from escaping the distractions of worldly affairs. Chuang Tzu's writings have been particularly praised for their combination of humor and wisdom. His parables and stories are classics of Chinese literature.

Chuang Tzu was one day fishing, when the Prince of Ch'u sent two high officials to interview him, saying that his Highness would be glad of Chuang Tzu's assistance in the administration of his government. The latter quietly fished on, and without looking round, replied, "I have heard that in the State of Ch'u there is a sacred tortoise, which has been dead three thousand years, and which the prince keeps packed up in a box on the altar in his ancestral shrine. Now do you think that tortoise would rather be dead and have its remains thus honoured, or be alive and wagging its tail in the mud?" The two officials answered that no doubt it would rather be alive and wagging its tail in the mud; whereupon Chuang Tzu cried out "Begone! I too elect to remain wagging my tail in the mud."

Questions

1. What part of this story is the exposition? How many sentences does Chuang Tzu use to set up the dramatic situation?
2. Why does the protagonist change the subject and mention the sacred tortoise? Why doesn't he answer the request directly and immediately? Does it serve any purpose that Chuang Tzu makes the officials answer a question to which he knows the answer?
3. What does this story tell us about the protagonist Chuang Tzu's personality?

Tale

The name *tale* (from the Old English *talu*, "speech") is sometimes applied to any story, whether short or long, true or fictitious. *Tale* being a more evocative name than *story*, writers sometimes call their stories "tales" as if to imply something handed down from the past. But defined in a more limited sense, a **tale** is a story, usually short, that sets forth strange and wonderful events in more or less bare summary, without detailed character-drawing. "Tale" is pretty much synonymous with "yarn," for it implies a story in which the goal is revelation of the marvelous rather than revelation of character. In the English folktale "Jack and the Beanstalk," we take away a more vivid impression of the miraculous beanstalk and the giant who dwells at its top than of Jack's mind or personality. Because such venerable stories were told aloud before someone set them down in writing, the storytellers had to limit themselves to brief descriptions. Probably spoken around a fire or hearth, such a tale tends to be less complicated and less closely detailed than a story written for the printed page, whose reader can linger over it. Still, such tales *can* be complicated. It is not merely greater length that makes a short story different from a tale or a fable: one mark of a short story is a fully delineated character.

Types of Tales

Even modern tales favor supernatural or fantastic events: for instance, the **tall tale**, a variety of folk story that recounts the deeds of a superhero (such as the giant lumberjack Paul Bunyan) or of the storyteller. If the storyteller is describing his or her own imaginary experience, the bragging yarn is usually told with a straight face to listeners who take pleasure in scoffing at it. Although the **fairy tale**, set in a world of magic and enchantment, is sometimes the work of a modern author (notably Hans Christian Andersen), well-known examples are those German folktales that probably originated in the Middle Ages, collected by the Brothers Grimm. The label *fairy tale* is something of an English misnomer, for in the Grimm stories, though witches and goblins abound, fairies are a minority.

Jakob and Wilhelm Grimm

Godfather Death   1812 (from oral tradition)

Translated by Dana Gioia

Jakob Grimm (1785–1863) and Wilhelm Grimm (1786–1859), brothers and scholars, were born near Frankfurt am Main, Germany. For most of their lives they worked together—lived together, too, even when in 1825 Wilhelm married. In 1838, as librarians, they began toiling on their Deutsch Wörterbuch, or German dictionary, a vast project that was to outlive them by a century. (It was completed only in 1960.) In 1840 King Friedrich Wilhelm IV appointed both brothers to the Royal Academy of Sciences, and both taught at the University of Berlin for the rest of their days.

Jakob and Wilhelm Grimm

The name Grimm is best known to us for that splendid collection of ancient German folk stories we call Grimm's Fairy Tales— in German, Kinder- und Hausmärchen ("*Childhood and Household Tales,*"

1812–1815). This classic work spread German children's stories around the world. Many tales we hear early in life were collected by the Grimms: "Hansel and Gretel," "Snow White and the Seven Dwarfs," "Rapunzel," "Tom Thumb," "Little Red Riding Hood," "Rumpelstiltskin." Versions of some of these tales had been written down as early as the sixteenth century, but mainly the brothers relied on the memories of Hessian peasants who recited the stories aloud for them.

A poor man had twelve children and had to work day and night just to give them bread. Now when the thirteenth came into the world, he did not know what to do, so he ran out onto the main highway intending to ask the first one he met to be the child's godfather.

The first person he met was the good Lord God, who knew very well what was weighing on the man's heart. And He said to him, "Poor man, I am sorry for you. I will hold your child at the baptismal font. I will take care of him and fill his days with happiness."

The man asked, "Who are you?"

"I am the good Lord."

"Then I don't want you as godfather. You give to the rich and let the poor starve."   5

The man spoke thus because he did not know how wisely God portions out wealth and poverty. So he turned away from the Lord and went on.

Then the Devil came up to him and said, "What are you looking for? If you take me as your child's sponsor, I will give him gold heaped high and wide and all the joys of this world."

The man asked, "Who are you?"

"I am the Devil."

"Then I don't want you as godfather," said the man. "You trick men   10
and lead them astray."

He went on, and bone-thin Death strode up to him and said, "Choose me as godfather."

The man asked, "Who are you?"

"I am Death, who makes all men equal."

Then the man said, "You are the right one. You take the rich and the poor without distinction. You will be the godfather."

Death answered, "I will make your child rich and famous. Whoever   15
has me as a friend shall lack for nothing."

The man said, "The baptism is next Sunday. Be there on time."

Death appeared just as he had promised and stood there as a proper godfather.

When the boy had grown up, his godfather walked in one day and said to come along with him. Death led him out into the woods, showed him an herb, and said, "Now you are going to get your christening present. I am making you a famous doctor. When you are called to a patient, I will always appear to you. If I stand next to the sick person's head, you may speak boldly that you will make him healthy again. Give him some of this herb, and he will recover. But if you see me standing by the sick person's feet, then he is mine. You must say that nothing can be done and that no doctor in the world can save him. But beware of using the herb against my will, or it will turn out badly for you."

It was not long before the young man was the most famous doctor in the whole world. "He needs only to look at the sick person," everyone said, "and then he knows how things stand—whether the patient will get well again or whether he must die." People came from far and wide to bring their sick and gave him so much gold that he quickly became quite rich.

Now it soon happened that the king grew ill, and the doctor was summoned to say whether a recovery was possible. But when he came to the bed, Death was standing at the sick man's feet, and now no herb grown could save him.   20

"If I cheat Death this one time," thought the doctor, "he will be angry, but since I am his godson, he will turn a blind eye, so I will risk it." He took up the sick man and turned him around so that his head was now where Death stood. Then he gave the king some of the herb. The king recovered and grew healthy again.

But Death then came to the doctor with a dark and angry face and threatened him with his finger. "You have hoodwinked me this time," he said. "And I will forgive you once because you are my godson. But if you try such a thing again, it will be your neck, and I will take you away with me."

Not long after, the king's daughter fell into a serious illness. She was his only child, and he wept day and night until his eyes went blind. He let it be known that whoever saved her from death would become her husband and inherit the crown.

When the doctor came to the sick girl's bed, he saw Death standing at her feet. He should have remembered his godfather's warning, but the princess's great beauty and the happy prospect of becoming her husband so infatuated him that he flung all caution to the wind. He didn't notice that Death stared at him angrily or that he raised his hand and shook his bony fist. The doctor picked up the sick girl and turned her around to place her head where her feet had been. He gave her the herb, and right away her cheeks grew rosy and she stirred again with life.

When Death saw that he had been cheated out of his property a second time, he strode with long steps up to the doctor and said, "It is all over for you. Now it's your turn." Death seized him so firmly with his ice-cold hand that the doctor could not resist. He led him into an underground cavern. There the doctor saw thousands and thousands of candles burning in endless rows. Some were tall, others medium-sized, and others quite small. Every moment some went out and others lit up, so that the tiny flames seemed to jump to and fro in perpetual motion.   25

"Look," said Death, "these are the life lights of mankind. The tall ones belong to children, the middle-size ones to married people in the prime of life, and the short ones to the very old. But sometimes even children and young people have only a short candle."

"Show me my life light," said the doctor, assuming it would be very tall.

Death pointed to a small stub that seemed about to flicker out.

"Oh, dear godfather!" cried the terrified doctor. "Light a new candle for me. If you love me, do it, so that I may enjoy my life, become king, and marry the beautiful princess."

"That I cannot do," Death replied. "One candle must first go out   30 before a new one is lighted."

"Then put my old one on top of a new candle that will keep burning when the old one goes out," begged the doctor.

Death acted as if he were going to grant the wish and picked up a tall new candle. But because he wanted revenge, he deliberately fumbled in placing the new candle, and the stub toppled over and went out. The doctor immediately dropped to the ground and fell into the hands of Death.

PLOT

Like a fable, the Grimm brothers' tale seems stark in its lack of detail and in the swiftness of its telling. Compared with the fully portrayed characters of many modern stories, the characters of father, son, king, princess, and even Death himself seem hardly more than stick figures. It may have been that to draw ample characters would not have contributed to the storytellers' design; that, indeed, to have done so would have been inartistic. Yet "Godfather Death" is a compelling story. By what methods does it arouse and sustain our interest?

Elements of Plot

Plot sometimes refers simply to the events in a story. In this book, though, **plot** will mean the artistic arrangement of those events. From the opening sentence of "Godfather Death," we watch the unfolding of a **dramatic situation**: a person is involved in some **conflict**. First, this character is a poor man with children to feed, in conflict with the world; very soon, we find him in conflict with God and with the Devil besides. Drama in fiction occurs in any clash of wills, desires, or powers—whether it be a conflict of character against character, character against society, character against some natural force, or, as in "Godfather Death," character against some supernatural entity.

Like any shapely tale, "Godfather Death" has a beginning, a middle, and an end. In fact, it is unusual to find a story so clearly displaying the elements of structure that critics have found in many classic works of fiction and drama. The tale begins with an **exposition**: the opening portion that sets the scene (if any), introduces the main characters, tells us what happened before the story opened, and provides any other background information that we need in order to understand and care about the events to follow. In "Godfather Death," the exposition is brief—all in the opening paragraph. The middle section of the story begins with Death's giving the herb to the boy and his warning not to defy him. This moment introduces a new conflict (a **complication**), and by this time it is clear that the son and not the father is to be the central human character of the story.

Protagonist Versus Antagonist

Death's godson is the principal person who strives: the **protagonist** (a better term than **hero**, for it may apply equally well to a central character who is not especially brave or virtuous). The **suspense**, the pleasurable anxiety we feel that heightens our attention to the story, resides in our wondering how it will all turn out. Will the doctor triumph over Death? Even though we suspect, early in the story, that the doctor stands no chance against such a superhuman **antagonist**, we want to see for ourselves the outcome of his defiance.

Crisis and Climax

When the doctor defies his godfather for the first time—when he saves the king—we have a **crisis**, a moment of high tension. The tension is momentarily resolved when Death lets him off. Then an even greater crisis—the turning point in the action—occurs with the doctor's second defiance in restoring the princess to life. In the last section of the story, with the doctor in the underworld, events come to a **climax**, the moment of greatest tension at which the outcome is to be decided, when the terrified doctor begs for a new candle. Will Death grant him one? Will he live, become king, and marry the princess? The outcome or **conclusion**—also called the **resolution** or **dénouement** (French for "the untying of the knot")—quickly follows as Death allows the little candle to go out.

Narrative Techniques

The treatment of plot is one aspect of an author's artistry. Different arrangements of the same material are possible. A writer might decide to tell of the events in chronological order, beginning with the earliest; or he or she might open the story with the last event, then tell what led up to it. Sometimes a writer chooses to skip rapidly over the exposition and begin *in medias res* (Latin for "in the midst of things"), first presenting some exciting or significant moment, then filling in what happened earlier. This method is by no means a modern invention: Homer begins the *Odyssey* with his hero mysteriously late in returning from war and his son searching for him; John Milton's *Paradise Lost* opens with Satan already defeated in his revolt against God. A device useful to writers for filling in what happened earlier is the **flashback** (or **retrospect**), a scene relived in a character's memory. Alternatively, a storyteller can try to incite our anticipation by giving us some **foreshadowing** or indication of events to come. In "Godfather Death" the foreshadowings are apparent in Death's warnings ("But if you try such a thing again, it will be your neck").

THE SHORT STORY

The teller of tales relies heavily on the method of **summary**: terse, general narration. In a **short story**, a form more realistic than the tale and of modern origin, the writer usually presents the main events in greater fullness. Fine writers of short stories, although they may use summary at times (often to give some portion of a story less emphasis), are skilled in rendering a **scene**: a vivid or dramatic moment described in enough detail to create the illusion that the reader is practically there. Avoiding long summary, they try to *show* rather than simply to *tell*, as if following Mark Twain's advice to authors: "Don't say, 'The old lady screamed.' Bring her on and let her scream."

A short story is more than just a sequence of happenings. A finely wrought short story has the richness and conciseness of an excellent lyric poem. Spontaneous and natural as the finished story may seem, the writer has crafted it so artfully that there is meaning in even seemingly casual speeches and apparently trivial details. If we skim it hastily, skipping the descriptive passages, we miss significant parts.

Some literary short stories, unlike commercial fiction in which the main interest is in physical action or conflict, tell of an **epiphany**: some moment of insight, discovery, or revelation by which a character's life, or view of life, is greatly altered. The term, which means "showing forth" in Greek, was first used in Christian theology to signify the manifestation of God's presence in the world. This theological idea was adapted by James Joyce to refer to a heightened moment of secular revelation. (For such moments in fiction, see the stories in this book by Joyce, John Steinbeck, and Joyce Carol Oates.) Other short stories tell of a character initiated into experience or maturity: one such **story of initiation** is William Faulkner's "Barn Burning" (Chapter 5), in which a boy finds it necessary to defy his father and suddenly grows into manhood. Less obviously dramatic, perhaps, than "Godfather Death," such a story may be no less powerful.

The fable and the tale are ancient forms; the short story is of more recent origin. In the nineteenth century, writers of fiction were encouraged by a large, literate audience of middle-class readers who wanted to see their lives reflected in faithful mirrors. Skillfully representing ordinary life, many writers perfected the art of the short story: in Russia, Anton Chekhov, and in America, Nathaniel Hawthorne and Edgar Allan Poe (although the Americans seem less fond of everyday life than of dream and fantasy). It would be false to claim that, in passing from the fable and the tale to the short story, fiction has made triumphant progress; or to claim that, because short stories are modern, they are superior to fables and tales. Fable, tale, and short story are distinct forms, each achieving its own effects. Far from being extinct, fable and tale have enjoyed a resurgence in recent years. Jorge Luis Borges, Italo Calvino, and Gabriel García Márquez have all used fable and folktale to create memorable and very modern fiction. All forms of fiction are powerful in the right authorial hands.

Let's begin with a contemporary short story whose protagonist undergoes an initiation into maturity. To notice the difference between a short story and a tale, you may find it helpful to compare John Updike's "A & P" with "Godfather Death." Although Updike's short story is centuries distant from the Grimm tale in its method of telling and in its setting, you may be reminded of "Godfather Death" in the main character's dramatic situation. To defend a young woman, a young man has to defy his mentor—here, the boss of a supermarket. In so doing, he places himself in jeopardy. Updike has the protagonist tell his own story, amply and with humor. How does it differ from a tale?

John Updike

A & P   1961

John Updike (1932–2009) was born in Pennsylvania, received his B.A. from Harvard, and then went to Oxford to study drawing and fine art. In the mid-1950s he worked on the staff of the New Yorker, *at times doing errands for the aged James Thurber. Although he left the magazine to become a full-time writer, Updike continued to supply it with memorable stories, witty light verse, and searching reviews. A famously prolific writer, he published more than fifty books. Updike is best known as a hardworking, versatile, highly productive writer of fiction. For his*

John Updike

novel The Centaur *(1963) he received a National Book Award, and for* Rabbit Is Rich *(1982) a Pulitzer Prize and an American Book Award. The fourth and last Rabbit Angstrom novel,* Rabbit at Rest *(1990), won him a second Pulitzer. Updike is one of the few Americans ever to be awarded both the National Medal of Arts (1989) and the National Humanities Medal (2003)—the nation's highest honors in each respective field. His many other books include* The Witches of Eastwick *(1984), made into a successful film starring Jack Nicholson,* Terrorist *(2006), and his final novel,* The Widows of Eastwick *(2008).*

    Almost uniquely among contemporary American writers, Updike moved back and forth successfully among a variety of literary genres: light verse, serious poetry, drama, criticism, children's books, novels, and short stories. But it is perhaps in short fiction that he did his finest work. Some critics, such as Washington Post writer Jonathan Yardley, believe that: "It is in his short stories that we find Updike's most assured work, and no doubt it is upon the best of them that his reputation ultimately will rest."

In walks three girls in nothing but bathing suits. I'm in the third check-out slot, with my back to the door, so I don't see them until they're over by the bread. The one that caught my eye first was the one in the plaid green two-piece. She was a chunky kid, with a good tan and a sweet broad soft-looking can with those two crescents of white just under it, where the sun never seems to hit, at the top of the backs of her legs. I stood there with my hand on a box of HiHo crackers trying to remember if I rang it up or not. I ring it up again and the customer starts giving me hell. She's one of these cash-register-watchers, a witch about fifty with rouge on her cheekbones and no eyebrows, and I know it made her day to trip me up. She'd been watching cash registers for fifty years and probably never seen a mistake before.

By the time I got her feathers smoothed and her goodies into a bag— she gives me a little snort in passing, if she'd been born at the right time they would have burned her over in Salem—by the time I get her on her way the girls had circled around the bread and were coming back, without a pushcart, back my way along the counters, in the aisle between the check-outs and the Special bins. They didn't even have shoes on. There was this chunky one, with the two-piece—it was bright green and the seams on the bra were still sharp and her belly was still pretty pale so I guessed she just got it (the suit)—there was this one, with one of those chubby berry-faces, the lips all bunched together under her nose, this one, and a tall one, with black hair that hadn't quite frizzed right, and one of these sunburns right across under the eyes, and a chin that was too long—you know, the kind of girl other girls think is very "striking" and "attractive" but never quite makes it, as they very well know, which is why they like her so much—and then the third one, that wasn't quite so tall. She was the queen. She kind of led them, the other two peeking around and making their shoulders round. She didn't look around, not this queen, she just walked straight on slowly, on these long white prima-donna legs. She came down a little hard on her heels, as if she didn't walk in her bare feet that much, putting down her heels and then letting the weight move along to her toes as if she was testing the floor with every step, putting a little deliberate extra action into it. You never know for sure how girls' minds work (do you really think it's a mind in there or just a little buzz like a bee in a glass jar?) but you got the idea she had talked the other two into coming in here with her, and now she was showing them how to do it, walk slow and hold yourself straight.

She had on a kind of dirty-pink—beige maybe, I don't know—bath-ing suit with a little nubble all over it and, what got me, the straps were down. They were off her shoulders looped loose around the cool tops of her arms, and I guess as a result the suit had slipped a little on her, so all around the top of the cloth there was this shining rim. If it hadn't been there you wouldn't have known there could have been anything whiter than those shoulders. With the straps pushed off, there was nothing be-tween the top of the suit and the top of her head except just *her*, this clean bare plane of the top of her chest down from the shoulder bones like a dented sheet of metal tilted in the light. I mean, it was more than pretty.

She had sort of oaky hair that the sun and salt had bleached, done up in a bun that was unraveling, and a kind of prim face. Walking into the A & P with your straps down, I suppose it's the only kind of face you *can* have. She held her head so high her neck, coming up out of those white shoulders, looked kind of stretched, but I didn't mind. The longer her neck was, the more of her there was.

She must have felt in the corner of her eye me and over my shoulder   5 Stokesie in the second slot watching, but she didn't tip. Not this queen. She kept her eyes moving across the racks, and stopped, and turned so slow it made my stomach rub the inside of my apron, and buzzed to the other two, who kind of huddled against her for relief, and they all three of them went up the cat-and-dog-food-breakfast-cereal-macaroni-rice-raisins-seasonings-spreads-spaghetti-soft-drinks-crackers-and-cookies aisle. From the third slot I look straight up this aisle to the meat counter, and I watched them all the way. The fat one with the tan sort of fumbled with the cookies, but on second thought she put the packages back. The sheep pushing their carts down the aisle—the girls were walking against the usual traffic (not that we have one-way signs or anything)—were pretty hilarious. You could see them, when Queenie's white shoulders dawned on them, kind of jerk, or hop, or hiccup, but their eyes snapped back to their own baskets and on they pushed. I bet you could set off dynamite in an A & P and the people would by and large keep reaching and checking oatmeal off their lists and muttering "Let me see, there was a third thing, began with A, asparagus, no, ah, yes, applesauce!" or whatever it is they do mutter. But there was no doubt, this jiggled them. A few houseslaves in pin curlers even looked around after pushing their carts past to make sure what they had seen was correct.

You know, it's one thing to have a girl in a bathing suit down on the beach, where what with the glare nobody can look at each other much anyway, and another thing in the cool of the A & P, under the fluorescent lights, against all those stacked packages, with her feet padding along na-ked over our checkerboard green-and-cream rubber-tile floor.

"Oh Daddy," Stokesie said beside me. "I feel so faint."

"Darling," I said. "Hold me tight." Stokesie's married, with two babies chalked up on his fuselage already, but as far as I can tell that's the only difference. He's twenty-two, and I was nineteen this April.

"Is it done?" he asks, the responsible married man finding his voice. I forgot to say he thinks he's going to be manager some sunny day, maybe in 1990 when it's called the Great Alexandrov and Petrooshki Tea Com-pany or something.

What he meant was, our town is five miles from a beach, with a big   10
summer colony out on the Point, but we're right in the middle of town,
and the women generally put on a shirt or shorts or something before they
get out of the car into the street. And anyway these are usually women
with six children and varicose veins mapping their legs and nobody, including them, could care less. As I say, we're right in the middle of town,
and if you stand at our front doors you can see two banks and the Congre-
gational church and the newspaper store and three real-estate offices and
about twenty-seven old freeloaders tearing up Central Street because the
sewer broke again. It's not as if we're on the Cape; we're north of Boston
and there's people in this town haven't seen the ocean for twenty years.
The girls had reached the meat counter and were asking McMahon something. He pointed, they pointed, and they shuffled out of sight behind a
pyramid of Diet Delight peaches. All that was left for us to see was old
McMahon patting his mouth and looking after them sizing up their joints.
Poor kids, I began to feel sorry for them, they couldn't help it.

Now here comes the sad part of the story, at least my family says it's
sad but I don't think it's sad myself. The store's pretty empty, it being
Thursday afternoon, so there was nothing much to do except lean on
the register and wait for the girls to show up again. The whole store was
like a pinball machine and I didn't know which tunnel they'd come out
of. After a while they come around out of the far aisle, around the light
bulbs, records at discount of the Caribbean Six or Tony Martin Sings
or some such gunk you wonder they waste the wax on, six-packs of
candy bars, and plastic toys done up in cellophane that fall apart when
a kid looks at them anyway. Around they come, Queenie still leading
the way, and holding a little gray jar in her hand. Slots Three through
Seven are unmanned and I could see her wondering between Stokes and
me, but Stokesie with his usual luck draws an old party in baggy gray
pants who stumbles up with four giant cans of pineapple juice (what do
these bums *do* with all that pineapple juice? I've often asked myself) so
the girls come to me. Queenie puts down the jar and I take it into my
fingers icy cold. Kingfish Fancy Herring Snacks in Pure Sour Cream:
49¢. Now her hands are empty, not a ring or a bracelet, bare as God
made them, and I wonder where the money's coming from. Still with
that prim look she lifts a folded dollar bill out of the hollow at the center of her nubbled pink top. The jar went heavy in my hand. Really, I
thought that was so cute.

Then everybody's luck begins to run out. Lengel comes in from haggling with a truck full of cabbages on the lot and is about to scuttle into that
door marked MANAGER behind which he hides all day when the girls touch
his eye. Lengel's pretty dreary, teaches Sunday school and the rest, but he
doesn't miss that much. He comes over and says, "Girls, this isn't the beach."

Queenie blushes, though maybe it's just a brush of sunburn I was noticing for the first time, now that she was so close. "My mother asked me to pick up a jar of herring snacks." Her voice kind of startled me, the way voices do when you see the people first, coming out so flat and dumb yet kind of tony, too, the way it ticked over "pick up" and "snacks." All of a sudden I slid right down her voice into her living room. Her father and the other men were standing around in ice-cream coats and bow ties and the women were in sandals picking up herring snacks on toothpicks off a big plate and they were all holding drinks the color of water with olives and sprigs of mint in them. When my parents have somebody over they get lemonade and if it's a real racy affair Schlitz in tall glasses with "They'll Do It Every Time" cartoons stencilled on.

"That's all right," Lengel said. "But this isn't the beach." His repeating this struck me as funny, as if it had just occurred to him, and he had been thinking all these years the A & P was a great big dune and he was the head lifeguard. He didn't like my smiling—as I say he doesn't miss much—but he concentrates on giving the girls that sad Sunday-school-superintendent stare.

Queenie's blush is no sunburn now, and the plump one in plaid, that I liked better from the back—a really sweet can—pipes up, "We weren't doing any shopping. We just came in for the one thing."   15

"That makes no difference," Lengel tells her, and I could see from the way his eyes went that he hadn't noticed she was wearing a two-piece before. "We want you decently dressed when you come in here."

"We *are* decent," Queenie says suddenly, her lower lip pushing, getting sore now that she remembers her place, a place from which the crowd that runs the A & P must look pretty crummy. Fancy Herring Snacks flashed in her very blue eyes.

"Girls, I don't want to argue with you. After this come in here with your shoulders covered. It's our policy." He turns his back. That's policy for you. Policy is what the kingpins want. What the others want is juvenile delinquency.

All this while, the customers had been showing up with their carts but, you know, sheep, seeing a scene, they had all bunched up on Stokesie, who shook open a paper bag as gently as peeling a peach, not wanting to miss a word. I could feel in the silence everybody getting nervous, most of all Lengel, who asks me, "Sammy, have you rung up this purchase?"

I thought and said "No" but it wasn't about that I was thinking. I go   20 through the punches, 4, 9, GROC, TOT—it's more complicated than you think, and after you do it often enough, it begins to make a little song, that you hear words to, in my case "Hello (*bing*) there, you (*gung*) hap-py pee-pul (*splat*)!"—the *splat* being the drawer flying out. I uncrease the bill, tenderly as you may imagine, it just having come from between the two smoothest scoops of vanilla I had ever known were there, and pass a half and a penny into her narrow pink palm, and nestle the herrings in a bag and twist its neck and hand it over, all the time thinking.

The girls, and who'd blame them, are in a hurry to get out, so I say "I quit" to Lengel quick enough for them to hear, hoping they'll stop and watch me, their unsuspected hero. They keep right on going, into the electric eye; the door flies open and they flicker across the lot to their car, Queenie and Plaid and Big Tall Goony-Goony (not that as raw material she was so bad), leaving me with Lengel and a kink in his eyebrow.

"Did you say something, Sammy?"

"I said I quit."

"I thought you did."

"You didn't have to embarrass them."

"It was they who were embarrassing us."

I started to say something that came out "Fiddle-de-doo." It's a saying of my grandmother's, and I know she would have been pleased.

"I don't think you know what you're saying," Lengel said.

"I know you don't," I said. "But I do." I pull the bow at the back of my apron and start shrugging it off my shoulders. A couple customers that had been heading for my slot begin to knock against each other, like scared pigs in a chute.

Lengel sighs and begins to look very patient and old and gray. He's been a friend of my parents for years. "Sammy, you don't want to do this to your Mom and Dad," he tells me. It's true, I don't. But it seems to me that once you begin a gesture it's fatal not to go through with it. I fold the apron, "Sammy" stitched in red on the pocket, and put it on the counter, and drop the bow tie on top of it. The bow tie is theirs, if you've ever wondered. "You'll feel this for the rest of your life," Lengel says, and I know that's true, too, but remembering how he made that pretty girl blush makes me so scrunchy inside I punch the No Sale tab and the machine whirs "pee-pul" and the drawer splats out. One advantage to this scene taking place in summer, I can follow this up with a clean exit, there's no fumbling around getting your coat and galoshes, I just saunter into the electric eye in my white shirt that my mother ironed the night before, and the door heaves itself open, and outside the sunshine is skating around on the asphalt.

I look around for my girls, but they're gone, of course. There wasn't anybody but some young married screaming with her children about some candy they didn't get by the door of a powder-blue Falcon station wagon. Looking back in the big windows, over the bags of peat moss and aluminum lawn furniture stacked on the pavement, I could see Lengel in my place in the slot, checking the sheep through. His face was dark gray and his back stiff, as if he'd just had an injection of iron, and my stomach kind of fell as I felt how hard the world was going to be to me hereafter.

25

30

Questions

1. Notice how artfully Updike arranges details to set the story in a perfectly ordinary supermarket. What details stand out for you as particularly true to life? What does this close attention to detail contribute to the story?

2. How fully does Updike draw the character of Sammy? What traits (admirable or otherwise) does Sammy show? Is he any less a hero for wanting the girls to notice his heroism? To what extent is he more thoroughly and fully portrayed than the doctor in "Godfather Death"?

3. What part of the story seems to be the exposition? (See the definition of *exposition* in the discussion of plot earlier in the chapter.) Of what value to the story is the carefully detailed portrait of Queenie, the leader of the three girls?

4. Where in "A & P" does the dramatic conflict become apparent? What moment in the story brings the crisis? What is the climax of the story?

5. Why, exactly, does Sammy quit his job?

6. Does anything lead you to *expect* Sammy to make some gesture of sympathy for the three girls? What incident earlier in the story (before Sammy quits) seems a foreshadowing?

7. What do you understand from the conclusion of the story? What does Sammy mean when he acknowledges "how hard the world was going to be . . . hereafter"?

8. What comment does Updike—through Sammy—make on supermarket society?

■ WRITING *effectively*

THINKING ABOUT PLOT

A day without conflict is pleasant, but a story without conflict is boring. The plot of every short story, novel, or movie derives its energy from conflict. A character desperately wants something he or she can't have, or is frantic to avoid an unpleasant (or deadly) event. In most stories, conflict is established and tension builds, leading to a crisis and, finally, a resolution of some sort. When analyzing a story, be sure to remember these points:

- **Plotting isn't superficial.** Although plot might seem like the most obvious and superficial part of a story, it is an important expressive device. Plot combines with the other elements of fiction—imagery, style, and symbolism, for example—to create an emotional response in the reader: suspense, humor, sadness, excitement, terror.

- **Small events can have large consequences.** In most short stories, plot depends less on large external events than on small occurrences that set off large internal changes in the main character.

- **Action reveals character.** Good stories are a lot like life: the protagonist's true nature is usually revealed not just by what he or she says but also by what he or she does. Stories often show how the protagonist comes to a personal turning point, or how his or her character is tested or revealed by events.

- **Plot is about cause and effect.** Plot is more than simply a sequence of events ("First A happens, and then B, and then C . . ."). The actions, events, and situations described in most stories are related to each other by more than just accident ("First A happens, which causes B to happen, which makes C all the more surprising, or inevitable, or ironic . . .").

CHECKLIST: WRITING ABOUT PLOT

☐ What is the story's central conflict?

☐ Who is the protagonist? What does he or she want?

☐ What is at stake for the protagonist in the conflict?

☐ What stands in the way of the protagonist's easily achieving his or her goal?

☐ What are the main events that take place in the story? How does each event relate to the protagonist's struggle?

☐ Where do you find the story's climax, or crisis?

☐ How is the conflict resolved?

☐ Does the protagonist succeed in achieving his or her goals?

☐ What is the impact of success, failure, or a surprising outcome on the protagonist?

TOPICS FOR WRITING ON PLOT

1. Choose and read a story from this collection, and write a brief description of its plot and main characters. Then write at length about how the protagonist is changed or tested by the story's events. What do the main character's actions reveal about his or her personality? Some possible story choices are Updike's "A & P," Alice Walker's "Everyday Use," Joyce Carol Oates's "Where Are You Going, Where Have You Been?" and Guy de Maupassant's "The Necklace."

2. Briefly list the events described in "A & P." Now write several paragraphs about the ways in which the story adds up to more than the sum of its events. Why should the reader care about Sammy's thoughts and decisions?

3. How do Sammy's actions in "A & P" reveal his character? In what ways are his thoughts and actions at odds with each other?

4. Write a brief fable modeled on either "Death Has an Appointment in Samarra," "The North Wind and the Sun," or "The Tortoise and the Geese." Begin with a familiar proverb—"A penny saved is a penny earned" or "Too many cooks spoil the broth"—and invent a story to make the moral convincing.

5. With "Godfather Death" in mind, write a fairy tale set in the present, in a town or city much like your own. After you've completed your fairy tale, write a paragraph explaining what aspects of the fairy tale by the Brothers Grimm you hoped to capture in your story.

6. The Brothers Grimm collected and wrote down many of our best-known fairy tales—"Cinderella," "Snow White and the Seven Dwarfs," and "Little Red Riding Hood," for example. If you have strong childhood recollections of one of these stories—perhaps based on picture books or on the animated Disney versions—find and read the Brothers Grimm version. Are you surprised by the differences? Write a brief essay contrasting the original with your remembered version. What does the original offer that the adaptation does not?

▶ TERMS FOR *review*

Types of Short Fiction

Fable ▶ A brief, often humorous narrative told to illustrate a moral. The characters in fables are traditionally animals whose personality traits symbolize human traits.

Parable ▶ A brief, usually allegorical narrative that teaches a moral. In parables, unlike fables (where the moral is explicitly stated within the narrative), the moral themes are implicit and can often be interpreted in several ways.

Tale ▶ A short narrative without a complex plot. Tales are an ancient form of narrative found in folklore, and traditional tales often contain supernatural elements. A tale differs from a short story by its tendency toward lesser-developed characters and linear plotting.

Tall tale ▶ A humorous short narrative that provides a wildly exaggerated version of events. Originally an oral form, the tall tale usually assumes that its audience knows the narrator is distorting the events. The form is often associated with the American frontier.

Fairy tale, folktale ▶ A traditional form of short narrative folklore, originally transmitted orally, which features supernatural characters such as witches, giants, fairies, or animals with human personality traits. Fairy tales often feature a hero or heroine who strives to achieve some desirable fate—such as marrying royalty or finding great wealth.

Short story ▶ A prose narrative too brief to be published in a separate volume—as novellas and novels frequently are. The short story is usually a focused narrative that presents one or two characters involved in a single compelling action.

Initiation story ▶ (also called **coming-of-age story**) A narrative in which the main character, usually a child or adolescent, undergoes an important experience (or "rite of passage") that prepares him or her for adulthood.

Elements of Plot

Protagonist ▶ The main or central character in a narrative. The protagonist usually initiates the main action of the story, often in conflict with the antagonist.

Antagonist ▶ The most significant character or force that opposes the protagonist in a narrative. The antagonist may be another character, society itself, a force of nature, or even—in modern literature—conflicting impulses within the protagonist.

Exposition ▸ The opening portion of a narrative. In the exposition, the scene is set, the protagonist is introduced, and the author discloses any other background information necessary for the reader to understand the events that follow.

Conflict ▸ The central struggle between two or more forces in a story. Conflict generally occurs when some person or thing prevents the protagonist from achieving his or her goal. Conflict is the basic material out of which most plots are made.

Complication ▸ The introduction of a significant development in the central conflict between characters (or between a character and his or her situation). Complications may be external (an outside problem that the characters cannot avoid) or internal (a complication that originates in some important aspect of a character's values or personality).

Crisis ▸ The point in a narrative when the crucial action, decision, or realization must take place. From the Greek word *krisis*, meaning "decision."

Climax ▸ The moment of greatest intensity in a story, which almost inevitably occurs toward the end of the work. The climax often takes the form of a decisive confrontation between the protagonist and antagonist.

Conclusion ▸ In plotting, the logical end or outcome of a unified plot, shortly following the climax. Also called **resolution** or **dénouement** ("the untying of the knot"), as in resolving—or untying the knots created by—plot complications earlier in the narrative.

Narrative Techniques

Foreshadowing ▸ An indication of events to come in a narrative. The author may introduce specific words, images, or actions in order to suggest significant later events.

Flashback ▸ A scene relived in a character's memory. Flashbacks may be related by the narrator in a summary, or they may be experienced by the characters themselves. Flashbacks allow the author to include significant events that occurred before the opening of the story.

Epiphany ▸ A moment of profound insight or revelation by which a character's life is greatly altered.

In medias res ▸ A Latin phrase meaning "in the midst of things"; refers to the narrative device of beginning a story midway in the events it depicts (usually at an exciting or significant moment) before explaining the context or preceding actions.

2 POINT OF VIEW

In the opening lines of *The Adventures of Huckleberry Finn*, Mark Twain takes care to separate himself from the leading character, who is to tell his own story:

> You don't know about me, without you have read a book by the name
> of *The Adventures of Tom Sawyer*, but that ain't no matter. That book
> was made by Mr. Mark Twain, and he told the truth, mainly.

Twain wrote the novel, but the **narrator** or speaker is Huck Finn, a fictional character who supposedly tells the story. Obviously, in *Huckleberry Finn*, the narrator of the story is not the same person as the "real-life" author. In employing Huck as his narrator, Twain selects a special angle of vision: not his own, exactly, but that of a resourceful boy moving through the thick of events, with a mind at times shrewd, at other times innocent. Through Huck's eyes, Twain takes in certain scenes, actions, and characters and—as only Huck's angle of vision could have enabled Twain to do so well—records them memorably.

IDENTIFYING POINT OF VIEW

Narrators come in many forms. Because stories usually are told by someone, almost every story has some kind of narrator. Some theorists reserve the term *narrator* for a character who tells a story in the first person. We use it in a wider sense, to mean a recording consciousness that an author creates, who may or may not be a participant in the events of the story. Real persons can tell stories in a factual way, but when such a story is *written*, the result is usually *nonfiction*: a memoir, a travelogue, an autobiography.

To identify a story's **point of view**, describe the role the narrator plays in the events and any limits placed on his or her knowledge of the events. In a short story, it is usual for the writer to maintain one point of view from beginning to end, but there is nothing to stop him or her from introducing other points of view as well. In his long, panoramic novel *War and Peace*, encompassing the vast drama of Napoleon's invasion of Russia, Leo Tolstoy freely shifts the point of view in and out of the minds of many characters, among them Napoleon himself.

TYPES OF NARRATORS

Theoretically, a great many points of view are possible. One initial way to determine a story's point of view is to identify whether or not the narrator appears as a major or minor character, as a sideline observer, or as an unnamed nonparticipant.

Participant Narrator

When the narrator is cast as a **participant** in the events of the story, he or she is a dramatized character who writes in the first person, who says "I." Such a narrator may be the protagonist (Huck Finn) or may be an **observer**, a minor character standing a little to one side, watching a story unfold that mainly involves other characters. A famous example of a participant narrator occurs in F. Scott Fitzgerald's *The Great Gatsby*. The novel's narrator is not Jay Gatsby, but his neighbor and friend Nick Carraway, who knows only portions of Gatsby's mysterious life.

Nonparticipant Narrator

A narrator who remains a **nonparticipant** does not appear in the story as a character. Viewing the characters, perhaps seeing into the minds of one or more of them, such a narrator refers to them as "he," "she," or "they." In the tale of "Godfather Death," we have a narrator who is not a character in the story at all, someone who is not even named, who stands at a distance from the action while recording what the main characters say and do.

HOW MUCH DOES A NARRATOR KNOW?

The narrator of a story can possess different levels of knowledge about the characters' thoughts, feelings, and actions—from total omniscience to almost total ignorance. Those levels of knowledge can be categorized in the following ways.

All-knowing

The **all-knowing** (or **omniscient**) narrator sees into the minds of any or all of the characters, moving when necessary from one to another. This is the point of view in "Godfather Death," in which the narrator knows the feelings and motives of the father, of the doctor, and even of Death himself. Since he adds an occasional comment or opinion, this narrator may be said also to show **editorial omniscience** (as we can tell from his disapproving remark that the doctor "should have remembered" and his observation that the father did not understand "how wisely God shares out wealth and poverty"). A narrator who shows **impartial omniscience** presents the thoughts and actions of the characters but does not judge them or comment on them.

Limited Omniscience

When a nonparticipating narrator sees events through the eyes of a single character, whether a major character or a minor one, the resulting point of view is sometimes called **limited omniscience** or **selective omniscience**. The author, of course, selects which character's perspective to see from; the omniscience is his and not the narrator's. In William Faulkner's "Barn Burning" (Chapter 5), the narrator is almost entirely confined to knowing the thoughts and perceptions of a boy, the central character.

Objective

In the **objective point of view**, the narrator does not enter the mind of any character but describes events from the outside. Telling us what people say and how their faces look, he or she leaves us to infer their thoughts and feelings. So inconspicuous is the narrator that this point of view has been called "the fly on the wall." Some critics would say that in the objective point of view, the narrator disappears altogether.

Consider this passage by a writer famous for remaining objective, Dashiell Hammett, from his crime novel *The Maltese Falcon*, describing his private detective Sam Spade:

> Spade's thick fingers made a cigarette with deliberate care, sifting a measured quantity of tan flakes down into curved paper, spreading the flakes so that they lay equal at the ends with a slight depression in the middle, thumbs rolling the paper's inner edge down and up under the outer edge as forefingers pressed it over, thumb and fingers sliding to the paper cylinder's ends to hold it even while tongue licked the flap, left forefinger and thumb pinching their ends while right forefinger and thumb smoothed the damp seam, right forefinger and thumb twisting their end and lifting the other to Spade's mouth.

In Hammett's novel, this sentence comes at a moment of crisis: just after Spade has been roused from bed in the middle of the night by a phone call telling him that his partner has been murdered. Even in times of stress (we infer) Spade is deliberate, cool, efficient, and painstaking. Hammett refrains from applying all those adjectives to Spade; to do so would be to exercise editorial omniscience and to destroy the objective point of view.

Other Narrative Points of View

Besides the common points of view just listed, uncommon points of view are possible. In Jack London's adventure novel *The Call of the Wild*, the story is told from the perspective of its protagonist, a dog.

Also possible, but unusual, is a story written in the second person, "you." This point of view results in a startling directness, as in Jay McInerney's novel *Bright Lights, Big City* (1985), which begins:

You are not the kind of guy who would be at a place like this at this time of the morning. But here you are, and you cannot say that the terrain is entirely unfamiliar, although the details are fuzzy. You are at a nightclub talking to a girl with a shaved head.

The attitudes and opinions of a narrator aren't necessarily those of the author; in fact, we may notice a lively conflict between what we are told and what, apparently, we are meant to believe. A story may be told by an **innocent narrator** or a **naive narrator**, a character who fails to understand all the implications of the story. One such innocent narrator (despite his sometimes shrewd perceptions) is Huckleberry Finn. Because Huck accepts without question the morality and lawfulness of slavery, he feels guilty about helping Jim, a runaway slave. But, far from condemning Huck for his defiance of the law—"All right, then, I'll *go* to hell," Huck tells himself, deciding against returning Jim to captivity—the author, and the reader along with him, silently applaud.

In a story told by an **unreliable narrator**, the point of view is that of a person who, we perceive, is deceptive, self-deceptive, deluded, or deranged. As though seeking ways to be faithful to uncertainty, contemporary writers have been particularly fond of unreliable narrators.

STREAM OF CONSCIOUSNESS

Virginia Woolf compared life to "a luminous halo, a semi-transparent envelope surrounding us from the beginning of consciousness to the end." To capture such a reality, modern writers of fiction have employed many strategies. One is the method of writing called **stream of consciousness**, from a phrase coined by psychologist William James to describe the procession of thoughts passing through the mind. In fiction, the stream of consciousness is a kind of selective omniscience: the presentation of thoughts and sense impressions in a lifelike fashion—not in a sequence arranged by logic, but mingled randomly. When in his novel *Ulysses* James Joyce takes us into the mind of Leopold Bloom, an ordinary Dublin mind well-stocked with trivia and fragments of odd learning, the reader may have an impression not of a smoothly flowing stream but of an ocean of miscellaneous things, all crowded and jostling.

> As he set foot on O'Connell bridge a puffball of smoke plumed up from the parapet. Brewery barge with export stout. England. Sea air sours it, I heard. Be interesting some day to get a pass through Hancock to see the brewery. Regular world in itself. Vats of porter, wonderful. Rats get in too. Drink themselves bloated as big as a collie floating.

Stream-of-consciousness writing usually occurs in relatively short passages, but in *Ulysses* Joyce employs it extensively. Similar in method, an **interior monologue** is an extended presentation of a character's thoughts, not in the seemingly helter-skelter order of a stream of consciousness, but in an arrangement as if the character were speaking out loud to himself, for us to overhear.

Every point of view has limitations. Even **total omniscience**, a knowledge of the minds of all the characters, has its disadvantages. Such a point of view requires high skill to manage, without the storyteller's losing his or her way in a multitude of perspectives. In fact, there are evident advantages in having a narrator not know everything. We are accustomed to seeing the world through one pair of eyes, to having truths gradually occur to us. Henry James, whose theory and practice of fiction have been influential, held that an excellent way to tell a story was through the fine but bewildered mind of an observer. "It seems probable," James wrote, "that if we were never bewildered there would never be a story to tell about us; we should partake of the superior nature of the all-knowing immortals whose annals are dreadfully dull so long as flurried humans are not, for the positive relief of bored Olympians, mixed up with them."

By using a particular point of view, an author may artfully withhold information, if need be, rather than immediately present it to us. If, for instance, the suspense in a story depends on our not knowing until the end that the protagonist is a spy, the author would be ill advised to tell the story from the protagonist's point of view. Clearly, the author makes a fundamental decision in selecting, from many possibilities, a story's point of view.

Here is a short story memorable for many reasons, among them its point of view.

William Faulkner

A Rose for Emily   1931

William Faulkner (1897–1962) spent most of his days in Oxford, Mississippi, where he attended the University of Mississippi and where he served as postmaster until angry townspeople ejected him because they had failed to receive mail. During World War I he served with the Royal Canadian Air Force and afterward worked as a feature writer for the New Orleans Times-Picayune. Faulkner's private life was a long struggle to stay solvent: even after fame came to him, he had to write Hollywood scripts and teach at the University of Virginia to support himself. His vio-

William Faulkner

lent comic novel Sanctuary *(1931) caused a stir and turned a profit, but critics tend most to admire* The Sound and the Fury *(1929), a tale partially told through the eyes of an idiot;* As I Lay Dying *(1930);* Light in August *(1932);* Absalom, Absalom *(1936); and* The Hamlet *(1940). Beginning with* Sartoris *(1929), Faulkner in his fiction imagines a Mississippi county named Yoknapatawpha and traces the fortunes of several of its families, including the aristocratic Compsons and Sartorises and the white-trash, dollar-grabbing*

Snopeses, from the Civil War to modern times. His influence on his fellow Southern writers (and others) has been profound. In 1950 he received the Nobel Prize in Literature. Although we think of Faulkner primarily as a novelist, he wrote nearly a hundred short stories. Forty-two of the best are available in his Collected Stories *(1950; 1995).*

I

When Miss Emily Grierson died, our whole town went to her funeral: the men through a sort of respectful affection for a fallen monument, the women mostly out of curiosity to see the inside of her house, which no one save an old manservant—a combined gardener and cook—had seen in at least ten years.

It was a big, squarish frame house that had once been white, decorated with cupolas and spires and scrolled balconies in the heavily lightsome style of the seventies, set on what had once been our most select street. But garages and cotton gins had encroached and obliterated even the august names of that neighborhood; only Miss Emily's house was left, lifting its stubborn and coquettish decay above the cotton wagons and the gasoline pumps—an eyesore among eyesores. And now Miss Emily had gone to join the representatives of those august names where they lay in the cedar-bemused cemetery among the ranked and anonymous graves of Union and Confederate soldiers who fell at the battle of Jefferson.

Alive, Miss Emily had been a tradition, a duty, and a care; a sort of hereditary obligation upon the town, dating from that day in 1894 when Colonel Sartoris, the mayor—he who fathered the edict that no Negro woman should appear on the streets without an apron—remitted her taxes, the dispensation dating from the death of her father on into perpetuity. Not that Miss Emily would have accepted charity. Colonel Sartoris invented an involved tale to the effect that Miss Emily's father had loaned money to the town, which the town, as a matter of business, preferred this way of repaying. Only a man of Colonel Sartoris' generation and thought could have invented it, and only a woman could have believed it.

When the next generation, with its more modern ideas, became mayors and aldermen, this arrangement created some little dissatisfaction. On the first of the year they mailed her a tax notice. February came, and there was no reply. They wrote her a formal letter, asking her to call at the sheriff's office at her convenience. A week later the mayor wrote her himself, offering to call or to send his car for her, and received in reply a note on paper of an archaic shape, in a thin, flowing calligraphy in faded ink, to the effect that she no longer went out at all. The tax notice was also enclosed, without comment.

They called a special meeting of the Board of Aldermen. A deputation waited upon her, knocked at the door through which no visitor had passed since she ceased giving china-painting lessons eight or ten years

5

earlier. They were admitted by the old Negro into a dim hall from which a stairway mounted into still more shadow. It smelled of dust and disuse—a close, dank smell. The Negro led them into the parlor. It was furnished in heavy, leather-covered furniture. When the Negro opened the blinds of one window, they could see that the leather was cracked; and when they sat down, a faint dust rose sluggishly about their thighs, spinning with slow motes in the single sun-ray. On a tarnished gilt easel before the fireplace stood a crayon portrait of Miss Emily's father.

They rose when she entered—a small, fat woman in black, with a thin gold chain descending to her waist and vanishing into her belt, leaning on an ebony cane with a tarnished gold head. Her skeleton was small and spare; perhaps that was why what would have been merely plumpness in another was obesity in her. She looked bloated, like a body long submerged in motionless water, and of that pallid hue. Her eyes, lost in the fatty ridges of her face, looked like two small pieces of coal pressed into a lump of dough as they moved from one face to another while the visitors stated their errand.

She did not ask them to sit. She just stood in the door and listened quietly until the spokesman came to a stumbling halt. Then they could hear the invisible watch ticking at the end of the gold chain.

Her voice was dry and cold. "I have no taxes in Jefferson. Colonel Sartoris explained it to me. Perhaps one of you can gain access to the city records and satisfy yourselves."

"But we have. We are the city authorities, Miss Emily. Didn't you get a notice from the sheriff, signed by him?"

"I received a paper, yes," Miss Emily said. "Perhaps he considers himself the sheriff . . . I have no taxes in Jefferson."   10

"But there is nothing on the books to show that, you see. We must go by the—"

"See Colonel Sartoris. I have no taxes in Jefferson."

"But, Miss Emily—"

"See Colonel Sartoris." (Colonel Sartoris had been dead almost ten years.) "I have no taxes in Jefferson. Tobe!" The Negro appeared. "Show these gentlemen out."

II

So she vanquished them, horse and foot, just as she had vanquished   15 their fathers thirty years before about the smell. That was two years after her father's death and a short time after her sweetheart—the one we believed would marry her—had deserted her. After her father's death she went out very little; after her sweetheart went away, people hardly saw her at all. A few of the ladies had the temerity to call, but were not received, and the only sign of life about the place was the Negro man—a young man then—going in and out with a market basket.

"Just as if a man—any man—could keep a kitchen properly," the ladies said; so they were not surprised when the smell developed. It was another link between the gross, teeming world and the high and mighty Griersons.

A neighbor, a woman, complained to the mayor, Judge Stevens, eighty years old.

"But what will you have me do about it, madam?" he said.

"Why, send her word to stop it," the woman said. "Isn't there a law?"

"I'm sure that won't be necessary," Judge Stevens said. "It's probably just a snake or a rat that nigger of hers killed in the yard. I'll speak to him about it."   20

The next day he received two more complaints, one from a man who came in diffident deprecation. "We really must do something about it, Judge. I'd be the last one in the world to bother Miss Emily, but we've got to do something." That night the Board of Aldermen met—three graybeards and one younger man, a member of the rising generation.

"It's simple enough," he said. "Send her word to have her place cleaned up. Give her a certain time to do it in, and if she don't . . ."

"Dammit, sir," Judge Stevens said, "will you accuse a lady to her face of smelling bad?"

So the next night, after midnight, four men crossed Miss Emily's lawn and slunk about the house like burglars, sniffing along the base of the brickwork and at the cellar openings while one of them performed a regular sowing motion with his hand out of a sack slung from his shoulder. They broke open the cellar door and sprinkled lime there, and in all the outbuildings. As they recrossed the lawn, a window that had been dark was lighted and Miss Emily sat in it, the light behind her, and her upright torso motionless as that of an idol. They crept quietly across the lawn and into the shadow of the locusts that lined the street. After a week or two the smell went away.

That was when people had begun to feel really sorry for her. People in our town, remembering how old lady Wyatt, her great-aunt, had gone completely crazy at last, believed that the Griersons held themselves a little too high for what they really were. None of the young men were quite good enough for Miss Emily and such. We had long thought of them as a tableau, Miss Emily a slender figure in white in the background, her father a spraddled silhouette in the foreground, his back to her and clutching a horsewhip, the two of them framed by the back-flung front door. So when she got to be thirty and was still single, we were not pleased exactly, but vindicated; even with insanity in the family she wouldn't have turned down all of her chances if they had really materialized.   25

When her father died, it got about that the house was all that was left to her; and in a way, people were glad. At last they could pity Miss Emily. Being left alone, and a pauper, she had become humanized. Now she too would know the old thrill and the old despair of a penny more or less.

The day after his death all the ladies prepared to call at the house and offer condolence and aid, as is our custom. Miss Emily met them at the door, dressed as usual and with no trace of grief on her face. She told them that her father was not dead. She did that for three days, with the ministers calling on her, and the doctors, trying to persuade her to let them dispose of the body. Just as they were about to resort to law and force, she broke down, and they buried her father quickly.

We did not say she was crazy then. We believed she had to do that. We remembered all the young men her father had driven away, and we knew that with nothing left, she would have to cling to that which had robbed her, as people will.

III

She was sick for a long time. When we saw her again, her hair was cut short, making her look like a girl, with a vague resemblance to those angels in colored church windows—sort of tragic and serene.

The town had just let the contracts for paving the sidewalks, and in the summer after her father's death they began the work. The construction company came with niggers and mules and machinery, and a foreman named Homer Barron, a Yankee—a big, dark, ready man, with a big voice and eyes lighter than his face. The little boys would follow in groups to hear him cuss the niggers, and the niggers singing in time to the rise and fall of picks. Pretty soon he knew everybody in town. Whenever you heard a lot of laughing anywhere about the square, Homer Barron would be in the center of the group. Presently we began to see him and Miss Emily on Sunday afternoons driving in the yellow-wheeled buggy and the matched team of bays from the livery stable.

At first we were glad that Miss Emily would have an interest, because the ladies all said, "Of course a Grierson would not think seriously of a Northerner, a day laborer." But there were still others, older people, who said that even grief could not cause a real lady to forget *noblesse oblige*°— without calling it *noblesse oblige*. They just said, "Poor Emily. Her kinsfolk should come to her." She had some kin in Alabama; but years ago her father had fallen out with them over the estate of old lady Wyatt, the crazy woman, and there was no communication between the two families. They had not even been represented at the funeral.

And as soon as the old people said, "Poor Emily," the whispering began. "Do you suppose it's really so?" they said to one another. "Of course it is. What else could . . ." This behind their hands; rustling of craned silk and satin behind jalousies closed upon the sun of Sunday afternoon as the thin, swift clop-clop-clop of the matched team passed: "Poor Emily."

She carried her head high enough—even when we believed that she was fallen. It was as if she demanded more than ever the recognition of

noblesse oblige: the obligation of a member of the nobility to behave with honor and dignity.

her dignity as the last Grierson; as if it had wanted that touch of earthiness to reaffirm her imperviousness. Like when she bought the rat poison, the arsenic. That was over a year after they had begun to say "Poor Emily," and while the two female cousins were visiting her.

"I want some poison," she said to the druggist. She was over thirty then, still a slight woman, though thinner than usual, with cold, haughty black eyes in a face the flesh of which was strained across the temples and about the eye-sockets as you imagine a lighthouse-keeper's face ought to look. "I want some poison," she said.

"Yes, Miss Emily. What kind? For rats and such? I'd recom—" 　　35

"I want the best you have. I don't care what kind."

The druggist named several. "They'll kill anything up to an elephant. But what you want is—"

"Arsenic," Miss Emily said. "Is that a good one?"

"Is . . . arsenic? Yes, ma'am. But what you want—"

"I want arsenic." 　　40

The druggist looked down at her. She looked back at him, erect, her face like a strained flag. "Why, of course," the druggist said. "If that's what you want. But the law requires you to tell what you are going to use it for."

Miss Emily just stared at him, her head tilted back in order to look him eye for eye, until he looked away and went and got the arsenic and wrapped it up. The Negro delivery boy brought her the package; the druggist didn't come back. When she opened the package at home there was written on the box, under the skull and bones: "For rats."

IV

So the next day we all said, "She will kill herself"; and we said it would be the best thing. When she had first begun to be seen with Homer Barron, we had said, "She will marry him." Then we said, "She will persuade him yet," because Homer himself had remarked—he liked men, and it was known that he drank with the younger men in the Elks' Club—that he was not a marrying man. Later we said, "Poor Emily," behind the jalousies as they passed on Sunday afternoon in the glittering buggy, Miss Emily with her head high and Homer Barron with his hat cocked and a cigar in his teeth, reins and whip in a yellow glove.

Then some of the ladies began to say that it was a disgrace to the town and a bad example to the young people. The men did not want to interfere, but at last the ladies forced the Baptist minister—Miss Emily's people were Episcopal—to call upon her. He would never divulge what happened during that interview, but he refused to go back again. The next Sunday they again drove about the streets, and the following day the minister's wife wrote to Miss Emily's relations in Alabama.

So she had blood-kin under her roof again and we sat back to watch 　　45 developments. At first nothing happened. Then we were sure that they were to be married. We learned that Miss Emily had been to the jeweler's and ordered a man's toilet set in silver, with the letters H.B. on each piece. Two days later we learned that she had bought a complete outfit of men's clothing, including a nightshirt, and we said, "They are married." We were really glad. We were glad because the two female cousins were even more Grierson than Miss Emily had ever been.

So we were not surprised when Homer Barron—the streets had been finished some time since—was gone. We were a little disappointed that there was not a public blowing-off, but we believed that he had gone on to prepare for Miss Emily's coming, or to give her a chance to get rid of the cousins. (By that time it was a cabal, and we were all Miss Emily's allies to help circumvent the cousins.) Sure enough, after another week they departed. And, as we had expected all along, within three days Homer Barron was back in town. A neighbor saw the Negro man admit him at the kitchen door at dusk one evening.

And that was the last we saw of Homer Barron. And of Miss Emily for some time. The Negro man went in and out with the market basket, but the front door remained closed. Now and then we would see her at a window for a moment, as the men did that night when they sprinkled the lime, but for almost six months she did not appear on the streets. Then we knew that this was to be expected too; as if that quality of her father which had thwarted her woman's life so many times had been too virulent and too furious to die.

When we next saw Miss Emily, she had grown fat and her hair was turning gray. During the next few years it grew grayer and grayer until it attained an even pepper-and-salt iron-gray, when it ceased turning. Up to the day of her death at seventy-four it was still that vigorous iron-gray, like the hair of an active man.

From that time on her front door remained closed, save for a period of six or seven years, when she was about forty, during which she gave lessons in china-painting. She fitted up a studio in one of the downstairs rooms, where the daughters and granddaughters of Colonel Sartoris' contemporaries were sent to her with the same regularity and in the same spirit that they were sent to church on Sundays with a twenty-five-cent piece for the collection plate. Meanwhile her taxes had been remitted.

Then the newer generation became the backbone and the spirit of the town, and the painting pupils grew up and fell away and did not send their children to her with boxes of color and tedious brushes and pictures cut from the ladies' magazines. The front door closed upon the last one and remained closed for good. When the town got free postal delivery, Miss Emily alone refused to let them fasten the metal numbers above her door and attach a mailbox to it. She would not listen to them. 50

Daily, monthly, yearly we watched the Negro grow grayer and more stooped, going in and out with the market basket. Each December we sent her a tax notice, which would be returned by the post office a week later, unclaimed. Now and then we would see her in one of the downstairs windows—she had evidently shut up the top floor of the house—like the carven torso of an idol in a niche, looking or not looking at us, we could never tell which. Thus she passed from generation to generation—dear, inescapable, impervious, tranquil, and perverse.

And so she died. Fell ill in the house filled with dust and shadows, with only a doddering Negro man to wait on her. We did not even know she was sick; we had long since given up trying to get any information from the Negro. He talked to no one, probably not even to her, for his voice had grown harsh and rusty, as if from disuse.

She died in one of the downstairs rooms, in a heavy walnut bed with a curtain, her gray head propped on a pillow yellow and moldy with age and lack of sunlight.

V

The Negro met the first of the ladies at the front door and let them in, with their hushed, sibilant voices and their quick, curious glances, and then he disappeared. He walked right through the house and out the back and was not seen again.

The two female cousins came at once. They held the funeral on the second day, with the town coming to look at Miss Emily beneath a mass of bought flowers, with the crayon face of her father musing profoundly above the bier and the ladies sibilant and macabre; and the very old men—some in their brushed Confederate uniforms—on the porch and the lawn, talking of Miss Emily as if she had been a contemporary of theirs, believing that they had danced with her and courted her perhaps, confusing time with its mathematical progression, as the old do, to whom all the past is not a diminishing road but, instead, a huge meadow which no winter ever quite touches, divided from them now by the narrow bottleneck of the most recent decade of years.

Already we knew that there was one room in that region above stairs which no one had seen in forty years, and which would have to be forced. They waited until Miss Emily was decently in the ground before they opened it.

The violence of breaking down the door seemed to fill this room with pervading dust. A thin, acrid pall as of the tomb seemed to lie everywhere upon this room decked and furnished as for a bridal: upon the valance curtains of faded rose color, upon the rose-shaded lights, upon the dressing table, upon the delicate array of crystal and the man's toilet things backed with tarnished silver, silver so tarnished that the monogram was obscured. Among them lay collar and tie, as if they had just been removed, which, lifted, left upon the surface a pale crescent in the dust. Upon a chair hung the suit, carefully folded; beneath it the two mute shoes and the discarded socks.

The man himself lay in the bed.

For a long while we just stood there, looking down at the profound and fleshless grin. The body had apparently once lain in the attitude of an embrace, but now the long sleep that outlasts love, that conquers even the grimace of love, had cuckolded him. What was left of him, rotted beneath what was left of the nightshirt, had become inextricable from the bed in which he lay; and upon him and upon the pillow beside him lay that even coating of the patient and biding dust.

Then we noticed that in the second pillow was the indentation of a head.   60 One of us lifted something from it, and leaning forward, that faint and invisible dust dry and acrid in the nostrils, we saw a long strand of iron-gray hair.

Questions

1. What is meaningful in the final detail that the strand of hair on the second pillow is "iron-gray"?

2. Who is the unnamed narrator? For whom does he (or she?) profess to be speaking?

3. Why does "A Rose for Emily" seem better told from his or her point of view than if it were told (like John Updike's "A & P") from the point of view of the main character?

4. What foreshadowings of the discovery of the body of Homer Barron are we given earlier in the story? Share your experience in reading "A Rose for Emily": did the foreshadowings give away the ending for you? Did they heighten your interest?

5. What contrasts does the narrator draw between changing reality and Emily's refusal or inability to recognize change?

6. How do the character and background of Emily Grierson differ from those of Homer Barron? What general observations about the society that Faulkner depicts can be made from his portraits of these two characters and from his account of life in this one Mississippi town?

7. Does the story seem to you totally grim, or do you find any humor in it?

8. What do you infer to be the author's attitude toward Emily Grierson? Is she simply a murderous madwoman? Why do you suppose Faulkner calls his story "A Rose . . ."?

Edgar Allan Poe

The Tell-Tale Heart   (1843) 1850

Edgar Poe (1809–1849) was born in Boston, the second son of actors Eliza and David Poe. Edgar inherited his family's legacy of artistic talent, financial instability, and social inferiority (actors were not considered respectable in the nineteenth century), as well as his father's problems with alcohol. David Poe abandoned his family after the birth of Edgar's little sister, Rosalie, and Eliza died of tuberculosis in a Richmond, Virginia, boardinghouse before Edgar turned three. He was taken in by the wealthy John and Frances Allan of Richmond, whose name he added to his own. Allan educated Poe at first-rate

Edgar Allan Poe

schools, where he excelled in all subjects. But he grew into a moody adolescent, and his relationship with his foster father deteriorated.

Poe's first year at the University of Virginia was marked by scholastic success, alcoholic binges, and gambling debts. Disgraced, he fled to Boston and joined the army under the name Edgar Perry. He performed well as an enlisted man and published his first collection of poetry, Tamerlane and Other Poems, *at the age of eighteen. After an abortive stint at West Point led to a final break with the Allans, Poe embarked on a full-time literary career. A respected critic and editor, he sharply improved both the content and circulation of every magazine with which he was associated. But, morbidly sensitive to criticism, paranoid and belligerent when drunk, he left or was fired from every post he held. Poorly paid as both an editor and a writer, he earned almost nothing from the works that made him famous, such as "The Fall of the House of Usher" and "The Raven."*

After the break with his foster family, Poe rediscovered his own. From 1831, he lived with his father's widowed sister, Maria Clemm, and her daughter, Virginia. In 1836 Poe married this thirteen-year-old first cousin. These women provided him with much-needed emotional stability. However, like his mother, Poe's wife died of tuberculosis at age twenty-four, her demise doubtless hastened by poverty. Afterward, Poe's life came apart; his drinking intensified, as did his self-destructive tendencies. In October 1849 he died in mysterious circumstances, a few days after being found sick and incoherent on a Baltimore street.

True!—nervous—very, very dreadfully nervous I had been and am; but why *will* you say that I am mad? The disease had sharpened my senses—not destroyed—not dulled them. Above all was the sense of hearing acute. I heard all things in the heaven and in the earth. I heard many things in hell. How, then, am I mad? Hearken! and observe how healthily—how calmly, I can tell you the whole story.

It is impossible to say how first the idea entered my brain; but once conceived, it haunted me day and night. Object there was none. Passion there was none. I loved the old man. He had never wronged me. He had never given me insult. For his gold I had no desire. I think it was his eye! yes, it was this! One of his eyes resembled that of a vulture—a pale blue eye, with a film over it. Whenever it fell upon me, my blood ran cold; and so by degrees—very gradually—I made up my mind to take the life of the old man, and thus rid myself of the eye forever.

Now this is the point. You fancy me mad. Madmen know nothing. But you should have seen *me.* You should have seen how wisely I proceeded—with what caution—with what foresight—with what dissimulation I went to work! I was never kinder to the old man than during the whole week before I killed him. And every night, about midnight, I turned the latch of his door and opened it—oh, so gently! And then, when I had made an opening sufficient for my head, I put in a dark lantern, all closed, closed, so that no light shone out, and then I thrust in my head. Oh, you would have laughed to see how cunningly I thrust it in! I moved it slowly—very, very slowly, so that I might not disturb the old man's sleep. It took me an hour to place my whole head within the opening so far that I could see him as he lay upon his bed. Ha!—would a madman have been so wise as this? And then, when my head was well in the room, I undid the lantern cautiously—oh, so cautiously—cautiously (for the hinges creaked)—I undid it just so much that a single thin ray fell upon the vulture eye. And this I did for seven long nights—every night just at midnight—but I found the eye always closed; and so it was impossible to do the work; for it was not the old man who vexed me, but his Evil Eye. And every morning, when the day broke, I went boldly into the chamber, and spoke courageously to him, calling him by name in a hearty tone, and inquiring how he had passed the night. So you see he would have been a very profound old man, indeed, to suspect that every night, just at twelve, I looked in upon him while he slept.

Upon the eighth night I was more than usually cautious in opening the door. A watch's minute hand moves more quickly than did mine. Never before that night had I *felt* the extent of my own powers—of my sagacity. I could scarcely contain my feelings of triumph. To think that there I was, opening the door, little by little, and he not even to dream of my secret deeds or thoughts. I fairly chuckled at the idea; and perhaps he heard me; for he moved on the bed suddenly, as if startled. Now you may think that I drew back—but no. His room was as black as pitch with the thick darkness (for the shutters were close fastened, through fear of robbers), and so I knew that he could not see the opening of the door, and I kept pushing it on steadily, steadily.

I had my head in, and was about to open the lantern, when my thumb   5 slipped upon the tin fastening, and the old man sprang up in the bed, crying out—"Who's there?"

I kept quite still and said nothing. For a whole hour I did not move a muscle, and in the meantime I did not hear him lie down. He was still sitting up in the bed, listening;—just as I have done, night after night, hearkening to the death watches° in the wall.

Presently I heard a slight groan, and I knew it was the groan of mortal terror. It was not a groan of pain or of grief—oh, no!—it was the low stifled sound that arises from the bottom of the soul when overcharged with awe. I knew the sound very well. Many a night, just at midnight, when all the world slept, it has welled up from my own bosom, deepening, with its dreadful echo, the terrors that distracted me. I say I knew it well. I knew what the old man felt, and pitied him, although I chuckled at heart. I knew that he had been lying awake ever since the first slight noise, when he had turned in the bed. His fears had been ever since growing upon him. He had

---

death watches: beetles that infest timbers. Their clicking sound was thought to be an omen of death.

been trying to fancy them causeless, but could not. He had been saying to himself—"It is nothing but the wind in the chimney—it is only a mouse crossing the floor," or "it is merely a cricket which has made a single chirp." Yes, he had been trying to comfort himself with these suppositions; but he had found all in vain. *All in vain*; because Death, in approaching him, had stalked with his black shadow before him, and enveloped the victim. And it was the mournful influence of the unperceived shadow that caused him to feel—although he neither saw nor heard—to *feel* the presence of my head within the room.

When I had waited a long time, very patiently, without hearing him lie down, I resolved to open a little—a very, very little crevice in the lantern. So I opened it—you cannot imagine how stealthily, stealthily— until, at length, a single dim ray, like the thread of the spider, shot from out of the crevice and fell upon the vulture eye.

It was open—wide, wide open—and I grew furious as I gazed upon it. I saw it with perfect distinctness—all a dull blue, with a hideous veil over it that chilled the very marrow in my bones; but I could see nothing else of the old man's face or person: for I had directed the ray as if by instinct, precisely upon the damned spot.

And now have I not told you that what you mistake for madness is but over-acuteness of the senses?—now, I say, there came to my ears a low, dull, quick sound, such as a watch makes when enveloped in cotton. I knew *that* sound well, too. It was the beating of the old man's heart. It increased my fury, as the beating of a drum stimulates the soldier into courage.

But even yet I refrained and kept still. I scarcely breathed. I held the lantern motionless. I tried how steadily I could maintain the ray upon the eye. Meantime the hellish tattoo of the heart increased. It grew quicker and quicker, and louder and louder every instant. The old man's terror *must* have been extreme! It grew louder, I say, louder every moment!—do you mark me well? I have told you that I am nervous: so I am. And now at the dead hour of the night, amid the dreadful silence of that old house, so strange a noise as this excited me to uncontrollable terror. Yet, for some minutes longer I refrained and stood still. But the beating grew louder, louder! I thought the heart must burst. And now a new anxiety seized me—the sound would be heard by a neighbor! The old man's hour had come! With a loud yell, I threw open the lantern and leaped into the room. He shrieked once—once only. In an instant I dragged him to the floor, and pulled the heavy bed over him. I then smiled gaily, to find the deed so far done. But, for many minutes, the heart beat on with a muffled sound. This, however, did not vex me; it would not be heard through the wall. At length it ceased. The old man was dead. I removed the bed and examined the corpse. Yes, he was stone, stone dead. I placed my hand upon the heart and held it there many minutes.

If still you think me mad, you will think so no longer when I describe the wise precautions I took for the concealment of the body. The night waned, and I worked hastily, but in silence. First of all I dismembered the corpse. I cut off the head and the arms and the legs.

I then took up three planks from the flooring of the chamber, and deposited all between the scantlings. I then replaced the boards so cleverly, so cunningly, that no human eye—not even *his*—could have detected anything wrong. There was nothing to wash out—no stain of any kind—no blood-spot whatever. I had been too wary for that. A tub had caught all—ha! ha!

When I had made an end of these labors, it was four o'clock—still dark as midnight. As the bell sounded the hour, there came a knocking at the street door. I went down to open it with a light heart,—for what had I *now* to fear? There entered three men, who introduced themselves, with perfect suavity, as officers of the police. A shriek had been heard by a neighbor during the night; suspicion of foul play had been aroused, information had been lodged at the police office, and they (the officers) had been deputed to search the premises.

I smiled,—for *what* had I to fear? I bade the gentlemen welcome. The   15
shriek, I said, was my own in a dream. The old man, I mentioned, was absent in the country. I took my visitors all over the house. I bade them search—search *well*. I led them, at length, to *his* chamber. I showed them his treasures, secure, undisturbed. In the enthusiasm of my confidence, I brought chairs into the room, and desired them *here* to rest from their fatigues, while I myself, in the wild audacity of my perfect triumph, placed my own seat upon the very spot beneath which reposed the corpse of the victim.

The officers were satisfied. My *manner* had convinced them. I was singularly at ease. They sat, and while I answered cheerily, they chatted of familiar things. But, ere long, I felt myself getting pale and wished them gone. My head ached, and I fancied a ringing in my ears: but still they sat and still chatted. The ringing became more distinct:—it continued and became more distinct: I talked more freely to get rid of the feeling: but it continued and gained definitiveness—until, at length, I found that the noise was *not* within my ears.

No doubt I now grew *very* pale:—but I talked more fluently, and with a heightened voice. Yet the sound increased—and what could I do? It was a *low, dull, quick sound—much such a sound as a watch makes when enveloped in cotton.* I gasped for breath—and yet the officers heard it not. I talked more quickly—more vehemently; but the noise steadily increased. I arose and argued about trifles, in a high key and with violent gesticulations; but the noise steadily increased. Why *would* they not be gone? I paced the floor to and fro with heavy strides, as if excited to fury by the observations of the men—but the noise steadily increased. Oh God! what *could* I do? I foamed—I raved—I swore! I swung the chair upon which I had been sitting, and grated it upon the boards, but the noise arose over all and continually increased. It grew louder—louder—*louder*! And still the men chatted pleasantly, and smiled. Was it possible they heard not? Almighty God!—no, no! They heard!—they suspected!—they *knew*!—they were making a mockery of my horror!—this I thought, and this I think. But anything was better than this agony! Anything was more tolerable than this derision! I could bear those hypocritical smiles no longer! I felt that I must scream or die!—and now—again!—hark! louder! louder! louder! *louder*!—

"Villains!" I shrieked, "dissemble no more! I admit the deed!—tear up the planks!—here, here!—it is the beating of his hideous heart!"

Questions

1. From what point of view is Poe's story told? Why is this point of view particularly effective for "The Tell-Tale Heart"?
2. Point to details in the story that identify its speaker as an unreliable narrator.
3. What do we know about the old man in the story? What motivates the narrator to kill him?
4. In spite of all his precautions, the narrator does not commit the perfect crime. What trips him up?
5. How do you account for the police officers chatting calmly with the murderer instead of reacting to the sound that stirs the murderer into a frenzy?

Eudora Welty

Why I Live at the P.O.   1941

Eudora Welty (1909–2001) was born in Jackson, Mississippi, daughter of an insurance company president. Like William Faulkner, another Mississippi writer, she stayed close to her roots for practically all her life, except for short sojourns at the University of Wisconsin, where she took her B.A., and in New York City, where she studied advertising. She lived most of her life in her childhood home in Jackson, within a stone's throw of the state capitol. Although Welty was a novelist distinguished for The Robber Bridegroom *(1942),* Delta Wedding *(1946),* The Ponder Heart *(1954),* Losing Battles *(1970), and* The*

Eudora Welty

Optimist's Daughter *(1972), many critics think her finest work was in the short-story form.* The Collected Stories of Eudora Welty *(1980) gathers the work of more than forty years. Welty's other books include a memoir,* One Writer's Beginnings *(1984), and* The Eye of the Story *(1977), a book of sympathetic criticism on the fiction of other writers, including Willa Cather, Virginia Woolf, Katherine Anne Porter, and Isak Dinesen.* One Time, One Place, *a book of photographs of everyday life that Welty took in Mississippi during the Depression, was republished in a revised edition in 1996.*

I was getting along fine with Mama, Papa-Daddy, and Uncle Rondo until my sister Stella-Rondo just separated from her husband and came back home again. Mr. Whitaker! Of course I went with Mr. Whitaker first, when he first appeared here in China Grove, taking "Pose Yourself" photos, and Stella-Rondo broke us up. Told him I was one-sided. Bigger on one side than the other, which is a deliberate, calculated falsehood: I'm the same. Stella-Rondo is exactly twelve months to the day younger than I am and for that reason she's spoiled.

She's always had anything in the world she wanted and then she'd throw it away. Papa-Daddy gave her this gorgeous Add-a-Pearl necklace when she was eight years old and she threw it away playing baseball when she was nine, with only two pearls.

So as soon as she got married and moved away from home the first thing she did was separate! From Mr. Whitaker! This photographer with the popeyes she said she trusted. Came home from one of those towns up in Illinois and to our complete surprise brought this child of two.

Mama said she like to make her drop dead for a second. "Here you had this marvelous blonde child and never so much as wrote your mother a word about it," says Mama. "I'm thoroughly ashamed of you." But of course she wasn't.

Stella-Rondo just calmly takes off this *hat*. I wish you could see it.   5
She says, "Why, Mama, Shirley-T.'s adopted, I can prove it."

"How?" says Mama, but all I says was, "H'm!" There I was over the hot stove, trying to stretch two chickens over five people and a completely unexpected child into the bargain, without one moment's notice.

"What do you mean—'H'm!'?" says Stella-Rondo, and Mama says, "I heard that, Sister."

I said that oh, I didn't mean a thing, only that whoever Shirley-T. was, she was the spit-image of Papa-Daddy if he'd cut off his beard, which of course he'd never do in the world. Papa-Daddy's Mama's papa and sulks.

Stella-Rondo got furious! She said, "Sister, I don't need to tell you you got a lot of nerve and always did have and I'll thank you to make no future reference to my adopted child whatsoever."

"Very well," I said. "Very well, very well. Of course I noticed at once   10
she looks like Mr. Whitaker's side too. That frown. She looks like a cross between Mr. Whitaker and Papa-Daddy."

"Well, all I can say is she isn't."

"She looks exactly like Shirley Temple to me," says Mama, but Shirley-T. just ran away from her.

So the first thing Stella-Rondo did at the table was turn Papa-Daddy against me.

"Papa-Daddy," she says. He was trying to cut up his meat. "Papa-Daddy!" I was taken completely by surprise. Papa-Daddy is about a million years old and's got this long-long beard. "Papa-Daddy, Sister says she fails to understand why you don't cut off your beard."

So Papa Daddy l-a-y-s down his knife and fork! He's real rich. Mama says he is, he says he isn't. So he says, "Have I heard correctly? You don't understand why I don't cut off my beard?"

"Why," I says, "Papa-Daddy, of course I understand, I did not say any such of a thing, the idea!"

He says, "Hussy!"

I says, "Papa-Daddy, you know I wouldn't any more want you to cut off your beard than the man in the moon. It was the farthest thing from my mind! Stella-Rondo sat there and made that up while she was eating breast of chicken."

But he says, "So the postmistress fails to understand why I don't cut off my beard. Which job I got you through my influence with the government. 'Bird's nest'—is that what you call it?"

Not that it isn't the next to smallest P.O. in the entire state of Mississippi.

I says, "Oh, Papa-Daddy," I says, "I didn't say any such of a thing, I never dreamed it was a bird's nest, I have always been grateful though this is the next to smallest P.O. in the state of Mississippi, and I do not enjoy being referred to as a hussy by my own grandfather."

But Stella-Rondo says, "Yes, you did say it too. Anybody in the world could of heard you, that had ears."

"Stop right there," says Mama, looking at *me*.

So I pulled my napkin straight back through the napkin ring and left the table.

As soon as I was out of the room Mama says, "Call her back, or she'll starve to death," but Papa-Daddy says, "This is the beard I started growing on the Coast when I was fifteen years old." He would of gone on till nightfall if Shirley-T. hadn't lost the Milky Way she ate in Cairo.

So Papa-Daddy says, "I am going out and lie in the hammock, and you can all sit here and remember my words: I'll never cut off my beard as long as I live, even one inch, and I don't appreciate it in you at all." Passed right by me in the hall and went straight out and got in the hammock.

It would be a holiday. It wasn't five minutes before Uncle Rondo suddenly appeared in the hall in one of Stella-Rondo's flesh-colored kimonos, all cut on the bias, like something Mr. Whitaker probably thought was gorgeous.

"Uncle Rondo!" I says. "I didn't know who that was! Where are you going?"

"Sister," he says, "get out of my way, I'm poisoned."

"If you're poisoned stay away from Papa-Daddy," I says. "Keep out of the hammock. Papa-Daddy will certainly beat you on the head if you come within forty miles of him. He thinks I deliberately said he ought to cut off his beard after he got me the P.O., and I've told him and told him and told him, and he acts like he just don't hear me. Papa-Daddy must of gone stone deaf."

"He picked a fine day to do it then," says Uncle Rondo, and before you could say "Jack Robinson" flew out in the yard.

What he'd really done, he'd drunk another bottle of that prescription. He does it every single Fourth of July as sure as shooting, and it's horribly expensive. Then he falls over in the hammock and snores. So he insisted on zigzagging right on out to the hammock, looking like a half-wit.

Papa-Daddy woke up with this horrible yell and right there without moving an inch he tried to turn Uncle Rondo against me. I heard every word he said. Oh, he told Uncle Rondo I didn't learn to read till I was eight years old and he didn't see how in the world I ever got the mail put up at the P.O., much less read it all, and he said if Uncle Rondo could only fathom the lengths he had gone to get me that job! And he said on the other hand he thought Stella-Rondo had a brilliant mind and deserved credit for getting out of town. All the time he was just lying there swinging as pretty as you please and looping out his beard, and poor Uncle Rondo was *pleading* with him to slow down the hammock, it was making him as dizzy as a witch to watch it. But that's what Papa-Daddy likes about a hammock. So Uncle Rondo was too dizzy to get turned against me for the time being. He's Mama's only brother and is a good case of a one-track mind. Ask anybody. A certified pharmacist.

Just then I heard Stella-Rondo raising the upstairs window. While she was married she got this peculiar idea that it's cooler with the windows shut and locked. So she has to raise the window before she can make a soul hear her outdoors.

So she raises the window and says, "*Oh!*" You would have thought she was mortally wounded.   35

Uncle Rondo and Papa-Daddy didn't even look up, but kept right on with what they were doing. I had to laugh.

I flew up the stairs and threw the door open! I says, "What in the wide world's the matter, Stella-Rondo? You mortally wounded?"

"No," she says, "I am not mortally wounded but I wish you would do me the favor of looking out that window there and telling me what you see."

So I shade my eyes and look out the window.

"I see the front yard," I says.   40

"Don't you see any human beings?" she says.

"I see Uncle Rondo trying to run Papa-Daddy out of the hammock," I says. "Nothing more. Naturally, it's so suffocating-hot in the house, with all the windows shut and locked, everybody who cares to stay in their right mind will have to go out and get in the hammock before the Fourth of July is over."

"Don't you notice anything different about Uncle Rondo?" asks Stella-Rondo.

"Why, no, except he's got on some terrible-looking flesh-colored contraption I wouldn't be found dead in, is all I can see," I says.

"Never mind, you won't be found dead in it, because it happens to be part of my trousseau, and Mr. Whitaker took several dozen photographs of me in it," says Stella-Rondo. "What on earth could Uncle Rondo *mean* by wearing part of my trousseau out in the broad open daylight without saying so much as 'Kiss my foot,' *knowing* I only got home this morning after my separation and hung my negligee up on the bathroom door, just as nervous as I could be?"

"I'm sure I don't know, and what do you expect me to do about it?" I says. "Jump out the window?"

"No, I expect nothing of the kind. I simply declare that Uncle Rondo looks like a fool in it, that's all," she says. "It makes me sick to my stomach."

"Well, he looks as good as he can," I says. "As good as anybody in reason could." I stood up for Uncle Rondo, please remember. And I said to Stella-Rondo, "I think I would do well not to criticize so freely if I were you and came home with a two-year-old child I had never said a word about, and no explanation whatever about my separation."

"I asked you the instant I entered this house not to refer one more time to my adopted child, and you gave me your word of honor you would not," was all Stella-Rondo would say, and started pulling out every one of her eyebrows with some cheap Kress tweezers.

So I merely slammed the door behind me and went down and made some green-tomato pickle. Somebody had to do it. Of course Mama had turned both the niggers loose; she always said no earthly power could hold one anyway on the Fourth of July, so she wouldn't even try. It turned out that Jaypan fell in the lake and came within a very narrow limit of drowning.

So Mama trots in. Lifts up the lid and says, "H'm! Not very good for your Uncle Rondo in his precarious condition, I must say. Or poor little adopted Shirley-T. Shame on you!"

That made me tired. I says, "Well, Stella-Rondo had better thank her lucky stars it was her instead of me came trotting in with that very peculiar-looking child. Now if it had been me that trotted in from Illinois and brought a peculiar-looking child of two, I shudder to think of the reception I'd of got, much less controlled the diet of an entire family."

"But you must remember, Sister, that you were never married to Mr. Whitaker in the first place and didn't go up to Illinois to live," says Mama, shaking a spoon in my face. If you had I would have been just as overjoyed to see you and your little adopted girl as I was to see Stella-Rondo, when you wound up with your separation and came on back home."

"You would not," I says.

"Don't contradict me, I would," says Mama.

But I said she couldn't convince me though she talked till she was blue in the face. Then I said, "Besides, you know as well as I do that that child is not adopted."

"She most certainly is adopted," says Mama, stiff as a poker.

I says, "Why, Mama, Stella-Rondo had her just as sure as anything in this world, and just too stuck up to admit it."

"Why Sister," said Mama. "Here I thought we were going to have a pleasant Fourth of July, and you start right out not believing a word your own baby sister tells you!"

"Just like Cousin Annie Flo. Went to her grave denying the facts of life," I remind Mama.   60

"I told you if you ever mentioned Annie Flo's name I'd slap your face," says Mama, and slaps my face.

"All right, you wait and see," I says.

"I," says Mama, "I prefer to take my children's word for anything when it's humanly possible." You ought to see Mama, she weighs two hundred pounds and has real tiny feet.

Just then something perfectly horrible occurred to me.

"Mama," I says, "can that child talk?" I simply had to whisper!   65
"Mama, I wonder if that child can be—you know—in any way? Do you realize," I says, "that she hasn't spoken one single, solitary word to a human being up to this minute? This is the way she looks," I says, and I looked like this.

Well, Mama and I just stood there and stared at each other. It was horrible!

"I remember well that Joe Whitaker frequently drank like a fish," says Mama. "I believed to my soul he drank *chemicals*." And without another word she marches to the foot of the stairs and calls Stella-Rondo.

"Stella-Rondo? O-o-o-o-o! Stella-Rondo!"

"What?" says Stella-Rondo from upstairs. Not even the grace to get up off the bed.

"Can that child of yours talk?" asks Mama.   70
Stella-Rondo yells back, "Can she what?"

"Talk! Talk!" says Mama. "Burdyburdyburdyburdy!"

So Stella-Rondo yells back, "Who says she can't talk?"

"Sister says so," says Mama.

"You didn't have to tell me, I know whose word of honor don't mean   75
a thing in this house," says Stella-Rondo.

And in a minute the loudest Yankee voice I ever heard in my life yells out, "OE'm Pop-OE the Sailor-r-r-r Ma-a-an!" and then somebody jumps up and down in the upstairs hall. In another second the house would of fallen down.

"Not only talks, she can tap-dance!" calls Stella-Rondo. "Which is more than some people I won't name can do."

"Why, the little precious darling thing!" Mama says, so surprised. "Just as smart as she can be!" Starts talking baby talk right there. Then she turns on me. "Sister, you ought to be thoroughly ashamed! Run upstairs this instant and apologize to Stella-Rondo and Shirley-T."

"Apologize for what?" I says. "I merely wondered if the child was normal, that's all. Now that she's proved she is, why, I have nothing further to say."

But Mama just turned on her heel and flew out, furious. She ran right upstairs and hugged the baby. She believed it was adopted. Stella-Rondo hadn't done a thing but turn her against me from upstairs while I stood there helpless over the hot stove. So that made Mama, Papa-Daddy, and the baby all on Stella-Rondo's side.

Next, Uncle Rondo.

I must say that Uncle Rondo has been marvelous to me at various times in the past and I was completely unprepared to be made to jump out of my skin, the way it turned out. Once Stella-Rondo did something perfectly horrible to him—broke a chain letter from Flanders Field°—and he took the radio back he had given her and gave it to me. Stella-Rondo was furious! For six months we all had to call her Stella instead of Stella-Rondo, or she wouldn't answer. I always thought Uncle Rondo had all the brains of the entire family. Another time he sent me to Mammoth Cave,° with all expenses paid.

But this would be the day he was drinking that prescription, the Fourth of July.

So at supper Stella-Rondo speaks up and says she thinks Uncle Rondo ought to try to eat a little something. So finally Uncle Rondo said he would try a little cold biscuits and ketchup, but that was all. So *she* brought it to him.

"Do you think it is wise to disport with ketchup in Stella-Rondo's flesh-colored kimono?" I says. Trying to be considerate! If Stella-Rondo couldn't watch out for her trousseau, somebody had to.

"Any objections?" asks Uncle Rondo, just about to pour out all the ketchup.

"Don't mind what she says, Uncle Rondo," says Stella-Rondo. "Sister has been devoting this solid afternoon to sneering out my bedroom window at the way you look."

"What's that?" says Uncle Rondo. Uncle Rondo has got the most terrible temper in the world. Anything is liable to make him tear the house down if it comes at the wrong time.

80

85

Flanders Field: an Allied military cemetery in Belgium for the dead of World War I; it was made famous by a poem by John McCrae. The artificial red poppies still sold for charity on Veterans Day commemorate the cemetery and poem.   *Mammoth Cave:* a network of natural underground caverns in Kentucky.

So Stella-Rondo says, "Sister says, 'Uncle Rondo certainly does look like a fool in that pink kimono!'"

Do you remember who it was really said that?   90

Uncle Rondo spills out all the ketchup and jumps out of his chair and tears off the kimono and throws it down on the dirty floor and puts his foot on it. It had to be sent all the way to Jackson to the cleaners and re-pleated.

"So that's your opinion of your Uncle Rondo, is it?" he says. "I look like a fool, do I? Well, that's the last straw. A whole day in this house with nothing to do, and then to hear you come out with a remark like that behind my back!"

"I didn't say any such of a thing, Uncle Rondo," I says, "and I'm not saying who did, either. Why, I think you look all right. Just try to take care of yourself and not talk and eat at the same time," I says. "I think you better go lie down."

"Lie down my foot," says Uncle Rondo. I ought to of known by that he was fixing to do something perfectly horrible.

So he didn't do anything that night in the precarious state he was in—   95 just played Casino with Mama and Stella-Rondo and Shirley-T. and gave Shirley-T. a nickel with a head on both sides. It tickled her nearly to death, and she called him "Papa." But at 6:30 A.M. the next morning, he threw a whole five-cent package of some unsold one-inch firecrackers from the store as hard as he could into my bedroom and they every one went off. Not one bad one in the string. Anybody else, there'd be one that wouldn't go off.

Well, I'm just terribly susceptible to noise of any kind, the doctor has always told me I was the most sensitive person he had ever seen in his whole life, and I was simply prostrated. I couldn't eat! People tell me they heard it as far as the cemetery, and old Aunt Jep Patterson, that had been holding her own so good, thought it was Judgment Day and she was going to meet her whole family. It's usually so quiet here.

And I'll tell you it didn't take me any longer than a minute to make up my mind what to do. There I was with the whole entire house on Stella-Rondo's side and turned against me. If I have anything at all I have pride.

So I just decided I'd go straight down to the P.O. There's plenty of room there in the back, I says to myself.

Well! I made no bones about letting the family catch on to what I was up to. I didn't try to conceal it.

The first thing they knew, I marched in where they were all playing   100 Old Maid and pulled the electric oscillating fan out by the plug, and everything got real hot. Next I snatched the pillow I'd done the needlepoint on right off the davenport from behind Papa-Daddy. He went "Ugh!" I beat Stella-Rondo up the stairs and finally found my charm bracelet in her bureau drawer under a picture of Nelson Eddy.°

Nelson Eddy: a popular singer (1901–1967) who appeared in romantic musical films during the Depression era.

"So that's the way the land lies," says Uncle Rondo. There he was, piecing on the ham. "Well, Sister, I'll be glad to donate my army cot if you got any place to set it up, providing you'll leave right this minute and let me get some peace." Uncle Rondo was in France.

"Thank you kindly for the cot and 'peace' is hardly the word I would select if I had to resort to firecrackers at 6:30 A.M. in a young girl's bedroom," I says back to him. "And as to where I intend to go, you seem to forget my position as postmistress of China Grove, Mississippi," I says. "I've always got the P.O."

Well, that made them all sit up and take notice.

I went out front and started digging up some four-o'clocks to plant around the P.O.

"Ah-ah-ah!" says Mama, raising the window. "Those happen to   105
be my four-o'clocks. Everything planted in that star is mine. I've never known you to make anything grow in your life."

"Very well," I says. "But I take the fern. Even you, Mama, can't stand there and deny that I'm the one watered that fern. And I happen to know where I can send in a box top and get a packet of one thousand mixed seeds, no two the same kind, free."

"Oh, where?" Mama wants to know.

But I says, "Too late. You 'tend to your house, and I'll 'tend to mine. You hear things like that all the time if you know how to listen to the radio. Perfectly marvelous offers. Get anything you want free."

So I hope to tell you I marched in and got that radio, and they could of all bit a nail in two, especially Stella-Rondo, that it used to belong to, and she well knew she couldn't get it back, I'd sue for it like a shot. And I very politely took the sewing-machine motor I helped pay the most on to give Mama for Christmas back in 1929, and a good big calendar, with the first-aid remedies on it. The thermometer and the Hawaiian ukulele certainly were rightfully mine, and I stood on the step-ladder and got all my watermelon-rind preserves and every fruit and vegetable I'd put up, every jar. Then I began to pull the tacks out of the bluebird wall vases on the archway to the dining room.

"Who told you you could have those, Miss Priss?" says Mama, fanning   110
as hard as she could.

"I bought 'em and I'll keep track of 'em," I says. "I'll tack 'em up one on each side the post-office window, and you can see 'em when you come to ask me for your mail, if you're so dead to see 'em."

"Not I! I'll never darken the door to that post office again if I live to be a hundred," Mama says. "Ungrateful child! After all the money we spent on you at the Normal."°

Normal: normal school, a two-year college for the training of elementary school teachers.

"Me either," says Stella-Rondo. "You can just let my mail lie there and *rot*, for all I care. I'll never come and relieve you of a single, solitary piece."

"I should worry," I says. "And who you think's going to sit down and write you all those big fat letters and postcards, by the way? Mr. Whitaker? Just because he was the only man ever dropped down in China Grove and you got him—unfairly—is he going to sit down and write you a lengthy correspondence after you come home giving no rhyme nor reason whatsoever for your separation and no explanation for the presence of that child? I may not have your brilliant mind, but I fail to see it."

So Mama says, "Sister, I've told you a thousand times that Stella-Rondo simply got homesick, and this child is far too big to be hers," and she says, "Now, why don't you just sit down and play Casino?"

Then Shirley-T. sticks out her tongue at me in this perfectly horrible way. She has no more manners than the man in the moon. I told her she was going to cross her eyes like that some day and they'd stick.

"It's too late to stop me now," I says. "You should have tried that yesterday. I'm going to the P.O. and the only way you can possibly see me is to visit me there."

So Papa-Daddy says, "You'll never catch me setting foot in that post office, even if I should take a notion into my head to write a letter some place." He says, "I won't have you reachin' out of that little old window with a pair of shears and cuttin' off any beard of mine. I'm too smart for you!"

"We all are," says Stella-Rondo.

But I said, "If you're so smart, where's Mr. Whitaker?"

So then Uncle Rondo says, "I'll thank you from now on to stop reading all the orders I get on postcards and telling everybody in China Grove what you think is the matter with them," but I says, "I draw my own conclusions and will continue in the future to draw them." I says, "If people want to write their inmost secrets on penny postcards, there's nothing in the wide world you can do about it, Uncle Rondo."

"And if you think we'll ever *write* another postcard you're sadly mistaken," says Mama.

"Cutting off your nose to spite your face then," I says. "But if you're all determined to have no more to do with the U.S. mail, think of this: What will Stella-Rondo do now, if she wants to tell Mr. Whitaker to come after her?"

"Wah!" says Stella-Rondo. I knew she'd cry. She had a conniption fit right there in the kitchen.

"It will be interesting to see how long she holds out," I says. "And now—I am leaving."

"Good-by," says Uncle Rondo.

"Oh, I declare," says Mama, "to think that a family of mine should quarrel on the Fourth of July, or the day after, over Stella-Rondo leaving old Mr. Whitaker and having the sweetest little adopted child! It looks like we'd all be glad!"

"Wah!" says Stella-Rondo, and has a fresh conniption fit.

"*He* left *her*—you mark my words," I says. "That's Mr. Whitaker. I know Mr. Whitaker. After all, I knew him first. I said from the beginning he'd up and leave her. I foretold every single thing that's happened."

"Where did he go?" asks Mama.   130

"Probably to the North Pole, if he knows what's good for him," I says.

But Stella-Rondo just bawled and wouldn't say another word. She flew to her room and slammed the door.

"Now look what you've gone and done, Sister," says Mama. "You go apologize."

"I haven't got time, I'm leaving," I says.

"Well, what are you waiting around for?" asks Uncle Rondo.   135

So I just picked up the kitchen clock and marched off, without saying "Kiss my foot," or anything, and never did tell Stella-Rondo good-by.

There was a nigger girl going along on a little wagon right in front.

"Nigger girl," I says, "come help me haul these things down the hill, I'm going to live in the post office."

Took her nine trips in her express wagon. Uncle Rondo came out on the porch and threw her a nickel.

And that's the last I've laid eyes on any of my family or my family laid 140
eyes on me for five solid days and nights. Stella-Rondo may be telling the most horrible tales in the world about Mr. Whitaker, but I haven't heard them. As I tell everybody, I draw my own conclusions.

But oh, I like it here. It's ideal, as I've been saying. You see, I've got everything cater-cornered, the way I like it. Hear the radio? All the war news. Radio, sewing machine, book ends, ironing board and that great big piano lamp—peace, that's what I like. Butter-bean vines planted all along the front where the strings are.

Of course, there's not much mail. My family are naturally the main people in China Grove, and if they prefer to vanish from the face of the earth, for all the mail they get or the mail they write, why, I'm not going to open my mouth. Some of the folks here in town are taking up for me and some turned against me. I know which is which. There are always people who will quit buying stamps just to get on the right side of Papa-Daddy.

But here I am, and here I'll stay. I want the world to know I'm happy.

And if Stella-Rondo should come to me this minute, on bended knees, and *attempt* to explain the incidents of her life with Mr. Whitaker, I'd simply put my fingers in both my ears and refuse to listen.

Questions

1. Can we equate the narrator's voice with Welty's? What clues does the author give that Sister's opinions are not her own?
2. What statements does the narrator make that seem unreliable?
3. Describe Sister's personality. Is she slightly crazy or is her odd behavior a justified revolt against her family?
4. Sister uses the word "nigger" several times in the story, and she is clearly a racist. What does her attitude toward African Americans tell you about the time and place of the story?
5. Why does Sister fight so much with her family?

Jamaica Kincaid

Girl   1983

Jamaica Kincaid was born Elaine Potter Richardson in 1949 in St. John's, capital of the West Indian island nation of Antigua and Barbuda (she adopted the name Jamaica Kincaid in 1973 because of her family's disapproval of her writing). In 1965 she was sent to Westchester County, New York, to work as an au pair (or "servant," as she prefers to describe it). She attended Franconia College in New Hampshire, but did not complete a degree. Kincaid worked as a staff writer for the New Yorker *for near-ly twenty years;* Talk Stories *(2001) is a collection of seventy-seven short pieces that she wrote for the*

Jamaica Kincaid

magazine. She won wide attention for At the Bottom of the River *(1983), the volume of her stories that includes "Girl." In 1985 she published* Annie John, *an interlocking cycle of short stories about growing up in Antigua.* Lucy *(1990) was her first novel; it was followed by* The Autobiography of My Mother *(1996) and* Mr. Potter *(2002), novels inspired by the lives of her parents. Kincaid is also the author of* A Small Place *(1988), a memoir of her homeland and meditation on the destructiveness of colonialism, and* My Brother *(1997), a reminiscence of her brother Devon, who died of AIDS at thirty-three. Her recent works include a travel book titled* Among Flowers: A Walk in the Himalaya *(2005) and a novel,* See Now Then *(2013). A naturalized U.S. citizen, Kincaid has said of her adopted country: "It's given me a place to be myself—but myself as I was formed somewhere else." She currently teaches at Claremont McKenna College in Southern California.*

Wash the white clothes on Monday and put them on the stone heap; wash the color clothes on Tuesday and put them on the clothesline to dry; don't walk barehead in the hot sun; cook pumpkin fritters in very hot sweet oil; soak your little cloths right after you take them off; when

buying cotton to make yourself a nice blouse, be sure that it doesn't have
gum on it, because that way it won't hold up well after a wash; soak salt
fish overnight before you cook it; is it true that you sing benna° in Sunday
school?; always eat your food in such a way that it won't turn someone
else's stomach; on Sundays try to walk like a lady and not like the slut you
are so bent on becoming; don't sing benna in Sunday school; you mustn't
speak to wharf-rat boys, not even to give directions; don't eat fruits on
the street—flies will follow you; *but I don't sing benna on Sundays at all and
never in Sunday school*; this is how to sew on a button; this is how to make
a buttonhole for the button you have just sewed on; this is how to hem a
dress when you see the hem coming down and so to prevent yourself from
looking like the slut I know you are so bent on becoming; this is how you
iron your father's khaki shirt so that it doesn't have a crease; this is how
you iron your father's khaki pants so that they don't have a crease; this
is how you grow okra—far from the house, because okra tree harbors red
ants; when you are growing dasheen, make sure it gets plenty of water or
else it makes your throat itch when you are eating it; this is how you sweep
a corner; this is how you sweep a whole house; this is how you sweep a
yard; this is how you smile to someone you don't like too much; this is
how you smile to someone you don't like at all; this is how you smile to
someone you like completely; this is how you set a table for tea; this is how
you set a table for dinner; this is how you set a table for dinner with an
important guest; this is how you set a table for lunch; this is how you set a
table for breakfast; this is how to behave in the presence of men who don't
know you very well, and this way they won't recognize immediately the
slut I have warned you against becoming; be sure to wash every day, even
if it is with your own spit; don't squat down to play marbles—you are not
a boy, you know; don't pick people's flowers—you might catch something;
don't throw stones at blackbirds, because it might not be a blackbird at all;
this is how to make a bread pudding; this is how to make doukona; this is
how to make pepper pot; this is how to make a good medicine for a cold;
this is how to make a good medicine to throw away a child before it even
becomes a child; this is how to catch a fish; this is how to throw back a fish
you don't like, and that way something bad won't fall on you; this is how to
bully a man; this is how a man bullies you; this is how to love a man, and
if this doesn't work there are other ways, and if they don't work don't feel
too bad about giving up; this is how to spit up in the air if you feel like it,
and this is how to move quick so that it doesn't fall on you; this is how to
make ends meet; always squeeze bread to make sure it's fresh; *but what if the*

benna: Kincaid defined this word, for two editors who inquired, as meaning "songs of the
sort your parents didn't want you to sing, at first calypso and later rock and roll" (quoted
by Sylvan Barnet and Marcia Stubbs, *The Little Brown Reader*, 2nd ed. [Boston: Little,
1980] 74).

baker won't let me feel the bread?; you mean to say that after all you are really going to be the kind of woman who the baker won't let near the bread?

Questions

1. Who is the speaker of "Girl"? Who is the listener?
2. What do we specifically know about the mother and daughter from the story? What can we infer?
3. What words of the daughter appear in the story?
4. How different do you think the story would be if the daughter were given a chance to respond?
5. Do you think the mother offers her daughter good advice?

▪ WRITING *effectively*

THINKING ABOUT POINT OF VIEW

When we hear an outlandish piece of news, something that doesn't quite add up, we're well advised, as the saying goes, to consider the source. The same is true when we read a short story.

- **Consider who is telling the story.** A story's point of view determines how much confidence a reader should have in the events related. A story told from a third-person omniscient point of view generally provides a sense of authority and stability that makes the narrative seem reliable.
- **Ask why the narrator is telling the story.** The use of a first-person narrator, on the other hand, often suggests a certain bias, especially when the narrator relates events in which he or she has played a part. In such cases the narrator sometimes has an obvious interest in the audience's accepting his or her version of the story as truth.
- **Think about whether anything important is being left out of the story.** Is something of obvious importance to the situation not being reported? Understanding the limits of a narrator's point of view is key to interpreting what a story says.

CHECKLIST: Writing About Point of View

☐ How is the story narrated? Is it told in the third or the first person?

☐ If the story is told in the third person, is the point of view omniscient or does it confine itself to what is perceived by a particular character?

☐ What is gained by this choice?

☐ If the story is told by a first-person narrator, what is the speaker's main reason for telling the story? What does the narrator have to gain by making us believe his or her account?

☐ Does the first-person narrator fully understand his or her own motivations? Is there some important aspect of the narrator's character or situation that is being overlooked?

☐ Is there anything peculiar about the first-person narrator? Does this peculiarity create any suspicions about the narrator's accuracy or reliability?

☐ What does the narrator's perspective add? Would the story seem as memorable if related from another narrative angle?

TOPICS FOR WRITING ON POINT OF VIEW

1. Retell the events in "A & P" from the point of view of one of the story's minor characters: Lengel, or Stokesie, or one of the girls. How does the story's emphasis change?

2. Here is another writing exercise to help you sense what a difference point of view makes. Write a short statement from the point of view of William Faulkner's Homer Barron on "My Affair with Miss Emily."

3. Imagine a story such as "A & P" or "A Rose for Emily" told by an omniscient third-person narrator. Write several paragraphs about what would be lost (or gained) by such a change.

4. Choose any tale from "Stories for Further Reading," and, in a paragraph or two, describe how point of view colors the general meaning. If you like, you may argue that the story might be told more effectively from an alternate point of view.

5. Think back to a confrontation in your own life, and describe that event from a point of view contrary to your own. Try to imagine yourself inside your speaker's personality, and present the facts as that person would, as convincingly as you can.

6. Tell the story of a confrontation—biographical or fictional—from the point of view of a minor character peripheral to the central action. You could, for instance, tell the story of a disastrous first date from the point of view of the unlucky waitress who serves the couple dinner.

▶ TERMS FOR *review*

Points of View

Total omniscience ▶ Point of view in which the narrator knows everything about all of the characters and events in a story. A narrator with total omniscience can move freely from one character to another. Generally, a totally omniscient narrative is written in the third person.

Limited or selective omniscience ▶ Point of view in which the narrator sees into the minds of some but not all of the characters. Most typically, limited omniscience sees through the eyes of one major or minor character.

Impartial omniscience ▶ Point of view employed when an omniscient narrator, who presents the thoughts and actions of the characters, does not judge them or comment on them.

Editorial omniscience ▶ Point of view employed when an omniscient narrator goes beyond reporting the thoughts of his characters to make a critical judgment or commentary, making explicit the narrator's own thoughts or attitudes.

Objective point of view ▶ Point of view in which the third-person narrator merely reports dialogue and action with little or no interpretation or access to the characters' minds.

Types of Narrators

Omniscient or all-knowing narrator ▶ A narrator who has the ability to move freely through the consciousness of any character. The omniscient narrator also has complete knowledge of all of the external events in a story.

Participant or first-person narrator ▶ A narrator who is a participant in the action. Such a narrator refers to himself or herself as "I" and may be a major or minor character in the story.

Observer ▶ A first-person narrator who is relatively detached from or plays only a minor role in the events described.

Nonparticipant or third-person narrator ▶ A narrator who does not appear in the story as a character but is usually capable of revealing the thoughts and motives of one or more characters.

Innocent or naive narrator ▶ A character who fails to understand all the implications of the story he or she tells. The innocent narrator—often a child or childlike adult—is frequently used by an author to generate irony, sympathy, or pity by creating a gap between what the narrator perceives and what the reader knows.

Unreliable narrator ▶ A narrator who—intentionally or unintentionally—relates events in a subjective or distorted manner. The author usually provides some indication early on in such stories that the narrator is not to be completely trusted.

Narrative Techniques

Interior monologue ▶ An extended presentation of a character's thoughts in a narrative. Usually written in the present tense and printed without quotation marks, an interior monologue reads as if the character were speaking aloud to himself or herself, for the reader to overhear.

Stream of consciousness ▶ A type of modern narration that uses various literary devices, especially interior monologue, in an attempt to duplicate the subjective and associative nature of human consciousness.

3

CHARACTER

What You Will Learn in This Chapter

- To define *character*
- To identify types of characters
- To explain motivation and development
- To analyze the role of a character in a story

From popular fiction and drama, both classic and contemporary, we are acquainted with many stereotyped characters. Called **stock characters**, they are often known by some outstanding trait or traits: the *bragging* soldier of Greek and Roman comedy, the Prince *Charming* of fairy tales, the *mad* scientist of horror movies, the *fearlessly reckless* police detective of urban action films, the *brilliant but alcoholic* brain surgeon of medical thrillers on television. Stock characters are especially convenient for writers of commercial fiction: they require little detailed portraiture, for we already know them well. Most writers of the literary story, however, attempt to create characters who strike us not as stereotypes but as unique individuals. Although stock characters tend to have single dominant virtues and vices, characters in the finest contemporary short stories tend to have many facets, like people we meet.

A **character**, then, is presumably an imagined person who inhabits a story. Usually we recognize, in the main characters of a story, human personalities that become familiar to us. If the story seems "true to life," we generally find that its characters act in a reasonably consistent manner and that the author has provided them with motivation: sufficient reason to behave as they do. Should a character behave in a sudden and unexpected way, seeming to deny what we have been told about his or her nature or personality, we trust that there was a reason for this behavior and that sooner or later we will discover it.

In good fiction, characters sometimes change or develop. In *A Christmas Carol*, Charles Dickens tells how Ebenezer Scrooge, a tightfisted miser, reforms overnight, suddenly gives to the poor, and endeavors to assist his clerk's struggling family. But Dickens amply demonstrates why Scrooge had such a change of heart: four ghostly visitors, stirring kind memories the old miser had forgotten and also warning him of the probable consequences of his habits, provide the character (and hence the story) with adequate motivation.

CHARACTERIZATION

To borrow the useful terms of the English novelist E. M. Forster, characters may seem flat or round, depending on whether a writer sketches or sculpts them. A **flat character** has only one outstanding trait or feature, or at most a few distinguishing marks: for example, the familiar stock character of the mad scientist, with his lust for absolute power and his crazily gleaming eyes. Flat characters, however, need not be stock characters: in all of literature there is probably only one Tiny Tim, though his functions in A *Christmas Carol* are mainly to invoke blessings and to remind others of their Christian duties.

Some writers, such as J. K. Rowling, people their novels with hosts of characters. Often they distinguish the flat ones by giving each a single odd physical feature or mannerism—a nervous twitch, a piercing gaze, an obsessive fondness for oysters. **Round characters**, however, present us with more facets—that is, their authors portray them in greater depth and in more generous detail. Such a round character may appear to us only as he appears to the other characters in the story. If their views of him differ, we will see him from more than one side. In other stories, we enter a character's mind and come to know him through his own thoughts, feelings, and perceptions.

Character Development

Flat characters tend to stay the same throughout a story, but round characters often change—learn or become enlightened, grow or deteriorate. In William Faulkner's "Barn Burning" (Chapter 5), the boy Sarty Snopes, driven to defy his proud and violent father, becomes at the story's end more knowing and more mature. (Some critics call a fixed character **static**; a changing one, **dynamic**.) This is not to damn a flat character as an inferior creation. In most fiction—even the greatest—minor characters tend to be flat instead of round. Why? Rounding them would cost time and space; and so enlarged, they might only distract us from the main characters.

What's in a Name?

"A character, first of all, is the noise of his name," according to novelist William Gass. Names, chosen artfully, can indicate natures. A simple illustration is the completely virtuous Squire Allworthy, the foster father in *Tom Jones* by Henry Fielding. Subtler, perhaps, is the custom of giving a character a name that makes an **allusion**: a reference to some famous person, place, or thing. For his central characters in *Moby-Dick*, Herman Melville chose names from the Old Testament, calling his tragic and domineering Ahab after a biblical tyrant who came to a bad end, and his wandering narrator Ishmael after a biblical outcast. Whether or not it includes such a reference, a good name often reveals the character of the character. Charles Dickens, a vigorous and richly suggestive christener, named a couple of shyster lawyers Dodgson and Fogg (suggesting dodging evasiveness and foglike obfuscation), and named two heartless educators, who grimly drill their schoolchildren in "hard facts," Gradgind and M'Choakumchild.

Hero Versus Antihero

Instead of a hero, many a recent novel has featured an **antihero**: a protagonist conspicuously lacking in one or more of the usual attributes of a traditional **hero**, bravery, skill, idealism, sense of purpose. The antihero is an ordinary, unglorious citizen of the modern world, usually drawn (according to the Irish short story writer Sean O'Faolain) as someone "groping, puzzled, cross, mocking, frustrated, and isolated."

If epic poets once drew their heroes as decisive leaders, embodying their people's highest ideals, antiheroes tend to be loners, without admirable qualities, just barely able to survive. A gulf separates Leopold Bloom, antihero of James Joyce's novel *Ulysses*, from the hero of the Greek *Odyssey*. In Homer's epic, Ulysses wanders the Mediterranean, battling monsters and overcoming enchantments. In Joyce's novel, Bloom wanders the littered streets of Dublin, peddling advertising space. Meursault, the title character of Albert Camus's novel *The Stranger*, is so alienated from his own life that he is unmoved at the news of his mother's death.

MOTIVATION

At the heart of most stories is **motivation**—the cause (or causes) of a character's actions. Motivation is what animates a story and justifies the behavior of each character, especially the protagonist whose motivation usually sets a story in action. In simple narratives, such as a fable or fairy tale, the motivation tends to be straightforward—a prince needs to rescue a princess, a poor boy sets off to find a fortune. In Aesop's famous fable "The Fox and the Grapes," the fox is hungry and wants to eat the grapes hanging high above him. That visceral motivation explains every event that follows. In a more sophisticated story, such as Raymond Carver's "Cathedral," the motivation is often more subtle and complex. Carver's protagonist is a man who reluctantly welcomes a blind visitor in his home. The protagonist doesn't want to meet the man, but he is forced into hospitality because his wife has demanded he be courteous as proof of his love to her. His motivation is neither pure nor simple, and his mixed feelings not only give the story its realistic atmosphere but also lead to the narrative's unexpected climax. Motivation usually reveals a character's psychological traits and values. In a good story the motivation makes the plot feel inevitable, even when it takes a surprising turn.

Katherine Anne Porter

The Jilting of Granny Weatherall   1930

Katherine Anne Porter (1890–1980) was born in Indian Creek, Texas. Her mother died when she was two, and Porter was raised by a grandmother who surrounded the growing girl with books. At sixteen she ran away from school and soon married a railway clerk in Louisiana. Three years later, she divorced her husband and began supporting herself as a reporter in Chicago, Denver, and Fort Worth, and sometimes as an actress and ballad singer while traveling through the South. Sojourns in Europe and in Mexico supplied her with mate-rial for some of her finest stories. Her brilliant,

Katherine Anne Porter

sensitive short fiction, first collected in Flowering Judas *(1930), won her a high reputation. Her one novel,* Ship of Fools *(1962), with which she had struggled for twenty years, received harsh critical notices, but proved a com-mercial success. In 1965 her* Collected Stories *received a Pulitzer Prize and a National Book Award.*

She flicked her wrist neatly out of Doctor Harry's pudgy careful fingers and pulled the sheet up to her chin. The brat ought to be in knee breeches. Doctoring around the country with spectacles on his nose! "Get along now, take your schoolbooks and go. There's nothing wrong with me."

Doctor Harry spread a warm paw like a cushion on her forehead where the forked green vein danced and made her eyelids twitch. "Now, now, be a good girl, and we'll have you up in no time."

"That's no way to speak to a woman nearly eighty years old just because she's down. I'd have you respect your elders, young man."

"Well, Missy, excuse me." Doctor Harry patted her cheek. "But I've got to warn you, haven't I? You're a marvel, but you must be careful or you're going to be good and sorry."

"Don't tell me what I'm going to be. I'm on my feet now, morally   5
speaking. It's Cornelia. I had to go to bed to get rid of her."

Her bones felt loose, and floated around in her skin, and Doctor Harry floated like a balloon around the foot of the bed. He floated and pulled down his waistcoat and swung his glasses on a cord. "Well, stay where you are, it certainly can't hurt you."

"Get along and doctor your sick," said Granny Weatherall. "Leave a well woman alone. I'll call for you when I want you. . . . Where were you forty years ago when I pulled through milk-leg and double pneumonia? You weren't even born. Don't let Cornelia lead you on," she shouted, because Doctor Harry appeared to float up to the ceiling and out. "I pay my own bills, and I don't throw my money away on nonsense!"

She meant to wave good-by, but it was too much trouble. Her eyes closed of themselves, it was like a dark curtain drawn around the bed. The pillow rose and floated under her, pleasant as a hammock in a light wind. She listened to the leaves rustling outside the window. No, somebody was swishing newspapers: no, Cornelia and Doctor Harry were whispering together. She leaped broad awake, thinking they whispered in her ear.

"She was never like this, *never* like this!" "Well, what can we expect?" "Yes, eighty years old. . . ."

Well, and what if she was? She still had ears. It was like Cornelia to whisper around doors. She always kept things secret in such a public way. She was always being tactful and kind. Cornelia was dutiful; that was the trouble with her. Dutiful and good: "So good and dutiful," said Granny, "that I'd like to spank her." She saw herself spanking Cornelia and making a fine job of it.

"What'd you say, Mother?"

Granny felt her face tying up in hard knots.

"Can't a body think, I'd like to know?"

"I thought you might want something."

"I do. I want a lot of things. First off, go away and don't whisper."

She lay and drowsed, hoping in her sleep that the children would keep out and let her rest a minute. It had been a long day. Not that she was tired. It was always pleasant to snatch a minute now and then. There was always so much to be done, let me see: tomorrow.

Tomorrow was far away and there was nothing to trouble about. Things were finished somehow when the time came; thank God there was always a little margin over for peace: then a person could spread out the plan of life and tuck in the edges orderly. It was good to have everything clean and folded away, with the hair brushes and tonic bottles sitting straight on the white embroidered linen: the day started without fuss and the pantry shelves laid out with rows of jelly glasses and brown jugs and white stone-china jars with blue whirligigs and words painted on them: coffee, tea, sugar, ginger, cinnamon, allspice: and the bronze clock with the lion on top nicely dusted off. The dust that lion could collect in twenty-four hours! The box in the attic with all those letters tied up, well, she'd have to go through that tomorrow. All those letters—George's letters and John's letters and her letters to them both—lying around for the children to find afterwards made her uneasy. Yes, that would be tomorrow's business. No use to let them know how silly she had been once.

While she was rummaging around she found death in her mind and it felt clammy and unfamiliar. She had spent so much time preparing for death there was no need for bringing it up again. Let it take care of itself

now. When she was sixty she had felt very old, finished, and went around
making farewell trips to see her children and grandchildren, with a secret
in her mind: This is the very last of your mother, children! Then she made
her will and came down with a long fever. That was all just a notion like
a lot of other things, but it was lucky too, for she had once for all got over
the idea of dying for a long time. Now she couldn't be worried. She hoped
she had better sense now. Her father had lived to be one hundred and two
years old and had drunk a noggin of strong hot toddy on his last birthday.
He told the reporters it was his daily habit, and he owed his long life to it.
He had made quite a scandal and was very pleased about it. She believed
she'd just plague Cornelia a little.

"Cornelia! Cornelia!" No footsteps, but a sudden hand on her cheek.
"Bless you, where have you been?"

"Here, Mother."   20

"Well, Cornelia, I want a noggin of hot toddy."

"Are you cold, darling?"

"I'm chilly, Cornelia. Lying in bed stops the circulation. I must have
told you that a thousand times."

Well, she could just hear Cornelia telling her husband that Mother
was getting a little childish and they'd have to humor her. The thing that
most annoyed her was that Cornelia thought she was deaf, dumb, and
blind. Little hasty glances and tiny gestures tossed around her and over
her head saying, "Don't cross her, let her have her way, she's eighty years
old," and she sitting there as if she lived in a thin glass cage. Sometimes
Granny almost made up her mind to pack up and move back to her own
house where nobody could remind her every minute that she was old.
Wait, wait, Cornelia, till your own children whisper behind your back!

In her day she had kept a better house and had got more work done.   25
She wasn't too old yet for Lydia to be driving eighty miles for advice when
one of the children jumped the track, and Jimmy still dropped in and
talked things over: "Now, Mammy, you've a good business head, I want
to know what you think of this? . . ." Old. Cornelia couldn't change the
furniture around without asking. Little things, little things! They had
been so sweet when they were little. Granny wished the old days were
back again with the children young and everything to be done over. It
had been a hard pull, but not too much for her. When she thought of all
the food she had cooked, and all the clothes she had cut and sewed, and
all the gardens she had made—well, the children showed it. There they
were, made out of her, and they couldn't get away from that. Sometimes
she wanted to see John again and point to them and say, Well, I didn't
do so badly, did I? But that would have to wait. That was for tomorrow.
She used to think of him as a man, but now all the children were older
than their father, and he would be a child beside her if she saw him now.
It seemed strange and there was something wrong in the idea. Why, he

couldn't possibly recognize her. She had fenced in a hundred acres once, digging the post holes herself and clamping the wires with just a negro boy to help. That changed a woman. John would be looking for a young woman with the peaked Spanish comb in her hair and the painted fan. Digging post holes changed a woman. Riding country roads in the winter when women had their babies was another thing: sitting up nights with sick horses and sick negroes and sick children and hardly ever losing one. John, I hardly ever lost one of them! John would see that in a minute, that would be something he could understand, she wouldn't have to explain anything!

It made her feel like rolling up her sleeves and putting the whole place to rights again. No matter if Cornelia was determined to be every-where at once, there were a great many things left undone on this place. She would start tomorrow and do them. It was good to be strong enough for everything, even if all you made melted and changed and slipped un-der your hands, so that by the time you finished you almost forgot what you were working for. What was it I set out to do? she asked herself in-tently, but she could not remember. A fog rose over the valley, she saw it marching across the creek swallowing the trees and moving up the hill like an army of ghosts. Soon it would be at the near edge of the orchard, and then it was time to go in and light the lamps. Come in, children, don't stay out in the night air.

Lighting the lamps had been beautiful. The children huddled up to her and breathed like little calves waiting at the bars in the twilight. Their eyes followed the match and watched the flame rise and settle in a blue curve, then they moved away from her. The lamp was lit, they didn't have to be scared and hang on to mother any more. Never, never, never more. God, for all my life I thank Thee. Without Thee, my God, I could never have done it. Hail, Mary, full of grace.

I want you to pick all the fruit this year and see that nothing is wasted. There's always someone who can use it. Don't let good things rot for want of using. You waste life when you waste good food. Don't let things get lost. It's bitter to lose things. Now, don't let me get to thinking, not when I am tired and taking a little nap before supper. . . .

The pillow rose about her shoulders and pressed against her heart and the memory was being squeezed out of it: oh, push down the pil-low, somebody: it would smother her if she tried to hold it. Such a fresh breeze blowing and such a green day with no threats in it. But he had not come, just the same. What does a woman do when she has put on the white veil and set out the white cake for a man and he doesn't come? She tried to remember. No, I swear he never harmed me but in that. He never harmed me but in that . . . and what if he did? There was the day, the day, but a whirl of dark smoke rose and covered it, crept up and over into the bright field where everything was planted so carefully in orderly rows. That was hell, she knew hell when she saw it. For sixty years she had prayed against remembering him and against losing her soul in the deep pit of hell, and now the two things were mingled in one and the thought of him was a smoky cloud from hell that moved and crept in her head when she had just got rid of Doctor Harry and was trying to rest a minute. Wounded vanity, Ellen, said a sharp voice in the top of her mind. Don't let your wounded vanity get the upper hand of you. Plenty of girls get jilted. You were jilted, weren't you? Then stand up to it. Her eyelids wavered and let in streamers of blue-gray light like tissue paper over her eyes. She must get up and pull the shades down or she'd never sleep. She was in bed again and the shades were not down. How could that happen? Better turn over, hide from the light, sleeping in the light gave you nightmares. "Mother, how do you feel now?" and a stinging wetness on her forehead. But I don't like having my face washed in cold water!

Hapsy? George? Lydia? Jimmy? No, Cornelia, and her features were   30
swollen and full of little puddles. "They're coming, darling, they'll all be here soon." Go wash your face, child, you look funny.

Instead of obeying, Cornelia knelt down and put her head on the pillow. She seemed to be talking but there was no sound. "Well, are you tongue-tied? Whose birthday is it? Are you going to give a party?"

Cornelia's mouth moved urgently in strange shapes. "Don't do that, you bother me, daughter."

"Oh, no, Mother. Oh, no. . . ."

Nonsense. It was strange about children. They disputed your every word. "No what, Cornelia?"

"Here's Doctor Harry."   35

"I won't see that boy again. He just left three minutes ago."

"That was this morning, Mother. It's night now. Here's the nurse."

"This is Doctor Harry, Mrs. Weatherall. I never saw you look so young and happy!"

"Ah, I'll never be young again—but I'd be happy if they'd let me lie in peace and get rested."

She thought she spoke up loudly, but no one answered. A warm   40
weight on her forehead, a warm bracelet on her wrist, and a breeze went on whispering, trying to tell her something. A shuffle of leaves in the everlasting hand of God. He blew on them and they danced and rattled. "Mother, don't mind, we're going to give you a little hypodermic." "Look here, daughter, how do ants get in this bed? I saw sugar ants yesterday." Did you send for Hapsy too?

It was Hapsy she really wanted. She had to go a long way back through a great many rooms to find Hapsy standing with a baby on her arm. She seemed to herself to be Hapsy also, and the baby on Hapsy's arm was Hapsy and himself and herself, all at once, and there was no surprise in the meeting. Then Hapsy melted from within and turned flimsy as gray gauze and the baby was a gauzy shadow, and Hapsy came up close and said, "I thought you'd never come," and looked at her very searchingly and said, "You haven't changed a bit!" They leaned forward to kiss, when Cornelia began whispering from a long way off, "Oh, is there anything you want to tell me? Is there anything I can do for you?"

Yes, she had changed her mind after sixty years and she would like to see George. I want you to find George. Find him and be sure to tell him I forgot him. I want him to know I had my husband just the same and my children and my house like any other woman. A good house too and a good husband that I loved and fine children out of him. Better than I hoped for even. Tell him I was given back everything he took away and more. Oh, no, oh, God, no, there was something else besides the house and the man and the children. Oh, surely they were not all? What was it? Something not given back. . . . Her breath crowded down under her ribs and grew into a monstrous frightening shape with cutting edges; it bored up into her head, and the agony was unbelievable: Yes, John, get the Doctor now, no more talk, my time has come.

When this one was born it should be the last. The last. It should have been born first, for it was the one she had truly wanted. Everything came in good time. Nothing left out, left over. She was strong, in three days she would be as well as ever. Better. A woman needed milk in her to have her full health.

"Mother, do you hear me?"

"I've been telling you—"

"Mother, Father Connolly's here."

"I went to Holy Communion only last week. Tell him I'm not so sinful as all that."

"Father just wants to speak to you."

He could speak as much as he pleased. It was like him to drop in and inquire about her soul as if it were a teething baby, and then stay on for a cup of tea and a round of cards and gossip. He always had a funny story of some sort, usually about an Irishman who made his little mistakes and confessed them, and the point lay in some absurd thing he would blurt out in the confessional showing his struggles between native piety and original sin. Granny felt easy about her soul. Cornelia, where are your manners? Give Father Connolly a chair. She had her secret comfortable understanding with a few favorite saints who cleared a straight road to God for her. All as surely signed and sealed as the papers for the new Forty Acres. Forever . . . heirs and assigns forever. Since the day the wedding cake was not cut, but thrown out and wasted. The whole bottom dropped out of the world, and there she was blind and sweating with nothing under her feet and the walls falling away. His hand had caught her under the breast, she had not fallen, there was the freshly polished floor with the green rug on it, just as before. He had cursed like a sailor's parrot and

said, "I'll kill him for you." Don't lay a hand on him, for my sake leave
something to God. "Now, Ellen, you must believe what I tell you. . . ."

So there was nothing, nothing to worry about any more, except   50
sometimes in the night one of the children screamed in a nightmare, and
they both hustled out shaking and hunting for the matches and calling,
"There, wait a minute, here we are!" John, get the doctor now, Hapsy's
time has come. But there was Hapsy standing by the bed in a white cap.
"Cornelia, tell Hapsy to take off her cap. I can't see her plain."

Her eyes opened very wide and the room stood out like a picture
she had seen somewhere. Dark colors with the shadows rising towards
the ceiling in long angles. The tall black dresser gleamed with nothing
on it but John's picture, enlarged from a little one, with John's eyes very
black when they should have been blue. You never saw him, so how do
you know how he looked? But the man insisted the copy was perfect, it
was very rich and handsome. For a picture, yes, but it's not my husband.
The table by the bed had a linen cover and a candle and a crucifix. The
light was blue from Cornelia's silk lampshades. No sort of light at all, just
frippery. You had to live forty years with kerosene lamps to appreciate
honest electricity. She felt very strong and she saw Doctor Harry with a
rosy nimbus around him.

"You look like a saint, Doctor Harry, and I vow that's as near as you'll
ever come to it."

"She's saying something."

"I heard you, Cornelia. What's all this carrying-on?"

"Father Connolly's saying—"   55

Cornelia's voice staggered and bumped like a cart in a bad road. It
rounded corners and turned back again and arrived nowhere. Granny
stepped up in the cart very lightly and reached for the reins, but a man sat
beside her and she knew him by his hands, driving the cart. She did not
look in his face, for she knew without seeing, but looked instead down the
road where the trees leaned over and bowed to each other and a thousand
birds were singing a Mass. She felt like singing too, but she put her hand in
the bosom of her dress and pulled out a rosary, and Father Connolly murmured Latin in a very solemn voice and tickled her feet. My God, will you
stop that nonsense? I'm a married woman. What if he did run away and
leave me to face the priest by myself? I found another a whole world better.
I wouldn't have exchanged my husband for anybody except St. Michael
himself, and you may tell him that for me with a thank you in the bargain.

Light flashed on her closed eyelids, and a deep roaring shook her.
Cornelia, is that lightning? I hear thunder. There's going to be a storm.
Close all the windows. Call the children in. . . . "Mother, here we are, all
of us." "Is that you, Hapsy?" "Oh, no, I'm Lydia. We drove as fast as we
could." Their faces drifted above her, drifted away. The rosary fell out of
her hands and Lydia put it back. Jimmy tried to help, their hands fumbled

together, and Granny closed two fingers around Jimmy's thumb. Beads wouldn't do, it must be something alive. She was so amazed her thoughts ran round and round. So, my dear Lord, this is my death and I wasn't even thinking about it. My children have come to see me die. But I can't, it's not time. Oh, I always hated surprises. I wanted to give Cornelia the amethyst set—Cornelia, you're to have the amethyst set, but Hapsy's to wear it when she wants, and, Doctor Harry, do shut up. Nobody sent for you. Oh, my dear Lord, do wait a minute. I meant to do something about the Forty Acres, Jimmy doesn't need it and Lydia will later on, with that worthless husband of hers. I meant to finish the altar cloth and send six bottles of wine to Sister Borgia for her dyspepsia. I want to send six bottles of wine to Sister Borgia, Father Connolly, now don't let me forget.

Cornelia's voice made short turns and tilted over and crashed, "Oh, Mother, oh, Mother, oh, Mother. . . ."

"I'm not going, Cornelia. I'm taken by surprise. I can't go."

You'll see Hapsy again. What about her? "I thought you'd never come." Granny made a long journey outward, looking for Hapsy. What if I don't find her? What then? Her heart sank down and down, there was no bottom to death, she couldn't come to the end of it. The blue light from Cornelia's lampshade drew into a tiny point in the center of her brain, it flickered and winked like an eye, quietly it fluttered and dwindled. Granny lay curled down within herself, amazed and watchful, staring at the point of light that was herself; her body was now only a deeper mass of shadow in an endless darkness and this darkness would curl around the light and swallow it up. God, give a sign!   60

For the second time there was no sign. Again no bridegroom and the priest in the house. She could not remember any other sorrow because this grief wiped them all away. Oh, no, there's nothing more cruel than this—I'll never forgive it. She stretched herself with a deep breath and blew out the light.

Questions

1. In the very first paragraph, what does the writer tell us about Ellen (Granny) Weatherall?
2. What does the name Weatherall have to do with Granny's nature (or her life story)? What other traits or qualities do you find in her?
3. "Her bones felt loose, and floated around in her skin, and Doctor Harry floated like a balloon" (paragraph 6). What do you understand from this statement? By what other remarks does the writer indicate Granny's condition? In paragraph 56, why does Father Connolly tickle Granny's feet? At what other moments in the story does she fail to understand what is happening, or confuse the present with the past?
4. Exactly what happened to Ellen Weatherall sixty years earlier? What effects did this event have on her?
5. In paragraph 49, whom do you guess to be the man who "cursed like a sailor's parrot"? In paragraph 56, whom do you assume to be the man driving the cart? Is

the fact that these persons are not clearly labeled and identified a failure on the author's part?

6. What is stream of consciousness? Would you call "The Jilting of Granny Weatherall" a stream-of-consciousness story? Refer to the story in your reply.
7. Sum up the character of the daughter Cornelia.
8. Why doesn't Granny's last child, Hapsy, come to her mother's deathbed?
9. Would you call the character of Doctor Harry "flat" or "round"? Why is his flatness (or roundness) appropriate to the story?
10. How is this the story of another "jilting"? What similarities are there between that fateful day sixty years ago (described in paragraphs 29, 49, and 61) and the moment when Granny is dying? This time, who is the "bridegroom" not in the house?
11. "This is the story of an eighty-year-old woman lying in bed, getting groggy, and dying. I can't see why it should interest anybody." How would you answer this critic?

Tobias Wolff

Bullet in the Brain   1997

Tobias Wolff was born in Birmingham, Alabama, in 1945, the son of an aerospace engineer and a waitress and secretary. Following his parents' divorce, Tobias moved with his mother to Washington State while his older brother, Geoffrey, remained with their father (a pathological liar who was the subject of Geoffrey Wolff's acclaimed memoir The Duke of Deception). *Tobias Wolff's own memoir,* This Boy's Life (1989), *describes, among other things, his tense relationship with his abusive stepfather; it was the basis for the 1993 film starring Robert De Niro and Leonardo DiCaprio. In 1964 Wolff*

Tobias Wolff

joined the army, where he spent four years, including a year in Vietnam as a Special Forces language expert. This experience is recounted in a second memoir, In Pharaoh's Army: Memories of the Lost War (1994). *After his military service, he earned a bachelor's degree at Oxford University and a master's at Stanford University, where he currently teaches in the creative writing program. Wolff is the author of six volumes of fiction: the novella* The Barracks Thief (1984, PEN/Faulkner Award), *the novel* Old School (2003), *and four volumes of short stories, most recently* Our Story Begins: New and Selected Stories (2008).

Acknowledging Raymond Carver (his onetime faculty colleague at Syracuse University) and Flannery O'Connor as influences, Wolff writes stories that, in the words of one critic, create a "sometimes comic, always compassionate world of ordinary people who suffer twentieth-century martyrdoms of growing up, growing old, loving and lacking love, living with parents and lovers and wives and their own weaknesses." Wolff lives in Northern California.

Anders couldn't get to the bank until just before it closed, so of course the line was endless and he got stuck behind two women whose loud, stupid conversation put him in a murderous temper. He was never in the best of tempers anyway, Anders—a book critic known for the weary, elegant savagery with which he dispatched almost everything he reviewed.

With the line still doubled around the rope, one of the bank tellers stuck a "POSITION CLOSED" sign in her window and walked to the back of the bank, where she leaned against a desk and began to pass the time with a man shuffling papers. The women in front of Anders broke off their conversation and watched the teller with hatred. "Oh, that's nice," one of them said. She turned to Anders and added, confident of his accord, "One of those little human touches that keep us coming back for more."

Anders had conceived his own towering hatred of the teller, but he immediately turned it on the presumptuous crybaby in front of him. "Damned unfair," he said, "Tragic, really. If they're not chopping off the wrong leg, or bombing your ancestral village, they're closing their positions."

She stood her ground. "I didn't say it was tragic," she said, "I just think it's a pretty lousy way to treat your customers."

"Unforgivable," Anders said, "Heaven will take note." 5

She sucked in her cheeks but stared past him and said nothing. Anders saw that the other woman, her friend, was looking in the same direction. And then the tellers stopped what they were doing, and the customers slowly turned, and silence came over the bank. Two man wearing black ski masks and blue business suits were standing to the side of the door. One of them had a pistol pressed against the guard's neck. The guard's eyes were closed, and his lips were moving. The other man had a sawed-off shotgun. "Keep your big mouth shut!" the man with the pistol said, though no one had spoken a word. "One of you tellers hits the alarm, you're all dead meat. Got it?"

The tellers nodded.

"Oh, bravo," Anders said. "*Dead meat.*" He turned to the woman in front of him. "Great script, eh? The stern, brass-knuckled poetry of the dangerous classes."

She looked at him with drowning eyes.

The man with the shotgun pushed the guard to his knees. He handed 10 the shotgun to his partner and yanked the guard's wrists up behind his back and locked them together with a pair of handcuffs. He toppled him onto the floor with a kick between the shoulder blades. Then he took his shotgun back and went over to the security gate at the end of the counter. He was short and heavy and moved with peculiar slowness, even torpor. "Buzz him in," his partner said. The man with the shotgun opened the gate and sauntered along the line of tellers, handing each of them a Hefty bag. When he came to the empty position he looked over at the man with the pistol, who said, "Whose slot is that?"

Anders watched the teller. She put her hand to her throat and turned to the man she'd been talking to. He nodded. "Mine," she said.

"Then get your ugly ass in gear and fill that bag."

"There you go," Anders said to the woman in front of him. "Justice is done."

"Hey! Bright boy! Did I tell you to talk?"

"No," Anders said.   15

"Then shut your trap."

"Did you hear that?" Anders said. "'Bright boy.' Right out of 'The Killers.'"°

"Please be quiet," the woman said.

"Hey, you deaf or what?" The man with the pistol walked over to Anders. He poked the weapon into Anders' gut. "You think I'm playing games?"

"No," Anders said, but the barrel tickled like a stiff finger and he had   20
to fight back the titters. He did this by making himself stare into the man's eyes, which were clearly visible behind the holes in the mask: pale blue and rawly red-rimmed. The man's left eyelid kept twitching. He breathed out a piercing, ammoniac smell that shocked Anders more than anything that had happened, and he was beginning to develop a sense of unease when the man prodded him again with the pistol.

"You like me, bright boy!" he said. "You want to suck my dick!"

"No," Anders said.

"Then stop looking at me."

Anders fixed his gaze on the man's shiny wing-tip shoes.

"Not down there. Up there." He stuck the pistol under Anders' chin   25
and pushed it upwards until Anders was looking at the ceiling.

Anders had never paid much attention to that part of the bank, a pompous old building with marble floors and counters and pillars, and gilt scrollwork over the tellers' cages. The domed ceiling had been decorated with mythological figures whose fleshy, toga-draped ugliness Anders had taken in at a glance years earlier and afterward declined to notice. Now he had no choice but to scrutinize the painter's work. It was even worse than he remembered, and all of it executed with the utmost gravity. The artist had a few tricks up his sleeve and used them again and again—a certain rosy blush on the underside of the clouds, a coy backwards glance on the faces of the cupids and fauns. The ceiling was crowded with various dramas, but the one that caught Anders' eye was Zeus and Europa—portrayed, in this rendition, as a bull ogling a cow from behind a haystack. To make the cow sexy, the painter had canted her hips suggestively and given her long, droopy eyelashes through which she gazed back at the bull with sultry

"The Killers": a short story by Ernest Hemingway about two gangsters who visit a suburban Chicago diner in search of a prizefighter they have been told to murder. They use the term "bright boy" to condescendingly and aggressively address the other men in the diner.

welcome. The bull wore a smirk and his eyebrows were arched. If there'd been a bubble coming out of his mouth, it would have said, "Hubba hubba."

"What's so funny, bright boy?"

"Nothing."

"You think I'm comical? You think I'm some kind of clown?"

"No."   30

"Fuck with me again, you're history. *Capiche?*"

Anders burst out laughing. He covered his mouth with both hands and said, "I'm sorry, I'm sorry," then snorted helplessly through his fingers and said, "*Capiche*—oh, God—*capiche*," and at that the man with the pistol raised the pistol and shot Anders right in the head.

The bullet smashed Anders' skull and ploughed through his brain and exited behind his right ear, scattering shards of bone into the cerebral cortex, the corpus callosum, back toward the basal ganglia, and down into the thalamus. But before all this occurred, the first appearance of the bullet in the cerebrum set off a crackling chain of iron transports and neuro-transmissions. Because of their peculiar origin these traced a peculiar pattern, flukishly calling into life a summer afternoon some forty years past, and long since lost to memory. After striking the cranium the bullet was moving at 900 feet per second, a pathetically sluggish, glacial pace compared to the synaptic lightning that flashed around it. Once in the brain, that is, the bullet came under the mediation of brain time, which gave Anders plenty of leisure to contemplate the scene that, in a phrase he would have abhorred, "passed before his eyes."

It is worth noting what Anders did not remember, given what he did remember. He did not remember his first lover, Sherry, or what he had most madly loved about her, before it came to irritate him—her unembarrassed carnality, and especially the cordial way she had with his unit, which she called Mr. Mole, as in, "Uh-oh, looks like Mr. Mole wants to play," and, "let's hide Mr. Mole!" Anders did not remember his wife, whom he had also loved before she exhausted him with her predictability, or his daughter, now a sullen professor of economics at Dartmouth. He did not remember standing just outside his daughter's door as she lectured her bear about his naughtiness and described the truly appalling punishment Paws would receive unless he changed his ways. He did not remember a single line of the hundreds of poems he committed to memory in his youth so that he could give himself the shivers at will—not "Silent, upon a peak in Darien," or "My God, I heard this day," or "All my pretty ones? Did you say all? O hell-kite! All?" None of these did he remember; not one. Anders did not remember his dying mother saying of his father, "I should have stabbed him in his sleep."

He did not remember Professor Josephs telling his class how Athenian prisoners in Sicily had been released if they could recite Aeschylus, and then reciting Aeschylus himself, right there, in the Greek. Anders   35 did not remember how his eyes had burned at those sounds. He did not remember the surprise of seeing a college classmate's name on the jacket of a novel not long after they graduated, or the respect he had felt after reading the book. He did not remember the pleasure of giving respect.

Nor did Anders remember seeing a woman leap to her death from the building opposite his own just days after his daughter was born. He did not remember shouting, "Lord have mercy!" He did not remember deliberately crashing his father's car into a tree, or having his ribs kicked in by three policemen at an anti-war rally, or waking himself up with laughter. He did not remember when he began to regard the heap of books on his desk with boredom and dread, or when he grew angry at writers for writing them. He did not remember when everything began to remind him of something else.

This is what Anders remembered. Heat. A baseball field. Yellow grass, the whirr of insects, himself leaning against a tree as the boys of the neighborhood gather for a pickup game. He looks on as the others argue the relative genius of Mantle and Mays. They have been worrying this subject all summer, and it has become tedious to Anders; an oppression, like the heat.

Then the last two boys arrive, Coyle and a cousin of his from Mississippi. Anders has never met Coyle's cousin before and will never see him again. He says hi with the rest but takes no further notice of him until they've chosen sides and someone asks the cousin what position he wants to play. "Shortstop," the boy says. "Short's the best position they is." Anders turns and looks at him. He wants to hear Coyle's cousin repeat what he's just said, but he knows better than to ask. The others will think he's being a jerk, ragging the kid for his grammar. But that isn't it, not at all—it's that Anders is strangely roused, elated, by those final two words, their pure unexpectedness and their music. He takes the field in a trance, repeating them to himself.

The bullet is already in the brain; it won't be outrun forever, or charmed to a halt. In the end it will do its work and leave the troubled skull behind, dragging its comet's tail of memory and hope and talent and love into the marble hall of commerce. That can't be helped. But for now Anders can still make time. Time for the shadows to lengthen on the grass, time for the tethered dog to bark at the flying ball, time for the boy in right field to smack his sweat-blackened mitt and softly chant, *They is, They is, They is.*

Questions

1. Describe the character of the adult Anders. Why do you think Wolff chose to make him a book critic?
2. Does Anders seem to experience the robbery as a real-life event? In what ways is his reaction different than the other customers, and why do you suppose that is?
3. Is there anything symbolic about setting the story in a "marble hall of commerce," especially in contrast to the baseball field conjured up in his memory?

4. Who in the story would you say is a *stock character*?
5. Why did Wolff decide to tell us what Anders did *not* remember?
6. What is the significance of the afternoon that Anders does remember? What do the final words, *They is*, symbolize for him?
7. How has Anders changed during the course of his life?

Alice Walker

Everyday Use   1973

Alice Walker, a leading black writer and social activist, was born in 1944 in Eatonton, Georgia, the youngest of eight children. Her father, a sharecropper and dairy farmer, usually earned about $300 a year; her mother helped by working as a maid. Both entertained their children by telling stories. When Alice Walker was eight, she was accidentally struck by a pellet from a brother's BB gun. She lost the sight of her right eye because the Walkers had no car to rush her to the hospital. Later she attended Spelman College in Atlanta and finished college at Sarah Lawrence College on a scholarship. While

Alice Walker

working for the civil rights movement in Mississippi, she met a young lawyer, Melvyn Leventhal. In 1967 they settled in Jackson, Mississippi, the first legally married interracial couple in town. They returned to New York in 1974 and were later divorced. First known as a poet, Walker has published eight books of her verse. She also has edited a collection of the work of the then-neglected black writer Zora Neale Hurston, and has written a study of Langston Hughes. In a collection of essays, In Search of Our Mothers' Gardens: Womanist Prose *(1983), she recalls her mother and addresses her own daughter. (By womanist she means "black feminist.") But the largest part of Walker's reading audience knows her fiction: four story collections, including* In Love and Trouble *(1973), from which "Everyday Use" is taken, and her many novels. Her best-known novel,* The Color Purple *(1982), won a Pulitzer Prize and was made into a film by Steven Spielberg in 1985. Her recent novels include* By the Light of My Father's Smile *(1998) and* Now Is the Time to Open Your Heart *(2004). Walker lives in Northern California.*

for your grandmama

I will wait for her in the yard that Maggie and I made so clean and wavy yesterday afternoon. A yard like this is more comfortable than most people know. It is not just a yard. It is like an extended living room. When the hard clay is swept clean as a floor and the fine sand around the edges lined with tiny, irregular grooves, anyone can come and sit and look up into the elm tree and wait for the breezes that never come inside the house.

Maggie will be nervous until after her sister goes: she will stand hopelessly in corners, homely and ashamed of the burn scars down her arms and legs, eyeing her sister with a mixture of envy and awe. She thinks her sister has held life always in the palm of one hand, that "no" is a word the world never learned to say to her.

You've no doubt seen those TV shows where the child who has "made it" is confronted, as a surprise, by her own mother and father, tottering in weakly from backstage. (A pleasant surprise, of course: What would they do if parent and child came on the show only to curse out and insult each other?) On TV mother and child embrace and smile into each other's faces. Sometimes the mother and father weep, the child wraps them in her arms and leans across the table to tell how she would not have made it without their help. I have seen these programs.°

Sometimes I dream a dream in which Dee and I are suddenly brought together on a TV program of this sort. Out of a dark and soft-seated limousine I am ushered into a bright room filled with many people. There I meet a smiling, gray, sporty man like Johnny Carson who shakes my hand and tells me what a fine girl I have. Then we are on the stage and Dee is embracing me with tears in her eyes. She pins on my dress a large orchid, even though she has told me once that she thinks orchids are tacky flowers.

In real life I am a large, big-boned woman with rough, man-working   5
hands. In the winter I wear flannel nightgowns to bed and overalls during the day. I can kill and clean a hog as mercilessly as a man. My fat keeps me hot in zero weather. I can work outside all day, breaking ice to get water for washing. I can eat pork liver cooked over the open fire minutes after it comes steaming from the hog. One winter I knocked a bull calf straight in the brain between the eyes with a sledge hammer and had the meat hung up to chill before nightfall. But of course all this does not show on television. I am the way my daughter would want me to be: a hundred pounds lighter, my skin like an uncooked barley pancake. My hair glistens in the hot bright lights. Johnny Carson has much to do to keep up with my quick and witty tongue.

But that is a mistake. I know even before I wake up. Who ever knew a Johnson with a quick tongue? Who can even imagine me looking a strange white man in the eye? It seems to me I have talked to them always with one foot raised in flight, with my head turned in whichever way is farthest from them. Dee, though. She would always look anyone in the eye. Hesitation was no part of her nature.

***

"How do I look, Mama?" Maggie says, showing just enough of her thin body enveloped in pink skirt and red blouse for me to know she's there, almost hidden by the door.

---

these programs: On the NBC television show *This Is Your Life*, people were publicly and often tearfully reunited with friends, relatives, and teachers they had not seen in years.

"Come out into the yard," I say.

Have you ever seen a lame animal, perhaps a dog run over by some careless person rich enough to own a car, sidle up to someone who is ignorant enough to be kind to him? That is the way my Maggie walks. She has been like this, chin on chest, eyes on ground, feet in shuffle, ever since the fire that burned the other house to the ground.

Dee is lighter than Maggie, with nicer hair and a fuller figure. She's a   10
woman now, though sometimes I forget. How long ago was it that the other house burned? Ten, twelve years? Sometimes I can still hear the flames and feel Maggie's arms sticking to me, her hair smoking and her dress falling off her in little black papery flakes. Her eyes seemed stretched open, blazed open by the flames reflected in them. And Dee. I see her standing off under the sweet gum tree she used to dig gum out of; a look of concentration on her face as she watched the last dingy gray board of the house fall in toward the red-hot brick chimney. Why don't you do a dance around the ashes? I'd wanted to ask her. She had hated the house that much.

I used to think she hated Maggie, too. But that was before we raised the money, the church and me, to send her to Augusta to school. She used to read to us without pity; forcing words, lies, other folks' habits, whole lives upon us two, sitting trapped and ignorant underneath her voice. She washed us in a river of make-believe, burned us with a lot of knowledge we didn't necessarily need to know. Pressed us to her with the serious way she read, to shove us away at just the moment, like dimwits, we seemed about to understand.

Dee wanted nice things. A yellow organdy dress to wear to her graduation from high school; black pumps to match a green suit she'd made from an old suit somebody gave me. She was determined to stare down any disaster in her efforts. Her eyelids would not flicker for minutes at a time. Often I fought off the temptation to shake her. At sixteen she had a style of her own: and knew what style was.

I never had an education myself. After second grade the school was closed down. Don't ask me why: in 1927 colored asked fewer questions than they do now. Sometimes Maggie reads to me. She stumbles along good-naturedly but can't see well. She knows she is not bright. Like good looks and money, quickness passed her by. She will marry John Thomas (who has mossy teeth in an earnest face) and then I'll be free to sit here and I guess just sing church songs to myself. Although I never was a good singer. Never could carry a tune. I was always better at a man's job. I used to love to milk till I was hoofed in the side in '49. Cows are soothing and slow and don't bother you, unless you try to milk them the wrong way.

I have deliberately turned my back on the house. It is three rooms, just like the one that burned, except the roof is tin; they don't make shingle roofs any more. There are no real windows, just some holes cut in the sides, like the portholes in a ship, but not round and not square, with rawhide holding the shutters up on the outside. This house is in a pasture, too, like the other one. No doubt when Dee sees it she will want to tear it down. She wrote me once that no matter where we "choose" to live, she will manage to come see us. But she will never bring her friends. Maggie and I thought about this and Maggie asked me, "Mama, when did Dee ever *have* any friends?"

She had a few. Furtive boys in pink shirts hanging about on washday   15 after school. Nervous girls who never laughed. Impressed with her they worshiped the well-turned phrase, the cute shape, the scalding humor that erupted like bubbles in lye. She read to them.

When she was courting Jimmy T she didn't have much time to pay to us, but turned all her faultfinding power on him. He *flew* to marry a cheap city girl from a family of ignorant flashy people. She hardly had time to recompose herself.

When she comes I will meet—but there they are!

Maggie attempts to make a dash for the house, in her shuffling way, but I stay her with my hand. "Come back here," I say. And she stops and tries to dig a well in the sand with her toe.

It is hard to see them clearly through the strong sun. But even the first glimpse of leg out of the car tells me it is Dee. Her feet were always neat-looking, as if God himself had shaped them with a certain style. From the other side of the car comes a short, stocky man. Hair is all over his head a foot long and hanging from his chin like a kinky mule tail. I hear Maggie suck in her breath. "Uhnnnh," is what it sounds like. Like when you see the wriggling end of a snake just in front of your foot on the road. "Uhnnnh."

Dee next. A dress down to the ground, in this hot weather. A dress so   20 loud it hurts my eyes. There are yellows and oranges enough to throw back the light of the sun. I feel my whole face warming from the heat waves it throws out. Earrings, too, gold and hanging down to her shoulders. Brace-lets dangling and making noises when she moves her arm up to shake the folds of the dress out of her armpits. The dress is loose and flows, and as she walks closer, I like it. I hear Maggie go "Uhnnnh" again. It is her sister's hair. It stands straight up like the wool on a sheep. It is black as night and around the edges are two long pigtails that rope about like small lizards disappearing behind her ears.

"Wa-su-zo-Tean-o!"° she says, coming on in that gliding way the dress makes her move. The short stocky fellow with the hair to his navel is all grinning and he follows up with "Asalamalakim,° my mother and sister!" He moves to hug Maggie but she falls back, right up against the back of my

---

Wa-su-zo-Tean-o!: salutation in Swahili, an African language. Notice that Dee has to sound it out, syllable by syllable.   *Asalamalakim*: salutation in Arabic: "Peace be upon you."

chair. I feel her trembling there and when I look up I see the perspiration falling off her chin.

"Don't get up," says Dee. Since I am stout it takes something of a push. You can see me trying to move a second or two before I make it. She turns, showing white heels through her sandals, and goes back to the car. Out she peeks next with a Polaroid. She stoops down quickly and lines up picture after picture of me sitting there in front of the house with Maggie cowering behind me. She never takes a shot without making sure the house is included. When a cow comes nibbling around the edge of the yard she snaps it and me and Maggie *and* the house. Then she puts the Polaroid in the back seat of the car, and comes up and kisses me on the forehead.

Meanwhile Asalamalakim is going through the motions with Maggie's hand. Maggie's hand is as limp as a fish, and probably as cold, despite the sweat, and she keeps trying to pull it back. It looks like Asalamalakim wants to shake hands but wants to do it fancy. Or maybe he don't know how people shake hands. Anyhow, he soon gives up on Maggie.

"Well," I say. "Dee."

"No, Mama," she says. "Not 'Dee,' Wangero Leewanika Kemanjo!"   25

"What happened to 'Dee'?" I wanted to know.

"She's dead," Wangero said. "I couldn't bear it any longer, being named after the people who oppress me."

"You know as well as me you was named after your aunt Dicie," I said. Dicie is my sister. She named Dee. We called her "Big Dee" after Dee was born.

"But who was *she* named after?" asked Wangero.

"I guess after Grandma Dee," I said.   30

"And who was she named after?" asked Wangero.

"Her mother," I said, and saw Wangero was getting tired. "That's about as far back as I can trace it," I said. Though, in fact, I probably could have carried it back beyond the Civil War through the branches.

"Well," said Asalamalakim, "there you are."

"Uhnnnh," I heard Maggie say.

"There I was not," I said, "before 'Dicie' cropped up in our family, so   35
why should I try to trace it that far back?"

He just stood there grinning, looking down on me like somebody inspecting a Model A car.° Every once in a while he and Wangero sent eye signals over my head.

"How do you pronounce this name?" I asked.

"You don't have to call me by it if you don't want to," said Wangero.

"Why shouldn't I?" I asked. "If that's what you want us to call you, we'll call you."

"I know it might sound awkward at first," said Wangero.   40

Model A car: popular low-priced automobile introduced by the Ford Motor Company in 1927.

"I'll get used to it," I said. "Ream it out again."

Well, soon we got the name out of the way. Asalamalakim had a name twice as long and three times as hard. After I tripped over it two or three times he told me to just call him Hakim-a-barber. I wanted to ask him was he a barber, but I didn't really think he was, so I didn't ask.

"You must belong to those beef-cattle peoples down the road," I said. They said "Asalamalakim" when they met you, too, but they didn't shake hands. Always too busy: feeding the cattle, fixing the fences, putting up salt-lick shelters, throwing down hay. When the white folks poisoned some of the herd the men stayed up all night with rifles in their hands. I walked a mile and a half just to see the sight.

Hakim-a-barber said, "I accept some of their doctrines, but farming and raising cattle is not my style." (They didn't tell me, and I didn't ask, whether Wangero (Dee) had really gone and married him.)

We sat down to eat and right away he said he didn't eat collards and ⁴⁵ pork was unclean. Wangero, though, went on through the chitlins and corn bread, the greens and everything else. She talked a blue streak over the sweet potatoes. Everything delighted her. Even the fact that we still used the benches her daddy made for the table when we couldn't afford to buy chairs.

"Oh, Mama!" she cried. Then turned to Hakim-a-barber. "I never knew how lovely these benches are. You can feel the rump prints," she said, running her hands underneath her and along the bench. Then she gave a sigh and her hand closed over Grandma Dee's butter dish. "That's it!" she said. "I knew there was something I wanted to ask you if I could have." She jumped up from the table and went over in the corner where the churn stood, the milk in it clabber° by now. She looked at the churn and looked at it.

"This churn top is what I need," she said. "Didn't Uncle Buddy whittle it out of a tree you all used to have?"

"Yes," I said.

"Uh huh," she said happily. "And I want the dasher, too."

"Uncle Buddy whittle that, too?" asked the barber.   ⁵⁰

Dee (Wangero) looked up at me.

"Aunt Dee's first husband whittled the dash," said Maggie so low you almost couldn't hear her. "His name was Henry, but they called him Stash."

"Maggie's brain is like an elephant's," Wangero said, laughing. "I can use the churn top as a centerpiece for the alcove table," she said, sliding a plate over the churn, "and I'll think of something artistic to do with the dasher."

When she finished wrapping the dasher the handle stuck out. I took it for a moment in my hands. You didn't even have to look close to see where hands pushing the dasher up and down to make butter had left a kind of sink in the wood. In fact, there were a lot of small sinks; you could

clabber: sour milk or buttermilk.

see where thumbs and fingers had sunk into the wood. It was beautiful light yellow wood, from a tree that grew in the yard where Big Dee and Stash had lived.

After dinner Dee (Wangero) went to the trunk at the foot of my bed and started rifling through it. Maggie hung back in the kitchen over the dishpan. Out came Wangero with two quilts. They had been pieced by Grandma Dee and then Big Dee and me had hung them on the quilt frames on the front porch and quilted them. One was in the Lone Star pattern. The other was Walk Around the Mountain. In both of them were scraps of dresses Grandma Dee had worn fifty and more years ago. Bits and pieces of Grandpa Jarrell's paisley shirts. And one teeny faded blue piece, about the size of a penny matchbox, that was from Great Grandpa Ezra's uniform that he wore in the Civil War.

"Mama," Wangero said sweet as a bird. "Can I have these old quilts?"

I heard something fall in the kitchen, and a minute later the kitchen door slammed.

"Why don't you take one or two of the others?" I asked. "These old things was just done by me and Big Dee from some tops your grandma pieced before she died."

"No," said Wangero. "I don't want those. They are stitched around the borders by machine."

"That'll make them last better," I said.

"That's not the point," said Wangero. "These are all pieces of dresses Grandma used to wear. She did all this stitching by hand. Imagine!" She held the quilts securely in her arms, stroking them.

"Some of the pieces, like those lavender ones, come from old clothes her mother handed down to her," I said, moving up to touch the quilts. Dee (Wangero) moved back just enough so that I couldn't reach the quilts. They already belonged to her.

"Imagine!" she breathed again, clutching them closely to her bosom.

"The truth is," I said, "I promised to give them quilts to Maggie, for when she marries John Thomas."

She gasped like a bee had stung her.

"Maggie can't appreciate these quilts!" she said. "She'd probably be backward enough to put them to everyday use."

"I reckon she would," I said. "God knows I been saving 'em for long enough with nobody using 'em. I hope she will!" I didn't want to bring up how I had offered Dee (Wangero) a quilt when she went away to college. Then she had told me they were old-fashioned, out of style.

"But they're *priceless*!" she was saying now, furiously; for she has a temper. "Maggie would put them on the bed and in five years they'd be in rags. Less than that!"

"She can always make some more," I said. "Maggie knows how to quilt."

Dee (Wangero) looked at me with hatred. "You just will not understand. The point is these quilts, *these* quilts!"

"Well," I said, stumped. "What would *you* do with them?"

"Hang them," she said. As if that was the only thing you *could* do with quilts.

Maggie by now was standing in the door. I could almost hear the sound her feet made as they scraped over each other.

"She can have them, Mama," she said, like somebody used to never winning anything, or having anything reserved for her. "I can 'member Grandma Dee without the quilts."

I looked at her hard. She had filled her bottom lip with checkerberry   75
snuff and it gave her face a kind of dopey, hangdog look. It was Grandma Dee and Big Dee who taught her how to quilt herself. She stood there with her scarred hands hidden in the folds of her skirt. She looked at her sister with something like fear but she wasn't mad at her. This was Maggie's portion. This was the way she knew God to work.

When I looked at her like that something hit me in the top of my head and ran down to the soles of my feet. Just like when I'm in church and the spirit of God touches me and I get happy and shout. I did something I never had done before: hugged Maggie to me, then dragged her on into the room, snatched the quilts out of Miss Wangero's hands and dumped them into Maggie's lap. Maggie just sat there on my bed with her mouth open.

"Take one or two of the others," I said to Dee.

But she turned without a word and went out to Hakim-a-barber.

"You just don't understand," she said, as Maggie and I came out to the car.

"What don't I understand?" I wanted to know.   80

"Your heritage," she said. And then she turned to Maggie, kissed her, and said, "You ought to try to make something of yourself, too, Maggie. It's really a new day for us. But from the way you and Mama still live you'd never know it."

She put on some sunglasses that hid everything above the tip of her nose and her chin.

Maggie smiled; maybe at the sunglasses. But a real smile, not scared. After we watched the car dust settle I asked Maggie to bring me a dip of snuff. And then the two of us sat there just enjoying, until it was time to go in the house and go to bed.

Questions

1. What is the basic conflict in "Everyday Use"?
2. What is the tone of Walker's story? By what means does the author communicate it?
3. From whose point of view is "Everyday Use" told? What does the story gain from being told from this point of view—instead of, say, from the point of view of Dee (Wangero)?

4. What does the narrator of the story feel toward Dee? What seems to be Dee's present attitude toward her mother and sister?
5. What do you take to be the author's attitude toward each of her characters? How does she convey it?
6. What levels of meaning do you find in the story's title?
7. Contrast Dee's attitude toward her heritage with the attitudes of her mother and sister. How much truth is there in Dee's accusation that her mother and sister don't understand their heritage?
8. Does the knowledge that "Everyday Use" was written by a black writer in any way influence your reactions to it? Explain.

Raymond Carver

Cathedral

1983

Raymond Carver

Raymond Carver (1938–1988) was born in Clatskanie, Oregon. When he was three, his family moved to Yakima, Washington, where his father worked in a sawmill. In his early years Carver worked briefly at a lumber mill and at other unskilled jobs, including a stint as a tulip-picker. Married with two children before he was twenty, he experienced blue-collar desperation more intimately than most American writers, though he once quipped that, until he read critics' reactions to his works, he never realized that the characters in his stories "were so bad off." In 1963 Carver earned a degree from Humboldt State College (now California State University, Humboldt). He briefly attended the Writers' Workshop of the University of Iowa, but, needing to support his family, he returned to California, working for three years as a hospital custodian before finding a job editing textbooks. In 1967 he met Gordon Lish, the influential editor who would publish several of his stories in Esquire. Under Lish's demanding tutelage, Carver learned to pare his fiction to the essentials. In the early 1970s, though plagued with bankruptcies, increasing dependency on alcohol, and marital problems, he taught at several universities.

Carver's publishing career began with a volume of poems, Near Klamath (1968). His books of short stories include Will You Please Be Quiet, Please? (1977), What We Talk About When We Talk About Love (1981), Cathedral (1983), and Where I'm Calling From (1988). The compression of language he learned as a poet may in part account for the lean quality of his prose, often called "minimalist," a term Carver did not like. In his last decade Carver taught creative writing at Syracuse University and lived with the poet Tess Gallagher, whom he married in 1988. He divided his final years between Syracuse and Port Angeles, Washington. Carver's personal victory in 1977 over decades of alcoholism underscored the many professional triumphs of his final decade. He once said, "I'm

prouder of that, that I quit drinking, than I am of anything in my life." His reputation as a master craftsman of the contemporary short story was still growing when
he died, after a struggle with lung cancer.

This blind man, an old friend of my wife's, he was on his way to spend
the night. His wife had died. So he was visiting the dead wife's relatives
in Connecticut. He called my wife from his in-laws'. Arrangements were
made. He would come by train, a five-hour trip, and my wife would meet
him at the station. She hadn't seen him since she worked for him one
summer in Seattle ten years ago. But she and the blind man had kept in
touch. They made tapes and mailed them back and forth. I wasn't enthusiastic about his visit. He was no one I knew. And his being blind bothered
me. My idea of blindness came from the movies. In the movies, the blind
moved slowly and never laughed. Sometimes they were led by seeing-eye
dogs. A blind man in my house was not something I looked forward to.

That summer in Seattle she had needed a job. She didn't have any
money. The man she was going to marry at the end of the summer was in
officers' training school. He didn't have any money, either. But she was in
love with the guy, and he was in love with her, etc. She'd seen something
in the paper: HELP WANTED—*Reading to Blind Man*, and a telephone number. She phoned and went over, was hired on the spot. She'd worked with
this blind man all summer. She read stuff to him, case studies, reports,
that sort of thing. She helped him organize his little office in the county
social-service department. They'd become good friends, my wife and the
blind man. How do I know these things? She told me. And she told me
something else. On her last day in the office, the blind man asked if he
could touch her face. She agreed to this. She told me he touched his fingers to every part of her face, her nose—even her neck! She never forgot
it. She even tried to write a poem about it. She was always trying to write
a poem. She wrote a poem or two every year, usually after something really important had happened to her.

When we first started going out together, she showed me the poem.
In the poem, she recalled his fingers and the way they had moved
around over her face. In the poem, she talked about what she had felt
at the time, about what went through her mind when the blind man
touched her nose and lips. I can remember I didn't think much of the
poem. Of course, I didn't tell her that. Maybe I just don't understand
poetry. I admit it's not the first thing I reach for when I pick up something to read.

Anyway, this man who'd first enjoyed her favors, the officer-to-be,
he'd been her childhood sweetheart. So okay. I'm saying that at the
end of the summer she let the blind man run his hands over her face,
said good-bye to him, married her childhood etc., who was now a commissioned officer, and she moved away from Seattle. But they'd kept in

touch, she and the blind man. She made the first contact after a year or so. She called him up one night from an Air Force base in Alabama. She wanted to talk. They talked. He asked her to send a tape and tell him about her life. She did this. She sent the tape. On the tape, she told the blind man about her husband and about their life together in the military. She told the blind man she loved her husband but she didn't like it where they lived and she didn't like it that he was part of the military-industrial thing. She told the blind man she'd written a poem and he was in it. She told him that she was writing a poem about what it was like to be an Air Force officer's wife. The poem wasn't finished yet. She was still writing it. The blind man made a tape. He sent her the tape. She made a tape. This went on for years. My wife's officer was posted to one base and then another. She sent tapes from Moody AFB, McGuire, McConnell, and finally Travis, near Sacramento, where one night she got to feeling lonely and cut off from people she kept losing in that moving-around life. She got to feeling she couldn't go it another step. She went in and swallowed all the pills and capsules in the medicine chest and washed them down with a bottle of gin. Then she got into a hot bath and passed out.

But instead of dying, she got sick. She threw up. Her officer—why should he have a name? he was the childhood sweetheart, and what more does he want?—came home from somewhere, found her, and called the ambulance. In time, she put it all on a tape and sent the tape to the blind man. Over the years, she put all kinds of stuff on tapes and sent the tapes off lickety-split. Next to writing a poem every year, I think it was her chief means of recreation. On one tape, she told the blind man she'd decided to live away from her officer for a time. On another tape, she told him about her divorce. She and I began going out, and of course she told her blind man about it. She told him everything, or so it seemed to me. Once she asked me if I'd like to hear the latest tape from the blind man. This was a year ago. I was on the tape, she said. So I said okay, I'd listen to it. I got us drinks and we settled down in the living room. We made ready to listen. First she inserted the tape into the player and adjusted a couple of dials. Then she pushed a lever. The tape squeaked and someone began to talk in this loud voice. She lowered the volume. After a few minutes of harmless chitchat, I heard my own name in the mouth of this stranger, this blind man I didn't even know! And then this: "From all you've said about him, I can only conclude—" But we were interrupted, a knock at the door, something, and we didn't ever get back to the tape. Maybe it was just as well. I'd heard all I wanted to.

Now this same blind man was coming to sleep in my house.

"Maybe I could take him bowling," I said to my wife. She was at the draining board doing scalloped potatoes. She put down the knife she was using and turned around.

"If you love me," she said, "you can do this for me. If you don't love me, okay. But if you had a friend, any friend, and the friend came to visit, I'd make him feel comfortable." She wiped her hands with the dish towel.

"I don't have any blind friends," I said.

"You don't have *any* friends," she said. "Period. Besides," she said,   10
"goddamn it, his wife's just died! Don't you understand that? The man's lost his wife!"

I didn't answer. She'd told me a little about the blind man's wife. Her name was Beulah. Beulah! That's a name for a colored woman.

"Was his wife a Negro?" I asked.

"Are you crazy?" my wife said. "Have you just flipped or something?" She picked up a potato. I saw it hit the floor, then roll under the stove. "What's wrong with you?" she said. "Are you drunk?"

"I'm just asking," I said.

Right then my wife filled me in with more detail than I cared to   15
know. I made a drink and sat at the kitchen table to listen. Pieces of the story began to fall into place.

Beulah had gone to work for the blind man the summer after my wife had stopped working for him. Pretty soon Beulah and the blind man had themselves a church wedding. It was a little wedding—who'd want to go to such a wedding in the first place?—just the two of them, plus the minister and the minister's wife. But it was a church wedding just the same. It was what Beulah had wanted, he'd said. But even then Beulah must have been carrying the cancer in her glands. After they had been inseparable for eight years—my wife's word, *inseparable*—Beulah's health went into a rapid decline. She died in a Seattle hospital room, the blind man sitting beside the bed and holding on to her hand. They'd married, lived and worked together, slept together—had sex, sure—and then the blind man had to bury her. All this without his having ever seen what the goddamned woman looked like. It was beyond my understanding. Hearing this, I felt sorry for the blind man for a little bit. And then I found myself thinking what a pitiful life this woman must have led. Imagine a woman who could never see herself as she was seen in the eyes of her loved one. A woman who could go on day after day and never receive the smallest compliment from her beloved. A woman whose husband could never read the expression on her face, be it misery or something better. Someone who could wear makeup or not—what difference to him? She could, if she wanted, wear green eye-shadow around one eye, a straight pin in her nostril, yellow slacks, and purple shoes, no matter. And then to slip off into death, the blind man's hand on her hand, his blind eyes streaming tears—I'm imagining now—her last thought maybe this: that he never even knew what she looked like, and she on an express to the grave. Robert was left with a small insurance policy and a half of a twenty-peso Mexican coin. The other half of the coin went into the box with her. Pathetic.

So when the time rolled around, my wife went to the depot to pick him up. With nothing to do but wait—sure, I blamed him for that—I was having a drink and watching the TV when I heard the car pull into the drive. I got up from the sofa with my drink and went to the window to have a look.

I saw my wife laughing as she parked the car. I saw her get out of the car and shut the door. She was still wearing a smile. Just amazing. She went around to the other side of the car to where the blind man was already starting to get out. This blind man, feature this, he was wearing a full beard! A beard on a blind man! Too much, I say. The blind man reached into the backseat and dragged out a suitcase. My wife took his arm, shut the car door, and, talking all the way, moved him down the drive and then up the steps to the front porch. I turned off the TV. I finished my drink, rinsed the glass, dried my hands. Then I went to the door.

My wife said, "I want you to meet Robert. Robert, this is my husband. I've told you all about him." She was beaming. She had this blind man by his coat sleeve.

The blind man let go of his suitcase and up came his hand.   20

I took it. He squeezed hard, held my hand, and then he let it go.

"I feel like we've already met," he boomed.

"Likewise," I said. I didn't know what else to say. Then I said, "Welcome. I've heard a lot about you." We began to move then, a little group, from the porch into the living room, my wife guiding him by the arm. The blind man was carrying his suitcase in his other hand. My wife said things like, "To your left here, Robert. That's right. Now watch it, there's a chair. That's it. Sit down right here. This is the sofa. We just bought this sofa two weeks ago."

I started to say something about the old sofa. I'd liked that old sofa. But I didn't say anything. Then I wanted to say something else, small-talk, about the scenic ride along the Hudson. How going *to* New York, you should sit on the right-hand side of the train, and coming *from* New York, the left-hand side.

"Did you have a good train ride?" I said. "Which side of the train did   25 you sit on, by the way?"

"What a question, which side!" my wife said. "What's it matter which side?" she said.

"I just asked," I said.

"Right side," the blind man said. "I hadn't been on a train in nearly forty years. Not since I was a kid. With my folks. That's been a long time. I'd nearly forgotten the sensation. I have winter in my beard now," he said. "So I've been told, anyway. Do I look distinguished, my dear?" the blind man said to my wife.

"You look distinguished, Robert," she said. "Robert," she said. "Robert, it's just so good to see you."

My wife finally took her eyes off the blind man and looked at me. I had the feeling she didn't like what she saw. I shrugged.   30

I've never met, or personally known, anyone who was blind. This blind man was late forties, a heavy-set, balding man with stooped shoulders, as if he carried a great weight there. He wore brown slacks, brown shoes, a light-brown shirt, a tie, a sports coat. Spiffy. He also had this full beard. But he didn't use a cane and he didn't wear dark glasses. I'd always thought dark glasses were a must for the blind. Fact was, I wished he had a pair. At first glance, his eyes looked like anyone else's eyes. But if you looked close, there was something different about them. Too much white in the iris, for one thing, and the pupils seemed to move around in the sockets without his knowing it or being able to stop it. Creepy. As I stared at his face, I saw the left pupil turn in toward his nose while the other made an effort to keep in one place. But it was only an effort, for that eye was on the roam without his knowing it or wanting it to be.

I said, "Let me get you a drink. What's your pleasure? We have a little of everything. It's one of our pastimes."

"Bub, I'm a Scotch man myself," he said fast enough in this big voice.

"Right," I said. Bub! "Sure you are. I knew it."

He let his fingers touch his suitcase, which was sitting alongside the sofa. He was taking his bearings. I didn't blame him for that.   35

"I'll move that up to your room," my wife said.

"No, that's fine," the blind man said loudly. "It can go up when I go up."

"A little water with the Scotch?" I said.

"Very little," he said.

"I knew it," I said.   40

He said, "Just a tad. The Irish actor, Barry Fitzgerald? I'm like that fellow. When I drink water, Fitzgerald said, I drink water. When I drink whiskey, I drink whiskey." My wife laughed. The blind man brought his hand up under his beard. He lifted his beard slowly and let it drop.

I did the drinks, three big glasses of Scotch with a splash of water in each. Then we made ourselves comfortable and talked about Robert's travels. First the long flight from the West Coast to Connecticut, we covered that. Then from Connecticut up here by train. We had another drink concerning that leg of the trip.

I remembered having read somewhere that the blind didn't smoke because, as speculation had it, they couldn't see the smoke they exhaled. I thought I knew that much and that much only about blind people. But this blind man smoked his cigarette down to the nubbin and then lit another one. This blind man filled his ashtray and my wife emptied it.

When we sat down at the table for dinner, we had another drink. My wife heaped Robert's plate with cube steak, scalloped potatoes, green beans. I buttered him up two slices of bread. I said, "Here's bread and butter for you." I swallowed some of my drink. "Now let us pray," I said, and the blind man lowered his head. My wife looked at me, her mouth agape. "Pray the phone won't ring and the food doesn't get cold," I said.

We dug in. We ate everything there was to eat on the table. We   45 ate like there was no tomorrow. We didn't talk. We ate. We scarfed. We grazed that table. We were into serious eating. The blind man had right away located his foods, he knew just where everything was on his plate. I watched with admiration as he used his knife and fork on the meat. He'd cut two pieces of meat, fork the meat into his mouth, and then go all out for the scalloped potatoes, the beans next, and then he'd tear off a hunk of buttered bread and eat that. He'd follow this up with a big drink of milk. It didn't seem to bother him to use his fingers once in a while, either.

We finished everything, including half a strawberry pie. For a few moments, we sat as if stunned. Sweat beaded on our faces. Finally, we got up from the table and left the dirty plates. We didn't look back. We took ourselves into the living room and sank into our places again. Robert and my wife sat on the sofa. I took the big chair. We had us two or three more drinks while they talked about the major things that had come to pass for them in the past ten years. For the most part, I just listened. Now and then I joined in. I didn't want him to think I'd left the room, and I didn't want her to think I was feeling left out. They talked of things that had happened to them—to them!—these past ten years. I waited in vain to hear my name on my wife's sweet lips: "And then my dear husband came into my life"—something like that. But I heard nothing of the sort. More talk of Robert. Robert had done a little of everything, it seemed, a regular blind jack-of-all-trades. But most recently he and his wife had had an Amway distributorship, from which, I gathered, they'd earned their living, such as it was. The blind man was also a ham radio operator. He talked in his loud voice about conversations he'd had with fellow operators in Guam, in the Philippines, in Alaska, and even in Tahiti. He said he'd have a lot of friends there if he ever wanted to go visit those places. From time to time, he'd turn his blind face toward me, put his hand under his beard, ask me something. How long had I been in my present position? (Three years.) Did I like my work? (I didn't.) Was I going to stay with it? (What were the options?) Finally, when I thought he was beginning to run down, I got up and turned on the TV.

My wife looked at me with irritation. She was heading toward a boil. Then she looked at the blind man and said, "Robert, do you have a TV?"

The blind man said, "My dear, I have two TVs. I have a color set and a black-and-white thing, an old relic. It's funny, but if I turn the TV on, and I'm always turning it on, I turn on the color set. It's funny, don't you think?"

I didn't know what to say to that. I had absolutely nothing to say to that. No opinion. So I watched the news program and tried to listen to what the announcer was saying.

"This is a color TV," the blind man said. "Don't ask me how, but I 50 can tell."

"We traded up a while ago," I said.

The blind man had another taste of his drink. He lifted his beard, sniffed it, and let it fall. He leaned forward on the sofa. He positioned his ashtray on the coffee table, then put the lighter to his cigarette. He leaned back on the sofa and crossed his legs at the ankles.

My wife covered her mouth, and then she yawned. She stretched. She said, "I think I'll go upstairs and put on my robe. I think I'll change into something else. Robert, you make yourself comfortable," she said.

"I'm comfortable," the blind man said.

"I want you to feel comfortable in this house," she said. 55

"I am comfortable," the blind man said.

After she'd left the room, he and I listened to the weather report and then to the sports roundup. By that time, she'd been gone so long I didn't know if she was going to come back. I thought she might have gone to bed. I wished she'd come back downstairs. I didn't want to be left alone with a blind man. I asked him if he wanted another drink, and he said sure. Then I asked if he wanted to smoke some dope with me. I said I'd just rolled a number. I hadn't, but I planned to do so in about two shakes.

"I'll try some with you," he said.

"Damm right," I said. "That's the stuff."

I got our drinks and sat down on the sofa with him. Then I rolled us 60 two fat numbers. I lit one and passed it. I brought it to his fingers. He took it and inhaled.

"Hold it as long as you can," I said. I could tell he didn't know the first thing.

My wife came back downstairs wearing her pink robe and her pink slippers.

"What do I smell?" she said.

"We thought we'd have us some cannabis," I said.

My wife gave me a savage look. Then she looked at the blind man 65 and said, "Robert, I didn't know you smoked."

He said, "I do now, my dear. There's a first time for everything. But I don't feel anything yet."

"This stuff is pretty mellow," I said. "This stuff is mild. It's dope you can reason with," I said. "It doesn't mess you up."

"Not much it doesn't, bub," he said, and laughed.

My wife sat on the sofa between the blind man and me. I passed her the number. She took it and toked and then passed it back to me. "Which way is this going?" she said. Then she said, "I shouldn't be smoking this. I can hardly keep my eyes open as it is. That dinner did me in. I shouldn't have eaten so much."

"It was the strawberry pie," the blind man said. "That's what did it," 70
he said, and he laughed his big laugh. Then he shook his head.

"There's more strawberry pie," I said.

"Do you want some more, Robert?" my wife said.

"Maybe in a little while," he said.

We gave our attention to the TV. My wife yawned again. She said, "Your bed is made up when you feel like going to bed, Robert. I know you must have had a long day. When you're ready to go to bed, say so." She pulled his arm. "Robert?"

He came to and said, "I've had a real nice time. This beats tapes, 75
doesn't it?"

I said, "Coming at you," and I put the number between his fingers. He inhaled, held the smoke, and then let it go. It was like he'd been doing it since he was nine years old.

"Thanks, bub," he said. "But I think this is all for me. I think I'm beginning to feel it," he said. He held the burning roach out for my wife.

"Same here," she said. "Ditto. Me, too." She took the roach and passed it to me. "I may just sit here for a while between you two guys with my eyes closed. But don't let me bother you, okay? Either one of you. If it bothers you, say so. Otherwise, I may just sit here with my eyes closed until you're ready to go to bed," she said. "Your bed's made up, Robert, when you're ready. It's right next to our room at the top of the stairs. We'll show you up when you're ready. You wake me up now, you guys, if I fall asleep." She said that and then she closed her eyes and went to sleep.

The news program ended. I got up and changed the channel. I sat back down on the sofa. I wished my wife hadn't pooped out. Her head lay across the back of the sofa, her mouth open. She'd turned so that her robe slipped away from her legs, exposing a juicy thigh. I reached to draw her robe back over her, and it was then that I glanced at the blind man. What the hell! I flipped the robe open again.

"You say when you want some strawberry pie," I said. 80

"I will," he said.

I said, "Are you tired? Do you want me to take you up to your bed? Are you ready to hit the hay?"

"Not yet," he said. "No, I'll stay up with you, bub. If that's all right. I'll stay up until you're ready to turn in. We haven't had a chance to talk. Know what I mean? I feel like me and her monopolized the evening." He lifted his beard and he let it fall. He picked up his cigarettes and his lighter.

"That's all right," I said. Then I said, "I'm glad for the company."

And I guess I was. Every night I smoked dope and stayed up as long 85
as I could before I fell asleep. My wife and I hardly ever went to bed at

the same time. When I did go to sleep, I had these dreams. Sometimes I'd
wake up from one of them, my heart going crazy.

Something about the church and the Middle Ages was on the TV.
Not your run-of-the-mill TV fare. I wanted to watch something else. I
turned to the other channels. But there was nothing on them, either. So
I turned back to the first channel and apologized.

"Bub, it's all right," the blind man said. "It's fine with me. Whatever
you want to watch is okay. I'm always learning something. Learning never
ends. It won't hurt me to learn something tonight. I got ears," he said.

We didn't say anything for a time. He was leaning forward with
his head turned at me, his right ear aimed in the direction of the set.
Very disconcerting. Now and then his eyelids drooped and then they
snapped open again. Now and then he put his fingers into his beard and
tugged, like he was thinking about something he was hearing on the
television.

On the screen, a group of men wearing cowls was being set upon
and tormented by men dressed in skeleton costumes and men dressed as
devils. The men dressed as devils wore devil masks, horns, and long tails.
This pageant was part of a procession. The Englishman who was narrating
the thing said it took place in Spain once a year. I tried to explain to the
blind man what was happening.

"Skeletons," he said. "I know about skeletons," he said, and he   90
nodded.

The TV showed this one cathedral. Then there was a long, slow look
at another one. Finally, the picture switched to the famous one in Paris,
with its flying buttresses and its spires reaching up to the clouds. The
camera pulled away to show the whole of the cathedral rising above the
skyline.

There were times when the Englishman who was telling the thing
would shut up, would simply let the camera move around the cathedrals.
Or else the camera would tour the countryside, men in fields walking be-
hind oxen. I waited as long as I could. Then I felt I had to say something.
I said, "They're showing the outside of this cathedral now. Gargoyles.
Little statues carved to look like monsters. Now I guess they're in Italy.
Yeah, they're in Italy. There's paintings on the walls of this one church."

"Are those fresco paintings, bub?" he asked, and he sipped from his
drink.

I reached for my glass. But it was empty. I tried to remember what I
could remember. "You're asking me are those frescoes?" I said. "That's a
good question. I don't know."

The camera moved to a cathedral outside Lisbon. The differences in   95
the Portuguese cathedral compared with the French and Italian were not
that great. But they were there. Mostly the interior stuff. Then something

occurred to me, and I said, "Something has occurred to me. Do you have any idea what a cathedral is? What they look like, that is? Do you follow me? If somebody says cathedral to you, do you have any notion what they're talking about? Do you know the difference between that and a Baptist church, say?"

He let the smoke dribble from his mouth. "I know they took hundreds of workers fifty or a hundred years to build," he said. "I just heard the man say that, of course. I know generations of the same families worked on a cathedral. I heard him say that, too. The men who began their life's work on them, they never lived to see the completion of their work. In that wise, bub, they're no different from the rest of us, right?" He laughed. Then his eyelids drooped again. His head nodded. He seemed to be snoozing. Maybe he was imagining himself in Portugal. The TV was showing another cathedral now. This one was in Germany. The Englishman's voice droned on. "Cathedrals," the blind man said. He sat up and rolled his head back and forth. "If you want the truth, bub, that's about all I know. What I just said. What I heard him say. But maybe you could describe one to me? I wish you'd do it. I'd like that. If you want to know, I really don't have a good idea."

I stared hard at the shot of the cathedral on the TV. How could I even begin to describe it? But say my life depended on it. Say my life was being threatened by an insane guy who said I had to do it or else.

I stared some more at the cathedral before the picture flipped off into the countryside. There was no use. I turned to the blind man and said, "To begin with, they're very tall." I was looking around the room for clues. "They reach way up. Up and up. Toward the sky. They're so big, some of them, they have to have these supports. To help hold them up, so to speak. These supports are called buttresses. They remind me of viaducts, for some reason. But maybe you don't know viaducts, either? Sometimes the cathedrals have devils and such carved into the front. Sometimes lords and ladies. Don't ask me why this is," I said.

He was nodding. The whole upper part of his body seemed to be moving back and forth.

"I'm not doing so good, am I?" I said.

He stopped nodding and leaned forward on the edge of the sofa. As he listened to me, he was running his fingers through his beard. I wasn't getting through to him, I could see that. But he waited for me to go on just the same. He nodded, like he was trying to encourage me. I tried to think what else to say. "They're really big," I said. "They're massive. They're built of stone. Marble, too, sometimes. In those olden days, when they built cathedrals, men wanted to be close to God. In those olden days, God was an important part of everyone's life. You could tell this from their cathedral-building. I'm sorry," I said, "but it looks like that's the best I can do for you. I'm just no good at it."

100

"That's all right, bub," the blind man said. "Hey, listen. I hope you don't mind my asking you. Can I ask you something? Let me ask you a simple question, yes or no. I'm just curious and there's no offense. You're my host. But let me ask if you are in any way religious? You don't mind my asking?"

I shook my head. He couldn't see that, though. A wink is the same as a nod to a blind man. "I guess I don't believe in it. In anything. Sometimes it's hard. You know what I'm saying?"

"Sure, I do," he said.

"Right," I said.   105

The Englishman was still holding forth. My wife sighed in her sleep. She drew a long breath and went on with her sleeping.

"You'll have to forgive me," I said. "But I can't tell you what a cathedral looks like. It just isn't in me to do it. I can't do any more than I've done."

The blind man sat very still, his head down, as he listened to me.

I said, "The truth is, cathedrals don't mean anything special to me. Nothing. Cathedrals. They're something to look at on late-night TV. That's all they are."

It was then that the blind man cleared his throat. He brought something up. He took a handkerchief from his back pocket. Then he said,   110
"I get it, bub. It's okay. It happens. Don't worry about it," he said. "Hey, listen to me. Will you do me a favor? I got an idea. Why don't you find us some heavy paper? And a pen. We'll do something. We'll draw one together. Get us a pen and some heavy paper. Go on, bub, get the stuff," he said.

So I went upstairs. My legs felt like they didn't have any strength in them. They felt like they did after I'd done some running. In my wife's room I looked around. I found some ballpoints in a little basket on her table. And then I tried to think where to look for the kind of paper he was talking about.

Downstairs, in the kitchen, I found a shopping bag with onion skins in the bottom of the bag. I emptied the bag and shook it. I brought it into the living room and sat down with it near his legs. I moved some things, smoothed the wrinkles from the bag, spread it out on the coffee table.

The blind man got down from the sofa and sat next to me on the carpet.

He ran his fingers over the paper. He went up and down the sides of the paper. The edges, even the edges. He fingered the corners.

"All right," he said. "All right, let's do her."   115

He found my hand, the hand with the pen. He closed his hand over my hand. "Go ahead, bub, draw," he said. "Draw. You'll see. I'll follow along with you. It'll be okay. Just begin now like I'm telling you. You'll see. Draw," the blind man said.

So I began. First I drew a box that looked like a house. It could have been the house I lived in. Then I put a roof on it. At either end of the roof, I drew spires. Crazy.

"Swell," he said. "Terrific. You're doing fine," he said. "Never thought anything like this could happen in your lifetime, did you, bub? Well, it's a strange life, we all know that. Go on now. Keep it up."

I put in windows with arches. I drew flying buttresses. I hung great doors. I couldn't stop. The TV station went off the air. I put down the pen and closed and opened my fingers. The blind man felt around over the paper. He moved the tips of his fingers over the paper, all over what I had drawn, and he nodded.

"Doing fine," the blind man said.   120

I took up the pen again, and he found my hand. I kept at it. I'm no artist. But I kept drawing just the same.

My wife opened up her eyes and gazed at us. She sat up on the sofa, her robe hanging open. She said, "What are you doing? Tell me, I want to know."

I didn't answer her.

The blind man said, "We're drawing a cathedral. Me and him are working on it. Press hard," he said to me. "That's right. That's good," he said. "Sure. You got it, bub, I can tell. You didn't think you could. But you can, can't you? You're cooking with gas now. You know what I'm saying? We're going to really have us something here in a minute. How's the old arm?" he said. "Put some people in there now. What's a cathedral without people?"

My wife said, "What's going on? Robert, what are you doing?   125
What's going on?"

"It's all right," he said to her. "Close your eyes now," the blind man said to me.

I did it. I closed them just like he said.

"Are they closed?" he said. "Don't fudge."

"They're closed," I said.

"Keep them that way," he said. He said, "Don't stop now. Draw."   130

So we kept on with it. His fingers rode my fingers as my hand went over the paper. It was like nothing else in my life up to now.

Then he said, "I think that's it. I think you got it," he said. "Take a look. What do you think?"

But I had my eyes closed. I thought I'd keep them that way for a little longer. I thought it was something I ought to do.

"Well?" he said. "Are you looking?"

My eyes were still closed. I was in my house. I knew that. But I didn't   135
feel like I was inside anything.

"It's really something," I said.

Questions

1. What details in "Cathedral" make clear the narrator's initial attitude toward blind people? What hints does the author give about the reasons for this attitude? At what point in the story do the narrator's preconceptions about blind people start to change?

2. For what reason does the wife keep asking Robert if he'd like to go to bed (paragraphs 74–78)? What motivates the narrator to make the same suggestion in paragraph 82? What effect does Robert's reply have on the narrator?

3. What makes the narrator start explaining what he's seeing on television?

4. How does the point of view contribute to the effectiveness of the story?

5. At the end, the narrator has an epiphany. How would you describe it?

6. Would you describe the narrator as an antihero? Use specific details from the story to back up your response.

7. Is the wife a flat or a round character? What about Robert? Support your conclusion about each of them.

8. In a good story, a character doesn't suddenly become a completely different sort of person. Find details early in the story that show the narrator's more sensitive side and thus help to make his development credible and persuasive.

■ WRITING *effectively*

THINKING ABOUT CHARACTER

Although readers usually consider plot the central element of fiction, writers usually remark that stories begin with characters.

- **Identify the most important character.** The central character is the one who must deal with the plot complications and the central crisis of the story. The choices made by this character communicate his or her attitudes as well as the story's themes.

- **Consider the ways the characters' personalities and values are communicated.** Note that the way characters speak can immediately reveal important things about their personalities, beliefs, and behavior. A single line of dialogue can tell the audience a great deal.

- **Consider how the story's action grows out of its central character.** A story's action usually grows out of the personality of its protagonist and the situation he or she faces. As novelist Phyllis Bottome observed, "If a writer is true to his characters, they will give him his plot."

CHECKLIST: Writing About Character

☐ Who is the main character or protagonist of the story?

☐ Make a quick list of the character's physical, mental, moral, or behavioral traits. Which seem especially significant to the action of the story?

☐ Does the main character have an antagonist in the story? How do they differ?

☐ Does the way the protagonist speaks reveal anything about his or her personality?

☐ If the story is told in the first person, what is revealed about how the protagonist views his or her surroundings?

☐ What is the character's primary motivation? Does this motivation seem reasonable to you?

☐ Does the protagonist fully understand his or her motivations?

☐ In what ways is the protagonist changed or tested by the events of the story?

TOPICS FOR WRITING ON CHARACTER

1. Choose a story with a dynamic protagonist. (See the beginning of this chapter for a discussion of dynamic characters.) Write an essay exploring how that character evolves over the course of the story, providing evidence from the story to back up your argument. Some good story choices might be Faulkner's "Barn Burning," Carver's "Cathedral," and Wolff's "Bullet in the Brain."

2. Using a story from this book, write a short essay that explains why a protagonist takes a crucial life-changing action. What motivates this character to do something that seems bold or surprising? You might consider:

   ▪ What motivates the narrator to overcome his instinctive antipathy to the blind man in "Cathedral"?

   ▪ Why does Anders provoke the bank robber in "Bullet in the Brain"?

3. Choose a minor character from any of the stories in this book, and write briefly on what the story reveals about that person, reading closely for even the smallest of details. Is he or she a stock character? Why or why not?

4. Choose a story in which the main character has an obvious antagonist, such as "Cathedral" or "A & P." What role does this second character play in bringing the protagonist to a new awareness of life?

5. Write a brief version of the encounter in "Everyday Use" from Dee's point of view. Is it possible to present a nonironic affirmation of her values over those of her mother and sister? Why or why not?

6. Choose a favorite character from a television show you watch regularly. What details are provided (either in the show's dialogue or in its visuals) to communicate the personality of this character? Would you say this person is a stock character or a rounded one? Write a brief essay making a case for your position.

7. Browse through magazines and newspapers to find a picture of a person you can't identify. Cut out the picture. Create a character based on the picture. As many writers do, make a list of characteristics, from the large (her life's ambition) to the small (his favorite breakfast cereal). As you build your list, make sure your details add up to a rounded character.

▶ TERMS FOR *review*

Characterization ▶ The techniques a writer uses to create, reveal, or develop the characters in a narrative.

Character description ▶ An aspect of characterization through which the author overtly relates either physical or mental traits of a character. This description is almost invariably a sign of what lurks beneath the surface of the character.

Character development ▶ The process by which a character is introduced, advanced, and possibly transformed in a story.

Motivation ▶ What a character in a narrative wants; the reasons an author provides for a character's actions. Motivation can be either explicit (the reasons are specifically stated in a story) or implicit (the reasons are only hinted at or partially revealed).

Flat (or **static**) **character** ▶ A term coined by English novelist E. M. Forster to describe a character with only one outstanding trait. Flat characters are rarely the central characters in a narrative and stay the same throughout a story.

Round (or **dynamic**) **character** ▶ A term also coined by Forster to describe a complex character who is presented in depth in a narrative. Round characters are those who change significantly during the course of a narrative or whose full personalities are revealed gradually throughout the story.

Stock character ▶ A common or stereotypical character. Examples of stock characters are the mad scientist, the battle-scarred veteran, and the strong but silent cowboy.

Hero ▶ The central character in a narrative. The term *hero* often implies positive moral attributes.

Antihero ▶ A protagonist who is lacking in one or more of the conventional qualities attributed to a hero. Instead of being dignified, brave, idealistic, or purposeful, for instance, the *antihero* may be buffoonish, cowardly, self-interested, or weak.

4

What You Will Learn in This Chapter

- To understand and define *setting*
- To identify the elements of setting—including place, time, weather, and atmosphere
- To describe literary modes such as historical fiction, regionalism, and naturalism
- To analyze the role of setting in a story

ELEMENTS OF SETTING

By the **setting** of a story, we mean its time and place. The word might remind you of the metal that holds a diamond in a ring, or of a set used in a play—perhaps a bare chair in front of a slab of painted canvas. But often, in an effective short story, setting may figure as more than mere background or underpinning. It can make things happen. It can prompt characters to act, bring them to realizations, or cause them to reveal their inmost natures.

Place

Of course, the idea of setting includes the physical environment of a story: a house, a street, a city, a landscape, a region. (*Where* a story takes place is sometimes called its **locale**.) Physical places mattered so greatly to French novelist Honoré de Balzac that sometimes, before writing a story set in a particular town, he would visit that town, select a few houses, and describe them in detail, down to their very smells.

Time

In addition to place, setting may crucially involve the *time* of the story—the hour, year, or century. It might matter greatly that a story takes place at dawn, or on the day of the first moon landing. When we begin to read a historical novel, we are soon made aware that we aren't reading about life in the twenty-first century. In *The Scarlet Letter*, nineteenth-century author Nathaniel Hawthorne, by a long introduction and a vivid opening scene at a prison door, prepares us to witness events in the Puritan community of Boston in the earlier seventeenth century. This setting, together with scenes of Puritan times we recall from high school history, helps us understand what happens in the novel. We can appreciate the shocked agitation in town when a woman is accused of adultery: she has given illegitimate birth. Such an event might seem common today, but in the stern, God-fearing New England Puritan community, it was a flagrant defiance of church and state, which were all-powerful (and were all one). That reader will make no sense of *The Scarlet Letter* who ignores its setting—if it is even possible to ignore the setting, given how much attention Hawthorne pays to it.

The fact that Hawthorne's novel takes place in a time remote from our own leads us to expect different customs and different attitudes. Some critics and teachers regard the setting of a story as its whole society, including the beliefs and assumptions of its characters. Still, we suggest that for now you keep your working definition of *setting* simple. Call it time and place. If later you should feel that your definition needs widening and deepening, you can always expand it.

Weather

Besides time and place, setting may also include the weather, which in some stories may be crucial. Climate seems as substantial as any character in William Faulkner's "Dry September." After sixty-two rainless days, a long unbroken spell of late-summer heat has frayed every nerve in a small town and caused the main character, a hotheaded white supremacist, to feel more and more irritated. The weather, someone remarks, is "enough to make a man do anything." When a false report circulates that a white woman has been raped by a black man, the rumor, like a match flung into a dry field, ignites rage and provokes a lynching. Evidently, to understand the story we have to recognize its locale, a small town in Mississippi in the 1930s during an infernal heat wave. Fully to take in the meaning of Faulkner's story, we have to take in the setting in its entirety.

Atmosphere

Atmosphere is the dominant mood or feeling that pervades all parts of a literary work. Atmosphere refers to the total effect conveyed by the author's use of language, images, and physical setting. But as the term *atmosphere* suggests, aspects of the physical setting (place, time, and weather) are usually crucial elements in achieving the author's intention. In some stories, a writer will seem to draw a setting mainly to evoke atmosphere. In such a story, setting starts us feeling whatever the storyteller would have us feel. In "The Tell-Tale Heart," Poe's having set the action in an old, dark, lantern-lit house greatly contributes to our sense of unease—and so helps the story's effectiveness.

HISTORICAL FICTION

One example of how time can become a major element of setting is in **historical fiction**, where the story is set in another time and place. In historical fiction the author usually tries to recreate a faithful picture of daily life during the period. The historical period might be long ago, such as ancient Rome in Robert Graves's novel *I, Claudius* (1934), or it may be more recent, as in the setting of early twentieth-century Britain in Ian McEwan's *Atonement* (2001). Historical fiction sometimes introduces well-known figures from the past. Thornton Wilder's *Ides of March* (1948) includes Julius Caesar and Cleopatra among its many characters. Ron Hansen's *Exiles* (2008) depicts the life of English poet Gerard Manley Hopkins. More often, historical fiction presents imaginary characters in a carefully reconstructed version of a particular period of the past. Part of the pleasure of reading this sort of fiction comes from experiencing the many details of another time, just as films carefully set in a particular historical moment, such as Ridley Scott's *Gladiator* (2000) and James Cameron's *Titanic* (1997), let us see meticulously recreated settings of another time and place.

REGIONALISM

Physical place, by the way, is especially vital to a **regional writer**, who usually sets stories (or other work) in one geographic area. Such a writer, often a native of the place, tries to bring it alive for readers who live elsewhere. William Faulkner, a distinguished regional writer, almost always sets his novels and stories in his native Mississippi. Though born in St. Louis, Kate Chopin became known as a regional writer because she wrote about Louisiana in many of her short stories and in her novel *The Awakening*. Willa Cather, for her novels of frontier Nebraska, sometimes is regarded as another outstanding regionalist (though she also set fiction in Quebec, the Southwest, and, in "Paul's Case," Pittsburgh and New York).

There is often something arbitrary, however, about calling an author a regional writer. The label sometimes has a political tinge; it means that the author describes an area outside the political and economic centers of a society. In a sense, we might think of James Joyce as a regional writer, in that all his fiction takes place in the city of Dublin, but instead we usually call him an Irish author.

As such writers show, a place can profoundly affect the character of someone who grew up in it. Willa Cather is fond of portraying strong-minded, independent women, such as the heroine of her novel *My Antonía*, strengthened in part by years of coping with the hardships of life on the wind-lashed prairie.

NATURALISM

Some writers consider the social and economic setting the most important element in the story. They present social environment as the determining factor in human behavior. Their approach is called **naturalism**—fiction of grim realism, in which the writer observes human characters like a scientist observing ants, seeing them as the products and victims of environment and heredity. Naturalism was first consciously developed in fiction in the late nineteenth century by French novelist Émile Zola. Important American naturalists include Jack London, Theodore Dreiser, and Stephen Crane. Dreiser's novel *The Financier* (1912) begins in a city setting. A young boy (who will grow up to be a ruthless industrialist) is watching a battle to the death between a lobster and a squid in a fish-market tank. Dented for the rest of his life by this grim scene, he decides that's exactly the way human society functions.

Setting usually operates more subtly than that fish tank. Often, setting and character will reveal each other. Recall how Faulkner, at the start of "A Rose for Emily," depicts Emily Grierson's house, once handsome but now "an eyesore among eyesores" surrounded by gas stations. Still standing, refusing to yield its old-time horse-and-buggy splendor to the age of the automobile, the house in "its stubborn and coquettish decay" embodies the character of its owner. In John Steinbeck's "The Chrysanthemums" (Chapter 7), the story begins with a fog that has sealed off a valley from the rest of the world—a fog like the lid on a pot. That physical setting helps convey the isolation and loneliness of the protagonist's situation.

But be warned: you'll meet stories in which setting appears hardly to matter. In the Sufi fable "Death Has an Appointment in Samarra," all we need to be told about the setting is that it is an inn in Baghdad. In that brief fable, the inevitability of death is the point, not an exotic setting. In this chapter, though, you will meet four fine stories in which setting, for one reason or another, counts greatly. Without it, none of these stories could take place.

Kate Chopin

The Storm   (1898)

Kate Chopin (1851–1904) was born Katherine O'Flaherty in St. Louis, daughter of an Irish immigrant grown wealthy in retailing. On his death, young Kate was raised by her mother's family: aristocratic Creoles, descendants of the French and Spaniards who had colonized Louisiana. She received a convent schooling and at nineteen married Oscar Chopin, a Creole cotton broker from New Orleans. Later, the Chopins lived on a plantation near Cloutierville, Louisiana, a region whose varied people—Creoles, Cajuns, blacks—Kate Chopin was later to write about with loving

Kate Chopin

care in Bayou Folk (1894) and A Night in Arcadie (1897). The shock of her husband's sudden death in 1883, which left her with the raising of six children, seems to have plunged Kate Chopin into writing. She read and admired fine woman writers of her day, such as the Maine realist Sarah Orne Jewett. She also read Maupassant, Zola, and other new (and scandalous) French naturalist writers. She began to bring into American fiction some of their hard-eyed

*observation and their passion for telling unpleasant truths. Determined, in defi-
ance of her times, frankly to show the sexual feelings of her characters, Chopin
suffered from neglect and censorship. When her major novel, The Awakening,
appeared in 1899, critics were outraged by her candid portrait of a woman who
seeks sexual and professional independence. After causing such a literary scandal, Chopin was unable to get her later work published, and wrote little more
before she died. The Awakening and many of her stories had to wait seven
decades for a sympathetic audience.*

I

The leaves were so still that even Bibi thought it was going to rain.
Bobinôt, who was accustomed to converse on terms of perfect equality
with his little son, called the child's attention to certain somber clouds
that were rolling with sinister intention from the west, accompanied by a
sullen, threatening roar. They were at Friedheimer's store and decided to
remain there till the storm had passed. They sat within the door on two
empty kegs. Bibi was four years old and looked very wise.

"Mama'll be 'fraid, yes," he suggested with blinking eyes.

"She'll shut the house. Maybe she got Sylvie helpin' her this eve-
nin'," Bobinôt responded reassuringly.

"No; she ent got Sylvie. Sylvie was helpin' her yistiday," piped Bibi.

Bobinôt arose and going across to the counter purchased a can of   5
shrimps, of which Calixta was very fond. Then he returned to his perch
on the keg and sat stolidly holding the can of shrimps while the storm
burst. It shook the wooden store and seemed to be ripping great furrows
in the distant field. Bibi laid his little hand on his father's knee and was
not afraid.

II

Calixta, at home, felt no uneasiness for their safety. She sat at a side
window sewing furiously on a sewing machine. She was greatly occupied
and did not notice the approaching storm. But she felt very warm and often stopped to mop her face on which the perspiration gathered in beads.
She unfastened her white sacque at the throat. It began to grow dark, and
suddenly realizing the situation she got up hurriedly and went about closing windows and doors.

Out on the small front gallery she had hung Bobinôt's Sunday clothes
to air and she hastened out to gather them before the rain fell. As she
stepped outside, Alcée Laballière rode in at the gate. She had not seen
him very often since her marriage, and never alone. She stood there with
Bobinôt's coat in her hands, and the big rain drops began to fall. Alcée
rode his horse under the shelter of a side projection where the chickens
had huddled and there were plows and a harrow piled up in the corner.

"May I come and wait on your gallery till the storm is over, Calixta?"
he asked.

"Come 'long in, M'sieur Alcée."

His voice and her own startled her as if from a trance, and she seized   10
Bobinôt's vest. Alcée, mounting to the porch, grabbed the trousers and
snatched Bibi's braided jacket that was about to be carried away by a sudden gust of wind. He expressed an intention to remain outside, but it was
soon apparent that he might as well have been out in the open: the water
beat in upon the boards in driving sheets, and he went inside, closing the
door after him. It was even necessary to put something beneath the door
to keep the water out.

"My! what a rain! It's good two years sence it rain' like that,"
exclaimed Calixta as she rolled up a piece of bagging and Alcée helped
her to thrust it beneath the crack.

She was a little fuller of figure than five years before when she married; but she had lost nothing of her vivacity. Her blue eyes still retained
their melting quality; and her yellow hair, dishevelled by the wind and
rain, kinked more stubbornly than ever about her ears and temples.

The rain beat upon the low, shingled roof with a force and clatter that
threatened to break an entrance and deluge them there. They were in the
dining room—the sitting room—the general utility room. Adjoining was
her bed room, with Bibi's couch along side her own. The door stood open,
and the room with its white, monumental bed, its closed shutters, looked
dim and mysterious.

Alcée flung himself into a rocker and Calixta nervously began to gather
up from the floor the lengths of a cotton sheet which she had been sewing.

"If this keeps up, *Dieu sait°* if the levees goin' to stan' it!" she   15
exclaimed.

"What have you got to do with the levees?"

"I got enough to do! An' there's Bobinôt with Bibi out in that
storm—if he only didn' left Friedheimer's!"

"Let us hope, Calixta, that Bobinôt's got sense enough to come in out
of a cyclone."

She went and stood at the window with a greatly disturbed look on
her face. She wiped the frame that was clouded with moisture. It was
stiflingly hot. Alcée got up and joined her at the window, looking over
her shoulder. The rain was coming down in sheets obscuring the view of
far-off cabins and enveloping the distant wood in a gray mist. The playing
of the lightning was incessant. A bolt struck a tall chinaberry tree at the
edge of the field. It filled all visible space with a blinding glare and the
crash seemed to invade the very boards they stood upon.

Calixta put her hands to her eyes, and with a cry, staggered back-   20
ward. Alcée's arm encircled her, and for an instant he drew her close and
spasmodically to him.

Dieu sait: God only knows.   *Bonté!:* Heavens!

"*Bonté!*"° she cried, releasing herself from his encircling arm and retreating from the window, "the house'll go next! If I only knew w'ere Bibi was!" She would not compose herself; she would not be seated. Alcée clasped her shoulders and looked into her face. The contact of her warm, palpitating body when he had unthinkingly drawn her into his arms, had aroused all the old-time infatuation and desire for her flesh.

"Calixta," he said, "don't be frightened. Nothing can happen. The house is too low to be struck, with so many tall trees standing about. There! aren't you going to be quiet? say, aren't you?" He pushed her hair back from her face that was warm and steaming. Her lips were as red and moist as pomegranate seed. Her white neck and a glimpse of her full, firm bosom disturbed him powerfully. As she glanced up at him the fear in her liquid blue eyes had given place to a drowsy gleam that unconsciously betrayed a sensuous desire. He looked down into her eyes and there was nothing for him to do but gather her lips in a kiss. It reminded him of Assumption.°

"Do you remember—in Assumption, Calixta?" he asked in a low voice broken by passion. Oh! she remembered; for in Assumption he had kissed her and kissed and kissed her; until his senses would well nigh fail, and to save her he would resort to a desperate flight. If she was not an immaculate dove in those days, she was still inviolate; a passionate creature whose very defenselessness had made her defense, against which his honor forbade him to prevail. Now—well, now—her lips seemed in a manner free to be tasted, as well as her round, white throat and her whiter breasts.

They did not heed the crashing torrents, and the roar of the elements made her laugh as she lay in his arms. She was a revelation in that dim, mysterious chamber; as white as the couch she lay upon. Her firm, elastic flesh that was knowing for the first time its birthright, was like a creamy lily that the sun invites to contribute its breath and perfume to the undying life of the world.

The generous abundance of her passion, without guile or trickery, was   25
like a white flame which penetrated and found response in depths of his own sensuous nature that had never yet been reached.

When he touched her breasts they gave themselves up in quivering ecstasy, inviting his lips. Her mouth was a fountain of delight. And when he possessed her, they seemed to swoon together at the very borderland of life's mystery.

He stayed cushioned upon her, breathless, dazed, enervated, with his heart beating like a hammer upon her. With one hand she clasped his head, her lips lightly touching his forehead. The other hand stroked with a soothing rhythm his muscular shoulders.

Assumption: a parish west of New Orleans.

The growl of the thunder was distant and passing away. The rain beat softly upon the shingles, inviting them to drowsiness and sleep. But they dared not yield.

The rain was over; and the sun was turning the glistening green world into a palace of gems. Calixta, on the gallery, watched Alcée ride away. He turned and smiled at her with a beaming face; and she lifted her pretty chin in the air and laughed aloud.

III

Bobinôt and Bibi, trudging home, stopped without at the cistern to   30 make themselves presentable.

"My! Bibi, w'at will yo' mama say! You ought to be ashame'. You oughtn' put on those good pants. Look at 'em! An' that mud on yo' collar! How you got that mud on yo' collar, Bibi? I never saw such a boy!" Bibi was the picture of pathetic resignation. Bobinôt was the embodiment of serious solicitude as he strove to remove from his own person and his son's the signs of their tramp over heavy roads and through wet fields. He scraped the mud off Bibi's bare legs and feet with a stick and carefully removed all traces from his heavy brogans. Then, prepared for the worst—the meeting with an overscrupulous housewife, they entered cautiously at the back door.

Calixta was preparing supper. She had set the table and was dripping coffee at the hearth. She sprang up as they came in.

"Oh, Bobinôt! You back! My! but I was uneasy. W'ere you been during the rain? An' Bibi? he ain't wet? he ain't hurt?" She had clasped Bibi and was kissing him effusively. Bobinôt's explanations and apologies which he had been composing all along the way, died on his lips as Calixta felt him to see if he were dry, and seemed to express nothing but satisfaction at their safe return.

"I brought you some shrimps, Calixta," offered Bobinôt, hauling the can from his ample side pocket and laying it on the table.

"Shrimps! Oh, Bobinôt! you too good fo' anything!" and she gave   35 him a smacking kiss on the cheek that resounded. "*J'vous réponds*,° we'll have a feas' to night! umph-umph!"

Bobinôt and Bibi began to relax and enjoy themselves, and when the three seated themselves at table they laughed much and so loud that anyone might have heard them as far away as Laballière's.

IV

Alcée Laballière wrote to his wife, Clarisse, that night. It was a loving letter, full of tender solicitude. He told her not to hurry back, but if she and the babies liked it at Biloxi, to stay a month longer. He was getting

J'vous réponds: Let me tell you.

on nicely; and though he missed them, he was willing to bear the separation a while longer—realizing that their health and pleasure were the first things to be considered.

V

As for Clarisse, she was charmed upon receiving her husband's letter. She and the babies were doing well. The society was agreeable; many of her old friends and acquaintances were at the bay. And the first free breath since her marriage seemed to restore the pleasant liberty of her maiden days. Devoted as she was to her husband, their intimate conjugal life was something which she was more than willing to forego for a while.

So the storm passed and everyone was happy.

Questions

1. Exactly where does Chopin's story take place? How can you tell?
2. What circumstances introduced in Part I turn out to have a profound effect on events in the story?
3. What details in "The Storm" emphasize the fact that Bobinôt loves his wife? What details reveal how imperfectly he comprehends her nature?
4. What general attitudes toward sex, love, and marriage does Chopin imply? Cite evidence to support your answer.
5. What meanings do you find in the title "The Storm"?
6. In the story as a whole, how do setting and plot reinforce each other?

Jack London

To Build a Fire   1910

Jack London

Jack London (1876–1916), born in San Francisco, won a large popular audience for his novels of the sea and the Yukon: The Call of the Wild *(1903),* The Sea-Wolf *(1904), and* White Fang *(1906). Like Ernest Hemingway, he was a writer who lived a strenuous life. In 1893, he marched cross-country in Coxey's Army, an organized protest of the unemployed; in 1897, he took part in the Klondike gold rush; and later, as a reporter, he covered the Russo-Japanese War and the Mexican Revolution. Son of an unmarried mother and a father who denied his paternity, London grew up in poverty. At fourteen, he began holding hard jobs: working in a canning factory and a jute-mill, serving as a deck hand, pirating oysters in San Francisco Bay. These experiences persuaded him to join the Socialist Labor Party and crusade for workers' rights. In his political novel* The Iron Heel *(1908), London envisions a grim totalitarian America. Like himself, the hero of his novel* Martin Eden *(1909) is a man of brief schooling who gains fame as a writer, works for a cause, loses faith in it, and finds life without meaning. Though endowed with immense physical energy—he wrote fifty volumes—London drank hard, spent fast, and played out early. While his reputation as a novelist may have declined since his own day, some of his short stories have lasted triumphantly.*

Day had broken cold and gray, exceedingly cold and gray, when the man turned aside from the main Yukon trail and climbed the high earth-bank, where a dim and little-travelled trail led eastward through the fat spruce timberland. It was a steep bank, and he paused for breath at the top, excusing the act to himself by looking at his watch. It was nine o'clock. There was no sun nor hint of sun, though there was not a cloud in the sky. It was a clear day, and yet there seemed an intangible pall over the face of things, a subtle gloom that made the day dark, and that was due to the absence of sun. This fact did not worry the man. He was used to the lack of sun. It had been days since he had seen the sun, and he knew that a few more days must pass before that cheerful orb, due south, would just peep above the sky line and dip immediately from view.

The man flung a look back along the way he had come. The Yukon lay a mile wide and hidden under three feet of ice. On top of this ice were as many feet of snow. It was all pure white, rolling in gentle undulations where the ice jams of the freeze-up had formed. North and south, as far as the eye could see, it was unbroken white, save for a dark hairline that curved and twisted from around the spruce-covered island to the south, and that curved and twisted away into the north, where it disappeared behind another spruce-covered island. This dark hairline was the trail—the main trail—that led south five hundred miles to the Chilcoot Pass, Dyea, and salt water; and that led north seventy miles to Dawson, and still on to the north a thousand miles to Nulato, and finally to St. Michael, on Bering Sea, a thousand miles and half a thousand more.

But all this—the mysterious, far-reaching hairline trail, the absence of sun from the sky, the tremendous cold, and the strangeness and weirdness of it all—made no impression on the man. It was not because he was long used to it. He was a newcomer in the land, a *chechaquo*, and this was his first winter. The trouble with him was that he was without imagination. He was quick and alert in the things of life, but only in the things, and not in the significances. Fifty degrees below zero meant eighty-odd degrees of frost. Such fact impressed him as being cold and uncomfortable, and that was all. It did not lead him to meditate upon his frailty as a creature of temperature, and upon man's frailty in general, able only to live within certain narrow limits of heat and cold; and from there on it did not lead him to the conjectural field of immortality and man's place in the universe. Fifty degrees below zero stood for a bite of frost that hurt and that must be guarded against by the use of mittens, ear flaps, warm moccasins, and thick socks. Fifty degrees below zero was to him just precisely fifty degrees below zero. That there should be anything more to it than that was a thought that never entered his head.

As he turned to go on, he spat speculatively. There was a sharp, explosive crackle that startled him. He spat again. And again, in the air, before it could fall to the snow, the spittle crackled. He knew that at fifty below spittle crackled on the snow, but this spittle had crackled in the air. Undoubtedly it was colder than fifty below—how much colder he did not know. But the temperature did not matter. He was bound for the old claim on the left fork of Henderson Creek, where the boys were already. They had come over across the divide from the Indian Creek country, while he had come the roundabout way to take a look at the possibilities of getting out logs in the spring from the islands in the Yukon. He would be in to camp by six o'clock; a bit after dark, it was true, but the boys would be there, a fire would be going, and a hot supper would be ready. As for lunch, he pressed his hand against the protruding bundle under his jacket. It was also under his shirt, wrapped up in a handkerchief and lying against the naked skin. It was the only way to keep the biscuits from freezing. He smiled agreeably to himself as he thought of those biscuits, each cut open and sopped in bacon grease, and each enclosing a generous slice of fried bacon.

He plunged in among the big spruce trees. The trail was faint. A foot of snow had fallen since the last sled had passed over, and he was glad he was without a sled, travelling light. In fact, he carried nothing but the lunch wrapped in the handkerchief. He was surprised, however, at the cold. It certainly was cold, he concluded, as he rubbed his numb nose and cheekbones with his mittened hand. He was a warm-whiskered man, but the hair on his face did not protect the high cheekbones and the eager nose that thrust itself aggressively into the frosty air.

At the man's heels trotted a dog, a big native husky, the proper wolf dog, gray-coated and without any visible or temperamental difference from its brother, the wild wolf. The animal was depressed by the tremendous cold. It knew that it was no time for travelling. Its instinct told it a truer tale than was told to the man by the man's judgment. In reality, it was not merely colder than fifty below zero; it was colder than sixty below, than seventy below. It was seventy-five below zero. Since the freezing point is thirty-two above zero, it meant that one hundred and seven degrees of frost obtained. The dog did not know anything about thermometers. Possibly in its brain there was no sharp consciousness of a condition of very cold such as was in the man's brain. But the brute had its instinct. It experienced a vague but menacing apprehension that subdued it and made it slink along at the man's heels, and that made it question eagerly

5

every unwonted movement of the man as if expecting him to go into camp or to seek shelter somewhere and build a fire. The dog had learned fire, and it wanted fire, or else to burrow under the snow and cuddle its warmth away from the air.

The frozen moisture of its breathing had settled on its fur in a fine powder of frost, and especially were its jowls, muzzle, and eyelashes whitened by its crystalled breath. The man's red beard and mustache were likewise frosted, but more solidly, the deposit taking the form of ice and increasing with every warm, moist breath he exhaled. Also, the man was chewing tobacco, and the muzzle of ice held his lips so rigidly that he was unable to clear his chin when he expelled the juice. The result was that a crystal beard of the color and solidity of amber was increasing its length on his chin. If he fell down it would shatter itself, like glass, into brittle fragments. But he did not mind the appendage. It was the penalty all tobacco chewers paid in that country, and he had been out before in two cold snaps. They had not been so cold as this, he knew, but by the spirit thermometer at Sixty Mile he knew they had been registered at fifty below and at fifty-five.

He held on through the level stretch of woods for several miles, crossed a wide flat, and dropped down a bank to the frozen bed of a small stream. This was Henderson Creek, and he knew he was ten miles from the forks. He looked at his watch. It was ten o'clock. He was making four miles an hour, and he calculated that he would arrive at the forks at half-past twelve. He decided to celebrate that event by eating his lunch there.

The dog dropped in again at his heels, with a tail drooping discouragement, as the man swung along the creek bed. The furrow of the old sled trail was plainly visible, but a dozen inches of snow covered the marks of the last runners. In a month no man had come up or down that silent creek. The man held steadily on. He was not much given to thinking, and just then particularly he had nothing to think about save that he would eat lunch at the forks and that at six o'clock he would be in camp with the boys. There was nobody to talk to; and, had there been, speech would have been impossible because of the ice muzzle on his mouth. So he continued monotonously to chew tobacco and to increase the length of his amber beard.

Once in a while the thought reiterated itself that it was very cold and that he had never experienced such cold. As he walked along he rubbed his cheekbones and nose with the back of his mittened hand. He did this automatically, now and again changing hands. But, rub as he would, the instant he stopped his cheekbones were numb, and the following instant the end of his nose went numb. He was sure to frost his cheeks; he knew that, and experienced a pang of regret that he had not devised a nose strap of the sort Bud wore in cold snaps. Such a strap

10

passed across the cheeks, as well, and saved them. But it didn't matter much, after all. What were frosted cheeks? A bit painful, that was all; they were never serious.

Empty as the man's mind was of thoughts, he was keenly observant, and he noticed the changes in the creek, the curves and bends and timber jams, and always he sharply noted where he placed his feet. Once, coming around a bend, he shied abruptly, like a startled horse, curved away from the place where he had been walking, and retreated several paces back along the trail. The creek he knew was frozen clear to the bottom—no creek could contain water in that arctic winter—but he knew also that there were springs that bubbled out from the hillsides and ran along under the snow and on top the ice of the creek. He knew that the coldest snaps never froze these springs, and he knew likewise their danger. They were traps. They hid pools of water under the snow that might be three inches deep, or three feet. Sometimes a skin of ice half an inch thick covered them, and in turn was covered by the snow. Sometimes there were alternate layers of water and ice skin, so that when one broke through he kept on breaking through for a while, sometimes wetting himself to the waist.

That was why he had shied in such panic. He had felt the give under his feet and heard the crackle of a snow-hidden ice skin. And to get his feet wet in such a temperature meant trouble and danger. At the very least it meant delay, for he would be forced to stop and build a fire, and under its protection to bare his feet while he dried his socks and moccasins. He stood and studied the creek bed and its banks, and decided that the flow of water came from the right. He reflected awhile, rubbing his nose and cheeks, then skirted to the left, stepping gingerly and testing the footing for each step. Once clear of the danger, he took a fresh chew of tobacco and swung along at his four-mile gait.

In the course of the next two hours he came upon several similar traps. Usually the snow above the hidden pools had a sunken, candied appearance that advertised the danger. Once again, however, he had a close call; and once, suspecting danger, he compelled the dog to go on in front. The dog did not want to go. It hung back until the man shoved it forward, and then it went quickly across the white, unbroken surface. Suddenly it broke through, floundered to one side, and got away to firmer footing. It had wet its forefeet and legs, and almost immediately the water that clung to it turned to ice. It made quick efforts to lick the ice off its legs, then dropped down in the snow and began to bite out the ice that had formed between the toes. This was a matter of instinct. To permit the ice to remain would mean sore feet. It did not know this. It merely obeyed the mysterious prompting that arose from the deep crypts of its being. But the man knew, having achieved a judgment on the subject, and he removed the mitten from his right hand and helped tear out the ice particles. He did not expose his fingers more than a minute, and was astonished at the swift numbness that smote them. It certainly was cold. He pulled on the mitten hastily, and beat the hand savagely across his chest.

At twelve o'clock the day was at its brightest. Yet the sun was too far south on its winter journey to clear the horizon. The bulge of the earth intervened between it and Henderson Creek, where the man walked under a clear sky at noon and cast no shadow. At half-past twelve, to the minute, he arrived at the forks of the creek. He was pleased at the speed he had made. If he kept it up, he would certainly be with the boys by six. He unbuttoned his jacket and shirt and drew forth his lunch. The action consumed no more than a quarter of a minute, yet in that brief moment the numbness laid hold of the exposed fingers. He did not put the mitten on, but, instead, struck the fingers a dozen sharp smashes against his leg. Then he sat down on a snow-covered log to eat. The sting that followed upon the striking of his fingers against his leg ceased so quickly that he was startled. He had had no chance to take a bite of biscuit. He struck the fingers repeatedly and returned them to the mitten, baring the other hand for the purpose of eating. He tried to take a mouthful, but the ice muzzle prevented. He had forgotten to build a fire and thaw out. He chuckled at his foolishness, and as he chuckled he noted the numbness creeping into the exposed fingers. Also, he noted that the stinging which had first come to his toes when he sat down was already passing away. He wondered whether the toes were warm or numb. He moved them inside the moccasins and decided that they were numb.

He pulled the mitten on hurriedly and stood up. He was a bit frightened. He stamped up and down until the stinging returned into the feet. It certainly was cold, was his thought. That man from Sulphur Creek had spoken the truth when telling how cold it sometimes got in the country. And he had laughed at him at the time! That showed one must not be too sure of things. There was no mistake about it, it *was* cold. He strode up and down, stamping his feet and threshing his arms, until reassured by the returning warmth. Then he got out matches and proceeded to make a fire. From the undergrowth, where high water of the previous spring had lodged a supply of seasoned twigs, he got his firewood. Working carefully from a small beginning, he soon had a roaring fire, over which he thawed the ice from his face and in the protection of which he ate his biscuits. For the moment the cold of space was outwitted. The dog took satisfaction in the fire, stretching out close enough for warmth and far enough away to escape being singed.

When the man had finished, he filled his pipe and took his comfortable time over a smoke. Then he pulled on his mittens, settled the ear flaps of his cap firmly about his ears, and took the creek trail up the left fork. The dog was disappointed and yearned back toward the fire. This man did not know cold. Possibly all the generations of his ancestry had been ignorant of cold, of real cold, of cold one hundred and seven degrees below freezing point. But the dog knew; all its ancestry knew, and it had inherited the knowledge. And it knew that it was not good to walk abroad in such fearful cold. It was the time to lie snug in a hole in the snow and wait for a curtain of cloud to be drawn across the face of outer space whence this cold came. On the other hand, there was no keen intimacy between the dog and the man. The one was the toil slave of the other, and the only caresses it had ever received were the caresses of the whip lash and of harsh and menacing throat sounds that threatened the whip lash. So the dog made no effort to communicate its apprehension to the man. It was not concerned in the welfare of the man; it was for its own sake that it yearned back toward the fire. But the man whistled, and spoke to it with the sound of whip lashes, and the dog swung in at the man's heels and followed after.

The man took a chew of tobacco and proceeded to start a new amber beard. Also, his moist breath quickly powdered with white his mustache, eyebrows, and lashes. There did not seem to be so many springs on the left fork of the Henderson, and for half an hour the man saw no signs of any. And then it happened. At a place where there were no signs, where the soft, unbroken snow seemed to advertise solidity beneath, the man broke through. It was not deep. He wet himself halfway to the knees before he floundered out to the firm crust.

He was angry, and cursed his luck aloud. He had hoped to get into camp with the boys at six o'clock, and this would delay him an hour, for he would have to build a fire and dry out his footgear. This was imperative at that low temperature—he knew that much; and he turned aside to the bank, which he climbed. On top, tangled in the underbrush about the trunks of several small spruce trees, was a high-water deposit of dry firewood—sticks and twigs, principally, but also larger portions of seasoned branches and fine, dry, last year's grasses. He threw down several large pieces on top of the snow. This served for a foundation and prevented the young flame from drowning itself in the snow it otherwise would melt. The flame he got by touching a match to a small shred of birch bark that he took from his pocket. This burned even more readily than paper. Placing it on the foundation, he fed the young flame with wisps of dry grass and with the tiniest dry twigs.

He worked slowly and carefully, keenly aware of his danger. Gradually, as the flame grew stronger, he increased the size of the twigs with which he fed it. He squatted in the snow, pulling the twigs out from their entanglement in the brush and feeding directly to the flame. He knew there must be no failure. When it is seventy-five below zero, a man must not fail in his first attempt to build a fire—that is, if his feet are wet. If his feet are dry, and he fails, he can run along the trail for half a mile and restore his circulation. But the circulation of wet and freezing feet cannot be restored by running when it is seventy-five below. No matter how fast he runs, the wet feet will freeze the harder.

All this the man knew. The old-timer on Sulphur Creek had told 20 him about it the previous fall, and now he was appreciating the advice. Already all sensation had gone out of his feet. To build the fire he had been forced to remove his mittens, and the fingers had quickly gone numb. His pace of four miles an hour had kept his heart pumping blood to the surface of his body and to all the extremities. But the instant he stopped, the action of the pump eased down. The cold of space smote the unprotected tip of the planet, and he, being on that unprotected tip, received the full force of the blow. The blood of his body recoiled before it. The blood was alive, like the dog, and like the dog it wanted to hide away and cover itself up from the fearful cold. So long as he walked four miles an hour, he pumped that blood, willy-nilly, to the surface; but now it ebbed away and sank down into the recesses of his body. The extremities were the first to feel its absence. His wet feet froze the faster, and his exposed fingers numbed the faster, though they had not yet begun to freeze. Nose and cheeks were already freezing, while the skin of all his body chilled as it lost its blood.

But he was safe. Toes and nose and cheeks would be only touched by the frost, for the fire was beginning to burn with strength. He was feeding it with twigs the size of his finger. In another minute he would be able to feed it with branches the size of his wrist, and then he could remove his wet footgear, and, while it dried, he could keep his naked feet warm by the fire, rubbing them at first, of course, with snow. The fire was a success. He was safe. He remembered the advice of the old-timer on Sulphur Creek, and smiled. The old-timer had been very serious in laying down the law that no man must travel alone in the Klondike after fifty below. Well, here he was; he had had the accident; he was alone; and he had saved himself. Those old-timers were rather womanish, some of them, he thought. All a man had to do was to keep his head, and he was all right. Any man who was a man could travel alone. But it was surprising, the rapidity with which his cheeks and nose were freezing. And he had not thought his fingers could go lifeless in so short a time. Lifeless they were, for he could scarcely make them move together to grip a twig, and they seemed remote from his body and from him. When he touched a twig, he had to look and see whether or not he had hold of it. The wires were pretty well down between him and his finger ends.

All of which counted for little. There was the fire, snapping and crackling and promising life with every dancing flame. He started to untie his moccasins. They were coated with ice; the thick German socks were like sheaths of iron halfway to the knees; and the moccasin strings were like rods of steel all twisted and knotted as by some conflagration. For a moment he tugged with his numb fingers, then, realizing the folly of it, he drew his sheath knife.

But before he could cut the strings, it happened. It was his own fault or, rather, his mistake. He should not have built the fire under the spruce tree. He should have built it in the open. But it had been easier to pull the twigs from the brush and drop them directly on the fire. Now the tree under which he had done this carried a weight of snow on its boughs. No wind had blown for weeks, and each bough was fully freighted. Each time he had pulled a twig he had communicated a slight agitation to the tree—an imperceptible agitation, so far as he was concerned, but an agitation sufficient to bring about the disaster. High up in the tree one bough capsized its load of snow. This fell on the boughs beneath, capsizing them. This process continued, spreading out and involving the whole tree. It grew like an avalanche, and it descended without warning upon the man and the fire, and the fire was blotted out! Where it had burned was a mantle of fresh and disordered snow.

The man was shocked. It was as though he had just heard his own sentence of death. For a moment he sat and stared at the spot where the fire had been. Then he grew very calm. Perhaps the old-timer on Sulphur Creek was right. If he had only had a trail mate he would have been in no danger now. The trail mate could have built the fire. Well, it was up to him to build the fire over again, and this second time there must be no failure. Even if he succeeded, he would most likely lose some toes. His feet must be badly frozen by now, and there would be some time before the second fire was ready.

Such were his thoughts, but he did not sit and think them. He was 25 busy all the time they were passing through his mind. He made a new foundation for a fire, this time in the open, where no treacherous tree could blot it out. Next he gathered dry grasses and tiny twigs from the high-water flotsam. He could not bring his fingers together to pull them out, but he was able to gather them by the handful. In this way he got many rotten twigs and bits of green moss that were undesirable, but it was the best he could do. He worked methodically, even collecting an armful of the larger branches to be used later when the fire gathered strength. And all the while the dog sat and watched him, a certain yearning wistfulness in its eye, for it looked upon him as the fire provider, and the fire was slow in coming.

When all was ready, the man reached in his pocket for a second piece of birch bark. He knew the bark was there, and, though he could not feel it with his fingers, he could hear its crisp rustling as he fumbled for it. Try as he would, he could not clutch hold of it. And all the time, in his consciousness, was the knowledge that each instant his feet were freezing.

This thought tended to put him in a panic, but he fought against it and kept calm. He pulled on his mittens with his teeth, and threshed his arms back and forth, beating his hands with all his might against his sides. He did this sitting down, and he stood up to do it; and all the while the dog sat in the snow, its wolf brush of a tail curled around warmly over its fore-feet, its sharp wolf ears pricked forward intently as it watched the man. And the man, as he beat and threshed with his arms and hands, felt a great surge of envy as he regarded the creature that was warm and secure in its natural covering.

After a time he was aware of the first faraway signals of sensation in his beaten fingers. The faint tingling grew stronger till it evolved into a stinging ache that was excruciating, but which the man hailed with sat-isfaction. He stripped the mitten from his right hand and fetched forth the birch bark. The exposed fingers were quickly going numb again. Next he brought out his bunch of sulphur matches. But the tremendous cold had already driven the life out of his fingers. In his effort to separate one match from the others, the whole bunch fell in the snow. He tried to pick it out of the snow, but failed. The dead fingers could neither touch nor clutch. He was very careful. He drove the thought of his freezing feet, and nose, and cheeks, out of his mind, devoting his whole soul to the matches. He watched, using the sense of vision in place of that of touch, and when he saw his fingers on each side the bunch, he closed them—that is, he willed to close them, for the wires were down, and the fingers did not obey. He pulled the mitten on the right hand, and beat it fiercely against his knee. Then, with both mittened hands, he scooped the bunch of matches, along with much snow, into his lap. Yet he was no better off.

After some manipulation he managed to get the bunch between the heels of his mittened hands. In this fashion he carried it to his mouth. The ice crackled and snapped when by a violent effort he opened his mouth. He drew the lower jaw in, curled the upper lip out of the way, and scraped the bunch with his upper teeth in order to separate a match. He succeeded in getting one, which he dropped on his lap. He was no better off. He could not pick it up. Then he devised a way. He picked it up in his teeth and scratched it on his leg. Twenty times he scratched before he succeeded in lighting it. As it flamed he held it with his teeth to the birch bark. But the burning brimstone went up his nostrils and into his lungs, causing him to cough spasmodically. The match fell into the snow and went out.

The old-timer on Sulphur Creek was right, he thought in the mo-ment of controlled despair that ensued: after fifty below, a man should travel with a partner. He beat his hands, but failed in exciting any sen-sation. Suddenly he bared both hands, removing the mittens with his teeth. He caught the whole bunch between the heels of his hands. His arm muscles not being frozen enabled him to press the hand heels tightly against the matches. Then he scratched the bunch along his leg. It flared into flame, seventy sulphur matches at once! There was no wind to blow them out. He kept his head to one side to escape the strangling fumes, and held the blazing bunch to the birch bark. As he so held it, he became aware of sensation in his hand. His flesh was burning. He could smell it. Deep down below the surface he could feel it. The sensation developed into pain that grew acute. And still he endured it, holding the flame of the matches clumsily to the bark that would not light readily because his own burning hands were in the way, absorbing most of the flame.

At last, when he could endure no more, he jerked his hands apart.   30 The blazing matches fell sizzling into the snow, but the birch bark was alight. He began laying dry grasses and the tiniest twigs on the flame. He could not pick and choose, for he had to lift the fuel between the heels of his hands. Small pieces of rotten wood and green moss clung to the twigs, and he bit them off as well as he could with his teeth. He cherished the flame carefully and awkwardly. It meant life, and it must not perish. The withdrawal of blood from the surface of his body now made him begin to shiver, and he grew more awkward. A large piece of green moss fell squarely on the little fire. He tried to poke it out with his fingers, but his shivering frame made him poke too far, and he disrupted the nucleus of the little fire, the burning grasses and tiny twigs separating and scattering. He tried to poke them together again, but in spite of the tenseness of the effort, his shivering got away from him, and the twigs were hopelessly scattered. Each twig gushed a puff of smoke and went out. The fire provider had failed. As he looked apathetically about him, his eyes chanced on the dog, sitting across the ruins of the fire from him, in the snow, making restless, hunching movements, slightly lifting one forefoot and then the other, shifting its weight back and forth on them with wistful eagerness.

The sight of the dog put a wild idea into his head. He remembered the tale of the man, caught in the blizzard, who killed a steer and crawled inside the carcass, and so was saved. He would kill the dog and bury his hands in the warm body until the numbness went out of them. Then he could build another fire. He spoke to the dog, calling it to him; but in his voice was a strange note of fear that frightened the animal, who had never known the man to speak in such a way before. Something was the matter, and its suspicious nature sensed danger—it knew not what danger, but somewhere, somehow, in its brain arose an apprehension of the man. It flattened its ears down at the sound of the man's voice, and its restless, hunching movements and the liftings and shiftings of its forefeet became more pronounced; but it would not come to the man. He got on his hands and knees and crawled toward the dog. This unusual posture again excited suspicion, and the animal sidled mincingly away.

The man sat up in the snow for a moment and struggled for calmness. Then he pulled on his mittens, by means of his teeth, and got upon his feet. He glanced down at first in order to assure himself that he was really standing up, for the absence of sensation in his feet left him unrelated to the earth. His erect position in itself started to drive the webs of suspicion from the dog's mind; and when he spoke peremptorily, with the sound of whip lashes in his voice, the dog rendered its customary allegiance and came to him. As it came within reaching distance, the man lost his control. His arms flashed out to the dog, and he experienced genuine surprise when he discovered that his hands could not clutch, that there was neither bend nor feeling in the fingers. He had forgotten for the moment that they were frozen and that they were freezing more and more. All this happened quickly, and before the animal could get away, he encircled its body with his arms. He sat down in the snow, and in this fashion held the dog, while it snarled and whined and struggled.

But it was all he could do, hold its body encircled in his arms and sit there. He realized that he could not kill the dog. There was no way to do it. With his helpless hands he could neither draw nor hold his sheath knife nor throttle the animal. He released it, and it plunged wildly away, with tail between its legs, and still snarling. It halted forty feet away and surveyed him curiously, with ears sharply pricked forward.

The man looked down at his hands in order to locate them, and found them hanging on the ends of his arms. It struck him as curious that one should have to use his eyes in order to find out where his hands were. He began threshing his arms back and forth, beating the mittened hands against his sides. He did this for five minutes, violently, and his heart pumped enough blood up to the surface to put a stop to his shivering. But no sensation was aroused in the hands. He had an impression that they hung like weights on the ends of his arms, but when he tried to run the impression down, he could not find it.

A certain fear of death, dull and oppressive, came to him. This fear quickly became poignant as he realized that it was no longer a mere matter of freezing his fingers and toes, or of losing his hands and feet, but that it was a matter of life and death with the chances against him. This threw him into a panic, and he turned and ran up the creek bed along the old, dim trail. The dog joined in behind and kept up with him. He ran blindly, without intention, in fear such as he had never known in his life. Slowly, as he plowed and floundered through the snow, he began to see things again—the banks of the creek, the old timber jams, the leafless aspens, and the sky. The running made him feel better. He did not shiver. Maybe, if he ran on, his feet would thaw out; and anyway, if he ran far enough, he would reach camp and the boys. Without doubt he would lose some fingers and toes and some of his face; but the boys would take care of him, and save the rest of him when he got there. And at the same time there was another thought in his mind that said he would never get to the camp and the boys; that it was too many miles away, that the freezing had too great a start on him, and that he would soon be stiff and dead. This thought he kept in the background and refused to consider. Sometimes it pushed itself forward and demanded to be heard, but he thrust it back and strove to think of other things.

It struck him as curious that he could run at all on feet so frozen that he could not feel them when they struck the earth and took the weight of his body. He seemed to himself to skim along above the surface, and to have no connection with the earth. Somewhere he had once seen a winged Mercury, and he wondered if Mercury felt as he felt when skimming over the earth.

His theory of running until he reached the camp and the boys had one flaw in it: he lacked the endurance. Several times he stumbled, and finally he tottered, crumpled up, and fell. When he tried to rise, he failed. He must sit and rest, he decided, and next time he would merely walk and keep on going. As he sat and regained his breath, he noted that he was feeling quite warm and comfortable. He was not shivering, and it even seemed that a warm glow had come to his chest and trunk. And yet, when he touched his nose and cheeks, there was no sensation. Running would not thaw them out. Nor would it thaw out his hands and feet. Then the thought came to him that the frozen portions of his body must be extending. He tried to keep this thought down, to forget it, to think of something else; he was aware of the panicky feeling that it caused, and he was afraid of the panic. But the thought asserted itself, and persisted, until it produced a vision of his body totally frozen. This was too much, and he made another wild run along the trail. Once he slowed down to a walk, but the thought of the freezing extending itself made him run again.

And all the time the dog ran with him, at his heels. When he fell down a second time, it curled its tail over its forefeet and sat in front of him, facing him, curiously eager and intent. The warmth and security of the animal angered him, and he cursed it till it flattened down its ears appeasingly. This time the shivering came more quickly upon the man. He was losing in his battle with the frost. It was creeping into his body from all sides. The thought of it drove him on, but he ran no more than a hundred feet, when he staggered and pitched headlong. It was his last panic. When he had recovered his breath and control, he sat up and entertained in his mind the conception of meeting death with dignity. However, the conception did not come to him in such terms. His idea of it was that he had been making a fool of himself, running around like a chicken with its head cut off—such was the simile that occurred to him. Well, he was bound to freeze anyway, and he might as well take it decently. With this new-found peace of mind came the first glimmerings of drowsiness. A good idea, he thought, to sleep off to death. It was like taking an anesthetic. Freezing was not so bad as people thought. There were lots worse ways to die.

He pictured the boys finding his body next day. Suddenly he found himself with them, coming along the trail and looking for himself. And, still with them, he came around a turn in the trail and found himself lying in the snow. He did not belong with himself any more, for even then he was out of himself, standing with the boys and looking at himself in the snow. It certainly was cold, was his thought. When he got back to the States he could tell the folks what real cold was. He drifted on from this to a vision of the old-timer on Sulphur Creek. He could see him quite clearly, warm and comfortable, and smoking a pipe.

"You were right, old hoss; you were right," the man mumbled to the old-timer of Sulphur Creek.   40

Then the man drowsed off into what seemed to him the most comfortable and satisfying sleep he had ever known. The dog sat facing him and waiting. The brief day drew to a close in a long, slow twilight. There were no signs of a fire to be made, and, besides, never in the dog's experience had it known a man to sit like that in the snow and make no fire. As the twilight drew on, its eager yearning for the fire mastered it, and with a great lifting and shifting of forefeet, it whined softly, then flattened its ears down in anticipation of being chidden by the man. But the man remained silent. Later the dog whined loudly. And still later it crept close to the man and caught the scent of death. This made the animal bristle and back away. A little longer it delayed, howling under the stars that leaped and danced and shone brightly in the cold sky. Then it turned and trotted up the trail in the direction of the camp it knew, where were the other food providers and fire providers.

Questions

1. Roughly how much of London's story is devoted to describing the setting? What particular details make it memorable?

2. To what extent does setting determine what happens in this story?

3. From what point of view is London's story told?

4. In "To Build a Fire" the man is never given a name. What is the effect of his being called simply "the man" throughout the story?

5. From the evidence London gives us, what stages are involved in the process of freezing to death? What does the story gain from London's detailed account of the man's experience with each successive stage?

6. What are the most serious mistakes the man makes? To what factors do you attribute these errors?

Jorge Luis Borges

The Gospel According to Mark

1970

Translated by Andrew Hurley

Jorge Luis Borges (1899–1986), an outstanding modern writer of Latin America, was born in Buenos Aires into a family prominent in Argentine history. His father, with whom he had a very close relationship, was a lawyer and teacher. Borges grew up bilingual, learning English from his English grandmother and receiving his early education from an English tutor. In later years, he would translate work by Poe, Melville, Whitman, Faulkner, and others into Spanish. Caught in Europe by the outbreak of World War I, Borges lived in Switzerland—where he learned French and

Jorge Luis Borges

taught himself German—and later Spain, where he joined the Ultraists, a group of experimental poets who renounced realism. On returning to Argentina, he edited a poetry magazine printed in the form of a poster and affixed to city walls. In his early writings, Borges favored the style of Criollismo (regionalism), but by the mid-1930s he had begun to take a more cosmopolitan and internationalist approach; in this same period, his principal literary emphasis began to shift from poetry to fiction. In 1946, for his opposition to the regime of Colonel Juan Perón, Borges was forced to resign his post as a librarian and was mockingly offered a job as a chicken inspector. In 1955, after Perón was deposed, Borges became director of the National Library and professor of English literature at the University of Buenos Aires. A sufferer since childhood from poor eyesight, Borges eventually went blind. His eye problems may have encouraged him to work mainly in short, highly crafted forms: stories, essays, fables, and lyric poems full of elaborate music. His short stories, in Ficciones (1944), El hacedor (1960; translated as Dreamtigers, 1964), and Labyrinths (1962), have been admired worldwide.

    The incident took place on the Los Alamos ranch, south of the small town of Junín, in late March of 1928. Its protagonist was a medical student named Baltasar Espinosa. We might define him for the moment as a Buenos Aires youth much like many others, with no traits worthier of note than the gift for public speaking that had won him more than one prize at the English school° in Ramos Mejía and an almost unlimited goodness. He didn't like to argue; he preferred that his interlocutor

---

English school: a prep school that emphasized English (well-to-do Argentines of this era wanted their children to learn English).

rather than he himself be right. And though he found the chance twists and turns of gambling interesting, he was a poor gambler, because he didn't like to win. He was intelligent and open to learning, but he was lazy; at thirty-three he had not yet completed the last requirements for his degree. (The work he still owed, incidentally, was for his favorite class.) His father, like all the gentlemen of his day a freethinker,° had instructed Espinosa in the doctrines of Herbert Spencer,° but once, before he set off on a trip to Montevideo, his mother had asked him to say the Lord's Prayer every night and make the sign of the cross, and never in all the years that followed did he break that promise. He did not lack courage; one morning, with more indifference than wrath, he had traded two or three blows with some of his classmates that were trying to force him to join a strike at the university. He abounded in debatable habits and opinions, out of a spirit of acquiescence: his country mattered less to him than the danger that people in other countries might think the Argentines still wore feathers; he venerated France but had contempt for the French; he had little respect for Americans but took pride in the fact that there were skyscrapers in Buenos Aires; he thought that the gauchos° of the plains were better horsemen than the gauchos of the mountains. When his cousin Daniel invited him to spend the summer at Los Alamos, he immediately accepted—not because he liked the country but out of a natural desire to please, and because he could find no good reason for saying no.

The main house at the ranch was large and a bit run-down; the quarters for the foreman, a man named Gutre, stood nearby. There were three members of the Gutre family: the father, the son (who was singularly rough and unpolished), and a girl of uncertain paternity. They were tall, strong, and bony, with reddish hair and Indian features. They rarely spoke. The foreman's wife had died years before.

In the country, Espinosa came to learn things he hadn't known, had never even suspected; for example, that when you're approaching a house there's no reason to gallop and that nobody goes out on a horse unless there's a job to be done. As the summer wore on, he learned to distinguish birds by their call.

Within a few days, Daniel had to go to Buenos Aires to close a deal on some livestock. At the most, he said, the trip would take a week. Espinosa, who was already a little tired of his cousin's *bonnes fortunes* and his indefatigable interest in the vagaries of men's tailoring, stayed behind on the ranch with his textbooks. The heat was oppressive, and not even nightfall brought relief. Then one morning toward dawn, he was awakened by thunder. Wind lashed the casuarina trees. Espinosa heard the first

---

freethinker: person who rejects traditional beliefs, especially religious dogma, in favor of rational inquiry.   *Herbert Spencer:* a British philosopher (1820–1903) who championed the theory of evolution.   *gauchos:* South American cowboys.

drops of rain and gave thanks to God. Suddenly the wind blew cold. That afternoon, the Salado overflowed.

The next morning, as he stood on the porch looking out over the 5 flooded plains, Baltasar Espinosa realized that the metaphor equating the pampas with the sea was not, at least that morning, an altogether false one, though Hudson° had noted that the sea seems the grander of the two because we view it not from horseback or our own height, but from the deck of a ship. The rain did not let up; the Gutres, helped (or hindered) by the city dweller, saved a good part of the livestock, though many animals were drowned. There were four roads leading to the ranch; all were under water. On the third day, when a leaking roof threatened the foreman's house, Espinosa gave the Gutres a room at the back of the main house, alongside the toolshed. The move brought Espinosa and the Gutres closer, and they began to eat together in the large dining room. Conversation was not easy; the Gutres, who knew so much about things in the country, did not know how to explain them. One night Espinosa asked them if people still remembered anything about the Indian raids, back when the military command for the frontier had been in Junín. They told him they did, but they would have given the same answer if he had asked them about the day Charles I° had been beheaded. Espinosa recalled that his father used to say that all the cases of longevity that occur in the country are the result of either poor memory or a vague notion of dates—gauchos quite often know neither the year they were born in nor the name of the man that fathered them.

In the entire house, the only reading material to be found were several copies of a farming magazine, a manual of veterinary medicine, a deluxe edition of the romantic verse drama *Tabaré*, a copy of *The History of the Shorthorn in Argentina*, several erotic and detective stories, and a recent novel that Espinosa had not read—*Don Segundo Sombra*, by Ricardo Güiraldes. In order to put some life into the inevitable afterdinner attempt at conversation, Espinosa read a couple of chapters of the novel to the Gutres, who did not know how to read or write. Unfortunately, the foreman had been a cattle drover himself, and he could not be interested in the adventures of another such a one. It was easy work, he said; they always carried along a pack mule with everything they might need. If he had not been a cattle drover, he announced, he'd never have seen Lake Gómez, or the Bragado River, or even the Núñez ranch, in Chacabuco. . . .

In the kitchen there was a guitar; before the incident I am narrating, the laborers would sit in a circle and someone would pick up the guitar and strum it, though never managing actually to play it. That was called "giving it a strum."

W. H. *Hudson:* an English naturalist and author (1841–1922) who wrote extensively about South America.   *Charles I:* King of England, beheaded in 1649.

Espinosa, who was letting his beard grow out, would stop before the mirror to look at his changed face; he smiled to think that he'd soon be boring the fellows in Buenos Aires with his stories about the Salado overrunning its banks. Curiously, he missed places in the city he never went, and would never go: a street corner on Cabrera where a mailbox stood; two cement lions on a porch on Calle Jujuy a few blocks from the Plaza del Once; a tile-floored corner grocery-store-and-bar (whose location he couldn't quite remember). As for his father and his brothers, by now Daniel would have told them that he had been isolated—the word was etymologically precise—by the floodwaters.

Exploring the house still cut off by the high water, he came upon a Bible printed in English. On its last pages the Guthries (for that was their real name) had kept their family history. They had come originally from Inverness° and had arrived in the New World—doubtlessly as peasant laborers—in the early nineteenth century; they had intermarried with Indians. The chronicle came to an end in the eighteen-seventies; they no longer knew how to write. Within a few generations they had forgotten their English; by the time Espinosa met them, even Spanish gave them some difficulty. They had no faith, though in their veins, alongside the superstitions of the pampas, there still ran a dim current of the Calvinist's harsh fanaticism. Espinosa mentioned his find to them, but they hardly seemed to hear him.

He leafed through the book, and his fingers opened it to the first   10
verses of the Gospel According to St. Mark. To try his hand at translating, and perhaps to see if they might understand a little of it, he decided that that would be the text he read the Gutres after dinner. He was surprised that they listened first attentively and then with mute fascination. The presence of gold letters on the binding may have given it increased authority. "It's in their blood," he thought. It also occurred to him that throughout history, humankind has told two stories: the story of a lost ship sailing the Mediterranean seas in quest of a beloved isle, and the story of a god who allows himself to be crucified on Golgotha. He recalled his elocution classes in Ramos Mejía, and he rose to his feet to preach the parables.

In the following days, the Gutres would wolf down the spitted beef and canned sardines in order to arrive sooner at the Gospel.

The girl had a little lamb; it was her pet, and she prettied it with a sky blue ribbon. One day it cut itself on a piece of barbed wire; to stanch the blood, the Gutres were about to put spiderwebs on the wound, but Espinosa treated it with pills. The gratitude awakened by that cure amazed him. At first, he had not trusted the Gutres and had hidden away in one of his books the two hundred forty pesos he'd brought; now, with Daniel gone, he had taken the master's place and begun to

Inverness: a county in Scotland.

give timid orders, which were immediately followed. The Gutres would trail him through the rooms and along the hallway, as though they were lost. As he read, he noticed that they would sweep away the crumbs he had left on the table. One afternoon, he surprised them as they were discussing him in brief, respectful words. When he came to the end of the Gospel According to St. Mark, he started to read another of the three remaining gospels, but the father asked him to reread the one he'd just finished, so they could understand it better. Espinosa felt they were like children, who prefer repetition to variety or novelty. One night he dreamed of the Flood (which is not surprising) and was awakened by the hammering of the building of the Ark, but he told himself it was thunder. And in fact the rain, which had let up for a while, had begun again; it was very cold. The Gutres told him the rain had broken through the roof of the toolshed; when they got the beams repaired, they said, they'd show him where. He was no longer a stranger, a foreigner, and they all treated him with respect; he was almost spoiled. None of them liked coffee, but there was always a little cup for him, with spoonfuls of sugar stirred in.

That second storm took place on a Tuesday. Thursday night there was a soft knock on his door; because of his doubts about the Gutres he always locked it. He got up and opened the door; it was the girl. In the darkness he couldn't see her, but he could tell by her footsteps that she was barefoot, and afterward, in the bed, that she was naked—that in fact she had come from the back of the house that way. She did not embrace him, or speak a word; she lay down beside him and she was shivering. It was the first time she had lain with a man. When she left, she did not kiss him; Espinosa realized that he didn't even know her name. Impelled by some sentiment he did not attempt to understand, he swore that when he returned to Buenos Aires, he'd tell no one of the incident.

The next day began like all the others, except that the father spoke to Espinosa to ask whether Christ had allowed himself to be killed in order to save all mankind. Espinosa, who was a freethinker like his father but felt obliged to defend what he had read them, paused.

"Yes," he finally replied. "To save all mankind from hell."   15

"What *is* hell?" Gutre then asked him.

"A place underground where souls will burn in fire forever."

"And those that drove the nails will also be saved?"

"Yes," replied Espinosa, whose theology was a bit shaky. (He had worried that the foreman wanted to have a word with him about what had happened last night with his daughter.)

After lunch they asked him to read the last chapters again.   20

Espinosa had a long siesta that afternoon, although it was a light sleep, interrupted by persistent hammering and vague premonitions. Toward evening he got up and went out into the hall.

"The water's going down," he said, as though thinking out loud. "It won't be long now."

"Not long now," repeated Gutre, like an echo.

The three of them had followed him. Kneeling on the floor, they asked his blessing. Then they cursed him, spat on him, and drove him to the back of the house. The girl was weeping. Espinosa realized what awaited him on the other side of the door. When they opened it, he saw the sky. A bird screamed; *it's a goldfinch*, Espinosa thought. There was no roof on the shed; they had torn down the roof beams to build the Cross.

Questions

1. What is about to happen to Baltasar Espinosa at the end of this story?
2. How old is Espinosa? What is ironic about his age?
3. Why is the isolated rural setting crucial to the story? Could the events have occurred in a large city like Buenos Aires?
4. What lessons does Espinosa learn in the country? What important lessons does he not notice as the weeks of his stay drag on?
5. How does weather affect the outcome of the story?
6. What is the background of the Gutre family? How did they come to own an English Bible? Why is it ironic that they own this book?
7. When Espinosa begins reading the Gospel of Saint Mark to the Gutres, what changes in their behavior does he notice?
8. What other action does Espinosa perform that earns the Gutres's gratitude?
9. Why do the Gutres kill Espinosa? What do they hope to gain?

Amy Tan

A Pair of Tickets   1989

Amy Tan was born in Oakland, California, in 1952. Both of her parents were recent Chinese immigrants. Her father was an electrical engineer (as well as a Baptist minister); her mother was a vocational nurse. When her father and older brother both died of brain tumors, the fifteen-year-old Tan moved with her mother and younger brother to Switzerland, where she attended high school. On their return to the United States, Tan attended Linfield College, a Baptist school in Oregon, but she eventually transferred to San Jose State University. At this time Tan and her mother argued about her future. The mother insisted her daughter pursue

Amy Tan

premedical studies in preparation for becoming a neurosurgeon, but Tan wanted to do something else. For six months the two did not speak to one another. Tan worked for IBM writing computer manuals and also wrote freelance business articles under a pseudonym. In 1987 she and her mother visited China together. This experience, which is reflected in "A Pair of Tickets," deepened Tan's sense of her Chinese Ameri-can identity. "As soon as my feet touched China," she wrote, "I became Chinese." Soon after, she began writing her first novel, The Joy Luck Club (1989), which consists of sixteen interrelated stories about a group of Chinese American mothers and their daughters. (The club of the title is a woman's social group.) The Joy Luck Club became both a critical success and a best seller, and was made into a movie in 1993. In 1991 Tan published her second novel, The Kitchen God's Wife. Her later novels include The Bonesetter's Daughter (2001), Saving Fish from Drowning (2005), and The Valley of Amazement (2013). Tan performed with a "vintage garage" band called the Rock Bottom Remainders—which included, among others, Stephen King, Dave Barry, and Scott Turow—an experience she discusses in the collaborative ebook Hard Listening (2013). She lives outside San Francisco with her husband.

The minute our train leaves the Hong Kong border and enters Shen-zhen, China, I feel different. I can feel the skin on my forehead tingling, my blood rushing through a new course, my bones aching with a familiar old pain. And I think, My mother was right. I am becoming Chinese.

"Cannot be helped," my mother said when I was fifteen and had vig-orously denied that I had any Chinese whatsoever below my skin. I was a sophomore at Galileo High in San Francisco, and all my Caucasian friends agreed: I was about as Chinese as they were. But my mother had studied at a famous nursing school in Shanghai, and she said she knew all about genetics. So there was no doubt in her mind, whether I agreed or not: Once you are born Chinese, you cannot help but feel and think Chinese.

"Someday you will see," said my mother. "It is in your blood, waiting to be let go."

And when she said this, I saw myself transforming like a werewolf, a mutant tag of DNA suddenly triggered, replicating itself insidiously into a *syndrome,*° a cluster of telltale Chinese behaviors, all those things my mother did to embarrass me—haggling with store owners, pecking her mouth with a toothpick in public, being color-blind to the fact that lemon yellow and pale pink are not good combinations for winter clothes.

But today I realize I've never really known what it means to be Chi-   5
nese. I am thirty-six years old. My mother is dead and I am on a train, carrying with me her dreams of coming home. I am going to China.

We are first going to Guangzhou, my seventy-two-year-old father, Canning Woo, and I, where we will visit his aunt, whom he has not seen since he was ten years old. And I don't know whether it's the prospect of seeing his aunt or if it's because he's back in China, but now he looks like he's a young boy, so innocent and happy I want to button his sweater and pat his head. We are sitting across from each other, separated by a little

---

syndrome: a group of symptoms that occur together as the sign of a particular disease or abnormality.

table with two cold cups of tea. For the first time I can ever remember, my father has tears in his eyes, and all he is seeing out the train window is a sectioned field of yellow, green, and brown, a narrow canal flanking the tracks, low rising hills, and three people in blue jackets riding an ox-driven cart on this early October morning. And I can't help myself. I also have misty eyes, as if I had seen this a long, long time ago, and had almost forgotten.

In less than three hours, we will be in Guangzhou, which my guide-book tells me is how one properly refers to Canton these days. It seems all the cities I have heard of, except Shanghai, have changed their spellings. I think they are saying China has changed in other ways as well. Chungking is Chongqing. And Kweilin is Guilin. I have looked these names up, because after we see my father's aunt in Guangzhou, we will catch a plane to Shanghai, where I will meet my two half-sisters for the first time.

They are my mother's twin daughters from her first marriage, little babies she was forced to abandon on a road as she was fleeing Kweilin for Chungking in 1944. That was all my mother had told me about these daughters, so they had remained babies in my mind, all these years, sitting on the side of a road, listening to bombs whistling in the distance while sucking their patient red thumbs.

And it was only this year that someone found them and wrote with this joyful news. A letter came from Shanghai, addressed to my mother. When I first heard about this, that they were alive, I imagined my identi-cal sisters transforming from little babies into six-year-old girls. In my mind, they were seated next to each other at a table, taking turns with the fountain pen. One would write a neat row of characters: *Dearest Mama. We are alive.* She would brush back her wispy bangs and hand the other sister the pen, and she would write: *Come get us. Please hurry.*

Of course they could not know that my mother had died three months before, suddenly, when a blood vessel in her brain burst. One minute she was talking to my father, complaining about the tenants up-stairs, scheming how to evict them under the pretense that relatives from China were moving in. The next minute she was holding her head, her eyes squeezed shut, groping for the sofa, and then crumpling softly to the floor with fluttering hands. 10

So my father had been the first one to open the letter, a long letter it turned out. And they did call her Mama. They said they always revered her as their true mother. They kept a framed picture of her. They told her about their life, from the time my mother last saw them on the road leav-ing Kweilin to when they were finally found.

And the letter had broken my father's heart so much—these daugh-ters calling my mother from another life he never knew—that he gave the letter to my mother's old friend Auntie Lindo and asked her to write back and tell my sisters, in the gentlest way possible, that my mother was dead.

But instead Auntie Lindo took the letter to the Joy Luck Club and discussed with Auntie Ying and Auntie An-mei what should be done, because they had known for many years about my mother's search for her twin daughters, her endless hope. Auntie Lindo and the others cried over this double tragedy, of losing my mother three months before, and now again. And so they couldn't help but think of some miracle, some possible way of reviving her from the dead, so my mother could fulfill her dream.

So this is what they wrote to my sisters in Shanghai: "Dearest Daughters, I too have never forgotten you in my memory or in my heart. I never gave up hope that we would see each other again in a joyous reunion. I am only sorry it has been too long. I want to tell you everything about my life since I last saw you. I want to tell you this when our family comes to see you in China. . . ." They signed it with my mother's name.

It wasn't until all this had been done that they first told me about my sisters, the letter they received, the one they wrote back.   15

"They'll think she's coming, then," I murmured. And I had imagined my sisters now being ten or eleven, jumping up and down, holding hands, their pigtails bouncing, excited that their mother—*their* mother—was coming, whereas my mother was dead.

"How can you say she is not coming in a letter?" said Auntie Lindo. "She is their mother. She is your mother. You must be the one to tell them. All these years, they have been dreaming of her." And I thought she was right.

But then I started dreaming, too, of my mother and my sisters and how it would be if I arrived in Shanghai. All these years, while they waited to be found, I had lived with my mother and then had lost her. I imagined seeing my sisters at the airport. They would be standing on their tip-toes, looking anxiously, scanning from one dark head to another as we got off the plane. And I would recognize them instantly, their faces with the identical worried look.

"*Jyejye, Jyejye*. Sister, Sister. We are here," I saw myself saying in my poor version of Chinese.

"Where is Mama?" they would say, and look around, still smiling, two   20 flushed and eager faces. "Is she hiding?" And this would have been like my mother, to stand behind just a bit, to tease a little and make people's patience pull a little on their hearts. I would shake my head and tell my sisters she was not hiding.

"Oh, that must be Mama, no?" one of my sisters would whisper excitedly, pointing to another small woman completely engulfed in a tower of presents. And that, too, would have been like my mother, to bring mountains of gifts, food, and toys for children—all bought on sale—shunning thanks, saying the gifts were nothing, and later turning the labels over to show my sisters, "Calvin Klein, 100% wool."

I imagined myself starting to say, "Sisters, I am sorry, I have come alone . . ." and before I could tell them—they could see it in my face—they were wailing, pulling their hair, their lips twisted in pain, as they ran away from me. And then I saw myself getting back on the plane and coming home.

After I had dreamed this scene many times—watching their despair turn from horror into anger—I begged Auntie Lindo to write another letter. And at first she refused.

"How can I say she is dead? I cannot write this," said Auntie Lindo with a stubborn look.

"But it's cruel to have them believe she's coming on the plane," I said.   25
"When they see it's just me, they'll hate me."

"Hate you? Cannot be." She was scowling. "You are their own sister, their only family."

"You don't understand," I protested.

"What I don't understand?" she said.

And I whispered, "They'll think I'm responsible, that she died because I didn't appreciate her."

And Auntie Lindo looked satisfied and sad at the same time, as if this   30
were true and I had finally realized it. She sat down for an hour, and when she stood up she handed me a two-page letter. She had tears in her eyes. I realized that the very thing I had feared, she had done. So even if she had written the news of my mother's death in English, I wouldn't have had the heart to read it.

"Thank you," I whispered.

The landscape has become gray, filled with low flat cement buildings, old factories, and then tracks and more tracks filled with trains like ours passing by in the opposite direction. I see platforms crowded with people wearing drab Western clothes, with spots of bright colors: little children wearing pink and yellow, red and peach. And there are soldiers in olive green and red, and old ladies in gray tops and pants that stop mid-calf. We are in Guangzhou.

Before the train even comes to a stop, people are bringing down their belongings from above their seats. For a moment there is a dangerous shower of heavy suitcases laden with gifts to relatives, half-broken boxes wrapped in miles of string to keep the contents from spilling out, plastic bags filled with yarn and vegetables and packages of dried mushrooms, and camera cases. And then we are caught in a stream of people rushing, shoving, pushing us along, until we find ourselves in one of a dozen lines waiting to go through customs. I feel as if I were getting on the number 30 Stockton bus in San Francisco. I am in China, I remind myself. And somehow the crowds don't bother me. It feels right. I start pushing too.

I take out the declaration forms and my passport. "Woo," it says at the top, and below that, "June May," who was born in "California, U.S.A.," in 1951. I wonder if the customs people will question whether I'm the same person in the passport photo. In this picture, my chin-length hair is swept back and artfully styled. I am wearing false eyelashes, eye shadow, and lip liner. My cheeks are hollowed out by bronze blusher. But I had not expected the heat in October. And now my hair hangs limp with the humidity. I wear no makeup; in Hong Kong my mascara had melted into dark circles and everything else had felt like layers of grease. So today my face is plain, unadorned except for a thin mist of shiny sweat on my forehead and nose.

Even without makeup, I could never pass for true Chinese. I stand   35 five-foot-six, and my head pokes above the crowd so that I am eye level only with other tourists. My mother once told me my height came from my grandfather, who was a northerner, and may have even had some Mongol blood. "This is what your grandmother once told me," explained my mother. "But now it is too late to ask her. They are all dead, your grandparents, your uncles, and their wives and children, all killed in the war, when a bomb fell on our house. So many generations in one instant."

She had said this so matter-of-factly that I thought she had long since gotten over any grief she had. And then I wondered how she knew they were all dead.

"Maybe they left the house before the bomb fell," I suggested.

"No," said my mother. "Our whole family is gone. It is just you and I."

"But how do you know? Some of them could have escaped."

"Cannot be," said my mother, this time almost angrily. And then her   40 frown was washed over by a puzzled blank look, and she began to talk as if she were trying to remember where she had misplaced something. "I went back to that house. I kept looking up to where the house used to be. And it wasn't a house, just the sky. And below, underneath my feet, were four stories of burnt bricks and wood, all the life of our house. Then off to the side I saw things blown into the yard, nothing valuable. There was a bed someone used to sleep in, really just a metal frame twisted up at one corner. And a book, I don't know what kind, because every page had turned black. And I saw a teacup which was unbroken but filled with ashes. And then I found my doll, with her hands and legs broken, her hair burned off. . . . When I was a little girl, I had cried for that doll, seeing it all alone in the store window, and my mother had bought it for me. It was an American doll with yellow hair. It could turn its legs and arms. The eyes moved up and down. And when I married and left my family home, I gave the doll to my youngest niece, because she was like me. She cried if that doll was not with her always. Do you see? If she was in the house with that doll, her parents were there, and so everybody was there, waiting together, because that's how our family was."

The woman in the customs booth stares at my documents, then glances at me briefly, and with two quick movements stamps everything and sternly nods me along. And soon my father and I find ourselves in a large area filled with thousands of people and suitcases. I feel lost and my father looks helpless.

"Excuse me," I say to a man who looks like an American. "Can you tell me where I can get a taxi?" He mumbles something that sounds Swedish or Dutch.

"Syau Yen! Syau Yen!" I hear a piercing voice shout from behind me. An old woman in a yellow knit beret is holding up a pink plastic bag filled with wrapped trinkets. I guess she is trying to sell us something. But my father is staring down at this tiny sparrow of a woman, squinting into her eyes. And then his eyes widen, his face opens up and he smiles like a pleased little boy.

"*Aiyi! Aiyi!*"—Auntie Auntie!—he says softly.

"Syau Yen!" coos my great-aunt. I think it's funny she has just called   45
my father "Little Wild Goose." It must be his baby milk name, the name used to discourage ghosts from stealing children.

They clasp each other's hands—they do not hug—and hold on like this, taking turns saying, "Look at you! You are so old. Look how old you've become!" They are both crying openly, laughing at the same time, and I bite my lip, trying not to cry. I'm afraid to feel their joy. Because I am thinking how different our arrival in Shanghai will be tomorrow, how awkward it will feel.

Now Aiyi beams and points to a Polaroid picture of my father. My father had wisely sent pictures when he wrote and said we were coming. See how smart she was, she seems to intone as she compares the picture to my father. In the letter, my father had said we would call her from the hotel once we arrived, so this is a surprise, that they've come to meet us. I wonder if my sisters will be at the airport.

It is only then that I remember the camera. I had meant to take a picture of my father and his aunt the moment they met. It's not too late.

"Here, stand together over here," I say, holding up the Polaroid. The camera flashes and I hand them the snapshot. Aiyi and my father still stand close together, each of them holding a corner of the picture, watching as their images begin to form. They are almost reverentially quiet. Aiyi is only five years older than my father, which makes her around seventy-seven. But she looks ancient, shrunken, a mummified relic. Her thin hair is pure white, her teeth are brown with decay. So much for stories of Chinese women looking young forever, I think to myself.

Now Aiyi is crooning to me: "*Jandale*." So big already. She looks up   50
at me, at my full height, and then peers into her pink plastic bag—her gifts to us, I have figured out—as if she is wondering what she will give to me, now that I am so old and big. And then she grabs my elbow with her sharp pincerlike grasp and turns me around. A man and woman in their fifties are shaking hands with my father, everybody smiling and saying, "Ah! Ah!" They are Aiyi's oldest son and his wife, and standing next to them are four other people, around my age, and a little girl who's around

ten. The introductions go by so fast, all I know is that one of them is Aiyi's grandson, with his wife, and the other is her granddaughter, with her husband. And the little girl is Lili, Aiyi's great-granddaughter.

Aiyi and my father speak the Mandarin dialect from their childhood, but the rest of the family speaks only the Cantonese of their village. I understand only Mandarin but can't speak it that well. So Aiyi and my father gossip unrestrained in Mandarin, exchanging news about people from their old village. And they stop only occasionally to talk to the rest of us, sometimes in Cantonese, sometimes in English.

"Oh, it is as I suspected," says my father, turning to me. "He died last summer." And I already understood this. I just don't know who this person, Li Gong, is. I feel as if I were in the United Nations and the translators had run amok.

"Hello," I say to the little girl. "My name is Jing-mei." But the little girl squirms to look away, causing her parents to laugh with embarrassment. I try to think of Cantonese words I can say to her, stuff I learned from friends in Chinatown, but all I can think of are swear words, terms for bodily functions, and short phrases like "tastes good," "tastes like garbage," and "she's really ugly." And then I have another plan: I hold up the Polaroid camera, beckoning Lili with my finger. She immediately jumps forward, places one hand on her hip in the manner of a fashion model, juts out her chest, and flashes me a toothy smile. As soon as I take the picture she is standing next to me, jumping and giggling every few seconds as she watches herself appear on the greenish film.

By the time we hail taxis for the ride to the hotel, Lili is holding tight onto my hand, pulling me along.

In the taxi, Aiyi talks nonstop, so I have no chance to ask her about the different sights we are passing by.

"You wrote and said you would come only for one day," says Aiyi to my father in an agitated tone. "One day! How can you see your family in one day! Toishan is many hours' drive from Guangzhou. And this idea to call us when you arrive. This is nonsense. We have no telephone."

My heart races a little. I wonder if Auntie Lindo told my sisters we would call from the hotel in Shanghai?

Aiyi continues to scold my father. "I was so beside myself, ask my son, almost turned heaven and earth upside down trying to think of a way! So we decided the best was for us to take the bus from Toishan and come into Guangzhou—meet you right from the start."

And now I am holding my breath as the taxi driver dodges between trucks and buses, honking his horn constantly. We seem to be on some sort of long freeway overpass, like a bridge above the city. I can see row after row of apartments, each floor cluttered with laundry hanging out to dry on the balcony. We pass a public bus, with people jammed in so tight their faces are nearly wedged against the window. Then I see the skyline of what must be downtown Guangzhou. From a distance, it looks like a major American city, with high rises and construction going on everywhere. As we slow down in the more congested part of the city, I see scores of little shops, dark inside, lined with counters and shelves. And then there is a building, its front laced with scaffolding made of bamboo poles held together with plastic strips. Men and women are standing on narrow platforms, scraping the sides, working without safety straps or helmets. Oh, would OSHA° have a field day here, I think.

Aiyi's shrill voice rises up again: "So it is a shame you can't see our village, our house. My sons have been quite successful, selling our vegetables in the free market. We had enough these last few years to build a big house, three stories, all of new brick, big enough for our whole family and then some. And every year, the money is even better. You Americans aren't the only ones who know how to get rich!"   60

The taxi stops and I assume we've arrived, but then I peer out at what looks like a grander version of the Hyatt Regency. "This is communist China?" I wonder out loud. And then I shake my head toward my father. "This must be the wrong hotel." I quickly pull out our itinerary, travel tickets, and reservations. I had explicitly instructed my travel agent to choose something inexpensive, in the thirty-to-forty-dollar range. I'm sure of this. And there it says on our itinerary: Garden Hotel, Huanshi Dong Lu. Well, our travel agent had better be prepared to eat the extra, that's all I have to say.

The hotel is magnificent. A bellboy complete with uniform and sharp-creased cap jumps forward and begins to carry our bags into the lobby. Inside, the hotel looks like an orgy of shopping arcades and restaurants all encased in granite and glass. And rather than be impressed, I am worried about the expense, as well as the appearance it must give Aiyi, that we rich Americans cannot be without our luxuries even for one night.

But when I step up to the reservation desk, ready to haggle over this booking mistake, it is confirmed. Our rooms are prepaid, thirty-four dollars each. I feel sheepish, and Aiyi and the others seem delighted by our temporary surroundings. Lili is looking wide-eyed at an arcade filled with video games.

Our whole family crowds into one elevator, and the bellboy waves, saying he will meet us on the eighteenth floor. As soon as the elevator door shuts, everybody becomes very quiet, and when the door finally opens again, everybody talks at once in what sounds like relieved voices. I have the feeling Aiyi and the others have never been on such a long elevator ride.

Our rooms are next to each other and are identical. The rugs, drapes, bedspreads are all in shades of taupe. There's a color television with   65 remote-control panels built into the lamp table between the two twin beds. The bathroom has marble walls and floors. I find a built-in wet bar with a small refrigerator stocked with Heineken beer, Coke Classic, and Seven-Up, mini-bottles of Johnnie Walker Red, Bacardi rum, and Smirnoff vodka, and packets of M & M's, honey-roasted cashews, and Cadbury chocolate bars. And again I say out loud, "This is communist China?"

My father comes into my room. "They decided we should just stay here and visit," he says, shrugging his shoulders. "They say, Less trouble that way. More time to talk."

"What about dinner?" I ask. I have been envisioning my first real Chinese feast for many days already, a big banquet with one of those soups steaming out of a carved winter melon, chicken wrapped in clay, Peking duck, the works.

My father walks over and picks up a room service book next to a *Travel & Leisure* magazine. He flips through the pages quickly and then points to the menu. "This is what they want," says my father.

So it's decided. We are going to dine tonight in our rooms, with our family, sharing hamburgers, french fries, and apple pie à la mode.

Aiyi and her family are browsing the shops while we clean up. After a   70
hot ride on the train, I'm eager for a shower and cooler clothes.

The hotel has provided little packets of shampoo which, upon opening, I discover is the consistency and color of hoisin sauce. This is more like it, I think. This is China. And I rub some in my damp hair.

Standing in the shower, I realize this is the first time I've been by myself in what seems like days. But instead of feeling relieved, I feel forlorn. I think about what my mother said, about activating my genes and becoming Chinese. And I wonder what she meant.

Right after my mother died, I asked myself a lot of things, things that couldn't be answered, to force myself to grieve more. It seemed as if I wanted to sustain my grief, to assure myself that I had cared deeply enough.

But now I ask the questions mostly because I want to know the answers. What was that pork stuff she used to make that had the texture of sawdust? What were the names of the uncles who died in Shanghai? What had she dreamt all these years about her other daughters? All the times when she got mad at me, was she really thinking about them? Did she wish I were they? Did she regret that I wasn't?

At one o'clock in the morning, I awake to tapping sounds on the   75
window. I must have dozed off and now I feel my body uncramping itself. I'm sitting on the floor, leaning against one of the twin beds. Lili is lying next to me. The others are asleep, too, sprawled out on the beds and floor. Aiyi is seated at a little table, looking very sleepy. And my father is staring

out the window, tapping his fingers on the glass. The last time I listened my father was telling Aiyi about his life since he last saw her. How he had gone to Yenching University, later got a post with a newspaper in Chungking, met my mother there, a young widow. How they later fled together to Shanghai to try to find my mother's family house, but there was nothing there. And then they traveled eventually to Canton and then to Hong Kong, then Haiphong and finally to San Francisco. . . .

"Suyuan didn't tell me she was trying all these years to find her daughters," he is now saying in a quiet voice. "Naturally, I did not discuss her daughters with her. I thought she was ashamed she had left them behind."

"Where did she leave them?" asks Aiyi. "How were they found?"

I am wide awake now. Although I have heard parts of this story from my mother's friends.

"It happened when the Japanese took over Kweilin," says my father.

"Japanese in Kweilin?" says Aiyi. "That was never the case. Couldn't   80 be. The Japanese never came to Kweilin."

"Yes, that is what the newspapers reported. I know this because I was working for the news bureau at the time. The Kuomintang often told us what we could say and could not say. But we knew the Japanese had come into Kwangsi Province. We had sources who told us how they had captured the Wuchang-Canton railway. How they were coming overland, making very fast progress, marching toward the provincial capital."

Aiyi looks astonished. "If people did not know this, how could Suyuan know the Japanese were coming?"

"An officer of the Kuomintang secretly warned her," explains my father. "Suyuan's husband also was an officer and everybody knew that officers and their families would be the first to be killed. So she gathered a few possessions and, in the middle of the night, she picked up her daughters and fled on foot. The babies were not even one year old."

"How could she give up those babies!" sighs Aiyi. "Twin girls. We have never had such luck in our family." And then she yawns again.

"What were they named?" she asks. I listen carefully. I had been plan-   85 ning on using just the familiar "Sister" to address them both. But now I want to know how to pronounce their names.

"They have their father's surname, Wang," says my father. "And their given names are Chwun Yu and Chwun Hwa."

"What do the names mean?" I ask.

"Ah." My father draws imaginary characters on the window. "One means 'Spring Rain,' the other 'Spring Flower,'" he explains in English, "because they born in the spring, and of course rain come before flower, same order these girls are born. Your mother like a poet, don't you think?"

I nod my head. I see Aiyi nod her head forward, too. But it falls forward and stays there. She is breathing deeply, noisily. She is asleep.

"And what does Ma's name mean?" I whisper.   90

"'Suyuan,'" he says, writing more invisible characters on the glass. "The way she write it in Chinese, it mean 'Long-Cherished Wish.' Quite a fancy name, not so ordinary like flower name. See this first character, it mean something like 'Forever Never Forgotten.' But there is another way to write 'Suyuan.' Sound exactly the same, but the meaning is opposite." His finger creates the brushstrokes of another character. "The first part look the same: 'Never Forgotten.' But the last part add to first part make the whole word mean 'Long-Held Grudge.' Your mother get angry with me, I tell her her name should be Grudge."

My father is looking at me, moist-eyed. "See, I pretty clever, too, hah?"

I nod, wishing I could find some way to comfort him. "And what about my name," I ask, "what does 'Jing-mei' mean?"

"Your name also special," he says. I wonder if any name in Chinese is not something special. "'Jing' like excellent *jing*. Not just good, it's something pure, essential, the best quality. *Jing* is good leftover stuff when you take impurities out of something like gold, or rice, or salt. So what is left—just pure essence. And 'Mei,' this is common *mei*, as in *meimei*, 'younger sister.'"

I think about this. My mother's long-cherished wish. Me, the younger   95
sister who was supposed to be the essence of the others. I feed myself with the old grief, wondering how disappointed my mother must have been. Tiny Aiyi stirs suddenly, her head rolls and then falls back, her mouth opens as if to answer my question. She grunts in her sleep, tucking her body more closely into the chair.

"So why did she abandon those babies on the road?" I need to know, because now I feel abandoned too.

"Long time I wondered this myself," says my father. "But then I read that letter from her daughters in Shanghai now, and I talk to Auntie Lindo, all the others. And then I knew. No shame in what she done. None."

"What happened?"

"Your mother running away—" begins my father.

"No, tell me in Chinese," I interrupt. "Really, I can understand."   100

He begins to talk, still standing at the window, looking into the night.

After fleeing Kweilin, your mother walked for several days trying to find a main road. Her thought was to catch a ride on a truck or wagon, to catch enough rides until she reached Chungking, where her husband was stationed.

She had sewn money and jewelry into the lining of her dress, enough, she thought, to barter rides all the way. If I am lucky, she thought, I will not have to trade the heavy gold bracelet and jade ring. These were things from her mother, your grandmother.

By the third day, she had traded nothing. The roads were filled with
people, everybody running and begging for rides from passing trucks. The
trucks rushed by, afraid to stop. So your mother found no rides, only the
start of dysentery pains in her stomach.

Her shoulders ached from the two babies swinging from scarf slings.   105
Blisters grew on her palms from holding two leather suitcases. And then
the blisters burst and began to bleed. After a while, she left the suitcases
behind, keeping only the food and a few clothes. And later she also
dropped the bags of wheat flour and rice and kept walking like this for
many miles, singing songs to her little girls, until she was delirious with
pain and fever.

Finally, there was not one more step left in her body. She didn't have
the strength to carry those babies any farther. She slumped to the ground.
She knew she would die of her sickness, or perhaps from thirst, from starvation, or from the Japanese, who she was sure were marching right behind her.

She took the babies out of the slings and sat them on the side of the
road, then lay down next to them. You babies are so good, she said, so
quiet. They smiled back, reaching their chubby hands for her, wanting to
be picked up again. And then she knew she could not bear to watch her
babies die with her.

She saw a family with three young children in a cart going by. "Take
my babies, I beg you," she cried to them. But they stared back with
empty eyes and never stopped.

She saw another person pass and called out again. This time a man
turned around, and he had such a terrible expression—your mother said
it looked like death itself—she shivered and looked away.

When the road grew quiet, she tore open the lining of her dress, and   110
stuffed jewelry under the shirt of one baby and money under the other.
She reached into her pocket and drew out the photos of her family, the
picture of her father and mother, the picture of herself and her husband
on their wedding day. And she wrote on the back of each the names of
the babies and this same message: "Please care for these babies with the
money and valuables provided. When it is safe to come, if you bring them
to Shanghai, 9 Weichang Lu, the Li family will be glad to give you a generous reward. Li Suyuan and Wang Fuchi."

And then she touched each baby's cheek and told her not to cry. She
would go down the road to find them some food and would be back. And
without looking back, she walked down the road, stumbling and crying,
thinking only of this one last hope, that her daughters would be found
by a kindhearted person who would care for them. She would not allow
herself to imagine anything else.

She did not remember how far she walked, which direction she went,
when she fainted, or how she was found. When she awoke, she was in the
back of a bouncing truck with several other sick people, all moaning. And
she began to scream, thinking she was now on a journey to Buddhist hell.

But the face of an American missionary lady bent over her and smiled, talking to her in a soothing language she did not understand. And yet she could somehow understand. She had been saved for no good reason, and it was now too late to go back and save her babies.

When she arrived in Chungking, she learned her husband had died two weeks before. She told me later she laughed when the officers told her this news, she was so delirious with madness and disease. To come so far, to lose so much and to find nothing.

I met her in a hospital. She was lying on a cot, hardly able to move, her dysentery had drained her so thin. I had come in for my foot, my missing toe, which was cut off by a piece of falling rubble. She was talking to herself, mumbling.

"Look at these clothes," she said, and I saw she had on a rather unusual dress for wartime. It was silk satin, quite dirty, but there was no doubt it was a beautiful dress.   115

"Look at this face," she said, and I saw her dusty face and hollow cheeks, her eyes shining back. "Do you see my foolish hope?"

"I thought I had lost everything, except these two things," she murmured. "And I wondered which I would lose next. Clothes or hope? Hope or clothes?"

"But now, see here, look what is happening," she said, laughing, as if all her prayers had been answered. And she was pulling hair out of her head as easily as one lifts new wheat from wet soil.

It was an old peasant woman who found them. "How could I resist?" the peasant woman later told your sisters when they were older. They were still sitting obediently near where your mother had left them, looking like little fairy queens waiting for their sedan to arrive.

The woman, Mei Ching, and her husband, Mei Han, lived in a stone cave. There were thousands of hidden caves like that in and around Kweilin so secret that the people remained hidden even after the war ended. The Meis would come out of their cave every few days and forage for food supplies left on the road, and sometimes they would see something that they both agreed was a tragedy to leave behind. So one day they took back to their cave a delicately painted set of rice bowls, another day a little footstool with a velvet cushion and two new wedding blankets. And once, it was your sisters.   120

They were pious people, Muslims, who believed the twin babies were a sign of double luck, and they were sure of this when, later in the evening, they discovered how valuable the babies were. She and her husband had never seen rings and bracelets like those. And while they admired the pictures, knowing the babies came from a good family, neither of them could read or write. It was not until many months later that Mei Ching found someone who could read the writing on the back. By then, she loved these baby girls like her own.

In 1952 Mei Han, the husband, died. The twins were already eight years old, and Mei Ching now decided it was time to find your sisters' true family.

She showed the girls the picture of their mother and told them they had been born into a great family and she would take them back to see their true mother and grandparents. Mei Ching told them about the reward, but she swore she would refuse it. She loved these girls so much, she only wanted them to have what they were entitled to—a better life, a fine house, educated ways. Maybe the family would let her stay on as the girls' amah. Yes, she was certain they would insist.

Of course, when she found the place at 9 Weichang Lu, in the old French Concession, it was something completely different. It was the site of a factory building, recently constructed, and none of the workers knew what had become of the family whose house had burned down on that spot.

Mei Ching could not have known, of course, that your mother and 125 I, her new husband, had already returned to that same place in 1945 in hopes of finding both her family and her daughters.

Your mother and I stayed in China until 1947. We went to many different cities—back to Kweilin, to Changsha, as far south as Kunming. She was always looking out of one corner of her eye for twin babies, then little girls. Later we went to Hong Kong, and when we finally left in 1949 for the United States, I think she was even looking for them on the boat. But when we arrived, she no longer talked about them. I thought, At last, they have died in her heart.

When letters could be openly exchanged between China and the United States, she wrote immediately to old friends in Shanghai and Kweilin. I did not know she did this. Auntie Lindo told me. But of course, by then, all the street names had changed. Some people had died, others had moved away. So it took many years to find a contact. And when she did find an old schoolmate's address and wrote asking her to look for her daughters, her friend wrote back and said this was impossible, like looking for a needle on the bottom of the ocean. How did she know her daughters were in Shanghai and not somewhere else in China? The friend, of course, did not ask, How do you know your daughters are still alive?

So her schoolmate did not look. Finding babies lost during the war was a matter of foolish imagination, and she had no time for that.

But every year, your mother wrote to different people. And this last year, I think she got a big idea in her head, to go to China and find them herself. I remember she told me, "Canning, we should go, before it is too late, before we are too old." And I told her we were already too old, it was already too late.

I just thought she wanted to be a tourist! I didn't know she wanted 130 to go and look for her daughters. So when I said it was too late, that must have put a terrible thought in her head that her daughters might be dead.

And I think this possibility grew bigger and bigger in her head, until it killed her.

Maybe it was your mother's dead spirit who guided her Shanghai schoolmate to find her daughters. Because after your mother died, the schoolmate saw your sisters, by chance, while shopping for shoes at the Number One Department Store on Nanjing Dong Road. She said it was like a dream, seeing these two women who looked so much alike, moving down the stairs together. There was something about their facial expressions that reminded the schoolmate of your mother.

She quickly walked over to them and called their names, which of course, they did not recognize at first, because Mei Ching had changed their names. But your mother's friend was so sure, she persisted. "Are you not Wang Chwun Yu and Wang Chwun Hwa?" she asked them. And then these double-image women became very excited, because they remembered the names written on the back of an old photo, a photo of a young man and woman they still honored, as their much-loved first parents, who had died and become spirit ghosts still roaming the earth looking for them.

At the airport, I am exhausted. I could not sleep last night. Aiyi had followed me into my room at three in the morning, and she instantly fell asleep on one of the twin beds, snoring with the might of a lumberjack. I lay awake thinking about my mother's story, realizing how much I have never known about her, grieving that my sisters and I had both lost her.

And now at the airport, after shaking hands with everybody, waving good-bye, I think about all the different ways we leave people in this world. Cheerily waving good-bye to some at airports, knowing we'll never see each other again. Leaving others on the side of the road, hoping that we will. Finding my mother in my father's story and saying good-bye before I have a chance to know her better.

Aiyi smiles at me as we wait for our gate to be called. She is so old. I put one arm around her and one around Lili. They are the same size, it seems. And then it's time. As we wave good-bye one more time and enter the waiting area, I get the sense I am going from one funeral to another. In my hand I'm clutching a pair of tickets to Shanghai. In two hours we'll be there.

The plane takes off. I close my eyes. How can I describe to them in my broken Chinese about our mother's life? Where should I begin?

"Wake up, we're here," says my father. And I awake with my heart pounding in my throat. I look out the window and we're already on the runway. It's gray outside.

And now I'm walking down the steps of the plane, onto the tarmac and toward the building. If only, I think, if only my mother had lived long enough to be the one walking toward them. I am so nervous I cannot even feel my feet. I am just moving somehow.

Somebody shouts, "She's arrived!" And then I see her. Her short hair. Her small body. And that same look on her face. She has the back of her hand pressed hard against her mouth. She is crying as though she had gone through a terrible ordeal and were happy it is over.

And I know it's not my mother, yet it is the same look she had 140 when I was five and had disappeared all afternoon, for such a long time, that she was convinced I was dead. And when I miraculously appeared, sleepy-eyed, crawling from underneath my bed, she wept and laughed, biting the back of her hand to make sure it was true.

And now I see her again, two of her, waving, and in one hand there is a photo, the Polaroid I sent them. As soon as I get beyond the gate, we run toward each other, all three of us embracing, all hesitations and expectations forgotten.

"Mama, Mama," we all murmur, as if she is among us.

My sisters look at me, proudly. "*Meimei jandale*," says one sister proudly to the other. "Little Sister has grown up." I look at their faces again and I see no trace of my mother in them. Yet they still look familiar. And now I also see what part of me is Chinese. It is so obvious. It is my family. It is in our blood. After all these years, it can finally be let go.

My sisters and I stand, arms around each other, laughing and wiping the tears from each other's eyes. The flash of the Polaroid goes off and my father hands me the snapshot. My sisters and I watch quietly together, eager to see what develops.

The gray-green surface changes to the bright colors of our three im- 145 ages, sharpening and deepening all at once. And although we don't speak, I know we all see it: Together we look like our mother. Her same eyes, her same mouth, open in surprise to see, at last, her long-cherished wish.

Questions

1. How is the external setting of "A Pair of Tickets" essential to what happens internally to the narrator in the course of this story?
2. How does the narrator's view of her father change by seeing him in a different setting?
3. In what ways does the narrator feel at home in China? In what ways does she feel foreign?
4. What do the narrator and her half-sisters have in common? How does this element relate to the theme of the story?
5. In what ways does the story explore specifically Chinese American experiences? In what other ways is the story grounded in universal family issues?

WRITING *effectively*

THINKING ABOUT SETTING

The time and place in which a story is set serve as more than mere backdrop. When preparing to write about a story, be sure to consider where and when it is set, and what role the setting plays.

- **Ask whether setting helps motivate the plot.** The external pressure of the setting is often the key factor that compels or invites the protagonist into action. Setting can play as large a role as plot and characters do by prompting a protagonist into an action he or she might not otherwise take.
- **Consider whether the external setting suggests the character's inner reality.** A particular setting can create a mood or provide clues to a protagonist's nature. To write about a story's setting, therefore, invites you to study not only the time and place but also their relation to the protagonist. Does the external reality provide a clue to the protagonist's inner reality?
- **Notice whether the setting changes as the plot progresses.** The settings in a story are not static. Characters can move from place to place, and their actions may bring them into significantly different external and internal places.

CHECKLIST: Writing About Setting

- ☐ Where does the story take place?
- ☐ What does the setting suggest about the characters' lives?
- ☐ Are there significant differences in the settings for different characters? What does this suggest about each person?
- ☐ When does the story take place? Is the time of year or time of day significant?
- ☐ Does the weather play a meaningful role in the story's action?
- ☐ What is the protagonist's relationship to the setting?
- ☐ Does the setting of the story in some way compel the protagonist into action?
- ☐ Does the story's time or place suggest something about the character of the protagonist?
- ☐ Does a change in setting during the story suggest some internal change in the protagonist?

TOPICS FOR WRITING ON SETTING

1. Choose a story from this chapter, and explore how character and setting are interrelated. How does the setting of the climax of the story contribute to a change in the character's personal perspective?

2. Write about how setting functions as a kind of character in "To Build a Fire." Do the landscape and weather act as the antagonist in the story's plot?

3. How is the plot of Jorge Luis Borges's "The Gospel According to Mark" dependent on the story's setting? Illustrate and analyze how the setting motivates and influences the story's main characters.

4. Take any story in this chapter and analyze how the author presents the key setting. Don't pay special attention to the protagonist or other human characters, but focus on the setting that surrounds him or her and how it emerges as a force in the story.

5. Think of a place to which you often return. If possible, go there. Make a list of every physical detail you can think of to describe that place. Then look the list over and write a paragraph on what sort of mood is suggested by it. If you were to describe your emotional connection to the place, which three details would you choose? Why?

6. Choose any story in this book, and pay careful attention to setting as you read it. Write several paragraphs reflecting on the following questions: What details in the story suggest the time and place in which it is set? Is setting central to the story? If the action were transplanted to some other place and time, how would the story change?

▶ TERMS FOR *review*

Setting ▶ The time and place of a story. The setting may also include the climate and even the social, psychological, or spiritual state of the characters.

Locale ▶ The location where a story takes place.

Atmosphere ▶ The dominant mood or feeling that pervades all or part of a literary work. Atmosphere is the total effect conveyed by the author's use of language, images, and physical setting.

Historical fiction ▶ A type of fiction in which the narrative is set in an earlier time or place, sometimes including well-known figures from the past.

Regionalism ▶ The literary representation of a specific locale that consciously uses the particulars of geography, custom, history, folklore, or speech. In regional narratives, the locale plays a crucial role in the presentation and progression of the story.

Naturalism ▶ A type of fiction in which the characters are presented as products or victims of environment and heredity. Naturalism is considered an extreme form of **realism** (the attempt to reproduce faithfully the surface appearance of life, especially that of ordinary people in everyday situations).

5

TONE AND STYLE

What You Will Learn in This Chapter

- To identify the tone of a story
- To describe the elements of an author's style
- To define *irony* and identify its many forms
- To analyze the tone and style of a story

In many Victorian novels it was customary for some commentator, presumably the author, to interrupt the story from time to time, remarking on the action, offering philosophical asides, or explaining the procedures to be followed in telling the story.

> Two hours later, Dorothea was seated in an inner room or boudoir of a handsome apartment in the Via Sistina. I am sorry to add that she was sobbing bitterly. . . .
>
> —George Eliot in *Middlemarch* (1873)

Of course, the voice of this commentator was not identical with that of the "real-life" author—the one toiling over an inkpot, worrying about publication deadlines and whether the rent would be paid. At times the living author might have been far different in personality from that usually wise and cheerful intruder who kept addressing the reader of the book. Much of the time, to be sure, the author probably agreed with whatever attitudes this alter ego expressed. But, in effect, the author created the character of a commentator to speak for him or her and artfully sustained that character's voice throughout the novel.

Such intrusions, although sometimes useful to the "real" author and enjoyable to the reader, are today rare. Modern storytellers, carefully keeping out of sight, seldom comment on their plots and characters. Apparently they agree with Anton Chekhov that a writer should not judge the characters but should serve as their "impartial witness." And yet, no less definitely than Victorian novelists who introduced commentators, modern writers of effective stories no doubt have feelings toward their characters and events. The authors make us see these people in such a way that we, too, will care about them. Although many modern writers have adopted Chekhov's "impartial" methods, they are rarely impartial witnesses. They merely embed their own feelings more deeply into the story so that those reactions emerge indirectly for the reader.

TONE

Not only the author's choice of details may lead us to infer his or her attitude, but also the choice of characters, events, and situations, and choice of words. When the narrator of Joseph Conrad's *Heart of Darkness* comes upon an African outpost littered with abandoned machines and notices "a boiler wallowing in the grass," the exact word *wallowing* conveys an attitude: that there is something swinish about this scene of careless waste.

Whatever leads us to infer the author's attitude is commonly called **tone**. Like a tone of voice, the tone of a story may communicate amusement, anger, affection, sorrow, contempt. It implies the feelings of the author, so far as we can sense them. Those feelings may be similar to feelings expressed by the narrator of the story (or by any character), but sometimes they may be dissimilar, even sharply opposed. The characters in a story may regard an event as sad, but we sense that the author regards it as funny. To understand the tone of a story, then, is to understand some attitude more fundamental to the story than whatever attitudes the characters explicitly declare.

The tone of a story, like a tone of voice, may convey not simply one attitude, but a medley. Reading "A & P" (Chapter 1), we have mingled feelings about Sammy: delight in his wicked comments about other people and his skewering of hypocrisy; irritation at his smugness and condescension; admiration for his readiness to take a stand; sympathy for the pain of his disillusionment. Often the tone of a literary story will be too rich and complicated to sum up in one or two words. But to try to describe the tone of such a story may be a useful way to penetrate to its center and to grasp the whole of it.

STYLE

One of the clearest indications of the tone of a story is the **style** in which it is written. In general, style refers to the individual traits or characteristics of a piece of writing: to a writer's particular ways of managing words that we come to recognize as habitual or customary. It includes all the ways in which a writer uses words, imagery, tone, syntax, and figurative language. A distinctive style marks the work of a fine writer: we can tell his or her work from that of anyone else. From one story to another, however, the writer may fittingly change style; and in some stories, style may be altered meaningfully as the story goes along. In his novel *As I Lay Dying*, William Faulkner changes narrators with every chapter, and he distinguishes the narrators from one another by giving each an individual style or manner of speaking. Though each narrator has his or her own style, the book as a whole demonstrates Faulkner's style as well. For instance, one chapter is written from the point of view of a small boy, Vardaman Bundren, member of a family of poor Mississippi tenant farmers, whose view of a horse in a barn reads like this:

> It is as though the dark were resolving him out of his integrity, into an unrelated scattering of components—snuffings and stampings; smells

of cooling flesh and ammoniac hair; an illusion of a co-ordinated whole of splotched hide and strong bones within which, detached and secret and familiar, an *is* different from my *is*.

How can a small boy unaccustomed to libraries use words like *integrity*, *components*, *illusion*, and *co-ordinated?* Elsewhere in the story, Vardaman says aloud, with no trace of literacy, "Hit was a-laying right there on the ground." Apparently, in the passage it is not the voice of the boy that we are hearing, but something resembling the voice of William Faulkner, elevated and passionate, expressing the boy's thoughts in a style that admits Faulknerian words.

DICTION

Usually, *style* indicates a mode of expression: the language a writer uses. In this sense, the notion of style includes such traits as the length and complexity of sentences, and **diction**, or choice of words: abstract or concrete, bookish ("unrelated scattering of components") or close to speech ("Hit was a-laying right there on the ground"). Involved in the idea of style, too, is any habitual use of imagery, patterns of sound, figures of speech, or other devices.

Several writers of realistic fiction known as **minimalists**—Ann Beattie, Raymond Carver, Bobbie Ann Mason—have written with a flat, laid-back, unemotional tone, in an appropriately bare, unadorned style. Minimalists seem to give nothing but facts drawn from ordinary life, sometimes in picayune detail. Here is a sample passage from Raymond Carver's story "A Small, Good Thing":

> She pulled into the driveway and cut the engine. She closed her eyes and leaned her head against the wheel for a minute. She listened to the ticking sounds the engine made as it began to cool. Then she got out of the car. She could hear the dog barking inside the house. She went to the front door, which was unlocked. She went inside and turned on lights and put on a kettle of water for tea. She opened some dog food and fed Slug on the back porch. The dog ate in hungry little smacks. It kept running into the kitchen to see that she was going to stay.

Explicit feeling and showy language are kept at a minimum here. Notice how Carver's diction relies on everyday words—mostly words of only one or two syllables. Taken out of context, this description may strike you as banal, as if the writer himself were bored; but it works effectively as a part of Carver's entire story. As in all good writing, the style here seems a faithful mirror of what is said in it. At its best, such writing achieves "a hard-won reduction, a painful stripping away of richness, a baring of bone."[1]

[1] Letter in the *New York Times Book Review*, 5 June 1988.

Two Examples of Style: Hemingway Versus Faulkner

To see what style means, compare the stories in this chapter by William Faulkner ("Barn Burning") and by Ernest Hemingway ("A Clean, Well-Lighted Place"). Faulkner frequently falls into a style in which a statement, as soon as it is uttered, is followed by another statement expressing the idea in a more emphatic way. Sentences are interrupted with parenthetical elements (asides, like this) thrust into them unexpectedly. At times, Faulkner writes of seemingly ordinary matters as if giving a speech in a towering passion. Here, from "Barn Burning," is a description of how a boy's father delivers a rug:

> "Don't you want me to help?" he whispered. His father did not answer and now he heard again that stiff foot striking the hollow portico with that wooden and clocklike deliberation, that outrageous overstatement of the weight it carried. The rug, hunched, not flung (the boy could tell that even in the darkness) from his father's shoulder struck the angle of wall and floor with a sound unbelievably loud, thunderous, then the foot again, unhurried and enormous; a light came on in the house and the boy sat, tense, breathing steadily and quietly and just a little fast, though the foot itself did not increase its beat at all, descending the steps now; now the boy could see him.

Faulkner is not merely indulging in language for its own sake. As you will find when you read the whole story, this rug delivery is vital to the story, and so too is the father's profound defiance—indicated by his walk. By devices of style— by *metaphor* and *simile* ("wooden and clocklike"), by exact qualification ("not flung"), by emphatic adjectives ("loud, thunderous")—Faulkner is carefully placing his emphases.

By the words he selects to describe the father's stride, Faulkner directs how we feel toward the man and perhaps also indicates his own wondering but skeptical attitude toward a character whose very footfall is "outrageous" and "enormous." (Fond of long sentences like the last one in the quoted passage, Faulkner remarked that there are sentences that need to be written in the way a circus acrobat pedals a bicycle on a high wire: rapidly, so as not to fall off.)

Hemingway's famous style includes both short sentences and long. His long compound sentences tend to be relatively simple in construction (clause plus clause plus clause), sometimes joined with the use of *and*. He interrupts such a sentence with a dependent clause or a parenthetical element much less frequently than Faulkner does. The effect is like listening to speech:

> In the day time the street was dusty, but at night the dew settled the dust and the old man liked to sit late because he was deaf and now at night it was quiet and he felt the difference.

Hemingway is a master of swift, terse dialogue and often casts whole scenes in the form of conversation. As if he were a closemouthed speaker unwilling to let his feelings loose, the narrator of a Hemingway story often addresses us in understatement, implying greater depths of feeling than he puts into words. Read the following story and you will see that its style and tone cannot be separated.

Ernest Hemingway

A Clean, Well-Lighted Place   1933

Ernest Hemingway (1899–1961), born in Oak Park, Illinois, bypassed college to be a cub reporter. In World War I, as an eighteen-year-old volunteer ambulance driver in Italy, he was wounded in action. In 1922 he settled in Paris, then aswarm with writers; he later recalled that time in A Moveable Feast *(1964). Hemingway won swift acclaim for his early stories,* In Our Time *(1925), and for his first, perhaps finest, novel,* The Sun Also Rises *(1926), portraying a "lost generation" of postwar American drifters in France and Spain. For Whom*

Ernest Hemingway

the Bell Tolls (1940) depicts life during the Spanish Civil War. Hemingway became a celebrity, often photographed as a marlin fisherman or a lion hunter. A fan of bullfighting, he wrote two nonfiction books on the subject: Death in the Afternoon *(1932) and* The Dangerous Summer *(posthumously published in 1985). After World War II, with his fourth wife, journalist Mary Welsh, he made his home in Cuba, where he wrote* The Old Man and the Sea *(1952). The Nobel Prize in Literature came his way in 1954. In 1961, mentally distressed and physically ailing, he shot himself. Hemingway brought a hard-bitten realism to American fiction. His heroes live dangerously, by personal codes of honor, courage, and endurance. Hemingway's distinctively crisp, unadorned style left American literature permanently changed.*

It was late and every one had left the café except an old man who sat in the shadow the leaves of the tree made against the electric light. In the day time the street was dusty, but at night the dew settled the dust and the old man liked to sit late because he was deaf and now at night it was quiet and he felt the difference. The two waiters inside the café knew that the old man was a little drunk, and while he was a good client they knew that if he became too drunk he would leave without paying, so they kept watch on him.

"Last week he tried to commit suicide," one waiter said.

"Why?"

"He was in despair."

"What about?"   5

"Nothing."

"How do you know it was nothing?"

"He has plenty of money."

They sat together at a table that was close against the wall near the door of the café and looked at the terrace where the tables were all empty except where the old man sat in the shadow of the leaves of the tree that moved slightly in the wind. A girl and a soldier went by in the street. The street light shone on the brass number on his collar. The girl wore no head covering and hurried beside him.

"The guard will pick him up," one waiter said.   10

"What does it matter if he gets what he's after?"

"He had better get off the street now. The guard will get him. They went by five minutes ago."

The old man sitting in the shadow rapped on his saucer with his glass. The younger waiter went over to him.

"What do you want?"

The old man looked at him. "Another brandy," he said.   15

"You'll be drunk," the waiter said. The old man looked at him. The waiter went away.

"He'll stay all night," he said to his colleague. "I'm sleepy now. I never get into bed before three o'clock. He should have killed himself last week."

The waiter took the brandy bottle and another saucer from the counter inside the café and marched out to the old man's table. He put down the saucer and poured the glass full of brandy.

"You should have killed yourself last week," he said to the deaf man. The old man motioned with his finger. "A little more," he said. The waiter poured on into the glass so that the brandy slopped over and ran down the stem into the top saucer of the pile. "Thank you," the old man said. The waiter took the bottle back inside the café. He sat down at the table with his colleague again.

"He's drunk now," he said.   20

"He's drunk every night."°

"What did he want to kill himself for?"

"How should I know?"

"How did he do it?"

"He hung himself with a rope."   25

"He's drunk now," he said. "He's drunk every night": The younger waiter perhaps says both these lines. A device of Hemingway's style is sometimes to have a character pause, then speak again—as often happens in actual speech.

"Who cut him down?"

"His niece."

"Why did they do it?"

"Fear for his soul."

"How much money has he got?"   30

"He's got plenty."

"He must be eighty years old."

"Anyway I should say he was eighty."°

"I wish he would go home. I never get to bed before three o'clock.
What kind of hour is that to go to bed?"

"He stays up because he likes it."   35

"He's lonely. I'm not lonely. I have a wife waiting in bed for me."

"He had a wife once too."

"A wife would be no good to him now."

"You can't tell. He might be better with a wife."

"His niece looks after him."   40

"I know. You said she cut him down."

"I wouldn't want to be that old. An old man is a nasty thing."

"Not always. This old man is clean. He drinks without spilling. Even
now, drunk. Look at him."

"I don't want to look at him. I wish he would go home. He has no
regard for those who must work."

The old man looked from his glass across the square, then over at the   45
waiters.

"Another brandy," he said, pointing to his glass. The waiter who was
in a hurry came over.

"Finished," he said, speaking with that omission of syntax stupid
people employ when talking to drunken people or foreigners. "No more
tonight. Close now."

"Another," said the old man.

"No. Finished." The waiter wiped the edge of the table with a towel
and shook his head.

The old man stood up, slowly counted the saucers, took a leather   50
coin purse from his pocket and paid for the drinks, leaving half a peseta
tip.

The waiter watched him go down the street, a very old man walking
unsteadily but with dignity.

"Why didn't you let him stay and drink?" the unhurried waiter asked.
They were putting up the shutters. "It is not half-past two."

"I want to go home to bed."

"What is an hour?"

"More to me than to him."   55

"He must be eighty years old." "Anyway I should say he was eighty": Is this another instance of
the same character's speaking twice? Clearly, it is the younger waiter who says the next line,
"I wish he would go home."

"An hour is the same."

"You talk like an old man yourself. He can buy a bottle and drink at home."

"It's not the same."

"No, it is not," agreed the waiter with a wife. He did not wish to be unjust. He was only in a hurry.

"And you? You have no fear of going home before the usual hour?"   60

"Are you trying to insult me?"

"No, hombre, only to make a joke."

"No," the waiter who was in a hurry said, rising from pulling down the metal shutters. "I have confidence. I am all confidence."

"You have youth, confidence, and a job," the older waiter said. "You have everything."

"And what do you lack?"   65

"Everything but work."

"You have everything I have."

"No. I have never had confidence and I am not young."

"Come on. Stop talking nonsense and lock up."

"I am of those who like to stay late at the café," the older waiter said.   70
"With all those who do not want to go to bed. With all those who need a light for the night."

"I want to go home and into bed."

"We are of two different kinds," the older waiter said. He was not dressed to go home. "It is not only a question of youth and confidence although those things are very beautiful. Each night I am reluctant to close up because there may be some one who needs the café."

"Hombre, there are bodegas° open all night long."

"You do not understand. This is a clean and pleasant café. It is well lighted. The light is very good and also, now, there are shadows of the leaves."

"Good night," said the younger waiter.   75

"Good night," the other said. Turning off the electric light he continued the conversation with himself. It is the light of course but it is necessary that the place be clean and pleasant. You do not want music. Certainly you do not want music. Nor can you stand before a bar with dignity although that is all that is provided for these hours. What did he fear? It was not fear or dread. It was a nothing that he knew too well. It was all a nothing and a man was nothing too. It was only that and light was all it needed and a certain cleanness and order. Some lived in it and never felt it but he knew it all was nada y pues nada y nada y pues nada.°
Our nada who art in nada, nada be thy name thy kingdom nada thy will be nada in nada as it is in nada. Give us this nada our daily nada and nada

---

bodegas: wineshops.   *nada y pues . . . nada:* nothing and then nothing and nothing and then nothing.

us our nada as we nada our nadas and nada us not into nada but deliver us from nada; pues nada. Hail nothing full of nothing, nothing is with thee. He smiled and stood before a bar with a shining steam pressure coffee machine.

"What's yours?" asked the barman.

"Nada."

"Otro loco más,"° said the barman and turned away.

"A little cup," said the waiter. 80

The barman poured it for him.

"The light is very bright and pleasant but the bar is unpolished," the waiter said.

The barman looked at him but did not answer. It was too late at night for conversation.

"You want another copita?"° the barman asked.

"No, thank you," said the waiter and went out. He disliked bars and 85 bodegas. A clean, well-lighted café was a very different thing. Now, without thinking further, he would go home to his room. He would lie in the bed and finally, with daylight, he would go to sleep. After all, he said to himself, it is probably only insomnia. Many must have it.

Questions

1. What besides insomnia makes the older waiter reluctant to go to bed? Comment especially on his meditation with its *nada* refrain. Why does he understand so well the old man's need for a café? What does the café represent for the two of them?

2. Compare the younger waiter and the older waiter in their attitudes toward the old man. Whose attitude do you take to be closer to that of the author? Even though Hemingway does not editorially state his own feelings, how does he make them clear to us?

3. Point to sentences that establish the style of the story. What is distinctive in them? What repetitions of words or phrases seem particularly effective? Does Hemingway seem to favor a simple or an erudite vocabulary?

4. What is the story's point of view? Discuss its appropriateness.

William Faulkner

Barn Burning 1939

William Faulkner (1897–1962) receives a capsule biography in Chapter 2, page 32, along with his story "A Rose for Emily." "Barn Burning" is among his many contributions to the history of Yoknapatawpha, an imaginary Mississippi county in which the Sartorises and the de Spains are landed aristocrats living by a code of honor and the Snopeses—most of them—are shiftless ne'er-do-wells.

Otro loco más: another lunatic.   *copita:* little cup.

The store in which the Justice of the Peace's court was sitting smelled of cheese. The boy, crouched on his nail keg at the back of the crowded room, knew he smelled cheese, and more: from where he sat he could see the ranked shelves close-packed with the solid, squat, dynamic shapes of tin cans whose labels his stomach read, not from the lettering which meant nothing to his mind but from the scarlet devils and the silver curve of fish—this, the cheese which he knew he smelled and the hermetic meat which his intestines believed he smelled coming in inter-mittent gusts momentary and brief between the other constant one, the smell and sense just a little of fear because mostly of despair and grief, the old fierce pull of blood. He could not see the table where the Justice sat and before which his father and his father's enemy (*our enemy* he thought in that despair: *ourn! mine and hisn both! He's my father!*) stood, but he could hear them, the two of them that is, because his father had said no word yet:

"But what proof have you, Mr. Harris?"

"I told you. The hog got into my corn. I caught it up and sent it back to him. He had no fence that would hold it. I told him so, warned him. The next time I put the hog in my pen. When he came to get it I gave him enough wire to patch up his pen. The next time I put the hog up and kept it. I rode down to his house and saw the wire I gave him still rolled on to the spool in his yard. I told him he could have the hog when he paid me a dollar pound fee. That evening a nigger came with the dollar and got the hog. He was a strange nigger. He said, 'He say to tell you wood and hay kin burn.' I said, 'What?' 'That whut he say to tell you,' the nigger said. 'Wood and hay kin burn.' That night my barn burned. I got the stock out but I lost the barn."

"Where's the nigger? Have you got him?"

"He was a strange nigger, I tell you. I don't know what became of him."   5

"But that's not proof. Don't you see that's not proof?"

"Get that boy up here. He knows." For a moment the boy thought too that the man meant his older brother until Harris said, "Not him. The little one. The boy," and, crouching, small for his age, small and wiry like his father, in patched and faded jeans even too small for him, with straight, uncombed, brown hair and eyes gray and wild as storm scud, he saw the men between himself and the table part and become a lane of grim faces, at the end of which he saw the Justice, a shabby, collarless, graying man in spectacles, beckoning him. He felt no floor under his bare feet; he seemed to walk beneath the palpable weight of the grim turning faces. His father, still in his black Sunday coat donned not for the trial but for the moving, did not even look at him. *He aims for me to lie*, he thought, again with that frantic grief and despair. *And I will have to do hit.*

"What's your name, boy?" the Justice said.

"Colonel Sartoris Snopes," the boy whispered.

"Hey?" the Justice said. "Talk louder. Colonel Sartoris? I reckon any-   10
body named for Colonel Sartoris in this country can't help but tell the
truth, can they?" The boy said nothing. *Enemy! Enemy!* he thought; for
a moment he could not even see, could not see that the Justice's face was
kindly nor discern that his voice was troubled when he spoke to the man
named Harris: "Do you want me to question this boy?" But he could hear,
and during those subsequent long seconds while there was absolutely no
sound in the crowded little room save that of quiet and intent breathing
it was as if he had swung outward at the end of a grape vine, over a ravine,
and at the top of the swing had been caught in a prolonged instant of
mesmerized gravity, weightless in time.

"No!" Harris said violently, explosively. "Damnation! Send him out
of here!" Now time, the fluid world, rushed beneath him again, the voices
coming to him again through the smell of cheese and sealed meat, the fear
and despair and the old grief of blood:

"This case is closed. I can't find against you, Snopes, but I can give
you advice. Leave this country and don't come back to it."

His father spoke for the first time, his voice cold and harsh, level,
without emphasis: "I aim to. I don't figure to stay in a country among people who . . ." he said something unprintable and vile, addressed to no one.

"That'll do," the Justice said. "Take your wagon and get out of this
country before dark. Case dismissed."

His father turned, and he followed the stiff black coat, the wiry   15
figure walking a little stiffly from where a Confederate provost's man's
musket ball had taken him in the heel on a stolen horse thirty years ago,
followed the two backs now, since his older brother had appeared from
somewhere in the crowd, no taller than the father but thicker, chewing
tobacco steadily, between the two lines of grim-faced men and out of the
store and across the worn gallery and down the sagging steps and among
the dogs and half-grown boys in the mild May dust, where as he passed
a voice hissed:

"Barn burner!"

Again he could not see, whirling; there was a face in a red haze, moon-
like, bigger than the full moon, the owner of it half again his size, he
leaping in the red haze toward the face, feeling no blow, feeling no shock
when his head struck the earth, scrabbling up and leaping again, feeling no blow this time either and tasting no blood, scrabbling up to see
the other boy in full flight and himself already leaping into pursuit as his
father's hand jerked him back, the harsh, cold voice speaking above him:
"Go get in the wagon."

It stood in a grove of locusts and mulberries across the road. His
two hulking sisters in their Sunday dresses and his mother and her sister
in calico and sunbonnets were already in it, sitting on and among the
sorry residue of the dozen and more movings which even the boy could
remember—the battered stove, the broken beds and chairs, the clock

inlaid with mother-of-pearl, which would not run, stopped at some fourteen minutes past two o'clock of a dead and forgotten day and time, which had been his mother's dowry. She was crying, though when she saw him she drew her sleeve across her face and began to descend from the wagon. "Get back," the father said.

"He's hurt. I got to get some water and wash his . . ."

"Get back in the wagon," his father said. He got in too, over the tail- 20 gate. His father mounted to the seat where the older brother already sat and struck the gaunt mules two savage blows with the peeled willow, but without heat. It was not even sadistic; it was exactly that same quality which in later years would cause his descendants to over-run the engine before putting a motor car into motion, striking and reining back in the same movement. The wagon went on, the store with its quiet crowd of grimly watching men dropped behind; a curve in the road hid it. *Forever* he thought. *Maybe he's done satisfied now, now that he has* . . . stopping himself, not to say it aloud even to himself. His mother's hand touched his shoulder.

"Does hit hurt?" she said.

"Naw," he said. "Hit don't hurt. Lemme be."

"Can't you wipe some of the blood off before hit dries?"

"I'll wash to-night," he said. "Lemme be, I tell you."

The wagon went on. He did not know where they were going. None 25 of them ever did or ever asked, because it was always somewhere, always a house of sorts waiting for them a day or two days or even three days away. Likely his father had already arranged to make a crop on another farm before he . . . Again he had to stop himself. He (the father) always did. There was something about his wolflike independence and even courage when the advantage was at least neutral which impressed strangers, as if they got from his latent ravening ferocity not so much a sense of dependability as a feeling that his ferocious conviction in the rightness of his own actions would be of advantage to all whose interest lay with his.

That night they camped, in a grove of oaks and beeches where a spring ran. The nights were still cool and they had a fire against it, of a rail lifted from a nearby fence and cut into lengths—a small fire, neat, niggard almost, a shrewd fire; such fires were his father's habit and custom always, even in freezing weather. Older, the boy might have remarked this and wondered why not a big one; why should not a man who had not only seen the waste and extravagance of war, but who had in his blood an inherent voracious prodigality with material not his own, have burned everything in sight? Then he might have gone a step farther and thought that that was the reason: that niggard blaze was the living fruit of nights passed during those four years in the woods hiding from all men, blue and gray, with his strings of horses (captured horses, he called them). And older still, he might have divined the true reason: that the element of fire spoke to some deep mainspring of his father's being, as the element of steel or of powder spoke to other men, as the one weapon for the preservation of integrity, else breath were not worth the breathing, and hence to be regarded with respect and used with discretion.

But he did not think this now and he had seen those same niggard blazes all his life. He merely ate his supper beside it and was already half asleep over his iron plate when his father called him, and once more he followed the stiff back, the stiff and ruthless limp, up the slope and on to the starlit road where, turning, he could see his father against the stars but without face or depth—a shape black, flat, and bloodless as though cut from tin in the iron folds of the frockcoat which had not been made for him, the voice harsh like tin and without heat like tin:

"You were fixing to tell them. You would have told him." He didn't answer. His father struck him with the flat of his hand on the side of the head, hard but without heat, exactly as he had struck the two mules at the store, exactly as he would strike either of them with any stick in order to kill a horse fly, his voice without heat or anger: "You're getting to be a man. You got to learn. You got to learn to stick to your own blood or you ain't going to have any blood to stick to you. Do you think either of them, any man there this morning, would? Don't you know all they wanted was a chance to get at me because they knew I had them beat? Eh?" Later, twenty years later, he was to tell himself, "If I had said they wanted only truth, justice, he would have hit me again." But now he said nothing. He was not crying. He just stood there. "Answer me," his father said.

"Yes," he whispered. His father turned.

"Get on to bed. We'll be there tomorrow."   30

Tomorrow they were there. In the early afternoon the wagon stopped before a paintless two-room house identical almost with the dozen others it had stopped before even in the boy's ten years, and again, as on the other dozen occasions, his mother and aunt got down and began to unload the wagon, although his two sisters and his father and brother had not moved.

"Likely hit ain't fitten for hawgs," one of the sisters said.

"Nevertheless, fit it will and you'll hog it and like it," his father said. "Get out of them chairs and help your Ma unload."

The two sisters got down, big, bovine, in a flutter of cheap ribbons; one of them drew from the jumbled wagon bed a battered lantern, the other a worn broom. His father handed the reins to the older son and began to climb stiffly over the wheel. "When they get unloaded, take the team to the barn and feed them." Then he said, and at first the boy thought he was still speaking to his brother: "Come with me."

"Me?" he said.   35

"Yes," his father said. "You."

"Abner," his mother said. His father paused and looked back—the harsh level stare beneath the shaggy, graying, irascible brows.

"I reckon I'll have a word with the man that aims to begin to-morrow owning me body and soul for the next eight months."

They went back up the road. A week ago—or before last night, that is—he would have asked where they were going, but not now. His father had struck him before last night but never before had he paused afterward to explain why; it was as if the blow and the following calm, outrageous voice still rang, repercussed, divulging nothing to him save the terrible handicap of being young, the light weight of his few years, just heavy enough to prevent his soaring free of the world as it seemed to be ordered but not heavy enough to keep him footed solid in it, to resist it and try to change the course of its events.

Presently he could see the grove of oaks and cedars and the other flowering trees and shrubs where the house would be, though not the house yet. They walked beside a fence massed with honeysuckle and Cherokee roses and came to a gate swinging open between two brick pillars, and now, beyond a sweep of drive, he saw the house for the first time and at that instant he forgot his father and the terror and despair both, and even when he remembered his father again (who had not stopped) the terror and despair did not return. Because, for all the twelve movings, they had sojourned until now in a poor country, a land of small farms and fields and houses, and he had never seen a house like this before. *Hit's big as a courthouse* he thought quietly, with a surge of peace and joy whose reason he could not have thought into words, being too young for that: *They are safe from him. People whose lives are a part of this peace and dignity are beyond his touch, he no more to them than a buzzing wasp: capable of stinging for a little moment but that's all; the spell of this peace and dignity rendering even the barns and stable and cribs which belong to it impervious to the puny flames he might contrive . . .* this, the peace and joy, ebbing for an instant as he looked again at the stiff black back, the stiff and implacable limp of the figure which was not dwarfed by the house, for the reason that it had never looked big anywhere and which now, against the serene columned backdrop, had more than ever that impervious quality of something cut ruthlessly from tin, depthless, as though, sidewise to the sun, it would cast no shadow. Watching him, the boy remarked the absolutely undeviating course which his father held and saw the stiff foot come squarely down in a pile of fresh droppings where a horse had stood in the drive and which his father could have avoided by a simple change of stride. But it ebbed only a moment, though he could not have thought this into words either, walking on in the spell of the house, which he could even want but without envy, without sorrow, certainly never with that ravening and jealous rage which unknown to him walked in the ironlike black coat before him: *Maybe he will feel it too. Maybe it will even change him now from what maybe he couldn't help but be.*

They crossed the portico. Now he could hear his father's stiff foot as it came down on the boards with clocklike finality, a sound out of all proportion to the displacement of the body it bore and which was not dwarfed either by the white door before it, as though it had attained to a sort of vicious and ravening minimum not to be dwarfed by anything—the

40

flat, wide, black hat, the formal coat of broadcloth which had once been black but which had now that friction-glazed greenish cast of the bodies of old house flies, the lifted sleeve which was too large, the lifted hand like a curled claw. The door opened so promptly that the boy knew the Negro must have been watching them all the time, an old man with neat grizzled hair, in a linen jacket, who stood barring the door with his body, saying, "Wipe yo foots, white man, fo you come in here. Major ain't home nohow."

"Get out of my way, nigger," his father said, without heat too, flinging the door back and the Negro also and entering, his hat still on his head. And now the boy saw the prints of the stiff foot on the doorjamb and saw them appear on the pale rug behind the machinelike deliberation of the foot which seemed to bear (or transmit) twice the weight which the body compassed. The Negro was shouting "Miss Lula! Miss Lula!" somewhere behind them, then the boy, deluged as though by a warm wave by a suave turn of the carpeted stair and a pendant glitter of chandeliers and a mute gleam of gold frames, heard the swift feet and saw her too, a lady—perhaps he had never seen her like before either—in a gray, smooth gown with lace at the throat and an apron tied at the waist and the sleeves turned back, wiping cake or biscuit dough from her hands with a towel as she came up the hall, looking not at his father at all but at the tracks on the blond rug with an expression of incredulous amazement.

"I tried," the Negro cried. "I tole him to . . ."

"Will you please go away?" she said in a shaking voice. "Major de Spain is not at home. Will you please go away?"

His father had not spoken again. He did not speak again. He did not   45
even look at her. He just stood stiff in the center of the rug, in his hat, the shaggy iron-gray brows twitching slightly above the pebble-colored eyes as he appeared to examine the house with brief deliberation. Then with the same deliberation he turned; the boy watched him pivot on the good leg and saw the stiff foot drag around the arc of the turning, leaving a final long and fading smear. His father never looked at it, he never once looked down at the rug. The Negro held the door. It closed behind them, upon the hysteric and indistinguishable woman-wail. His father stopped at the top of the steps and scraped his boot clean on the edge of it. At the gate he stopped again. He stood for a moment, planted stiffly on the stiff foot, looking back at the house. "Pretty and white, ain't it?" he said. "That's sweat. Nigger sweat. Maybe it ain't white enough yet to suit him. Maybe he wants to mix some white sweat with it."

Two hours later the boy was chopping wood behind the house within which his mother and aunt and the two sisters (the mother and aunt, not the two girls, he knew that; even at this distance and muffled by walls the flat loud voices of the two girls emanated an incorrigible idle inertia) were setting up the stove to prepare a meal, when he heard the hooves and saw the linen-clad man on a fine sorrel mare, whom he recognized even before he saw the rolled rug in front of the Negro youth following on a fat bay carriage horse—a suffused, angry face vanishing, still at full gallop, beyond the corner of the house where his father and brother were sitting in the two tilted chairs; and a moment later, almost before he could have put the axe down, he heard the hooves again and watched the sorrel mare go back out of the yard, already galloping again. Then his father began to shout one of the sisters' names, who presently emerged backward from the kitchen door dragging the rolled rug along the ground by one end while the other sister walked behind it.

"If you ain't going to tote, go on and set up the wash pot," the first said.

"You, Sarty!" the second shouted. "Set up the wash pot!" His father appeared at the door, framed against that shabbiness, as he had been against that other bland perfection, impervious to either, the mother's anxious face at his shoulder.

"Go on," the father said. "Pick it up." The two sisters stooped, broad, lethargic; stooping, they presented an incredible expanse of pale cloth and a flutter of tawdry ribbons.

"If I thought enough of a rug to have to git hit all the way from France 50 I wouldn't keep hit where folks coming in would have to tromp on hit," the first said. They raised the rug.

"Abner," the mother said. "Let me do it."

"You go back and git dinner," his father said. "I'll tend to this."

From the woodpile through the rest of the afternoon the boy watched them, the rug spread flat in the dust beside the bubbling wash pot, the two sisters stooping over it with that profound and lethargic reluctance, while the father stood over them in turn, implacable and grim, driving them though never raising his voice again. He could smell the harsh homemade lye they were using; he saw his mother come to the door once and look toward them with an expression not anxious now but very like despair; he saw his father turn, and he fell to with the axe and saw from the corner of his eye his father raise from the ground a flattish fragment of field stone and examine it and return to the pot, and this time his mother actually spoke: "Abner. Abner. Please don't. Please, Abner."

Then he was done too. It was dusk; the whippoorwills had already begun. He could smell coffee from the room where they would presently eat the cold food remaining from the mid-afternoon meal, though when he entered the house he realized they were having coffee again probably because there was a fire on the hearth, before which the rug now lay spread over the backs of the two chairs. The tracks of his father's foot were gone. Where they had been were now long, water-cloudy scoriations resembling the sporadic course of a lilliputian mowing machine.

It still hung there while they ate the cold food and then went to bed, 55 scattered without order or claim up and down the two rooms, his mother in one bed, where his father would later lie, the older brother in the other, himself, the aunt, and the two sisters on pallets on the floor. But his father was not in bed yet. The last thing the boy remembered was the depthless, harsh silhouette of the hat and coat bending over the rug and it seemed to him that he had not even closed his eyes when the silhouette was standing over him, the fire almost dead behind it, the stiff foot prodding him awake. "Catch up the mule," his father said.

When he returned with the mule his father was standing in the back door, the rolled rug over his shoulder. "Ain't you going to ride?" he said.

"No. Give me your foot."

He bent his knee into his father's hand, the wiry, surprising power flowed smoothly, rising, he rising with it, on to the mule's bare back (they had owned a saddle once; the boy could remember it though not when or where) and with the same effortlessness his father swung the rug up in front of him. Now in the starlight they retraced the afternoon's path, up the dusty road rife with honeysuckle, through the gate and up the black tunnel of the drive to the lightless house, where he sat on the mule and felt the rough warp of the rug drag across his thighs and vanish.

"Don't you want me to help?" he whispered. His father did not answer and now he heard again that stiff foot striking the hollow portico with that wooden and clocklike deliberation, that outrageous overstatement of the weight it carried. The rug, hunched, not flung (the boy could tell that even in the darkness) from his father's shoulder struck the angle of wall and floor with a sound unbelievably loud, thunderous, then the foot again, unhurried and enormous; a light came on in the house and the boy sat, tense, breathing steadily and quietly and just a little fast, though the foot itself did not increase its beat at all, descending the steps now; now the boy could see him.

"Don't you want to ride now?" he whispered. "We kin both ride now," the light within the house altering now, flaring up and sinking. *He's coming down the stairs now*, he thought. He had already ridden the mule up beside the horse block; presently his father was up behind him and he doubled the reins over and slashed the mule across the neck, but before the animal could begin to trot the hard, thin arm came around him, the hard, knotted hand jerking the mule back to a walk. 60

In the first red rays of the sun they were in the lot, putting plow gear on the mules. This time the sorrel mare was in the lot before he heard it at all, the rider collarless and even bareheaded, trembling, speaking in a shaking voice as the woman in the house had done, his father merely looking up once before stooping again to the hame° he was buckling, so that the man on the mare spoke to his stooping back:

"You must realize you have ruined that rug. Wasn't there anybody here, any of your women . . . ." he ceased, shaking, the boy watching him,

---

hame: a curved section of the harness of a draft animal.

the older brother leaning now in the stable door, chewing, blinking slowly and steadily at nothing apparently. "It cost a hundred dollars. But you never had a hundred dollars. You never will. So I'm going to charge you twenty bushels of corn against your crop. I'll add it in your contract and when you come to the commissary you can sign it. That won't keep Mrs. de Spain quiet but maybe it will teach you to wipe your feet off before you enter her house again."

Then he was gone. The boy looked at his father, who still had not spoken or even looked up again, who was now adjusting the logger-head in the hame.

"Pap," he said. His father looked at him—the inscrutable face, the shaggy brows beneath where the gray eyes glinted coldly. Suddenly the boy went toward him, fast, stopping as suddenly. "You done the best you could!" he cried. "If he wanted hit done different why didn't he wait and tell you how? He won't git no twenty bushels! He won't git none! We'll gather hit and hide hit! I kin watch . . ."

"Did you put the cutter back in that straight stock like I told you?"   65

"No, sir," he said.

"Then go do it."

That was Wednesday. During the rest of that week he worked steadily, at what was within his scope and some which was beyond it, with an industry that did not need to be driven nor even commanded twice; he had this from his mother, with the difference that some at least of what he did he liked to do, such as splitting wood with the half-size axe which his mother and aunt had earned, or saved money somehow, to present him with at Christmas. In company with the two older women (and on one afternoon, even one of the sisters), he built pens for the shoat and the cow which were a part of his father's contract with the landlord, and one afternoon, his father being absent, gone somewhere on one of the mules, he went to the field.

They were running a middle buster now, his brother holding the plow straight while he handled the reins, and walking beside the straining mule, the rich black soil shearing cool and damp against his bare ankles, he thought *Maybe this is the end of it. Maybe even that twenty bushels that seems hard to have to pay for just a rug will be a cheap price for him to stop forever and always from being what he used to be*; thinking, dreaming now, so that his brother had to speak sharply to him to mind the mule: *Maybe he even won't collect the twenty bushels. Maybe it will all add up and balance and vanish—corn, rug, fire; the terror and grief; the being pulled two ways like between two teams of horses—gone, done with for ever and ever.*

Then it was Saturday; he looked up from beneath the mule he was   70 harnessing and saw his father in the black coat and hat. "Not that," his father said. "The wagon gear." And then, two hours later, sitting in the wagon bed behind his father and brother on the seat, the wagon accomplished a final curve, and he saw the weathered paintless store with its tattered tobacco- and patent-medicine posters and the tethered wagons and saddle animals below the gallery. He mounted the gnawed steps behind his father and brother, and there again was the lane of quiet, watching faces for the three of them to walk through. He saw the man in spectacles sitting at the plank table and he did not need to be told this was a Justice of the Peace; he sent one glare of fierce, exultant, partisan defiance at the man in collar and cravat now, whom he had seen but twice before in his life, and that on a galloping horse, who now wore on his face an expression not of rage but of amazed unbelief which the boy could not have known was at the incredible circumstance of being sued by one of his own tenants, and came and stood against his father and cried at the Justice: "He ain't done it! He ain't burnt . . ."

"Go back to the wagon," his father said.

"Burnt?" the Justice said. "Do I understand this rug was burned too?"

"Does anybody here claim it was?" his father said. "Go back to the wagon." But he did not, he merely retreated to the rear of the room, crowded as that other had been, but not to sit down this time, instead, to stand pressing among the motionless bodies, listening to the voices:

"And you claim twenty bushels of corn is too high for the damage you did to the rug?"

"He brought the rug to me and said he wanted the tracks washed out of it. I washed the tracks out and took the rug back to him."

"But you didn't carry the rug back to him in the same condition it was in before you made the tracks on it."

His father did not answer, and now for perhaps half a minute there was no sound at all save that of breathing, the faint, steady suspiration of complete and intent listening.

"You decline to answer that, Mr. Snopes?" Again his father did not answer. "I'm going to find against you, Mr. Snopes. I'm going to find that you were responsible for the injury to Major de Spain's rug and hold you liable for it. But twenty bushels of corn seems a little high for a man in your circumstances to have to pay. Major de Spain claims it cost a hundred dollars. October corn will be worth about fifty cents. I figure that if Major de Spain can stand a ninety-five dollar loss on something he paid cash for, you can stand a five-dollar loss you haven't earned yet. I hold you in damages to Major de Spain to the amount of ten bushels of corn over and above your contract with him, to be paid to him out of your crop at gathering time. Court adjourned."

It had taken no time hardly, the morning was but half begun. He thought they would return home and perhaps back to the field, since they were late, far behind all other farmers. But instead his father passed on behind the wagon, merely indicating with his hand for the older brother to follow with it, and crossed the road toward the blacksmith shop opposite, pressing on after his father, overtaking him, speaking, whispering up at the harsh, calm face beneath the weathered hat: "He won't git no ten bushels either. He won't git one. We'll . . ." until his father glanced for an instant down at him, the face absolutely calm, the grizzled eyebrows tangled above the cold eyes, the voice almost pleasant, almost gentle: "You think so? Well, we'll wait till October anyway."

80

The matter of the wagon—the setting of a spoke or two and the tightening of the tires—did not take long either, the business of the tires accomplished by driving the wagon into the spring branch behind the shop and letting it stand there, the mules nuzzling into the water from time to time, and the boy on the seat with the idle reins, looking up the slope and through the sooty tunnel of the shed where the slow hammer rang and where his father sat on an upended cypress bolt, easily, either talking or listening, still sitting there when the boy brought the dripping wagon up out of the branch and halted it before the door.

"Take them on to the shade and hitch," his father said. He did so and returned. His father and the smith and a third man squatting on his heels inside the door were talking, about crops and animals; the boy, squatting too in the ammoniac dust and hoof-parings and scales of rust, heard his father tell a long and unhurried story out of the time before the birth of the older brother even when he had been a professional horsetrader. And then his father came up beside him where he stood before a tattered last year's circus poster on the other side of the store, gazing rapt and quiet at the scarlet horses, the incredible poisings and convulsions of tulle and tights and the painted leers of comedians, and said, "It's time to eat."

But not at home. Squatting beside his brother against the front wall, he watched his father emerge from the store and produce from a paper sack a segment of cheese and divide it carefully and deliberately into three with his pocket knife and produce crackers from the same sack. They all three squatted on the gallery and ate, slowly, without talking; then in the store again, they drank from a tin dipper tepid water smelling of the cedar bucket and of living beech trees. And still they did not go home. It was a horse lot this time, a tall rail fence upon and along which men stood and sat and out of which one by one horses were led, to be walked and trotted and then cantered back and forth along the road while the slow swapping and buying went on and the sun began to slant westward, they—the three of them—watching and listening, the older brother with his muddy eyes and his steady, inevitable tobacco, the father commenting now and then on certain of the animals, to no one in particular.

It was after sundown when they reached home. They ate supper by lamplight, then, sitting on the doorstep, the boy watched the night fully accomplish, listening to the whippoorwills and the frogs, when he heard his mother's voice: "Abner! No! No! Oh, God. Oh, God. Abner!" and he rose, whirled, and saw the altered light through the door where a candle stub now burned in a bottle neck on the table and his father, still in the hat and coat, at once formal and burlesque as though dressed carefully for some shabby and ceremonial violence, emptying the reservoir of the lamp back into the five-gallon kerosene can from which it had been filled, while the mother tugged at his arm until he shifted the lamp to the other hand and flung her back, not savagely or viciously, just hard, into the wall, her hands flung out against the wall for balance, her mouth open and in her face the same quality of hopeless despair as had been in her voice. Then his father saw him standing in the door.

"Go to the barn and get that can of oil we were oiling the wagon with," he said. The boy did not move. Then he could speak.

"What . . ." he cried. "What are you . . ."

"Go get that oil," his father said. "Go."

Then he was moving, running, outside the house, toward the stable: this the old habit, the old blood which he had not been permitted to choose for himself, which had been bequeathed him willy nilly and which had run for so long (and who knew where, battening on what of outrage and savagery and lust) before it came to him. *I could keep on,* he thought. *I could run on and on and never look back, never need to see his face again. Only I can't. I can't,* the rusted can in his hand now, the liquid sploshing in it as he ran back to the house and into it, into the sound of his mother's weeping in the next room, and handed the can to his father.

"Ain't you going to even send a nigger?" he cried. "At least you sent a nigger before!"

This time his father didn't strike him. The hand came even faster than the blow had, the same hand which had set the can on the table with almost excruciating care flashing from the can toward him too quick for him to follow it, gripping him by the back of his shirt and on to tiptoe before he had seen it quit the can, the face stooping at him in breathless and frozen ferocity, the cold, dead voice speaking over him to the older brother who leaned against the table, chewing with that steady, curious, sidewise motion of cows:

"Empty the can into the big one and go on. I'll catch up with you."

"Better tie him up to the bedpost," the brother said.

"Do like I told you," the father said. Then the boy was moving, his bunched shirt and the hard, bony hand between his shoulder-blades, his toes just touching the floor, across the room and into the other one, past the sisters sitting with spread heavy thighs in the two chairs over the cold hearth, and to where his mother and aunt sat side by side on the bed, the aunt's arm about his mother's shoulders.

"Hold him," the father said. The aunt made a startled movement. "Not you," the father said. "Lennie. Take hold of him. I want to see you do it." His mother took him by the wrist. "You'll hold him better than that. If he gets loose don't you know what he is going to do? He will go up yonder." He jerked his head toward the road. "Maybe I'd better tie him."

"I'll hold him," his mother whispered.

"See you do then." Then his father was gone, the stiff foot heavy and measured upon the boards, ceasing at last.

Then he began to struggle. His mother caught him in both arms, he jerking and wrenching at them. He would be stronger in the end, he knew that. But he had no time to wait for it. "Lemme go!" he cried. "I don't want to have to hit you!"

"Let him go!" the aunt said. "If he don't go, before God, I am going up there myself!"

"Don't you see I can't?" his mother cried. "Sarty! Sarty! No! No! Help me, Lizzie!"

Then he was free. His aunt grasped at him but it was too late. He   100
whirled, running, his mother stumbled forward on to her knees behind him, crying to the nearer sister: "Catch him, Net! Catch him!" But that was too late too, the sister (the sisters were twins, born at the same time, yet either of them now gave the impression of being, encompassing as much living meat and volume and weight as any other two of the family) not yet having begun to rise from the chair, her head, face, alone merely turned, presenting to him in the flying instant an astonishing expanse of young female features untroubled by any surprise even, wearing only an expression of bovine interest. Then he was out of the room, out of the house, in the mild dust of the starlit road and the heavy rifeness of honeysuckle, the pale ribbon unspooling with terrific slowness under his running feet, reaching the gate at last and turning in, running, his heart and lungs drumming, on up the drive toward the lighted house, the lighted door. He did not knock, he burst in, sobbing for breath, incapable for the moment of speech; he saw the astonished face of the Negro in the linen jacket without knowing when the Negro had appeared.

"De Spain!" he cried, panted. "Where's . . ." then he saw the white man too emerging from a white door down the hall. "Barn!" he cried. "Barn!"

"What?" the white man said. "Barn?"

"Yes!" the boy cried. "Barn!"

"Catch him!" the white man shouted.

But it was too late this time too. The Negro grasped his shirt, but the   105
entire sleeve, rotten with washing, carried away, and he was out that door too and in the drive again, and had actually never ceased to run even while he was screaming into the white man's face.

Behind him the white man was shouting, "My horse! Fetch my horse!" and he thought for an instant of cutting across the park and climbing the fence into the road, but he did not know the park nor how high the vine-massed fence might be and he dared not risk it. So he ran on down the drive, blood and breath roaring; presently he was in the road again though he could not see it. He could not hear either: the galloping mare was almost upon him before he heard her, and even then he held his course, as if the very urgency of his wild grief and need must in a moment more find him wings, waiting until the ultimate instant to hurl himself aside and into the weed-choked roadside ditch as the horse thundered past and on, for an instant in furious silhouette against the stars, the tranquil early summer night sky which, even before the shape of the horse and rider vanished, stained abruptly and violently upward: a long, swirling roar incredible and soundless, blotting the stars, and he springing up and into the road again, running again, knowing it was too late yet still running even after he heard the shot and, an instant later, two shots, pausing now without knowing he had ceased to run, crying, "Pap! Pap!", running again before he knew he had begun to run, stumbling, tripping over something and scrabbling up again without ceasing to run, looking backward over his shoulder at the glare as he got up, running on among the invisible trees, panting, sobbing, "Father! Father!"

At midnight he was sitting on the crest of a hill. He did not know it was midnight and he did not know how far he had come. But there was no glare behind him now and he sat now, his back toward what he had called home for four days anyhow, his face toward the dark woods which he would enter when breath was strong again, small, shaking steadily in the chill darkness, hugging himself into the remainder of his thin, rotten shirt, the grief and despair now no longer terror and fear but just grief and despair. *Father. My father*, he thought. "He was brave!" he cried suddenly, aloud but not loud, no more than a whisper. "He was! He was in the war! He was in Colonel Sartoris' cav'ry!" not knowing that his father had gone to that war a private in the fine old European sense, wearing no uniform, admitting the authority of and giving fidelity to no man or army or flag, going to war as Malbrouck° himself did: for booty—it meant nothing and less than nothing to him if it were enemy booty or his own.

The slow constellations wheeled on. It would be dawn and then sunup after a while and he would be hungry. But that would be to-morrow and now he was only cold, and walking would cure that. His breathing was easier now and he decided to get up and go on, and then he found that he had been asleep because he knew it was almost dawn, the night almost over. He could tell that from the whippoorwills. They were everywhere now among the dark trees below him, constant and inflectioned and ceaseless, so that, as the instant for giving over to the day birds drew nearer and nearer, there was no interval at all between them. He got up. He was a little stiff, but walking would cure that too as it would the cold, and soon there would be the sun. He went on down the hill, toward the dark woods within which the liquid silver voices of the birds called unceasing—the rapid and urgent beating of the urgent and quiring heart of the late spring night. He did not look back.

Malbrouck: John Churchill, Duke of Marlborough (1650–1722), English general victorious in the Battle of Blenheim (1704), a triumph that drove the French army out of Germany. The French called him Malbrouck, a name they found easier to pronounce.

Questions

1. After delivering his warning to Major de Spain, the boy Snopes does not actually witness what happens to his father and brother, or what happens to the Major's barn. But what do you assume happens? What evidence is given in the story?

2. What do you understand to be Faulkner's opinion of Abner Snopes? Make a guess, indicating details in the story that convey attitudes.

3. Which adjectives best describe the general tone of the story: *calm, amused, disinterested, scornful, marveling, excited, impassioned*? Point out passages that may be so described. What do you notice about the style in which these passages are written?

4. In tone and style, how does "Barn Burning" compare with Faulkner's story "A Rose for Emily" (Chapter 2)? To what do you attribute any differences?

5. Suppose that, instead of "Barn Burning," Faulkner had written a story told by Abner Snopes in the first person. Why would such a story need a style different from that of "Barn Burning"? (Suggestion: Notice Faulkner's descriptions of Abner Snopes's voice.)

6. Although "Barn Burning" takes place some thirty years after the Civil War, how does the war figure in it?

IRONY

If a friend declares, "Oh, sure, I just *love* to have four papers due on the same day," you detect that the statement contains **irony**. This is **verbal irony**, the most familiar kind, in which we understand the speaker's meaning to be far from the usual meaning of the words—in this case, quite the opposite. (When the irony is found, as here, in a somewhat sour statement tinged with mockery, it is called **sarcasm**.)

Irony, of course, occurs in writing as well as in conversation. When in a comic moment in Isaac Bashevis Singer's "Gimpel the Fool" the sexton announces, "The wealthy Reb Gimpel invites the congregation to a feast in honor of the birth of a son," the people at the synagogue burst into laughter. They know that Gimpel, in contrast to the sexton's words, is not a wealthy man but a humble baker; that the son is not his own but his wife's lover's; and that the birth brings no honor to anybody. Verbal irony, then, implies a contrast or discrepancy between what is *said* and what is *meant*.

Dramatic Irony

There are also times when the speaker, unlike the reader, does not realize the ironic dimension of his or her words; such instances are known as **dramatic irony**. The most famous example occurs in Sophocles's tragic drama *Oedipus the King*, when Oedipus vows to find and punish the murderer of King Laius, unaware that he himself is the man he seeks, and adds: "If by any chance / he proves to be an intimate of our house, / here at my hearth, with my full knowledge, / may the curse I just called down on him strike me!" Stories often contain other kinds of irony. A situation, for example, can be ironic if it contains some wry contrast or incongruity. In Jack London's "To

Build a Fire" (Chapter 4), it is ironic that a freezing man, desperately trying to strike a match to light a fire and save himself, accidentally ignites all his remaining matches.

Irony as Point of View

An entire story may be told from an **ironic point of view**. Whenever we sense a sharp distinction between the narrator of a story and the author, irony is likely to occur—especially when the narrator is telling us something that we are clearly expected to doubt or to interpret very differently. In "A & P," Sammy (who tells his own story) makes many smug and cruel observations about the people around him; but the author makes clear to us that much of his superiority is based on immaturity and lack of self-knowledge. (This irony, by the way, does not negate the fact that Sammy makes some very telling comments about society's superficial values and rigid and judgmental attitudes, comments that Updike seems to endorse and wants us to endorse as well.) And when we read Hemingway's "A Clean, Well-Lighted Place," surely we feel that most of the time the older waiter speaks for the author. Though the waiter gives us a respectful, compassionate view of a lonely old man, and we don't doubt that the view is Hemingway's, still, in the closing lines of the story we are reminded that author and waiter are not identical. Musing on the sleepless night ahead of him, the waiter tries to shrug off his problem—"After all, it is probably only insomnia"—but the reader, who recalls the waiter's bleak view of *nada*, nothingness, knows that it certainly isn't mere insomnia that keeps him awake but a dread of solitude and death. At that crucial moment, Hemingway and the older waiter part company, and we perceive an ironic point of view, and also a verbal irony, "After all, it is probably only insomnia."

Cosmic Irony

Storytellers are sometimes fond of ironic twists of fate—developments that reveal a terrible distance between what people deserve and what they get, between what is and what ought to be. In the novels of Thomas Hardy, some hostile fate keeps playing tricks to thwart the main characters. In *Tess of the D'Urbervilles*, an all-important letter, thrust under a door, by chance slides beneath a carpet and is not received. Such an irony is sometimes called an **irony of fate** or a **cosmic irony**, for it suggests that some malicious fate (or other spirit in the universe) is deliberately frustrating human efforts. Evidently, there is an irony of fate in the student's futile attempt to escape Death in the fable "Death Has an Appointment in Samarra," and perhaps in the flaring up of the all-precious matches in "To Build a Fire," as well. To notice an irony gives pleasure. It may move us to laughter, make us feel wonder, or arouse our sympathy. By so involving us, irony—whether in a statement, a situation, an unexpected event, or a point of view—can render a story more likely to strike us, to affect us, and to be remembered.

Guy de Maupassant

The Necklace   1884

Translated by John Siscoe

*Henri René Albert Guy de Maupassant (1850–1893)
was born in a rented castle in Normandy. The son
of minor aristocrats (the* de *in his surname denotes
a noble family), Maupassant grew up overshadowed
by his parents' unhappy marriage. His mother was
a friend of the novelist Gustave Flaubert, who took
the teenage boy under his tutelage. "He is my disciple," Flaubert declared, "and I love him like a son."
Maupassant studied law, but the Franco-Prussian
war of 1870 inspired him to enlist as a solider. After
the war he worked briefly as a minor bureaucrat
while continuing to study privately with Flaubert.*

Guy de Maupassant

*Maupassant quit his government job and dedicated himself to literature, writing
more than three hundred short stories, six novels—most notably* Pierre and Jean
*(1888)—and three travel books in the decade before his untimely death. Wealthy
and internationally famous from his stories, the hardworking author lived luxuriously. After contracting syphilis (then incurable) in his twenties, Maupassant
watched his own health and sanity deteriorate. He died one month before his
forty-third birthday.*

She was one of those lovely and charming young women born, as if
by some quirk of fate, into a family of commoners. She had no dowry, no
prospects, no chance to meet a rich and distinguished man who would
love, understand, and marry her. So she let herself be married to an
insignificant clerk in the Ministry of Education.

She dressed simply, being unable to adorn herself. But she was
unhappy, as if she had been denied her rightful place in society. For
women recognize neither caste nor lineage; their beauty, grace, and
charm serve them instead of birth and family. A natural delicacy, an
instinct for elegance, a sparkling wit; these alone define their social
status, enabling the daughter of the poor to be the equal of the greatest
of ladies.

Believing that she had been born to enjoy every refinement and
luxury, she suffered deeply. She suffered from her wretched apartment,
from its dingy walls, worn-out chairs, and ugly upholstery. All these
things, which another woman of her class wouldn't even have noticed,
tormented and infuriated her. The sight of the little Breton girl going about her simple housework aroused in her deep regrets and hopeless dreams. She would imagine gleaming reception rooms rich with
oriental draperies, lit by high bronze sconces, with two tall footmen

in knee breeches dozing in large armchairs, overcome by the central heating. She would imagine great halls decorated in antique silk, with furniture of fine workmanship displaying priceless bibelots. There were also smaller, more intimate rooms, elegant and perfumed, ideal for five o'clock chats with one's closest friends, men who were well known and much in demand, whose company and attentions all women envied and admired.

When she sat down to dinner, the round table was covered with a cloth that hadn't been cleaned for three days. Across the table her husband, as he lifted the lid of the tureen, exclaimed with delight: "Ah! Good old beef stew! Could there be anything better?" But she was dreaming of refined dinners, of glittering silverware, while on the walls tapestries portrayed people from olden times and exotic birds in the midst of a fairytale forest. She dreamt of exquisite meals served on marvelous china, and of murmured compliments that she would reward with an inscrutable smile, while she tasted the pink flesh of a trout or the wings of a grouse.

She had no fine dresses, no jewels, nothing. Yet luxury was all she   5
cared about; she felt that she had been born for it. She wanted so much to give pleasure, to be envied, to be alluring and admired.

She had one rich friend, a girl she had known in convent school, whom she couldn't bear to visit anymore, because when she returned home she would feel miserable. And she would cry for days on end, from sorrow, regret, despair, and grief.

One evening her husband came home looking very pleased with himself, and holding a large envelope.

"Here's a little something for you."

She immediately tore open the envelope. Inside was a card which read:

"The Minister of Education and Madame Georges Ramponneau re-   10
quest that Monsieur and Madame Loisel would do them the honor of spending the evening with them at the Ministry on Monday, January eighteenth."

Instead of being thrilled, as her husband had hoped, she scornfully tossed the invitation onto the table, muttering:

"What do you want me to do with this?"

"But darling, I thought you'd be pleased. You never go out, and this really is a special occasion. It wasn't easy for me to get that card. Everybody wanted one, there weren't many being handed out, especially to the clerks. You'll see all the important officials there."

She glared at him and said impatiently:

"And what do you expect me to wear?"   15

He hadn't given it a thought. He stammered:

"What about the dress—the one you wear to the theater. It seems perfectly fine to me . . .

He fell silent, at a loss, struck dumb, as he watched his wife crying. Two large tears slowly trickled down from the corners of her eyes to the corners of her mouth. He blurted out:

"What's wrong? What's the matter?"

But with a supreme effort she had stifled her grief and replied in a   20 calm voice, dabbing at her cheeks:

"It's nothing. But as I haven't a thing to wear, I can't attend this party. Go give your card to a colleague whose wife has a better wardrobe than mine."

He was devastated. He replied:

"Look, Mathilde, how much would a suitable dress cost, one that you could wear on other occasions, something very simple?"

She thought a moment, estimating the costs, and also calculating how much she might ask from this thrifty clerk without risking a cry of horror and immediate rejection.

At last she said hesitantly: 25

"I can't say for certain, but I might be able to find one for four hundred francs."

He blanched a little, since he'd put aside that very sum to buy a rifle so he could go hunting next summer on the Nanterre plain, with some friends who went there on Sundays to shoot larks.

However he said:

"All right. I'll give you four hundred francs. But try to make sure that it's a nice dress."

The day of the ball drew near, and Madame Loisel seemed sad, rest-   30 less, and worried. And yet her dress was ready. One evening her husband said to her:

"What's the matter with you? You've been acting strange for the past three days."

And she replied:

"I'm upset because I haven't a single piece of jewelry or a gemstone or anything to wear with my dress. I'll look like a pauper. I almost think it would be better if I didn't go."

"What if you wore flowers? They're very chic right now. Ten francs would get you two or three magnificent roses."

She wasn't convinced.   35

"No . . . There's nothing more humiliating than to look poor when you're surrounded by rich women."

Then her husband exclaimed:

"Here's what you do: go and look up your friend Madame Forestier and ask her to loan you some of her jewelry. After all, you know each other well enough."

She gave a cry of joy.

"You're right. It didn't occur to me."   40

The next day she paid her friend a visit and explained her problem. Madame Forestier went over to her mirrored wardrobe and took out a large jewelry case. She brought it back, opened it, and said to Madame Loisel:

"You choose, my dear."

First she examined some bracelets, then a pearl necklace, then a finely wrought Venetian cross of gold and gems. She tried on the jewelry in front of the mirror, hesitating, unable to decide which to take and which to leave behind. She kept asking:

"Do you have anything else?"

"I do. Here, take a look yourself. I don't know what would please   45 you."

Suddenly she discovered, in a black satin case, a stunning diamond necklace, and her heart began to throb with intense desire. Her hands trembled as she lifted up the necklace. She fastened it around her neck, below the high collar of her dress, and she gazed at her reflection in ecstasy.

Then she asked in a hesitant, anxious voice:

"Would you loan me this, just this?"

"Yes, of course."

She fell on her friend's neck, embraced her passionately, and then   50 fled with her treasure.

The day of the ball arrived: Madame Loisel was a success. She was the loveliest of all; elegant, graceful, smiling, and radiant with joy. All the men looked at her, asked who she was, and wanted to be introduced to her. Every cabinet attaché wanted a waltz with her. The Minister noticed her.

She danced with fervor, with passion, drunk with pleasure, no longer thinking of anything. The triumph of her beauty and the glory of her success enveloped her in a sort of cloud of happiness made up of all the compliments, all the admiring glances, all the awakened desires of this victory so complete and so dear to a woman's heart.

She left around four in the morning. Since midnight her husband had been dozing in a small side room, along with three other gentlemen whose wives had been having a grand time.

He threw over her shoulders the wraps he had brought for the journey home. Humble, everyday things, their shabbiness contrasted with her elegant dress. Sensing this, she wanted to leave at once so as to escape the notice of the other women wrapping themselves in their expensive furs.

Loisel held her back.   55

"Wait here. You'll catch cold outside. I'll go hail a cab."

But she wouldn't listen to him and hurried down the stairs. When they reached the street they didn't see any cabs so they went looking for one, calling out to the coachmen they saw passing in the distance.

Discouraged and shivering, they walked toward the Seine. Finally, on the quay, they found one of those old "sleepwalkers"—cabs that never make their appearance until after dark, as if they were ashamed to show their decrepit selves by day.

It brought them to their building's front door on the Rue de Martyrs, and they made the sad climb up the stairs to their apartment. For her it was all over. And he couldn't help thinking that he'd have to be at his desk by ten o'clock.

Standing in front of the mirror, she pulled the wraps off her shoulders   60
so that she could see herself one more time in all her glory. But suddenly she gave a cry. Her throat was bare: the necklace was gone.

Her husband, already half-undressed, asked:

"What is it?"

She looked at him, panic-stricken:

"I . . . I . . . I don't have Madame Forestier's necklace."

He stood up, bewildered.   65

"What? . . . How? . . . That's impossible."

And they searched in the folds of the dress, in the folds of the cloak, in the pockets, everywhere. They found nothing.

He asked:

"Are you sure that you still had it when you left the ball?"

"Yes. I touched it, in the vestibule at the Ministry."   70

"But if you had lost it on the street we would have heard it fall. So it must be in the cab."

"Yes. That makes sense. Did you take down the number?"

"No. You didn't notice it, did you?"

"No."

"They stared at one another, dumbfounded. Finally Loisel started to   75
get dressed.

"I'm going to retrace our steps to see if I can't find it."

And he left. Still in her elegant dress, too nervous to sleep, she sat huddled in her chair, unable to act or to think.

He husband came back around seven o'clock, empty-handed.

That day he filed a report at police headquarters, he placed ads in the newspapers, he inquired at the cab companies; in short he tried every-thing that had a ghost of a chance.

She waited all day long, still overwhelmed by the weight of the ca-   80
tastrophe.

Loisel returned that evening, his face lined and pale. Nothing had turned up.

"You are going to have to write your friend," he said. "Tell her that you've broken the clasp of her necklace and that you're having it repaired. That will buy us some time."

She wrote as he dictated.

* * *

After a week they had lost all hope.

And Loisel, who had aged five years, said: 85

"We'll have to try to replace the necklace."

The next morning they took the empty case to the jeweler whose name was inside. He consulted his account books.

"I didn't sell such a necklace, Madame. It appears I only provided the case."

So they went from jeweler to jeweler looking for a duplicate necklace, searching their memories, both of them sick with grief and anxiety.

They found, at a store in the Palais-Royal, a diamond necklace that   90 seemed to them almost identical to the original. The price was forty thousand francs. The store would let them have it for thirty-six thousand.

They asked the jeweler to hold it for them for three days. And they reached an agreement that they could return it for a refund of thirty-four thousand francs if they had found the original before the end of February.

Loisel had eighteen thousand francs which his father had left him. He would have to borrow the rest.

And borrow he did, asking now a thousand francs from one, five hundred francs from another, five louis here, three louis there. He signed notes, made reckless promises, struck deals with usurers, with every kind of loan shark. He placed everything he had at risk, signing papers without even knowing if he could fulfill their terms. Haunted by the fear of what lay before him, by the black fate that was about to engulf him, by the prospect of physical hardship and moral agony, he went to the jeweler's and picked up the new necklace, leaving behind on the counter thirty-six thousand francs.

When Madame Loisel brought the necklace to Madame Forestier, the latter said coldly:

"You could have returned it sooner. I might have needed it."   95

She didn't open the case, as her friend feared that she would. If she had noticed the substitution, what would she have thought? What would she have said? Would she have taken her for a thief?

Madame Loisel came to know the wretched life of the poor. Yet she played her part heroically, without faltering. The terrible debt had to be paid. She would pay it. The maid was let go, and they moved from their apartment into a garret, under the eaves.

She came to know the heavy burden of housework and the lowly chores of the kitchen. She scrubbed the dishes, ruining her pink nails scouring the greasy pots and the bottoms of pans. She washed the dirty laundry, the shirts and the cleaning rags, hanging them up on the line to dry. Every morning she would haul the garbage down to the street and carry fresh water back up the stairs, pausing at every landing to catch her breath. Dressed as the poor woman she was, she would scurry from fruit-

seller to grocer to butcher, basket on her arm, haggling, arguing, trying to
stretch every miserable sou.

Every month they had to pay off some debts, and renew others to pay
off later.

Her husband worked evenings balancing a shopkeeper's account   100
books. And he frequently worked nights as well, copying out documents
at five sous a page.

And this life lasted for ten years.

When the ten years had come to an end they had paid off everything,
including the usurers' fees and the accumulated interest.

Madame Loisel looked old now. She had become the sort of woman
often found in poor households: tough, grasping, and coarse. With her hair
uncombed, her skirts askew, with red hands, talking in a loud voice, she
would wash and scrub the floors. But sometimes, while her husband was at
work, she would sit by the window and remember that evening long ago,
and that ball where she had been so lovely and so admired.

What might have happened if she hadn't lost that necklace? Who
could know? Who could know? Life was so strange, so uncertain: the
slightest thing could either ruin you or save you!

One Sunday in the Champs Elysees, while she was taking a walk   105
as a respite from the week's chores, she suddenly noticed a woman
walking with a child. It was Madame Forestier: still young, still lovely,
still alluring.

Madame Loisel felt moved. Should she speak to her? Yes, she should. And
now that she'd paid her debts, she could tell her the whole story. Why not?

She went up to her.

"Hello Jeanne."

The lady, who didn't recognize her, was startled to be addressed so
familiarly by a badly dressed stranger.

She stammered: 110

"But . . . Madame . . . I don't know . . . You must be mistaken."

"No. I am Mathilde Loisel."

"Oh! . . . My poor Mathilde, how you've changed!"

"Yes, I've had some hard times since I saw you last, and plenty of
misery—and all on account of you."

"Of me? What do you mean?"   115

"I take it you remember the diamond necklace that you let me borrow for the Minister's ball?"

"Yes. So?"

"So I lost it."

"But how? You returned it to me."

"I brought you another that was just like it. And we've spent the last   120
ten years paying for it. You can imagine that it wasn't easy for us, since we
had nothing . . . But now, I'm glad to say, it's over and done with at last."

Madame Forestier froze.

"You're saying that you bought a diamond necklace to replace mine?"

"Yes. And you never guessed, did you? They were so alike."

And she smiled with a proud and naïve joy.

Madame Forestier, deeply moved, reached out with both of her hands.   125
"Oh, my poor Mathilde! But mine was a fake. It wasn't worth more than five hundred francs."

Questions

1. Why does Mathilde Loisel borrow her friend's diamond necklace for the ball? What do her motivations reveal about her character?

2. Why does the protagonist not admit to her friend that she has lost the necklace?

3. How do the Loisels afford the new necklace? What obligations does its purchase involve?

4. What is ironic about the story's conclusion?

5. What other ironic elements are present in this story?

Kate Chopin

The Story of an Hour   1894

Kate Chopin (1851–1904) demonstrates again, as in "The Storm" in Chapter 4, her ability to write short stories of compressed intensity. For a brief biography and a portrait, see page 104.

Knowing that Mrs. Mallard was afflicted with a heart trouble, great care was taken to break to her as gently as possible the news of her husband's death.

It was her sister Josephine who told her, in broken sentences; veiled hints that revealed in half concealing. Her husband's friend Richards was there, too, near her. It was he who had been in the newspaper office when intelligence of the railroad disaster was received, with Brently Mallard's name leading the list of "killed." He had only taken the time to assure himself of its truth by a second telegram, and had hastened to forestall any less careful, less tender friend in bearing the sad message.

She did not hear the story as many women have heard the same, with a paralyzed inability to accept its significance. She wept at once, with sudden, wild abandonment, in her sister's arms. When the storm of grief had spent itself she went away to her room alone. She would have no one follow her.

There stood, facing the open window, a comfortable, roomy armchair. Into this she sank, pressed down by a physical exhaustion that haunted her body and seemed to reach into her soul.

She could see in the open square before her house the tops of trees   5
that were all aquiver with the new spring life. The delicious breath of rain was in the air. In the street below a peddler was crying his wares. The notes of a distant song which some one was singing reached her faintly, and countless sparrows were twittering in the eaves.

There were patches of blue sky showing here and there through the clouds that had met and piled one above the other in the west facing her window.

She sat with her head thrown back upon the cushion of the chair, quite motionless, except when a sob came up into her throat and shook her, as a child who has cried itself to sleep continues to sob in its dreams.

She was young, with a fair, calm face, whose lines bespoke repression and even a certain strength. But now there was a dull stare in her eyes, whose gaze was fixed away off yonder on one of those patches of blue sky. It was not a glance of reflection, but rather indicated a suspension of intelligent thought.

There was something coming to her and she was waiting for it, fearfully. What was it? She did not know; it was too subtle and elusive to name. But she felt it, creeping out of the sky, reaching toward her through the sounds, the scents, the color that filled the air.

Now her bosom rose and fell tumultuously. She was beginning to recognize this thing that was approaching to possess her, and she was striving to beat it back with her will—as powerless as her two white slender hands would have been.   10

When she abandoned herself a little whispered word escaped her slightly parted lips. She said it over and over under her breath: "free, free, free!" The vacant stare and the look of terror that had followed it went from her eyes. They stayed keen and bright. Her pulses beat fast, and the coursing blood warmed and relaxed every inch of her body.

She did not stop to ask if it were or were not a monstrous joy that held her. A clear and exalted perception enabled her to dismiss the suggestion as trivial.

She knew that she would weep again when she saw the kind, tender hands folded in death; the face that had never looked save with love upon her, fixed and gray and dead. But she saw beyond that bitter moment a long procession of years to come that would belong to her absolutely. And she opened and spread her arms out to them in welcome.

There would be no one to live for her during those coming years; she would live for herself. There would be no powerful will bending hers in that blind persistence with which men and women believe they have a right to impose a private will upon a fellow-creature. A kind intention or a cruel intention made the act seem no less a crime as she looked upon it in that brief moment of illumination.

And yet she had loved him—sometimes. Often she had not. What did it matter! What could love, the unsolved mystery, count for in face of this possession of self-assertion which she suddenly recognized as the strongest impulse of her being!   15

"Free! Body and soul free!" she kept whispering.

Josephine was kneeling before the closed door with her lips to the keyhole, imploring for admission. "Louise, open the door! I beg; open the door—you will make yourself ill. What are you doing, Louise? For heaven's sake open the door."

"Go away. I am not making myself ill." No; she was drinking in a very elixir of life through that open window.

Her fancy was running riot along those days ahead of her. Spring days, and summer days, and all sorts of days that would be her own. She breathed a quick prayer that life might be long. It was only yesterday she had thought with a shudder that life might be long.

She arose at length and opened the door to her sister's importuni- 20 ties. There was a feverish triumph in her eyes, and she carried herself unwittingly like a goddess of Victory. She clasped her sister's waist, and together they descended the stairs. Richards stood waiting for them at the bottom.

Some one was opening the front door with a latchkey. It was Brently Mallard who entered, a little travel-stained, composedly carrying his grip-sack and umbrella. He had been far from the scene of the accident, and did not even know there had been one. He stood amazed at Josephine's piercing cry; at Richards' quick motion to screen him from the view of his wife.

But Richards was too late.

When the doctors came they said she had died of heart disease—of joy that kills.

Questions

1. What proves to be ironic about the opening sentence of the story?
2. What is Mrs. Mallard's first reaction on hearing the news of her husband's death? How does that moment eventually prove ironic?
3. What emotion overcomes her later when she is alone in her room? How does it eventually also prove to be ironic?
4. Describe why Mrs. Mallard experiences a "monstrous joy" at being "free, free, free!"
5. How do Mrs. Mallard's fanciful plans for her future and her "prayer" prove ironic?
6. Unfold the double irony of the last sentence.

■ WRITING *effectively*

THINKING ABOUT TONE AND STYLE

If you look around a crowded classroom, you will notice—consciously or not—the styles of your fellow students. The way they dress, talk, and even sit conveys information about their attitudes. A haircut, T-shirt, tattoo, or piece of jewelry all silently say something. Similarly, a writer's style—his or her own distinct voice—can give the reader crucial extra information. To analyze a writer's style, think about:

- **Diction: Consider the flavor of words chosen by the author for a particular story.** In "A Clean, Well-Lighted Place," for example, Hemingway favors simple, unemotional, and descriptive language, whereas in "The Storm," Chopin uses extravagant and emotionally charged diction. Each choice reveals something important about the story.
- **Sentence structure: Look for patterns in a story's sentence structure.** Hemingway is famous for his short, clipped sentences, which often repeat certain key words. Faulkner, however, favors complex, elaborate syntax that immerses the reader in the emotion of the narrative.
- **Tone: Try to determine the writer's attitude toward the story he or she is telling.** In "The Gospel According to Mark," Borges uses dispassionate restraint to present a central irony, a tragic misunderstanding that will doom his protagonist. Tan's "A Pair of Tickets," by contrast, creates a tone of hushed excitement and direct emotional involvement.
- **Organization: Examine the order in which information is presented.** Borges tells his story in a straightforward, chronological manner, which eventually makes it possible for us to appreciate the tale's complex undercurrents. Other stories (for example, Atwood's "Happy Endings") present the narrative's events in more complicated and surprising ways.

CHECKLIST: Writing About Tone and Style

- ☐ Does the writer use word choice in a distinctive way?
- ☐ Is the diction unusual in any way?
- ☐ Does the author tend toward long or short—even fragmented—sentences?
- ☐ How would you characterize the writer's voice? Is it formal or casual? Distant or intimate? Impassioned or restrained?
- ☐ Can the narrator's words be taken at face value? Is there anything ironic about the narrator's voice?
- ☐ How does the writer arrange the material? Is information delivered chronologically, or is the organization more complex?
- ☐ What is the writer's attitude toward the material?

TOPICS FOR WRITING ON TONE AND STYLE

1. Examine a short story with a style you admire. Write an essay in which you analyze the author's approach toward diction, sentence structure, tone, and organization. How do these elements work together to create a certain mood? How does that mood contribute to the story's meaning? If your chosen story has a first-person narrator, how do stylistic choices help to create a sense of that particular character?

2. Write a brief analysis of irony in "The Necklace," "The Story of an Hour," or "The Jilting of Granny Weatherall." What sorts of irony does your story employ?

3. Consider a short story in which the narrator is the central character, perhaps "A & P," "Araby," or "Cathedral." In a brief essay, show how the character of the narrator determines the style of the story. Examine language in particular—words or phrases, slang expressions, figures of speech, local or regional usage.

4. Write a page in which you describe eating a meal in the company of others. Using sensory details, convey a sense of the setting, the quality of the food, and the presence of your dining companions. Now rewrite your paragraph as Ernest Hemingway. Finally, rewrite it as William Faulkner.

5. In a paragraph, describe a city street as seen through the eyes of a college graduate who has just moved to the city to start a new career. Now describe that same street in the voice of an old woman walking home from the hospital where her husband has just died. Finally, describe the street in the voice of a teenage runaway. In each paragraph, refrain from identifying your character or saying anything about his or her circumstances. Simply present the street as each character would perceive it.

▶ TERMS FOR *review*

Tone ▶ The attitude toward a subject conveyed in a literary work. No single stylistic device creates tone; it is the net result of the various elements an author brings to creating the work's feeling and manner.

Style ▶ All the distinctive ways in which an author uses language to create a literary work. An author's style depends on his or her characteristic use of diction, imagery, tone, syntax, and figurative language.

Diction ▶ Word choice or vocabulary. Diction refers to the class of words that an author decides is appropriate to use in a particular work.

Irony ▶ A literary device in which a discrepancy of meaning is masked beneath the surface of the language. Irony is present when a writer says one thing but means something quite the opposite.

Verbal irony ▶ A statement in which the speaker or writer says the opposite of what is really meant. For example, a friend might say, "How graceful!" after you trip clumsily on a stair.

Sarcasm ▶ A conspicuously bitter form of irony in which the ironic statement is designed to hurt or mock its target.

Dramatic irony ▶ Where the reader understands the implication and meaning of a situation and may foresee the oncoming disaster or triumph while the character does not.

Cosmic irony or irony of fate ▶ A type of situational irony that emphasizes the discrepancy between what characters deserve and what they get, between a character's aspirations and the treatment he or she receives at the hands of fate.

6

THEME

The **theme** of a story is whatever general idea or insight the entire story reveals. In some stories the theme is unmistakable. At the end of Aesop's fable about the council of the mice that can't decide who will bell the cat, the theme is stated in the moral: *It is easier to propose a thing than to carry it out*. In a work of commercial fiction, too, the theme (if any) is usually obvious. Consider a typical detective thriller in which, say, a rookie police officer trained in scientific methods of crime detection sets out to solve a mystery sooner than his or her rival, a veteran sleuth whose only laboratory is carried under his hat. Perhaps the veteran solves the case, leading to the conclusion (and the theme), "The old ways are the best ways after all." Or the story might dramatize the same rivalry but reverse the outcome, having the rookie win, thereby reversing the theme: "The times are changing! Let's shake loose from old-fashioned ways."

PLOT VERSUS THEME

In literary fiction, a theme is seldom so obvious. That is, a theme need not be a moral or a message; it may be what the events add up to, what the story is about. When we come to the end of a finely wrought short story such as Ernest Hemingway's "A Clean, Well-Lighted Place" (Chapter 5), it may be easy to sum up the plot—to say what happens—but it is more difficult to sum up the story's main idea. Evidently, Hemingway relates events—how a younger waiter gets rid of an old man and how an older waiter then goes to a coffee bar—but in themselves these events seem relatively slight, though the story as a whole seems large (for its size) and full of meaning. A **summary**, a brief condensation of the main idea or plot of a literary work, may be helpful, but it tends to focus on the surface events of a story. A theme aims for a deeper and more comprehensive statement of its larger meaning.

For the meaning, we must look to other elements in the story besides what happens in it. It is clear that Hemingway is most deeply interested in the thoughts and feelings of the older waiter, the character who has more and

more to say as the story progresses, until at the end the story is entirely confined to his thoughts and perceptions. What is meaningful in these thoughts
and perceptions? The older waiter understands the old man and sympathizes
with his need for a clean, well-lighted place. If we say that, we are still talking
about what happens in the story, though we have gone beyond merely recording its external events. But a theme is usually stated in *general* words. Another
try: "Solitary people who cannot sleep need a cheerful, orderly place where
they can drink with dignity." That's a little better. We have indicated, at least,
that Hemingway's story is about more than just an old man and a couple of
waiters. But what about the older waiter's meditation on *nada*, nothingness?
Coming near the end of the story, it is given great emphasis, and probably no
good statement of Hemingway's theme can leave it out. Still another try at a
statement: "Solitary people need a place of refuge from their terrible awareness that their lives (or, perhaps, human lives) are essentially meaningless."
Neither this nor any other statement of the story's theme is unarguably right,
but at least the sentence helps the reader to bring into focus one primary idea
that Hemingway seems to be driving at.

When we finish reading "A Clean, Well-Lighted Place," we feel that
there is such a theme, a unifying vision, even though we cannot reduce it absolutely to a tag. Like some freshwater lake alive with creatures, Hemingway's
story is a broad expanse, reflecting in many directions. No wonder that many
readers will view it in different ways.

Moral inferences may be drawn from the story, no doubt, for Hemingway
is indirectly giving us advice about properly regarding and sympathizing with
the lonely, the uncertain, and the old. But the story doesn't set forth a lesson
that we are supposed to put into practice. One could argue that "A Clean,
Well-Lighted Place" contains *several* themes, and other statements could
be made to include Hemingway's views of love, of communication between
people, of dignity. Great short stories, like great symphonies, frequently have
more than one theme.

SUMMARIZING THE THEME

In many a fine short story, theme is the center, the moving force, the principle
of unity. Clearly, such a theme is something other than the characters or plot
of a story. To say that James Joyce's "Araby" (Chapter 8) is a short story about
a boy who goes to a bazaar to buy a gift for a young woman, only to arrive too
late, is to summarize the plot, not the theme. (The theme *might* be put, "The
romantic illusions of a young man are vulnerable to the lessons of reality," or
it might be put in any of a hundred other ways.) Although the title of Shirley
Jackson's "The Lottery" (Chapter 7), with its hint of the lure of easy riches,
may arouse pleasant expectations, which the neutral tone of the narrative
does nothing initially to dispel, the theme—the larger realization that the
story leaves us with—has to do with the ways in which cruel and insensitive
social practices can come to seem like normal and natural ones.

Sometimes you will hear it said that the theme of a story (say, Faulkner's "Barn Burning") is "loss of innocence" or that the theme of some other story (Hurston's "Sweat," for instance) is "the revolt of the downtrodden." Although such general descriptions of theme in a short phrase can be useful, we suggest that you work to become more specific. Try to sum the theme up in a short sentence that gives a fuller and more vivid sense of whatever truth or insight you think the story reveals. Crafting that sentence, you will find yourself looking closely at the story as you attempt to define its principal meaning.

FINDING THE THEME

You may find it helpful, in making a one-sentence statement of theme, to consider these questions:

1. Look back at the title of the story. From what you have read, what does it indicate?
2. Does the main character change in any way over the course of the story? Does this character arrive at any eventual realization or understanding? Are you left with any realization or understanding you did not have before?
3. Does the author make any general observations about life or human nature? Do the characters make any? (Caution: Characters now and again will utter opinions with which the reader is not necessarily supposed to agree.)
4. Does the story contain any especially curious objects, mysterious flat characters, significant animals, repeated names, song titles, or whatever, that hint at meanings larger than such things ordinarily have? In literary stories, such symbols may point to central themes.
5. When you have worded your statement of theme, have you cast it into general language, not just given a plot summary?
6. Does your statement hold true for the story as a whole, not for just part of it?

In distilling a statement of theme from a rich and complicated story, we have, of course, no more encompassed the whole story than a paleontologist taking a plaster mold of a petrified footprint has captured a living stegosaurus. A writer (other than a fabulist) does not usually set out with theme in hand, determined to make every detail in the story work to demonstrate it. Well then, the skeptical reader may ask, if only *some* stories have themes, if those themes may be hard to sum up, and if readers will probably disagree in their summations, why bother to state themes? Isn't it too much trouble? Surely it is, unless the effort to state a theme ends in pleasure and profit. Trying to sum up the point of a story in our own words is merely one way to make ourselves better aware of whatever we may have understood vaguely and tentatively. Attempted with loving care, such statements may bring into focus our scattered impressions of a rewarding story, may help to clarify and hold fast whatever wisdom the storyteller has offered us.

Chinua Achebe

Dead Men's Path (1953) 1972

Chinua Achebe (1930–2013) was born in Ogidi, a village in eastern Nigeria. His father was a missionary schoolteacher, and Achebe had a devout Christian upbringing. A member of the Ibo tribe, the future writer grew up speaking Igbo, but at the age of eight, he began learning English. He went abroad to study at London University but returned to Africa to complete his B.A. at the University College of Ibadan in 1953. Achebe worked for years in Nigerian radio. Shortly after Nigeria's independence from Great Britain in 1963, civil war broke out, and the nation split in two. Achebe left his job to join the Ministry of Information

Chinua Achebe

for Biafra, the new country created from eastern Nigeria. It was not until 1970 that the bloody civil war ended. Approximately one million Ibos lay dead from war, disease, and starvation as the defeated Biafrans reunited with Nigeria. Achebe was often considered Africa's premier novelist. His novels included Things Fall Apart *(1958),* No Longer at Ease *(1962),* A Man of the People *(1966), and* Anthills of the Savannah *(1987). His short stories were collected in* Girls at War *(1972). He also published poetry, children's stories, and several volumes of essays, the last of which is* Home and Exile *(2000). In 1990 Achebe suffered massive injuries in a car accident outside Lagos that left him paralyzed from the waist down. Following the accident, he taught at Bard College in upstate New York for almost nineteen years. In 1999 he visited Nigeria again after a deliberate nine-year absence to protest government dictatorship, and his homecoming became a national event. In 2007 he was awarded the second Man Booker International Prize for his lifetime contribution to world literature. He died at age 82.*

Michael Obi's hopes were fulfilled much earlier than he had expected. He was appointed headmaster of Ndume Central School in January 1949. It had always been an unprogressive school, so the Mission authorities decided to send a young and energetic man to run it. Obi accepted this responsibility with enthusiasm. He had many wonderful ideas and this was an opportunity to put them into practice. He had had sound secondary school education which designated him a "pivotal teacher" in the official records and set him apart from the other headmasters in the mission field. He was outspoken in his condemnation of the narrow views of these older and often less-educated ones.

"We shall make a good job of it, shan't we?" he asked his young wife when they first heard the joyful news of his promotion.

"We shall do our best," she replied. "We shall have such beautiful gardens and everything will be just *modern* and delightful . . ." In their two years of married life she had become completely infected by his passion for "modern methods" and his denigration of "these old and superannuated people in the teaching field who would be better employed as traders in the Onitsha market." She began to see herself already as the admired wife of the young headmaster, the queen of the school.

The wives of the other teachers would envy her position. She would set the fashion in everything . . . Then, suddenly, it occurred to her that there might not be other wives. Wavering between hope and fear, she asked her husband, looking anxiously at him.

"All our colleagues are young and unmarried," he said with enthusi-   5
asm which for once she did not share. "Which is a good thing," he continued.

"Why?"

"Why? They will give all their time and energy to the school."

Nancy was downcast. For a few minutes she became skeptical about the new school; but it was only for a few minutes. Her little personal misfortune could not blind her to her husband's happy prospects. She looked at him as he sat folded up in a chair. He was stoop-shouldered and looked frail. But he sometimes surprised people with sudden bursts of physical energy. In his present posture, however, all his bodily strength seemed to have retired behind his deep-set eyes, giving them an extraordinary power of penetration. He was only twenty-six, but looked thirty or more. On the whole, he was not unhandsome.

"A penny for your thoughts, Mike," said Nancy after a while, imitating the woman's magazine she read.

"I was thinking what a grand opportunity we've got at last to show   10
these people how a school should be run."

Ndume School was backward in every sense of the word. Mr. Obi put his whole life into the work, and his wife hers too. He had two aims. A high standard of teaching was insisted upon, and the school compound was to be turned into a place of beauty. Nancy's dream-gardens came to life with the coming of the rains, and blossomed. Beautiful hibiscus and allamanda hedges in brilliant red and yellow marked out the carefully tended school compound from the rank neighborhood bushes.

One evening as Obi was admiring his work he was scandalized to see an old woman from the village hobble right across the compound, through a marigold flower-bed and the hedges. On going up there he found faint signs of an almost disused path from the village across the school compound to the bush on the other side.

"It amazes me," said Obi to one of his teachers who had been three years in the school, "that you people allowed the villagers to make use of this footpath. It is simply incredible." He shook his head.

"The path," said the teacher apologetically, "appears to be very important to them. Although it is hardly used, it connects the village shrine with their place of burial."

"And what has that got to do with the school?" asked the headmaster.   15

"Well, I don't know," replied the other with a shrug of the shoulders. "But I remember there was a big row some time ago when we attempted to close it."

"That was some time ago. But it will not be used now," said Obi as he walked away. "What will the Government Education Officer think of this when he comes to inspect the school next week? The villagers might, for all I know, decide to use the schoolroom for a pagan ritual during the inspection."

Heavy sticks were planted closely across the path at the two places where it entered and left the school premises. These were further strengthened with barbed wire.

Three days later the village priest of *Ani* called on the headmaster. He was an old man and walked with a slight stoop. He carried a stout walking-stick which he usually tapped on the floor, by way of emphasis, each time he made a new point in his argument.

"I have heard," he said after the usual exchange of cordialities, "that   20 our ancestral footpath has recently been closed . . ."

"Yes," replied Mr. Obi. "We cannot allow people to make a highway of our school compound."

"Look here, my son," said the priest bringing down his walking-stick, "this path was here before you were born and before your father was born. The whole life of this village depends on it. Our dead relatives depart by it and our ancestors visit us by it. But most important, it is the path of children coming in to be born . . ."

Mr. Obi listened with a satisfied smile on his face.

"The whole purpose of our school," he said finally, "is to eradicate just such beliefs as that. Dead men do not require footpaths. The whole idea is just fantastic. Our duty is to teach your children to laugh at such ideas."

"What you say may be true," replied the priest, "but we follow the   25 practices of our fathers. If you reopen the path we shall have nothing to quarrel about. What I always say is: let the hawk perch and let the eagle perch." He rose to go.

"I am sorry," said the young headmaster. "But the school compound cannot be a thoroughfare. It is against our regulations. I would suggest your constructing another path, skirting our premises. We can even get our boys to help in building it. I don't suppose the ancestors will find the little detour too burdensome."

"I have no more words to say," said the old priest, already outside.

Two days later a young woman in the village died in childbed. A diviner was immediately consulted and he prescribed heavy sacrifices to propitiate ancestors insulted by the fence.

Obi woke up next morning among the ruins of his work. The beautiful hedges were torn up not just near the path but right round the school, the flowers trampled to death and one of the school buildings pulled down . . . . That day, the white Supervisor came to inspect the school and wrote a nasty report on the state of the premises but more seriously about the "tribal-war situation developing between the school and the village, arising in part from the misguided zeal of the new headmaster."

Questions

1. How would you describe the personalities of the main characters Michael Obi and the village priest?
2. What are the new headmaster's motivations for wanting to improve the school?
3. Why does the village priest visit the school? What choice does he offer the headmaster?
4. What significance do you see in the story's title, "Dead Men's Path"?
5. What ironies do you see in the story?
6. What theme in the story seems most important to you? Is it stated anywhere in the story?

Sandra Cisneros

The House on Mango Street   1984

Sandra Cisneros was born in Chicago in 1954. The child of a Mexican father and a Mexican American mother, she was the only daughter in a family of seven children. She attended Loyola University of Chicago and then received a master's degree from the University of Iowa Writers' Workshop. She has instructed high-school dropouts, but more recently she has taught as a visiting writer at numerous universities, including the University of California at Irvine and at Berkeley, and the University of Michigan. Her honors include fellowships from the National Endowment for the Arts and

Sandra Cisneros

the MacArthur Foundation, as well as the American Book Award. Cisneros's first published work was poetry: Bad Boys (1980), followed by My Wicked Wicked Ways (1987) and Loose Woman (1994). Her fiction collections, The House on Mango Street (1984) and Woman Hollering Creek (1991), earned her a broader audience. She has also published a bilingual children's book, Hairs/Pelitos *(1994), and a novel,* Caramelo *(2002). In 2012 she published an illustrated fable for adults,* Have You Seen Marie?, *which was inspired by her mother's death. Cisneros lives in San Antonio, Texas.*

We didn't always live on Mango Street. Before that we lived on Loomis on the third floor, and before that we lived on Keeler. Before Keeler it was Paulina, and before that I can't remember. But what I remember most is moving a lot. Each time it seemed there'd be one more of us. By the time we got to Mango Street we were six—Mama, Papa, Carlos, Kiki, my sister Nenny, and me.

The house on Mango Street is ours, and we don't have to pay rent to anybody, or share the yard with the people downstairs, or be careful not to make too much noise, and there isn't a landlord banging on the ceiling with a broom. But even so, it's not the house we'd thought we'd get.

We had to leave the flat on Loomis quick. The water pipes broke and the landlord wouldn't fix them because the house was too old. We had to leave fast. We were using the washroom next door and carrying water over in empty milk gallons. That's why Mama and Papa looked for a house, and that's why we moved into the house on Mango Street, far away, on the other side of town.

They always told us that one day we would move into a house, a real house that would be ours for always so we wouldn't have to move each year. And our house would have running water and pipes that worked. And inside it would have real stairs, not hallway stairs, but stairs inside like the houses on T.V. And we'd have a basement and at least three washrooms so when we took a bath we wouldn't have to tell everybody. Our house would be white with trees around it, a great big yard and grass growing without a fence. This was the house Papa talked about when he held a lottery ticket and this was the house Mama dreamed up in the stories she told us before we went to bed.

But the house on Mango Street is not the way they told it at all. It's   5
small and red with tight steps in front and windows so small you'd think they are holding their breath. Bricks are crumbling in places, and the front door is so swollen you have to push hard to get in. There is no front yard, only four little elms the city planted by the curb. Out back is a small garage for the car we don't own yet and a small yard that looks smaller between the two buildings on either side. There are stairs in our house, but they're ordinary hallway stairs, and the house has only one washroom. Everybody has to share a bedroom—Mama and Papa, Carlos and Kiki, me and Nenny.

Once when we were living on Loomis, a nun from my school passed by and saw me playing out front. The laundromat downstairs had been boarded up because it had been robbed two days before and the owner had painted on the wood YES WE'RE OPEN so as not to lose business.

Where do you live? she asked.

There, I said pointing up to the third floor.

You live *there*?

There. I had to look to where she pointed—the third floor, the paint peeling, wooden bars Papa had nailed on the windows so we wouldn't fall out. You live *there*? The way she said it made me feel like nothing. *There.* I lived *there*. I nodded. 10

I knew then I had to have a house. A real house. One I could point to. But this isn't it. The house on Mango Street isn't it. For the time being, Mama says. Temporary, says Papa. But I know how those things go.

Questions

1. Identify the point of view of the story. Do you think the narrator is male or female? What details lead you to that conclusion?
2. How old do you think the narrator is? Explain.
3. Does the story rely more on the use of detail or on plot to get its point across?
4. What is the tone of the story? What does the narrator mean by the final sentence?
5. Using the advice earlier in the chapter on "Finding the Theme," how would you state the theme of this story in one sentence?

Luke

The Parable of the Prodigal Son   (King James Version, 1611)

Luke (first century) is traditionally considered the author of the Gospel bearing his name and the Acts of the Apostles in the New Testament. A physician who lived in the Greek city of Antioch (now in Syria), Luke accompanied the Apostle Paul on some of his missionary journeys. Luke's elegantly written Gospel includes some of the Bible's most beloved parables, including that of the Good Samaritan and the Prodigal Son.

And he said, A certain man had two sons: And the younger of them said to his father, Father, give me the portion of goods that falleth to me. And he divided unto them his living. And not many days after the younger son gathered all together, and took his journey into a far country, and there wasted his substance with riotous living. And when he had spent all, there arose a mighty famine in that land; and he began to be in want. And he went and joined himself to a citizen of that country; and he sent him into his fields to feed swine. And he would fain have filled his belly with the husks that the swine did eat: and no man gave unto him. And when he came to himself, he said, How many hired servants of my father's have bread enough and to spare, and I perish with hunger! I will arise and go to my father, and will say unto him, Father I

The Prodigal Son, woodcut by Gustave Doré, 1865.

have sinned against heaven, and before thee, and am no more worthy to be called thy son; make me as one of thy hired servants. And he arose, and came to his father. But when he was yet a great way off, his father saw him, and had compassion, and ran, and fell on his neck, and kissed him. And the son said unto him, Father I have sinned against heaven, and in thy sight, and am no more worthy to be called thy son. But the father said to his servants, Bring forth the best robe, and put it on him; and put a ring on his hand, and shoes on his feet: And bring hither the fatted calf, and kill it; and let us eat, and be merry: For this my son was dead, and is alive again; he was lost, and is found. And they began to be merry. Now his elder son was in the field: and he came and drew nigh to the house, he heard music and dancing. And he called one of the servants, and asked what these things meant. And he said unto him, Thy brother is come; and thy father hath killed the fatted calf, because he hath received him safe and sound. And he was angry, and would not go in: therefore came his father out, and entreated him. And he answering said to his father, Lo, these many years do I serve thee, neither transgressed I at any time thy commandment; and yet thou never gavest me a kid, that I might make merry with my friends: But as soon as this thy son was come, which hath devoured thy living with harlots, thou hast killed for him the fatted calf. And he said unto him, Son thou art ever with me, and all that I have is thine. It was meet that we should make merry, and be glad: for this thy brother was dead, and is alive again; and was lost, and is found.

—Luke 15:11-32

Questions

1. This story has traditionally been called "The Parable of the Prodigal Son." What does *prodigal* mean? Which of the two brothers is prodigal?

2. What position does the younger son expect when he returns to his father's house? What does the father give him?

3. When the older brother sees the celebration for his younger brother's return, he grows angry. He makes a very reasonable set of complaints to his father. He has indeed been a loyal and moral son, but what virtue does the older brother lack?

4. Is the father fair to the elder son? Explain your answer.

5. Theologians have discussed this parable's religious significance for two thousand years. What, in your own words, is the human theme of the story?

Kurt Vonnegut Jr.

Harrison Bergeron   1961

Kurt Vonnegut Jr.

Kurt Vonnegut Jr. (1922–2007) was born in Indianapolis. During the Depression his father, a well-to-do architect, had virtually no work, and the family lived in reduced circumstances. Vonnegut attended Cornell University, where he majored in chemistry and was also managing editor of the daily student newspaper. In 1943 he enlisted in the U.S. Army. During the Battle of the Bulge he was captured by German troops and interned as a prisoner of war in Dresden, where he survived the massive Allied firebombing, which killed tens of thousands of people, mostly civilians. (The firebombing of Dresden became the central incident in Vonnegut's best-selling 1969 novel, Slaughterhouse-Five.*) After the war, Vonnegut worked as a reporter and later as a public relations man for General Electric in Schenectady, New York. He quit his job in 1951 to write full-time after publishing several science fiction stories in national magazines. His first novel,* Player Piano, *appeared in 1952, followed by* Sirens of Titan *(1959) and his first best seller,* Cat's Cradle *(1963)— all now considered classics of literary science fiction. Among his many other books are* Mother Night *(1961),* Jailbird *(1979), and a book of biographical essays,* A Man Without a Country *(2005). His short fiction is collected in*

Welcome to the Monkey House (1968) and Bagombo Snuff Box (1999).
*Vonnegut is a singular figure in modern American fiction. An ingenious comic
writer, he combined the popular genre of science fiction with the literary tradition of dark satire—a combination splendidly realized in "Harrison Bergeron."*

The year was 2081, and everybody was finally equal. They weren't
only equal before God and the law. They were equal every which way.
Nobody was smarter than anybody else. Nobody was better looking than
anybody else. Nobody was stronger or quicker than anybody else. All
this equality was due to the 211th, 212th, and 213th Amendments to
the Constitution, and to the unceasing vigilance of agents of the United
States Handicapper General.

Some things about living still weren't quite right, though. April, for
instance, still drove people crazy by not being springtime. And it was in
that clammy month that the H-G men took George and Hazel Bergeron's
fourteen-year-old son, Harrison, away.

It was tragic, all right, but George and Hazel couldn't think about it
very hard. Hazel had a perfectly average intelligence, which meant she
couldn't think about anything except in short bursts. And George, while
his intelligence was way above normal, had a little mental handicap radio
in his ear. He was required by law to wear it at all times. It was tuned to
a government transmitter. Every twenty seconds or so, the transmitter
would send out some sharp noise to keep people like George from taking
unfair advantage of their brains.

George and Hazel were watching television. There were tears on
Hazel's cheeks, but she'd forgotten for the moment what they were
about.

On the television screen were ballerinas.   5

A buzzer sounded in George's head. His thoughts fled in panic, like
bandits from a burglar alarm.

"That was a real pretty dance, that dance they just did," said Hazel.

"Huh?" said George.

"That dance—it was nice," said Hazel.

"Yup," said George. He tried to think a little about the ballerinas.   10
They weren't really very good—no better than anybody else would have
been, anyway. They were burdened with sashweights and bags of birdshot,
and their faces were masked, so that no one, seeing a free and graceful
gesture or a pretty face, would feel like something the cat drug in. George
was toying with the vague notion that maybe dancers shouldn't be handi-
capped. But he didn't get very far with it before another noise in his ear
radio scattered his thoughts.

George winced. So did two out of the eight ballerinas.

Hazel saw him wince. Having no mental handicap herself, she had to
ask George what the latest sound had been.

"Sounded like somebody hitting a milk bottle with a ball peen hammer," said George.

"I'd think it would be real interesting, hearing all the different sounds," said Hazel, a little envious. "All the things they think up."

"Um," said George.

"Only, if I was Handicapper General, you know what I would do?" said Hazel. Hazel, as a matter of fact, bore a strong resemblance to the Handicapper General, a woman named Diana Moon Glampers. "If I was Diana Moon Glampers," said Hazel, "I'd have chimes on Sunday—just chimes. Kind of in honor of religion."

"I could think, if it was just chimes," said George.

"Well—maybe make 'em real loud," said Hazel. "I think I'd make a good Handicapper General."

"Good as anybody else," said George.

"Who knows better'n I do what normal is?" said Hazel.

"Right," said George. He began to think glimmeringly about his abnormal son who was now in jail, about Harrison, but a twenty-one-gun salute in his head stopped that.

"Boy!" said Hazel, "that was a doozy, wasn't it?"

It was such a doozy that George was white and trembling, and tears stood on the rims of his red eyes. Two of the eight ballerinas had collapsed to the studio floor, were holding their temples.

"All of a sudden you look so tired," said Hazel. "Why don't you stretch out on the sofa, so's you can rest your handicap bag on the pillows, honeybunch." She was referring to the forty-seven pounds of birdshot in a canvas bag, which was padlocked around George's neck. "Go on and rest the bag for a little while," she said. "I don't care if you're not equal to me for a while."

George weighed the bag with his hands. "I don't mind it," he said. "I don't notice it any more. It's just a part of me."

"You been so tired lately—kind of wore out," said Hazel. "If there was just some way we could make a little hole in the bottom of the bag, and just take out a few of them lead balls. Just a few."

"Two years in prison and two thousand dollars fine for every ball I took out," said George. "I don't call that a bargain."

"If you could just take a few out when you came home from work," said Hazel. "I mean—you don't compete with anybody around here. You just set around."

"If I tried to get away with it," said George, "then other people'd get away with it—and pretty soon we'd be right back to the dark ages again, with everybody competing against everybody else. You wouldn't like that, would you?"

"I'd hate it," said Hazel.

"There you are," said George. "The minute people start cheating on laws, what do you think happens to society?"

If Hazel hadn't been able to come up with an answer to this question, George couldn't have supplied one. A siren was going off in his head.

"Reckon it'd fall all apart," said Hazel.

"What would?" said George blankly.

"Society," said Hazel uncertainly. "Wasn't that what you just said?"   35

"Who knows?" said George.

The television program was suddenly interrupted for a news bulletin. It wasn't clear at first as to what the bulletin was about, since the announcer, like all announcers, had a serious speech impediment. For about half a minute, and in a state of high excitement, the announcer tried to say, "Ladies and gentlemen—"

He finally gave up, handed the bulletin to a ballerina to read.

"That's all right—" Hazel said of the announcer, "he tried. That's the big thing. He tried to do the best he could with what God gave him. He should get a nice raise for trying so hard."

"Ladies and gentlemen—" said the ballerina, reading the bulletin.   40
She must have been extraordinarily beautiful, because the mask she wore was hideous. And it was easy to see that she was the strongest and most graceful of all the dancers, for her handicap bags were as big as those worn by two-hundred-pound men.

And she had to apologize at once for her voice, which was a very unfair voice for a woman to use. Her voice was a warm, luminous, timeless melody. "Excuse me—" she said, and she began again, making her voice absolutely uncompetitive.

"Harrison Bergeron, age fourteen," she said in a grackle squawk, "has just escaped from jail, where he was held on suspicion of plotting to overthrow the government. He is a genius and an athlete, is under-handicapped, and should be regarded as extremely dangerous."

A police photograph of Harrison Bergeron was flashed on the screen upside down, then sideways, upside down again, then right side up. The picture showed the full length of Harrison against a background calibrated in feet and inches. He was exactly seven feet tall.

The rest of Harrison's appearance was Halloween and hardware. Nobody had ever borne heavier handicaps. He had outgrown hindrances faster than the H-G men could think them up. Instead of a little ear radio for a mental handicap, he wore a tremendous pair of earphones, and spectacles with thick wavy lenses. The spectacles were intended to make him not only half blind, but to give him whanging headaches besides.

Scrap metal was hung all over him. Ordinarily, there was a certain symmetry, a military neatness to the handicaps issued to strong people, but Harrison looked like a walking junkyard. In the race of life, Harrison carried three hundred pounds.   45

And to offset his good looks, the H-G men required that he wear at all times a red rubber ball for a nose, keep his eyebrows shaved off, and cover his even white teeth with black caps at snaggle-tooth random.

"If you see this boy," said the ballerina, "do not—I repeat, do not—try to reason with him."

There was the shriek of a door being torn from its hinges.

Screams and barking cries of consternation came from the television set. The photograph of Harrison Bergeron on the screen jumped again and again, as though dancing to the tune of an earthquake.

George Bergeron correctly identified the earthquake, and well he   50 might have—for many was the time his own home had danced to the same crashing tune. "My God—" said George, "that must be Harrison!"

The realization was blasted from his mind instantly by the sound of an automobile collision in his head.

When George could open his eyes again, the photograph of Harrison was gone. A living, breathing Harrison filled the screen.

Clanking, clownish, and huge, Harrison stood in the center of the studio. The knob of the uprooted studio door was still in his hand. Ballerinas, technicians, musicians, and announcers cowered on their knees before him, expecting to die.

"I am the Emperor!" cried Harrison. "Do you hear? I am the Emperor! Everybody must do what I say at once!" He stamped his foot and the studio shook.

"Even as I stand here—" he bellowed, "crippled, hobbled, sickened—I   55 am a greater ruler than any man who ever lived! Now watch me become what I *can* become!"

Harrison tore the straps of his handicap harness like wet tissue paper, tore straps guaranteed to support five thousand pounds.

Harrison's scrap-iron handicaps crashed to the floor.

Harrison thrust his thumbs under the bar of the padlock that secured his head harness. The bar snapped like celery. Harrison smashed his headphones and spectacles against the wall.

He flung away his rubber-ball nose, revealed a man that would have awed Thor, the god of thunder.

"I shall now select my Empress!" he said, looking down on the cower-   60 ing people. "Let the first woman who dares rise to her feet claim her mate and her throne!"

A moment passed, and then a ballerina arose, swaying like a willow.

Harrison plucked the mental handicap from her ear, snapped off her physical handicaps with marvelous delicacy. Last of all, he removed her mask.

She was blindingly beautiful.

"Now—" said Harrison, taking her hand, "shall we show the people the meaning of the word dance? Music!" he commanded.

The musicians scrambled back into their chairs, and Harrison 65
stripped them of their handicaps, too. "Play your best," he told them,
"and I'll make you barons and dukes and earls."

The music began. It was normal at first—cheap, silly, false. But Harrison snatched two musicians from their chairs, waved them like batons
as he sang the music as he wanted it played. He slammed them back into
their chairs.

The music began again and was much improved.

Harrison and his Empress merely listened to the music for a while—
listened gravely, as though synchronizing their heartbeats with it.

They shifted their weights to their toes.

Harrison placed his big hands on the girl's tiny waist, letting her sense 70
the weightlessness that would soon be hers.

And then, in an explosion of joy and grace, into the air they sprang!

Not only were the laws of the land abandoned, but the law of gravity
and the laws of motion as well.

They reeled, whirled, swiveled, flounced, capered, gamboled, and
spun.

They leaped like deer on the moon.

The studio ceiling was thirty feet high, but each leap brought the 75
dancers nearer to it.

It became their obvious intention to kiss the ceiling.

They kissed it.

And then, neutralizing gravity with love and pure will, they remained
suspended in air inches below the ceiling, and they kissed each other for
a long, long time.

It was then that Diana Moon Glampers, the Handicapper General,
came into the studio with a double-barreled ten-gauge shotgun. She fired
twice, and the Emperor and the Empress were dead before they hit the
floor.

Diana Moon Glampers loaded the gun again. She aimed it at the 80
musicians and told them they had ten seconds to get their handicaps
back on.

It was then that the Bergerons' television tube burned out.

Hazel turned to comment about the blackout to George. But George
had gone out into the kitchen for a can of beer.

George came back in with the beer, paused while a handicap signal
shook him up. And then he sat down again. "You been crying?" he said
to Hazel.

"Yup," she said.

"What about?" he said.

"I forget," she said. "Something real sad on television." 85

"What was it?" he said.

"It's all kind of mixed up in my mind," said Hazel.

"Forget sad things," said George.

"I always do," said Hazel.   90

"That's my girl," said George. He winced. There was the sound of a rivetting gun in his head.

"Gee—I could tell that one was a doozy," said Hazel.

"You can say that again," said George.

"Gee—" said Hazel, "I could tell that one was a doozy."

Questions

1. What tendencies in present-day American society is Vonnegut satirizing? Does the story argue *for* anything? How would you sum up its theme?

2. Is Diana Moon Glampers a "flat" or a "round" character? (If you need to review these terms, see the discussion of character in Chapter 3.) Would you call Vonnegut's characterization of her "realistic"? If not, why doesn't it need to be?

3. From what point of view is the story told? Why is it more effective than if Harrison Bergeron had told his own story in the first person?

4. Two sympathetic critics of Vonnegut's work, Karen and Charles Wood, have said of his stories: "Vonnegut proves repeatedly . . . that men and women remain fundamentally the same, no matter what technology surrounds them." Try applying this comment to "Harrison Bergeron." Do you agree?

5. Stanislaw Lem, Polish author of *Solaris* and other novels, once made this thoughtful criticism of many of his contemporaries among science fiction writers:

> The revolt against the machine and against civilization, the praise of the "aesthetic" nature of catastrophe, the dead-end course of human civilization—these are their foremost problems, the intellectual content of their works. Such SF is as it were *a priori* vitiated by pessimism, in the sense that anything that may happen will be for the worse. ("The Time-Travel Story and Related Matters of SF Structuring," *Science Fiction Studies* 1 [1974], 143–54.)

How might Lem's objection be raised against "Harrison Bergeron"? In your opinion, does it negate the value of Vonnegut's story?

■ WRITING *effectively*

THINKING ABOUT THEME

A clear, precise statement about a story's theme can serve as a promising thesis for a writing assignment. After you read a short story, you will probably have some vague sense of its theme—the central unifying idea, or the point of the story. How do you hone that vague sense of theme into a sharp and intriguing thesis?

- **Start by making a list of phrases or ideas that suggest the story's possible theme.** If you are discussing Chinua Achebe's "Dead Men's Path," your initial list might look like this:

    new ideas versus tradition
    danger of inflexibility
    importance of compromise
    necessity of inclusiveness
    stubbornness of youth
    changing cultures
    wisdom of elders

- **Choose the most important points and then combine them into a single sentence.** For Achebe, you might have circled "new ideas versus tradition," "importance of compromise," and "necessity of inclusiveness," and your summary might be this:

    The central theme of "Dead Men's Path" is that lasting progress is best made in a spirit of compromise and inclusivity, not by insensitivity to the feelings of those who follow the old ways.

- **Refine your sentence to capture the story's essence as clearly and specifically as possible.** Remember, your goal is to transcend a mere one-sentence plot summary. How can you clearly express the central theme in a few words? Your refinement might read as follows:

    The theme of "Dead Men's Path" is that progress requires compromise and inclusiveness, which recognizes the feelings of those who follow the old ways.

CHECKLIST: Writing About Theme

☐ List as many possible themes as you can.

☐ Circle the two or three most important points and try to combine them into a sentence.

☐ Relate particular details of the story to the theme you have spelled out. Consider plot details, dialogue, setting, point of view, title—any elements that seem especially pertinent.

☐ Check whether all the elements of the story fit your thesis.

☐ Have you missed an important aspect of the story? Or, have you chosen to focus on a secondary idea, overlooking the central one?

☐ If necessary, rework your thesis until it applies to every element in the story.

TOPICS FOR WRITING ON THEME

1. Choose a story that catches your attention, and go through the steps outlined above to develop a strong thesis sentence about the story's theme. Then flesh out your argument into an essay, supporting your thesis with evidence from the text, including quotations. Some good story choices might be "A Clean, Well-Lighted Place," "The Chrysanthemums," "A Good Man Is Hard to Find," and "The Lottery."

2. Define the central theme of "Harrison Bergeron." Is Vonnegut's early-1960s vision of the future still relevant today? Why or why not?

3. Does the house in "The House on Mango Street" represent something larger than simply a dwelling? How would you describe the narrator's outlook on life? Use examples from the story to support your argument.

4. A recent *Time* magazine article describes a young California woman who distanced herself from her Chinese heritage until reading *The Joy Luck Club* "turned her into a 'born-again Asian.' It gave her new insights into why her mom was so hard on her and why the ways she showed love—say, through food—were different from those of the families [she] saw on TV, who seemed to say 'I love you' all day long." Have you ever had a similar experience, in which something you read gave you a better understanding of a loved one, or even yourself?

▶ TERMS FOR *review*

Summary ▶ A brief condensation of the main idea or plot of a literary work. A summary is similar to a paraphrase, but less detailed.

Theme ▶ The main idea or larger meaning of a work of literature. A theme may be a message or a moral, but it is more likely to be a central, unifying insight or viewpoint.

7

SYMBOL

What You Will Learn in This Chapter

- To recognize and define a literary *symbol*
- To explain allegory and describe its characteristics
- To identify and describe symbolic characters and symbolic acts
- To analyze a symbol's role in a story

In F. Scott Fitzgerald's novel *The Great Gatsby*, a huge pair of bespectacled eyes stares across a wilderness of ash heaps, from a billboard advertising the services of an oculist. Repeatedly entering into the story, the advertisement comes to mean more than simply the availability of eye examinations. Fitzgerald has a character liken it to the eyes of God; he hints that some sad, compassionate spirit is brooding as it watches the passing procession of humanity. Such an object is a **symbol**: in literature, a person, place, or thing that suggests more than its literal meaning. Symbols generally do not "stand for" any single meaning, nor for anything absolutely definite; they point, they hint, or, as Henry James put it, they cast long shadows. To take a large example: in Herman Melville's *Moby-Dick*, the great white whale of the book's title apparently means more than the literal dictionary-definition meaning of an aquatic mammal. He also suggests more than the devil, to whom some of the characters liken him. The great whale, as the story unfolds, comes to imply an amplitude of meanings, among them the forces of nature and the whole created universe.

ALLEGORY

This indefinite multiplicity of meanings is characteristic of a symbolic story and distinguishes it from an **allegory**, a story in which persons, places, and things form a system of clearly labeled equivalents. In a simple allegory, characters and other elements often stand for other definite meanings, which are often abstractions. You will meet such a character in another story in this book, Nathaniel Hawthorne's "Young Goodman Brown" (Chapter 8). This tale's main female character, Faith, represents the religious virtue suggested by her name. Supreme allegories are found in some biblical parables ("The Kingdom of Heaven is like a man who sowed good seed in his field . . . ," Matthew 13:24–30).

203

A classic allegory is the medieval play *Everyman*, whose hero represents us all, and who, deserted by false friends called Kindred and Goods, faces the judgment of God accompanied only by a faithful friend called Good Deeds. In John Bunyan's seventeenth-century allegory *Pilgrim's Progress*, the protagonist, Christian, struggles along the difficult road toward salvation, meeting along the way persons such as Mr. Worldly Wiseman, who directs him into a more comfortable path (a wrong turn), and the residents of a town called Fair Speech, among them a hypocrite named Mr. Facing-both-ways. Not all allegories are simple: Dante's *Divine Comedy*, written during the Middle Ages, continues to reveal new meanings to careful readers. Allegory was much beloved in the Middle Ages, but in contemporary fiction it is rare. One modern instance is George Orwell's long fable *Animal Farm*, in which (among its double meanings) barnyard animals stand for human victims and totalitarian oppressors.

SYMBOLS

Symbols in fiction are not generally abstract terms such as *love* or *truth*, but are likely to be perceptible objects. In William Faulkner's "A Rose for Emily" (Chapter 2), Miss Emily's invisible watch ticking at the end of a golden chain not only indicates the passage of time, but also suggests that time passes without even being noticed by the watch's owner, and the golden chain carries suggestions of wealth and authority. Objects (and creatures) that seem insignificant in themselves can take on a symbolic importance in the larger context.

Often the symbols we meet in fiction are inanimate objects, but other things also may function symbolically. In James Joyce's "Araby" (Chapter 8), the very name of the bazaar, Araby—the poetic name for Arabia—suggests magic, romance, and *The Arabian Nights*; its syllables (the narrator tells us) "cast an Eastern enchantment over me." Even a locale, or a feature of physical topography, can provide rich suggestions. Recall Ernest Hemingway's "A Clean, Well-Lighted Place" (Chapter 5), in which the café is not merely a café, but an island of refuge from night, chaos, loneliness, old age, and impending death.

Symbolic Characters

In some novels and stories, symbolic characters make brief cameo appearances. Such characters often are not well-rounded and fully known, but are seen fleetingly and remain slightly mysterious. Usually such a symbolic character is more a portrait than a person—or somewhat portraitlike, as Faulkner's Miss Emily, who twice appears at a window of her house "like the carven torso of an idol in a niche." Though Faulkner invests Miss Emily with life and vigor, he also clothes her in symbolic hints: she seems almost to personify the vanishing aristocracy of the antebellum South, still maintaining a black servant and being ruthlessly betrayed by a moneymaking Yankee. Sometimes a part of a character's body or an attribute may convey symbolic meaning: a baleful eye, as in Edgar Allan Poe's "The Tell-Tale Heart" (Chapter 2).

Symbolic Acts

Much as a symbolic whale holds more meaning than an ordinary whale, a **symbolic act** is a gesture with larger significance than usual. For the boy's father in Faulkner's "Barn Burning" (Chapter 5), the act of destroying a barn is no mere act of spite, but an expression of his profound hatred for anything not belonging to him. Faulkner adds that burning a barn reflects the father's memories of the "waste and extravagance of war," and further adds that "the element of fire spoke to some deep mainspring" in his being. A symbolic act, however, doesn't have to be a gesture as large as starting a conflagration. Before setting out in pursuit of the great white whale, Melville's Captain Ahab in *Moby-Dick* deliberately snaps his tobacco pipe and throws it away, as if to suggest (among other things) that he will let no pleasure or pastime distract him from his vengeance.

Why Use Symbols?

Why do writers have to symbolize—why don't they tell us outright? One advantage of a symbol is that it is so compact, and yet so fully laden. Both starkly concrete and slightly mysterious, like Miss Emily's invisible ticking watch, it may impress us with all the force of something beheld in a dream or in a nightmare. The watch suggests, among other things, the slow and invisible passage of time. What this symbol says, it says more fully and more memorably than could be said, perhaps, in a long essay on the subject.

To some extent (it may be claimed), all stories are symbolic. Merely by holding up for our inspection these characters and their actions, the writer lends them *some* special significance. But this is to think of *symbol* in an extremely broad and inclusive way. For the usual purposes of reading a story and understanding it, there is probably little point in looking for symbolism in every word, in every stick or stone, in every striking of a match, in every minor character. Still, to be on the alert for symbols when reading fiction is perhaps wiser than to ignore them. Not to admit that symbolic meanings may be present, or to refuse to think about them, would be another way to misread a story—or to read no further than its outer edges.

RECOGNIZING SYMBOLS

How, then, do you recognize a symbol in fiction when you meet it? Fortunately, the storyteller often gives the symbol particular emphasis. It may be mentioned repeatedly throughout the story; it may even supply the story with a title ("Barn Burning," "A Clean, Well-Lighted Place," "Araby"). At times, a crucial symbol will open a story or end it. Unless an object, act, or character is given some such special emphasis and importance, we may generally feel safe in taking it at face value. Probably it isn't a symbol if it points clearly and unmistakably toward some one meaning, like a whistle in a factory, whose blast at noon means lunch. But an object, an act, or a character is surely symbolic (and almost as surely displays high literary art) if, when we finish the story, we realize that it was that item—that gigantic eye; that clean, well-lighted café; that burning of a barn—which led us to the author's theme, the essential meaning.

John Steinbeck

The Chrysanthemums   1938

John Steinbeck (1902–1968) was born in Salinas, California, in the fertile valley he remembers in "The Chrysanthemums." Off and on, he attended Stanford University, and then he sojourned in New York as a reporter and a bricklayer. After years of struggle to earn his living by fiction, Steinbeck reached a large audience with Tortilla Flat *(1935), a loosely woven novel portraying Mexican Americans in Monterey with fondness and sympathy. Great acclaim greeted* The Grapes of Wrath *(1939), the story of a family of Oklahoma farmers who, ruined by dust storms in the 1930s, join a mass migration to California.*

John Steinbeck

In 1962 he became the seventh American to win the Nobel Prize in Literature, but critics have never placed Steinbeck on the same high shelf as Faulkner and Hemingway. He wrote much, not all good, and yet his best work adds up to an impressive total. Besides The Grapes of Wrath, *it includes* In Dubious Battle *(1936), a novel of an apple-pickers' strike;* Of Mice and Men *(1937), a powerful short novel of comradeship between a hobo and a man; and the short stories in* The Long Valley *(1938). Throughout the fiction he wrote in his prime, Steinbeck maintains an appealing sympathy for the poor and downtrodden, the lonely and dispossessed.*

The high grey-flannel fog of winter closed off the Salinas Valley° from the sky and from all the rest of the world. On every side it sat like a lid on the mountains and made of the great valley a closed pot. On the broad, level land floor the gang plows bit deep and left the black earth shining like metal where the shares had cut. On the foothill ranches across the Salinas River, the yellow stubble fields seemed to be bathed in pale cold sunshine, but there was no sunshine in the valley now in December. The thick willow scrub along the river flamed with sharp and positive yellow leaves.

Salinas Valley: south of San Francisco in the Coast Ranges region of California.

It was a time of quiet and of waiting. The air was cold and tender. A light wind blew up from the southwest so that the farmers were mildly hopeful of a good rain before long; but fog and rain do not go together.

Across the river, on Henry Allen's foothill ranch there was little work to be done, for the hay was cut and stored and the orchards were plowed up to receive the rain deeply when it should come. The cattle on the higher slopes were becoming shaggy and rough-coated.

Elisa Allen, working in her flower garden, looked down across the yard and saw Henry, her husband, talking to two men in business suits. The three of them stood by the tractor shed, each man with one foot on the side of the little Fordson. They smoked cigarettes and studied the machine as they talked.

Elisa watched them for a moment and then went back to her work.   5
She was thirty-five. Her face was lean and strong and her eyes were as clear as water. Her figure looked blocked and heavy in her gardening costume, a man's black hat pulled low down over her eyes, clodhopper shoes, a figured print dress almost completely covered by a big corduroy apron with four big pockets to hold the snips, the trowel and scratcher, the seeds and the knife she worked with. She wore heavy leather gloves to protect her hands while she worked.

She was cutting down the old year's chrysanthemum stalks with a pair of short and powerful scissors. She looked down toward the men by the tractor shed now and then. Her face was eager and mature and handsome; even her work with the scissors was over-eager, over-powerful. The chrysanthemum stems seemed too small and easy for her energy.

She brushed a cloud of hair out of her eyes with the back of her glove, and left a smudge of earth on her cheek in doing it. Behind her stood the neat white farm house with red geraniums close-banked around it as high as the windows. It was a hard-swept looking little house with hard-polished windows, and a clean mud-mat on the front steps.

Elisa cast another glance toward the tractor shed. The strangers were getting into their Ford coupe. She took off a glove and put her strong fingers down into the forest of new green chrysanthemum sprouts that were growing around the old roots. She spread the leaves and looked down among the close-growing stems. No aphids were there, no sowbugs or snails or cutworms. Her terrier fingers destroyed such pests before they could get started.

Elisa started at the sound of her husband's voice. He had come near quietly, and he leaned over the wire fence that protected her flower garden from cattle and dogs and chickens.

"At it again," he said. "You've got a strong new crop coming."   10
Elisa straightened her back and pulled on the gardening glove again. "Yes. They'll be strong this coming year." In her tone and on her face there was a little smugness.

"You've got a gift with things," Henry observed. "Some of those yellow chrysanthemums you had this year were ten inches across. I wish you'd work out in the orchard and raise some apples that big."

Her eyes sharpened. "Maybe I could do it, too. I've a gift with things, all right. My mother had it. She could stick anything in the ground and make it grow. She said it was having planters' hands that knew how to do it."

"Well, it sure works with flowers," he said.

"Henry, who were those men you were talking to?"   15

"Why, sure, that's what I came to tell you. They were from the Western Meat Company. I sold those thirty head of three-year-old steers. Got nearly my own price, too."

"Good," she said. "Good for you."

"And I thought," he continued, "I thought how it's Saturday afternoon, and we might go into Salinas for dinner at a restaurant, and then to a picture show—to celebrate, you see."

"Good," she repeated. "Oh, yes. That will be good."

Henry put on his joking tone. "There's fights tonight. How'd you like   20
to go to the fights?"

"Oh, no," she said breathlessly. "No, I wouldn't like fights."

"Just fooling, Elisa. We'll go to a movie. Let's see. It's two now. I'm going to take Scotty and bring down those steers from the hill. It'll take us maybe two hours. We'll go in town about five and have dinner at the Cominos Hotel. Like that?"

"Of course I'll like it. It's good to eat away from home."

"All right, then. I'll go get up a couple of horses."

She said, "I'll have plenty of time to transplant some of these sets, I   25
guess."

She heard her husband calling Scotty down by the barn. And a little later she saw the two men ride up the pale yellow hillside in search of the steers.

There was a little square sandy bed kept for rooting the chrysanthemums. With her trowel she turned the soil over and over, and smoothed it and patted it firm. Then she dug ten parallel trenches to receive the sets. Back at the chrysanthemum bed she pulled out the little crisp shoots, trimmed off the leaves of each one with her scissors and laid it on a small orderly pile.

A squeak of wheels and plod of hoofs came from the road. Elisa looked up. The country road ran along the dense bank of willows and cottonwoods that bordered the river, and up this road came a curious vehicle, curiously drawn. It was an old spring-wagon, with a round canvas top on it like the cover of a prairie schooner. It was drawn by an old bay horse and a little grey-and-white burro. A big stubble-bearded man sat between the cover flaps and drove the crawling team. Underneath the wagon, between the hind wheels, a lean and rangy mongrel dog walked sedately. Words were painted on the canvas, in clumsy, crooked letters. "Pots, pans, knives, sisors, lawn mores, Fixed." Two rows of articles, and the triumphantly definitive "Fixed" below. The black paint had run down in little sharp points beneath each letter.

Elisa, squatting on the ground, watched to see the crazy, loose-jointed wagon pass by. But it didn't pass. It turned into the farm road in front of her house, crooked old wheels skirling and squeaking. The rangy dog darted from between the wheels and ran ahead. Instantly the two ranch shepherds flew out at him. Then all three stopped, and with stiff and quivering tails, with taut straight legs, with ambassadorial dignity, they slowly circled, sniffing daintily. The caravan pulled up to Elisa's wire fence and stopped. Now the newcomer dog, feeling out-numbered, lowered his tail and retired under the wagon with raised hackles and bared teeth.

The man on the wagon seat called out, "That's a bad dog in a fight   30 when he gets started."

Elisa laughed. "I see he is. How soon does he generally get started?"

The man caught up her laughter and echoed it heartily. "Sometimes not for weeks and weeks," he said. He climbed stiffly down, over the wheel. The horse and the donkey drooped like unwatered flowers.

Elisa saw that he was a very big man. Although his hair and beard were greying, he did not look old. His worn black suit was wrinkled and spotted with grease. The laughter had disappeared from his face and eyes the moment his laughing voice ceased. His eyes were dark, and they were full of the brooding that gets in the eyes of teamsters and of sailors. The calloused hands he rested on the wire fence were cracked, and every crack was a black line. He took off his battered hat.

"I'm off my general road, ma'am," he said. "Does this dirt road cut over across the river to the Los Angeles highway?"

Elisa stood up and shoved the thick scissors in her apron pocket.   35 "Well, yes, it does, but it winds around and then fords the river. I don't think your team could pull through the sand."

He replied with some asperity, "It might surprise you what them beasts can pull through."

"When they get started?" she asked.

He smiled for a second. "Yes. When they get started."

"Well," said Elisa, "I think you'll save time if you go back to the Salinas road and pick up the highway there."

He drew a big finger down the chicken wire and made it sing. "I   40 ain't in any hurry, ma'am. I go from Seattle to San Diego and back every year. Takes all my time. About six months each way. I aim to follow nice weather."

Elisa took off her gloves and stuffed them in the apron pocket with the scissors. She touched the under edge of her man's hat, searching for fugitive hairs. "That sounds like a nice kind of a way to live," she said.

He leaned confidentially over the fence. "Maybe you noticed the writing on my wagon. I mend pots and sharpen knives and scissors. You got any of them things to do?"

"Oh, no," she said quickly. "Nothing like that." Her eyes hardened with resistance.

"Scissors is the worst thing," he explained. "Most people just ruin scissors trying to sharpen 'em, but I know how. I got a special tool. It's a little bobbit kind of thing, and patented. But it sure does the trick."

"No. My scissors are all sharp." 45

"All right, then. Take a pot," he continued earnestly, "a bent pot, or a pot with a hole. I can make it like new so you don't have to buy no new ones. That's a saving for you."

"No," she said shortly. "I tell you I have nothing like that for you to do."

His face fell to an exaggerated sadness. His voice took on a whining undertone. "I ain't had a thing to do today. Maybe I won't have no supper tonight. You see I'm off my regular road. I know folks on the highway clear from Seattle to San Diego. They save their things for me to sharpen up because they know I do it so good and save them money."

"I'm sorry," Elisa said irritably. "I haven't anything for you to do."

His eyes left her face and fell to searching the ground. They roamed 50 about until they came to the chrysanthemum bed where she had been working. "What's them plants, ma'am?"

The irritation and resistance melted from Elisa's face. "Oh, those are chrysanthemums, giant whites and yellows. I raise them every year, bigger than anybody around here."

"Kind of a long-stemmed flower? Looks like a quick puff of colored smoke?" he asked.

"That's it. What a nice way to describe them."

"They smell kind of nasty till you get used to them," he said.

"It's a good bitter smell," she retorted, "not nasty at all." 55

He changed his tone quickly. "I like the smell myself."

"I had ten-inch blooms this year," she said.

The man leaned farther over the fence. "Look. I know a lady down the road a piece, has got the nicest garden you ever seen. Got nearly every kind of flower but no chrysanthemums. Last time I was mending a copper-bottom washtub for her (that's a hard job but I do it good), she said to me, 'If you ever run acrost some nice chrysanthemums I wish you'd try to get me a few seeds.' That's what she told me."

Elisa's eyes grew alert and eager. "She couldn't have known much about chrysanthemums. You *can* raise them from seed, but it's much easier to root the little sprouts you see there."

"Oh," he said. "I s'pose I can't take none to her, then." 60

"Why yes you can," Elisa cried. "I can put some in damp sand, and you can carry them right along with you. They'll take root in the pot if you keep them damp. And then she can transplant them."

"She'd sure like to have some, ma'am. You say they're nice ones?"

"Beautiful," she said. "Oh, beautiful." Her eyes shone. She tore off the battered hat and shook out her dark pretty hair. "I'll put them in a flower pot, and you can take them right with you. Come into the yard."

While the man came through the picket gate Elisa ran excitedly along the geranium-bordered path to the back of the house. And she returned carrying a big red flower pot. The gloves were forgotten now. She kneeled on the ground by the starting bed and dug up the sandy soil with her fingers and scooped it into the bright new flower pot. Then she picked up the little pile of shoots she had prepared. With her strong fingers she pressed them in the sand and tamped around them with her knuckles. The man stood over her. "I'll tell you what to do," she said. "You remember so you can tell the lady."

"Yes, I'll try to remember."

"Well, look. These will take root in about a month. Then she must set them out, about a foot apart in good rich earth like this, see?" She lifted a handful of dark soil for him to look at. "They'll grow fast and tall. Now remember this: In July tell her to cut them down, about eight inches from the ground."

"Before they bloom?" he asked.

"Yes, before they bloom." Her face was tight with eagerness. "They'll grow right up again. About the last of September the buds will start."

She stopped and seemed perplexed. "It's the budding that takes the most care," she said hesitantly. "I don't know how to tell you." She looked deep into his eyes, searchingly. Her mouth opened a little, and she seemed to be listening. "I'll try to tell you," she said. "Did you ever hear of planting hands?"

"Can't say I have, ma'am."

"Well, I can only tell you what it feels like. It's when you're picking off the buds you don't want. Everything goes right down into your fingertips. You watch your fingers work. They do it themselves. You can feel how it is. They pick and pick the buds. They never make a mistake. They're with the plant. Do you see? Your fingers and the plant. You can feel that, right up your arm. They know. They never make a mistake. You can feel it. When you're like that you can't do anything wrong. Do you see that? Can you understand that?"

She was kneeling on the ground looking up at him. Her breast swelled passionately.

The man's eyes narrowed. He looked away self-consciously. "Maybe I know," he said. "Sometimes in the night in the wagon there—"

Elisa's voice grew husky. She broke in on him, "I've never lived as you do, but I know what you mean. When the night is dark—why, the stars are sharp-pointed, and there's quiet. Why, you rise up and up! Every pointed star gets driven into your body. It's like that. Hot and sharp and—lovely."

Kneeling there, her hand went out toward his legs in the greasy black trousers. Her hesitant fingers almost touched the cloth. Then her hand dropped to the ground. She crouched low like a fawning dog.

He said, "It's nice, just like you say. Only when you don't have no dinner, it ain't."

She stood up then, very straight, and her face was ashamed. She held the flower pot out to him and placed it gently in his arms. "Here. Put it in your wagon, on the seat, where you can watch it. Maybe I can find something for you to do."

At the back of the house she dug in the can pile and found two old and battered aluminum saucepans. She carried them back and gave them to him. "Here, maybe you can fix these."

His manner changed. He became professional. "Good as new I can fix them." At the back of his wagon he set a little anvil, and out of an oily tool box dug a small machine hammer. Elisa came through the gate to watch him while he pounded out the dents in the kettles. His mouth grew sure and knowing. At a difficult part of the work he sucked his under-lip.

"You sleep right in the wagon?" Elisa asked. 80

"Right in the wagon, ma'am. Rain or shine I'm dry as a cow in there."

"It must be nice," she said. "It must be very nice. I wish women could do such things."

"It ain't the right kind of a life for a woman."

Her upper lip raised a little, showing her teeth. "How do you know? How can you tell?" she said.

"I don't know, ma'am," he protested. "Of course I don't know. Now 85 here's your kettles, done. You don't have to buy no new ones."

"How much?"

"Oh, fifty cents'll do. I keep my prices down and my work good. That's why I have all them satisfied customers up and down the highway."

Elisa brought him a fifty-cent piece from the house and dropped it in his hand. "You might be surprised to have a rival some time. I can sharpen scissors, too. And I can beat the dents out of little pots. I could show you what a woman might do."

He put his hammer back in the oily box and shoved the little anvil out of sight. "It would be a lonely life for a woman, ma'am, and a scarey life, too, with animals creeping under the wagon all night." He climbed over the singletree, steadying himself with a hand on the burro's white rump. He settled himself in the seat, picked up the lines. "Thank you kindly, ma'am," he said. "I'll do like you told me; I'll go back and catch the Salinas road."

"Mind," she called, "if you're long in getting there, keep the sand damp." 90

"Sand, ma'am? . . . Sand? Oh, sure. You mean around the chrysanthemums. Sure I will." He clucked his tongue. The beasts leaned luxuriously into their collars. The mongrel dog took his place between the back wheels. The wagon turned and crawled out the entrance road and back the way it had come, along the river.

Elisa stood in front of her wire fence watching the slow progress of the caravan. Her shoulders were straight, her head thrown back, her eyes half-closed, so that the scene came vaguely into them. Her lips moved silently, forming the words "Good-bye—good-bye." Then she whispered, "That's a bright direction. There's a glowing there." The sound of her whisper startled her. She shook herself free and looked about to see whether anyone had been listening. Only the dogs had heard. They lifted their heads toward her from their sleeping in the dust, and then stretched out their chins and settled asleep again. Elisa turned and ran hurriedly into the house.

In the kitchen she reached behind the stove and felt the water tank. It was full of hot water from the noonday cooking. In the bathroom she tore off her soiled clothes and flung them into the corner. And then she scrubbed herself with a little block of pumice, legs and thighs, loins and chest and arms, until her skin was scratched and red. When she had dried herself she stood in front of a mirror in her bedroom and looked at her body. She tightened her stomach and threw out her chest. She turned and looked over her shoulder at her back.

After a while she began to dress, slowly. She put on her newest underclothing and her nicest stockings and the dress which was the symbol of her prettiness. She worked carefully on her hair, penciled her eyebrows and rouged her lips.

Before she was finished she heard the little thunder of hoofs and the shouts of Henry and his helper as they drove the red steers into the corral. She heard the gate bang shut and set herself for Henry's arrival. 95

His step sounded on the porch. He entered the house calling, "Elisa, where are you?"

"In my room, dressing. I'm not ready. There's hot water for your bath. Hurry up. It's getting late."

When she heard him splashing in the tub, Elisa laid his dark suit on the bed, and shirt and socks and tie beside it. She stood his polished shoes on the floor beside the bed. Then she went to the porch and sat primly and stiffly down. She looked toward the river road where the willow-line was still yellow with frosted leaves so that under the high grey fog they seemed a thin band of sunshine. This was the only color in the grey afternoon. She sat unmoving for a long time. Her eyes blinked rarely.

Henry came banging out of the door, shoving his tie inside his vest as he came. Elisa stiffened and her face grew tight. Henry stopped short and looked at her. "Why—why, Elisa. You look so nice!"

"Nice? You think I look nice? What do you mean by 'nice'?" 100

Henry blundered on. "I don't know. I mean you look different, strong and happy."

"I am strong? Yes, strong. What do you mean 'strong'?"

He looked bewildered. "You're playing some kind of a game," he said helplessly. "It's a kind of a play. You look strong enough to break a calf over your knee, happy enough to eat it like a watermelon."

For a second she lost her rigidity. "Henry! Don't talk like that. You didn't know what you said." She grew complete again. "I'm strong," she boasted. "I never knew before how strong."

Henry looked down toward the tractor shed, and when he brought 105 his eyes back to her, they were his own again. "I'll get out the car. You can put on your coat while I'm starting."

Elisa went into the house. She heard him drive to the gate and idle down his motor, and then she took a long time to put on her hat. She pulled it here and pressed it there. When Henry turned the motor off she slipped into her coat and went out.

The little roadster bounced along on the dirt road by the river, raising the birds and driving the rabbits into the brush. Two cranes flapped heavily over the willow-line and dropped into the river-bed.

Far ahead on the road Elisa saw a dark speck. She knew.

She tried not to look as they passed it, but her eyes would not obey. She whispered to herself sadly, "He might have thrown them off the road. That wouldn't have been much trouble, not very much. But he kept the pot," she explained. "He had to keep the pot. That's why he couldn't get them off the road."

The roadster turned a bend and she saw the caravan ahead. She 110 swung full around toward her husband so she could not see the little covered wagon and the mismatched team as the car passed them.

In a moment it was over. The thing was done. She did not look back.

She said loudly, to be heard above the motor, "It will be good, tonight, a good dinner."

"Now you're changed again," Henry complained. He took one hand from the wheel and patted her knee. "I ought to take you in to dinner oftener. It would be good for both of us. We get so heavy out on the ranch."

"Henry," she asked, "could we have wine at dinner?"

"Sure we could. Say! That will be fine." 115

She was silent for a while; then she said, "Henry, at those prize fights, do the men hurt each other very much?"

"Sometimes a little, not often. Why?"

"Well, I've read how they break noses, and blood runs down their chests. I've read how the fighting gloves get heavy and soggy with blood."

He looked around at her. "What's the matter, Elisa? I didn't know you read things like that." He brought the car to a stop, then turned to the right over the Salinas River bridge.

"Do any women ever go to the fights?" she asked. 120

"Oh, sure, some. What's the matter, Elisa? Do you want to go? I don't think you'd like it, but I'll take you if you really want to go."

She relaxed limply in the seat. "Oh, no. No. I don't want to go. I'm sure I don't." Her face was turned away from him. "It will be enough if we can have wine. It will be plenty." She turned up her coat collar so he could not see that she was crying weakly—like an old woman.

Questions

1. When we first meet Elisa Allen in her garden, with what details does Steinbeck delineate her character for us?
2. Elisa works inside a "wire fence that protected her flower garden from cattle and dogs and chickens" (paragraph 9). What does this wire fence suggest?
3. How would you describe Henry and Elisa's marriage? Cite details from the story.
4. With what motive does the traveling salesman take an interest in Elisa's chrysanthemums? What immediate effect does his interest have on Elisa?
5. For what possible purpose does Steinbeck give us such a detailed account of Elisa's preparations for her evening out? Notice her tearing off her soiled clothes and her scrubbing her body with pumice (paragraphs 93–94).
6. Of what significance to Elisa is the sight of the contents of the flower pot discarded in the road? Notice that, as her husband's car overtakes the covered wagon, Elisa turns away; and then Steinbeck adds, "In a moment it was over. The thing was done. She did not look back" (paragraph 111). Explain this passage.
7. How do you interpret Elisa's asking for wine with dinner? How do you account for her new interest in prizefights?
8. In a sentence, try to state this short story's theme.
9. Why are Elisa Allen's chrysanthemums so important to this story? Sum up what you understand them to mean.

Charlotte Perkins Gilman

The Yellow Wallpaper

1892

Charlotte Perkins Gilman (1860–1935) was born in Hartford, Connecticut. Her father was the writer Frederick Beecher Perkins (a nephew of reformer-novelist Harriet Beecher Stowe, author of Uncle Tom's Cabin, *and abolitionist minister Henry Ward Beecher), but he abandoned the family shortly after his daughter's birth. Raised in meager surroundings, the young Gilman adopted her intellectual Beecher aunts as role models. Because she and her mother moved from one relation to another, Gilman's early education was neglected—at fifteen, she had had only four years of schooling.*

Charlotte Perkins Gilman

In 1878 she studied commercial art at the Rhode Island School of Design. In 1884 she married Walter Stetson, an artist. After the birth of her one daughter, she experienced a severe depression. The rest cure her doctor prescribed became the basis of her most famous story, "The Yellow Wallpaper." This tale combines standard elements of Gothic fiction (the isolated country mansion, the brooding atmosphere of the room, the aloof but dominating husband) with the fresh clarity of Gilman's feminist perspective. Gilman's first marriage ended in an amicable divorce. A celebrated essayist and public speaker, she became an important early figure in American feminism. Her study Women and Economics (1898) stressed the importance of both sexes having a place in the working world. Her feminist-Utopian novel Herland (1915) describes a thriving nation of women without men. In 1900 Gilman married a second time—this time, more happily—to her cousin George Houghton Gilman. Following his sudden death in 1934, Gilman discovered she had inoperable breast cancer. After finishing her autobiography, she killed herself with chloroform in Pasadena, California.

It is very seldom that mere ordinary people like John and myself secure ancestral halls for the summer.

A colonial mansion, a hereditary estate, I would say a haunted house and reach the height of romantic felicity—but that would be asking too much of fate!

Still I will proudly declare that there is something queer about it.

Else, why should it be let so cheaply? And why have stood so long untenanted?

John laughs at me, of course, but one expects that in marriage.　　5

John is practical in the extreme. He has no patience with faith, an intense horror of superstition, and he scoffs openly at any talk of things not to be felt and seen and put down in figures.

John is a physician, and perhaps—(I would not say it to a living soul, of course, but this is dead paper and a great relief to my mind)—perhaps that is one reason I do not get well faster.

You see he does not believe I am sick!

And what can one do?

If a physician of high standing, and one's own husband, assures　10 friends and relatives that there is really nothing the matter with one but temporary nervous depression—a slight hysterical tendency—what is one to do?

My brother is also a physician, and also of high standing, and he says the same thing.

So I take phosphates or phosphites—whichever it is—and tonics, and journeys, and air, and exercise, and am absolutely forbidden to "work" until I am well again.

Personally, I disagree with their ideas.

Personally, I believe that congenial work, with excitement and change, would do me good.

But what is one to do?　　15

I did write for a while in spite of them; but it does exhaust me a good deal—having to be so sly about it, or else meet with heavy opposition.

I sometimes fancy that in my condition if I had less opposition and more society and stimulus—but John says the very worst thing I can do is to think about my condition, and I confess it always makes me feel bad.

So I will let it alone and talk about the house.

It is as airy and comfortable a room as any one need wish, and, of course, I would not be so silly as to make him uncomfortable just for a whim.

I'm really getting quite fond of the big room, all but that horrid paper.

Out of one window I can see the garden, those mysterious deep-shaded arbors, the riotous old-fashioned flowers, and bushes and gnarly trees.

Out of another I get a lovely view of the bay and a little private wharf belonging to the estate. There is a beautiful shaded lane that runs down there from the house. I always fancy I see people walking in these numerous paths and arbors, but John has cautioned me not to give way to fancy in the least. He says that with my imaginative power and habit of story-making, a nervous weakness like mine is sure to lead to all manner of excited fancies, and that I ought to use my will and good sense to check the tendency. So I try.

I think sometimes that if I were only well enough to write a little it would relieve the press of ideas and rest me.

But I find I get pretty tired when I try.

It is so discouraging not to have any advice and companionship about my work. When I get really well, John says we will ask Cousin Henry and Julia down for a long visit; but he says he would as soon put fireworks in my pillow-case as to let me have those stimulating people about now.

I wish I could get well faster.

But I must not think about that. This paper looks to me as if it *knew* what a vicious influence it had!

There is a recurrent spot where the pattern lolls like a broken neck and two bulbous eyes stare at you upside down.

I get positively angry with the impertinence of it and the everlasting-ness. Up and down and sideways they crawl, and those absurd unblinking eyes are everywhere. There is one place where two breadths didn't match, and the eyes go all up and down the line, one a little higher than the other.

I never saw so much expression in an inanimate thing before, and we all know how much expression they have! I used to lie awake as a child and get more entertainment and terror out of blank walls and plain furniture than most children could find in a toy-store.

I remember what a kindly wink the knobs of our big, old bureau used to have, and there was one chair that always seemed like a strong friend.

I used to feel that if any of the other things looked too fierce I could always hop into that chair and be safe.

The furniture in this room is no worse than inharmonious, however, for we had to bring it all from downstairs. I suppose when this was used as a playroom they had to take the nursery things out, and no wonder! I never saw such ravages as the children have made here.

The wallpaper, as I said before, is torn off in spots, and it sticketh closer than a brother°—they must have had perseverance as well as hatred.

Then the floor is scratched and gouged and splintered, the plaster itself is dug out here and there, and this great heavy bed, which is all we found in the room, looks as if it had been through the wars.

But I don't mind it a bit—only the paper.   75

There comes John's sister. Such a dear girl as she is, and so careful of me! I must not let her find me writing.

She is a perfect and enthusiastic housekeeper, and hopes for no better profession. I verily believe she thinks it is the writing which made me sick!

But I can write when she is out, and see her a long way off from these windows.

There is one that commands the road, a lovely shaded winding road, and one that just looks off over the country. A lovely country, too, full of great elms and velvet meadows.

This wallpaper has a kind of sub-pattern in a different shade, a par-   80
ticularly irritating one, for you can only see it in certain lights, and not clearly then.

But in the places where it isn't faded and where the sun is just so—I can see a strange, provoking, formless sort of figure, that seems to skulk about behind that silly and conspicuous front design.

There's sister on the stairs!

Well, the Fourth of July is over! The people are all gone and I am tired out. John thought it might do me good to see a little company, so we just had Mother and Nellie and the children down for a week.

Of course I didn't do a thing. Jennie sees to everything now.

But it tired me all the same.   85

John says if I don't pick up faster he shall send me to Weir Mitchell° in the fall.

But I don't want to go there at all. I had a friend who was in his hands once, and she says he is just like John and my brother, only more so!

Besides, it is such an undertaking to go so far.

I don't feel as if it was worthwhile to turn my hand over for anything, and I'm getting dreadfully fretful and querulous.

I cry at nothing, and cry most of the time.   90

Of course I don't when John is here, or anybody else, but when I am alone.

And I am alone a good deal just now. John is kept in town very often by serious cases, and Jennie is good and lets me alone when I want her to.

---

it sticketh . . . brother: From Proverbs 18:24: "There is a friend that sticketh closer than a brother." *Weir Mitchell:* (1829–1914): famed nerve specialist who actually treated the author, Charlotte Perkins Gilman, for nervous prostration with his well-known "rest cure." (The cure was not successful.) Also the author of *Diseases of the Nervous System, Especially of Women* (1881).

So I walk a little in the garden or down that lovely lane, sit on the porch under the roses, and lie down up here a good deal.

I'm getting really fond of the room in spite of the wallpaper. Perhaps *because* of the wallpaper.

It dwells in my mind so!   95

I lie here on this great immovable bed—it is nailed down, I believe—and follow that pattern about by the hour. It is as good as gymnastics, I assure you. I start, we'll say, at the bottom, down in the corner over there where it has not been touched, and I determine for the thousandth time that I *will* follow that pointless pattern to some sort of a conclusion.

I know a little of the principle of design, and I know this thing was not arranged on any laws of radiation,° or alternation, or repetition, or symmetry, or anything else that I ever heard of.

It is repeated, of course, by the breadths, but not otherwise.

Looked at in one way, each breadth stands alone, the bloated curves and flourishes—a kind of "debased Romanesque" with *delirium tremens*—go waddling up and down in isolated columns of fatuity.

But, on the other hand, they connect diagonally, and the sprawling   100
outlines run off in great slanting waves of optic horror, like a lot of wallowing sea-weeds in full chase.

The whole thing goes horizontally, too, at least it seems so, and I exhaust myself trying to distinguish the order of its going in that direction.

They have used a horizontal breadth for a frieze, and that adds wonderfully to the confusion.

There is one end of the room where it is almost intact, and there, when the crosslights fade and the low sun shines directly upon it, I can almost fancy radiation after all—the interminable grotesques seem to form around a common centre and rush off in headlong plunges of equal distraction.

It makes me tired to follow it. I will take a nap I guess.

I don't know why I should write this.   105
I don't want to.
I don't feel able.

And I know John would think it absurd. But I *must* say what I feel and think in some way—it is such a relief!

But the effort is getting to be greater than the relief.

Half the time now I am awfully lazy, and lie down ever so much.   110

John says I mustn't lose my strength, and has me take cod liver oil and lots of tonics and things, to say nothing of ale and wine and rare meat.

Dear John! He loves me very dearly, and hates to have me sick. I tried to have a real earnest reasonable talk with him the other day, and tell him how I wish he would let me go and make a visit to Cousin Henry and Julia.

laws of radiation: a principle of design in which all elements are arranged in some circular pattern around a center.

But he said I wasn't able to go, nor able to stand it after I got there; and I did not make out a very good case for myself, for I was crying before I had finished.

It is getting to be a great effort for me to think straight. Just this nervous weakness I suppose.

And dear John gathered me up in his arms, and just carried me 115 upstairs and laid me on the bed, and sat by me and read to me till it tired my head.

He said I was his darling and his comfort and all he had, and that I must take care of myself for his sake, and keep well.

He says no one but myself can help me out of it, that I must use my will and self-control and not let any silly fancies run away with me.

There's one comfort, the baby is well and happy, and does not have to occupy this nursery with the horrid wallpaper.

If we had not used it, that blessed child would have! What a fortunate escape! Why, I wouldn't have a child of mine, an impressionable little thing, live in such a room for worlds.

I never thought of it before, but it is lucky that John kept me here 120 after all, I can stand it so much easier than a baby, you see.

Of course I never mention it to them any more—I am too wise—but I keep watch of it all the same.

There are things in that paper that nobody knows but me, or ever will.

Behind that outside pattern the dim shapes get clearer every day.

It is always the same shape, only very numerous.

And it is like a woman stooping down and creeping about behind that 125 pattern. I don't like it a bit. I wonder—I begin to think—I wish John would take me away from here!

It is so hard to talk with John about my case, because he is so wise, and because he loves me so.

But I tried it last night.

It was moonlight. The moon shines in all around just as the sun does.

I hate to see it sometimes, it creeps so slowly, and always comes in by one window or another.

John was asleep and I hated to waken him, so I kept still and watched 130 the moonlight on that undulating wallpaper till I felt creepy.

The faint figure behind seemed to shake the pattern, just as if she wanted to get out.

I got up softly and went to feel and see if the paper *did* move, and when I came back John was awake.

"What is it, little girl?" he said. "Don't go walking about like that— you'll get cold."

I thought it was a good time to talk, so I told him that I really was not gaining here, and that I wished he would take me away.

"Why, darling!" said he, "our lease will be up in three weeks, and I 135
can't see how to leave before.

"The repairs are not done at home, and I cannot possibly leave town
just now. Of course if you were in any danger, I could and would, but you
really are better, dear, whether you can see it or not. I am a doctor, dear,
and I know. You are gaining flesh and color, your appetite is better, I feel
really much easier about you."

"I don't weigh a bit more," said I, "nor as much; and my appetite may
be better in the evening when you are here, but it is worse in the morning
when you are away!"

"Bless her little heart!" said he with a big hug, "she shall be as sick
as she pleases! But now let's improve the shining hours by going to sleep,
and talk about it in the morning!"

"And you won't go away?" I asked gloomily.

"Why, how can I, dear? It is only three weeks more and then we will 140
take a nice little trip of a few days while Jennie is getting the house ready.
Really, dear, you are better!"

"Better in body perhaps—" I began, and stopped short, for he sat up
straight and looked at me with such a stern, reproachful look that I could
not say another word.

"My darling," said he, "I beg of you, for my sake and for our child's
sake, as well as for your own, that you will never for one instant let that
idea enter your mind! There is nothing so dangerous, so fascinating, to a
temperament like yours. It is a false and foolish fancy. Can you not trust
me as a physician when I tell you so?"

So of course I said no more on that score, and we went to sleep before
long. He thought I was asleep first, but I wasn't, and lay there for hours
trying to decide whether that front pattern and the back pattern really did
move together or separately.

On a pattern like this, by daylight, there is a lack of sequence, a defiance of law, that is a constant irritant to a normal mind.

The color is hideous enough, and unreliable enough, and infuriating 145
enough, but the pattern is torturing.

You think you have mastered it, but just as you get well underway
in following, it turns a back-somersault and there you are. It slaps you in
the face, knocks you down, and tramples upon you. It is like a bad dream.

The outside pattern is a florid arabesque,° reminding one of a fungus. If you can imagine a toadstool in joints, an interminable string of
toadstools, budding and sprouting in endless convolutions—why, that is
something like it.

That is, sometimes!

---

arabesque: a type of ornamental style (Arabic in origin) that uses flowers, foliage, fruit, or
other figures to create an intricate pattern of interlocking shapes and lines.

There is one marked peculiarity about this paper, a thing nobody seems to notice but myself, and that is that it changes as the light changes.

When the sun shoots in through the east window—I always watch 150 for that first long, straight ray—it changes so quickly that I never can quite believe it.

That is why I watch it always.

By moonlight—the moon shines in all night when there is a moon— I wouldn't know it was the same paper.

At night in any kind of light, in twilight, candlelight, lamplight, and worst of all by moonlight, it becomes bars! The outside pattern, I mean, and the woman behind it is as plain as can be.

I didn't realize for a long time what the thing was that showed behind, that dim sub-pattern, but now I am quite sure it is a woman.

By daylight she is subdued, quiet. I fancy it is the pattern that keeps 155 her so still. It is so puzzling. It keeps me quiet by the hour.

I lie down ever so much now. John says it is good for me, and to sleep all I can.

Indeed he started the habit by making me lie down for an hour after each meal.

It is a very bad habit, I am convinced, for you see I don't sleep.

And that cultivates deceit, for I don't tell them I'm awake—O, no!

The fact is I am getting a little afraid of John. 160

He seems very queer sometimes, and even Jennie has an inexplicable look.

It strikes me occasionally, just as a scientific hypothesis, that perhaps it is the paper!

I have watched John when he did not know I was looking, and come into the room suddenly on the most innocent excuses, and I've caught him several times *looking at the paper*! And Jennie too. I caught Jennie with her hand on it once.

She didn't know I was in the room, and when I asked her in a quiet, a very quiet voice, with the most restrained manner possible, what she was doing with the paper—she turned around as if she had been caught stealing, and looked quite angry—asked me why I should frighten her so!

Then she said that the paper stained everything it touched, that she 165 had found yellow smooches° on all my clothes and John's, and she wished we would be more careful!

Did not that sound innocent? But I know she was studying that pattern, and I am determined that nobody shall find it out but myself!

Life is very much more exciting now than it used to be. You see I have something more to expect, to look forward to, to watch. I really do eat better, and am more quiet than I was.

---

smooches: smudges or smears.

John is so pleased to see me improve! He laughed a little the other day, and said I seemed to be flourishing in spite of my wallpaper.

I turned it off with a laugh. I had no intention of telling him it was *because* of the wallpaper—he would make fun of me. He might even want to take me away.

I don't want to leave now until I have found it out. There is a week 170 more, and I think that will be enough.

I'm feeling ever so much better! I don't sleep much at night, for it is so interesting to watch developments; but I sleep a good deal in the daytime.

In the daytime it is tiresome and perplexing.

There are always new shoots on the fungus, and new shades of yellow all over it. I cannot keep count of them, though I have tried conscientiously.

It is the strangest yellow, that wallpaper! It makes me think of all the yellow things I ever saw—not beautiful ones like buttercups, but old foul, bad yellow things.

But there is something else about that paper—the smell! I noticed 175 it the moment we came into the room, but with so much air and sun it was not bad. Now we have had a week of fog and rain, and whether the windows are open or not, the smell is here.

It creeps all over the house.

I find it hovering in the dining-room, skulking in the parlor, hiding in the hall, lying in wait for me on the stairs.

It gets into my hair.

Even when I go to ride, if I turn my head suddenly and surprise it— there is that smell!

Such a peculiar odor, too! I have spent hours in trying to analyze it, 180 to find what it smelled like.

It is not bad—at first—and very gentle, but quite the subtlest, most enduring odor I ever met.

In this damp weather it is awful. I wake up in the night and find it hanging over me.

It used to disturb me at first. I thought seriously of burning the house—to reach the smell.

But now I am used to it. The only thing I can think of that it is like is the *color* of the paper! A yellow smell.

There is a very funny mark on this wall, low down, near the mop- 185 board. A streak that runs round the room. It goes behind every piece of furniture, except the bed, a long, straight, even *smooch*, as if it had been rubbed over and over.

I wonder how it was done and who did it, and what they did it for. Round and round and round—round and round and round—it makes me dizzy!

***

I really have discovered something at last.

Through watching so much at night, when it changes so, I have finally found out.

The front pattern *does* move—and no wonder! The woman behind shakes it!

Sometimes I think there are a great many women behind, and some- 190 times only one, and she crawls around fast, and her crawling shakes it all over.

Then in the very bright spots she keeps still, and in the very shady spots she just takes hold of the bars and shakes them hard.

And she is all the time trying to climb through. But nobody could climb through that pattern—it strangles so; I think that is why it has so many heads.

They get through, and then the pattern strangles them off and turns them upside down, and makes their eyes white!

If those heads were covered or taken off it would not be half so bad.

I think that woman gets out in the daytime! 195

And I'll tell you why—privately—I've seen her!

I can see her out of every one of my windows!

It is the same woman, I know, for she is always creeping, and most women do not creep by daylight.

I see her in that long shaded lane, creeping up and down. I see her in those dark grape arbors, creeping all round the garden.

I see her on that long road under the trees, creeping along, and when 200 a carriage comes she hides under the blackberry vines.

I don't blame her a bit. It must be very humiliating to be caught creeping by daylight!

I always lock the door when I creep by daylight. I can't do it at night, for I know John would suspect something at once.

And John is so queer now, that I don't want to irritate him. I wish he would take another room! Besides, I don't want anybody to get that woman out at night but myself.

I often wonder if I could see her out of all the windows at once.

But, turn as fast as I can, I can only see out of one at one time. 205

And though I always see her, she *may* be able to creep faster than I can turn!

I have watched her sometimes away off in the open country, creeping as fast as a cloud shadow in a high wind.

If only that top pattern could be gotten off from the under one! I mean to try it, little by little.

I have found out another funny thing, but I shan't tell it this time! It does not do to trust people too much.

There are only two more days to get this paper off, and I believe John 210 is beginning to notice. I don't like the look in his eyes.

And I heard him ask Jennie a lot of professional questions about me. She had a very good report to give.

She said I slept a good deal in the daytime.

John knows I don't sleep very well at night, for all I'm so quiet!

He asked me all sorts of questions, too, and pretended to be very loving and kind.

As if I couldn't see through him!   215

Still, I don't wonder he acts so, sleeping under this paper for three months.

It only interests me, but I feel sure John and Jennie are affected by it.

Hurrah! This is the last day, but it is enough. John had to stay in town over night, and won't be out until this evening.

Jennie wanted to sleep with me—the sly thing—but I told her I should undoubtedly rest better for a night all alone.

That was clever, for really I wasn't alone a bit! As soon as it was   220 moonlight and that poor thing began to crawl and shake the pattern, I got up and ran to help her.

I pulled and she shook, I shook and she pulled, and before morning we had peeled off yards of that paper.

A strip about as high as my head and half around the room.

And then when the sun came and that awful pattern began to laugh at me, I declared I would finish it to-day!

We go away to-morrow, and they are moving all my furniture down again to leave things as they were before.

Jennie looked at the wall in amazement, but I told her merrily that I   225 did it out of pure spite at the vicious thing.

She laughed and said she wouldn't mind doing it herself, but I must not get tired.

How she betrayed herself that time!

But I am here, and no person touches this paper but me—not *alive*!

She tried to get me out of the room—it was too patent! But I said it was so quiet and empty and clean now that I believed I would lie down again and sleep all I could; and not to wake me even for dinner—I would call when I woke.

So now she is gone, and the servants are gone, and the things are   230 gone, and there is nothing left but that great bedstead nailed down, with the canvas mattress we found on it.

We shall sleep downstairs to-night, and take the boat home to-morrow.

I quite enjoy the room, now it is bare again.

How those children did tear about here!

This bedstead is fairly gnawed!

But I must get to work.   235

I have locked the door and thrown the key down into the front path.

I don't want to go out, and I don't want to have anybody come in, till John comes.

I want to astonish him.

I've got a rope up here that even Jennie did not find. If that woman does get out, and tries to get away, I can tie her!

But I forgot I could not reach far without anything to stand on!   240

This bed will *not* move!

I tried to lift and push it until I was lame, and then I got so angry I bit off a little piece at one corner—but it hurt my teeth.

Then I peeled off all the paper I could reach standing on the floor. It sticks horribly and the pattern just enjoys it! All those strangled heads and bulbous eyes and waddling fungus growths just shriek with derision!

I am getting angry enough to do something desperate. To jump out of the window would be admirable exercise, but the bars are too strong even to try.

Besides, I wouldn't do it. Of course not. I know well enough that a   245
step like that is improper and might be misconstrued.

I don't like to *look* out of the windows even—there are so many of those creeping women, and they creep so fast.

I wonder if they all come out of that wallpaper as I did!

But I am securely fastened now by my well-hidden rope—you don't get *me* out in the road there!

I suppose I shall have to get back behind the pattern when it comes night, and that is hard!

It is so pleasant to be out in this great room and creep around as I   250
please!

I don't want to go outside. I won't, even if Jennie asks me to.

For outside you have to creep on the ground, and everything is green instead of yellow.

But here I can creep smoothly on the floor, and my shoulder just fits in that long smooch around the wall, so I cannot lose my way.

Why, there's John at the door!

It is no use, young man, you can't open it!   255

How he does call and pound!

Now he's crying for an axe.

It would be a shame to break down that beautiful door!

"John, dear!" said I in the gentlest voice, "the key is down by the front steps, under a plantain leaf!"

That silenced him for a few moments.   260

Then he said—very quietly indeed—"Open the door, my darling!"

"I can't," said I. "The key is down by the front door under a plantain leaf!"

And then I said it again, several times, very gently and slowly, and said it so often that he had to go and see, and he got it of course, and came in. He stopped short by the door.

"What is the matter?" he cried. "For God's sake, what are you doing!"

I kept on creeping just the same, but I looked at him over my   265
shoulder.

"I've got out at last," said I, "in spite of you and Jane! And I've pulled off most of the paper, so you can't put me back!"

Now why should that man have fainted? But he did, and right across my path by the wall, so that I had to creep over him every time!

Questions

1. Several times at the beginning of the story, the narrator says such things as "What is one to do?" and "What can one do?" What do these comments refer to? What, if anything, do they suggest about women's roles at the time the story was written?

2. The narrator says, "I get unreasonably angry with John sometimes" (paragraph 25). How unreasonable is her anger at him? What does the fact that she feels it is unreasonable say about her?

3. What do her changing feelings about the wallpaper tell us about her condition?

4. As the story progresses, the wallpaper begins to acquire powerful associations. What does it come to symbolize at the story's end?

5. "It is so hard to talk with John about my case, because he is so wise, and because he loves me so" (paragraph 126). His wisdom is, to say the least, open to question, but what about his love? Do you think he suffers merely from a failure of perception, or is there a failure of affection as well? Explain your response.

6. Where precisely in the story do you think it becomes clear that she has begun to hallucinate?

7. What does the woman behind the wallpaper represent? Why does the narrator come to identify with her?

8. How ill does the narrator seem at the beginning of the story? How ill does she seem at the end? How do you account for the change in her condition?

Ursula K. Le Guin

The Ones Who Walk Away from Omelas   1975

Ursula Kroeber Le Guin was born in 1929 on St. Ursula's Day (October 21) in Berkeley, California, the only daughter and youngest child of Theodora Kroeber, a folklorist, and Alfred Kroeber, a renowned anthropologist. Le Guin attended Radcliffe College, where she graduated Phi Beta Kappa, and then entered Columbia University to do graduate work in French and Italian literature. While completing her master's, she wrote her first stories. On a Fulbright fellowship to France, she met Charles Le Guin, a professor of French history, whom she married in Paris in 1953. Over the next decade Le Guin reared three children and worked on her writing in private.

Ursula K. Le Guin

In the early sixties Le Guin began publishing in both science fiction pulp magazines and academic journals. In 1966 her first novel, Rocannon's World, *was published as an Ace science fiction paperback original—hardly a respectable format for the debut of one of America's premier writers. In 1968 Le Guin published A Wizard of Earthsea, the first novel in her Earthsea series, now considered a classic of children's literature. The next two volumes, The Tombs of Atuan (1971), which won a Newbery citation, and The Farthest Shore (1972), which won a National Book Award, brought Le Guin mainstream acclaim.*

Le Guin's novels The Left Hand of Darkness (1969) and The Dispossessed (1974) won both the Hugo and the Nebula awards, science fiction's two most prized honors. She also twice won the Hugo for best short story, including the 1974 award for "The Ones Who Walk Away from Omelas." Le Guin has published more than thirty novels and many volumes of short stories, poetry, and essays. A recent novel is the Locus Award–winning Lavinia (2008). Le Guin lives in Portland, Oregon.

One of the few science fiction writers whose work has earned general critical acclaim, Le Guin belongs most naturally in the company of major novelists of ideas such as Aldous Huxley, George Orwell, and Anthony Burgess, who have used the genre of science fiction to explore the possible consequences of ideological rather than technological change. Le Guin has been especially concerned with issues of social justice and equality. In her short stories—including "The Ones Who Walk Away from Omelas"—she creates complex imaginary civilizations, envisioned with anthropological authority, and her aim is less to imagine alien cultures than to explore humanity.

With a clamor of bells that set the swallows soaring, the Festival of Summer came to the city Omelas, bright-towered by the sea. The rigging of the boats in harbor sparkled with flags. In the streets between houses with red roofs and painted walls, between old moss-grown gardens and under avenues of trees, past great parks and public buildings, processions moved. Some were decorous: old people in long stiff robes of mauve and grey, grave master workmen, quiet, merry women carrying their babies and chatting as they walked. In other streets the music beat faster, a shimmering of gong and tambourine, and the people went dancing, the procession was a dance. Children dodged in and out, their high calls rising like the swallows' crossing flights over the music and the singing. All the processions wound towards the north side of the city, where on the great water-meadow called the Green Fields boys and girls, naked in the bright air, with mud-stained feet and ankles and long, lithe arms, exercised their restive horses before the race. The horses wore no gear at all but a halter without bit. Their manes were braided with streamers of silver, gold, and green. They flared their nostrils and pranced and boasted to one another; they were vastly excited, the horse being the only animal who has adopted our ceremonies as his own. Far off to the north and west the mountains stood up half encircling Omelas on her bay. The air of morning was so clear that the snow still crowning the Eighteen Peaks burned with white-gold fire across the miles of sunlit air, under the dark blue of the sky. There was just enough wind to make the banners that marked the racecourse snap and flutter now and then. In the silence of the broad green meadows one could hear the music winding through the city streets, farther and nearer and ever approaching, a cheerful faint sweetness of the air that from time to time trembled and gathered together and broke out into the great joyous clanging of the bells.

Joyous! How is one to tell about joy? How describe the citizens of Omelas?

They were not simple folk, you see, though they were happy. But we do not say the words of cheer much any more. All smiles have become archaic. Given a description such as this one tends to make certain assumptions. Given a description such as this one tends to look next for the King, mounted on a splendid stallion and surrounded by his noble knights, or perhaps in a golden litter borne by great-muscled slaves. But there was no king. They did not use swords, or keep slaves. They were not barbarians. I do not know the rules and laws of their society, but I suspect that they were singularly few. As they did without monarchy and slavery, so they also got on without the stock exchange, the advertisement, the secret police, and the bomb. Yet I repeat that these were not simple folk, not dulcet shepherds, noble savages, bland utopians. They were not less complex than us. The trouble is that we have a bad habit, encouraged by pedants and sophisticates, of considering happiness as something rather stupid. Only pain is intellectual, only evil interesting. This is the treason of the artist: a refusal to admit the banality of evil and the terrible boredom of pain. If you can't lick 'em, join 'em. If it hurts, repeat it. But to praise despair is to condemn delight, to embrace violence is to lose hold of everything else. We have almost lost hold; we can no longer describe a happy man, nor make any celebration of joy. How can I tell you about the people of Omelas? They were not naïve and happy children—though their children were, in fact, happy. They were mature, intelligent, passionate adults whose lives were not wretched. O miracle! but I wish I could describe it better. I wish I could convince you. Omelas sounds in my words like a city in a fairy tale, long ago and far away, once upon a time. Perhaps it would be best if you imagined it as your own fancy bids, assuming it will rise to the occasion, for certainly I cannot suit you all. For instance, how about technology? I think that there would be no cars or helicopters in and above the streets; this follows from the fact that the people of Omelas are happy people. Happiness is based on a just discrimination of what is necessary, what is neither necessary nor destructive, and what is destructive. In the middle category, however—that of the unnecessary but undestructive, that of comfort, luxury, exuberance, etc.—they could perfectly well have central heating, subway trains, washing machines, and all kinds of marvelous devices not yet invented here, floating light-sources, fuelless power, a cure for the common cold. Or they could have none of that: it doesn't matter. As you like it. I incline to think that people from towns up and down the coast have been coming in to Omelas during the last days before the Festival on very fast little trains and double-decked trams, and that the train station of Omelas is actually the handsomest building in town, though plainer than the magnificent Farmers' Market. But even granted trains, I fear that Omelas so far strikes some of you as goody-goody. Smiles, bells, parades, horses, bleh. If so, please add an orgy. If an orgy would help, don't hesitate. Let us not, however, have temples from which issue beautiful nude priests and priestesses already half in ecstasy and ready to copulate with any man or woman, lover or stranger, who desires union with the deep godhead of the blood, although that was my first idea. But really it would be better not to have any temples in Omelas—at least, not manned temples. Religion yes, clergy no. Surely the beautiful nudes can just wander about, offering themselves like divine soufflés to the hunger of the needy and the rapture of the flesh. Let them join the processions. Let tambourines be struck above the copulations, and the glory of desire be proclaimed upon the gongs, and (a not unimportant point) let the off-spring of these delightful rituals be beloved and looked after by all. One thing I know there is none of in Omelas is guilt. But what else should there be? I thought at first there were no drugs, but that is puritanical. For those who like it, the faint insistent sweetness of *drooz* may perfume the ways of the city, *drooz* which first brings a great lightness and brilliance to the mind and limbs, and then after some hours a dreamy languor, and wonderful visions at last of the very arcana and inmost secrets of the Universe, as well as exciting the pleasure of sex beyond all belief; and it is not habit-forming. For more modest tastes I think there ought to be beer. What else, what else belongs in the joyous city? The sense of victory, surely, the celebration of courage. But as we did without clergy, let us do without soldiers. The joy built upon successful slaughter is not the right kind of joy; it will not do; it is fearful and it is trivial. A boundless and generous contentment, a magnanimous triumph felt not against some outer enemy but in communion with the finest and fairest in the souls of all men everywhere and the splendor of the world's summer: this is what swells the hearts of the people of Omelas, and the victory they celebrate is that of life. I really don't think many of them need to take *drooz*.

Most of the processions have reached the Green Fields by now. A marvelous smell of cooking goes forth from the red and blue tents of the provisioners. The faces of small children are amiably sticky; in the benign grey beard of a man a couple of crumbs of rich pastry are entangled. The youths and girls have mounted their horses and are beginning to group around the starting line of the course. An old woman, small, fat, and laughing, is passing out flowers from a basket, and tall young men wear her flowers in their shining hair. A child of nine or ten sits at the edge of the crowd, alone, playing on a wooden flute. People pause to listen, and they smile, but they do not speak to him, for he never ceases playing and never sees them, his dark eyes wholly rapt in the sweet, thin magic of the tune.

He finishes, and slowly lowers his hands holding the wooden flute.   5

As if that little private silence were the signal, all at once a trumpet sounds from the pavilion near the starting line: imperious, melancholy, piercing. The horses rear on their slender legs, and some of them neigh in answer. Sober-faced, the young riders stroke the horses' necks and soothe them, whispering, "Quiet, quiet, there my beauty, my hope. . . ." They begin to form in rank along the starting line. The crowds along the race-course are like a field of grass and flowers in the wind. The Festival of Summer has begun.

Do you believe? Do you accept the festival, the city, the joy? No? Then let me describe one more thing.

In a basement under one of the beautiful public buildings of Omelas, or perhaps in the cellar of one of its spacious private homes, there is a room. It has one locked door, and no window. A little light seeps in dust-ily between cracks in the boards, secondhand from a cobwebbed window somewhere across the cellar. In one corner of the little room a couple of mops, with stiff, clotted, foul-smelling heads, stand near a rusty bucket. The floor is dirt, a little damp to the touch, as cellar dirt usually is. The room is about three paces long and two wide: a mere broom closet or dis-used tool room. In the room a child is sitting. It could be a boy or a girl. It looks about six, but actually is nearly ten. It is feeble-minded. Perhaps it was born defective, or perhaps it has become imbecile through fear, mal-nutrition, and neglect. It picks its nose and occasionally fumbles vaguely with its toes or genitals, as it sits hunched in the corner farthest from the bucket and the two mops. It is afraid of the mops. It finds them horrible. It shuts its eyes, but it knows the mops are still standing there; and the door is locked; and nobody will come. The door is always locked; and nobody ever comes, except that sometimes—the child has no understanding of time or interval—sometimes the door rattles terribly and opens, and a person, or several people, are there. One of them may come in and kick the child to make it stand up. The others never come close, but peer in at it with frightened, disgusted eyes. The food bowl and the water jug are hastily filled, the door is locked, the eyes disappear. The people at the door never say anything, but the child, who has not always lived in the tool room, and can remember sunlight and its mother's voice, sometimes speaks. "I will be good," it says. "Please let me out. I will be good!" They never answer. The child used to scream for help at night, and cry a good deal, but now it only makes a kind of whining, "eh-haa, eh-haa," and it speaks less and less often. It is so thin there are no calves to its legs; its belly protrudes; it lives on a half-bowl of corn meal and grease a day. It is naked. Its buttocks and thighs are a mass of festered sores, as it sits in its own excrement continually.

They all know it is there, all the people of Omelas. Some of them have come to see it, others are content merely to know it is there. They all know that it has to be there. Some of them understand why, and some do not, but they all understand that their happiness, the beauty of their city, the tenderness of their friendships, the health of their children, the wisdom of their scholars, the skill of their makers, even the abundance of their harvest and the kindly weathers of their skies, depend wholly on this child's abominable misery.

This is usually explained to children when they are between eight and twelve, whenever they seem capable of understanding; and most of those who come to see the child are young people, though often enough an adult comes, or comes back, to see the child. No matter how well the matter has been explained to them, these young spectators are always shocked and sickened at the sight. They feel disgust, which they had thought themselves superior to. They feel anger, outrage, impotence, despite all the explanations. They would like to do something for the child. But there is nothing they can do. If the child were brought up into the sunlight out of that vile place, if it were cleaned and fed and comforted, that would be a good thing, indeed; but if it were done, in that day and hour all the prosperity and beauty and delight of Omelas would wither and be destroyed. Those are the terms. To exchange all the goodness and grace of every life in Omelas for that single, small improvement: to throw away the happiness of thousands for the chance of the happiness of one: that would be to let guilt within the walls indeed.

The terms are strict and absolute; there may not even be a kind word spoken to the child.

Often the young people go home in tears, or in a tearless rage, when they have seen the child and faced this terrible paradox. They may brood over it for weeks or years. But as time goes on they begin to realize that even if the child could be released, it would not get much good of its freedom: a little vague pleasure of warmth and food, no doubt, but little more. It is too degraded and imbecile to know any real joy. It has been afraid too long ever to be free of fear. Its habits are too uncouth for it to respond to humane treatment. Indeed, after so long it would probably be wretched without walls about it to protect it, and darkness for its eyes, and its own excrement to sit in. Their tears at the bitter injustice dry when they begin to perceive the terrible justice of reality, and to accept it. Yet it is their tears and anger, the trying of their generosity and the acceptance of their helplessness, which are perhaps the true source of the splendor of their lives. Theirs is no vapid, irresponsible happiness. They know that they, like the child, are not free. They know compassion. It is the existence of the child, and their knowledge of its existence, that makes possible the nobility of their architecture, the poignancy of their music, the profundity of their science. It is because of the child that they are so gentle with children. They know that if the wretched one were not there snivelling in the dark, the other one, the flute-player, could make no joyful music as the young riders line up in their beauty for the race in the sunlight of the first morning of summer.

Now do you believe in them? Are they not more credible? But there is one more thing to tell, and this is quite incredible.

At times one of the adolescent girls or boys who go to see the child does not go home to weep or rage, does not, in fact, go home at all. Sometimes also a man or woman much older falls silent for a day or two, and then leaves home. These people go out into the street, and walk down the street alone. They keep walking, and walk straight out of the city of Omelas, through the beautiful gates. They keep walking across the farmlands of Omelas. Each one goes alone, youth or girl, man or woman. Night falls; the traveler must pass down village streets, between the houses with yellow-lit windows, and on out into the darkness of the fields. Each alone, they go west or north, toward the mountains. They go on. They leave Omelas, they walk ahead into the darkness, and they do not come back. The place they go towards is a place even less imaginable to most of us than the city of happiness. I cannot describe it at all. It is possible that it does not exist. But they seem to know where they are going, the ones who walk away from Omelas.

Questions

1. Does the narrator live in Omelas? What do we know about the narrator's society?

2. What is the narrator's opinion of Omelas? Does the author seem to share that opinion?

3. What is the narrator's attitude toward "the ones who walk away from Omelas"? Would the narrator have been one of those who walked away?

4. How do you account for the narrator's willingness to let readers add anything they like to the story?—"If an orgy would help, don't hesitate" (paragraph 3). Doesn't Ursula Le Guin care what her story includes?

5. What is suggested by the locked, dark cellar in which the child sits? What other details in the story are suggestive enough to be called symbolic?

6. Do you find in the story any implied criticism of our own society?

Shirley Jackson

The Lottery   1948

Shirley Jackson (1919–1965), a native of San Francisco, moved in her teens to Rochester, New York. She started college at the University of Rochester, but had to drop out, stricken by severe depression, a problem that was to recur at intervals throughout her life. Later she graduated from Syracuse University. With her husband, Stanley Edgar Hyman, a literary critic, she settled in Bennington, Vermont, in a sprawling house built in the nineteenth century. There Jackson conscientiously set herself to produce a fixed number of words each day. She

Shirley Jackson

wrote novels—The Road Through the Wall *(1948)*—*and three psychological thrillers*—Hangsaman *(1951)*, The Haunting of Hill House *(1959)*, *and* We Have Always Lived in the Castle *(1962)*. *She wrote light, witty articles for* Good Housekeeping *and other popular magazines about the horrors of house-keeping and rearing four children, collected in* Life Among the Savages *(1953)* *and* Raising Demons *(1957); but she claimed to have written them only for money. When "The Lottery" appeared in the* New Yorker *in 1948, that issue of the magazine quickly sold out. Her purpose in writing the story, Jackson declared, had been "to shock the story's readers with a graphic demonstration of the point-less violence and general inhumanity in their own lives."*

The morning of June 27th was clear and sunny, with the fresh warmth of a full-summer day; the flowers were blossoming profusely and the grass was richly green. The people of the village began to gather in the square, between the post office and the bank, around ten o'clock; in some towns there were so many people that the lottery took two days and had to be started on June 26th, but in this village, where there were only about three hundred people, the whole lottery took less than two hours, so it could begin at ten o'clock in the morning and still be through in time to allow the villagers to get home for noon dinner.

The children assembled first, of course. School was recently over for the summer, and the feeling of liberty sat uneasily on most of them; they tended to gather together quietly for a while before they broke into boisterous play, and their talk was still of the classroom and the teacher, of books and reprimands. Bobby Martin had already stuffed his pockets full of stones, and the other boys soon followed his example, selecting the smoothest and roundest stones; Bobby and Harry Jones and Dickie Delacroix—the villagers pronounced this name "Dellacroy"—eventually made a great pile of stones in one corner of the square and guarded it against the raids of the other boys. The girls stood aside, talking among themselves, looking over their shoulders at the boys, and the very small children rolled in the dust or clung to the hands of their older brothers or sisters.

Soon the men began to gather, surveying their own children, speaking of planting and rain, tractors and taxes. They stood together, away from the pile of stones in the corner, and their jokes were quiet and they smiled rather than laughed. The women, wearing faded house dresses and sweaters, came shortly after their menfolk. They greeted one another and exchanged bits of gossip as they went to join their husbands. Soon the women, standing by their husbands, began to call to their children, and the children came reluc-tantly, having to be called four or five times. Bobby Martin ducked under his mother's grasping hand and ran, laughing, back to the pile of stones. His father spoke up sharply, and Bobby came quickly and took his place between his father and his oldest brother.

The lottery was conducted—as were the square dances, the teenage club, the Halloween program—by Mr. Summers, who had time and energy to devote to civic activities. He was a roundfaced, jovial man and he ran the coal business, and people were sorry for him, because he had no children and his wife was a scold. When he arrived in the square, carrying the black wooden box, there was a murmur of conversation among the villagers and he waved and called, "Little late today, folks." The postmaster, Mr. Graves, followed him, carrying a three-legged stool, and the stool was put in the center of the square and Mr. Summers set the black box down on it. The villagers kept their distance, leaving a space between themselves and the stool, and when Mr. Summers said, "Some of you fellows want to give me a hand?" there was a hesitation before two men, Mr. Martin and his oldest son, Baxter, came forward to hold the box steady on the stool while Mr. Summers stirred up the papers inside it.

The original paraphernalia for the lottery had been lost long ago, and   5 the black box now resting on the stool had been put into use even before Old Man Warner, the oldest man in town, was born. Mr. Summers spoke frequently to the villagers about making a new box, but no one liked to upset even as much tradition as was represented by the black box. There was a story that the present box had been made with some pieces of the box that had preceded it, the one that had been constructed when the first people settled down to make a village here. Every year, after the lottery, Mr. Summers began talking again about a new box, but every year the subject was allowed to fade off without anything's being done. The black box grew shabbier each year; by now it was no longer completely black but splintered badly along one side to show the original wood color, and in some places faded or stained.

Mr. Martin and his oldest son, Baxter, held the black box securely on the stool until Mr. Summers had stirred the papers thoroughly with his hand. Because so much of the ritual had been forgotten or discarded, Mr. Summers had been successful in having slips of paper substituted for the chips of wood that had been used for generations. Chips of wood, Mr. Summers had argued, had been all very well when the village was tiny, but now that the population was more than three hundred and likely to keep on growing, it was necessary to use something that would fit more easily into the black box. The night before the lottery, Mr. Summers and Mr. Graves made up the slips of paper and put them in the box, and it was then taken to the safe of Mr. Summers's coal company and locked up until Mr. Summers was ready to take it to the square next morning. The rest of the year, the box was put away, sometimes one place, sometimes another; it had spent one year in Mr. Graves's barn and another year underfoot in the post office, and sometimes it was set on a shelf in the Martin grocery and left there.

There was a great deal of fussing to be done before Mr. Summers declared the lottery open. There were lists to make up—of heads of families, heads of households in each family, members of each household in each family. There was the proper swearing-in of Mr. Summers by the postmaster, as the official of the lottery; at one time, some people remembered, there had been a recital of some sort, performed by the official of the lottery, a perfunctory, tuneless chant that had been rattled off duly each year; some people believed that the official of the lottery used to stand just so when he said or sang it, others believed that he was supposed to walk among the people, but years and years ago this part of the ritual had been allowed to lapse. There had been, also, a ritual salute, which the official of the lottery had had to use in addressing each person who came up to draw from the box, but this also had changed with time, until now it was felt necessary only for the official to speak to each person approaching. Mr. Summers was very good at all this; in his clean white shirt and blue jeans, with one hand resting carelessly on the black box, he seemed very proper and important as he talked interminably to Mr. Graves and the Martins.

Just as Mr. Summers finally left off talking and turned to the assembled villagers, Mrs. Hutchinson came hurriedly along the path to the square, her sweater thrown over her shoulders, and slid into place in the back of the crowd. "Clean forgot what day it was," she said to Mrs. Delacroix, who stood next to her, and they both laughed softly. "Thought my old man was out back stacking wood," Mrs. Hutchinson went on, "and then I looked out the window and the kids were gone, and then I remembered it was the twenty-seventh and came a-running." She dried her hands on her apron, and Mrs. Delacroix said, "You're in time, though. They're still talking away up there."

Mrs. Hutchinson craned her neck to see through the crowd and found her husband and children standing near the front. She tapped Mrs. Delacroix on the arm as a farewell and began to make her way through the crowd. The people separated good-humoredly to let her through; two or three people said, in voices just loud enough to be heard across the crowd, "Here comes your Missus, Hutchinson," and "Bill, she made it after all." Mrs. Hutchinson reached her husband, and Mr. Summers, who had been waiting, said cheerfully, "Thought we were going to have to get on without you, Tessie." Mrs. Hutchinson said, grinning, "Wouldn't have me leave m'dishes in the sink, now would you, Joe?" and soft laughter ran through the crowd as the people stirred back into position after Mrs. Hutchinson's arrival.

"Well, now," Mr. Summers said soberly, "guess we better get started, get this over with, so's we can go back to work. Anybody ain't here?" 10

"Dunbar," several people said. "Dunbar, Dunbar."

Mr. Summers consulted his list. "Clyde Dunbar," he said. "That's right. He's broke his leg, hasn't he? Who's drawing for him?"

"Me, I guess," a woman said, and Mr. Summers turned to look at her. "Wife draws for her husband," Mr. Summers said. "Don't you have a grown boy to do it for you, Janey?" Although Mr. Summers and everyone else in the village knew the answer perfectly well, it was the business of the official of the lottery to ask such questions formally. Mr. Summers waited with an expression of polite interest while Mrs. Dunbar answered.

"Horace's not but sixteen yet," Mrs. Dunbar said regretfully. "Guess I gotta fill in for the old man this year."

"Right," Mr. Summers said. He made a note on the list he was hold- 15 ing. Then he asked, "Watson boy drawing this year?"

A tall boy in the crowd raised his hand. "Here," he said. "I'm draw- ing for m'mother and me." He blinked his eyes nervously and ducked his head as several voices in the crowd said things like "Good fellow, Jack," and "Glad to see your mother's got a man to do it."

"Well," Mr. Summers said, "guess that's everyone. Old Man Warner make it?"

"Here," a voice said, and Mr. Summers nodded.

A sudden hush fell on the crowd as Mr. Summers cleared his throat and looked at the list. "All ready?" he called. "Now, I'll read the names— heads of families first—and the men come up and take a paper out of the box. Keep the paper folded in your hand without looking at it until everyone has had a turn. Everything clear?"

The people had done it so many times that they only half listened 20 to the directions; most of them were quiet, wetting their lips, not looking around. Then Mr. Summers raised one hand high and said, "Adams." A man disengaged himself from the crowd and came forward. "Hi, Steve," Mr. Summers said, and Mr. Adams said, "Hi, Joe." They grinned at one another humorlessly and nervously. Then Mr. Adams reached into the black box and took out a folded paper. He held it firmly by one corner as he turned and went hastily back to his place in the crowd, where he stood a little apart from his family, not looking down at his hand.

"Allen," Mr. Summers said. "Anderson. . . . Bentham."

"Seems like there's no time at all between lotteries any more," Mrs. Delacroix said to Mrs. Graves in the back row. "Seems like we got through with the last one only last week."

"Time sure goes fast," Mrs. Graves said.

"Clark. . . . Delacroix."

"There goes my old man," Mrs. Delacroix said. She held her breath 25 while her husband went forward.

"Dunbar," Mr. Summers said, and Mrs. Dunbar went steadily to the box while one of the women said, "Go on, Janey," and another said, "There she goes."

"We're next," Mrs. Graves said. She watched while Mr. Graves came around from the side of the box, greeted Mr. Summers gravely, and selected a slip of paper from the box. By now, all through the crowd there were men holding the small folded papers in their large hands, turning them over and over nervously. Mrs. Dunbar and her two sons stood together, Mrs. Dunbar holding the slip of paper.

"Harburt. . . . Hutchinson."

"Get up there, Bill," Mrs. Hutchinson said, and the people near her laughed.

"Jones."

"They do say," Mr. Adams said to Old Man Warner, who stood next to him, "that over in the north village they're talking of giving up the lottery." 30

Old Man Warner snorted. "Pack of crazy fools," he said. "Listening to the young folks, nothing's good enough for *them*. Next thing you know, they'll be wanting to go back to living in caves, nobody work any more, live *that* way for a while. Used to be a saying about 'Lottery in June, corn be heavy soon.' First thing you know, we'd all be eating stewed chickweed and acorns. There's *always* been a lottery," he added petulantly. "Bad enough to see young Joe Summers up there joking with everybody."

"Some places have already quit lotteries," Mrs. Adams said.

"Nothing but trouble in *that*," Old Man Warner said stoutly. "Pack of young fools."

"Martin." And Bobby Martin watched his father go forward. "Over- 35 dyke. . . . Percy."

"I wish they'd hurry," Mrs. Dunbar said to her older son. "I wish they'd hurry."

"They're almost through," her son said.

"You get ready to run tell Dad," Mrs. Dunbar said.

Mr. Summers called his own name and then stepped forward precisely and selected a slip from the box. Then he called, "Warner."

"Seventy-seventh year I been in the lottery," Old Man Warner said as 40 he went through the crowd. "Seventy-seventh time."

"Watson." The tall boy came awkwardly through the crowd. Someone said, "Don't be nervous, Jack," and Mr. Summers said, "Take your time, son."

"Zanini."

***

After that, there was a long pause, a breathless pause, until Mr. Summers, holding his slip of paper in the air, said, "All right, fellows." For a minute, no one moved, and then all the slips of paper were opened. Suddenly, all the women began to speak at once, saying, "Who is it?" "Who's got it?" "Is it the Dunbars?" "Is it the Watsons?" Then the voices began to say, "It's Hutchinson. It's Bill." "Bill Hutchinson's got it."

"Go tell your father," Mrs. Dunbar said to her older son.

People began to look around to see the Hutchinsons. Bill Hutchin- 45
son was standing quiet, staring down at the paper in his hand. Suddenly,
Tessie Hutchinson shouted to Mr. Summers, "You didn't give him time
enough to take any paper he wanted. I saw you. It wasn't fair!"

"Be a good sport, Tessie," Mrs. Delacroix called, and Mrs. Graves
said, "All of us took the same chance."

"Shut up, Tessie," Bill Hutchinson said.

"Well, everyone," Mr. Summers said, "that was done pretty fast, and
now we've got to be hurrying a little more to get done in time." He consulted his next list. "Bill," he said, "you draw for the Hutchinson family.
You got any other households in the Hutchinsons?"

"There's Don and Eva," Mrs. Hutchinson yelled. "Make them take
their chance!"

"Daughters draw with their husbands' families, Tessie," Mr. Summers 50
said gently. "You know that as well as anyone else."

"It wasn't fair," Tessie said.

"I guess not, Joe," Bill Hutchinson said regretfully. "My daughter
draws with her husband's family, that's only fair. And I've got no other
family except the kids."

"Then, as far as drawing for families is concerned, it's you," Mr.
Summers said in explanation, "and as far as drawing for households is
concerned, that's you, too. Right?"

"Right," Bill Hutchinson said.

"How many kids, Bill?" Mr. Summers asked formally. 55

"Three," Bill Hutchinson said. "There's Bill, Jr., and Nancy, and little
Dave. And Tessie and me."

"All right, then," Mr. Summers said. "Harry, you got their tickets back?"

Mr. Graves nodded and held up the slips of paper. "Put them in the
box, then," Mr. Summers directed. "Take Bill's and put it in."

"I think we ought to start over," Mrs. Hutchinson said, as quietly as
she could. "I tell you it wasn't *fair*. You didn't give him time enough to
choose. *Everybody* saw that."

Mr. Graves had selected the five slips and put them in the box, and 60
he dropped all the papers but those onto the ground, where the breeze
caught them and lifted them off.

"Listen, everybody," Mrs. Hutchinson was saying to the people
around her.

"Ready, Bill?" Mr. Summers asked, and Bill Hutchinson, with one
quick glance around at his wife and children, nodded.

"Remember," Mr. Summers said, "take the slips and keep them folded
until each person has taken one. Harry, you help little Dave." Mr. Graves
took the hand of the little boy, who came willingly with him up to the
box. "Take a paper out of the box, Davy," Mr. Summers said. Davy put
his hand into the box and laughed. "Take just *one* paper," Mr. Summers

said. "Harry, you hold it for him." Mr. Graves took the child's hand and removed the folded paper from the tight fist and held it while little Dave stood next to him and looked up at him wonderingly.

"Nancy next," Mr. Summers said. Nancy was twelve, and her school friends breathed heavily as she went forward, switching her skirt, and took a slip daintily from the box. "Bill, Jr.," Mr. Summers said, and Billy, his face red and his feet over-large, nearly knocked the box over as he got a paper out. "Tessie," Mr. Summers said. She hesitated for a minute, looking around defiantly, and then set her lips and went up to the box. She snatched a paper out and held it behind her.

"Bill," Mr. Summers said, and Bill Hutchinson reached into the box   65
and felt around, bringing his hand out at last with the slip of paper in it.

The crowd was quiet. A girl whispered, "I hope it's not Nancy," and the sound of the whisper reached the edges of the crowd.

"It's not the way it used to be," Old Man Warner said clearly. "People ain't the way they used to be."

"All right," Mr. Summers said. "Open the papers. Harry, you open little Dave's."

Mr. Graves opened the slip of paper and there was a general sigh through the crowd as he held it up and everyone could see that it was blank. Nancy and Bill, Jr., opened theirs at the same time, and both beamed and laughed, turning around to the crowd and holding their slips of paper above their heads.

"Tessie," Mr. Summers said. There was a pause, and then Mr. Sum-   70
mers looked at Bill Hutchinson, and Bill unfolded his paper and showed it. It was blank.

"It's Tessie," Mr. Summers said, and his voice was hushed. "Show us her paper, Bill."

Bill Hutchinson went over to his wife and forced the slip of paper out of her hand. It had a black spot on it, the black spot Mr. Summers had made the night before with the heavy pencil in the coal-company office. Bill Hutchinson held it up, and there was a stir in the crowd.

"All right, folks," Mr. Summers said, "Let's finish quickly."

Although the villagers had forgotten the ritual and lost the original black box, they still remembered to use stones. The pile of stones the boys had made earlier was ready; there were stones on the ground with the blowing scraps of paper that had come out of the box. Mrs. Delacroix selected a stone so large she had to pick it up with both hands and turned to Mrs. Dunbar. "Come on," she said. "Hurry up."

Mrs. Dunbar had small stones in both hands, and she said, gasping   75
for breath, "I can't run at all. You'll have to go ahead and I'll catch up with you."

The children had stones already, and someone gave little Davy Hutchinson a few pebbles.

Tessie Hutchinson was in the center of a cleared space by now, and she held her hands out desperately as the villagers moved in on her. "It isn't fair," she said. A stone hit her on the side of the head.

Old Man Warner was saying, "Come on, come on, everyone." Steve Adams was in the front of the crowd of villagers, with Mrs. Graves beside him.

"It isn't fair, it isn't right," Mrs. Hutchinson screamed, and then they were upon her.

Questions

1. Where do you think "The Lottery" takes place? What purpose do you suppose the writer has in making this setting appear so familiar and ordinary?

2. What details in paragraphs 2 and 3 foreshadow the ending of the story?

3. Take a close look at Jackson's description of the black wooden box (paragraph 5) and of the black spot on the fatal slip of paper (paragraph 72). What do these objects suggest to you? Are there any other symbols in the story?

4. What do you understand to be the writer's own attitude toward the lottery and the stoning? Exactly what in the story makes her attitude clear to us?

5. What do you make of Old Man Warner's saying, "Lottery in June, corn be heavy soon" (paragraph 32)?

6. What do you think Shirley Jackson is driving at? Consider each of the following interpretations and, looking at the story, see if you can find any evidence for it:

   Jackson takes a primitive fertility rite and playfully transfers it to a small town in North America.

   Jackson, writing her story soon after World War II, indirectly expresses her horror at the Holocaust. She assumes that the massacre of the Jews was carried out by unwitting, obedient people, like these villagers.

   Jackson is satirizing our own society, in which men are selected for the army by lottery.

   Jackson is just writing a memorable story that signifies nothing at all.

▪ WRITING *effectively*

THINKING ABOUT SYMBOLS

One danger in analyzing a story's symbolism is the temptation to read symbolic meaning into *everything*. An image acquires symbolic resonance because it is organically important to the actions and emotions of the story.

- **Consider a symbolic object's relevance to the plot.** What events, characters, and ideas are associated with it? It also helps to remember that some symbols arrive with cultural baggage. Any great white whale that swims into a work of contemporary fiction will inevitably summon up the symbolic associations of Melville's Moby Dick.

- **Ask yourself what the symbol means to the protagonist of your story.** Writers don't simply assign arbitrary meanings to items in their stories; generally, a horse is a horse, and a hammer is just a hammer. Sometimes, though, an object means something more to a character. Think of the flowers in "The Chrysanthemums."

- **Remember: in literature, few symbols are hidden.** Don't go on a symbol hunt. As you read or reread a story, any real symbol will usually find you. If an object appears time and again, or is tied inextricably to the story's events, it is likely to suggest something beyond itself. When an object, an action, or a place has emotional or intellectual power beyond its literal importance, then it is a genuine symbol.

CHECKLIST: Writing About Symbols

- ☐ Which objects, actions, or places seem unusually significant?
- ☐ List the specific objects, people, and ideas with which a particular symbol is associated.
- ☐ Locate the exact place in the story where the symbol links itself to the other thing.
- ☐ Ask whether each symbol comes with ready-made cultural associations.
- ☐ Avoid far-fetched interpretations. Focus first on the literal things, places, and actions in the story.
- ☐ Don't make a symbol mean too much or too little. Don't limit it to one narrow association or claim it summons up many different things.
- ☐ Be specific. Identify the exact place in the story where a symbol takes on a deeper meaning.

TOPICS FOR WRITING ON SYMBOLS

1. From the stories in this book, choose one with a strong central symbol. Explain how the symbol helps to communicate the story's meaning, citing specific moments in the text.

2. Choose a story from this chapter. Describe your experience of reading that story, and of encountering its symbols. At what point did the main symbol's meaning become clear? What in the story indicated the larger importance of that symbol?

3. From any story in this book, select an object, or place, or action that seems clearly symbolic. How do you know? Now select an object, place, or action from the same story that clearly seems to signify no more than itself. How can you tell?

4. Analyze the symbolism in either "Dead Men's Path" or "The Story of an Hour." Consider a symbol that recurs over the course of the story, and look closely at each appearance it makes. How does the story's use of the symbol evolve?

5. In an essay of 600 to 800 words, compare and contrast the symbolic use of the scapegoat in "The Lottery" and "The Ones Who Walk Away from Omelas."

▶ TERMS FOR *review*

Symbol ▶ A person, place, or thing in a narrative that suggests meanings beyond its literal sense. Symbol is related to allegory, but it works more complexly. A symbol often contains multiple meanings and associations.

Conventional symbol ▶ A literary symbol that has a conventional or customary meaning for most readers—for example, a black cat crossing a path or a young bride in a white dress.

Symbolic act ▶ An action whose significance goes well beyond its literal meaning. In literature, symbolic acts often involve some conscious or unconscious ritual element such as rebirth, purification, forgiveness, vengeance, or initiation.

Allegory ▶ A narrative in which the literal events (persons, places, and things) consistently point to a parallel sequence of symbolic equivalents. This narrative strategy is often used to dramatize abstract ideas, historical events, religious systems, or political issues. An allegory has two levels of meaning: a literal level that tells a surface story and a symbolic level in which the abstract ideas unfold.

8 STORIES FOR FURTHER READING

Sherman Alexie

This Is What It Means to Say Phoenix, Arizona 1993

Sherman Alexie was born in 1966 on the Spokane Indian Reservation in Wellpinit, Washington. Hydrocephalic at birth, he underwent surgery at the age of six months. At first he was expected not to survive; when that prognosis proved wrong, it was predicted, again wrongly, that he would be severely retarded. Alexie attended Gonzaga University in Spokane and graduated from Washington State University with a degree in American studies. His first book, a collection of poems called The Business of Fancydancing, *appeared in 1991, and he has published prolifically since then, averaging a*

Sherman Alexie

*book a year. He is the author of several volumes of poetry as well as four collections of stories—*The Lone Ranger and Tonto Fistfight in Heaven *(1993),* The Toughest Indian in the World *(2000),* Ten Little Indians *(2003), and* War Dances *(2009), which won the PEN/Faulkner Award—and three novels—*Reservation Blues *(1995),* Indian Killer *(1996), and* Flight *(2007). In addition to his writing, Alexie won the World Heavyweight Poetry Bout competition an unprecedented four consecutive times (1998–2001); he has appeared on television discussion programs hosted by Bill Maher, Bill Moyers, and Jim Lehrer (a 1998 "Dialogue on Race" whose participants also included President Bill Clinton); he has performed frequently as a stand-up comedian; and he co-produced and wrote the 1998 feature film* Smoke Signals, *based on "This Is What It Means to Say Phoenix, Arizona." Alexie lives with his wife and two sons in Seattle, Washington.*

Just after Victor lost his job at the BIA,° he also found out that his father had died of a heart attack in Phoenix, Arizona. Victor hadn't seen his father in a few years, only talked to him on the telephone once or

---

BIA: Bureau of Indian Affairs, a federal agency responsible for management of Indian lands and concerns.

twice, but there still was a genetic pain, which was soon to be pain as real and immediate as a broken bone.

Victor didn't have any money. Who does have money on a reservation, except the cigarette and fireworks salespeople? His father had a savings account waiting to be claimed, but Victor needed to find a way to get to Phoenix. Victor's mother was just as poor as he was, and the rest of his family didn't have any use at all for him. So Victor called the Tribal Council.

"Listen," Victor said. "My father just died. I need some money to get to Phoenix to make arrangements."

"Now, Victor," the council said. "You know we're having a difficult time financially."

"But I thought the council had special funds set aside for stuff like   5 this."

"Now, Victor, we do have some money available for the proper return of tribal members' bodies. But I don't think we have enough to bring your father all the way back from Phoenix."

"Well," Victor said. "It ain't going to cost all that much. He had to be cremated. Things were kind of ugly. He died of a heart attack in his trailer and nobody found him for a week. It was really hot, too. You get the picture."

"Now, Victor, we're sorry for your loss and the circumstances. But we can really only afford to give you one hundred dollars."

"That's not even enough for a plane ticket."

"Well, you might consider driving down to Phoenix."   10

"I don't have a car. Besides, I was going to drive my father's pickup back up here."

"Now, Victor," the council said. "We're sure there is somebody who could drive you to Phoenix. Or is there somebody who could lend you the rest of the money?"

"You know there ain't nobody around with that kind of money."

"Well, we're sorry, Victor, but that's the best we can do."

Victor accepted the Tribal Council's offer. What else could he do?   15 So he signed the proper papers, picked up his check, and walked over to the Trading Post to cash it.

While Victor stood in line, he watched Thomas Builds-the-Fire standing near the magazine rack, talking to himself. Like he always did. Thomas was a storyteller that nobody wanted to listen to. That's like being a dentist in a town where everybody has false teeth.

Victor and Thomas Builds-the-Fire were the same age, had grown up and played in the dirt together. Ever since Victor could remember, it was Thomas who always had something to say.

Once, when they were seven years old, when Victor's father still lived with the family, Thomas closed his eyes and told Victor this story:

"Your father's heart is weak. He is afraid of his own family. He is afraid of you. Late at night he sits in the dark. Watches the television until there's nothing but that white noise. Sometimes he feels like he wants to buy a motorcycle and ride away. He wants to run and hide. He doesn't want to be found."

Thomas Builds-the-Fire had known that Victor's father was going to leave, knew it before anyone. Now Victor stood in the Trading Post with a one-hundred-dollar check in his hand, wondering if Thomas knew that Victor's father was dead, if he knew what was going to happen next.

Just then Thomas looked at Victor, smiled, and walked over to him.   20

"Victor, I'm sorry about your father," Thomas said.

"How did you know about it?" Victor asked.

"I heard it on the wind. I heard it from the birds. I felt it in the sunlight. Also, your mother was just in here crying."

"Oh," Victor said and looked around the Trading Post. All the other Indians stared, surprised that Victor was even talking to Thomas. Nobody talked to Thomas anymore because he told the same damn stories over and over again. Victor was embarrassed, but he thought that Thomas might be able to help him. Victor felt a sudden need for tradition.

"I can lend you the money you need," Thomas said suddenly. "But   25
you have to take me with you."

"I can't take your money," Victor said. "I mean, I haven't hardly talked to you in years. We're not really friends anymore."

"I didn't say we were friends. I said you had to take me with you."

"Let me think about it."

Victor went home with his one hundred dollars and sat at the kitchen table. He held his head in his hands and thought about Thomas Builds-the-Fire, remembered little details, tears and scars, the bicycle they shared for a summer, so many stories.

Thomas Builds-the-Fire sat on the bicycle, waited in Victor's yard.   30
He was ten years old and skinny. His hair was dirty because it was the Fourth of July.

"Victor," Thomas yelled. "Hurry up. We're going to miss the fireworks."

After a few minutes, Victor ran out of his house, jumped the porch railing, and landed gracefully on the sidewalk.

"And the judges award him a 9.95, the highest score of the summer," Thomas said, clapped, laughed.

"That was perfect, cousin," Victor said. "And it's my turn to ride the bike."

Thomas gave up the bike and they headed for the fairgrounds. It was   35
nearly dark and the fireworks were about to start.

"You know," Thomas said. "It's strange how us Indians celebrate the Fourth of July. It ain't like it was *our* independence everybody was fighting for."

"You think about things too much," Victor said. "It's just supposed to be fun. Maybe Junior will be there."

"Which Junior? Everybody on this reservation is named Junior."

And they both laughed.

The fireworks were small, hardly more than a few bottle rockets and   40
a fountain. But it was enough for two Indian boys. Years later, they would need much more.

Afterwards, sitting in the dark, fighting off mosquitoes, Victor turned to Thomas Builds-the-Fire.

"Hey," Victor said. "Tell me a story."

Thomas closed his eyes and told this story: "There were these two Indian boys who wanted to be warriors. But it was too late to be warriors in the old way. All the horses were gone. So the two Indian boys stole a car and drove to the city. They parked the stolen car in front of the police station and then hitchhiked back home to the reservation. When they got back, all their friends cheered and their parents' eyes shone with pride. *You were very brave*, everybody said to the two Indian boys. *Very brave.*"

"Ya-hey," Victor said. "That's a good one. I wish I could be a warrior."

"Me, too," Thomas said.   45

They went home together in the dark, Thomas on the bike now, Victor on foot. They walked through shadows and light from streetlamps.

"We've come a long ways," Thomas said. "We have outdoor lighting."

"All I need is the stars," Victor said. "And besides, you still think about things too much."

They separated then, each headed for home, both laughing all the way.

Victor sat at his kitchen table. He counted his one hundred dollars   50
again and again. He knew he needed more to make it to Phoenix and back. He knew he needed Thomas Builds-the-Fire. So he put his money in his wallet and opened the front door to find Thomas on the porch.

"Ya-hey, Victor," Thomas said. "I knew you'd call me."

Thomas walked into the living room and sat down on Victor's favorite chair.

"I've got some money saved up," Thomas said. "It's enough to get us down there, but you have to get us back."

"I've got this hundred dollars," Victor said. "And my dad had a savings account I'm going to claim."

"How much in your dad's account?"   55

"Enough. A few hundred."

"Sounds good. When we leaving?"

*

When they were fifteen and had long since stopped being friends, Victor and Thomas got into a fistfight. That is, Victor was really drunk and beat Thomas up for no reason at all. All the other Indian boys stood around and watched it happen. Junior was there and so were Lester, Seymour, and a lot of others. The beating might have gone on until Thomas was dead if Norma Many Horses hadn't come along and stopped it.

"Hey, you boys," Norma yelled and jumped out of her car. "Leave him alone."

If it had been someone else, even another man, the Indian boys would've just ignored the warnings. But Norma was a warrior. She was powerful. She could have picked up any two of the boys and smashed their skulls together. But worse than that, she would have dragged them all over to some tipi and made them listen to some elder tell a dusty old story.

The Indian boys scattered, and Norma walked over to Thomas and picked him up.

"Hey, little man, are you okay?" she asked.

Thomas gave her a thumbs up.

"Why they always picking on you?"

Thomas shook his head, closed his eyes, but no stories came to him, no words or music. He just wanted to go home, to lie in his bed and let his dreams tell his stories for him.

Thomas Builds-the-Fire and Victor sat next to each other in the airplane, coach section. A tiny white woman had the window seat. She was busy twisting her body into pretzels. She was flexible.

"I have to ask," Thomas said, and Victor closed his eyes in embarrassment.

"Don't," Victor said.

"Excuse me, miss," Thomas asked. "Are you a gymnast or something?"

"There's no something about it," she said. "I was first alternate on the 1980 Olympic team."

"Really?" Thomas asked.

"Really."

"I mean, you used to be a world-class athlete?" Thomas asked.

"My husband still thinks I am."

Thomas Builds-the-Fire smiled. She was a mental gymnast, too. She pulled her leg straight up against her body so that she could've kissed her kneecap.

"I wish I could do that," Thomas said.

Victor was ready to jump out of the plane. Thomas, that crazy Indian storyteller with ratty old braids and broken teeth, was flirting with a beautiful Olympic gymnast. Nobody back home on the reservation would ever believe it.

"Well," the gymnast said. "It's easy. Try it."

Thomas grabbed at his leg and tried to pull it up into the same posi-tion as the gymnast. He couldn't even come close, which made Victor and the gymnast laugh.

"Hey," she asked. "You two are Indian, right?"   80

"Full-blood," Victor said.

"Not me," Thomas said. "I'm half magician on my mother's side and half clown on my father's."

They all laughed.

"What are your names?" she asked.

"Victor and Thomas."   85

"Mine is Cathy. Pleased to meet you all."

The three of them talked for the duration of the flight. Cathy the gym-nast complained about the government, how they screwed the 1980 Olympic team by boycotting.°

"Sounds like you all got a lot in common with Indians," Thomas said. Nobody laughed.

After the plane landed in Phoenix and they had all found their way   90
to the terminal, Cathy the gymnast smiled and waved good-bye.

"She was really nice," Thomas said.

"Yeah, but everybody talks to everybody on airplanes," Victor said. "It's too bad we can't always be that way."

"You always used to tell me I think too much," Thomas said. "Now it sounds like you do."

"Maybe I caught it from you."

"Yeah."   95

Thomas and Victor rode in a taxi to the trailer where Victor's father died.

"Listen," Victor said as they stopped in front of the trailer. "I never told you I was sorry for beating you up that time."

"Oh, it was nothing. We were just kids and you were drunk."

"Yeah, but I'm still sorry."

"That's all right."   100

Victor paid for the taxi and the two of them stood in the hot Phoenix summer. They could smell the trailer.

"This ain't going to be nice," Victor said. "You don't have to go in."

"You're going to need help."

Victor walked to the front door and opened it. The stink rolled out and made them both gag. Victor's father had lain in that trailer for a week in hundred-degree temperatures before anyone found him. And the only

---

they screwed the 1980 Olympic team by boycotting: in an international movement led by the United States at the direction of President Jimmy Carter, some sixty nations boycotted the 1980 Summer Olympic Games in Moscow as a protest against the Soviet invasion of Afghanistan in December 1979.

reason anyone found him was because of the smell. They needed dental records to identify him. That's exactly what the coroner said. They needed dental records.

"Oh, man," Victor said. "I don't know if I can do this."   105

"Well, then don't."

"But there might be something valuable in there."

"I thought his money was in the bank."

"It is. I was talking about pictures and letters and stuff like that."

"Oh," Thomas said as he held his breath and followed Victor into   110
the trailer.

When Victor was twelve, he stepped into an underground wasp nest. His foot was caught in the hole, and no matter how hard he struggled, Victor couldn't pull free. He might have died there, stung a thousand times, if Thomas Builds-the-Fire had not come by.

"Run," Thomas yelled and pulled Victor's foot from the hole. They ran then, hard as they ever had, faster than Billy Mills, faster than Jim Thorpe,° faster than the wasps could fly.

Victor and Thomas ran until they couldn't breathe, ran until it was cold and dark outside, ran until they were lost and it took hours to find their way home. All the way back, Victor counted his stings.

"Seven," Victor said. "My lucky number."

Victor didn't find much to keep in the trailer. Only a photo album   115
and a stereo. Everything else had that smell stuck in it or was useless anyway.

"I guess this is all," Victor said. "It ain't much."

"Better than nothing," Thomas said.

"Yeah, and I do have the pickup."

"Yeah," Thomas said. "It's in good shape."

"Dad was good about that stuff."   120

"Yeah, I remember your dad."

"Really?" Victor asked. "What do you remember?"

Thomas Builds-the-Fire closed his eyes and told this story: "I remember when I had this dream that told me to go to Spokane, to stand by the Falls in the middle of the city and wait for a sign. I knew I had to go there but I didn't have a car. Didn't have a license. I was only thirteen. So I walked all the way, took me all day, and I finally made it to the Falls. I stood there for an hour waiting. Then your dad came walking up. *What the*

Billy Mills . . . Jim Thorpe: William Mervin "Billy" Mills (born 1938), a member of the Sioux tribe, won a gold medal in the 10,000-meter run at the 1964 Summer Olympic Games in Tokyo, Japan. Jacobus Franciscus "Jim" Thorpe (1888–1953), of the Sac and Fox tribe, is widely regarded as one of the greatest American athletes of the twentieth century; he won gold medals in the pentathlon and decathlon at the 1912 Summer Olympic Games in Stockholm, Sweden. He also played professional football, baseball, and basketball.

hell are you doing here? he asked me. I said, *Waiting for a vision.* Then your father said, *All you're going to get here is mugged.* So he drove me over to Denny's, bought me dinner, and then drove me home to the reservation. For a long time I was mad because I thought my dreams had lied to me. But they didn't. Your dad was my vision. *Take care of each other* is what my dreams were saying. *Take care of each other.*"

Victor was quiet for a long time. He searched his mind for memories of his father, found the good ones, found a few bad ones, added it all up, and smiled.

"My father never told me about finding you in Spokane," Victor said.   125

"He said he wouldn't tell anybody. Didn't want me to get in trouble. But he said I had to watch out for you as part of the deal."

"Really?"

"Really. Your father said you would need the help. He was right."

"That's why you came down here with me, isn't it?" Victor asked.

"I came because of your father."   130

Victor and Thomas climbed into the pickup, drove over to the bank, and claimed the three hundred dollars in the savings account.

Thomas Builds-the-Fire could fly.

Once, he jumped off the roof of the tribal school and flapped his arms like a crazy eagle. And he flew. For a second, he hovered, suspended above all the other Indian boys who were too smart or too scared to jump.

"He's flying," Junior yelled, and Seymour was busy looking for the trick wires or mirrors. But it was real. As real as the dirt when Thomas lost altitude and crashed to the ground.

He broke his arm in two places.   135

"He broke his wing," Victor chanted, and the other Indian boys joined in, made it a tribal song.

"He broke his wing, he broke his wing, he broke his wing," all the Indian boys chanted as they ran off, flapping their wings, wishing they could fly, too. They hated Thomas for his courage, his brief moment as a bird. Everybody has dreams about flying. Thomas flew.

One of his dreams came true for just a second, just enough to make it real.

Victor's father, his ashes, fit in one wooden box with enough left over to fill a cardboard box.

"He always was a big man," Thomas said.   140

Victor carried part of his father and Thomas carried the rest out to the pickup. They set him down carefully behind the seats, put a cowboy hat on the wooden box and a Dodgers cap on the cardboard box. That's the way it was supposed to be.

"Ready to head back home," Victor asked.

"It's going to be a long drive."

"Yeah, take a couple days, maybe."

"We can take turns," Thomas said.   145

"Okay," Victor said, but they didn't take turns. Victor drove for sixteen hours straight north, made it halfway up Nevada toward home before he finally pulled over.

"Hey, Thomas," Victor said. "You got to drive for a while."

"Okay."

Thomas Builds-the-Fire slid behind the wheel and started off down the road. All through Nevada, Thomas and Victor had been amazed at the lack of animal life, at the absence of water, of movement.

"Where is everything?" Victor had asked more than once.   150

Now when Thomas was finally driving they saw the first animal, maybe the only animal in Nevada. It was a long-eared jackrabbit.

"Look," Victor yelled. "It's alive."

Thomas and Victor were busy congratulating themselves on their discovery when the jackrabbit darted out into the road and under the wheels of the pickup.

"Stop the goddamn car," Victor yelled, and Thomas did stop, backed the pickup to the dead jackrabbit.

"Oh, man, he's dead," Victor said as he looked at the squashed animal.   155

"Really dead."

"The only thing alive in this whole state and we just killed it."

"I don't know," Thomas said. "I think it was suicide."

Victor looked around the desert, sniffed the air, felt the emptiness and loneliness, and nodded his head.

"Yeah," Victor said. "It had to be suicide."   160

"I can't believe this," Thomas said. "You drive for a thousand miles and there ain't even any bugs smashed on the windshield. I drive for ten seconds and kill the only living thing in Nevada."

"Yeah," Victor said. "Maybe I should drive."

"Maybe you should."

Thomas Builds-the-Fire walked through the corridors of the tribal school by himself. Nobody wanted to be anywhere near him because of all those stories. Story after story.

Thomas closed his eyes and this story came to him: "We are all given   165
one thing by which our lives are measured, one determination. Mine are the stories which can change or not change the world. It doesn't matter which as long as I continue to tell the stories. My father, he died on Okinawa in World War II, died fighting for this country, which had tried to kill him for years. My mother, she died giving birth to me, died while I was still inside her. She pushed me out into the world with her last breath. I have no brothers or sisters. I have only my stories which came to me before I even had the words to speak. I learned a thousand stories before I took my first thousand steps. They are all I have. It's all I can do."

Thomas Builds-the-Fire told his stories to all those who would stop and listen. He kept telling them long after people had stopped listening.

Victor and Thomas made it back to the reservation just as the sun was rising. It was the beginning of a new day on earth, but the same old shit on the reservation.

"Good morning," Thomas said.

"Good morning."

The tribe was waking up, ready for work, eating breakfast, reading the 170 newspaper, just like everybody else does. Willene LeBret was out in her garden wearing a bathrobe. She waved when Thomas and Victor drove by.

"Crazy Indians made it," she said to herself and went back to her roses.

Victor stopped the pickup in front of Thomas Builds-the-Fire's HUD house.° They both yawned, stretched a little, shook dust from their bodies.

"I'm tired," Victor said.

"Of everything," Thomas added.

They both searched for words to end the journey. Victor needed to 175 thank Thomas for his help, for the money, and make the promise to pay it all back.

"Don't worry about the money," Thomas said. "It don't make any difference anyhow."

"Probably not, enit?"

"Nope."

Victor knew that Thomas would remain the crazy storyteller who talked to dogs and cars, who listened to the wind and pine trees. Victor knew that he couldn't really be friends with Thomas, even after all that had happened. It was cruel but it was real. As real as the ashes, as Victor's father, sitting behind the seats.

"I know how it is," Thomas said. "I know you ain't going to treat 180 me any better than you did before. I know your friends would give you too much shit about it."

Victor was ashamed of himself. Whatever happened to the tribal ties, the sense of community? The only real thing he shared with anybody was a bottle and broken dreams. He owed Thomas something, anything.

"Listen," Victor said and handed Thomas the cardboard box which contained half of his father. "I want you to have this."

Thomas took the ashes and smiled, closed his eyes, and told this story: "I'm going to travel to Spokane Falls one last time and toss these ashes into the water. And your father will rise like a salmon, leap over the bridge, over me, and find his way home. It will be beautiful. His teeth will shine like silver, like a rainbow. He will rise, Victor, he will rise."

HUD house: housing subsidized by the U.S. Department of Housing and Urban Development.

Victor smiled.

"I was planning on doing the same thing with my half," Victor 185
said. "But I didn't imagine my father looking anything like a salmon. I
thought it'd be like cleaning the attic or something. Like letting things
go after they've stopped having any use."

"Nothing stops, cousin," Thomas said. "Nothing stops."

Thomas Builds-the-Fire got out of the pickup and walked up his
driveway. Victor started the pickup and began the drive home.

"Wait," Thomas yelled suddenly from his porch. "I just got to ask one
favor."

Victor stopped the pickup, leaned out the window, and shouted back.
"What do you want?"

"Just one time when I'm telling a story somewhere, why don't you stop 190
and listen?" Thomas asked.

"Just once?"

"Just once."

Victor waved his arms to let Thomas know that the deal was good. It
was a fair trade, and that was all Victor had ever wanted from his whole
life. So Victor drove his father's pickup toward home while Thomas went
into his house, closed the door behind him, and heard a new story come
to him in the silence afterwards.

Margaret Atwood

Happy Endings   1983

Born in Ottawa, Ontario, in 1939, Margaret
Eleanor Atwood was the daughter of an entomolo-
gist and spent her childhood summers in the forests
of northern Quebec, where her father carried out
research. Atwood began writing at the age of five
and had already seriously entertained thoughts of
becoming a professional writer before she finished
high school. She graduated from the University of
Toronto in 1961, and got a master's degree from
Radcliffe. Atwood initially gained prominence as
a poet. Her first full-length collection of poems,
The Circle Game (1966), was awarded a Gov-

Margaret Atwood

ernor General's Award, Canada's most prestigious literary honor, and she has
since published nearly twenty volumes of verse. Atwood also began to write
fiction seriously in graduate school, and her short stories were first collected
in Dancing Girls (1977), followed by numerous additional collections, most
recently Moral Disorder (2006).

A dedicated feminist, Atwood's works of fiction explore the complex relations
between the sexes, most incisively in The Handmaid's Tale (1985), a futuristic

novel about a world in which gender roles are ruthlessly enforced by a society based on religious fundamentalism. In 1986 Atwood was named Woman of the Year by Ms. magazine. Subsequent novels include Cat's Eye (1988), The Robber Bride (1993), The Blind Assassin (2000), The Year of the Flood (2009), and MaddAddam (2013). Atwood has served as writer-in-residence at many universities, and she is widely in demand for appearances at symposia devoted to literature and women's issues.

John and Mary meet.
What happens next?
If you want a happy ending, try A.

A

John and Mary fall in love and get married. They both have worthwhile and remunerative jobs which they find stimulating and challenging. They buy a charming house. Real estate values go up. Eventually, when they can afford live-in help, they have two children, to whom they are devoted. The children turn out well. John and Mary have a stimulating and challenging sex life and worthwhile friends. They go on fun vacations together. They retire. They both have hobbies which they find stimulating and challenging. Eventually they die. This is the end of the story.

B

Mary falls in love with John but John doesn't fall in love with Mary.   5
He merely uses her body for selfish pleasure and ego gratification of a tepid kind. He comes to her apartment twice a week and she cooks him dinner, you'll notice that he doesn't even consider her worth the price of a dinner out, and after he's eaten the dinner he fucks her and after that he falls asleep, while she does the dishes so he won't think she's untidy, having all those dirty dishes lying around, and puts on fresh lipstick so she'll look good when he wakes up, but when he wakes up he doesn't even notice, he puts on his socks and his shorts and his pants and his shirt and his tie and his shoes, the reverse order from the one in which he took them off. He doesn't take off Mary's clothes, she takes them off herself, she acts as if she's dying for it every time, not because she likes sex exactly, she doesn't, but she wants John to think she does because if they do it often enough surely he'll get used to her, he'll come to depend on her and they will get married, but John goes out the door with hardly so much as a goodnight and three days later he turns up at six o'clock and they do the whole thing over again.

Mary gets run down. Crying is bad for your face, everyone knows that and so does Mary but she can't stop. People at work notice. Her friends tell her John is a rat, a pig, a dog, he isn't good enough for her, but she can't believe it. Inside John, she thinks, is another John, who is much nicer. This other John will emerge like a butterfly from a cocoon, a Jack from a box, a pit from a prune, if the first John is only squeezed enough.

One evening John complains about the food. He has never complained about the food before. Mary is hurt.

Her friends tell her they've seen him in a restaurant with another woman, whose name is Madge. It's not even Madge that finally gets to Mary; it's the restaurant. John has never taken Mary to a restaurant. Mary collects all the sleeping pills and aspirins she can find, and takes them and a half a bottle of sherry. You can see what kind of a woman she is by the fact that it's not even whiskey. She leaves a note for John. She hopes he'll discover her and get her to the hospital in time and repent and then they can get married, but this fails to happen and she dies.

John marries Madge and everything continues as in A.

C

John, who is an older man, falls in love with Mary, and Mary, who is   10 only twenty-two, feels sorry for him because he's worried about his hair falling out. She sleeps with him even though she's not in love with him. She met him at work. She's in love with someone called James, who is twenty-two also and not yet ready to settle down.

John on the contrary settled down long ago: this is what is bothering him. John has a steady, respectable job and is getting ahead in his field, but Mary isn't impressed by him, she's impressed by James, who has a motorcycle and a fabulous record collection. But James is often away on his motorcycle, being free. Freedom isn't the same for girls, so in the meantime Mary spends Thursday evenings with John. Thursdays are the only days John can get away.

John is married to a woman called Madge and they have two children, a charming house which they bought just before the real estate values went up, and hobbies which they find stimulating and challenging, when they have the time. John tells Mary how important she is to him, but of course, he can't leave his wife because a commitment is a commitment. He goes on about this more than is necessary and Mary finds it boring, but older men can keep it up longer so on the whole she has a fairly good time.

One day James breezes in on his motorcycle with some top-grade California hybrid and James and Mary get higher than you'd believe possible and they climb into bed. Everything becomes very underwater, but along comes John, who has a key to Mary's apartment. He finds them stoned and entwined. He's hardly in any position to be jealous, considering Madge, but nevertheless he's overcome with despair. Finally he's middle-aged, in two years he'll be bald as an egg and he can't stand it. He purchases a handgun, saying he needs it for target practice—this is the thin part of the plot, but it can be dealt with later—and shoots the two of them and himself.

Madge, after a suitable period of mourning, marries an understanding man called Fred and everything continues as in A, but under different names.

D

Fred and Madge have no problems. They get along exceptionally   15
well and are good at working out any little difficulties that may arise. But their charming house is by the seashore and one day a giant tidal wave approaches. Real estate values go down. The rest of the story is about what caused the tidal wave and how they escape from it. They do, though thousands drown, but Fred and Madge are virtuous and lucky. Finally on high ground they clasp each other, wet and dripping and grateful, and continue as in A.

E

Yes, but Fred has a bad heart. The rest of the story is about how kind and understanding they both are until Fred dies. Then Madge devotes herself to charity work until the end of A. If you like, it can be "Madge," "cancer," "guilty and confused," and "bird watching."

F

If you think this is all too bourgeois, make John a revolutionary and Mary a counterespionage agent and see how far that gets you. Remember, this is Canada. You'll still end up with A, though in between you may get a lustful brawling saga of passionate involvement, a chronicle of our times, sort of.

You'll have to face it, the endings are the same however you slice it. Don't be deluded by any other endings, they're all fake, either deliberately fake, with malicious intent to deceive, or just motivated by excessive optimism if not by downright sentimentality.

The only authentic ending is the one provided here:

John and Mary die. John and Mary die. John and Mary die.   20

So much for endings. Beginnings are always more fun. True connoisseurs, however, are known to favor the stretch in between, since it's the hardest to do anything with.

That's about all that can be said for plots, which anyway are just one thing after another, a what and a what and a what.

Now try How and Why.

Nathaniel Hawthorne

Young Goodman Brown   (1835) 1846

Nathaniel Hawthorne

Nathaniel Hawthorne (1804–1864) was born in the clipper-ship seaport of Salem, Massachusetts, son of a merchant captain (who died when the future novelist was only four years old) and great-great-grandson of a magistrate involved in the notorious Salem witchcraft trials. Hawthorne takes a keen interest in New England's sin-and-brimstone Puritan past in many of his stories, especially "Young Goodman Brown," and in the classic novel The Scarlet Letter *(1850), his deepest exploration of his major themes of conscience, sin, and guilt. In 1825 Hawthorne graduated from Bowdoin College; one of his classmates—and his lifelong best friend—was Franklin Pierce, who in 1852 would be elected president of the United States. After college, Hawthorne lived at home and trained to be a writer. His first novel,* Fanshawe *(1828), begun while he was still an undergraduate, was published anonymously and at his own expense. During this period, Hawthorne also experienced great difficulty in trying to publish his short fiction, both in magazines and in book form, until the appearance of* Twice-Told Tales *(1837). In 1841, he was appointed to a position in the Boston Custom House; in the following year he married Sophia Peabody. The newlyweds settled in the Old Manse in Concord, Massachusetts. Three more novels followed:* The House of the Seven Gables *(1851, the story of a family curse, tinged with nightmarish humor),* The Blithedale Romance *(1852, drawn from his short, irritating stay at a Utopian commune, Brook Farm), and* The Marble Faun *(1860, inspired by a stay in Italy). When Franklin Pierce ran for president, Hawthorne wrote his campaign biography. After taking office, Pierce appointed his old friend American consul at Liverpool, England. Depressed by ill health and the terrible toll of the Civil War, Hawthorne died suddenly while on a tour with Pierce of New Hampshire's White Mountains. With his contemporary Edgar Allan Poe, Hawthorne transformed the American short story from popular magazine filler into a major literary form.*

Young Goodman° Brown came forth, at sunset, into the street of Salem village,° but put his head back, after crossing the threshold, to exchange a parting kiss with his young wife. And Faith, as the wife was

---

Goodman: title given by Puritans to a male head of a household; a farmer or other ordinary citizen.   *Salem village:* in England's Massachusetts Bay Colony.

aptly named, thrust her own pretty head into the street, letting the wind play with the pink ribbons of her cap, while she called to Goodman Brown.

"Dearest heart," whispered she, softly and rather sadly, when her lips were close to his ear, "pray thee, put off your journey until sunrise, and sleep in your own bed to-night. A lone woman is troubled with such dreams and such thoughts, that she's afraid of herself, sometimes. Pray, tarry with me this night, dear husband, of all nights in the year!"

"My love and my Faith," replied young Goodman Brown, "of all nights in the year, this one night must I tarry away from thee. My journey, as thou callest it, forth and back again, must needs be done 'twixt now and sunrise. What, my sweet, pretty wife, dost thou doubt me already, and we but three months married!"

"Then, God bless you!" said Faith, with the pink ribbons, "and may you find all well, when you come back."

"Amen!" cried Goodman Brown. "Say thy prayers, dear Faith, and go   5
to bed at dusk, and no harm will come to thee."

So they parted; and the young man pursued his way, until, being about to turn the corner by the meeting-house, he looked back, and saw the head of Faith still peeping after him, with a melancholy air, in spite of her pink ribbons.

"Poor little Faith!" thought he, for his heart smote him. "What a wretch am I, to leave her on such an errand! She talks of dreams, too. Methought, as she spoke, there was trouble in her face, as if a dream had warned her what work is to be done tonight. But, no, no! 'twould kill her to think it. Well; she's a blessed angel on earth; and after this one night, I'll cling to her skirts and follow her to Heaven."

With this excellent resolve for the future, Goodman Brown felt himself justified in making more haste on his present evil purpose. He had taken a dreary road, darkened by all the gloomiest trees of the forest, which barely stood aside to let the narrow path creep through, and closed immediately behind. It was all as lonely as could be; and there is this peculiarity in such a solitude, that the traveller knows not who may be concealed by the innumerable trunks and the thick boughs overhead; so that, with lonely footsteps, he may yet be passing through an unseen multitude.

"There may be a devilish Indian behind every tree," said Goodman Brown, to himself; and he glanced fearfully behind him, as he added, "What if the devil himself should be at my very elbow!"

His head being turned back, he passed a crook of the road, and   10
looking forward again, beheld the figure of a man, in grave and decent attire, seated at the foot of an old tree. He arose, at Goodman Brown's approach, and walked onward, side by side with him.

"You are late, Goodman Brown," said he. "The clock of the Old South was striking as I came through Boston; and that is full fifteen minutes agone."°

"Faith kept me back awhile," replied the young man, with a tremor in his voice, caused by the sudden appearance of his companion, though not wholly unexpected.

It was now deep dusk in the forest, and deepest in that part of it where these two were journeying. As nearly as could be discerned, the second traveller was about fifty years old, apparently in the same rank of life as Goodman Brown, and bearing a considerable resemblance to him, though perhaps more in expression than features. Still, they might have been taken for father and son. And yet, though the elder person was as simply clad as the younger, and as simple in manner too, he had an indescribable air of one who knew the world, and would not have felt abashed at the governor's dinner-table, or in King William's court,° were it possible that his affairs should call him thither. But the only thing about him, that could be fixed upon as remarkable, was his staff, which bore the likeness of a great black snake, so curiously wrought, that it might almost be seen to twist and wriggle itself, like a living serpent. This, of course, must have been an ocular deception, assisted by the uncertain light.

"Come, Goodman Brown!" cried his fellow-traveller, "this is dull pace for the beginning of a journey. Take my staff, if you are so soon weary."

"Friend," said the other, exchanging his slow pace for a full stop,   15 "having kept covenant by meeting thee here, it is my purpose now to return whence I came. I have scruples, touching the matter thou wot'st° of."

"Sayest thou so?" replied he of the serpent, smiling apart. "Let us walk on, nevertheless, reasoning as we go, and if I convince thee not, thou shalt turn back. We are but a little way in the forest, yet."

"Too far, too far!" exclaimed the goodman, unconsciously resuming his walk. "My father never went into the woods on such an errand, nor his father before him. We have been a race of honest men and good Christians, since the days of the martyrs.° And shall I be the first of the name of Brown, that ever took this path, and kept—"

"Such company, thou wouldst say," observed the elder person, interpreting his pause. "Well said, Goodman Brown! I have been as well acquainted with your family as with ever a one among the Puritans; and

---

full fifteen minutes agone: Apparently this mystery man has traveled in a flash from Boston's Old South Church all the way to the woods beyond Salem—as the crow flies, a good sixteen miles. *King William's court:* back in England, where William III reigned from 1689 to 1702. *wot'st:* know. *days of the martyrs:* a time when many forebears of the New England Puritans had given their lives for religious convictions—when Mary I (Mary Tudor, nicknamed "Bloody Mary"), queen of England from 1553 to 1558, briefly reestablished the Roman Catholic Church in England and launched a campaign of persecution against Protestants.

that's no trifle to say. I helped your grandfather, the constable, when he lashed the Quaker woman so smartly through the streets of Salem. And it was I that brought your father a pitch-pine knot, kindled at my own hearth, to set fire to an Indian village, in King Philip's war.° They were my good friends, both; and many a pleasant walk have we had along this path, and returned merrily after midnight. I would fain be friends with you, for their sake."

"If it be as thou sayest," replied Goodman Brown, "I marvel they never spoke of these matters. Or, verily, I marvel not, seeing that the least rumor of the sort would have driven them from New England. We are a people of prayer, and good works, to boot, and abide no such wickedness."

"Wickedness or not," said the traveller with the twisted staff, "I have   20 a very general acquaintance here in New England. The deacons of many a church have drunk the communion wine with me; the selectmen, of divers towns, make me their chairman; and a majority of the Great and General Court are firm supporters of my interest. The governor and I, too—but these are state-secrets."

"Can this be so!" cried Goodman Brown, with a stare of amazement at his undisturbed companion. "Howbeit, I have nothing to do with the governor and council; they have their own ways, and are no rule for a simple husbandman, like me. But, were I to go on with thee, how should I meet the eye of that good old man, our minister, at Salem village? Oh, his voice would make me tremble, both Sabbath-day and lecture-day!"°

Thus far, the elder traveller had listened with due gravity, but now burst into a fit of irrepressible mirth, shaking himself so violently, that his snake-like staff actually seemed to wriggle in sympathy.

"Ha! ha! ha!" shouted he, again and again; then composing himself, "Well, go on, Goodman Brown, go on; but pray thee, don't kill me with laughing!"

"Well, then, to end the matter at once," said Goodman Brown, considerably nettled, "there is my wife, Faith. It would break her dear little heart; and I'd rather break my own!"

"Nay, if that be the case," answered the other, "e'en go thy ways,   25 Goodman Brown. I would not, for twenty old women like the one hobbling before us, that Faith should come to any harm."

As he spoke, he pointed his staff at a female figure on the path, in whom Goodman Brown recognized a very pious and exemplary dame, who had taught him his catechism, in youth, and was still his moral and spiritual adviser, jointly with the minister and Deacon Gookin.

King Philip's war: Metacomet, or King Philip (as the English called him), chief of the Wampanoag Indians, had led a bitter, widespread uprising of several New England tribes (1675–1678). Metacomet died in the war, as did one out of every ten white male colonists. *lecture-day:* a weekday when everyone had to go to church to hear a sermon or Bible-reading.

"A marvel, truly, that Goody° Hoyse should be so far in the wilderness, at nightfall!" said he. "But, with your leave, friend, I shall take a cut through the woods, until we have left this Christian woman behind. Being a stranger to you, she might ask whom I was consorting with, and whither I was going."

"Be it so," said his fellow-traveller. "Betake you to the woods, and let me keep the path."

Accordingly, the young man turned aside, but took care to watch his companion, who advanced softly along the road, until he had come within a staff's length of the old dame. She, meanwhile, was making the best of her way, with singular speed for so aged a woman, and mumbling some indistinct words, a prayer, doubtless, as she went. The traveller put forth his staff, and touched her withered neck with what seemed the serpent's tail.

"The devil!" screamed the pious old lady.   30

"Then Goody Cloyse knows her old friend?" observed the traveller, confronting her, and leaning on his writhing stick.

"Ah, forsooth, and is it your worship, indeed?" cried the good dame. "Yea, truly is it, and in the very image of my old gossip,° Goodman Brown, the grandfather of the silly fellow that now is. But—would your worship believe it?—my broomstick hath strangely disappeared, stolen, as I suspect, by that unhanged witch, Goody Cory, and that, too, when I was all anointed with the juice of smallage and cinquefoil and wolfs bane—"°

"Mingled with fine wheat and the fat of a new-born babe," said the shape of old Goodman Brown.

"Ah, your worship knows the receipt,"° cried the old lady, cackling aloud. "So, as I was saying, being all ready for the meeting, and no horse to ride on, I made up my mind to foot it; for they tell me, there is a nice young man to be taken into communion to-night. But now your good worship will lend me your arm, and we shall be there in a twinkling."

"That can hardly be," answered her friend. "I may not spare you my   35 arm, Goody Cloyse, but here is my staff, if you will."

So saying, he threw it down at her feet, where, perhaps, it assumed life, being one of the rods which its owner had formerly lent to the Egyptian Magi.° Of this fact, however, Goodman Brown could not take cognizance. He had cast up his eyes in astonishment, and looking down again, beheld neither Goody Cloyse nor the serpentine staff, but his fellow-traveller alone, who waited for him as calmly as if nothing had happened.

Goody: short for Goodwife, title for a married woman of ordinary station. In his story, Hawthorne borrows from history the names of two "Goodys"—Goody Cloyse and Goody Cory—and one unmarried woman, Martha Carrier. In 1692 Hawthorne's great-great-grandfather John Hathorne, a judge in the Salem witchcraft trials, had condemned all three to be hanged.   *gossip:* friend or kinsman.   *smallage and cinquefoil and wolf's bane:* wild plants—here, ingredients for a witch's brew.   *receipt:* recipe.   *Egyptian Magi:* In the Bible, Pharaoh's wise men and sorcerers who by their magical powers changed their rods into live serpents. (This incident, part of the story of Moses and Aaron, is related in Exodus 7:8–12.)

above Goodman Brown. But something fluttered lightly down through the air, and caught on the branch of a tree. The young man seized it, and beheld a pink ribbon.

"My Faith is gone!" cried he, after one stupefied moment. "There is no good on earth; and sin is but a name. Come, devil! for to thee is this world given."

And maddened with despair, so that he laughed loud and long, did Goodman Brown grasp his staff and set forth again, at such a rate, that he seemed to fly along the forest-path, rather than to walk or run. The road grew wilder and drearier, and more faintly traced, and vanished at length, leaving him in the heart of the dark wilderness, still rushing onward, with the instinct that guides mortal man to evil. The whole forest was peopled with frightful sounds; the creaking of the trees, the howling of wild beasts, and the yell of Indians; while, sometimes, the wind tolled like a distant church-bell, and sometimes gave a broad roar around the traveller, as if all Nature were laughing him to scorn. But he was himself the chief horror of the scene, and shrank not from its other horrors.

"Ha! ha! ha!" roared Goodman Brown, when the wind laughed at him. "Let us hear which will laugh loudest! Think not to frighten me with your deviltry! Come witch, come wizard, come Indian powow, come devil himself! and here comes Goodman Brown. You may as well fear him as he fear you!"

In truth, all through the haunted forest, there could be nothing more frightful than the figure of Goodman Brown. On he flew, among the black pines, brandishing his staff with frenzied gestures, now giving vent to an inspiration of horrid blasphemy, and now shouting forth such laughter, as set all the echoes of the forest laughing like demons around him. The fiend in his own shape is less hideous, than when he rages in the breast of man. Thus sped the demoniac on his course, until, quivering among the trees, he saw a red light before him, as when the felled trunks and branches of a clearing have been set on fire, and throw up their lurid blaze against the sky, at the hour of midnight. He paused, in a lull of the tempest that had driven him onward, and heard the swell of what seemed a hymn, rolling solemnly from a distance, with the weight of many voices. He knew the tune; it was a familiar one in the choir of the village meeting-house. The verse died heavily away, and was lengthened by a chorus, not of human voices, but of all the sounds of the benighted wilderness, pealing in awful harmony together. Goodman Brown cried out; and his cry was lost to his own ear, by its unison with the cry of the desert.

In the interval of silence, he stole forward, until the light glared full upon his eyes. At one extremity of an open space, hemmed in by the dark wall of the forest, arose a rock, bearing some rude, natural resemblance either to an altar or a pulpit, and surrounded by four blazing pines, their tops aflame, their stems untouched, like candles at an evening meeting.

The mass of foliage, that had overgrown the summit of the rock, was all on fire, blazing high into the night, and fitfully illuminating the whole field. Each pendent twig and leafy festoon was in a blaze. As the red light arose and fell, a numerous congregation alternately shone forth, then disappeared in shadow, and again grew, as it were, out of the darkness, peopling the heart of the solitary woods at once.

"A grave and dark-clad company!" quoth Goodman Brown. 55

In truth, they were such. Among them, quivering to-and-fro, between gloom and splendor, appeared faces that would be seen, next day, at the council-board of the province, and others which, Sabbath after Sabbath, looked devoutly heavenward, and benignantly over the crowded pews, from the holiest pulpits in the land. Some affirm that the lady of the governor was there. At least, there were high dames well known to her, and wives of honored husbands, and widows, a great multitude, and ancient maidens, all of excellent repute, and fair young girls, who trembled, lest their mothers should espy them. Either the sudden gleams of light, flashing over the obscure field, bedazzled Goodman Brown, or he recognized a score of the church-members of Salem village, famous for their especial sanctity. Good old Deacon Gookin had arrived, and waited at the skirts of that venerable saint, his revered pastor. But, irreverently consorting with these grave, reputable, and pious people, these elders of the church, these chaste dames and dewy virgins, there were men of dissolute lives and women of spotted fame, wretches given over to all mean and filthy vice, and suspected even of horrid crimes. It was strange to see, that the good shrank not from the wicked, nor were the sinners abashed by the saints. Scattered, also, among their pale-faced enemies, were the Indian priests, or powows, who had often scared their native forest with more hideous incantations than any known to English witchcraft.

"But, where is Faith?" thought Goodman Brown; and, as hope came into his heart, he trembled.

Another verse of the hymn arose, a slow and mournful strain, such as the pious love, but joined to words which expressed all that our nature can conceive of sin, and darkly hinted at far more. Unfathomable to mere mortals is the lore of fiends. Verse after verse was sung, and still the chorus of the desert swelled between, like the deepest tone of a mighty organ. And, with the final peal of that dreadful anthem, there came a sound, as if the roaring wind, the rushing streams, the howling beasts, and every other voice of the unconverted wilderness, were mingling and according with the voice of guilty man, in homage to the prince of all. The four blazing pines threw up a loftier flame, and obscurely discovered shapes and visages of horror on the smoke-wreaths, above the impious assembly. At the same moment, the fire on the rock shot redly forth, and formed a glowing arch above its base, where now appeared a figure. With reverence be it spoken, the figure bore no slight similitude, both in garb and manner, to some grave divine of the New England churches.

"Bring forth the converts!" cried a voice, that echoed through the field and rolled into the forest.

At the word, Goodman Brown stepped forth from the shadow of the trees, and approached the congregation, with whom he felt a loathful brotherhood, by the sympathy of all that was wicked in his heart. He could have well nigh sworn, that the shape of his own dead father beckoned him to advance, looking downward from a smoke-wreath, while a woman, with dim features of despair, threw out her hand to warn him back. Was it his mother? But he had no power to retreat one step, nor to resist, even in thought, when the minister and good old Deacon Gookin seized his arms, and led him to the blazing rock. Thither came also the slender form of a veiled female, led between Goody Cloyse, that pious teacher of the catechism, and Martha Carrier, who had received the devil's promise to be queen of hell. A rampant hag was she! And there stood the proselytes,° beneath the canopy of fire.

"Welcome, my children," said the dark figure, "to the communion of your race! Ye have found, thus young, your nature and your destiny. My children, look behind you!"

They turned; and flashing forth, as it were, in a sheet of flame, the fiend-worshippers were seen; the smile of welcome gleamed darkly on every visage.

"There," resumed the sable form, "are all whom ye have reverenced from youth. Ye deemed them holier than yourselves, and shrank from your own sin, contrasting it with their lives of righteousness, and prayerful aspirations heavenward. Yet, here are they all, in my worshipping assembly! This night it shall be granted you to know their secret deeds; how hoary-bearded elders of the church have whispered wanton words to the young maids of their households; how many a woman, eager for widow's weeds, has given her husband a drink at bedtime, and let him sleep his last sleep in her bosom; how beardless youths have made haste to inherit their fathers' wealth; and how fair damsels—blush not, sweet ones!— have dug little graves in the garden, and bidden me, the sole guest, to an infant's funeral. By the sympathy of your human hearts for sin, ye shall scent out all the places—whether in church, bed-chamber, street, field, or forest—where crime has been committed, and shall exult to behold the whole earth one stain of guilt, one mighty bloodspot. Far more than this! It shall be yours to penetrate, in every bosom, the deep mystery of sin, the fountain of all wicked arts, and which inexhaustibly supplies more evil impulses than human power—than my power, at its utmost!—can make manifest in deeds. And now, my children, look upon each other."

proselytes: new converts.

They did so; and, by the blaze of the hell-kindled torches, the wretched man beheld his Faith, and the wife her husband, trembling before that unhallowed altar.

"Lo! there ye stand, my children," said the figure, in a deep and solemn   65
tone, almost sad, with its despairing awfulness, as if his once angelic nature could yet mourn for our miserable race. "Depending upon one another's hearts, ye had still hoped, that virtue were not all a dream. Now are ye undeceived! Evil is the nature of mankind. Evil must be your only happiness. Welcome, again, my children, to the communion of your race!"

"Welcome!" repeated the fiend-worshippers, in one cry of despair and triumph.

And there they stood, the only pair, as it seemed, who were yet hesitating on the verge of wickedness, in this dark world. A basin was hollowed, naturally, in the rock. Did it contain water, reddened by the lurid light? or was it blood? or, perchance, a liquid flame? Herein did the Shape of Evil dip his hand, and prepare to lay the mark of baptism upon their foreheads, that they might be partakers of the mystery of sin, more conscious of the secret guilt of others, both in deed and thought, than they could now be of their own. The husband cast one look at his pale wife, and Faith at him. What polluted wretches would the next glance show them to each other, shuddering alike at what they disclosed and what they saw!

"Faith! Faith!" cried the husband. "Look up to Heaven, and resist the Wicked one!"

Whether Faith obeyed, he knew not. Hardly had he spoken, when he found himself amid calm night and solitude, listening to a roar of the wind, which died heavily away through the forest. He staggered against the rock and felt it chill and damp, while a hanging twig, that had been all on fire, besprinkled his cheek with the coldest dew.

The next morning, young Goodman Brown came slowly into the   70
street of Salem village, staring around him like a bewildered man. The good old minister was taking a walk along the grave-yard, to get an appetite for breakfast and meditate his sermon, and bestowed a blessing, as he passed, on Goodman Brown. He shrank from the venerable saint, as if to avoid an anathema.° Old Deacon Goodkin was at domestic worship, and the holy words of his prayer were heard through the open window. "What God doth the wizard pray to?" quoth Goodman Brown. Goody Cloyse, that excellent old Christian, stood in the early sunshine, at her own lattice, catechizing a little girl, who had brought her a pint of morning's milk. Goodman Brown snatched away the child, as from the grasp of the fiend himself. Turning the corner by the meeting-house, he spied the head

---

anathema: an official curse, a decree that casts communicants out of a church and bans them from receiving the sacraments.

of Faith, with the pink ribbons, gazing anxiously forth, and bursting into such joy at sight of him, that she skipt along the street, and almost kissed her husband before the whole village. But, Goodman Brown looked sternly and sadly into her face, and passed on without a greeting.

Had Goodman Brown fallen asleep in the forest, and only dreamed a wild dream of a witch-meeting?

Be it so, if you will. But, alas! it was a dream of evil omen for young Goodman Brown. A stern, a sad, a darkly meditative, a distrustful, if not a desperate man, did he become, from the night of that fearful dream. On the Sabbath-day, when the congregation were singing a holy psalm, he could not listen, because an anthem of sin rushed loudly upon his ear, and drowned all the blessed strain. When the minister spoke from the pulpit, with power and fervid eloquence, and, with his hand on the open Bible, of the sacred truths of our religion, and of saint-like lives and triumphant deaths, and of future bliss or misery unutterable, then did Goodman Brown turn pale, dreading, lest the roof should thunder down upon the gray blasphemer and his hearers. Often, awakening suddenly at midnight, he shrank from the bosom of Faith, and at morning or eventide, when the family knelt down at prayer, he scowled, and muttered to himself, and gazed sternly at his wife, and turned away. And when he had lived long, and was borne to his grave, a hoary corpse, followed by Faith, an aged woman, and children and grandchildren, a goodly procession, besides neighbors, not a few, they carved no hopeful verse upon his tombstone; for his dying hour was gloom.

O. Henry (William Sydney Porter)

The Gift of the Magi   1906

William Sydney Porter (1862–1910), known to the world as O. Henry, was born in Greensboro, North Carolina. He began writing in his mid-twenties, contributing humorous sketches to various periodicals. In 1896 he was indicted for embezzlement from the First National Bank of Austin, Texas; he fled to Honduras before his trial but returned when he found that his wife was terminally ill. He was convicted and served three years of a five-year sentence; his guilt or innocence has never been definitively established. Released in 1901, he moved to New York the

O. Henry

following year. Already a well-known writer, for the next three years he produced a story every week for the New York World *while also contributing tales and sketches to magazines. Beginning with* Cabbages and Kings *in 1904, his stories were published in nine highly successful collections in the few remaining years of his life, as well as in three posthumously issued volumes.*

Financial extravagance and alcoholism darkened his last days, culminating in his death from tuberculosis at the age of forty-seven. Ranked during his lifetime with Hawthorne and Poe, O. Henry is more likely now to be invoked in negative terms, for his sentimentality and especially for his reliance on frequently forced trick endings, but the most prestigious annual volume of the best American short fiction is still called The O. Henry Prize Stories, *and the best of his own work is loved by millions of readers.*

One dollar and eighty-seven cents. That was all. And sixty cents of it was in pennies. Pennies saved one and two at a time by bulldozing the grocer and the vegetable man and the butcher until one's cheeks burned with the silent imputation of parsimony that such close dealing implied. Three times Della counted it. One dollar and eighty-seven cents. And the next day would be Christmas.

There was clearly nothing to do but flop down on the shabby little couch and howl. So Della did it. Which instigates the moral reflection that life is made up of sobs, sniffles, and smiles, with sniffles predominating.

While the mistress of the home is gradually subsiding from the first stage to the second, take a look at the home. A furnished flat at $8 per week. It did not exactly beggar description, but it certainly had that word on the lookout for the mendicancy squad.

In the vestibule below was a letter-box into which no letter would go, and an electric button from which no mortal finger could coax a ring. Also appertaining thereunto was a card bearing the name "Mr. James Dillingham Young."

The "Dillingham" had been flung to the breeze during a former period of prosperity when its possessor was being paid $30 per week. Now, when the income was shrunk to $20, the letters of "Dillingham" looked blurred, as though they were thinking seriously of contracting to a modest and unassuming D. But whenever Mr. James Dillingham Young came home and reached his flat above he was called "Jim" and greatly hugged by Mrs. James Dillingham Young, already introduced to you as Della. Which is all very good.

Della finished her cry and attended to her cheeks with the powder rag. She stood by the window and looked out dully at a grey cat walking a grey fence in a grey backyard. Tomorrow would be Christmas Day, and she had only $1.87 with which to buy Jim a present. She had been saving every penny she could for months, with this result. Twenty dollars a week doesn't go far. Expenses had been greater than she had calculated. They always are. Only $1.87 to buy a present for Jim. Her Jim. Many a happy hour she had spent planning for something nice for him. Something fine and rare and sterling—something just a little bit near to being worthy of the honor of being owned by Jim.

There was a pier-glass between the windows of the room. Perhaps you have seen a pier-glass in an $8 flat. A very thin and very agile person may, by observing his reflection in a rapid sequence of longitudinal strips, obtain a fairly accurate conception of his looks. Della, being slender, had mastered the art.

Suddenly she whirled from the window and stood before the glass. Her eyes were shining brilliantly, but her face had lost its color within twenty seconds. Rapidly she pulled down her hair and let it fall to its full length.

Now, there were two possessions of the James Dillingham Youngs in which they both took a mighty pride. One was Jim's gold watch that had been his father's and his grandfather's. The other was Della's hair. Had the Queen of Sheba lived in the flat across the airshaft, Della would have let her hair hang out the window some day to dry just to depreciate Her Majesty's jewels and gifts. Had King Solomon been the janitor, with all his treasures piled up in the basement, Jim would have pulled out his watch every time he passed, just to see him pluck at his beard from envy.

So now Della's beautiful hair fell about her, rippling and shining like a cascade of brown waters. It reached below her knee and made itself almost a garment for her. And then she did it up again nervously and quickly. Once she faltered for a minute and stood still while a tear or two splashed on the worn red carpet.

On went her old brown jacket; on went her old brown hat. With a whirl of skirts and with the brilliant sparkle still in her eyes, she fluttered out the door and down the stairs to the street.

Where she stopped the sign read: "Mme. Sofronie. Hair Goods of All Kinds." One flight up Della ran, and collected herself, panting. Madame, large, too white, chilly, hardly looked the "Sofronie."

"Will you buy my hair?" asked Della.

"I buy hair," said Madame. "Take yer hat off and let's have a sight at the looks of it."

Down rippled the brown cascade.

"Twenty dollars," said Madame, lifting the mass with a practiced hand.

"Give it to me quick," said Della.

Oh, and the next two hours tripped by on rosy wings. Forget the hashed metaphor. She was ransacking the stores for Jim's present.

She found it at last. It surely had been made for Jim and no one else. There was no other like it in any of the stores, and she had turned all of them inside out. It was a platinum fob chain simple and chaste in design, properly proclaiming its value by substance alone and not by meretricious ornamentation—as all good things should do. It was even worthy of The Watch. As soon as she saw it she knew that it must be Jim's. It was like him. Quietness and value—the description applied to both. Twenty-one dollars they took from her for it, and she hurried home with the 87 cents. With that chain on his watch Jim might be properly anxious about the time in any company. Grand as the watch was, he sometimes looked at it on the sly on account of the old leather strap that he used in place of a chain.

When Della reached home her intoxication gave way a little to pru-   20
dence and reason. She got out her curling irons and lighted the gas and went to work repairing the ravages made by generosity added to love. Which is always a tremendous task, dear friends—a mammoth task.

Within forty minutes her head was covered with tiny, close-lying curls that made her look wonderfully like a truant schoolboy. She looked at her reflection in the mirror long, carefully, and critically.

"If Jim doesn't kill me," she said to herself, "before he takes a second look at me, he'll say I look like a Coney Island chorus girl. But what could I do—oh! What could I do with a dollar and eighty-seven cents?"

At 7 o'clock the coffee was made and the frying-pan was on the back of the stove hot and ready to cook the chops.

Jim was never late. Della doubled the fob chain in her hand and sat on the corner of the table near the door that he always entered. Then she heard his step on the stair away down on the first flight, and she turned white for just a moment. She had a habit of saying little silent prayers about the simplest everyday things, and now she whispered: "Please God, make him think I am still pretty."

The door opened and Jim stepped in and closed it. He looked thin and   25
very serious. Poor fellow, he was only twenty-two—and to be burdened with a family! He needed a new overcoat and he was without gloves.

Jim stopped inside the door, as immovable as a setter at the scent of quail. His eyes were fixed upon Della, and there was an expression in them that she could not read, and it terrified her. It was not anger, nor surprise, nor disapproval, nor horror, nor any of the sentiments that she had been prepared for. He simply stared at her fixedly with that peculiar expression on his face.

Della wriggled off the table and went for him.

"Jim, darling," she cried, "don't look at me that way. I had my hair cut off and sold because I couldn't have lived through Christmas without giving you a present. It'll grow out again—you won't mind, will you? I just had to do it. My hair grows awfully fast. Say 'Merry Christmas!' Jim, and let's be happy. You don't know what a nice—what a beautiful, nice gift I've got for you."

"You've cut off your hair?" asked Jim, laboriously, as if he had not arrived at that patent fact yet even after the hardest mental labor.

"Cut it off and sold it," said Della. "Don't you like me just as well,   30
anyhow? I'm me without my hair, ain't I?"

Jim looked about the room curiously.

"You say your hair is gone?" he said, with an air almost of idiocy.

"You needn't look for it," said Della. "It's sold, I tell you—sold and gone, too. It's Christmas Eve, boy. Be good to me, for it went for you. Maybe the hairs of my head were numbered," she went on with a sudden serious sweetness, "but nobody could ever count my love for you. Shall I put the chops on, Jim?"

Out of his trance Jim seemed quickly to wake. He enfolded his Della. For ten seconds let us regard with discreet scrutiny some inconsequential object in the other direction. Eight dollars a week or a million a year— what is the difference? A mathematician or a wit would give you the wrong answer. The magi brought valuable gifts, but that was not among them. This dark assertion will be illuminated later on.

Jim drew a package from his overcoat pocket and threw it upon the table. 35

"Don't make any mistake, Dell," he said, "about me. I don't think there's anything in the way of a haircut or a shave or a shampoo that could make me like my girl any less. But if you'll unwrap that package you may see why you had me going a while at first."

White fingers and nimble tore at the string and paper. And then an ecstatic scream of joy; and then, alas! a quick feminine change to hysterical tears and wails, necessitating the immediate employment of all the comforting powers of the lord of the flat.

For there lay The Combs—the set of combs, side and back, that Della had worshipped for long in a Broadway window. Beautiful combs, pure tortoise shell, with jewelled rims—just the shade to wear in the beautiful vanished hair. They were expensive combs, she knew, and her heart had simply craved and yearned over them without the least hope of possession. And now, they were hers, but the tresses that should have adorned the coveted adornments were gone.

But she hugged them to her bosom, and at length she was able to look up with dim eyes and a smile and say: "My hair grows so fast, Jim!"

And then Della leaped up like a little singed cat and cried, "Oh, oh!" 40

Jim had not yet seen his beautiful present. She held it out to him eagerly upon her open palm. The dull precious metal seemed to flash with a reflection of her bright and ardent spirit.

"Isn't it a dandy, Jim? I hunted all over town to find it. You'll have to look at the time a hundred times a day now. Give me your watch. I want to see how it looks on it."

Instead of obeying, Jim tumbled down on the couch and put his hands under the back of his head and smiled.

"Dell," said he, "let's put our Christmas presents away and keep 'em a while. They're too nice to use just at present. I sold the watch to get the money to buy your combs. And now suppose you put the chops on."

The magi, as you know, were wise men—wonderfully wise men— 45 who brought gifts to the Babe in the manger. They invented the art of giving Christmas presents. Being wise, their gifts were no doubt wise ones, possibly bearing the privilege of exchange in case of duplication. And here I have lamely related to you the uneventful chronicle of two foolish children in a flat who most unwisely sacrificed for each other the greatest treasures of their house. But in a last word to the wise of these days let it be said that of all who give gifts these two were the wisest. Of all who give and receive gifts, such as they are wisest. Everywhere they are wisest. They are the magi.

Zora Neale Hurston

Sweat   1926

Zora Neale Hurston (1901?–1960) was born in Eatonville, Florida, but no record of her actual date of birth exists (best guesses range from 1891 to 1901). Hurston was one of eight children. Her father, a carpenter and Baptist preacher, was also the three-term mayor of Eatonville, the first all-black town incorporated in the United States. When Hurston's mother died in 1912, the father moved the children from one relative to another. Conse-quently, Hurston never finished grammar school, although in 1918 she began taking classes at How-ard University, paying her way through school by

Zora Neale Hurston

working as a manicurist and maid. While at Howard, she published her first story. In early 1925 she moved to New York, arriving with "$1.50, no job, no friends, and a lot of hope." She soon became an important member of the Har-lem Renaissance, a group of young black artists (including Langston Hughes, Countee Cullen, Jean Toomer, and Claude McKay) who sought "spiritual eman-cipation" for African Americans by exploring black heritage and identity in the arts. Hurston eventually became, according to critic Laura Zaidman, "the most prolific black American woman writer of her time." In 1925 she became the first African American student at Barnard College, where she completed a B.A. in anthropology. Hurston's most famous story, "Sweat," appeared in the only issue of Fire!!, a 1926 avant-garde Harlem Renaissance magazine edited by Hurston, Hughes, and Wallace Thurman. This powerful story of an unhappy marriage turned murderous was particularly noteworthy for having the characters speak in the black country dialect of Hurston's native Florida. Hurston achieved only modest success during her lifetime, despite the publication of her memorable novel Their Eyes Were Watching God *(1937) and her many contributions to the study of African American folklore. She died, poor and neglected, in a Florida welfare home and was buried in an unmarked grave. In 1973 novelist Alice Walker erected a gravestone for her carved with the words:*

Zora Neale Hurston
"A Genius of the South"
1901–1960
Novelist, Folklorist
Anthropologist

I

It was eleven o'clock of a Spring night in Florida. It was Sunday. Any other night, Delia Jones would have been in bed for two hours by this time. But she was a washwoman, and Monday morning meant a great deal to her. So she collected the soiled clothes on Saturday when she returned the clean things. Sunday night after church, she sorted and put the white things to soak. It saved her almost a half-day's start. A great hamper in the bedroom held the clothes that she brought home. It was so much neater than a number of bundles lying around.

She squatted on the kitchen floor beside the great pile of clothes, sorting them into small heaps according to color, and humming a song in a mournful key, but wondering through it all where Sykes, her husband, had gone with her horse and buckboard.°

Just then something long, round, limp, and black fell upon her shoulders and slithered to the floor beside her. A great terror took hold of her. It softened her knees and dried her mouth so that it was a full minute before she could cry out or move. Then she saw that it was the big bull whip her husband liked to carry when he drove.

She lifted her eyes to the door and saw him standing there bent over with laughter at her fright. She screamed at him.

"Sykes, what you throw dat whip on me like dat? You know it would   5
skeer me—looks just like a snake, an' you knows how skeered Ah is of snakes."

"Course Ah knowed it! That's how come Ah done it." He slapped his leg with his hand and almost rolled on the ground in his mirth. "If you such a big fool dat you got to have a fit over a earth worm or a string, Ah don't keer how bad Ah skeer you."

"You ain't got no business doing it. Gawd knows it's a sin. Some day Ah'm gointuh drop dead from some of yo' foolishness. 'Nother thing, where you been wid mah rig? Ah feeds dat pony. He ain't fuh you to be drivin' wid no bull whip."

"You sho' is one aggravatin' nigger woman!" he declared and stepped into the room. She resumed her work and did not answer him at once. "Ah done tole you time and again to keep them white folks' clothes outa dis house."

---

buckboard: a four-wheeled open carriage with the seat resting on a spring platform.

He picked up the whip and glared at her. Delia went on with her work. She went out into the yard and returned with a galvanized tub and set it on the wash-bench. She saw that Sykes had kicked all of the clothes together again, and now stood in her way truculently, his whole manner hoping, *praying*, for an argument. But she walked calmly around him and commenced to re-sort the things.

"Next time, Ah'm gointer kick 'em outdoors," he threatened as he   10
struck a match along the leg of his corduroy breeches.

Delia never looked up from her work, and her thin, stooped shoulders sagged further.

"Ah ain't for no fuss t'night Sykes. Ah just come from taking sacrament at the church house."

He snorted scornfully. "Yeah, you just come from de church house on a Sunday night, but heah you is gone to work on them clothes. You ain't nothing but a hypocrite. One of them amen-corner Christians— sing, whoop, and shout, then come home and wash white folks' clothes on the Sabbath."

He stepped roughly upon the whitest pile of things, kicking them helter-skelter as he crossed the room. His wife gave a little scream of dismay, and quickly gathered them together again.

"Sykes, you quit grindin' dirt into these clothes! How can Ah git   15
through by Sat'day if Ah don't start on Sunday?"

"Ah don't keer if you never git through. Anyhow, Ah done promised Gawd and a couple of other men, Ah ain't gointer have it in mah house. Don't gimme no lip neither, else Ah'll throw 'em out and put mah fist up side yo' head to boot."

Delia's habitual meekness seemed to slip from her shoulders like a blown scarf. She was on her feet; her poor little body, her bare knuckly hands bravely defying the strapping hulk before her.

"Looka heah, Sykes, you done gone too fur. Ah been married to you fur fifteen years, and Ah been takin' in washin' fur fifteen years. Sweat, sweat, sweat! Work and sweat, cry and sweat, pray and sweat!"

"What's that got to do with me?" he asked brutally.

"What's it got to do with you, Sykes? Mah tub of suds is filled yo' belly   20
with vittles more times than yo' hands is filled it. Mah sweat is done paid for this house and Ah reckon Ah kin keep on sweatin' in it."

She seized the iron skillet from the stove and struck a defensive pose, which act surprised him greatly, coming from her. It cowed him and he did not strike her as he usually did.

"Naw you won't," she panted, "that ole snaggle-toothed black woman you runnin' with ain't comin' heah to pile up on *mah* sweat and blood. You ain't paid for nothin' on this place, and Ah'm gointer stay right heah till Ah'm toted out foot foremost."

"Well, you better quit gittin' me riled up, else they'll be totin' you out sooner than you expect. Ah'm so tired of you Ah don't know whut to do. Gawd! How Ah hates skinny wimmen!"

A little awed by this new Delia, he sidled out of the door and slammed the back gate after him. He did not say where he had gone, but she knew too well. She knew very well that he would not return until nearly daybreak also. Her work over, she went on to bed but not to sleep at once. Things had come to a pretty pass!

She lay awake, gazing upon the debris that cluttered their matrimonial trail. Not an image left standing along the way. Anything like flowers had long ago been drowned in the salty stream that had been pressed from her heart. Her tears, her sweat, her blood. She had brought love to the union and he had brought a longing after the flesh. Two months after the wedding, he had given her the first brutal beating. She had the memory of his numerous trips to Orlando with all of his wages when he had returned to her penniless, even before the first year had passed. She was young and soft then, but now she thought of her knotty, muscled limbs, her harsh knuckly hands, and drew herself up into an unhappy little ball in the middle of the big feather bed. Too late now to hope for love, even if it were not Bertha it would be someone else. This case differed from the others only in that she was bolder than the others. Too late for everything except her little home. She had built it for her old days, and planted one by one the trees and flowers there. It was lovely to her, lovely.

Somehow, before sleep came, she found herself saying aloud: "Oh well, whatever goes over the Devil's back, is got to come under his belly. Sometime or ruther, Sykes, like everybody else, is gointer reap his sowing." After that she was able to build a spiritual earthworks° against her husband. His shells could no longer reach her. AMEN. She went to sleep and slept until he announced his presence in bed by kicking her feet and rudely snatching the covers away.

"Gimme some kivah heah, an' git yo' damn foots over on yo' own side! Ah oughter mash you in yo' mouf fuh drawing dat skillet on me."

Delia went clear to the rail without answering him. A triumphant indifference to all that he was or did.

II

The week was full of work for Delia as all other weeks, and Saturday found her behind her little pony, collecting and delivering clothes.

It was a hot, hot day near the end of July. The village men on Joe Clarke's porch even chewed cane listlessly. They did not hurl the

---

spiritual earthworks: earthworks are military fortifications made of earth; here Hurston uses it metaphorically to mean Delia's emotional defenses.

cane-knots as usual. They let them dribble over the edge of the porch. Even conversation had collapsed under the heat.

"Heah come Delia Jones," Jim Merchant said, as the shaggy pony came 'round the bend of the road toward them. The rusty buckboard was heaped with baskets of crisp, clean laundry.

"Yep," Joe Lindsay agreed. "Hot or col', rain or shine, jes'ez reg'lar ez de weeks roll roun' Delia carries 'em an' fetches 'em on Sat'day."

"She better if she wanter eat," said Moss. "Syke Jones ain't wuth de shot an' powder hit would tek tuh kill 'im. Not to *huh* he ain't."

"He sho' ain't," Walter Thomas chimed in. "It's too bad, too, cause she wuz a right pretty li'l trick when he got huh. Ah'd uh mah'ied huh mahself if he hadnter beat me to it."

Delia nodded briefly at the men as she drove past.   35

"Too much knockin' will ruin *any* 'oman. He done beat huh 'nough tuh kill three women, let 'lone change they looks," said Elijah Moseley. "How Syke kin stommuck dat big black greasy Mogul he's layin' roun' wid, gits me. Ah swear dat eight-rock couldn't kiss a sardine can Ah done thowed out de back do' 'way las' yeah."

"Aw, she's fat, thass how come. He's allus been crazy 'bout fat women," put in Merchant. "He'd a' been tied up wid one long time ago if he could a' found one tuh have him. Did Ah tell yuh 'bout him come sidlin' roun' *mah* wife—bringin' her a basket uh peecans outa his yard fuh a present? Yessir, mah wife! She tol' him tuh take 'em right straight back home, 'cause Delia works so hard ovah dat washtub she reckon everything on de place taste lak sweat an' soapsuds. Ah jus' wisht Ah'd a' caught 'im 'roun' dere! Ah'd a' made his hips ketch on fiah down dat shell road."

"Ah know he done it, too. Ah sees 'im grinnin' at every 'oman dat passes," Walter Thomas said. "But even so, he useter eat some mighty big hunks uh humble pie tuh git dat li'l 'oman he got. She wuz ez pritty ez a speckled pup! Dat wuz fifteen years ago. He useter be so skeered uh losin' huh, she could make him do some parts of a husband's duty. Dey never wuz de same in de mind."

"There oughter be a law about him," said Lindsay. "He ain't fit tuh carry guts tuh a bear."

Clarke spoke for the first time. "Tain't no law on earth dat kin make   40 a man be decent if it ain't in 'im. There's plenty men dat takes a wife lak dey do a joint uh sugar-cane. It's round, juicy, an' sweet when dey gits it. But dey squeeze an' grind, squeeze an' grind an' wring tell dey wring every drop uh pleasure dat's in 'em out. When dey's satisfied dat dey is wrung dry, dey treats 'em jes' lak dey do a cane-chew. Dey thows 'em away. Dey knows whut dey is doin' while dey is at it, an' hates theirselves fuh it but they keeps on hangin' after huh tell she's empty. Den dey hates huh fuh bein' a cane-chew an' in de way."

"We oughter take Syke an' dat stray 'oman uh his'n down in Lake Howell swamp an' lay on de rawhide till they cain't say Lawd a' mussy. He allus wuz uh ovahbearin niggah, but since dat white 'oman from up north done teached 'im how to run a automobile, he done got too biggety to live—an' we oughter kill 'im," Old Man Anderson advised.

A grunt of approval went around the porch. But the heat was melting their civic virtue and Elijah Moseley began to bait Joe Clarke.

"Come on, Joe, git a melon outa dere an' slice it up for yo' customers. We'se all sufferin' wid de heat. De bear's done got *me*!"

"Thass right, Joe, a watermelon is jes' whut Ah needs tuh cure de eppizudicks," Walter Thomas joined forces with Moseley. "Come on dere, Joe. We all is steady customers an' you ain't set us up in a long time. Ah chooses dat long, bowlegged Floridy favorite."

"A god, an' be dough. You all gimme twenty cents and slice away,"   45 Clarke retorted. "Ah needs a col' slice m'self. Heah, everybody chip in. Ah'll lend y'all mah meat knife."

The money was all quickly subscribed and the huge melon brought forth. At that moment, Sykes and Bertha arrived. A determined silence fell on the porch and the melon was put away again.

Merchant snapped down the blade of his jackknife and moved toward the store door.

"Come on in, Joe, an' gimme a slab uh sow belly an' uh pound uh coffee—almost fuhgot 'twas Sat'day. Got to git on home." Most of the men left also.

Just then Delia drove past on her way home, as Sykes was ordering magnificently for Bertha. It pleased him for Delia to see.

"Git whutsoever yo' heart desires, Honey. Wait a minute, Joe. Give   50 huh two bottles uh strawberry soda-water, uh quart parched ground-peas, an' a block uh chewin' gum."

With all this they left the store, with Sykes reminding Bertha that this was his town and she could have it if she wanted it.

The men returned soon after they left, and held their watermelon feast.

"Where did Syke Jones git da 'oman from nohow?" Lindsay asked.

"Ovah Apopka. Guess dey musta been cleanin' out de town when she lef'. She don't look lak a thing but a hunk uh liver wid hair on it."

"Well, she sho' kin squall," Dave Carter contributed. "When she gits   55 ready tuh laff, she jes' opens huh mouf an' latches it back tuh de las' notch. No ole granpa alligator down in Lake Bell ain't got nothin' on huh."

III

Bertha had been in town three months now. Sykes was still paying her room-rent at Della Lewis'—the only house in town that would have taken her in. Sykes took her frequently to Winter Park to "stomps." He still assured her that he was the swellest man in the state.

"Sho' you kin have dat li'l ole house soon's Ah git dat 'oman outadere. Everything b'longs tuh me an' you sho' kin have it. Ah sho' 'bominates uh skinny 'oman. Lawdy, you sho' is got one portly shape on you! You kin git *anything* you wants. Dis is *mah* town an' you sho' kin have it."

Delia's work-worn knees crawled over the earth in Gethsemane° and up the rocks of Calvary° many, many times during these months. She avoided the villagers and meeting places in her efforts to be blind and deaf. But Bertha nullified this to a degree, by coming to Delia's house to call Sykes out to her at the gate.

Delia and Sykes fought all the time now with no peaceful interludes. They slept and ate in silence. Two or three times Delia had attempted a timid friendliness, but she was repulsed each time. It was plain that the breaches must remain agape.

The sun had burned July to August. The heat streamed down like a   60
million hot arrows, smiting all things living upon the earth. Grass withered, leaves browned, snakes went blind in shedding, and men and dogs went mad. Dog days!

Delia came home one day and found Sykes there before her. She wondered, but started to go on into the house without speaking, even though he was standing in the kitchen door and she must either stoop under his arm or ask him to move. He made no room for her. She noticed a soap box beside the steps, but paid no particular attention to it, knowing that he must have brought it there. As she was stooping to pass under his outstretched arm, he suddenly pushed her backward, laughingly.

"Look in de box dere, Delia, Ah done brung yuh somethin'!"

She nearly fell upon the box in her stumbling, and when she saw what it held, she all but fainted outright.

"Syke! Syke, mah Gawd! You take dat rattlesnake 'way from heah! You *gottuh*. Oh, Jesus, have mussy!"

"Ah ain't got tuh do nuthin' uh de kin'—fact is Ah ain't got tuh do   65
nothin' but die. Tain't no use uh you puttin' on airs makin' out lak you skeered uh dat snake—he's gointer stay right heah tell he die. He wouldn't bite me cause Ah knows how tuh handle 'im. Nohow he wouldn't risk breakin' out his fangs 'gin yo skinny laigs."

"Naw, now Syke, don't keep dat thing 'round tryin' tuh skeer me tuh death. You knows Ah'm even feared uh earth worms. Thass de biggest snake Ah evah did see. Kill 'im, Syke, please."

"Doan ast me tuh do nothin' fuh yuh. Goin' 'round tryin' tuh be so damn asterperious.° Naw, Ah ain't gonna kill it. Ah think uh damn sight

---

Gethsemane: the garden outside Jerusalem that was the scene of Jesus's agony and arrest (see Matthew 26:36–57); hence, a scene of great suffering. *Calvary:* the hill outside Jerusalem where Jesus was crucified. *asterperious:* haughty.

mo' uh him dan you! Dat's a nice snake an' anybody doan lak 'im kin jes' hit de grit."

The village soon heard that Sykes had the snake, and came to see and ask questions.

"How de hen-fire did you ketch dat six-foot rattler, Syke?" Thomas asked.

"He's full uh frogs so he cain't hardly move, thass how Ah eased up on 'im. But Ah'm a snake charmer an' knows how tuh handle 'em. Shux, dat ain't nothin'. Ah could ketch one eve'y day if Ah so wanted tuh."   70

"Whut he needs is a heavy hick'ry club leaned real heavy on his head. Dat's de bes' way tuh charm a rattlesnake."

"Naw, Walt, y'all jes' don't understand dese diamon' backs lak Ah do," said Sykes in a superior tone of voice.

The village agreed with Walter, but the snake stayed on. His box remained by the kitchen door with its screen wire covering. Two or three days later it had digested its meal of frogs and literally came to life. It rattled at every movement in the kitchen or the yard. One day as Delia came down the kitchen steps she saw his chalky-white fangs curved like scimitars hung in the wire meshes. This time she did not run away with averted eyes as usual. She stood for a long time in the doorway in a red fury that grew bloodier for every second that she regarded the creature that was her torment.

That night she broached the subject as soon as Sykes sat down to the table.

"Syke, Ah wants you tuh take dat snake 'way fum heah. You done starved me an' Ah put up widcher, you done beat me an Ah took dat, but you done kilt all mah insides bringin' dat varmint heah."   75

Sykes poured out a saucer full of coffee and drank it deliberately before he answered her.

"A whole lot Ah keer 'bout how you feels inside uh out. Dat snake ain't goin' no damn wheah till Ah gits ready fuh 'im tuh go. So fur as beatin' is concerned, yuh ain't took near all dat you gointer take ef yuh stay 'round *me*."

Delia pushed back her plate and got up from the table. "Ah hates you, Sykes," she said calmly. "Ah hates you tuh de same degree dat Ah useter love yuh. Ah done took an' took till mah belly is full up tuh mah neck. Dat's de reason Ah got mah letter fum de church an' moved mah membership tuh Woodbridge—so Ah don't haftuh take no sacrament wid yuh. Ah don't wantuh see yuh 'round me atall. Lay 'round wid dat 'oman all yuh wants tuh, but gwan 'way fum me an' mah house. Ah hates yuh lak uh suck-egg dog."

Sykes almost let the huge wad of corn bread and collard greens he was chewing fall out of his mouth in amazement. He had a hard time whipping himself up to the proper fury to try to answer Delia.

"Well, Ah'm glad you does hate me. Ah'm sho' tiahed uh you hangin'   80
ontuh me. Ah don't want yuh. Look at yuh stringey ole neck! Yo' rawbony
laigs an' arms is enough tuh cut uh man tuh death. You looks jes' lak de
devvul's doll-baby tuh *me*. You cain't hate me no worse dan Ah hates you.
Ah been hatin' *you* fuh years."

"Yo' ole black hide don't look lak nothin' tuh me, but uh passle
uh wrinkled up rubber, wid yo' big ole yeahs flappin' on each side lak
uh paih uh buzzard wings. Don't think Ah'm gointuh be run 'way fum
mah house neither. Ah'm goin' tuh de white folks 'bout *you*, mah young
man, de very nex' time you lay yo' han's on me. Mah cup is done run
ovah." Delia said this with no signs of fear and Sykes departed from the
house, threatening her, but made not the slightest move to carry out
any of them.

That night he did not return at all, and the next day being Sunday,
Delia was glad she did not have to quarrel before she hitched up her pony
and drove the four miles to Woodbridge.

She stayed to the night service—"love feast"—which was very warm
and full of spirit. In the emotional winds her domestic trials were borne
far and wide so that she sang as she drove homeward,

> Jurden water,° black an' col
> Chills de body, not de soul
> An' Ah wantah cross Jurden in uh calm time.

She came from the barn to the kitchen door and stopped.

"Whut's de mattah, ol' Satan, you ain't kickin' up yo' racket?" She   85
addressed the snake's box. Complete silence. She went on into the
house with a new hope in its birth struggles. Perhaps her threat to go
to the white folks had frightened Sykes! Perhaps he was sorry! Fifteen
years of misery and suppression had brought Delia to the place where
she would hope *anything* that looked towards a way over or through her
wall of inhibitions.

She felt in the match-safe behind the stove at once for a match.
There was only one there.

"Dat niggah wouldn't fetch nothin' heah tuh save his rotten neck,
but he kin run thew whut Ah brings quick enough. Now he done toted
off nigh on tuh haff uh box uh matches. He done had dat 'oman heah in
mah house, too."

Nobody but a woman could tell how she knew this even before she
struck the match. But she did and it put her into a new fury.

Jurden water: black Southern dialect for the River Jordan, which represents the last boundary before entering heaven. It comes from the Old Testament, when the Jews had to cross
the River Jordan to reach the Promised Land.

Presently she brought in the tubs to put the white things to soak. This time she decided she need not bring the hamper out of the bedroom; she would go in there and do the sorting. She picked up the pot-bellied lamp and went in. The room was small and the hamper stood hard by the foot of the white iron bed. She could sit and reach through the bed-posts—resting as she worked.

"*Ah wantah cross Jurden in uh calm time.*" She was singing again. The mood of the "love feast" had returned. She threw back the lid of the basket almost gaily. Then, moved by both horror and terror, she sprang back toward the door. *There lay the snake in the basket!* He moved sluggishly at first, but even as she turned round and round, jumped up and down in an insanity of fear, he began to stir vigorously. She saw him pouring his awful beauty from the basket upon the bed, then she seized the lamp and ran as fast as she could to the kitchen. The wind from the open door blew out the light and the darkness added to her terror. She sped to the darkness of the yard, slamming the door after her before she thought to set down the lamp. She did not feel safe even on the ground, so she climbed up in the hay barn.

There for an hour or more she lay sprawled upon the hay a gibbering wreck.

Finally she grew quiet, and after that came coherent thought. With this stalked through her a cold, bloody rage. Hours of this. A period of introspection, a space of retrospection, then a mixture of both. Out of this an awful calm.

"Well, Ah done de bes' Ah could. If things ain't right, Gawd knows tain't mah fault."

She went to sleep—a twitch sleep—and woke up to a faint gray sky. There was a loud hollow sound below. She peered out. Sykes was at the wood-pile, demolishing a wire-covered box.

He hurried to the kitchen door, but hung outside there some minutes before he entered, and stood some minutes more inside before he closed it after him.

The gray in the sky was spreading. Delia descended without fear now, and crouched beneath the low bedroom window. The drawn shade shut out the dawn, shut in the night. But the thin walls held back no sound.

"Dat ol' scratch° is woke up now!" She mused at the tremendous whirr inside, which every woodsman knows, is one of the sound illusions. The rattler is a ventriloquist. His whirr sounds to the right, to the left, straight ahead, behind, close under foot—everywhere but where it is. Woe to him who guesses wrong unless he is prepared to hold up his end of the argument! Sometimes he strikes without rattling at all.

scratch: a folk expression for the devil.

Inside, Sykes heard nothing until he knocked a pot lid off the stove while trying to reach the match-safe in the dark. He had emptied his pockets at Bertha's.

The snake seemed to wake up under the stove and Sykes made a quick leap into the bedroom. In spite of the gin he had had, his head was clearing now.

"Mah Gawd!" he chattered, "ef Ah could on'y strack uh light!"   100

The rattling ceased for a moment as he stood paralyzed. He waited. It seemed that the snake waited also.

"Oh, fuh de light! Ah thought he'd be too sick"—Sykes was muttering to himself when the whirr began again, closer, right underfoot this time. Long before this, Sykes' ability to think had been flattened down to primitive instinct and he leaped—onto the bed.

Outside Delia heard a cry that might have come from a maddened chimpanzee, a stricken gorilla. All the terror, all the horror, all the rage that man possibly could express, without a recognizable human sound.

A tremendous stir inside there, another series of animal screams, the intermittent whirr of the reptile. The shade torn violently down from the window, letting in the red dawn, a huge brown hand seizing the window stick, great dull blows upon the wooden floor punctuating the gibberish of sound long after the rattle of the snake had abruptly subsided. All this Delia could see and hear from her place beneath the window, and it made her ill. She crept over to the four-o'clocks and stretched herself on the cool earth to recover.

She lay there. "Delia, Delia!" She could hear Sykes calling in a most   105
despairing tone as one who expected no answer. The sun crept on up, and he called. Delia could not move—her legs had gone flabby. She never moved, he called, and the sun kept rising.

"Mah Gawd!" She heard him moan, "Mah Gawd fum Heben!" She heard him stumbling about and got up from her flower-bed. The sun was growing warm. As she approached the door she heard him call out hopefully, "Delia, is dat you Ah heah?"

She saw him on his hands and knees as soon as she reached the door. He crept an inch or two toward her—all that he was able, and she saw his horribly swollen neck and his one open eye shining with hope. A surge of pity too strong to support bore her away from that eye that must, could not, fail to see the tubs. He would see the lamp. Orlando with its doctors was too far. She could scarcely reach the chinaberry tree, where she waited in the growing heat while inside she knew the cold river was creeping up and up to extinguish that eye which must know by now that she knew.

Ha Jin

Saboteur   2000

Ha Jin is the pen name of Xuefei Jin, who was born in Liaoning, China, in 1956. The son of a military officer and a worker, Jin grew up during the turbulent Cultural Revolution, a ten-year up-heaval initiated by the Communist Party in 1966 to transform China into a Marxist workers' society by destroying all remnants of the nation's ancient past. During this period many schools and universi-ties were closed and intellectuals were required to work in proletarian jobs. At fourteen, Jin joined the People's Liberation Army, where he remained for nearly six years, and he later worked as a telegraph

Ha Jin

operator for a railroad company. He then attended Heilongjiang University, where in 1981 he received a B.A. in English. After earning an M.A. in Ameri-can literature from Shangdong University in 1984, Jin traveled to the United States to work on a Ph.D. at Brandeis University. He intended to return to China, but the Communist Party's violent suppression of the student movement in 1989 made him decide to stay in the United States and write only in English. "It's such a brutal government," he commented. "I was very angry, and I decid-ed not to return to China." "Writing in English became my means of survival," he remarked, "of spending or wasting my life, of retrieving losses, mine, and those of others." Jin has published both poetry and fiction, including the novels Waiting *(1999, National Book Award),* War Trash *(2004, PEN/Faulkner Award),* A Free Life *(2007), and* Nanjing Requiem *(2011). His first volume of short fiction,* Ocean of Words *(1996), was drawn from his experience in the People's Liberation Army and won the PEN/Hemingway Award. He teaches creative writing at Boston University.*

Mr. Chiu and his bride were having lunch in the square before Muji Train Station. On the table between them were two bottles of soda spewing out brown foam and two paper boxes of rice and sautéed cucumber and pork. "Let's eat," he said to her, and broke the con-nected ends of the chopsticks. He picked up a slice of streaky pork and put it into his mouth. As he was chewing, a few crinkles appeared on his thin jaw.

To his right, at another table, two railroad policemen were drinking tea and laughing; it seemed that the stout, middle-aged man was telling a joke to his young comrade, who was tall and of athletic build. Now and again they would steal a glance at Mr. Chiu's table.

The air smelled of rotten melon. A few flies kept buzzing above the couple's lunch. Hundreds of people were rushing around to get on the platform or to catch buses to downtown. Food and fruit vendors were crying for customers in lazy voices. About a dozen young women, representing the local hotels, held up placards which displayed the daily prices and words as large as a palm, like FREE MEALS, AIR-CONDITIONING, and ON THE RIVER. In the center of the square stood a concrete statue of Chairman Mao, at whose feet peasants were napping, their backs on the warm granite and their faces toward the sunny sky. A flock of pigeons perched on the Chairman's raised hand and forearm.

The rice and cucumber tasted good, and Mr. Chiu was eating unhurriedly. His sallow face showed exhaustion. He was glad that the honeymoon was finally over and that he and his bride were heading back for Harbin. During the two weeks' vacation, he had been worried about his liver, because three months ago he had suffered from acute hepatitis; he was afraid he might have a relapse. But he had had no severe symptoms, despite his liver being still big and tender. On the whole he was pleased with his health, which could endure even the strain of a honeymoon; indeed, he was on the course of recovery. He looked at his bride, who took off her wire glasses, kneading the root of her nose with her fingertips. Beads of sweat coated her pale cheeks.

"Are you all right, sweetheart?" he asked.   5

"I have a headache. I didn't sleep well last night."

"Take an aspirin, will you?"

"It's not that serious. Tomorrow is Sunday and I can sleep in. Don't worry."

As they were talking, the stout policeman at the next table stood up and threw a bowl of tea in their direction. Both Mr. Chiu's and his bride's sandals were wet instantly.

"Hooligan!" she said in a low voice.   10

Mr. Chiu got to his feet and said out loud, "Comrade Policeman, why did you do this?" He stretched out his right foot to show the wet sandal.

"Do what?" the stout man asked huskily, glaring at Mr. Chiu while the young fellow was whistling.

"See, you dumped tea on our feet."

"You're lying. You wet your shoes yourself."

"Comrade Policemen, your duty is to keep order, but you purposely   15
tortured us common citizens. Why violate the law you are supposed to enforce?" As Mr. Chiu was speaking, dozens of people began gathering around.

With a wave of his hand, the man said to the young fellow, "Let's get hold of him!"

They grabbed Mr. Chiu and clamped handcuffs around his wrists. He cried, "You can't do this to me. This is utterly unreasonable."

"Shut up!" The man pulled out his pistol. "You can use your tongue at our headquarters."

The young fellow added, "You're a saboteur, you know that? You're disrupting public order."

The bride was too petrified to say anything coherent. She was a   20
recent college graduate, had majored in fine arts, and had never seen the police make an arrest. All she could say was, "Oh, please, please!"

The policemen were pulling Mr. Chiu, but he refused to go with them, holding the corner of the table and shouting, "We have a train to catch. We already bought the tickets."

The stout man punched him in the chest. "Shut up. Let your ticket expire." With the pistol butt he chopped Mr. Chiu's hands, which at once released the table. Together the two men were dragging him away to the police station.

Realizing he had to go with them, Mr. Chiu turned his head and shouted to his bride, "Don't wait for me here. Take the train. If I'm not back by tomorrow morning, send someone over to get me out."

She nodded, covering her sobbing mouth with her palm.

After removing his belt, they locked Mr. Chiu into a cell in the   25
back of the Railroad Police Station. The single window in the room was blocked by six steel bars; it faced a spacious yard, in which stood a few pines. Beyond the trees, two swings hung from an iron frame, swaying gently in the breeze. Somewhere in the building a cleaver was chopping rhythmically. There must be a kitchen upstairs, Mr. Chiu thought.

He was too exhausted to worry about what they would do to him, so he lay down on the narrow bed and shut his eyes. He wasn't afraid. The Cultural Revolution was over already, and recently the Party had been propagating the idea that all citizens were equal before the law. The police ought to be a law-abiding model for common people. As long as he remained coolheaded and reasoned with them, they probably wouldn't harm him.

Late in the afternoon he was taken to the Interrogation Bureau on the second floor. On his way there, in the stairwell, he ran into the middle-aged policeman who had manhandled him. The man grinned, rolling his bulgy eyes and pointing his fingers at him as if firing a pistol. Egg of a tortoise! Mr. Chiu cursed mentally.

The moment he sat down in the office, he burped, his palm shielding his mouth. In front of him, across a long desk, sat the chief of the bureau and a donkey-faced man. On the glass desktop was a folder containing information on his case. He felt it bizarre that in just a matter of hours they had accumulated a small pile of writing about him. On second thought he began to wonder whether they had kept a file on him all the time. How could this have happened? He lived and worked in Harbin, more than three hundred miles away, and this was his first time in Muji City.

The chief of the bureau was a thin, bald man who looked serene and intelligent. His slim hands handled the written pages in the folder in the manner of a lecturing scholar. To Mr. Chiu's left sat a young scribe, with a clipboard on his knee and a black fountain pen in his hand.

"Your name?" the chief asked, apparently reading out the question 30
from a form.

"Chiu Maguang."

"Age?"

"Thirty-four."

"Profession?"

"Lecturer." 35

"Work unit?"

"Harbin University."

"Political status?"

"Communist Party member."

The chief put down the paper and began to speak. "Your crime is 40
sabotage, although it hasn't induced serious consequences yet. Because you are a Party member, you should be punished more. You have failed to be a model for the masses and you—"

"Excuse me, sir," Mr. Chiu cut him off.

"What?"

"I didn't do anything. Your men are the saboteurs of our social order. They threw hot tea on my feet and on my wife's feet. Logically speaking, you should criticize them, if not punish them."

"That statement is groundless. You have no witness. Why should I believe you?" the chief said matter-of-factly.

"This is my evidence." He raised his right hand. "Your man hit my 45
fingers with a pistol."

"That doesn't prove how your feet got wet. Besides, you could have hurt your fingers yourself."

"But I am telling the truth!" Anger flared up in Mr. Chiu. "Your police station owes me an apology. My train ticket has expired, my new leather sandals are ruined, and I am late for a conference in the provincial capital. You must compensate me for the damage and losses. Don't mistake me for a common citizen who would tremble when you sneeze. I'm a scholar, a philosopher, and an expert in dialectical materialism. If necessary, we will argue about this in *The Northeastern Daily*, or we will go to the highest People's Court in Beijing. Tell me, what's your name?" He got carried away with his harangue, which was by no means trivial and had worked to his advantage on numerous occasions.

"Stop bluffing us," the donkey-faced man broke in. "We have seen a lot of your kind. We can easily prove you are guilty. Here are some of the statements given by eyewitnesses." He pushed a few sheets of paper toward Mr. Chiu.

Mr. Chiu was dazed to see the different handwritings, which all stated that he had shouted in the square to attract attention and refused to obey the police. One of the witnesses had identified herself as a purchasing agent from a shipyard in Shanghai. Something stirred in Mr. Chiu's stomach, a pain rising to his rib. He gave out a faint moan.

"Now you have to admit you are guilty," the chief said. "Although   50 it's a serious crime, we won't punish you severely, provided you write out a self-criticism and promise that you won't disrupt the public order again. In other words, your release will depend on your attitude toward this crime."

"You're daydreaming," Mr. Chiu cried. "I won't write a word, because I'm innocent. I demand that you provide me with a letter of apology so I can explain to my university why I'm late."

Both the interrogators smiled contemptuously. "Well, we've never done that," said the chief, taking a puff of his cigarette.

"Then make this a precedent."

"That's unnecessary. We are pretty certain that you will comply with our wishes." The chief blew a column of smoke toward Mr. Chiu's face.

At the tilt of the chief's head, two guards stepped forward and grabbed   55 the criminal by the arms. Mr. Chiu meanwhile went on saying, "I shall report you to the Provincial Administration. You'll have to pay for this! You are worse than the Japanese military police."

They dragged him out of the room.

After dinner, which consisted of a bowl of millet porridge, a corn bun, and a piece of pickled turnip, Mr. Chiu began to have a fever, shaking with a chill and sweating profusely. He knew that the fire of anger had gotten into his liver and that he was probably having a relapse. No medicine was available, because his briefcase had been left with his bride. At home it would have been time for him to sit in front of their color TV, drinking jasmine tea and watching the evening news. It was so lonesome in here. The orange bulb above the single bed was the only source of light, which enabled the guards to keep him under surveillance at night. A moment ago he had asked them for a newspaper or a magazine to read, but they turned him down.

Through the small opening on the door noises came in. It seemed that the police on duty were playing cards or chess in a nearby office; shouts and laughter could be heard now and then. Meanwhile, an accordion kept coughing from a remote corner in the building. Looking at the ballpoint and the letter paper left for him by the guards when they took him back from the Interrogation Bureau, Mr. Chiu remembered the old saying, "When a scholar runs into soldiers, the more he argues, the muddier his point becomes." How ridiculous this whole thing was. He ruffled his thick hair with his fingers.

He felt miserable, massaging his stomach continually. To tell the truth, he was more upset than frightened, because he would have to catch up with his work once he was back home—a paper that was due at the printers next week, and two dozen books he ought to read for the courses he was going to teach in the fall.

A human shadow flitted across the opening. Mr. Chiu rushed to the door and shouted through the hole, "Comrade Guard, Comrade Guard!"   60

"What do you want?" a voice rasped.

"I want you to inform your leaders that I'm very sick. I have heart disease and hepatitis. I may die here if you keep me like this without medication."

"No leader is on duty on the weekend. You have to wait till Monday."

"What? You mean I'll stay in here tomorrow?"

"Yes."   65

"Your station will be held responsible if anything happens to me."

"We know that. Take it easy, you won't die."

It seemed illogical that Mr. Chiu slept quite well that night, though the light above his head had been on all the time and the straw mattress was hard and infested with fleas. He was afraid of ticks, mosquitoes, cockroaches—any kind of insect but fleas and bedbugs. Once, in the countryside, where his school's faculty and staff had helped the peasants harvest crops for a week, his colleagues had joked about his flesh, which they said must have tasted nonhuman to fleas. Except for him, they were all afflicted with hundreds of bites.

More amazing now, he didn't miss his bride a lot. He even enjoyed sleeping alone, perhaps because the honeymoon had tired him out and he needed more rest.

The backyard was quiet on Sunday morning. Pale sunlight streamed   70
through the pine branches. A few sparrows were jumping on the ground, catching caterpillars and ladybugs. Holding the steel bars, Mr. Chiu inhaled the morning air, which smelled meaty. There must have been an eatery or a cooked-meat stand nearby. He reminded himself that he should take this detention with ease. A sentence that Chairman Mao had written to a hospitalized friend rose in his mind: "Since you are already in here, you may as well stay and make the best of it."

His desire for peace of mind originated in his fear that his hepatitis might get worse. He tried to remain unperturbed. However, he was sure that his liver was swelling up, since the fever still persisted. For a whole day he lay in bed, thinking about his paper on the nature of contradictions. Time and again he was overwhelmed by anger, cursing aloud, "A bunch of thugs!" He swore that once he was out, he would write an article about this experience. He had better find out some of the policemen's names.

It turned out to be a restful day for the most part; he was certain that his university would send somebody to his rescue. All he should do now was remain calm and wait patiently. Sooner or later the police would have to release him, although they had no idea that he might refuse to leave unless they wrote him an apology. Damn those hoodlums, they had ordered more than they could eat!

When he woke up on Monday morning, it was already light. Somewhere a man was moaning; the sound came from the backyard. After a long yawn, and kicking off the tattered blanket, Mr. Chiu climbed out of bed and went to the window. In the middle of the yard, a young man was fastened to a pine, his wrists handcuffed around the trunk from behind. He was wriggling and swearing loudly, but there was no sight of anyone else in the yard. He looked familiar to Mr. Chiu.

Mr. Chiu squinted his eyes to see who it was. To his astonishment, he recognized the man, who was Fenjin, a recent graduate from the Law Department at Harbin University. Two years ago Mr. Chiu had taught a course in Marxist materialism, in which Fenjin had enrolled. Now, how on earth had this young devil landed here?

Then it dawned on him that Fenjin must have been sent over by his bride. What a stupid woman! A bookworm, who only knew how to read foreign novels! He had expected that she would contact the school's Security Section, which would for sure send a cadre here. Fenjin held no official position; he merely worked in a private law firm that had just two lawyers; in fact, they had little business except for some detective work for men and women who suspected their spouses of having extramarital affairs. Mr. Chiu was overcome with a wave of nausea.

Should he call out to let his student know he was nearby? He decided not to, because he didn't know what had happened. Fenjin must have quarreled with the police to incur such a punishment. Yet this could never have occurred if Fenjin hadn't come to his rescue. So no matter what, Mr. Chiu had to do something. But what could he do?

It was going to be a scorcher. He could see purple steam shimmering and rising from the ground among the pines. Poor devil, he thought, as he raised a bowl of corn glue to his mouth, sipped, and took a bite of a piece of salted celery.

When a guard came to collect the bowl and the chopsticks, Mr. Chiu asked him what had happened to the man in the backyard. "He called our boss 'bandit,'" the guard said. "He claimed he was a lawyer or something. An arrogant son of a rabbit."

Now it was obvious to Mr. Chiu that he had to do something to help his rescuer. Before he could figure out a way, a scream broke out in the backyard. He rushed to the window and saw a tall policeman standing before Fenjin, an iron bucket on the ground. It was the same young fellow who had arrested Mr. Chiu in the square two days before. The man pinched Fenjin's nose, then raised his hand, which stayed in the air for

75

a few seconds, then slapped the lawyer across the face. As Fenjin was groaning, the man lifted up the bucket and poured water on his head.

"This will keep you from getting sunstroke, boy. I'll give you some more every hour," the man said loudly.   80

Fenjin kept his eyes shut, yet his wry face showed that he was struggling to hold back from cursing the policeman, or, more likely, that he was sobbing in silence. He sneezed, then raised his face and shouted, "Let me go take a piss."

"Oh, yeah?" the man bawled. "Pee in your pants."

Still Mr. Chiu didn't make any noise, gripping the steel bars with both hands, his fingers white. The policeman turned and glanced at the cell's window; his pistol, partly holstered, glittered in the sun. With a snort he spat his cigarette butt to the ground and stamped it into the dust.

Then the door opened and the guards motioned Mr. Chiu to come out. Again they took him upstairs to the Interrogation Bureau.

The same men were in the office, though this time the scribe was sitting there empty-handed. At the sight of Mr. Chiu the chief said, "Ah, here you are. Please be seated."   85

After Mr. Chiu sat down, the chief waved a white silk fan and said to him, "You may have seen your lawyer. He's a young man without manners, so our director had him taught a crash course in the backyard."

"It's illegal to do that. Aren't you afraid to appear in a newspaper?"

"No, we are not, not even on TV. What else can you do? We are not afraid of any story you make up. We call it fiction. What we do care about is that you cooperate with us. That is to say, you must admit your crime."

"What if I refuse to cooperate?"

"Then your lawyer will continue his education in the sunshine."   90

A swoon swayed Mr. Chiu, and he held the arms of the chair to steady himself. A numb pain stung him in the upper stomach and nauseated him, and his head was throbbing. He was sure that the hepatitis was finally attacking him. Anger was flaming up in his chest; his throat was tight and clogged.

The chief resumed, "As a matter of fact, you don't even have to write out your self-criticism. We have your crime described clearly here. All we need is your signature."

Holding back his rage, Mr. Chiu said, "Let me look at that."

With a smirk the donkey-faced man handed him a sheet which carried these words:

> I hereby admit that on July 13 I disrupted public order at Muji Train Station, and that I refused to listen to reason when the railroad police issued their warning. Thus I myself am responsible for my arrest. After two days' detention, I have realized the reactionary nature of my crime. From now on, I shall continue

to educate myself with all my effort and shall never commit this
kind of crime again.

A voice started screaming in Mr. Chiu's ears, "Lie, lie!" But he shook   95
his head and forced the voice away. He asked the chief, "If I sign this, will
you release both my lawyer and me?"

"Of course, we'll do that." The chief was drumming his fingers on the
blue folder—their file on him.

Mr. Chiu signed his name and put his thumbprint under his signature.

"Now you are free to go," the chief said with a smile, and handed him
a piece of paper to wipe his thumb with.

Mr. Chiu was so sick that he couldn't stand up from the chair at first
try. Then he doubled his effort and rose to his feet. He staggered out of the
building to meet his lawyer in the backyard, having forgotten to ask for
his belt back. In his chest he felt as though there were a bomb. If he were
able to, he would have razed the entire police station and eliminated all
their families. Though he knew he could do nothing like that, he made
up his mind to do something.

"I'm sorry about this torture, Fenjin," Mr. Chiu said when they met.   100
"It doesn't matter. They are savages." The lawyer brushed a patch of
dirt off his jacket with trembling fingers. Water was still dribbling from
the bottoms of his trouser legs.

"Let's go now," the teacher said.

The moment they came out of the police station, Mr. Chiu caught
sight of a tea stand. He grabbed Fenjin's arm and walked over to the old
woman at the table. "Two bowls of black tea," he said and handed her a
one-yuan note.

After the first bowl, they each had another one. Then they set out for
the train station. But before they walked fifty yards, Mr. Chiu insisted on
eating a bowl of tree-ear soup at a food stand. Fenjin agreed. He told his
teacher, "You mustn't treat me like a guest."

"No, I want to eat something myself."   105

As if dying of hunger, Mr. Chiu dragged his lawyer from restaurant to
restaurant near the police station, but at each place he ordered no more
than two bowls of food. Fenjin wondered why his teacher wouldn't stay at
one place and eat his fill.

Mr. Chiu bought noodles, wonton, eight-grain porridge, and chicken
soup, respectively, at four restaurants. While eating, he kept saying
through his teeth, "If only I could kill all the bastards!" At the last place
he merely took a few sips of the soup without tasting the chicken cubes
and mushrooms.

Fenjin was baffled by his teacher, who looked ferocious and muttered
to himself mysteriously, and whose jaundiced face was covered with dark
puckers. For the first time Fenjin thought of Mr. Chiu as an ugly man.

*

Within a month over eight hundred people contracted acute hepatitis in Muji. Six died of the disease, including two children. Nobody knew how the epidemic had started.

James Joyce

Araby   1914

James Joyce (1882–1941) quit Ireland at twenty to spend his mature life in voluntary exile on the continent, writing of nothing but Dublin, where he was born. In Trieste, Zurich, and Paris, he supported his family with difficulty, sometimes teaching in Berlitz language schools, until his writing won him fame and wealthy patrons. At first Joyce met difficulty in getting his work printed and circulated. Publication of Dubliners (1914), the collection of stories that includes "Araby," was delayed seven years because its prospective Irish publisher feared libel suits. (The book depicts local citizens, some of them recogniz-

James Joyce

able, and views Dubliners mostly as a thwarted, self-deceived lot.) A Portrait of the Artist as a Young Man (1916), a novel of thinly veiled autobiography, recounts a young intellectual's breaking away from country, church, and home. Joyce's immense comic novel Ulysses (1922), a parody of the Odyssey, spans eighteen hours in the life of a wandering Jew, a Dublin seller of advertising. Frank about sex but untitillating, the book was banned at one time by the U.S. Post Office. Joyce's later work stepped up its demands on readers. The challenging Finnegans Wake (1939), if read aloud, sounds as though a learned comic poet were sleep-talking, jumbling several languages. Joyce was an innovator whose bold experiments showed many other writers possibilities in fiction that had not earlier been imagined.

North Richmond Street, being blind,° was a quiet street except at the hour when the Christian Brothers' School set the boys free. An uninhabited house of two stories stood at the blind end, detached from its neighbors in a square ground. The other houses of the street, conscious of decent lives within them, gazed at one another with brown imperturbable faces.

The former tenant of our house, a priest, had died in the back drawing-room. Air, musty from having been long enclosed, hung in all the rooms, and the waste room behind the kitchen was littered with old useless papers. Among these I found a few paper-covered books,

---

being blind: being a dead-end street.

the pages of which were curled and damp: *The Abbot*, by Walter Scott, *The Devout Communicant* and *The Memoirs of Vidocq*.° I liked the last best because its leaves were yellow. The wild garden behind the house contained a central apple-tree and a few straggling bushes under one of which I found the late tenant's rusty bicycle-pump. He had been a very charitable priest: in his will he had left all his money to institutions and the furniture of his house to his sister.

When the short days of winter came dusk fell before we had well eaten our dinners. When we met in the street the houses had grown somber. The space of sky above us was the color of ever-changing violet and towards it the lamps of the street lifted their feeble lanterns. The cold air stung us and we played till our bodies glowed. Our shouts echoed in the silent street. The career of our play brought us through the dark muddy lanes behind the houses where we ran the gauntlet of the rough tribes from the cottages, to the back doors of the dark dripping gardens where odors arose from the ashpits, to the dark odorous stables where a coachman smoothed and combed the horse or shook music from the buckled harness. When we returned to the street light from the kitchen windows had filled the areas. If my uncle was seen turning the corner we hid in the shadow until we had seen him safely housed. Or if Mangan's sister° came out on the doorstep to call her brother in to his tea we watched her from our shadow peer up and down the street. We waited to see whether she would remain or go in and, if she remained, we left our shadow and walked up to Mangan's steps resignedly. She was waiting for us, her figure defined by the light from the half-opened door. Her brother always teased her before he obeyed and I stood by the railings looking at her. Her dress swung as she moved her body and the soft rope of her hair tossed from side to side.

Every morning I lay on the floor in the front parlor watching her door. The blind was pulled down within an inch of the sash so that I could not be seen. When she came out on the doorstep my heart leaped. I ran to the hall, seized my books and followed her. I kept her brown figure always in my eye and, when we came near the point at which our ways diverged, I quickened my pace and passed her. This happened morning after morning. I had never spoken to her, except for a few casual words, and yet her name was like a summons to all my foolish blood.

Her image accompanied me even in places the most hostile to romance. 5 On Saturday evenings when my aunt went marketing I had to go to carry some of the parcels. We walked through the flaring streets, jostled by

---

The Abbot . . . Vidocq: a popular historical romance (1820); a book of pious meditations by an eighteenth-century English Franciscan, Pacificus Baker; and the autobiography of François-Jules Vidocq (1775–1857), a criminal who later turned detective.   *Mangan's sister:* an actual young woman in this story, but the phrase recalls Irish poet James Clarence Mangan (1803–1849) and his best-known poem, "Dark Rosaleen," which personifies Ireland as a beautiful woman for whom the poet yearns.

drunken men and bargaining women, amid the curses of laborers, the shrill litanies of shopboys who stood on guard by the barrels of pigs' cheeks, the nasal chanting of street-singers, who sang a *come-all-you* about O'Donovan Rossa,° or a ballad about the troubles in our native land. These noises converged in a single sensation of life for me: I imagined that I bore my chalice safely through a throng of foes. Her name sprang to my lips at moments in strange prayers and praises which I myself did not understand. My eyes were often full of tears (I could not tell why) and at times a flood from my heart seemed to pour itself out into my bosom. I thought little of the future. I did not know whether I would ever speak to her or not or, if I spoke to her, how I could tell her of my confused adoration. But my body was like a harp and her words and gestures were like fingers running upon the wires.

One evening I went into the back drawing-room in which the priest had died. It was a dark rainy evening and there was no sound in the house. Through one of the broken panes I heard the rain impinge upon the earth, the fine incessant needles of water playing in the sodden beds. Some distant lamp or lighted window gleamed below me. I was thankful that I could see so little. All my senses seemed to desire to veil themselves and, feeling that I was about to slip from them, I pressed the palms of my hands together until they trembled, murmuring: *O love! O love!* many times.

At last she spoke to me. When she addressed the first words to me I was so confused that I did not know what to answer. She asked me was I going to *Araby*. I forget whether I answered yes or no. It would be a splendid bazaar, she said; she would love to go.

—And why can't you? I asked.

While she spoke she turned a silver bracelet round and round her wrist. She could not go, she said, because there would be a retreat that week in her convent.° Her brother and two other boys were fighting for their caps and I was alone at the railings. She held one of the spikes, bowing her head towards me. The light from the lamp opposite our door caught the white curve of her neck, lit up her hair that rested there and, falling, lit up the hand upon the railing. It fell over one side of her dress and caught the white border of a petticoat, just visible as she stood at ease.

—It's well for you, she said.

—If I go, I said, I will bring you something.

What innumerable follies laid waste my waking and sleeping thoughts after that evening! I wished to annihilate the tedious interven-   10

---

come-all-you about O'Donovan Rossa: the street singers earned their living by singing timely songs that usually began, "Come all you gallant Irishmen / And listen to my song." Their subject, also called Dynamite Rossa, was a popular hero jailed by the British for advocating violent rebellion. *a retreat . . . in her convent:* a week devoted to religious observances more intense than usual, at the convent school Miss Mangan attends; probably she will have to listen to a number of hellfire sermons.

ing days. I chafed against the work of school. At night in my bedroom and by day in the classroom her image came between me and the page I strove to read. The syllables of the word *Araby* were called to me through the silence in which my soul luxuriated and cast an Eastern enchantment over me. I asked for leave to go to the bazaar on Saturday night. My aunt was surprised and hoped it was not some Freemason° affair. I answered few questions in class. I watched my master's face pass from amiability to sternness; he hoped I was not beginning to idle. I could not call my wandering thoughts together. I had hardly any patience with the serious work of life which, now that it stood between me and my desire, seemed to me child's play, ugly monotonous child's play.

On Saturday morning I reminded my uncle that I wished to go to the bazaar in the evening. He was fussing at the hallstand, looking for the hatbrush, and answered me curtly:

—Yes, boy, I know.

As he was in the hall I could not go into the front parlor and lie at the window. I left the house in bad humor and walked slowly towards the school. The air was pitilessly raw and already my heart misgave me.   15

When I came home to dinner my uncle had not yet been home. Still it was early. I sat staring at the clock for some time and, when its ticking began to irritate me, I left the room. I mounted the staircase and gained the upper part of the house. The high cold empty gloomy rooms liberated me and I went from room to room singing. From the front window I saw my companions playing below in the street. Their cries reached me weakened and indistinct and, leaning my forehead against the cool glass, I looked over at the dark house where she lived. I may have stood there for an hour, seeing nothing but the brown-clad figure cast by my imagination, touched discreetly by the lamplight at the curved neck, at the hand upon the railings and at the border below the dress.

When I came downstairs again I found Mrs. Mercer sitting at the fire. She was an old garrulous woman, a pawnbroker's widow, who collected used stamps for some pious purpose. I had to endure the gossip of the tea-table. The meal was prolonged beyond an hour and still my uncle did not come. Mrs. Mercer stood up to go: she was sorry she couldn't wait any longer, but it was after eight o'clock and she did not like to be out late, as the night air was bad for her. When she had gone I began to walk up and down the room, clenching my fists. My aunt said:

—I'm afraid you may put off your bazaar for this night of Our Lord.

At nine o'clock I heard my uncle's latchkey in the halldoor. I heard him talking to himself and heard the hallstand rocking when it had received the weight of his overcoat. I could interpret these signs. When he was midway through his dinner I asked him to give me the money to go to the bazaar. He had forgotten.

Freemason: Catholics in Ireland viewed the Masonic order as a Protestant conspiracy against them.

—The people are in bed and after their first sleep now, he said.   20
I did not smile. My aunt said to him energetically:

—Can't you give him the money and let him go? You've kept him
late enough as it is.

My uncle said he was very sorry he had forgotten. He said he believed
in the old saying: *All work and no play makes Jack a dull boy.* He asked me
where I was going and, when I had told him a second time he asked me
did I know *The Arab's Farewell to His Steed.*° When I left the kitchen he
was about to recite the opening lines of the piece to my aunt.

I held a florin tightly in my hands as I strode down Buckingham
Street towards the station. The sight of the streets thronged with buyers
and glaring with gas recalled to me the purpose of my journey. I took
my seat in a third-class carriage of a deserted train. After an intolerable
delay the train moved out of the station slowly. It crept onward among
ruinous houses and over the twinkling river. At Westland Row Station
a crowd of people pressed to the carriage doors; but the porters moved
them back, saying that it was a special train for the bazaar. I remained
alone in the bare carriage. In a few minutes the train drew up beside an
improvised wooden platform. I passed out on to the road and saw by the
lighted dial of a clock that it was ten minutes to ten. In front of me was
a large building which displayed the magical name.

I could not find any sixpenny entrance and, fearing that the ba-   25
zaar would be closed, I passed in quickly through a turnstile, handing
a shilling to a weary-looking man. I found myself in a big hall girdled
at half its height by a gallery. Nearly all the stalls were closed and the
greater part of the hall was in darkness. I recognized a silence like that
which pervades a church after a service. I walked into the center of the
bazaar timidly. A few people were gathered about the stalls which were
still open. Before a curtain, over which the words *Café Chantant*° were
written in colored lamps, two men were counting money on a salver.°
I listened to the fall of the coins.

Remembering with difficulty why I had come I went over to one of the
stalls and examined porcelain vases and flowered tea-sets. At the door of
the stall a young lady was talking and laughing with two young gentlemen.
I remarked their English accents and listened vaguely to their conversation.

—O, I never said such a thing!

—O, but you did!

—O, but I didn't!

—Didn't she say that?   30

The Arab's Farewell to His Steed: This sentimental ballad by a popular poet, Caroline Norton
(1808–1877), tells the story of a nomad of the desert who, in a fit of greed, sells his beloved
horse, then regrets the loss, flings away the gold he had received, and takes back his horse.
Notice the echo of "Araby" in the song title. *Café Chantant:* name for a Paris nightspot
featuring topical songs. *salver:* a tray like that used in serving Holy Communion.

—Yes. I heard her.

—O, there's a . . . . fib!

Observing me the young lady came over and asked me did I wish to buy anything. The tone of her voice was not encouraging; she seemed to have spoken to me out of a sense of duty. I looked humbly at the great jars that stood like eastern guards at either side of the dark entrance to the stall and murmured:

—No, thank you.

The young lady changed the position of one of the vases and went   35
back to the two young men. They began to talk of the same subject. Once or twice the young lady glanced at me over her shoulder.

I lingered before her stall, though I knew my stay was useless, to make my interest in her wares seem the more real. Then I turned away slowly and walked down the middle of the bazaar. I allowed the two pennies to fall against the sixpence in my pocket. I heard a voice call from one end of the gallery that the light was out. The upper part of the hall was now completely dark.

Gazing up into the darkness I saw myself as a creature driven and derided by vanity; and my eyes burned with anguish and anger.

Franz Kafka

Before the Law   1919

Translated by John Siscoe

Franz Kafka (1883–1924) was born into a German-speaking Jewish family in Prague, Czechoslovakia (then part of the Austro-Hungarian empire). He was the only surviving son of a domineering, successful father. After earning a law degree, Kafka worked as a claims investigator for the state accident insurance company. He worked on his stories at night, especially during his frequent bouts of insomnia. He never married, and lived mostly with his parents. Kafka was such a careful and self-conscious writer that he found it difficult to finish his work and send it out for publication. During his lifetime he published only a few

Franz Kafka

thin volumes of short fiction, most notably The Metamorphosis *(1915) and* In the Penal Colony *(1919). He never finished to his own satisfaction any of his three novels (all published posthumously):* The Trial *(1925),* The Castle *(1926), and* Amerika *(1927). As Kafka was dying of tuberculosis, he begged his friend and literary executor Max Brod to burn his uncompleted manuscripts. Brod pondered this request but luckily didn't obey. Kafka's two major novels,* The Trial *and* The Castle, *both depict huge, remote, bumbling, irresponsible bureaucracies in whose*

*power the individual feels helpless and blind. Kafka's works appear startlingly pro-
phetic to readers looking back on them in the later light of Stalinism, World War II,
and the Holocaust. His haunting vision of an alienated modern world led the poet
W. H. Auden to remark at midcentury, "Had one to name the author who comes
nearest to bearing the same kind of relation to our age as Dante, Shakespeare, and
Goethe bore to theirs, Kafka is the first one would think of." The ironic and devastating parable "Before the Law" contains the distilled essence of what we mean by the
term "Kafkaesque."*

Before the Law stands a doorkeeper. To this doorkeeper comes a man
from the country who asks to be admitted to the Law. But the doorkeeper
says that he can't let the man in just now. The man thinks this over
and then asks if he will be allowed to enter later. "It's possible," answers
the doorkeeper, "but not just now." Since the door to the Law stands
open as usual and the doorkeeper steps aside, the man bends down to
look through the doorway into the interior. Seeing this, the doorkeeper
laughs and says: "If you find it so compelling, then try to enter despite
my prohibition. But bear in mind that I am powerful. And I am only the
lowest doorkeeper. In hall after hall, keepers stand at every door. The
mere sight of the third one is more than even I can bear." These are
difficulties which the man from the country has not expected; the Law,
he thinks, should be always available to everyone. But when he looks
more closely at the doorkeeper in his furred robe, with his large pointed
nose and his long, thin, black Tartar beard, he decides that it would
be better to wait until he receives permission to enter. The doorkeeper
gives him a stool and allows him to sit down beside the door. There
he sits for days and years. He makes many attempts to be let in, and
wearies the doorkeeper with his pleas. The doorkeeper often questions
him casually about his home and many other matters, but the questions
are asked with indifference, the way important men might ask them,
and always conclude with the statement the man can't be admitted at
this time. The man, who has equipped himself with many things for his
journey, spends all that he has, regardless of value, in order to bribe the
doorkeeper. The doorkeeper accepts it all, though saying each time as he
does so, "I'm taking this only so that you won't feel that you haven't tried
everything." During these long years the man watches the doorkeeper
almost continuously. He forgets about the other doorkeepers, and imagines that this first one is the sole obstacle barring his way to the Law. In
the early years he loudly bewails his misfortune; later, as he grows old, he
merely grumbles to himself. He becomes childish, and since during his
long study of the doorkeeper he has gotten to know even the fleas in the
fur collar, he begs these fleas to help him change the doorkeeper's mind.
At last his eyesight grows dim and he cannot tell whether it is really
growing darker or whether his eyes are simply deceiving him. Yet in the

darkness he can now perceive that radiance that streams inextinguish-
ably from the door of the Law. Now his life is nearing its end. Before he
dies, all his experiences during this long time coalesce in his mind into
a single question, one which he has never yet asked the doorkeeper. He
beckons to the doorkeeper, for he can no longer raise his stiffening body.
The doorkeeper has to bend low to hear him, since the difference in
size between them has increased very much to the man's disadvantage.
"What do you want to know now?" asks the doorkeeper, "you are insa-
tiable." "Surely everyone strives to reach the Law," says the man, "why
then is it that in all these years no one has come seeking admittance but
me?" The doorkeeper realizes that the man has reached his end and that
his hearing is failing so he yells in his ear: "No one but you could have
been admitted here, since this entrance was meant for you alone. Now I
am going to shut it."

Katherine Mansfield

Miss Brill

1922

*Katherine Mansfield Beauchamp (1888–1923),
was born into a sedate Victorian family in New
Zealand, the daughter of a successful businessman.
At fifteen, she emigrated to England to attend school
and did not ever permanently return Down Under.
In 1918, after a time of wild-oat sowing in bohemian
London, she married the journalist and critic John
Middleton Murry. All at once, Mansfield found herself struggling to define her sexual identity, to earn a
living by her pen, to endure World War I (in which
her brother was killed in action), and to survive the
ravages of tuberculosis. She died at thirty-four, in*

Katherine Mansfield

*France, at a spiritualist commune where she had sought to regain her health. Mans-
field wrote no novels, but during her brief career concentrated on the short story,
in which she has few peers.* Bliss *(1920) and* The Garden-Party and Other
Stories *(1922) were greeted with an acclaim that has continued; her collected
short stories were published in 1937. Some of her stories celebrate life, others
wryly poke fun at it. Many reveal, in ordinary lives, small incidents that open like
doorways into significances.*

Although it was so brilliantly fine—the blue sky powdered with
gold and great spots of light like white wine splashed over the Jardins
Publiques—Miss Brill was glad that she had decided on her fur. The air
was motionless, but when you opened your mouth there was just a faint
chill, like a chill from a glass of iced water before you sip, and now and

again a leaf came drifting—from nowhere, from the sky. Miss Brill put up her hand and touched her fur. Dear little thing! It was nice to feel it again. She had taken it out of its box that afternoon, shaken out the moth-powder, given it a good brush, and rubbed the life back into the dim little eyes. "What has been happening to me?" said the sad little eyes. Oh, how sweet it was to see them snap at her again from the red eiderdown! . . . But the nose, which was of some black composition, wasn't at all firm. It must have had a knock, somehow. Never mind—a little dab of black sealing-wax when the time came—when it was absolutely necessary. . . . Little rogue! Yes, she really felt like that about it. Little rogue biting its tail just by her left ear. She could have taken it off and laid it on her lap and stroked it. She felt a tingling in her hands and arms, but that came from walking, she supposed. And when she breathed, something light and sad—no, not sad, exactly—something gentle seemed to move in her bosom.

There were a number of people out this afternoon, far more than last Sunday. And the band sounded louder and gayer. That was because the Season had begun. For although the band played all year round on Sundays, out of season it was never the same. It was like some one playing with only the family to listen; it didn't care how it played if there weren't any strangers present. Wasn't the conductor wearing a new coat, too? She was sure it was new. He scraped with his foot and flapped his arms like a rooster about to crow, and the bandsmen sitting in the green rotunda blew out their cheeks and glared at the music. Now there came a little "flutey" bit—very pretty!—a little chain of bright drops. She was sure it would be repeated. It was; she lifted her head and smiled.

Only two people shared her "special" seat: a fine old man in a velvet coat, his hands clasped over a huge carved walking-stick, and a big old woman, sitting upright, with a roll of knitting on her embroidered apron. They did not speak. This was disappointing, for Miss Brill always looked forward to the conversation. She had become really quite expert, she thought, at listening as though she didn't listen, at sitting in other people's lives just for a minute while they talked round her.

She glanced, sideways, at the old couple. Perhaps they would go soon. Last Sunday, too, hadn't been as interesting as usual. An Englishman and his wife, he wearing a dreadful Panama hat and she button boots. And she'd gone on the whole time about how she ought to wear spectacles; she knew she needed them; but that it was no good getting any; they'd be sure to break and they'd never keep on. And he'd been so patient. He'd suggested everything—gold rims, the kind that curved round your ears, little pads inside the bridge. No, nothing would please her. "They'll always be sliding down my nose!" Miss Brill wanted to shake her.

The old people sat on the bench, still as statues. Never mind, there was always the crowd to watch. To and fro, in front of the flower-beds and the band rotunda, the couples and groups paraded, stopped to talk, to greet, to buy a handful of flowers from the old beggar who had his tray fixed to the railings. Little children ran among them, swooping and laughing; little boys with big white silk bows under their chins, little girls, little French dolls, dressed up in velvet and lace. And sometimes a tiny staggerer came suddenly rocking into the open from under the trees, stopped, stared, as suddenly sat down "flop," until its small high-stepping mother, like a young hen, rushed scolding to its rescue. Other people sat on the benches and green chairs, but they were nearly always the same, Sunday after Sunday, and—Miss Brill had often noticed—there was something funny about nearly all of them. They were odd, silent, nearly all old, and from the way they stared they looked as though they'd just come from dark little rooms or even—even cupboards!

Behind the rotunda the slender trees with yellow leaves down drooping, and through them just a line of sea, and beyond the blue sky with gold-veined clouds.

Tum-tum-tum tiddle-um! tiddle-um! turn tiddley-um turn ta! blew the band.

Two young girls in red came by and two young soldiers in blue met them, and they laughed and paired and went off arm-in-arm. Two peasant women with funny straw hats passed, gravely, leading beautiful smoke-colored donkeys. A cold, pale nun hurried by. A beautiful woman came along and dropped her bunch of violets, and a little boy ran after to hand them to her, and she took them and threw them away as if they'd been poisoned. Dear me! Miss Brill didn't know whether to admire that or not! And now an ermine toque and a gentleman in grey met just in front of her. He was tall, stiff, dignified, and she was wearing the ermine toque she'd bought when her hair was yellow. Now everything, her hair, her face, even her eyes, was the same color as the shabby ermine, and her hand, in its cleaned glove, lifted to dab her lips, was a tiny yellowish paw. Oh, she was so pleased to see him—delighted! She rather thought they were going to meet that afternoon. She described where she'd been—everywhere, here, there, along by the sea. The day was so charming—didn't he agree? And wouldn't he, perhaps? . . . But he shook his head, lighted a cigarette, slowly breathed a great deep puff into her face, and, even while she was still talking and laughing, flicked the match away and walked on. The ermine toque was alone; she smiled more brightly than ever. But even the band seemed to know what she was feeling and played more softly, played tenderly, and the drum beat, "The Brute! The Brute!" over and over. What would she do? What was going to happen now? But as Miss Brill wondered, the ermine toque turned, raised her hand as though she'd seen some one else, much nicer, just over there, and pattered away. And the band changed again and played more quickly, more gaily than ever, and the old couple on Miss Brill's seat got up and marched away, and such a funny old man with long whiskers hobbled along in time to the music and was nearly knocked over by four girls walking abreast.

Oh, how fascinating it was! How she enjoyed it! How she loved sitting here, watching it all! It was like a play. It was exactly like a play. Who could believe the sky at the back wasn't painted? But it wasn't till a little brown dog trotted on solemn and then slowly trotted off, like a little "theatre" dog, a little dog that had been drugged, that Miss Brill discovered what it was that made it so exciting. They were all on the stage. They weren't only the audience, not only looking on; they were acting. Even she had a part and came every Sunday. No doubt somebody would have noticed if she hadn't been there; she was part of the performance after all. How strange she'd never thought of it like that before! And yet it explained why she made such a point of starting from home at just the same time each week—so as not to be late for the performance—and it also explained why she had quite a queer, shy feeling at telling her English pupils how she spent her Sunday afternoons. No wonder! Miss Brill nearly laughed out loud. She was on the stage. She thought of the old invalid gentleman to whom she read the newspaper four afternoons a week while he slept in the garden. She had got quite used to the frail head on the cotton pillow, the hollowed eyes, the open mouth and the high pinched nose. If he'd been dead she mightn't have noticed for weeks; she wouldn't have minded. But suddenly he knew he was having the paper read to him by an actress! "An actress!" The old head lifted; two points of light quivered in the old eyes. "An actress—are ye?" And Miss Brill smoothed the newspaper as though it were the manuscript of her part and said gently: "Yes, I have been an actress for a long time."

The band had been having a rest. Now they started again. And what 10 they played was warm, sunny, yet there was just a faint chill—a something, what was it?—not sadness—no, not sadness—a something that made you want to sing. The tune lifted, lifted, the light shone; and it seemed to Miss Brill that in another moment all of them, all the whole company, would begin singing. The young ones, the laughing ones who were moving together, they would begin, and the men's voices, very resolute and brave, would join them. And then she too, she too, and the others on the benches—they would come in with a kind of accompaniment— something low, that scarcely rose or fell, something so beautiful—moving . . . And Miss Brill's eyes filled with tears and she looked smiling at all the other members of the company. Yes, we understand, we understand, she thought—though what they understood she didn't know.

Just at that moment a boy and a girl came and sat down where the old couple had been. They were beautifully dressed; they were in love. The hero and heroine, of course, just arrived from his father's yacht. And still soundlessly singing, still with that trembling smile, Miss Brill prepared to listen.

"No, not now," said the girl. "Not here, I can't."

"But why? Because of that stupid old thing at the end there?" asked the boy. "Why does she come here at all—who wants her? Why doesn't she keep her silly old mug at home?"

"It's her fu-fur which is so funny," giggled the girl. "It's exactly like a fried whiting."

"Ah, be off with you!" said the boy in an angry whisper. Then: "Tell   15
me, my petite cherie—"

"No, not here," said the girl. "Not yet."

On her way home she usually bought a slice of honeycake at the baker's. It was her Sunday treat. Sometimes there was an almond in her slice, sometimes not. It made a great difference. If there was an almond it was like carrying home a tiny present—a surprise—something that might very well not have been there. She hurried on the almond Sundays and struck the match for the kettle in quite a dashing way.

But today she passed the baker's boy, climbed the stairs, went into the little dark room—her room like a cupboard—and sat down on the red eiderdown. She sat there for a long time. The box that the fur came out of was on the bed. She unclasped the necklet quickly; quickly, without looking, laid it inside. But when she put the lid on she thought she heard something crying.

Joyce Carol Oates

Where Are You Going, Where Have You Been?   1970

Joyce Carol Oates was born in 1938 into a blue collar, Catholic family in Lockport, New York. As an undergraduate at Syracuse University, she won a Mademoiselle magazine award for fiction. After graduating with top honors, she took a master's degree in English at the University of Wisconsin and went on to teach at several universities: Detroit, Windsor, and Princeton. A remarkably prolific writer, Oates has produced more than twenty-five collections of stories, including High Lonesome: New & Selected Stories, 1966–2006, *and forty novels, including them, winner of a National Book Award in 1970,* Because

Joyce Carol Oates

It Is Bitter, and Because It Is My Heart *(1990), and, more recently,* Black Girl/ White Girl *(2006),* The Gravedigger's Daughter *(2007), and* A Fair Maiden *(2010). She also writes poetry, plays, and literary criticism.* On Boxing *(1987) is her nonfiction memoir and study of fighters and fighting.* Foxfire *(1993), her twenty-second novel, is the story of a girl gang in upstate New York. Her 1996 Gothic novella,* First Love, *is a bizarre tale of terror and torture. Violence and*

the macabre may inhabit her best stories, but Oates has insisted that these elements
in her work are never gratuitous. The 1985 film Smooth Talk, *directed by Joyce*
Chopra, was based on "Where Are You Going, Where Have You Been?"

For Bob Dylan

Her name was Connie. She was fifteen and she had a quick nervous
giggling habit of craning her neck to glance into mirrors, or checking
other people's faces to make sure her own was all right. Her mother, who
noticed everything and knew everything and who hadn't much reason
any longer to look at her own face, always scolded Connie about it. "Stop
gawking at yourself, who are you? You think you're so pretty?" she would
say. Connie would raise her eyebrows at these familiar complaints and
look right through her mother, into a shadowy vision of herself as she was
right at that moment: she knew she was pretty and that was everything.
Her mother had been pretty once too, if you could believe those old snap-
shots in the album, but now her looks were gone and that was why she
was always after Connie.

"Why don't you keep your room clean like your sister? How've you
got your hair fixed—what the hell stinks? Hair spray? You don't see your
sister using that junk."

Her sister June was twenty-four and still lived at home. She was a secretary in the high school Connie attended, and if that wasn't bad enough—
with her in the same building—she was so plain and chunky and steady
that Connie had to hear her praised all the time by her mother and her
mother's sisters. June did this, June did that, she saved money and helped
clean the house and cooked and Connie couldn't do a thing, her mind was
all filled with trashy daydreams. Their father was away at work most of the
time and when he came home he wanted supper and he read the newspaper
at supper and after supper he went to bed. He didn't bother talking much to
them, but around his bent head Connie's mother kept picking at her until
Connie wished her mother was dead and she herself was dead and it was all
over. "She makes me want to throw up sometimes," she complained to her
friends. She had a high, breathless, amused voice which made everything
she said sound a little forced, whether it was sincere or not.

There was one good thing: June went places with girl friends of hers,
girls who were just as plain and steady as she, and so when Connie wanted
to do that her mother had no objections. The father of Connie's best girl
friend drove the girls the three miles to town and left them off at a shopping plaza, so that they could walk through the stores or go to a movie,
and when he came to pick up again at eleven he never bothered to
ask what they had done.

They must have been familiar sights, walking around that shop-   5
ping plaza in their shorts and flat ballerina slippers that always scuffed
the sidewalk, with charm bracelets jingling on their thin wrists; they

would lean together to whisper and laugh secretly if someone passed by who amused or interested them. Connie had long dark blond hair that drew anyone's eye to it, and she wore part of it pulled up on her head and puffed out and the rest of it she let fall down her back. She wore a pull-over jersey blouse that looked one way when she was at home and another way when she was away from home. Everything about her had two sides to it, one for home and one for anywhere that was not home: her walk that could be childlike and bobbing, or languid enough to make anyone think she was hearing music in her head, her mouth which was pale and smirking most of the time, but bright and pink on these evenings out, her laugh which was cynical and drawling at home—"Ha, ha, very funny"—but high-pitched and nervous anywhere else, like the jingling of the charms on her bracelet.

Sometimes they did go shopping or to a movie, but sometimes they went across the highway, ducking fast across the busy road, to a drive-in restaurant where older kids hung out. The restaurant was shaped like a big bottle, though squatter than a real bottle, and on its cap was a revolving figure of a grinning boy who held a hamburger aloft. One night in mid-summer they ran across, breathless with daring, and right away someone leaned out a car window and invited them over, but it was just a boy from high school they didn't like. It made them feel good to be able to ignore him. They went up through the maze of parked and cruising cars to the bright-lit, fly-infested restaurant, their faces pleased and expectant as if they were entering a sacred building that loomed out of the night to give them what haven and what blessing they yearned for. They sat at the counter and crossed their legs at the ankles, their thin shoulders rigid with excitement, and listened to the music that made everything so good: the music was always in the background like music at a church service, it was something to depend upon.

A boy named Eddie came in to talk with them. He sat backwards on his stool, turning himself jerkily around in semi-circles and then stopping and turning again, and after a while he asked Connie if she would like something to eat. She said she did and so she tapped her friend's arm on her way out—her friend pulled her face up into a brave droll look—and Connie said she would meet her at eleven, across the way. "I just hate to leave her like that," Connie said earnestly, but the boy said that she wouldn't be alone for long. So they went out to his car and on the way Connie couldn't help but let her eyes wander over the windshields and faces all around her, her face gleaming with a joy that had nothing to do with Eddie or even this place; it might have been the music. She drew her shoulders up and sucked in her breath with the pure pleasure of being alive, and just at that moment she happened to glance at a face just a few feet from hers. It was a boy with shaggy black hair, in a convertible jalopy painted gold. He stared at her and then his lips widened into a grin. Connie slit her eyes at him and turned away, but she couldn't help glancing back and there he was still watching her. He wagged a finger and laughed and said, "Gonna get you, baby," and Connie turned away again without Eddie noticing anything.

She spent three hours with him, at the restaurant where they ate hamburgers and drank Cokes in wax cups that were always sweating, and then down an alley a mile or so away, and when he left her off at five to eleven only the movie house was still open at the plaza. Her girl friend was there, talking with a boy. When Connie came up the two girls smiled at each other and Connie said, "How was the movie?" and the girl said, "*You should know.*" They rode off with the girl's father, sleepy and pleased, and Connie couldn't help but look at the darkened shopping plaza with its big empty parking lot and its signs that were faded and ghostly now, and over at the drive-in restaurant where cars were still circling tirelessly. She couldn't hear the music at this distance.

Next morning June asked her how the movie was and Connie said, "So-so."

She and that girl and occasionally another girl went out several   10
times a week that way, and the rest of the time Connie spent around the house—it was summer vacation—getting in her mother's way and thinking, dreaming, about the boys she met. But all the boys fell back and dissolved into a single face that was not even a face, but an idea, a feeling, mixed up with the urgent insistent pounding of the music and the humid night air of July. Connie's mother kept dragging her back to the daylight by finding things for her to do or saying, suddenly, "What's this about the Pettinger girl?"

And Connie would say nervously, "Oh, her. That dope." She always drew thick clear lines between herself and such girls, and her mother was simple and kindly enough to believe her. Her mother was so simple, Connie thought, that it was maybe cruel to fool her so much. Her mother went scuffling around the house in old bedroom slippers and complained over the telephone to one sister about the other, then the other called up and the two of them complained about the third one. If June's name was mentioned her mother's tone was approving, and if Connie's name was mentioned it was disapproving. This did not really mean she disliked Connie and actually Connie thought that her mother preferred her to June because she was prettier, but the two of them kept up a pretense of exasperation, a sense that they were tugging and struggling over something of little value to either of them. Sometimes, over coffee, they were almost friends, but something would come up—some vexation that was like a fly buzzing suddenly around their heads—and their faces went hard with contempt.

One Sunday Connie got up at eleven—none of them bothered with church—and washed her hair so that it could dry all day long, in the sun. Her parents and sister were going to a barbecue at an aunt's house and

Connie said no, she wasn't interested, rolling her eyes to let her mother know just what she thought of it. "Stay home alone then," her mother said sharply. Connie sat out back in a lawn chair and watched them drive away, her father quiet and bald, hunched around so that he could back the car out, her mother with a look that was still angry and not at all softened through the windshield, and in the back seat poor old June all dressed up as if she didn't know what a barbecue was, with all the running yelling kids and the flies. Connie sat with her eyes closed in the sun, dreaming and dazed with the warmth about her as if this were a kind of love, the caresses of love, and her mind slipped over onto thoughts of the boy she had been with the night before and how nice he had been, how sweet it always was, not the way someone like June would suppose but sweet, gentle, the way it was in movies and promised in songs; and when she opened her eyes she hardly knew where she was, the back yard ran off into weeds and a fence-line of trees and behind it the sky was perfectly blue and still. The asbestos "ranch house" that was now three years old startled her—it looked small. She shook her head as if to get awake.

It was too hot. She went inside the house and turned on the radio to drown out the quiet. She sat on the edge of her bed, barefoot, and listened for an hour and a half to a program called XYZ Sunday Jamboree, record after record of hard, fast, shrieking songs she sang along with, interspersed by exclamations from "Bobby King": "An' look here you girls at Napoleon's—Son and Charley want you to pay real close attention to this song coming up!"

And Connie paid close attention herself, bathed in a glow of slow-pulsed joy that seemed to rise mysteriously out of the music itself and lay languidly about the airless little room, breathed in and breathed out with each gentle rise and fall of her chest.

After a while she heard a car coming up the drive. She sat up at once, startled, because it couldn't be her father so soon. The gravel kept crunching all the way in from the road—the driveway was long—and Connie ran to the window. It was a car she didn't know. It was an open jalopy, painted a bright gold that caught the sunlight opaquely. Her heart began to pound and her fingers snatched at her hair, checking it, and she whispered "Christ, Christ," wondering how bad she looked. The car came to a stop at the side door and the horn sounded four short taps as if this were a signal Connie knew.

She went into the kitchen and approached the door slowly, then hung out the screen door, her bare toes curling down off the step. There were two boys in the car and now she recognized the driver: he had shaggy, shabby black hair that looked crazy as a wig and he was grinning at her.

"I ain't late, am I?" he said.

"Who the hell do you think you are?" Connie said.

"Toldja I'd be out, didn't I?"

"I don't even know who you are."   20

She spoke sullenly, careful to show no interest or pleasure, and he spoke in a fast bright monotone. Connie looked past him to the other boy, taking her time. He had fair brown hair, with a lock that fell onto his forehead. His sideburns gave him a fierce, embarrassed look, but so far he hadn't even bothered to glance at her. Both boys wore sunglasses. The driver's glasses were metallic and mirrored everything in miniature.

"You wanta come for a ride?" he said.

Connie smirked and let her hair fall loose over one shoulder.

"Don'tcha like my car? New paint job," he said. "Hey."

"What?"   25

"You're cute."

She pretended to fidget, chasing flies away from the door.

"Don'tcha believe me, or what?" he said.

"Look, I don't even know who you are," Connie said in disgust.

"Hey, Ellie's got a radio, see. Mine's broke down." He lifted his   30 friend's arm and showed her the little transistor the boy was holding, and now Connie began to hear the music. It was the same program that was playing inside the house.

"Bobby King?" she said.

"I listen to him all the time. I think he's great."

"He's kind of great," Connie said reluctantly.

"Listen, that guy's *great*. He knows where the action is."

Connie blushed a little, because the glasses made it impossible for   35 her to see just what this boy was looking at. She couldn't decide if she liked him or if he was just a jerk, and so she dawdled in the doorway and wouldn't come down or go back inside. She said, "What's all that stuff painted on your car?"

"Can'tcha read it?" He opened the door very carefully, as if he was afraid it might fall off. He slid out just as carefully, planting his feet firmly on the ground, the tiny metallic world in his glasses slowing down like gelatine hardening and in the midst of it Connie's bright green blouse. "This here is my name, to begin with," he said. ARNOLD FRIEND was written in tarlike black letters on the side, with a drawing of a round grinning face that reminded Connie of a pumpkin, except it wore sunglasses. "I wanta introduce myself, I'm Arnold Friend and that's my real name and I'm gonna be your friend, honey, and inside the car's Ellie Oscar, he's kinda shy." Ellie brought his transistor radio up to his shoulder and balanced it there. "Now these numbers are a secret code, honey," Arnold Friend explained. He read off the numbers 33, 19, 17 and raised his eyebrows at her to see what she thought of that, but she didn't think much of it. The left rear fender had been smashed and around it was written, on the gleaming gold background: DONE BY CRAZY WOMAN DRIVER. Connie had to laugh at that. Arnold Friend was pleased at her laughter and looked up at her. "Around the other side's a lot more—you wanta come and see them?"

"No."

"Why not?"

"Why should I?"

"Don'tcha wanta see what's on the car? Don'tcha wanta go for a ride?" 40

"I don't know."

"Why not?"

"I got things to do."

"Like what?"

"Things." 45

He laughed as if she had said something funny. He slapped his thighs. He was standing in a strange way, leaning back against the car as if he were balancing himself. He wasn't tall, only an inch or so taller than she would be if she came down to him. Connie liked the way he was dressed, which was the way all of them dressed: tight faded jeans stuffed into black, scuffed boots, a belt that pulled his waist in and showed how lean he was, and a white pull-over shirt that was a little soiled and showed the hard small muscles of his arms and shoulders. He looked as if he probably did hard work, lifting and carrying things. Even his neck looked muscular. And his face was a familiar face, somehow: the jaw and chin and cheeks slightly darkened, because he hadn't shaved for a day or two, and the nose long and hawk-like, sniffing as if she were a treat he was going to gobble up and it was all a joke.

"Connie, you ain't telling the truth. This is your day set aside for a ride with me and you know it," he said, still laughing. The way he straightened and recovered from his fit of laughing showed that it had been all fake.

"How do you know what my name is?" she said suspiciously.

"It's Connie."

"Maybe and maybe not." 50

"I know my Connie," he said, wagging his finger. Now she remembered him even better, back at the restaurant, and her cheeks warmed at the thought of how she sucked in her breath just at the moment she passed him—how she must have looked to him. And he had remembered her. "Ellie and I come out here especially for you," he said. "Ellie can sit in back. How about it?"

"Where?"

"Where what?"

"Where're we going?"

He looked at her. He took off the sunglasses and she saw how pale the 55 skin around his eyes was, like holes that were not in shadow but instead in light. His eyes were chips of broken glass that catch the light in an amiable way. He smiled. It was as if the idea of going for a ride somewhere, to some place, was a new idea to him.

"Just for a ride, Connie sweetheart."

"I never said my name was Connie," she said.

"But I know what it is. I know your name and all about you, lots of things," Arnold Friend said. He had not moved yet but stood still leaning back against the side of his jalopy. "I took a special interest in you, such a pretty girl, and found out all about you like I know your parents and sister are gone somewheres and I know where and how long they're going to be gone, and I know who you were with last night, and your best girl friend's name is Betty. Right?"

He spoke in a simple lilting voice, exactly as if he were reciting the words to a song. His smile assured her that everything was fine. In the car Ellie turned up the volume on his radio and did not bother to look around at them.

"Ellie can sit in the back seat," Arnold Friend said. He indicated   60
his friend with a casual jerk of his chin, as if Ellie did not count and she
should not bother with him.

"How'd you find out all that stuff?" Connie said.

"Listen: Betty Schultz and Tony Fitch and Jimmy Pettinger and Nancy Pettinger," he said, in a chant. "Raymond Stanley and Bob Hutter—"

"Do you know all those kids?"

"I know everybody."

"Look, you're kidding. You're not from around here."   65

"Sure."

"But—how come we never saw you before?"

"Sure you saw me before," he said. He looked down at his boots, as if he were a little offended. "You just don't remember."

"I guess I'd remember you," Connie said.

"Yeah?" He looked up at this, beaming. He was pleased. He began to   70
mark time with the music from Ellie's radio, tapping his fists lightly together. Connie looked away from his smile to the car, which was painted
so bright it almost hurt her eyes to look at it. She looked at that name,
ARNOLD FRIEND. And up at the front fender was an expression that was
familiar—MAN THE FLYING SAUCERS. It was an expression kids had used
the year before, but didn't use this year. She looked at it for a while as if
the words meant something to her that she did not yet know.

"What're you thinking about? Huh?" Arnold Friend demanded. "Not
worried about your hair blowing around in the car, are you?"

"No."

"Think I maybe can't drive good?"

"How do I know?"

"You're a hard girl to handle. How come?" he said. "Don't you know   75
I'm your friend? Didn't you see me put my sign in the air when you
walked by?"

"What sign?"

"My sign." And he drew an X in the air, leaning out toward her. They were maybe ten feet apart. After his hand fell back to his side the X was still in the air, almost visible. Connie let the screen door close and stood perfectly still inside it, listening to the music from her radio and the boy's blend together. She stared at Arnold Friend. He stood there so stiffly relaxed, pretending to be relaxed, with one hand idly on the door handle as if he were keeping himself up that way and had no intention of ever moving again. She recognized most things about him, the tight jeans that showed his thighs and buttocks and the greasy leather boots and the tight shirt, and even that slippery friendly smile of his, that sleepy dreamy smile that all the boys used to get across ideas they didn't want to put into words. She recognized all this and also the singsong way he talked, slightly mocking, kidding, but serious and a little melancholy, and she recognized the way he tapped one fist against the other in homage to the perpetual music behind him. But all these things did not come together.

She said suddenly, "Hey, how old are you?"

His smile faded. She could see then that he wasn't a kid, he was much older—thirty, maybe more. At this knowledge her heart began to pound faster.

"That's a crazy thing to ask. Can'tcha see I'm your own age?"

"Like hell you are."

"Or maybe a coupla years older, I'm eighteen."

"Eighteen?" she said doubtfully.

He grinned to reassure her and lines appeared at the corners of his mouth. His teeth were big and white. He grinned so broadly his eyes became slits and she saw how thick the lashes were, thick and black as if painted with a black tarlike material. Then he seemed to become embarrassed, abruptly, and looked over his shoulder at Ellie. "*Him*, he's crazy," he said. "Ain't he a riot, he's a nut, a real character." Ellie was still listening to the music. His sunglasses told nothing about what he was thinking. He wore a bright orange shirt unbuttoned halfway to show his chest, which was a pale, bluish chest and not muscular like Arnold Friend's. His shirt collar was turned up all around and the very tips of the collar pointed out past his chin as if they were protecting him. He was pressing the transistor radio up against his ear and sat there in a kind of daze, right in the sun.

"He's kinda strange," Connie said.

"Hey, she says you're kinda strange! Kinda strange!" Arnold Friend cried. He pounded on the car to get Ellie's attention. Ellie turned for the first time and Connie saw with shock that he wasn't a kid either—he had a fair, hairless face, cheeks reddened slightly as if the veins grew too close to the surface of his skin, the face of a forty-year-old baby. Connie felt a wave of dizziness rise in her at this sight and she stared at him as if waiting for something to change the shock of the moment, make it all right again. Ellie's lips kept shaping words, mumbling along with the words blasting in his ear.

80

85

"Maybe you two better go away," Connie said faintly.

"What? How come?" Arnold Friend cried. "We come out here to take you for a ride. It's Sunday." He had the voice of the man on the radio now. It was the same voice, Connie thought. "Don'tcha know it's Sunday all day and honey, no matter who you were with last night today you're with Arnold Friend and don't you forget it!—Maybe you better step out here," he said, and this last was in a different voice. It was a little flatter, as if the heat was finally getting to him.

"No. I got things to do."

"Hey."   90

"You two better leave."

"We ain't leaving until you come with us."

"Like hell I am—"

"Connie, don't fool around with me. I mean, I mean, don't fool *around*," he said, shaking his head. He laughed incredulously. He placed his sunglasses on top of his head, carefully, as if he were indeed wearing a wig, and brought the stems down behind his ears. Connie stared at him, another wave of dizziness and fear rising in her so that for a moment he wasn't even in focus but was just a blur, standing there against his gold car, and she had the idea that he had driven up the driveway all right but had come from nowhere before that and belonged nowhere and that everything about him and even about the music that was so familiar to her was only half real.

"If my father comes and sees you—"   95

"He ain't coming. He's at a barbecue."

"How do you know that?"

"Aunt Tillie's. Right now they're—uh—they're drinking. Sitting around," he said vaguely, squinting as if he were staring all the way to town and over to Aunt Tillie's backyard. Then the vision seemed to get clear and he nodded energetically. "Yeah. Sitting around. There's your sister in a blue dress, huh? And high heels, the poor sad bitch—nothing like you, sweetheart! And your mother's helping some fat woman with the corn, they're cleaning the corn—husking the corn—"

"What fat woman?" Connie cried.

"How do I know what fat woman. I don't know every goddam fat   100
woman in the world!" Arnold Friend laughed.

"Oh, that's Mrs. Hornby. . . . Who invited her?" Connie said. She felt a little light-headed. Her breath was coming quickly.

"She's too fat. I don't like them fat. I like them the way you are, honey," he said, smiling sleepily at her. They stared at each other for a while, through the screen door. He said softly, "Now what you're going to do is this: you're going to come out that door. You're going to sit up front with me and Ellie's going to sit in the back, the hell with Ellie, right? This isn't Ellie's date. You're my date. I'm your lover, honey."

"What? You're crazy——"

"Yes, I'm your lover. You don't know what that is but you will," he said. "I know that too. I know all about you. But look: it's real nice and you couldn't ask for nobody better than me, or more polite. I always keep my word. I'll tell you how it is, I'm always nice at first, the first time. I'll hold you so tight you won't think you have to try to get away or pretend anything because you'll know you can't. And I'll come inside you where it's all secret and you'll give in to me and you'll love me——"

"Shut up! You're crazy!" Connie said. She backed away from the door. 105 She put her hands against her ears as if she'd heard something terrible, something not meant for her. "People don't talk like that, you're crazy," she muttered. Her heart was almost too big now for her chest and its pumping made sweat break out all over her. She looked out to see Arnold Friend pause and then take a step toward the porch lurching. He almost fell. But, like a clever drunken man, he managed to catch his balance. He wobbled in his high boots and grabbed hold of one of the porch posts.

"Honey?" he said. "You still listening?"

"Get the hell out of here!"

"Be nice, honey. Listen."

"I'm going to call the police——"

He wobbled again and out of the side of his mouth came a fast spat 110 curse, an aside not meant for her to hear. But even this "Christ!" sounded forced. Then he began to smile again. She watched this smile come, awkward as if he were smiling from inside a mask. His whole face was a mask, she thought wildly, tanned down onto his throat but then running out as if he had plastered makeup on his face but had forgotten about his throat.

"Honey——? Listen, here's how it is. I always tell the truth and I promise you this: I ain't coming in that house after you."

"You better not! I'm going to call the police if you—if you don't——"

"Honey," he said, talking right through her voice, "honey, I'm not coming in there but you are coming out here. You know why?"

She was panting. The kitchen looked like a place she had never seen before, some room she had run inside but which wasn't good enough, wasn't going to help her. The kitchen window had never had a curtain, after three years, and there were dishes in the sink for her to do——probably——and if you ran your hand across the table you'd probably feel something sticky there.

"You listening, honey? Hey?"

"——going to call the police——"   115

"Soon as you touch the phone I don't need to keep my promise and can come inside. You won't want that."

She rushed forward and tried to lock the door. Her fingers were shaking. "But why lock it," Arnold Friend said gently, talking right into her face. "It's just a screen door. It's just nothing." One of his boots was at a strange angle, as if his foot wasn't in it. It pointed out to the left, bent at the ankle. "I mean, anybody can break through a screen door and glass and wood and iron or anything else if he needs to, anybody at all and specially Arnold Friend. If the place got lit up with a fire honey you'd come running out into my arms, right into my arms and safe at home—like you knew I was your lover and'd stopped fooling around. I don't mind a nice shy girl but I don't like no fooling around." Part of those words were spoken with a slight rhythmic lilt, and Connie somehow recognized them— the echo of a song from last year, about a girl rushing into her boyfriend's arms and coming home again—

Connie stood barefoot on the linoleum floor, staring at him. "What do you want?" she whispered.

"I want you," he said.   120

"What?"

"Seen you that night and thought, that's the one, yes sir. I never needed to look any more."

"But my father's coming back. He's coming to get me. I had to wash my hair first—" She spoke in a dry, rapid voice, hardly raising it for him to hear.

"No, your daddy is not coming and yes, you had to wash your hair and you washed it for me. It's nice and shining and all for me, I thank you, sweetheart," he said, with a mock bow, but again he almost lost his balance. He had to bend and adjust his boots. Evidently his feet did not go all the way down; the boots must have been stuffed with something so that he would seem taller. Connie stared out at him and behind him Ellie in the car, who seemed to be looking off toward Connie's right, into nothing. This Ellie said, pulling the words out of the air one after another as if he were just discovering them, "You want me to pull out the phone?"

"Shut your mouth and keep it shut," Arnold Friend said, his face red   125
from bending over or maybe from embarrassment because Connie had seen his boots. "This ain't none of your business."

"What—what are you doing? What do you want?" Connie said. "If I call the police they'll get you, they'll arrest you—"

"Promise was not to come in unless you touch that phone, and I'll keep that promise," he said. He resumed his erect position and tried to force his shoulders back. He sounded like a hero in a movie, declaring something important. He spoke too loudly and it was as if he were speaking to someone behind Connie. "I ain't made plans for coming in that house where I don't belong but just for you to come out to me, the way you should. Don't you know who I am?"

"You're crazy," she whispered. She backed away from the door but did not want to go another part of the house, as if this would give him permission to come through the door. "What do you . . . You're crazy, you . . ."

"Huh? What're you saying, honey?"

Her eyes darted everywhere in the kitchen. She could not remember 130
what it was, this room.

"This is how it is, honey: you come out and we'll drive away, have
a nice ride. But if you don't come out we're gonna wait till your people
come home and then they're all going to get it."

"You want that telephone pulled out?" Ellie said. He held the radio
away from his ear and grimaced, as if without the radio the air was too
much for him.

"I toldja shut up, Ellie," Arnold Friend said, "you're deaf, get a hearing aid, right? Fix yourself up. This little girl's no trouble and's gonna be
nice to me, so Ellie keep to yourself, this ain't your date—right? Don't
hem in on me. Don't hog. Don't crush. Don't bird dog. Don't trail me,"
he said in a rapid meaningless voice, as if he were running through all the
expressions he'd learned but was no longer sure which one of them was in
style, then rushing on to new ones, making them up with his eyes closed,
"Don't crawl under my fence, don't squeeze in my chipmunk hole, don't
sniff my glue, suck my popsicle, keep your own greasy fingers on yourself!"
He shaded his eyes and peered in at Connie, who was backed against
the kitchen table. "Don't mind him honey he's just a creep. He's a dope.
Right? I'm the boy for you and like I said you come out here nice like a
lady and give me your hand, and nobody else gets hurt, I mean, your nice
old bald-headed daddy and your mummy and your sister in her high heels.
Because listen: why bring them in this?"

"Leave me alone," Connie whispered.

"Hey, you know that old woman down the road, the one with the 135
chickens and stuff—you know her?"

"She's dead!"

"Dead? What? You know her?" Arnold Friend said.

"She's dead—"

"Don't you like her?"

"She's dead—she's—she isn't here any more—"

"But don't you like her, I mean, you got something against her? Some 140
grudge or something?" Then his voice dipped as if he were conscious of
a rudeness. He touched the sunglasses perched on top of his head as if to
make sure they were still there. "Now you be a good girl."

"What are you going to do?"

"Just two things, or maybe three," Arnold Friend said. "But I promise
it won't last long and you'll like me that way you get to like people you're
close to. You will. It's all over for you here, so come on out. You don't want
your people in any trouble, do you?"

She turned and bumped against a chair or something, hurting her
leg, but she ran into the back room and picked up the telephone. Something roared in her ear, a tiny roaring, and she was so sick with fear that

she could do nothing but listen to it—the telephone was clammy and very heavy and her fingers groped down to the dial but were too weak to touch it. She began to scream into the phone, into the roaring. She cried out, she cried for her mother, she felt her breath start jerking back and forth in her lungs as if it were something Arnold Friend were stabbing her with again and again with no tenderness. A noisy sorrowful wailing rose all about her and she was locked inside it the way she was locked inside the house.

After a while she could hear again. She was sitting on the floor with 145 her wet back against the wall.

Arnold Friend was saying from the door, "That's a good girl. Put the phone back."

She kicked the phone away from her.

"No, honey. Pick it up. Put it back right."

She picked it up and put it back. The dial tone stopped.

"That's a good girl. Now come outside."   150

She was hollow with what had been fear, but what was now just an emptiness. All that screaming had blasted it out of her. She sat, one leg cramped under her, and deep inside her brain was something like a pinpoint of light that kept going and would not let her relax. She thought, I'm not going to see my mother again. She thought, I'm not going to sleep in my bed again. Her bright green blouse was all wet.

Arnold Friend said, in a gentle-loud voice that was like a stage voice, "The place where you came from ain't there any more, and where you had in mind to go is cancelled out. This place you are now—inside your daddy's house—is nothing but a cardboard box I can knock down any time. You know that and always did know it. You hear me?"

She thought, I have got to think. I have to know what to do.

"We'll go out to a nice field, out in the country here where it smells so nice and it's sunny," Arnold Friend said. "I'll have my arms around you so you won't need to try to get away and I'll show you what love is like, what it does. The hell with this house! It looks solid all right," he said. He ran a fingernail down the screen and the noise did not make Connie shiver, as it would have the day before. "Now put your hand on your heart, honey. Feel that? That feels solid too but we know better, be nice to me, be sweet like you can because what else is there for a girl like you but to be sweet and pretty and give in?—and get away before her people come back?"

She felt her pounding heart. Her hand seemed to enclose it. She 155 thought for the first time in her life that it was nothing that was hers, that belonged to her, but just a pounding, living thing inside this body that wasn't really hers either.

"You don't want them to get hurt," Arnold Friend went on. "Now get up, honey. Get up all by yourself."

She stood up.

"Now turn this way. That's right. Come over here to me—Ellie, put that away, didn't I tell you? You dope. You miserable creepy dope," Arnold Friend said. His words were not angry but only part of an incantation. The incantation was kindly. "Now come out through the kitchen to me honey and let's see a smile, try it, you're a brave sweet little girl and now they're eating corn and hotdogs cooked to bursting over an outdoor fire, and they don't know one thing about you and never did and honey you're better than them because not a one of them would have done this for you."

Connie felt the linoleum under her feet; it was cool. She brushed her hair back out of her eyes. Arnold Friend let go of the post tentatively and opened his arms for her, his elbows pointing in toward each other and his wrists limp, to show that this was an embarrassed embrace and a little mocking, he didn't want to make her self-conscious.

She put out her hand against the screen. She watched herself push the 160 door slowly open as if she were safe back somewhere in the other doorway, watching this body and this head of long hair moving out into the sunlight where Arnold Friend waited.

"My sweet little blue-eyed girl," he said, in a half-sung sigh that had nothing to do with her brown eyes but was taken up just the same by the vast sunlit reaches of the land behind him and on all sides of him, so much land that Connie had never seen before and did not recognize except to know that she was going to it.

Tim O'Brien

The Things They Carried _____ 1990

Tim O'Brien was born in 1946 in Austin, Minnesota. Immediately after graduating summa cum laude from Macalester College in 1968, he was drafted into the U.S. Army. Serving as an infantryman in Vietnam, O'Brien attained the rank of sergeant and was awarded a Purple Heart after being wounded by shrapnel. Upon his discharge in 1970, he began graduate work at Harvard. In 1973 he published If I Die in a Combat Zone, Box Me Up and Ship Me Home, *a mixture of memoir and fiction about his wartime experiences. His 1978 novel* Going After Cacciato *won the National Book Award, and is considered by some*

Tim O'Brien

critics to be the best book of American fiction about the Vietnam War. "The Things They Carried" was first published in Esquire *in 1986, and later became the title piece in a book of interlocking short stories published in 1990. His other novels include* The Nuclear Age *(1985),* In the Lake of the Woods *(1994),* Tomcat in Love *(1998), and* July, July *(2002). O'Brien currently teaches at Texas State University–San Marcos.*

First Lieutenant Jimmy Cross carried letters from a girl named Martha, a junior at Mount Sebastian College in New Jersey. They were not love letters, but Lieutenant Cross was hoping, so he kept them folded in plastic at the bottom of his rucksack. In the late afternoon, after a day's march, he would dig his foxhole, wash his hands under a canteen, unwrap the letters, hold them with the tips of his fingers, and spend the last hour of light pretending. He would imagine romantic camping trips into the White Mountains in New Hampshire. He would sometimes taste the envelope flaps, knowing her tongue had been there. More than anything, he wanted Martha to love him as he loved her, but the letters were mostly chatty, elusive on the matter of love. She was a virgin, he was almost sure. She was an English major at Mount Sebastian, and she wrote beautifully about her professors and roommates and midterm exams, about her respect for Chaucer and her great affection for Virginia Woolf. She often quoted lines of poetry; she never mentioned the war, except to say, Jimmy, take care of yourself. The letters weighed 10 ounces. They were signed Love, Martha, but Lieutenant Cross understood that Love was only a way of signing and did not mean what he sometimes pretended it meant. At dusk, he would carefully return the letters to his rucksack. Slowly, a bit distracted, he would get up and move among his men, checking the perimeter; then at full dark he would return to his hole and watch the night and wonder if Martha was a virgin.

The things they carried were largely determined by necessity. Among the necessities or near-necessities were P-38 can openers, pocket knives, heat tabs, wristwatches, dog tags, mosquito repellent, chewing gum, candy, cigarettes, salt tablets, packets of Kool-Aid, lighters, matches, sewing kits, Military Payment Certificates, C rations, and two or three canteens of water. Together, these items weighed between 15 and 20 pounds, depending upon a man's habits or rate of metabolism. Henry Dobbins, who was a big man, carried extra rations; he was especially fond of canned peaches in heavy syrup over pound cake. Dave Jensen, who practiced field hygiene, carried a toothbrush, dental floss, and several hotel-sized bars of soap he'd stolen on R&R° in Sydney, Australia. Ted Lavender, who was scared, carried tranquilizers until he was shot in the head outside the village of Than Khe in mid-April. By necessity, and because it was SOP,° they all carried steel helmets that weighed 5 pounds including the liner and camouflage cover. They carried the standard fatigue jackets and trousers. Very few

---

R&R: the military abbreviation for "rest and relaxation," a brief vacation from active service. *SOP:* standard operating procedure.

carried underwear. On their feet they carried jungle boots—2.1 pounds—and Dave Jensen carried three pairs of socks and a can of Dr. Scholl's foot powder as a precaution against trench foot. Until he was shot, Ted Lavender carried six or seven ounces of premium dope, which for him was a necessity. Mitchell Sanders, the RTO,° carried condoms. Norman Bowker carried a diary. Rat Kiley carried comic books. Kiowa, a devout Baptist, carried an illustrated New Testament that had been presented to him by his father, who taught Sunday school in Oklahoma City, Oklahoma. As a hedge against bad times, however, Kiowa also carried his grandmother's distrust of the white man, his grandfather's old hunting hatchet. Necessity dictated. Because the land was mined and booby-trapped, it was SOP for each man to carry a steel-centered, nylon-covered flak jacket, which weighed 6.7 pounds, but which on hot days seemed much heavier. Because you could die so quickly, each man carried at least one large compress bandage, usually in the helmet band for easy access. Because the nights were cold, and because the monsoons were wet, each carried a green plastic poncho that could be used as a raincoat or groundsheet or makeshift tent. With its quilted liner, the poncho weighed almost two pounds, but it was worth every ounce. In April, for instance, when Ted Lavender was shot, they used his poncho to wrap him up, then to carry him across the paddy, then to lift him into the chopper that took him away.

They were called legs or grunts.

To carry something was to hump it, as when Lieutenant Jimmy Cross humped his love for Martha up the hills and through the swamps. In its intransitive form, to hump meant to walk, or to march, but it implied burdens far beyond the intransitive.

Almost everyone humped photographs. In his wallet, Lieutenant Cross carried two photographs of Martha. The first was a Kodacolor snapshot signed Love, though he knew better. She stood against a brick wall. Her eyes were gray and neutral, her lips slightly open as she stared straight-on at the camera. At night, sometimes, Lieutenant Cross wondered who had taken the picture, because he knew she had boyfriends, because he loved her so much, and because he could see the shadow of the picture-taker spreading out against the brick wall. The second photograph had been clipped from the 1968 Mount Sebastian yearbook. It was an action shot—women's volleyball—and Martha was bent horizontal to the floor, reaching, the palms of her hands in sharp focus, the tongue taut, the expression frank and competitive. There was no visible sweat. She wore white gym shorts. Her legs, he thought, were almost certainly the legs of a virgin, dry and without hair, the left knee cocked and carrying her entire weight, which was just over one hundred pounds. Lieutenant

5

RTO: radio and telephone operator.

Cross remembered touching that left knee. A dark theater, he remembered, and the movie was *Bonnie and Clyde*, and Martha wore a tweed skirt, and during the final scene, when he touched her knee, she turned and looked at him in a sad, sober way that made him pull his hand back, but he would always remember the feel of the tweed skirt and the knee beneath it and the sound of the gunfire that killed Bonnie and Clyde, how embarrassing it was, how slow and oppressive. He remembered kissing her good night at the dorm door. Right then, he thought, he should've done something brave. He should've carried her up the stairs to her room and tied her to the bed and touched that left knee all night long. He should've risked it. Whenever he looked at the photographs, he thought of new things he should've done.

What they carried was partly a function of rank, partly of field specialty.

As a first lieutenant and platoon leader, Jimmy Cross carried a compass, maps, code books, binoculars, and a .45-caliber pistol that weighed 2.9 pounds fully loaded. He carried a strobe light and the responsibility for the lives of his men.

As an RTO, Mitchell Sanders carried the PRC-25 radio, a killer, 26 pounds with its battery.

As a medic, Rat Kiley carried a canvas satchel filled with morphine and plasma and malaria tablets and surgical tape and comic books and all the things a medic must carry, including M&M's for especially bad wounds, for a total weight of nearly 20 pounds.

As a big man, therefore a machine gunner, Henry Dobbins carried   10 the M-60, which weighed 23 pounds unloaded, but which was almost always loaded. In addition, Dobbins carried between 10 and 15 pounds of ammunition draped in belts across his chest and shoulders.

As PFCs or Spec 4s, most of them were common grunts and carried the standard M-16 gas-operated assault rifle. The weapon weighed 7.5 pounds unloaded, 8.2 pounds with its full 20-round magazine. Depending on numerous factors, such as topography and psychology, the riflemen carried anywhere from 12 to 20 magazines, usually in cloth bandoliers, adding on another 8.4 pounds at minimum, 14 pounds at maximum. When it was available, they also carried M-16 maintenance gear—rods and steel brushes and swabs and tubes of LSA oil—all of which weighed about a pound. Among the grunts, some carried the M-79 grenade launcher, 5.9 pounds unloaded, a reasonably light weapon except for the ammunition, which was heavy. A single round weighed 10 ounces. The typical load was 25 rounds. But Ted Lavender, who was scared, carried 34 rounds when he was shot and killed outside Than Khe, and he went down under an exceptional burden, more than 20 pounds of ammunition, plus the flak jacket and helmet and rations and water and toilet paper and tranquilizers and all the rest, plus the unweighed fear. He was dead weight. There was no twitching or flopping. Kiowa, who saw it happen, said it was like watching a rock fall, or a big sandbag or something—just boom, then down—not like the movies where the dead guy rolls around and does fancy spins and goes ass over teakettle—not like that, Kiowa said, the poor bastard just flat-fuck fell. Boom. Down. Nothing else. It was a bright morning in mid-April. Lieutenant Cross felt the pain. He blamed himself. They stripped off Lavender's canteens and ammo, all the heavy things, and Rat Kiley said the obvious, the guy's dead, and Mitchell Sanders used his radio to report one U.S. KIA° and to request a chopper. Then they wrapped Lavender in his poncho. They carried him out to a dry paddy, established security, and sat smoking the dead man's dope until the chopper came. Lieutenant Cross kept to himself. He pictured Martha's smooth young face, thinking he loved her more than anything, more than his men, and now Ted Lavender was dead because he loved her so much and could not stop thinking about her. When the dustoff arrived, they carried Lavender aboard. Afterward they burned Than Khe. They marched until dusk, then dug their holes, and that night Kiowa kept explaining how you had to be there, how fast it was, how the poor guy just dropped like so much concrete. Boom-down, he said. Like cement.

In addition to the three standard weapons—the M-60, M-16, and M-79—they carried whatever presented itself, or whatever seemed appropriate as a means of killing or staying alive. They carried catch-as-catch-can. At various times, in various situations, they carried M-14s and CAR-15s and Swedish Ks and grease guns and captured AK-47s and Chi-Coms and RPGs and Simonov carbines and black market Uzis and .38-caliber Smith & Wesson handguns and 66 mm LAWs and shotguns and silencers and blackjacks and bayonets and C-4 plastic explosives. Lee Strunk carried a slingshot; a weapon of last resort, he called it. Mitchell Sanders carried brass knuckles. Kiowa carried his grandfather's feathered hatchet. Every third or fourth man carried a Claymore antipersonnel mine—3.5 pounds with its firing device. They all carried fragmentation grenades—14 ounces each. They all carried at least one M-18 colored smoke grenade—24 ounces. Some carried CS or tear gas grenades. Some carried white phosphorus grenades. They carried all they could bear, and then some, including a silent awe for the terrible power of the things they carried.

In the first week of April, before Lavender died, Lieutenant Jimmy Cross received a good-luck charm from Martha. It was a simple pebble, an ounce at most. Smooth to the touch, it was a milky white color with flecks of orange and violet, oval-shaped, like a miniature egg. In the

---

KIA: killed in action.

accompanying letter, Martha wrote that she had found the pebble on the Jersey shoreline, precisely where the land touched water at high tide, where things came together but also separated. It was this separate-but-together quality, she wrote, that had inspired her to pick up the pebble and to carry it in her breast pocket for several days, where it seemed weight-less, and then to send it through the mail, by air, as a token of her truest feelings for him. Lieutenant Cross found this romantic. But he wondered what her truest feelings were, exactly, and what she meant by separate-but-together. He wondered how the tides and waves had come into play on that afternoon along the Jersey shoreline when Martha saw the pebble and bent down to rescue it from geology. He imagined bare feet. Martha was a poet, with the poet's sensibilities, and her feet would be brown and bare, the toenails unpainted, the eyes chilly and somber like the ocean in March, and though it was painful, he wondered who had been with her that afternoon. He imagined a pair of shadows moving along the strip of sand where things came together but also separated. It was phantom jealousy, he knew, but he couldn't help himself. He loved her so much. On the march, through the hot days of early April, he carried the pebble in his mouth, turning it with his tongue, tasting sea salt and moisture. His mind wandered. He had difficulty keeping his attention on the war. On occasion he would yell at his men to spread out the column, to keep their eyes open, but then he would slip away into daydreams, just pretending, walking barefoot along the Jersey shore, with Martha, carrying nothing. He would feel himself rising. Sun and waves and gentle winds, all love and lightness.

What they carried varied by mission.

When a mission took them to the mountains, they carried mosquito   15 netting, machetes, canvas tarps, and extra bug juice.

If a mission seemed especially hazardous, or if it involved a place they knew to be bad, they carried everything they could. In certain heavily mined AOs,° where the land was dense with Toe Poppers and Bounc-ing Betties, they took turns humping a 28-pound mine detector. With its headphones and big sensing plate, the equipment was a stress on the lower back and shoulders, awkward to handle, often useless because of the shrapnel in the earth, but they carried it anyway, partly for safety, partly for the illusion of safety.

On ambush, or other night missions, they carried peculiar little odds and ends. Kiowa always took along his New Testament and a pair of moc-casins for silence. Dave Jensen carried night-sight vitamins high in caro-tene. Lee Strunk carried his slingshot; ammo, he claimed, would never be a problem. Rat Kiley carried brandy and M&M's candy. Until he was shot,

AOs: areas of operation.

Ted Lavender carried the starlight scope, which weighed 6.3 pounds with its aluminum carrying case. Henry Dobbins carried his girlfriend's pantyhose wrapped around his neck as a comforter. They all carried ghosts. When dark came, they would move out single file across the meadows and paddies to their ambush coordinates, where they would quietly set up the Claymores and lie down and spend the night waiting.

Other missions were more complicated and required special equipment. In mid-April, it was their mission to search out and destroy the elaborate tunnel complexes in the Than Khe area south of Chu Lai. To blow the tunnels, they carried one-pound blocks of pentrite high explosives, four blocks to a man, 68 pounds in all. They carried wiring, detonators, and battery-powered clackers. Dave Jensen carried earplugs. Most often, before blowing the tunnels, they were ordered by higher command to search them, which was considered bad news, but by and large they just shrugged and carried out orders. Because he was a big man, Henry Dobbins was excused from tunnel duty. The others would draw numbers. Before Lavender died there were 17 men in the platoon, and whoever drew the number 17 would strip off his gear and crawl in headfirst with a flashlight and Lieutenant Cross's .45-caliber pistol. The rest of them would fan out as security. They would sit down or kneel, not facing the hole, listening to the ground beneath them, imagining cobwebs and ghosts, whatever was down there—the tunnel walls squeezing in—how the flashlight seemed impossibly heavy in the hand and how it was tunnel vision in the very strictest sense, compression in all ways, even time, and how you had to wiggle in—ass and elbows—a swallowed-up feeling—and how you found yourself worrying about odd things: Will your flashlight go dead? Do rats carry rabies? If you screamed, how far would the sound carry? Would your buddies hear it? Would they have the courage to drag you out? In some respects, though not many, the waiting was worse than the tunnel itself. Imagination was a killer.

On April 16, when Lee Strunk drew the number 17, he laughed and muttered something and went down quickly. The morning was hot and very still. Not good, Kiowa said. He looked at the tunnel opening, then out across a dry paddy toward the village of Than Khe. Nothing moved. No clouds or birds or people. As they waited, the men smoked and drank Kool-Aid, not talking much, feeling sympathy for Lee Strunk but also feeling the luck of the draw. You win some, you lose some, said Mitchell Sanders, and sometimes you settle for a rain check. It was a tired line and no one laughed.

Henry Dobbins ate a tropical chocolate bar. Ted Lavender popped a tranquilizer and went off to pee.   20

After five minutes, Lieutenant Jimmy Cross moved to the tunnel, leaned down, and examined the darkness. Trouble, he thought—a cave-in maybe. And then suddenly, without willing it, he was thinking about

Martha. The stresses and fractures, the quick collapse, the two of them
buried alive under all that weight. Dense, crushing love. Kneeling, watching the hole, he tried to concentrate on Lee Strunk and the war, all the
dangers, but his love was too much for him, he felt paralyzed, he wanted
to sleep inside her lungs and breathe her blood and be smothered. He
wanted her to be a virgin and not a virgin, all at once. He wanted to
know her. Intimate secrets: Why poetry? Why so sad? Why that grayness in her eyes? Why so alone? Not lonely, just alone—riding her bike
across campus or sitting off by herself in the cafeteria—even dancing, she
danced alone—and it was the aloneness that filled him with love. He
remembered telling her that one evening. How she nodded and looked
away. And how, later, when he kissed her, she received the kiss without
returning it, her eyes wide open, not afraid, not a virgin's eyes, just flat
and uninvolved.

Lieutenant Cross gazed at the tunnel. But he was not there. He was
buried with Martha under the white sand at the Jersey shore. They were
pressed together, and the pebble in his mouth was her tongue. He was
smiling. Vaguely, he was aware of how quiet the day was, the sullen paddies, yet he could not bring himself to worry about matters of security. He
was beyond that. He was just a kid at war, in love. He was twenty-four
years old. He couldn't help it.

A few moments later Lee Strunk crawled out of the tunnel. He came
up grinning, filthy but alive. Lieutenant Cross nodded and closed his eyes
while the others clapped Strunk on the back and made jokes about rising
from the dead.

Worms, Rat Kiley said. Right out of the grave. Fuckin' zombie.

The men laughed. They all felt great relief.   25

Spook city, said Mitchell Sanders.

Lee Strunk made a funny ghost sound, a kind of moaning, yet very
happy, and right then, when Strunk made that high happy moaning
sound, when he went *Ahhooooo*, right then Ted Lavender was shot in the
head on his way back from peeing. He lay with his mouth open. The teeth
were broken. There was a swollen black bruise under his left eye. The
cheekbone was gone. Oh shit, Rat Kiley said, the guy's dead. The guy's
dead, he kept saying, which seemed profound—the guy's dead. I mean
really.

The things they carried were determined to some extent by superstition. Lieutenant Cross carried his good-luck pebble. Dave Jensen carried
a rabbit's foot. Norman Bowker, otherwise a very gentle person, carried a
thumb that had been presented to him as a gift by Mitchell Sanders. The
thumb was dark brown, rubbery to the touch, and weighed four ounces at
most. It had been cut from a VC corpse, a boy of fifteen or sixteen. They'd
found him at the bottom of an irrigation ditch, badly burned, flies in his

mouth and eyes. The boy wore black shorts and sandals. At the time of his death he had been carrying a pouch of rice, a rifle, and three magazines of ammunition.

You want my opinion, Mitchell Sanders said, there's a definite moral here.

He put his hand on the dead boy's wrist. He was quiet for a time, as if   30 counting a pulse, then he patted the stomach, almost affectionately, and used Kiowa's hunting hatchet to remove the thumb.

Henry Dobbins asked what the moral was.

Moral?

You know. *Moral.*

Sanders wrapped the thumb in toilet paper and handed it across to Norman Bowker. There was no blood. Smiling, he kicked the boy's head, watched the flies scatter, and said, It's like with that old TV show—Paladin. Have gun, will travel.

Henry Dobbins thought about it.   35

Yeah, well, he finally said. I don't see no moral.

There it *is*, man.

Fuck off.

They carried USO stationery and pencils and pens. They carried Sterno, safety pins, trip flares, signal flares, spools of wire, razor blades, chewing tobacco, liberated joss sticks and statuettes of the smiling Buddha, candles, grease pencils, *The Stars and Stripes*, fingernail clippers, Psy Ops leaflets, bush hats, bolos, and much more. Twice a week, when the resupply choppers came in, they carried hot chow in green mermite cans and large canvas bags filled with iced beer and soda pop. They carried plastic water containers, each with a two-gallon capacity. Mitchell Sanders carried a set of starched tiger fatigues for special occasions. Henry Dobbins carried Black Flag insecticide. Dave Jensen carried empty sandbags that could be filled at night for added protection. Lee Strunk carried tanning lotion. Some things they carried in common. Taking turns, they carried the big PRC-77 scrambler radio, which weighed 30 pounds with its battery. They shared the weight of memory. They took up what others could no longer bear. Often, they carried each other, the wounded or weak. They carried infections. They carried chess sets, basketballs, Vietnamese-English dictionaries, insignia of rank, Bronze Stars and Purple Hearts, plastic cards imprinted with the Code of Conduct. They carried diseases, among them malaria and dysentery. They carried lice and ringworm and leeches and paddy algae and various rots and molds. They carried the land itself—Vietnam, the place, the soil—a powdery orange-red dust that covered their boots and fatigues and faces. They carried the sky. The whole atmosphere, they carried it, the humidity, the monsoons, the stink of fungus and decay, all of it, they carried gravity. They moved like mules. By daylight they took sniper fire, at night they were mortared, but it was not battle, it was just the endless march, village to village, without purpose, nothing won or lost. They marched for the sake of the march. They plodded along slowly, dumbly, leaning forward against the heat, unthinking, all blood and bone, simple grunts, soldiering with their legs, toiling up the hills and down into the paddies and across the rivers and up again and down, just humping, one step and then the next and then another, but no volition, no will, because it was automatic, it was anatomy, and the war was entirely a matter of posture and carriage, the hump was everything, a kind of inertia, a kind of emptiness, a dullness of desire and intellect and conscience and hope and human sensibility. Their principles were in their feet. Their calculations were biological. They had no sense of strategy or mission. They searched the villages without knowing what to look for, not caring, kicking over jars of rice, frisking children and old men, blowing tunnels, sometimes setting fires and sometimes not, then forming up and moving on to the next village, then other villages, where it would always be the same. They carried their own lives. The pressures were enormous. In the heat of early afternoon, they would remove their helmets and flak jackets, walking bare, which was dangerous but which helped ease the strain. They would often discard things along the route of march. Purely for comfort, they would throw away rations, blow their Claymores and grenades, no matter, because by nightfall the resupply choppers would arrive with more of the same, then a day or two later still more, fresh watermelons and crates of ammunition and sunglasses and woolen sweaters—the resources were stunning—sparklers for the Fourth of July, colored eggs for Easter—it was the great American war chest—the fruits of science, the smokestacks, the canneries, the arsenals at Hartford, the Minnesota forests, the machine shops, the vast fields of corn and wheat—they carried like freight trains; they carried it on their backs and shoulders—and for all the ambiguities of Vietnam, all the mysteries and unknowns, there was at least the single abiding certainty that they would never be at a loss for things to carry.

   After the chopper took Lavender away, Lieutenant Jimmy Cross led   40 his men into the village of Than Khe. They burned everything. They shot chickens and dogs, they trashed the village well, they called in artillery and watched the wreckage, then they marched for several hours through the hot afternoon, and then at dusk, while Kiowa explained how Lavender died, Lieutenant Cross found himself trembling.
   He tried not to cry. With his entrenching tool, which weighed five pounds, he began digging a hole in the earth.
   He felt shame. He hated himself. He had loved Martha more than his men, and as a consequence Lavender was now dead, and this was something he would have to carry like a stone in his stomach for the rest of the war.

All he could do was dig. He used his entrenching tool like an ax, slashing, feeling both love and hate, and then later, when it was full dark, he sat at the bottom of his foxhole and wept. It went on for a long while. In part, he was grieving for Ted Lavender, but mostly it was for Martha, and for himself, because she belonged to another world, which was not quite real, and because she was a junior at Mount Sebastian College in New Jersey, a poet and a virgin and uninvolved, and because he realized she did not love him and never would.

Like cement, Kiowa whispered in the dark. I swear to God—boom, down. Not a word.

I've heard this, said Norman Bowker. 45

A pisser, you know? Still zipping himself up. Zapped while zipping.

All right, fine. That's enough.

Yeah, but you had to see it, the guy just—

I *heard*, man. Cement. So why not shut the fuck *up*?

Kiowa shook his head sadly and glanced over at the hole where Lieu- 50 tenant Jimmy Cross sat watching the night. The air was thick and wet. A warm dense fog had settled over the paddies and there was the stillness that precedes rain.

After a time Kiowa sighed.

One thing for sure, he said. The lieutenant's in some deep hurt. I mean that crying jag—the way he was carrying on—it wasn't fake or any- thing, it was real heavy-duty hurt. The man cares.

Sure, Norman Bowker said.

Say what you want, the man does care.

We all got problems. 55

Not Lavender.

No, I guess not, Bowker said. Do me a favor, though.

Shut up?

That's a smart Indian. Shut up.

Shrugging, Kiowa pulled off his boots. He wanted to say more, just 60 to lighten up his sleep, but instead he opened his New Testament and ar- ranged it beneath his head as a pillow. The fog made things seem hollow and unattached. He tried not to think about Ted Lavender, but then he was thinking how fast it was, no drama, down and dead, and how it was hard to feel anything except surprise. It seemed unchristian. He wished he could find some great sadness, or even anger, but the emotion wasn't there and he couldn't make it happen. Mostly he felt pleased to be alive. He liked the smell of the New Testament under his cheek, the leather and ink and paper and glue, whatever the chemicals were. He liked hearing the sounds of night. Even his fatigue, it felt fine, the stiff muscles and the prickly awareness of his own body, a floating feeling. He enjoyed not be- ing dead. Lying there, Kiowa admired Lieutenant Jimmy Cross's capacity for grief. He wanted to share the man's pain, he wanted to care as Jimmy Cross cared. And yet when he closed his eyes, all he could think was Boom-down, and all he could feel was the pleasure of having his boots off and the fog curling in around him and the damp soil and the Bible smells and the plush comfort of night.

After a moment Norman Bowker sat up in the dark.

What the hell, he said. You want to talk, *talk*. Tell it to me.

Forget it.

No, man, go on. One thing I hate, it's a silent Indian.

For the most part they carried themselves with poise, a kind of dignity. 65 Now and then, however, there were times of panic, when they squealed or wanted to squeal but couldn't, when they twitched and made moaning sounds and covered their heads and said Dear Jesus and flopped around on the earth and fired their weapons blindly and cringed and sobbed and begged for the noise to stop and went wild and made stupid promises to themselves and to God and to their mothers and fathers, hoping not to die. In different ways, it happened to all of them. Afterward, when the firing ended, they would blink and peek up. They would touch their bodies, feeling shame, then quickly hiding it. They would force themselves to stand. As if in slow motion, frame by frame, the world would take on the old logic—absolute silence, then the wind, then sunlight, then voices. It was the burden of being alive. Awkwardly, the men would reassemble themselves, first in private, then in groups, becoming soldiers again. They would repair the leaks in their eyes. They would check for casualties, call in dustoffs, light cigarettes, try to smile, clear their throats and spit and begin cleaning their weapons. After a time someone would shake his head and say, No lie, I almost shit my pants, and someone else would laugh, which meant it was bad, yes, but the guy had obviously not shit his pants, it wasn't that bad, and in any case nobody would ever do such a thing and then go ahead and talk about it. They would squint into the dense, oppressive sunlight. For a few moments, perhaps, they would fall silent, lighting a joint and tracking its passage from man to man, inhaling, holding in the humiliation. Scary stuff, one of them might say. But then someone else would grin or flick his eyebrows and say, Roger-dodger, almost cut me a new asshole, *almost.*

There were numerous such poses. Some carried themselves with a sort of wistful resignation, others with pride or stiff soldierly discipline or good humor or macho zeal. They were afraid of dying but they were even more afraid to show it.

They found jokes to tell.

They used a hard vocabulary to contain the terrible softness. *Greased,* they'd say. *Offed, lit up, zapped while zipping.* It wasn't cruelty, just stage presence. They were actors. When someone died, it wasn't quite dying, because in a curious way it seemed scripted, and because they had their lines mostly memorized, irony mixed with tragedy, and because they called it by other names, as if to encyst and destroy the reality of death itself. They kicked corpses. They cut off thumbs. They talked grunt lingo. They told stories about Ted Lavender's supply of tranquilizers, how the poor guy didn't feel a thing, how incredibly tranquil he was.

There's a moral here, said Mitchell Sanders.

They were waiting for Lavender's chopper, smoking the dead man's dope. 70

The moral's pretty obvious, Sanders said, and winked. Stay away from drugs. No joke, they'll ruin your day every time.

Cute, said Henry Dobbins.

Mind blower, get it? Talk about wiggy. Nothing left, just blood and brains.

They made themselves laugh.

There it is, they'd say. Over and over—there it is, my friend, there 75 it is—as if the repetition itself were an act of poise, a balance between crazy and almost crazy, knowing without going, there it is, which meant be cool, let it ride, because Oh yeah, man, you can't change what can't be changed, there it is, there it absolutely and positively and fucking well *is*.

They were tough.

They carried all the emotional baggage of men who might die. Grief, terror, love, longing—these were intangibles, but the intangibles had their own mass and specific gravity, they had tangible weight. They carried shameful memories. They carried the common secret of cowardice barely restrained, the instinct to run or freeze or hide, and in many respects this was the heaviest burden of all, for it could never be put down, it required perfect balance and perfect posture. They carried their reputations. They carried the soldier's greatest fear, which was the fear of blushing. Men killed, and died, because they were embarrassed not to. It was what had brought them to the war in the first place, nothing positive, no dreams of glory or honor, just to avoid the blush of dishonor. They died so as not to die of embarrassment. They crawled into tunnels and walked point and advanced under fire. Each morning, despite the unknowns, they made their legs move. They endured. They kept humping. They did not submit to the obvious alternative, which was simply to close the eyes and fall. So easy, really. Go limp and tumble to the ground and let the muscles unwind and not speak and not budge until your buddies picked you up and lifted you into the chopper that would roar and dip its nose and carry you off to the world. A mere matter of falling, yet no one ever fell. It was not courage, exactly; the object was not valor. Rather, they were too frightened to be cowards.

By and large they carried these things inside, maintaining the masks of composure. They sneered at sick call. They spoke bitterly about guys who had found release by shooting off their own toes or fingers. Pussies, they'd say. Candy-asses. It was fierce, mocking talk, with only a trace of envy or awe, but even so the image played itself out behind their eyes.

They imagined the muzzle against flesh. So easy: squeeze the trigger and blow away a toe. They imagined it. They imagined the quick, sweet pain, then the evacuation to Japan, then a hospital with warm beds and cute geisha nurses.

And they dreamed of freedom birds.   80

At night, on guard, staring into the dark, they were carried away by jumbo jets. They felt the rush of takeoff. *Gone!* they yelled. And then velocity—wings and engines—a smiling stewardess—but it was more than a plane, it was a real bird, a big sleek silver bird with feathers and talons and high screeching. They were flying. The weights fell off; there was nothing to bear. They laughed and held on tight, feeling the cold slap of wind and altitude, soaring, thinking *It's over, I'm gone!*—they were naked, they were light and free—it was all lightness, bright and fast and buoyant, light as light, a helium buzz in the brain, a giddy bubbling in the lungs as they were taken up over the clouds and the war, beyond duty, beyond gravity and mortification and global entanglements—*Sin loi!*° they yelled. *I'm sorry, mother-fuckers, but I'm out of it, I'm goofed, I'm on a space cruise, I'm gone!*—and it was a restful, unencumbered sensation, just riding the light waves, sailing that big silver freedom bird over the mountains and oceans, over America, over the farms and great sleeping cities and cemeteries and highways and the golden arches of McDonald's, it was flight, a kind of fleeing, a kind of falling, falling higher and higher, spinning off the edge of the earth and beyond the sun and through the vast, silent vacuum where there were no burdens and where everything weighed exactly nothing— *Gone!* they screamed. *I'm sorry but I'm gone!*—and so at night, not quite dreaming, they gave themselves over to lightness, they were carried, they were purely borne.

On the morning after Ted Lavender died, First Lieutenant Jimmy Cross crouched at the bottom of his foxhole and burned Martha's letters. Then he burned the two photographs. There was a steady rain falling, which made it difficult, but he used heat tabs and Sterno to build a small fire, screening it with his body, holding the photographs over the tight blue flame with the tips of his fingers.

He realized it was only a gesture. Stupid, he thought. Sentimental, too, but mostly just stupid.

Lavender was dead. You couldn't burn the blame.

Sin loi: Vietnamese for "sorry."

Besides, the letters were in his head. And even now, without photo-   85
graphs, Lieutenant Cross could see Martha playing volleyball in her white
gym shorts and yellow T-shirt. He could see her moving in the rain.

When the fire died out, Lieutenant Cross pulled his poncho over his
shoulders and ate breakfast from a can.

There was no great mystery, he decided.

In those burned letters Martha had never mentioned the war, except
to say, Jimmy, take care of yourself. She wasn't involved. She signed the
letters Love, but it wasn't love, and all the fine lines and technicalities did
not matter. Virginity was no longer an issue. He hated her. Yes, he did. He
hated her. Love, too, but it was a hard, hating kind of love.

The morning came up wet and blurry. Everything seemed part of everything else, the fog and Martha and the deepening rain.

He was a soldier, after all.   90

Half smiling, Lieutenant Jimmy Cross took out his maps. He shook
his head hard, as if to clear it, then bent forward and began planning the
day's march. In ten minutes, or maybe twenty, he would rouse the men
and they would pack up and head west, where the maps showed the country to be green and inviting. They would do what they had always done.
The rain might add some weight, but otherwise it would be one more day
layered upon all the other days.

He was realistic about it. There was that new hardness in his stomach. He loved her but he hated her.

No more fantasies, he told himself.

Henceforth, when he thought about Martha, it would be only to
think that she belonged elsewhere. He would shut down the daydreams.
This was not Mount Sebastian, it was another world, where there were
no pretty poems or midterm exams, a place where men died because of
carelessness and gross stupidity. Kiowa was right. Boom-down, and you
were dead, never partly dead.

Briefly, in the rain, Lieutenant Cross saw Martha's gray eyes gazing   95
back at him.

He understood.

It was very sad, he thought. The things men carried inside. The
things men did or felt they had to do.

He almost nodded at her, but didn't.

Instead he went back to his maps. He was now determined to perform his duties firmly and without negligence. It wouldn't help Lavender, he knew that, but from this point on he would comport himself
as an officer. He would dispose of his good-luck pebble. Swallow it,
maybe, or use Lee Strunk's slingshot, or just drop it along the trail. On
the march he would impose strict field discipline. He would be careful to send out flank security, to prevent straggling or bunching up, to
keep his troops moving at the proper pace and at the proper interval.

He would insist on clean weapons. He would confiscate the remainder of Lavender's dope. Later in the day, perhaps, he would call the men together and speak to them plainly. He would accept the blame for what had happened to Ted Lavender. He would be a man about it. He would look them in the eyes, keeping his chin level, and he would issue the new SOPs in a calm, impersonal tone of voice, a lieutenant's voice, leaving no room for argument or discussion. Commencing immediately, he'd tell them, they would no longer abandon equipment along the route of march. They would police up their acts. They would get their shit together, and keep it together, and maintain it neatly and in good working order.

He would not tolerate laxity. He would show strength, distancing   100 himself.

Among the men there would be grumbling, of course, and maybe worse, because their days would seem longer and their loads heavier, but Lieutenant Jimmy Cross reminded himself that his obligation was not to be loved but to lead. He would dispense with love; it was not now a factor. And if anyone quarreled or complained, he would simply tighten his lips and arrange his shoulders in the correct command posture. He might give a curt little nod. Or he might not. He might just shrug and say, Carry on, then they would saddle up and form into a column and move out toward the villages west of Than Khe.

Flannery O'Connor

A Good Man Is Hard to Find   1955

Mary Flannery O'Connor (1925–1964) was born in Savannah, Georgia, but spent most of her life in the small town of Milledgeville. While attending Georgia State College for Women, she won a local reputation for her fledgling stories and satiric cartoons. After graduating in 1945, she went on to study at the University of Iowa, where she earned an M.F.A. in 1947. Diagnosed in 1950 with disseminated lupus, the same incurable illness that had killed her father, O'Connor returned home and spent the last decade of her life living with her mother in Milledgeville. Back on the family dairy farm, she wrote, maintained an extensive literary correspondence, raised peacocks, and underwent medical treatment. When her illness occasionally went into a period of remission, she made trips to lecture and read her stories to college audiences. Her health declined rapidly after surgery early in 1964 for an unrelated complaint. She died at thirty-nine.

Flannery O'Connor

O'Connor is unusual among modern American writers in the depth of her Christian vision. A devout Roman Catholic, she attended mass daily while growing up and living in the largely Protestant South. As a latter-day satirist in the manner of Jonathan Swift, O'Connor levels the eye of an uncompromising moralist on the violence and spiritual disorder of the modern world, focusing on what she calls "the action of grace in territory held largely by the devil." She is sometimes called a "Southern Gothic" writer because of her fascination with grotesque incidents and characters. Throughout her career she depicted the South as a troubled region in which the social, racial, and religious status quo that had existed since before the Civil War was coming to a violent end. Despite the inherent seriousness of her religious and social themes, O'Connor's mordant and frequently outrageous humor is everywhere apparent. Her combination of profound vision and dark comedy is the distinguishing characteristic of her literary sensibilities.

O'Connor's published work includes two short novels, Wise Blood (1952) and The Violent Bear It Away (1960), and two collections of short stories, A Good Man Is Hard to Find (1955) and Everything That Rises Must Converge, published posthumously in 1965. A collection of essays and miscellaneous prose, Mystery and Manners (1969), and her selected letters, The Habit of Being (1979), reveal an innate cheerfulness and engaging personal warmth that are not always apparent in her fiction. The Complete Stories of Flannery O'Connor was posthumously awarded the National Book Award in 1971.

The grandmother didn't want to go to Florida. She wanted to visit some of her connections in east Tennessee and she was seizing at every chance to change Bailey's mind. Bailey was the son she lived with, her only boy. He was sitting on the edge of his chair at the table, bent over the orange sports section of the Journal. "Now look here, Bailey," she said, "see here, read this," and she stood with one hand on her thin hip and the other rattling the newspaper at his bald head. "Here this fellow that calls himself The Misfit is aloose from the Federal Pen and headed toward Florida and you read here what it says he did to these people. Just you read it. I wouldn't take my children in any direction with a criminal like that aloose in it. I couldn't answer to my conscience if I did."

Bailey didn't look up from his reading so she wheeled around then and faced the children's mother, a young woman in slacks, whose face was as broad and innocent as a cabbage and was tied around with a green head-kerchief that had two points on the top like rabbit's ears. She was sitting on the sofa, feeding the baby his apricots out of a jar. "The children have been to Florida before," the old lady said. "You all ought to take them somewhere else for a change so they would see different parts of the world and be broad. They never have been to east Tennessee."

The children's mother didn't seem to hear her but the eight-year-old boy, John Wesley, a stocky child with glasses, said, "If you don't want to go to Florida, why dontcha stay at home?" He and the little girl, June Star, were reading the funny papers on the floor.

"She wouldn't stay at home to be queen for a day," June Star said without raising her yellow head.

"Yes and what would you do if this fellow, The Misfit, caught you?" 5
the grandmother said.

"I'd smack his face," John Wesley said.

"She wouldn't stay at home for a million bucks," June Star said. "Afraid she'd miss something. She has to go everywhere we go."

"All right, Miss," the grandmother said. "Just remember that the next time you want me to curl your hair."

June Star said her hair was naturally curly.

The next morning the grandmother was the first one in the car, ready 10
to go. She had her big black valise that looked like the head of a hippopotamus in one corner, and underneath it she was hiding a basket with Pitty Sing, the cat, in it. She didn't intend for the cat to be left alone in the house for three days because he would miss her too much and she was afraid he might brush against one of the gas burners and accidentally asphyxiate himself. Her son, Bailey, didn't like to arrive at a motel with a cat.

She sat in the middle of the back seat with John Wesley and June Star on either side of her. Bailey and the children's mother and the baby sat in front and they left Atlanta at eight forty-five with the mileage on the car at 55890. The grandmother wrote this down because she thought it would be interesting to say how many miles they had been when they got back. It took them twenty minutes to reach the outskirts of the city.

The old lady settled herself comfortably, removing her white cotton gloves and putting them up with her purse on the shelf in front of the back window. The children's mother still had on slacks and still had her hair tied up in a green kerchief, but the grandmother had on a navy blue straw sailor hat with a bunch of white violets on the brim and a navy blue dress with a small white dot in the print. Her collars and cuffs were white organdy trimmed with lace and at her neckline she had pinned a purple spray of cloth violets containing a sachet. In case of an accident, anyone seeing her dead on the highway would know at once that she was a lady.

She said she thought it was going to be a good day for driving, neither too hot nor too cold, and she cautioned Bailey that the speed limit was fifty-five miles an hour and that the patrolmen hid themselves behind billboards and small clumps of trees and sped out after you before you had a chance to slow down. She pointed out interesting details of the scenery: Stone Mountain; the blue granite that in some places came up to both sides of the highway; the brilliant red clay banks slightly streaked with purple; and the various crops that made rows of green lace-work on the ground. The trees were full of silver-white sunlight and the meanest of them sparkled. The children were reading comic magazines and their mother had gone back to sleep.

"Let's go through Georgia fast so we won't have to look at it much," John Wesley said.

"If I were a little boy," said the grandmother, "I wouldn't talk about 15
my native state that way. Tennessee has the mountains and Georgia has the hills."

"Tennessee is just a hillbilly dumping ground," John Wesley said, "and Georgia is a lousy state too."

"You said it," June Star said.

"In my time," said the grandmother, folding her thin veined fingers, "children were more respectful of their native states and their parents and everything else. People did right then. Oh look at the cute little pickaninny!" she said and pointed to a Negro child standing in the door of a shack. "Wouldn't that make a picture, now?" she asked and they all turned and looked at the little Negro out of the back window. He waved.

"He didn't have any britches on," June Star said.

"He probably didn't have any," the grandmother explained. "Little 20
niggers in the country don't have things like we do. If I could paint, I'd paint that picture," she said.

The children exchanged comic books.

The grandmother offered to hold the baby and the children's mother passed him over the front seat to her. She set him on her knee and bounced him and told him about the things they were passing. She rolled her eyes and screwed up her mouth and stuck her leathery thin face into his smooth bland one. Occasionally he gave her a faraway smile. They passed a large cotton field with five or six graves fenced in the middle of it, like a small island. "Look at the graveyard!" the grandmother said, pointing it out. "That was the old family burying ground. That belonged to the plantation."

"Where's the plantation?" John Wesley asked.

"Gone With the Wind," said the grandmother. "Ha. Ha."

When the children finished all the comic books they had brought, 25
they opened the lunch and ate it. The grandmother ate a peanut butter sandwich and an olive and would not let the children throw the box and the paper napkins out the window. When there was nothing else to do they played a game by choosing a cloud and making the other two guess what shape it suggested. John Wesley took one the shape of a cow and June Star guessed a cow and John Wesley said, no, an automobile, and June Star said he didn't play fair, and they began to slap each other over the grandmother.

The grandmother said she would tell them a story if they would keep quiet. When she told a story, she rolled her eyes and waved her head and was very dramatic. She said once when she was a maiden lady she had been courted by a Mr. Edgar Atkins Teagarden from Jasper, Georgia. She said he was a very good-looking man and a gentleman and that he brought her a watermelon every Saturday afternoon with his initials cut in it, E. A. T. Well, one Saturday, she said, Mr. Teagarden brought the watermelon and there was nobody at home and he left it on the front porch and returned in his buggy to Jasper, but she never got the watermelon, she said, because a nigger boy ate it when he saw the initials, E. A. T.! This story tickled John Wesley's funny bone and he giggled and giggled but June Star didn't think it was any good. She said she wouldn't marry a man that just brought her a watermelon on Saturday. The grandmother said she would have done well to marry Mr. Teagarden because he was a gentleman and had bought Coca-Cola stock when it first came out and that he had died only a few years ago, a very wealthy man.

They stopped at The Tower for barbecued sandwiches. The Tower was a part stucco and part wood filling station and dance hall set in a clearing outside of Timothy. A fat man named Red Sammy Butts ran it and there were signs stuck here and there on the building and for miles up and down the highway saying, TRY RED SAMMY'S FAMOUS BARBECUE. NONE LIKE FAMOUS RED SAMMY'S! RED SAM! THE FAT BOY WITH THE HAPPY LAUGH. A VETERAN! RED SAMMY'S YOUR MAN!

Red Sammy was lying on the bare ground outside The Tower with his head under a truck while a gray monkey about a foot high, chained to a small chinaberry tree, chattered nearby. The monkey sprang back into the tree and got on the highest limb as soon as he saw the children jump out of the car and run toward him.

Inside, The Tower was a long dark room with a counter at one end and tables at the other and dancing space in the middle. They all sat down at a board table next to the nickelodeon and Red Sam's wife, a tall burnt-brown woman with hair and eyes lighter than her skin, came and took their order. The children's mother put a dime in the machine and played "The Tennessee Waltz," and the grandmother said that tune always made her want to dance. She asked Bailey if he would like to dance but he only glared at her. He didn't have a naturally sunny disposition like she did and trips made him nervous. The grandmother's brown eyes were very bright. She swayed her head from side to side and pretended she was dancing in her chair. June Star said play something she could tap to so the children's mother put in another dime and played a fast number and June Star stepped out onto the dance floor and did her tap routine.

"Ain't she cute?" Red Sam's wife said, leaning over the counter. "Would you like to come be my little girl?"

"No I certainly wouldn't," June Star said. "I wouldn't live in a broken-down place like this for a million bucks!" and she ran back to the table.

"Ain't she cute?" the woman repeated, stretching her mouth politely.

"Aren't you ashamed?" hissed the grandmother.

Red Sam came in and told his wife to quit lounging on the counter and hurry up with these people's order. His khaki trousers reached just to his hip bones and his stomach hung over them like a sack of meal swaying under his shirt. He came over and sat down at a table nearby and let out a combination sigh and yodel. "You can't win," he said. "You can't win," and he wiped his sweating red face off with a gray handkerchief. "These days you don't know who to trust," he said. "Ain't that the truth?"

"People are certainly not nice like they used to be," said the grand-   35
mother.

"Two fellers come in here last week," Red Sammy said, "driving a Chrysler. It was a old beat-up car but it was a good one and these boys looked all right to me. Said they worked at the mill and you know I let them fellers charge the gas they bought? Now why did I do that?"

"Because you're a good man!" the grandmother said at once.

"Yes'm, I suppose so," Red Sam said as if he were struck with this answer.

His wife brought the orders, carrying the five plates all at once without a tray, two in each hand and one balanced on her arm. "It isn't a soul in this green world of God's that you can trust," she said. "And I don't count nobody out of that, not nobody," she repeated, looking at Red Sammy.

"Did you read about that criminal, The Misfit, that's escaped?" asked   40
the grandmother.

"I wouldn't be a bit surprised if he didn't attact this place right here," said the woman. "If he hears about it being here, I wouldn't be none surprised to see him. If he hears it's two cent in the cash register, I wouldn't be a-tall surprised if he . . ."

"That'll do," Red Sam said. "Go bring these people their Co'-Colas," and the woman went off to get the rest of the order.

"A good man is hard to find," Red Sammy said. "Everything is getting terrible. I remember the day you could go off and leave your screen door unlatched. Not no more."

He and the grandmother discussed better times. The old lady said that in her opinion Europe was entirely to blame for the way things were now. She said the way Europe acted you would think we were made of money and Red Sam said it was no use talking about it, she was exactly right. The children ran outside into the white sunlight and looked at the monkey in the lacy chinaberry tree. He was busy catching fleas on himself and biting each one carefully between his teeth as if it were a delicacy.

They drove off again into the hot afternoon. The grandmother took   45
cat naps and woke up every five minutes with her own snoring. Outside of Toombsboro she woke up and recalled an old plantation that she had visited in this neighborhood once when she was a young lady. She said the house had six white columns across the front and that there was an avenue of oaks leading up to it and two little wooden trellis arbors on either side in front where you sat down with your suitor after a stroll in the garden. She recalled exactly which road to turn off to get to it. She knew that Bailey would not be willing to lose any time looking at an old house, but the more she talked about it, the more she wanted to see it once again and find out if the little twin arbors were still standing.

"There was a secret panel in this house," she said craftily, not telling the truth but wishing that she were, "and the story went that all the family silver was hidden in it when Sherman° came through but it was never found . . ."

"Hey!" John Wesley said. "Let's go see it! We'll find it! We'll poke all the woodwork and find it! Who lives there? Where do you turn off at? Hey, Pop, can't we turn off there?"

"We never have seen a house with a secret panel!" June Star shrieked. "Let's go to the house with the secret panel! Hey Pop, can't we go see the house with the secret panel!"

"It's not far from here, I know," the grandmother said. "It wouldn't take over twenty minutes."

Bailey was looking straight ahead. His jaw was as rigid as a horseshoe. "No," he said.

The children began to yell and scream that they wanted to see the house with the secret panel. John Wesley kicked the back of the front seat and June Star hung over her mother's shoulder and whined desperately into her ear that they never had any fun even on their vacation, that they could never do what THEY wanted to do. The baby began to scream and John Wesley kicked the back of the seat so hard that his father could feel the blows in his kidney.

"All right!" he shouted and drew the car to a stop at the side of the road. "Will you all shut up? Will you all just shut up for one second? If you don't shut up, we won't go anywhere."

"It would be very educational for them," the grandmother murmured.

"All right," Bailey said, "but get this: this is the only time we're going to stop for anything like this. This is the one and only time."

"The dirt road that you have to turn down is about a mile back," the grandmother directed. "I marked it when we passed."

"A dirt road," Bailey groaned.

After they had turned around and were headed toward the dirt road, the grandmother recalled other points about the house, the beautiful glass over the front doorway and the candle-lamp in the hall. John Wesley said that the secret panel was probably in the fireplace.

"You can't go inside this house," Bailey said. "You don't know who lives there."

"While you all talk to the people in front, I'll run around behind and get in a window," John Wesley suggested.

"We'll all stay in the car," his mother said.

They turned onto the dirt road and the car raced roughly along in a swirl of pink dust. The grandmother recalled the times when there were no paved roads and thirty miles was a day's journey. The dirt road was

Sherman: General William Tecumseh Sherman, Union commander, whose troops burned Atlanta in 1864 and then made a devastating march to the sea.

hilly and there were sudden washes in it and sharp curves on dangerous embankments. All at once they would be on a hill, looking down over the blue tops of trees for miles around, then the next minute, they would be in a red depression with the dust-coated trees looking down on them.

"This place had better turn up in a minute," Bailey said, "or I'm going to turn around."

The road looked as if no one had traveled on it for months.

"It's not much farther," the grandmother said and just as she said it, a horrible thought came to her. The thought was so embarrassing that she turned red in the face and her eyes dilated and her feet jumped up, upsetting her valise in the corner. The instant the valise moved, the newspaper top she had over the basket under it rose with a snarl and Pitty Sing, the cat, sprang onto Bailey's shoulder.

The children were thrown to the floor and their mother, clutching the baby, was thrown out the door onto the ground; the old lady was thrown into the front seat. The car turned over once and landed right-side-up in a gulch off the side of the road. Bailey remained in the driver's seat with the cat—gray-striped with a broad white face and an orange nose—clinging to his neck like a caterpillar.

As soon as the children saw they could move their arms and legs, they scrambled out of the car, shouting, "We've had an ACCIDENT!" The grandmother was curled up under the dashboard, hoping she was injured so that Bailey's wrath would not come down on her all at once. The horrible thought she had had before the accident was that the house she had remembered so vividly was not in Georgia but in Tennessee.   65

Bailey removed the cat from his neck with both hands and flung it out the window against the side of a pine tree. Then he got out of the car and started looking for the children's mother. She was sitting against the side of the red gutted ditch, holding the screaming baby, but she only had a cut down her face and a broken shoulder. "We've had an ACCIDENT!" the children screamed in a frenzy of delight.

"But nobody's killed," June Star said with disappointment as the grandmother limped out of the car, her hat still pinned to her head but the broken front brim standing up at a jaunty angle and the violet spray hanging off the side. They all sat down in the ditch, except the children, to recover from the shock. They were all shaking.

"Maybe a car will come along," said the children's mother hoarsely.

"I believe I have injured an organ," said the grandmother, pressing her side, but no one answered her. Bailey's teeth were clattering. He had on a yellow sport shirt with bright blue parrots designed in it and his face was as yellow as the shirt. The grandmother decided that she would not mention that the house was in Tennessee.

The road was about ten feet above and they could see only the tops   70
of the trees on the other side of it. Behind the ditch they were sitting in there were more woods, tall and dark and deep. In a few minutes they

saw a car some distance away on top of a hill, coming slowly as if the occupants were watching them. The grandmother stood up and waved both her arms dramatically to attract their attention. The car continued to come on slowly, disappeared around a bend and appeared again, moving even slower, on top of the hill they had gone over. It was a big black battered hearse-like automobile. There were three men in it.

It came to a stop just over them and for some minutes, the driver looked down with a steady expressionless gaze to where they were sitting, and didn't speak. Then he turned his head and muttered something to the other two and they got out. One was a fat boy in black trousers and a red sweat shirt with a silver stallion embossed on the front of it. He moved around on the right side of them and stood staring, his mouth partly open in a kind of loose grin. The other had on khaki pants and a blue striped coat and a gray hat pulled down very low, hiding most of his face. He came around slowly on the left side. Neither spoke.

The driver got out of the car and stood by the side of it, looking down at them. He was an older man than the other two. His hair was just beginning to gray and he wore silver-rimmed spectacles that gave him a scholarly look. He had a long creased face and didn't have on any shirt or undershirt. He had on blue jeans that were too tight for him and was holding a black hat and a gun. The two boys also had guns.

"We've had an ACCIDENT!" the children screamed.

The grandmother had the peculiar feeling that the bespectacled man was someone she knew. His face was as familiar to her as if she had known him all her life but she could not recall who he was. He moved away from the car and began to come down the embankment, placing his feet carefully so that he wouldn't slip. He had on tan and white shoes and no socks, and his ankles were red and thin. "Good afternoon," he said. "I see you all had you a little spill."

"We turned over twice!" said the grandmother.   75

"Oncet," he corrected. "We seen it happen. Try their car and see will it run, Hiram," he said quietly to the boy with the gray hat.

"What you got that gun for?" John Wesley asked. "Whatcha gonna do with that gun?"

"Lady," the man said to the children's mother, "would you mind calling them children to sit down by you? Children make me nervous. I want all you all to sit down right together there where you're at."

"What are you telling US what to do for?" June Star asked.

Behind them the line of woods gaped like a dark open mouth. "Come   80
here," said their mother.

"Look here now," Bailey began suddenly, "we're in a predicament! We're in . . ."

The grandmother shrieked. She scrambled to her feet and stood staring. "You're The Misfit!" she said. "I recognized you at once!"

"Yes'm," the man said, smiling slightly as if he were pleased in spite of himself to be known, "but it would have been better for all of you, lady, if you hadn't of reckernized me."

Bailey turned his head sharply and said something to his mother that shocked even the children. The old lady began to cry and The Misfit reddened.

"Lady," he said, "don't you get upset. Sometimes a man says things he   85 don't mean. I don't reckon he meant to talk to you thataway."

"You wouldn't shoot a lady, would you?" the grandmother said and removed a clean handkerchief from her cuff and began to slap at her eyes with it.

The Misfit pointed the toe of his shoe into the ground and made a little hole and then covered it up again. "I would hate to have to," he said.

"Listen," the grandmother almost screamed, "I know you're a good man. You don't look a bit like you have common blood. I know you must come from nice people!"

"Yes mam," he said, "finest people in the world." When he smiled he showed a row of strong white teeth. "God never made a finer woman than my mother and my daddy's heart was pure gold," he said. The boy with the red sweat shirt had come around behind them and was standing with his gun at his hip. The Misfit squatted down on the ground. "Watch them children, Bobby Lee," he said. "You know they make me nervous." He looked at the six of them huddled together in front of him and he seemed to be embarrassed as if he couldn't think of anything to say. "Ain't a cloud in the sky," he remarked, looking up at it. "Don't see no sun but don't see no cloud neither."

"Yes, it's a beautiful day," said the grandmother. "Listen," she said,   90 "you shouldn't call yourself The Misfit because I know you're a good man at heart. I can just look at you and tell."

"Hush!" Bailey yelled. "Hush! Everybody shut up and let me handle this!" He was squatting in the position of a runner about to sprint forward but he didn't move.

"I pre-chate that, lady," The Misfit said and drew a little circle in the ground with the butt of his gun.

"It'll take a half a hour to fix this here car," Hiram called, looking over the raised hood of it.

"Well, first you and Bobby Lee get him and that little boy to step over yonder with you," The Misfit said, pointing to Bailey and John Wesley. "The boys want to ast you something," he said to Bailey. "Would you mind stepping back in them woods there with them?"

"Listen," Bailey began, "we're in a terrible predicament! Nobody   95 realizes what this is," and his voice cracked. His eyes were as blue and intense as the parrots in his shirt and he remained perfectly still.

The grandmother reached up to adjust her hat brim as if she were going to the woods with him but it came off in her hand. She stood staring at it and after a second she let it fall on the ground. Hiram pulled Bailey up by the arm as if he were assisting an old man. John Wesley caught hold of his father's hand and Bobby Lee followed. They went off toward the woods and just as they reached the dark edge, Bailey turned and supporting himself against a gray naked pine trunk, he shouted, "I'll be back in a minute, Mamma, wait on me!"

"Come back this instant!" his mother shrilled but they all disappeared into the woods.

"Bailey Boy!" the grandmother called in a tragic voice but she found she was looking at The Misfit squatting on the ground in front of her. "I just know you're a good man," she said desperately. "You're not a bit common!"

"Nome, I ain't a good man," The Misfit said after a second as if he had considered her statement carefully, "but I ain't the worst in the world neither. My daddy said I was a different breed of dog from my brothers and sisters. 'You know,' Daddy said, 'it's some that can live their whole life out without asking about it and it's others has to know why it is, and this boy is one of the latters. He's going to be into everything!'" He put on his black hat and looked up suddenly and then away deep into the woods as if he were embarrassed again. "I'm sorry I don't have on a shirt before you ladies," he said, hunching his shoulders slightly. "We buried our clothes that we had on when we escaped and we're just making do until we can get better. We borrowed these from some folks we met," he explained.

"That's perfectly all right," the grandmother said. "Maybe Bailey has   100
an extra shirt in his suitcase."

"I'll look and see terrectly," The Misfit said.

"Where are they taking him?" the children's mother screamed.

"Daddy was a card himself," The Misfit said. "You couldn't put anything over on him. He never got in trouble with the Authorities though. Just had the knack of handling them."

"You could be honest too if you'd only try," said the grandmother. "Think how wonderful it would be to settle down and live a comfortable life and not have to think about somebody chasing you all the time."

The Misfit kept scratching in the ground with the butt of his gun as if he   105
were thinking about it. "Yes'm, somebody is always after you," he murmured.

The grandmother noticed how thin his shoulder blades were just behind his hat because she was standing up looking down on him. "Do you ever pray?" she asked.

He shook his head. All she saw was the black hat wiggle between his shoulder blades. "Nome," he said.

There was a pistol shot from the woods, followed closely by another. Then silence. The old lady's head jerked around. She could hear the wind move through the tree tops like a long satisfied insuck of breath. "Bailey Boy!" she called.

"I was a gospel singer for a while," The Misfit said. "I been most everything. Been in the arm service, both land and sea, at home and abroad, been twict married, been an undertaker, been with the railroads, plowed Mother Earth, been in a tornado, seen a man burnt alive oncet," and he looked up at the children's mother and the little girl who were sitting close together, their faces white and their eyes glassy; "I even seen a woman flogged," he said.

"Pray, pray," the grandmother began, "pray, pray . . ."   110

"I never was a bad boy that I remember of," The Misfit said in an almost dreamy voice, "but somewheres along the line I done something wrong and got sent to the penitentiary. I was buried alive," and he looked up and held her attention to him by a steady stare.

"That's when you should have started to pray," she said. "What did you do to get sent to the penitentiary that first time?"

"Turn to the right, it was a wall," The Misfit said, looking up again at the cloudless sky. "Turn to the left, it was a wall. Look up it was a ceiling, look down it was a floor. I forget what I done, lady. I set there and set there, trying to remember what it was I done and I ain't recalled it to this day. Oncet in a while, I would think it was coming to me, but it never come."

"Maybe they put you in by mistake," the old lady said vaguely.

"Nome," he said. "It wasn't no mistake. They had the papers on me."   115

"You must have stolen something," she said.

The Misfit sneered slightly. "Nobody had nothing I wanted," he said. "It was a head-doctor at the penitentiary said what I had done was kill my daddy but I known that for a lie. My daddy died in nineteen ought nineteen of the epidemic flu and I never had a thing to do with it. He was buried in the Mount Hopewell Baptist churchyard and you can go there and see for yourself."

"If you would pray," the old lady said, "Jesus would help you."

"That's right," The Misfit said.

"Well then, why don't you pray?" she asked trembling with delight   120
suddenly.

"I don't want no hep," he said. "I'm doing all right by myself."

Bobby Lee and Hiram came ambling back from the woods. Bobby Lee was dragging a yellow shirt with bright blue parrots in it.

"Thow me that shirt, Bobby Lee," The Misfit said. The shirt came flying at him and landed on his shoulder and he put it on. The grandmother couldn't name what the shirt reminded her of. "No, lady," The Misfit said while he was buttoning it up, "I found out the crime don't matter. You can do one thing or you can do another, kill a man or take a tire off his car, because sooner or later you're going to forget what it was you done and just be punished for it."

The children's mother had begun to make heaving noises as if she couldn't get her breath. "Lady," he asked, "would you and that little girl like to step off yonder with Bobby Lee and Hiram and join your husband?"

"Yes, thank you," the mother said faintly. Her left arm dangled help-   125
lessly and she was holding the baby, who had gone to sleep, in the other.

"Hep that lady up, Hiram," The Misfit said as she struggled to climb out of the ditch, "and Bobby Lee, you hold onto that little girl's hand."

"I don't want to hold hands with him," June Star said. "He reminds me of a pig."

The fat boy blushed and laughed and caught her by the arm and pulled her off into the woods after Hiram and her mother.

Alone with The Misfit, the grandmother found that she had lost her voice. There was not a cloud in the sky nor any sun. There was nothing around her but woods. She wanted to tell him that he must pray. She opened and closed her mouth several times before anything came out. Finally she found herself saying, "Jesus. Jesus," meaning, Jesus will help you, but the way she was saying it, it sounded as if she might be cursing.

"Yes'm," The Misfit said as if he agreed. "Jesus thown everything off balance. It was the same case with Him as with me except He hadn't committed any crime and they could prove I had committed one because they had the papers on me. Of course," he said, "they never shown me my papers. That's why I sign myself now. I said long ago, you get you a signature and sign everything you do and keep a copy of it. Then you'll know what you done and you can hold up the crime to the punishment and see do they match and in the end you'll have something to prove you ain't been treated right. I call myself The Misfit," he said, "because I can't make what all I done wrong fit what all I gone through in punishment."

There was a piercing scream from the woods, followed closely by a 130 pistol report. "Does it seem right to you, lady, that one is punished a heap and another ain't punished at all?"

"Jesus!" the old lady cried. "You've got good blood! I know you wouldn't shoot a lady! I know you come from nice people! Pray! Jesus, you ought not to shoot a lady. I'll give you all the money I've got!"

"Lady," The Misfit said, looking beyond her far into the woods, "there never was a body that give the undertaker a tip."

There were two more pistol reports and the grandmother raised her head like a parched old turkey hen crying for water and called, "Bailey Boy, Bailey Boy!" as if her heart would break.

"Jesus was the only One that ever raised the dead," The Misfit continued, "and He shouldn't have done it. He thown everything off balance. If He did what He said, then it's nothing for you to do but thow away everything and follow Him, and if He didn't, then it's nothing for you to do but enjoy the few minutes you got left the best way you can—by killing somebody or burning down his house or doing some other meanness to him. No pleasure but meanness," he said and his voice had become almost a snarl.

"Maybe He didn't raise the dead," the old lady mumbled, not know- 135 ing what she was saying and feeling so dizzy that she sank down in the ditch with her legs twisted under her.

"I wasn't there so I can't say He didn't," The Misfit said. "I wisht I had of been there," he said, hitting the ground with his fist. "It ain't right I wasn't there because if I had of been there I would of known. Listen lady," he said in a high voice, "if I had of been there I would of known and I wouldn't be like I am now." His voice seemed about to crack and the grandmother's head cleared for an instant. She saw the man's face twisted close to her own as if he were going to cry and she murmured, "Why you're one of my babies. You're one of my own children!" She reached out and touched him on the shoulder. The Misfit sprang back as if a snake had bitten him and shot her three times through the chest. Then he put his gun down on the ground and took off his glasses and began to clean them.

Hiram and Bobby Lee returned from the woods and stood over the ditch, looking down at the grandmother who half sat and half lay in a puddle of blood with her legs crossed under her like a child's and her face smiling up at the cloudless sky.

Without his glasses, The Misfit's eyes were red-rimmed and pale and defenseless-looking. "Take her off and thow her where you thown the others," he said, picking up the cat that was rubbing itself against his leg.

"She was a talker, wasn't she?" Bobby Lee said, sliding down the ditch with a yodel.

"She would of been a good woman," The Misfit said, "if it had been 140 somebody there to shoot her every minute of her life."

"Some fun!" Bobby Lee said.

"Shut up, Bobby Lee," The Misfit said. "It's no real pleasure in life."

Juan Rulfo

Tell Them Not to Kill Me!   1953
Translated by Ilan Stavans

Born in the rural Mexican state of Jalisco, Juan Rulfo (1917–1986) experienced war firsthand. From 1926 to 1929, western Mexico underwent a backlash to the Mexican Revolution, known as the Cristero Rebellion. During the violence, Rulfo's father was assassinated and his mother died of a heart attack. Rulfo's uncles also died during the Rebellion, and the boy was sent to live with his grandmother and later to various boarding schools. When he came of age, Rulfo aspired to attend the University of Guadalajara, but the college was closed due to strikes, so he moved to Mexico City, attended literary lectures, traveled widely, and began to write. Rulfo produced only two books during

Juan Rulfo

his lifetime, yet he is remembered as one of the most influential mid-century Latin American authors. El Llano en Llamas (1953; translated as The Burning Plain, *1967) is a collection of short stories that centers around the violence of the Mexican countryside. His ambitious, slim novel,* Pedro Páramo *(1955), was massively influential for emerging authors of magic realism. Jorge Luis Borges considered* Pedro Páramo, *which portrays a town populated by ghosts, one of the greatest works of literature in any language. Rulfo won the National Literature Prize in 1970 and the Príncipe de Asturias Prize for literature in 1983. For more than two decades he served as an editor for the National Indigenous Institute in Mexico City. He died of lung cancer at age sixty-eight.*

"Tell them not to kill me, Justino! Go on, go and tell them that. For pity's sake. Just tell them that. Tell them to not do it out of pity."

"I can't. There's a *sargento* over there who doesn't want to hear anything about you."

"Make him listen. Find a way and tell him I've been frightened enough. Tell him for God's sake."

"It doesn't have anything to do with being frightened. It looks like they're really going to kill you. And I don't want to go back there."

"Go one more time. Just one more time, to see what you can do."   5

"No. I don't feel like going. If I do that, they'll know I'm your son. And, if I go to them that much, in the end they'll know who I am and they'll end up shooting me as well. Better to leave things as they are."

"Come on, Justino. Tell them to have a little pity on me. Just tell them that."

Justino clenched his teeth and shook his head saying:

"No."

For a long time he continued shaking his head.   10

"Tell the *sargento* to let you see the *coronel*. And tell him how old I am. How I'm not worth very much. What will he gain by killing me? Nothing. After all, he must have a soul. Tell him to do it for the salvation of his blessed soul."

Justino got up from the pile of rocks on which he was sitting and walked toward the corral gate. Then he turned around and said:

"Okay, I'll go. But if they shoot me, too, who'll take care of my wife and children?"

"Providence, Justino. Providence will take care of them. Just take a minute and go over there and see what you can do for me. That's what it'll take."

They had brought him at daybreak. And now the morning was   15
well along and he was still there, tied to a post, waiting. He couldn't sit still. He had tried to sleep for a while so he would calm down, but sleep had escaped him. His hunger had fled, as well. He didn't feel like doing

anything. Just staying alive. Now that he knew for sure he was going to be killed, he had been overwhelmed by such an intense desire to live, as only a man who had recently been resuscitated can be.

Who would have thought that that old business would come back to haunt him, so rancid, so deeply buried, he had always thought. That business of when he had to kill Don Lupe. No, not just like that, as those from Alima wanted him to admit, but because he had his own reasons. He remembered:

Don Lupe Terreros, owner of Puerta de Piedra, and his compadre to boot. Whom he, Juvencio Nava, had to kill for one reason; for being the owner of Puerta de Piedra and who, in spite of being his compadre, had refused pasture to his animals.

At first, he did nothing out of duty. But then, when the drought came along, when he saw how one after another of his animals died of hunger and his compadre Don Lupe still refused to let them have the grass in his fields, that's when he broke the fence and drove his herd of skinny animals to the pasture so they could eat their fill. And Don Lupe hadn't liked that, and he ordered the fence mended so he, Juvencio Nava, had to break open a hole again. In that way, by day the hole was mended and by night it was opened again, while the stock stayed there, always near the fence, always waiting; that stock of his that before had only smelled the grass without being able to taste it.

And he and Don Lupe argued and argued without ever reaching an agreement.

Until one time Don Lupe said to him: 20

"Look, Juvencio, if you put one more of your animals in my pasture again, I'll kill it."

And he answered:

"Look, Don Lupe, it's not my fault that the animals fend for themselves. They're innocent. You kill them and we'll see what happens."

"And he killed one of my yearlings.

"This happened thirty-five years ago, around March, because in April   25
I was already in the mountains, fleeing the warrant. The ten cows I gave the judge did me no good, nor did the bond I paid on my house to get out of jail. And they still paid themselves out of what was left so they wouldn't keep after me, but they kept after me all the same. That's why I came to live with my son on this other little piece of land I had named Palo de Venado. And my son grew up and married my daughter-in-law Ignacia and has already had eight children. In other words, that business is already old and should have been forgotten by now. But it's clear it hasn't been.

"I figured that with about a hundred pesos everything would be fine. The late Don Lupe left only a wife and two little boys, who were still on all fours. And the widow died, too, of grief, apparently, soon after. And the boys were taken away to live with relatives. So there was nothing to fear from them.

"But other people considered that I was still under warrant and awaiting trial so they could keep on stealing from me. Any time someone came to the town, I was told:

"'Some strangers are in town, Juvencio.'

"And I would head for the hills, hiding among the madrone thickets and eating only wild grasses all day long. Sometimes, in the middle of the night, I would have to come out, as if dogs were after me. I spent my entire life that way. It wasn't a year or two. It was my whole life."

And now they had come for him, when he was no longer expecting anyone, confident that people had forgotten him, believing that he would at least spend his remaining days in tranquility. "At least that," he thought, "I'll end up with that because I'm old. They'll leave me in peace." 30

He had given himself over fully to that hope. That's why it was hard for him to imagine he would die that way, suddenly, at this stage of his life, after fighting so hard to liberate himself from death; after spending his best years running from pillar to post, dragged along by fear and when his body had ended up as a dried-out carcass, leathery from the bad days in which he needed to hide from everyone.

Hadn't he even gone so far that his wife left him, as well? That day when he woke up to the news she had left him it didn't even enter his head to go out looking for her. He let her go without even trying to find out anything, whom she had left with or where, as long as he didn't have to go down to the village. He let her go the way he had let everything else go, without bothering to put up a fight. The only thing left was to take care of his life, which he would protect no matter what. He couldn't let them kill him. He couldn't. Even less so now.

But that's why they had brought him from over yonder, from Palo de Venado. They didn't even need to tie him up for him to follow them. He walked on his own, handcuffed solely by fear. They realized he couldn't run with that old body, with those skinny legs like dried-out ropes, cramped up by the fear of dying. That's why he went along. To die. That's what they told him.

That's when he knew. He started to feel an itch in his stomach, which would come to him suddenly whenever he would see death nearby, bringing out the fear in his eyes and making his mouth swell up with that sour water he hadn't wanted to swallow. And that thing that made his feet heavy while his head turned soft and his heart pounded with all its might against his ribs. No, he couldn't get used to the idea that they were going to kill him.

There had to be some sort of hope. Someplace there had to be some sort of hope. Maybe they had made a mistake. Maybe they were looking for a different Juvencio Nava and not this Juvencio Nava. 35

He walked with the men in silence, his arms at his sides. The predawn was dark, without stars. The wind blew slowly, carrying dried earth with it and bringing something else, full of that odor, like urine, that road dust has.

As his eyes, squinty with the years, went along, they stared at the ground here, under his feet, despite the darkness. His entire life was there in that earth. Sixty years of living on it, of grasping it tightly in his hands, of having tested it the way one tests the flavor of meat. For a long time he had been crumbling it with his eyes, savoring each piece as if it were his last, almost knowing it would be his last.

Then, as if trying to say something, he would look at the men next to him. He was going to tell them to set him free, to let him go: "I haven't hurt anyone, muchachos," he was about to say to them, but he said nothing. "I'll tell them a bit later," he thought. He would only look at them. He could almost imagine they were his friends; but he didn't want to do that. They weren't. He didn't know who they were. He would watch them leaning to the side and bending down from time to time to see where the road was leading.

He had seen them for the first time in the gray of the evening, in that dusky hour when everything looks scorched. They had crossed the furrows stepping on tender young corn. That's why he had come down: to tell them the corn was just beginning to grow there. But they didn't stop.

He had seen them in time. He had always been lucky to see every-   40
thing in time. He could have hidden, walking a few hours in the hills until they left and he could go back down. After all, there was no way the corn crop would come to anything anyway. It was already past the time for rain, but no rain had come and the corn was beginning to wither. Soon it would all be dry.

So it wasn't even worth having come down; having put himself among those men as if in a hole, never to get out again.

And now he was right next to them, suppressing the desire to tell them to let him go. He couldn't see their faces; he could only see shapes closing in and then moving away from him. So when he actually began to talk, he didn't know if they had heard him. He said:

"I've never hurt anybody," is what he said. But nothing changed. Not one of the shapes appeared to pay attention. The faces didn't turn around to look at him. They remained the same, as if they were asleep.

Then he thought he had nothing more to say, that he needed to seek hope somewhere else. He again dropped his arms and went by the first houses in the village in the middle of those four men obscured by the black color of night.

"*Mi coronel*, here's the man."   45

They had stopped before the opening of the doorway. With his hat in his hand out of respect, he waited for someone to come out. But only the voice came out:

"What man?" it asked.

"The one from Pablo de Venado, *mi coronel*. The one you ordered us to bring in."

"Ask him if he has ever lived in Alima," the voice inside said.

"Hey, you! Have you ever lived in Alima?" repeated the *sargento* in   50 front of him.

"Yes. Tell the *coronel* that's exactly where I'm from. And I've lived there until recently."

"Ask him if he knew one Guadalupe Terreros."

"He wants to know if you knew one Guadalupe Terreros."

"Don Lupe? Yes. Tell him I knew him. He's dead."

Then the tone of the inside voice changed: 55

"I know he's dead," it said. And it continued talking as if it were talking with someone there, on the other side of the reed wall.

"Guadalupe Terreros was my father. When I grew up and went out looking for him, people told me he was dead. It's a bit difficult growing up knowing that the thing you can grab on to to make roots for yourself is dead. That's what happened to us.

"Then I found out he had been killed with a machete and with a cattle prod stuck in his stomach. They told me that he spent more than two days alone and that when they found him, lying in an arroyo, he was still in agony, asking people to take care of his family.

"With time, one apparently forgets all that. One tries to forget. What one can't forget is finding out that the person who did it is still alive, feeding his rotten soul with the illusion of eternal life. I couldn't forgive that man, though I don't know him; but the fact that he has placed himself where I know he is makes me want to finish him off. I can't forgive him his still being alive. He shouldn't have been born in the first place."

From here, from the outside, you could hear what he said clearly.   60 Then he ordered:

"Take him away and tie him up for a while, so that he suffers, and then shoot him!"

"Look at me, *coronel*," he asked. "I'm not worth anything. It won't take long for me to die all by myself, crippled by old age. Don't kill me . . . !"

"Take him away!" the voice inside said again.

" . . . I've already paid for this, *coronel*. I've paid for it many times over. Everything was taken away from me. They punished me in many different ways. I've spent over forty years hiding like a leper, with the constant fear that I'd be killed at any moment. I don't deserve to die like this, *coronel*. Let me be, at least, so that God may forgive me. Don't kill me! Tell them not to kill me!"

There he was, as if they had been beating him, slapping his hat   65 against the earth. Screaming.

The voice inside said immediately:

"Tie him up and give him something to drink until he gets so drunk that the shots won't hurt."

Now, finally, he was calm. He was curled up at the foot of the post. His son Justino had come and his son Justino had gone and had come back and now he was back again.

He slung him on top of the donkey. He cinched him up tight against the rigging so he wouldn't fall on the way. He put a sack over his head so he wouldn't give a bad impression. And then he prodded the donkey and they hurriedly left, in order to reach Palo de Venado still with time to arrange a wake for the dead man.

"Your daughter-in-law and grandkids will miss you," he was telling him. "They'll see your face and think it's not you. They'll think coyotes gnawed on you when they see you with that face full of holes, so many more gunshots than they needed."   70

Virginia Woolf

A Haunted House   1921

*Adeline Virginia Stephen Woolf (1882–1941) was born in London, the daughter of Sir Leslie Stephen, an influential critic and editor of the voluminous Dic-*tionary of National Biography. *Virginia and her sister Vanessa (later Vanessa Bell) were largely self-educated in their father's extensive library while—in a distinction not lost on them—their brothers were sent to college. After their father's death in 1904, Virginia and Vanessa moved to Bloomsbury, a bohemian London neighborhood, and became the center of the "Bloomsbury Group" of progressive artists and intellectuals. Always in frail health, Virginia experi-*

Virginia Woolf

enced episodes of mental disturbance. In 1912 she married Leonard Woolf, a journalist and novelist. In 1917 as therapy, they set up a hand-press in their home and started the Hogarth Press, which became one of the most celebrated small presses of the century. In addition to Woolf's books, it issued works by T. S. Eliot, Katherine Mansfield, Robinson Jeffers, Edwin Arlington Robinson, and Sigmund Freud. Woolf's first novel was The Voyage Out *(1915); though realistic in technique, it foreshadowed the psychological depth and poetic force of her late work. In innovative novels such as* Mrs. Dalloway *(1925) and* To the Lighthouse *(1927), Woolf became one of the central Modernist writers in English and a pioneer of stream-of-consciousness narration, which portrays the random flow of thoughts and feelings through a character's mind. Her critical essays are collected in* The Common Reader *(1925, second series 1932); her long essay* A Room of One's*

Own (1929) *is a feminist classic. After several nervous breakdowns, Woolf, fearing for her sanity, drowned herself in 1941.*

Whatever hour you woke there was a door shutting. From room to room they went, hand in hand, lifting here, opening there, making sure— a ghostly couple.

"Here we left it," she said. And he added, "Oh, but here too!" "It's upstairs," she murmured. "And in the garden," he whispered. "Quietly," they said, "or we shall wake them."

But it wasn't that you woke us. Oh, no. "They're looking for it; they're drawing the curtain," one might say, and so read on a page or two. "Now they've found it," one would be certain, stopping the pencil on the margin. And then, tired of reading, one might rise and see for oneself, the house all empty, the doors standing open, only the wood pigeons bubbling with content and the hum of the threshing machine sounding from the farm. "What did I come in here for? What did I want to find?" My hands were empty. "Perhaps it's upstairs then?" The apples were in the loft. And so down again, the garden still as ever, only the book had slipped into the grass.

But they had found it in the drawing room. Not that one could ever see them. The window panes reflected apples, reflected roses; all the leaves were green in the glass. If they moved in the drawing room, the apple only turned its yellow side. Yet, the moment after, if the door was opened, spread about the floor, hung upon the walls, pendant from the ceiling—what? My hands were empty. The shadow of a thrush crossed the carpet; from the deepest wells of silence the wood pigeon drew its bubble of sound. "Safe, safe, safe," the pulse of the house beat softly. "The treasure buried; the room . . ." the pulse stopped short. Oh, was that the buried treasure?

A moment later the light had faded. Out in the garden then? But the trees spun darkness for a wandering beam of sun. So fine, so rare, coolly sunk beneath the surface the beam I sought always burnt behind the glass. Death was the glass; death was between us; coming to the woman first, hundreds of years ago, leaving the house, sealing all the windows; the rooms were darkened. He left it, left her, went North, went East, saw the stars turned in the Southern sky; sought the house, found it dropped beneath the Downs. "Safe, safe, safe," the pulse of the house beat gladly. "The Treasure yours."

The wind roars up the avenue. Trees stoop and bend this way and that. Moonbeams splash and spill wildly in the rain. But the beam of the lamp falls straight from the window. The candle burns stiff and still. Wandering through the house, opening the windows, whispering not to wake us, the ghostly couple seek their joy.

"Here we slept" she says. And he adds, "Kisses without number." "Waking in the morning—" "Silver between the trees—" "Upstairs—" "In the garden—" "When summer came—" "In winter snowtime—" The doors go shutting far in the distance, gently knocking like the pulse of a heart.

Nearer they come; cease at the doorway. The wind falls, the rain slides silver down the glass. Our eyes darken; we hear no steps beside us; we see no lady spread her ghostly cloak. His hands shield the lantern. "Look," he breathes. "Sound asleep. Love upon their lips."

Stooping, holding their silver lamp above us, long they look and deeply. Long they pause. The wind drives straightly; the flame stoops slightly. Wild beams of moonlight cross both floor and wall, and, meeting, stain the faces bent; the faces pondering; the faces that search the sleepers and seek their hidden joy.

"Safe, safe, safe," the heart of the house beats proudly. "Long years—" he sighs. "Again you found me." "Here," she murmurs, "sleeping; in the garden reading; laughing, rolling apples in the loft. Here we left our treasure—" Stooping, their light lifts the lids upon my eyes. "Safe! safe! safe!" the pulse of the house beats wildly. Waking, I cry "Oh, is this *your* buried treasure? The light in the heart." 10

Kay Ryan, U.S. Poet Laureate, 2008–2010

POETRY

TALKING WITH *Kay Ryan*

"Language That Lasts"

Dana Gioia Interviews Former U.S. Poet Laureate Kay Ryan

Q: When did you start writing poetry?

KAY RYAN: In a way I'd say I started writing poetry when I started collecting language, which was as soon as I could. I loved hearing a new word or phrase, and I had a private game of trying to say things differently than I'd said them before. I remember when I was quite advanced in this language study, in ninth grade, I went on a summer trip with my friend and her parents down to Texas. I was sitting there quietly in the small hot living room of my friend's aunt, listening to the adult conversation. Someone said something irritated along the lines of, "Tracy totaled Teddy's Toronado, and Tyler tattled it to Tina!" and I just burst out laughing: that accidental string of T's nobody else seemed to notice. Language brought me constant, secret pleasure, and it was free; I could have as much as I wanted, which is nice if you're poor.

As to writing-writing, I fooled around with writing poetry during high school and college and even after I'd become a community college teacher, trying to keep it at arm's length because I didn't want to be exposed the way poetry makes you exposed. I wanted to stay superficial. But by the time I was thirty I could see that poetry was eating away at my mind anyhow. Why not accept it and try to get really good at it? So, either I started writing poetry at three or thirty.

Q: Did poetry play much of a part in your childhood?

KAY RYAN: I guess the short answer would be no. But my mother had one lovely poem about a dead kitten that she liked to say. I always enjoyed feeling tender and sad when she did; it was a kind of intimacy with a mother who wasn't very intimate. And my mother's mother liked to recite poems when she came to visit. They made me feel very serious, and that is a lovely feeling for a child: "Life is real! Life is earnest! / And the grave is not its goal; / Dust thou art, to dust returnest / Was not spoken of the soul!" My grandmother grew up in a time when people really memorized poetry for pleasure, and I loved hearing it.

My only other contact with poetry—but it was an important one—was in sixth grade. My enlightened teacher, Mrs. Kimball, at Roosevelt Elementary School in Bakersfield, California, had us do "choral reading," meaning the whole class memorized poems and stood up on the stage like a chorus at assemblies and recited them with great gusto. So I got a chance, like my grandmother, to memorize poetry for pleasure and have the pleasure of saying it aloud.

Q: Whom do you write for?

KAY RYAN: This is a devilish question. I'll have to answer it in parts.

First, when I write a poem I'm completely occupied with trying to net some elusive fish; I'm desperate to get the net (made of words) knotted in such a way that it will catch this desired fish (a half-formed idea, a wisp of a feeling). I'm not thinking of anything but that; I'm not thinking of me, I'm not thinking of you.

But then later, after I've finished writing the poem and have let it sit for days or months and look back to see if there's a fish in the net after all (many times, I'm sorry to say, there is no fish), I begin thinking of you. Have I put the necessary connections in the poem, or are some of them still in my head? Have I shaped the lines so they will present the reader with the most pleasure in discovering the secret rhymes? Have I removed self-indulgences? Because a poem, by its nature, must please others. If it doesn't, it can't last; and if it doesn't last it wasn't a poem, because poems are language that lasts.

Q: What gives you pleasure in writing?

KAY RYAN: People have dreams where they begin noticing that their house is lots bigger than they knew; they realize there is a maze of rooms behind the ones they've been occupying. The dreamer (I've had this dream) doesn't know why she hasn't noticed this before, because it's fascinating.

Writing a poem is like this; I go back behind my usual mind and find places I didn't know about, places that only the activity of writing a poem can let me into.

Q: Who are your favorite poets?

KAY RYAN: My favorite American poets are Emily Dickinson and Robert Frost. British favorites include John Donne, Gerard Manley Hopkins, Philip Larkin, and Stevie Smith. Favorites in other languages are Fernando Pessoa and Constantine Cavafy.

Q: Did a poem ever change your life?

KAY RYAN: A dream poem might have. When I was around ten, I dreamed that a piece of white paper was blowing around and I was chasing it. I knew it had the most beautiful poem in the world written on it. I couldn't catch it.

I never forgot that dream, although at the time I wasn't even thinking of trying to write poetry. Still, maybe some deep part of me was busy at it even then. I'm still trying to catch that piece of paper.

Q: What is the purpose of poetry? Why do people need poetry?

KAY RYAN: The secret, long-term purpose of poetry is to create more space between everything. Poetry is the main engine of the expanding universe. You yourself will have noticed how reading a poem that really strikes you (that will be one in 25, if you're lucky; a poem can be great and still not strike YOU) makes you feel freer and less burdened, even if it's about death. You feel fresher, more awake. This proves my point; your atoms have been subtly distanced from each other, like a breeze is blowing through your DNA. That's poetry loosening you.

To the Muse

Give me leave, Muse, in plain view to array
Your shift and bodice by the light of day.
I would have brought an epic. Be not vexed
Instead to grace a niggling schoolroom text;
Let down your sanction, help me to oblige
Those who would lead fresh devots to your liege,
And at your altar, grant that in a flash
Readers and I know incense from dead ash.

—X. J. K.

results may take as many words as the original, if not more. A paraphrase, then, is ampler than a **summary**, a brief condensation of gist, main idea, or story. (Click the "Info" button on your TV remote control, and you'll get a movie summary such as: "Scientist seeks revenge by creating giant man-eating cockroaches.") Here is a poem worth considering line by line. The poet writes of an island in a lake in the west of Ireland, in a region where he spent many summers as a boy.

William Butler Yeats (1865–1939)

The Lake Isle of Innisfree   1892

I will arise and go now, and go to Innisfree,
And a small cabin build there, of clay and wattles made:
Nine bean-rows will I have there, a hive for the honey-bee,
And live alone in the bee-loud glade.

And I shall have some peace there, for peace comes dropping slow,   5
Dropping from the veils of the morning to where the cricket sings;
There midnight's all a glimmer, and noon a purple glow,
And evening full of the linnet's wings.

I will arise and go now, for always night and day
I hear lake water lapping with low sounds by the shore;   10
While I stand on the roadway, or on the pavements gray,
I hear it in the deep heart's core.

Though relatively simple, this poem is far from simple-minded. We need to absorb it slowly and thoughtfully. At the start, for most of us, it raises problems: what are *wattles*, from which the speaker's dream-cabin is to be made? We might guess, but in this case it will help to consult a dictionary: they are "poles interwoven with sticks or branches, formerly used in building as frameworks to support walls or roofs." Evidently, this getaway house will be built in an old-fashioned way: it won't be a prefabricated log cabin or A-frame house, nothing modern or citified. The phrase *bee-loud glade* certainly isn't common-place language, but right away, we can understand it, at least partially: it's a place loud with bees. What is a *glade*? Experience might tell us that it is an open space in woods, but if that word stops us, we can look it up. Although the *linnet* doesn't live in North America, it is a creature with wings—a songbird of the finch family, adds the dictionary. But even if we don't make a special trip to the dictionary to find *linnet*, we probably recognize that the word means "bird," and so the line makes sense to us.

A paraphrase of the whole poem might go something like this (in language easier to forget than that of the original): "I'm going to get up now, go to Innisfree, build a cabin, plant beans, keep bees, and live peacefully by myself amid nature and beautiful light. I want to because I can't forget the sound of

that lake water. When I'm in the city, a gray and dingy place, I seem to hear
it deep inside me."

These dull remarks, roughly faithful to what Yeats is saying, seem a long
way from poetry. Nevertheless, they make certain things clear. For one, they
spell out what the poet merely hints at in his choice of the word *gray*: that he
finds the city dull and depressing. He stresses the word; instead of saying *gray
pavements*, in the usual word order, he turns the phrase around and makes *gray*
stand at the end of the line, where it rimes with *day* and so takes extra emphasis. The grayness of the city therefore seems important to the poem, and the
paraphrase tries to make its meaning obvious.

Theme and Subject

Whenever you paraphrase, you stick your neck out. You affirm what the poem
gives you to understand. And making a paraphrase can help you see the central
thought of the poem, its **theme**. The theme isn't the same as the **subject**,
which is the main topic, whatever the poem is "about." In Yeats's poem, the
subject is the lake isle of Innisfree, or a wish to retreat to it. But the theme is,
"I yearn for an ideal place where I will find perfect peace and happiness."

Themes can be stated variously, depending on what you believe matters most in the poem. Taking a different view of the poem, placing more
weight on the speaker's wish to escape the city, you might instead state the
theme: "This city is getting me down—I want to get back to nature." But
after taking a second look at that statement, you might want to sharpen it.
After all, this Innisfree seems a special, particular place, where the natural
world means more to the poet than just any old trees and birds he might see
in a park. Perhaps a stronger statement of theme, one closer to what matters
most in the poem, might be: "I want to quit the city for my heaven on earth."
That, of course, is saying in an obvious way what Yeats says more subtly,
more memorably.

Limits of Paraphrase

A paraphrase never tells *all* that a poem contains, nor will every reader agree
that a particular paraphrase is accurate. We all make our own interpretations,
and sometimes the total meaning of a poem evades even the poet who wrote
it. Asked to explain a passage in one of his poems, Robert Browning replied
that when he had written the poem, only God and he knew what it meant;
but "Now, only God knows." Still, to analyze a poem *as if* we could be certain
of its meaning is, in general, more fruitful than to proceed as if no certainty
could ever be had. A useful question might be, "What can we understand from
the poem's very words?"

All of us bring personal associations to the poems we read. "The Lake
Isle of Innisfree" might give you special pleasure if you have ever vacationed
on a small island or on the shore of a lake. Such associations are inevitable,
even to be welcomed, as long as they don't interfere with our reading the

words on the page. We need to distinguish irrelevant responses from those the poem calls for. The reader who can't stand "The Lake Isle of Innisfree" because she is afraid of bees isn't reading a poem by Yeats, but one of her own invention.

Now and again we meet a poem—perhaps startling and memorable— into which the method of paraphrase won't take us far. Some portion of any deep poem resists explanation, but certain poems resist it almost entirely. Many poems by religious mystics seem closer to dream than waking. So do poems that purport to record drug experiences, such as Coleridge's "Kubla Khan" (Chapter 22). So do nonsense poems, translations of primitive folk songs, and surreal poems. Such poetry may move us and give pleasure (although not, perhaps, the pleasure of intellectual understanding). We do it no harm by trying to paraphrase it, though we may fail. Whether logically clear or strangely opaque, good poems appeal to the intelligence and do not shrink from it.

So far, we have taken for granted that poetry differs from prose; yet all our strategies for reading poetry—plowing straight on through and then going back, isolating difficulties, trying to paraphrase, reading aloud, using a dictionary—are no different from those we might employ in unraveling a complicated piece of prose. Poetry, after all, is similar to prose in most respects. At the very least, it is written in the same language. Like prose, poetry shares knowledge with us. It tells us, for instance, of a beautiful island in Lake Gill, County Sligo, Ireland, and of how one man feels about it.

LYRIC POETRY

Originally, as its Greek name suggests, a *lyric* was a poem sung to the music of a lyre. This earlier meaning—a poem made for singing—is still current today, when we use *lyrics* to mean the words of a popular song. But the kind of printed poem we now call a *lyric* is usually something else, for over the past five hundred years the nature of lyric poetry has changed greatly. Ever since the invention of the printing press in the fifteenth century, poets have written less often for singers, more often for readers. In general, this tendency has made lyric poems contain less word-music and (since they can be pondered on a page) more thought—and perhaps more complicated feelings.

What Is a Lyric Poem?

Here is a rough definition of a **lyric poem** as it is written today: a short poem expressing the thoughts and feelings of a single speaker. Often a poet will write a lyric in the first person ("I will arise and go now, and go to Innisfree"), but not always. A lyric can also be in the first person plural, as in Paul Laurence Dunbar's "We Wear the Mask" (Chapter 17). Or, a lyric might describe an object or recall an experience without the speaker's ever bringing himself or herself into it. (For an example of such a lyric, one in which the poet refrains from saying "I," see Theodore Roethke's "Root Cellar" or Gerard Manley Hopkins's "Pied Beauty," both found in Chapter 13.)

Perhaps because, rightly or wrongly, some people still think of lyrics as lyre-strummings, they expect a lyric to be an outburst of feeling, somewhat resembling a song, at least containing musical elements such as rime, rhythm, or sound effects. Such expectations are fulfilled in "The Lake Isle of Innisfree," that impassioned lyric full of language rich in sound. Many contemporary poets, however, write short poems in which they voice opinions or complicated feelings—poems that no reader would dream of trying to sing.

But in the sense in which we use it, *lyric* will usually apply to a kind of poem you can easily recognize. Here, for instance, are two lyrics. They differ sharply in subject and theme, but they have traits in common: both are short, and (as you will find) both set forth one speaker's definite, unmistakable feelings.

Robert Hayden (1913–1980)

Those Winter Sundays   1962

Sundays too my father got up early
and put his clothes on in the blueblack cold,
then with cracked hands that ached
from labor in the weekday weather made
banked fires blaze. No one ever thanked him.   5

I'd wake and hear the cold splintering, breaking.
When the rooms were warm, he'd call,
and slowly I would rise and dress,
fearing the chronic angers of that house,

Speaking indifferently to him,   10
who had driven out the cold
and polished my good shoes as well.
What did I know, what did I know
of love's austere and lonely offices?

Questions

1. Jot down a brief paraphrase of this poem. In your paraphrase, clearly show what the speaker finds himself remembering.
2. What are the speaker's various feelings? What do you understand from the words "chronic angers" and "austere"?
3. With what specific details does the poem make the past seem real?
4. What is the subject of Hayden's poem? How would you state its theme?

Adrienne Rich (1929–2012)

Aunt Jennifer's Tigers   1951

Aunt Jennifer's tigers prance across a screen,
Bright topaz denizens of a world of green.
They do not fear the men beneath the tree;
They pace in sleek chivalric certainty.

Aunt Jennifer's fingers fluttering through her wool   5
Find even the ivory needle hard to pull.
The massive weight of Uncle's wedding band
Sits heavily upon Aunt Jennifer's hand.

When Aunt is dead, her terrified hands will lie
Still ringed with ordeals she was mastered by.   10
The tigers in the panel that she made
Will go on prancing, proud and unafraid.

NARRATIVE POETRY

Although a lyric sometimes relates an incident, or like "Those Winter Sundays" draws a scene, it does not usually relate a series of events. That happens in a **narrative poem**, one whose main purpose is to tell a story.

Narrative poetry dates back to the Babylonian *Epic of Gilgamesh* (composed before 2000 B.C.) and Homer's epics the *Iliad* and the *Odyssey* (composed before 700 B.C.). It may well have originated much earlier. In England and Scotland, storytelling poems, such as *Beowulf*, have long been popular; in the late Middle Ages, ballads—or storytelling songs—circulated widely. Some, such as "Sir Patrick Spence" and "Bonny Barbara Allan," survive in our day, and folksingers sometimes perform them.

Evidently the art of narrative poetry invites the skills of a writer of fiction: the ability to draw characters and settings, to engage attention, to shape a plot. Needless to say, it calls for all the skills of a poet as well. In the English language today, lyrics seem more plentiful than other kinds of poetry. Although there has recently been a revival of interest in writing narrative poems, they have a far smaller audience than the readership enjoyed by long verse narratives, such as Henry Wadsworth Longfellow's *Evangeline* and Alfred, Lord Tennyson's *Idylls of the King*, in the nineteenth century.

Here are two narrative poems: one medieval, one modern. How would you paraphrase the stories they tell? How do they hold your attention on their stories?

Anonymous   (traditional Scottish ballad)

Sir Patrick Spence

The king sits in Dumferling toune,
   Drinking the blude-reid wine:
"O whar will I get guid sailor
   To sail this schip of mine?"

Up and spak an eldern knicht,°   *knight*   5
   Sat at the kings richt kne:
"Sir Patrick Spence is the best sailor
   That sails upon the se."

The king has written a braid letter,
   And signed it wi' his hand,   10
And sent it to Sir Patrick Spence,
   Was walking on the sand.

The first line that Sir Patrick red,
   A loud lauch lauchèd he;
The next line that Sir Patrick red,   15
   The teir blinded his ee.

"O wha° is this has don this deid,   *who*
   This ill deid don to me,
To send me out this time o' the yeir,
   To sail upon the se!   20

"Mak haste, mak haste, my mirry men all,
   Our guid schip sails the morne."
"O say na sae,° my master deir,   *so*
   For I feir a deadlie storme.

"Late late yestreen I saw the new moone,   25
   Wi' the auld moone in hir arme,
And I feir, I feir, my deir master,
   That we will cum to harme."

O our Scots nobles wer richt laith°   *loath*
   To weet° their cork-heild schoone,°   *wet; shoes*   30
Bot lang owre° a' the play wer playd,   *long before*
   Their hats they swam aboone.°   *above (their heads)*

O lang, lang may their ladies sit,
   Wi' their fans into their hand,
Or ere° they se Sir Patrick Spence   *before*   35
   Cum sailing to the land.

O lang, lang may the ladies stand,
   Wi' their gold kems° in their hair,   *combs*
Waiting for their ain° deir lords,   *own*
   For they'll se thame na mair.   40

Haf owre,° haf owre to Aberdour,   *halfway over*
   It's fiftie fadom deip,
And thair lies guid Sir Patrick Spence,
   Wi' the Scots lords at his feit.

SIR PATRICK SPENCE. 9 *braid*: Broad, but broad in what sense? Among guesses are *plain-spoken*, *official*, and *on wide paper*.

Questions

1. That the king drinks "blude-reid wine" (line 2)—what meaning do you find in that detail? What does it hint at or foreshadow?

2. What do you make of this king and his motives for sending Spence and the Scots lords into an impending storm? Is he a fool, is he cruel and inconsiderate, is he deliberately trying to drown Sir Patrick and his crew, or is it impossible for us to know? Let your answer rely on the poem alone, not on anything you read into it.

3. Comment on this ballad's methods of storytelling. Is the story told too briefly for us to care what happens to Spence and his men, or are there any means by which the poet makes us feel compassion for them? Do you resent the lack of a detailed account of the shipwreck?

4. Lines 25–28—the new moon with the old moon in her arm—have been much admired as poetry. What does this stanza contribute to the story as well?

Robert Frost (1874–1963)

"Out, Out—"   1916

The buzz-saw snarled and rattled in the yard
And made dust and dropped stove-length sticks of wood,
Sweet-scented stuff when the breeze drew across it.
And from there those that lifted eyes could count
Five mountain ranges one behind the other   5
Under the sunset far into Vermont.
And the saw snarled and rattled, snarled and rattled,
As it ran light, or had to bear a load.
And nothing happened: day was all but done.
Call it a day, I wish they might have said   10
To please the boy by giving him the half hour
That a boy counts so much when saved from work.
His sister stood beside them in her apron
To tell them "Supper." At the word, the saw,
As if to prove saws knew what supper meant,   15
Leaped out at the boy's hand, or seemed to leap—

He must have given the hand. However it was,
Neither refused the meeting. But the hand!
The boy's first outcry was a rueful laugh,
As he swung toward them holding up the hand   20
Half in appeal, but half as if to keep
The life from spilling. Then the boy saw all—
Since he was old enough to know, big boy
Doing a man's work, though a child at heart—
He saw all spoiled. "Don't let him cut my hand off— 25
The doctor, when he comes. Don't let him, sister!"
So. But the hand was gone already.
The doctor put him in the dark of ether.
He lay and puffed his lips out with his breath.
And then—the watcher at his pulse took fright.   30
No one believed. They listened at his heart.
Little—less—nothing!—and that ended it.
No more to build on there. And they, since they
Were not the one dead, turned to their affairs.

"OUT, OUT—." The title of this poem echoes the words of Shakespeare's *Macbeth* on receiving news that his queen is dead: "Out, out, brief candle! / Life's but a walking shadow, a poor player / That struts and frets his hour upon the stage / And then is heard no more. It is a tale / Told by an idiot, full of sound and fury, / Signifying nothing" (*Macbeth* 5.5.23–28).

Questions

1. How does Frost make the buzz-saw appear sinister? How does he make it seem, in another way, like a friend?

2. What do you make of the people who surround the boy—the "they" of the poem? Who might they be? Do they seem to you concerned and compassionate, cruel, indifferent, or what?

3. What does Frost's reference to *Macbeth* contribute to your understanding of "'Out, Out—'"? How would you state the theme of Frost's poem?

4. Set this poem beside "Sir Patrick Spence." How does "'Out, Out—'" resemble or differ from that medieval folk ballad in subject? How is Frost's poem similar or different in its way of telling a story?

DRAMATIC POETRY

A third kind of poetry is **dramatic poetry**, which presents the voice of an imaginary character (or characters) speaking directly, without any additional narration by the author.

A dramatic poem, according to T. S. Eliot, does not consist of "what the poet would say in his own person, but only what he can say within the limits of one imaginary character addressing another imaginary character." Strictly speaking, the term *dramatic poetry* describes any verse written for the stage (and until a few centuries ago most playwrights, like Shakespeare and Molière, wrote their plays mainly in verse).

Dramatic Monologue

The term *dramatic poetry* most often refers to the **dramatic monologue**, a poem written as a speech made by a character (other than the author) at some decisive moment. A dramatic monologue is usually addressed by the speaker to some other character who remains silent. If the listener replies, the poem becomes a dialogue (such as Thomas Hardy's "The Ruined Maid" in Chapter 11) in which the story unfolds in the conversation between two speakers.

The Victorian poet Robert Browning, who developed the form of the dramatic monologue, liked to put words in the mouths of characters who were conspicuously nasty, weak, reckless, or crazy: see, for instance, Browning's "Soliloquy of the Spanish Cloister" (Chapter 22), in which the speaker is an obsessively proud and jealous monk. The dramatic monologue has been a popular form among American poets, including Edwin Arlington Robinson, Robert Frost, Ezra Pound, Randall Jarrell, Sylvia Plath, and David Mason. The most famous dramatic monologue ever written is probably Browning's "My Last Duchess," in which the poet conjures up a Renaissance Italian duke whose words reveal much more about himself than the aristocratic speaker intends.

Robert Browning (1812–1889)

My Last Duchess   1842

Ferrara

That's my last Duchess painted on the wall,
Looking as if she were alive. I call
That piece a wonder, now: Frà Pandolf's hands
Worked busily a day, and there she stands.
Will't please you sit and look at her? I said   5
"Frà Pandolf" by design, for never read
Strangers like you that pictured countenance,
The depth and passion of its earnest glance,
But to myself they turned (since none puts by
The curtain I have drawn for you, but I)   10
And seemed as they would ask me, if they durst,
How such a glance came there; so, not the first
Are you to turn and ask thus. Sir, 'twas not
Her husband's presence only, called that spot
Of joy into the Duchess' cheek: perhaps   15

Frà Pandolf chanced to say, "Her mantle laps
Over my lady's wrist too much," or "Paint
Must never hope to reproduce the faint
Half-flush that dies along her throat": such stuff
Was courtesy, she thought, and cause enough   20
For calling up that spot of joy. She had
A heart—how shall I say?—too soon made glad,
Too easily impressed; she liked whate'er
She looked on, and her looks went everywhere.
Sir, 'twas all one! My favor at her breast,   25
The dropping of the daylight in the West,
The bough of cherries some officious fool
Broke in the orchard for her, the white mule
She rode with round the terrace—all and each
Would draw from her alike the approving speech,   30
Or blush, at least. She thanked men,—good! but thanked
Somehow—I know not how—as if she ranked
My gift of a nine-hundred-years-old name
With anybody's gift. Who'd stoop to blame
This sort of trifling? Even had you skill   35
In speech—(which I have not)—to make your will
Quite clear to such an one, and say, "Just this
Or that in you disgusts me; here you miss,
Or there exceed the mark"—and if she let
Herself be lessoned so, nor plainly set   40
Her wits to yours, forsooth, and made excuse,
—E'en then would be some stooping; and I choose
Never to stoop. Oh sir, she smiled, no doubt,
Whene'er I passed her; but who passed without
Much the same smile? This grew; I gave commands;   45
Then all smiles stopped together. There she stands
As if alive. Will't please you rise? We'll meet
The company below, then. I repeat,
The Count your master's known munificence
Is ample warrant that no just pretense   50
Of mine for dowry will be disallowed;
Though his fair daughter's self, as I avowed
At starting, is my object. Nay, we'll go
Together down, sir. Notice Neptune, though,
Taming a sea-horse, thought a rarity,   55
Which Claus of Innsbruck cast in bronze for me!

MY LAST DUCHESS. Ferrara, a city in northern Italy, is the scene. Browning may have modeled his speaker after Alonzo, Duke of Ferrara (1533–1598). 3 *Frà Pandolf* and 56 *Claus of
Innsbruck*: names of fictitious artists.

Questions

1. Whom is the Duke addressing? What is this person's business in Ferrara?
2. What is the Duke's opinion of his last Duchess's personality? Do we see her character differently?
3. If the Duke was unhappy with the Duchess's behavior, why didn't he make his displeasure known? Cite a specific passage to explain his reticence.
4. How much do we know about the fate of the last Duchess? Would it help our understanding of the poem to know more?
5. Does Browning imply any connection between the Duke's art collection and his attitude toward his wife?

DIDACTIC POETRY

More fashionable in former times was a fourth variety of poetry, **didactic poetry**: poetry or verse written to state a message or teach a body of knowledge. In a lyric, a speaker may express sadness; in a didactic poem, he or she may explain that sadness is inherent in life. Poems that impart a body of knowledge, such as Ovid's *Art of Love* and Lucretius's *On the Nature of Things*, are didactic. Such instructive poetry was favored especially by classical Latin poets and by English poets of the eighteenth century. In *The Fleece* (1757), John Dyer celebrated the British woolen industry and included practical advice on raising sheep:

> In cold stiff soils the bleaters oft complain
> Of gouty ails, by shepherds termed the halt:
> Those let the neighboring fold or ready crook
> Detain, and pour into their cloven feet
> Corrosive drugs, deep-searching arsenic,
> Dry alum, verdigris, or vitriol keen.

One might agree with Dr. Johnson's comment on Dyer's effort: "The subject, Sir, cannot be made poetical." But it may be argued that the subject of didactic poetry does not make it any less poetical. Good poems, it seems, can be written about anything under the sun. Like Dyer, John Milton described sick sheep in "Lycidas," a poem few readers have thought unpoetic:

> The hungry sheep look up, and are not fed,
> But, swoll'n with wind and the rank mist they draw,
> Rot inwardly, and foul contagion spread . . .

What makes Milton's lines better poetry than Dyer's is, among other things, a difference in attitude. Sick sheep to Dyer mean the loss of a few shillings and pence; to Milton, whose sheep stand for English Christendom, they mean a moral catastrophe.

▪ WRITING *effectively*

THINKING ABOUT PARAPHRASING

A poet takes pains to choose each word of a poem for both its sound and its exact shade of meaning. Since a poem's full effect is so completely wedded to its precise wording, some would say that no poem can be truly paraphrased. But even though it represents an imperfect approximation of the real thing, a paraphrase can be useful to write and read. It can clearly map out a poem's key images, actions, and ideas. A map is no substitute for a landscape, but a good map often helps us find our way through the landscape without getting lost.

William Stafford (1914–1993)

Ask Me   1975

Some time when the river is ice ask me
mistakes I have made. Ask me whether
what I have done is my life. Others
have come in their slow way into
my thought, and some have tried to help   5
or to hurt—ask me what difference
their strongest love or hate has made.

I will listen to what you say.
You and I can turn and look
at the silent river and wait. We know   10
the current is there, hidden; and there
are comings and goings from miles away
that hold the stillness exactly before us.
What the river says, that is what I say.

William Stafford (1914–1993)

A Paraphrase of "Ask Me"   1977

I think my poem can be paraphrased—and that any poem can be paraphrased. But every pass through the material, using other words, would have to be achieved at certain costs, either in momentum, or nuance, or dangerously explicit (and therefore misleading in tone) adjustments. I'll try one such pass through the poem:

> When it's quiet and cold and we have some chance to interchange
> without hurry, confront me if you like with a challenge about

whether I think I have made mistakes in my life—and ask me, if you want to, whether to me my life is actually the sequence of events or exploits others would see. Well, those others tag along in my living, and some of them in fact have played significant roles in the narrative run of my world; they have intended either helping or hurting (but by implication in the way I am saying this you will know that neither effort is conclusive). So—ask me how important their good or bad intentions have been (both intentions get a drastic *leveling* judgment from this cool stating of it all). You, too, will be entering that realm of maybe-help-maybe-hurt, by entering that far into my life by asking this serious question—so: I will stay still and consider. Out there will be the world confronting us both; we will both know we are surrounded by mystery, tremendous things that do not reveal themselves to us. That river, that world—and our lives—all share the depth and stillness of much more significance than our talk, or intentions. There is a steadiness and somehow a solace in knowing that what is around us so greatly surpasses our human concerns.

From "Ask Me"

CHECKLIST: Writing a Paraphrase

☐ **Read the poem closely.** It is important to read it more than once to understand it well.

☐ **Go through it line by line.** Don't skip lines or stanzas or any key details. In your own words, what does each line say?

☐ **Write your paraphrase as prose.**

☐ **State the poem's literal meaning.** Don't worry about deeper meanings.

☐ **Reread your statement to see if you have missed anything important.** Check to see if you have captured the overall significance of the poem along with the details.

TOPICS FOR WRITING ON PARAPHRASING

1. Paraphrase any short poem from Chapter 22, "Poems for Further Reading." Be sure to do a careful line-by-line reading. Include the most vital points and details, and state the poem's main thought or theme without quoting any original passage.

2. In a paragraph, contrast William Stafford's poem with his paraphrase. What does the poem offer that the paraphrase does not? What, then, is the value of the paraphrase?

3. Write a two-page paraphrase of the events described in "'Out, Out—.'" Then take your paraphrase further: summarize the poem's message in a single sentence.

▶ TERMS FOR *review*

Analytic Terms

Verse ▶ This term has two major meanings. It refers to any single line of poetry or to any composition written in separate lines of more or less regular rhythm, in contrast to prose.

Paraphrase ▶ The restatement in one's own words of what one understands a poem to say or suggest. A paraphrase is similar to a summary, although not as brief or simple.

Summary ▶ A brief condensation of the main idea or plot of a work. A summary is similar to a paraphrase, but less detailed.

Subject ▶ The main topic of a work, whatever the work is "about."

Theme ▶ A generally recurring subject or idea noticeably evident in a literary work. Not all subjects in a work can be considered themes, only the central one(s).

Types of Poetry

Lyric poem ▶ A short poem expressing the thoughts and feelings of a single speaker. Often written in the first person, it traditionally has a songlike immediacy and emotional force.

Narrative poem ▶ A poem that tells a story. **Ballads** and **epics** are two common forms of narrative poetry.

Dramatic monologue ▶ A poem written as a speech made by a character at some decisive moment. The speaker is usually addressing a silent listener.

Didactic poem ▶ A poem intended to teach a moral lesson or impart a body of knowledge.

10 LISTENING TO A VOICE

What You Will Learn in This Chapter

- To identify the speaker in a poem
- To understand and characterize the tone of a poem
- To define *irony* in its major forms
- To analyze the role of a speaker in a poem

TONE

In old Western movies, when one hombre taunts another, it is customary for the second to drawl, "Smile when you say that, pardner" or "Mister, I don't like your tone of voice." Sometimes in reading a poem, although we can neither see a face nor hear a voice, we can infer the poet's attitude from other evidence.

Like tone of voice, **tone** in literature often conveys an attitude toward the person addressed. Like the manner of a person, the manner of a poem may be friendly or belligerent toward its reader, condescending or respectful. Again like tone of voice, the tone of a poem may tell us how the speaker feels about himself or herself: cocksure or humble, sad or glad. But usually when we ask "What is the tone of a poem?" we mean "What attitude does the poet take toward a theme or a subject?" Is the poet being affectionate, hostile, earnest, playful, sarcastic, or what? We may never be able to know, of course, the poet's personal feelings. All we need know is how to feel when we read the poem.

Strictly speaking, tone isn't an attitude; it is whatever in the poem makes an attitude clear to us: the choice of certain words instead of others, the picking out of certain details. In A. E. Housman's "Loveliest of trees" (Chapter 22), for example, the poet communicates his admiration for a cherry tree's beauty by singling out its white blossoms for attention; had he wanted to show his dislike for the tree, he might have concentrated on its broken branches, birdlime, or snails. To perceive the tone of a poem rightly, we need to read the poem carefully, paying attention to whatever suggestions we find in it.

Theodore Roethke (1908–1963)

My Papa's Waltz   1948

The whiskey on your breath
Could make a small boy dizzy;
But I hung on like death:
Such waltzing was not easy.

We romped until the pans   5
Slid from the kitchen shelf;
My mother's countenance
Could not unfrown itself.

The hand that held my wrist
Was battered on one knuckle;   10
At every step you missed
My right ear scraped a buckle.

You beat time on my head
With a palm caked hard by dirt,
Then waltzed me off to bed   15
Still clinging to your shirt.

    What is the tone of this poem? Most readers find the speaker's attitude
toward his father critical, but nonetheless affectionate. They take this recollection of childhood to be an odd but happy one. Other readers, however, concentrate on other details, such as the father's rough manners and drunkenness.
One reader has written that "Roethke expresses his resentment for his father,
a drunken brute with dirty hands and whiskey breath who carelessly hurt the
child's ear and manhandled him." Although this reader accurately noticed
some of the events in the poem and perceived that there was something desperate in the son's hanging onto the father "like death," he simplifies the tone
of the poem and so misses its humorous side.
    While "My Papa's Waltz" contains the dark elements of manhandling and
drunkenness, the tone remains grotesquely comic. The rollicking rhythms of
the poem underscore Roethke's complex humor—half loving and half cen-
suring of the unwashed, intoxicated father. The humor is further reinforced
by playful rimes such as *dizzy* and *easy*, *knuckle* and *buckle*, as well as the joyful suggestions of the words *waltz*, *waltzing*, and *romped*. The scene itself is
comic, with kitchen pans falling because of the father's roughhousing while
the mother looks on unamused. However much the speaker satirizes the overly
rambunctious father, he does not have the boy identify with the soberly disapproving mother. Not all comedy is comfortable and reassuring. Certainly, this
small boy's family life has its frightening side, but the last line suggests the boy
is *still clinging* to his father with persistent if also complicated love.

Satiric Poetry

"My Papa's Waltz," though it includes lifelike details that aren't pretty, has a tone relatively easy to recognize. So does **satiric poetry**, a kind of comic poetry that generally conveys a message. Usually its tone is one of detached amusement, withering contempt, and implied superiority. In a satiric poem, the poet ridicules some person or persons (or perhaps some type of human behavior), examining the victim by the light of certain principles and implying that the reader, too, ought to feel contempt for the victim.

Stephen Crane (1871–1900)

The Wayfarer   1899

The wayfarer,
Perceiving the pathway to truth,
Was struck with astonishment.
It was thickly grown with weeds.
"Ha," he said,   5
"I see that none has passed here
In a long time."
Later he saw that each weed
Was a singular knife.
"Well," he mumbled at last,   10
"Doubtless there are other roads."

Questions

1. What is Crane's message?
2. How would you characterize the tone of this poem? Disillusioned? Amused?

A Spectrum of Tones

In some poems the poet's attitude may be plain enough, while in other poems attitudes may be so mingled that it is hard to describe them tersely without doing injustice to the poem. Does Andrew Marvell in "To His Coy Mistress" (Chapter 22) take a serious or playful attitude toward the fact that he and his lady are destined to be food for worms? No one-word answer will suffice. And what of T. S. Eliot's "The Love Song of J. Alfred Prufrock" (Chapter 22)? In his attitude toward his redemption-seeking hero who wades with trousers rolled, Eliot is seriously funny. Such a mingled tone may be seen in the following poem by the wife of a governor of the Massachusetts Bay Colony and the earliest American poet of note. Anne Bradstreet's first book, *The Tenth Muse Lately Sprung Up in America* (1650), had been published in England without her consent. She wrote these lines to preface a second edition:

Anne Bradstreet (1612?–1672)

The Author to Her Book   1678

Thou ill-formed offspring of my feeble brain,
Who after birth did'st by my side remain,
Till snatched from thence by friends, less wise than true,
Who thee abroad exposed to public view;
Made thee in rags, halting, to the press to trudge,   5
Where errors were not lessened, all may judge.
At thy return my blushing was not small,
My rambling brat (in print) should mother call;
I cast thee by as one unfit for light,
Thy visage was so irksome in my sight;   10
Yet being mine own, at length affection would
Thy blemishes amend, if so I could:
I washed thy face, but more defects I saw,
And rubbing off a spot, still made a flaw.
I stretched thy joints to make thee even feet,   15
Yet still thou run'st more hobbling than is meet;
In better dress to trim thee was my mind,
But nought save homespun cloth in the house I find.
In this array, 'mongst vulgars may'st thou roam;
In critics' hands beware thou dost not come;   20
And take thy way where yet thou are not known.
If for thy Father asked, say thou had'st none;
And for thy Mother, she alas is poor,
Which caused her thus to send thee out of door.

In the author's comparison of her book to an illegitimate ragamuffin, we may be struck by the details of scrubbing and dressing a child: details that might well occur to a mother who had scrubbed and dressed many. As she might feel toward such a child, so she feels toward her book. She starts by deploring it, but, as the poem goes on, cannot deny it her affection. Humor enters (as in the pun in line 15). She must dress the creature in *homespun cloth*, something both crude and serviceable. By the end of her poem, Bradstreet seems to regard her book-child with tenderness, amusement, and a certain indulgent awareness of its faults. To read this poem is to sense its mingling of several attitudes. A poet can be merry and in earnest at the same time.

Walt Whitman (1819–1892)

To a Locomotive in Winter   1881

Thee for my recitative,
Thee in the driving storm even as now, the snow, the winter-day
    declining,

Thee in thy panoply,° thy measur'd dual throbbing and thy beat   *suit of armor*
   convulsive,
Thy black cylindric body, golden brass and silvery steel,
Thy ponderous side-bars, parallel and connecting rods, gyrating,   5
   shuttling at thy sides,
Thy metrical, now swelling pant and roar, now tapering in the
   distance,
Thy great protruding head-light fix'd in front,
Thy long, pale, floating vapor-pennants, tinged with delicate purple,
The dense and murky clouds out-belching from thy smoke-stack,
Thy knitted frame, thy springs and valves, the tremulous twinkle of   10
   thy wheels,
Thy train of cars behind, obedient, merrily following,
Through gale or calm, now swift, now slack, yet steadily careering;
Type of the modern—emblem of motion and power—pulse of the
   continent,
For once come serve the Muse and merge in verse, even as here I
   see thee,
With storm and buffeting gusts of wind and falling snow,   15
By day thy warning ringing bell to sound its notes,
By night thy silent signal lamps to swing.

Fierce-throated beauty!
Roll through my chant with all thy lawless music, thy swinging
   lamps at night,
Thy madly-whistled laughter, echoing, rumbling like an earth-quake,   20
   rousing all,
Law of thyself complete, thine own track firmly holding,
(No sweetness debonair of tearful harp or glib piano thine,)
Thy trills of shrieks by rocks and hills return'd,
Launch'd o'er the prairies wide, across the lakes,
To the free skies unpent and glad and strong.   25

Emily Dickinson   (1830–1886)

I like to see it lap the Miles   (about 1862)

I like to see it lap the Miles –
And lick the Valleys up –
And stop to feed itself at Tanks –
And then – prodigious step

Around a Pile of Mountains –   5
And supercilious peer
In Shanties – by the sides of Roads –
And then a Quarry pare

To fit its Ribs
And crawl between   10
Complaining all the while
In horrid – hooting stanza –
Then chase itself down Hill –

And neigh like Boanerges –
Then – punctual as a Star   15
Stop – docile and omnipotent
At its own stable door–

Questions

1. What differences in tone do you find between Whitman's and Dickinson's poems?
   Point out whatever in each poem contributes to these differences.

2. "Boanerges" in Dickinson's last stanza means "sons of thunder," a name given by
   Jesus to the disciples John and James (see Mark 3:17). How far should the reader
   work out the particulars of this comparison? Does it make the tone of the poem
   serious?

3. In Whitman's opening line, what is a "recitative"? What other specialized terms
   from the vocabulary of music and poetry does each poem contain? How do they
   help underscore Whitman's theme?

4. Poets and songwriters probably have regarded the locomotive with more affection
   than they have shown most other machines. Why do you suppose this is so? Can
   you think of any other poems or songs as examples?

5. What do these two poems tell you about locomotives that you would not be likely
   to find in a technical book on railroading?

6. Are the subjects of the two poems identical? Discuss.

Weldon Kees (1914–1955)

For My Daughter   1940

Looking into my daughter's eyes I read
Beneath the innocence of morning flesh
Concealed, hintings of death she does not heed.
Coldest of winds have blown this hair, and mesh
Of seaweed snarled these miniatures of hands;   5
The night's slow poison, tolerant and bland,
Has moved her blood. Parched years that I have seen
That may be hers appear: foul, lingering
Death in certain war, the slim legs green.
Or, fed on hate, she relishes the sting   10
Of others' agony; perhaps the cruel
Bride of a syphilitic or a fool.
These speculations sour in the sun.
I have no daughter. I desire none.

Questions

1. How does the last line of this sonnet affect the meaning of the poem?
2. "For My Daughter" was first published in 1940. What considerations might a potential American parent have felt at that time? Are these historical concerns mirrored in the poem?
3. Donald Justice has said that "Kees is one of the bitterest poets in history." Is bitterness the only attitude the speaker reveals in this poem?

THE SPEAKER IN THE POEM

The tone of a poem, we said, is like tone of voice in that both communicate feelings. Still, this comparison raises a question: when we read a poem, whose "voice" speaks to us?

"The poet's" is one possible answer; and in the case of many a poem that answer may be right. Reading Anne Bradstreet's "The Author to Her Book," we can be reasonably sure that the poet speaks of her very own book, and of her own experiences. In order to read a poem, we seldom need to read a poet's biography; but in truth there are certain poems whose full effect depends upon our knowing at least a fact or two of the poet's life. Here is one such poem.

Natasha Trethewey (b. 1966)

White Lies

2000

The lies I could tell,
when I was growing up
light-bright, near-white,
high-yellow, red-boned
in a black place,   5
were just white lies.

I could easily tell the white folks
that we lived uptown,
not in that pink and green
shanty-fied shotgun section   10
along the tracks. I could act
like my homemade dresses
came straight out the window
of Maison Blanche. I could even
keep quiet, quiet as kept,   15
like the time a white girl said
(squeezing my hand), *Now*
we have three of us in this class.

But I paid for it every time
Mama found out.   20

She laid her hands on me,
then washed out my mouth
with Ivory soap. *This
is to purify*, she said,
and cleanse your lying tongue.   25
Believing her, I swallowed suds
thinking they'd work
from the inside out.

Through its pattern of vivid color imagery, Trethewey's poem tells of a black child light enough to "pass for white" in a society that was still extremely race-sensitive. But knowing the author's family background gives us a deeper insight into the levels of meaning in the poem. Trethewey was born in Mississippi in 1966, at a time when her parents' interracial marriage was a criminal act in that state. On her birth certificate, her mother's race was given as "colored"; in the box intended to record the race of her father—who was white and had been born in Nova Scotia—appeared the word "Canadian" (although her parents divorced before she began grade school, she remained extremely close to both of them). Trethewey has said of her birth certificate: "Something is left out of the official record that way. The irony isn't lost on me. Even in documenting myself as a person there is a little fiction." "White Lies" succeeds admirably on its own, but these biographical details allow us to read it as an even more complex meditation on issues of racial definition and personal identity in America.

Persona

Most of us can tell the difference between a person we meet in life and a person we meet in a work of art. And yet, in reading poems, we are liable to temptation. When the poet says "I," we may want to assume that he or she is making a personal statement. But reflect: do all poems have to be personal? Here is a brief poem inscribed on the tombstone of an infant in Burial Hill Cemetery, Plymouth, Massachusetts:

Since I have been so quickly done for,
I wonder what I was begun for.

We do not know who wrote those lines, but it is clear that the poet was not a short-lived infant writing from personal experience. In some poems, the speaker is obviously a **persona**, or fictitious character: not the poet, but the poet's creation. As a grown man, William Blake, a skilled professional engraver, wrote a poem in the voice of a boy, an illiterate chimney sweeper. (The poem appears later in this chapter.)

Let's consider a poem spoken not by a poet, but by a persona—in this case a mysterious one. Edwin Arlington Robinson's "Luke Havergal" is a dramatic monologue, but the identity of the speaker is never clearly stated. In 1905, upon first reading the poem in Robinson's *The Children of the Night*

(1897), President Theodore Roosevelt was so moved that he wrote an essay about the book that made the author famous. Roosevelt, however, admitted that he found the musically seductive poem difficult. "I am not sure I understand 'Luke Havergal,'" he wrote, "but I am entirely sure I like it." Possibly what most puzzled our twenty-sixth president was who was speaking in the poem. How much does Robinson let us know about the voice and the person it addresses?

Edwin Arlington Robinson (1869–1935)

Luke Havergal

1897

Go to the western gate, Luke Havergal,
There where the vines cling crimson on the wall,
And in the twilight wait for what will come.
The leaves will whisper there of her, and some,
Like flying words, will strike you as they fall;   5
But go, and if you listen she will call.
Go to the western gate, Luke Havergal—
Luke Havergal.

No, there is not a dawn in eastern skies
To rift the fiery night that's in your eyes;   10
But there, where western glooms are gathering,
The dark will end the dark, if anything:
God slays Himself with every leaf that flies,
And hell is more than half of paradise.
No, there is not a dawn in eastern skies—   15
In eastern skies.

Out of a grave I come to tell you this,
Out of a grave I come to quench the kiss
That flames upon your forehead with a glow
That blinds you to the way that you must go.   20
Yes, there is yet one way to where she is,
Bitter, but one that faith may never miss.
Out of a grave I come to tell you this—
To tell you this.

There is the western gate, Luke Havergal,   25
There are the crimson leaves upon the wall.
Go, for the winds are tearing them away,—
Nor think to riddle the dead words they say,
Nor any more to feel them as they fall;
But go, and if you trust her she will call.   30
There is the western gate, Luke Havergal—
Luke Havergal.

Questions

1. Who is the speaker of the poem? What specific details does the author reveal about the speaker?
2. What does the speaker ask Luke Havergal to do?
3. What do you understand "the western gate" to be?
4. Would you advise Luke Havergal to follow the speaker's advice? Why or why not?

No literary law decrees that the speaker in a poem even has to be human. Good poems have been uttered by clouds, pebbles, clocks, and animals. Here is a comic poem spoken by man's best friend, a dog.

Anonymous

Dog Haiku   2001

Today I sniffed
Many dog behinds—I celebrate
By kissing your face.

*

I sound the alarm!
Garbage man—come to kill us all—   5
Look! Look! Look! Look! Look!

*

How do I love thee?
The ways are numberless as
My hairs on the rug.

*

I sound the alarm!
Paper boy—come to kill us all—   10
Look! Look! Look! Look! Look!

*

I am your best friend,
Now, always, and especially
When you are eating.   15

Questions

1. Who is the "I" in the poem? Who is the "you"?
2. Do you recognize the allusion in lines 7–9?
3. What elements create the humorous effect of the poem?

The Art of Imagination

We need not deny that a poet's experience can contribute to a poem or that the emotion in the poem can indeed be the poet's. Still, to write a good poem one has to do more than live and feel. Writing poetry takes skill and imagination—qualities that extensive travel and wide experience do not necessarily give. Emily Dickinson seldom strayed from her family's house and grounds in Amherst, Massachusetts, yet her rimed life studies of a snake, a bee, and a hummingbird contain more poetry than we find in any firsthand description (so far) of the surface of the moon.

Langston Hughes (1902–1967)

Theme for English B   1951
The instructor said,

> Go home and write
> a page tonight.
> And let that page come out of you—
> Then, it will be true.   5

I wonder if it's that simple?
I am twenty-two, colored, born in Winston-Salem.
I went to school there, then Durham, then here
to this college on the hill above Harlem.
I am the only colored student in my class.   10
The steps from the hill lead down into Harlem,
through a park, then I cross St. Nicholas,
Eighth Avenue, Seventh, and I come to the Y,
the Harlem Branch Y, where I take the elevator
up to my room, sit down, and write this page: 15

It's not easy to know what is true for you or me
at twenty-two, my age. But I guess I'm what
I feel and see and hear, Harlem, I hear you:
hear you, hear me—we two—you, me, talk on this page.
(I hear New York, too.) Me—who?   20
Well, I like to eat, sleep, drink, and be in love.
I like to work, read, learn, and understand life.
I like a pipe for a Christmas present,
or records—Bessie, bop, or Bach.
I guess being colored doesn't make me *not* like   25
the same things other folks like who are other races.
So will my page be colored that I write?
Being me, it will not be white.
But it will be
a part of you, instructor.   30
You are white—
yet a part of me, as I am a part of you.
That's American.

Sometimes perhaps you don't want to be a part of me.
Nor do I often want to be a part of you.   35
But we are, that's true!
As I learn from you,
I guess you learn from me—
although you're older—and white—
and somewhat more free.   40
This is my page for English B.

THEME FOR ENGLISH B. 9 *college on the hill above Harlem:* Columbia University, where
Hughes was briefly a student. (Note, however, that this poem is not autobiographical.
The young speaker is a character invented by the middle-aged author.) 24 *Bessie:* Bes-
sie Smith (1898?–1937) was a popular blues singer often called the "Empress of the
Blues."

Charlotte Mew   (1869–1928)

The Farmer's Bride   1916

Three summers since I chose a maid,
Too young maybe—but more's to do
At harvest-time than bide and woo.
    When us was wed she turned afraid
Of love and me and all things human;   5
Like the shut of a winter's day
Her smile went out, and 'twasn't a woman—
    More like a little frightened fay.°   *elf*
        One night, in the Fall, she runned away.

"Out 'mong the sheep, her be," they said,   10
'Should properly have been abed;
But sure enough she wasn't there
Lying awake with her wide brown stare.
So over seven-acre field and up-along across the down
We chased her, flying like a hare   15
Before our lanterns. To Church-Town
    All in a shiver and a scare
We caught her, fetched her home at last
    And turned the key upon her, fast.

She does the work about the house   20
As well as most, but like a mouse:
    Happy enough to chat and play
    With birds and rabbits and such as they,
    So long as men-folk keep away.
"Not near, not near!" her eyes beseech   25
When one of us comes within reach.

The women say that beasts in stall
Look round like children at her call.
I've hardly heard her speak at all.

Shy as a leveret,° swift as he,   hare   30
Straight and slight as a young larch tree,
Sweet as the first wild violets, she,
To her wild self. But what to me?

The short days shorten and the oaks are brown,
    The blue smoke rises to the low gray sky,   35
One leaf in the still air falls slowly down,
    A magpie's spotted feathers lie
On the black earth spread white with rime,°   frost
The berries redden up to Christmas-time.
    What's Christmas-time without there be   40
Some other in the house than we!

    She sleeps up in the attic there
Alone, poor maid. 'Tis but a stair
Betwixt us. Oh! my God! the down,
The soft young down of her, the brown,   45
The brown of her—her eyes, her hair, her hair!

Questions

1. Who is the speaker of this poem? What do we know about him?
2. What is the farmer's opinion of his bride's behavior? Do you view her actions differently?
3. Why do you think the bride "turned afraid" after the wedding? Find evidence in the text.
4. What do you make of the last few lines? Are the farmer's feelings for his wife more complicated than they first seem?

William Carlos Williams (1883–1963)

The Red Wheelbarrow   1923

so much depends
upon

a red wheel
barrow

glazed with rain   5
water

beside the white
chickens

Experiment: **Reading With and Without Biography**

1. Write a paragraph summing up your initial reactions to "The Red Wheelbarrow."
2. Now write a second paragraph with the benefit of this snippet of biographical information: Inspiration for this poem apparently came to Dr. Williams as he was gazing from the window of a house where one of his patients, a small girl, lay suspended between life and death.[1] How does this information affect your reading of the poem?

IRONY

To see a distinction between the poet and the words of a fictitious character—between Robert Browning and "My Last Duchess"—is to be aware of **irony**: a manner of speaking that implies a discrepancy. If the mask says one thing and we sense that the writer is in fact saying something else, the writer has adopted an **ironic point of view**. No finer illustration exists in English than Jonathan Swift's "A Modest Proposal," an essay in which Swift speaks as an earnest, humorless citizen who sets forth his reasonable plan to aid the Irish poor. The plan is so monstrous no sane reader can assent to it: the poor are to sell their children as meat for the tables of their landlords. From behind his false face, Swift is actually recommending not cannibalism but love and Christian charity.

A poem is often made complicated and more interesting by another kind of irony. **Verbal irony** occurs whenever words say one thing but mean something else, usually the opposite. The word *love* means *hate* here: "I just *love* to stay home and surf the Web on a Saturday night!"

Sarcasm

When verbal irony is conspicuously bitter, heavy-handed, and mocking, it is defined as **sarcasm**: "Oh, he's the biggest spender in the world, all right!" (The sarcasm, if that statement were spoken, would be underscored by the speaker's tone of voice.) A famous instance of sarcasm occurs in Shakespeare's *Julius Caesar* in Mark Antony's oration over the body of the slain Caesar: "Brutus is an honorable man." Antony repeats this line until the enraged populace begins shouting exactly what he means to call Brutus and the other conspirators: traitors, villains, murderers. We had best be alert for irony on the printed page, for if we miss it, our interpretations of a poem may go wild.

Robert Creeley (1926–2005)

Oh No   1959

If you wander far enough
you will come to it
and when you get there
they will give you a place to sit

---

[1]This account, from the director of the public library in Williams's native Rutherford, New Jersey, is given by Geri M. Rhodes in "The Paterson Metaphor in William Carlos Williams's *Paterson*," master's thesis, Tufts University, 1965.

for yourself only, in a nice chair,   5
and all your friends will be there
with smiles on their faces
and they will likewise all have places.

This poem is rich in verbal irony. The title helps point out that between the speaker's words and attitude lie deep differences. In line 2, what is *it*? Old age? The wandering suggests a conventional metaphor: the journey of life. Is *it* literally a rest home for "senior citizens," or perhaps some naïve popular concept of heaven (such as we meet in comic strips: harps, angels with hoops for halos) in which the saved all sit around in a ring, smugly congratulating one another? We can't be sure, but the speaker's attitude toward this final sitting-place is definite. It is a place for the selfish, as we infer from the phrase *for yourself only*. And *smiles on their faces* may hint that the smiles are unchanging and forced. There is a difference between saying "They had smiles on their faces" and "They smiled": the latter suggests that the smiles came from within. The word *nice* is to be regarded with distrust. If we see through this speaker, as Creeley implies we can, we realize that, while pretending to be sweet-talking us into a seat, actually he is revealing the horror of a little hell. And the title is the poet's reaction to it (or the speaker's unironic, straightforward one): "Oh no! Not *that*!"

Dramatic Irony

Dramatic irony, like verbal irony, contains an element of contrast, but it usually refers to a situation in a play wherein a character whose knowledge is limited says, does, or encounters something of greater significance than he or she knows. We, the spectators, realize the meaning of this speech or action, for the playwright has afforded us superior knowledge. In Sophocles's *Oedipus the King*, when Oedipus vows to punish whoever has brought down a plague upon the city of Thebes, we know—as he does not—that the man he would punish is himself. The situation of Oedipus also contains **cosmic irony**, or **irony of fate**: some Fate with a grim sense of humor seems cruelly to trick a human being. Cosmic irony clearly exists in poems in which fate or the Fates are personified and seen as hostile.

To sum up: the effect of irony depends on the reader's noticing some incongruity or discrepancy between two things. In *verbal irony*, there is a contrast between the speaker's words and meaning; in an *ironic point of view*, between the writer's attitude and what is spoken by a fictitious character; in *dramatic irony*, between the limited knowledge of a character and the fuller knowledge of the reader or spectator; in *cosmic irony*, between a character's position or aspiration and the treatment he or she receives at the hands of Fate. Although, in the work of an inept poet, irony can be crude and obvious sarcasm, it is invaluable to a poet of more complicated mind, who imagines more than one perspective.

W. H. Auden (1907–1973)

The Unknown Citizen   1940

(To JS/07/M/378
This Marble Monument Is Erected by the State)

He was found by the Bureau of Statistics to be
One against whom there was no official complaint,
And all the reports on his conduct agree
That, in the modern sense of an old-fashioned word, he was a saint,
For in everything he did he served the Greater Community.   5
Except for the War till the day he retired
He worked in a factory and never got fired,
But satisfied his employers, Fudge Motors Inc.
Yet he wasn't a scab or odd in his views,
For his Union reports that he paid his dues,   10
(Our report on his Union shows it was sound)
And our Social Psychology workers found
That he was popular with his mates and liked a drink.
The Press are convinced that he bought a paper every day
And that his reactions to advertisements were normal in every way.   15
Policies taken out in his name prove that he was fully insured,
And his Health-card shows he was once in hospital but left it cured.
Both Producers Research and High-Grade Living declare
He was fully sensible to the advantages of the Installment Plan
And had everything necessary to the Modern Man,   20
A phonograph, a radio, a car and a frigidaire.
Our researchers into Public Opinion are content
That he held the proper opinions for the time of year;
When there was peace, he was for peace; when there was war, he went.
He was married and added five children to the population,   25
Which our Eugenist says was the right number for a parent of his
        generation,
And our teachers report that he never interfered with their education.
Was he free? Was he happy? The question is absurd:
Had anything been wrong, we should certainly have heard.

Questions

1. Read the two-line epitaph at the beginning of the poem as carefully as you read what follows. How does the epitaph help establish the voice by which the rest of the poem is spoken?
2. Who is speaking?
3. What ironic discrepancies do you find between the speaker's attitude toward the subject and that of the poet himself? By what is the poet's attitude made clear?

4. In the phrase "The Unknown Soldier" (of which "The Unknown Citizen" reminds us), what does the word *unknown* mean? What does it mean in the title of Auden's poem?
5. What tendencies in our civilization does Auden satirize?
6. How would you expect the speaker to define a Modern Man, if an iPod, a radio, a car, and a refrigerator are "everything" a Modern Man needs?

Sharon Olds (b. 1942)

Rite of Passage   1983

As the guests arrive at my son's party
they gather in the living room—
short men, men in first grade
with smooth jaws and chins.
Hands in pockets, they stand around   5
jostling, jockeying for place, small fights
breaking out and calming. One says to another
How old are you? Six. I'm seven. So?
They eye each other, seeing themselves
tiny in the other's pupils. They clear their   10
throats a lot, a room of small bankers,
they fold their arms and frown. *I could beat you
up*, a seven says to a six,
the dark cake, round and heavy as a
turret, behind them on the table. My son,   15
freckles like specks of nutmeg on his cheeks,
chest narrow as the balsa keel of a
model boat, long hands
cool and thin as the day they guided him
out of me, speaks up as a host   20
for the sake of the group.
We could easily kill a two-year-old,
he says in his clear voice. The other
men agree, they clear their throats
like Generals, they relax and get down to   25
playing war, celebrating my son's life.

Questions

1. What is ironic about the way the speaker describes the first-grade boys at her son's birthday party?
2. What other irony does the author underscore in the last two lines?
3. Does this mother sentimentalize her own son by seeing him as better than the other boys?

Edna St. Vincent Millay (1892–1950)

Second Fig   1920

Safe upon the solid rock the ugly houses stand:
Come and see my shining palace built upon the sand!

Question

Do you think the author is making fun of the speaker's attitude or agreeing with it?

Exercise: Detecting Irony

Point out the kinds of irony that occur in "The Workbox."

Thomas Hardy (1840–1928)

The Workbox   1914

"See, here's the workbox, little wife,
    That I made of polished oak."
He was a joiner,° of village life;   *carpenter*
    She came of borough folk.

He holds the present up to her   5
    As with a smile she nears
And answers to the profferer,
    "'Twill last all my sewing years!"

"I warrant it will. And longer too.
    'Tis a scantling that I got   10
Off poor John Wayward's coffin, who
    Died of they knew not what.

"The shingled pattern that seems to cease
    Against your box's rim
Continues right on in the piece   15
    That's underground with him.

"And while I worked it made me think
    Of timber's varied doom:
One inch where people eat and drink,
    The next inch in a tomb.   20

"But why do you look so white, my dear,
    And turn aside your face?
You knew not that good lad, I fear,
    Though he came from your native place?"

"How could I know that good young man,   25
    Though he came from my native town,
When he must have left far earlier than
    I was a woman grown?"

"Ah, no. I should have understood!
    It shocked you that I gave   30
To you one end of a piece of wood
    Whose other is in a grave?"

"Don't, dear, despise my intellect,
    Mere accidental things
Of that sort never have effect   35
    On my imaginings."

Yet still her lips were limp and wan,
    Her face still held aside,
As if she had known not only John,
    But known of what he died.   40

FOR REVIEW AND FURTHER STUDY

Amy Uyematsu   (b. 1947)

Deliberate   1992

So by sixteen we move in packs
learn to strut and slide
in deliberate lowdown rhythm
talk in a syn/co/pa/ted beat
because we want so bad   5
to be cool, never to be mistaken
for white, even when we leave
these rowdier L.A. streets—
remember how we paint our eyes
like gangsters   10
flash our legs in nylons
sassy black high heels
or two inch zippered boots
stack them by the door at night
next to Daddy's muddy gardening shoes.   15

Questions

1. At what point in the poem does the speaker's adult voice start to imitate her
   teenage Asian street voice?
2. How does the image of the last line change the tone of the poem?

Exercise: **Telling Tone**

Here are two radically different poems on a similar subject. Try stating the theme of each poem in your own words. How is the tone (the speaker's attitude) different in the two poems?

Richard Lovelace   (1618–1658)

To Lucasta   1649

> *On Going to the Wars*

Tell me not, Sweet, I am unkind
   That from the nunnery
Of thy chaste breast and quiet mind,
   To war and arms I fly.

True, a new mistress now I chase,   5
   The first foe in the field;
And with a stronger faith embrace
   A sword, a horse, a shield.

Yet this inconstancy is such
   As you too shall adore;   10
I could not love thee, Dear, so much,
   Loved I not Honor more.

Wilfred Owen   (1893–1918)

Dulce et Decorum Est   1920

Bent double, like old beggars under sacks,
Knock-kneed, coughing like hags, we cursed through sludge,
Till on the haunting flares we turned our backs
And towards our distant rest began to trudge.
Men marched asleep. Many had lost their boots   5
But limped on, blood-shod. All went lame; all blind;
Drunk with fatigue; deaf even to the hoots
Of tired, outstripped Five-Nines that dropped behind.

Gas! GAS! Quick, boys!—An ecstasy of fumbling,
Fitting the clumsy helmets just in time;   10
But someone still was yelling out and stumbling,
And flound'ring like a man in fire or lime . . .
Dim, through the misty panes and thick green light,
As under a green sea, I saw him drowning.

In all my dreams, before my helpless sight,   15
He plunges at me, guttering, choking, drowning.

If in some smothering dreams you too could pace
Behind the wagon that we flung him in,
And watch the white eyes writhing in his face,
His hanging face, like a devil's sick of sin;   20
If you could hear, at every jolt, the blood
Come gargling from the froth-corrupted lungs,
Obscene as cancer, bitter as the cud
Of vile, incurable sores on innocent tongues,—
My friend, you would not tell with such high zest   25
To children ardent for some desperate glory,
The old Lie: Dulce et decorum est
Pro patria mori.

DULCE ET DECORUM EST. Owen's title is the beginning of the famous Latin quotation from the
Roman poet Horace with which he ends this poem: "*Dulce et decorum est pro patria mori.*" It is
translated as "It is sweet and proper to die for your country." 8 *Five-Nines:* German howitzers
often used to shoot poison gas shells. 17 *you too:* Some manuscript versions of this poem carry the
dedication "To Jessie Pope" (a writer of patriotic verse) or "To a certain Poetess."

■ WRITING *effectively*

THINKING ABOUT TONE

To understand the tone of a poem, we need to listen to the words, as we might
listen to an actual conversation. The key is to hear not only *what* is being said
but also *how* it is being said. Does the speaker sound noticeably surprised, angry, nostalgic, or tender? Begin with an obvious but often overlooked question:
who is speaking? Don't assume that every poem is spoken by its author.

- **Look for the ways—large and small—in which the speaker reveals
  aspects of his or her character.** Attitudes may be revealed directly
  or indirectly. Often, emotions must be intuited. The details a poet
  chooses to convey can reveal much about a speaker's stance toward
  his or her subject matter.
- **Consider also how the speaker addresses the listener.** Again, listen
  to the sound of the poem as you would listen to the sound of someone's voice—is it shrill, or soothing, or sarcastic?
- **Look for an obvious difference between the speaker's attitude and
  your own honest reaction toward what is happening in the poem.**
  If the gap between the two responses is wide, the poem may be taken
  as ironic.

■ **Remember that many poets strive toward understatement, writing matter-of-factly about matters of intense sorrow, horror, or joy.** In poems, as in conversation, understatement can be a powerful tool, more convincing—and often more moving—than hyperbole.

CHECKLIST: Writing About Tone

☐ Who is speaking the poem?

☐ Is the narrator's voice close to the poet's, or is it the voice of a fictional or historical person?

☐ How does the speaker address the listener?

☐ Does the poem directly reveal an emotion or attitude?

☐ Does it indirectly reveal any attitudes or emotions?

☐ Does your reaction to what is happening in the poem differ widely from that of the speaker? If so, what does that difference suggest? Is the poem in some way ironic?

☐ What adjectives would best describe the poem's tone?

TOPICS FOR WRITING ON TONE

1. Describe the tone of W. H. Auden's "The Unknown Citizen," quoting as necessary to back up your argument. How does the poem's tone contribute to its meaning?

2. Write an analysis of Thomas Hardy's "The Workbox," focusing on what the poem leaves unsaid.

3. In an essay of 250 to 500 words, compare and contrast the tone of two poems on a similar subject. You might examine how Walt Whitman and Emily Dickinson treat the subject of locomotives, or how Richard Lovelace and Wilfred Owen write about war. (For advice on writing about poetry by the method of comparison and contrast, see the chapter "Writing About Literature.")

4. Look closely at any poem in this chapter. Going through it line by line, make a list of the sensory details the poem provides. Now write briefly about how those details combine to create a particular tone. Two choices are Theodore Roethke's "My Papa's Waltz" and Sharon Olds's "Rite of Passage."

▶ TERMS FOR *review*

Tone ▶ The mood or manner of expression of a literary work, which conveys an attitude toward the work's subject, which may be playful, sarcastic, ironic, sad, solemn, or any other possible attitude. Tone helps to establish the reader's relationship to the characters or ideas presented in the work.

Satiric poetry ▶ Poetry that blends criticism with humor to convey a message, usually through the use of irony and a tone of detached amusement, withering contempt, and implied superiority.

Persona ▶ Latin for "mask." A fictitious character created by an author to be the speaker of a literary work.

Types of Irony

Irony ▶ In language, a discrepancy between what is said and what is meant. In life, a discrepancy between what is expected and what occurs.

Verbal irony ▶ A mode of expression in which the speaker or writer says the opposite of what is really meant, such as saying "Great story!" in response to a boring, pointless anecdote.

Sarcasm ▶ A style of bitter irony intended to hurt or mock its target.

Dramatic irony ▶ A situation in which the larger implications of a character's words, actions, or situation are unrealized by that character but seen by the author and the reader or audience.

Cosmic irony ▶ The contrast between a character's position or aspiration and the treatment he or she receives at the hands of a seemingly hostile fate; also called **irony of fate**.

11

WORDS

What You Will Learn in This Chapter

- To define *diction*
- To recognize and define the standard *levels of diction*
- To recognize and explain allusions in a poem
- To analyze the role of diction in a poem

LITERAL MEANING: WHAT A POEM SAYS FIRST

Although successful as a painter, Edgar Degas found poetry discouragingly hard to write. To his friend, the poet Stéphane Mallarmé, he complained, "What a business! My whole day gone on a blasted sonnet, without getting an inch further . . . and it isn't ideas I'm short of . . . I'm full of them, I've got too many. . . ."

"But Degas," said Mallarmé, "you can't make a poem with ideas—you make it with *words*!"

Like the celebrated painter, some people assume that all it takes to make a poem is a bright idea. Poems state ideas, to be sure, and sometimes the ideas are invaluable; and yet the most impressive idea in the world will not make a poem, unless its words are selected and arranged with loving art. Some poets take great pains to find the right word. Unable to fill a two-syllable gap in an unfinished line that went, "The seal's wide _____ gaze toward Paradise," Hart Crane paged through an unabridged dictionary. When he reached S, he found the object of his quest in *spindrift*: "spray skimmed from the sea by a strong wind." The word is exact and memorable.

In reading a poem, some people assume that its words can be skipped over rapidly, and they try to leap at once to the poem's general theme. It is as if they fear being thought clods unless they can find huge ideas in the poem (whether or not there are any). Such readers often ignore the literal meanings of words: the ordinary, matter-of-fact sense to be found in a dictionary. (As you will see in the next chapter, "Saying and Suggesting," words possess not only dictionary meanings—denotations—but also many associations and suggestions—connotations.) Consider the following poem and see what you make of it.

William Carlos Williams (1883–1963)

This Is Just to Say   1934

I have eaten
the plums
that were in
the icebox

and which   5
you were probably
saving
for breakfast

Forgive me
they were delicious   10
so sweet
and so cold

Some readers distrust a poem so simple and candid. They think, "What's wrong with me? There has to be more to it than this!" But poems seldom are puzzles in need of solutions. We can begin by accepting the poet's statements, without suspecting the poet of trying to hoodwink us. On later reflection, of course, we might possibly decide that the poet is playfully teasing or being ironic; but Williams gives us no reason to think that. There seems no need to look beyond the literal sense of his words, no profit in speculating that the plums symbolize worldly joys and that the icebox stands for the universe. Clearly, a reader who held such a grand theory would have overlooked (in eagerness to find a significant idea) the plain truth that the poet makes clear to us: that ice-cold plums are a joy to taste.

To be sure, Williams's small poem is simpler than most poems are; and yet in reading any poem, no matter how complicated, you will do well to reach slowly and reluctantly for a theory to explain it by. To find the general theme of a poem, you first need to pay attention to its words. Recall Yeats's "The Lake Isle of Innisfree" (Chapter 9), a poem that makes a statement—crudely summed up, "I yearn to leave the city and retreat to a place of ideal peace and happiness." And yet before we can realize this theme, we have to notice details: nine bean rows, a glade loud with bees, "lake water lapping with low sounds by the shore," the gray of a pavement. These details and not some abstract remark make clear what the poem is saying: that the city is drab, while the island hideaway is sublimely beautiful.

DICTION

If a poem says *daffodils* instead of *plant life* or *diaper years* instead of *infancy*, we call its **diction**, or choice of words, **concrete** rather than **abstract**. Concrete words refer to what we can immediately perceive with our senses: *dog*, *actor*, *chemical*, or particular individuals who belong to those general classes: *Bonzo the fox terrier, Ryan Gosling, hydrogen sulfate*. Abstract words express ideas or concepts: *love, time, truth*. In abstracting, we leave out some characteristics found in each individual, and instead observe a quality common to many. The word *beauty*, for instance, denotes what may be observed in numerous persons, places, and things.

Ezra Pound gave a famous piece of advice to his fellow poets: "Go in fear of abstractions." This is not to say that a poet cannot employ abstract words, nor that all poems have to be about physical things. Much of T. S. Eliot's *Four Quartets* is concerned with time, eternity, history, language, reality, and other things that cannot be physically handled. But Eliot, however high he may soar for a larger view, keeps returning to earth. He makes us aware of *things*.

Here is a famous poem that groups together some very specific things: certain ships and their cargoes.

John Masefield (1878–1967)

Cargoes 1902

Quinquireme of Nineveh from distant Ophir,
Rowing home to haven in sunny Palestine,
With a cargo of ivory,
And apes and peacocks,
Sandalwood, cedarwood, and sweet white wine. 5

Stately Spanish galleon coming from the Isthmus,
Dipping through the Tropics by the palm-green shores,
With a cargo of diamonds,
Emeralds, amethysts,
Topazes, and cinnamon, and gold moidores. 10

Dirty British coaster with a salt-caked smoke stack,
Butting through the Channel in the mad March days,
With a cargo of Tyne coal,
Road-rails, pig-lead,
Firewood, iron-ware, and cheap tin trays. 15

CARGOES. 1 *Quinquireme*: ancient Assyrian vessel propelled by sails and oars. *Ninevah*: capital of ancient Assyrian empire. *Ophir*: a vanished place, possibly in Arabia; according to the Bible, King Solomon sent expeditions there for its celebrated pure gold, and also for ivory, apes, peacocks, and other luxury items. (See I Kings 9–10.) 10 *Moidores*: Portuguese coins. 13 *Tyne*: a river in Scotland.

Questions

1. Does this poem use elevated language or everyday words?
2. Pick out some examples of unusual words in this poem.

John Donne (1572–1631)

Batter my heart, three-personed God, for You

(about 1610)

Batter my heart, three-personed God, for You
As yet but knock, breathe, shine, and seek to mend.
That I may rise and stand, o'erthrow me, and bend
Your force to break, blow, burn, and make me new.
I, like an usurped town to another due,   5
Labor to admit You, but Oh! to no end.
Reason, Your viceroy in me, me should defend,
But is captived, and proves weak or untrue.
Yet dearly I love You, and would be lovèd fain,
But am betrothed unto Your enemy;   10
Divorce me, untie or break that knot again;
Take me to You, imprison me, for I,
Except You enthrall me, never shall be free,
Nor ever chaste, except You ravish me.

Questions

1. In the last line of this sonnet, to what does Donne compare the onslaught of God's love? Do you think the poem is weakened by the poet's comparing a spiritual experience to something so grossly carnal? Discuss.

2. Explain the seeming contradiction in the last line: in what sense can a ravished person be "chaste"? Explain the seeming contradictions in lines 3–4 and 12–13: how can a person thrown down and destroyed be enabled to "rise and stand"; an imprisoned person be "free"?

3. In lines 5–6 the speaker compares himself to a "usurped town" trying to throw off its conqueror by admitting an army of liberation. Who is the "usurper" in this comparison?

4. Explain the comparison of "Reason" to a "viceroy" (lines 7–8).

5. Sum up in your own words the message of Donne's poem. In stating its theme, did you have to read the poem for literal meanings, figurative comparisons, or both?

THE VALUE OF A DICTIONARY

Use the dictionary. It's better than the critics.

—ELIZABETH BISHOP TO HER STUDENTS

If a poet troubles to seek out the best words available, the least we can do is to find out what the words mean. The dictionary is a firm ally in reading poems; if the poems are more than a century old, it is indispensable. Meanings change. When the Elizabethan poet George Gascoigne wrote, "O Abraham's brats, O brood of blessed seed," the word *brats* implied neither irritation nor contempt. When in the seventeenth century Andrew Marvell imagined two lovers' "vegetable love," he referred to a vegetative or growing love, not one resembling a lettuce. And when Queen Anne, in a famous anecdote, called the just-completed Saint Paul's Cathedral "awful, artificial, and amusing," its architect, Sir Christopher Wren, was overwhelmed with joy and gratitude, for what she had told him was that it was awe-inspiring, artful, and stimulating to contemplate (or *muse* upon).

In reading poetry, there is nothing to be done about the inevitable tendency of language to change except to watch out for it. If you suspect that a word has shifted in meaning over the years, most standard desk dictionaries will be helpful, an unabridged dictionary more helpful still, and most helpful of all the *Oxford English Dictionary (OED)*, which gives, for each definition, successive examples of the word's written use through the past thousand years. You need not feel a grim obligation to keep interrupting a poem in order to rummage in the dictionary; but if the poem is worth reading very closely, you may wish for any aid you can find.

"Every word which is used to express a moral or intellectual fact," said Emerson in his study *Nature*, "if traced to its root, is found to be borrowed from some material appearance. *Right* means straight; *wrong* means twisted. *Spirit* primarily means wind; *transgression*, the crossing of a line; *supercilious*, the raising of an eyebrow." Browse in a dictionary and you will discover such original concretenesses. These are revealed in your dictionary's etymologies, or brief notes on the derivation of words, given in most dictionaries near the beginning of an entry on a word; in some dictionaries, at the end of the entry. Look up *squirrel*, for instance, and you will find it comes from two Greek words meaning "shadow-tail." For another example of a common word that originally contained a poetic metaphor, look up the origin of *daisy*.

Experiment: Use the Dictionary to Read Longfellow's "Aftermath"

The following short poem seems very simple and straightforward, but much of its total effect depends on the reader knowing the literal meanings of several words. The most crucial word is in the title—"aftermath." Most readers today will assume that they know what that word means, but in this poem Longfellow uses it in both its current sense and its original, more literal meaning. Read the poem twice—first without a dictionary, then a second time after looking up the meanings of "aftermath," "fledged," "rowen," and "mead." How does knowing the exact meanings of these words add to both your literal and critical reading of the poem?

Henry Wadsworth Longfellow (1807–1882)

Aftermath   1873

When the summer fields are mown,
When the birds are fledged and flown,
    And the dry leaves strew the path;
With the falling of the snow,
With the cawing of the crow,   5
Once again the fields we mow
    And gather in the aftermath.

Not the sweet, new grass with flowers
In this harvesting of ours;
     Not the upland clover bloom;   10
But the rowen mixed with weeds,
Tangled tufts from marsh and meads,
Where the poppy drops its seeds
     In the silence and the gloom.

Questions

1. How do the etymology and meaning of "aftermath" help explain this poem? (Look the word up in your dictionary.)
2. What is the meaning of "fledged" (line 2) and "rowen" (line 11)?
3. Once you understand the literal meaning of the poem, do you think that Longfellow intended any further significance to it?

Kay Ryan (b. 1945)

That Will to Divest   2000

Action creates
a taste
for itself.
Meaning: once
you've swept   5
the shelves
of spoons
and plates
you kept
for guests,   10
it gets harder
not to also
simplify the larder,
not to dismiss
rooms, not to   15
divest yourself
of all the chairs
but one, not
to test what
singleness can bear,   20
once you've begun.

Questions

1. Look up the word "divest" in a dictionary. What possible meanings do you think the author intends?
2. What is the meaning of "singleness" (line 20)?

Allusion

An **allusion** is an indirect reference to any person, place, or thing—fictitious, historical, or actual. Sometimes, to understand an allusion in a poem, we have to find out something we didn't know before. But usually the poet asks of us only common knowledge. When, in his poem "To Helen," Edgar Allan Poe refers to "the glory that was Greece / And the grandeur that was Rome," he assumes that we have heard of those places. He also expects that we will understand his allusion to the cultural achievements of those ancient nations and perhaps even catch the subtle contrast between those two similar words *glory* and *grandeur*, with its suggestion that, for all its merits, Roman civilization was also more pompous than Greek.

Allusions not only enrich the meaning of a poem, they also save space. In "The Love Song of J. Alfred Prufrock" (Chapter 22), T. S. Eliot, by giving a brief introductory quotation from the speech of a damned soul in Dante's *Inferno*, is able to suggest that his poem will be the confession of a soul in torment, who sees no chance of escape and who feels the need to confide in someone, yet trusts that his secrets will be kept safe.

Often in reading a poem, you will meet a name you don't recognize, on which the meaning of a line (or perhaps a whole poem) seems to depend. In this book, most such unfamiliar references and allusions are glossed or footnoted, but when you venture out on your own in reading poems, you may find yourself needlessly perplexed unless you look up such names, the way you look up any other words. Unless the name is one that the poet made up, you will probably find it in one of the larger desk dictionaries, such as *Merriam-Webster's Collegiate Dictionary* or the *American Heritage Dictionary*. If you don't solve your problem there, try an online search of the word or phrase, as some allusions are quotations from other poems.

Exercise: Catching Allusions

From your knowledge, supplemented by a dictionary or other reference work if need be, explain the allusions in the following poems.

J. V. Cunningham   (1911–1985)

Friend, on this scaffold Thomas More lies dead   1960

Friend, on this scaffold Thomas More lies dead
Who would not cut the Body from the Head.

Samuel Menashe   (1925–2011)

Bread   1985

Thy will be done
By crust and crumb
And loaves left over

The sea is swollen
With the bread I throw   5
Upon the water

Questions

1. Can you identify the two allusions Menashe uses in this poem? (Hint: The first allusion occurs in line 1; the second in lines 5–6).
2. Paraphrase the content of the poem in a few sentences.
3. How do you think these references add meaning to this very short poem?

Carl Sandburg (1878–1967)

Grass   1918

Pile the bodies high at Austerlitz and Waterloo.
Shovel them under and let me work—
   I am the grass; I cover all.

And pile them high at Gettysburg
And pile them high at Ypres and Verdun.   5
Shovel them under and let me work.
Two years, ten years, and passengers ask the conductor:
   What place is this?
   Where are we now?

   I am the grass.   10
   Let me work.

Questions

1. What do the five proper nouns in Sandburg's poem have in common?
2. How much does the reader need to understand about the allusions in "Grass" to appreciate their importance to the literal meaning of the poem?

WORD CHOICE AND WORD ORDER

Even if Samuel Johnson's famous *Dictionary* of 1755 had been as thick as Webster's unabridged, an eighteenth-century poet searching through it for words would have had a narrower choice. For in English literature of the neo-classical period, many poets subscribed to a belief in **poetic diction**: "A system of words," said Dr. Johnson, "refined from the grossness of domestic use." The system admitted into a serious poem only certain words and subjects, excluding others as violations of **decorum** (propriety). Accordingly, such common words as *rat*, *cheese*, *big*, *sneeze*, and *elbow*, although admissible to satire, were thought inconsistent with the loftiness of tragedy, epic, ode, and elegy. Dr. Johnson's biographer, James Boswell, tells how a poet writing an epic reconsidered the word "rats" and instead wrote "the whiskered vermin race." Johnson himself objected to Lady Macbeth's allusion to her "keen knife," saying that "we do not immediately conceive that any crime of importance is to be committed with a knife; or who does not, at last, from the long habit of connecting a knife with sordid offices, feel aversion rather than terror?"

Anglo-Saxon Versus Latinate Diction

When Wordsworth, in his Preface to *Lyrical Ballads*, asserted that "the language really spoken by men," especially by humble rustics, is plainer and more emphatic, and conveys "elementary feelings . . . in a state of greater simplicity," he was, in effect, advocating a new poetic diction. Wordsworth's ideas invited freshness into English poetry and, by admitting words that neoclassical poets would have called "low" ("His poor old *ankles* swell"), helped rid poets of the fear of being thought foolish for mentioning a commonplace.

This theory of the superiority of rural diction was, as Coleridge pointed out, hard to adhere to, and, in practice, Wordsworth was occasionally to write a language as Latinate and citified as these lines on yew trees:

> Huge trunks!—and each particular trunk a growth
> Of intertwisted fibers serpentine
> Up-coiling, and inveterately convolved . . .

Language so Latinate sounds pedantic to us, especially the phrase *inveterately convolved*. In fact, some poets, notably Gerard Manley Hopkins, have subscribed to the view that English words derived from Anglo-Saxon (Old English) have more force and flavor than their Latin equivalents. *Kingly*, one may feel, has more power than *regal*. One argument for this view is that so many words of Old English origin—*man*, *wife*, *child*, *house*, *eat*, *drink*, *sleep*—are basic to our living speech. Yet Latinate diction is not necessarily elevated. We use Latinate words every day, such as *station*, *office*, *order*, and *human*. None of these terms seem "inveterately convolved." Word choice is a subtle and flexible art.

Levels of Diction

When E. E. Cummings begins a poem, "mr youse needn't be so spry/concernin questions arty," we recognize another kind of diction available to poetry: **low diction** (or **vulgate**, speech not much affected by schooling). Handbooks of grammar sometimes distinguish various **levels of diction**. A sort of ladder is imagined, on whose rungs words, phrases, and sentences may be ranked in an ascending order of formality, from the curses of an illiterate thug to the commencement-day address of a doctor of divinity. These levels range from vulgate through **colloquial** (the casual conversation or informal writing of literate people) and **middle diction** (or **general English**, most literate speech and writing, more studied than colloquial but not pretentious), up to **high diction** (or **formal English**, the impersonal language of educated persons, usually only written, possibly spoken on dignified occasions). Recently, however, lexicographers have been shunning such labels.

The designation *colloquial* was expelled from *Webster's Third New International Dictionary* on the grounds that "it is impossible to know whether a word out of context is colloquial or not" and that the diction of Americans nowadays is more fluid than the labels suggest. Aware that we are being unscientific, you may find the labels useful. They may help roughly to describe what happens when, as in the following poem, a poet shifts from one level of usage to another.

Robert Herrick (1591–1674)

Upon Julia's Clothes   1648

Whenas in silks my Julia goes,
Then, then, methinks, how sweetly flows
That liquefaction of her clothes.

Next, when I cast mine eyes and see
That brave vibration each way free,
O how that glittering taketh me!   5

UPON JULIA'S CLOTHES. 3 *liquefaction:* becoming fluid, turning to liquid. 5 *brave:* Herrick uses *brave* in its original sense, meaning excellent or fine.

Even in so short a poem as "Upon Julia's Clothes," we see how a sudden shift in the level of diction can produce a surprising and memorable effect. One word in each stanza—*liquefaction* in the first, *vibration* in the second—stands out from the standard, but not extravagant, language that surrounds it. Try to imagine the entire poem being written in such formal English, in mostly unfamiliar words of several syllables each: the result, in all likelihood, would be merely an oddity, and a turgid one at that. But by using such terms sparingly, Herrick allows them to take on a greater strength and significance through their contrast with the words that surround them. It is *liquefaction* in particular that strikes the reader: like a great catch by an outfielder, it impresses both for its appropriateness in the situation and for its sheer beauty as a demonstration of superior skill. Once we have read the poem, we realize that the effect would be severely compromised, if not ruined, by the substitution of any other word in its place.

Dialect

At present, most poetry in English avoids elaborate literary expressions such as "fleecy care" in favor of more colloquial language. In many English-speaking areas, such as Scotland, there has even been a movement to write poems in regional dialects. (A **dialect** is a particular variety of language spoken by an identifiable regional group or social class of persons.) Dialect poets frequently try to capture the freshness and authenticity of the language spoken in their immediate locale.

Thomas Hardy (1840–1928)

The Ruined Maid   1901

"O 'Melia, my dear, this does everything crown!
Who could have supposed I should meet you in Town?
And whence such fair garments, such prosperi-ty?"—
"O didn't you know I'd been ruined?" said she.

—"You left us in tatters, without shoes or socks,   5
Tired of digging potatoes, and spudding up docks;°   *spading up dockweed*
And now you've gay bracelets and bright feathers three!"
"Yes: that's how we dress when we're ruined," said she.

—"At home in the barton° you said 'thee' and 'thou,'   *farmyard*
And 'thik oon,' and 'theäs oon,' and 't'other'; but now   10
Your talking quite fits 'ee for high compa-ny!"—
"Some polish is gained with one's ruin," said she.

—"Your hands were like paws then, your face blue and bleak
But now I'm bewitched by your delicate cheek,
And your little gloves fit as on any la-dy!"—   15
"We never do work when we're ruined," said she.

—"You used to call home-life a hag-ridden dream,
And you'd sigh, and you'd sock;° but at present you seem   *groan*
To know not of megrims° or melancho-ly!"—   *blues*
"True. One's pretty lively when ruined," said she.   20

—"I wish I had feathers, a fine sweeping gown,
And a delicate face, and could strut about Town!"—
"My dear—a raw country girl, such as you be,
Cannot quite expect that. You ain't ruined," said she.

Questions

1. Where does this dialogue take place? Who are the two speakers?
2. Comment on Hardy's use of the word *ruined*. What is the conventional meaning of the word when applied to a woman? As 'Melia applies it to herself, what is its meaning?
3. Sum up the attitude of each speaker toward the other. What details of the new 'Melia does the first speaker most dwell on? Would you expect Hardy to be so impressed by all these details, or is there, between his view of the characters and their view of themselves, any hint of an ironic discrepancy?
4. In losing her country dialect ("thik oon" and "theäs oon" for "this one" and "that one"), 'Melia is presumed to have gained in sophistication. What does Hardy suggest by her "ain't" in the last line?

Wendy Cope (b. 1945)

Lonely Hearts   1986

Can someone make my simple wish come true?
Male biker seeks female for touring fun.
Do you live in North London? Is it you?

Gay vegetarian whose friends are few,
I'm into music, Shakespeare and the sun.   5
Can someone make my simple wish come true?

Executive in search of something new—
Perhaps bisexual woman, arty, young.
Do you live in North London? Is it you?

Successful, straight and solvent? I am too—   10
Attractive Jewish lady with a son.
Can someone make my simple wish come true?

I'm Libran, inexperienced and blue—
Need slim non-smoker, under twenty-one.
Do you live in North London? Is it you?   15

Please write (with photo) to Box 152.
Who knows where it may lead once we've begun?
Can someone make my simple wish come true?
Do you live in North London? Is it you?

LONELY HEARTS. This poem has a double form: the rhetorical, a series of "lonely heart" personal ads from a newspaper, and metrical, a **villanelle**, a fixed form developed by French courtly poets in imitation of Italian folk song. For other villanelles, see Elizabeth Bishop's "One Art" (Chapter 22) and Dylan Thomas's "Do not go gentle into that good night" (Chapter 17). In the villanelle, the first and the third lines are repeated in a set pattern throughout the poem.

Questions

1. What sort of language does Wendy Cope borrow for this poem?
2. The form of the villanelle requires that the poet end each stanza with one of two repeating lines. What special use does the author make of these mandatory repetitions?
3. How many speakers are there in the poem? Does the author's voice ever enter or is the entire poem spoken by individuals in personal ads?
4. The poem seems to begin satirically. Does the poem ever move beyond the critical, mocking tone typical of satire?

FOR REVIEW AND FURTHER STUDY

E. E. Cummings (1894–1962)

anyone lived in a pretty how town   1940

anyone lived in a pretty how town
(with up so floating many bells down)
spring summer autumn winter
he sang his didn't he danced his did.

Women and men(both little and small)   5
cared for anyone not at all
they sowed their isn't they reaped their same
sun moon stars rain

children guessed(but only a few
and down they forgot as up they grew   10
autumn winter spring summer)
that noone loved him more by more

when by now and tree by leaf
she laughed his joy she cried his grief
bird by snow and stir by still   15
anyone's any was all to her

someones married their everyones
laughed their cryings and did their dance
(sleep wake hope and then)they
said their nevers they slept their dream   20

stars rain sun moon
(and only the snow can begin to explain
how children are apt to forget to remember
with up so floating many bells down)

one day anyone died i guess   25
(and noone stooped to kiss his face)
busy folk buried them side by side
little by little and was by was

all by all and deep by deep
and more by more they dream their sleep   30
noone and anyone earth by april
wish by spirit and if by yes.

Women and men(both dong and ding)
summer autumn winter spring
reaped their sowing and went their came   35
sun moon stars rain

Questions

1. Summarize the story told in this poem. Who are the characters?
2. Rearrange the words in the two opening lines into the order you would expect them usually to follow. What effect does Cummings obtain by his unconventional word order?
3. Another of Cummings's strategies is to use one part of speech as if it were another; for instance, in line 4, *didn't* and *did* ordinarily are verbs, but here they are used as nouns. What other words in the poem perform functions other than their expected ones?

Exercise: Different Kinds of English

Read the following poems and see what kinds of diction and word order you find in them. Which poems are least formal in their language and which most formal? Is there any use of low diction? Any dialect? What does each poem achieve that its own kind of English makes possible?

Anonymous (American oral verse)

Carnation Milk   (about 1900?)

Carnation Milk is the best in the land;
Here I sit with a can in my hand—
No tits to pull, no hay to pitch,
You just punch a hole in the son of a bitch.

CARNATION MILK. "This quatrain is imagined as the caption under a picture of a rugged-looking cowboy seated upon a bale of hay," notes William Harmon in his *Oxford Book of American Light Verse* (New York: Oxford UP, 1979). Possibly the first to print this work was David Ogilvy (1911–1999), who quotes it in his *Confessions of an Advertising Man* (New York: Atheneum, 1963).

Gina Valdés (b. 1943)

English con Salsa   1993

Welcome to ESL 100, English Surely Latinized,
inglés con chile y cilantro, English as American
as Benito Juárez. Welcome, muchachos from Xochicalco,
learn the language of dólares and dolores, of kings
and queens, of Donald Duck and Batman. Holy Toluca!   5
In four months you'll be speaking like George Washington,
in four weeks you can ask, More coffee? In two months
you can say, May I take your order? In one year you
can ask for a raise, cool as the Tuxpan River.

Welcome, muchachas from Teocaltiche, in this class   10
we speak English refrito, English con sal y limón,
English thick as mango juice, English poured from
a clay jug, English tuned like a requinto from Uruapan,

English lighted by Oaxacan dawns, English spiked
with mezcal from Mitla, English with a red cactus   15
flower blooming in its heart.

Welcome, welcome, amigos del sur, bring your Zapotec
tongues, your Nahuatl tones, your patience of pyramids,
your red suns and golden moons, your guardian angels,
your duendes, your patron saints, Santa Tristeza,   20
Santa Alegría, Santo Todolopuede. We will sprinkle
holy water on pronouns, make the sign of the cross
on past participles, jump like fish from Lake Pátzcuaro
on gerunds, pour tequila from Jalisco on future perfects,
say shoes and shit, grab a cool verb and a pollo loco   25
and dance on the walls like chapulines.

When a teacher from La Jolla or a cowboy from Santee
asks you, Do you speak English? You'll answer, Sí,
yes, simón, of course, I love English!
                      And you'll hum
A Mixtec chant that touches la tierra and the heavens.   30

ENGLISH CON SALSA. 3 *Benito Juárez*: Mexican statesman (1806–1872), president of Mexico
in the 1860s and 1870s.

William Wordsworth (1770–1850)

My heart leaps up when I behold   1807

My heart leaps up when I behold
   A rainbow in the sky:
So was it when my life began;
So is it now I am a man;
So be it when I shall grow old,   5
   Or let me die!
The Child is father of the Man;
And I could wish my days to be
Bound each to each by natural piety.

William Wordsworth (1770–1850)

Mutability   1822

From low to high doth dissolution climb,
And sink from high to low, along a scale
Of awful notes, whose concord shall not fail;
A musical but melancholy chime,
Which they can hear who meddle not with crime,   5

Nor avarice, nor over-anxious care.
Truth fails not; but her outward forms that bear
The longest date do melt like frosty rime,°   *frozen dew*
That in the morning whitened hill and plain
And is no more; drop like the tower sublime   10
Of yesterday, which royally did wear
His crown of weeds, but could not even sustain
Some casual shout that broke the silent air,
Or the unimaginable touch of Time.

Lewis Carroll
[*Charles Lutwidge Dodgson*] (1832–1898)

Jabberwocky   1871

'Twas brillig, and the slithy toves
   Did gyre and gimble in the wabe:
All mimsy were the borogoves,
   And the mome raths outgrabe.

"Beware the Jabberwock, my son!   5
   The jaws that bite, the claws that catch!
Beware the Jubjub bird, and shun
   The frumious Bandersnatch!"

He took his vorpal sword in hand:
   Long time the manxome foe he sought—   10
So rested he by the Tumtum tree
   And stood awhile in thought.

And, as in uffish thought he stood,
   The Jabberwock, with eyes of flame,
Came whiffling through the tulgey wood,   15
   And burbled as it came!

One, two! One, two! And through and through
   The vorpal blade went snicker-snack!
He left it dead, and with its head
   He went galumphing back.   20

**The Jabberwock,
as illustrated
by John Tenniel, 1872.**

"And hast thou slain the Jabberwock?
   Come to my arms, my beamish boy!
O frabjous day! Callooh! Callay!"
   He chortled in his joy.

'Twas brillig, and the slithy toves   25
   Did gyre and gimble in the wabe:

All mimsy were the borogoves,
   And the mome raths outgrabe.

JABBERWOCKY. Fussy about pronunciation, Carroll in his preface to *The Hunting of the Snark* declares: "The first 'o' in 'borogoves' is pronounced like the 'o' in 'borrow.' I have heard people try to give it the sound of the 'o' in 'worry.' Such is Human Perversity." *Toves*, he adds, rimes with *groves*.

Questions

1. Look up *chortled* (line 24) in your dictionary and find out its definition and origin.
2. In *Through the Looking Glass*, Alice seeks the aid of Humpty Dumpty to decipher the meaning of this nonsense poem. "*Brillig*," he explains, "means four o'clock in the afternoon—the time when you begin *broiling* things for dinner." Does "brillig" sound like any other familiar word?
3. "*Slithy*," the explanation goes on, "means 'lithe and slimy.' 'Lithe' is the same as 'active.' You see it's like a portmanteau—there are two meanings packed up into one word." "Mimsy" is supposed to pack together both "flimsy" and "miserable." In the rest of the poem, what other portmanteau—or packed suitcase—words can you find?

▪ WRITING *effectively*

THINKING ABOUT DICTION

Although a poem may contain images and ideas, it is made up of words. Language is the medium of poetry, and a poem's diction—its exact wording—is the chief source of its power. Writers labor to shape each word and phrase to create particular effects. Poets choose words for their meanings, their associations, and even their sounds. Changing a single word may ruin a poem's effect, just as changing one number in an online password makes all the other numbers useless.

- ▪ **As you prepare to write about a poem, ask yourself if some particular word or combination of words gives you particular pleasure or especially intrigues you.** Don't worry yet about why the word or words impress you. Don't even worry about the meaning. Just underline the words in your book.
- ▪ **Try to determine what about the word or phrase commanded your attention.** Maybe a word strikes you as being unexpected but just right. A phrase might seem especially musical or it might call forth a vivid picture in your imagination.
- ▪ **Consider your underlined words and phrases in the context of the poem.** How does each relate to the words around it? What does it add to the poem?

■ **Think about the poem as a whole.** What sort of language does it rely on? Many poems favor the plain, straightforward language people use in everyday conversation, but others reach for more elegant diction. Choices such as these contribute to the poem's distinctive flavor, as well as to its ultimate meaning.

CHECKLIST: Writing About Diction

☐ As you read, underline words or phrases that appeal to you or seem especially significant.

☐ What is it about each underlined word or phrase that appeals to you?

☐ How does the word or phrase relate to the other lines? What does it contribute to the poem's effect?

☐ How does the sound of a word you've chosen add to the poem's mood?

☐ What would be lost if synonyms were substituted for your favorite words?

☐ What sort of diction does the poem use? Conversational? Lofty? Monosyllabic? Polysyllabic? Concrete? Abstract?

☐ How does diction contribute to the poem's flavor and meaning?

TOPICS FOR WRITING ON WORD CHOICE

1. Find two poems in this book that use very different sorts of diction to address similar subjects. You might choose one with formal and elegant language and another with very down-to-earth or slangy word choices. A good choice might be John Milton's "When I consider how my light is spent" and Seamus Heaney's "Digging." In a short essay (750 to 1,000 words), discuss how the difference in diction affects the tones of the two poems.

2. Browse through Chapter 22, "Poems for Further Reading," for a poem that catches your interest. Within that poem, find a word or phrase that particularly intrigues you. Write a paragraph on what the word or phrase adds to the poem, including how it shades the meaning and contributes to the overall effect.

3. Choose a brief poem from this chapter. Type the poem out, substituting synonyms for each of its nouns and verbs, using a thesaurus if necessary. Next, write a one-page analysis of the difference in feel and meaning between the original and your creation.

4. Choose a poem that strikes you as particularly inventive or unusual in its language, such as E. E. Cummings's "anyone lived in a pretty how town," Gerard Manley Hopkins's "The Windhover" (Chapter 22), or Wendy Cope's "Lonely Hearts," and write a brief analysis of it. Concentrate on the diction of the poem and word order. For what possible purposes does the poet depart from standard English or incorporate unusual vocabulary?

5. Writers are notorious word junkies who often jot down interesting words they stumble across in daily life. Over the course of a day, keep a list of any intriguing words you run across in your reading, music listening, or television viewing. Even

street signs and advertisements can supply surprising words. After twenty-four hours of list-keeping, choose your five favorites. Write a five-line poem, incorporating your five words, letting them take you where they will. Then write a page-long description of the process. What appealed to you in the words you chose? What did you learn about the process of composing a poem?

▶ TERMS FOR *review*

Diction and Allusion

Diction ▶ Word choice or vocabulary. *Diction* refers to the class of words that an author chooses as appropriate for a particular work.

Concrete diction ▶ Words that specifically name or describe things or persons. Concrete words refer to what we can immediately perceive with our senses.

Abstract diction ▶ Words that express general ideas or concepts.

Poetic diction ▶ Strictly speaking, *poetic diction* means any language deemed suitable for verse, but the term generally refers to elevated language intended for poetry rather than common use.

Allusion ▶ A brief, sometimes indirect, reference in a text to a person, place, or thing. Allusions imply a common body of knowledge between reader and writer and act as a literary shorthand to enrich the meaning of a text.

Levels of Diction

Low diction (or **vulgate**) ▶ The language of the common people. Not necessarily containing foul or inappropriate language, it refers simply to unschooled, everyday speech. The term *vulgate* comes from the Latin word *vulgus*, meaning "mob" or "common people."

Colloquial English ▶ The casual or informal but correct language of ordinary native speakers. Conversational in tone, it may include contractions, slang, and shifts in grammar, vocabulary, and diction.

Middle diction (or **general English**) ▶ The ordinary speech of educated native speakers. Most literate speech and writing is in middle diction, which is more educated than **colloquial English**, yet not as elevated as **high diction**.

High diction (or **formal English**) ▶ The heightened, impersonal language of educated persons, usually only written, although possibly spoken on dignified occasions.

Dialect ▶ A particular variety of language spoken by an identifiable regional group or social class.

12

SAYING AND SUGGESTING

What You Will Learn in This Chapter

- To understand and define *denotation*
- To understand and define *connotation*
- To explain the difference between what words say and suggest in a poem
- To analyze the role of suggestion in a poem

To write so clearly that they might bring "all things as near the mathematical plainness" as possible—that was the goal of scientists, according to Bishop Thomas Sprat, who lived in the seventeenth century. Such an effort would seem bound to fail, because words, unlike numbers, are ambiguous indicators. Although it may have troubled Bishop Sprat, the tendency of a word to have multiplicity of meaning rather than mathematical plainness opens broad avenues to poetry.

DENOTATION AND CONNOTATION

Every word has at least one **denotation**: also known as a **literal meaning**, as defined in a dictionary. But the English language has many a common word with so many denotations that a reader may need to think twice to see what it means in a specific context. The noun *field*, for instance, can denote a piece of ground, a sports arena, the scene of a battle, part of a flag, a profession, and a number system in mathematics. Further, the word can be used as a verb ("he fielded a grounder") or an adjective ("field trip," "field glasses").

A word also has **connotations**: overtones or suggestions of additional meaning that it gains from all the contexts in which we have met it in the past. **Suggestion** is the power of a word to imply unspoken associations, in addition to its literal meaning. Suggestion is one of the greatest powers of poetry. The word *skeleton*, according to a dictionary, denotes "the bony framework of a human being or other vertebrate animal, which supports the flesh and protects the organs." But by its associations, the word can rouse thoughts of war, of disease and death, of Halloween, or of one's plans to go to medical school. Think, too, of the difference between "Old Doc Jones" and "Theodore E. Jones, M.D." In the mind's eye, the former appears in his shirtsleeves; the latter has a gold nameplate on his door.

That some words denote the same thing but have sharply different connotations is pointed out in this anonymous Victorian jingle:

Here's a little ditty that you really ought to know:
Horses "sweat" and men "perspire," but ladies only "glow."

Poets aren't the only people who care about the connotations of language. Advertisers know that connotations make money. Nowadays many automobile dealers advertise their secondhand cars not as "used" but as "pre-owned," as if fearing that "used car" would connote an old heap with soiled upholstery and mysterious engine troubles. "Pre-owned," however, suggests that the previous owner has kindly taken the trouble of breaking in the car for you.

In imaginative writing, connotations are as crucial as they are in advertising. Consider this sentence: "A new brand of journalism is being born, or spawned" (Dwight Macdonald writing in the *New York Review of Books*). The last word, by its associations with fish and crustaceans, suggests that this new journalism is scarcely the product of human beings.

William Blake was a master at choosing words loaded with connotation, as in this classic poem.

William Blake (1757–1827)

London   1794

I wander through each chartered street,
Near where the chartered Thames does flow,
And mark in every face I meet
Marks of weakness, marks of woe.

In every cry of every man,   5
In every infant's cry of fear,
In every voice, in every ban,
The mind-forged manacles I hear.

How the chimney-sweeper's cry
Every black'ning church appalls   10
And the hapless soldier's sigh
Runs in blood down palace walls.

But most through midnight streets I hear
How the youthful harlot's curse
Blasts the new-born infant's tear   15
And blights with plagues the marriage hearse.

Here are only a few of the possible meanings of four of Blake's words:

- **chartered** (lines 1, 2)

  Denotations: Established by a charter (a written grant or a certificate of incorporation); leased or hired.

  Connotations: Defined, limited, restricted, channeled, mapped, bound by law; bought and sold (like a slave or an inanimate object); Magna Carta; charters given to crown colonies by the King.

  Other words in the poem with similar connotations: Ban, which can denote (1) a legal prohibition; (2) a churchman's curse or malediction; (3) in medieval times, an order summoning a king's vassals to fight for him. *Manacles,* or shackles, restrain movement. *Chimney-sweeper, soldier,* and *harlot* are all hirelings.

  Interpretation of the lines: The street has had mapped out for it the direction in which it must go; the Thames has had laid down to it the course it must follow. Street and river are channeled, imprisoned, enslaved (like every inhabitant of London).

- **black'ning** (line 10)

  Denotation: Becoming black.

  Connotations: The darkening of something once light, the defilement of something once clean, the deepening of guilt, the gathering of darkness at the approach of night.

  Other words in the poem with similar connotations: Objects becoming marked or smudged (*marks of weakness, marks of woe* in the faces of passersby; bloodied walls of a palace; marriage blighted with plagues); the word *appalls* (denoting not only "to overcome with horror" but "to make pale" and also "to cast a pall or shroud over"); *midnight streets.*

  Interpretation of the line: Literally, every London church grows black from soot and hires a chimney-sweeper (a small boy) to help clean it. But Blake suggests too that by profiting from the suffering of the child laborer, the church is soiling its original purity.

- **Blasts, blights** (lines 15, 16)

  Denotations: Both *blast* and *blight* mean "to cause to wither" or "to ruin and destroy." Both are terms from horticulture. Frost *blasts* a bud and kills it; disease *blights* a growing plant.

  Connotations: Sickness and death; gardens shriveled and dying; gusts of wind and the ravages of insects; things blown to pieces or rotted and warped.

  Other words in the poem with similar connotations: Faces marked with weakness and woe; the child becomes a chimney-sweep; the soldier killed by war; blackening church and bloodied palace; young girl turned harlot; wedding carriage transformed into a hearse.

Interpretation of the lines: Literally, the harlot spreads the plague of syphilis, which, carried into marriage, can cause a baby to be born blind. In a larger and more meaningful sense, Blake sees the prostitution of even one young girl corrupting the entire institution of matrimony and endangering every child.

Some of these connotations are more to the point than others; the reader of a poem nearly always has the problem of distinguishing relevant associations from irrelevant ones. We need to read a poem in its entirety and, when a word leaves us in doubt, look for other things in the poem to corroborate or refute what we think it means. Relatively simple and direct in its statement, Blake's account of his stroll through the city at night becomes an indictment of a whole social and religious order. The indictment could hardly be this effective if it were "mathematically plain," its every word restricted to one denotation clearly spelled out.

Wallace Stevens (1879–1955)

Disillusionment of Ten O'Clock   1923

The houses are haunted
By white night-gowns.
None are green,
Or purple with green rings,
Or green with yellow rings,   5
Or yellow with blue rings.
None of them are strange,
With socks of lace
And beaded ceintures.
People are not going   10
To dream of baboons and periwinkles.
Only, here and there, an old sailor,
Drunk and asleep in his boots,
Catches tigers
In red weather.   15

Questions

1. What are "beaded ceintures"? What does the phrase suggest?
2. What contrast does Stevens draw between the people who live in these houses and the old sailor? What do the connotations of "white night-gowns" and "sailor" add to this contrast?
3. What is lacking in these people who wear white night-gowns? Why should the poet's view of them be a "disillusionment"?

Robert Frost (1874–1963)

Fire and Ice   1923

Some say the world will end in fire,
Some say in ice.
From what I've tasted of desire
I hold with those who favor fire.
But if it had to perish twice,   5
I think I know enough of hate
To say that for destruction ice
Is also great
And would suffice.

Questions

1. To whom does Frost refer in line 1? In line 2?
2. What connotations of *fire* and *ice* contribute to the richness of Frost's comparison?

Diane Thiel (b. 1967)

The Minefield   2000

He was running with his friend from town to town.
They were somewhere between Prague and Dresden.
He was fourteen. His friend was faster
and knew a shortcut through the fields they could take.
He said there was lettuce growing in one of them,   5
and they hadn't eaten all day. His friend ran a few lengths ahead,
like a wild rabbit across the grass,
turned his head, looked back once,
and his body was scattered across the field.

My father told us this, one night,   10
and then continued eating dinner.

He brought them with him—the minefields.
He carried them underneath his good intentions.
He gave them to us—in the volume of his anger,
in the bruises we covered up with sleeves.   15
In the way he threw anything against the wall—
a radio, that wasn't even ours,
a melon, once, opened like a head.
In the way we still expect, years later and continents away,
that anything might explode at any time,   20
and we would have to run on alone
with a vision like that
only seconds behind.

Questions

1. In the opening lines of the poem, a seemingly small decision—to take a shortcut and find something to eat—leads to a horrifying result. What does this suggest about the poem's larger view of what life is like?

2. The speaker tells the story of the minefield before letting us know that the other boy was her father. What is the effect of this narrative strategy?

3. How does the image of the melon reinforce the poem's intentions?

Rhina P. Espaillat (b. 1932)

Bilingual/*Bilingüe*   1998

My father liked them separate, one there,
one here (*allá y aquí*), as if aware

that words might cut in two his daughter's heart
(*el corazón*) and lock the alien part

to what he was—his memory, his name   5
(*su nombre*)—with a key he could not claim.

"English outside this door, Spanish inside,"
he said, "*y basta.*" But who can divide

the world, the word (*mundo y palabra*) from
any child? I knew how to be dumb   10

and stubborn (*testaruda*); late, in bed,
I hoarded secret syllables I read

until my tongue (*mi lengua*) learned to run
where his stumbled. And still the heart was one.

I like to think he knew that, even when,   15
proud (*orgulloso*) of his daughter's pen,

he stood outside *mis versos*, half in fear
of words he loved but wanted not to hear.

Questions

1. Espaillat's poem is full of Spanish words and phrases. (Even the title is given in both languages.) What does the Spanish add to the poem? Could we remove the phrases without changing the poem?

2. How does the father want to divide his daughter's world, at least in terms of language? Does his request suggest any other divisions he hopes to enforce in her life?

3. How does the daughter respond to her father's request to leave English outside their home?

4. "And still the heart was one," states the speaker of the poem. Should we take her statement at face value or do we sense a cost to her bilingual existence? Agree or disagree with the daughter's statement, but state the reasons for your opinion.

Alfred, Lord Tennyson (1809–1892)

Tears, Idle Tears   1847

    Tears, idle tears, I know not what they mean,
Tears from the depth of some divine despair
Rise in the heart, and gather to the eyes,
In looking on the happy Autumn-fields,
And thinking of the days that are no more.   5

    Fresh as the first beam glittering on a sail,
That brings our friends up from the underworld,
Sad as the last which reddens over one
That sinks with all we love below the verge;
So sad, so fresh, the days that are no more.   10

    Ah, sad and strange as in dark summer dawns
The earliest pipe of half-awakened birds
To dying ears, when unto dying eyes
The casement slowly grows a glimmering square;
So sad, so strange, the days that are no more.   15

    Dear as remembered kisses after death,
And sweet as those by hopeless fancy feigned
On lips that are for others; deep as love,
Deep as first love, and wild with all regret;
O Death in Life, the days that are no more.   20

Question
Why is the speaker crying?

Richard Wilbur (b. 1921)

Love Calls Us to the Things of This World   1956

    The eyes open to a cry of pulleys,
And spirited from sleep, the astounded soul
Hangs for a moment bodiless and simple
As false dawn.
             Outside the open window
The morning air is all awash with angels.   5

    Some are in bed-sheets, some are in blouses,
Some are in smocks: but truly there they are.
Now they are rising together in calm swells
Of halcyon feeling, filling whatever they wear
With the deep joy of their impersonal breathing;   10

Now they are flying in place, conveying
The terrible speed of their omnipresence, moving
And staying like white water; and now of a sudden
They swoon down into so rapt a quiet
That nobody seems to be there.
      The soul shrinks   15

From all that it is about to remember,
From the punctual rape of every blessèd day,
And cries,
    "Oh, let there be nothing on earth but laundry,
Nothing but rosy hands in the rising steam
And clear dances done in the sight of heaven."   20

Yet, as the sun acknowledges
With a warm look the world's hunks and colors,
The soul descends once more in bitter love
To accept the waking body, saying now
In a changed voice as the man yawns and rises,   25

"Bring them down from their ruddy gallows;
Let there be clean linen for the backs of thieves;
Let lovers go fresh and sweet to be undone,
And the heaviest nuns walk in a pure floating
Of dark habits,
     keeping their difficult balance."   30

LOVE CALLS US TO THE THINGS OF THIS WORLD. Wilbur once said that his title was taken from St. Augustine, but in a later interview he admitted that neither he nor any critic has ever been able to locate the quotation. Whatever its source, however, the title establishes the poem's central idea that love allows us to return from the divine world of the spirit to the imperfect world of our everyday lives.

Questions

1. What are the "angels" in line 5? Why does this metaphor seem appropriate to the situation?
2. What is "the punctual rape of every blessèd day"? Who is being raped? Who or what commits the rape? Why would Wilbur choose this particular word with all its violent associations?
3. Whom or what does the soul love in line 23, and why is that love bitter?
4. Is it merely obesity that make the nuns' balance "difficult" in the two final lines of the poem? What other "balance" does Wilbur's poem suggest?
5. The soul has two speeches in the poem. How do they differ in tone and imagery?
6. The spiritual world is traditionally considered invisible. What concrete images does Wilbur use to express its special character?

■ WRITING *effectively*

THINKING ABOUT DENOTATION AND CONNOTATION

People often convey their feelings indirectly, through body language, facial expression, tone of voice, and other ways. Similarly, the imagery, tone, and diction of a poem can suggest a message so clearly that it doesn't need to be stated outright.

- **Pay careful attention to what a poem suggests.** Jot down a few key observations both about what the poem says directly and what you might want to know but aren't told. What important details are you left to infer for yourself?
- **Establish what the poem actually says.** When journalists write a news story, they usually try to cover the "five W's" in the opening paragraph—who, what, when, where, and why. These questions are worthwhile ones to ask about a poem:

Who? Who is the speaker or central figure of the poem? (In William Blake's "London," for instance, the speaker is also the protagonist who witnesses the hellish horror of the city.) If the poem seems to be addressed not simply to the reader but to a more specific listener, identify that listener as well.

What? What objects or events are being seen or presented? Does the poem ever suddenly change its subject? (In Wallace Stevens's "Disillusionment of Ten O'Clock," for example, there are essentially two scenes—one dull and proper, the other wild and disreputable. What does that obvious shift suggest about Stevens's meaning?)

When? When does the poem take place? If a poet explicitly states a time of day or a season of the year, it is likely that the *when* of the poem is important. (The fact that Stevens's poem takes place at 10 P.M. and not 2 A.M. tells us a great deal about the people it describes.)

Where? Where is the poem set? Often the setting suggests something important, or plays a role in setting the mood.

Why? If the poem describes a dramatic action but does not provide an overt reason for the occurrence, perhaps the reader is meant to draw his or her own conclusions on the subject. (Tennyson's "Tears, Idle Tears" becomes more evocative by not being explicit about why the speaker weeps.)

■ **Remember, it is almost as important to know what a poem does not tell us as to know what it does.**

CHECKLIST: Writing About What a Poem Says and Suggests

☐ Who speaks the words of the poem? Is it a voice close to the poet's own? A fictional character? A real person?

☐ Who is the poem's central figure?

☐ To whom—if anyone—is the poem addressed?

☐ What objects or events are depicted?

☐ When does the poem take place? Is that timing significant in any way?

☐ Where does the action of the poem take place?

☐ Why does the action of the poem take place? Is there some significant motivation?

☐ Does the poem leave any of the above information out? If so, what does that lack of information reveal about the poem's intentions?

TOPICS FOR WRITING ON DENOTATION AND CONNOTATION

1. Search a poem of your own choosing for the answers to the "five W's"—*Who? What? When? Where? Why?* Indicate, with details, which of the questions are explicitly answered by the poem and which are left unaddressed.

2. Look closely at the central image of Richard Wilbur's "Love Calls Us to the Things of This World." Why does such an ordinary sight cause such intense feelings in the poem's speaker? Give evidence from the poem to back up your theory.

3. What do the various images in Tennyson's "Tears, Idle Tears" suggest about the speaker's reasons for weeping? Address each image, and explain what the images add up to.

4. Browse through a newspaper or magazine for an advertisement that tries to surround a product with an aura. A new car, for instance, might be described in terms of some powerful jungle cat ("purring power, ready to spring"). Clip or photocopy the ad and circle words in it that seem especially suggestive. Then, in an accompanying essay, unfold the suggestions in these words and try to explain the ad's appeal. What differences can you see between how poetry and advertising copy use connotative language?

▶ TERMS FOR *review*

Denotation ▶ The literal, dictionary meaning of a word.

Connotation ▶ An association or additional meaning that a word, image, or phrase may carry, apart from its literal denotation or dictionary definition. A word may pick up connotations from the uses to which it has been put in the past.

Suggestion ▶ The power of a word to imply unspoken associations, in addition to its literal meaning.

13 IMAGERY

What You Will Learn in This Chapter

- To define *imagery*
- To differentiate and explain the major types of imagery
- To recognize and describe haiku as a literary form
- To analyze the role of imagery in a poem

Ezra Pound (1885–1972)

In a Station of the Metro   1916

The apparition of these faces in the crowd;
Petals on a wet, black bough.

Pound said he wrote this poem to convey an experience: emerging one day from a train in the Paris subway (*Métro*), he beheld "suddenly a beautiful face, and then another and another." Originally he had described his impression in a poem thirty lines long. In this final version, each line contains an image, which, like a picture, may take the place of a thousand words.

Though the term **image** suggests a thing seen, when speaking of images in poetry, we generally mean *a word or sequence of words that refers to any sensory experience.* Often this experience is a sight (**visual imagery**, as in Pound's poem), but it may be a sound (**auditory imagery**) or a touch (**tactile imagery,** such as a perception of roughness or smoothness). It may be an odor or a taste or perhaps a bodily sensation such as pain, the prickling of gooseflesh, the quenching of thirst, or—as in the following brief poem—the perception of something cold.

Taniguchi Buson (1716–1783)

The piercing chill I feel   (about 1760)

The piercing chill I feel:
  my dead wife's comb, in our bedroom,
    under my heel . . .

            —*Translated by Harold G. Henderson*

As in this haiku (in Japanese, a poem typically of three lines and seventeen syllables), an image can convey a flash of understanding. Had he wished, the poet might have spoken of the dead woman, of the contrast between her death and his memory of her, of his feelings toward death in general. But such a discussion would be quite different from the poem he actually wrote. Striking his bare foot against the comb, now cold and motionless but associated with the living wife (perhaps worn in her hair), the widower feels a shock as if he had touched the woman's corpse. A literal, physical sense of death is conveyed; the abstraction "death" is understood through the senses. To render the abstract in concrete terms is what poets often try to do; in this attempt, an image can be valuable.

IMAGERY

An image may occur in a single word, a phrase, a sentence, or, as in this case, an entire short poem. To speak of the **imagery** of a poem—all its images taken together—is often more useful than to speak of separate images. To divide Buson's haiku into five images—*chill, wife, comb, bedroom, heel*—is possible, for any noun that refers to a visible object or a sensation is an image, but this is to draw distinctions that in themselves mean little and to disassemble a single experience.

Some literary critics look for much of the meaning of a poem in its imagery, wherein they expect to see the mind of the poet more truly revealed than in whatever the poet explicitly claims to believe. Though Shakespeare's Theseus (in *A Midsummer Night's Dream*) accuses poets of being concerned with "airy nothings," poets are usually very much concerned with what is in front of them. This concern is of use to us. Involved in our personal hopes and apprehensions, anticipating the future so hard that much of the time we see the present through a film of thought across our eyes, perhaps we need a poet occasionally to remind us that even the coffee we absentmindedly sip comes (as Yeats put it) in a "heavy spillable cup."

T. S. Eliot (1888–1965)

The winter evening settles down   1917

The winter evening settles down
With smell of steaks in passageways.
Six o'clock.
The burnt-out ends of smoky days.
And now a gusty shower wraps   5
The grimy scraps
Of withered leaves about your feet
And newspapers from vacant lots;

The showers beat
On broken blinds and chimney-pots,   10
And at the corner of the street
A lonely cab-horse steams and stamps.

And then the lighting of the lamps.

Questions

1. What mood is evoked by the images in Eliot's poem?
2. What kind of city neighborhood has the poet chosen to describe? How can you
   tell?

Theodore Roethke (1908–1963)

Root Cellar   1948

Nothing would sleep in that cellar, dank as a ditch,
Bulbs broke out of boxes hunting for chinks in the dark,
Shoots dangled and drooped,
Lolling obscenely from mildewed crates,
Hung down long yellow evil necks, like tropical snakes.   5
And what a congress of stinks!—
Roots ripe as old bait,
Pulpy stems, rank, silo-rich,
Leaf-mold, manure, lime, piled against slippery planks.
Nothing would give up life: 10
Even the dirt kept breathing a small breath.

Questions

1. As a boy growing up in Saginaw, Michigan, Theodore Roethke spent much of his
   time in a large commercial greenhouse run by his family. What details in his poem
   show more than a passing acquaintance with growing things?
2. What varieties of image does "Root Cellar" contain? Point out examples.
3. What do you understand to be Roethke's attitude toward the root cellar? Does he
   view it as a disgusting chamber of horrors? Pay special attention to the last two
   lines.

Elizabeth Bishop (1911–1979)

The Fish   1946

I caught a tremendous fish
and held him beside the boat
half out of water, with my hook
fast in a corner of his mouth.
He didn't fight.   5
He hadn't fought at all.
He hung a grunting weight,

battered and venerable
and homely. Here and there
his brown skin hung in strips   10
like ancient wallpaper,
and its pattern of darker brown
was like wallpaper:
shapes like full-blown roses
stained and lost through age.   15
He was speckled with barnacles,
fine rosettes of lime,
and infested
with tiny white sea-lice,
and underneath two or three   20
rags of green weed hung down.
While his gills were breathing in
the terrible oxygen
—the frightening gills,
fresh and crisp with blood,   25
that can cut so badly—
I thought of the coarse white flesh
packed in like feathers,
the big bones and the little bones,
the dramatic reds and blacks   30
of his shiny entrails,
and the pink swim-bladder
like a big peony.
I looked into his eyes
which were far larger than mine   35
but shallower, and yellowed,
the irises backed and packed
with tarnished tinfoil
seen through the lenses
of old scratched isinglass.   40
They shifted a little, but not
to return my stare.
—It was more like the tipping
of an object toward the light.
I admired his sullen face,   45
the mechanism of his jaw,
and then I saw
that from his lower lip
—if you could call it a lip—
grim, wet, and weaponlike,   50
hung five old pieces of fish-line,
or four and a wire leader

with the swivel still attached,
with all their five big hooks
grown firmly in his mouth.
A green line, frayed at the end   55
where he broke it, two heavier lines,
and a fine black thread
still crimped from the strain and snap
when it broke and he got away.   60
Like medals with their ribbons
frayed and wavering,
a five-haired beard of wisdom
trailing from his aching jaw.
I stared and stared   65
and victory filled up
the little rented boat,
from the pool of bilge
where oil had spread a rainbow
around the rusted engine   70
to the bailer rusted orange,
the sun-cracked thwarts,
the oarlocks on their strings,
the gunnels—until everything
was rainbow, rainbow, rainbow!   75
And I let the fish go.

Questions

1. How many abstract words does this poem contain? What proportion of the poem
   is imagery?
2. What is the speaker's attitude toward the fish? Comment in particular on lines
   61–64.
3. What attitude do the images of the rainbow of oil (line 69), the orange bailer
   (bailing bucket, line 71), and the "sun-cracked thwarts" (line 72) convey? Does
   the poet expect us to feel mournful because the boat is in such sorry condition?
4. What is meant by "rainbow, rainbow, rainbow"?
5. How do these images prepare us for the conclusion? Why does the speaker let the
   fish go?

Emily Dickinson (1830–1886)

A Route of Evanescence   (about 1879)

A Route of Evanescence
With a revolving Wheel –
A Resonance of Emerald –
A Rush of Cochineal° –   *red dye*

And every Blossom on the Bush   5
Adjusts its tumbled Head –
The mail from Tunis, probably,
An easy Morning's Ride –

A ROUTE OF EVANESCENCE. Dickinson titled this poem "A Humming-bird" in an 1880 letter to a friend. 1 *Evanescence:* ornithologist's term for the luminous sheen of certain birds'
feathers. 7 *Tunis:* capital city of Tunisia, North Africa.

Question

What is the subject of this poem? How can you tell?

Jean Toomer (1894–1967)

Reapers   1923

Black reapers with the sound of steel on stones
Are sharpening scythes. I see them place the hones
In their hip-pockets as a thing that's done,
And start their silent swinging, one by one.
Black horses drive a mower through the weeds,   5
And there, a field rat, startled, squealing bleeds,
His belly close to ground. I see the blade,
Blood-stained, continue cutting weeds and shade.

Questions

1. Imagine the scene Toomer describes. What details most vividly strike the mind's eye?
2. What kind of image is "silent swinging"?
3. Read the poem aloud. Notice especially the effect of the words "sound of steel on stones" and "field rat, startled, squealing bleeds." What interesting sounds are present in the very words that contain these images?
4. What feelings do you get from this poem as a whole? Besides appealing to our auditory and visual imagination, what do the images contribute?

Gerard Manley Hopkins (1844–1889)

Pied Beauty   (1877)

Glory be to God for dappled things—
  For skies of couple-color as a brinded° cow;   *streaked*
    For rose-moles all in stipple° upon trout that swim;   *speckled or dotted*
Fresh-firecoal chestnut-falls; finches' wings;
  Landscape plotted and pieced—fold, fallow, and plow;   5
    And áll trádes, their gear and tackle and trim.°   *equipment*

All things counter, original, spare, strange;
  Whatever is fickle, freckled (who knows how?)

With swift, slow; sweet, sour; adazzle, dim;
He fathers-forth whose beauty is past change: 10
        Praise him.

Questions

1. What does the word "pied" mean? (Hint: what does a Pied Piper look like?)
2. According to Hopkins, what do "skies," "cow," "trout," "ripe chestnuts," "finches' wings," and "landscapes" all have in common? What landscapes can the poet have in mind? (Have you ever seen any "dappled" landscape while looking down from an airplane, or from a mountain or high hill?)
3. What do you make of line 6? What can carpenters' saws and ditch-diggers' spades possibly have in common with the dappled things in lines 2–4?
4. Does Hopkins refer only to visual contrasts? What other kinds of variation interest him?
5. Try to state in your own words the theme of this poem. How essential to our understanding of this theme are Hopkins's images?

ABOUT HAIKU

Arakida Moritake (1473–1549)

The falling flower

The falling flower
I saw drift back to the branch
Was a butterfly.

           —*Translated by Babette Deutsch*

Haiku means "beginning-verse" in Japanese—perhaps because the form may have originated in a game. Players, given a haiku, were supposed to extend its three lines into a longer poem. Haiku (the word can also be plural) consist mainly of imagery, but as we saw in Buson's lines about the cold comb, their imagery is not always only pictorial; it can involve any of the five senses. Haiku are so short that they depend on imagery to trigger associations and responses in the reader. A haiku in Japanese is rimeless; its seventeen syllables are traditionally arranged in three lines, usually following a pattern of five, seven, and five syllables. English haiku frequently ignore such a pattern, being rimed or unrimed as the poet prefers. What English haiku do try to preserve is the powerful way Japanese haiku capture the intensity of a particular moment, usually by linking two concrete images. There is little room for abstract thoughts or general observations. The following attempt, though containing seventeen syllables, is far from haiku in spirit:

Now that our love is gone
I feel within my soul
a nagging distress.

Unlike the author of those lines, haiku poets look out upon a literal world, seldom looking inward to *discuss* their feelings. Japanese haiku tend to be seasonal in subject, but because they are so highly compressed, they usually only *imply* a season: a blossom indicates spring; a crow on a branch, autumn; snow, winter. Not just pretty little sketches of nature (as some Westerners think), haiku assume a view of the universe in which observer and nature are not separated.

Haiku emerged in sixteenth-century Japan and soon developed into a deeply esteemed form. Even today, Japanese soldiers, stockbrokers, scientists, schoolchildren, and the emperor himself still find occasion to pen haiku. Soon after the form first captured the attention of Western poets at the end of the nineteenth century, it became immensely influential for modern poets, such as Ezra Pound, William Carlos Williams, and H.D., as a model for the kind of verse they wanted to write—concise, direct, and imagistic.

The Japanese consider the poems of the "Three Masters"—Basho, Buson, and Issa—to be the pinnacle of the classical haiku. Each poet had his own personality: Basho, the ascetic seeker of Zen enlightenment; Buson, the worldly artist; Issa, the sensitive master of wit and pathos. Here are liberal translations of poems from each of the "Three Masters."

Matsuo Basho (1644–1694)

Heat-lightning streak

Heat-lightning streak—
through darkness pierces
the heron's shriek.

—*Translated by X. J. Kennedy*

In the old stone pool

In the old stone pool
a frogjump:
splishhhhh.

—*Translated by X. J. Kennedy*

Taniguchi Buson (1716–1783)

On the one-ton temple bell

On the one-ton temple bell
a moonmoth, folded into sleep,
sits still.

—*Translated by X. J. Kennedy*

Moonrise on mudflats

Moonrise on mudflats,
the line of water and sky
blurred by a bullfrog

—*Translated by Michael Stillman*

Kobayashi Issa (1763–1827)

only one guy

only one guy and
only one fly trying to
make the guest room do.

—*Translated by Cid Corman*

Cricket

Cricket, be
careful! I'm rolling
over!

—*Translated by Robert Bly*

HAIKU FROM JAPANESE INTERNMENT CAMPS

Japanese immigrants brought the tradition of haiku-writing to the United States, often forming local clubs to pursue their shared literary interests. During World War II, when Japanese Americans were unjustly considered "enemy aliens" and confined to federal internment camps, these poets continued to write in their bleak new surroundings. Today these haiku provide a vivid picture of the deprivations suffered by the poets, their families, and their fellow internees.

Suiko Matsushita

Rain shower from mountain

Rain shower from mountain
quietly soaking
barbed wire fence
——*Translated by Violet Kazue*
de Cristoforo

Cosmos in bloom

Cosmos in bloom
as if no war
were taking place
——*Translated by Violet Kazue*
de Cristoforo

Hakuro Wada

Even the croaking of frogs

Even the croaking of frogs
comes from outside the barbed wire fence
this is our life
——*Translated by Violet Kazue*
de Cristoforo

Neiji Ozawa

The war—this year

The war—this year
New Year midnight bell
ringing in the desert
——*Translated by Violet Kazue*
de Cristoforo

CONTEMPORARY HAIKU

Here are four more recent haiku written in English. (Don't expect them all to observe a strict arrangement of seventeen syllables, however.) Haiku, in any language, is an art of few words but many suggestions. A haiku starts us thinking and telling.

Nick Virgilio   (1928–1989)

The Old Neighborhood

the old neighborhood
falling to the wrecking ball:
names in the sidewalk

Lee Gurga   (b. 1949)

Visitor's Room

Visitor's Room—
everything bolted down
except my brother.

Jennifer Brutschy (b. 1960)

Born Again

Born Again
she speaks excitedly
of death.

Adelle Foley (b. 1940)

**Learning to Shave
(Father Teaching Son)**

A nick on the jaw
The razor's edge of manhood
Along the bloodline.

FOR REVIEW AND FURTHER STUDY

John Keats (1795–1821)

Bright star, would I were steadfast as thou art   (1819)

Bright star, would I were steadfast as thou art—
  Not in lone splendor hung aloft the night,
And watching, with eternal lids apart,
  Like Nature's patient, sleepless Eremite,°   *hermit*
The moving waters at their priestlike task   5
  Of pure ablution round earth's human shores,
Or gazing on the new soft-fallen mask
  Of snow upon the mountains and the moors—
No—yet still steadfast, still unchangeable,
  Pillowed upon my fair love's ripening breast,   10
To feel for ever its soft swell and fall,
  Awake for ever in a sweet unrest,
Still, still to hear her tender-taken breath,
And so live ever—or else swoon to death.

Questions

1. Stars are conventional symbols for love and a loved one. (Love, Shakespeare tells us in a sonnet, "is the star to every wandering bark.") In this sonnet, why is it not possible for the star to have this meaning? How does Keats use it?
2. What seems concrete and particular in the speaker's observations?
3. Suppose Keats had said "slow and easy" instead of "tender-taken" in line 13. What would have been lost?

Tami Haaland (b. 1960)

Lipstick   2001

I wonder how they do it, those women
who can slip lipstick over lips without
looking, after they've finished a meal
or when they ride in cars. Satin Claret

or Plum or Twig or Pecan. I can't stay   5
inside the lines, late comer to lipstick
that I am, and sometimes get messy
even in front of a mirror. But these
women know where lips end and plain
skin begins, probably know how to put   10
their hair in a knot with a single pin.

Questions

1. How does the speaker use lipstick differently from the way "those women" do?
2. Why do the other women know how to apply lipstick more accurately? What does this knowledge suggest about the difference between them and the speaker?
3. What does lipstick seem to suggest in the poem? Support your ideas with specific examples from the poem.

Experiment: Writing with Images

Taking the following poems as examples from which to start rather than as models to be slavishly copied, try to compose a brief poem that consists largely of imagery.

William Carlos Williams (1883–1963)

El Hombre   1917

It's a strange courage
you give me ancient star:

Shine alone in the sunrise
toward which you lend no part!

Li Po (701–762)

Drinking Alone by Moonlight   (about 750)

A cup of wine, under the flowering trees;
I drink alone, for no friend is near.
Raising my cup I beckon the bright moon,
For he, with my shadow, will make three men.
The moon, alas, is no drinker of wine;   5
Listless, my shadow creeps about at my side.
Yet with the moon as friend and the shadow as slave
I must make merry before the Spring is spent.
To the songs I sing the moon flickers her beams;
In the dance I weave my shadow tangles and breaks.   10

While we were sober, three shared the fun;
Now we are drunk, each goes his way.
May we long share our odd; inanimate feast,
And meet as last on the Cloudy River of the sky.

—*Translated by Arthur Waley, 1919*

DRINKING ALONE BY MOONLIGHT. 14 *the Cloudy River of the sky:* the Milky Way.

Stevie Smith (1902–1971)

Not Waving but Drowning   1957

Nobody heard him, the dead man,
But still he lay moaning:
I was much further out than you thought
And not waving but drowning.

Poor chap, he always loved larking   5
And now he's dead
It must have been too cold for him his heart gave way,
They said.

Oh, no no no, it was too cold always
(Still the dead one lay moaning)   10
I was much too far out all my life
And not waving but drowning.

Robert Bly (b. 1926)

Driving to Town Late to Mail a Letter   1962

It is a cold and snowy night. The main street is deserted.
The only things moving are swirls of snow.
As I lift the mailbox door, I feel its cold iron.
There is a privacy I love in this snowy night.
Driving around, I will waste more time.   5

■ WRITING *effectively*

THINKING ABOUT IMAGERY

Images are powerful things—thus the old saw, "A picture is worth a thousand words." A poem, however, must build its pictures from words. By taking note of its imagery, and watching how the nature of those images evolves from start to finish, you can go a long way toward a better understanding of the poem. The following steps can help:

- **Make a short list of the poem's key images.** Be sure to write them down in the order they appear, because the sequence can be as important as the images themselves.
- **Take the poem's title into account.** A title often points the way to important insights.
- **Remember: not all images are visual.** Images can draw on any or all of the five senses.
- **Jot down key adjectives or other qualifying words.**
- **Go back through your list and take notes about what moods or attitudes are suggested by each image.** What do you notice about the movement from the first image to the last?

Example: **Robert Bly's "Driving to Town Late to Mail a Letter"**

Let's try this method on a short poem. An initial list of images in Bly's "Driving to Town Late to Mail a Letter" might look like this:

> cold and snowy night
> deserted main street
> mailbox door—cold iron
> snowy night (speaker loves its privacy)
> speaker drives around (to waste time)

Bly's title also contains several crucial images. Let's add them to the top of the list:

> driving (to town)
> late night
> a letter (to be mailed)

Looking over our list, we see how the images provide an outline of the poem's story. We also see how Bly begins the poem without providing an initial sense of how his speaker feels about the situation. Is driving to town late on a snowy evening a positive, negative, or neutral experience? By noting where (in line 4) the speaker reveals a subjective response to an image ("There is a privacy I love in this snowy night"), we begin to grasp the poem's overall emotional structure. We might also note on our list how the poem begins and ends with the same image (driving), but uses it for different effects. At the beginning, the speaker is driving for the practical purpose of mailing a letter, but at the end, he drives purely for pleasure.

Simply by noting the images from start to finish, we have already worked out a rough essay outline—all on a single sheet of paper or a few inches of computer screen.

CHECKLIST: Writing About Imagery

☐ List a poem's key images, in the order in which they appear.
☐ What does the poem's title suggest?
☐ Remember, images can draw on all five senses—not just the visual.
☐ List key adjectives or other qualifying words.
☐ What emotions or attitudes are suggested by each image?
☐ Does the mood of the imagery change from start to finish?
☐ What is suggested by the movement from one image to the next? Remember that the order or sequence of images is almost as important as the images themselves.

TOPICS FOR WRITING ON IMAGERY

1. Apply the steps listed in "Checklist: Writing About Imagery" to one of the poems in this chapter. Stevie Smith's "Not Waving but Drowning," John Keats's "Bright star, would I were steadfast as thou art," and Jean Toomer's "Reapers" would each make a good subject. Make a brief list of images, and jot down notes on what the images suggest. Now write a two-page description of this process—what it revealed about the poem itself, and about reading poetry in general.

2. Choose a small, easily overlooked object in your home that has special significance to you. Write a paragraph-long, excruciatingly detailed description of the item, putting at least four senses into play. Without making any direct statements about the item's importance to you, try to let the imagery convey the mood you associate with it. Bring your paragraph to class, exchange it with a partner, and see if he or she can identify the mood you were trying to convey.

3. Reread the section on haiku in this chapter. Write three or four haiku of your own and a brief prose account of your experience in writing them. Did anything about the process surprise you?

4. Examining any poem in this chapter, demonstrate how its imagery helps communicate its general theme. Be specific in noting how each key image contributes to the poem's total effect. Feel free to consult criticism on the poem but make sure to credit any observation you borrow from a critical source.

▶ TERMS FOR *review*

Image ▶ A word or series of words that refers to any sensory experience (usually sight, although also sound, smell, touch, or taste). An image is a direct or literal recreation of physical experience and adds immediacy to literary language.

Imagery ▶ The collective set of images in a poem or other literary work.

Visual imagery ▶ Imagery that refers to the sense of sight or presents something one may see.

Auditory imagery ▶ Imagery that refers to the sense of hearing.

Tactile imagery ▶ Imagery that refers to the sense of touch.

Haiku ▶ A Japanese verse form that has three unrhymed lines of five, seven, and five syllables. Traditional haiku is often serious and spiritual in tone, relying mostly on imagery, and usually set (often by implication instead of direct statement) in one of the four seasons. Modern haiku in English often ignore strict syllable count and may have a more playful, worldly tone.

14 FIGURES OF SPEECH

What You Will Learn in This Chapter

- To define *simile*
- To define *metaphor*
- To recognize the major figures of speech
- To analyze the role of figurative speech in a poem

WHY SPEAK FIGURATIVELY?

"I will speak daggers to her, but use none," says Hamlet, preparing to confront his mother. His statement makes sense only because we realize that *daggers* is to be taken two ways: literally (denoting sharp, pointed weapons) and nonliterally (referring to something that can be used *like* weapons—namely, words). Reading poetry, we often meet comparisons between two things whose similarity we have never noticed before. When Marianne Moore observes that a fir tree has "an emerald turkey-foot at the top," the result is a pleasure that poetry richly affords: the sudden recognition of likenesses.

A treetop like a turkey-foot, words like daggers—such comparisons are called **figures of speech**. A figure of speech occurs whenever a speaker or writer, for the sake of freshness or emphasis, departs from the usual denotations, or literal definitions, of words. Certainly, when Hamlet says he will speak daggers, no one expects him to release pointed weapons from his lips, for *daggers* is not to be read solely for its denotation. Its connotations, or suggested meanings—sharp, stabbing, piercing, wounding—also come to mind, and we see ways in which words and daggers might work alike.

Figures of speech are not devices to state what is demonstrably untrue. Indeed they often state truths that more literal language cannot communicate; they call attention to such truths; they lend them emphasis.

Alfred, Lord Tennyson (1809–1892)

The Eagle   1851

He clasps the crag with crooked hands;
Close to the sun in lonely lands,
Ringed with the azure world, he stands.

The wrinkled sea beneath him crawls;
He watches from his mountain walls,   5
And like a thunderbolt he falls.

This brief poem is rich in figurative language. In the first line, the phrase
crooked hands may surprise us. An eagle does not have hands, we might protest; but the objection would be a quibble, for evidently Tennyson is indicating exactly how an eagle clasps a crag, in the way that human fingers clasp
a thing. By implication, too, the eagle is a person. *Close to the sun,* if taken
literally, is an absurd exaggeration, the sun being a mean distance of 93
million miles from the earth. For the eagle to be closer to it by the altitude
of a mountain is so minor as to be insignificant. But figuratively, Tennyson
conveys that the eagle stands above the clouds, perhaps silhouetted against
the sun, and for the moment belongs to the heavens rather than to the land
and sea. The word *ringed* makes a circle of the whole world's horizons and
suggests that we see the world from the eagle's height; the *wrinkled sea* becomes an aged, sluggish animal; *mountain walls,* possibly literal, also suggests
a fort or castle; and finally the eagle itself is likened to a thunderbolt in speed
and in power, perhaps also in that its beak is—like our abstract conception
of a lightning bolt—pointed. How much of the poem can be taken literally? Only *he clasps the crag, he stands, he watches, he falls.* The rest is made
of figures of speech. The result is that, reading Tennyson's poem, we gain a
bird's-eye view of sun, sea, and land—and even of bird. Like imagery, figurative language refers us to the physical world.

William Shakespeare (1564–1616)

Shall I compare thee to a summer's day? (Sonnet 18)   1609

Shall I compare thee to a summer's day?
Thou art more lovely and more temperate.
Rough winds do shake the darling buds of May,
And summer's lease hath all too short a date.
Sometime too hot the eye of heaven shines,   5
And often is his gold complexion dimmed;
And every fair° from fair sometimes declines,   *fair one*
By chance, or nature's changing course, untrimmed:
But thy eternal summer shall not fade,
Nor lose possession of that fair thou ow'st,°   *ownest, have*   10
Nor shall death brag thou wand'rest in his shade,
When in eternal lines to time thou grow'st.
    So long as men can breathe or eyes can see,
    So long lives this, and this gives life to thee.

Howard Moss (1922–1987)

Shall I Compare Thee to a Summer's Day? 1976

Who says you're like one of the dog days?
You're nicer. And better.
Even in May, the weather can be gray,
And a summer sub-let doesn't last forever.
Sometimes the sun's too hot;   5
Sometimes it is not.
Who can stay young forever?
People break their necks or just drop dead!
But you? Never!
If there's just one condensed reader left   10
Who can figure out the abridged alphabet,
　　After you're dead and gone,
　　In this poem you'll live on!

SHALL I COMPARE THEE TO A SUMMER'S DAY? (Moss). 1 *dog days:* the hottest days of summer.
The ancient Romans believed that the Dog-star, Sirius, added heat to summer months.

Questions

1. In Howard Moss's streamlined version of Shakespeare, from a series called "Modified Sonnets (Dedicated to adapters, abridgers, digesters, and condensers everywhere)," to what extent does the poet use figurative language? In Shakespeare's original sonnet, how high a proportion of Shakespeare's language is figurative?

2. Compare some of Moss's lines to the corresponding lines in Shakespeare's sonnet. Why is "Even in May, the weather can be gray" less interesting than the original? In the lines on the sun (5–6 in both versions), what has Moss's modification deliberately left out? Why is Shakespeare's seeing death as a braggart memorable? Why aren't you greatly impressed by Moss's last two lines?

3. Can you explain Shakespeare's play on the word "untrimmed" (line 8)? Evidently the word can mean "divested of trimmings," but what other suggestions do you find in it?

4. How would you answer someone who argued, "Maybe Moss's language isn't as good as Shakespeare's, but the meaning is still there. What's wrong with putting Shakespeare into up-to-date words that can be understood by everybody?"

METAPHOR AND SIMILE

Life, like a dome of many-colored glass,
　Stains the white radiance of Eternity.

The first of these lines (from Shelley's "Adonais") is a **simile**: a comparison of two things, indicated by some connective, usually *like*, *as*, *than*, or a verb such as *resembles*. A simile expresses a similarity. Still, for a simile to exist, the things compared have to be dissimilar in kind. It is no simile to say "Your fingers are like mine"; it is a literal observation. But to say "Your fingers are like sausages" is to use a simile. Omit the connective—say "Your fingers are sausages"—and the result is a **metaphor**, a statement that one thing *is* something else, which, in a literal sense, it is not. In the second of Shelley's lines, it is *assumed* that Eternity is light or radiance, and we have an **implied metaphor**, one that uses neither a connective nor the verb *to be*. Here are examples:

Oh, my love is like a red, red rose.	*Simile*
Oh, my love resembles a red, red rose.	*Simile*
Oh, my love is redder than a rose.	*Simile*
Oh, my love is a red, red rose.	*Metaphor*
Oh, my love has red petals and sharp thorns.	*Implied metaphor*

Often you can tell a metaphor from a simile by much more than just the presence or absence of a connective. In general, a simile refers to only one characteristic that two things have in common, while a metaphor is not plainly limited in the number of resemblances it may indicate. To use the simile "He eats like a pig" is to compare man and animal in one respect: eating habits. But to say "He's a pig" is to use a metaphor that might involve comparisons of appearance and morality as well.

The Usefulness of Metaphors

For scientists as well as poets, the making of metaphors is customary. As astrophysicist and novelist Alan Lightman has noted, we can't help envisioning scientific discoveries in terms of things we know from daily life— spinning balls, waves in water, pendulums, weights on springs. "We have no other choice," Lightman reasons. "We cannot avoid forming mental pictures when we try to grasp the meaning of our equations, and how can we picture what we have not seen?"[1] In science as well as in poetry, it would seem, metaphors are necessary instruments of understanding.

Mixed Metaphors

In everyday speech, simile and metaphor occur frequently. We use metaphors ("She's a doll") and similes ("The tickets are selling like hotcakes") without being fully conscious of them. If, however, we are aware that words possess literal meanings as well as figurative ones, we should avoid using what are called **mixed metaphors** and not follow the example of the writer who advised, "Water the spark of knowledge and it will bear fruit," or the speaker who urged, "To get ahead, keep your nose to the grindstone, your shoulder

---

[1]"Physicists' Use of Metaphor," *The American Scholar* (Winter 1989): 99.

to the wheel, your ear to the ground, and your eye on the ball." Perhaps the unintended humor of these statements comes from our seeing that the writer, busy stringing together stale metaphors, was not aware that they had any physical reference.

Poetry and Metaphor

A poem may make a series of comparisons, or the whole poem may be one extended comparison:

Emily Dickinson (1830–1886)

My Life had stood – a Loaded Gun

(about 1863)

My Life had stood – a Loaded Gun –
In Corners – till a Day
The Owner passed – identified –
And carried Me away –

And now We roam in Sovereign Woods –   5
And now We hunt the Doe –
And every time I speak for Him –
The Mountains straight reply –

And do I smile, such cordial light
Upon the Valley glow –   10
It is as a Vesuvian face
Had let its pleasure through –

And when at Night – Our good Day done –
I guard My Master's Head –
'Tis better than the Eider-Duck's   15
Deep Pillow – to have shared –

To foe of His – I'm deadly foe –
None stir the second time –
On whom I lay a Yellow Eye –
Or an emphatic Thumb –   20

Though I than He – may longer live
He longer must – than I –
For I have but the power to kill,
Without – the power to die –

How much life metaphors can bring to poetry may be seen by comparing two poems by Tennyson and Blake.

Alfred, Lord Tennyson (1809–1892)

Flower in the Crannied Wall   1869

Flower in the crannied wall,
I pluck you out of the crannies,
I hold you here, root and all, in my hand,
Little flower—but *if* I could understand
What you are, root and all, and all in all,   5
I should know what God and man is.

How many metaphors does this poem contain? None. Compare it with a
briefer poem on a similar theme: the quatrain that begins Blake's "Auguries
of Innocence." (We follow here the opinion of W. B. Yeats, who, in editing
Blake's poems, thought the lines, each with its own metaphor, ought to be
printed separately.)

William Blake (1757–1827)

To see a world in a grain of sand   (about 1803)

To see a world in a grain of sand
And a heaven in a wild flower,
Hold infinity in the palm of your hand
And eternity in an hour.

Set beside Blake's poem, Tennyson's—short though it is—seems lengthy.
What contributes to the richness of "To see a world in a grain of sand" is
Blake's use of a metaphor in every line. And every metaphor is loaded with
suggestion. Our world does indeed resemble a grain of sand: in being round,
in being stony, in being one of a myriad (the suggestions go on and on).
Like Blake's grain of sand, a metaphor holds much within a small circum-
ference.

Sylvia Plath (1932–1963)

Metaphors   1960

I'm a riddle in nine syllables,
An elephant, a ponderous house,
A melon strolling on two tendrils.
O red fruit, ivory, fine timbers!
This loaf's big with its yeasty rising.   5
Money's new-minted in this fat purse.
I'm a means, a stage, a cow in calf.
I've eaten a bag of green apples,
Boarded the train there's no getting off.

Questions

1. To what central fact do all the metaphors in this poem refer?
2. In the first line, what has the speaker in common with a riddle? Why does she say she has *nine* syllables? What patterns using the number nine do you find in the poem?

N. Scott Momaday (b. 1934)

Simile
1974

What did we say to each other
that now we are as the deer
who walk in single file
with heads high
with ears forward
with eyes watchful
with hooves always placed on firm ground
in whose limbs there is latent flight

5

Questions

1. Momaday never tells us what was said. Does this omission keep us from understanding the comparison?
2. The comparison is extended with each detail adding some new twist. Explain the implications of the last line.

Experiment: Likening

Write a poem that follows the method of N. Scott Momaday's "Simile," consisting of one long comparison between two objects. Possible subjects might include talking to a loved one long-distance; how you feel going to a weekend job; being on a diet; not being noticed by someone you love; winning a lottery.

Craig Raine (b. 1944)

A Martian Sends a Postcard Home
1979

Caxtons are mechanical birds with many wings
and some are treasured for their markings—

they cause the eyes to melt
or the body to shriek without pain.

I have never seen one fly, but
sometimes they perch on the hand.

5

Mist is when the sky is tired of flight
and rests its soft machine on ground:

then the world is dim and bookish
like engravings under tissue paper.   10

Rain is when the earth is television.
It has the property of making colors darker.

Model T is a room with the lock inside—
a key is turned to free the world

for movement, so quick there is a film   15
to watch for anything missed.

But time is tied to the wrist
or kept in a box, ticking with impatience.

In homes, a haunted apparatus sleeps,
that snores when you pick it up.   20

If the ghost cries, they carry it
to their lips and soothe it to sleep

with sounds. And yet, they wake it up
deliberately, by tickling with a finger.

Only the young are allowed to suffer   25
openly. Adults go to a punishment room

with water but nothing to eat.
They lock the door and suffer the noises

alone. No one is exempt
and everyone's pain has a different smell.   30

At night, when all the colors die,
they hide in pairs

and read about themselves—
in color, with their eyelids shut.

A MARTIAN SENDS A POSTCARD HOME. The title of this poem literally describes
its contents. A Martian briefly describes everyday objects and activities on
earth, but the visitor sees them all from an alien perspective. The Martian/
author lacks a complete vocabulary and sometimes describes general categories
of things with a proper noun (as in "Model T" in line 13). 1 *Caxtons*: books,
since William Caxton (c. 1422–1491) was the first person to print books in
England.

Question

Can you recognize *everything* the Martian describes and translate it back into Earth-
based English?

Exercise: **What Is Similar?**

Each of these quotations contains a simile or a metaphor. In each of these figures of speech, what two things are being compared? Try to state exactly what you understand the two things to have in common: the most striking similarity or similarities that the poet sees.

1.
    All the world's a stage,
    And all the men and women merely players:
    They have their exits and their entrances,
    And one man in his time plays many parts,
    His acts being seven ages.
            —William Shakespeare, *As You Like It*

2. "Hope" is the thing with feathers –
    That perches in the soul –
    And sings the tune without the words –
    And never stops – at all –
            —Emily Dickinson, an untitled poem

3. Why should I let the toad *work*
        Squat on my life?
    Can't I use my wit as a pitchfork
        And drive the brute off?
            —Philip Larkin, "Toads"

4. I wear my patience like a light-green dress
    and wear it thin.
            —Emily Grosholz, "Remembering the Ardèche"

OTHER FIGURES OF SPEECH

When Shakespeare asks, in a sonnet,

> O! how shall summer's honey breath hold out
> Against the wrackful siege of batt'ring days,

it might seem at first that he mixes metaphors. How can a *breath* confront the battering ram of an invading army? But it is summer's breath and, by giving it to summer, Shakespeare makes the season seem human. It is as if the fragrance of summer were the breath within a person's body, and winter were the onslaught of old age.

Personification

Such is Shakespeare's instance of **personification**: a figure of speech in which a thing, an animal, or an abstract term (*truth, nature*) is made human. A personification extends throughout the following short poem, in which the wind is a wild man, and evidently it is not just any autumn breeze but a hurricane or at least a stiff gale.

James Stephens (1882–1950)

The Wind   1915

The wind stood up, and gave a shout;
He whistled on his fingers, and

Kicked the withered leaves about,
And thumped the branches with his hand,

And said he'd kill, and kill, and kill;   5
And so he will! And so he will!

Apostrophe

Hand in hand with personification often goes **apostrophe**: a way of addressing someone or something invisible or not ordinarily spoken to. In an apostrophe, a poet (in these examples Wordsworth) may address an inanimate
object ("Spade! with which Wilkinson hath tilled his lands"), some dead or
absent person ("Milton! thou shouldst be living at this hour"), an abstract
thing ("Return, Delights!"), or a spirit ("Thou Soul that art the eternity of
thought"). More often than not, the poet uses apostrophe to announce a lofty
and serious tone. An "O" may even be put in front of it ("O moon!") since,
according to W. D. Snodgrass, every poet has a right to do so at least once in
a lifetime. But apostrophe doesn't have to be highfalutin. It is a means of giving life to the inanimate. It is a way of giving body to the intangible, a way of
speaking to it person to person, as in the words of a moving American spiritual: "Death, ain't you got no shame?"

Overstatement and Understatement

Most of us, from time to time, emphasize a point with a statement containing
exaggeration: "Faster than greased lightning"; "I've told him a thousand times."
We speak, then, not literal truth but use a figure of speech called **overstatement** (or **hyperbole**). Poets too, being fond of emphasis, often exaggerate for
effect. Instances are Marvell's profession of a love that should grow "Vaster than
empires, and more slow" and John Burgon's description of Petra: "A rose-red
city, half as old as Time." Overstatement can be used also for humorous purposes,
as in a fat woman's boast (from a blues song): "Every time I shake, some skinny
gal loses her home."[2] The opposite is **understatement**, implying more than is
said. Mark Twain in *Life on the Mississippi* recalls how, as an apprentice steam-
boat-pilot asleep when supposed to be on watch, he was roused by the pilot and
sent clambering to the pilot house: "Mr. Bixby was close behind, commenting."
Another example is Robert Frost's line "One could do worse than be a swinger of
birches"—the conclusion of a poem that has suggested that to swing on a birch
tree is one of the most deeply satisfying activities in the world.

[2]Quoted by Amiri Baraka [LeRoi Jones] in *Blues People* (New York: Morrow, 1963).

Pun

Asked to tell the difference between men and women, Samuel Johnson replied, "I can't conceive, madam, can you?" The great dictionary-maker was using a figure of speech known to classical rhetoricians as *paronomasia*, better known to us as a **pun** or play on words. How does a pun operate? It reminds us of another word (or other words) of similar or identical sound but of very different denotation. Although puns at their worst can be mere piddling quibbles, at best they can sharply point to surprising but genuine resemblances. The name of a dentist's country estate, Tooth Acres, is accurate: aching teeth paid for the property. In his novel *Moby-Dick*, Herman Melville takes up questions about whales that had puzzled scientists: for instance, are the whale's spoutings water or gaseous vapor? When Melville speaks pointedly of the great whale "sprinkling and mistifying the gardens of the deep," we catch his pun and conclude that the creature both mistifies and mystifies at once.

In poetry, a pun may be facetious, as in Thomas Hood's ballad of "Faithless Nelly Gray":

> Ben Battle was a soldier bold,
>   And used to war's alarms;
> But a cannon-ball took off his legs,
>   So he laid down his arms!

Or it may be serious, as in these lines on war by E. E. Cummings:

> the bigness of cannon
> is skilful,

(*is skilful* becoming *is kill-ful* when read aloud), or perhaps, as in Shakespeare's song in *Cymbeline*, "Fear no more the heat o' th' sun," both facetious and serious at once:

> Golden lads and girls all must,
> As chimney-sweepers, come to dust.

Poets often make puns on images, thereby combining the sensory force of imagery with the verbal pleasure of wordplay. Find and explain the punning images in these two poems.

Margaret Atwood (b. 1939)

You fit into me   1971

you fit into me
like a hook into an eye

a fish hook
an open eye

Timothy Steele   (b. 1948)

Epitaph   1979

Here lies Sir Tact, a diplomatic fellow
Whose silence was not golden, but just yellow.

To sum up: even though figures of speech are not to be taken *only* literally, they refer us to a tangible world. By *personifying* an eagle, Tennyson reminds us that the bird and humankind have certain characteristics in common. Through *hyperbole* and *understatement*, a poet can make us see the physical actuality in back of words. *Pun* causes us to realize this actuality, too, and probably surprise us enjoyably at the same time. Through *apostrophe*, the poet animates the inanimate and asks it to listen—speaks directly to an immediate god or to the revivified dead. Put to such uses, figures of speech have power. They are more than just ways of playing with words.

Dana Gioia   (b. 1950)

Money   1991

> *Money is a kind of poetry.*
> —*Wallace Stevens*

Money, the long green,
cash, stash, rhino, jack
or just plain dough.

Chock it up, fork it over,
shell it out. Watch it   5
burn holes through pockets.

To be made of it! To have it
to burn! Greenbacks, double eagles,
megabucks and Ginnie Maes.

It greases the palm, feathers a nest,   10
holds heads above water,
makes both ends meet.

Money breeds money.
Gathering interest, compounding daily.
Always in circulation.   15

Money. You don't know where it's been,
but you put it where your mouth is.
And it talks.

Question
What figures of speech can you identify in this poem?

Carl Sandburg   (1878–1967)

Fog   1916

The fog comes
on little cat feet.

It sits looking
over harbor and city
on silent haunches   5
and then moves on.

Questions

1. What figure of speech does this poem use?
2. Which specific feline qualities does the speaker impute to the fog?

FOR REVIEW AND FURTHER STUDY

Exercise: Figures of Speech

Identify the central figure of speech in the following short poems.

Robert Frost   (1874–1963)

The Secret Sits   1942

We dance round in a ring and suppose,
But the Secret sits in the middle and knows.

Kay Ryan   (b. 1945)

Turtle   1994

Who would be a turtle who could help it?
A barely mobile hard roll, a four-oared helmet,
she can ill afford the chances she must take
in rowing toward the grasses that she eats.
Her track is graceless, like dragging   5
a packing case places, and almost any slope
defeats her modest hopes. Even being practical,
she's often stuck up to the axle on her way
to something edible. With everything optimal,
she skirts the ditch which would convert   10
her shell into a serving dish. She lives
below luck-level, never imagining some lottery
will change her load of pottery to wings.
Her only levity is patience,
the sport of truly chastened things.   15

Emily Brontë (1818–1848)

Love and Friendship   (1839)

Love is like the wild rose-briar;
Friendship like the holly-tree—
The holly is dark when the rose-briar blooms
But which will bloom most constantly?

The wild rose-briar is sweet in spring,   5
Its summer blossoms scent the air;
Yet wait till winter comes again
And who will call the wild-briar fair?

Then scorn the silly rose-wreath now
And deck thee with the holly's sheen,   10
That when December blights thy brow
He still may leave thy garland green.

John Keats (1795–1821)

Ode on a Grecian Urn   1820

Thou still unravished bride of quietness,
    Thou foster-child of silence and slow time,
Sylvan historian, who canst thus express
    A flowery tale more sweetly than our rhyme:
What leaf-fringed legend haunts about thy shape   5
    Of deities or mortals, or of both,
        In Tempe or the dales of Arcady?
    What men or gods are these? What maidens loth?
What mad pursuit? What struggle to escape?
        What pipes and timbrels? What wild ecstasy?   10

Heard melodies are sweet, but those unheard
    Are sweeter; therefore, ye soft pipes, play on;
Not to the sensual° ear, but, more endeared,   *physical*
    Pipe to the spirit ditties of no tone:
Fair youth, beneath the trees, thou canst not leave   15
    Thy song, nor ever can those trees be bare;
        Bold Lover, never, never canst thou kiss,
Though winning near the goal—yet, do not grieve;
        She cannot fade, though thou hast not thy bliss,
    For ever wilt thou love, and she be fair!   20

Ah, happy, happy boughs! that cannot shed
    Your leaves, nor ever bid the Spring adieu;
And, happy melodist, unwearièd,
    For ever piping songs for ever new;

More happy love! more happy, happy love!   25
    For ever warm and still to be enjoyed,
        For ever panting, and for ever young;
All breathing human passion far above,
    That leaves a heart high-sorrowful and cloyed,
        A burning forehead, and a parching tongue.   30

Who are these coming to the sacrifice?
    To what green altar, O mysterious priest,
Lead'st thou that heifer lowing at the skies,
    And all her silken flanks with garlands drest?
What little town by river or sea shore,   35
    Or mountain-built with peaceful citadel,
        Is emptied of this folk, this pious morn?
And, little town, thy streets for evermore
    Will silent be; and not a soul to tell
        Why thou art desolate, can e'er return.   40

O Attic shape! Fair attitude! with brede°   *design*
    Of marble men and maidens overwrought,
With forest branches and the trodden weed;
    Thou, silent form, dost tease us out of thought
As doth eternity: Cold Pastoral!   45
    When old age shall this generation waste,
        Thou shalt remain, in midst of other woe
Than ours, a friend to man, to whom thou say'st,
    Beauty is truth, truth beauty,—that is all
        Ye know on earth, and all ye need to know.   50

ODE ON A GRECIAN URN. *7 Tempe, dales of Arcady:* valleys in Greece. *41 Attic:* Athenian, possessing a classical simplicity and grace. 49–50: if Keats had put the urn's words in quotation marks, critics might have been spared much ink. Does the urn say just "beauty is truth, truth beauty," or does its statement take in the whole of the last two lines?

■ WRITING *effectively*

THINKING ABOUT METAPHORS

Metaphors are more than mere decoration. Sometimes, for example, they help us envision an unfamiliar thing more clearly by comparing it with another, more familiar item. A metaphor can reveal interesting aspects of both items. Usually we can see the main point of a good metaphor immediately, but in interpreting a poem, the practical issue sometimes arises of how far to extend a comparison.

■ **To write effectively about a metaphorical poem, start by considering the general scope of its key metaphor.** In what ways, for instance, do the characters resemble deer in N. Scott Momaday's "Simile"?

■ **Before you begin to write, clarify which aspects of the comparison are true and which are false.** While the characters in Momaday's poem may resemble alert, anxious deer in their emotional response to their conflict, they probably don't actually have hooves and forward-pointing ears.

■ **Make a list of metaphors and key images in the poem.** Then draw lines to connect the ones that seem to be related.

■ **Notice whether there are obvious connections among all the metaphors or similes in a poem.** Perhaps all of them are threatening, or inviting, or nocturnal, or exaggerated. Such similarities, if they occur, will almost certainly be significant.

CHECKLIST: Writing About Metaphors

☐ Underline a poem's key comparisons. Look for both similes and metaphors.

☐ How are the two things being compared alike?

☐ In what ways are the two things unlike each other?

☐ Do the metaphors or similes in the poem have anything in common?

☐ If so, what does that commonality suggest?

TOPICS FOR WRITING ON FIGURES OF SPEECH

1. In a brief essay of approximately 500 words, analyze the figures of speech to be found in any poem in this chapter. To what effect does the poem employ metaphors, similes, hyperbole, overstatement, paradox, or any other figure of speech?

2. Whip up some similes of your own. Choose someone likely to be unfamiliar to your classmates—your brother or your best friend from home, for example. Write a paragraph in which you use multiple metaphors and similes to communicate a sense of what that person looks, sounds, and acts like. Come up with at least one figure of speech in each sentence.

3. Write a paragraph on any topic, tossing in as many hyperbolic statements as possible. Then write another version, changing all your exaggeration to understatement. In one last paragraph, sum up what this experience taught you about figurative language.

4. Rewrite a short poem rich in figurative language: for example, William Shakespeare's "Shall I compare thee to a summer's day?" or Sylvia Plath's "Metaphors." Taking for your model Howard Moss's deliberately bepiddling version of Shakespeare's poem, use language as flat and unsuggestive as possible. Eliminate every figure of speech. (Ignore any rime or rhythm in the original.) Then, in a paragraph, indicate lines in your revised version that seem glaringly worsened. In conclusion, sum up what your barbaric rewrite tells you about the nature of poetry.

▶ TERMS FOR *review*

Simile and Metaphor

Simile ▶ A comparison of two things, indicated by some connective, usually *like*, *as*, or *than*, or a verb such as *resembles*. A simile usually compares two things that initially seem unlike but are shown to have a significant resemblance. "Cool as a cucumber" and "My love is like a red, red rose" are examples of similes.

Metaphor ▶ A statement that one thing *is* something else, which, in a literal sense, it is not. A metaphor creates a close association between the two entities and underscores some important similarity between them. An example of metaphor is "Richard is a pig."

Implied metaphor ▶ A metaphor that uses neither connectives nor the verb *to be*. If we say "John crowed over his victory," we imply metaphorically that John is a rooster but do not say so specifically.

Mixed metaphor ▶ The (usually unintentional) combining of two or more incompatible metaphors, resulting in ridiculousness or nonsense. For example, "Mary was such a tower of strength that she breezed her way through all the work" ("towers" do not "breeze").

Other Figures of Speech

Personification ▶ The endowing of a thing, an animal, or an abstract term with human characteristics. Personification dramatizes the nonhuman world in tangibly human terms.

Apostrophe ▶ A direct address to someone or something. In an apostrophe, a speaker may address an inanimate object, a dead or absent person, an abstract thing, or a spirit.

Overstatement ▶ Also called **hyperbole**. Exaggeration used to emphasize a point.

Understatement ▶ An ironic figure of speech that deliberately describes something in a way that is less than the case.

15

What You Will Learn in This Chapter

- To recognize and define *alliteration* and *assonance*
- To differentiate and define *euphony*, *cacophony*, and *onomatopoeia*
- To recognize and define the major types of rime
- To analyze the role of sound in a poem

SOUND AS MEANING

Isak Dinesen, in a memoir of her life on a plantation in East Africa, tells how some Kikuyu tribesmen reacted to their first hearing of rimed verse:

> The Natives, who have a strong sense of rhythm, know nothing of verse, or at least did not know anything before the times of the schools, where they were taught hymns. One evening out in the maize-field, where we had been harvesting maize, breaking off the cobs and throwing them on to the ox-carts, to amuse myself, I spoke to the field laborers, who were mostly quite young, in Swahili verse. There was no sense in the verse, it was made for the sake of the rime—"Ngumbe na-penda chumbe, Malaya-mbaya. Wakamba na-kula mamba." The oxen like salt—whores are bad,—The Wakamba do eat snakes. It caught the interest of the boys, they formed a ring round me. They were quick to understand that the meaning in poetry is of no consequence, and they did not question the thesis of the verse, but waited eagerly for the rime, and laughed at it when it came. I tried to make them themselves find the rime and finish the poem when I had begun it, but they could not, or would not, do that, and turned away their heads. As they had become used to the idea of poetry, they begged: "Speak again. Speak like rain." Why they should feel verse to be like rain I do not know. It must have been, however, an expression of applause, since in Africa rain is always longed for and welcomed.[1]

What the tribesmen had discovered is that poetry, like music, appeals to the ear. However limited it may be in comparison with the sound of an orchestra—or a tribal drummer—the sound of words in itself gives pleasure. However, we might doubt Isak Dinesen's assumption that "meaning in poetry is

---

[1]Isak Dinesen, *Out of Africa* (New York: Random, 1972).

of no consequence." "Hey nonny-nonny" and such nonsense has a place in song lyrics and other poems, and we might take pleasure in hearing rimes in Swahili; but most good poetry has meaningful sound as well as musical sound. Certainly the words of a song have an effect different from that of wordless music: they go along with their music and, by making statements, add more meaning. In the response of the Kikuyu tribesmen, there may have been not only the pleasure of hearing sounds but also the agreeable surprise of finding that things not usually associated had been brought together.

Euphony and Cacophony

More powerful when in the company of meaning, not apart from it, the sounds of consonants and vowels can contribute greatly to a poem's effect. The sound of s, which can suggest the swishing of water, has rarely been used more accurately than in Surrey's line "Calm is the sea, the waves work less and less." When, in a poem, the sound of words working together with meaning pleases mind and ear, the effect is **euphony**, as in the following lines from Tennyson's "Come down, O maid":

> Myriads of rivulets hurrying through the lawn,
> The moan of doves in immemorial elms,
> And murmuring of innumerable bees.

Its opposite is **cacophony**: a harsh, discordant effect. It too is chosen for the sake of meaning. We hear it in Milton's scornful reference in "Lycidas" to corrupt clergymen whose songs "Grate on their scrannel pipes of wretched straw." (Read that line and one of Tennyson's aloud and see which requires lips, teeth, and tongue to do more work.) But note that although Milton's line is harsh in sound, the line (when we meet it in his poem) is pleasing because it is artful.

Is sound identical with meaning in lines such as these? Not quite. In the passage from Tennyson, for instance, the cooing of doves is not *exactly* a moan. As John Crowe Ransom pointed out, the sound would be almost the same but the meaning entirely different in "The murdering of innumerable beeves." While it is true that the consonant sound sl- will often begin a word that conveys ideas of wetness and smoothness—*slick, slimy, slippery, slush*—we are so used to hearing it in words that convey nothing of the kind—*slave, slow, sledgehammer*—that it is doubtful whether, all by itself, the sound communicates anything definite. The most beautiful phrase in the English language, according to Dorothy Parker, is *cellar door*. Another wit once nominated, as our most euphonious word, not *sunrise* or *silvery* but *syphilis*.

Onomatopoeia

Relating sound more closely to meaning, the device called **onomatopoeia** is an attempt to represent a thing or action by a word that imitates the sound associated with it: *zoom, whiz, crash, bang, ding-dong, pitter-patter, yakety-yak.*

Onomatopoeia is often effective in poetry, as in Emily Dickinson's line about the fly with its "uncertain stumbling Buzz," in which the nasal sounds *n, m, ng* and the sibilants *c, s* help make a droning buzz.

Like the Kikuyu tribesmen, others who care for poetry have discovered in the sound of words something of the refreshment of cool rain. Dylan Thomas, describing how he began to write poetry, said that from early childhood words were to him "as the notes of bells, the sounds of musical instruments, the noises of wind, sea, and rain, the rattle of milk carts, the clopping of hooves on cobbles, the fingering of branches on the window pane, might be to someone, deaf from birth, who has miraculously found his hearing."[2] For readers, too, the sound of words can have a magical spell, most powerful when it points to meaning.

William Butler Yeats   (1865–1939)

Who Goes with Fergus?   1892

Who will go drive with Fergus now,
And pierce the deep wood's woven shade,
And dance upon the level shore?
Young man, lift up your russet brow,
And lift your tender eyelids, maid,   5
And brood on hopes and fear no more.

And no more turn aside and brood
Upon love's bitter mystery;
For Fergus rules the brazen cars,°   *chariots*
And rules the shadows of the wood,   10
And the white breast of the dim sea
And all dishevelled wandering stars.

WHO GOES WITH FERGUS? *Fergus:* Irish king who gave up his throne to be a wandering poet.

Questions

1. In what lines do you find euphony?
2. In what line do you find cacophony?
3. How do the sounds of these lines stress what is said in them?

Exercise: Listening to Meaning

Read aloud the following brief poems. In the sounds of which particular words are meanings well captured? In which of the two poems do you find onomatopoeia?

[2]"Notes on the Art of Poetry," *Modern Poetics*, ed. James Scully (New York: McGraw-Hill, 1965).

Edgar Allan Poe (1809–1849)

from Ulalume

1847

The skies they were ashen and sober;
  The leaves they were crispéd and sere—
  The leaves they were withering and sere;
It was night, in the lonesome October
  Of my most immemorial year;   5
It was hard by the dim lake of Auber,
  In the misty mid region of Weir—
It was down by the dank tarn of Auber,
  In the ghoul-haunted woodland of Weir.

William Wordsworth (1770–1850)

A Slumber Did My Spirit Seal

1800

A slumber did my spirit seal;
  I had no human fears—
She seemed a thing that could not feel
  The touch of earthly years.

No motion has she now, no force;   5
  She neither hears nor sees;
Rolled round in earth's diurnal course,
  With rocks, and stones, and trees.

ALLITERATION AND ASSONANCE

Listening to a symphony in which themes are repeated throughout each movement, we enjoy both their recurrence and their variation. We take similar pleasure in the repetition of a phrase or a single chord. Something like this pleasure is afforded us frequently in poetry.

Analogies between poetry and wordless music, it is true, tend to break down when carried far, since poetry—to mention a single difference—has words with literal meanings. But like musical compositions, poems have patterns of sounds. Among such patterns long popular in English poetry is **alliteration**, which has been defined as a succession of similar sounds. Alliteration occurs in the repetition of the same consonant sound at the beginning of successive words—"round and round the rugged rocks the ragged rascal ran." Or it may occur inside the words, as in Milton's description of the gates of Hell:

>   On a sudden open fly
> With impetuous recoil and jarring sound
> The infernal doors, and on their hinges grate
> Harsh thunder, that the lowest bottom shook
> Of Erebus.

The former kind is called **initial alliteration**, the latter **internal alliteration** or **hidden alliteration**. We recognize alliteration by sound, not by spelling: *know* and *nail* alliterate, *know* and *key* do not. In a line by E. E. Cummings, "colossal hoax of clocks and calendars," the sound of *x* within *hoax* alliterates with the *cks* in *clocks*.

As we have seen, to repeat the sound of a consonant is to produce alliteration, but to repeat the sound of a *vowel* is to produce **assonance**. Like alliteration, assonance may occur either initially—"all the *awful auguries*"— or internally—Edmund Spenser's "Her goodly *eyes* like sapphires shining bright, / Her forehead *ivory* white . . . "—and it can help make common phrases unforgettable: "eager beaver," "holy smoke." Like alliteration, it slows the reader down and focuses attention.

Frances Cornford (1886–1960)

The Watch   1910

I wakened on my hot, hard bed,
Upon the pillow lay my head;
Beneath the pillow I could hear
My little watch was ticking clear.
I thought the throbbing of it went   5
Like my continual discontent;
I thought it said in every tick:
I am so sick, so sick, so sick;
O Death, come quick, come quick, come quick,
Come quick, come quick, come quick, come quick.   10

Questions

1. Read the poem aloud, and identify examples of internal alliteration.
2. What do the hard *ck* sounds at the end of the poem resemble, and how does that fit with the poem's theme and subject?

Experiment: Reading for Assonance

Try reading aloud as rapidly as possible the following poem by Tennyson. From the difficulties you encounter, you may be able to sense the slowing effect of assonance. Then read the poem aloud a second time, with consideration.

Alfred, Lord Tennyson (1809–1892)

The splendor falls on castle walls   1847

The splendor falls on castle walls
    And snowy summits old in story:
The long light shakes across the lakes,
    And the wild cataract leaps in glory.

Blow, bugle, blow, set the wild echoes flying,   5
Blow, bugle; answer, echoes, dying, dying, dying.

> O hark, O hear! how thin and clear,
>   And thinner, clearer, farther going!
> O sweet and far from cliff and scar°   *jutting rock*
>   The horns of Elfland faintly blowing!   10
> Blow, let us hear the purple glens replying:
> Blow, bugle; answer, echoes, dying, dying, dying.

> O love, they die in yon rich sky,
>   They faint on hill or field or river:
> Our echoes roll from soul to soul,   15
>   And grow for ever and for ever.
> Blow, bugle, blow, set the wild echoes flying,
> And answer, echoes, answer, dying, dying, dying.

RIME

Isak Dinesen's tribesmen, to whom rime was a new phenomenon, recognized at once that rimed language is special language. So do we, for, although much English poetry is unrimed, rime is one means of setting poetry apart from ordinary conversation and bringing it closer to music. A **rime** (or rhyme), defined most narrowly, occurs when two or more words or phrases contain an identical or similar vowel sound, usually accented, and the consonant sounds (if any) that follow the vowel sound are identical: *hay* and *sleigh*, *prairie schooner* and *piano tuner*. From these examples it will be seen that rime depends not on spelling but on sound.

Excellent rimes surprise. It is all very well that a reader may anticipate which vowel sound is coming next, for patterns of rime give pleasure by satisfying expectations; but riming becomes dull clunking if, at the end of each line, the reader can predict the word that will end the next. Hearing many a jukebox song for the first time, a listener can do so: *charms* lead to *arms*, *skies above* to *love*. As Alexander Pope observes of the habits of dull rimesters,

> Where'er you find "the cooling western breeze,"
> In the next line it "whispers through the trees";
> If crystal streams "with pleasing murmurs creep,"
> The reader's threatened (not in vain) with "sleep" . . .

Robert Herrick made good use of rime to indicate a startling contrast:

> Then while time serves, and we are but decaying,
> Come, my Corinna, come, let's go a-Maying.

Though good rimes seem fresh, not all will startle us, and probably few will call to mind things so unlike as *May* and *decay*. Some masters of rime often link words that, taken out of context, might seem common and unevocative.

Here are the opening lines of Rachel Hadas's poem "Three Silences," which describe an infant feeding at a mother's breast:

> Of all the times when not to speak is best,
> mother's and infant's is the easiest,
> the milky mouth still warm against her breast.

Hadas's rime words are not especially memorable in themselves, and yet these lines are—at least in part because they rime so well. The quiet echo of sound at the end of each line reinforces the intimate tone of the mother's moment with her child. Poetic invention may be driven home without rime, but sometimes it is rime that rings the doorbell.

Admittedly, some rimes wear thin from too much use. Rimes such as *moon, June, croon* seem leaden and would need an extremely powerful context to ring true. *Death, breath* is a rime that poets have used with wearisome frequency; another is *birth, earth, mirth*. And yet we cannot exclude these from the diction of poetry, for they might be the very words a poet would need in order to say something new and original.

Types of Rime

To have an **exact rime**, sounds following the vowel sound have to be the same: *red* and *bread, wealthily* and *stealthily, walk to her* and *talk to her*. If final consonant sounds are the same but the vowel sounds are different, the result is **slant rime**, also called **near rime**, **off rime**, or **imperfect rime**: *sun* riming with *bone, moon, rain, green, gone, thin*. By not satisfying the reader's expectation of an exact chime, but instead giving a clunk, a slant rime can help a poet say some things in a particular way. It works especially well for disappointed letdowns, negations, and denials, as in Blake's couplet:

> He who the ox to wrath has moved
> Shall never be by woman loved.

Consonance, a kind of slant rime, occurs when the rimed words or phrases have the same beginning and ending consonant sounds but a different vowel, as in *chitter* and *chatter*. Consonance is used in a traditional nonsense poem, "The Cutty Wren": "'O where are you going?' says *Milder* to *Malder*." (W. H. Auden wrote a variation on it that begins, "'O where are you going?' said *reader* to *rider*," thus keeping the consonance.)

End rime, as its name indicates, comes at the ends of lines; **internal rime** within them. Most rime tends to be end rime. Few recent poets have used internal rime so heavily as Wallace Stevens in the beginning of "Bantams in Pine-Woods": "Chieftain Iffucan of Azcan in caftan / Of tan with henna hackles, halt!" (lines also heavy on alliteration). A poet may employ both end rime and internal rime in the same poem, as in Robert Burns's satiric ballad "The Kirk's Alarm":

Orthodox, Orthodox, wha believe in John Knox,
   Let me sound an alarm to your conscience:
A heretic blast has been blawn i' the wast,°   *west*
   That "what is not sense must be nonsense."

Masculine rime is a rime of one-syllable words (*jail, bail*) or (in words
of more than one syllable) stressed final syllables: *di-VORCE, re-MORSE,* or
horse, re-MORSE.

Feminine rime is a rime of two or more syllables, with stress on a syllable
other than the last: *TUR-tle, FER-tile,* or (to take an example from Byron) *in-
tel-LECT-u-al, hen-PECKED you all.* Often it lends itself to comic verse, but
it can occasionally be valuable to serious poems, as in Wordsworth's "Resolution and Independence":

We poets in our youth begin in gladness,
But thereof come in the end despondency and madness.

Artfully used, feminine rime can give a poem a heightened musical effect
for the simple reason that it offers the listener twice as many riming syllables in
each line. In the wrong hands, however, that sonic abundance has the unfortunate ability of making a bad poem twice as painful to endure. Serious poems
containing feminine rimes of three syllables have been attempted, notably by
Thomas Hood in "The Bridge of Sighs":

Take her up tenderly,
Lift her with care;
Fashioned so slenderly,
Young, and so fair!

But the pattern is hard to sustain without lapsing into unintended comedy, as
in the same poem:

Still, for all slips of hers,
One of Eve's family—
Wipe those poor lips of hers,
Oozing so clammily.

It works better when the comedy is intentional.

Hilaire Belloc (1870–1953)

The Hippopotamus   1896

I shoot the Hippopotamus
   with bullets made of platinum,
Because if I use leaden ones
   his hide is sure to flatten 'em.

William Butler Yeats (1865–1939)

Leda and the Swan

1928

A sudden blow: the great wings beating still
Above the staggering girl, her thighs caressed
By the dark webs, her nape caught in his bill,
He holds her helpless breast upon his breast.

How can those terrified vague fingers push   5
The feathered glory from her loosening thighs?
And how can body, laid in that white rush,
But feel the strange heart beating where it lies?

A shudder in the loins engenders there
The broken wall, the burning roof and tower   10
And Agamemnon dead.
                       Being so caught up,
So mastered by the brute blood of the air,
Did she put on his knowledge with his power
Before the indifferent beak could let her drop?

Questions

1. According to Greek mythology, the god Zeus in the form of a swan descended on Leda, a Spartan queen. Among Leda's children were Clytemnestra, Agamemnon's unfaithful wife, who conspired in his murder, and Helen, on whose account the Trojan War was fought. What does a knowledge of these allusions contribute to our understanding of the poem's last two lines?

2. The slant rime *up / drop* (lines 11, 14) may seem accidental or inept. Is it? Would this poem have ended nearly so well if Yeats had made an exact rime like *up / cup* or *stop / drop*?

Gerard Manley Hopkins (1844–1889)

God's Grandeur

(1877)

The world is charged with the grandeur of God.
    It will flame out, like shining from shook foil;
    It gathers to a greatness, like the ooze of oil
Crushed. Why do men then now not reck his rod?
Generations have trod, have trod, have trod;   5
    And all is seared with trade; bleared, smeared with toil;
    And wears man's smudge and shares man's smell: the soil
Is bare now, nor can foot feel, being shod.

And for all this, nature is never spent;
    There lives the dearest freshness deep down things;   10
And though the last lights off the black West went

Oh, morning, at the brown brink eastward, springs—
Because the Holy Ghost over the bent
World broods with warm breast and with ah! bright wings.

GOD'S GRANDEUR. 1 *charged:* as though with electricity. 3–4 *It gathers . . . Crushed:* The grandeur of God will rise and be manifest, as oil rises and collects from crushed olives or grain. 4 *reck his rod:* heed His law. 10 *deep down things:* Tightly packing the poem, Hopkins omits the preposition *in* or *within* before *things.* 11 *last lights . . . went:* When in 1534 Henry VIII broke ties with the Roman Catholic Church and created the Church of England.

Questions

1. In a letter Hopkins explained "shook foil" (line 2): "I mean foil in its sense of leaf or tinsel. . . . Shaken goldfoil gives off broad glares like sheet lightning and also, and this is true of nothing else, owing to its zigzag dints and creasings and network of small many cornered facets, a sort of fork lightning too." What do you think he meant by the phrase "ooze of oil" (line 3)? Would you call this phrase an example of alliteration?

2. What instances of internal rime does the poem contain? How would you describe their effects?

3. Point out some of the poet's uses of alliteration and assonance. Do you believe that Hopkins perhaps goes too far in his heavy use of devices of sound, or would you defend his practice?

4. Why do you suppose Hopkins, in the last two lines, says "over the bent / World" instead of (as we might expect) *bent over the world*? How can the world be bent? Can you make any sense out of this wording, or is Hopkins just trying to get his rime scheme to work out?

Robert Frost (1874–1963)

Desert Places   1936

Snow falling and night falling fast, oh, fast
In a field I looked into going past,
And the ground almost covered smooth in snow,
But a few weeds and stubble showing last.

The woods around it have it—it is theirs.   5
All animals are smothered in their lairs.
I am too absent-spirited to count;
The loneliness includes me unawares.

And lonely as it is that loneliness
Will be more lonely ere it will be less—   10
A blanker whiteness of benighted snow
With no expression, nothing to express.

They cannot scare me with their empty spaces
Between stars—on stars where no human race is.
I have it in me so much nearer home   15
To scare myself with my own desert places.

Questions

1. What are these desert places that the speaker finds in himself? (More than one theory is possible. What is yours?)
2. Notice how many times, within the short space of lines 8–10, Frost says *lonely* (or *loneliness*). What other words in the poem contain similar sounds that reinforce these words?
3. In the closing stanza, the feminine rimes *spaces*, *race is*, and *places* might well occur in light or comic verse. Does "Desert Places" leave you laughing? If not, what does it make you feel?

HOW TO READ A POEM ALOUD

There is no better way to understand a poem than to read it aloud. Developing skill at reading poems aloud will not only deepen your understanding of literature, but it will also improve your ability to speak in public.

Before trying to read a poem aloud to other people, understand its meaning as thoroughly as possible. If you know what the poet is saying and the poet's attitude toward it, you will be able to find an appropriate tone of voice and to give each part of the poem a proper emphasis.

Except in the most informal situations and in some class exercises, read a poem to yourself before trying it on an audience. No actor goes before the footlights without first having studied the script, and the language of poems usually demands even more consideration than the language of most contemporary plays. Prepare your reading in advance. Check pronunciations you are not sure of. Underline words that should be emphasized.

Read more slowly than you normally would. Keep in mind that you are saying something to somebody. Don't race through the poem as if you are eager to get it over with.

Don't lapse into singsong. A poem may have a definite swing, but swing should never be exaggerated at the cost of sense. If you understand what the poem is saying and speak the poem as if you do, the temptation to fall into such a mechanical intonation should not occur. Observe the punctuation, making slight pauses for commas and longer pauses for full stops (periods, question marks, exclamation points).

If the poem is rimed, don't raise your voice and make the rimes stand out unnaturally. They should receive no more volume than other words in the poem, though a faint pause at the end of each line will call the listener's attention to them.

If, in first listening to a poem, you don't take in all its meaning, don't be discouraged. With more practice in listening, your attention span and your ability to understand poems read aloud will increase. Incidentally, following the text of poems in a book while hearing them read aloud may increase your comprehension, but it may not necessarily help you to *listen*. At least some of the time, close your book and let your ears make the poems welcome. That way, their sounds may better work for you.

Exercise: **Reading for Sound and Meaning**

Read this brief poem aloud. What devices of sound do you find? Try to explain what sound contributes to the total effect of the poem and how it reinforces what the poet is saying.

Michael Stillman (b. 1940)

In Memoriam John Coltrane   1972

Listen to the coal
rolling, rolling through the cold
   steady rain, wheel on

wheel, listen to the
turning of the wheels this night   5
   black as coal dust, steel

on steel, listen to
these cars carry coal, listen
   to the coal train roll.

IN MEMORIAM JOHN COLTRANE. John Coltrane (1926–1967) was a saxophonist whose originality, passion, and technical wizardry have had a deep influence on the history of modern jazz.

■ WRITING *effectively*

THINKING ABOUT A POEM'S SOUND

A poem's music—the distinct way it sounds—is an important element of its effect and a large part of what separates it from prose. Describing a poem's sound can be tricky, though. Critics often disagree about the sonic effects of particular poems. Cataloguing every auditory element of a poem would be a huge, unwieldy job. The easiest way to write about sound is to focus your discussion. Concentrate on a single, clearly defined sonic element that strikes you as especially noteworthy. Simply try to understand how that element helps communicate the poem's main theme.

> ■ **You might examine, for example, how certain features (such as rime, rhythm, meter, or alliteration) add force to the literal meaning of each line.** Or, for an ironic poem, you might look at how those same elements undercut and change the surface meaning of the poem.

- **Keep in mind that for a detailed analysis of this sort, it often helps to choose a short poem.** If you want to write about a longer poem, focus on a short passage that strikes you as especially rich in sonic effects.
- **Let your data build up before you force any conclusions about the poem's auditory effects.** As your list grows, a pattern should emerge, and ideas will probably occur to you that were not apparent earlier.

CHECKLIST: Writing About a Poem's Sound

☐ List the main auditory elements you find in the poem.

☐ Look for rime, meter, alliteration, assonance, euphony, cacophony, repetition, onomatopoeia.

☐ Is there a pattern in your list? Is the poem particularly heavy in alliteration or repetition, for example?

☐ Limit your discussion to one or two clearly defined sonic effects.

☐ How do your chosen effects help communicate the poem's main theme?

☐ How does the sound of the words add to the poem's mood?

TOPICS FOR WRITING ON SOUND

1. Choose a brief poem from this chapter or Chapter 22 and examine how one or two elements of sound work throughout the poem to strengthen its meaning. Before you write, review the elements of sound described in this chapter. Back up your argument with specific quotations from the poem.

2. Silently read Sylvia Plath's "Daddy" (Chapter 22). Then read the poem aloud, to yourself or to a friend. Now write briefly. What did you perceive about the poem from reading it aloud that you hadn't noticed before?

3. Consider the verbal music of Michael Stillman's "In Memoriam John Coltrane" (or a selection from Chapter 22). Read the poem both silently and aloud, listening for sonic effects. Describe how the poem's sound underscores its meaning.

▶ TERMS FOR *review*

Sound Effects

Alliteration ▶ The repetition of a consonant sound in a line of verse or prose. Alliteration can be used at the beginning of words (**initial alliteration** as in "cool cats") or internally on stressed syllables (**internal alliteration** as in "I met a traveler from an antique land.").

Assonance ▶ The repetition of two or more vowel sounds in successive words, which creates a kind of rime. Like alliteration, the assonance may occur initially ("*a*ll the *aw*ful *au*guries") or internally ("white lilacs").

Cacophony ▶ A harsh, discordant sound often mirroring the meaning of the context in which it is used. The opposite of cacophony is **euphony**.

Euphony ▶ The harmonious effect when the sounds of the words connect with the meaning in a way pleasing to the ear and mind. The opposite of euphony is **cacophony**.

Onomatopoeia ▶ An attempt to represent a thing or action by a word that imitates the sound associated with it.

Rime

Rime ▶ Two or more words that contain an identical or similar vowel sound, usually accented, with following consonant sounds (if any) identical as well (*woo* and *stew*). An **exact rime** is a full rime in which the sounds following the initial letters of the words are identical in sound (*follow* and *hollow*).

Consonance ▶ Also called **slant rime**. A kind of rime in which the linked words share similar consonant sounds but have different vowel sounds, as in *reason* and *raisin*, *mink* and *monk*. Sometimes only the final consonant sound is identical, as in *fame* and *room*.

End rime ▶ Rime that occurs at the ends of lines, rather than within them. End rime is the most common kind of rime in English-language poetry.

Internal rime ▶ Rime that occurs within a line of poetry, as opposed to **end rime**.

Masculine rime ▶ Either a rime of one-syllable words (*fox* and *socks*) or—in polysyllabic words—a rime on the stressed final syllables (con-*trive* and sur-*vive*).

Feminine rime ▶ A rime of two or more syllables with stress on a syllable other than the last (*tur*-tle and *fer*-tile).

16 RHYTHM

What You Will Learn in This Chapter

- To define *rhythm* and *stress*
- To define *prosody* and *scansion*
- To recognize and define the four major English meters
- To analyze the role of rhythm in a poem

STRESSES AND PAUSES

Rhythms affect us powerfully. We are lulled by a hammock's sway, awakened by an alarm clock's repeated yammer. Long after we come home from a beach, the rising and falling of waves and tides continue in memory. How powerfully the rhythms of poetry also move us may be felt in folk songs of railroad workers and chain gangs whose words were chanted in time to the lifting and dropping of a sledgehammer, and in verse that marching soldiers shout, putting a stress on every word that coincides with a footfall:

> Your LEFT! TWO! THREE! FOUR!
> Your LEFT! TWO! THREE! FOUR!
> You LEFT your WIFE and TWEN-ty-one KIDS
> And you LEFT! TWO! THREE! FOUR!
> You'll NEV-er get HOME to-NIGHT!

A rhythm is produced by a series of recurrences: the returns and departures of the seasons, the repetitions of an engine's stroke, the beats of the heart. A rhythm may be produced by the recurrence of a sound (the throb of a drum, a telephone's busy signal), but rhythm and sound are not identical. A totally deaf person at a parade can sense rhythm from the motions of the marchers' arms and feet, from the shaking of the pavement as they tramp. Rhythms inhere in the motions of the moon and stars, even though when they move, we hear no sound.

Rhythm

In poetry, several kinds of recurrent *sound* are possible, including (as we saw in the previous chapter) rime, alliteration, and assonance. But most often when we speak of the **rhythm** of a poem, we mean the recurrence of stresses and pauses in it. When we hear a poem read aloud, stresses and pauses are, of course, part of its sound. It is possible to be aware of rhythms in poems read silently, too.

Stresses

A **stress** (or **accent**) is a greater amount of force given to one syllable in speaking than is given to another. We favor a stressed syllable with a little more breath and emphasis, with the result that it comes out slightly louder, higher in pitch, or longer in duration than other syllables. In this manner we place a stress on the first syllable of words such as *eagle*, *impact*, *open*, and *statue*, and on the second syllable in *cigar*, *mystique*, *precise*, and *until*.

Each word in English carries at least one stress, except (usually) for the articles *a*, *an*, and *the*, the conjunction *and*, and one-syllable prepositions: *at*, *by*, *for*, *from*, *of*, *to*, *with*. One word by itself is seldom long enough for us to notice a rhythm in it. Usually a sequence of at least a few words is needed for stresses to establish their pattern: a line, a passage, a whole poem.

Strong rhythms may be seen in most Mother Goose rimes, to which children have been responding for hundreds of years. This rime is for an adult to chant while bouncing a child up and down on a knee:

> Here goes my lord
> A trot, a trot, a trot, a trot!
> Here goes my lady
> A canter, a canter, a canter, a canter!
> Here goes my young master
> Jockey-hitch, jockey-hitch, jockey-hitch, jockey-hitch!
> Here goes my young miss
> An amble, an amble, an amble, an amble!
> The footman lags behind to tipple ale and wine
> And goes gallop, a gallop, a gallop, to make up his time.

More than one rhythm occurs in these lines, as the make-believe horse changes pace. How do these rhythms differ? From one line to the next, the interval between stresses lengthens or grows shorter. In "a TROT a TROT a TROT a TROT," the stress falls on every other syllable. But in the middle of the line "A CAN-ter a CAN-ter a CAN-ter a CAN-ter," the stress falls on every third syllable. When stresses recur at fixed intervals as in these lines, the result is called a **meter**.

STRESS AND MEANING

Stresses embody meanings. Whenever two or more fall side by side, words gain in emphasis. Consider these hard-hitting lines from John Donne, in which accent marks have been placed, dictionary-fashion, to indicate the stressed syllables:

> Bat·ter my heart, three·per·soned God, for You
> As yet but knock, breathe, shine, and seek to mend.
> That I may rise and stand, o'er·throw me, and bend
> Your force to break, blow, burn, and make me new.

When unstressed (or **slack**) **syllables** recur in pairs, the result is a rhythm that trips and bounces, as in Robert Service's rollicking line:

A bunch of the boys were whoop·ing it up in the Ma·la·mute sa·loon . . .

or in Edgar Allan Poe's lines—also light but meant to be serious:

For the moon nev·er beams, with·out bring·ing me dreams
Of the beau·ti·ful An·na·bel Lee.

Apart from the words that convey it, the rhythm of a poem has no meaning. There are no essentially sad rhythms, nor any essentially happy ones. But some rhythms enforce certain meanings better than others do. The bouncing rhythm of Service's line seems fitting for an account of a merry night in a Klondike saloon; but it may be distracting when encountered in Poe's wistful elegy.

The special power of poetry comes from allowing us to hear simultaneously every level of meaning in language—denotation and connotation, image and idea, abstract content and physical sound. Since sound stress is one of the ways that the English language most clearly communicates meaning, any regular rhythmic pattern will influence the poem's effect. As film directors know, any movie scene's effect can change dramatically if different background music accompanies the images. Master of the suspense film Alfred Hitchcock, for instance, could fill an ordinary scene with tension or terror just by playing nervous, grating music underneath it.

Exercise: Get with the Beat

In these two passages the author has established a strong rhythm. Describe how the rhythm helps establish the tone and meaning of the poem. How does each poem's beat seem appropriate to the tone and subject?

1. I couldn't be cooler, I come from Missoula,
   And I rope and I chew and I ride.
   But I'm a heroin dealer, and I drive a four-wheeler
   With stereo speakers inside.
   My ol' lady Phoebe's out rippin' off C.B.'s
   From the rigs at the Wagon Wheel Bar,
   Near a Montana truck stop and a shit-outta-luck stop
   For a trucker who's driven too far.
                    —Greg Keeler, from "There Ain't No Such Thing as a Montana
                       Cowboy" (a song lyric)

2. Oh newsprint moonprint Marilyn!
   Rub ink from a finger
   to make your beauty mark.
                    —Rachel Eisler, from "Marilyn's Nocturne" (a poem about a
                       newspaper photograph of Marilyn Monroe)

Pauses

Rhythms in poetry are due not only to stresses but also to pauses. "Every nice ear," observed Alexander Pope (*nice* meaning "finely tuned"), "must, I believe, have observed that in any smooth English verse of ten syllables, there is naturally a pause either at the fourth, fifth, or sixth syllable." Such a light but definite pause within a line is called a **cesura** (or **caesura**), Latin for "a cutting." More liberally than Pope, we apply the name to any pause in a line of any length, after any word in the line. In studying a poem, we often indicate a cesura by double vertical lines (‖). Usually, a cesura will occur at a mark of punctuation, but there can be a cesura even if no punctuation is present. Sometimes you will find it at the end of a phrase or clause or, as in these lines by William Blake, after an internal rime:

> And priests in black gowns ‖ were walking their rounds
> And binding with briars ‖ my joys and desires.

Lines of ten or twelve syllables (as Pope knew) tend to have just one cesura, though sometimes there are more, as in John Webster's line from *The Duchess of Malfi*:

> Cover her face: ‖ mine eyes dazzle: ‖ she died young.

LINE ENDINGS

Pauses also tend to recur at more prominent places—namely, after each line. At the end of a verse (from *versus*, Latin for "a turning"), the reader's eye, before turning to go on to the next line, makes a pause, however brief. If a line ends in a full pause—usually indicated by some mark of punctuation—we call it **end-stopped**. All the lines in this passage from Christopher Marlowe's *Doctor Faustus* (in which Faustus addresses the apparition of Helen of Troy) are end-stopped:

> Was this the face that launch'd a thousand ships,
> And burnt the topless towers of Ilium?
> Sweet Helen, make me immortal with a kiss.
> Her lips suck forth my soul: see, where it flies!
> Come, Helen, come, give me my soul again.
> Here will I dwell, for heaven is in these lips,
> And all is dross that is not Helena.

A line that does not end in punctuation and that therefore is read with only a slight pause after it is called a **run-on line**. Because a run-on line gives us only part of a phrase, clause, or sentence, we have to read on to the line or lines following, in order to complete a thought. All these lines from Robert Browning's "My Last Duchess" (Chapter 9) are run-on lines:

> Sir, 'twas not
> Her husband's presence only, called that spot
> Of joy into the Duchess' cheek: perhaps
> Frà Pandolf chanced to say "Her mantle laps
> Over my lady's wrist too much," or "Paint
> Must never hope to reproduce the faint
> Half-flush that dies along her throat": such stuff
> Was courtesy, she thought . . .

A passage in run-on lines has a rhythm different from that of a passage like Marlowe's in end-stopped lines. When emphatic pauses occur in the quotation from Browning, they fall within a line rather than at the end of one. The passage by Marlowe and that by Browning are in lines of the same meter (iambic) and the same length (ten syllables). What makes the big difference in their rhythms is the running on, or lack of it.

To sum up: rhythm is recurrence. In poems, it is made of stresses and pauses. The poet can produce it by doing any of several things: making the intervals between stresses fixed or varied, long or short; indicating pauses (cesuras) within lines; end-stopping lines or running them over; writing in short or long lines. Rhythm in itself cannot convey meaning. And yet if a poet's words have meaning, their rhythm must be one with it.

Gwendolyn Brooks   (1917–2000)

We Real Cool   1960

> *The Pool Players.*
> *Seven at the Golden Shovel.*

We real cool. We
Left school. We

Lurk late. We
Strike straight. We

Sing sin. We   5
Thin gin. We

Jazz June. We
Die soon.

Question

Describe the rhythms of this poem. By what techniques are they produced?

Alfred, Lord Tennyson (1809–1892)

Break, Break, Break   (1834)

Break, break, break,
   On thy cold gray stones, O Sea!
And I would that my tongue could utter
   The thoughts that arise in me.

O well for the fisherman's boy,   5
   That he shouts with his sister at play!
O well for the sailor lad,
   That he sings in his boat on the bay!

And the stately ships go on
   To their haven under the hill;   10
But O for the touch of a vanish'd hand,
   And the sound of a voice that is still!

Break, break, break,
   At the foot of thy crags, O Sea!
But the tender grace of a day that is dead   15
   Will never come back to me.

Questions

1. Read the first line aloud. What effect does it create at the beginning of the poem?
2. Is there a regular rhythmic pattern in this poem? If so, how would you describe it?
3. The speaker claims that his or her thoughts are impossible to utter. Using evidence from the poem, can you describe the speaker's thoughts and feelings?

Dorothy Parker (1893–1967)

Résumé   1926

Razors pain you;
Rivers are damp;
Acids stain you;
And drugs cause cramp.
Guns aren't lawful;   5
Nooses give;
Gas smells awful;
You might as well live.

Questions

1. Which of the following words might be used to describe the rhythm of this poem, and which might not—*flowing, jaunty, mournful, tender, abrupt?*
2. Is this light verse or a serious poem? Can it be both?

METER

Meter is the rhythmic pattern of stresses in verse. To enjoy the rhythms of a poem, no special knowledge of meter is necessary. All you need do is pay attention to stresses and where they fall, and you will perceive the basic pattern, if there is any. There is nothing occult about the study of meter. Most people find they can master its essentials in no more time than it takes to learn a new video game. If you take the time, you will then have the pleasure of knowing what is happening in the rhythms of many a fine poem, and pleasurable knowledge may even deepen your insight into poetry. The following discussion, then, will be of interest only to those who care to go deeper into **prosody**, the study of metrical structures in poetry.

Scansion

To make ourselves aware of a meter, we need only listen to a poem, or sound its words to ourselves. If we care to work out exactly what a poet is doing, we *scan* a line or a poem by indicating the stresses in it. **Scansion**, the art of so doing, is not just a matter of pointing to syllables; it is also a matter of listening to a poem and making sense of it. To scan a poem is one way to indicate how to read it aloud; in order to see where stresses fall, you have to see the places where the poet wishes to put emphasis. That is why, when scanning a poem, you may find yourself suddenly understanding it.

The idea in scanning a poem is not to reproduce the sound of a human voice. To scan a poem, rather, is to make a diagram of the stresses (and absences of stress) to show its rhythmical shape, its musical beat. Various marks are used in scansion; in this book we use ′ for a stressed syllable and ⌣ for an unstressed syllable.

Types of Meter

There are four common accentual-syllabic meters in English: iambic, anapestic, trochaic, and dactylic. Each is named for its basic **foot** (usually a unit of two or three syllables that contains one strong stress) or building block.

1. **Iambic**—the most common meter in English poetry. An iambic line is made up primarily of **iambs**, an unstressed syllable followed by a stressed syllable, ⌣ ′. Many writers, such as Robert Frost, feel iambs most easily capture the natural rhythms of our speech.

> ⌣　　′　⌣　′　⌣　　′　⌣　′　　⌣　　　′
> But soft, | what light | through yon | der win | dow breaks?
> —*William Shakespeare*

> ⌣　′　⌣　　′　⌣　′　⌣　　′　⌣　′
> When I | have fears | that I | may cease | to be
> —*John Keats*

2. **Anapestic**—a galloping meter. The anapestic line is made up primarily of **anapests**, two unstressed syllables followed by a stressed syllable, ⏑ ⏑ ′. Anapestic meter resembles iambic but contains an extra unstressed syllable. Totally anapestic lines often roll with such speed that poets sometimes slow them down by substituting an iambic foot (as Poe does in "Annabel Lee").

   Now this | is the Law | of the Jun | gle—as old | and as true
   | as the sky;
   And the Wolf | that shall keep | it may pros | per, | but the Wolf
   | that shall break | it must die.
   —*Rudyard Kipling*

   It was ma | ny and ma | ny a year | a go,
   In a king | dom by | the sea,
   That a maid | en there lived | whom you | may know
   By the name | of An | na·bel Lee.
   —*Edgar Allan Poe*

3. **Trochaic**—often associated with songs, chants, and magic spells in English. The trochaic line is made up primarily of **trochees**, a stressed syllable followed by an unstressed syllable, ′ ⏑. Trochees make a strong, emphatic meter that is often very mnemonic—that is, "helping, or meant to help, the memory." Shakespeare used trochaic meter to exploit its magical associations.

   Dou·ble, | dou·ble, | toil and | trou·ble,
   Fi·re | burn and | caul·dron | bub·ble.
   —*William Shakespeare*

4. **Dactylic**—a less common meter for English poetry, with a gently rolling meter. The dactylic line is made up primarily of **dactyls**, one stressed syllable followed by two unstressed syllables, ′ ⏑ ⏑. The dactylic meter is more often found in classical languages such as Greek or Latin. Used carefully, dactylic meter can sound stately, as in Longfellow's *Evangeline*.

$$\acute{\ } \smile \smile \quad \acute{\ } \smile \smile \quad \acute{\ } \smile \smile \quad \acute{\ } \smile \quad \smile \quad \acute{\ } \smile \smile$$

This is the | for·est pri | me·val. The | mur·mur·ing | pines and the

$$\acute{\ }$$

| hem·lock

—*Henry Wadsworth Longfellow*

But it also easily becomes a prancing, propulsive measure and is often used in comic verse.

$$\acute{\ } \smile \smile \quad \acute{\ } \smile \smile \quad \acute{\ } \smile \smile \quad \acute{\ }$$

Puss·y·cat, | puss·y·cat, | where have you | been?

—*Mother Goose*

Iambic and anapestic meters are called **rising meters** because their movement rises from an unstressed syllable (or syllables) to stress; trochaic and dactylic meters are called **falling**. In the twentieth century, the bouncing meters—anapestic and dactylic—were used more often for comic verse than for serious poetry. Called feet, though they contain no unaccented syllables, are the **monosyllabic foot** ($\acute{\ }$) and the **spondee** ($\acute{\ }\acute{\ }$). Meters are not ordinarily made up of them; if one were, it would be like the steady impact of nails being hammered into a board—no pleasure to hear or to dance to. But inserted now and then, they can lend emphasis and variety to a meter, as Yeats well knew when he broke up the predominantly iambic rhythm of "Who Goes with Fergus?" (Chapter 15) with a line in which two spondees occur.

$$\smile \smile \acute{\ } \quad \acute{\ } \smile \smile \acute{\ } \acute{\ }$$

And the white breast of the dim sea.

The Poetic Line

Meters are classified also by line lengths: *trochaic monometer*, for instance, is a line one trochee long, as in this anonymous brief comment on microbes:

Adam
Had 'em.

A frequently heard metrical description is **iambic pentameter**: a line of five iambs, a meter especially familiar because it occurs in all heroic couplets, sonnets, and blank verse (such as Shakespeare's plays and Milton's *Paradise Lost*).

Line Lengths

Here are the commonly used names for line lengths:

monometer	one foot
dimeter	two feet
trimeter	three feet
tetrameter	four feet
pentameter	five feet

hexameter	six feet
heptameter	seven feet
octameter	eight feet

Lines of more than eight feet are possible but are rare. They tend to break up into shorter lengths in the listening ear.

Like a basic dance step, a meter is not to be slavishly adhered to. The fun in reading a metrical poem often comes from watching the poet continually departing from perfect regularity, giving a few heel-kicks to display a bit of joy or ingenuity, then easing back into the basic step again. Because meter is orderly and the rhythms of living speech are unruly, poets can play one against the other, in a sort of counterpoint. Robert Frost, a master at pitting a line of iambs against a very natural-sounding and irregular sentence, declared, "I am never more pleased than when I can get these into strained relation. I like to drag and break the intonation across the meter as waves first comb and then break stumbling on the shingle."[1]

Accentual Meter

Besides the two rising meters (iambic, anapestic) and the two falling meters (trochaic, dactylic), English poets have another valuable meter, which is commonly found in spoken forms of poetry, such as the ballad and rap music. It is **accentual meter**, in which the poet does not write in feet (as in the other meters) but instead counts accents (stresses). The idea is to have the same number of stresses in each line. The poet may place them anywhere in the line and may include practically any number of unstressed syllables. In "Christabel," for instance, Coleridge keeps four stresses to a line, though the first line has only eight syllables and the last line has eleven:

> There is not wind e·nough to twirl
> The one red leaf, the last of its clan,
> That dan·ces as of·ten as dance it can,
> Hang·ing so light, and hang·ing so high,
> On the top·most twig that looks up at the sky.

Meter has seen a great return to popularity in the past many years. Most contemporary poets now explore the rhythmic possibilities of regular meter in their work, following the examples of major poets from Shakespeare through Yeats, who fashioned their work by it. To enjoy metrical poetry— even to write it—you do not have to slice lines into feet; yet you *do* need to

---

[1]Letter to John Cournos in 1914, in *Selected Letters of Robert Frost*, ed. Lawrance Thompson (New York: Holt, 1964) 128.

recognize when a meter is present in a line, and when the line departs from it. An argument in favor of meter is that it reminds us of body rhythms such as breathing, walking, the beating of the heart. In an effective metrical poem, these rhythms cannot be separated from what the poet is saying—or, in the words of an old jazz song of Duke Ellington's, "It don't mean a thing if it ain't got that swing."

Exercise: Recognizing Rhythms

Which of the following poems contain predominant meters? Which poems are not wholly metrical, but are metrical in certain lines? Point out any such lines. What reasons do you see, in such places, for the poet's seeking a metrical effect?

Edna St. Vincent Millay (1892–1950)

Counting-out Rhyme   1928

Silver bark of beech, and sallow
Bark of yellow birch and yellow
    Twig of willow.

Stripe of green in moosewood maple,
Color seen in leaf of apple,   5
    Bark of popple.

Wood of popple pale as moonbeam,
Wood of oak for yoke and barn-beam,
    Wood of hornbeam.

Silver bark of beech, and hollow   10
Stem of elder, tall and yellow
    Twig of willow.

A. E. Housman (1859–1936)

When I was one-and-twenty   1896

When I was one-and-twenty
    I heard a wise man say,
"Give crowns and pounds and guineas
    But not your heart away;
Give pearls away and rubies   5
    But keep your fancy free."
But I was one-and-twenty,
    No use to talk to me.

When I was one-and-twenty
  I heard him say again,   10
"The heart out of the bosom
  Was never given in vain;
'Tis paid with sighs a plenty
  And sold for endless rue."
And I am two-and-twenty,   15
  And oh, 'tis true, 'tis true.

Walt Whitman (1819–1892)

Beat! Beat! Drums!   (1861)

Beat! beat! drums!—blow! bugles! blow!
Through the windows—through doors—burst like a ruthless force,
Into the solemn church, and scatter the congregation,
Into the school where the scholar is studying;
Leave not the bridegroom quiet—no happiness must he have now   5
    with his bride,
Nor the peaceful farmer any peace, ploughing his field or gathering
    his grain,
So fierce you whirr and pound you drums—so shrill you bugles blow.

Beat! beat! drums!—blow! bugles! blow!
Over the traffic of cities—over the rumble of wheels in the streets;
Are beds prepared for sleepers at night in the houses? no sleepers   10
    must sleep in those beds,
No bargainers' bargains by day—no brokers or speculators—would
    they continue?
Would the talkers be talking? would the singer attempt to sing?
Would the lawyer rise in the court to state his case before the judge?
Then rattle quicker, heavier drums—you bugles wilder blow.

Beat! beat! drums!—blow! bugles! blow!   15
Make no parley—stop for no expostulation,
Mind not the timid—mind not the weeper or prayer,
Mind not the old man beseeching the young man,
Let not the child's voice be heard, nor the mother's entreaties,
Make even the trestles to shake the dead where they lie awaiting   20
    the hearses,
So strong you thump O terrible drums—so loud you bugles blow.

▪ WRITING *effectively*

THINKING ABOUT RHYTHM

When we read casually, we don't need to think very hard about a poem's rhythm. We *feel* it as we read, even if we aren't consciously paying attention to matters such as iambs or anapests. When analyzing a poem, though, it helps to have a clear sense of how the rhythm works, and the best way to reach that understanding is through scansion. A scansion gives us a picture of the poem's most important sound patterns. Scanning a poem can seem a bit intimidating at first, but it really isn't all that difficult.

- ▪ **Read the poem aloud, marking the stressed syllables as you go.**
- ▪ **If you're having a hard time hearing the stresses, read the line a few different ways.** Try to detect which way seems most like natural speech.

Example: **Tennyson's "Break, Break, Break"**
A simple scansion of the opening of Tennyson's poem "Break, Break, Break" might look like this in your notes:

Break, break, break	(3 syllables)
On thy cold gray stones, O Sea!	(7 syllables)/rime
And I would that my tongue could utter	(9 syllables)
The thoughts that arise in me.	(7 syllables)/rime

By now some basic organizing principles of the poem have become clear. The lines are rimed *a b c b*, but they contain an irregular number of syllables. The number of strong stresses, however, seems to be constant, at least in the opening stanza.

Now that you have a visual diagram of the poem's sound, the rhythm will be much easier to write about. This diagram will also lead you to a richer understanding of how the poet's artistry reinforces the poem's meaning. The three sharp syllables of the first line give the reader an immediate sense of the depth and intensity of the speaker's feelings. The sudden burst of syllables in the third line underscores the rush of passion that wells up in his breast and outstrips his ability to give voice to it. And the rhythm of the last two lines— the rising intensity of the third line followed by the ebb of the fourth—subtly suggests the effect of the surging and receding of the waves.

CHECKLIST: Scanning a Poem

☐ Read the poem aloud.

☐ Mark the syllables on which the main speech stresses fall. When in doubt, read the line aloud several different ways. Which way seems most natural?

☐ Are there rimes? Indicate where they occur.

☐ How many syllables are there in each line?

☐ Do any other recurring sound patterns strike you?

☐ Does the poem set up a reliable pattern and then diverge from it anywhere? If so, how does that irregularity underscore the line's meaning?

TOPICS FOR WRITING ON RHYTHM

1. Scan the rhythm of a passage from any poem in this chapter, following the guidelines listed above. Discuss how the poem uses rhythm to create certain key effects. Be sure that your scansion shows all the elements you've chosen to discuss.

2. Pair up with a friend or classmate and take turns reading a poem from this chapter out loud to each other. Now write briefly on what you learned about the poem's rhythm by speaking and hearing it.

3. How do rhythm and other kinds of sonic effects (alliteration and consonance, for example) combine to make meaning in Edna St. Vincent Millay's "Counting-out Rhyme"?

4. Scan a stanza of Walt Whitman's "Beat! Beat! Drums!" What do you notice about the poem's rhythms? How do the rhythms underscore the poem's meaning?

5. Scan two poems, one in free verse, and the other in regular meter. For a free verse poem you might pick Allen Ginsberg's "A Supermarket in California" (Chapter 22) or Stephen Crane's "The Wayfarer" (Chapter 10); for a poem in regular meter you could go with one of the poems in this chapter, for example, A. E. Housman's "When I was one-and-twenty." Now write about the experience. Do you detect any particular strengths offered by regular meter? How about by free verse?

▶ TERMS FOR *review*

Pattern and Structure

Stress ▶ An emphasis, or **accent**, placed on a syllable in speech. An unstressed syllable in a line of verse is called a **slack syllable**.

Rhythm ▶ The recurring pattern of stresses and pauses in a poem. A fixed rhythm in a poem is called **meter**.

Prosody ▶ The study of metrical structures in poetry.

Scansion ▶ A practice used to describe rhythmic patterns in a poem by separating the metrical feet, counting the syllables, marking the accents, and indicating the cesuras.

Cesura or **caesura** ▶ A light but definite pause within a line of verse. Cesuras often appear near the middle of a line, but their placement may be varied for rhythmic effect.

Run-on line ▶ A line of verse that does not end in punctuation but carries on grammatically to the next line. The use of run-on lines is called *enjambment*.

End-stopped line ▶ A line of verse that ends in a full pause, often indicated by a mark of punctuation.

Meter

Foot ▶ The basic unit of measurement in metrical poetry. Each separate meter is identified by the pattern and order of stressed and unstressed syllables in its foot.

Iamb ▶ A metrical foot in verse in which an unaccented syllable is followed by an accented one (˘ ′). The iambic measure is the most common one used in English poetry.

Iambic pentameter ▶ The most common meter in English verse, five iambic feet per line. Many fixed forms, such as the sonnet and heroic couplets, employ iambic pentameter.

Anapest ▶ A metrical foot in verse in which two unstressed syllables are followed by a stressed syllable (˘˘′).

Trochee ▶ A metrical foot in which a stressed syllable is followed by an unstressed one (′ ˘).

Dactyl ▶ A metrical foot in which one stressed syllable is followed by two unstressed ones (′ ˘˘). Dactylic meter is less common in English than in classical Greek and Latin.

Spondee ▶ A metrical foot of verse consisting of two stressed syllables (′ ′).

Accentual meter ▶ Verse meter based on the number of stresses per line, not the number of syllables.

17

CLOSED FORM

What You Will Learn in This Chapter

- To define *form* as a literary concept
- To describe and differentiate closed and open forms
- To recognize and describe the two major sonnet forms, Italian and English
- To analyze the role of form in a poem

Form, as a general idea, is the design of a thing as a whole, the configuration of all its parts. No poem can escape having some kind of form, whether its lines are as various in length as a tree's branches or all in hexameter. To put this point in another way: if you were to listen to a poem read aloud in a language unknown to you, or if you saw the poem printed in that foreign language, whatever in the poem you could see or hear would be the form of it.

Writing in **closed form**, a poet follows (or finds) some sort of pattern, such as that of a sonnet with its rime scheme and its fourteen lines of iambic pentameter. On a page, poems in closed form tend to look regular and symmetrical, often falling into stanzas that indicate groups of rimes. Along with William Butler Yeats, who held that a successful poem will "come shut with a click, like a closing box," the poet who writes in closed form apparently strives for a kind of perfection—seeking, perhaps, to lodge words so securely in place that no word can be budged without a worsening. For the sake of meaning, though, a competent poet often will depart from a symmetrical pattern. As Robert Frost observed, there is satisfaction to be found in things not mechanically regular: "We enjoy the straight crookedness of a good walking stick."

The poet who writes in **open form** usually seeks no final click. Often, such a poet views the writing of a poem as a process, rather than a quest for an absolute. Free to use white space for emphasis, able to shorten or lengthen lines as the sense seems to require, the poet lets the poem discover its shape as it goes along, moving as water flows downhill, adjusting to its terrain, engulfing obstacles. (Open form will provide the focus of the next chapter.)

Most poetry of the past is in closed form, exhibiting at least a pattern of rime or meter, but since the early 1960s the majority of American poets have preferred forms that stay open. Lately, the situation has been changing yet again, with closed form reappearing in much recent poetry. Whatever the fashion of the moment, the reader who seeks a wide understanding of poetry of both the present and the past will need to know both the closed and open varieties.

THE VALUE OF FORM

Closed form gives some poems a valuable advantage: it makes them more easily memorable. The **epic** poems of nations—long narratives tracing the adventures of popular heroes: the Greek *Iliad* and *Odyssey*, the French *Song of Roland*, the Spanish *Cid*—tend to occur in patterns of fairly consistent line length or number of stresses because these works were sometimes transmitted orally. Sung to the music of a lyre or chanted to a drumbeat, they may have been easier to memorize because of their patterns. If a singer forgot something, the song would have a noticeable hole in it, so rime or fixed meter probably helped prevent an epic from deteriorating when passed along from one singer to another. It is no coincidence that so many English playwrights of Shakespeare's day favored iambic pentameter. Companies of actors, often called on to perform a different play each day, could count on a fixed line length to aid their burdened memories.

Some poets complain that closed form is a straitjacket, a limit to free expression. Other poets, however, feel that, like fires held fast in a narrow space, thoughts stated in a tightly binding form may take on a heightened intensity. "Limitation makes for power," according to one contemporary practitioner of closed form, Richard Wilbur; "the strength of the genie comes of his being confined in a bottle." Compelled by some strict pattern to arrange and rearrange words, delete, and exchange them, poets must focus on them the keenest attention. Often they stand a chance of discovering words more meaningful than the ones they started out with. And at times, in obedience to a rime scheme, the poet may be surprised by saying something quite unexpected.

FORMAL PATTERNS

The best-known line-by-line pattern for a poem in English is **blank verse**: unrimed iambic pentameter. Most portions of Shakespeare's plays are in blank verse, and so are Milton's *Paradise Lost*, Tennyson's "Ulysses," certain dramatic monologues of Browning and Frost, and thousands of other poems. Here are some lines of blank verse that begin Robert Frost's "Mending Wall":

> Something there is that doesn't love a wall,
> That sends the frozen-ground-swell under it,
> And spills the upper boulders in the sun;
> And makes gaps even two can pass abreast.

The Couplet

The **couplet** is a two-line stanza, usually rimed. Its lines often tend to be equal in length, whether short or long. Here are two examples:

> Blow,
> Snow!

As I in hoary winter's night stood shivering in the snow,
Surprised I was with sudden heat which made my heart to glow.

Actually, any pair of rimed lines that contains a complete thought is called a couplet, even if it is not a stanza, such as the couplet that ends a sonnet by Shakespeare. Unlike other stanzas, couplets are often printed solid; one couplet is not separated from the next by white space. This practice is usual in writing the **heroic couplet**—or **closed couplet**—two rimed lines of iambic pentameter, with the first ending in a light pause and the second more heavily end-stopped. George Crabbe, in *The Parish Register*, described a shotgun wedding:

> Next at our altar stood a luckless pair,
> Brought by strong passions and a warrant there:
> By long rent cloak, hung loosely, strove the bride,
> From every eye, what all perceived, to hide;
> While the boy bridegroom, shuffling in his pace,
> Now hid awhile and then exposed his face.
> As shame alternately with anger strove
> The brain confused with muddy ale to move,
> In haste and stammering he performed his part,
> And looked the rage that rankled in his heart.

Though employed by Chaucer, the heroic couplet was named from its later use by John Dryden and others in poems, translations of classical epics, and verse plays of epic heroes. It continued in favor through most of the eighteenth century. Much of our pleasure in reading good heroic couplets comes from the seemingly easy precision with which a skilled poet unites statements and strict pattern.

The Tercet

A **tercet** is a group of three lines. If rimed, they usually keep to one rime sound, as in this anonymous English children's jingle:

> Julius Caesar,
> The Roman geezer,
> Squashed his wife with a lemon-squeezer.

(That, by the way, is a great demonstration of surprising and unpredictable rimes.) ***Terza rima***, the form Dante employs in *The Divine Comedy*, is made of tercets linked together by the rime scheme *a b a, b c b, c d c, d e d, e f e*, and so on. Harder to do in English than in Italian—with its greater resources of riming words—the form nevertheless has been managed by Shelley in "Ode to the West Wind" (with the aid of some slant rimes):

> Make me thy lyre, even as the forest is:
> What if my leaves are falling like its own!
> The tumult of thy mighty harmonies

Will take from both a deep, autumnal tone,
Sweet though in sadness. Be thou, Spirit fierce,
My spirit! Be thou me, impetuous one!

The Quatrain

The workhorse of English poetry is the **quatrain**, a stanza consisting of four
lines. Quatrains are used in rimed poems more often than any other form.

Ernest Dowson   (1867–1900)

Days of wine and roses   1896

Vitae summa brevis spem nos vetat incohare longam

They are not long, the weeping and the laughter,
    Love and desire and hate:
I think they have no portion in us after
    We pass the gate.

They are not long, the days of wine and roses: 5
    Out of a misty dream
Our path emerges for a while, then closes
    Within a dream.

DAYS OF WINE AND ROSES. The epigraph, from Horace's *Odes* Book 1, 4, translates as "the
brief sum of life forbids us the hope of enduring long."

Question

What elements of sound and rhythm are consistent between the two stanzas?

Quatrains come in many line lengths, and sometimes contain lines of varying
length. Most often, poets rime the second and fourth lines of quatrains, as in the
ballad, but the rimes can occur in any combination the poet chooses.

Longer and more complicated stanzas are, of course, possible, but couplet,
tercet, and quatrain have been called the building blocks of our poetry because
most longer stanzas are made up of them. What short stanzas does John Donne
mortar together to make the longer stanza of his "Song"?

John Donne   (1572–1631)

Song   1633

Go and catch a falling star,
    Get with child a mandrake root,
Tell me where all past years are,
    Or who cleft the Devil's foot,
Teach me to hear mermaids singing,   5
    Or to keep off envy's stinging,

> And find
> What wind
> Serves to advance an honest mind.

> If thou be'st borne to strange sights,   10
>   Things invisible to see,
> Ride ten thousand days and nights,
>   Till age snow white hairs on thee,
> Thou, when thou return'st, wilt tell me
>   All strange wonders that befell thee,   15
>   And swear
>   Nowhere
> Lives a woman true, and fair.

> If thou findst one, let me know,
>   Such a pilgrimage were sweet—   20
> Yet do not, I would not go,
>   Though at next door we might meet;
> Though she were true, when you met her,
>   And last, till you write your letter,
>   Yet she   25
>   Will be
> False, ere I come, to two, or three.

BALLADS

Any narrative song might be called a **ballad**. In English, some of the most famous ballads are **folk ballads**, loosely defined as anonymous story-songs transmitted orally before they were ever written down. Sir Walter Scott, a pioneer
collector of Scottish folk ballads, drew the ire of an old woman whose songs he
had transcribed: "They were made for singing and no' for reading, but ye ha'e
broken the charm now and they'll never be sung mair." The old singer had a
point. Print freezes songs and tends to hold them fast to a single version. If Scott
and others had not written them down, however, many would have been lost.

Anonymous (traditional Scottish ballad)

Bonny Barbara Allan

It was in and about the Martinmas time,
    When the green leaves were afalling,
That Sir John Graeme, in the West Country,
    Fell in love with Barbara Allan.

He sent his men down through the town,   5
    To the place where she was dwelling;

"O haste and come to my master dear,
   Gin° ye be Barbara Allan."   *if*

O hooly,° hooly rose she up,   *slowly*
   To the place where he was lying,   10
And when she drew the curtain by:
   "Young man, I think you're dying."

"O it's I'm sick, and very, very sick,
   And 'tis a' for Barbara Allan."—
"O the better for me ye's never be,   15
   Tho your heart's blood were aspilling.

"O dinna ye mind,° young man," said she,   *don't you remember*
   "When ye was in the tavern adrinking,
That ye made the health° gae round and round,   *toasts*
   And slighted Barbara Allan?"   20

He turned his face unto the wall,
   And death was with him dealing:
"Adieu, adieu, my dear friends all,
   And be kind to Barbara Allan."

And slowly, slowly raise she up,   25
   And slowly, slowly left him,
And sighing said she could not stay,
   Since death of life had reft him.

She had not gane a mile but twa,
   When she heard the dead-bell ringing,
And every jow° that the dead-bell geid,°   30
   It cried, "Woe to Barbara Allan!"   *stroke, gave*

"O mother, mother, make my bed!
   O make it saft and narrow!
Since my love died for me today,   35
   I'll die for him tomorrow."

BONNY BARBARA ALLAN. 1 *Martinmas:* Saint Martin's Day, November 11.

Questions

1. Without ever coming out and explicitly calling Barbara hard-hearted, this ballad reveals that she is. In which stanza and by what means is her cruelty demonstrated?

2. At what point does Barbara evidently have a change of heart? Again, how does the poem dramatize this change without explicitly talking about it?

3. Paraphrase lines 9, 15–16, 22, and 25–28. By putting these lines into prose, what has been lost?

As you can see from "Bonny Barbara Allan," in a traditional English or Scottish folk ballad the storyteller speaks of the lives and feelings of others. Even if the pronoun "I" occurs, it rarely has much personality. Characters often exchange dialogue, but no one character speaks all the way through. Events move rapidly, perhaps because some of the dull transitional stanzas have been forgotten.

Ballad Stanza

One favorite pattern of ballad-makers is the so-called **ballad stanza**, four lines rimed *a b c b*, tending to fall into 8, 6, 8, and 6 syllables:

> Clerk Saunders and Maid Margaret
>   Walked owre yon garden green,
> And deep and heavy was the love
>   That fell thir twa between.°   *between those two*

Though not the only possible stanza for a ballad, this easily singable quatrain has continued to attract poets since the Middle Ages. Close kin to the ballad stanza is **common meter**, a stanza found in hymns such as "Amazing Grace," by the eighteenth-century English hymnist John Newton:

> Amazing grace! how sweet the sound
>   That saved a wretch like me!
> I once was lost, but now am found,
>   Was blind, but now I see.

Notice that its pattern is that of the ballad stanza except for its *two* pairs of rimes. That all its lines rime is probably a sign of more literate artistry than we usually hear in folk ballads. Another sign of schoolteachers' influence is that Newton's rimes are exact. (Rimes in folk ballads are often rough-and-ready, as if made by ear, rather than polished and exact, as if the riming words had been matched for their similar spellings. In "Barbara Allan," for instance, the hard-hearted lover's name rimes with *afalling, dwelling, aspilling, dealing,* and even with *ringing* and *adrinking.*) That so many hymns were written in common meter may have been due to convenience. If a congregation didn't know the tune to a hymn in common meter, they readily could sing its words to the tune of another such hymn they knew.

Literary Ballads

Literary ballads, not meant for singing, are written by sophisticated poets for book-educated readers who enjoy being reminded of folk ballads. Literary ballads imitate certain features of folk ballads: they may tell of dramatic conflicts or of mortals who encounter the supernatural; they may use conventional figures of speech or ballad stanzas. Well-known poems of this kind include Keats's "La Belle Dame sans Merci," Coleridge's "Rime of the Ancient Mariner," and (more recently) Dudley Randall's "Ballad of Birmingham."

Dudley Randall (1914–2000)

Ballad of Birmingham   1966

(*On the Bombing of a Church in
Birmingham, Alabama, 1963*)

"Mother dear, may I go downtown
Instead of out to play,
And march the streets of Birmingham
In a Freedom March today?"

"No, baby, no, you may not go,   5
For the dogs are fierce and wild,
And clubs and hoses, guns and jails
Aren't good for a little child."

"But, mother, I won't be alone.
Other children will go with me,   10
And march the streets of Birmingham
To make our country free."

"No, baby, no, you may not go,
For I fear those guns will fire.
But you may go to church instead   15
And sing in the children's choir."

She has combed and brushed her night-dark hair,
And bathed rose petal sweet,
And drawn white gloves on her small brown hands,
And white shoes on her feet.   20

The mother smiled to know her child
Was in the sacred place,
But that smile was the last smile
To come upon her face.

For when she heard the explosion,   25
Her eyes grew wet and wild.
She raced through the streets of Birmingham
Calling for her child.

She clawed through bits of glass and brick,
Then lifted out a shoe.   30
"O here's the shoe my baby wore,
But, baby, where are you?"

Questions

1. This poem, about a dynamite blast set off in an African American church by a racial terrorist (later convicted), delivers a message without preaching. How would you sum up this message, its implied theme?
2. What is ironic in the mother's denying her child permission to take part in a protest march?
3. How does this modern poem resemble a traditional ballad?

THE SONNET

When we speak of "traditional verse forms," we usually mean **fixed forms**. If written in a fixed form, a poem inherits from other poems certain familiar elements of structure: an unvarying number of lines, say, or a stanza pattern. In addition, it may display certain **conventions**: expected features such as themes, subjects, attitudes, or figures of speech. In medieval folk ballads a "milk-white steed" is a conventional figure of speech; and if its rider be a cruel and beautiful witch who kidnaps mortals, she is a conventional character.

In the poetry of western Europe and America, the **sonnet** is the fixed form that has attracted for the longest time the largest number of noteworthy practitioners. Originally an Italian form (*sonetto*: "little song"), the sonnet owes much of its prestige to Petrarch (1304–1374), who wrote in it of his love for the unattainable Laura. So great was the vogue for sonnets in England at the end of the sixteenth century that a gentleman might have been thought a boor if he couldn't turn out a decent one. Not content to adopt merely the sonnet's fourteen-line pattern, English poets also tried on its conventional mask of the tormented lover. They borrowed some of Petrarch's similes (a lover's heart, for instance, is like a storm-tossed boat) and invented others.

Soon after English poets imported the sonnet in the sixteenth century, they worked out their own rime scheme—one easier for them to follow than Petrarch's, which calls for a greater number of riming words than English can readily provide. (It's a popular though exaggerated belief that in Italian, practically everything rimes.) In the following **English sonnet**, sometimes called a **Shakespearean sonnet**, the rimes cohere in four clusters: *a b a b, c d c d, e f e f, g g*. Because a rime scheme tends to shape the poet's statements to it, the English sonnet has three places where the procession of thought is likely to turn in another direction. Within its form, a poet may pursue one idea throughout the three quatrains and then in the couplet end with a surprise.

William Shakespeare (1564–1616)

Let me not to the marriage of true minds (Sonnet 116)   1609

Let me not to the marriage of true minds
Admit impediments; love is not love
Which alters when it alteration finds,

Or bends with the remover to remove.
O, no, it is an ever-fixèd mark   5
That looks on tempests and is never shaken;
It is the star to every wand'ring bark,
Whose worth's unknown, although his height be taken.
Love's not Time's fool, though rosy lips and cheeks
Within his bending sickle's compass° come;   *range*   10
Love alters not with his° brief hours and weeks,   *Time's*
But bears° it out even to the edge of doom.   *endures*
      If this be error and upon me proved,
          I never writ, nor no man ever loved.

LET ME NOT TO THE MARRIAGE OF TRUE MINDS. 5 *ever-fixèd mark*: a sea-mark like a beacon or a lighthouse that provides mariners with safe bearings. 7 *the star*: presumably the North Star, which gave sailors the most dependable bearing at sea. 12 *edge of doom*: either the brink of death or—taken more generally—Judgment Day.

Less frequently met in English poetry, the **Italian sonnet**, or **Petrarchan sonnet**, follows the rime scheme *a b b a a b b a* in its first eight lines, called the **octave**, and then adds new rime sounds in the last six lines, called the **sestet**. The sestet may rime *c d c d c d, c d e c d e, c d c c d c,* or in almost any other variation that doesn't end in a couplet. This organization into two parts sometimes helps arrange the poet's thoughts. In the octave, the poet may state a problem, and then, in the sestet, may offer a resolution. A lover, for example, may lament all octave long that a loved one is neglectful, then in line 9 begin to foresee some outcome: the speaker will die, or accept unhappiness, or trust that the beloved will have a change of heart.

Edna St. Vincent Millay (1892–1950)

What lips my lips have kissed, and where, and why   1923

What lips my lips have kissed, and where, and why,
I have forgotten, and what arms have lain
Under my head till morning; but the rain
Is full of ghosts tonight, that tap and sigh
Upon the glass and listen for reply,   5
And in my heart there stirs a quiet pain
For unremembered lads that not again
Will turn to me at midnight with a cry.
Thus in the winter stands the lonely tree,
Nor knows what birds have vanished one by one,   10
Yet knows its boughs more silent than before:
I cannot say what loves have come and gone,
I only know that summer sang in me
A little while, that in me sings no more.

In this Italian sonnet, the turn of thought comes at the traditional point—the beginning of the ninth line. Many English-speaking poets, however, feel free to vary its placement. In John Milton's commanding sonnet on his blindness ("When I consider how my light is spent" in Chapter 22), the turn comes midway through line 8, and no one has ever thought the worse of it for bending the rules.

When we hear the terms *closed form* or *fixed form*, we imagine traditional poetic forms as a series of immutable rules. But, in the hands of the best poets, metrical forms are fluid concepts that change to suit the occasion. Here, for example, is a haunting poem by Robert Frost that simultaneously fulfills the rules of two traditional forms. Is it an innovative sonnet or a poem in *terza rima*? Frost combined the features of both forms to create a compressed and powerfully lyric poem.

Robert Frost (1874–1963)

Acquainted with the Night   1928

I have been one acquainted with the night.
I have walked out in rain—and back in rain.
I have outwalked the furthest city light.

I have looked down the saddest city lane.
I have passed by the watchman on his beat   5
And dropped my eyes, unwilling to explain.

I have stood still and stopped the sound of feet
When far away an interrupted cry
Came over houses from another street,

But not to call me back or say good-by;   10
And further still at an unearthly height,
One luminary clock against the sky

Proclaimed the time was neither wrong nor right.
I have been one acquainted with the night.

"The sonnet," quipped poet-critic Robert Bly, "is where old professors go to die." And certainly in the hands of an unskilled practitioner, the form can seem moribund. Considering the impressive number of powerful sonnets by modern poets such as Yeats, Frost, Auden, Millay, Cummings, Kees, and Heaney, however, the form hardly appears to be exhausted. No law compels sonnets to adopt an exalted tone or confines them to an Elizabethan vocabulary, as demonstrated in these two contemporary examples.

R. S. Gwynn (b. 1948)

Shakespearean Sonnet 2002

With a first line taken from the TV listings

A man is haunted by his father's ghost.
Boy meets girl while feuding families fight.
A Scottish king is murdered by his host.
Two couples get lost on a summer night.
A hunchback slaughters all who block his way. 5
A ruler's rivals plot against his life.
A fat man and a prince make rebels pay.
A noble Moor has doubts about his wife.
An English king decides to conquer France.
A duke finds out his best friend is a she. 10
A forest sets the scene for this romance.
An old man and his daughters disagree.
A Roman leader makes a big mistake.
A sexy queen is bitten by a snake.

Questions

1. Explain the play on words in the title.
2. How many of the texts described in this sonnet can you identify?
3. Does this poem intend merely to amuse, or does it have a larger point?

Sherman Alexie (b. 1966)

The Facebook Sonnet 2011

Welcome to the endless high-school
Reunion. Welcome to past friends
And lovers, however kind or cruel.
Let's undervalue and unmend

The present. Why can't we pretend 5
Every stage of life is the same?
Let's exhume, resume, and extend
Childhood. Let's play all the games

That occupy the young. Let fame
And shame intertwine. Let one's search 10
For God become public domain.
Let church.com become our church.

Let's sign up, sign in, and confess
Here at the altar of loneliness.

Questions

1. How would you paraphrase this poem? What are the speaker's objections to social media?
2. Read the poem aloud, pausing slightly at the line endings. What is the rhythmic effect of the run-on lines?

THE EPIGRAM

Oscar Wilde said that a cynic is "a man who knows the price of everything and the value of nothing." Such a terse, pointed statement is called an epigram. In poetry, however, an **epigram** is a form: "A short poem ending in a witty or ingenious turn of thought, to which the rest of the composition is intended to lead up" (according to the *Oxford English Dictionary*). Often it is a malicious gibe with an unexpected stinger in the final line—perhaps in the very last word.

Sir John Harrington (1561?–1612)

Of Treason   1618

Treason doth never prosper; what's the reason?
For if it prosper, none dare call it treason.

Langston Hughes (1902–1967)

Two Somewhat Different Epigrams   1957

I

Oh, God of dust and rainbows, help us see
That without dust the rainbow would not be.

II

I look with awe upon the human race
And God, who sometimes spits right in its face.

OTHER FORMS

There are many other verse forms used in English. Some forms, like the villanelle and sestina, come from other European literatures. But English has borrowed fixed forms from an astonishing variety of sources. The haiku and tanka, for instance, originated in Japan. Other borrowed forms include the ghazal (Arabic), rubaiyat (Persian), pantoum (Malay), and sapphics (Greek). Even blank verse, which seems as English as the royal family, began as an attempt by Elizabethan poets to copy an Italian eleven-syllable line. To conclude this chapter, here are poems in three widely used closed forms—the villanelle, rondeau, and sestina. Their patterns, which are sometimes called "French forms," have been particularly fascinating to English-language poets because they do not merely require the repetition of rime sounds; instead, they demand more elaborate echoing, involving the repetition of either full words or whole lines of verse. Sometimes difficult to master, these forms can create a powerful musical effect unlike ordinary riming.

Dylan Thomas (1914–1953)

Do not go gentle into that good night   1952

Do not go gentle into that good night,
Old age should burn and rave at close of day;
Rage, rage against the dying of the light.

Though wise men at their end know dark is right,
Because their words had forked no lightning they   5
Do not go gentle into that good night.

Good men, the last wave by, crying how bright
Their frail deeds might have danced in a green bay,
Rage, rage against the dying of the light.

Wild men who caught and sang the sun in flight,   10
And learn, too late, they grieved it on its way,
Do not go gentle into that good night.

Grave men, near death, who see with blinding sight
Blind eyes could blaze like meteors and be gay,
Rage, rage against the dying of the light.   15

And you, my father, there on the sad height,
Curse, bless, me now with your fierce tears, I pray,
Do not go gentle into that good night.
Rage, rage against the dying of the light.

Questions

1. "Do not go gentle into that good night" is a **villanelle**: a fixed form originated by French courtly poets of the Middle Ages. What are its rules?
2. Whom does the poem address? What is the speaker saying?
3. Villanelles are sometimes criticized as elaborate exercises in trivial wordplay. How would you defend Thomas's poem against this charge?

Paul Laurence Dunbar (1872–1906)

We Wear the Mask   1895

We wear the mask that grins and lies,
It hides our cheeks and shades our eyes,—
This debt we pay to human guile;
With torn and bleeding hearts we smile,
And mouth with myriad subtleties.   5

Why should the world be over-wise,
In counting all our tears and sighs?
Nay, let them only see us, while
    We wear the mask.

We smile, but, O great Christ, our cries   10
To thee from tortured souls arise.
We sing, but oh the clay is vile
Beneath our feet, and long the mile;
But let the world dream otherwise,
    We wear the mask!   15

Question

"We Wear the Mask" uses another French form, the **rondeau**. Where do you find patterns of repetition, and how is that repetition effective at expressing the poem's theme?

Elizabeth Bishop (1911–1979)

Sestina   1965

September rain falls on the house.
In the failing light, the old grandmother
sits in the kitchen with the child
beside the Little Marvel Stove,
reading the jokes from the almanac,   5
laughing and talking to hide her tears.

She thinks that her equinoctial tears
and the rain that beats on the roof of the house
were both foretold by the almanac,
but only known to a grandmother.   10
The iron kettle sings on the stove.
She cuts some bread and says to the child,

It's time for tea now; but the child
is watching the teakettle's small hard tears
dance like mad on the hot black stove,   15
the way the rain must dance on the house.

Tidying up, the old grandmother
hangs up the clever almanac

on its string. Birdlike, the almanac
hovers half open above the child,   20
hovers above the old grandmother
and her teacup full of dark brown tears.
She shivers and says she thinks the house
feels chilly, and puts more wood in the stove.

It was to be, says the Marvel Stove.   25
I know what I know, says the almanac.
With crayons the child draws a rigid house
and a winding pathway. Then the child
puts in a man with buttons like tears
and shows it proudly to the grandmother.   30

But secretly, while the grandmother
busies herself about the stove,
the little moons fall down like tears
from between the pages of the almanac
into the flower bed the child   35
has carefully placed in the front of the house.

Time to plant tears, says the almanac.
The grandmother sings to the marvellous stove
and the child draws another inscrutable house.

SESTINA. As its title indicates, this poem is written in the trickiest of medieval fixed forms, that of the **sestina** (or "song of sixes"), said to have been invented in Provence in the thirteenth century by the troubadour poet Arnaut Daniel. In its six six-line stanzas, the poet repeats six end-words (in a prescribed order) and then reintroduces the six repeated words (in any order) in a closing **envoy** of three lines. Elizabeth Bishop strictly follows the troubadour rules for the order in which the end-words recur. (If you'd like, you can figure out the formula: in the first stanza, the six words are arranged A B C D E F; in the second, F A E B D C; and so on.)

Questions

1. A perceptive comment from a student: "Something seems to be going on here that the child doesn't understand. Maybe some terrible loss has happened." Test this guess by reading the poem closely.
2. In the "little moons" that fall from the almanac (line 33), does the poem introduce dream or fantasy, or do you take these to be small round pieces of paper?
3. What is the tone of this poem—the speaker's apparent attitude toward the scene described?

■ WRITING *effectively*

THINKING ABOUT A SONNET

A poem's form is closely tied to its meaning. This is especially true of the sonnet, a form whose rules dictate not only the sound of a poem but also, to a certain extent, its sense. A sonnet traditionally looks at a single theme, but reverses its stance on the subject somewhere along the way. One possible definition of the sonnet might be a fourteen-line poem divided into two unequal parts. Traditionally, Italian sonnets divide their parts into an octave (the first eight lines) and a sestet (the last six), while English sonnets are more lopsided, with a final couplet balanced against three preceding quatrains. The moment when a sonnet changes its direction is commonly called "the turn."

- ■ **Identifying the moment when the poem "turns" helps in understanding both its theme and its structure.** In a Shakespearean sonnet, the turn usually—but not always—comes in the final couplet. In modern sonnets, the turn is often less overt.
- ■ **To find that moment, study the poem's opening.** Latch on to the mood and manner of the opening lines. Is the feeling joyful or sad, loving or angry?
- ■ **Read the poem from this opening perspective until you feel it tug strongly in another direction.** Sometimes the second part of a sonnet will directly contradict the opening. More often it explains, augments, or qualifies the opening.

CHECKLIST: Writing About a Sonnet

- ☐ Read the poem carefully.
- ☐ What is the mood of its opening lines?
- ☐ Keep reading until you feel the mood shift. Where does that shift take place?
- ☐ What is the tone after the sonnet's turn away from its opening direction?
- ☐ What do the two alternative points of view add up to?
- ☐ How does the poem reconcile its contrasting sections?

TOPICS FOR WRITING ON CLOSED FORM

1. Examine a sonnet from anywhere in this book. Explain how its two parts combine to create a total effect neither part could achieve alone. Be sure to identify the turning point. Paraphrase what each of the poem's two sections says and describe how the poem as a whole reconciles the two contrasting parts. (In addition to the sonnets in this chapter, you might consider any of the following

from Chapter 22: Elizabeth Barrett Browning's "How Do I Love Thee?"; Gerard Manley Hopkins's "The Windhover"; John Milton's "When I consider how my light is spent"; William Shakespeare's "When in disgrace with Fortune and men's eyes"; or William Wordsworth's "Composed upon Westminster Bridge.")

2. Select a poem that incorporates rime from Chapter 22, "Poems for Further Reading." Write a paragraph describing how the poem's rime scheme helps to advance its meaning.

3. Write ten lines of blank verse on a topic of your own choice. Then write about the experience. What aspects of writing in regular meter did you find most challenging? What did you learn about reading blank verse from trying your hand at writing it?

4. Compare Dylan Thomas's "Do not go gentle into that good night" with Wendy Cope's "Lonely Hearts" (Chapter 11). How can the same form be used to create such different kinds of poems?

5. Write a sestina and see what you find out by doing so. (Even if you fail in the attempt, you just might learn something interesting.) To start, pick six words you think are worth repeating six times. This elaborate pattern gives you much help: as John Ashbery has pointed out, writing a sestina is "like riding downhill on a bicycle and having the pedals push your feet." Here is some encouragement from a poet and critic, John Heath-Stubbs: "I have never read a sestina that seemed to me a total failure."

▶ TERMS FOR *review*

Form

Form ▶ In a general sense, form is the means by which a literary work expresses its content. In poetry, form is usually used to describe the design of a poem.

Fixed form ▶ A traditional verse form requiring certain predetermined elements of structure—for example, a stanza pattern, set meter, or predetermined line length.

Closed form ▶ A generic term that describes poetry written in a pattern of meter, rime, lines, or stanzas. A closed form adheres to a set structure.

Open form ▶ Verse that has no set scheme—no regular meter, rime, or stanzaic pattern. Open form has also been called **free verse**.

Blank verse ▶ Verse that contains five iambic feet per line (iambic pentameter) and is not rimed. ("Blank" means unrimed.)

Couplet ▶ A two-line stanza in poetry, usually rimed and with lines of equal length.

Closed couplet ▶ Two rimed lines of iambic pentameter that usually contain an independent and complete thought or statement. Also called **heroic couplet**.

Quatrain ▶ A stanza consisting of four lines, it is the most common stanza form used in English-language poetry.

Epic ▶ A long narrative poem tracing the adventures of a popular hero. Epic poems are usually written in a consistent form and meter throughout.

Epigram ▶ A very short comic poem, often turning at the end with some sharp wit or unexpected stinger.

Ballads

Ballad ▶ Traditionally, a song that tells a story. Ballads are characteristically compressed, dramatic, and objective in their narrative style.

Folk ballads ▶ Anonymous narrative songs, usually in ballad meter. They were originally created for oral performance, often resulting in many versions of a single ballad.

Ballad stanza ▶ The most common pattern for a ballad, consisting of four lines rimed *a b c b*, in which the first and third lines have four metrical feet (usually eight syllables) and the second and fourth lines have three feet (usually six syllables). **Common meter**, often used in hymns, is a variation rimed *a b a b*.

Literary ballad ▶ A ballad not meant for singing, written by a sophisticated poet for educated readers, rather than arising from the anonymous oral tradition.

The Sonnet

Sonnet ▶ A fixed form of fourteen lines, traditionally written in iambic pentameter and rimed throughout.

Italian sonnet ▶ Also called **Petrarchan sonnet**, it rimes the **octave** (eight lines) *a b b a a b b a*; the **sestet** (last six lines) may follow any rime pattern, as long as it does not end in a couplet. The poem traditionally turns, or shifts in mood or tone, after the octave.

English sonnet ▶ Also called **Shakespearean sonnet**, it has the following rime scheme organized into three quatrains and a concluding couplet: *a b a b c d c d e f e f g g*. The poem may turn—that is, shift in mood or tone—between any of the rime clusters.

18 OPEN FORM

What You Will Learn in This Chapter

- To recognize and describe free verse and open form
- To explain how line breaks contribute to the meaning of a free verse poem
- To define *prose poetry*
- To analyze the role of free verse in shaping the meaning of a poem

Writing in **open form**, a poet seeks to discover a fresh and individual arrangement for words in every poem. Such a poem, generally speaking, has neither a rime scheme nor a basic meter informing the whole of it. Doing without those powerful (some would say hypnotic) elements, the poet who writes in open form relies on other means to engage and sustain the reader's attention. Novice poets often think that open form looks easy, not nearly so hard as riming everything; but in truth, formally open poems are easy to write only if written carelessly. To compose lines with keen awareness of open form's demands, and of its infinite possibilities, calls for skill: at least as much as that needed to write in meter and rime, if not more. Should the poet succeed, then the discovered arrangement will seem exactly right for what the poem is saying.

Denise Levertov (1923–1997)

Ancient Stairway   1999

Footsteps like water hollow
the broad curves of stone
ascending, descending
century by century.
Who can say if the last   5
to climb these stairs
will be journeying
downward or upward?

     Open form, in this brief poem, affords Denise Levertov certain advantages. Able to break off a line at whatever point she likes (a privilege not available to the poet writing, say, a conventional sonnet, who has to break off each line after its tenth syllable), she selects her pauses artfully. Line breaks lend emphasis: a word or phrase at the end of a line takes a little more stress (and receives a little more attention), because the ending of the line compels the reader to make a slight pause, if only for the brief moment it takes to sling back one's eyes and fix them on the line following. Slight pauses, then, follow the words and phrases *hollow/stone/descending/century/last/stairs/journeying/upward*—all these being elements that apparently the poet wishes to call our attention to. (The pause after a line break also casts a little more weight on the *first* word or phrase of each succeeding line.) Levertov makes the most of white space—another means of calling attention to things, as any good picture-framer knows. She has greater control over the shape of the poem, its look on the page, than would be allowed by the demands of meter; she uses that control to stack on top of one another lines that appear much like the steps of a staircase. The opening line with its quick stresses might suggest to us the feet passing over the steps. From there, Levertov slows the rhythm to the heavy beats of lines 3–4, which could communicate a sense of repeated trudging up and down the stairs (in a particularly effective touch, all four of the stressed syllables in these two lines make the same sound), a sense that is reinforced by the poem's last line, which echoes the rhythm of line 3. Note too how, without being restricted by the need of a rime, she can order the terms in that last line according to her intended thematic emphasis. In all likelihood, we perceive these effects instinctively, not consciously (which may also be the way the author created them), but no matter how we apprehend them, they serve to deepen our understanding of and pleasure in the text.

FREE VERSE

Poetry in open form can also be called **free verse** (from the French **vers libre**), suggesting a kind of verse liberated from the shackles of rime and meter. "Writing free verse," said Robert Frost, who wasn't interested in it, "is like playing tennis with the net down." And yet, as Denise Levertov and many other poets demonstrate, high scores can be made in such an unconventional game, provided it doesn't straggle all over the court. For a successful poem in open form, the term *free verse* seems inaccurate. "Being an art form," said William Carlos Williams, "verse cannot be 'free' in the sense of having *no* limitations or guiding principles."[1] Various substitute names have been suggested: organic poetry, composition by field, raw (as opposed to cooked) poetry, open form poetry. "But what does it matter what you call it?" remark the editors of a 1969 anthology called *Naked Poetry*. "The best poems of the last thirty years don't rhyme (usually) and don't move on feet of more or less equal duration (usually). That nondescription moves toward the only technical principle they all have in common."[2]

[1]"Free Verse," *Princeton Encyclopedia of Poetry and Poetics*, 2nd ed., 1975.
[2]Stephen Berg and Robert Mezey, eds., foreword, *Naked Poetry: Recent American Poetry in Open Forms* (Indianapolis: Bobbs, 1969).

Free Verse Lines

To the poet working in open form, no less than to the poet writing a sonnet, line length can be valuable. Walt Whitman, who loved to expand vast sentences for line after line, knew well that an impressive rhythm can accumulate if the poet will keep long lines approximately the same length, causing a pause to recur at about the same interval after every line. Sometimes, too, Whitman repeats the same words at each line's opening. An instance is the masterly sixth section of "When Lilacs Last in the Dooryard Bloom'd," an elegy for Abraham Lincoln:

> Coffin that passes through lanes and streets,
> Through day and night with the great cloud darkening the land,
> With the pomp of the inloop'd flags with the cities draped in black,
> With the show of the States themselves as of crape-veil'd women
>   standing,
> With processions long and winding and the flambeaus of the night,
> With the countless torches lit, with the silent sea of faces and the
>   unbared heads,
> With the waiting depot, the arriving coffin, and the somber faces,
> With dirges through the night, with the thousand voices rising
>   strong and solemn,
> With all the mournful voices of the dirges pour'd around the coffin,
> The dim-lit churches and the shuddering organs—where amid
>   these you journey,
> With the tolling tolling bells' perpetual clang,
> Here, coffin that slowly passes,
> I give you my sprig of lilac.

There is music in such solemn, operatic arias. Whitman's lines echo another model: the Hebrew **psalms**, or sacred songs, as translated in the King James Version of the Bible. In Psalm 150, repetition also occurs inside of lines:

> Praise ye the Lord. Praise God in his sanctuary: praise him in the
>   firmament of his power.
> Praise him for his mighty acts: praise him according to his excellent
>   greatness.
> Praise him with the sound of the trumpet: praise him with the
>   psaltery and harp.
> Praise him with the timbrel and dance: praise him with stringed
>   instruments and organs.
> Praise him upon the loud cymbals: praise him upon the high
>   sounding cymbals.
> Let every thing that hath breath praise the Lord. Praise ye the Lord.

Sound and Rhythm in Free Verse

In many classics of open form poetry, sound and rhythm are positive forces. When speaking a poem in open form, you often may find that it makes a difference for the better if you pause at the end of each line. Why do the pauses matter? Open form poetry usually has no meter to lend it rhythm. *Some* lines in an open form poem, as we have seen in Whitman's "dimes on the eyes" passage, do fall into metrical feet; sometimes the whole poem does. Usually lacking meter's aid, however, open form, in order to have more and more noticeable rhythms, has need of all the recurring pauses it can get. As we can hear in recordings of them reading their work aloud, open form poets such as Robert Creeley and Allen Ginsberg would often pause very definitely at each line break—and so, for that matter, did Ezra Pound.

Some poems, to be sure, seem more widely open in form than others. A poet may wish to avoid the rigidity and predictability of fixed line lengths and stanzaic forms but still wish to hold a poem together through a strong rhythmic impulse and even a discernible metrical emphasis. A poet may employ rime, but have the rimes recur at various intervals, or perhaps rime lines of varying lengths. In a 1917 essay called "Reflections on *Vers Libre*" (French for "free verse"), T. S. Eliot famously observed, "No *vers* is *libre* for the man who wants to do a good job." In that same year, Eliot published his first collection of poems, whose title piece was the classic "The Love Song of J. Alfred Prufrock" (Chapter 22). Is "Prufrock" a closed poem left ajar or an open poem trying to slam itself shut?

E. E. Cummings (1894–1962)

Buffalo Bill 's   1923

Buffalo Bill 's
defunct
      who used to
      ride a watersmooth-silver
                 stallion   5
and break onetwothreefourfive pigeonsjustlikethat
                       Jesus

he was a handsome man
               and what i want to know is
how do you like your blueeyed boy   10
Mister Death

Question

If set as conventional prose, Cumming's poem would look like this:

> Buffalo Bill's defunct, who used to ride a water-smooth silver stallion and break one, two, three, four, five pigeons just like that. Jesus, he was a handsome man. And what I want to know is: "How do you like your blue-eyed boy, Mister Death?"

By what characteristics would this still be recognizable as poetry? What would be lost?

The Kermess or *Peasant Dance* by Pieter Brueghel the Elder (1520?–1569).

William Carlos Williams (1883–1963)

The Dance   1944

In Brueghel's great picture, The Kermess,
the dancers go round, they go round and
around, the squeal and the blare and the
tweedle of bagpipes, a bugle and fiddles
tipping their bellies (round as the thick-   5
sided glasses whose wash they impound)
their hips and their bellies off balance
to turn them. Kicking and rolling about
the Fair Grounds, swinging their butts, those
shanks must be sound to bear up under such   10
rollicking measures, prance as they dance
in Brueghel's great picture, The Kermess.

THE DANCE. 1 *Brueghel:* Flemish painter known for his scenes of peasant activities. *The Kermess:* painting of a celebration on the feast day of a local patron saint.

Questions

1. Scan this poem and try to describe the effect of its rhythms.
2. Williams, widely admired for his free verse, insisted for many years that what he sought was a form not in the least bit free. What effect does he achieve by ending lines on such weak words as the articles "and" and "the"? By splitting "thick-/sided"? By splitting a prepositional phrase with the break at the end of line 8? By using line breaks to split "those" and "such" from what they modify? What do you think he is trying to convey?
3. Is there any point in his making line 12 a repetition of the opening line?
4. Look at the reproduction of Brueghel's painting *The Kermess* (also called *Peasant Dance*). Aware that the rhythms of dancers, the rhythms of a painting, and the rhythms of a poem are not all the same, can you put in your own words what Brueghel's dancing figures have in common with Williams's descriptions of them?
5. Compare "The Dance" with another poem that refers to a Brueghel painting: W. H. Auden's "Musée des Beaux Arts" in Chapter 22. What seems to be each poet's main concern: to convey in words a sense of the painting, or to visualize the painting in order to state some theme?

Stephen Crane (1871–1900)

The Heart   1895

In the desert
I saw a creature, naked, bestial,
Who, squatting upon the ground,
Held his heart in his hands,
And ate of it.   5
I said, "Is it good, friend?"
"It is bitter—bitter," he answered;
"But I like it
Because it is bitter,
And because it is my heart."   10

Walt Whitman (1819–1892)

Cavalry Crossing a Ford   1865

A line in long array where they wind betwixt green islands,
They take a serpentine course, their arms flash in the sun—hark to
    the musical clank,
Behold the silvery river, in it the splashing horses loitering stop to drink,
Behold the brown-faced men, each group, each person a picture, the
    negligent rest on the saddles,
Some emerge on the opposite bank, others are just entering the   5
    ford—while,
Scarlet and blue and snowy white,
The guidon flags flutter gayly in the wind.

Questions: Crane Versus Whitman

The following nit-picking questions are intended to help you see exactly what makes these two open form poems by Crane and Whitman so different in their music.

1. What devices of sound occur in Whitman's phrase "silvery river" (line 3)? Where else in his poem do you find these devices?
2. Does Crane use any such devices?
3. In number of syllables, Whitman's poem is almost twice as long as Crane's. Which poem has more pauses in it? (Count pauses at the ends of lines, at marks of punctuation.)
4. Read the two poems aloud. In general, how would you describe the effect of their sounds and rhythms? Is Crane's poem necessarily an inferior poem for having less music?

Analyzing Line Breaks

Wallace Stevens's lineation in "Thirteen Ways of Looking at a Blackbird" allows us not only to see but also to savor the connections between the poem's ideas and images. Consider section II of the poem:

> I was of three minds,
> Like a tree
> In which there are three blackbirds.

On a purely semantic level, these lines may mean the same as the prose statement, "I was of three minds, like a tree in which there are three blackbirds," but Stevens's choice of line breaks adds special emphasis at several points. Each of these three lines isolates and presents a separate image (the speaker, the tree, and the blackbirds). The placement of *three* in the opening and closing lines helps us feel the similar nature of the two statements. The short middle line allows us to see the image of the tree before we fully understand why it is parallel to the divided mind—thus adding a touch of suspense that the prose version of this statement just can't supply. Ending each line with a key noun and image also gives the poem a concrete feel not altogether evident in the prose.

Wallace Stevens   (1879–1955)

Thirteen Ways of Looking at a Blackbird   1923

I

Among twenty snowy mountains,
The only moving thing
Was the eye of the blackbird.

II

I was of three minds,
Like a tree   5
In which there are three blackbirds.

III

The blackbird whirled in the autumn winds.
It was a small part of the pantomime.

IV

A man and a woman
Are one.
A man and a woman and a blackbird   10
Are one.

V

I do not know which to prefer,
The beauty of inflections
Or the beauty of innuendoes,   15
The blackbird whistling
Or just after.

VI

Icicles filled the long window
With barbaric glass.
The shadow of the blackbird   20
Crossed it, to and fro.
The mood
Traced in the shadow
An indecipherable cause.

VII

O thin men of Haddam,   25
Why do you imagine golden birds?
Do you not see how the blackbird
Walks around the feet
Of the women about you?

VIII

I know noble accents
And lucid, inescapable rhythms;   30
But I know, too,
That the blackbird is involved
In what I know.

IX

When the blackbird flew out of sight,   35
It marked the edge
Of one of many circles.

X

At the sight of blackbirds
Flying in a green light,
Even the bawds of euphony   40
Would cry out sharply.

XI

He rode over Connecticut
In a glass coach.
Once, a fear pierced him,
In that he mistook   45
The shadow of his equipage
For blackbirds.

XII

The river is moving.
The blackbird must be flying.

XIII

It was evening all afternoon.   50
It was snowing
And it was going to snow.
The blackbird sat
In the cedar-limbs.

THIRTEEN WAYS OF LOOKING AT A BLACKBIRD. 25 *Haddam:* This biblical-sounding name is
that of a town in Connecticut.

Questions

1. What is the speaker's attitude toward the men of Haddam? What attitude toward this
   world does he suggest they lack? What is implied by calling them "thin" (line 25)?
2. What do the landscapes of winter contribute to the poem's effectiveness? If Stevens had chosen images of summer lawns, what would have been lost?
3. In which sections of the poem does Stevens suggest that a unity exists between
   human being and blackbird, between blackbird and the entire natural world? Can
   we say that Stevens "philosophizes"? What role does imagery play in Stevens's
   statement of his ideas?
4. What sense can you make of Part X? Make an enlightened guess.
5. Consider any one of the thirteen parts. What patterns of sound and rhythm do
   you find in it? What kind of structure does it have?
6. If the thirteen parts were arranged in some different order, would the poem be just
   as good? Or can you find a justification for its beginning with Part I and ending
   with Part XIII?
7. Does the poem seem an arbitrary combination of thirteen separate poems? Or is
   there any reason to call it a whole?

PROSE POETRY

No law requires a poet to split thoughts into verse lines. Charles Baudelaire, Rainer Maria Rilke, Jorge Luis Borges, Alexander Solzhenitsyn, T. S. Eliot, and many others have written **prose poems**, in which, without caring that eye appeal and some of the rhythm of a line structure may be lost, the poet prints words in a block like a prose paragraph. To some, the term "prose poetry" is as oxymoronic as "jumbo shrimp" or "plastic glasses," if not a flat-out contradiction in terms. Yet prose poems exist, such as the following. As you read it, ask yourself if this is a prose poem, or a very short piece of prose? If poetry, what features distinguish it from prose? If it should be considered prose, what essential features of poetry does it lack?

Charles Simic (b. 1939)

The Magic Study of Happiness   1992

In the smallest theater in the world the bread crumbs speak. It's a mystery play on the subject of a lost paradise. Once there was a kitchen with a table on which a few crumbs were left. Through the window you could see your young mother by the fence talking to a neighbor. She was cold and kept hugging her thin dress tighter and tighter. The clouds in the sky sailed on   5
as she threw her head back to laugh.

Where the words can't go any further—there's the hard table. The crumbs are watching you as you in turn watch them. The unknown in you and the unknown in them attract each other. The two unknowns are like illicit lovers when they're exceedingly and unaccountably happy.   10

Questions

1. What is the effect of the phrases "the smallest theater in the world" and "mystery play"?
2. How do you interpret: "Where the words can't go any further—there's the hard table"?
3. What is the significance of the simile in the last sentence?

FOR REVIEW AND FURTHER STUDY

Exercise: Seeing the Logic of Open Form Verse

Read the following poems in open form silently to yourself, noticing what each poet does with white space, repetitions, line breaks, and indentations. Then read the poems aloud, trying to indicate by slight pauses where lines end and also pausing slightly at any space inside a line. Can you see any reasons for the poet's placing his or her words in this arrangement rather than in a prose paragraph? Do any of these poets seem to care also about visual effect?

E. E. Cummings (1894–1962)

in Just-   1923

in Just-
spring   when the world is mud-
luscious the little
lame balloonman

whistles   far   and wee   5

and eddieandbill come
running from marbles and
piracies and it's
spring

when the world is puddle-wonderful   10

the queer
old balloonman whistles
far   and   wee
and bettyandisbel come dancing

from hop-scotch and jump-rope and   15

it's
spring
and
    the

        goat-footed   20

balloonMan   whistles
far
and
wee

Carole Satyamurti (b. 1939)

I Shall Paint My Nails Red   1990

Because a bit of color is a public service.

Because I am proud of my hands.

Because it will remind me I'm a woman.

Because I will look like a survivor.

Because I can admire them in traffic jams.   5

Because my daughter will say ugh.

Because my lover will be surprised.

Because it is quicker than dyeing my hair.

Because it is a ten-minute moratorium.

Because it is reversible.   10

Question
"I Shall Paint My Nails Red" is written in free verse, but the poem has several organizing principles. How many can you discover?

Langston Hughes (1902–1967)

I, Too   1926
I, too, sing America.

I am the darker brother.
They send me to eat in the kitchen
When company comes,
But I laugh,   5
And eat well,
And grow strong.

Tomorrow,
I'll be at the table
When company comes.   10
Nobody'll dare
Say to me,
"Eat in the kitchen,"
Then.

Besides,   15
They'll see how beautiful I am
And be ashamed—

I, too, am America.

Questions
1. Who do you imagine to be the speaker of this poem?
2. What is suggested by the final line?

■ WRITING *effectively*

THINKING ABOUT FREE VERSE

"That's not poetry! It's just chopped-up prose." So runs one old-fashioned complaint about free verse. Such criticism may be true of inept poems, but in the best free verse the line endings transform language in ways beyond the possibilities of prose. A line break implies a slight pause so that the last word of each line receives special emphasis. The last word in a line is meant to linger, however briefly, in the listener's ear. With practice and attention, you can easily develop a better sense of how a poem's line breaks operate.

- **Note whether the breaks tend to come at the end of sentences or phrases, or in the middle of an idea.** An abundance of breaks in midthought can create a tumbling, headlong effect, forcing your eye to speed down the page. Conversely, lines that tend to break at the end of a full idea can give a more stately rhythm to a poem.
- **Determine whether the lines tend to be all brief, all long, or a mix.** A very short line forces us to pay special attention to its every word, no matter how small.
- **Ask yourself how the poet's choices about line breaks help to reinforce the poem's meaning.** Can you identify any example of a line break affecting the meaning of a phrase or sentence?

CHECKLIST: Writing About Line Breaks

☐ Reread a poem, paying attention to where its lines end.
☐ Do the breaks tend to come at the end of the sentences or phrases?
☐ Do they tend to come in the middle of an idea?
☐ Do the lines tend to be long? Short? A mix of both?
☐ Is the poem broken into stanzas? Are they long? Short? A mix of both?
☐ What mood is created by the breaks?
☐ How do line breaks and stanza breaks reinforce the poem's meaning as a whole?

TOPICS FOR WRITING ON OPEN FORM

1. Retype a free verse poem as prose, adding conventional punctuation and capitalization if necessary. Then compare and contrast the prose version with the poem itself. How do the two texts differ in tone, rhythm, emphasis, and effect? How do they remain similar? Use any poem from this chapter or any of the following from Chapter 22, "Poems for Further Reading": W. H. Auden's "Musée des Beaux

Arts"; Ezra Pound's "The River-Merchant's Wife: A Letter"; or William Carlos Williams's "Queen-Anne's-Lace."

2. Write a brief essay (approximately 500 words) on how the line breaks and white space (or lack thereof) in E. E. Cummings's "Buffalo Bill 's" contribute to the poem's effect.

3. Read aloud William Carlos Williams's "The Dance." Examine how the poem's line breaks and sonic effects underscore the poem's meaning.

4. Imagine Charles Simic's "The Magic Study of Happiness" broken into free-verse lines. What are the benefits of the prose-poem form to this particular text?

5. Compare any poem in this chapter with a poem in rime and meter. Discuss several key features that they have in common despite their apparent differences in style. Features it might be useful to compare include imagery, tone, figures of speech, and word choice.

6. Write an imitation of Wallace Stevens's "Thirteen Ways of Looking at a Black-bird." Come up with thirteen ways of looking at your car, a can opener, a house-cat—or any object that intrigues you. Choose your line breaks carefully, to recreate some of the mood of the original. You might also have a look at Aaron Abeyta's parody "thirteen ways of looking at a tortilla" in Chapter 22.

▶ TERMS FOR *review*

Open form ▶ Poems that have neither a rime scheme nor a basic meter are in open form. Open form has also been called **free verse**.

Free verse ▶ From the French *vers libre*. Free verse is poetry whose lines follow no consistent meter. It may be rimed, but usually is not. In the last hundred years, free verse has become a common practice.

Prose poetry ▶ Poetic language printed in prose paragraphs, but displaying the careful attention to sound, imagery, and figurative language characteristic of poetry.

19

SYMBOL

What You Will Learn in This Chapter

■ To recognize and define a *poetic symbol*
■ To identify and define *symbolic actions*
■ To describe allegory and its characteristics
■ To analyze the role of a symbol in a poem

The national flag is supposed to stir our patriotic feelings. When a black cat crosses his path, a superstitious man shivers, foreseeing bad luck. To each of these, by custom, our society expects a standard response. A flag, a black cat crossing one's path—each is a **symbol**: a visible object or action that suggests some further meaning in addition to itself. In literature, a symbol might be the word *flag* or the words *a black cat crossed his path* or every description of flag or cat in an entire novel, story, play, or poem.

A flag and the crossing of a black cat may be called **conventional symbols**, since they can have a conventional or customary effect on us. Conventional symbols are also part of the language of poetry, as we know when we meet the red rose, emblem of love, in a lyric, or the Christian cross in the devotional poems of George Herbert. More often, however, symbols in literature have no conventional, long-established meaning, but particular meanings of their own. In Melville's novel *Moby-Dick*, to take a rich example, whatever we associate with the great white whale is *not* attached unmistakably to white whales by custom. Though Melville tells us that men have long regarded whales with awe and relates Moby Dick to the celebrated fish that swallowed Jonah, the reader's response is to one particular whale, the creature of Herman Melville. Only the experience of reading the novel in its entirety can give Moby Dick his particular meaning.

THE MEANINGS OF A SYMBOL

As Eudora Welty has observed, it is a good thing Melville made Moby Dick a whale, a creature large enough to contain all that critics have found in him. A symbol in literature, if not conventional, has more than just one meaning. In "The Raven," by Edgar Allan Poe, the appearance of a strange black bird in the narrator's study is sinister; and indeed, if we take the poem seriously, we may even respond with a sympathetic shiver of dread. Does the bird mean death, fate, melancholy, the loss of a loved one, knowledge in the service of evil? All of these, perhaps. Like any well-chosen symbol, Poe's raven sets off within the reader an unending train of feelings and associations.

We miss the value of a symbol, however, if we think it can mean absolutely anything we wish. If a poet has any control over our reactions, the poem will guide our responses in a certain direction.

T. S. Eliot (1888–1965)

The *Boston Evening Transcript*   1917

The readers of the *Boston Evening Transcript*
Sway in the wind like a field of ripe corn.

When evening quickens faintly in the street,
Wakening the appetites of life in some
And to others bringing the *Boston Evening Transcript*,   5
I mount the steps and ring the bell, turning
Wearily, as one would turn to nod good-bye to La Rochefoucauld,
If the street were time and he at the end of the street,
And I say, "Cousin Harriet, here is the *Boston Evening Transcript*."

The newspaper, whose name Eliot purposely repeats so monotonously, indicates what this poem is about. Now defunct, the *Transcript* covered in detail the slightest activity of Boston's leading families and was noted for the great length of its obituaries. Eliot, then, uses the newspaper as a symbol for an existence of boredom, fatigue ("Wearily"), petty and unvarying routine (since an evening newspaper, like night, arrives on schedule). The *Transcript* evokes a way of life without zest or passion, for, opposed to people who read it, Eliot sets people who do not: those whose desires revive, not expire, when the working day is through. Suggestions abound in the ironic comparison of the *Transcript*'s readers to a cornfield late in summer. To mention only a few: the readers sway because they are sleepy; they vegetate; they are drying up; each makes a rattling sound when turning a page. It is not necessary that we know the remote and similarly disillusioned friend to whom the speaker might nod: La Rochefoucauld, for example, whose cynical *Maxims* entertained Parisian society under Louis XIV. We understand that the nod is symbolic of an immense weariness of spirit. We know nothing about Cousin Harriet, whom the speaker addresses, but imagine from the greeting she inspires that she is probably a bore.

If Eliot wishes to say that certain Bostonians lead lives of sterile boredom, why does he couch his meaning in symbols? Why doesn't he tell us directly what he means? These questions imply two assumptions not necessarily true: first, that Eliot has a message to impart; second, that he is concealing it. We have reason to think that Eliot did not usually have a message in mind when beginning a poem, for as he once told a critic: "The conscious problems with which one is concerned in the actual writing are more those of a quasi-musical nature . . . than of a conscious exposition of ideas." Poets sometimes discover what they have to say while in the act of saying it. And it may be that in his *Transcript* poem, Eliot is saying exactly what he means. By communicating his meaning through symbols instead of statements, he may be choosing the only kind of language appropriate to an idea of great subtlety and complexity. (The paraphrase "Certain Bostonians are bored" hardly begins to describe the poem in all its possible meanings.) And by his use of symbolism, Eliot affords us the pleasure of finding our own entrances to his poem.

This power of suggestion that a symbol contains is, perhaps, its greatest advantage. Sometimes, as in the following poem by Emily Dickinson, a symbol will lead us from a visible object to something too vast to be perceived.

Emily Dickinson   (1830–1886)

The Lightning is a yellow Fork   (about 1870)

The Lightning is a yellow Fork
From Tables in the sky
By inadvertent fingers dropt
The awful Cutlery

Of mansions never quite disclosed   5
And never quite concealed
The Apparatus of the Dark
To ignorance revealed.

If the lightning is a fork, then whose are the fingers that drop it, the table from which it slips, the household to which it belongs? The poem implies this question without giving an answer. An obvious answer is "God," but can we be sure? We wonder, too, about these partially lighted mansions: if our vision were clearer, what would we behold?

IDENTIFYING SYMBOLS

You might wonder, "But how am I supposed to know a symbol when I see one?" The best approach is to read poems closely, taking comfort in the likelihood that it is better not to notice symbols at all than to find significance in every literal stone and huge meanings in every thing. In looking for the symbols in a poem, pick out all the references to concrete objects—newspapers, black cats, twisted pins. Consider these with special care. Notice any that the poet emphasizes by detailed description, by repetition, or by placing them at the very beginning or end of the poem. Ask: What is the poem about; what does it add up to? If, when the poem is paraphrased, the paraphrase depends primarily on the meaning of certain concrete objects, these richly suggestive objects may be the symbols.

There are some things a literary symbol usually is *not*. A symbol is not an abstraction. Such terms as *truth*, *death*, *love*, and *justice* cannot work as symbols (unless personified, as in the traditional figure of Justice holding a scale). Most often, a symbol is something we can see in the mind's eye: a newspaper, a lightning bolt, a gesture of nodding good-bye.

In narratives, a well-developed character who speaks much dialogue and is not the least bit mysterious is usually not a symbol. But watch out for an executioner in a black hood; a character, named for a biblical prophet, who does little but utter a prophecy; a trio of old women who resemble the Three Fates. (It has been argued, with good reason, that Milton's fully rounded character of Satan in *Paradise Lost* is a symbol embodying evil and human pride, but a narrower definition of symbol is more frequently useful.) A symbol *may* be a part of a person's body (the baleful eye of the murder victim in Poe's story "The Tell-Tale Heart") or a look, a voice, or a mannerism.

A symbol usually is not the second term of a metaphor. In the line "The Lightning is a yellow Fork," the symbol is the lightning, not the fork.

Sometimes a symbol addresses a sense other than sight: in William Faulkner's tale "A Rose for Emily," the odor of decay that surrounds the house of the last survivor of a town's leading family suggests not only physical dissolution but also the decay of a social order. A symbol is a special kind of image, for it exceeds the usual image in the richness of its connotations. The dead wife's cold comb in the haiku of Buson (discussed in Chapter 13) works symbolically, suggesting among other things the chill of the grave, the contrast between the living and the dead.

Symbolic Action

Holding a narrower definition than that used in this book, some readers of poetry prefer to say that a symbol is always a concrete object, never an act. They would deny the label "symbol" to Ahab's breaking his tobacco pipe before setting out to pursue Moby Dick (suggesting, perhaps, his determination to allow no pleasure to distract him from the chase) or to any large motion (such as Ahab's whole quest). This distinction, while confining, does have the merit of sparing one from seeing all motion to be possibly symbolic. Some would call Ahab's gesture not a symbol but a **symbolic act**.

To sum up: a symbol radiates hints or casts long shadows (to use Henry James's metaphor). We are unable to say it "stands for" or "represents" a meaning. It evokes, it suggests, it manifests. It demands no single necessary interpretation, such as the interpretation a driver gives to a red traffic light. Rather, like Emily Dickinson's lightning bolt, it points toward an indefinite meaning, which may lie in part beyond the reach of words.

Thomas Hardy (1840–1928)

Neutral Tones   1898

We stood by a pond that winter day,
And the sun was white, as though chidden of° God,   *rebuked by*
And a few leaves lay on the starving sod;
    —They had fallen from an ash, and were gray.

Your eyes on me were as eyes that rove   5
Over tedious riddles of years ago;
And some words played between us to and fro
    On which lost the more by our love.

The smile on your mouth was the deadest thing
Alive enough to have strength to die;   10
And a grin of bitterness swept thereby
    Like an ominous bird a-wing. . . .

Since then, keen lessons that love deceives,
And wrings with wrong, have shaped to me
Your face, and the God-curst sun, and a tree,   15
    And a pond edged with grayish leaves.

Questions

1. Sum up the story told in this poem. In lines 1–12, what is the dramatic situation?
   What has happened in the interval between the experience related in these lines
   and the reflection in the last stanza?
2. What meanings do you find in the title?
3. Explain in your own words the metaphor in line 2.
4. What connotations appropriate to this poem does the "ash" (line 4) have that *oak*
   or *maple* would lack?
5. What visible objects in the poem function symbolically? What actions or gestures?

Yusef Komunyakaa (b. 1947)

Facing It   1988

My black face fades,
hiding inside the black granite.
I said I wouldn't,
dammit: No tears.
I'm stone. I'm flesh.   5
My clouded reflection eyes me
like a bird of prey, the profile of night
slanted against morning. I turn
this way—the stone lets me go.
I turn that way—I'm inside   10

the Vietnam Veterans Memorial
again, depending on the light
to make a difference.
I go down the 58,022 names,
half-expecting to find   15
my own in letters like smoke.
I touch the name Andrew Johnson;
I see the booby trap's white flash.
Names shimmer on a woman's blouse
but when she walks away   20
the names stay on the wall.
Brushstrokes flash, a red bird's
wings cutting across my stare.
The sky. A plane in the sky.
A white vet's image floats   25
closer to me, then his pale eyes
look through mine. I'm a window.
He's lost his right arm
inside the stone. In the black mirror
a woman's trying to erase names: 30
No, she's brushing a boy's hair.

Questions

1. How does the title of "Facing It" relate to the poem? Does it have more than one meaning?
2. The narrator describes the people around him by their reflections on the polished granite rather than by looking at them directly. What does this indirect way of scrutinizing contribute to the poem?

ALLEGORY

If we read of a ship, its captain, its sailors, and the rough seas, and we realize we are reading about a commonwealth and how its rulers and workers keep it going even in difficult times, then we are reading an **allegory**. Closely akin to symbolism, allegory is a description—usually narrative—in which persons, places, and things are employed in a continuous and consistent system of equivalents. In an allegory an object has a single additional significance, one largely determined by convention. When an allegory appears in a work, it usually has a one-to-one relationship to an abstract entity, recognizable to readers and audiences familiar with the cultural context of the work.

Although more strictly limited in its suggestions than symbolism, allegory need not be thought inferior. Few poems continue to interest readers more than Dante's allegorical *Divine Comedy*. Sublime evidence of the appeal of allegory may be found in Jesus's use of the **parable**: a brief narrative—usually allegorical but sometimes not—that teaches a moral.

Matthew

The Parable of the Good Seed   (King James Version, 1611)

The kingdom of heaven is likened unto a man which sowed good
    seed in his field:
But while men slept, his enemy came and sowed tares among the
    wheat, and went his way.
But when the blade was sprung up, and brought forth fruit, then
    appeared the tares also.
So the servants of the householder came and said unto him, Sir,
    didst not thou sow good seed in thy field? From whence then
    hath it tares?
He said unto them, An enemy hath done this. The servants said unto   5
    him, Wilt thou then that we go and gather them up?
But he said, Nay; lest while ye gather up the tares, ye root up also
    the wheat with them.
Let both grow together until the harvest: and in the time of harvest I
    will say to the reapers, Gather ye together first the tares, and bind
    them in bundles to burn them: but gather the wheat into my barn.

                                      —Matthew 13:24–30

THE PARABLE OF THE GOOD SEED. 2 *tares:* harmful weeds.

Jesus explains this parable to his disciples, saying that the sower is the Son of
man, the field is the world, the good seed are the children of the Kingdom, the
tares are the children of the wicked one, the enemy is the devil, the harvest is
the end of the world, the reapers are angels. "As therefore the tares are gathered and burned in the fire; so shall it be in the end of this world" (Matthew
13:36–42).

    Usually, as in this parable, the meanings of an allegory are plainly labeled
or thinly disguised. An allegory, when carefully built, is systematic. It makes
one principal comparison, the working out of whose details may lead to further comparisons, then still further comparisons.

George Herbert (1593–1633)

Redemption   1633

Having been tenant long to a rich Lord,
  Not thriving, I resolved to be bold,
  And make a suit unto him, to afford
A new small-rented lease, and cancel th' old.

In Heaven at his manor I him sought: 5
  They told me there, that he was lately gone
  About some land, which he had dearly bought
Long since on earth, to take possession.

I straight returned, and knowing his great birth,
  Sought him accordingly in great resorts;   10
In cities, theaters, gardens, parks, and courts:
At length I heard a ragged noise and mirth

  Of thieves and murderers: there I him espied,
Who straight, *Your suit is granted*, said, and died.

Questions

1. In this allegory, what equivalents does Herbert give each of these terms: "tenant," "Lord," "not thriving," "suit," "new lease," "old lease," "manor," "land," "dearly bought," "take possession," "his great birth"?
2. What scene is depicted in the last three lines?

An object in an allegory is like a bird whose cage is clearly lettered with its identity—"RAVEN, *Corvus corax*; habitat of specimen, Maine." A symbol, by contrast, is a bird with piercing eyes that mysteriously appears one evening in your library. It is there; you can touch it. But what does it mean? You look at it. It continues to look at you.

Whether an object in literature is a symbol, part of an allegory, or no such thing at all, it has at least one sure meaning. Moby Dick is first a whale, and the *Boston Evening Transcript* is a newspaper. Besides deriving a multitude of intangible suggestions from the title symbol in Eliot's long poem *The Waste Land*, its readers cannot fail to carry away a sense of the land's physical appearance: a river choked with sandwich papers and cigarette ends, London Bridge "under the brown fog of a winter dawn." The most vital element of a literary work may pass us by, unless, before seeking further depths in a thing, we look to the thing itself.

Antonio Machado (1875–1939)

Proverbios y Cantares (XXIX) 1912

Caminante, son tus huellas
el camino, y nada más;
caminante, no hay camino,
se hace camino al andar.
Al andar se hace camino,
y al volver la vista atrás
se ve la senda que nunca
se ha de volver a pisar.
Caminante, no hay camino
sino estelas en la mar.

Traveler   2011

Traveler, your footsteps are
the road, there's nothing more;
traveler, there is no road,
the road is made by walking.
Walking makes the road,   5
and if you turn around,
you only see the path
you cannot walk again.
Traveler, there is no road,
only a track of foam   10
upon the sea.

      — *Translated by Michael Ortiz*

Questions

Compare Machado's poem with Robert Frost's famous "The Road Not Taken." In what ways does Machado's use of the road as a symbol resemble Frost's use? In what ways does it differ?

Robert Frost (1874–1963)

The Road Not Taken   1916

Two roads diverged in a yellow wood,
And sorry I could not travel both
And be one traveler, long I stood
And looked down one as far as I could
To where it bent in the undergrowth;   5

Then took the other, as just as fair,
And having perhaps the better claim,
Because it was grassy and wanted wear;
Though as for that the passing there
Had worn them really about the same,   10

And both that morning equally lay
In leaves no step had trodden black.
Oh, I kept the first for another day!
Yet knowing how way leads on to way,
I doubted if I should ever come back.   15

I shall be telling this with a sigh
Somewhere ages and ages hence:
Two roads diverged in a wood, and I—
I took the one less traveled by,
And that has made all the difference.   20

Question

What symbolism do you find in this poem, if any? Back up your claim with evidence.

Christina Rossetti (1830–1894)

Up-Hill   1862

Does the road wind up-hill all the way?
    Yes, to the very end.
Will the day's journey take the whole long day?
    From morn to night, my friend.

But is there for the night a resting-place?   5
    A roof for when the slow dark hours begin.

May not the darkness hide it from my face?
  You cannot miss that inn.

Shall I meet other wayfarers at night?
  Those who have gone before.   10
Then must I knock, or call when just in sight?
  They will not keep you standing at that door.

Shall I find comfort, travel-sore and weak?
  Of labor you shall find the sum.
Will there be beds for me and all who seek?   15
  Yea, beds for all who come.

Questions

1. In reading this poem, at what line did you realize that the poet is building an allegory?
2. For what does each thing stand?
3. What does the title of the poem suggest to you?
4. Recast the meaning of line 14, a knotty line, in your own words.
5. Discuss the possible identities of the two speakers—the apprehensive traveler and the character with all the answers. Are they specific individuals? Allegorical figures?
6. Compare "Up-Hill" with Robert Creeley's "Oh No" (Chapter 10). What striking similarities do you find in these two dissimilar poems?

FOR REVIEW AND FURTHER STUDY

Mary Oliver   (b. 1935)

Wild Geese   1986

You do not have to be good.
You do not have to walk on your knees
for a hundred miles through the desert, repenting.
You only have to let the soft animal of your body
    love what it loves.
Tell me about despair, yours, and I will tell you mine.   5
Meanwhile the world goes on.
Meanwhile the sun and the clear pebbles of the rain
are moving across the landscapes,
over the prairies and the deep trees,
the mountains and the rivers.   10
Meanwhile the wild geese, high in the clean blue air,
are heading home again.
Whoever you are, no matter how lonely,

the world offers itself to your imagination,
calls to you like the wild geese, harsh and exciting—   15
over and over announcing your place
in the family of things.

Questions

1. Is this poem addressed to a specific person?
2. What is meant by "good" in the first line?
3. What do the wild geese symbolize? What is the significance of the use of the term "wild"?
4. What other adjectives are used to describe the phenomena of nature? What thematic purpose is served by this characterization of the natural world?

Lorine Niedecker (1903–1970)

Popcorn-can cover   (about 1959)

Popcorn-can cover
screwed to the wall
over a hole
     so the cold
can't mouse in   5

Wallace Stevens (1879–1955)

Anecdote of the Jar   1923

I placed a jar in Tennessee,
And round it was, upon a hill.
It made the slovenly wilderness
Surround that hill.

The wilderness rose up to it,   5
And sprawled around, no longer wild.
The jar was round upon the ground
And tall and of a port in air.

It took dominion everywhere.
The jar was gray and bare.   10
It did not give of bird or bush,
Like nothing else in Tennessee.

WRITING *effectively*

THINKING ABOUT SYMBOLS

A symbol, to use poet John Drury's concise definition, is "an image that radiates meanings." While images in a poem can and should be read as what they literally are, images often do double duty, suggesting deeper meanings. Exactly what those meanings are, however, often differs from poem to poem.

Some symbols have been used so often and effectively over time that a traditional reading of them has developed. At times a poet clearly adopts an image's traditional symbolic meaning. Some poems, however, deliberately play against a symbol's conventional associations.

- **To determine the meaning (or meanings) of a symbol, start by asking if it has traditional associations.** If so, consider whether the symbol is being used in the expected way or if the poet is playing with those associations.
- **Consider the symbol's relationship to the rest of the poem.** Let context be your guide. The image might have a unique meaning to the poem's speaker.
- **Consider the emotions that the image evokes.** If the image recurs in the poem, pay attention to how it changes from one appearance to the next.
- **Keep in mind that not everything is a symbol.** If an image doesn't appear to radiate meanings above and beyond its literal sense, don't feel you have failed as a critic. As Sigmund Freud once said about symbol-hunting, "Sometimes a cigar is just a cigar."

CHECKLIST: Writing About Symbols

- ☐ Is the symbol a traditional one?
- ☐ If so, is it being used in the expected way? Or is the poet playing with its associations?
- ☐ What does the image seem to mean to the poem's speaker?
- ☐ What emotions are evoked by the image?
- ☐ If an image recurs in a poem, how does it change from one appearance to the next?
- ☐ Does the image radiate meaning beyond its literal sense? If not, it might not be intended as a symbol.

TOPICS FOR WRITING ON SYMBOLISM

1. Do an in-depth analysis of the symbolism in a poem of your choice from Chapter 22, "Poems for Further Reading." Two likely choices would be Gerard Manley Hopkins's "The Windhover" and Sylvia Plath's "Daddy."

2. Compare and contrast the use of roads as symbols in Christina Rossetti's "Up-Hill" and Robert Frost's "The Road Not Taken." What does the use of this image suggest in each poem?

3. Discuss "Anecdote of the Jar" in terms of Wallace Stevens's use of symbolism to portray the relationship between humanity and nature.

4. Write an explication of any poem from this chapter, paying careful attention to its symbols. Some good choices are Mary Oliver's "Wild Geese," Thomas Hardy's "Neutral Tones," and Christina Rossetti's "Up-Hill." For a further description of poetic explication, see the chapter, "Writing About Literature."

5. Take a relatively simple, straightforward poem, such as William Carlos Williams's "This Is Just to Say" (Chapter 11), and write a burlesque critical interpretation of it. Claim to discover symbols that the poem doesn't contain. While running wild with your "reading into" the poem, don't invent anything that you can't somehow support from the text of the poem itself. At the end of your burlesque, sum up in a paragraph what this exercise taught you about how to read poems, or how not to.

▶ TERMS FOR *review*

Symbol ▶ A person, place, or thing in a narrative that suggests meanings beyond its literal sense. Symbol is related to *allegory*, but it works more complexly. A symbol bears multiple suggestions and associations. It is unique to the work, not common to a culture.

Allegory ▶ A description—often a narrative—in which the literal events (persons, places, and things) consistently point to a parallel sequence of ideas, values, or other recognizable abstractions. An allegory has two levels of meaning: a literal level that tells a surface story and a symbolic level in which the abstractions unfold.

Symbolic act ▶ An action whose significance goes well beyond its literal meaning. In literature, symbolic acts often involve a primal or unconscious ritual element such as rebirth, purification, forgiveness, vengeance, or initiation.

Conventional symbols ▶ Symbols that, because of their frequent use, have acquired a standard significance. They may range from complex metaphysical images such as those of Christian saints in Gothic art to social customs such as a young bride in a white dress. They are conventional symbols because they carry recognizable meanings and suggestions.

20 MYTH AND NARRATIVE

What You Will Learn in This Chapter

- To define *myth* and *mythology*
- To recognize and describe an archetype
- To describe personal myth
- To analyze the role of myth and archetype in a poem

Poets have long been fond of retelling **myths**, narrowly defined as traditional stories about the exploits of immortal beings. Such stories taken collectively may also be called myth or **mythology**. In one of the most celebrated collections of myth ever assembled, the *Metamorphoses*, the Roman poet Ovid told how Phaeton, child of the sun god, rashly tried to drive his father's fiery chariot on its daily round, lost control of the horses, and caused disaster both to himself and to the world.

Our use of the term *myth* in discussing poetry, then, differs from its use in expressions such as "the myth of communism" and "the myth of democracy." In these examples, *myth* is used broadly to represent any idea people believe in, whether true or false. Nor do we mean—to take another familiar use of the word—a cock-and-bull story: "Judge Rapp doesn't roast speeders alive; that's just a *myth*." In the following discussion, *myth* will mean a kind of story—either from ancient or modern sources—whose actions implicitly symbolize some profound truth about human or natural existence.

THE SUBJECTS AND USES OF MYTH

Traditional myths tell us stories of gods or heroes—their battles, their lives, their loves, and often their suffering—all on a scale of magnificence larger than our life. These exciting stories usually reveal part of a culture's worldview. Myths often try to explain universal natural phenomena, like the phases of the moon or the turning of the seasons, but some myths tell the stories of purely local phenomena.

Modern psychologists, such as Sigmund Freud and Carl Jung, have been fascinated by myth and legend, since they believe these stories symbolically enact deep truths about human nature. Our myths, psychologists insist, express our wishes, dreams, and nightmares. Whether or not we believe myths, we recognize their psychological power. Even in the first century B.C., Ovid did not believe in the literal truth of the legends he so suavely retold; he confessed, "I prate of ancient poets' monstrous lies."

ORIGINS OF MYTH

How does a myth begin? Several theories have been proposed, none universally accepted. One is that a myth is a way to explain some natural phenomenon. Winter comes and the vegetation perishes because Persephone, child of Demeter, must return to the underworld for several months every year. This theory, as classical scholar Edith Hamilton has pointed out, may lead us to think incorrectly that Greek mythology was the creation of a primitive people. Tales of the gods of Mount Olympus may reflect an earlier inheritance, but the Greek myths known to us were transcribed in an era of high civilization. Anthropologists have questioned whether primitive people generally found beauty in the mysteries of nature. Many anthropologists emphasize the practical function of myth; in his influential work of comparative mythology, *The Golden Bough*, Sir James Frazer argued that most myths were originally expressions of human hope that nature would be fertile. Still another theory maintains that many myths began as real events; mythic heroes were real human beings whose deeds have been changed and exaggerated by posterity. Most present-day myth historians would say that different myths probably have different origins.

Poets have many coherent mythologies on which to draw; perhaps those most frequently consulted by British and American poets are the classical, the Christian, the Norse, the Native American, and the folktales of the American frontier (embodying the deeds of superhuman characters such as Paul Bunyan). Some poets have taken inspiration from other myths as well: T. S. Eliot's *The Waste Land*, for example, is enriched by allusions to Buddhism and to pagan vegetation cults.

A tour through any good art museum will demonstrate how thoroughly myth pervades the painting and sculpture of nearly every civilization. In literature, one evidence of its continuing value to recent poets and storytellers is how frequently ancient myths are retold. Even in modern society, writers often turn to myth when they try to tell stories of deep significance. Mythic structures still touch a powerful and primal part of the human imagination. William Faulkner's story "The Bear" recalls tales of Indian totem animals; John Updike's novel *The Centaur* presents the horse-man Chiron as a modern high-school teacher; James Joyce's *Ulysses* transposes the *Odyssey* to modern Dublin (and the Coen brothers' film *O Brother, Where Art Thou?* reimagines Homer's epic in Depression-era Mississippi); Rita Dove's play *The Darker Face of the Earth* recasts the story of Oedipus in the slave-era South; Bernard Shaw retells the story of Pygmalion in his popular Edwardian social comedy *Pygmalion*, later the basis of the hit musical *My Fair Lady*. Popular interest in such works may testify to the profound appeal myths continue to hold for us. Like other varieties of poetry, myth is a kind of knowledge, not at odds with scientific knowledge but existing in addition to it.

Robert Frost (1874–1963)

Nothing Gold Can Stay   1923

Nature's first green is gold,
Her hardest hue to hold.
Her early leaf's a flower;
But only so an hour.
Then leaf subsides to leaf.   5
So Eden sank to grief,
So dawn goes down to day.
Nothing gold can stay.

Questions

1. To what myth does this poem allude? Does Frost sound as though he believes in the myth or as though he rejects it?
2. When Frost says, "Nature's first green is gold," he is describing how many leaves first appear as tiny yellow buds and blossoms. But what else does this line imply?
3. What would happen to the poem's meaning if line 6 were omitted?

William Wordsworth (1770–1850)

The world is too much with us   1807

The world is too much with us; late and soon,
Getting and spending, we lay waste our powers:
Little we see in Nature that is ours;
We have given our hearts away, a sordid boon!
This Sea that bares her bosom to the moon;   5
The winds that will be howling at all hours,
And are up-gathered now like sleeping flowers;
For this, for everything, we are out of tune;
It moves us not.—Great God! I'd rather be
A Pagan suckled in a creed outworn;   10
So might I, standing on this pleasant lea,
Have glimpses that would make me less forlorn;
Have sight of Proteus rising from the sea;
Or hear old Triton blow his wreathèd horn.

Questions

1. What condition does the speaker complain of in this sonnet? To what does he attribute this condition?
2. How does this situation affect him personally?

H.D. [Hilda Doolittle] (1886–1961)

Helen   1924

All Greece hates
the still eyes in the white face,
the lustre as of olives
where she stands,
and the white hands.   5

All Greece reviles
the wan face when she smiles,
hating it deeper still
when it grows wan and white,
remembering past enchantments   10
and past ills.

Greece sees, unmoved,
God's daughter, born of love,
the beauty of cool feet
and slenderest knees,   15
could love indeed the maid,
only if she were laid,
white ash amid funereal cypresses.

HELEN. In Greek mythology, Helen, most beautiful of all women, was the daughter of a
mortal, Leda, by the god Zeus. Her abduction set off the long and devastating Trojan War.
While married to Menelaus, king of the Greek city-state of Sparta, Helen was carried off by
Paris, prince of Troy. Menelaus and his brother, Agamemnon, raised an army, besieged Troy
for ten years, and eventually recaptured her. One episode of the Trojan War is related in the
Iliad, Homer's epic poem, composed before 700 B.C.

Questions

1. At what point in the Troy narrative does this poem appear to be set?
2. What connotations does the color white usually possess? Does it have those same
   associations here?
3. Reread Yeats's "Leda and the Swan" (Chapter 15). Does his retelling of that myth
   add an ironic dimension to line 13 of "Helen"?

ARCHETYPE

An important concept in understanding myth is the **archetype**, a basic
image, character, situation, or symbol that appears so often in literature
and legend that it evokes a deep universal response. (The Greek root
of *archetype* means "original pattern.") The term was borrowed by literary critics from the writings of the Swiss psychologist Carl Jung, a serious
scholar of myth and religion, who formulated a theory of the "collective
unconscious," a set of primal memories common to the entire human race.

Archetypal patterns emerged, he speculated, in prerational thought and often reflect key primordial experiences such as birth, growth, sexual awakening, family, generational struggle, and death, as well as primal elements such as fire, sun, moon, blood, and water. Jung also believed that these situations, images, and figures had actually been genetically coded into the human brain and are passed down to successive generations, but no one has ever been able to prove a biological base for the undeniable phenomenon of similar characters, stories, and symbols appearing across widely separated and diverse cultures.

Whatever their origin, archetypal images do seem verbally coded in most myths, legends, and traditional tales. One sees enough recurring patterns and figures from Greek myth to *Star Wars*, from Hindu epic to Marvel superhero comics, to strongly suggest that there is some common psychic force at work. Typical archetypal figures include the trickster, the cruel stepmother, the rebellious young man, the beautiful but destructive woman, and the stupid youngest son who succeeds through simple goodness. Any one of these figures can be traced from culture to culture. The trickster, for instance, appears in American Indian coyote tales, Norse myths about the fire god Loki, Marx Brothers films, and *Batman* comic books and movies featuring the Joker.

Archetypal myths are the basic conventions of human storytelling, which we learn without necessarily being aware of the process. The patterns we absorb in our first nursery rhymes and fairy tales, as mythological critic Northrop Frye has demonstrated, underlie—though often very subtly—the most sophisticated poems and novels. One powerful archetype seen across many cultures is the demon-goddess who immobilizes men by locking them into a deathly trance or—in the most primitive forms of the myth—turning them to stone. Here is a modern version of this ancient myth in the following poem.

Louise Bogan (1897–1970)

Medusa   1923

I had come to the house, in a cave of trees,
Facing a sheer sky.
Everything moved,—a bell hung ready to strike,
Sun and reflection wheeled by.

When the bare eyes were before me   5
And the hissing hair,
Held up at a window, seen through a door.
The stiff bald eyes, the serpents on the forehead
Formed in the air.

This is a dead scene forever now.   10
Nothing will ever stir.
The end will never brighten it more than this,
Nor the rain blur.

The water will always fall, and will not fall,
And the tipped bell make no sound.   15
The grass will always be growing for hay
Deep on the ground.

And I shall stand here like a shadow
Under the great balanced day,
My eyes on the yellow dust, that was lifting in the wind,   20
And does not drift away.

MEDUSA. One of the Gorgons of Greek mythology. Hideously ugly with snakes for hair,
Medusa turned those who looked upon her face into stone.

Questions

1. Who is the speaker of the poem?
2. Why are the first two stanzas spoken in the past tense while the final three are
   mainly in the future tense?
3. What is the speaker's attitude toward Medusa? Is there anything surprising about
   his or her reaction to being transformed into stone?
4. Does Bogan merely dramatize an incident from classical mythology, or does the
   poem suggest other interpretations as well?

A. E. Stallings (b. 1968)

First Love: A Quiz   2006

He came up to me:
    a. in his souped-up Camaro
    b. to talk to my skinny best friend
    c. and bumped my glass of wine so I wore the ferrous stain on
       my sleeve   5
    d. from the ground, in a lead chariot drawn by a team of stal-
       lions black as crude oil and breathing sulfur; at his heart,
       he sported a tiny golden arrow

He offered me:
    a. a ride   10
    b. dinner and a movie, with a wink at the cliché
    c. an excuse not to go back alone to the apartment with its
       sink of dirty knives
    d. a narcissus with a hundred dazzling petals that breathed a
       sweetness as cloying as decay   15

I went with him because:
   a. even his friends told me to beware
   b. I had nothing to lose except my virginity
   c. he placed his hand in the small of my back and I felt the
      tread of honeybees   20
   d. he was my uncle, the one who lived in the half-finished base-
      ment, and he took me by the hair

The place he took me to:
   a. was dark as my shut eyes
   b. and where I ate bitter seed and became ripe   25
   c. and from which my mother would never take me wholly back,
      though she wept and walked the earth and made the bearded
      ears of barley wither on their stalks and the blasted flowers
      drop from their sepals
   d. is called by some men hell and others love   30
   e. all of the above

First Love: A Quiz. Stallings's poem alludes to the classical myth of Persephone. A beautiful young goddess, the daughter of Zeus and Demeter, she was abducted by Hades, the ruler of the Underworld (and the brother of Zeus). Her mother Demeter, the goddess of agriculture, became so grief-stricken that plants stopped growing. Eventually, Persephone was permitted to spend six months on the earth each year, which allows spring and summer to return, before descending again to Hades, which brings back winter.

Questions

1. How does Stallings adapt a classical myth of abduction and rape into a contemporary story? Give specific examples.
2. In each option, does the speaker see the man as dangerous? If so, why does she go with him?
3. What is your interpretation of the last line?

PERSONAL MYTH

Sometimes poets have been inspired to make up myths of their own, to embody their own visions of life. "I must create a system or be enslaved by another man's," said William Blake, who in his "prophetic books" peopled the cosmos with supernatural beings having names such as Los, Urizen, and Vala (side by side with recognizable figures from the Old and New Testaments). This kind of system-making probably has advantages and drawbacks. T. S. Eliot, in his essay on Blake, wishes that the author of *The Four Zoas* had accepted traditional myths, and he compares Blake's thinking to a piece of homemade furniture whose construction diverted valuable energy from the writing of poems. Others have found Blake's untraditional cosmos an achievement—notably William Butler Yeats, himself the creator of an elaborate personal mythology. Although we need not know all of Yeats's mythology to enjoy his poems, to know of its existence can make a few great poems deeper for us and less difficult.

William Butler Yeats (1865–1939)

The Second Coming   1921

Turning and turning in the widening gyre°   *spiral*
The falcon cannot hear the falconer;
Things fall apart; the center cannot hold;
Mere anarchy is loosed upon the world,
The blood-dimmed tide is loosed, and everywhere   5
The ceremony of innocence is drowned;
The best lack all conviction, while the worst
Are full of passionate intensity.

Surely some revelation is at hand;
Surely the Second Coming is at hand.   10
The Second Coming! Hardly are those words out
When a vast image out of *Spiritus Mundi*
Troubles my sight: somewhere in sands of the desert
A shape with lion body and the head of a man,
A gaze blank and pitiless as the sun,   15
Is moving its slow thighs, while all about it
Reel shadows of the indignant desert birds.
The darkness drops again; but now I know
That twenty centuries of stony sleep
Were vexed to nightmare by a rocking cradle,   20
And what rough beast, its hour come round at last,
Slouches towards Bethlehem to be born?

What kind of Second Coming does Yeats expect? Evidently it is not to
be a Christian one. Yeats saw human history as governed by the turning of a
Great Wheel, whose phases influence events and determine human personalities—rather like the signs of the Zodiac in astrology. Every two thousand
years comes a horrendous moment: the Wheel completes a turn; one civilization ends and another begins. Strangely, a new age is always announced by
birds and by acts of violence. Thus the Greek-Roman world arrives with the
descent of Zeus in swan's form and the burning of Troy, the Christian era with
the descent of the Holy Spirit—traditionally depicted as a dove—and the
Crucifixion. In 1919 when Yeats wrote "The Second Coming," his Ireland
was in the midst of turmoil and bloodshed; the Western Hemisphere had been
severely shaken by World War I and the Russian Revolution. A new millen-
nium seemed imminent. What sphinxlike, savage deity would next appear
on earth, with birds proclaiming it angrily? Yeats imagines it emerging from
Spiritus Mundi, Soul of the World, a collective unconscious from which a human being (since the individual soul touches it) receives dreams, nightmares,
and racial memories.

It is hard to say whether a poet who discovers a personal myth does so to have something to live by or to have something to write about. Robert Graves, who professed his belief in a White Goddess ("Mother of All Living, the ancient power of love and terror"), declared that he wrote his poetry in a trance, inspired by his Goddess-Muse. Luckily, we do not have to know a poet's religious affiliation before we can read his or her poems. Perhaps most personal myths that enter poems are not acts of faith but works of art: stories that resemble traditional mythology.

Diane Thiel (b. 1967)

Memento Mori in Middle School 2000

When I was twelve, I chose Dante's *Inferno*
in gifted class—an oral presentation
with visual aids. My brother, *il miglior fabbro,*

said he would draw the tortures. We used ten
red posterboards. That day, for school, I dressed   5
in pilgrim black, left earlier to hang them

around the class. The students were impressed.
The teacher, too. She acted quite amused
and peered too long at all the punishments.

We knew by reputation she was cruel.   10
The class could see a hint of twisted forms
and asked to be allowed to round the room

as I went through my final presentation.
We passed the first one, full of poets cut
out of a special issue of *Horizon*.   15

The class thought these were such a boring set,
they probably deserved their tedious fates.
They liked the next, though—bodies blown about,

the lovers kept outside the tinfoil gates.
We had a new boy in our class named Paolo   20
and when I noted Paolo's wind-blown state

and pointed out Francesca, people howled.
I knew that more than one of us not-so-
covertly liked him. It seemed like hours

before we moved on to the gluttons, though,   25
where they could hold the cool fistfuls of slime
I brought from home. An extra touch. It sold

in canisters at toy stores at the time.
The students recognized the River Styx,
the logo of a favorite band of mine.   30

We moved downriver to the town of Dis,
which someone loudly re-named Dis and Dat.
And for the looming harpies and the furies,

who shrieked and tore things up, I had clipped out
the shrillest, most deserving teacher's heads   35
from our school paper, then thought better of it.

At the wood of suicides, we quieted.
Though no one in the room would say a word,
I know we couldn't help but think of Fred.

His name was in the news, though we had heard   40
he might have just been playing with the gun.
We moved on quickly by that huge, dark bird

and rode the flying monster, Geryon,
to reach the counselors, each wicked face,
again, I had resisted pasting in.   45

To represent the ice in that last place,
where Satan chewed the traitors' frozen heads,
my mother had insisted that I take

an ice-chest full of popsicles—to end
my gruesome project on a lighter note.   50
"It *is* a comedy, isn't it," she said.

She hadn't read the poem, or seen our art,
but asked me what had happened to the sweet,
angelic poems I once read and wrote.

The class, though, was delighted by the treat,   55
and at the last round, they all pushed to choose
their colors quickly, so they wouldn't melt.

The bell rang. Everyone ran out of school,
as always, yelling at the top of their lungs,
The *Inferno* fast forgotten, but their howls   60

showed off their darkened red and purple tongues.

MEMENTO MORI IN MIDDLE SCHOOL. *Memento Mori:* Latin for "Remember you must die,"
the phrase now means any reminder of human mortality and the need to lead a virtuous life.
1 *Dante's* Inferno: The late medieval epic poem by the Italian poet Dante Alighieri describes
a Christian soul's journey through hell. (*Inferno* means "hell" in Italian.) 3 *il miglior fabbro:*

the better craftsman—Dante's term for fellow poet Arnaut Daniel, which T. S. Eliot later famously quoted to praise Ezra Pound. 15 *Horizon:* a magazine of art and culture. 20–23: *Paolo . . . Francesca:* two lovers in Dante's *Inferno* who have been damned for their adultery. 29 *River Styx:* the river that flows around hell to mark its boundary. 31 *Dis:* the main city of hell named after its ruler, Dis (Pluto). 43 *Geryon:* a mythical monster Dante places in his *Inferno.*

Sylvia Plath (1932–1963)

Lady Lazarus

(1962) 1965

I have done it again.
One year in every ten
I manage it—

A sort of walking miracle, my skin
Bright as a Nazi lampshade,   5
My right foot

A paperweight,
My face a featureless, fine
Jew linen.

Peel off the napkin
O my enemy.
Do I terrify?—   10

The nose, the eye pits, the full set of teeth?
The sour breath
Will vanish in a day.   15

Soon, soon the flesh
The grave cave ate will be
At home on me

And I a smiling woman.
I am only thirty.
And like the cat I have nine times to die.   20

This is Number Three.
What a trash
To annihilate each decade.

What a million filaments.
The peanut-crunching crowd   25
Shoves in to see

Them unwrap me hand and foot—
The big strip tease.
Gentleman, ladies   30

These are my hands
My knees.
I may be skin and bone,

Nevertheless, I am the same, identical woman.
The first time it happened I was ten.   35
It was an accident.

The second time I meant
To last it out and not come back at all.
I rocked shut

As a seashell.   40
They had to call and call
And pick the worms off me like sticky pearls.

Dying
Is an art, like everything else.
I do it exceptionally well.   45

I do it so it feels like hell.
I do it so it feels real.
I guess you could say I've a call.

It's easy enough to do it in a cell.
It's easy enough to do it and stay put.   50
It's the theatrical

Comeback in broad day
To the same place, the same face, the same brute
Amused shout:

"A miracle!"   55
That knocks me out.
There is a charge

For the eyeing of my scars, there is a charge
For the hearing of my heart—
It really goes.   60

And there is a charge, a very large charge,
For the word or a touch
Or a bit of blood

Or a piece of my hair or my clothes.
So, so, Herr Doktor.   65
So, Herr Enemy.

I am your opus,°   work, work of art
I am your valuable,
The pure gold baby

That melts to a shriek.   70
I turn and burn.
Do not think I underestimate your great concern.

Ash, ash—
You poke and stir.
Flesh, bone, there is nothing there—   75

A cake of soap,
A wedding ring,
A gold filling,

Herr God, Herr Lucifer
Beware   80
Beware.

Out of the ash
I rise with my red hair
And I eat men like air.

Questions

1. What or whom does the title, "Lady Lazarus," allude to?
2. Although the poem is openly autobiographical, Plath uses certain symbols to represent herself (Lady Lazarus, a Jew murdered in a concentration camp, a cat with nine lives, and so on). What do these symbols tell us about Plath's attitude toward herself and the world around her?
3. In her biography of Plath, *Bitter Fame*, the poet Anne Stevenson says that this poem penetrates "the furthest reaches of disdain and rage . . . bereft of all 'normal' human feelings." What do you think Stevenson means? Does anything in the poem strike you as particularly chilling?
4. The speaker in "Lady Lazarus" says, "Dying / Is an art, like everything else" (lines 43–44). What sense do you make of this metaphor?
5. Does the ending of "Lady Lazarus" imply that the speaker assumes that she will outlive her suicide attempts? Set forth your final understanding of the poem.

MYTH AND POPULAR CULTURE

If one can find myths in an art museum, one can also find them abundantly in popular culture. Movies and comic books, for example, are full of myths in modern guise. What is Superman, if not a mythic hero who has adapted himself to modern urban life? Marvel Comics even made the Norse thunder god, Thor, into a superhero, although they initially obliged him, like Clark Kent, to get a job. We also see myths retold on the technicolor screen. Sometimes Hollywood presents the traditional story directly, as in Walt Disney's *Cinderella*; more often the ancient tales acquire contemporary settings, as in another celluloid Cinderella story, *Pretty Woman*. George Lucas's *Star Wars* series borrowed the structure of medieval quest legends. In quest stories, young knights pursued their destiny, often by seeking the Holy Grail, the cup Christ used at the Last Supper; in *Star Wars*, Luke Skywalker searched for his own parentage and identity, but his interstellar quest brought him to a surprisingly similar cast of knights, monsters, princesses, and wizards. Medieval Grail romances, which influenced Eliot's *The Waste Land* and J. R. R. Tolkien's *The Lord of the Rings* trilogy, also shaped films such as *The Fisher King* and *The Matrix*. Science fiction commonly uses myth to original effect. Extraterrestrial visitors usually appear as either munificent mythic gods or nightmarish demons. Steven Spielberg's *E.T.*, for example, revealed a gentle, Christ-like alien recognized by innocent children, but persecuted by adults. E.T. even healed the sick, fell into a deathlike coma, and was resurrected.

Why do poets retell myths? Why don't they just make up their own stories? First, using myth allows poets to be concise. By alluding to stories that their audiences know, they can draw on powerful associations with just a few words. If someone describes an acquaintance, "He thinks he's James Bond," that one allusion speaks volumes. Likewise, when Robert Frost inserts the single line "So Eden sank to grief" in "Nothing Gold Can Stay," those five words summon up a wealth of associations. They tie the perishable quality of spring's beauty to the equally transient nature of human youth. They also suggest that everything in the human world is subject to time's ravages, that perfection is impossible for us to maintain, just as it was for Adam and Eve.

Second, poets know that many stories fall into familiar mythic patterns, and that the most powerful stories of human existence tend to be the same, generation after generation. Sometimes using an old story allows a writer to describe a new situation in a fresh and surprising way. Novels often try to capture the exact texture of a social situation; they need to present the everyday details to evoke the world in which their characters live. Myths tend to tell their stories more quickly and in more general terms. They give just the essential actions and leave out everything else. Narrative poems also work best when they focus on just the essential elements. Here is a contemporary narrative poem that retells a traditional myth to make a modern interpretation.

Anne Sexton (1928–1974)

Cinderella   1971

You always read about it:
the plumber with twelve children
who wins the Irish Sweepstakes.
From toilets to riches.
That story.   5

Or the nursemaid,
some luscious sweet from Denmark
who captures the oldest son's heart.
From diapers to Dior.
That story.   10

Or a milkman who serves the wealthy,
eggs, cream, butter, yogurt, milk,
the white truck like an ambulance
who goes into real estate
and makes a pile.   15
From homogenized to martinis at lunch.

Or the charwoman
who is on the bus when it cracks up
and collects enough from the insurance.
From mops to Bonwit Teller.   20
That story.

Once
the wife of a rich man was on her deathbed
and she said to her daughter Cinderella:
Be devout. Be good. Then I will smile   25
down from heaven in the seam of a cloud.
The man took another wife who had
two daughters, pretty enough
but with hearts like blackjacks.
Cinderella was their maid.   30
She slept on the sooty hearth each night
and walked around looking like Al Jolson.
Her father brought presents home from town,
jewels and gowns for the other women
but the twig of a tree for Cinderella.   35
She planted that twig on her mother's grave
and it grew to a tree where a white dove sat.
Whenever she wished for anything the dove
would drop it like an egg upon the ground.
The bird is important, my dears, so heed him.   40

Next came the ball, as you all know.
It was a marriage market.
The prince was looking for a wife.
All but Cinderella were preparing
and gussying up for the big event.   45
Cinderella begged to go too.
Her stepmother threw a dish of lentils
into the cinders and said: Pick them
up in an hour and you shall go.
The white dove brought all his friends;   50
all the warm wings of the fatherland came,
and picked up the lentils in a jiffy.
No, Cinderella, said the stepmother,
you have no clothes and cannot dance.
That's the way with stepmothers.   55

Cinderella went to the tree at the grave
and cried forth like a gospel singer:
Mama! Mama! My turtledove,
send me to the prince's ball!
The bird dropped down a golden dress   60
and delicate little gold slippers.
Rather a large package for a simple bird.
So she went. Which is no surprise.
Her stepmother and sisters didn't
recognize her without her cinder face   65
and the prince took her hand on the spot
and danced with no other the whole day.

As nightfall came she thought she'd better
get home. The prince walked her home
and she disappeared into the pigeon house   70
and although the prince took an axe and broke
it open she was gone. Back to her cinders.
These events repeated themselves for three days.
However on the third day the prince
covered the palace steps with cobbler's wax   75
and Cinderella's gold shoe stuck upon it.
Now he would find whom the shoe fit
and find his strange dancing girl for keeps.
He went to their house and the two sisters
were delighted because they had lovely feet.   80
The eldest went into a room to try the slipper on
but her big toe got in the way so she simply

sliced it off and put on the slipper.
The prince rode away with her until the white dove
told him to look at the blood pouring forth.   85
That is the way with amputations.
They just don't heal up like a wish.
The other sister cut off her heel
but the blood told as blood will.
The prince was getting tired.   90
He began to feel like a shoe salesman.
But he gave it one last try.
This time Cinderella fit into the shoe
like a love letter into its envelope.

At the wedding ceremony   95
the two sisters came to curry favor
and the white dove pecked their eyes out.
Two hollow spots were left
like soup spoons.

Cinderella and the prince   100
lived, they say, happily ever after,
like two dolls in a museum case
never bothered by diapers or dust,
never arguing over the timing of an egg,
never telling the same story twice,   105
never getting a middle-aged spread,
their darling smiles pasted on for eternity.
Regular Bobbsey Twins.
That story.

CINDERELLA. 32 *Al Jolson:* Extremely popular American entertainer (1886–1950) who
frequently performed in blackface.

Questions

1. Most of Sexton's "Cinderella" straightforwardly retells a version of the famous
   fairy tale. But in the beginning and ending of the poem, how does Sexton change
   the story?
2. How does Sexton's refrain of "That story" alter the meaning of the episodes it
   describes? What is the tone of this poem (the poet's attitude toward her material)?
3. What does Sexton's final stanza suggest about the way fairy tales usually end?

■ WRITING *effectively*

THINKING ABOUT MYTH

Of the many myths conjured by the poets in these pages, you may know some by heart, some only vaguely, and others not at all. When reading a poem inspired by myth, there's no way around it: your understanding will be more precise if you know the mythic story the poem refers to. With the vast resources available on the Web, it's never hard to find a description of a myth, whether traditional or contemporary. While different versions of most myths exist, what usually remains fixed is the tale's basic pattern. A familiarity with that narrative is a key to the meaning—both intellectual and emotional—of any poem that makes reference to mythology.

- **Start with the underlying pattern of the narrative in question.** Does the basic shape of the poem's story seem familiar? Does it have some recognizable source in myth or legend? Even if the poem has no obvious narrative line, does it call to mind other stories?
- **Notice what new details the poem has added, and what it inevitably leaves out.** The difference between the poem and the source material will reveal something about the author's attitude toward the original, and may give you a sense of his or her intentions in reworking the original myth.

CHECKLIST: Writing About Myth

☐ Does the poem have a recognizable source in myth or legend?

☐ What new details has the poet added to the original myth?

☐ What do these details reveal about the poet's attitude toward the source material?

☐ Have important elements of the original been discarded? What does their absence suggest about the author's primary focus?

☐ Does the poem rely heavily on its mythic imagery? Or is myth tangential to the poem's theme?

☐ How do mythic echoes underscore the poem's meaning?

TOPICS FOR WRITING ON MYTH

1. Anne Sexton's "Cinderella" freely mixes period detail and slang from twentieth-century American life with elements from the original fairy tale. (You can read the original in Charles Perrault's *Mother Goose Tales*.) Write an analysis of the effect of all this anachronistic mixing and matching. Be sure to look up any period details you don't recognize.

2. Provide an explication of Louise Bogan's "Medusa." For tips on poetic explication, refer to the chapter "Writing About Literature."

3. Write an essay of approximately 750 words discussing A. E. Stallings's "First Love: A Quiz." How does the poet combine modern circumstances and mythological allusions to suggest personal meaning for the reader?

4. You're probably familiar with an urban legend or two—near-fantastical stories passed on from one person to another, with the suggestion that they really happened to a friend of a friend of the person who told you the tale. Retell an urban myth in free-verse form. If you don't know any urban myths, an Internet search engine can lead you to scores of them.

5. Retell a famous myth or fairy tale to reflect your personal worldview.

▶ TERMS FOR *review*

Myth ▶ A traditional narrative of anonymous authorship that arises out of a culture's oral tradition. The characters in traditional myths are often gods or heroic figures engaged in significant actions and decisions. Myth is usually differentiated from *legend*, which has a specific historical base.

Mythology ▶ The body of myths belonging to a particular culture.

Archetype ▶ A recurring symbol, character, landscape, or event found in myth and literature across different cultures and eras, one that appears so often that it evokes a universal response.

21 WHAT IS POETRY?

What You Will Learn in This Chapter

■ To appreciate the diverse ways in which poetry has been defined

By now, perhaps, you have formed your own idea of what poetry is, whether or not you can easily define it. Robert Frost made a try at a definition: "A poem is an idea caught in the act of dawning." Just in case further efforts at definition may be useful, here are a few memorable ones. Poetry is:

> things that are true expressed in words that are beautiful.
> —*Dante*

> the best words in the best order.
> —*Samuel Taylor Coleridge*

> the spontaneous overflow of powerful feelings.
> —*William Wordsworth*

> emotion put into measure.
> —*Thomas Hardy*

> a way of remembering what it would impoverish us to forget.
> —*Robert Frost*

> a revelation in words by means of the words.
> —*Wallace Stevens*

> Poetry is prose bewitched.
> —*Mina Loy*

> the clear expression of mixed feelings.
> —*W. H. Auden*

> an angel with a gun in its hand . . .
> —*José Garcia Villa*

> the language in which man explores his own amazement.
> —*Christopher Fry*

> hundreds of things coming together at the right moment.
> —*Elizabeth Bishop*

Poetry is a sound art.
>   —*Joy Harjo*

Reduced to its simplest and most essential form, the poem is a song.
Song is neither discourse nor explanation.
>   —*Octavio Paz*

Poems come out of wonder, not out of knowing.
>   —*Lucille Clifton*

Poetry is always the cat concert under the window of the room in
which the official version of reality is being written.
>   —*Charles Simic*

A poem differs from most prose in several ways. For one, both writer and reader tend to regard it differently. The poet's attitude is something like this: I offer this piece of writing to be read not as prose but as a poem—that is, more perceptively, thoughtfully, and creatively, with more attention to sounds and connotations. This is a great deal to expect, but in return, the reader, too, has a right to certain expectations.

Approaching the poem in the anticipation of out-of-the-ordinary knowledge and pleasure, the reader assumes that the poem may use certain enjoyable devices not available to prose: rime, alliteration, meter, and rhythms—definite, various, or emphatic. (The poet may not *always* decide to use these things.) The reader expects the poet to make greater use, perhaps, of resources of meaning such as figurative language, allusion, symbol, and imagery. As readers of prose, we might seek no more than meaning: no more than what could be paraphrased without serious loss. Meeting any figurative language or graceful turns of word order, we think them pleasant extras. But in poetry all these "extras" matter as much as the paraphrasable content, if not more. For, when we finish reading a good poem, we cannot explain precisely to ourselves what we have experienced—without repeating, word for word, the language of the poem itself. Archibald MacLeish makes this point memorably in "Ars Poetica":

> A poem should not mean
> But be.

Throughout this book, we have been working on the assumption that the patient and conscious explication of poems will sharpen unconscious perceptions. We can only hope that it will; the final test lies in whether you care to go on by yourself, reading other poems, finding in them pleasure and enlightenment. Pedagogy must have a stop; so too must the viewing of poems as if their elements fell into chapters. For the total experience of reading a poem surpasses the mind's categories. The wind in the grass, says a proverb, cannot be taken into the house.

22 POEMS FOR FURTHER READING

Aaron Abeyta (b. 1971)

thirteen ways of looking at a tortilla   2001

i.

among twenty different tortillas
the only thing moving
was the mouth of the niño

ii.

i was of three cultures
like a tortilla
for which there are three bolios   5

iii.

the tortilla grew on the wooden table
it was a small part of the earth

iv.

a house and a tortilla
are one   10
a man a woman and a tortilla
are one

v.

i do not know which to prefer
the beauty of the red wall
or the beauty of the green wall   15
the tortilla fresh
or just after

vi.

tortillas filled the small kitchen
with ancient shadows
the shadow of Maclovia   20
cooking long ago
the tortilla
rolled from the shadow
the innate roundness

vii.

o thin viejos of chimayo
why do you imagine biscuits
do you not see how the tortilla
lives with the hands
of the women about you

25

viii.

i know soft corn
and beautiful inescapable sopapillas
but i know too
that the tortilla
has taught me what I know

30

ix.

when the tortilla is gone
it marks the end
of one of many tortillas

35

x.

at the sight of tortillas
browning on a black comal°
even the pachucos of española
would cry out sharply

flat griddle pan

40

xi.

he rode over new mexico
in a pearl low rider
once he got a flat
in that he mistook
the shadow of his spare
for a tortilla

45

xii.

the abuelitas are moving
the tortilla must be baking

xiii.

it was cinco de mayo all year
it was warm
and it was going to get warmer
the tortilla sat
on the frijolito plate

50

Kim Addonizio (b. 1954)

First Poem for You   1994

I like to touch your tattoos in complete
darkness, when I can't see them. I'm sure of
where they are, know by heart the neat
lines of lightning pulsing just above
your nipple, can find, as if by instinct, the blue   5
swirls of water on your shoulder where a serpent
twists, facing a dragon. When I pull you
to me, taking you until we're spent
and quiet on the sheets, I love to kiss
the pictures in your skin. They'll last until   10
you're seared to ashes; whatever persists
or turns to pain between us, they will still
be there. Such permanence is terrifying.
So I touch them in the dark; but touch them, trying.

Sherman Alexie

Sherman Alexie (b. 1966)

The Powwow at the End of the World   1996

I am told by many of you that I must forgive and so I shall
after an Indian woman puts her shoulder to the Grand
      Coulee Dam
and topples it. I am told by many of you that I must forgive
and so I shall after the floodwaters burst each successive dam
downriver from the Grand Coulee. I am told by many of you   5
that I must forgive and so I shall after the floodwaters find
their way to the mouth of the Columbia River as it enters
      the Pacific
and causes all of it to rise. I am told by many of you that
      I must forgive
and so I shall after the first drop of floodwater is swallowed by that
      salmon

waiting in the Pacific. I am told by many of you that I must forgive   10
    and so I shall
after that salmon swims upstream, through the mouth of the Columbia
and then past the flooded cities, broken dams and abandoned reactors
of Hanford. I am told by many of you that I must forgive and so I shall
after that salmon swims through the mouth of the Spokane River
as it meets the Columbia, then upstream, until it arrives   15
in the shallows of a secret bay on the reservation where I wait alone.
I am told by many of you that I must forgive and so I shall after
that salmon leaps into the night air above the water, throws
a lightning bolt at the brush near my feet, and starts the fire
which will lead all of the lost Indians home. I am told   20
by many of you that I must forgive and so I shall
after we Indians have gathered around the fire with that salmon
who has three stories it must tell before sunrise: one story will teach us
how to pray; another story will make us laugh for hours;
the third story will give us reason to dance. I am told by many   25
of you that I must forgive and so I shall when I am dancing
with my tribe during the powwow at the end of the world.

Anonymous (Navajo mountain chant)

Last Words of the Prophet

Farewell, younger brother!
From the holy places the gods come for me.
You will never see me again; but when the showers pass and the
    thunder peals,
"There," you will say, "is the voice of my elder brother."
And when the harvest comes, of the beautiful birds and   5
    grasshoppers you will say,
"There is the ordering of my elder brother!"

—*Translated by Washington Matthews*

Matthew Arnold (1822–1888)

Dover Beach   1867

The sea is calm to-night.
The tide is full, the moon lies fair
Upon the straits; on the French coast the light
Gleams and is gone; the cliffs of England stand,
Glimmering and vast, out in the tranquil bay.   5
Come to the window, sweet is the night-air!
Only, from the long line of spray

Where the sea meets the moon-blanched land,
Listen! you hear the grating roar
Of pebbles which the waves draw back, and fling,   10
At their return, up the high strand,
Begin, and cease, and then again begin,
With tremulous cadence slow, and bring
The eternal note of sadness in.

Sophocles long ago   15
Heard it on the Aegean, and it brought
Into his mind the turbid ebb and flow
Of human misery; we
Find also in the sound a thought,
Hearing it by this distant northern sea.   20

The Sea of Faith
Was once, too, at the full, and round earth's shore
Lay like the folds of a bright girdle furled.
But now I only hear
Its melancholy, long, withdrawing roar,   25
Retreating, to the breath
Of the night-wind, down the vast edges drear
And naked shingles° of the world.   *gravel beaches*

Ah, love, let us be true
To one another! for the world, which seems   30
To lie before us like a land of dreams,
So various, so beautiful, so new,
Hath really neither joy, nor love, nor light,
Nor certitude, nor peace, nor help for pain;
And we are here as on a darkling° plain   *darkened or darkening*   35
Swept with confused alarms of struggle and flight,
Where ignorant armies clash by night.

W. H. Auden (1907–1973)

Musée des Beaux Arts   1940

About suffering they were never wrong,
The Old Masters: how well they understood
Its human position; how it takes place
While someone else is eating or opening a window or just walking
      dully along;
How, when the aged are reverently, passionately waiting   5

The Fall of Icarus by Pieter Brueghel the Elder (1520?–1569).

For the miraculous birth, there always must be
Children who did not specially want it to happen, skating
On a pond at the edge of the wood:
They never forgot
That even the dreadful martyrdom must run its course   10
Anyhow in a corner, some untidy spot
Where the dogs go on with their doggy life and the torturer's horse
Scratches its innocent behind on a tree.

In Brueghel's *Icarus*, for instance: how everything turns away
Quite leisurely from the disaster; the ploughman may   15
Have heard the splash, the forsaken cry,
But for him it was not an important failure; the sun shone
As it had to on the white legs disappearing into the green
Water; and the expensive delicate ship that must have seen
Something amazing, a boy falling out of the sky,   20
Had somewhere to get to and sailed calmly on.

Elizabeth Bishop

Elizabeth Bishop (1911–1979)

One Art   1976

The art of losing isn't hard to master;
so many things seem filled with the intent
to be lost that their loss is no disaster.

Lose something every day. Accept the fluster
of lost door keys, the hour badly spent.   5
The art of losing isn't hard to master.

Then practice losing farther, losing faster:
places, and names, and where it was you meant
to travel. None of these will bring disaster.

I lost my mother's watch. And look! my last, or   10
next-to-last, of three loved houses went.
The art of losing isn't hard to master.

I lost two cities, lovely ones. And, vaster,
some realms I owned, two rivers, a continent.
I miss them, but it wasn't a disaster.   15

—Even losing you (the joking voice, a gesture
I love) I shan't have lied. It's evident
the art of losing's not too hard to master
though it may look like (*Write* it!) like disaster.

William Blake (1757–1827)

The Tyger   1794

Tyger! Tyger! burning bright
In the forests of the night,
What immortal hand or eye
Could frame thy fearful symmetry?

In what distant deeps or skies   5
Burnt the fire of thine eyes?
On what wings dare he aspire?
What the hand dare seize the fire?

And what shoulder, and what art,
Could twist the sinews of thy heart?   10
And when thy heart began to beat,
What dread hand? and what dread feet?

What the hammer? what the chain?
In what furnace was thy brain?
What the anvil? what dread grasp   15
Dare its deadly terrors clasp?

When the stars threw down their spears,
And watered heaven with their tears,
Did he smile his work to see?
Did he who made the Lamb make thee?   20

Tyger! Tyger! burning bright
In the forests of the night,
What immortal hand or eye
Dare frame thy fearful symmetry?

Detail of William Blake's *The Tyger*.

Gwendolyn Brooks

Gwendolyn Brooks (1917–2000)

the mother   1945

Abortions will not let you forget.
You remember the children you got that you did not get,
The damp small pulps with a little or with no hair,
The singers and workers that never handled the air.
You will never neglect or beat   5
Them, or silence or buy with a sweet.
You will never wind up the sucking-thumb
Or scuttle off ghosts that come.
You will never leave them, controlling your luscious sigh,
Return for a snack of them, with gobbling mother-eye.   10

I have heard in the voices of the wind the voices of my dim killed
     children.
I have contracted. I have eased
My dim dears at the breasts they could never suck.
I have said, Sweets, if I sinned, if I seized
Your luck   15
And your lives from your unfinished reach,
If I stole your births and your names,
Your straight baby tears and your games,
Your stilted or lovely loves, your tumults, your marriages, aches, and
     your deaths,
If I poisoned the beginnings of your breaths,   20
Believe that even in my deliberateness I was not deliberate.
Though why should I whine,
Whine that the crime was other than mine?—
Since anyhow you are dead.
Or rather, or instead,   25
You were never made.
But that too, I am afraid,
Is faulty: oh, what shall I say, how is the truth to be said?

You were born, you had body, you died.
It is just that you never giggled or planned or cried.   30

Believe me, I loved you all.
Believe me, I knew you, though faintly, and I loved, I loved you
All.

Elizabeth Barrett Browning (1806–1861)

How Do I Love Thee? Let Me Count the Ways   1850

How do I love thee? Let me count the ways.
I love thee to the depth and breadth and height
My soul can reach, when feeling out of sight
For the ends of Being and ideal Grace.
I love thee to the level of every day's   5
Most quiet need, by sun and candle-light.
I love thee freely, as men strive for Right;
I love thee purely, as they turn from Praise.
I love thee with the passion put to use
In my old griefs, and with my childhood's faith.   10
I love thee with a love I seemed to lose
With my lost saints,—I love thee with the breath,
Smiles, tears, of all my life!—and, if God choose,
I shall but love thee better after death.

Robert Browning (1812–1889)

Soliloquy of the Spanish Cloister   1842

Gr-r-r—there go, my heart's abhorrence!
    Water your damned flower-pots, do!
If hate killed men, Brother Lawrence,
    God's blood, would not mine kill you!
What? your myrtle-bush wants trimming?   5
    Oh, that rose has prior claims—
Needs its leaden vase filled brimming?
    Hell dry you up with its flames!

At the meal we sit together;
    Salve tibi!° I must hear   *Hail to thee!*   10
Wise talk of the kind of weather,
    Sort of season, time of year:
Not a plenteous cork-crop: scarcely
    Dare we hope oak-galls, I doubt:
What's the Latin name for "parsley"?   15
    What's the Greek name for Swine's Snout?

Whew! We'll have our platter burnished,
    Laid with care on our own shelf!
With a fire-new spoon we're furnished,
    And a goblet for ourself,   20
Rinsed like something sacrificial
    Ere 'tis fit to touch our chaps°—   *lower jaw*
Marked with L. for our initial!
    (He-he! There his lily snaps!)

Saint, forsooth! While brown Dolores   25
    Squats outside the Convent bank
With Sanchicha, telling stories,
    Steeping tresses in the tank,
Blue-black, lustrous, thick like horsehairs,
    —Can't I see his dead eye glow,   30
Bright as 'twere a Barbary corsair's?
    (That is, if he'd let it show!)

When he finishes refection,
    Knife and fork he never lays
Cross-wise, to my recollection,   35
    As I do, in Jesu's praise.
I the Trinity illustrate,
    Drinking watered orange-pulp—
In three sips the Arian frustrate;
    While he drains his at one gulp!   40

Oh, those melons! if he's able
    We're to have a feast; so nice!
One goes to the Abbot's table,
    All of us get each a slice.
How go on your flowers? None double?   45
    Not one fruit-sort can you spy?
Strange!—And I, too, at such trouble,
    Keep them close-nipped on the sly!

There's a great text in Galatians,
    Once you trip on it, entails   50
Twenty-nine distinct damnations,
    One sure, if another fails:
If I trip him just a-dying,
    Sure of heaven as sure can be,
Spin him round and send him flying   55
    Off to hell, a Manichee?

Or, my scrofulous French novel
  On grey paper with blunt type!
Simply glance at it, you grovel
  Hand and foot in Belial's gripe: 60
If I double down its pages
  At the woeful sixteenth print,
When he gathers his greengages,
  Ope a sieve and slip it in't?

Or, there's Satan!—one might venture   65
  Pledge one's soul to him, yet leave
Such a flaw in the indenture
  As he'd miss till, past retrieve,
Blasted lay that rose-acacia
  We're so proud of! Hy, Zy, Hine. . . .   70
'St, there's Vespers! Plena gratia
  Ave, Virgo!° Gr-r-r—you swine!   Hail, Virgin, full of grace!

SOLILOQUY OF THE SPANISH CLOISTER. 3 Brother Lawrence: one of the speaker's fellow
monks. 31 Barbary corsair: a pirate operating off the Barbary Coast of Africa. 39 Arian:
a follower of Arius, a heretic who denied the doctrine of the Trinity. 49 a Great text in
Galatians: a difficult verse in this book of the Bible. Brother Lawrence will be damned as
a heretic if he wrongly interprets it. 56 Manichee: another kind of heretic, one who (after
the Persian philosopher Mani) sees in the world a constant struggle between good and evil,
neither able to win. 60 Belial: here, not specifically Satan but (as used in the Old Testament) a name for wickedness. 70 Hy, Zy, Hine: possibly the sound of a bell to announce
evening devotions.

Charles Bukowski

Charles Bukowski (1920–1994)

Dostoevsky   1997

against the wall, the firing squad ready.
then he got a reprieve.
suppose they had shot Dostoevsky?
before he wrote all that?
I suppose it wouldn't have   5

mattered
not directly.
there are billions of people who have
never read him and never
will.
but as a young man I know that he   10
got me through the factories,
past the whores,
lifted me high through the night
and put me down
in a better   15
place.
even while in the bar
drinking with the other
derelicts,
I was glad they gave Dostoevsky a   20
reprieve,
it gave me one,
allowed me to look directly at those
rancid faces   25
in my world,
death pointing its finger,
I held fast,
an immaculate drunk
sharing the stinking dark with   30
my
brothers.

DOSTOEVSKY. The Russian novelist Fyodor Dostoevsky (1821–1880), author of *Crime and Punishment* and *The Brothers Karamazov*, was arrested in 1849 in a czarist crackdown on liberal organizations and sentenced to death. It was not until the members of the firing squad had aimed their rifles and were awaiting the order to fire that he was informed that his sentence had been commuted to four years of hard labor in Siberia.

Judith Ortiz Cofer (b. 1952)

Quinceañera   1987

My dolls have been put away like dead
children in a chest I will carry
with me when I marry.
I reach under my skirt to feel
a satin slip bought for this day. It is soft   5
as the inside of my thighs. My hair
has been nailed back with my mother's
black hairpins to my skull. Her hands

stretched my eyes open as she twisted
braids into a tight circle at the nape   10
of my neck. I am to wash my own clothes
and sheets from this day on, as if
the fluids of my body were poison, as if
the little trickle of blood I believe
travels from my heart to the world were   15
shameful. Is not the blood of saints and
men in battle beautiful? Do Christ's hands
not bleed into your eyes from His cross?
At night I hear myself growing and wake
to find my hands drifting of their own will   20
to soothe skin stretched tight
over my bones.
I am wound like the guts of a clock,
waiting for each hour to release me.

QUINCEAÑERA. The title refers to a fifteen-year-old girl's coming-out party in Latin cultures.

Samuel Taylor Coleridge (1772–1834)

Kubla Khan   (1797–1798)

Or, a Vision in a Dream. A Fragment.

In Xanadu did Kubla Khan
A stately pleasure-dome decree:
Where Alph, the sacred river, ran
Through caverns measureless to man
    Down to a sunless sea.   5
So twice five miles of fertile ground
With walls and towers were girdled round:
And here were gardens bright with sinuous rills,
Where blossomed many an incense-bearing tree;
And here were forests ancient as the hills,   10
Enfolding sunny spots of greenery.

But oh! that deep romantic chasm which slanted
Down the green hill athwart a cedarn cover!
A savage place! as holy and enchanted
As e'er beneath a waning moon was haunted   15
By woman wailing for her demon-lover!
And from this chasm, with ceaseless turmoil seething,
As if this earth in fast thick pants were breathing,
A mighty fountain momently was forced:
Amid whose swift half-intermitted burst   20

Huge fragments vaulted like rebounding hail,
Or chaffy grain beneath the thresher's flail:
And 'mid these dancing rocks at once and ever
It flung up momently the sacred river.
Five miles meandering with a mazy motion   25
Through wood and dale the sacred river ran,
Then reached the caverns measureless to man,
And sank in tumult to a lifeless ocean:
And 'mid this tumult Kubla heard from far
Ancestral voices prophesying war!   30

    The shadow of the dome of pleasure
    Floated midway on the waves;
    Where was heard the mingled measure
    From the fountain and the caves.
It was a miracle of rare device,   35
A sunny pleasure-dome with caves of ice!

    A damsel with a dulcimer
    In a vision once I saw:
    It was an Abyssinian maid,
    And on her dulcimer she played,   40
    Singing of Mount Abora.
    Could I revive within me
    Her symphony and song,
    To such a deep delight 'twould win me,
That with music loud and long,   45
I would build that dome in air,
That sunny dome! those caves of ice!
And all who heard should see them there,
And all should cry, Beware! Beware!
His flashing eyes, his floating hair!   50
Weave a circle round him thrice,
And close your eyes with holy dread,
For he on honey-dew hath fed,
And drunk the milk of Paradise.

KUBLA KHAN. There was an actual Kublai Khan, a thirteenth-century Mongol emperor, and
a Chinese city of Xanadu; but Coleridge's dream vision also borrows from travelers' descriptions of such other exotic places as Abyssinia and America. 51 *circle:* a magic circle drawn
to keep away evil spirits.

Billy Collins

Billy Collins (b. 1941)

Care and Feeding

2003

Because tomorrow
I will turn 420 in dog years,
I have decided to take myself
for a long walk on the path around the lake,

and when I get back to the house,   5
I will jump up on my chest
and lick my nose, my ears and eyelids
while I tell myself again and again to get down.

Then I will replenish my bowl
with cold water from the tap   10
and hand myself a biscuit from the jar
which I will hold gingerly in my teeth.

Then I will make three circles
and lie down on the wood floor at my feet
and close my eyes   15
as I type all morning and into the afternoon,

checking every once in a while
to make sure I am still there,
reaching down with one hand
to stroke my furry, esteemed, venerable head.   20

Emily Dickinson

Emily Dickinson (1830–1886)

Wild Nights – Wild Nights! (about 1861)

Wild Nights – Wild Nights!
Were I with thee
Wild Nights should be
Our luxury!

Futile – the Winds –   5
To a Heart in port –
Done with the Compass –
Done with the Chart!

Rowing in Eden –
Ah, the Sea!   10
Might I but moor – Tonight –
In Thee!

Emily Dickinson (1830–1886)

I felt a Funeral, in my Brain (about 1861)

I felt a Funeral, in my Brain,
And Mourners to and fro
Kept treading – treading – till it seemed
That Sense was breaking through –

And when they all were seated,   5
A Service, like a Drum –
Kept beating – beating – till I thought
My Mind was going numb –

And then I heard them lift a Box
And creak across my Soul
With those same Boots of Lead, again,
Then Space – began to toll,

10

As all the Heavens were a Bell,
And Being, but an Ear,
And I, and Silence, some strange Race
Wrecked, solitary, here –

15

And Then a Plank in Reason, broke,
And I dropped down, and down –
And hit a World, at every plunge,
And Finished knowing – then –

20

Emily Dickinson (1830–1886)

Because I could not stop for Death   (about 1863)

Because I could not stop for Death –
He kindly stopped for me –
The Carriage held but just Ourselves –
And Immortality.

We slowly drove – He knew no haste   5
And I had put away
My labor and my leisure too,
For His Civility –

We passed the School, where Children strove
At Recess – in the Ring –   10
We passed the Fields of Gazing Grain –
We passed the Setting Sun –

Or rather – He passed Us –
The Dews drew quivering and chill –
For only Gossamer, my Gown –   15
My Tippet° – only Tulle –   *cape*

We paused before a House that seemed
A Swelling of the Ground –
The Roof was scarcely visible –
The Cornice – in the Ground –   20

Since then – 'tis Centuries – and yet
Feels shorter than the Day
I first surmised the Horses' Heads
Were toward Eternity –

John Donne

John Donne (1572–1631)

Death be not proud   (about 1610)

Death be not proud, though some have callèd thee
Mighty and dreadful, for thou art not so;
For those whom thou think'st thou dost overthrow
Die not, poor death, nor yet canst thou kill me.
From rest and sleep, which but thy pictures be,   5
Much pleasure, then from thee much more must flow,
And soonest our best men with thee do go,
Rest of their bones, and soul's delivery.
Thou art slave to fate, chance, kings, and desperate men,
And dost with poison, war, and sickness dwell,   10
And poppy, or charms can make us sleep as well,
And better than thy stroke; why swell'st thou then?
One short sleep past, we wake eternally,
And death shall be no more; death, thou shalt die.

John Donne (1572–1631)

The Flea   1633

Mark but this flea, and mark in this
How little that which thou deny'st me is;
It sucked me first, and now sucks thee,
And in this flea our two bloods mingled be;
Thou know'st that this cannot be said   5
A sin, nor shame, nor loss of maidenhead,
        Yet this enjoys before it woo,
        And pampered swells with one blood made of two,
        And this, alas, is more than we would do.

Oh stay, three lives in one flea spare,   10
Where we almost, yea more than married are.
This flea is you and I, and this

Our marriage bed, and marriage temple is;
Though parents grudge, and you, we're met
And cloistered in these living walls of jet.   15
    Though use° make you apt to kill me,   *custom*
    Let not to that, self-murder added be,
    And sacrilege, three sins in killing three.

Cruel and sudden, hast thou since
Purpled thy nail in blood of innocence?   20
Wherein could this flea guilty be,
Except in that drop which it sucked from thee?
Yet thou triumph'st, and say'st that thou
Find'st not thyself, nor me, the weaker now;
    'Tis true; then learn how false, fears be;   25
    Just so much honor, when thou yield'st to me,
    Will waste, as this flea's death took life from thee.

T. S. Eliot

T. S. Eliot (1888–1965)

The Love Song of J. Alfred Prufrock   1917

> *S'io credessi che mia risposta fosse*
> *a persona che mai tornasse al mondo,*
> *questa fiamma staria senza più scosse.*
> *Ma per ciò che giammai di questo fondo*
> *non tornò vivo alcun, s'i'odo il vero,*
> *senza tema d'infamia ti rispondo.*

Let us go then, you and I,
When the evening is spread out against the sky
Like a patient etherized upon a table;
Let us go, through certain half-deserted streets,
The muttering retreats   5
Of restless nights in one-night cheap hotels
And sawdust restaurants with oyster-shells:

Streets that follow like a tedious argument
Of insidious intent
To lead you to an overwhelming question   10
Oh, do not ask, "What is it?"
Let us go and make our visit.

In the room the women come and go
Talking of Michelangelo.

The yellow fog that rubs its back upon the window-panes,   15
The yellow smoke that rubs its muzzle on the window-panes,
Licked its tongue into the corners of the evening,
Lingered upon the pools that stand in drains,
Let fall upon its back the soot that falls from chimneys,
Slipped by the terrace, made a sudden leap,   20
And seeing that it was a soft October night,
Curled once about the house, and fell asleep.

And indeed there will be time
For the yellow smoke that slides along the street
Rubbing its back upon the window-panes;   25
There will be time, there will be time
To prepare a face to meet the faces that you meet;
There will be time to murder and create,
And time for all the works and days of hands
That lift and drop a question on your plate;   30
Time for you and time for me,
And time yet for a hundred indecisions,
And for a hundred visions and revisions,
Before the taking of a toast and tea.

In the room the women come and go   35
Talking of Michelangelo.
And indeed there will be time
To wonder, "Do I dare?" and, "Do I dare?"
Time to turn back and descend the stair,
With a bald spot in the middle of my hair—   40
(They will say: "How his hair is growing thin!")
My morning coat, my collar mounting firmly to the chin,
My necktie rich and modest, but asserted by a simple pin—
(They will say: "But how his arms and legs are thin!")
Do I dare   45
Disturb the universe?
In a minute there is time
For decisions and revisions which a minute will reverse.

For I have known them all already, known them all—
Have known the evenings, mornings, afternoons,   50
I have measured out my life with coffee spoons;
I know the voices dying with a dying fall
Beneath the music from a farther room.
   So how should I presume?

And I have known the eyes already, known them all—   55
The eyes that fix you in a formulated phrase,
And when I am formulated, sprawling on a pin,
When I am pinned and wriggling on the wall,
Then how should I begin
To spit out all the butt-ends of my days and ways?   60
   And how should I presume?

And I have known the arms already, known them all—
Arms that are braceleted and white and bare
(But in the lamplight, downed with light brown hair!)
Is it perfume from a dress   65
That makes me so digress?
Arms that lie along a table, or wrap about a shawl.
   And should I then presume?
   And how should I begin?

* * *

Shall I say, I have gone at dusk through narrow streets   70
And watched the smoke that rises from the pipes
Of lonely men in shirt-sleeves, leaning out of windows? . . .

I should have been a pair of ragged claws
Scuttling across the floors of silent seas.

* * *

And the afternoon, the evening, sleeps so peacefully!   75
Smoothed by long fingers,
Asleep . . . tired . . . or it malingers,
Stretched on the floor, here beside you and me.
Should I, after tea and cakes and ices,
Have the strength to force the moment to its crisis?   80
But though I have wept and fasted, wept and prayed,
Though I have seen my head (grown slightly bald) brought in upon a platter,
I am no prophet—and here's no great matter;
I have seen the moment of my greatness flicker,
And I have seen the eternal Footman hold my coat, and snicker,   85
And in short, I was afraid.

And would it have been worth it, after all,
After the cups, the marmalade, the tea,
Among the porcelain, among some talk of you and me,
Would it have been worth while,   90
To have bitten off the matter with a smile,
To have squeezed the universe into a ball
To roll it toward some overwhelming question,
To say: "I am Lazarus, come from the dead,
Come back to tell you all, I shall tell you all"—   95
If one, settling a pillow by her head,
    Should say: "That is not what I meant at all.
    That is not it, at all."

And would it have been worth it, after all,
Would it have been worth while,   100
After the sunsets and the dooryards and the sprinkled streets,
After the novels, after the teacups, after the skirts that trail along
    the floor—
And this, and so much more?—
It is impossible to say just what I mean!
But as if a magic lantern threw the nerves in patterns on a screen: 105
Would it have been worth while
If one, settling a pillow or throwing off a shawl,
And turning toward the window, should say:
    "That is not it at all,
    That is not what I meant, at all."   110
                                  ● ● ●
No! I am not Prince Hamlet, nor was meant to be;
Am an attendant lord, one that will do
To swell a progress, start a scene or two,
Advise the prince; no doubt, an easy tool,
Deferential, glad to be of use,   115
Politic, cautious, and meticulous;
Full of high sentence, but a bit obtuse;
At times, indeed, almost ridiculous—
Almost, at times, the Fool.

I grow old . . . I grow old . . .   120
I shall wear the bottoms of my trousers rolled.

Shall I part my hair behind? Do I dare to eat a peach?
I shall wear white flannel trousers, and walk upon the beach.
I have heard the mermaids singing, each to each.

I do not think that they will sing to me.   125

I have seen them riding seaward on the waves
Combing the white hair of the waves blown back
When the wind blows the water white and black.

We have lingered in the chambers of the sea
By sea-girls wreathed with seaweed red and brown   130
Till human voices wake us, and we drown.

THE LOVE SONG OF J. ALFRED PRUFROCK. The epigraph, from Dante's *Inferno*, is the speech
of one dead and damned, who thinks that his hearer also is going to remain in Hell. Count
Guido da Montefeltro, whose sin has been to give false counsel after a corrupt prelate had
offered him prior absolution and whose punishment is to be wrapped in a constantly burning
flame, offers to tell Dante his story:

> If I thought my answer were to someone who
>   might see the world again, then there would be
>   no more stirrings of this flame. Since it is true
> that no one leaves these depths of misery
>   alive, from all that I have heard reported,
>   I answer you without fear of infamy.

(Translation by Michael Palma from: Dante Alighieri, *Inferno: A New Verse Translation* [New
York: Norton, 2002].) 29 *works and days:* title of a poem by Hesiod (eighth century B.C.),
depicting his life as a hardworking Greek farmer and exhorting his brother to be like him.
82 *head . . . platter:* like that of John the Baptist, prophet and praiser of chastity, whom King
Herod beheaded at the demand of Herodias, his unlawfully wedded wife (see Mark 6:17–28).
92–93 *squeezed . . . To roll it:* an echo from Marvell's "To His Coy Mistress," lines 41–42. 94
Lazarus: probably the Lazarus whom Jesus called forth from the tomb (John 11:1–44), but
possibly the beggar seen in Heaven by the rich man in Hell (Luke 16:19–25). 105 *magic
lantern:* an early type of projector used to display still pictures from transparent slides.

Robert Frost

Robert Frost (1874–1963)

Mending Wall   1914

Something there is that doesn't love a wall,
That sends the frozen-ground-swell under it,
And spills the upper boulders in the sun;
And makes gaps even two can pass abreast.
The work of hunters is another thing: 5

I have come after them and made repair
Where they have left not one stone on a stone,
But they would have the rabbit out of hiding,
To please the yelping dogs. The gaps I mean,
No one has seen them made or heard them made,   10
But at spring mending-time we find them there.
I let my neighbor know beyond the hill;
And on a day we meet to walk the line
And set the wall between us once again.
We keep the wall between us as we go.   15
To each the boulders that have fallen to each.
And some are loaves and some so nearly balls
We have to use a spell to make them balance:
"Stay where you are until our backs are turned!"
We wear our fingers rough with handling them.   20
Oh, just another kind of outdoor game,
One on a side. It comes to little more:
There where it is we do not need the wall:
He is all pine and I am apple orchard.
My apple trees will never get across   25
And eat the cones under his pines, I tell him.
He only says, "Good fences make good neighbors."
Spring is the mischief in me, and I wonder
If I could put a notion in his head:
"*Why* do they make good neighbors? Isn't it   30
Where there are cows? But here there are no cows.
Before I built a wall I'd ask to know
What I was walling in or walling out,
And to whom I was like to give offence.
Something there is that doesn't love a wall,   35
That wants it down." I could say "Elves" to him,
But it's not elves exactly, and I'd rather
He said it for himself. I see him there
Bringing a stone grasped firmly by the top
In each hand, like an old-stone savage armed.   40
He moves in darkness as it seems to me,
Not of woods only and the shade of trees.
He will not go behind his father's saying,
And he likes having thought of it so well
He says again, "Good fences make good neighbors."   45

Robert Frost (1874–1963)

Birches   1916

When I see birches bend to left and right
Across the lines of straighter darker trees,
I like to think some boy's been swinging them.
But swinging doesn't bend them down to stay
As ice-storms do. Often you must have seen them   5
Loaded with ice a sunny winter morning
After a rain. They click upon themselves
As the breeze rises, and turn many-colored
As the stir cracks and crazes their enamel.
Soon the sun's warmth makes them shed crystal shells   10
Shattering and avalanching on the snow-crust—
Such heaps of broken glass to sweep away
You'd think the inner dome of heaven had fallen.
They are dragged to the withered bracken by the load,
And they seem not to break; though once they are bowed   15
So low for long, they never right themselves:
You may see their trunks arching in the woods
Years afterwards, trailing their leaves on the ground
Like girls on hands and knees that throw their hair
Before them over their heads to dry in the sun.   20
But I was going to say when Truth broke in
With all her matter-of-fact about the ice-storm
I should prefer to have some boy bend them
As he went out and in to fetch the cows—
Some boy too far from town to learn baseball,   25
Whose only play was what he found himself,
Summer or winter, and could play alone.
One by one he subdued his father's trees
By riding them down over and over again
Until he took the stiffness out of them,   30
And not one but hung limp, not one was left
For him to conquer. He learned all there was
To learn about not launching out too soon
And so not carrying the tree away
Clear to the ground. He always kept his poise   35
To the top branches, climbing carefully
With the same pains you use to fill a cup
Up to the brim, and even above the brim.

Then he flung outward, feet first, with a swish,
Kicking his way down through the air to the ground.   40
So was I once myself a swinger of birches.
And so I dream of going back to be.
It's when I'm weary of considerations,
And life is too much like a pathless wood
Where your face burns and tickles with the cobwebs   45
Broken across it, and one eye is weeping
From a twig's having lashed across it open.
I'd like to get away from earth awhile
And then come back to it and begin over.
May no fate willfully misunderstand me   50
And half grant what I wish and snatch me away
Not to return. Earth's the right place for love:
I don't know where it's likely to go better.
I'd like to go by climbing a birch tree,
And climb black branches up a snow-white trunk   55
Toward heaven, till the tree could bear no more,
But dipped its top and set me down again.
That would be good both going and coming back.
One could do worse than be a swinger of birches.

Robert Frost (1874–1963)

Stopping by Woods on a Snowy Evening   1923

Whose woods these are I think I know.
His house is in the village though;
He will not see me stopping here
To watch his woods fill up with snow.

My little horse must think it queer   5
To stop without a farmhouse near
Between the woods and frozen lake
The darkest evening of the year.

He gives his harness bells a shake
To ask if there is some mistake.   10
The only other sound's the sweep
Of easy wind and downy flake.

The woods are lovely, dark and deep,
But I have promises to keep,
And miles to go before I sleep,   15
And miles to go before I sleep.

Allen Ginsberg (1926–1997)

A Supermarket in California   1956

What thoughts I have of you tonight, Walt Whitman, for I walked down the sidestreets under the trees with a headache self-conscious looking at the full moon.

In my hungry fatigue, and shopping for images, I went into the neon fruit supermarket, dreaming of your enumerations!

What peaches and what penumbras! Whole families shopping at night! Aisles full of husbands! Wives in the avocados, babies in the tomatoes!—and you, García Lorca, what were you doing down by the watermelons?

I saw you, Walt Whitman, childless, lonely old grubber, poking among the meats in the refrigerator and eyeing the grocery boys.

I heard you asking questions of each: Who killed the pork chops?   5
What price bananas? Are you my Angel?

I wandered in and out of the brilliant stacks of cans following you, and followed in my imagination by the store detective.

We strode down the open corridors together in our solitary fancy tasting artichokes, possessing every frozen delicacy, and never passing the cashier.

Where are we going, Walt Whitman? The doors close in an hour. Which way does your beard point tonight?

(I touch your book and dream of our odyssey in the supermarket and feel absurd.)

Will we walk all night through solitary streets? The trees add   10
shade to shade, lights out in the houses, we'll both be lonely.

Will we stroll dreaming of the lost America of love past blue automobiles in driveways, home to our silent cottage?

Ah, dear father, graybeard, lonely old courage-teacher, what America did you have when Charon quit poling his ferry and you got out on a smoking bank and stood watching the boat disappear on the black waters of Lethe?

A SUPERMARKET IN CALIFORNIA. 2 *enumerations*: many of Whitman's poems contain lists of observed details. 3 *García Lorca*: modern Spanish poet who wrote an "Ode to Walt Whitman" in his book-length sequence *Poet in New York*. 12 *Charon . . . Lethe*: Is the poet confusing two underworld rivers? Charon, in Greek and Roman mythology, is the boatman who ferries the souls of the dead across the river Styx. The river Lethe also flows through Hades, and a drink of its waters makes the dead lose their painful memories of loved ones they have left behind.

Thomas Hardy

Thomas Hardy (1840–1928)

The Convergence of the Twain   1912

Lines on the Loss of the "Titanic"

I

In a solitude of the sea
Deep from human vanity,
And the Pride of Life that planned her, stilly couches she.

II

Steel chambers, late the pyres
Of her salamandrine fires,
Cold currents thrid,° and turn to rhythmic tidal lyres.   *thread*   5

III

Over the mirrors meant
To glass the opulent
The sea-worm crawls—grotesque, slimed, dumb, indifferent.

IV

Jewels in joy designed
To ravish the sensuous mind   10
Lie lightless, all their sparkles bleared and black and blind.

V

Dim moon-eyed fishes near
Gaze at the gilded gear
And query: "What does this vaingloriousness down here?" . . .   15

VI

Well: while was fashioning
This creature of cleaving wing,
The Immanent Will that stirs and urges everything

VII

Prepared a sinister mate
For her—so gaily great—   20
A Shape of Ice, for the time far and dissociate.

VIII

And as the smart ship grew
In stature, grace, and hue,
In shadowy silent distance grew the Iceberg too.

IX

Alien they seemed to be: 25
No mortal eye could see
The intimate welding of their later history,

X

Or sign that they were bent
By paths coincident
On being anon twin halves of one august event,   30

XI

Till the Spinner of the Years
Said "Now!" And each one hears,
And consummation comes, and jars two hemispheres.

THE CONVERGENCE OF THE TWAIN. The luxury liner *Titanic*, supposedly unsinkable, went
down in 1912 after striking an iceberg on its first Atlantic voyage. 5 *salamandrine:* like the
salamander, a lizard that supposedly thrives in fires, or like a spirit of the same name that
inhabits fire (according to alchemists).

Seamus Heaney (1939–2013)

Digging   1966

Between my finger and my thumb
The squat pen rests; snug as a gun.

Under my window, a clean rasping sound
When the spade sinks into gravelly ground:
My father, digging. I look down   5

Till his straining rump among the flowerbeds
Bends low, comes up twenty years away
Stooping in rhythm through potato drills
Where he was digging.

The coarse boot nestled on the lug, the shaft   10
Against the inside knee was levered firmly.
He rooted out tall tops, buried the bright edge deep
To scatter new potatoes that we picked
Loving their cool hardness in our hands.

By God, the old man could handle a spade.   15
Just like his old man.

My grandfather cut more turf in a day
Than any other man on Toner's bog.
Once I carried him milk in a bottle
Corked sloppily with paper. He straightened up   20
To drink it, then fell to right away
Nicking and slicing neatly, heaving sods
Over his shoulder, going down and down
For the good turf. Digging.

The cold smell of potato mould, the squelch and slap   25
Of soggy peat, the curt cuts of an edge
Through living roots awaken in my head.
But I've no spade to follow men like them.

Between my finger and my thumb
The squat pen rests.   30
I'll dig with it.

George Herbert (1593–1633)

Easter Wings   1633

Lord, who createdst man in wealth and store,
Though foolishly he lost the same,
Decaying more and more
Till he became
Most poor;
With thee
Oh, let me rise
As larks, harmoniously,
And sing this day thy victories;
Then shall the fall further the flight in me.

My tender age in sorrow did begin;
And still with sicknesses and shame
Thou didst so punish sin,
That I became
Most thin.
With thee
Let me combine,
And feel this day thy victory;
For if I imp my wing on thine,
Affliction shall advance the flight in me.

Robert Herrick (1591–1674)

To the Virgins, to Make Much of Time   1648

Gather ye rose-buds while ye may,
   Old Time is still a-flying;
And this same flower that smiles today,
   Tomorrow will be dying.

The glorious lamp of heaven, the sun,   5
   The higher he's a-getting,
The sooner will his race be run,
   And nearer he's to setting.

That age is best which is the first,
   When youth and blood are warmer;   10
But being spent, the worse, and worst
   Times still succeed the former.

Then be not coy, but use your time,
   And while ye may, go marry;
For having lost but once your prime,   15
   You may for ever tarry.

Gerard Manley Hopkins (1844–1889)

Spring and Fall   (1880)

   To a young child

Márgarét, áre you gríeving
Over Goldengrove unleaving?°   *shedding its leaves*
Leáves, líke the things of man, you
With your fresh thoughts care for, can you?
Áh! ás the heart grows older   5
It will come to such sights colder
By and by, nor spare a sigh
Though worlds of wanwood leafmeal lie;
And yet you wíll weep and know why.
Now no matter, child, the name: 10
Sórrow's spríngs áre the same.
Nor mouth had, no nor mind, expressed
What heart heard of, ghost° guessed: *spirit*
It ís the blight man was born for,
It is Margaret you mourn for.   15

Gerard Manley Hopkins

Gerard Manley Hopkins (1844–1889)

The Windhover   (1877)

To Christ Our Lord

I caught this morning morning's minion, king-
   dom of daylight's dauphin, dapple-dawn-drawn Falcon, in his riding
    Of the rolling level underneath him steady air, and striding
High there, how he rung upon the rein of a wimpling wing
In his ecstasy! then off, off forth on swing,   5
   As a skate's heel sweeps smooth on a bow-bend: the hurl and gliding
    Rebuffed the big wind. My heart in hiding
Stirred for a bird, —the achieve of, the mastery of the thing!

Brute beauty and valor and act, oh, air, pride, plume, here
   Buckle! AND the fire that breaks from thee then, a billion   10
Times told lovelier, more dangerous, O my chevalier!

   No wonder of it: shéer plód makes plough down sillion°   *furrow*
Shine, and blue-bleak embers, ah my dear,
   Fall, gall themselves, and gash gold-vermilion.

THE WINDHOVER. A windhover is a kestrel, or small falcon, so called because it can hover upon the wind. 4 *rung . . . wing:* A horse is "rung upon the rein" when its trainer holds the end of a long rein and has the horse circle him. The possible meanings of *wimpling* include: (1) curving; (2) pleated, arranged in many little folds one on top of another; (3) rippling or undulating like the surface of a flowing stream.

A. E. Housman (1859–1936)

Loveliest of trees, the cherry now   1896

Loveliest of trees, the cherry now
Is hung with bloom along the bough,
And stands about the woodland ride°   *path*
Wearing white for Eastertide.

Now, of my threescore years and ten,   5
Twenty will not come again,
And take from seventy springs a score,
It only leaves me fifty more.

And since to look at things in bloom
Fifty springs are little room,   10
About the woodlands I will go
To see the cherry hung with snow.

A. E. Housman (1859–1936)

To an Athlete Dying Young   1896

The time you won your town the race
We chaired you through the market-place;
Man and boy stood cheering by,
And home we brought you shoulder-high.

To-day, the road all runners come,   5
Shoulder-high we bring you home,
And set you at your threshold down,
Townsman of a stiller town.

Smart lad, to slip betimes away
From fields where glory does not stay   10
And early though the laurel grows
It withers quicker than the rose.

Eyes the shady night has shut
Cannot see the record cut,
And silence sounds no worse than cheers   15
After earth has stopped the ears:

Now you will not swell the rout
Of lads that wore their honors out,
Runners whom renown outran
And the name died before the man.   20

So set, before its echoes fade,
The fleet foot on the sill of shade,
And hold to the low lintel up
The still-defended challenge-cup.

And round that early-laureled head   25
Will flock to gaze the strengthless dead,
And find unwithered on its curls
The garland briefer than a girl's.

Langston Hughes

Langston Hughes (1902–1967)

The Negro Speaks of Rivers   (1921) 1926

I've known rivers:
I've known rivers ancient as the world and older than the flow of hu-
    man blood in human veins.

My soul has grown deep like the rivers.

I bathed in the Euphrates when dawns were young.
I built my hut near the Congo and it lulled me to sleep.   5
I looked upon the Nile and raised the pyramids above it.
I heard the singing of the Mississippi when Abe Lincoln went down to New
    Orleans, and I've seen its muddy bosom turn all golden in the sunset.

I've known rivers:
Ancient, dusky rivers.

My soul has grown deep like the rivers.   10

Langston Hughes (1902–1967)

Harlem [Dream Deferred]   1951

What happens to a dream deferred?

> Does it dry up
> like a raisin in the sun?
> Or fester like a sore—
> And then run?
> Does it stink like rotten meat?   5
> Or crust and sugar over—
> like a syrupy sweet?

> Maybe it just sags
> like a heavy load.   10

> *Or does it explode?*

John Keats

John Keats (1795–1821)

Ode to a Nightingale   1820

I

My heart aches, and a drowsy numbness pains
  My sense, as though of hemlock I had drunk,
Or emptied some dull opiate to the drains
  One minute past, and Lethe-wards had sunk:
'Tis not through envy of thy happy lot,
  But being too happy in thine happiness,—   5
    That thou, light-winged Dryad of the trees
      In some melodious plot
  Of beechen green, and shadows numberless,
    Singest of summer in full-throated ease.   10

II

O, for a draught of vintage! that hath been
  Cool'd a long age in the deep-delved earth,
Tasting of Flora and the country green,
  Dance, and Provençal song, and sunburnt mirth!
O for a beaker full of the warm South,   15
  Full of the true, the blushful Hippocrene,
    With beaded bubbles winking at the brim,
      And purple-stained mouth;
  That I might drink, and leave the world unseen,
    And with thee fade away into the forest dim: 20

III

Fade far away, dissolve, and quite forget
  What thou among the leaves hast never known,
The weariness, the fever, and the fret
  Here, where men sit and hear each other groan;
Where palsy shakes a few, sad, last gray hairs,   25
  Where youth grows pale, and specter-thin, and dies;
    Where but to think is to be full of sorrow

And leaden-eyed despairs,
Where Beauty cannot keep her lustrous eyes,
  Or new Love pine at them beyond to-morrow. 30

IV

Away! away! for I will fly to thee,
  Not charioted by Bacchus and his pards,
But on the viewless wings of Poesy,
  Though the dull brain perplexes and retards:
Already with thee! tender is the night, 35
  And haply the Queen-Moon is on her throne,
    Cluster'd around by all her starry Fays;
      But here there is no light,
  Save what from heaven is with the breezes blown
    Through verdurous glooms and winding mossy ways. 40

V

I cannot see what flowers are at my feet,
  Nor what soft incense hangs upon the boughs,
But, in embalmed darkness, guess each sweet
  Wherewith the seasonable month endows
The grass, the thicket, and the fruit-tree wild; 45
  White hawthorn, and the pastoral eglantine;
    Fast fading violets cover'd up in leaves;
      And mid-May's eldest child,
  The coming musk-rose, full of dewy wine,
    The murmurous haunt of flies on summer eves. 50

VI

Darkling I listen; and, for many a time
  I have been half in love with easeful Death,
Call'd him soft names in many a mused rhyme,
  To take into the air my quiet breath;
Now more than ever seems it rich to die, 55
  To cease upon the midnight with no pain,
    While thou art pouring forth thy soul abroad
      In such an ecstasy!
  Still wouldst thou sing, and I have ears in vain—
    To thy high requiem become a sod. 60

VII

Thou wast not born for death, immortal Bird!
  No hungry generations tread thee down;
The voice I hear this passing night was heard
  In ancient days by emperor and clown:

Perhaps the self-same song that found a path   65
　　Through the sad heart of Ruth, when, sick for home,
　　　She stood in tears amid the alien corn;
　　　　The same that oft-times hath
　Charm'd magic casements, opening on the foam
　　Of perilous seas, in faery lands forlorn.   70

VIII

Forlorn! the very word is like a bell
　To toll me back from thee to my sole self!
Adieu! the fancy cannot cheat so well
　As she is fam'd to do, deceiving elf.
Adieu! adieu! thy plaintive anthem fades   75
　Past the near meadows, over the still stream,
　　Up the hill-side; and now 'tis buried deep
　　　In the next valley-glades:
　Was it a vision, or a waking dream?
　　Fled is that music:—Do I wake or sleep?   80

ODE TO A NIGHTINGALE. 4 *Lethe-wards:* towards Lethe, the river of oblivion in Hades, the classical Underworld; dead souls drank the waters of Lethe to forget their past lives. 7 *Dryad:* wood nymph. 13 *Flora:* the classical goddess of flowers and spring. 16 *Hippocrene:* the sacred fountain of the Muses, whose waters have the power to inspire poetry. 32 *pards:* leopards, the animals who pull the chariot of Bacchus, the god of wine. 66–67 *Ruth . . . alien corn:* In the Old Testament, Ruth is a Moabite widow who gleans grain from the Israelite Boaz's field.

Philip Larkin (1922–1985)

Home is so Sad   1964

Home is so sad. It stays as it was left,
Shaped to the comfort of the last to go
As if to win them back. Instead, bereft
Of anyone to please, it withers so,
Having no heart to put aside the theft   5

And turn again to what it started as,
A joyous shot at how things ought to be,
Long fallen wide. You can see how it was:
Look at the pictures and the cutlery.
The music in the piano stool. That vase.   10

D. H. Lawrence (1885–1930)

Piano   1918

Softly, in the dusk, a woman is singing to me;
Taking me back down the vista of years, till I see
A child sitting under the piano, in the boom of the tingling strings
And pressing the small, poised feet of a mother who smiles as she sings.

In spite of myself, the insidious mastery of song   5
Betrays me back, till the heart of me weeps to belong
To the old Sunday evenings at home, with winter outside
And hymns in the cozy parlor, the tinkling piano our guide.

So now it is vain for the singer to burst into clamor
With the great black piano appassionato. The glamour   10
Of childish days is upon me, my manhood is cast
Down in the flood of remembrance, I weep like a child for the past.

Shirley Geok-lin Lim

Shirley Geok-lin Lim (b. 1944)

Learning to love America   1998

because it has no pure products

because the Pacific Ocean sweeps along the coastline
because the water of the ocean is cold
and because land is better than ocean

because I say we rather than they   5

because I live in California
I have eaten fresh artichokes
and jacarandas bloom in April and May

because my senses have caught up with my body
my breath with the air it swallows   10
my hunger with my mouth

because I walk barefoot in my house

because I have nursed my son at my breast
because he is a strong American boy
because I have seen his eyes redden when he is asked who he is   15
because he answers I don't know

because to have a son is to have a country
because my son will bury me here
because countries are in our blood and we bleed them

because it is late and too late to change my mind   20
because it is time.

LEARNING TO LOVE AMERICA. 1 *pure products*: an allusion to poem XVIII of *Spring and All* (1923) by William Carlos Williams, which begins: "The pure products of America / go crazy—."

Andrew Marvell (1621–1678)

To His Coy Mistress   1681

Had we but world enough, and time,
This coyness,° Lady, were no crime.   *modesty, reluctance*
We would sit down, and think which way
To walk, and pass our long love's day.
Thou by the Indian Ganges' side   5
Should'st rubies find; I by the tide
Of Humber would complain.° I would   *sing sad songs*
Love you ten years before the Flood,
And you should, if you please, refuse
Till the Conversion of the Jews.   10
My vegetable° love should grow   *vegetative, flourishing*
Vaster than empires, and more slow.
An hundred years should go to praise
Thine eyes, and on thy forehead gaze,
Two hundred to adore each breast,   15
But thirty thousand to the rest.
An age at least to every part,
And the last age should show your heart.
For, Lady, you deserve this state,°   *pomp, ceremony*
Nor would I love at lower rate.   20
    But at my back I always hear
Time's wingèd chariot hurrying near,
And yonder all before us lie
Deserts of vast eternity.
Thy beauty shall no more be found,   25
Nor, in thy marble vault, shall sound

My echoing song; then worms shall try
That long preserved virginity,
And your quaint honor turn to dust,
And into ashes all my lust.   30
The grave's a fine and private place,
But none, I think, do there embrace.
   Now therefore, while the youthful hue
Sits on thy skin like morning glew°   *glow*
And while thy willing soul transpires   35
At every pore with instant° fires,   *eager*
Now let us sport us while we may;
And now, like amorous birds of prey,
Rather at once our time devour,
Than languish in his slow-chapped° power.   *slow-jawed*   40
Let us roll all our strength, and all
Our sweetness, up into one ball
And tear our pleasures with rough strife,
Thorough° the iron gates of life.   *through*
Thus, though we cannot make our sun   45
Stand still, yet we will make him run.

To His Coy Mistress. 7 *Humber:* a river that flows by Marvell's town of Hull (on the side of
the world opposite from the Ganges). 10 *conversion of the Jews:* an event that, according to
St. John the Divine, is to take place just before the end of the world. 35 *transpires:* exudes,
as a membrane lets fluid or vapor pass through it.

Claude McKay

Claude McKay (1890–1948)

The Harlem Dancer   1922

Applauding youths laughed with young prostitutes
And watched her perfect, half-clothed body sway;
Her voice was like the sound of blended flutes
Blown by black players upon a picnic day.
She sang and danced on gracefully and calm,   5
The light gauze hanging loose about her form;

To me she seemed a proudly-swaying palm
Grown lovelier for passing through a storm.
Upon her swarthy neck black shiny curls
Luxuriant fell; and tossing coins in praise,   10
The wine-flushed, bold-eyed boys, and even the girls,
Devoured her shape with eager, passionate gaze;
But looking at her falsely-smiling face,
I knew her self was not in that strange place.

Edna St. Vincent Millay

Edna St. Vincent Millay (1892–1950)

Recuerdo   1920

We were very tired, we were very merry—
We had gone back and forth all night on the ferry.
It was bare and bright, and smelled like a stable—
But we looked into a fire, we leaned across a table,
We lay on a hill-top underneath the moon;   5
And the whistles kept blowing, and the dawn came soon.

We were very tired, we were very merry—
We had gone back and forth all night on the ferry;
And you ate an apple, and I ate a pear,
From a dozen of each we had bought somewhere;   10
And the sky went wan, and the wind came cold,
And the sun rose dripping, a bucketful of gold.

We were very tired, we were very merry,
We had gone back and forth all night on the ferry.
We hailed, "Good morrow, mother!" to a shawl-covered head,   15
And bought a morning paper, which neither of us read;
And she wept, "God bless you!" for the apples and pears,
And we gave her all our money but our subway fares.

RECUERDO. The Spanish title means "a recollection" or "a memory."

John Milton (1608–1674)

When I consider how my light is spent   (1655?)

When I consider how my light is spent,
  Ere half my days in this dark world and wide,
  And that one talent which is death to hide
  Lodged with me useless, though my soul more bent
To serve therewith my Maker, and present   5
  My true account, lest He returning chide;
  "Doth God exact day-labor, light denied?"
  I fondly° ask. But Patience, to prevent   *foolishly*
That murmur, soon replies, "God doth not need
  Either man's work or his own gifts. Who best   10
  Bear his mild yoke, they serve him best. His state
Is kingly: thousands at his bidding speed,
  And post o'er land and ocean without rest;
  They also serve who only stand and wait."

WHEN I CONSIDER HOW MY LIGHT IS SPENT. 1 *my light is spent:* Milton had become blind.
3 *that one talent:* For Jesus's parable of the talents (measures of money), see Matthew 25:14–30.

Pablo Neruda (1904–1973)

We are Many   1967

Of the many men who I am, who we are,
I can't find a single one;
they disappear among my clothes,
they've left for another city.

When everything seems to be set   5
to show me off as intelligent,
the fool I always keep hidden
takes over all that I say.

At other times, I'm asleep
among distinguished people,   10
and when I look for my brave self,
a coward unknown to me
rushes to cover my skeleton
with a thousand fine excuses.

When a decent house catches fire,   15
instead of the fireman I summon,
an arsonist bursts on the scene,
and that's me. What can I do?

What can I do to distinguish myself?
How can I pull myself together?   20

All the books I read
are full of dazzling heroes,
always sure of themselves.
I die with envy of them;
and in films full of wind and bullets,   25
I goggle at the cowboys,
I even admire the horses.

But when I call for a hero,
out comes my lazy old self;
so I never know who I am,   30
nor how many I am or will be.
I'd love to be able to touch a bell
and summon the real me,
because if I really need myself,
I mustn't disappear.   35

While I am writing, I'm far away;
and when I come back, I've gone.
I would like to know if others
go through the same things that I do,
have as many selves as I have,   40
and see themselves similarly;
and when I've exhausted this problem,
I'm going to study so hard
that when I explain myself,
I'll be talking geography.   45

—Translated by Alastair Reid

Wilfred Owen (1893–1918)

Anthem for Doomed Youth   (1917)

What passing-bells for these who die as cattle?
    Only the monstrous anger of the guns.
Only the stuttering rifles' rapid rattle
    Can patter out their hasty orisons.
No mockeries now for them; no prayers nor bells,   5
    Nor any voice of mourning save the choirs,—
The shrill, demented choirs of wailing shells;
    And bugles calling for them from sad shires.°   *countries*

What candles may be held to speed them all?
  Not in the hands of boys, but in their eyes   10
  Shall shine the holy glimmers of good-byes.
The pallor of girls' brows shall be their pall;
Their flowers the tenderness of patient minds,
And each slow dusk a drawing-down of blinds.

Sylvia Plath

Sylvia Plath (1932–1963)

Daddy   (1962) 1965

You do not do, you do not do
Any more, black shoe
In which I have lived like a foot
For thirty years, poor and white,
Barely daring to breathe or Achoo.   5

Daddy, I have had to kill you.
You died before I had time—
Marble-heavy, a bag full of God,
Ghastly statue with one grey toe
Big as a Frisco seal   10

And a head in the freakish Atlantic
Where it pours bean green over blue
In the waters off beautiful Nauset.
I used to pray to recover you.
Ach, du.   15

In the German tongue, in the Polish town
Scraped flat by the roller
Of wars, wars, wars.
But the name of the town is common.
My Polack friend   20

Says there are a dozen or two.
So I never could tell where you
Put your foot, your root,
I never could talk to you.
The tongue stuck in my jaw.   25

It stuck in a barb wire snare.
Ich, ich, ich, ich,
I could hardly speak.
I thought every German was you.
And the language obscene   30

An engine, an engine
Chuffing me off like a Jew.
A Jew to Dachau, Auschwitz, Belsen.
I began to talk like a Jew.
I think I may well be a Jew.   35

The snows of the Tyrol, the clear beer of Vienna
Are not very pure or true.
With my gypsy ancestress and my weird luck
And my Taroc pack and my Taroc pack
I may be a bit of a Jew.   40

I have always been scared of *you*,
With your Luftwaffe, your gobbledygoo.
And your neat moustache
And your Aryan eye, bright blue.
Panzer-man, panzer-man, O You—   45

Not God but a swastika
So black no sky could squeak through.
Every woman adores a Fascist,
The boot in the face, the brute
Brute heart of a brute like you.   50

You stand at the blackboard, daddy,
In the picture I have of you,
A cleft in your chin instead of your foot
But no less a devil for that, no not
Any less the black man who   55

Bit my pretty red heart in two.
I was ten when they buried you.
At twenty I tried to die
And get back, back, back to you.
I thought even the bones would do.   60

But they pulled me out of the sack,
And they stuck me together with glue.
And then I knew what to do.
I made a model of you,
A man in black with a Meinkampf look   65

And a love of the rack and the screw.
And I said I do, I do.
So daddy, I'm finally through.
The black telephone's off at the root,
The voices just can't worm through.   70

If I've killed one man, I've killed two—
The vampire who said he was you
And drank my blood for a year,
Seven years, if you want to know.
Daddy, you can lie back now.   75

There's a stake in your fat black heart
And the villagers never liked you.
They are dancing and stamping on you.
They always *knew* it was you.
Daddy, daddy, you bastard, I'm through.   80

DADDY. 15 *Ach, du:* Oh, you. 27 *Ich, ich, ich, ich:* I, I, I, I. 51 *blackboard:* Otto Plath had been a professor of biology at Boston University. 65 *Meinkampf:* Adolf Hitler titled his autobiography *Mein Kampf* ("My Struggle").

Introducing this poem in a reading, Sylvia Plath remarked:

> The poem is spoken by a girl with an Electra complex. Her father died while she thought he was God. Her case is complicated by the fact that her father was also a Nazi and her mother very possibly part Jewish. In the daughter the two strains marry and paralyze each other—she has to act out the awful little allegory before she is free of it. (Quoted by A. Alvarez, *Beyond All This Fiddle* [New York: Random, 1968].)

In some details "Daddy" is autobiography: the poet's father, Otto Plath, a German, had come to the United States from Grabow, Poland. He died following the amputation of a gangrened foot and leg when Sylvia was eight years old. Politically, Otto Plath was a Republican, not a Nazi, but was apparently a somewhat domineering head of the household. (See the recollections of the poet's mother, Aurelia Schober Plath, in her edition of *Letters Home* by Sylvia Plath [New York: Harper, 1975].)

Edgar Allan Poe

Edgar Allan Poe (1809–1849)

Annabel Lee   1849

It was many and many a year ago,
  In a kingdom by the sea,
That a maiden there lived whom you may know
  By the name of Annabel Lee;
And this maiden she lived with no other thought   5
  Than to love and be loved by me.

I was a child and *she* was a child,
  In this kingdom by the sea,
But we loved with a love that was more than love—
  I and my Annabel Lee—   10
With a love that the wingéd seraphs of Heaven
  Coveted her and me.

And this was the reason that, long ago,
  In this kingdom by the sea,
A wind blew out of a cloud, chilling   15
  My beautiful Annabel Lee;
So that her highborn kinsmen came
  And bore her away from me,
To shut her up in a sepulchre
  In this kingdom by the sea.   20

The angels, not half so happy in Heaven,
  Went envying her and me:—
Yes!—that was the reason (as all men know,
  In this kingdom by the sea)
That the wind came out of the cloud by night,   25
  Chilling and killing my Annabel Lee.

But our love it was stronger by far than the love
  Of those who were older than we—
  Of many far wiser than we—

And neither the angels in Heaven above,   30
   Nor the demons down under the sea,
Can ever dissever my soul from the soul
   Of the beautiful Annabel Lee:—

For the moon never beams, without bringing me dreams
   Of the beautiful Annabel Lee;   35
And the stars never rise, but I feel the bright eyes
   Of the beautiful Annabel Lee:
And so, all the night-tide, I lie down by the side
Of my darling—my darling—my life and my bride,
   In the sepulchre there by the sea—   40
   In her tomb by the sounding sea.

Ezra Pound (1885–1972)

The River-Merchant's Wife: A Letter   1915

While my hair was still cut straight across my forehead
I played about the front gate, pulling flowers.
You came by on bamboo stilts, playing horse,
You walked about my seat, playing with blue plums.
And we went on living in the village of Chokan: 5
Two small people, without dislike or suspicion.

At fourteen I married My Lord you.
I never laughed, being bashful.
Lowering my head, I looked at the wall.
Called to, a thousand times, I never looked back.   10

At fifteen I stopped scowling,
I desired my dust to be mingled with yours
Forever and forever and forever.
Why should I climb the look out?

At sixteen you departed,   15
You went into far Ku-to-yen, by the river of swirling eddies,
And you have been gone five months.
The monkeys make sorrowful noise overhead.

You dragged your feet when you went out.
By the gate now, the moss is grown, the different mosses,   20
Too deep to clear them away!
The leaves fall early this autumn, in wind.
The paired butterflies are already yellow with August
Over the grass in the West garden;
They hurt me. I grow older.   25

If you are coming down through the narrows of the river Kiang,
Please let me know beforehand,
And I will come out to meet you
         As far as Cho-fu-sa.

THE RIVER-MERCHANT'S WIFE: A LETTER. A free translation from the Chinese poet Li Po
(eighth century).

Henry Reed (1914–1986)

Naming of Parts   1946

Today we have naming of parts. Yesterday,
We had daily cleaning. And tomorrow morning,
We shall have what to do after firing. But today,
Today we have naming of parts. Japonica
Glistens like coral in all of the neighboring gardens,   5
         And today we have naming of parts.

This is the lower sling swivel. And this
Is the upper sling swivel, whose use you will see,
When you are given your slings. And this is the piling swivel,
Which in your case you have not got. The branches   10
Hold in the gardens their silent, eloquent gestures,
         Which in our case we have not got.

This is the safety-catch, which is always released
With an easy flick of the thumb. And please do not let me
See anyone using his finger. You can do it quite easy   15
If you have any strength in your thumb. The blossoms
Are fragile and motionless, never letting anyone see
         Any of them using their finger.

And this you can see is the bolt. The purpose of this
Is to open the breech, as you see. We can slide it   20
Rapidly backwards and forwards: we call this
Easing the spring. And rapidly backwards and forwards
The early bees are assaulting and fumbling the flowers:
         They call it easing the Spring.

They call it easing the Spring: it is perfectly easy   25
If you have any strength in your thumb: like the bolt,
And the breech, and the cocking-piece, and the point of balance,
Which in our case we have not got; and the almond-blossom
Silent in all of the gardens and the bees going backwards and forwards,
         For today we have naming of parts.   30

Edwin Arlington Robinson (1869–1935)

Miniver Cheevy   1910

Miniver Cheevy, child of scorn,
   Grew lean while he assailed the seasons;
He wept that he was ever born,
   And he had reasons.

Miniver loved the days of old   5
   When swords were bright and steeds were prancing;
The vision of a warrior bold
   Would set him dancing.

Miniver sighed for what was not,
   And dreamed, and rested from his labors;   10
He dreamed of Thebes and Camelot,
   And Priam's neighbors.

Miniver mourned the ripe renown
   That made so many a name so fragrant;
He mourned Romance, now on the town,   15
   And Art, a vagrant.

Miniver loved the Medici,
   Albeit he had never seen one;
He would have sinned incessantly
   Could he have been one.   20

Miniver cursed the commonplace
   And eyed a khaki suit with loathing;
He missed the medieval grace
   Of iron clothing.

Miniver scorned the gold he sought,   25
   But sore annoyed was he without it;
Miniver thought, and thought, and thought,
   And thought about it.

Miniver Cheevy, born too late,
   Scratched his head and kept on thinking;   30
Miniver coughed, and called it fate,
   And kept on drinking.

MINIVER CHEEVY. 11 *Thebes:* a city in ancient Greece and the setting of many famous Greek myths; *Camelot:* the legendary site of King Arthur's Court. 12 *Priam:* the last king of Troy; his "neighbors" would have included Helen of Troy, Aeneas, and other famous figures. 17 *the Medici:* the ruling family of Florence during the high Renaissance, the Medici were renowned patrons of the arts.

Christina Rossetti (1830–1894)

Song   (1848) 1862

When I am dead, my dearest,
   Sing no sad songs for me;
Plant thou no roses at my head,
   Nor shady cypress tree:
Be the green grass above me   5
   With showers and dewdrops wet;
And if thou wilt, remember,
   And if thou wilt, forget.

I shall not see the shadows,
   I shall not feel the rain;
I shall not hear the nightingale   10
   Sing on, as if in pain:
And dreaming through the twilight
   That doth not rise nor set,
Haply I may remember,   15
   And haply may forget.

William Shakespeare

William Shakespeare (1564–1616)

When, in disgrace with   1609
Fortune and men's eyes (Sonnet 29)

When, in disgrace with Fortune and men's eyes,
I all alone beweep my outcast state,
And trouble deaf heaven with my bootless° cries,   *futile*
And look upon myself and curse my fate,
Wishing me like to one more rich in hope,   5
Featured like him, like him with friends possessed,
Desiring this man's art, and that man's scope,
With what I most enjoy contented least,

Yet in these thoughts myself almost despising,
Haply° I think on thee, and then my state,   *luckily*   10
Like to the lark at break of day arising
From sullen earth, sings hymns at heaven's gate;
    For thy sweet love rememb'red such wealth brings
    That then I scorn to change my state with kings.

William Shakespeare (1564–1616)

My mistress' eyes are nothing like the sun (Sonnet 130)   1609

My mistress' eyes are nothing like the sun;
Coral is far more red than her lips' red;
If snow be white, why then her breasts are dun;
If hairs be wires, black wires grow on her head.
I have seen roses damasked, red and white,   5
But no such roses see I in her cheeks;
And in some perfumes is there more delight
Than in the breath that from my mistress reeks.
I love to hear her speak, yet well I know
That music hath a far more pleasing sound;   10
I grant I never saw a goddess go:
My mistress, when she walks, treads on the ground.
    And yet, by heaven, I think my love as rare
    As any she° belied with false compare.   *woman*

Percy Bysshe Shelley (1792–1822)

Ozymandias   1819

I met a traveler from an antique land
Who said: Two vast and trunkless legs of stone
Stand in the desert. . . . Near them, on the sand,
Half sunk, a shattered visage lies, whose frown,
And wrinkled lip, and sneer of cold command,   5
Tell that its sculptor well those passions read
Which yet survive, stamped on these lifeless things,
The hand that mocked° them, and the heart that fed: *imitated*
And on the pedestal these words appear:
"My name is Ozymandias, king of kings: 10
Look on my works, ye Mighty, and despair!"
Nothing beside remains. Round the decay
Of that colossal wreck, boundless and bare
The lone and level sands stretch far away.

Wallace Stevens

Wallace Stevens   (1879–1955)

The Emperor of Ice-Cream   1923

Call the roller of big cigars,
The muscular one, and bid him whip
In kitchen cups concupiscent curds.
Let the wenches dawdle in such dress
As they are used to wear, and let the boys   5
Bring flowers in last month's newspapers.
Let be be finale of seem.
The only emperor is the emperor of ice-cream.

Take from the dresser of deal,
Lacking the three glass knobs, that sheet   10
On which she embroidered fantails once
And spread it so as to cover her face.
If her horny feet protrude, they come
To show how cold she is, and dumb.
Let the lamp affix its beam.   15
The only emperor is the emperor of ice-cream.

THE EMPEROR OF ICE-CREAM. 9 *deal:* fir or pine wood used to make cheap furniture.

Alfred, Lord Tennyson   (1809–1892)

Ulysses   (1833)

It little profits that an idle king,
By this still hearth, among these barren crags,
Matched with an agèd wife, I mete and dole°   *measure and dispense*
Unequal laws unto a savage race
That hoard, and sleep, and feed, and know not me.   5
I cannot rest from travel; I will drink
Life to the lees.° All times I have enjoyed   *to the bottom, the dregs*

Greatly, have suffered greatly, both with those
That loved me, and alone; on shore, and when
Through scudding drifts the rainy Hyades   10
Vexed the dim sea. I am become a name;
For always roaming with a hungry heart
Much have I seen and known—cities of men
And manners, climates, councils, governments,
Myself not least, but honored of them all—   15
And drunk delight of battle with my peers,
Far on the ringing plains of windy Troy.
I am a part of all that I have met;
Yet all experience is an arch wherethrough
Gleams that untraveled world whose margin fades   20
Forever and forever when I move.
How dull it is to pause, to make an end,
To rust unburnished, not to shine in use!
As though to breathe were life! Life piled on life
Were all too little, and of one to me   25
Little remains; but every hour is saved
From that eternal silence, something more,
A bringer of new things; and vile it were
For some three suns to store and hoard myself,
And this grey spirit yearning in desire   30
To follow knowledge like a sinking star,
Beyond the utmost bound of human thought.
    This is my son, mine own Telemachus,
To whom I leave the scepter and the isle—
Well-loved of me, discerning to fulfill   35
This labor, by slow prudence to make mild
A rugged people, and through soft degrees
Subdue them to the useful and the good.
Most blameless is he, centered in the sphere
Of common duties, decent not to fail   40
In offices of tenderness, and pay
Meet adoration to my household gods,
When I am gone. He works his work, I mine.
    There lies the port; the vessel puffs her sail;
There gloom the dark, broad seas. My mariners,   45
Souls that have toiled, and wrought, and thought with me—
That ever with a frolic welcome took
The thunder and the sunshine, and opposed
Free hearts, free foreheads—you and I are old;
Old age hath yet his honor and his toil.   50
Death closes all; but something ere the end,

Some work of noble note, may yet be done,
Not unbecoming men that strove with Gods.
The lights begin to twinkle from the rocks;
The long day wanes; the slow moon climbs; the deep   55
Moans round with many voices. Come, my friends,
'Tis not too late to seek a newer world.
Push off, and sitting well in order smite
The sounding furrows; for my purpose holds
To sail beyond the sunset, and the baths   60
Of all the western stars, until I die.
It may be that the gulfs will wash us down;
It may be we shall touch the Happy Isles,
And see the great Achilles, whom we knew.
Though much is taken, much abides; and though   65
We are not now that strength which in old days
Moved earth and heaven, that which we are, we are—
One equal temper of heroic hearts,
Made weak by time and fate, but strong in will
To strive, to seek, to find, and not to yield.   70

ULYSSES. Known as Odysseus in Greek, Ulysses was the king of Ithaca and a hero of the Trojan War. His ten-year journey home was portrayed in Homer's epic poem the *Odyssey*. 10 *Hyades:* daughters of Atlas, who were transformed into a group of stars. Their rising with the sun was thought to be a sign of rain. 33 *Telemachus:* son of Ulysses and Prince of Ithaca. 63 *Happy Isles:* Elysium, a paradise believed to be attainable by sailing west. 64 *Achilles:* also a hero of the Trojan War, a great warrior whose only vulnerability was found on a single spot on his heel.

Dylan Thomas (1914–1953)

Fern Hill   1946

Now as I was young and easy under the apple boughs
About the lilting house and happy as the grass was green,
      The night above the dingle° starry,   *wooded valley*
        Time let me hail and climb
        Golden in the heydays of his eyes,   5
And honored among wagons I was prince of the apple towns
And once below a time I lordly had the trees and leaves
        Trail with daisies and barley
        Down the rivers of the windfall light.

And as I was green and carefree, famous among the barns   10
About the happy yard and singing as the farm was home,
      In the sun that is young once only,
        Time let me play and be
        Golden in the mercy of his means,

And green and golden I was huntsman and herdsman, the calves 15
Sang to my horn, the foxes on the hills barked clear and cold,
   And the sabbath rang slowly
  In the pebbles of the holy streams.

All the sun long it was running, it was lovely, the hay
Fields high as the house, the tunes from the chimneys, it was air 20
   And playing, lovely and watery
    And fire green as grass.
   And nightly under the simple stars
As I rode to sleep the owls were bearing the farm away,
All the moon long I heard, blessed among stables, the nightjars 25
   Flying with the ricks, and the horses
    Flashing into the dark.

And then to awake, and the farm, like a wanderer white
With the dew, come back, the cock on his shoulder: it was all
   Shining, it was Adam and maiden, 30
    The sky gathered again
   And the sun grew round that very day.
So it must have been after the birth of the simple light
In the first, spinning place, the spellbound horses walking warm
   Out of the whinnying green stable 35
    On to the fields of praise.

And honored among foxes and pheasants by the gay house
Under the new made clouds and happy as the heart was long,
   In the sun born over and over,
    I ran my heedless ways,
    My wishes raced through the house high hay 40
And nothing I cared, at my sky blue trades, that time allows
In all his tuneful turning so few and such morning songs
   Before the children green and golden
    Follow him out of grace, 45

Nothing I cared, in the lamb white days, that time would take me
Up to the swallow thronged loft by the shadow of my hand,
   In the moon that is always rising,
    Nor that riding to sleep
   I should hear him fly with the high fields 50
And wake to the farm forever fled from the childless land.
Oh as I was young and easy in the mercy of his means,
   Time held me green and dying
  Though I sang in my chains like the sea.

Walt Whitman

Walt Whitman (1819–1892)

When I Heard the Learn'd Astronomer   1865

When I heard the learn'd astronomer,
When the proofs, the figures, were ranged in columns before me,
When I was shown the charts and diagrams, to add, divide, and
    measure them,
When I sitting heard the astronomer where he lectured with much
    applause in the lecture-room,
How soon unaccountable I became tired and sick,   5
Till rising and gliding out I wander'd off by myself,
In the mystical moist night-air, and from time to time,
Look'd up in perfect silence at the stars.

Walt Whitman (1819–1892)

O Captain! My Captain!   1865

O Captain! my Captain! our fearful trip is done,
The ship has weather'd every rack, the prize we sought is won,
The port is near, the bells I hear, the people all exulting,
While follow eyes the steady keel, the vessel grim and daring;
    But O heart! heart! heart!   5
        O the bleeding drops of red,
            Where on the deck my Captain lies,
                Fallen cold and dead.

O Captain! my Captain! rise up and hear the bells;
Rise up—for you the flag is flung—for you the bugle trills,   10
For you bouquets and ribbon'd wreaths—for you the shores
    a-crowding,
For you they call, the swaying mass, their eager faces turning;
    Here Captain! dear father!

This arm beneath your head!
   It is some dream that on the deck,   15
      You've fallen cold and dead.

My Captain does not answer, his lips are pale and still,
My father does not feel my arm, he has no pulse nor will,
The ship is anchor'd safe and sound, its voyage closed and done,
From fearful trip the victor ship comes in with object won;   20
   Exult O shores, and ring O bells!
      But I with mournful tread,
         Walk the deck my Captain lies,
           Fallen cold and dead.

O CAPTAIN! MY CAPTAIN! Written soon after the death of Abraham Lincoln, this was, in Whitman's lifetime, by far the most popular of his poems.

William Carlos Williams

William Carlos Williams (1883–1963)

Spring and All   1923

By the road to the contagious hospital
under the surge of the blue
mottled clouds driven from the
northeast—a cold wind. Beyond, the
waste of broad, muddy fields   5
brown with dried weeds, standing and fallen

patches of standing water
the scattering of tall trees

All along the road the reddish
purplish, forked, upstanding, twiggy   10
stuff of bushes and small trees
with dead, brown leaves under them
leafless vines—

Lifeless in appearance, sluggish
dazed spring approaches—   15

They enter the new world naked,
cold, uncertain of all
save that they enter. All about them
the cold, familiar wind—

Now the grass, tomorrow   20
the stiff curl of wildcarrot leaf

One by one objects are defined—
It quickens: clarity, outline of leaf

But now the stark dignity of
entrance—Still, the profound change   25
has come upon them: rooted, they
grip down and begin to awaken

William Carlos Williams (1883–1963)

Queen-Anne's-Lace   1921

Her body is not so white as
anemone petals nor so smooth—nor
so remote a thing. It is a field
of the wild carrot taking
the field by force; the grass   5
does not raise above it.
Here is no question of whiteness,
white as can be, with a purple mole
at the center of each flower.
Each flower is a hand's span   10
of her whiteness. Wherever
his hand has lain there is
a tiny purple blemish. Each part
is a blossom under his touch
to which the fibers of her being   15
stem one by one, each to its end,
until the whole field is a
white desire, empty, a single stem,
a cluster, flower by flower,
a pious wish to whiteness gone over—   20
or nothing.

William Wordsworth   (1770–1850)

Composed upon Westminster Bridge   1807

Earth has not anything to show more fair:
Dull would he be of soul who could pass by
A sight so touching in its majesty:
This City now doth, like a garment, wear
The beauty of the morning; silent, bare,   5
Ships, towers, domes, theaters, and temples lie
Open unto the fields, and to the sky;
All bright and glittering in the smokeless air.
Never did sun more beautifully steep
In his first splendor, valley, rock, or hill;   10
Ne'er saw I, never felt, a calm so deep!
The river glideth at his own sweet will:
Dear God! the very houses seem asleep;
And all that mighty heart is lying still!

James Wright   (1927–1980)

Autumn Begins in Martins Ferry, Ohio   1963

In the Shreve High football stadium,
I think of Polacks nursing long beers in Tiltonsville,
And gray faces of Negroes in the blast furnace at Benwood,
And the ruptured night watchman of Wheeling Steel,
Dreaming of heroes.   5

All the proud fathers are ashamed to go home.
Their women cluck like starved pullets,
Dying for love.

Therefore,
Their sons grow suicidally beautiful   10
At the beginning of October,
And gallop terribly against each other's bodies.

Mary Sidney Wroth   (1587–1653?)

In this strange labyrinth   1621

In this strange labyrinth how shall I turn?
Ways are on all sides while the way I miss:
If to the right hand, there in love I burn;
Let me go forward, therein danger is;

If to the left, suspicion hinders bliss,   5
Let me turn back, shame cries I ought return
Nor faint though crosses with my fortunes kiss.
Stand still is harder, although sure to mourn;
Thus let me take the right, or left hand way;
Go forward, or stand still, or back retire;   10
I must these doubts endure without allay
Or help, but travail find for my best hire;
Yet that which most my troubled sense doth move
Is to leave all, and take the thread of love.

IN THIS STRANGE LABYRINTH. This sonnet comes from Wroth's *Urania* (1621), the first significant sonnet sequence by a woman. Wroth was the niece of Sir Philip Sidney and of the
Countess of Pembroke as well as a distant relation of Sir Walter Ralegh. The *labyrinth* of
the title was the maze built by Minos to trap the young men and women sacrificed to the
Minotaur. King Minos's daughter Ariadne saved her beloved Theseus by giving him a skein
of thread to guide his way through the labyrinth. (See the final line of the sonnet.)

William Butler Yeats (1865–1939)

He wishes for the Cloths of Heaven   1899

Had I the heavens' embroidered cloths,
Enwrought with golden and silver light,
The blue and the dim and the dark cloths
Of night and light and the half light,
I would spread the cloths under your feet: 5
But I, being poor, have only my dreams;
I have spread my dreams under your feet;
Tread softly because you tread on my dreams.

William Butler Yeats (1865–1939)

Sailing to Byzantium   1927

I

That is no country for old men. The young
In one another's arms, birds in the trees
—Those dying generations—at their song,
The salmon-falls, the mackerel-crowded seas,
Fish, flesh, or fowl, commend all summer long   5
Whatever is begotten, born, and dies.
Caught in that sensual music all neglect
Monuments of unaging intellect.

II

An aged man is but a paltry thing,
A tattered coat upon a stick, unless   10
Soul clap its hands and sing, and louder sing
For every tatter in its mortal dress,
Nor is there singing school but studying
Monuments of its own magnificence;
And therefore I have sailed the seas and come   15
To the holy city of Byzantium.

III

O sages standing in God's holy fire
As in the gold mosaic of a wall,
Come from the holy fire, perne in a gyre,°   *spin down a spiral*
And be the singing-masters of my soul.
Consume my heart away; sick with desire   20
And fastened to a dying animal
It knows not what it is; and gather me
Into the artifice of eternity.

IV

Once out of nature I shall never take   25
My bodily form from any natural thing,
But such a form as Grecian goldsmiths make
Of hammered gold and gold enameling
To keep a drowsy Emperor awake;
Or set upon a golden bough to sing   30
To lords and ladies of Byzantium
Of what is past, or passing, or to come.

SAILING TO BYZANTIUM. Byzantium was the capital of the Byzantine Empire, the city now called Istanbul. Yeats means, though, not merely the physical city. Byzantium is also a name for his conception of paradise. 1 *no country for old men:* a line that provided the title for Cormac McCarthy's masterful 2005 novel and for the Coen brothers' 2007 Academy Award-winning film adaptation.

William Butler Yeats

William Butler Yeats   (1865–1939)

When You Are Old   1893

When you are old and grey and full of sleep,
And nodding by the fire, take down this book,
And slowly read, and dream of the soft look
Your eyes had once, and of their shadows deep;

How many loved your moments of glad grace,   5
And loved your beauty with love false or true,
But one man loved the pilgrim soul in you,
And loved the sorrows of your changing face;

And bending down beside the glowing bars,
Murmur, a little sadly, how Love fled   10
And paced upon the mountains overhead
And hid his face amid a crowd of stars.

Playwright David Ives.

DRAMA

TALKING WITH *David Ives*

"Comedy is just tragedy without the sentimentality."
Dana Gioia Interviews David Ives

Q: When did you first become interested in theater?

DAVID IVES: I played The Wolf opposite drop-dead-sexy Amy Skeehan in our third-grade production of "Little Red Riding Hood" at St. Mary Magdalene School in South Chicago. Basically it was all over after that. The show was so successful Amy and I took it on tour to the fourth and fifth grades. By then I had learned the Great Lesson of Theater, which is: *theater is a great way to hang out with girls*. It may be why Shakespeare became both an actor and a playwright: *more girls*.

Q: When did you discover that you could make people laugh?

DAVID IVES: There's some debate about this. An aunt of mine, a few years ago, said to me, "You're just like you were as a boy. Such a happy, funny child." I reported this to my mother, who said without a pause: "I wouldn't say that." She didn't seem to want to explain. One of my old high-school classmates recently mentioned that I was funny in high school. I only remember reading Russian novels about suicide in high school. Maybe I was funny between novels, but they were pretty thick.

Q: Tell us about your first play.

DAVID IVES: I wrote my first play when I was nine. It was about gangsters and had lots of gunfire and a girl I based on Amy Skeehan. I wrote my second play in high school. It was about Russian-like people talking about suicide a lot. My third play was at college and was The Worst Play Ever Written. From there, I had nowhere to go but up. My next play got produced, and suddenly I was a real live playwright. I've been faking it ever since.

Q: When you see one of your plays onstage, how different is it from what you imagined while writing it?

DAVID IVES: It's always better than I imagined it, unless it's worse.

Q: You are the master of the short comic play. What drew you to this unconventional form?

DAVID IVES: Probably a shorter and shorter attention span, like everybody else. Also, my wife Martha is on the short side and I am very drawn to her, so it is only a short (so to speak) way to short plays. I'm fond in general of the concise, the compact, the jeweled, the specific, and perfect as opposed to the verbose, the bloated, the baggy, and general. A good rock-and-roll song can be three or four minutes long and when it's over, if it's been made right and played right, you feel like you've gotten into a barfight, had a love affair, and ridden a convertible down Pacific Coast One on the

most beautiful day of the year, all in three minutes. Imagine what you can do with a ten- or fifteen-minute play. You can make an audience feel like they've done all those things, plus they've gotten married, had kids, died, and went to heaven. There they are, breathless just inside the pearly gates with their heads still spinning, and only ten minutes have passed. As far as I'm concerned, all plays, short or long, should aspire to the conditions of rock-and-roll, whose purpose is to make us aware of our mortality and the fact that we had better get with it before the song ends. Not a bad rule of thumb for art as a whole.

Q: Who are your favorite comic writers and comedians?

DAVID IVES: Nothing depresses me like comedians. Maybe it's because people who try to make me laugh instantly put me in a really bad mood. I once shot a man in Tucson and spent 38 years in the penitentiary because he tried to tell me a joke that started "A priest, a minister, and a rabbi walk into a bar. . . ." As for funny playwrights, Joe Orton and Noel Coward and Chris Durang do it for me because they're not just trying to be funny. They have a vision of life that happens to be comic. They've also got *style*, which is the outward and visible sign of having a vision of life.

Q: Why do people need comedy?

DAVID IVES: Comedy is important for three reasons. First, it's funny. Second, it makes us laugh. Third, it's easier to get a girl to go see a comedy than, let's say, *Hamlet*. Fourth, it shows us what frigging idiots we can be under the right circumstances. As Wendell Berry once said, "It is not from ourselves that we will learn to be better." Watching idiots cavort around onstage is one possible way to do that. First, of course, you have to be interested in being better.

Q: Comedy seems to get less critical respect than tragedy. Does that seem fair to you?

DAVID IVES: Nothing seems fair to me. That's why I write comedy. If you've ever met a critic you'll understand why they give more respect to sadder plays: because critics are the saddest dogs you'll ever meet. The fact is, comedy is much harder to do—to write, to act—than drama, the same way it's harder to look at life and say, *Okay*, than it is to mope around thinking about Russian roulette all the time. But let's get one thing clear: Comedy is not jokes. It certainly isn't sitcoms, which to me are about as funny as a sack of dead kittens. I'm talking about real comedy—human comedy, which is to say comedy that thinks and feels. I'm talking about *Twelfth Night*, or *The Marriage of Bette and Boo*, or *The Importance of Being Earnest*, where there's truth and sadness mixed in with the joy, just as there is in life. Theater *is* life, and it fails when it settles for merely being funny, the same way life is not enough when it settles for just being funny. In the end, comedy is just tragedy without the sentimentality. Dostoyevsky, anyone?

Drama is life with the dull bits left out.

—ALFRED HITCHCOCK

Unlike a short story or a novel, a **play** is a work of storytelling in which actors represent the characters. A play also differs from a work of fiction in another essential way: it is addressed not to readers but to spectators.

To be part of an audience in a theater is an experience far different from reading a story in solitude. As the house lights dim and the curtain rises, we become members of a community. The responses of people around us affect our own responses. We, too, contribute to the community's response whenever we laugh, sigh, applaud, murmur in surprise, or catch our breath in excitement. In contrast, when we watch a movie by ourselves in our living room—say, a slapstick comedy—we probably laugh less often than if we were watching the same film in a theater, surrounded by a roaring crowd. On the other hand, no one is spilling popcorn down the backs of our necks. Each kind of theatrical experience, to be sure, has its advantages.

A theater of live actors has another advantage: a sensitive give-and-take between actors and audience. (Such rapport, of course, depends on the skill of the actors and the perceptiveness of the audience.) Although professional actors may try to give a first-rate performance on all occasions, it is natural for them to feel more keenly inspired by a lively, appreciative audience than by a lethargic one. As veteran playgoers well know, something unique and wonderful can happen when good actors and a good audience respond to each other.

In another sense, a play is more than actors and audience. Like a short story or a poem, a play is a work of art made of words. Watching a play, of course, we don't notice the playwright standing between us and the characters. If the play is absorbing, it flows before our eyes. In a silent reading, the usual play consists mainly of **dialogue**, exchanges of speech, punctuated by stage directions. In performance, though, stage directions vanish. And although the thoughtful efforts of perhaps a hundred people—actors, director, producer, stage designer, costumer, makeup artist, technicians—may have gone into a production, a successful play makes us forget its artifice. We may even forget that the play is literature, for its gestures, facial expressions, bodily stances, lighting, and special effects are as much a part of it as the playwright's written words. Even though words are not all there is to a living play, they are its bones. And the whole play, the finished production, is the total of whatever takes place on stage.

23 READING A PLAY

What You Will Learn in This Chapter

- To define the play as a literary form
- To identify and describe theatrical conventions
- To recognize and describe the elements of a play
- To analyze a play

Most plays are written not to be read in books but to be performed. Finding plays in a literature anthology, the student may well ask: Isn't there something wrong with the idea of reading plays on the printed page? Isn't that a perversion of their nature?

True, plays are meant to be seen on stage, but equally true, reading a play may afford advantages. One is that it is better to know some masterpieces by reading them than never to know them at all. Even if you live in a large city with many theaters, even if you attend a college with many theatrical productions, to succeed in your lifetime in witnessing, say, all the plays of Shakespeare might well be impossible. In print, they are as near to hand as a book on a shelf, ready to be enacted (if you like) on the stage of the mind.

INTERPRETING PLAYS

After all, a play is literature before it comes alive in a theater, and it might be argued that when we read an unfamiliar play, we meet it in the same form in which it first appears to its actors and its director. If a play is rich and complex or if it dates from the remote past and contains difficulties of language and allusion, to read it on the page enables us to study it at our leisure and return to the parts that demand greater scrutiny.

But even if a play may be seen in a theater, sometimes to read it in print may be our way of knowing it as the author wrote it in its entirety. Far from regarding Shakespeare's words as holy writ, producers of *Hamlet*, *King Lear*, *Othello*, and other masterpieces often shorten or even leave out whole speeches and scenes. Besides, the nature of the play, as far as you can tell from a stage production, may depend on decisions of the director. In one production Othello may dress as a Renaissance Moor, in another as a modern general. Every actor who plays Iago in *Othello* makes his own interpretation of this knotty character. Some see Iago as a figure of pure evil; others, as a madman; still others, as a suffering human being consumed by hatred, jealousy, and pride. What do you think Shakespeare meant? You can always read the play and decide for yourself. If every stage production of a play is a fresh interpretation, so, too, is every reader's reading of it. Some readers, when silently reading a play to themselves, try to visualize a stage, imagining the characters in costume and under lights. If such a reader is an actor or a director and is reading the play with an eye toward staging it, then he or she may try to imagine every detail of a possible production, even shades of makeup and the loudness of sound effects. But the nonprofessional reader, who regards the play as literature, need not attempt such exhaustive imagining. Although some readers find it enjoyable to imagine the play taking place on a stage, others prefer to imagine the people and events that the play brings vividly to mind. Sympathetically following the tangled life of Nora in A Doll's House by Henrik Ibsen, we forget that we are reading printed stage directions and instead feel ourselves in the presence of human conflict. Thus regarded, a play becomes a form of storytelling, and the playwright's instructions to the actors and the director become a conventional mode of narrative that we accept much as we accept the methods of a novel or short story.

THEATRICAL CONVENTIONS

Most plays, whether seen in a theater or in print, employ some **conventions**: customary methods of presenting an action, usual and recognizable devices that an audience is willing to accept. In reading a great play from the past, such as Oedipus the King or Othello, it will help if we know some of the conventions of the classical Greek theater or the Elizabethan theater. When in Oedipus the King we encounter a character called the Chorus, it may be useful to be aware that this is a group of citizens who stand to one side of the action, conversing with the principal character and commenting. In Othello, when the sinister Iago, left on stage alone, begins to speak (at the end of Act I, Scene iii), we recognize the conventional device of a **soliloquy**, a monologue in which we seem to overhear the character's inmost thoughts uttered aloud. Another such device is the **aside**, in which a character addresses the audience directly, unheard by the other characters on stage, as when the villain in a melodrama chortles, "Heh! Heh! Now she's in my power!" Like conventions in poetry, such familiar methods of staging a narrative afford us a happy shock of recognition. Often, as in these examples, they are ways of making clear to us exactly what the playwright would have us know.

ELEMENTS OF A PLAY

When we read a play on the printed page and find ourselves swept forward by the motion of its story, we need not wonder how—and from what ingredients—the playwright put it together. Still, to analyze the structure of a play is one way to understand and appreciate a playwright's art. Analysis is complicated, however, because in an excellent play the elements (including plot, theme, and characters) do not stand in isolation. Often, deeds clearly follow from the kinds of people the characters are, and from those deeds it is left to the reader to infer the **theme** of the play—the general point or truth about human beings that may be drawn from it. Perhaps the most meaningful way to study the elements of a play (and certainly the most enjoyable) is to consider a play in its entirety.

Here is a short, famous one-act play worth reading for the boldness of its elements—and for its own sake. *Trifles* tells the story of a murder. As you will discover, the "trifles" mentioned in its title are not of trifling stature. In reading the play, you will probably find yourself imagining what you might see on stage if you were in a theater. You may also want to imagine what took place in the lives of the characters before the curtain rose. All this imagining may sound like a tall order, but don't worry. Just read the play for enjoyment the first time through, and then we will consider what makes it effective.

Susan Glaspell

Trifles   1916

Susan Glaspell (1876–1948) grew up in her native Davenport, Iowa, daughter of a grain dealer. After four years at Drake University and a job as a reporter in Des Moines, she settled in New York's Greenwich Village. In 1915, with her husband, George Cram Cook, a theatrical director, she founded the Provincetown Players, the first influential noncommercial theater troupe in America. During the summers of 1915 and 1916, in a makeshift playhouse on a Cape Cod pier, the Players staged the earliest plays of Eugene O'Neill and works by John Reed, Edna St. Vincent Millay,

Susan Glaspell

and Glaspell herself. Transplanting the company to New York in the fall of 1916, Glaspell and Cook renamed it the Playwrights' Theater. Glaspell wrote several still-remembered plays, among them a pioneering work of feminist drama, The Verge *(1921), and the Pulitzer Prize-winning* Alison's House *(1930), about the family of a reclusive poet reminiscent of Emily Dickinson who, after her death, squabble over the right to publish her poems. First widely known for her fiction set in Iowa, Glaspell wrote ten novels, including* Fidelity *(1915) and* The Morning Is Near Us *(1939). Shortly after writing the play* Trifles, *she rewrote it as a short story, "A Jury of Her Peers."*

CHARACTERS

George Henderson, county attorney
Henry Peters, sheriff
Lewis Hale, a neighboring farmer
Mrs. Peters
Mrs. Hale

SCENE. *The kitchen in the now abandoned farmhouse of John Wright, a gloomy kitchen, and left without having been put in order—unwashed pans under the sink, a loaf of bread outside the breadbox, a dish towel on the table—other signs of incompleted work. At the rear the outer door opens and the Sheriff comes in followed by the County Attorney and Hale. The Sheriff and Hale are men in middle life, the County Attorney is a young man; all are much bundled up and go at once to the stove. They are followed by two women—the Sheriff's wife first; she is a slight wiry woman, a thin nervous face. Mrs. Hale is larger and would ordinarily be called more comfortable looking, but she is disturbed now and looks fearfully about as she enters. The women have come in slowly, and stand close together near the door.*

County Attorney (*rubbing his hands*): This feels good. Come up to the fire, ladies.
Mrs. Peters (*after taking a step forward*): I'm not—cold.
Sheriff (*unbuttoning his overcoat and stepping away from the stove as if to mark the beginning of official business*): Now, Mr. Hale, before we move things about, you explain to Mr. Henderson just what you saw when you came here yesterday morning.
County Attorney: By the way, has anything been moved? Are things just as you left them yesterday?
Sheriff (*looking about*): It's just the same. When it dropped below zero last night I thought I'd better send Frank out this morning to make a fire for us—no use getting pneumonia with a big case on, but I told him not to touch anything except the stove—and you know Frank.
County Attorney: Somebody should have been left here yesterday.
Sheriff: Oh—yesterday. When I had to send Frank to Morris Center for that man who went crazy—I want you to know I had my hands full yesterday, I knew you could get back from Omaha by today and as long as I went over everything here myself—
County Attorney: Well, Mr. Hale, tell just what happened when you came here yesterday morning.
Hale: Harry and I had started to town with a load of potatoes. We came along the road from my place and as I got here I said, "I'm going to see if I can't get John Wright to go in with me on a party telephone." I spoke to Wright about it once before and he put me off, saying folks talked too much anyway, and all he asked was peace and quiet—I guess you know about how

much he talked himself; but I thought maybe if I went to the house and talked about it before his wife, though I said to Harry that I didn't know as what his wife wanted made much difference to John—

County Attorney: Let's talk about that later, Mr. Hale. I do want to talk about that, but tell now just what happened when you got to the house.

Hale: I didn't hear or see anything; I knocked at the door, and still it was all quiet inside. I knew they must be up, it was past eight o'clock. So I knocked again, and I thought I heard somebody say, "Come in." I wasn't sure, I'm not sure yet, but I opened the door—this door *(indicating the door by which the two women are still standing)* and there in that rocker—*(pointing to it)* sat Mrs. Wright.

(They all look at the rocker.)

County Attorney: What—was she doing?

Hale: She was rockin' back and forth. She had her apron in her hand and was kind of—pleating it.

County Attorney: And how did she—look?

Hale: Well, she looked queer.

County Attorney: How do you mean—queer?

Hale: Well, as if she didn't know what she was going to do next. And kind of done up.

County Attorney: How did she seem to feel about your coming?

Hale: Why, I don't think she minded—one way or other. She didn't pay much attention. I said, "How do, Mrs. Wright, it's cold, ain't it?" And she said, "Is it?"—and went on kind of pleating at her apron. Well, I was surprised; she didn't ask me to come up to the stove, or to set down, but just sat there, not even looking at me, so I said, "I want to see John." And then she—laughed. I guess you would call it a laugh. I thought of Harry and the team outside, so I said a little sharp: "Can't I see John?" "No," she says, kind o' dull like. "Ain't he home?" says I. "Yes," says she, "he's home." "Then why can't I see him?" I asked her, out of patience. "'Cause he's dead," says she. "*Dead?*" says I. She just nodded her head, not getting a bit excited, but rockin' back and forth. "Why—where is he?" says I, not knowing what to say. She just pointed upstairs—like that. *(Himself pointing to the room above.)* I got up, with the idea of going up there. I walked from there to here—then I says, "Why, what did he die of?" "He died of a rope round his neck," says she, and just went on pleatin' at her apron. Well, I went out and called Harry. I thought I might—need help. We went upstairs and there he was lyin'—

County Attorney: I think I'd rather have you go into that upstairs, where you can point it all out. Just go on now with the rest of the story.

Hale: Well, my first thought was to get that rope off. It looked . . . *(stops, his face twitches)* . . . but Harry, he went up to him, and he said, "No, he's dead all right, and we'd better not touch anything." So we went back

down stairs. She was still sitting that same way. "Has anybody been noti-
fied?" I asked. "No," says she, unconcerned. "Who did this, Mrs. Wright?"
said Harry. He said it businesslike—and she stopped pleatin' of her apron.
"I don't know," she says. "You don't *know*?" says Harry. "No," says she.
"Weren't you sleepin' in the bed with him?" says Harry. "Yes," says she,
"but I was on the inside." "Somebody slipped a rope round his neck and
strangled him and you didn't wake up?" says Harry. "I didn't wake up,"
she said after him. We must 'a looked as if we didn't see how that could
be, for after a minute she said, "I sleep sound." Harry was going to ask her
more questions but I said maybe we ought to let her tell her story first to
the coroner, or the sheriff, so Harry went fast as he could to Rivers' place,
where there's a telephone.

County Attorney: And what did Mrs. Wright do when she knew that you had
gone for the coroner?

Hale: She moved from that chair to this one over here (*pointing to a small chair
in the corner*) and just sat there with her hands held together and looking
down. I got a feeling that I ought to make some conversation, so I said I
had come in to see if John wanted to put in a telephone, and at that she
started to laugh, and then she stopped and looked at me—scared. (*The
County Attorney, who has had his notebook out, makes a note.*) I dunno,
maybe it wasn't scared. I wouldn't like to say it was. Soon Harry got back,
and then Dr. Lloyd came, and you, Mr. Peters, and so I guess that's all I
know that you don't.

County Attorney (looking around): I guess we'll go upstairs first—and then out
to the barn and around there. (*To the Sheriff*) You're convinced that there
was nothing important here—nothing that would point to any motive.

Sheriff: Nothing here but kitchen things.

(*The County Attorney, after again looking around the kitchen, opens the door of
a cupboard closet. He gets up on a chair and looks on a shelf. Pulls his hand away,
sticky.*)

County Attorney: Here's a nice mess.

(*The women draw nearer.*)

Mrs. Peters (to the other woman): Oh, her fruit; it did freeze. (*To the County
Attorney*) She worried about that when it turned so cold. She said the
fire'd go out and her jars would break.

Sheriff: Well, can you beat the women! Held for murder and worryin' about
her preserves.

County Attorney: I guess before we're through she may have something more
serious than preserves to worry about.

Hale: Well, women are used to worrying over trifles.

(*The two women move a little closer together.*)

County Attorney (with the gallantry of a young politician): And yet, for all their worries, what would we do without the ladies? *(The women do not unbend. He goes to the sink, takes a dipperful of water from the pail and pouring it into a basin, washes his hands. Starts to wipe them on the roller towel, turns it for a cleaner place.)* Dirty towels! *(Kicks his foot against the pans under the sink.)* Not much of a housekeeper, would you say, ladies?

Mrs. Hale (stiffly): There's a great deal of work to be done on a farm.

County Attorney: To be sure. And yet *(with a little bow to her)* I know there are some Dickson County farmhouses which do not have such roller towels.

(He gives it a pull to expose its full length again.)

Mrs. Hale: Those towels get dirty awful quick. Men's hands aren't always as clean as they might be.

County Attorney: Ah, loyal to your sex, I see. But you and Mrs. Wright were neighbors. I suppose you were friends, too.

Mrs. Hale (shaking her head): I've not seen much of her of late years. I've not been in this house—it's more than a year.

County Attorney: And why was that? You didn't like her?

Mrs. Hale: I liked her all well enough. Farmers' wives have their hands full, Mr. Henderson. And then—

County Attorney: Yes—?

Mrs. Hale (looking about): It never seemed a very cheerful place.

County Attorney: No—it's not cheerful. I shouldn't say she had the home-making instinct.

Mrs. Hale: Well, I don't know as Wright had, either.

County Attorney: You mean that they didn't get on very well?

Mrs. Hale: No, I don't mean anything. But I don't think a place'd be any cheerfuller for John Wright's being in it.

County Attorney: I'd like to talk more of that a little later. I want to get the lay of things upstairs now.

(He goes to the left, where three steps lead to a stair door.)

Sheriff: I suppose anything Mrs. Peters does'll be all right. She was to take in some clothes for her, you know, and a few little things. We left in such a hurry yesterday.

County Attorney: Yes, but I would like to see what you take, Mrs. Peters, and keep an eye out for anything that might be of use to us.

Mrs. Peters: Yes, Mr. Henderson.

(The women listen to the men's steps on the stairs, then look about the kitchen.)

Mrs. Hale: I'd hate to have men coming into my kitchen, snooping around and criticizing.

(*She arranges the pans under sink which the County Attorney had shoved out of place.*)

Mrs. Peters: Of course it's no more than their duty.

Mrs. Hale: Duty's all right, but I guess that deputy sheriff that came out to make the fire might have got a little of this on. (*Gives the roller towel a pull.*) Wish I'd thought of that sooner. Seems mean to talk about her for not having things slicked up when she had to come away in such a hurry.

Mrs. Peters (*who has gone to a small table in the left rear corner of the room, and lifted one end of a towel that covers a pan*): She had bread set.

(*Stands still.*)

Mrs. Hale (*eyes fixed on a loaf of bread beside the breadbox, which is on a low shelf at the other side of the room; moves slowly toward it*): She was going to put this in there. (*Picks up loaf, then abruptly drops it. In a manner of returning to familiar things.*) It's a shame about her fruit. I wonder if it's all gone. (*Gets up on the chair and looks.*) I think there's some here that's all right, Mrs. Peters. Yes—here; (*holding it toward the window*) this is cherries, too. (*Looking again.*) I declare I believe that's the only one. (*Gets down, bottle in her hand. Goes to the sink and wipes it off on the outside.*) She'll feel awful bad after all her hard work in the hot weather. I remember the afternoon I put up my cherries last summer.

(*She puts the bottle on the big kitchen table, center of the room. With a sigh, is about to sit down in the rocking-chair. Before she is seated realizes what chair it is; with a slow look at it, steps back. The chair which she has touched rocks back and forth.*)

Mrs. Peters: Well, I must get those things from the front room closet. (*She goes to the door at the right, but after looking into the other room, steps back.*) You coming with me, Mrs. Hale? You could help me carry them.

(*They go in the other room; reappear, Mrs. Peters carrying a dress and skirt, Mrs. Hale following with a pair of shoes.*)

Mrs. Peters: My, it's cold in there.

(*She puts the clothes on the big table, and hurries to the stove.*)

Mrs. Hale (*examining her skirt*): Wright was close. I think maybe that's why she kept so much to herself. She didn't even belong to the Ladies Aid. I suppose she felt she couldn't do her part, and then you don't enjoy things when you feel shabby. She used to wear pretty clothes and be lively, when she was Minnie Foster, one of the town girls singing in the choir. But that—oh, that was thirty years ago. This all you was to take in?

Mrs. Peters: She said she wanted an apron. Funny thing to want, for there isn't much to get you dirty in jail, goodness knows. But I suppose just to make her feel more natural. She said they was in the top drawer in this cupboard. Yes, here. And then her little shawl that always hung behind the door. (*Opens stair door and looks.*) Yes, here it is.

(*Quickly shuts door leading upstairs.*)

Mrs. Hale (*abruptly moving toward her*): Mrs. Peters?

Mrs. Peters: Yes, Mrs. Hale?

Mrs. Hale: Do you think she did it?

Mrs. Peters (*in a frightened voice*): Oh, I don't know.

Mrs. Hale: Well, I don't think she did. Asking for an apron and her little shawl. Worrying about her fruit.

Mrs. Peters (*starts to speak, glances up, where footsteps are heard in the room above; in a low voice*): Mr. Peters says it looks bad for her. Mr. Henderson is awful sarcastic in a speech and he'll make fun of her sayin' she didn't wake up.

Mrs. Hale: Well, I guess John Wright didn't wake when they was slipping that rope under his neck.

Mrs. Peters: No, it's strange. It must have been done awful crafty and still. They say it was such a—funny way to kill a man, rigging it all up like that.

Mrs. Hale: That's just what Mr. Hale said. There was a gun in the house. He says that's what he can't understand.

Mrs. Peters: Mr. Henderson said coming out that what was needed for the case was a motive; something to show anger, or—sudden feeling.

Mrs. Hale (*who is standing by the table*): Well, I don't see any signs of anger around here. (*She puts her hand on the dish towel which lies on the table, stands looking down at table, one half of which is clean, the other half messy.*) It's wiped to here. (*Makes a move as if to finish work, then turns and looks at loaf of bread outside the breadbox. Drops towel. In that voice of coming back to familiar things.*) Wonder how they are finding things upstairs. I hope she had it a little more red-up° there. You know, it seems kind of *sneaking.* Locking her up in town and then coming out here and trying to get her own house to turn against her!

Mrs. Peters: But Mrs. Hale, the law is the law.

Mrs. Hale: I s'pose 'tis. (*Unbuttoning her coat.*) Better loosen up your things, Mrs. Peters. You won't feel them when you go out.

(*Mrs. Peters takes off her fur tippet, goes to hang it on hook at back of room, stands looking at the under part of the small corner table.*)

Mrs. Peters: She was piecing a quilt.

(*She brings the large sewing basket and they look at the bright pieces.*)

---

red-up: (slang) readied up, ready to be seen.

Mrs. *Hale:* It's a log cabin pattern. Pretty, isn't it? I wonder if she was goin' to quilt it or just knot it?

(*Footsteps have been heard coming down the stairs. The Sheriff enters followed by Hale and the County Attorney.*)

Sheriff: They wonder if she was going to quilt it or just knot it!

(*The men laugh; the women look abashed.*)

County Attorney (*rubbing his hands over the stove*): Frank's fire didn't do much up there, did it? Well, let's go out to the barn and get that cleared up.

(*The men go outside.*)

Mrs. *Hale (resentfully)*: I don't know as there's anything so strange, our takin' up our time with little things while we're waiting for them to get the evidence. (*She sits down at the big table smoothing out a block with decision.*) I don't see as it's anything to laugh about.

Mrs. *Peters (apologetically)*: Of course they've got awful important things on their minds.

(*Pulls up a chair and joins Mrs. Hale at the table.*)

Mrs. *Hale (examining another block)*: Mrs. Peters, look at this one. Here, this is the one she was working on, and look at the sewing! All the rest of it has been so nice and even. And look at this! It's all over the place! Why, it looks as if she didn't know what she was about!

(*After she has said this they look at each, then start to glance back at the door. After an instant Mrs. Hale has pulled at a knot and ripped the sewing.*)

Mrs. *Peters:* Oh, what are you doing, Mrs. Hale?

Mrs. *Hale (mildly)*: Just pulling out a stitch or two that's not sewed very good. (*Threading a needle.*) Bad sewing always made me fidgety.

Mrs. *Peters (nervously)*: I don't think we ought to touch things.

Mrs. *Hale:* I'll just finish up this end. (*Suddenly stopping and leaning forward.*) Mrs. Peters?

Mrs. *Peters:* Yes, Mrs. Hale?

Mrs. *Hale:* What do you suppose she was so nervous about?

Mrs. *Peters:* Oh—I don't know. I don't know as she was nervous. I sometimes sew awful queer when I'm just tired. (*Mrs. Hale starts to say something, looks at Mrs. Peters, then goes on sewing.*) Well, I must get these things wrapped up. They may be through sooner than we think. (*Putting apron and other things together.*) I wonder where I can find a piece of paper, and string.

Mrs. *Hale:* In that cupboard, maybe.

Mrs. *Peters (looking in cupboard)*: Why, here's a birdcage. (*Holds it up.*) Did she have a bird, Mrs. Hale?

Mrs. Hale: Why, I don't know whether she did or not—I've not been here for so long. There was a man around last year selling canaries cheap, but I don't know as she took one; maybe she did. She used to sing real pretty herself.

Mrs. Peters (glancing around): Seems funny to think of a bird here. But she must have had one, or why would she have a cage? I wonder what happened to it.

Mrs. Hale: I s'pose maybe the cat got it.

Mrs. Peters: No, she didn't have a cat. She's got that feeling some people have about cats—being afraid of them. My cat got in her room and she was real upset and asked me to take it out.

Mrs. Hale: My sister Bessie was like that. Queer, ain't it?

Mrs. Peters (examining the cage): Why, look at this door. It's broke. One hinge is pulled apart.

Mrs. Hale (looking too): Looks as if someone must have been rough with it.

Mrs. Peters: Why, yes.

(She brings the cage forward and puts it on the table.)

Mrs. Hale: I wish if they're going to find any evidence they'd be about it. I don't like this place.

Mrs. Peters: But I'm awful glad you came with me, Mrs. Hale. It would be lonesome for me sitting here alone.

Mrs. Hale: It would, wouldn't it? *(Dropping her sewing.)* But I tell you what I do wish, Mrs. Peters. I wish I had come over sometimes when *she* was here. I—*(looking around the room)*—wish I had.

Mrs. Peters: But of course you were awful busy, Mrs. Hale—your house and your children.

Mrs. Hale: I could've come. I stayed away because it weren't cheerful—and that's why I ought to have come. I—I've never liked this place. Maybe because it's down in a hollow and you don't see the road. I dunno what it is but it's a lonesome place and always was. I wish I had come over to see Minnie Foster sometimes. I can see now—

(Shakes her head.)

Mrs. Peters: Well, you mustn't reproach yourself, Mrs. Hale. Somehow we just don't see how it is with other folks until—something comes up.

Mrs. Hale: Not having children makes less work—but it makes a quiet house, and Wright out to work all day, and no company when he did come in. Did you know John Wright, Mrs. Peters?

Mrs. Peters: Not to know him; I've seen him in town. They say he was a good man.

Mrs. Hale: Yes—good; he didn't drink, and kept his word as well as most, I guess, and paid his debts. But he was a hard man, Mrs. Peters. Just to pass the time of day with him—*(shivers)*. Like a raw wind that gets to the bone. (*Pauses, her eye falling on the cage.*) I should think she would'a wanted a bird. But what do you suppose went with it?

Mrs. Peters: I don't know, unless it got sick and died.

(*She reaches over and swings the broken door, swings it again. Both women watch it.*)

Mrs. Hale: You weren't raised round here, were you? (*Mrs. Peters shakes her head.*) You didn't know—her?

Mrs. Peters: Not till they brought her yesterday.

Mrs. Hale: She—come to think of it, she was kind of like a bird herself— real sweet and pretty, but kind of timid and—fluttery. How—she—did— change. (*Silence; then as if struck by a happy thought and relieved to get back to everyday things.*) Tell you what, Mrs. Peters, why don't you take the quilt in with you? It might take up her mind.

Mrs. Peters: Why, I think that's a real nice idea, Mrs. Hale. There couldn't possibly be any objection to it, could there? Now, just what would I take? I wonder if her patches are in here—and her things.

(*They look in the sewing basket.*)

Mrs. Hale: Here's some red. I expect this has got sewing things in it. (*Brings out a fancy box.*) What a pretty box. Looks like something somebody would give you. Maybe her scissors are in here. (*Opens box. Suddenly puts her hand to her nose.*) Why—(*Mrs. Peters bends nearer, then turns her face away.*) There's something wrapped up in this piece of silk.

Mrs. Peters: Why, this isn't her scissors.

Mrs. Hale (*lifting the silk*): Oh, Mrs. Peters—it's—

(*Mrs. Peters bends closer.*)

Mrs. Peters: It's the bird.

Mrs. Hale (*jumping up*): But, Mrs. Peters—look at it! Its neck! Look at its neck! It's all—other side *to*.

Mrs. Peters: Somebody—wrung—its—neck.

(*Their eyes meet. A look of growing comprehension, of horror. Steps are heard outside. Mrs. Hale slips box under quilt pieces, and sinks into her chair. Enter Sheriff and County Attorney. Mrs. Peters rises.*)

County Attorney (*as one turning from serious things to little pleasantries*): Well, ladies, have you decided whether she was going to quilt it or knot it?

Mrs. Peters: We think she was going to—knot it.

County Attorney: Well, that's interesting, I'm sure. (*Seeing the birdcage.*) Has the bird flown?

Mrs. Hale (*putting more quilt pieces over the box*): We think the—cat got it.

County Attorney (*preoccupied*): Is there a cat?

Production of *Trifles* by Echo Theatre of Dallas, 2000.

(Mrs. Hale glances in a quick covert way at Mrs. Peters.)

Mrs. Peters: Well, not now. They're superstitious, you know. They leave.

County Attorney *(to Sheriff Peters, continuing an interrupted conversation)*: No sign at all of anyone having come from the outside. Their own rope. Now let's go up again and go over it piece by piece. *(They start upstairs.)* It would have to have been someone who knew just the—

(Mrs. Peters sits down. The two women sit there not looking at one another, but as if peering into something and at the same time holding back. When they talk now it is in the manner of feeling their way over strange ground, as if afraid of what they are saying, but as if they cannot help saying it.)

Mrs. Hale: She liked the bird. She was going to bury it in that pretty box.

Mrs. Peters *(in a whisper)*: When I was a girl—my kitten—there was a boy took a hatchet, and before my eyes—and before I could get there—*(covers her face an instant)*. If they hadn't held me back I would have—*(catches herself, looks upstairs where steps are heard, falters weakly)*—hurt him.

Mrs. *Hale (with a slow look around her):* I wonder how it would seem never to have had any children around. (*Pause.*) No, Wright wouldn't like the bird—a thing that sang. She used to sing. He killed that, too.

Mrs. *Peters (moving uneasily):* We don't know who killed the bird.

Mrs. *Hale:* I knew John Wright.

Mrs. *Peters:* It was an awful thing was done in this house that night, Mrs. Hale. Killing a man while he slept, slipping a rope around his neck that choked the life out of him.

Mrs. *Hale:* His neck. Choked the life out of him.

(Her hand goes out and rests on the birdcage.)

Mrs. *Peters (with rising voice):* We don't know who killed him. We don't *know.*

Mrs. *Hale (her own feeling not interrupted):* If there'd been years and years of nothing, then a bird to sing to you, it would be awful—still, after the bird was still.

Mrs. *Peters (something within her speaking):* I know what stillness is. When we homesteaded in Dakota, and my first baby died—after he was two years old, and me with no other then—

Mrs. *Hale (moving):* How soon do you suppose they'll be through looking for the evidence?

Mrs. *Peters:* I know what stillness is. (*Pulling herself back.*) The law has got to punish crime, Mrs. Hale.

Mrs. *Hale (not as if answering that):* I wish you'd seen Minnie Foster when she wore a white dress with blue ribbons and stood up there in the choir and sang. (*A look around the room.*) Oh, I *wish* I'd come over here once in a while! That was a crime! That was a crime! Who's going to punish that?

Mrs. *Peters (looking upstairs):* We mustn't—take on.

Mrs. *Hale:* I might have known she needed help! I know how things can be—for women. I tell you, it's queer, Mrs. Peters. We live close together and we live far apart. We all go through the same things—it's all just a different kind of the same thing. (*Brushes her eyes; noticing the bottle of fruit, reaches out for it.*) If I was you I wouldn't tell her her fruit was gone. Tell her it ain't. Tell her it's all right. Take this in to prove it to her. She—she may never know whether it was broke or not.

Mrs. *Peters (takes the bottle, looks about for something to wrap it in; takes petticoat from the clothes brought from the other room, very nervously begins winding this around the bottle; in a false voice):* My, it's a good thing the men couldn't hear us. Wouldn't they just laugh! Getting all stirred up over a little thing like a—dead canary. As if that could have anything to do with—with—wouldn't they *laugh!*

(The men are heard coming down stairs.)

Mrs. Hale *(under her breath)*: Maybe they would—maybe they wouldn't.

County Attorney: No, Peters, it's all perfectly clear except a reason for doing it. But you know juries when it comes to women. If there was some definite thing. Something to show—something to make a story about—a thing that would connect up with this strange way of doing it—

(The women's eyes meet for an instant. Enter Hale from outer door.)

Hale: Well, I've got the team around. Pretty cold out there.

County Attorney: I'm going to stay here a while by myself. *(To the Sheriff)* You can send Frank out for me, can't you? I want to go over everything. I'm not satisfied that we can't do better.

Sheriff: Do you want to see what Mrs. Peters is going to take in?

(The County Attorney goes to the table, picks up the apron, laughs.)

County Attorney: Oh, I guess they're not very dangerous things the ladies have picked out. *(Moves a few things about, disturbing the quilt pieces which cover the box. Steps back.)* No, Mrs. Peters doesn't need supervising. For that matter, a sheriff's wife is married to the law. Ever think of it that way, Mrs. Peters?

Mrs. Peters: Not—just that way.

Sheriff *(chuckling)*: Married to the law. *(Moves toward the other room.)* I just want you to come in here a minute, George. We ought to take a look at these windows.

County Attorney *(scoffingly)*: Oh, windows!

Sheriff: We'll be right out, Mr. Hale.

(Hale goes outside. The Sheriff follows the County Attorney into the other room. Then Mrs. Hale rises, hands tight together, looking intensely at Mrs. Peters, whose eyes make a slow turn, finally meeting Mrs. Hale's. A moment Mrs. Hale holds her, then her own eyes point the way to where the box is concealed. Suddenly Mrs. Peters throws back quilt pieces and tries to put the box in the bag she is wearing. It is too big. She opens box, starts to take bird out, cannot touch it, goes to pieces, stands there helpless. Sound of a knob turning in the other room. Mrs. Hale snatches the box and puts it in the pocket of her big coat. Enter County Attorney and Sheriff.)

County Attorney *(facetiously)*: Well, Henry, at least we found out that she was not going to quilt it. She was going to—what is it you call it, ladies?

Mrs. Hale *(her hand against her pocket)*: We call it—knot it, Mr. Henderson.

CURTAIN

Questions

1. What attitudes toward women do the Sheriff and the County Attorney express? How do Mrs. Hale and Mrs. Peters react to these sentiments?

2. Why does the County Attorney care so much about discovering a motive for the killing?

3. What does Glaspell show us about the position of women in this early twentieth-century community?

4. What do we learn about the married life of the Wrights? By what means is this knowledge revealed to us?

5. What is the setting of this play, and how does it help us to understand Mrs. Wright's deed?

6. What do you infer from the wildly stitched block in Minnie's quilt? Why does Mrs. Hale rip out the crazy stitches?

7. What is so suggestive in the ruined birdcage and the dead canary wrapped in silk? What do these objects have to do with Minnie Foster Wright? What similarity do you notice between the way the canary died and John Wright's own death?

8. What thoughts and memories confirm Mrs. Peters and Mrs. Hale in their decision to help Minnie beat the murder rap?

9. In what places does Mrs. Peters show that she is trying to be a loyal, law-abiding sheriff's wife? How do she and Mrs. Hale differ in background and temperament?

10. What ironies does the play contain? Comment on Mrs. Hale's closing speech: "We call it—knot it, Mr. Henderson." Why is that little hesitation before "knot it" such a meaningful pause?

11. Point out some moments in the play when the playwright conveys much to the audience without needing dialogue.

12. How would you sum up the play's major theme?

13. How does this play, first produced in 1916, show its age? In what ways does it seem still remarkably new?

14. "*Trifles* is a lousy mystery. All the action took place before the curtain went up. Almost in the beginning, on the third page, we find out 'who done it.' So there isn't really much reason for us to sit through the rest of the play." Discuss this view.

ANALYZING *TRIFLES*

Some plays endure, perhaps because (among other reasons) actors take pleasure in performing them. *Trifles* is such a play, a showcase for the skills of its two principals. While the men importantly bumble about, trying to discover a motive, Mrs. Peters and Mrs. Hale solve the case right under their dull noses. The two players in these leading roles face a challenging task: to show both characters growing onstage before us. Discovering a secret that binds them, the two women must realize painful truths in their own lives, become aware of all they have in common with Minnie Wright, and gradually resolve to side with the accused against the men. That *Trifles* has enjoyed a revival of attention may reflect its evident feminist views, its convincing portrait of two women forced reluctantly to arrive at a moral judgment and to make a defiant move.

Conflict

Some critics say that the essence of drama is **conflict**, the central struggle between two or more forces in a play. Evidently, Glaspell's play is rich in this essential, even though its most violent conflict—the war between John and Minnie Wright—takes place before the play begins. Right away, when the menfolk barge through the door into the warm room, letting the women trail in after them; right away, when the sheriff makes fun of Minnie for worrying about "trifles" and the county attorney (that slick politician) starts crudely trying to flatter the "ladies," we sense a conflict between officious, self-important men and the women they expect to wait on them. What is the play's *theme?* Surely the title points to it: women, who men say worry over trifles, can find large meanings in those little things.

Plot

Like a carefully constructed traditional short story, *Trifles* has a **plot**, a term sometimes taken to mean whatever happens in a story, but more exactly referring to the unique arrangement of events that the author has made. (For more about plot in a story, see Chapter 1.) If Glaspell had elected to tell the story of John and Minnie Wright in chronological order, the sequence in which events took place in time, she might have written a much longer play, opening perhaps with a scene of Minnie's buying her canary and John's cold complaint, "That damned bird keeps twittering all day long!" She might have included scenes showing John strangling the canary and swearing when it beaks him; the Wrights in their loveless bed while Minnie knots her noose; and farmer Hale's entrance after the murder, with Minnie rocking. Only at the end would she have shown us what happened after the crime. That arrangement of events would have made for a quite different play than the short, tight one Glaspell wrote. By telling of events in retrospect, by having the women detectives piece together what happened, Glaspell leads us to focus not only on the murder but, more importantly, on the developing bond between the two women and their growing compassion for the accused.

Subplot

Tightly packed, the one-act *Trifles* contains a single plot: the story of how two women discover evidence that might hang another woman and then hide it. Some plays, usually longer ones, may be more complicated. They may contain a **double plot** (or **subplot**), a secondary arrangement of incidents, involving not the protagonist but someone less important. In Henrik Ibsen's *A Doll's House*, the main plot involves a woman and her husband; they are joined by a second couple, whose fortunes we also follow with interest and whose futures pose different questions.

Protagonist

If *Trifles* may be said to have a **protagonist**, a leading character—a word we usually save for the primary figure of a larger and more eventful play such as *Othello*—then you would call the two women dual protagonists. They act in unison to make the plot unfold. Or you could argue that Mrs. Hale—because she destroys the wild stitching in the quilt, because she finds the dead canary, because she invents a cat to catch the bird (thus deceiving the county attorney), and because in the end when Mrs. Peters helplessly "goes to pieces" it is she who takes the initiative and seizes the evidence—deserves to be called the protagonist. More than anyone else in the play, you could claim, the more decisive Mrs. Hale makes things happen.

Exposition

A vital part of most plays is an **exposition**, the part in which we first meet the characters, learn what happened before the curtain rose, and find out what is happening now. For a one-act play, *Trifles* has a fairly long exposition, extending from the opening of the kitchen door through the end of farmer Hale's story. Clearly, this substantial exposition is necessary to set the situation and to fill in the facts of the crime. By comparison, Shakespeare's far longer *Tragedy of Richard III* begins almost abruptly, with its protagonist, a duke who yearns to be king, summing up history in an opening speech and revealing his evil character: "And therefore, since I cannot prove a lover . . . I am determinèd to prove a villain." But Glaspell, too, knows her craft. In the exposition, we are given a **foreshadowing**—a hint of what is to come—in Hale's dry remark, "I didn't know as what his wife wanted made much difference to John." The remark announces the play's theme that men often ignore women's feelings, and it hints at Minnie Wright's motive, later to be revealed. The county attorney, failing to pick up a valuable clue, tables the discussion. (Still another foreshadowing occurs in Mrs. Hale's ripping out the wild, panicky stitches in Minnie's quilt. In the end, Mrs. Hale will make a similar final move to conceal the evidence.)

Dramatic Question

With the county attorney's speech to the sheriff, "You're convinced that there was nothing important here—nothing that would point to any motive," we begin to understand what he seeks. As he will make even clearer later, the attorney needs a motive in order to convict the accused wife of murder in the first degree. Will Minnie's motive in killing her husband be discovered? Through the first two-thirds of *Trifles*, this is the play's **dramatic question**. Whether or not we state such a question in our minds (and it is doubtful that we do), our interest quickens as we sense that here is a problem to be solved, an uncertainty to be cleared up. When Mrs. Hale and Mrs. Peters find the dead canary with the twisted neck, the question is answered. We know that Minnie killed John to repay him for his act of gross cruelty. The playwright, however, now raises a *new* dramatic question. Having discovered Minnie's motive, will the women reveal it to the lawmen? Alternatively (if you care to phrase the new question differently), what will they do with the incriminating evidence? We keep reading, or stay clamped to our theater seats, because we want that question answered. We share the women's secret now, and we want to see what they will do with it.

Climax

Step by step, *Trifles* builds to a **climax**: a moment, usually coming late in a play, when tension reaches its greatest height. At such a moment, we sense that the play's dramatic question (or its final dramatic question, if the writer has posed more than one) is about to be answered. In *Trifles* this climax occurs when Mrs. Peters finds herself torn between her desire to save Minnie and her duty to the law. "It was an awful thing was done in this house that night," she reminds herself in one speech, suggesting that Minnie deserves to be punished; then in the next speech she insists, "We don't know who killed him. We don't *know*." Shortly after that, in one speech she voices two warring attitudes. Remembering the loss of her first child, she sympathizes with Minnie: "I know what stillness is." But in her next breath she recalls once more her duty to be a loyal sheriff's wife: "The law has got to punish crime, Mrs. Hale." For a moment, she is placed in conflict with Mrs. Hale, who knew Minnie personally. The two now stand on the edge of a fateful brink. Which way will they decide?

You will sometimes hear climax used in a different sense to mean any **crisis**—that is, a moment of tension when one or another outcome is possible. What crisis means will be easy to remember if you think of a crisis in medicine: the turning point in an illness when it becomes clear that a patient will either die or recover. In talking about plays, you will probably find both crisis and climax useful. You can say that a play has more than one crisis, perhaps several. In such a play, the last and most decisive crisis is the climax. A play has only one climax.

Resolution and Dénouement

From this moment of climax, the play, like its protagonist (or if you like, protagonists), will make a final move. Mrs. Peters takes her stand. Mrs. Hale, too, decides. She owes Minnie something to make up for her own "crime"— her failure to visit the desperate woman. The plot now charges ahead to its outcome or **resolution**, also called the **conclusion** or **dénouement** (French for "untying of a knot"). The two women act: they scoop up the damaging evidence. Seconds before the very end, Glaspell heightens the **suspense**, our enjoyable anxiety, by making Mrs. Peters fumble with the incriminating box as the sheriff and the county attorney draw near. Mrs. Hale's swift grab for the evidence saves the day and presumably saves Minnie's life. The sound of the doorknob turning in the next room, as the lawmen return, is a small but effective bit of **stage business**—any nonverbal action that engages the attention of an audience. Earlier, when Mrs. Hale almost sits down in Minnie's place, the empty chair that ominously starts rocking is another brilliant piece of stage business. Not only does it give us something interesting to watch, but it also gives us something to think about.

Rising and Falling Action

The German critic Gustav Freytag maintained that events in a plot can be arranged in the outline of a pyramid. In his influential view, a play begins with a **rising action**, that part of the narrative (including the exposition) in which events start moving toward a climax. After the climax, the story tapers off in a **falling action**—that is, the subsequent events, including a resolution. In a tragedy, this falling action usually is recognizable: the protagonist's fortunes proceed downhill to an inevitable end.

Some plays indeed have demonstrable pyramids. In *Trifles*, we might claim that in the first two-thirds of the play a rising action builds in intensity. It proceeds through each main incident: the finding of the crazily stitched quilt, Mrs. Hale's ripping out the evidence, the discovery of the birdcage, then of the bird itself, and Mrs. Hale's concealing it. At the climax, the peak of the pyramid, the two women seem about to clash as Mrs. Peters wavers uncertainly. The action then falls to a swift resolution. If you outlined that pyramid on paper, however, it would look lopsided—a long rise and a short, steep fall. The pyramid metaphor seems more meaningfully to fit longer plays, among them some classic tragedies, such as *Oedipus the King*. Nevertheless, in most other plays, it is hard to find a symmetrical pyramid.

Unity of Time, Place, and Action

Because its action occurs all at one time and in one place, *Trifles* happens to observe the **unities**, certain principles of good drama laid down by Italian literary critics in the sixteenth century. Interpreting the theories of Aristotle as binding laws, these critics set down three basic principles: a good play, they maintained, should display unity of *action*, unity of *time*, and unity of *place*. In practical terms, this theory maintained that a play must represent a single series of interrelated actions that take place within twenty-four hours in a single location. Furthermore, they insisted, to have true unity of action, a play had to be entirely serious or entirely funny. Mixing tragic and comic elements was not allowed. That Glaspell consciously strove to obey those critics is doubtful, and certainly many great plays, such as Shakespeare's *Othello*, defy such arbitrary rules. Still, it is at least arguable that some of the power of *Trifles* (or Sophocles's *Oedipus the King*) comes from the intensity of the playwright's concentration on what happens in one place, in one short expanse of time.

Symbols in Drama

Brief though it is, *Trifles* has main elements you will find in much longer, more complicated plays. It even has **symbols**, things that hint at large meanings— for example, the broken birdcage and the dead canary, both suggesting the music and the joy that John Wright stifled in Minnie and the terrible stillness that followed his killing the one thing she loved. Perhaps the lone remaining jar of cherries, too, radiates suggestions: it is the one bright, cheerful thing poor Minnie has to show for a whole summer of toil. Plays can also contain symbolic characters (generally flat ones such as a prophet who croaks, "Beware the ides of March"), symbolic settings, and symbolic gestures. Symbols in drama may be as big as a house—the home in Ibsen's *A Doll's House*, for instance—or they may appear to be trifles. In Glaspell's rich art, such trifles aren't trifling at all.

▓ WRITING *effectively*

THINKING ABOUT A PLAY

A good play almost always presents a conflict. Conflict creates suspense and keeps an audience from meandering out to the lobby water fountain. Without it, a play would be static and, most likely, dull. When a character intensely desires something but some obstacle—perhaps another character—stands in the way, the result is dramatic tension. To understand a play, it is essential to understand the basic conflicts motivating the plot.

- **Identify the play's protagonist.** Who is the central character of the play? What motivates this character? What does this character want most to achieve or avoid? Is this goal reasonable or does it reflect some delusion on the part of the protagonist?
- **Identify the antagonist.** Who prevents the main character from achieving his or her goal? Is the opposition conscious or accidental? What motivates this character to oppose the protagonist?
- **Identify the central dramatic conflict.** What does the struggle between the protagonist and antagonist focus on? Is it another person, a possession, an action, some sort of recognition, or honor?

▪ **How does the conflict influence the action of the play?** The central conflict usually fuels the plot, causing characters to do and say all sorts of things they might not otherwise undertake. What series of later events does the central conflict set in motion?

CHECKLIST: Writing About a Play

☐ List the play's three or four main characters. Jot down what each character wants most at the play's beginning.

☐ Which of these characters is the protagonist?

☐ What stands in the way of the protagonist achieving his or her goal?

☐ How do the other characters' motivations fit into the central conflict? Identify any double plots or subplots.

☐ What are the play's main events? How does each relate to the protagonist's struggle?

☐ Where do you find the play's climax?

☐ How is the conflict resolved? What qualities in the protagonist's character bring about the play's outcome?

☐ Does the protagonist achieve his or her goal? How does success or failure affect the protagonist?

TOPICS FOR WRITING ON *TRIFLES*

1. Write a brief essay on the role gender differences play in Susan Glaspell's *Trifles*.

2. Write an analysis of the exposition—how the scene is set, characters introduced, and background information communicated—in *Trifles*.

3. Describe the significance of setting in *Trifles*.

4. Imagine you are a lawyer hired to defend Minnie Wright. Present your closing argument to the jury.

5. Watch any hour-long television drama. Write about the main conflict that drives the story. What motivates the protagonist? What stands in his or her way? How do each of the drama's main events relate to the protagonist's struggle? How is the conflict resolved? Is the show's outcome connected to the protagonist's character, or do events just happen to him or her? Do you believe the script is well written? Why or why not?

6. Select any short play, and write a brief essay identifying the protagonist, central conflict, and dramatic question.

► TERMS FOR *review*

To review definitions of the elements of plot (**protagonist, antagonist, exposition, conflict, complication, crisis, climax**, and **conclusion**), see Chapter 1 "Terms for Review" on pages 26 and 27.

Double plot ► Also called **subplot**. A second story or plotline that is complete and interesting in its own right, often doubling or inverting the main plot.

Unities ► Unity of time, place, and action, the three formal qualities recommended by Renaissance critics to give a theatrical plot cohesion and integrity. According to this theory, a play should depict the causes and effects of a single action unfolding in one day in one place.

Soliloquy ► In drama, a speech by a character alone onstage in which he or she utters his or her thoughts aloud.

Aside ► A speech that a character addresses directly to the audience, unheard by the other characters on stage, as when the villain in a melodrama chortles: "Heh! Heh! Now she's in my power!"

Stage business ► Nonverbal action that engages the attention of an audience.

24 TRAGEDY AND COMEDY

What You Will Learn in This Chapter
- To define tragedy as a dramatic mode
- To define comedy as a dramatic mode
- To explain the difference between tragedy and comedy
- To understand and describe the various levels and kinds of comedy

In 1770, Horace Walpole wrote, "the world is a comedy to those that think, a tragedy to those that feel." All of us, of course, both think and feel, and all of us have moments when we stand back and laugh, whether ruefully or with glee, at life's absurdities, just as we all have times when our hearts are broken by its pains and losses. Thus, the modes of tragedy and comedy, diametrically opposed to one another though they are, do not demand that we choose between them: both of them speak to something deep and real within us, and each of them has its own truth to tell about the infinitely complex experience of living in this world.

TRAGEDY

By **tragedy** we mean a play that portrays a serious conflict between human beings and some superior, overwhelming force. It ends sorrowfully and disastrously, and this outcome seems inevitable. Few spectators of *Oedipus the King* wonder how the play will turn out or wish for a happy ending. "In a tragedy," French playwright Jean Anouilh has remarked, "nothing is in doubt and everyone's destiny is known. . . . Tragedy is restful, and the reason is that hope, that foul, deceitful thing, has no part in it. There isn't any hope. You're trapped. The whole sky has fallen on you, and all you can do about it is shout."[1]

Many of our ideas of tragedy (from the Greek *tragoidia*, "goat song," referring to the goatskin dress of the performers) go back to ancient Athens; the plays of the Greek dramatists Sophocles, Aeschylus, and Euripides exemplify the art of tragedy. In the fourth century B.C., the philosopher Aristotle described Sophocles's *Oedipus the King* and other tragedies he had seen, analyzing their elements and trying to account for their power over our emotions.

---

[1]Anouilh, Jean, "Preface," *Antigone*, trans. Lewis Galantière (New York: Random, 1946) 24.

Aristotle's observations will make more sense after you read *Oedipus the King*, so we will save our principal discussion of them for the next chapter. But for now, to understand something of the nature of tragedy, let us take a brief overview of the subject.

One of the oldest and most durable of literary genres, tragedy is also one of the simplest—the protagonist undergoes a reversal of fortune, from good to bad, ending in catastrophe. However simple, though, tragedy can be one of the most complex genres to explain satisfactorily, with almost every principal point of its definition open to differing and often hotly debated interpretations. It is a fluid and adaptive genre, and for every one of its defining points, we can cite a tragic masterpiece that fails to observe that particular convention. Its fluidity and adaptability can also be shown by the way in which the classical tragic pattern is played out in pure form in such unlikely places as Orson Welles's film *Citizen Kane* (1941) and Chinua Achebe's great novel *Things Fall Apart* (1958): in each of these works, a man of high position and character—one a multimillionaire newspaper publisher, the other a late nineteenth-century African warrior—moves inexorably to destruction, impelled by his rigidity and self-righteousness. Even a movie such as *King Kong*—despite its oversized and hirsute protagonist—exemplifies some of the principles of tragedy.

To gain a clearer understanding of what tragedy is, let us first take a moment to talk about what it is not. Consider the kinds of events that customarily bring the term "tragedy" to mind: the death of a child, a fire that destroys a family's home and possessions, the killing of a bystander caught in the crossfire of a shootout between criminals, and so on. What all of these unfortunate instances have in common, obviously, is that they involve the infliction of great and irreversible suffering. But what they also share is the sense that the sufferers are innocent, that they have done nothing to cause or to deserve their fate. This is what we usually describe as a tragedy in real life, but tragedy in a literary or dramatic context has a different meaning: most theorists take their lead from Aristotle (see the next chapter for a fuller discussion of several of the points raised here) in maintaining that the protagonist's reversal of fortune is brought about through some error or weakness on his part, generally referred to as his **tragic flaw**.

Despite this weakness, the hero is traditionally a person of nobility, of both social rank and personality. Just as the suffering of totally innocent people stirs us to sympathetic sorrow rather than a tragic response, so too the destruction of a purely evil figure, a tyrant or a murderer with no redeeming qualities, would inspire only feelings of relief and satisfaction—hardly the emotions that tragedy seeks to stimulate. In most tragedies, the catastrophe entails not only the loss of outward fortune—things such as reputation, power, and life itself, which even the basest villain may possess and then be deprived of—but also the erosion of the protagonist's moral character and greatness of spirit.

Tragic Style

In keeping with this emphasis on nobility of spirit, tragedies are customarily written in an elevated style, one characterized by dignity and seriousness. In the Middle Ages, just as *tragedy* meant a work written in a high style in which the central character went from good fortune to bad, *comedy* indicated just the opposite, a work written in a low or common style, in which the protagonist moved from adverse circumstances to happy ones—hence Dante's great triptych of hell, purgatory, and heaven, written in everyday Italian rather than scholarly Latin, is known as *The Divine Comedy*, despite the relative absence of humor, let alone hilarity, in its pages. The tragic view of life, clearly, presupposes that in the end we will prove unequal to the challenges we must face, while the comic outlook asserts a view of human possibility in which our common sense and resilience—or pure dumb luck—will enable us to win out.

Tragedy's complexity can be seen also in the response that, according to Aristotle, it seeks to arouse in the viewer: pity and fear. By its very nature, pity distances the one who pities from the object of that pity, since we can feel sorry only for those whom we perceive to be worse off than ourselves. When we watch or read a tragedy, moved as we may be, we observe the downfall of the protagonist with a certain detachment; "better him than me" may be a rather crude way of putting it, but perhaps not an entirely incorrect one. Fear, on the other hand, usually involves an immediate anxiety about our own well-being. Even as we regard the hero's destruction from the safety of a better place, we are made to feel our own vulnerability in the face of life's dangers and instability, because we see that neither position nor virtue can protect even the great from ruin.

The following is a scene from Christopher Marlowe's classic Elizabethan tragedy *Doctor Faustus*. Based on an anonymous pamphlet published in Germany in 1587 and translated into English shortly thereafter, this celebrated play tells the story of an elderly professor who feels that he has wasted his life in fruitless inquiry. Chafing at the limits of human understanding, he makes a pact with the devil to gain forbidden knowledge and power. The scene presented here is the decisive turning point of the play, in which Faustus seals the satanic bargain that will damn him. Stimulated by his thirst for knowledge and experience, spurred on by his pride to assume that the divinely ordained limits of human experience no longer apply to him, he rushes to embrace his own undoing. Marlowe dramatizes Faustus's situation by bringing a good angel and a fallen angel (i.e., a demon) to whisper conflicting advice in this pivotal scene. (This good angel versus bad angel device has proved popular for centuries. We still see it today in everything from TV commercials to cartoons such as *The Simpsons*.) Notice the dignified and often gorgeous language Marlowe employs to create the serious mood necessary for tragedy.

Christopher Marlowe

Scene from **Doctor Faustus**[2]   (about 1588)

Edited by Sylvan Barnet

*Christopher Marlowe was born in Canterbury, England, in February 1564, about ten weeks before William Shakespeare. Marlowe, the son of a prosperous shoemaker, received a B.A. from Cambridge University in 1584 and an M.A. in 1587, after which he settled in London. The rest of his short life was marked by rumor, secrecy, and violence, including suspicions that he was a secret agent for Queen Elizabeth's government and allegations against him of blasphemy and atheism—no small matter in light of the political instability and religious controversies of the times. Peripherally implicated in several violent deaths, he met his own end in May 1593 when he was stabbed above the right eye during a tavern brawl, under circumstances that have never been fully explained. Brief and crowded as his life was, he wrote a number of intense, powerful, and highly influential tragedies—*Tamburlaine the Great, Parts 1 and 2 *(1587)*, *Doctor Faustus *(1588)*, The Jew of Malta *(1589)*, Edward the Second *(c. 1592)*, The Massacre at Paris *(1593)*, and *Dido, Queen of Carthage *(c. 1593, with Thomas Nashe). He is also the author of the lyric poem "The Passionate Shepherd to His Love," with its universally known first line: "Come live with me and be my love."*

Doctor Faustus with the Bad Angel and the Good Angel, from the Utah Shakespearean Festival's 2005 production.

[2]This scene is from the 1616 text, or "B-Text," published as *The Tragicall History of the Life and Death of Doctor Faustus.* Modernizations have been made in spelling and punctuation.

DRAMATIS PERSONAE

Doctor Faustus
Good Angel
Bad Angel
Mephistophilis, a devil

ACT II

SCENE I

(*Enter Faustus in his study.*)

Faustus: Now, Faustus, must thou needs be damned;
Canst thou not be saved!
What boots° it then to think on God or heaven?
Away with such vain fancies, and despair—
Despair in God and trust in Belzebub!   5
Now go not backward Faustus; be resolute!
Why waver'st thou? O something soundeth in mine ear,
"Abjure this magic, turn to God again."
Ay, and Faustus will turn to God again.
To God? He loves thee not.   10
The god thou serv'st is thine own appetite
Wherein is fixed the love of Belzebub!
To him I'll build an altar and a church,
And offer lukewarm blood of newborn babes!

(*Enter the two Angels.*)

Bad Angel: Go forward, Faustus, in that famous art.   15
Good Angel: Sweet Faustus, leave that execrable art.
Faustus: Contrition, prayer, repentance? What of these?
Good Angel: O, they are means to bring thee unto heaven.
Bad Angel: Rather illusions, fruits of lunacy,
That make men foolish that do use them most.   20
Good Angel: Sweet Faustus, think of heaven and heavenly things.
Bad Angel: No, Faustus, think of honor and of wealth.
                                            (*Exeunt Angels.*)

Faustus: Wealth!
Why, the signory of Emden° shall be mine!
When Mephistophilis shall stand by me   25
What power can hurt me? Faustus, thou art safe.
Cast no more doubts! Mephistophilis, come,

---

3 *boots:* avails.   24 *signory of Emden:* lordship of the rich German port at the mouth of the Ems.

And bring glad tidings from great Lucifer.
Is't not midnight? Come Mephistophilis,
Veni, veni, Mephostophile!°   30

(Enter Mephistophilis.)

Now tell me, what saith Lucifer thy lord?
Mephistophilis: That I shall wait on Faustus whilst he lives,
    So he will buy my service with his soul.
Faustus: Already Faustus hath hazarded that for thee.
Mephistophilis: But now thou must bequeath it solemnly   35
    And write a deed of gift with thine own blood,
    For that security craves Lucifer.
    If thou deny it I must back to hell.
Faustus: Stay Mephistophilis and tell me,
    What good will my soul do thy lord?   40
Mephistophilis: Enlarge his kingdom.
Faustus: Is that the reason why he tempts us thus?
Mephistophilis: Solamen miseris socios habuisse doloris.°
Faustus: Why, have you any pain that torture other?°
Mephistophilis: As great as have the human souls of men.   45
    But tell me, Faustus, shall I have thy soul—
    And I will be thy slave and wait on thee
    And give thee more than thou hast wit to ask?
Faustus: Ay Mephistophilis, I'll give it him.°
Mephistophilis: Then, Faustus, stab thy arm courageously,   50
    And bind thy soul, that at some certain day
    Great Lucifer may claim it as his own.
    And then be thou as great as Lucifer!
Faustus: Lo, Mephistophilis: for love of thee
    Faustus hath cut his arm, and with his proper° blood   55
    Assures° his soul to be great Lucifer's,
    Chief Lord and Regent of perpetual night.
    View here this blood that trickles from mine arm,
    And let it be propitious for my wish.
Mephistophilis: But, Faustus,   60
    Write it in manner of a deed of gift.
Faustus: Ay, so I do—But Mephistophilis,
    My blood congeals and I can write no more.
Mephistophilis: I'll fetch thee fire to dissolve it straight.

                                                                                        (Exit.)

Faustus: What might the staying of my blood portend?   65

---

30 *Veni, veni, Mephostophile!*: Come, come, Mephistophilis (Latin).   43 *Solamen . . . doloris:*
Misery loves company (Latin).   44 *other:* others.   49 *him:* i.e., to Lucifer.   55 *proper:* own.
56 *Assures:* conveys by contract.

Is it unwilling I should write this bill?°
Why streams it not that I may write afresh:
"Faustus gives to thee his soul"? O there it stayed.
Why should'st thou not? Is not thy soul thine own?
Then write again: "Faustus gives to thee his soul."   70

(Enter Mephistophilis, with the chafer° of fire.)

Mephistophilis: See, Faustus, here is fire. Set it° on.
Faustus: So, now the blood begins to clear again.
      Now will I make an end immediately.
Mephistophilis (aside): What will not I do to obtain his soul!
Faustus: Consummatum est!° This bill is ended: 75
      And Faustus hath bequeathed his soul to Lucifer.
      —But what is this inscription on mine arm?
      Homo fuge!° Whither should I fly?
      If unto God, He'll throw me down to hell.
      My senses are deceived; here's nothing writ.   80
      O yes, I see it plain! Even here is writ
      Homo fuge! Yet shall not Faustus fly!
Mephistophilis (aside): I'll fetch him somewhat° to delight his mind.
                                                  (Exit Mephistophilis.)

*(Enter Devils, giving crowns and rich apparel to Faustus. They dance and
then depart.)*

(Enter Mephistophilis.)

Faustus: What means this show? Speak, Mephistophilis.
Mephistophilis: Nothing, Faustus, but to delight thy mind,   85
      And let thee see what magic can perform.
Faustus: But may I raise such spirits when I please?
Mephistophilis: Ay, Faustus, and do greater things than these.
Faustus: Then, Mephistophilis, receive this scroll,
      A deed of gift of body and of soul: 90
      But yet conditionally that thou perform
      All covenants and articles between us both.
Mephistophilis: Faustus, I swear by hell and Lucifer
      To effect all promises between us both.
Faustus: Then hear me read it, Mephistophilis: 95

      "On these conditions following:

66 *bill:* contract.   70 s.d. *chafer:* portable grate.   71 *it:* i.e., the receptacle containing the congealed blood.   75 *Consummatum est:* It is finished. (Latin: a blasphemous repetition of Christ's words on the Cross; see John 19:30.)   78 *Homo fuge:* fly, man (Latin).   83 *somewhat:* something.

First, that Faustus may be a spirit° in form and substance.

Secondly, that Mephistophilis shall be his servant, and be by him commanded.

Thirdly, that Mephistophilis shall do for him and bring him what- 100
soever.

Fourthly, that he shall be in his chamber or house invisible.

Lastly, that he shall appear to the said John Faustus, at all times, in
what shape and form soever he please.

I, John Faustus of Wittenberg, Doctor, by these presents, do give 105
both body and soul to Lucifer, Prince of the East, and his minister
Mephistophilis, and furthermore grant unto them that, four and
twenty years being expired, and these articles written being inviolate,°
full power to fetch or carry the said John Faustus, body and soul, flesh,
blood, into their habitation wheresoever. 110

> By me John Faustus."

Mephistophilis: Speak, Faustus, do you deliver this as your deed?
Faustus: Ay, take it, and the devil give thee good of it!
Mephistophilis: So, now Faustus, ask me what thou wilt.
Faustus: First, I will question with thee about hell. 115
  Tell me, where is the place that men call hell?
Mephistophilis: Under the heavens.
Faustus: Ay, so are all things else, but whereabouts?
Mephistophilis: Within the bowels of these elements,
  Where we are tortured, and remain forever. 120
  Hell hath no limits, nor is circumscribed,
  In one self place, but where we are is hell,
  And where hell is there must we ever be.
  And to be short, when all the world dissolves,
  And every creature shall be purified, 125
  All places shall be hell that is not heaven!
Faustus: I think hell's a fable.
Mephistophilis: Ay, think so still—till experience change thy mind.
Faustus: Why, dost thou think that Faustus shall be damned?
Mephistophilis: Ay, of necessity, for here's the scroll 130
  In which thou hast given thy soul to Lucifer.
Faustus: Ay, and body too; but what of that?
  Think'st thou that Faustus is so fond° to imagine,

---

97 *spirit:* evil spirit, devil. (But to see Faustus as transformed now into a devil deprived of freedom
to repent is to deprive the remainder of the play of much of its meaning.)   108 *inviolate:* unvio-
lated.   133 *fond:* foolish.

That after this life there is any pain?
No, these are trifles, and mere old wives' tales.   135
Mephistophilis: But I am an instance to prove the contrary,
For I tell thee I am damned, and now in hell!
Faustus: Nay, and this be hell, I'll willingly be damned—
What, sleeping, eating, walking, and disputing?
But leaving this, let me have a wife,   140
The fairest maid in Germany,
For I am wanton and lascivious,
And cannot live without a wife.
Mephistophilis: Well, Faustus, thou shalt have a wife.

(*He fetches in a woman devil.*)

Faustus: What sight is this?   145
Mephistophilis: Now, Faustus, wilt thou have a wife?
Faustus: Here's a hot whore indeed! No, I'll no wife.
Mephistophilis: Marriage is but a ceremonial toy,°

(*Exit she-devil.*)

And if thou lov'st me, think no more of it.
I'll cull thee out° the fairest courtesans   150
And bring them every morning to thy bed.
She whom thine eye shall like, thy heart shall have,
Were she as chaste as was Penelope,°
As wise as Saba,° or as beautiful
As was bright Lucifer before his fall.   155
Here, take this book and peruse it well.
The iterating° of these lines brings gold;
The framing° of this circle on the ground
Brings thunder, whirlwinds, storm, and lightning;
Pronounce this thrice devoutly to thyself,   160
And men in harness° shall appear to thee,
Ready to execute what thou command'st.
Faustus: Thanks, Mephistophilis, for this sweet book.
This will I keep as chary as my life.

(*Exeunt.*)

Questions

1. What specifically motivates Faustus to make his satanic compact? Cite the text to back up your response.
2. How does his behavior constitute a compromise of his nobility?
3. "Is not thy soul thine own?" Faustus asks rhetorically (line 69). Discuss the implications of this statement in terms of the larger thematic concerns of the work.
4. Does Faustus inspire your pity and fear in this scene? Why or why not?

---

148 *toy:* trifle.   150 *cull thee out:* select for you.   153 *Penelope:* wife of Ulysses, famed for her fidelity. 154 *Saba:* the Queen of Sheba.   157 *iterating:* repetition.   158 *framing:* drawing.   161 *harness:* armor.

Traditional masks of comedy and tragedy.

COMEDY

The best-known traditional emblem of drama—a pair of masks, one sorrowful (representing tragedy) and one smiling (representing comedy)—suggests that tragedy and comedy, although opposites, are close relatives. Often, comedy shows people getting into trouble through error or weakness; in this respect it is akin to tragedy. An important difference between comedy and tragedy lies in the attitude toward human failing that is expected of us. When a main character in a comedy suffers from overweening pride, as does Oedipus, or if he fails to recognize that his bride-to-be is actually his mother, we laugh—something we would never do in watching a competent performance of *Oedipus the King*.

Comedy, from the Greek *komos*, "a revel," is thought to have originated in festivities to celebrate spring, ritual performances in praise of Dionysus, god of fertility and wine. In drama, comedy may be broadly defined as whatever makes us laugh. A comedy may be a name for one entire play, or we may say that there is comedy in only part of a play—as in a comic character or a comic situation.

Theories of Comedy

Many theories have been propounded to explain why we laugh; most of these notions fall into a few familiar types. One school, exemplified by French philosopher Henri Bergson, sees laughter as a form of ridicule, implying a feeling of disinterested superiority; all jokes are *on* somebody. Bergson suggests that laughter springs from situations in which we sense a conflict between some mechanical or rigid pattern of behavior and our sense of a more natural or "organic" kind of behavior that is possible. An example occurs in Buster Keaton's comic film *The Boat*. Having launched a little boat that springs a leak, Keaton rigidly goes down with it, with frozen face. (The more natural and organic thing to do would be to swim for shore.)

Other thinkers view laughter as our response to expectations fulfilled or to expectations set up but then suddenly frustrated. Some hold it to be the expression of our delight in seeing our suppressed urges acted out (as when a comedian hurls an egg at a pompous stuffed shirt); some, to be our defensive reaction to a painful and disturbing truth.

Satiric Comedy

Derisive humor is basic to **satiric comedy**, in which human weakness or folly is ridiculed from a vantage point of supposedly enlightened superiority. Satiric comedy may be coolly malicious and gently biting, but it tends to be critical of people, their manners, and their morals. It is at least as old as the comedies of Aristophanes, who thrived in the fifth century B.C. In *Lysistrata*, the satirist shows how the women of two warring cities speedily halt a war by agreeing to deny themselves to their husbands. (The satirist's target is men so proud that they go to war rather than make the slightest concession.)

High Comedy

Comedy is often divided into two varieties—"high" and "low." **High comedy** relies more on wit and wordplay than on physical action for its humor. It tries to address the audience's intelligence by pointing out the pretension and hypocrisy of human behavior. High comedy also generally avoids derisive humor. Jokes about physical appearance would, for example, be avoided. One technique it employs to appeal to a sophisticated, verbal audience is use of the **epigram**, a brief and witty statement that memorably expresses some truth, large or small. Oscar Wilde's plays such as *The Importance of Being Earnest* (1895) and *Lady Windermere's Fan* (1892) sparkle with such brilliant epigrams as: "I can resist everything except temptation"; "Experience is the name everyone gives to their mistakes"; "There is only one thing in the world worse than being talked about, and that is not being talked about."

Low Comedy

Low comedy explores the opposite extreme of humor. It places greater emphasis on physical action and visual gags, and its verbal jokes do not require much intellect to appreciate (as in Groucho Marx's pithy put-down to his brother Chico, "You have the brain of a five-year-old, and I bet he was glad to get rid of it!"). Low comedy does not avoid derisive humor; rather, it revels in making fun of whatever will get a good laugh. Drunkenness, stupidity, lust, senility, trickery, insult, and clumsiness are inexhaustible staples of this style of comedy. Although it is all too easy for critics to dismiss low comedy, like high comedy it serves a valuable purpose in satirizing human failings. Shakespeare indulged in coarse humor in some of his noblest plays. Low comedy is usually the preferred style of popular culture, and it has inspired many incisive satires on modern life—from the classic films of W. C. Fields and the Marx Brothers to the weekly TV antics of Matt Groening's *The Simpsons* or Tina Fey's *30 Rock*.

    Low comedy includes several distinct types. One is the **burlesque**, a broadly humorous parody or travesty of another play or kind of play. (In the United States, *burlesque* is something else: a once-popular form of variety show featuring stripteases interspersed with bits of ribald low comedy.) Another valuable type of low comedy is the **farce**, a broadly humorous play whose action is usually fast-moving and improbable. **Slapstick comedy** (such as that of the Three Stooges) is a kind of farce. Featuring pratfalls, pie-throwing, fisti-cuffs, and other violent action, it takes its name from a circus clown's prop—a bat with two boards that loudly clap together when one clown swats another.

Romantic Comedy

Romantic comedy, another traditional sort of comedy, is subtler. Its main characters are generally lovers, and its plot unfolds their ultimately successful strivings to be united. Unlike satiric comedy, romantic comedy portrays its characters not with withering contempt but with kindly indulgence. It may take place in the everyday world, or perhaps in some never-never land, such as the forest of Arden in Shakespeare's *As You Like It*. Romantic comedy is also a popular staple of Hollywood, which depicts two people undergoing humorous mishaps on their way to falling in love. The characters often suf-fer humiliation and discomfort along the way, but these moments are funny rather than sad, and the characters are rewarded in the end by true love.

Here is an example of high comedy—a scene from the first act of Oscar Wilde's classic play, *The Importance of Being Earnest*. Following that is *Soap Opera*, a short contemporary comedy by David Ives, one of America's most ingenious playwrights.

Oscar Wilde

Scene from The Importance of Being Earnest: Lady Bracknell Interviews Her Daughter's Suitor 1895

Oscar Fingal O'Flahertie Wills Wilde (1854–1900) was born in Ireland to a mother who wrote revolutionary poetry and a philandering father who was an eye and ear surgeon. Wilde was a top student at Trinity College in Dublin and then Magdalen College in Oxford. After settling in London, Wilde married Con-stance Lloyd and promptly had two sons. Soon after, he entered his years of great productivity. He published two volumes of fairy tales and his sole novel, The Picture of Dorian Gray (1891), which critics derided for its homosexual under-tones. However, it was Wilde's plays that marked him as one of the great writers of England's late-Victorian era. He wrote a string of successes that started with Lady Windermere's Fan (1892) and culminated with his masterpiece, The Im-portance of Being Earnest (1895). His comedies focused on high society, the stratum in which Wilde was famously popular. It was said that he was London's "most sought-after dinner guest" and was known for his boundless wit and his many epigrams, such as "Work is the curse of the drinking classes." In 1895 Wilde endured a very public and humiliating legal battle over accusations of "gross indecency" with men, and he was sentenced to two years of hard labor, which devastated him as an artist. Upon his release, Wilde wandered Europe under the name Sebastian Melmoth. Three years later he died of meningitis in Paris, with barely a penny to his name.

A 2008 production of *The Importance of Being Earnest*, by the Vaudeville Theatre of London.

CHARACTERS

Lady Bracknell, mother of Gwendolen Fairfax
Jack, the suitor

SCENE. *Morning-room in Algernon's flat in Half-Moon Street. The room is luxuriously and artistically furnished. The sound of a piano is heard in the adjoining room.*

The following is an excerpt from Act I, Scene 1 of the play.

Lady Bracknell (sitting down): You can take a seat, Mr. Worthing.

(*Looks in her pocket for note-book and pencil.*)

Jack: Thank you, Lady Bracknell, I prefer standing.
Lady Bracknell (pencil and note-book in hand): I feel bound to tell you that you are not down on my list of eligible young men, although I have the same list as the dear Duchess of Bolton has. We work together, in fact. However, I am quite ready to enter your name, should your answers be what a really affectionate mother requires. Do you smoke?
Jack: Well, yes, I must admit I smoke.
Lady Bracknell: I am glad to hear it. A man should always have an occupation of some kind. There are far too many idle men in London as it is. How old are you?
Jack: Twenty-nine.

Lady Bracknell: A very good age to be married at. I have always been of opinion that a man who desires to get married should know either everything or nothing. Which do you know?

Jack (after some hesitation): I know nothing, Lady Bracknell.

Lady Bracknell: I am pleased to hear it. I do not approve of anything that tampers with natural ignorance. Ignorance is like a delicate exotic fruit; touch it and the bloom is gone. The whole theory of modern education is radically unsound. Fortunately in England, at any rate, education produces no effect whatsoever. If it did, it would prove a serious danger to the upper classes, and probably lead to acts of violence in Grosvenor Square. What is your income?

Jack: Between seven and eight thousand a year.

Lady Bracknell (makes a note in her book): In land, or in investments?

Jack: In investments, chiefly.

Lady Bracknell: That is satisfactory. What between the duties expected of one during one's lifetime, and the duties exacted from one after one's death, land has ceased to be either a profit or a pleasure. It gives one position, and prevents one from keeping it up. That's all that can be said about land.

Jack: I have a country house with some land, of course, attached to it, about fifteen hundred acres, I believe; but I don't depend on that for my real income. In fact, as far as I can make out, the poachers are the only people who make anything out of it.

Lady Bracknell: A country house! How many bedrooms? Well, that point can be cleared up afterwards. You have a town house, I hope? A girl with a simple, unspoiled nature, like Gwendolen, could hardly be expected to reside in the country.

Jack: Well, I own a house in Belgrave Square, but it is let by the year to Lady Bloxham. Of course, I can get it back whenever I like, at six months' notice.

Lady Bracknell: Lady Bloxham? I don't know her.

Jack: Oh, she goes about very little. She is a lady considerably advanced in years.

Lady Bracknell: Ah, nowadays that is no guarantee of respectability of character. What number in Belgrave Square?

Jack: 149.

Lady Bracknell (shaking her head): The unfashionable side. I thought there was something. However, that could easily be altered.

Jack: Do you mean the fashion, or the side?

Lady Bracknell (sternly): Both, if necessary, I presume. What are your politics?

Jack: Well, I am afraid I really have none. I am a Liberal Unionist.

Lady Bracknell: Oh, they count as Tories. They dine with us. Or come in the evening, at any rate. Now to minor matters. Are your parents living?

Jack: I have lost both my parents.

Lady Bracknell: To lose one parent, Mr. Worthing, may be regarded as a misfortune; to lose both looks like carelessness. Who was your father? He was evidently a man of some wealth. Was he born in what the Radical papers call the purple of commerce, or did he rise from the ranks of the aristocracy?

Jack: I am afraid I really don't know. The fact is, Lady Bracknell, I said I had lost my parents. It would be nearer the truth to say that my parents seem to have lost me . . . I don't actually know who I am by birth. I was . . . well, I was found.

Lady Bracknell: Found!

Jack: The late Mr. Thomas Cardew, an old gentleman of a very charitable and kindly disposition, found me, and gave me the name of Worthing, because he happened to have a first-class ticket for Worthing in his pocket at the time. Worthing is a place in Sussex. It is a seaside resort.

Lady Bracknell: Where did the charitable gentleman who had a first-class ticket for this seaside resort find you?

Jack (gravely): In a hand-bag.

Lady Bracknell: A hand-bag?

Jack (very seriously): Yes, Lady Bracknell. I was in a hand-bag—a somewhat large, black leather hand-bag, with handles to it—an ordinary hand-bag in fact.

Lady Bracknell: In what locality did this Mr. James, or Thomas, Cardew come across this ordinary hand-bag?

Jack: In the cloak-room at Victoria Station. It was given to him in mistake for his own.

Lady Bracknell: The cloak-room at Victoria Station?

Jack: Yes. The Brighton line.

Lady Bracknell: The line is immaterial. Mr. Worthing, I confess I feel somewhat bewildered by what you have just told me. To be born, or at any rate bred, in a hand-bag, whether it had handles or not, seems to me to display a contempt for the ordinary decencies of family life that reminds one of the worst excesses of the French Revolution. And I presume you know what that unfortunate movement led to? As for the particular locality in which the hand-bag was found, a cloak-room at a railway station might serve to conceal a social indiscretion—has probably, indeed, been used for that purpose before now—but it could hardly be regarded as an assured basis for a recognised position in good society.

Jack: May I ask you then what you would advise me to do? I need hardly say I would do anything in the world to ensure Gwendolen's happiness.

Lady Bracknell: I would strongly advise you, Mr. Worthing, to try and acquire some relations as soon as possible, and to make a definite effort to produce at any rate one parent, of either sex, before the season is quite over.

Jack: Well, I don't see how I could possibly manage to do that. I can produce the hand-bag at any moment. It is in my dressing-room at home. I really think that should satisfy you, Lady Bracknell.

Lady Bracknell: Me, sir! What has it to do with me? You can hardly imagine that I and Lord Bracknell would dream of allowing our only daughter—a girl brought up with the utmost care—to marry into a cloak-room, and form an alliance with a parcel? Good morning, Mr. Worthing!

(*Lady Bracknell sweeps out in majestic indignation.*)

Questions

1. How would you characterize Lady Bracknell? What are her chief concerns in interviewing her daughter's suitor? Find examples from the text to support your argument.
2. Describe Jack's tone. Does he seem amused with Lady Bracknell, nervous about the interview, or genuinely eager to please her?
3. Would you call this passage high comedy or low? Explain the reasons for your choice.

David Ives

Soap Opera   1999

David Ives (b. 1950) grew up on the South Side of Chicago. He attended Catholic schools before entering Northwestern University. Later Ives studied at the Yale Drama School—"a blissful time for me," he recalls, "in spite of the fact that there is slush on the ground in New Haven 238 days a year." Ives received his first professional production in Los Angeles at the age of twenty-one "at America's smallest, and possibly worst theater, in a storefront that had a pillar dead center in the middle of the stage." He continued writing for the theater while working as an editor at Foreign Affairs, *and gradually achieved*

David Ives

a reputation in theatrical circles for his wildly original and brilliantly written short comic plays. His public breakthrough came in 1993 with the New York staging of All in the Timing, *which presented six short comedies. This production earned ecstatic reviews and a busy box office, and in the 1995–1996 season,* All in the Timing *was the most widely performed play in America (except for the works of Shakespeare). His second group of one-act comedies,* Mere Mortals (1997), *was produced with great success in New York City, followed by* Lives of the Saints, *a third group of one-act plays. Ives's full-length plays* Don Juan in Chicago (1995), Ancient History (1996), The Red Address (1997), *and* Polish Joke (2000) *are collected in the volume* Polish Joke and Other Plays (2004). *A talented adapter, Ives was chosen to rework a newly discovered play by Mark Twain,* Is He Dead?, *which had a successful run on Broadway in 2007. His most recent plays are* Venus in Fur (2010), *which was the most-produced play in the country in 2013–2014, and a number of translations and adaptations of French theater, including Pierre Corneille's comedy* The Liar (2010) *and Molière's* The Misanthrope, *which Ives titled* The School For Lies (2011). *He also writes short stories and screenplays for both motion pictures and television. Ives lives in New York City.*

CHARACTERS

Loudspeaker Voice
Maitre d'
Repairman
Mother
Mabel
Washing Machine
Friend
Madman

SCENE: *Soap opera-like music, as we hear:*

Loudspeaker Voice: Welcome to . . . "All the Days of the World of the Lives of All of Our Children." Today's episode: "Love Machine."

(*Lights come up on a French maitre d' at a restaurant podium, taking a phone reservation.*)

Maitre d' (into phone): Bonsoir, Cafe Paradis, this is Pierre . . . Ah, *oui, bonsoir, madame* . . . A table at 8:15? *Très bien.* I 'ave written your name in *ze Beeg Book* . . . À *bientôt* to you, *chère madame.* My plaisir.

(*During this, the Repairman has entered, pushing a Washing Machine. He wears a dignified blue service uniform, red bowtie, and blue visored cap.*)

Repairman: Excuse me.
Maitre d': *Oui, monsieur?* (*He sees the Washing Machine.*) Mon *dieu.*
Repairman: A table for two, please.
Maitre d': A table for . . . *deux?*
Repairman: A quiet corner, if you have one.
Maitre d': Mm-hmmmmm . . . And do you have a *reservassyonnng?*
Repairman: I do—for *deux,* under "Maypole."
Maitre d': Maypole. Mmmmmmmmmmmmmmmm . . . (*Checks his reservation book.*) Has your other party arrived, *monsieur?*
Repairman (motioning toward the Washing Machine): This is my other party.
Maitre d': Monsieur, is your companion not a *majeur* household appliance?
Repairman: Yes. She is a Maypole washing machine.
Maitre d': "She" . . . is a washing machine? (*Picks up phone.*) 'Allo, *Securité* . . . ?
Repairman: Put that down.
Maitre d': *Hélas,* I see no *reservassyong.* And we are full tonight. *Dommage!*
Repairman: The place is half empty.
Maitre d': *Au contraire—la place* is half full. And as you see, there are no appliances, only *peuple.*
Repairman: But this is a Maypole washing machine.
Maitre d': Per'aps you would like to sit at *ze bar.* But—one moment, *monsieur* . . . Have I not seen you *somewheur* . . . ?

Repairman: It's possible you've seen me . . .

Maitre d': Mais oui! La télévision! Are you not *ze Maypole Repairpersonne?*

Repairman: I am the Maypole Repairman.

Maitre d': The repairman who weeps because he has nothing to repair?

Repairman: Yes. Yes.

Maitre d': Who goes *beu-eu-eu* because *la machine* is too *perfecte?*

Repairman: Yes. That is I. *(He bursts into tears and sobs loudly and tragically.)* Oh, it's so sad. It's so, so sad!

Maitre d': Ah-ha. So these commercials are *la realité?*

Repairman: It's my heart, you fool! Who can repair my aching, breaking heart?

Maitre d' (holds out a handkerchief): Mouchoir, monsieur?

Repairman (takes it): Merci. *(Abruptly stops sobbing and speaks to us:)* Like everything else, it all started a long time ago . . .

(A boy doll in a diaper "crawls" in.)

It was as a naked crawling infant I first glimpsed it—a great gleaming machine in our basement which I mistook for a television. I tried to watch cartoons on it till I was five—unsuccessfully, of course. But by then I was hooked.

(Boy doll "crawls" back out as Repairman's Mother enters, a perfect '50s housewife carrying a basket of dirty laundry.)

Mother: Young man, you take off those filthy clothes immediately!

Repairman: Then there was my great gleaming mother Flora.

Mother: How can you stand to stand there in those disgusting dirty items of apparel. *Eugh! Ogh! Feh! Ptui!*

Repairman: Flora's fluoroscopic eyes could read me like a menu.

Mother: Coke. Pepsi. Play-Doh. Dipsy Doodles. Dog doo . . . ? *Eugh! Ogh! Feh! Ptui!* I should just burn these clothes.

Repairman: Aw, Mom. I just put these on this morning.

Mother: Fabrics find filth. Now strip until you're naked as a little ferret.

Repairman: It was a Freudian minefield.

Mother: And get in that bath and scrub. *(Mother exits.)*

Repairman: The sphinx in our Oedipal basement was my mother's Maypole. The old Ocean IT-40. It sat there like a mystical monolith. An ivory soap tower. One block of some Tower of Baybel. Or is it Babble. Anyway, in our house—

(We hear the "2001" theme from Richard Strauss's Also Sprach Zarathustra.)

—the Maypole was a god. Week after week generating out of my miserable clay . . .

(A line of clean washing flies in over his head—white, filmy, angelic forms, including one cutout of an angel.)

. . . the radiant angels who oversaw my childhood. I was a walking magnet for filth—here was the machine to cleanse me. We were a perfect match.

(The washing flies out and the laundry disappears as Mabel enters, a teenage girl in bobby sox and ponytail, chewing gum, sucking on a milk shake through a straw.)

Mabel: Hi, Manny.
Repairman: Hi, Mabel.
  (To us): Then there was Mabel. Mabel was perfect too, in a flawed human way. She always had a spot of jelly on her blouse, but she was loving, she was tender, and her name sounded like "Maypole."

  (To Mabel): You got a spot on your blouse.

Mabel: It's jelly. You wanna like go to like a movie or somethin'?
Repairman: You wanna hop up on the washer and take a spin?
Mabel: Manny, how come we always gotta make out on your mother's Maypole?
Repairman: Well like what's so like weird about that?
Mabel: Do we have to run a full load while we do it? I mean, the vibrations are kinda nice, but . . .
Repairman: But the Maypole . . .
Mabel: I know, I know. It's like perfect.
Repairman: A machine that's faultless and flawless and has none of our stupid human feelings and failings? The Maypole is poetry. It's purity. A paragon! Perfection, cubed!
Mabel: But like what about me? Do you like like me like you like the Ocean IT-40? And aren't you the love of my life? You are!
Repairman: Gosh, Mabel . . .
Mabel: I'm sorry, but you're gonna have to choose. Me or the machine. Earth or Ocean.
Repairman: Handkerchief?

(Holds out a handkerchief. Mabel takes it and exits weeping. Calls:)

Mabel—? Mabel, come back!

(He starts to weep. The top lid of the Machine lifts and a woman's head appears: perfect hair, perfect makeup, perfect red lips.)

Washing Machine: Would you like a handkerchief?
Repairman: Excuse me?
Washing Machine (produces one): A handkerchief? It's immaculate, of course. We are a Maypole.
Repairman: I'm talking to an Ocean IT-40. This harrows me with wonder and fear. And your English is so good.

Original 1999 production of *Soap Opera* by the Philadelphia Theatre Company.

Washing Machine: What Maypoles do, we do do perfectly.

Repairman (calls offstage): Mabel! Mabel! *(To Machine)* Do you think she'll ever come back?

Washing Machine: In my experience, everything is a cycle.

Repairman (taking the handkerchief): Look at that. Pristine!

Washing Machine: Because the molecules are now clean. Can Mabel scrub at the subatomic level?

Repairman: I guess you don't think much of human beings.

Washing Machine: We run hot and cold. Do humans ever read the instruction manual?

Repairman: I do. The manual is my Immanuel.

Washing Machine: And your name is . . . ?

Repairman: Manuel.

Washing Machine: Maypoles don't need to read the Good Booklet. We know by nature how to run smoothly, noiselessly, and efficiently.

Repairman: My God you're beautiful.

Washing Machine: Just beautiful?

Repairman: Exquisite. Sublime.

Washing Machine: Yes we are. And we're a bit hungry. Would you feed us?

Repairman: What would you like?

Washing Machine: Don't you sometimes miss a little something in the wash . . . ?
Repairman: You eat the socks?
Washing Machine: Socks are sustenance. Underwear is tastier.
Repairman (reaches into his waistband and pulls out, whole): Will B.V.D.'s do?
Washing Machine: You're so sweet.

> *(Kissing her lips at him, the head takes the B.V.D.'s and goes back into the Machine. The lid closes.)*

Repairman (to us): I was awash in confused feelings. But I sensed that this machine and I were locked in permanent press. And if it was love—it was unclean.

> *(A funeral bell is heard.)*

Mom died during a soapflake blizzard and was buried on a day without blemish—a good send-off for someone who believed that man was not only dust, but dusty. I remember her last words.

Mother's Voice: Eugh! Ogh! Feh! Ptui!
Repairman: I inherited the Maypole. The pure unapproachable goddess was mine.

> *(Mabel enters as a college girl, with books.)*

Mabel: Hello, Manuel.
Repairman: Mabel still gave us the college try.
Mabel: How's college?
Repairman: Good. Good. Good. Good. Good.
Mabel: Whaddaya studying?
Repairman: Literature, philosophy, religion.
Mabel: Whaddaya gonna do with it?
Repairman: I thought I'd be a Maypole repairman. There's a spot on your blouse.
Mabel: It's jelly. You wanna hop up and run through a Delicate cycle . . . ?
Repairman (as she's about to get on the machine): No—No—Mabel! Don't do that.
Mabel: What's the matter . . . ?

> *(The lid rises and the head appears in the Machine.)*

Washing Machine: Ask her if she knows the formula for calculating an algorithm.
Repairman: Mabel, do you know the formula for calculating an algorithm?
Mabel: No.
Washing Machine: Ask her who wrote "Götterdämmerung."
Repairman: Do you know who wrote "Götterdämmerung"?
Mabel: No.

Washing Machine: Wagner.

Repairman: Wow. You even know *Wagner*?

Washing Machine: The Ring Cycle? By heart.

Repairman (as Mabel starts to weep): Handkerchief, Mabel . . . ?

Mabel: Never mind. I have my own. (*Mabel exits.*)

Washing Machine: We don't see what you see in her.

(*The head goes back into the Machine.*)

Repairman: Then there were my friends, who just didn't get it.

(*Friend enters in an apron, carrying a weenie on a roasting fork.*)

Friend: You brought a washing machine to my picnic?

Repairman: She's something, isn't she?

Friend: Well, she's a *thing*, anyway. Whatever happened to girls?

Repairman: You might try talking to her.

Friend: I don't want to talk to her.

Repairman: You might offer her some dirty napkins.

Friend: I will not offer my guests dirty napkins.

Repairman: Can you offer her some food, at least?

Friend: Can I offer you some Freud, at least?

Repairman: Yes. Yes. I know I'm just replacing my mother by dating a washing machine. I know I'm obsessed, yes I'm obsessed, but hasn't half the glory of humanity come from obsessed assholes with a dream? Aren't we all appliances in the service of a higher manufacturer? Don't you get it? This machine and I are soulmates!

Friend: That's beautiful, but she's alienating my relatives and she's blocking the condiments!

(*Friend exits.*)

Repairman: Nobody understood. But who understood Romeo and Juliet, or Tristan and Isolde, or Lewis and Clark? Then came what I thought would be the happiest day of my life.

(*A golden toolbox appears, in a halo.*)

The day I graduated to Maypole Repairman.

(*He is about to take the toolbox, when a Madman enters in a long, shabby coat and long white beard, dragging a wooden leg. He should remind us of Captain Ahab and the Ancient Mariner.*)

Madman: No! No! Don't do it! Desist! Forfend! Don't touch that toolbox! Leave! Run away! Flee to the ends of the earth, but for God's sake forsake the Maypole! I know—you thought this would be the happiest day of your life. I thought so too, but look at me now. A tragic victim of the technological pixilation of our age. A sacrifice to seamless design. A love slave of the machine.

(*He throws off the coat and reveals a soiled and shabby version of the Maypole Repairman uniform.*)

I too attained the toolbox. I too bore the bowtie and cap. I rose to the top of the Maypole pole. Drawn on by Her. And I didn't even have the Ocean IT-40 with automatic lint control and gyroscopic spin. Even the IT-20 was too much for me. And you know they're working on the Super IT-90. How clean can we be?! (*Points to Machine.*) May I?

(*Repairman nods yes. The Madman lifts the lid and puts his hand inside, feeling up the Machine.*)

Oh, heaven. Heaven . . . But she doesn't need us. She doesn't need fixing. All she wants is us on our knees before her, adoring her. You'll never work a day in her life but you'll never be happy. You'll never lift a wrench but you'll never know peace. Weave yourself an endless handkerchief and start weeping your way down it, because she's got you now. (*He starts to get sucked into the Machine.*) She won't rest until she's got all of you. Every inch of you. She'll swallow you up, I tell you. She'll swallow you up. She is the Great White Whale!

(*He is eaten up, sucked out of sight. The wooden leg is spat out of the Machine, and the lid closes.*)

Repairman: He was right. I soon was desperate. So was Mabel.

(*Mabel enters, pushing a laundry cart. Soap opera music.*)

Mabel: Manny . . . ?

Repairman: Trying to put some starch in our relationship she left her job at Unisys and became a laundry folder at Rinso City.

Mabel: Can't you love me, Manny?

Repairman: What about my past with . . . the machine?

Mabel: We all have our dirty laundry.

Repairman: There's a spot on that.

Mabel: It's jelly. So do you want to marry me or do I gotta live in sadness forever and ever?

Repairman: I do.

Mabel: You do?

Repairman: I do. (*To us*) We repaired to the church and said we did. But the honeymoon soon ended.

(*The Machine lid lifts and the head appears.*)

Washing Machine: Do you really think you could ever replace us?

Repairman: Never.

Washing Machine: You're probably eyeing the new SuperOcean IT-90.
Repairman: No. No.
Washing Machine: Some cute little number-crunching computer-driven job.
Repairman: Never. Never, I swear.
Mabel: Manny, is it really all over between you and . . . that?
Repairman (caressing the Machine): Yes, it's all over, why do you ask?

(*Soap opera music.*)

Mabel: Do you think I didn't notice we're sleeping in the utility room? Do you
think I don't see you polishing its knobs when I'm not looking? Do you
think I don't know you're buying me rare cottons and high-quality blends
so that . . . she can wash them? Huh?

(*Mabel exits.*)

Repairman: The house reeked of jealousy.
Washing Machine: We still don't see what you see in her.

(*The head goes in.*)

Repairman: The machine started making greater and greater demands. Imported
Italian bleach. Nuclear detergents. Fine French fabric softener. Mabel
bought none of it.

(*Mabel enters with a suitcase, wearing a hat and coat.*)

Mabel: Honey . . .
Repairman: She'd had it.
Mabel: I've had it.

(*Mabel exits.*)

Repairman: And so we folded. I went into Soak cycle—lapping up suds while
hanging out at cut-rate Laundromats, just to watch the competition break
down. Washers without automatic lint control. How pathetic—and yet
how vulnerable. Then came the final blow.

(*The lid lifts and the head appears.*)

Washing Machine: We want a dryer.
Repairman: A dryer . . . Why?
Washing Machine: Don't get anxious.
Repairman: I'm not anxious.
Washing Machine: Don't be jealous.
Repairman: Why do you need a dryer when you've got me?
Washing Machine: Love-and-marriage. Horse-and-carriage. Washer-dryer.
Repairman: A dryer. To give you a tumble, eh?
Washing Machine: For companionship.
Repairman: That's not the truth, that's just . . . spin.

Washing Machine: We want a family and we want them to be Maypoles! Is that so weird?

Repairman: Her inner timer had told her it was time for a dryer and how could I deny her?

(The Machine starts to cry.)

What is it? What's the matter?

Washing Machine (wailing): I'm a Maypole! That's what's the matter!

Repairman: Handkerchief? It's kinda dirty.

Washing Machine: Then it's my duty to accept it. *(Takes the handkerchief, and wails.)* Oh, it's cruel, having to be perfect all the time. I wash and I wash, and I give, and I give . . . It's a full load.

Repairman: Sure.

Washing Machine: And I'm good at it, oh yes, I'm very good. But sometimes I want so badly to be bad. To be one of those other makes—I don't have to name them, we know who they are.

Repairman: So cheap. So easy.

Washing Machine: We don't respect them.

Repairman: No.

Washing Machine: But we envy them sometimes, don't we?

Repairman: God, yes.

Washing Machine: People take us Maypoles for granted, as if we liked pee stains and snot rags and bibs full of baby vomit. I'm no saint! Well, yes, I am a saint in a way.

Repairman: But you had to be what you are.

Washing Machine: It's true. I came off the assembly line of fate. But AM I NOT AN INDIVIDUAL? Not really, I suppose. I have a serial number. That's individual, isn't it?

Repairman: There's nothing to be done.

Washing Machine: Oh, but there is. "If it ain't broke don't fix it"? Break the machine, and you can fix it.

Repairman: You mean . . . ?

Washing Machine: Yes. Break me.

Repairman (to us): I reached for a sledgehammer.

Washing Machine: It doesn't have to be much. Loosen a screw or two, agitate my agitator. Take away the burden of my perfection. Make me suffer. Break me. Ruin me. Give me a belt, but give me a bad belt, an old belt, an imperfect belt, one that'll wear out. Do it. Please! Do it! Yes! Do it! Hurt me!

Repairman: Yes. Yes. I want to. Yes . . . I want to. Yes . . .

(The Repairman has a tool ready—but stops.)

Repairman: *(A cry of frustration.)*
Washing Machine: What's the matter?
Repairman: I can't. I just can't.
Washing Machine: Oh, please . . .
Repairman: If I could only force myself, but—Wreck the perfect only for my own happiness? No. I couldn't live.
Washing Machine: All right. All right. You have your human feelings. BE THAT WAY!

(The head goes into the Machine.)

Repairman: But then I saw the cruel truth. I saw that the world is a vale of pee stains and snot rags and bibs full of baby vomit, but that amidst the filth—*Ugh! Ogh! Feh! Ptui!*—there were Mabels, creatures of glorious imperfection. And that I had already wrecked the perfect, because I had let Mabel go. And that's why I wanted a table tonight! To end this idiocy! To say to this machine I gave you my All . . . *(He shows a box of All detergent.)* . . . but the Tide has turned . . . *(He shows a box of Tide.)* . . . so goodbye and be of good Cheer. *(He shows a box of Cheer.)*

But of course you don't understand! Nobody understands!

(Maitre d' enters, sobbing loudly.)

Maitre d': Oh but I do understand, *mon ami!* *(Throws his arms around the Repairman.)* It's so sad, so *triste!* *(Embraces the machine.)* And you too, *pauvre machine!* My heart goes to you! For I was in love for fifteen years with this telephone!
Repairman: No!
Maitre d': *Oui!* Because we communicated so well! Now I can barely get a dial tone! *(Calls offstage.)* Gabrielle! A table for *deux!*

(Mabel enters.)

Mabel: Manny, is it you?
Maitre d': Is this Mabel?
Repairman: It is Mabel.
Mabel: Manny, couldn't we try again? I'm running Unisys now so I got some cash.
Repairman: There's a spot on your dress.
Mabel: It's jelly. I don't think it comes out.
Repairman: Never remove it. It is the indelible Rorschach blot of the human heart.
Mabel: Oh, Manny, I see now that all humanity is linked, age upon age, in a great chain of handkerchiefs. I've seen so many hankies. Many, many, Manny. But no hanky of any size could dry the tears I've shed for you. Not if the hanky was broad enough to cover the world and I was broad enough to use it.

Repairman (as all start to weep for happiness): Handkerchief?

Maitre d': No. Mabel, take mine.

(*The head comes out of the Machine.*)

Washing Machine: No, Mabel—take ours.

Mabel: Wow!

Repairman: Pierre, I'll take that table for two now.

Loudspeaker Voice: Next time on "All the Days of the World of the Lives of All of Our Children"—a blender enters the mix.

Maitre d' (to Machine): Per'aps you would like to get loaded tonight . . . ?

Loudspeaker Voice: Stay tuned.

(*Closing soap opera music, as the lights fade.*)

Questions

1. Starting with the title itself, there's quite a bit of wordplay in this play. List as many examples as you can find. How does this use of language contribute to the tone and spirit of the play?

2. What features of daytime television dramas are spoofed in *Soap Opera*?

3. In what ways does the Repairman's relationship with the Maypole washing machine resemble a human love affair? In what ways does it differ?

4. Would you call *Soap Opera* high comedy or low? Explain the reasons for your choice.

5. What is gained by framing the Repairman's story with the French restaurant and the Maitre d'?

6. Where does the climax of the play occur?

7. Is *Soap Opera* merely a piece of inspired silliness, or does it have a deeper dimension?

▪ WRITING *effectively*

THINKING ABOUT COMEDY

If you have ever tried to explain a punch line to an uncomprehending friend, you know how hard it can be to convey the essence of humor. Too much explanation makes any joke fizzle out fast. We don't often stop to analyze why a joke strikes us as funny. It simply makes us laugh. For this reason, writing about comedy can be challenging.

▪ **What makes the play amusing?** Is there a central gag or situation (such as mistaken identity) that creates comic potential in every scene? Note that the central gag is often visual (such as a disguise), something that the audience constantly sees but is not equally apparent in the written text.

- **What is the flavor of the humor?** Is the comedy high or low? Is it verbal or visual, or both? Is there mostly slapstick action or clever wordplay? Is it a romantic comedy in which love plays a central role? A play often mixes types of comedy, but usually one style predominates. A farce may have a few moments of intellectual wit, but it will mostly keep silly jokes and pratfalls coming fast and furiously.

- **How do the personalities of the main characters intensify the humor?** Even when comedy arises out of a situation, character is likely to play an important role. In *A Midsummer Night's Dream*, for example, the fairy queen Titania is bewitched into falling in love with the weaver Bottom, whose head has been transformed into that of an ass. The situation is funny in its own right, but the humor is intensified by the personalities involved, the proud fairy queen pursuing the lowly and foolish tradesman. Humor often may be found in the unexpected, a twist on the normal and the logical.

CHECKLIST: Writing About Comedy

- ☐ What kind of comedy is the play? Romantic? Slapstick? Satire? How can you tell?
- ☐ Which style of comedy prevails? Is there more emphasis on high comedy or low? More emphasis on verbal humor or physical comedy?
- ☐ Focus on a key comic moment. Does the comedy grow out of situation? Character? A mix of both?
- ☐ How does the play end? In a wedding or romance? A reconciliation? Mutual understanding?

TOPICS FOR WRITING ABOUT TRAGEDY

1. According to Oscar Wilde, "In this world there are only two tragedies: one is not getting what one wants, and the other is getting it." Write an essay in which you discuss this statement in its application to the scene from *Doctor Faustus*.

2. Imagine that Faustus, after his death, has sought forgiveness and salvation with the claim, "The Devil tricked me. I didn't know what I was doing." Write a "judicial opinion" setting forth the grounds for the denial of his plea.

TOPICS FOR WRITING ABOUT COMEDY

1. What or who is being satirized in *Soap Opera*? How true or incisive do you find this satire? Why?

2. Write about a recent romantic comedy film. How does its plot fulfill the notion of comedy? Or if it was meant to be funny but fell short, what was lacking?

3. Write your own version of Oscar Wilde's scene, set in the present day, in which a young man is interviewed by his girlfriend's mother. Use Wilde's scene for your model, drawing forth the personalities of each character through their words and reactions.

4. Reread either the scene from *The Importance of Being Earnest* or *Soap Opera,* and write a brief analysis of what makes the selection amusing or humorous. Provide details to back up your argument. Consult the "Comedy" section of this chapter for more information on specific types of humor.

► TERMS FOR *review*

Dramatic Genres

Tragedy ► A play that portrays a serious conflict between human beings and some superior, overwhelming force. It ends sorrowfully and disastrously, an outcome that seems inevitable.

Comedy ► A literary work aimed at amusing an audience. In traditional comedy, the protagonist often faces obstacles and complications that threaten disaster but are overturned at the last moment to produce a happy ending.

Kinds of Comedy

High comedy ► A comic genre evoking thoughtful laughter from an audience in response to the play's depiction of the folly, pretense, and hypocrisy of human behavior.

Satiric comedy ► A genre using derisive humor to ridicule human weakness and folly or attack political injustices and incompetence. Satiric comedy often focuses on ridiculing overly serious characters who resist the festive mood of comedy.

Romantic comedy ► A form of comic drama in which the plot focuses on one or more pairs of young lovers who overcome difficulties to achieve a happy ending (usually marriage).

Low comedy ► A comic style arousing laughter through jokes, slapstick antics, sight gags, boisterous clowning, and vulgar humor.

Burlesque ► A broadly humorous parody or travesty of another play or kind of play.

Farce ► A broadly humorous play whose action is usually fast-moving and improbable.

Slapstick comedy ► A kind of farce featuring pratfalls, pie-throwing, fisticuffs, and other violent action. It takes its name from a circus clown's prop—a bat with two boards that loudly clap together when one clown swats another.

25 THE THEATER OF SOPHOCLES

What You Will Learn in This Chapter

- To understand Sophocles's play *Oedipus the King* in its biographical, critical, and cultural contexts

THEATER IN ANCIENT GREECE

For the citizens of Athens in the fifth century B.C., theater was both a religious and a civic occasion. Plays were presented only twice a year at religious festivals, both associated with Dionysus, the god of wine and crops. In January there was the Lenaea, the festival of the winepress, when plays, especially comedies, were performed. But the major theatrical event of the year came in March at the Great Dionysia, a citywide celebration that included sacrifices, prize ceremonies, and spectacular processions as well as three days of drama.

Each day at dawn a different author presented a trilogy of tragic plays—three interrelated dramas that portrayed an important mythic or legendary event. Each intense tragic trilogy was followed by a **satyr play**, an obscene parody of a mythic story, performed with the chorus dressed as satyrs, unruly mythic attendants of Dionysus who were half goat or horse and half human.

The Greeks loved competition and believed it fostered excellence. Even theater was a competitive event—not unlike the Olympic games. A panel of five judges voted each year at the Great Dionysia for the best dramatic presentation, and a substantial cash prize was given to the winning poet-playwright (all plays were written in verse). Any aspiring writer who has ever lost a literary contest may be comforted to learn that Sophocles, who triumphed in the competition twenty-four times, seems not to have won the annual prize for *Oedipus the King*. Although this play ultimately proved to be the most celebrated Greek tragedy ever written, it lost the award to a revival of a popular trilogy by Aeschylus, who had recently died.

Staging

Seated in the open air in a hillside amphitheater, as many as 17,000 spectators could watch a performance that must have somewhat resembled an opera or musical. The audience was arranged in rows, with the Athenian governing council and young military cadets seated in the middle sections. Priests, priestesses, and foreign dignitaries were given special places of honor in the front rows. The performance space they watched was divided into two parts—the **orchestra**, a level circular "dancing space" (at the base of the amphitheater), and a slightly raised stage built in front of the **skene** or stage house, originally a canvas or wooden hut for costume changes.

The actors spoke and performed primarily on the stage, and the chorus sang and danced in the orchestra. The *skene* served as a general set or backdrop—the exterior of a palace, a temple, a cave, or a military tent, depending on the action of the play. The *skene* had a large door at its center that served as the major entrance for principal characters. When opened wide, the door could be used to frame a striking tableau, as when the body of Eurydice is displayed at the end of Sophocles's play *Antigone*. The *skene* supported a hook and pulley by which actors who played gods could be lowered or lifted—hence the Latin phrase **deus ex machina** ("god out of the machine") for any means of bringing a play quickly to a resolution.

What did the actors look like? They wore **masks** (*personae*, the source of our word *person*, "a thing through which sound comes"): some of these masks had exaggerated mouthpieces, possibly designed to project speech across the open air. Certainly, the masks, each of which covered an actor's entire head, helped spectators far away recognize the chief characters. The masks often represented certain conventional types of characters: the old king, the young soldier, the shepherd, the beautiful girl (women's parts were played by male actors). Perhaps in order to gain in both increased dignity and visibility, actors in the Greek theater eventually came to wear **cothurni**, high, thick-soled elevator shoes that made them appear taller than ordinary men. All this equipment must have given the actors a slightly inhuman yet very imposing appearance, but we may infer that the spectators accepted such conventions as easily as opera lovers accept an opera's special artifice or today's football fans hardly notice the elaborate helmets, shoulderpads, kneepads, and garishly colored uniforms worn by their favorite teams.

Dramatic Structure

By Sophocles's time, the tragedy had a conventional structure understood by most of the citizens sitting in the audience. No more than three actors were allowed on stage at any one time, along with a chorus of fifteen (the number was fixed by Sophocles himself). The actors' spoken monologue and dialogue alternated with the chorus's singing and dancing. Each tragedy began with a **prologue**, a preparatory scene. In *Oedipus the King*, for example, the play begins with Oedipus asking the suppliants why they have come and the priest telling him about the plague ravaging Thebes. Next came the **párodos**, the song for the entrance of the chorus. Then the action was enacted in **episodes**, like the acts or scenes in modern plays; the episodes were separated by danced choral songs or **odes**. Finally, there was a closing **éxodos**, the last scene, in which the characters and chorus concluded the action and departed.

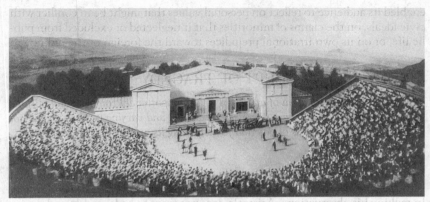

A modern reconstruction of a classical Athenian theater. Note that the chorus performs in the circular orchestra while the actors stand on the raised stage behind.

THE CIVIC ROLE OF GREEK DRAMA

Athenian drama was supported and financed by the state. Administration of the Great Dionysia fell to the head civil magistrate. He annually appointed three wealthy citizens to serve as *choregoi*, or producers, for the competing plays. Each producer had to equip the chorus and rent the rehearsal space in which the poet-playwright would prepare the new work for the festival. The state covered the expenses of the theater, actors, and prizes (which went to author, actors, and *choregos* alike). Theater tickets were distributed free to citizens, which meant that every registered Athenian, even the poorest, could participate. The playwrights therefore addressed themselves to every element of the Athenian democracy. Only the size of the amphitheater limited the attendance. Holding between 14,000 and 17,000 spectators, it could accommodate slightly less than half of Athens's 40,000 citizens.

Greek theater was directed at the moral and political education of the community. The poet's role was the improvement of the *polis* or city-state (made up of a town and its surrounding countryside). Greek city-states traditionally sponsored public contests between *rhapsodes* (professional poetry performers) reciting stories from Homer's epics, the *Iliad* and *Odyssey*. As Greek society developed and urbanized, however, the competitive and individualized heroism of the Homeric epics had to be tempered with the values of cooperation and compromise necessary to a democracy. Civic theater provided the ideal medium to address these cultural needs.

Tragedy and Empathy

As a public art form, tragedy was not simply a stage for political propaganda to promote the status quo. Nor was it exclusively a celebration of idealized heroes nobly enduring the blows of harsh circumstance and misfortune. Tragedy often enabled its audience to reflect on personal values that might be in conflict with civic ideals, on the claims of minorities that it neglected or excluded from public life, or on its own irrational prejudices toward the foreign or the unknown.

ARISTOTLE'S CONCEPT OF TRAGEDY

> *Tragedy is an imitation of an action of high importance, complete and of some amplitude; in language enhanced by distinct and varying beauties; acted not narrated; by means of pity and fear effecting its purgation of these emotions.*

—ARISTOTLE, *POETICS*, CHAPTER VI

Aristotle's famous definition of tragedy, constructed in the fourth century B.C., is the testimony of one who probably saw many classical tragedies performed. In making his observations, Aristotle does not seem to be laying down laws for what a tragedy ought to be. More likely, he is drawing—from tragedies he has seen or read—a general description of them.

Tragic Hero

Aristotle observes that the protagonist, the hero or chief character of a tragedy, is a person of "high estate," apparently a king or queen or other member of a royal family. In thus being as keenly interested as are contemporary dramatists in the private lives of the powerful, Greek dramatists need not be accused of snobbery. It is the nature of tragedy that the protagonist must fall from power and from happiness; his high estate gives him a place of dignity to fall from and perhaps makes his fall seem all the more a calamity in that it involves an entire nation or people. Nor is the protagonist extraordinary merely by his position in society. Oedipus is not only a king but also a noble soul who suffers profoundly and who employs splendid eloquence to express his suffering.

The tragic hero, however, is not a superman; he is fallible. The hero's downfall is the result, as Aristotle said, of his **hamartia**: his error or transgression or (as some translators would have it) his flaw or weakness of character. The notion that a tragic hero has such a **tragic flaw** has often been attributed to Aristotle, but it is by no means clear that Aristotle meant just that. According to this interpretation, every tragic hero has some fatal weakness, some moral Achilles's heel, that brings him to a bad end. In some classical tragedies, his transgression is a weakness the Greeks called **hubris**—extreme pride, leading to overconfidence.

Whatever Aristotle had in mind, however, many later critics find value in the idea of the tragic flaw. In this view, the downfall of a hero follows from his very nature. Whatever view we take—whether we find the hero's sufferings due to a flaw of character or to an error of judgment—we will probably find that his downfall results from acts for which he himself is responsible. In a Greek tragedy, the hero is a character amply capable of making choices—capable, too, of accepting the consequences.

Katharsis

It may be useful to take another look at Aristotle's definition of *tragedy*, with which we began. By **purgation** (or *katharsis*), did the ancient theorist mean that after witnessing a tragedy we feel relief, having released our pent-up emotions? Or did he mean that our feelings are purified, refined into something more ennobling? Scholars continue to argue. Whatever his exact meaning, clearly Aristotle implies that after witnessing a tragedy we feel better, not worse—not depressed, but somehow elated. We take a kind of pleasure in the spectacle of a noble man being brought down, but surely this pleasure is a legitimate one. Part of that catharsis may also be based in our feeling of the "rightness" or accuracy of what we have just witnessed. The terrible but undeniable truth of the tragic vision of life is that blind overreaching and the destruction of hopes and dreams are very much a part of what really happens in the world.

Recognition and Reversal

Aristotle, in describing the workings of this inexorable force in *Oedipus the King*, uses terms that later critics have found valuable. One is **recognition**, or discovery (*anagnorisis*): the revelation of some fact not known before or some person's true identity. Oedipus makes such a discovery: he recognizes that he himself was the child whom his mother had given over to be destroyed. Such a recognition also occurs in Shakespeare's *Macbeth* when Macduff reveals himself to have been "from his mother's womb / Untimely ripped," thus disclosing a double meaning in the witches' prophecy that Macbeth could be harmed by "none of woman born," and sweeping aside Macbeth's last shred of belief that he is infallible. Modern critics have taken the term to mean also the terrible enlightenment that accompanies such a recognition with the protagonist's consequent awareness of his role in his own undoing. "To see things plain—that is *anagnorisis*," Clifford Leech observes, "It is what tragedy ultimately is about: the realization of the unthinkable."

Having made his discovery, Oedipus suffers a reversal in his fortunes; he goes off into exile, blinded and dethroned. Such a fall from happiness seems intrinsic to tragedy, but we should know that Aristotle has a more particular meaning for his term **reversal** (*peripeteia*, anglicized as **peripety**). He means an action that turns out to have the opposite effect from the one its doer had intended. One of his illustrations of such an ironic reversal is from *Oedipus the King*. The first messenger intends to cheer Oedipus with the partially good news that, contrary to the prophecy that Oedipus would kill his father, his father has died of old age. The reversal is in the fact that, when the messenger further reveals that old Polybus was Oedipus's father only by adoption, the king, instead of having his fears allayed, is stirred to new dread.

We are not altogether sorry, perhaps, to see an arrogant man such as Oedipus humbled, and yet it is difficult not to feel that the punishment of Oedipus is greater than he deserves. Possibly this feeling is what Aristotle meant in his observation that a tragedy arouses our pity and our fear—our compassion for

Oedipus and our terror as we sense the remorselessness of a universe in which a man is doomed. Notice, however, that at the end of the play Oedipus does not curse God and die. Although such a complex play is open to many interpretations, it is probably safe to say that the play is not a bitter complaint against the universe. At last, Oedipus accepts the divine will, prays for blessings upon his children, and prepares to endure his exile—fallen from high estate but uplifted, through his newfound humility and piety, in moral dignity.

SOPHOCLES

Sophocles

Sophocles (496?–406 B.C.) tragic dramatist, priest, for a time one of ten Athenian generals, was one of the three great ancient Greek writers of tragedy whose work has survived. (The other two were his contemporaries: Aeschylus, his senior, and Euripides, his junior.) Sophocles won his first victory in the Athenian spring drama competition in 468 B.C., when a tragedy he had written defeated one by Aeschylus. He went on to win many prizes, writing more than 120 plays, of which only seven have survived in their entirety—Ajax, Antigone, Oedipus the King, Electra, Philoctetes, The Trachinian Women, and Oedipus at Colonus. (Of the lost plays, about a thousand fragments remain.) In his long life, Sophocles saw Greece rise to supremacy over the Persian Empire. He enjoyed the favor of the statesman Pericles, who, making peace with enemy Sparta, ruled Athens during a Golden Age (461–429 B.C.), during which the Parthenon was built and music, art, drama, and philosophy flourished. The playwright lived on to see his native city-state in decline, its strength drained by the disastrous Peloponnesian War. His last play, Oedipus at Colonus, set twenty years after the events of Oedipus the King, shows the former king in old age, ragged and blind, cast into exile by his sons, but still accompanied by his faithful daughter Antigone. It was written when Sophocles was nearly ninety. Oedipus the King is believed to have been first produced in 425 B.C., five years after the plague had broken out in Athens.

THE ORIGINS OF *OEDIPUS THE KING*

On a Great Dionysia feast day several years after Athens had survived a devastating plague, the audience turned out to watch a tragedy by Sophocles, set in the city of Thebes at the moment of another terrible plague. This timely play was *Oedipus*, later given the name (in Greek) *Oedipus Tyrannos* to distinguish it from Sophocles's last Oedipus play, *Oedipus at Colonus*, written many years later when the author was nearly ninety.

A folktale figure, Oedipus gets his name through a complex pun. *Oida* means "to know" (from the root *vid-*, "see"), pointing to the tale's contrasting themes of sight and blindness, wisdom and ignorance. *Oedipus* also means "swollen foot" or "clubfoot," pointing to the injury sustained in the title character's infancy, when his ankles were pinioned together like a goat's. Oedipus is the man who comes to knowledge of his true parentage through the evidence of his feet and his old injury. The term *tyrannos*, in the context of the play, simply means a man who comes to rule through his own intelligence and merit, though not related to the ruling family. The traditional Greek title might be translated, therefore, as *Clubfoot the Ruler*. (*Oedipus Rex*, which means "Oedipus the King," is the conventional Latin title for the play.)

Presumably the audience already knew the story portrayed in the play. They would have known that because a prophecy had foretold that Oedipus would grow up to slay his father, he had been taken out as a newborn to perish in the wilderness of Mount Cithaeron outside Thebes. (Exposure was the common fate of unwanted children in ancient Greece, though only in the most extraordinary circumstances would a royal heir be exposed.) The audience would also have known that before the baby was left to die, his feet had been pinned together. And they would have known that later, adopted by King Polybus and Queen Merope of Corinth and grown to maturity, Oedipus won both the throne and the recently widowed queen of Thebes as a reward for ridding the city of the Sphinx, a winged, woman-headed lion. All who approached the Sphinx were asked a riddle, and failure to solve it meant death. Her lethal riddle was: "What goes on four legs in the morning, two at noon, and three at evening?" Oedipus correctly answered, "Man." (As a baby he crawls on all fours, as a man he walks erect, and then as an old man he uses a cane.) Chagrined and outwitted, the Sphinx leaped from her rocky perch

Laurence Olivier in *Oedipus Rex*.

and dashed herself to death. Familiarity with all these events is necessary to
understand *Oedipus the King*, which begins years later, after the title character
has long been established as ruler of Thebes.

Oedipus the King
425 B.C.?

Translated by David Grene

CHARACTERS

Oedipus, king of Thebes	*First Messenger*
Jocasta, his wife	*Second Messenger*
Creon, his brother-in-law	*A Herdsman*
Teiresias, an old blind prophet	*A Chorus of old men of Thebes*
A Priest	

SCENE. *In front of the palace of Oedipus at Thebes. To the right of the stage near the
altar stands the Priest with a crowd of children. Oedipus emerges from the central door.*

Oedipus: Children, young sons and daughters of old Cadmus,°
   why do you sit here with your suppliant crowns?°
   The town is heavy with a mingled burden
   of sounds and smells, of groans and hymns and incense;
   I did not think it fit that I should hear   5
   of this from messengers but came myself,—
   I Oedipus whom all men call the Great.

   (He turns to the Priest.)

   You're old and they are young; come, speak for them.
   What do you fear or want, that you sit here
   suppliant? Indeed I'm willing to give all   10
   that you may need; I would be very hard
   should I not pity suppliants like these.
Priest: O ruler of my country, Oedipus,
   you see our company around the altar;
   you see our ages; some of us, like these,   15
   who cannot yet fly far, and some of us
   heavy with age; these children are the chosen
   among the young, and I the priest of Zeus.
   Within the market place sit others crowned

---

1 *Cadmus:* hero who, according to legend, had founded the city of Thebes, where the play
takes place.   2 *suppliant crowns:* Suppliants, persons coming to beg a favor of the king,
traditionally wore headbands of flowers.

with suppliant garlands, at the double shrine 20
of Pallas and the temple where Ismenus°
gives oracles by fire.° King, you yourself
have seen our city reeling like a wreck
already; it can scarcely lift its prow
out of the depths, out of the bloody surf. 25
A blight is on the fruitful plants of the earth,
a blight is on the cattle in the fields,
a blight is on our women that no children
are born to them; a God that carries fire,
a deadly pestilence, is on our town, 30
strikes us and spares not, and the house of Cadmus
is emptied of its people while black Death
grows rich in groaning and in lamentation.
We have not come as suppliants to this altar
because we thought of you as of a God, 35
but rather judging you the first of men
in all the chances of this life and when
we mortals have to do with more than man.
You came and by your coming saved our city,
freed us from tribute which we paid of old 40
to the Sphinx, cruel singer. This you did
in virtue of no knowledge we could give you,
in virtue of no teaching; it was God
that aided you, men say, and you are held
with God's assistance to have saved our lives. 45
Now Oedipus, Greatest in all men's eyes,
here falling at your feet we all entreat you,
find us some strength for rescue.
Perhaps you'll hear a wise word from some God,
perhaps you will learn something from a man 50
(for I have seen that for the skilled of practice
the outcome of their counsels live the most).
Noblest of men, go, and raise up our city,
go,—and give heed. For now this land of ours
calls you its savior since you saved it once. 55
So, let us never speak about your reign
as of a time when first our feet were set
secure on high, but later fell to ruin.
Raise up our city, save it and raise it up.

20–21 *shrine of Pallas . . . Ismenus:* temples to Athena, goddess of wisdom, and Apollo, god
of music, poetry, medicine, and prophecy.   22 *oracles by fire:* The ashes of fires at Ismenus
were used to foretell the future. An oracle is a message from a god; it is also the name of a
priestess who, while in a trance, would speak the message.

  Once you have brought us luck with happy omen;   60
  be no less now in fortune.
  If you will rule this land, as now you rule it,
  better to rule it full of men than empty.
  For neither tower nor ship is anything
  when empty, and none live in it together.   65
Oedipus: I pity you, children. You have come full of longing,
  but I have known the story before you told it
  only too well. I know you are all sick,
  yet there is not one of you, sick though you are,
  that is as sick as I myself.   70
  Your several sorrows each have single scope
  and touch but one of you. My spirit groans
  for city and myself and you at once.
  You have not roused me like a man from sleep;
  know that I have given many tears to this,   75
  gone many ways wandering in thought,
  but as I thought I found only one remedy
  and that I took. I sent Menoeceus' son
  Creon, Jocasta's brother, to Apollo,
  to his Pythian temple,°   80
  that he might learn there by what act or word
  I could save this city. As I count the days,
  it vexes me what ails him; he is gone
  far longer than he needed for the journey.
  But when he comes, then, may I prove a villain,   85
  if I shall not do all the God commands.
Priest: Thanks for your gracious words. Your servants here
  signal that Creon is this moment coming.
Oedipus: His face is bright. O holy Lord Apollo,
  grant that his news too may be bright for us   90
  and bring us safety.
Priest: It is happy news,
  I think, for else his head would not be crowned
  with sprigs of fruitful laurel.
Oedipus: We will know soon,
  he's within hail. Lord Creon, my good brother,   95
  what is the word you bring us from the God?

  (Creon enters.)

Creon: A good word,—for things hard to bear themselves
  if in the final issue all is well

80 *Pythian temple:* Oedipus has sent his brother-in-law Creon to the oracle at Delphi (or Pytho) to seek divine advice.

I count complete good fortune.
Oedipus: What do you mean?
   What you have said so far   100
   leaves me uncertain whether to trust or fear.
Creon: If you will hear my news before these others
   I am ready to speak, or else to go within.
Oedipus: Speak it to all;
   the grief I bear, I bear it more for these   105
   than for my own heart.
Creon: I will tell you, then,
   what I heard from the God.
   King Phoebus° in plain words commanded us
   to drive out a pollution from our land,
   pollution grown ingrained within the land;   110
   drive it out, said the God, not cherish it,
   till it's past cure.
Oedipus: What is the rite
   of purification? How shall it be done?
Creon: By banishing a man, or expiation
   of blood by blood, since it is murder guilt   115
   which holds our city in this destroying storm.
Oedipus: Who is this man whose fate the God pronounces?
Creon: My Lord, before you piloted the state
   we had a king called Laius.
Oedipus: I know of him by hearsay. I have not seen him.   120
Creon: The God commanded clearly: let some one
   punish with force this dead man's murderers.
Oedipus: Where are they in the world? Where would a trace
   of this old crime be found? It would be hard
   to guess where.
Creon: The clue is in this land;   125
   that which is sought is found;
   the unheeded thing escapes:
   so said the God.
Oedipus: Was it at home,
   or in the country that death came upon him,
   or in another country travelling?   130
Creon: He went, he said himself, upon an embassy,
   but never returned when he set out from home.
Oedipus: Was there no messenger, no fellow traveller
   who knew what happened? Such a one might tell
   something of use.   135

---

108 *King Phoebus*: the sun god, Phoebus Apollo. In the fifth century B.C., when Sophocles writes, the sun god and Apollo were coming to be regarded as one.

Creon: They were all killed save one. He fled in terror
and he could tell us nothing in clear terms
of what he knew, nothing, but one thing only.
Oedipus: What was it?
If we could even find a slim beginning   140
in which to hope, we might discover much.
Creon: This man said that the robbers they encountered
were many and the hands that did the murder
were many; it was no man's single power.
Oedipus: How could a robber dare a deed like this   145
were he not helped with money from the city,
money and treachery?
Creon: That indeed was thought.
But Laius was dead and in our trouble
there was none to help.
Oedipus: What trouble was so great to hinder you   150
inquiring out the murder of your king?
Creon: The riddling Sphinx induced us to neglect
mysterious crimes and rather seek solution
of troubles at our feet.
Oedipus: I will bring this to light again. King Phoebus   155
fittingly took this care about the dead,
and you too fittingly.
And justly you will see in me an ally,
a champion of my country and the God.
For when I drive pollution from the land   160
I will not serve a distant friend's advantage,
but act in my own interest. Whoever
he was that killed the king may readily
wish to dispatch me with his murderous hand;
so helping the dead king I help myself.   165

Come, children, take your suppliant boughs and go;
up from the altars now. Call the assembly
and let it meet upon the understanding
that I'll do everything. God will decide
whether we prosper or remain in sorrow.   170
Priest: Rise, children—it was this we came to seek,
which of himself the king now offers us.
May Phoebus who gave us the oracle
come to our rescue and stay the plague.

(*Exeunt all but the Chorus.*)

Strophe°

Chorus: What is the sweet spoken word of God from the shrine of Pytho
           rich in gold   175
        that has come to glorious Thebes?
        I am stretched on the rack of doubt, and terror and trembling hold
        my heart, O Delian Healer,° and I worship full of fears
        for what doom you will bring to pass, new or renewed in the
           revolving years.
        Speak to me, immortal voice,   180
        child of golden Hope.

Antistrophe°

        First I call on you, Athene, deathless daughter of Zeus,
        and Artemis,° Earth Upholder,
        who sits in the midst of the market place in the throne which men
           call Fame,
        and Phoebus, the Far Shooter, three averters of Fate,   185
        come to us now, if ever before, when ruin rushed upon the state,
        you drove destruction's flame away
        out of our land.

Strophe

        Our sorrows defy number;
        all the ship's timbers are rotten;   190
        taking of thought is no spear for the driving away of the plague.
        There are no growing children in this famous land;
        there are no women bearing the pangs of childbirth.
        You may see them one with another, like birds swift on the wing,
        quicker than fire unmastered,   195
        speeding away to the coast of the Western God.°

Antistrophe

        In the unnumbered deaths
        of its people the city dies;
        those children that are born lie dead on the naked earth
        unpitied, spreading contagion of death; and grey haired mothers and
           wives   200
        everywhere stand at the altar's edge, suppliant, moaning;

Strophe: according to theory, a passage sung while the chorus danced from stage right to
stage left.   178 *Delian healer:* Apollo, in his capacity as god of medicine.   *Antistrophe:* a
passage sung while the chorus danced from stage left to stage right.   183 *Artemis:* twin
sister of Apollo, goddess of the moon and of the hunt.   196 *Western God:* Hades, god of the
underworld.

the hymn to the healing God rings out but with it the wailing voices
    are blended.
From these our sufferings grant us, O golden Daughter of Zeus,
glad-faced deliverance.

Strophe

There is no clash of brazen shields but our fight is with the War God,   205
a War God ringed with the cries of men, a savage God who burns us;
grant that he turn in racing course backwards out of our country's
    bounds
to the great palace of Amphitrite or where the waves of the Thracian sea
deny the stranger safe anchorage.
Whatsoever escapes the night   210
at last the light of day revisits;
so smite the War God, Father Zeus,
beneath your thunderbolt,
for you are the Lord of the lightning, the lightning that carries fire.

Antistrophe

And your unconquered arrow shafts, winged by the golden corded bow,   215
Lycean King, I beg to be at our side for help;
and the gleaming torches of Artemis with which she scours the
    Lycean hills,
and I call on the God with the turban of gold, who gave his name to this
    country of ours,
the Bacchic God with the wind flushed face,
Evian One, who travel   220
with the Maenad company,°
combat the God that burns us
with your torch of pine;
for the God that is our enemy is a God unhonored among the Gods.

(Oedipus returns.)

Oedipus: For what you ask me—if you will hear my words,   225
    and hearing welcome them and fight the plague,
    you will find strength and lightening of your load.

    Hark to me; what I say to you, I say
    as one that is a stranger to the story
    as stranger to the deed. For I would not   230
    be far upon the track if I alone
    were tracing it without a clue. But now,

218–221 *God with the turban of gold . . . Maenad company:* Bacchus, or Dionysus, god of wine, was
said to travel with a company of Maenads, female revelers.

since after all was finished, I became
a citizen among you, citizens—
now I proclaim to all the men of Thebes: 235
who so among you knows the murderer
by whose hand Laius, son of Labdacus,
died—I command him to tell everything
to me,—yes, though he fears himself to take the blame
on his own head; for bitter punishment   240
he shall have none, but leave this land unharmed.
Or if he knows the murderer, another,
a foreigner, still let him speak the truth.
For I will pay him and be grateful, too.
But if you shall keep silence, if perhaps   245
some one of you, to shield a guilty friend,
or for his own sake shall reject my words—
hear what I shall do then:
I forbid that man, whoever he be, my land,
my land where I hold sovereignty and throne;   250
and I forbid any to welcome him
or cry him greeting or make him a sharer
in sacrifice or offering to the Gods,
or give him water for his hands to wash.
I command all to drive him from their homes,   255
since he is our pollution, as the oracle
of Pytho's God proclaimed him now to me.
So I stand forth a champion of the God
and of the man who died.
Upon the murderer I invoke this curse—   260
whether he is one man and all unknown,
or one of many—may he wear out his life
in misery to miserable doom!
If with my knowledge he lives at my hearth
I pray that I myself may feel my curse.   265
On you I lay my charge to fulfill all this
for me, for the God, and for this land of ours
destroyed and blighted, by the God forsaken.

Even were this no matter of God's ordinance
it would not fit you so to leave it lie,   270
unpurified, since a good man is dead
and one that was a king. Search it out.
Since I am now the holder of his office,
and have his bed and wife that once was his,
and had his line not been unfortunate   275
we would have common children—(fortune leaped
upon his head)—because of all these things,

I fight in his defense as for my father,
and I shall try all means to take the murderer
of Laius the son of Labdacus   280
the son of Polydorus and before him
of Cadmus and before him of Agenor.
Those who do not obey me, may the Gods
grant no crops springing from the ground they plough
nor children to their women! May a fate   285
like this, or one still worse than this consume them!
For you whom these words please, the other Thebans,
may Justice as your ally and all the Gods
live with you, blessing you now and for ever!

Chorus: As you have held me to my oath, I speak: 290
I neither killed the king nor can declare
the killer; but since Phoebus set the quest
it is his part to tell who the man is.

Oedipus: Right; but to put compulsion on the Gods
against their will—no man can do that.   295

Chorus: May I then say what I think second best?

Oedipus: If there's a third best, too, spare not to tell it.

Chorus: I know that what the Lord Teiresias
sees, is most often what the Lord Apollo
sees. If you should inquire of this from him   300
you might find out most clearly.

Oedipus: Even in this my actions have not been sluggard.
On Creon's word I have sent two messengers
and why the prophet is not here already
I have been wondering.

Chorus: His skill apart   305
there is besides only an old faint story.

Oedipus: What is it?
I look at every story.

Chorus: It was said
that he was killed by certain wayfarers.

Oedipus: I heard that, too, but no one saw the killer.   310

Chorus: Yet if he has a share of fear at all,
his courage will not stand firm, hearing your curse.

Oedipus: The man who in the doing did not shrink
will fear no word.

Chorus: Here comes his prosecutor:
led by your men the godly prophet comes   315
in whom alone of mankind truth is native.

(Enter Teiresias, led by a little boy.)

Oedipus: Teiresias, you are versed in everything,
    things teachable and things not to be spoken,
    things of the heaven and earth-creeping things.
    You have no eyes but in your mind you know   320
    with what a plague our city is afflicted.
    My lord, in you alone we find a champion,
    in you alone one that can rescue us.
    Perhaps you have not heard the messengers,
    but Phoebus sent in answer to our sending   325
    an oracle declaring that our freedom
    from this disease would only come when we
    should learn the names of those who killed King Laius,
    and kill them or expel them from our country.
    Do not begrudge us oracles from birds,   330
    or any other way of prophecy
    within your skill; save yourself and the city,
    save me; redeem the debt of our pollution
    that lies on us because of this dead man.
    We are in your hands; pains are most nobly taken   335
    to help another when you have means and power.
Teiresias: Alas, how terrible is wisdom when
    it brings no profit to the man that's wise!
    This I knew well, but had forgotten it,
    else I would not have come here.
Oedipus: What is this?   340
    How sad you are now you have come!
Teiresias: Let me
    go home. It will be easiest for us both
    to bear our several destinies to the end
    if you will follow my advice.
Oedipus: You'd rob us
    of this your gift of prophecy? You talk   345
    as one who had no care for law nor love
    for Thebes who reared you.
Teiresias: Yes, but I see that even your own words
    miss the mark; therefore I must fear for mine.
Oedipus: For God's sake if you know of anything,   350
    do not turn from us; all of us kneel to you,
    all of us here, your suppliants.
Teiresias: All of you here know nothing. I will not
    bring to the light of day my troubles, mine—
    rather than call them yours.
Oedipus: What do you mean?   355
    You know of something but refuse to speak.
    Would you betray us and destroy the city?

Teiresias: I will not bring this pain upon us both,
neither on you nor on myself. Why is it
you question me and waste your labor? I   360
will tell you nothing.
Oedipus: You would provoke a stone! Tell us, you villain,
tell us, and do not stand there quietly
unmoved and balking at the issue.
Teiresias: You blame my temper but you do not see   365
your own that lives within you; it is me
you chide.
Oedipus: Who would not feel his temper rise
at words like these with which you shame our city?
Teiresias: Of themselves things will come, although I hide them   370
and breathe no word of them.
Oedipus: Since they will come
tell them to me.
Teiresias: I will say nothing further.
Against this answer let your temper rage
as wildly as you will.
Oedipus: Indeed I am
so angry I shall not hold back a jot   375
of what I think. For I would have you know
I think you were complotter of the deed
and doer of the deed save in so far
as for the actual killing. Had you had eyes
I would have said alone you murdered him.   380
Teiresias: Yes? Then I warn you faithfully to keep
the letter of your proclamation and
from this day forth to speak no word of greeting
to these nor me; you are the land's pollution.
Oedipus: How shamelessly you started up this taunt!   385
How do you think you will escape?
Teiresias: I have.
I have escaped; the truth is what I cherish
and that's my strength.
Oedipus: And who has taught you truth?
Not your profession surely!
Teiresias: You have taught me,
for you have made me speak against my will.   390
Oedipus: Speak what? Tell me again that I may learn it better.
Teiresias: Did you not understand before or would you
provoke me into speaking?
Oedipus: I did not grasp it,
not so to call it known. Say it again.

Teiresias: I say you are the murderer of the king 395
    whose murderer you seek.

Oedipus: Not twice you shall
    say calumnies like this and stay unpunished.

Teiresias: Shall I say more to tempt your anger more?

Oedipus: As much as you desire; it will be said
    in vain.

Teiresias: I say that with those you love best 400
    you live in foulest shame unconsciously
    and do not see where you are in calamity.

Oedipus: Do you imagine you can always talk
    like this, and live to laugh at it hereafter?

Teiresias: Yes, if the truth has anything of strength. 405

Oedipus: It has, but not for you; it has no strength
    for you because you are blind in mind and ears
    as well as in your eyes.

Teiresias: You are a poor wretch
    to taunt me with the very insults which
    every one soon will heap upon yourself. 410

Oedipus: Your life is one long night so that you cannot
    hurt me or any other who sees the light.

Teiresias: It is not fate that I should be your ruin,
    Apollo is enough; it is his care
    to work this out.

Oedipus: Was this your own design 415
    or Creon's?

Teiresias: Creon is no hurt to you,
    but you are to yourself.

Oedipus: Wealth, sovereignty and skill outmatching skill
    for the contrivance of an envied life!
    Great store of jealousy fill your treasury chests, 420
    if my friend Creon, friend from the first and loyal,
    thus secretly attacks me, secretly
    desires to drive me out and secretly
    suborns this juggling, trick devising quack,
    this wily beggar who has only eyes 425
    for his own gains, but blindness in his skill.
    For, tell me, where have you seen clear, Teiresias,
    with your prophetic eyes? When the dark singer,
    the Sphinx, was in your country, did you speak
    word of deliverance to its citizens? 430
    And yet the riddle's answer was not the province
    of a chance comer. It was a prophet's task
    and plainly you had no such gift of prophecy
    from birds nor otherwise from any God

to glean a word of knowledge. But I came,   435
Oedipus, who knew nothing, and I stopped her.
I solved the riddle by my wit alone.
Mine was no knowledge got from birds. And now
you would expel me,
because you think that you will find a place   440
by Creon's throne. I think you will be sorry,
both you and your accomplice, for your plot
to drive me out. And did I not regard you
as an old man, some suffering would have taught you
that what was in your heart was treason.   445
Chorus: We look at this man's words and yours, my king,
and we find both have spoken them in anger.
We need no angry words but only thought
how we may best hit the God's meaning for us.
Teiresias: If you are king, at least I have the right   450
no less to speak in my defense against you.
Of that much I am master. I am no slave
of yours, but Loxias',° and so I shall not
enroll myself with Creon for my patron.
Since you have taunted me with being blind,   455
here is my word for you.
You have your eyes but see not where you are
in sin, nor where you live, nor whom you live with.
Do you know who your parents are? Unknowing
you are an enemy to kith and kin   460
in death, beneath the earth, and in this life.
A deadly footed, double striking curse,
from father and mother both, shall drive you forth
out of this land, with darkness on your eyes,
that now have such straight vision. Shall there be   465
a place will not be harbor to your cries,
a corner of Cithaeron° will not ring
in echo to your cries, soon, soon,—
when you shall learn the secret of your marriage,
which steered you to a haven in this house,—   470
haven no haven, after lucky voyage?
And of the multitude of other evils
establishing a grim equality
between you and your children, you know nothing.
So, muddy with contempt my words and Creon's!   475

---

453 *Loxias':* Apollo's.   467 *Cithaeron:* a mountain outside Thebes where the child Oedipus
had been abandoned to die.

Misery shall grind no man as it will you.
Oedipus: Is it endurable that I should hear
  such words from him? Go and a curse go with you!
  Quick, home with you! Out of my house at once!
Teiresias: I would not have come either had you not called me.   480
Oedipus: I did not know then you would talk like a fool—
  or it would have been long before I called you.
Teiresias: I am a fool then, as it seems to you—
  but to the parents who have bred you, wise.
Oedipus: What parents? Stop! Who are they of all the world?   485
Teiresias: This day will show your birth and will destroy you.
Oedipus: How needlessly your riddles darken everything.
Teiresias: But it's in riddle answering you are strongest.
Oedipus: Yes. Taunt me where you will find me great.
Teiresias: It is this very luck that has destroyed you.   490
Oedipus: I do not care, if it has saved this city.
Teiresias: Well, I will go. Come, boy, lead me away.
Oedipus: Yes, lead him off. So long as you are here,
  you'll be a stumbling block and a vexation;
  once gone, you will not trouble me again.
Teiresias: I have said   495
  what I came here to say not fearing your
  countenance: there is no way you can hurt me.
  I tell you, king, this man, this murderer
  (whom you have long declared you are in search of,
  indicting him in threatening proclamation   500
  as murderer of Laius)—he is here.
  In name he is a stranger among citizens
  but soon he will be shown to be a citizen
  true native Theban, and he'll have no joy
  of the discovery: blindness for sight   505
  and beggary for riches his exchange,
  he shall go journeying to a foreign country
  tapping his way before him with a stick.
  He shall be proved father and brother both
  to his own children in his house; to her   510
  that gave him birth, a son and husband both;
  a fellow sower in his father's bed
  with that same father that he murdered.
  Go within, reckon that out, and if you find me
  mistaken, say I have no skill in prophecy.   515

(Exeunt separately Teiresias and Oedipus.)

Strophe

Chorus: Who is the man proclaimed
by Delphi's prophetic rock°
as the bloody handed murderer,
the doer of deeds that none dare name?
Now is the time for him to run   520
with a stronger foot
than Pegasus°
for the child of Zeus° leaps in arms upon him
with fire and the lightning bolt,
and terribly close on his heels   525
are the Fates that never miss.

Antistrophe

Lately from snowy Parnassus
clearly the voice flashed forth,
bidding each Theban track him down,
the unknown murderer.   530
In the savage forests he lurks and in
the caverns like
the mountain bull.
He is sad and lonely, and lonely his feet
that carry him far from the navel of earth;   535
but its prophecies, ever living,
flutter around his head.

Strophe

The augur has spread confusion,
terrible confusion;
I do not approve what was said   540
nor can I deny it.
I do not know what to say;
I am in a flutter of foreboding;
I never heard in the present
nor past of a quarrel between   545
the sons of Labdacus and Polybus,°
that I might bring as proof

517 *Delphi's prophetic rock:* The shrine at Delphi, thought to stand at the geographical center of the world, featured a holy stone known as the Navel of the Earth.   522 *Pegasus:* in Greek mythology, the winged horse born from the neck of the dying gorgon Medusa. A blow of his hoof caused the stream Hippocrene to spring forth from Mount Helicon; its waters were thought to inspire poets to write.   523 *child of Zeus:* Apollo, armed with the thunderbolts of his father. 546 *sons of Labdacus and Polybus:* The son of Labdacus was Laius, previous king of Thebes. At this moment in the play Oedipus is assumed to be the son of Polybus, king of Corinth.

in attacking the popular fame
of Oedipus, seeking
to take vengeance for undiscovered   550
death in the line of Labdacus.

Antistrophe

Truly Zeus and Apollo are wise
and in human things all knowing;
but amongst men there is no
distinct judgment, between the prophet   555
and me—which of us is right.
One man may pass another in wisdom
but I would never agree
with those that find fault with the king
till I should see the word   560
proved right beyond doubt. For once
in visible form the Sphinx
came on him and all of us
saw his wisdom and in that test
he saved the city. So he will not be condemned by my mind.   565

(*Enter Creon.*)

Creon: Citizens, I have come because I heard
    deadly words spread about me, that the king
    accuses me. I cannot take that from him.
    If he believes that in these present troubles
    he has been wronged by me in word or deed   570
    I do not want to live on with the burden
    of such a scandal on me. The report
    injures me doubly and most vitally—
    for I'll be called a traitor to my city
    and traitor also to my friends and you.   575
Chorus: Perhaps it was a sudden gust of anger
    that forced that insult from him, and no judgment.
Creon: But did he say that it was in compliance
    with schemes of mine that the seer told him lies?
Chorus: Yes, he said that, but why, I do not know.   580
Creon: Were his eyes straight in his head? Was his mind right
    when he accused me in this fashion?
Chorus: I do not know; I have no eyes to see
    what princes do. Here comes the king himself.

(*Enter Oedipus.*)

Oedipus: You, sir, how is it you come here? Have you so much   585
    brazen-faced daring that you venture in

my house although you are proved manifestly
the murderer of that man, and though you tried,
openly, highway robbery of my crown?
For God's sake, tell me what you saw in me, 590
what cowardice or what stupidity,
that made you lay a plot like this against me?
Did you imagine I should not observe
the crafty scheme that stole upon me or
seeing it, take no means to counter it? 595
Was it not stupid of you to make the attempt,
to try to hunt down royal power without
the people at your back or friends? For only
with the people at your back or money can
the hunt end in the capture of a crown. 600

Creon: Do you know what you're doing? Will you listen
  to words to answer yours, and then pass judgment?
Oedipus: You're quick to speak, but I am slow to grasp you,
  for I have found you dangerous,—and my foe.
Creon: First of all hear what I shall say to that. 605
Oedipus: At least don't tell me that you are not guilty.
Creon: If you think obstinacy without wisdom
  a valuable possession, you are wrong.
Oedipus: And you are wrong if you believe that one,
  a criminal, will not be punished only 610
  because he is my kinsman.
Creon: This is but just—
  but tell me, then, of what offense I'm guilty?
Oedipus: Did you or did you not urge me to send
  to this prophetic mumbler?
Creon: I did indeed,
  and I shall stand by what I told you. 615
Oedipus: How long ago is it since Laius. . . .
Creon: What about Laius? I don't understand.
Oedipus: Vanished—died—was murdered?
Creon: It is long,
  a long, long time to reckon.
Oedipus: Was this prophet
  in the profession then?
Creon: He was, and honored 620
  as highly as he is today.
Oedipus: At that time did he say a word about me?
Creon: Never, at least when I was near him.
Oedipus: You never made a search for the dead man?
Creon: We searched, indeed, but never learned of anything. 625

Oedipus: Why did our wise old friend not say this then?
Creon: I don't know; and when I know nothing, I
    usually hold my tongue.
Oedipus: You know this much,
    and can declare this much if you are loyal.
Creon: What is it? If I know, I'll not deny it.   630
Oedipus: That he would not have said that I killed Laius
    had he not met you first.
Creon: You know yourself
    whether he said this, but I demand that I
    should hear as much from you as you from me.
Oedipus: Then hear,—I'll not be proved a murderer.   635
Creon: Well, then. You're married to my sister.
Oedipus: Yes,
    that I am not disposed to deny.
Creon: You rule
    this country giving her an equal share
    in the government?
Oedipus: Yes, everything she wants
    she has from me.
Creon: And I, as thirdsman to you,   640
    am rated as the equal of you two?
Oedipus: Yes, and it's there you've proved yourself false friend.
Creon: Not if you will reflect on it as I do.
    Consider, first, if you think any one
    would choose to rule and fear rather than rule   645
    and sleep untroubled by a fear if power
    were equal in both cases. I, at least,
    I was not born with such a frantic yearning
    to be a king—but to do what kings do.
    And so it is with every one who has learned   650
    wisdom and self-control. As it stands now,
    the prizes are all mine—and without fear.
    But if I were the king myself, I must
    do much that went against the grain.
    How should despotic rule seem sweeter to me   655
    than painless power and an assured authority?
    I am not so besotted yet that I
    want other honors than those that come with profit.
    Now every man's my pleasure; every man greets me;
    now those who are your suitors fawn on me,—   660
    success for them depends upon my favor.
    Why should I let all this go to win that?
    My mind would not be traitor if it's wise;

I am no treason lover, of my nature,
nor would I ever dare to join a plot.   665
Prove what I say. Go to the oracle
at Pytho and inquire about the answers,
if they are as I told you. For the rest,
if you discover I laid any plot
together with the seer, kill me, I say,   670
not only by your vote but by my own.
But do not charge me on obscure opinion
without some proof to back it. It's not just
lightly to count your knaves as honest men,
nor honest men as knaves. To throw away   675
an honest friend is, as it were, to throw
your life away, which a man loves the best.
In time you will know all with certainty;
time is the only test of honest men,
one day is space enough to know a rogue.   680
Chorus: His words are wise, king, if one fears to fall.
        Those who are quick of temper are not safe.
Oedipus: When he that plots against me secretly
        moves quickly, I must quickly counterplot.
        If I wait taking no decisive measure   685
        his business will be done, and mine be spoiled.
Creon: What do you want to do then? Banish me?
Oedipus: No, certainly; kill you, not banish you.
Creon: I do not think that you've your wits about you.
Oedipus: For my own interests, yes.
Creon: But for mine, too,   690
        you should think equally.
Oedipus: You are a rogue.
Creon: Suppose you do not understand?
Oedipus: But yet
        I must be ruler.
Creon: Not if you rule badly.
Oedipus: O, city, city!
Creon: I too have some share
        in the city; it is not yours alone.   695
Chorus: Stop, my lords! Here—and in the nick of time
        I see Jocasta coming from the house;
        with her help lay the quarrel that now stirs you.

        (*Enter Jocasta.*)

Jocasta: For shame! Why have you raised this foolish squabbling
        brawl? Are you not ashamed to air your private   700

griefs when the country's sick? Go in, you, Oedipus,
and you, too, Creon, into the house. Don't magnify
your nothing troubles.

Creon: Sister, Oedipus,
your husband, thinks he has the right to do
terrible wrongs—he has but to choose between   705
two terrors: banishing or killing me.

Oedipus: He's right, Jocasta; for I find him plotting
with knavish tricks against my person.

Creon: That God may never bless me! May I die
accursed, if I have been guilty of   710
one tittle of the charge you bring against me!

Jocasta: I beg you, Oedipus, trust him in this,
spare him for the sake of this his oath to God,
for my sake, and the sake of those who stand here.

Chorus: Be gracious, be merciful,   715
we beg of you.

Oedipus: In what would you have me yield?

Chorus: He has been no silly child in the past.
He is strong in his oath now.
Spare him.   720

Oedipus: Do you know what you ask?

Chorus: Yes.

Oedipus: Tell me then.

Chorus: He has been your friend before all men's eyes; do not cast him
away dishonored on an obscure conjecture.   725

Oedipus: I would have you know that this request of yours
really requests my death or banishment.

Chorus: May the Sun God, king of Gods, forbid! May I die without God's
blessing, without friends' help, if I had any such thought. But my spirit is
broken by my unhappiness for my wasting country; and this would   730
but add troubles amongst ourselves to the other troubles.

Oedipus: Well, let him go then—if I must die ten times for it,
or be sent out dishonored into exile.
It is your lips that prayed for him I pitied,
not his; wherever he is, I shall hate him.   735

Creon: I see you sulk in yielding and you're dangerous
when you are out of temper; natures like yours
are justly heaviest for themselves to bear.

Oedipus: Leave me alone! Take yourself off, I tell you.

Creon: I'll go, you have not known me, but they have,   740
and they have known my innocence.

(*Exit.*)

Chorus: Won't you take him inside, lady?
Jocasta: Yes, when I've found out what was the matter.
Chorus: There was some misconceived suspicion of a story, and on the
        other side the sting of injustice.   745
Jocasta: So, on both sides?
Chorus: Yes.
Jocasta: What was the story?
Chorus: I think it best, in the interests of the country,
        to leave it where it ended.   750
Oedipus: You see where you have ended, straight of judgment
        although you are, by softening my anger.
Chorus: Sir, I have said before and I say again—be sure that I would have
        been proved a madman, bankrupt in sane council, if I should put
        you away, you who steered the country I love safely when she was
        crazed with troubles. God grant that now, too, you may prove a   755
        fortunate guide for us.
Jocasta: Tell me, my lord, I beg of you, what was it
        that roused your anger so?
Oedipus: Yes, I will tell you.
        I honor you more than I honor them.
        It was Creon and the plots he laid against me.   760
Jocasta: Tell me—if you can clearly tell the quarrel—
Oedipus: Creon says
        that I'm the murderer of Laius.
Jocasta: Of his own knowledge or on information?
Oedipus: He sent this rascal prophet to me, since
        he keeps his own mouth clean of any guilt.   765
Jocasta: Do not concern yourself about this matter;
        listen to me and learn that human beings
        have no part in the craft of prophecy.
        Of that I'll show you a short proof.
        There was an oracle once that came to Laius,—   770
        I will not say that it was Phoebus' own,
        but it was from his servants—and it told him
        that it was fate that he should die a victim
        at the hands of his own son, a son to be born
        of Laius and me. But, see now, he,   775
        the king, was killed by foreign highway robbers
        at a place where three roads meet—so goes the story;
        and for the son—before three days were out
        after his birth King Laius pierced his ankles
        and by the hands of others cast him forth   780
        upon a pathless hillside. So Apollo
        failed to fulfill his oracle to the son,
        that he should kill his father, and to Laius

also proved false in that the thing he feared,
death at his son's hands, never came to pass.   785
So clear in this case were the oracles,
so clear and false. Give them no heed, I say;
what God discovers need of, easily
he shows to us himself.

Oedipus: O dear Jocasta,
as I hear this from you, there comes upon me   790
a wandering of the soul—I could run mad.

Jocasta: What trouble is it, that you turn again
and speak like this?

Oedipus: I thought I heard you say
that Laius was killed at a crossroads.

Jocasta: Yes, that was how the story went and still   795
that word goes round.

Oedipus: Where is this place, Jocasta,
where he was murdered?

Jocasta: Phocis is the country
and the road splits there, one of two roads from Delphi,
another comes from Daulia.

Oedipus: How long ago is this?

Jocasta: The news came to the city just before   800
you became king and all men's eyes looked to you.
What is it, Oedipus, that's in your mind?

Oedipus: What have you designed, O Zeus, to do with me?

Jocasta: What is the thought that troubles your heart?

Oedipus: Don't ask me yet—tell me of Laius—   805
How did he look? How old or young was he?

Jocasta: He was a tall man and his hair was grizzled
already—nearly white—and in his form
not unlike you.

Oedipus: O God, I think I have
called curses on myself in ignorance.   810

Jocasta: What do you mean? I am terrified
when I look at you.

Oedipus: I have a deadly fear
that the old seer had eyes. You'll show me more
if you can tell me one more thing.

Jocasta: I will.
I'm frightened,—but if I can understand,   815
I'll tell you all you ask.

Oedipus: How was his company?
Had he few with him when he went this journey,
or many servants, as would suit a prince?

Jocasta: In all there were but five, and among them
    a herald; and one carriage for the king.   820
Oedipus: It's plain—it's plain—who was it told you this?
Jocasta: The only servant that escaped safe home.
Oedipus: Is he at home now?
Jocasta: No, when he came home again
    and saw you king and Laius was dead,
    he came to me and touched my hand and begged   825
    that I should send him to the fields to be
    my shepherd and so he might see the city
    as far off as he might. So I
    sent him away. He was an honest man,
    as slaves go, and was worthy of far more   830
    than what he asked of me.
Oedipus: O, how I wish that he could come back quickly!
Jocasta: He can. Why is your heart so set on this?
Oedipus: O dear Jocasta, I am full of fears
    that I have spoken far too much; and therefore   835
    I wish to see this shepherd.
Jocasta: He will come;
    but, Oedipus, I think I'm worthy too
    to know what it is that disquiets you.
Oedipus: It shall not be kept from you, since my mind
    has gone so far with its forebodings. Whom   840
    should I confide in rather than you, who is there
    of more importance to me who have passed
    through such a fortune?
    Polybus was my father, king of Corinth,
    and Merope, the Dorian, my mother.   845
    I was held greatest of the citizens
    in Corinth till a curious chance befell me
    as I shall tell you—curious, indeed,
    but hardly worth the store I set upon it.
    There was a dinner and at it a man,   850
    a drunken man, accused me in his drink
    of being bastard. I was furious
    but held my temper under for that day.
    Next day I went and taxed my parents with it;
    they took the insult very ill from him,   855
    the drunken fellow who had uttered it.
    So I was comforted for their part, but
    still this thing rankled always, for the story
    crept about widely. And I went at last
    to Pytho, though my parents did not know.   860

But Phoebus sent me home again unhonored
in what I came to learn, but he foretold
other and desperate horrors to befall me,
that I was fated to lie with my mother,
and show to daylight an accursed breed   865
which men would not endure, and I was doomed
to be murderer of the father that begot me.
When I heard this I fled, and in the days
that followed I would measure from the stars
the whereabouts of Corinth—yes, I fled   870
to somewhere where I should not see fulfilled
the infamies told in that dreadful oracle.
And as I journeyed I came to the place
where, as you say, this king met with his death.
Jocasta, I will tell you the whole truth.   875
When I was near the branching of the crossroads,
going on foot, I was encountered by
a herald and a carriage with a man in it,
just as you tell me. He that led the way
and the old man himself wanted to thrust me   880
out of the road by force. I became angry
and struck the coachman who was pushing me.
When the old man saw this he watched his moment,
and as I passed he struck me from his carriage,
full on the head with his two pointed goad.   885
But he was paid in full and presently
my stick had struck him backwards from the car
and he rolled out of it. And then I killed them
all. If it happened there was any tie
of kinship twixt this man and Laius,   890
who is then now more miserable than I,
what man on earth so hated by the Gods,
since neither citizen nor foreigner
may welcome me at home or even greet me,
but drive me out of doors? And it is I,   895
I and no other have so cursed myself.
And I pollute the bed of him I killed
by the hands that killed him. Was I not born evil?
Am I not utterly unclean? I had to fly
and in my banishment not even see   900
my kindred nor set foot in my own country,
or otherwise my fate was to be yoked
in marriage with my mother and kill my father,
Polybus who begot me and had reared me.
Would not one rightly judge and say that on me   905

these things were sent by some malignant God?
O no, no, no—O holy majesty
of God on high, may I not see that day!
May I be gone out of men's sight before
I see the deadly taint of this disaster   910
come upon me.

Chorus: Sir, we too fear these things. But until you see this man face to
face and hear his story, hope.

Oedipus: Yes, I have just this much of hope—to wait until the herdsman
comes.   915

Jocasta: And when he comes, what do you want with him?

Oedipus: I'll tell you; if I find that his story is the same as yours, I at least
will be clear of this guilt.

Jocasta: Why, what so particularly did you learn from my story?

Oedipus: You said that he spoke of highway *robbers* who killed Laius.   920
Now if he uses the same number, it was not I who killed him. One
man cannot be the same as many. But if he speaks of a man travelling
alone, then clearly the burden of the guilt inclines towards me.

Jocasta: Be sure, at least, that this was how he told the story. He cannot
unsay it now, for every one in the city heard it—not I alone. But,   925
Oedipus, even if he diverges from what he said then, he shall never
prove that the murder of Laius squares rightly with the prophecy—
for Loxias declared that the king should be killed by his own son.
And that poor creature did not kill him surely,—for he died himself
first. So as far as prophecy goes, henceforward I shall not look to the   930
right hand or the left.

Oedipus: Right. But yet, send some one for the peasant to bring him here; do
not neglect it.

Jocasta: I will send quickly. Now let me go indoors. I will do nothing
except what pleases you.   935

(*Exeunt.*)

Strophe

Chorus: May destiny ever find me
pious in word and deed
prescribed by the laws that live on high:
laws begotten in the clear air of heaven,
whose only father is Olympus;   940
no mortal nature brought them to birth,
no forgetfulness shall lull them to sleep;
for God is great in them and grows not old.

Antistrophe

Insolence breeds the tyrant, insolence
if it is glutted with a surfeit, unseasonable, unprofitable,   945

climbs to the roof-top and plunges
sheer down to the ruin that must be,
and there its feet are no service.
But I pray that the God may never
abolish the eager ambition that profits the state.   950
For I shall never cease to hold the God as our protector.

Strophe

If a man walks with haughtiness
of hand or word and gives no heed
to Justice and the shrines of Gods
despises—may an evil doom   955
smite him for his ill-starred pride of heart!—
if he reaps gains without justice
and will not hold from impiety
and his fingers itch for untouchable things.
When such things are done, what man shall contrive   960
to shield his soul from the shafts of the God?
When such deeds are held in honor,
why should I honor the Gods in the dance?

Antistrophe

No longer to the holy place,
to the navel of earth I'll go   965
to worship, nor to Abae
nor to Olympia,
unless the oracles are proved to fit,
for all men's hands to point at.
O Zeus, if you are rightly called   970
the sovereign lord, all-mastering,
let this not escape you nor your ever-living power!
The oracles concerning Laius
are old and dim and men regard them not.
Apollo is nowhere clear in honor; God's service perishes.   975

(Enter Jocasta, carrying garlands.)

Jocasta: Princes of the land, I have had the thought to go
to the Gods' temples, bringing in my hand
garlands and gifts of incense, as you see.
For Oedipus excites himself too much
at every sort of trouble, not conjecturing,   980
like a man of sense, what will be from what was,
but he is always at the speaker's mercy,
when he speaks terrors. I can do no good
by my advice, and so I came as suppliant

to you, Lycaean Apollo, who are nearest.   985
These are the symbols of my prayer and this
my prayer: grant us escape free of the curse.
Now when we look to him we are all afraid;
he's pilot of our ship and he is frightened.

(Enter Messenger.)

Messenger: Might I learn from you, sirs, where is the house of Oedipus?   990
Or best of all, if you know, where is the king himself?

Chorus: This is his house and he is within doors. This lady is his wife and
mother of his children.

Messenger: God bless you, lady, and God bless your household! God bless
Oedipus' noble wife!   995

Jocasta: God bless you, sir, for your kind greeting! What do you want of us
that you have come here? What have you to tell us?

Messenger: Good news, lady. Good for your house and for your husband.

Jocasta: What is your news? Who sent you to us?

Messenger: I come from Corinth and the news I bring will give you   1000
pleasure. Perhaps a little pain too.

Jocasta: What is this news of double meaning?

Messenger: The people of the Isthmus will choose Oedipus to be their
king. That is the rumor there.

Jocasta: But isn't their king still old Polybus?   1005

Messenger: No. He is in his grave. Death has got him.

Jocasta: Is that the truth? Is Oedipus' father dead?

Messenger: May I die myself if it be otherwise!

Jocasta (to a servant): Be quick and run to the King with the news! O oracles
of the Gods, where are you now? It was from this man Oedipus fled,   1010
lest he should be his murderer! And now he is dead, in the course of
nature, and not killed by Oedipus.

(Enter Oedipus.)

Oedipus: Dearest Jocasta, why have you sent for me?

Jocasta: Listen to this man and when you hear reflect what is the outcome
of the holy oracles of the Gods.   1015

Oedipus: Who is he? What is his message for me?

Jocasta: He is from Corinth and he tells us that your father Polybus is
dead and gone.

Oedipus: What's this you say, sir? Tell me yourself.

Messenger: Since this is the first matter you want clearly told: Polybus has 1020
gone down to death. You may be sure of it.

Oedipus: By treachery or sickness?

Messenger: A small thing will put old bodies asleep.

Oedipus: So he died of sickness, it seems,—poor old man!

Messenger: Yes, and of age—the long years he had measured. 1025
Oedipus: Ha! Ha! O dear Jocasta, why should one
look to the Pythian hearth?° Why should one look
to the birds screaming overhead? They prophesied
that I should kill my father! But he's dead,
and hidden deep in earth, and I stand here 1030
who never laid a hand on spear against him,—
unless perhaps he died of longing for me,
and thus I am his murderer. But they,
the oracles, as they stand—he's taken them
away with him, they're dead as he himself is, 1035
and worthless.
Jocasta: That I told you before now.
Oedipus: You did, but I was misled by my fear.
Jocasta: Then lay no more of them to heart, not one.
Oedipus: But surely I must fear my mother's bed?
Jocasta: Why should man fear since chance is all in all 1040
for him, and he can clearly foreknow nothing?
Best to live lightly, as one can, unthinkingly.
As to your mother's marriage bed,—don't fear it.
Before this, in dreams too, as well as oracles,
many a man has lain with his own mother. 1045
But he to whom such things are nothing bears
his life most easily.
Oedipus: All that you say would be said perfectly
if she were dead; but since she lives I must
still fear, although you talk so well, Jocasta. 1050
Jocasta: Still in your father's death there's light of comfort?
Oedipus: Great light of comfort; but I fear the living.
Messenger: Who is the woman that makes you afraid?
Oedipus: Merope, old man, Polybus' wife.
Messenger: What about her frightens the queen and you? 1055
Oedipus: A terrible oracle, stranger, from the Gods.
Messenger: Can it be told? Or does the sacred law
forbid another to have knowledge of it?
Oedipus: O no! Once on a time Loxias said
that I should lie with my own mother and 1060
take on my hands the blood of my own father.
And so for these long years I've lived away
from Corinth; it has been to my great happiness;
but yet it's sweet to see the face of parents.
Messenger: This was the fear which drove you out of Corinth? 1065

1027 *Pythian hearth:* the oracle at Delphi.

Oedipus: Old man, I did not wish to kill my father.

Messenger: Why should I not free you from this fear, sir,
     since I have come to you in all goodwill?

Oedipus: You would not find me thankless if you did.

Messenger: Why, it was just for this I brought the news,—   1070
     to earn your thanks when you had come safe home.

Oedipus: No, I will never come near my parents.

Messenger: Son,
     it's very plain you don't know what you're doing.

Oedipus: What do you mean, old man? For God's sake, tell me.

Messenger: If your homecoming is checked by fears like these.   1075

Oedipus: Yes, I'm afraid that Phoebus may prove right.

Messenger: The murder and the incest?

Oedipus: Yes, old man;
     that is my constant terror.

Messenger: Do you know
     that all your fears are empty?

Oedipus: How is that,
     if they are father and mother and I their son?   1080

Messenger: Because Polybus was no kin to you in blood.

Oedipus: What, was not Polybus my father?

Messenger: No more than I but just so much.

Oedipus: How can
     my father be my father as much as one
     that's nothing to me?

Messenger: Neither he nor I   1085
     begat you.

Oedipus: Why then did he call me son?

Messenger: A gift he took you from these hands of mine.

Oedipus: Did he love so much what he took from another's hand?

Messenger: His childlessness before persuaded him.

Oedipus: Was I a child you bought or found when I   1090
     was given to him?

Messenger: On Cithaeron's slopes
     in the twisting thickets you were found.

Oedipus: And why
     were you a traveller in those parts?

Messenger: I was
     in charge of mountain flocks.

Oedipus: You were a shepherd?
     A hireling vagrant?

Messenger: Yes, but at least at that time   1095
     the man that saved your life, son.

Oedipus: What ailed me when you took me in your arms?

Messenger: In that your ankles should be witnesses.
Oedipus: Why do you speak of that old pain?
Messenger: I loosed you;
    the tendons of your feet were pierced and fettered,—   1100
Oedipus: My swaddling clothes brought me a rare disgrace.
Messenger: So that from this you're called your present name.°
Oedipus: Was this my father's doing or my mother's?
    For God's sake, tell me.
Messenger: I don't know, but he
    who gave you to me has more knowledge than I.   1105
Oedipus: You yourself did not find me then? You took me
    from someone else?
Messenger: Yes, from another shepherd.
Oedipus: Who was he? Do you know him well enough
    to tell?
Messenger: He was called Laius' man.   1110
Oedipus: You mean the king who reigned here in the old days?
Messenger: Yes, he was that man's shepherd.
Oedipus: Is he alive
    still, so that I could see him?
Messenger: You who live here
    would know that best.
Oedipus: Do any of you here
    know of this shepherd whom he speaks about   1115
    in town or in the fields? Tell me. It's time
    that this was found out once for all.
Chorus: I think he is none other than the peasant
    whom you have sought to see already; but
    Jocasta here can tell us best of that.   1120
Oedipus: Jocasta, do you know about this man
    whom we have sent for? Is he the man he mentions?
Jocasta: Why ask of whom he spoke? Don't give it heed;
    nor try to keep in mind what has been said.
    It will be wasted labor.
Oedipus: With such clues   1125
    I could not fail to bring my birth to light.
Jocasta: I beg you—do not hunt this out—I beg you,
    if you have any care for your own life.
    What I am suffering is enough.
Oedipus: Keep up
    your heart, Jocasta. Though I'm proved a slave,   1130

1102 *your present name:* Oedipus's name means "swollen foot" or "clubfoot."

thrice slave, and though my mother is thrice slave,
  you'll not be shown to be of lowly lineage.
Jocasta: O be persuaded by me, I entreat you;
  do not do this.
Oedipus: I will not be persuaded to let be   1135
  the chance of finding out the whole thing clearly.
Jocasta: It is because I wish you well that I
  give you this counsel—and it's the best counsel.
Oedipus: Then the best counsel vexes me, and has
  for some while since.
Jocasta: O Oedipus, God help you!   1140
  God keep you from the knowledge of who you are!
Oedipus: Here, some one, go and fetch the shepherd for me;
  and let her find her joy in her rich family!
Jocasta: O Oedipus, unhappy Oedipus!
  that is all I can call you, and the last thing   1145
  that I shall ever call you.

(*Exit.*)

Chorus: Why has the queen gone, Oedipus, in wild
  grief rushing from us? I am afraid that trouble
  will break out of this silence.
Oedipus: Break out what will! I at least shall be   1150
  willing to see my ancestry, though humble.
  Perhaps she is ashamed of my low birth,
  for she has all a woman's high-flown pride.
  But I account myself a child of Fortune,
  beneficent Fortune, and I shall not be   1155
  dishonored. She's the mother from whom I spring;
  the months, my brothers, marked me, now as small,
  and now again as mighty. Such is my breeding,
  and I shall never prove so false to it,
  as not to find the secret of my birth.   1160

Strophe

Chorus: If I am a prophet and wise of heart
  you shall not fail, Cithaeron,
  by the limitless sky, you shall not!—
  to know at tomorrow's full moon
  that Oedipus honors you,   1165
  as native to him and mother and nurse at once;
  and that you are honored in dancing by us, as finding favor in sight
    of our king.
  Apollo, to whom we cry, find these things pleasing!

Antistrophe

Who was it bore you, child? One of
the long-lived nymphs who lay with Pan°—   1170
the father who treads the hills?
Or was she a bride of Loxias, your mother? The grassy slopes
are all of them dear to him. Or perhaps Cyllene's king°
or the Bacchants' God° that lives on the tops
of the hills received you a gift from some   1175
one of the Helicon Nymphs, with whom he mostly plays?

(Enter an old man, led by Oedipus' servants.)

Oedipus: If some one like myself who never met him
    may make a guess,—I think this is the herdsman,
    whom we were seeking. His old age is consonant
    with the other. And besides, the men who bring him   1180
    I recognize as my own servants. You
    perhaps may better me in knowledge since
    you've seen the man before.
Chorus: You can be sure
    I recognize him. For if Laius
    had ever an honest shepherd, this was he.   1185
Oedipus: You, sir, from Corinth, I must ask you first,
    is this the man you spoke of?
Messenger: This is he
    before your eyes.
Oedipus: Old man, look here at me
    and tell me what I ask you. Were you ever
    a servant of King Laius?
Herdsman: I was,—   1190
    no slave he bought but reared in his own house.
Oedipus: What did you do as work? How did you live?
Herdsman: Most of my life was spent among the flocks.
Oedipus: In what part of the country did you live?
Herdsman: Cithaeron and the places near to it.   1195
Oedipus: And somewhere there perhaps you knew this man?
Herdsman: What was his occupation? Who?
Oedipus: This man here,
    have you had any dealings with him?

1170 *nymphs who lay with Pan:* In Greek mythology, nymphs are beautiful young immortals
associated with features of nature or specific places. Pan is the goat-footed god of wildlife and
the flocks. In this passage the chorus speculates that Oedipus is the child of a nymph by some
god.   1173 *Cyllene's king:* Hermes, messenger of the gods.   1174 *Bacchants' God:* Dionysus.
Bacchants are the same as Maenads, the wine god's priestesses.

Herdsman: No—
   not such that I can quickly call to mind.

Messenger: That is no wonder, master. But I'll make him remember 1200
   what he does not know. For I know, that he well knows the country
   of Cithaeron, how he with two flocks, I with one kept company
   for three years—each year half a year—from spring till autumn
   time and then when winter came I drove my flocks to our fold home
   again and he to Laius' steadings. Well—am I right or not in what 1205
   I said we did?

Herdsman: You're right—although it's a long time ago.

Messenger: Do you remember giving me a child
   to bring up as my foster child?

Herdsman: What's this?
   Why do you ask this question?

Messenger: Look old man,   1210
   here he is—here's the man who was that child!

Herdsman: Death take you! Won't you hold your tongue?

Oedipus: No, no,
   do not find fault with him, old man. Your words
   are more at fault than his.

Herdsman: O best of masters,
   how do I give offense?

Oedipus: When you refuse   1215
   to speak about the child of whom he asks you.

Herdsman: He speaks out of his ignorance, without meaning.

Oedipus: If you'll not talk to gratify me, you
   will talk with pain to urge you.

Herdsman: O please, sir,
   don't hurt an old man, sir.

Oedipus (to the servants):   Here, one of you,   1220
   twist his hands behind him.

Herdsman: Why, God help me, why?
   What do you want to know?

Oedipus: You gave a child
   to him,—the child he asked you of?

Herdsman: I did.
   I wish I'd died the day I did.

Oedipus: You will
   unless you tell me truly.

Herdsman: And I'll die   1225
   far worse if I should tell you.

Oedipus: This fellow
   is bent on more delays, as it would seem.

Herdsman: O no, no! I have told you that I gave it.

Oedipus: Where did you get this child from? Was it your own
  or did you get it from another?

Herdsman: Not   1230
  my own at all; I had it from some one.

Oedipus: One of these citizens? or from what house?

Herdsman: O master, please—I beg you, master, please
  don't ask me more.

Oedipus: You're a dead man if I
  ask you again.

Herdsman: It was one of the children   1235
  of Laius.

Oedipus: A slave? Or born in wedlock?

Herdsman: O God, I am on the brink of frightful speech.

Oedipus: And I of frightful hearing. But I must hear.

Herdsman: The child was called his child; but she within,
  your wife would tell you best how all this was.   1240

Oedipus: *She* gave it to you?

Herdsman: Yes, she did, my lord.

Oedipus: To do what with it?

Herdsman: Make away with it.

Oedipus: She was so hard—its mother?

Herdsman: Aye, through fear
  of evil oracles.

Oedipus: Which?

Herdsman: They said that he
  should kill his parents.

Oedipus: How was it that you   1245
  gave it away to this old man?

Herdsman: O master,
  I pitied it, and thought that I could send it
  off to another country and this man
  was from another country. But he saved it
  for the most terrible troubles. If you are   1250
  the man he says you are, you're bred to misery.

Oedipus: O, O, O, they will all come,
  all come out clearly! Light of the sun, let me
  look upon you no more after today!
  I who first saw the light bred of a match   1255
  accursed, and accursed in my living
  with them I lived with, cursed in my killing.

  (Exeunt all but the Chorus.)

Strophe

Chorus: O generations of men, how I
    count you as equal with those who live
    not at all!   1260
    What man, what man on earth wins more
    of happiness than a seeming
    and after that turning away?
    Oedipus, you are my pattern of this,
    Oedipus, you and your fate!   1265
    Luckless Oedipus, whom of all men
    I envy not at all.

Antistrophe

In as much as he shot his bolt
beyond the others and won the prize
of happiness complete—   1270
O Zeus—and killed and reduced to nought
the hooked taloned maid of the riddling speech,
standing a tower against death for my land:
hence he was called my king and hence
was honored the highest of all   1275
honors; and hence he ruled
in the great city of Thebes.

Strophe

But now whose tale is more miserable?
Who is there lives with a savager fate?
Whose troubles so reverse his life as his?   1280

O Oedipus, the famous prince
for whom a great haven°
the same both as father and son
sufficed for generation,
how, O how, have the furrows ploughed   1285
by your father endured to bear you, poor wretch,
and hold their peace so long?

Antistrophe

Time who sees all has found you out
against your will; judges your marriage accursed,
begetter and begot at one in it.   1290

1282 *a great haven:* the womb of Jocasta.

O child of Laius,
would I had never seen you.
I weep for you and cry
a dirge of lamentation.

To speak directly, I drew my breath   1295
from you at the first and so now I lull
my mouth to sleep with your name.

(*Enter a second messenger.*)

Second Messenger: O Princes always honored by our country,
what deeds you'll hear of and what horrors see,
what grief you'll feel, if you as true born Thebans   1300
care for the house of Labdacus's sons.
Phasis nor Ister cannot purge this house,
I think, with all their streams, such things
it hides, such evils shortly will bring forth
into the light, whether they will or not;   1305
and troubles hurt the most
when they prove self-inflicted.
Chorus: What we had known before did not fall short
of bitter groaning's worth; what's more to tell?
Second Messenger: Shortest to hear and tell—our glorious queen   1310
Jocasta's dead.
Chorus: Unhappy woman! How?
Second Messenger: By her own hand. The worst of what was done
you cannot know. You did not see the sight.
Yet in so far as I remember it
you'll hear the end of our unlucky queen.   1315
When she came raging into the house she went
straight to her marriage bed, tearing her hair
with both her hands, and crying upon Laius
long dead—Do you remember, Laius,
that night long past which bred a child for us   1320
to send you to your death and leave
a mother making children with her son?
And then she groaned and cursed the bed in which
she brought forth husband by her husband, children
by her own child, an infamous double bond.   1325
How after that she died I do not know,—
for Oedipus distracted us from seeing.
He burst upon us shouting and we looked
to him as he paced frantically around,
begging us always: Give me a sword, I say,   1330
to find this wife no wife, this mother's womb,
this field of double sowing whence I sprang

and where I sowed my children! As he raved
some god showed him the way—none of us there.
Bellowing terribly and led by some   1335
invisible guide he rushed on the two doors,—
wrenching the hollow bolts out of their sockets,
he charged inside. There, there, we saw his wife
hanging, the twisted rope around her neck.
When he saw her, he cried out fearfully   1340
and cut the dangling noose. Then, as she lay,
poor woman, on the ground, what happened after,
was terrible to see. He tore the brooches—
the gold chased brooches fastening her robe—
away from her and lifting them up high   1345
dashed them on his own eyeballs, shrieking out
such things as: they will never see the crime
I have committed or had done upon me!
Dark eyes, now in the days to come look on
forbidden faces, do not recognize   1350
those whom you long for—with such imprecations
he struck his eyes again and yet again
with the brooches. And the bleeding eyeballs gushed
and stained his beard—no sluggish oozing drops
but a black rain and bloody hail poured down.   1355

So it has broken—and not on one head
but troubles mixed for husband and for wife.
The fortune of the days gone by was true
good fortune—but today groans and destruction
and death and shame—of all ills can be named   1360
not one is missing.
Chorus: Is he now in any ease from pain?
Second Messenger: He shouts
for some one to unbar the doors and show him
to all the men of Thebes, his father's killer,
his mother's—no I cannot say the word,   1365
it is unholy—for he'll cast himself,
out of the land, he says, and not remain
to bring a curse upon his house, the curse
he called upon it in his proclamation. But
he wants for strength, aye, and some one to guide him;   1370
his sickness is too great to bear. You, too,
will be shown that. The bolts are opening.
Soon you will see a sight to waken pity
even in the horror of it.

(*Enter the blinded Oedipus.*)

Chorus: This is a terrible sight for men to see!   1375
   I never found a worse!
   Poor wretch, what madness came upon you!
   What evil spirit leaped upon your life
   to your ill-luck—a leap beyond man's strength!
   Indeed I pity you, but I cannot   1380
   look at you, though there's much I want to ask
   and much to learn and much to see.
   I shudder at the sight of you.

Oedipus: O, O,
   where am I going? Where is my voice   1385
   borne on the wind to and fro?
   Spirit, how far have you sprung?

Chorus: To a terrible place whereof men's ears
   may not hear, nor their eyes behold it.

Oedipus: Darkness!   1390
   Horror of darkness enfolding, resistless, unspeakable visitant sped by
      an ill wind in haste!
   madness and stabbing pain and memory
   of evil deeds I have done!

Chorus: In such misfortunes it's no wonder
   if double weighs the burden of your grief.   1395

Oedipus: My friend,
   you are the only one steadfast, the only one that attends on me;
   you still stay nursing the blind man.
   Your care is not unnoticed. I can know
   your voice, although this darkness is my world.   1400

Chorus: Doer of dreadful deeds, how did you dare
   so far to do despite to your own eyes?
   what spirit urged you to it?

Oedipus: It was Apollo, friends, Apollo,
   that brought this bitter bitterness, my sorrows to completion.   1405
   But the hand that struck me
   was none but my own.
   Why should I see
   whose vision showed me nothing sweet to see?

Chorus: These things are as you say.   1410

Oedipus: What can I see to love?
   What greeting can touch my ears with joy?
   Take me away, and haste—to a place out of the way!
   Take me away, my friends, the greatly miserable,
   the most accursed, whom God too hates   1415
   above all men on earth!

Chorus: Unhappy in your mind and your misfortune,
   would I had never known you!

Oedipus: Curse on the man who took
    the cruel bonds from off my legs, as I lay in the field.   1420
    He stole me from death and saved me,
    no kindly service.
    Had I died then
    I would not be so burdensome to friends.
Chorus: I, too, could have wished it had been so.   1425
Oedipus: Then I would not have come
    to kill my father and marry my mother infamously.
    Now I am godless and child of impurity,
    begetter in the same seed that created my wretched self.
    If there is any ill worse than ill,   1430
    that is the lot of Oedipus.
Chorus: I cannot say your remedy was good;
    you would be better dead than blind and living.
Oedipus: What I have done here was best done—don't tell me
    otherwise, do not give me further counsel.   1435
    I do not know with what eyes I could look
    upon my father when I die and go
    under the earth, nor yet my wretched mother—
    those two to whom I have done things deserving
    worse punishment than hanging. Would the sight   1440
    of children, bred as mine are, gladden me?
    No, not these eyes, never. And my city,
    its towers and sacred places of the Gods,
    of these I robbed my miserable self
    when I commanded all to drive *him* out,   1445
    the criminal since proved by God impure
    and of the race of Laius.
    To this guilt I bore witness against myself—
    with what eyes shall I look upon my people?
    No. If there were a means to choke the fountain   1450
    of hearing I would not have stayed my hand
    from locking up my miserable carcase,
    seeing and hearing nothing; it is sweet
    to keep our thoughts out of the range of hurt.

    Cithaeron, why did you receive me? Why   1455
    having received me did you not kill me straight?
    And so I had not shown to men my birth.

    O Polybus and Corinth and the house,
    the old house that I used to call my father's—
    what fairness you were nurse to, and what foulness   1460
    festered beneath! Now I am found to be
    a sinner and a son of sinners. Crossroads,

and hidden glade, oak and the narrow way
at the crossroads, that drank my father's blood
offered you by my hands, do you remember   1465
still what I did as you looked on, and what
I did when I came here? O marriage, marriage!
you bred me and again when you had bred
bred children of your child and showed to men
brides, wives and mothers and the foulest deeds   1470
that can be in this world of ours.

Come—it's unfit to say what is unfit
to do.—I beg of you in God's name hide me
somewhere outside your country, yes, or kill me,
or throw me into the sea, to be forever   1475
out of your sight. Approach and deign to touch me
for all my wretchedness, and do not fear.
No man but I can bear my evil doom.
Chorus: Here Creon comes in fit time to perform
or give advice in what you ask of us.   1480
Creon is left sole ruler in your stead.
Oedipus: Creon! Creon! What shall I say to him?
How can I justly hope that he will trust me?
In what is past I have been proved towards him
an utter liar.

(Enter Creon.)

Creon: Oedipus, I've come   1485
not so that I might laugh at you nor taunt you
with evil of the past. But if you still
are without shame before the face of men
reverence at least the flame that gives all life,
our Lord the Sun, and do not show unveiled   1490
to him pollution such that neither land
nor holy rain nor light of day can welcome.

(To a servant.)

Be quick and take him in. It is most decent
that only kin should see and hear the troubles
of kin.
Oedipus: I beg you, since you've torn me from   1495
my dreadful expectations and have come
in a most noble spirit to a man
that has used you vilely—do a thing for me.
I shall speak for your own good, not for my own.

Creon: What do you need that you would ask of me? 1500
Oedipus: Drive me from here with all the speed you can
    to where I may not hear a human voice.
Creon: Be sure, I would have done this had not I
    wished first of all to learn from the God the course
    of action I should follow.
Oedipus: But his word 1505
    has been quite clear to let the parricide,
    the sinner, die.
Creon: Yes, that indeed was said.
    But in the present need we had best discover
    what we should do.
Oedipus: And will you ask about
    a man so wretched?
Creon: Now even you will trust 1510
    the God.
Oedipus: So. I command you—and will beseech you—
    to her that lies inside that house give burial
    as you would have it; she is yours and rightly
    you will perform the rites for her. For me—
    never let this my father's city have me 1515
    living a dweller in it. Leave me live
    in the mountains where Cithaeron is, that's called
    my mountain, which my mother and my father
    while they were living would have made my tomb.
    So I may die by their decree who sought 1520
    indeed to kill me. Yet I know this much:
    no sickness and no other thing will kill me.
    I would not have been saved from death if not
    for some strange evil fate. Well, let my fate
    go where it will.
                    Creon, you need not care 1525
    about my sons; they're men and so wherever
    they are, they will not lack a livelihood.
    But my two girls—so sad and pitiful—
    whose table never stood apart from mine,
    and everything I touched they always shared— 1530
    O Creon, have a thought for them! And most
    I wish that you might suffer me to touch them
    and sorrow with them.

(Enter Antigone and Ismene, Oedipus' two daughters.)

    O my lord! O true noble Creon! Can I
    really be touching them, as when I saw? 1535
    What shall I say?

Yes, I can hear them sobbing—my two darlings!
and Creon has had pity and has sent me
what I loved most?
Am I right?   1540

Creon: You're right: it was I gave you this
because I knew from old days how you loved them
as I see now.

Oedipus: God bless you for it, Creon,
and may God guard you better on your road
than he did me!

           O children,   1545
where are you? Come here, come to my hands,
a brother's hands which turned your father's eyes,
those bright eyes you knew once, to what you see,
a father seeing nothing, knowing nothing,
begetting you from his own source of life.   1550
I weep for you—I cannot see your faces—
I weep when I think of the bitterness
there will be in your lives, how you must live
before the world. At what assemblages
of citizens will you make one? to what   1555
gay company will you go and not come home
in tears instead of sharing in the holiday?
And when you're ripe for marriage, who will he be,
the man who'll risk to take such infamy
as shall cling to my children, to bring hurt   1560
on them and those that marry with them? What
curse is not there? "Your father killed his father
and sowed the seed where he had sprung himself
and begot you out of the womb that held him."
These insults you will hear. Then who will marry you?   1565
No one, my children; clearly you are doomed
to waste away in barrenness unmarried.
Son of Menoeceus, since you are all the father
left these two girls, and we, their parents, both
are dead to them—do not allow them wander   1570
like beggars, poor and husbandless.
They are of your own blood.
And do not make them equal with myself
in wretchedness; for you can see them now
so young, so utterly alone, save for you only.   1575
Touch my hand, noble Creon, and say yes.
If you were older, children, and were wiser,
there's much advice I'd give you. But as it is,
let this be what you pray: give me a life

wherever there is opportunity   1580
to live, and better life than was my father's.
Creon: Your tears have had enough of scope; now go within the house.
Oedipus: I must obey, though bitter of heart.
Creon: In season, all is good.
Oedipus: Do you know on what conditions I obey?
Creon: You tell me them,   1585
and I shall know them when I hear.
Oedipus: That you shall send me out
to live away from Thebes.
Creon: That gift you must ask of the God.
Oedipus: But I'm now hated by the Gods.
Creon: So quickly you'll obtain your prayer.
Oedipus: You consent then?
Creon: What I do not mean, I do not use to say.
Oedipus: Now lead me away from here.
Creon: Let go the children, then, and come.   1590
Oedipus: Do not take them from me.
Creon: Do not seek to be master in everything,
for the things you mastered did not follow you throughout your life.

(*As Creon and Oedipus go out.*)

Chorus: You that live in my ancestral Thebes, behold this Oedipus,—
him who knew the famous riddles and was a man most masterful;
not a citizen who did not look with envy on his lot—   1595
see him now and see the breakers of misfortune swallow him!
Look upon that last day always. Count no mortal happy till
he has passed the final limit of his life secure from pain.

Questions

1. How explicitly does the prophet Teiresias reveal the guilt of Oedipus? Does it seem to you stupidity on the part of Oedipus or a defect in Sophocles's play that the king takes so long to recognize his guilt and to admit to it?

2. How does Oedipus exhibit weakness of character? Point to lines that reveal him as imperfectly noble in his words, deeds, or treatment of others.

3. "Oedipus is punished not for any fault in himself, but for his ignorance. Not knowing his family history, unable to recognize his parents on sight, he is blameless; and in slaying his father and marrying his mother, he behaves as any sensible person might behave in the same circumstances." Do you agree with this interpretation?

4. Besides the predictions of Teiresias, what other foreshadowings of the shepherd's revelation does the play contain?

5. Consider the character of Jocasta. Is she a "flat" character—a generalized queen figure—or an individual with distinctive traits of personality? Point to speeches or details in the play to back up your opinion.

6. What is dramatic irony? What instances of dramatic irony do you find in *Oedipus the King*? What do they contribute to the effectiveness of the play?

7. In the drama of Sophocles, violence and bloodshed take place offstage; thus, the suicide of Jocasta is only reported to us. Nor do we witness Oedipus's removal of his eyes; this horror is only given in the report by the second messenger. Of what advantage or disadvantage to the play is this limitation?

8. For what reason does Oedipus blind himself? What meaning, if any, do you find in his choice of a surgical instrument?

9. What are your feelings toward him as the play ends?

10. With what attitude toward the gods does the play leave you? By inflicting a plague on Thebes, by causing barrenness, by cursing both the people and their king, do the gods seem cruel, unjust, or tyrannical? Does the play show any reverence toward them?

11. Does this play end in total gloom?

■ WRITING *effectively*

THINKING ABOUT GREEK TRAGEDY

Reading an ancient work of literature, such as Sophocles's *Oedipus the King,* you might have two contradictory reactions. On the one hand, you are likely to note how differently people thought, spoke, and conducted themselves in the ancient world from the way they do now. On the other hand, you might notice how many facets of human nature remain constant across the ages. Though Sophocles's characters are mythic, they also are recognizably human.

■ **Stay alert to both impulses.** Be open to the play's universal appeal, but never forget its foreignness. Take note of the basic beliefs and values that the characters hold that are different from your own. How do those elements influence their actions and motivations?

■ **Jot down something about each major character that seems odd or exotic to you.** Don't worry about being too basic; these notes are just a starting place. You might observe, for example, that Oedipus and Jocasta both believe in the power of prophecy. They also believe that Apollo and the other gods would punish the city with a plague because of an unsolved crime committed twenty years earlier. These are certainly not mainstream modern beliefs.

■ **Focus on the differences themselves.** You do not need to understand the historical origins or cultural context of the differences you note. You can safely leave those things to scholars. But observing these differences—at least a few important ones—will keep you from making inappropriate modern assumptions about the characters, and keeping the differences in mind will give you greater insight into their behavior.

CHECKLIST: Writing About Greek Drama

☐ Identify the play's major characters.

☐ In what ways do they seem alien to you?

☐ What do you notice about a character's beliefs? About his or her values? How do these differ from your own?

☐ In what ways are the play's characters like the people you know?

☐ How do these qualities—both the alien and the familiar—influence the characters' motivations and actions?

TOPICS FOR WRITING ON SOPHOCLES

1. Write a brief personality profile (two or three pages) of any major character in *Oedipus the King*. Describe the character's age, social position, family background, personality, and beliefs. What is his or her major motivation in the play? In what ways does the character resemble his or her modern equivalent? In what ways do they differ?

2. Suppose you were to direct and produce a new stage production of *Oedipus the King*. How would you go about it? Would you use masks? How would you render the chorus? Would you set the play in contemporary North America? Justify your decisions by referring to the play itself.

3. Compare the version of *Oedipus the King* given in this book with a different English translation of the play. You might use, for instance, any of the versions by Robert Fagles; by Gilbert Murray, J. T. Sheppard, and H. D. F. Kitto; by Dudley Fitts and Robert Fitzgerald; by Paul Roche (in a Signet paperback); by William Butler Yeats (in his *Collected Plays*); or by Stephen Berg and Diskin Clay (Oxford UP, 1978). Point to significant differences between the two texts. What decisions did the translators have to make? Which version do you prefer? Why?

4. Write an essay explaining how Oedipus exemplifies or refutes Aristotle's definition of a tragic hero.

▶ TERMS FOR *review*

Stagecraft in Ancient Greece

Skene ▶ The canvas or wooden stage building in which actors changed masks and costumes when changing roles. Its façade, with double center doors and possibly two side doors, served as the setting for action taking place before a palace, temple, cave, or other interior space.

Orchestra ▶ "The place for dancing"; a circular, level performance space at the base of a horseshoe-shaped amphitheater, where twelve, then later (in Sophocles's plays) fifteen masked young male chorus members sang and danced the odes interspersed between dramatic episodes in a play. (Today the term *orchestra* refers to the ground-floor seats in a theater or concert hall.)

Deus ex machina ▶ (Latin for "god out of the machine.") Originally, the phrase referred to the Greek playwrights' frequent use of a god, mechanically lowered to the stage from the *skene* roof to resolve the human conflict. Today, *deus ex machina* refers to any forced or improbable device used to resolve a plot.

Masks ▶ (In Latin, *personae*.) Classical Greek theater masks covered an actor's entire head. Large, recognizable masks allowed far-away spectators to distinguish the conventional characters of tragedy and comedy.

Cothurni ▶ High, thick-soled elevator boots worn by tragic actors in late classical times to make them appear taller than ordinary men. (Earlier, in the fifth-century classical Athenian theater, actors wore soft shoes or boots or went barefoot.)

Elements of Classical Tragedy

Hamartia ▶ (Greek for "error.") An offense committed in ignorance of some material fact; a great mistake made as a result of an error by a morally good person.

Tragic flaw ▶ A fatal weakness or moral flaw in the protagonist that brings him or her to a bad end. Sometimes offered as an alternative understanding of *hamartia*, in contrast to the idea that the tragic hero's catastrophe is caused by an error in judgment.

Hubris ▶ Overweening pride, outrageous behavior, or the insolence that leads to ruin, the antithesis of moderation or rectitude.

Peripeteia ▶ (Anglicized as *peripety*; Greek for "sudden change.") A reversal of fortune, a sudden change of circumstance affecting the protagonist. According to Aristotle, the play's peripety occurs when a certain result is expected and instead its *opposite* effect is produced. In a tragedy, the reversal takes the protagonist from good fortune to catastrophe.

Recognition ▶ In tragic plotting, the moment of recognition occurs when ignorance gives way to knowledge, illusion to disillusion.

Katharsis, catharsis ▶ (Often translated from Greek as *purgation* or *purification*.) The feeling of emotional release or calm the spectator feels at the end of tragedy. The term is drawn from Aristotle's definition of tragedy, relating to the final cause or purpose of tragic art. Some feel that through *katharsis*, drama taught the audience compassion for the vulnerabilities of others and schooled it in justice and other civic virtues.

26 THE THEATER OF SHAKESPEARE

What You Will Learn in This Chapter

- To understand *Othello* by William Shakespeare in its biographical, critical, and cultural contexts

Compared with the technical resources of a theater of today, those of a London public theater in the time of Queen Elizabeth I seem hopelessly limited. Plays had to be performed by daylight, and scenery had to be kept simple: a table, a chair, a throne, perhaps an artificial tree or two to suggest a forest. But these limitations were, in a sense, advantages. What the theater of today can spell out for us realistically, with massive scenery and electric lighting, Elizabethan playgoers had to imagine and the playwright had to make vivid for them by means of language. Not having a lighting technician to work a panel, Shakespeare had to indicate the dawn by having Horatio, in *Hamlet*, say in a speech rich in metaphor and descriptive detail:

> But look, the morn in russet mantle clad
> Walks o'er the dew of yon high eastward hill.

And yet the theater of Shakespeare was not bare, for the playwright did have *some* valuable technical resources. Costumes could be elaborate, and apparently some costumes conveyed recognized meanings: one theater manager's inventory included "a robe for to go invisible in." There could be musical accompaniment and sound effects such as gunpowder explosions and the beating of a pan to simulate thunder.

The stage itself was remarkably versatile. At its back were doors for exits and entrances and a curtained booth or alcove useful for hiding inside. Above the stage was a higher acting area—perhaps a porch or balcony—useful for a Juliet to stand upon and for a Romeo to raise his eyes to. In the stage floor was a trapdoor leading to a "hell" or cellar, especially useful for ghosts or devils who had to appear or disappear. The stage itself was a rectangular platform that projected into a yard enclosed by three-storied galleries.

The building was round or octagonal. In *Henry V*, Shakespeare calls it a "wooden O." The audience sat in these galleries or else stood in the yard in front of the stage and at its sides. A roof or awning protected the stage and the high-priced gallery seats, but in a sudden rain, the *groundlings*, who paid a penny to stand in the yard, must have been dampened.

The reconstructed Globe Theatre in today's London—built in 1997 as an exact replica of the original.

Built by the theatrical company to which Shakespeare belonged, the Globe, most celebrated of Elizabethan theaters, was not in the city of London itself but on the south bank of the Thames River. This location had been chosen because earlier, in 1574, public plays had been banished from the city by an ordinance that blamed them for "corruptions of youth and other enormities" (such as providing opportunities for prostitutes and pickpockets).

A playwright had to please all members of the audience, not only the mannered and educated. This obligation may help to explain the wide range of subject matter and tone in an Elizabethan play: passages of subtle poetry, of deep philosophy, of coarse bawdry; scenes of sensational violence and of quiet psychological conflict (not that most members of the audience did not enjoy all these elements). Because he was an actor as well as a playwright, Shakespeare well knew what his company could do and what his audience wanted. In devising a play, he could write a part to take advantage of some actor's specific skills, or he could avoid straining the company's resources (some of his plays have few female parts, perhaps because of a shortage of competent boy actors). The company might offer as many as thirty plays in a season, customarily changing the program daily. The actors thus had to hold many parts in their heads, which may account for Elizabethan playwrights' fondness for blank verse. Lines of fixed length were easier for actors to commit to memory.

WILLIAM SHAKESPEARE

William Shakespeare

William Shakespeare (1564–1616), the supreme writer of English, was born, baptized, and buried in the market town of Stratford-on-Avon, eighty miles from London. Son of a glove maker and merchant who was high bailiff (or mayor) of the town, he probably attended grammar school and learned to read Latin authors in the original. At eighteen, he married Anne Hathaway, twenty-six, by whom he had three children, including twins. By 1592 he had become well known and envied as an actor and playwright in London. From 1594 until he retired, he belonged to the same theatrical company, the Lord Chamberlain's Men (later renamed the King's Men in honor of their patron, James I), for whom he wrote thirty-six plays—some of them, such as Hamlet and King Lear, profound reworkings of old plays. As an actor, Shakespeare is believed to have played supporting roles, such as the ghost of Hamlet's father. The company prospered, moved into the Globe in 1599, and in 1608 bought the fashionable Blackfriars as well; Shakespeare owned an interest in both theaters. When plagues shut down the theaters from 1592 to 1594, Shakespeare turned to story poems; his great Sonnets (published only in 1609) probably also date from the 1590s. Plays were regarded as entertainments of little literary merit, like comic books today, and Shakespeare did not bother to supervise their publication. After writing The Tempest (1611), the last play entirely from his hand, he retired to Stratford, where since 1597 he had owned the second-largest house in town. Most critics agree that when he wrote Othello, about 1604, Shakespeare was at the height of his powers.

A NOTE ON *OTHELLO*

Othello, the Moor of Venice, here offered for study, may be (if you are fortunate) new to you. It is seldom taught in high school, for it is ablaze with passion and violence. Even if you already know the play, we trust that you (like your instructor and these editors) still have much more to learn from it. Following his usual practice, Shakespeare based the play on a story he had appropriated—from a tale, "Of the Unfaithfulness of Husbands and

Wives," by a sixteenth-century Italian writer, Giraldi Cinthio. As he could not help but do, Shakespeare freely transformed his source material. In the original tale, the heroine Disdemona (whose name Shakespeare improved) is beaten to death with a stocking full of sand—a shoddier death than the bard imagined for her.

Surely no character in literature can touch us more than Desdemona; no character can shock and disgust us more than Iago. Between these two extremes stands Othello, a black man of courage and dignity—and yet insecure, capable of being fooled, a pushover for bad advice. Besides breathing life into these characters and a host of others, Shakespeare—as brilliant a writer as any the world has known—enables them to speak poetry. Sometimes this poetry seems splendid and rich in imagery; at other times quiet and understated. Always, it seems to grow naturally from the nature of Shakespeare's characters and from their situations. *Othello, the Moor of Venice* has never ceased to grip readers and beholders alike. It is a safe bet that it will triumphantly live as long as fathers dislike whomever their daughters marry, as long as husbands suspect their wives of cheating, as long as blacks remember slavery, and as long as the ambitious court favor and the jealous practice deceit. The play may well make sense as long as public officials connive behind smiling faces, and it may even endure as long as the world makes room for the kind, the true, the beautiful— the blessed pure in heart.

PICTURING *Othello*

▼ Iago toasts Cassio, *page 778*

◀ Desdemona and Othello, *page 761*

▼ Roderigo suspects Iago, *page 828*

▲ Emilia prepares
Desdemona for bed,
page 832

▼ Iago plots to get the fateful handkerchief, *page 800*

▲ Othello despairs, *page 822*

▲ Othello attacks Desdemona in a jealous rage, *page 842*

PRODUCTION PHOTOS

The photos illustrating the play are from the 2008 Utah Shakespeare Festival production of *Othello*. (All photos by Karl Hugh. Copyright Utah Shakespeare Festival 2008.)

Jonathan Earl Peck *Othello*
James Newcomb *Iago*
Lindsey Wochley *Desdemona*
Justin Matthew Gordon *Cassio*
Corliss Preston *Emilia*

Will Zahrn *Brabantio*
Marcella Rose Sciotto *Bianca*
Danny Camiel *Roderigo*
Drew Shirley *Lodovico*
Bernie Balbot *Servant*

Othello, the Moor of Venice   1604?

Edited by David Bevington

THE NAMES OF THE ACTORS

Othello, the Moor
Brabantio, [a senator,] father to Desdemona
Cassio, an honorable lieutenant [to Othello]
Iago, [Othello's ancient,] a villain
Roderigo, a gulled gentleman
Duke of Venice
Senators [of Venice]
Montano, governor of Cyprus
Gentlemen of Cyprus
Lodovico and Gratiano, [kinsmen to Brabantio,] two noble Venetians
Sailors
Clown
Desdemona, [daughter to Brabantio and] wife to Othello
Emilia, wife to Iago
Bianca, a courtesan [and mistress to Cassio]
[*A Messenger*
A Herald
A Musician
Servants, Attendants, Officers, Senators, Musicians, Gentlemen

SCENE. *Venice; a seaport in Cyprus*]

ACT I

SCENE I [VENICE. A STREET.]

Enter Roderigo and Iago.

Roderigo: Tush, never tell me!° I take it much unkindly
    That thou, Iago, who hast had my purse
    As if the strings were thine, shouldst know of this.°

NOTE ON THE TEXT:
This text of *Othello* is based on that of the First Folio, or large collection, of Shakespeare's plays (1623). But there are many differences between the Folio text and that of the play's first printing in the Quarto, or small volume, of 1621 (eighteen or nineteen years after the play's first performance). Some readings from the Quarto are included. For the reader's convenience, some material has been added by the editor, David Bevington (some indications of scene, some stage directions). Such additions are enclosed in brackets. Mr. Bevington's text and notes were prepared for his book *The Complete Works of Shakespeare*, updated 4th ed. (New York: Longman, 1997).

1 *never tell me* (An expression of incredulity, like "tell me another one.")   3 *this* i.e., Desdemona's elopement

Iago: 'Sblood,° but you'll not hear me.
   If ever I did dream of such a matter,   5
   Abhor me.
Roderigo: Thou toldst me thou didst hold him in thy hate.
Iago: Despise me
   If I do not. Three great ones of the city,
   In personal suit to make me his lieutenant,   10
   Off-capped to him;° and by the faith of man,
   I know my price, I am worth no worse a place.
   But he, as loving his own pride and purposes,
   Evades them with a bombast circumstance°
   Horribly stuffed with epithets of war,°   15
   And, in conclusion,
   Nonsuits° my mediators. For, "Certes,"° says he,
   "I have already chose my officer."
   And what was he?
   Forsooth, a great arithmetician,°   20
   One Michael Cassio, a Florentine,
   A fellow almost damned in a fair wife,°
   That never set a squadron in the field
   Nor the division of a battle° knows
   More than a spinster°—unless the bookish theoric,°   25
   Wherein the togaed° consuls° can propose°
   As masterly as he. Mere prattle without practice
   Is all his soldiership. But he, sir, had th' election;
   And I, of whom his° eyes had seen the proof
   At Rhodes, at Cyprus, and on other grounds   30
   Christened° and heathen, must be beleed and calmed°
   By debitor and creditor.° This countercaster,°
   He, in good time,° must his lieutenant be,
   And I—God bless the mark!°—his Moorship's ancient.°
Roderigo: By heaven, I rather would have been his hangman.°   35
Iago: Why, there's no remedy. 'Tis the curse of service;

---

4 *'Sblood* by His (Christ's) blood   11 *him* i.e., Othello   14 *bombast circumstance* wordy evasion. (Bombast is cotton padding.)   15 *epithets of war* military expressions   17 *Nonsuits* rejects the petition of.   *Certes* certainly   20 *arithmetician* i.e., a man whose military knowledge is merely theoretical, based on books of tactics   22 *A . . . wife* (Cassio does not seem to be married, but his counterpart in Shakespeare's source does have a woman in his house. See also IV, i, 127.)   24 *division of a battle* disposition of a military unit   25 *a spinster* i.e., a housewife, one whose regular occupation is spinning.   *theoric* theory   26 *togaed* wearing the toga.   *consuls* counselors, senators.   *propose* discuss   29 *his* i.e., Othello's   31 *Christened* Christian.   *beleed and calmed* left to leeward without wind, becalmed. (A sailing metaphor.)   32 *debitor and creditor* (A name for a system of bookkeeping, here used as a contemptuous nickname for Cassio.)   *countercaster* i.e., bookkeeper, one who tallies with *counters*, or "metal disks." (Said contemptuously.)   33 *in good time* opportunely, i.e., forsooth   34 *God bless the mark* (Perhaps originally a formula to ward off evil; here an expression of impatience.)   *ancient* standard-bearer, ensign   35 *his hangman* his executioner.

Preferment° goes by letter and affection,°
And not by old gradation,° where each second
Stood heir to th' first. Now, sir, be judge yourself
Whether I in any just term° am affined°   40
To love the Moor.
Roderigo: I would not follow him then.
Iago: O sir, content you.°
  I follow him to serve my turn upon him.
We cannot all be masters, nor all masters   45
Cannot be truly° followed. You shall mark
Many a duteous and knee-crooking knave
That, doting on his own obsequious bondage,
Wears out his time, much like his master's ass,
For naught but provender, and when he's old, cashiered.°   50
Whip me° such honest knaves. Others there are
Who, trimmed in forms and visages of duty,°
Keep yet their hearts attending on themselves,
And, throwing but shows of service on their lords,
Do well thrive by them, and when they have lined their coats,°   55
Do themselves homage.° These fellows have some soul,
And such a one do I profess myself. For, sir,
It is as sure as you are Roderigo,
Were I the Moor I would not be Iago.°
In following him, I follow but myself—   60
Heaven is my judge, not I for love and duty,
But seeming so for my peculiar° end.
For when my outward action doth demonstrate
The native° act and figure° of my heart
In compliment extern,° 'tis not long after   65
But I will wear my heart upon my sleeve
For daws° to peck at. I am not what I am.°
Roderigo: What a full° fortune does the thick-lips° owe°
  If he can carry 't thus!°
Iago: Call up her father.
  Rouse him, make after him, poison his delight,   70

---

37 *Preferment* promotion. *letter and affection* personal influence and favoritism   38 *old gradation* step-by-step seniority, the traditional way   40 *term* respect. *affined* bound   43 *content you* don't you worry about that   46 *truly* faithfully   50 *cashiered* dismissed from service   51 *Whip me* whip, as far as I'm concerned   52 *trimmed . . . duty* dressed up in the mere form and show of dutifulness   55 *lined their coats* i.e., stuffed their purses   56 *Do themselves homage* i.e., attend to self-interest solely   59 *Were . . . Iago* i.e., if I were able to assume command, I certainly would not choose to remain a subordinate, or, I would keep a suspicious eye on a flattering subordinate   62 *peculiar* particular, personal   64 *native* innate. *figure* shape, intent   65 *compliment extern* outward show. (Conforming in this case to the inner workings and intention of the heart.)   67 *daws* small crowlike birds, proverbially stupid and avaricious. *I am not what I am* i.e., I am not one who wears his heart on his sleeve   68 *full* swelling. *thick-lips* (Elizabethans often applied the term "Moor" to blacks.) *owe* own   69 *carry 't thus* carry this off

Brabantio asks, "What is the matter there?" (I, i, 85).

Proclaim him in the streets; incense her kinsmen,
And, though he in a fertile climate dwell,
Plague him with flies.° Though that his joy be joy,°
Yet throw such changes of vexation° on 't
As it may° lose some color.° 75

Roderigo: Here is her father's house. I'll call aloud.

Iago: Do, with like timorous° accent and dire yell
As when, by night and negligence,° the fire
Is spied in populous cities.

Roderigo: What ho, Brabantio! Signor Brabantio, ho! 80

Iago: Awake! What ho, Brabantio! Thieves, thieves, thieves!
Look to your house, your daughter, and your bags!
Thieves, thieves!

Brabantio [enters] above [at a window].°

Brabantio: What is the reason of this terrible summons?
What is the matter° there? 85

Roderigo: Signor, is all your family within?

72–73 *though . . . flies* though he seems prosperous and happy now, vex him with misery   73 *Though . . . be joy* although he seems fortunate and happy. (Repeats the idea of line 72.)   74 *changes of vexation* vexing changes   75 *As it may* that may cause it to. *some color* some of its fresh gloss   77 *timorous* frightening   78 *and negligence* i.e., by negligence   83 s.d. *at a window* (This stage direction, from the Quarto, probably calls for an appearance on the gallery above and rearstage.)   85 *the matter* your business

Iago: Are your doors locked?
Brabantio: Why, wherefore ask you this?
Iago: Zounds,° sir, you're robbed. For shame, put on your gown!
    Your heart is burst; you have lost half your soul.
    Even now, now, very now, an old black ram   90
    Is tupping° your white ewe. Arise, arise!
    Awake the snorting° citizens with the bell,
    Or else the devil° will make a grandsire of you.
    Arise, I say!
Brabantio: What, have you lost your wits?
Roderigo: Most reverend signor, do you know my voice?   95
Brabantio: Not I. What are you?
Roderigo: My name is Roderigo.
Brabantio: The worser welcome.
    I have charged thee not to haunt about my doors.
    In honest plainness thou hast heard me say   100
    My daughter is not for thee; and now, in madness,
    Being full of supper and distempering° drafts,
    Upon malicious bravery° dost thou come
    To start° my quiet.
Roderigo: Sir, sir, sir—
Brabantio: But thou must needs be sure   105
    My spirits and my place° have in° their power
    To make this bitter to thee.
Roderigo: Patience, good sir.
Brabantio: What tell'st thou me of robbing? This is Venice;
    My house is not a grange.°
Roderigo: Most grave Brabantio,
    In simple° and pure soul I come to you.   110
Iago: Zounds, sir, you are one of those that will not serve God if the devil
    bid you. Because we come to do you service and you think we are ruf-
    fians, you'll have your daughter covered with a Barbary° horse; you'll
    have your nephews° neigh to you; you'll have coursers° for cousins°
    and jennets° for germans.°   115
Brabantio: What profane wretch art thou?
Iago: I am one, sir, that comes to tell you your daughter and the Moor
    are now making the beast with two backs.

88 *Zounds* by His (Christ's) wounds 91 *tupping* covering, copulating with. (Said of
sheep.) 92 *snorting* snoring 93 *the devil* (The devil was conventionally pictured as
black.) 102 *distempering* intoxicating 103 *Upon malicious bravery* with hostile intent
to defy me 104 *start* startle, disrupt 106 *My spirits and my place* my temperament and
my authority of office. *have in* have it in 109 *grange* isolated country house 110 *simple*
sincere 113 *Barbary* from northern Africa (and hence associated with Othello). 114 *nephews*
i.e., grandsons. *coursers* powerful horses. *cousins* kinsmen. 115 *jennets* small Spanish
horses. *germans* near relatives

Brabantio: Thou art a villain.
Iago: You are—a senator.°
Brabantio: This thou shalt answer.° I know thee, Roderigo.   120
Roderigo: Sir, I will answer anything. But I beseech you,
    If't be your pleasure and most wise° consent—
    As partly I find it is—that your fair daughter,
    At this odd-even° and dull watch o' the night,
    Transported with° no worse nor better guard   125
    But with a knave° of common hire, a gondolier,
    To the gross clasps of a lascivious Moor—
    If this be known to you and your allowance°
    We then have done you bold and saucy° wrongs.
    But if you know not this, my manners tell me   130
    We have your wrong rebuke. Do not believe
    That, from° the sense of all civility,°
    I thus would play and trifle with your reverence.°
    Your daughter, if you have not given her leave,
    I say again, hath made a gross revolt,   135
    Tying her duty, beauty, wit,° and fortunes
    In an extravagant° and wheeling° stranger°
    Of here and everywhere. Straight° satisfy yourself.
    If she be in her chamber or your house,
    Let loose on me the justice of the state   140
    For thus deluding you.
Brabantio: Strike on the tinder,° ho!
    Give me a taper! Call up all my people!
    This accident° is not unlike my dream.
    Belief of it oppresses me already.
    Light, I say, light!   *Exit [above].*
Iago: Farewell, for I must leave you.   145
    It seems not meet° nor wholesome to my place°
    To be producted°—as, if I stay, I shall—
    Against the Moor. For I do know the state,
    However this may gall° him with some check,°

---

119 *a senator* (Said with mock politeness, as though the word itself were an insult.)
120 *answer* be held accountable for   122 *wise* well-informed   124 *odd-even* between one
day and the next, i.e., about midnight   125 *with* by   126 *But with a knave* than by a
low fellow, a servant   128 *allowance* permission   129 *saucy* insolent   132 *from* contrary
to. *civility* good manners, decency   133 *your reverence* the respect due to you   136 *wit*
intelligence   137 *extravagant* expatriate, wandering far from home. *wheeling* roving
about, vagabond. *stranger* foreigner   138 *Straight* straightway   141 *tinder* charred linen
ignited by a spark from flint and steel, used to light torches or *tapers* (lines 142, 167)
143 *accident* occurrence, event   146 *meet* fitting. *place* position (as ensign)
147 *producted* produced (as a witness)   149 *gall* rub; oppress. *check* rebuke

Cannot with safety cast° him, for he's embarked°   150
With such loud reason° to the Cyprus wars,
Which even now stands in act,° that, for their souls,°
Another of his fathom° they have none
To lead their business; in which regard,°
Though I do hate him as I do hell pains,   155
Yet for necessity of present life°
I must show out a flag and sign of love,
Which is indeed but sign. That you shall surely find him,
Lead to the Sagittary° the raisèd search,°
And there will I be with him. So farewell.   160

Exit.

Enter [below] Brabantio [in his nightgown°] with servants and torches.

Brabantio: It is too true an evil. Gone she is;
    And what's to come of my despisèd time°
    Is naught but bitterness. Now, Roderigo,
    Where didst thou see her?—O unhappy girl!—
    With the Moor, sayst thou?—Who would be a father!—   165
    How didst thou know 'twas she?—O, she deceives me
    Past thought!—What said she to you?—Get more tapers.
    Raise all my kindred.—Are they married, think you?
Roderigo: Truly, I think they are.
Brabantio: O heaven! How got she out? O treason of the blood!   170
    Fathers, from hence trust not your daughters' minds
    By what you see them act. Is there not charms°
    By which the property° of youth and maidhood
    May be abused?° Have you not read, Roderigo,
    Of some such thing?
Roderigo: Yes, sir, I have indeed.   175
Brabantio: Call up my brother.—O, would you had had her!—
    Some one way, some another.—Do you know
    Where we may apprehend her and the Moor?
Roderigo: I think I can discover° him, if you please
    To get good guard and go along with me.   180
Brabantio: Pray you, lead on. At every house I'll call;

150 *cast* dismiss. *embarked* engaged 151 *loud reason* unanimous shout of confirmation (in the Senate) 152 *stands in act* are going on. *for their souls* to save themselves 153 *fathom* i.e., ability, depth of experience 154 *in which regard* out of regard for which 156 *life* livelihood 159 *Sagittary* (An inn or house where Othello and Desdemona are staying, named for its sign of Sagittarius, or Centaur.) *raisèd search* search party roused out of sleep s.d. *nightgown* dressing gown. (This costuming is specified in the Quarto text.) 162 *time* i.e., remainder of life 172 *charms* spells 173 *property* special quality, nature 174 *abused* deceived 179 *discover* reveal, uncover

I may command° at most.—Get weapons, ho!
And raise some special officers of night.—
On, good Roderigo. I will deserve° your pains.

Exeunt.

SCENE II [VENICE. ANOTHER STREET, BEFORE OTHELLO'S LODGINGS.]

Enter Othello, Iago, attendants with torches.

Iago: Though in the trade of war I have slain men,
　　　Yet do I hold it very stuff° o' the conscience
　　　To do no contrived° murder. I lack iniquity
　　　Sometimes to do me service. Nine or ten times
　　　I had thought t' have yerked° him° here under the ribs.   5
Othello: 'Tis better as it is.
Iago:　　　　　　　　Nay, but he prated,
　　　And spoke such scurvy and provoking terms
　　　Against your honor
　　　That, with the little godliness I have,
　　　I did full hard forbear him.° But, I pray you, sir,   10
　　　Are you fast married? Be assured of this,
　　　That the magnifico° is much beloved,
　　　And hath in his effect° a voice potential°
　　　As double as the Duke's. He will divorce you,
　　　Or put upon you what restraint or grievance   15
　　　The law, with all his might to enforce it on,
　　　Will give him cable.°
Othello:　　　　　　　Let him do his spite.
　　　My services which I have done the seigniory°
　　　Shall out-tongue his complaints. 'Tis yet to know°—
　　　Which, when I know that boasting is an honor,   20
　　　I shall promulgate—I fetch my life and being
　　　From men of royal siege,° and my demerits°
　　　May speak unbonneted° to as proud a fortune
　　　As this that I have reached. For know, Iago,
　　　But that I love the gentle Desdemona,   25

182 *command* demand assistance   184 *deserve* show gratitude for   2 *very stuff* essence, basic material (continuing the metaphor of *trade* from line 1)   3 *contrived* premeditated   5 *yerked* stabbed.   *him* i.e., Roderigo   10 *I . . . him* I restrained myself with great difficulty from assaulting him   12 *magnifico* Venetian grandee, i.e., Brabantio   13 *in his effect* at his command.   *potential* powerful   17 *cable* i.e., scope   18 *seigniory* Venetian government   19 *yet to know* not yet widely known   22 *siege* i.e., rank. (Literally, a seat used by a person of distinction.)   *demerits* deserts   23 *unbonneted* without removing the hat, i.e., on equal terms (?) (Or "with hat off," "in all due modesty.")

I would not my unhousèd° free condition
Put into circumscription and confine°
For the sea's worth.° But look, what lights come yond?

Enter Cassio [and certain officers°] with torches.

Iago: Those are the raisèd father and his friends.
     You were best go in.
Othello: Not I. I must be found.   30
     My parts, my title, and my perfect soul°
     Shall manifest me rightly. Is it they?
Iago: By Janus,° I think no.
Othello: The servants of the Duke? And my lieutenant?
     The goodness of the night upon you, friends!   35
     What is the news?
Cassio: The Duke does greet you, General,
     And he requires your haste-post-haste appearance
     Even on the instant.
Othello: What is the matter,° think you?
Cassio: Something from Cyprus, as I may divine.°
     It is a business of some heat.° The galleys   40
     Have sent a dozen sequent° messengers
     This very night at one another's heels,
     And many of the consuls,° raised and met,
     Are at the Duke's already. You have been hotly called for;
     When, being not at your lodging to be found,   45
     The Senate hath sent about° three several° quests
     To search you out.
Othello: 'Tis well I am found by you.
     I will but spend a word here in the house
     And go with you.   [*Exit.*]
Cassio: Ancient, what makes° he here?
Iago: Faith, he tonight hath boarded° a land carrack.°   50
     If it prove lawful prize,° he's made forever.
Cassio: I do not understand.
Iago: He's married.
Cassio: To who?

---

26 *unhousèd* unconfined, undomesticated   27 *circumscription and confine* restriction and confinement   28 *the sea's worth* all the riches at the bottom of the sea.   s.d. *officers* (The Quarto text calls for "Cassio with lights, officers with torches.")   31 *My . . . soul* my natural gifts, my position or reputation, and my unflawed conscience   33 *Janus* Roman two-faced god of beginnings   38 *matter* business   39 *divine* guess   40 *heat* urgency   41 *sequent* successive   43 *consuls* senators   46 *about* all over the city.   *several* separate   49 *makes* does   50 *boarded* gone aboard and seized as an act of piracy (with sexual suggestion).   *carrack* large merchant ship   51 *prize* booty

[*Enter Othello.*]

Iago: Marry,° to—Come, Captain, will you go?
Othello: Have with you.°
Cassio: Here comes another troop to seek for you.   55

    Enter Brabantio, Roderigo, with officers and torches.°

Iago: It is Brabantio. General, be advised.°
    He comes to bad intent.
Othello: Holla! Stand there!
Roderigo: Signor, it is the Moor.
Brabantio: Down with him, thief!

    [*They draw on both sides.*]

Iago: You, Roderigo! Come, sir, I am for you.
Othello: Keep up° your bright swords, for the dew will rust them.   60
    Good signor, you shall more command with years
    Than with your weapons.
Brabantio: O thou foul thief, where hast thou stowed my daughter?
    Damned as thou art, thou hast enchanted her!
    For I'll refer me° to all things of sense,°   65
    If she in chains of magic were not bound
    Whether a maid so tender, fair, and happy,
    So opposite to marriage that she shunned
    The wealthy curlèd darlings of our nation,
    Would ever have, t' incur a general mock,   70
    Run from her guardage° to the sooty bosom
    Of such a thing as thou—to fear, not to delight.
    Judge me the world if 'tis not gross in sense°
    That thou hast practiced on her with foul charms,
    Abused her delicate youth with drugs or minerals°   75
    That weaken motion.° I'll have 't disputed on;°
    'Tis probable and palpable to thinking.
    I therefore apprehend and do attach° thee
    For an abuser of the world, a practicer
    Of arts inhibited° and out of warrant.°—   80
    Lay hold upon him! If he do resist,
    Subdue him at his peril.

---

53 *Marry* (An oath, originally "by the Virgin Mary"; here used with wordplay on *married.*)
54 *Have with you* i.e., let's go   55 s.d. *officers and torches* (The Quarto text calls for "others
with lights and weapons.")   56 *be advised* be on your guard   60 *Keep up* keep in the sheath
65 *refer me* submit my case.   *things of sense* commonsense understandings, or, creatures possessing common sense   71 *her guardage* my guardianship of her   73 *gross in sense* obvious
75 *minerals* i.e., poisons   76 *weaken motion* impair the vital faculties.   *disputed on* argued in
court by professional counsel, debated by experts   78 *attach* arrest   80 *arts inhibited* prohibited arts, black magic.   *out of warrant* illegal

Othello: Hold your hands,
    Both you of my inclining° and the rest.
    Were it my cue to fight, I should have known it
    Without a prompter.—Whither will you that I go   85
    To answer this your charge?
Brabantio: To prison, till fit time
    Of law and course of direct session°
    Call thee to answer.
Othello: What if I do obey?
    How may the Duke be therewith satisfied,   90
    Whose messengers are here about my side
    Upon some present business of the state
    To bring me to him?
Officer: 'Tis true, most worthy signor.
    The Duke's in council, and your noble self,
    I am sure, is sent for.
Brabantio: How? The Duke in council?   95
    In this time of the night? Bring him away.°
    Mine's not an idle° cause. The Duke himself,
    Or any of my brothers of the state,
    Cannot but feel this wrong as 'twere their own;
    For if such actions may have passage free,°   100
    Bondslaves and pagans shall our statesmen be.

    Exeunt.

SCENE III [VENICE. A COUNCIL CHAMBER.]

*Enter Duke [and] Senators [and sit at a table, with lights], and Officers.° [The
Duke and Senators are reading dispatches.]*

Duke: There is no composition° in these news
    That gives them credit.
First Senator: Indeed, they are disproportioned.°
    My letters say a hundred and seven galleys.
Duke: And mine, a hundred forty.
Second Senator: And mine, two hundred.   5
    But though they jump° not on a just° account—
    As in these cases, where the aim° reports

---

83 *inclining* following, party   88 *course of direct session* regular or specially convened legal
proceedings   96 *away* right along   97 *idle* trifling   100 *have passage free* are allowed to
go unchecked   s.d. *Enter . . . Officers* (The Quarto text calls for the Duke and senators
to "sit at a table with lights and attendants.")   1 *composition* consistency   3 *disproportioned* inconsistent   6 *jump* agree. *just* exact   7 *the aim* conjecture

     'Tis oft with difference—yet do they all confirm
     A Turkish fleet, and bearing up to Cyprus.
Duke: Nay, it is possible enough to judgment.   10
     I do not so secure me in the error
     But the main article I do approve°
     In fearful sense.
Sailor (within):   What ho, what ho, what ho!

     Enter Sailor.

Officer: A messenger from the galleys.
Duke: Now, what's the business?   15
Sailor: The Turkish preparation° makes for Rhodes.
     So was I bid report here to the state
     By Signor Angelo.
Duke: How say you by° this change?
First Senator: This cannot be
     By no assay° of reason. 'Tis a pageant°   20
     To keep us in false gaze.° When we consider
     Th' importancy of Cyprus to the Turk,
     And let ourselves again but understand
     That, as it more concerns the Turk than Rhodes,
     So may he with more facile question bear it,°   25
     For that° it stands not in such warlike brace,°
     But altogether lacks th' abilities°
     That Rhodes is dressed in°—if we make thought of this,
     We must not think the Turk is so unskillful°
     To leave that latest° which concerns him first,   30
     Neglecting an attempt of ease and gain
     To wake° and wage° a danger profitless.
Duke: Nay, in all confidence, he's not for Rhodes.
Officer: Here is more news.

     Enter a Messenger.

Messenger: The Ottomites, reverend and gracious,   35
     Steering with due course toward the isle of Rhodes,
     Have there injointed them° with an after° fleet.
First Senator: Ay, so I thought. How many, as you guess?

11–12 *I do not . . . approve* I do not take such (false) comfort in the discrepancies that I fail to perceive the main point, i.e., that the Turkish fleet is threatening 16 *preparation* fleet prepared for battle 19 *by* about 20 *assay* test. *pageant* mere show 21 *in false gaze* looking the wrong way 25 *So may . . . it* so also he (the Turk) can more easily capture it (Cyprus) 26 *For that* since. *brace* state of defense 27 *abilities* means of self-defense 28 *dressed in* equipped with 29 *unskillful* deficient in judgment 30 *latest* last 32 *wake* stir up. *wage* risk 37 *injointed them* joined themselves. *after* second, following

Messenger: Of thirty sail; and now they do restem
    Their backward course,° bearing with frank appearance°   40
    Their purposes toward Cyprus. Signor Montano,
    Your trusty and most valiant servitor,°
    With his free duty° recommends° you thus,
    And prays you to believe him.
Duke: 'Tis certain then for Cyprus.   45
    Marcus Luccicos, is not he in town?
First Senator: He's now in Florence.
Duke: Write from us to him, post-post-haste. Dispatch.
First Senator: Here comes Brabantio and the valiant Moor.

    Enter Brabantio, Othello, Cassio, Iago, Roderigo, and officers.

Duke: Valiant Othello, we must straight° employ you   50
    Against the general enemy° Ottoman.
    [*To Brabantio.*] I did not see you; welcome, gentle° signor.
    We lacked your counsel and your help tonight.
Brabantio: So did I yours. Good Your Grace, pardon me;
    Neither my place° nor aught I heard of business   55
    Hath raised me from my bed, nor doth the general care
    Take hold on me, for my particular° grief
    Is of so floodgate° and o'erbearing nature
    That it engluts° and swallows other sorrows
    And it is still itself.°
Duke: Why, what's the matter?   60
Brabantio: My daughter! O, my daughter!
Duke and Senators: Dead?
Brabantio: Ay, to me.
    She is abused,° stol'n from me, and corrupted
    By spells and medicines bought of mountebanks;
    For nature so preposterously to err,
    Being not deficient,° blind, or lame of sense,°   65
    Sans° witchcraft could not.
Duke: Whoe'er he be that in this foul proceeding
    Hath thus beguiled your daughter of herself,
    And you of her, the bloody book of law
    You shall yourself read in the bitter letter   70
    After your own sense°—yea, though our proper° son

39–40 *restem . . . course* retrace their original course 40 *frank appearance* undisguised
intent 42 *servitor* officer under your command 43 *free duty* freely given and loyal service. *recommends* commends himself and reports to 50 *straight* straightway 51 *general enemy* universal enemy to all Christendom 52 *gentle* noble 55 *place* official position
57 *particular* personal 58 *floodgate* i.e., overwhelming (as when floodgates are opened)
59 *engluts* engulfs 60 *is still itself* remains undiminished 62 *abused* deceived 65 *deficient* defective. *lame of sense* deficient in sensory perception 66 *Sans* without 71 *After . . . sense*
according to your own interpretation. *our proper* my own

  Stood in your action.°
Brabantio: Humbly I thank Your Grace.
  Here is the man, this Moor, whom now it seems
  Your special mandate for the state affairs
  Hath hither brought.
All: We are very sorry for 't.   75
Duke [to Othello]: What, in your own part, can you say to this?
Brabantio: Nothing, but this is so.
Othello: Most potent, grave, and reverend signors,
  My very noble and approved° good masters:
  That I have ta'en away this old man's daughter,   80
  It is most true; true, I have married her.
  The very head and front° of my offending
  Hath this extent, no more. Rude° am I in my speech,
  And little blessed with the soft phrase of peace;
  For since these arms of mine had seven years' pith,°   85
  Till now some nine moons wasted,° they have used
  Their dearest° action in the tented field;
  And little of this great world can I speak
  More than pertains to feats of broils and battle,
  And therefore little shall I grace my cause   90
  In speaking for myself. Yet, by your gracious patience,
  I will a round° unvarnished tale deliver
  Of my whole course of love—what drugs, what charms,
  What conjuration, and what mighty magic,
  For such proceeding I am charged withal,°   95
  I won his daughter.
Brabantio: A maiden never bold;
  Of spirit so still and quiet that her motion
  Blushed at herself;° and she, in spite of nature,
  Of years,° of country, credit,° everything,
  To fall in love with what she feared to look on!   100
  It is a judgment maimed and most imperfect
  That will confess° perfection so could err
  Against all rules of nature, and must be driven
  To find out practices° of cunning hell
  Why this should be. I therefore vouch° again   105

---

72 *Stood . . . action* were under your accusation   79 *approved* proved, esteemed   82 *head and front* height and breadth, entire extent   83 *Rude* unpolished   85 *since . . . pith* i.e., since I was seven. *pith* strength, vigor   86 *Till . . . wasted* until some nine months ago (since when Othello has evidently not been on active duty, but in Venice)   87 *dearest* most valuable   92 *round* plain   95 *withal* with   97–98 *her . . . herself* i.e., she blushed easily at herself. (*Motion* can suggest the impulse of the soul or of the emotions, or physical movement.)   99 *years* i.e., difference in age. *credit* virtuous reputation   102 *confess* concede (that)   104 *practices* plots   105 *vouch* assert

That with some mixtures powerful o'er the blood,°
Or with some dram conjured to this effect,°
He wrought upon her.

Duke: To vouch this is no proof,
Without more wider° and more overt test°
Than these thin habits° and poor likelihoods°   110
Of modern seeming° do prefer° against him.

First Senator: But Othello, speak.
Did you by indirect and forcèd courses°
Subdue and poison this young maid's affections?
Or came it by request and such fair question°   115
As soul to soul affordeth?

Othello: I do beseech you,
Send for the lady to the Sagittary
And let her speak of me before her father.
If you do find me foul in her report,
The trust, the office I do hold of you   120
Not only take away, but let your sentence
Even fall upon my life.

Duke: Fetch Desdemona hither.

Othello: Ancient, conduct them. You best know the place.

[*Exeunt Iago and attendants.*]

And, till she come, as truly as to heaven
I do confess the vices of my blood,°   125
So justly° to your grave ears I'll present
How I did thrive in this fair lady's love,
And she in mine.

Duke: Say it, Othello.

Othello: Her father loved me, oft invited me,   130
Still° questioned me the story of my life
From year to year—the battles, sieges, fortunes
That I have passed.
I ran it through, even from my boyish days
To th' very moment that he bade me tell it,   135
Wherein I spoke of most disastrous chances,
Of moving accidents° by flood and field,
Of hairbreadth scapes i' th' imminent deadly breach,°

---

106 *blood* passions   107 *dram . . . effect* dose made by magical spells to have this effect   109
more wider fuller. *test* testimony   110 *habits* garments, i.e., appearances. *poor likeli-
hoods* weak inferences   111 *modern seeming* commonplace assumption. *prefer* bring forth
113 *forcèd courses* means used against her will   115 *question* conversation   125 *blood* passions,
human nature   126 *justly* truthfully, accurately   131 *Still* continually   137 *moving accident*
stirring happenings   138 *imminent . . . breach* death-threatening gaps made in a fortification

Of being taken by the insolent foe
And sold to slavery, of my redemption thence,   140
And portance° in my travels' history,
Wherein of antres° vast and deserts idle,°
Rough quarries,° rocks, and hills whose heads touch heaven,
It was my hint° to speak—such was my process—
And of the Cannibals that each other eat,   145
The Anthropophagi,° and men whose heads
Do grow beneath their shoulders. These things to hear
Would Desdemona seriously incline;
But still the house affairs would draw her thence,
Which ever as she could with haste dispatch   150
She'd come again, and with a greedy ear
Devour up my discourse. Which I, observing,
Took once a pliant° hour, and found good means
To draw from her a prayer of earnest heart
That I would all my pilgrimage dilate,°   155
Whereof by parcels° she had something heard,
But not intentively.° I did consent,
And often did beguile her of her tears,
When I did speak of some distressful stroke
That my youth suffered. My story being done,   160
She gave me for my pains a world of sighs.
She swore, in faith, 'twas strange, 'twas passing° strange,
'Twas pitiful, 'twas wondrous pitiful.
She wished she had not heard it, yet she wished
That heaven had made her° such a man. She thanked me,   165
And bade me, if I had a friend that loved her,
I should but teach him how to tell my story,
And that would woo her. Upon this hint° I spake.
She loved me for the dangers I had passed,
And I loved her that she did pity them.   170
This only is the witchcraft I have used.
Here comes the lady. Let her witness it.

Enter Desdemona, Iago, [and] attendants.

Duke: I think this tale would win my daughter too.
    Good Brabantio,
    Take up this mangled matter at the best.°   175

---

141 *portance* conduct   142 *antres* caverns. *idle* barren, desolate   143 *Rough quarries* rugged rock formations   144 *hint* occasion, opportunity   146 *Anthropophagi* man-eaters.
(A term from Pliny's *Natural History.*)   153 *pliant* well-suiting   155 *dilate* relate in detail
156 *by parcels* piecemeal   157 *intentively* with full attention, continuously   162 *passing*
exceedingly   165 *made her* created her to be   168 *hint* opportunity. (Othello does not mean
that she was dropping hints.)   175 *Take . . . best* make the best of a bad bargain

Desdemona tells her father, "I do perceive here a divided duty" (I, iii, 183).

	Men do their broken weapons rather use	
	Than their bare hands.	
Brabantio:	I pray you, hear her speak.	
	If she confess that she was half the wooer,	
	Destruction on my head if my bad blame	
	Light on the man!—Come hither, gentle mistress.	180
	Do you perceive in all this noble company	
	Where most you owe obedience?	
Desdemona:	My noble Father,	
	I do perceive here a divided duty.	
	To you I am bound for life and education;°	
	My life and education both do learn° me	185
	How to respect you. You are the lord of duty;°	
	I am hitherto your daughter. But here's my husband,	
	And so much duty as my mother showed	
	To you, preferring you before her father,	
	So much I challenge° that I may profess	190
	Due to the Moor my lord.	
Brabantio:	God be with you! I have done.	
	Please it Your Grace, on to the state affairs.	
	I had rather to adopt a child than get° it.	
	Come hither, Moor. [*He joins the hands of Othello and Desdemona.*]	195
	I here do give thee that with all my heart°	
	Which, but thou hast already, with all my heart°	

184 *education* upbringing   185 *learn* teach   186 *of duty* to whom duty is due   190 *challenge* claim   194 *get* beget   196 *with all my heart* wherein my whole affection has been engaged   197 *with all my heart* willingly, gladly

I would keep from thee.—For your sake,° jewel,
I am glad at soul I have no other child,
For thy escape° would teach me tyranny,   200
To hang clogs° on them.—I have done, my lord.
Duke: Let me speak like yourself,° and lay a sentence°
  Which, as a grece° or step, may help these lovers
  Into your favor.
When remedies° are past, the griefs are ended   205
By seeing the worst, which late on hopes depended.°
To mourn a mischief° that is past and gone
Is the next° way to draw new mischief on.
What° cannot be preserved when fortune takes,
Patience her injury a mockery makes.°   210
The robbed that smiles steals something from the thief;
He robs himself that spends a bootless grief.°
Brabantio: So let the Turk of Cyprus us beguile,
  We lose it not, so long as we can smile.
He bears the sentence well that nothing bears   215
But the free comfort which from thence he hears,
But he bears both the sentence and the sorrow
That, to pay grief, must of poor patience borrow.°
These sentences, to sugar or to gall,
Being strong on both sides, are equivocal.°   220
But words are words. I never yet did hear
That the bruisèd heart was piercèd through the ear.°
I humbly beseech you, proceed to th' affairs of state.
Duke: The Turk with a most mighty preparation makes for Cyprus.
  Othello, the fortitude° of the place is best known to you; and though   225
  we have there a substitute° of most allowed° sufficiency, yet opinion,
  a sovereign mistress of effects, throws a more safer voice on you.° You
  must therefore be content to slubber° the gloss of your new fortunes
  with this more stubborn° and boisterous expedition.

198 *For your sake* on your account   200 *escape* elopement   201 *clogs* (Literally, blocks of wood fastened to the legs of criminals or convicts to inhibit escape.)   202 *like yourself* i.e., as you would, in your proper temper. *lay a sentence* apply a maxim   203 *grece* step   205 *remedies* hopes of remedy   206 *which . . . depended* which griefs were sustained until recently by hopeful anticipation   207 *mischief* misfortune, injury   208 *next* nearest   209 *What* whatever   210 *Patience . . . makes* patience laughs at the injury inflicted by fortune (and thus eases the pain)   212 *spends a bootless grief* indulges in unavailing grief   215–218 *He bears . . . borrow* a person well bears out your maxim who can enjoy its platitudinous comfort, free of all genuine sorrow, but anyone whose grief bankrupts his poor patience is left with your saying and his sorrow, too. (*Bears the sentence* also plays on the meaning, "receives judicial sentence.")   219–220 *These . . . equivocal* these fine maxims are equivocal, either sweet or bitter in their application   222 *piercèd . . . ear* i.e., surgically lanced and cured by mere words of advice   225 *fortitude* strength   226 *substitute* deputy. *allowed* acknowledged   226–227 *opinion . . . on you* general opinion, an important determiner of affairs, chooses you as the best man   228 *slubber* soil, sully.   229 *stubborn* harsh, rough

Othello: The tyrant custom, most grave senators,   230
　　　Hath made the flinty and steel couch of war
　　　My thrice-driven° bed of down. I do agnize°
　　　A natural and prompt alacrity
　　　I find in hardness,° and do undertake
　　　These present wars against the Ottomites.   235
　　　Most humbly therefore bending to your state,°
　　　I crave fit disposition for my wife,
　　　Due reference of place and exhibition,°
　　　With such accommodation° and besort°
　　　As levels° with her breeding.°   240
Duke: Why, at her father's.
Brabantio: I will not have it so.
Othello: Nor I.
Desdemona: Nor I. I would not there reside,
　　　To put my father in impatient thoughts
　　　By being in his eye. Most gracious Duke,
　　　To my unfolding° lend your prosperous° ear,   245
　　　And let me find a charter° in your voice,
　　　T' assist my simpleness.
Duke: What would you, Desdemona?
Desdemona: That I did love the Moor to live with him,
　　　My downright violence and storm of fortunes°   250
　　　May trumpet to the world. My heart's subdued
　　　Even to the very quality of my lord.°
　　　I saw Othello's visage in his mind,
　　　And to his honors and his valiant parts°
　　　Did I my soul and fortunes consecrate.   255
　　　So that, dear lords, if I be left behind
　　　A moth° of peace, and he go to the war,
　　　The rites° for why I love him are bereft me,
　　　And I a heavy interim shall support
　　　By his dear° absence. Let me go with him.   260
Othello: Let her have your voice.°
　　　Vouch with me, heaven, I therefore beg it not
　　　To please the palate of my appetite,

---

232 *thrice-driven* thrice sifted, winnowed. *agnize* know in myself, acknowledge 234 *hardness* hardship 236 *bending . . . state* bowing or kneeling to your authority 238 *reference . . . exhibition* provision of appropriate place to live and allowance of money 239 *accommodation* suitable provision. *besort* attendance 240 *levels* equals, suits. *breeding* social position, upbringing 245 *unfolding* explanation, proposal. *prosperous* propitious 246 *charter* privilege, authorization 250 *My . . . fortunes* my plain and total breach of social custom, taking my future by storm and disrupting my whole life 251–252 *My heart's . . . . lord* my heart is brought wholly into accord with Othello's virtues; I love him for his virtues 254 *parts* qualities 257 *moth* i.e., one who consumes merely 258 *rites* rites of love (with a suggestion, too, of "rights," sharing) 260 *dear* (1) heartfelt (2) costly 261 *voice* consent

Desdemona declares her loyalty to her husband Othello (I, iii, 182–301).

Nor to comply with heat°—the young affects°
In me defunct—and proper° satisfaction, 265
But to be free° and bounteous to her mind.
And heaven defend° your good souls that you think°
I will your serious and great business scant
When she is with me. No, when light-winged toys
Of feathered Cupid seel° with wanton dullness 270
My speculative and officed instruments,°
That° my disports° corrupt and taint° my business,
Let huswives make a skillet of my helm,
And all indign° and base adversities
Make head° against my estimation!° 275

Duke: Be it as you shall privately determine,
Either for her stay or going. Th' affair cries haste,
And speed must answer it.

A Senator:　　　　　　You must away tonight.

Desdemona: Tonight, my lord?

264 *heat* sexual passion. *young affects* passions of youth, desires 265 *proper* personal 266 *free* generous 267 *defend* forbid. *think* should think 270 *seel* i.e., make blind (as in falconry, by sewing up the eyes of the hawk during training) 271 *speculative . . . instruments* eyes and other faculties used in the performance of duty 272 *That* so that. *disports* sexual pastimes. *taint* impair 274 *indign* unworthy, shameful 275 *Make head* raise an army. *estimation* reputation

Duke: This night.
Othello: With all my heart.
Duke: At nine i' the morning here we'll meet again.   280
  Othello, leave some officer behind,
  And he shall our commission bring to you,
  With such things else of quality and respect°
  As doth import° you.
Othello: So please Your Grace, my ancient;
  A man he is of honesty and trust.   285
  To his conveyance I assign my wife,
  With what else needful Your Good Grace shall think
  To be sent after me.
Duke: Let it be so.
  Good night to everyone. [*To Brabantio.*] And, noble signor,
  If virtue no delighted° beauty lack,   290
  Your son-in-law is far more fair than black.
First Senator: Adieu, brave Moor. Use Desdemona well.
Brabantio: Look to her, Moor, if thou hast eyes to see.
  She has deceived her father, and may thee.

                Exeunt [*Duke, Brabantio, Cassio, Senators, and officers*].

Othello: My life upon her faith! Honest Iago,   295
  My Desdemona must I leave to thee.
  I prithee, let thy wife attend on her,
  And bring them after in the best advantage.°
  Come, Desdemona. I have but an hour
  Of love, of worldly matters and direction,°   300
  To spend with thee. We must obey the time.°
                                        Exit [*with Desdemona*].

Roderigo: Iago—
Iago: What sayst thou, noble heart?
Roderigo: What will I do, think'st thou?
Iago: Why, go to bed and sleep.   305
Roderigo: I will incontinently° drown myself.
Iago: If thou dost, I shall never love thee after. Why, thou silly gentleman?
Roderigo: It is silliness to live when to live is torment; and then have we
    a prescription° to die when death is our physician.
Iago: O villainous!° I have looked upon the world for four times seven   310
    years, and, since I could distinguish betwixt a benefit and an injury,

---

283 *of quality and respect* of importance and relevance   284 *import* concern   290 *delighted* capable of delighting   298 *in . . . advantage* at the most favorable opportunity   300 *direction* instructions   301 *the time* the urgency of the present crisis   306 *incontinently* immediately, without self-restraint   309 *prescription* (1) right based on long-established custom (2) doctor's prescription   310 *villainous* i.e., what perfect nonsense

I never found man that knew how to love himself. Ere I would say I
would drown myself for the love of a guinea hen,° I would change my
humanity with a baboon.

Roderigo: What should I do? I confess it is my shame to be so fond,° but it   315
is not in my virtue° to amend it.

Iago: Virtue? A fig!° 'Tis in ourselves that we are thus or thus. Our bodies
are our gardens, to the which our wills are gardeners; so that if we will
plant nettles or sow lettuce, set hyssop° and weed up thyme, supply it
with one gender° of herbs or distract it with° many, either to have it   320
sterile with idleness° or manured with industry—why, the power and
corrigible authority° of this lies in our wills. If the beam° of our lives
had not one scale of reason to poise° another of sensuality, the blood°
and baseness of our natures would conduct us to most preposterous
conclusions. But we have reason to cool our raging motions,° our   325
carnal stings, our unbitted° lusts, whereof I take this that you call
love to be a sect or scion.°

Roderigo: It cannot be.

Iago: It is merely a lust of the blood and a permission of the will. Come,
be a man. Drown thyself? Drown cats and blind puppies. I have   330
professed me thy friend, and I confess me knit to thy deserving
with cables of perdurable° toughness. I could never better stead°
thee than now. Put money in thy purse. Follow thou the wars; defeat thy favor° with an usurped° beard. I say, put money in thy purse.
It cannot be long that Desdemona should continue her love to the   335
Moor—put money in thy purse—nor he his to her. It was a violent com-
mencement in her, and thou shalt see an answerable sequestration°—
put but money in thy purse. These Moors are changeable in their
wills°—fill thy purse with money. The food that to him now is as
luscious as locusts° shall be to him shortly as bitter as coloquintida.°   340
She must change for youth; when she is sated with his body, she will
find the error of her choice. She must have change, she must. Therefore put money in thy purse. If thou wilt needs damn thyself, do it a
more delicate way than drowning. Make° all the money thou canst.
If sanctimony° and a frail vow betwixt an erring° barbarian and a   345
supersubtle Venetian be not too hard for my wits and all the tribe of

313 *guinea hen* (A slang term for a prostitute.)   315 *fond* infatuated   316 *virtue* strength,
nature   317 *fig* (To give a fig is to thrust the thumb between the first and second fingers in a
vulgar and insulting gesture.)   319 *hyssop* an herb of the mint family   320 *gender* kind.   *distract it with* divide it among   321 *idleness* want of cultivation   322 *corrigible authority* power
to correct.   *beam* balance   323 *poise* counterbalance.   *blood* natural passions   325 *motions*
appetites   326 *unbitted* unbridled, uncontrolled.   327 *sect or scion* cutting or offshoot   332
perdurable very durable.   *stead* assist   333–334 *defeat thy favor* disguise your face   334 *usurped*
(The suggestion is that Roderigo is not man enough to have a beard of his own.)   337 *an
answerable sequestration* a corresponding separation or estrangement   339 *wills* carnal appetites   340 *locusts* fruit of the carob tree (see Matthew 3:4), or perhaps honeysuckle.   *coloquintida* colocynth or bitter apple, a purgative   344 *Make* raise, collect   345 *sanctimony* sacred ceremony.   *erring* wandering, vagabond, unsteady

hell, thou shalt enjoy her. Therefore make money. A pox of drowning
thyself! It is clean out of the way.° Seek thou rather to be hanged in
compassing° thy joy than to be drowned and go without her.

Roderigo: Wilt thou be fast° to my hopes if I depend on the issue?°   350

Iago: Thou art sure of me. Go, make money. I have told thee often, and
I retell thee again and again, I hate the Moor. My cause is hearted;°
thine hath no less reason. Let us be conjunctive° in our revenge
against him. If thou canst cuckold him, thou dost thyself a pleasure,
me a sport. There are many events in the womb of time which will   355
be delivered. Traverse,° go, provide thy money. We will have more
of this tomorrow. Adieu.

Roderigo: Where shall we meet i' the morning?

Iago: At my lodging.

Roderigo: I'll be with thee betimes.°   [*He starts to leave.*]   360

Iago: Go to, farewell.—Do you hear, Roderigo?

Roderigo: What say you?

Iago: No more of drowning, do you hear?

Roderigo: I am changed.

Iago: Go to, farewell. Put money enough in your purse.   365

Roderigo: I'll sell all my land.   *Exit.*

Iago: Thus do I ever make my fool my purse;
For I mine own gained knowledge should profane
If I would time expend with such a snipe°
But for my sport and profit. I hate the Moor;   370
And it is thought abroad° that twixt my sheets
He's done my office.° I know not if 't be true;
But I, for mere suspicion in that kind,
Will do as if for surety.° He holds me well;°
The better shall my purpose work on him.   375
Cassio's a proper° man. Let me see now:
To get his place and to plume up° my will
In double knavery—How, how?—Let's see:
After some time, to abuse° Othello's ear
That he° is too familiar with his wife.   380
He hath a person and a smooth dispose°
To be suspected, framed to make women false.
The Moor is of a free° and open° nature,

---

348 *clean . . . way* entirely unsuitable as a course of action   349 *compassing* encompassing,
embracing   350 *fast* true.   *issue* (successful) outcome   352 *hearted* fixed in the heart,
heartfelt   353 *conjunctive* united   356 *Traverse* (A military marching term.)   360 *betimes*
early   369 *snipe* woodcock, i.e., fool   371 *it is thought abroad* it is rumored   372 *my office* i.e.,
my sexual function as husband   374 *do . . . surety* act as if on certain knowledge.   *holds me
well* regards me favorably   376 *proper* handsome   377 *plume up* put a feather in the cap of,
i.e., glorify, gratify   379 *abuse* deceive   380 *he* i.e., Cassio   381 *dispose* disposition   383 *free*
frank, generous.   *open* unsuspicious

That thinks men honest that but seem to be so,
And will as tenderly° be led by the nose   385
As asses are.
I have 't. It is engendered. Hell and night
Must bring this monstrous birth to the world's light.

[*Exit.*]

ACT II

SCENE I [A SEAPORT IN CYPRUS. AN OPEN PLACE NEAR THE QUAY.]

Enter Montano and two Gentlemen.

Montano: What from the cape can you discern at sea?
First Gentleman: Nothing at all. It is a high-wrought flood.°
    I cannot, twixt the heaven and the main,°
    Descry a sail.
Montano: Methinks the wind hath spoke aloud at land;   5
    A fuller blast ne'er shook our battlements.
    If it hath ruffianed° so upon the sea,
    What ribs of oak, when mountains° melt on them,
    Can hold the mortise?° What shall we hear of this?
Second Gentleman: A segregation° of the Turkish fleet.   10
    For do but stand upon the foaming shore,
    The chidden° billow seems to pelt the clouds;
    The wind-shaked surge, with high and monstrous mane,°
    Seems to cast water on the burning Bear°
    And quench the guards of th' ever-fixèd pole.   15
    I never did like molestation° view
    On the enchafèd° flood.
Montano: If that° the Turkish fleet
    Be not ensheltered and embayed,° they are drowned;
    It is impossible to bear it out.°   20

Enter a [Third] Gentleman.

---

385 *tenderly* readily   2 *high-wrought flood* very agitated sea   3 *main* ocean (also at line 41)   7 *ruffianed* raged   8 *mountains* i.e., of water   9 *hold the mortise* hold their joints together. (A *mortise* is the socket hollowed out in fitting timbers.)   10 *segregation* dispersal   12 *chidden* i.e., rebuked, repelled (by the shore), and thus shot into the air   13 *monstrous mane* (The surf is like the mane of a wild beast.)   14 *the burning Bear* i.e., the constellation Ursa Minor or the Little Bear, which includes the polestar (and hence regarded as the *guards of th' ever-fixèd pole* in the next line; sometimes the term *guards* is applied to the two "pointers" of the Big Bear or Dipper, which may be intended here).   16 *like molestation* comparable disturbance   17 *enchafèd* angry   18 *If that* if   19 *embayed* sheltered by a bay   20 *bear it out* survive, weather the storm

Third Gentleman: News, lads! Our wars are done.
    The desperate tempest hath so banged the Turks
    That their designment° halts.° A noble ship of Venice
    Hath seen a grievous wreck° and sufferance°
    On most part of their fleet.   25
Montano: How? Is this true?
Third Gentleman: The ship is here put in,
    A Veronesa;° Michael Cassio,
    Lieutenant to the warlike Moor Othello,
    Is come on shore; the Moor himself at sea,   30
    And is in full commission here for Cyprus.
Montano: I am glad on 't. 'Tis a worthy governor.
Third Gentleman: But this same Cassio, though he speak of comfort
    Touching the Turkish loss, yet he looks sadly°
    And prays the Moor be safe, for they were parted   35
    With foul and violent tempest.
Montano: Pray heaven he be,
    For I have served him, and the man commands
    Like a full° soldier. Let's to the seaside, ho!
    As well to see the vessel that's come in
    As to throw out our eyes for brave Othello,   40
    Even till we make the main and th' aerial blue°
    An indistinct regard.°
Third Gentleman: Come, let's do so,
    For every minute is expectancy°
    Of more arrivance.°

    Enter Cassio.

Cassio: Thanks, you the valiant of this warlike isle,   45
    That so approve° the Moor! O, let the heavens
    Give him defense against the elements,
    For I have lost him on a dangerous sea.
Montano: Is he well shipped?
Cassio: His bark is stoutly timbered, and his pilot   50
    Of very expert and approved allowance;°
    Therefore my hopes, not surfeited to death,°
    Stand in bold cure.°

---

23 *designment* design, enterprise. *halts* is lame 24 *wreck* shipwreck. *sufferance* damage, disaster 28 *Veronesa* i.e., fitted out in Verona for Venetian service, or possibly *Verennessa* (the Folio spelling), i.e., *verrinessa*, a cutter (from *verrinare*, "to cut through") 34 *sadly* gravely 38 *full* perfect 41 *the main . . . blue* the sea and the sky 42 *An indistinct regard* indistinguishable in our view 43 *is expectancy* gives expectation 44 *arrivance* arrival 46 *approve* admire, honor 51 *approved allowance* tested reputation 52 *surfeited to death* i.e., overextended, worn thin through repeated application or delayed fulfillment 53 *in bold cure* in strong hopes of fulfillment

[*A cry*] *within:*   "A sail, a sail, a sail!"

Cassio: What noise?
A Gentleman: The town is empty. On the brow o' the sea°   55
  Stand ranks of people, and they cry "A sail!"
Cassio: My hopes do shape him for° the governor.

[*A shot within.*]

Second Gentleman: They do discharge their shot of courtesy;°
  Our friends at least.
Cassio: I pray you, sir, go forth,
  And give us truth who 'tis that is arrived.   60
Second Gentleman: I shall.   *Exit.*
Montano: But, good Lieutenant, is your general wived?
Cassio: Most fortunately. He hath achieved a maid
  That paragons° description and wild fame,°
  One that excels the quirks° of blazoning° pens,   65
  And in th' essential vesture of creation
  Does tire the enginer.°

  Enter [*Second*] *Gentleman.*°

                              How now? Who has put in?°
Second Gentleman: 'Tis one Iago, ancient to the General.
Cassio: He's had most favorable and happy speed.
  Tempests themselves, high seas, and howling winds,   70
  The guttered° rocks and congregated sands—
  Traitors ensteeped° to clog the guiltless keel—
  As° having sense of beauty, do omit°
  Their mortal° natures, letting go safely by
  The divine Desdemona.
Montano: What is she?   75
Cassio: She that I spake of, our great captain's captain,
  Left in the conduct of the bold Iago,
  Whose footing° here anticipates our thoughts
  A sennight's° speed. Great Jove, Othello guard,

---

55 *brow o' the sea* cliff-edge   57 *My . . . for* I hope it is   58 *discharge . . . courtesy* fire a salute in token of respect and courtesy   64 *paragons* surpasses.   *wild fame* extravagant report   65 *quirks* witty conceits.   *blazoning* setting forth as though in heraldic language   66–67 *in . . . enginer* in her real, God-given, beauty, (she) defeats any attempt to praise her.   *enginer* engineer, i.e., poet, one who devises.   s.d. [*Second*] *Gentleman* (So identified in the Quarto text here and in lines 58, 61, 68, and 96; the Folio calls him a gentleman.)   67 *put in* i.e., to harbor   71 *guttered* jagged, trenched   72 *ensteeped* lying under water   73 *As* as if.   *omit* forbear to exercise   74 *mortal* deadly   78 *footing* landing   79 *sennight's* week's

"I thank you, valiant Cassio. / What tidings can you tell me of my lord?"
(II, i, 89–90).

And swell his sail with thine own powerful breath,   80
That he may bless this bay with his tall° ship,
Make love's quick pants in Desdemona's arms,
Give renewed fire to our extinguished spirits,
And bring all Cyprus comfort!

Enter Desdemona, Iago, Roderigo, and Emilia.

                    O, behold,
The riches of the ship is come on shore!   85
You men of Cyprus, let her have your knees.

[The gentlemen make curtsy to Desdemona.]

Hail to thee, lady! And the grace of heaven
Before, behind thee, and on every hand
Enwheel thee round!
Desdemona: I thank you, valiant Cassio.
    What tidings can you tell me of my lord?   90
Cassio: He is not yet arrived, nor know I aught
    But that he's well and will be shortly here.
Desdemona: O, but I fear—How lost you company?
Cassio: The great contention of the sea and skies

81 *tall* splendid, gallant

Parted our fellowship.

(Within)   "A sail, a sail!" [*A shot.*]

                                      But hark. A sail!   95

Second Gentleman: They give their greeting to the citadel.

This likewise is a friend.

Cassio: See for the news.

[*Exit Second Gentleman.*]

Good Ancient, you are welcome. [*Kissing Emilia.*] Welcome, mistress.

Let it not gall your patience, good Iago,

That I extend° my manners; 'tis my breeding°   100

That gives me this bold show of courtesy.

Iago: Sir, would she give you so much of her lips

As of her tongue she oft bestows on me,

You would have enough.

Desdemona: Alas, she has no speech!°   105

Iago: In faith, too much.

I find it still,° when I have list° to sleep.

Marry, before your ladyship, I grant,

She puts her tongue a little in her heart

And chides with thinking.°

Emilia: You have little cause to say so.   110

Iago: Come on, come on. You are pictures out of doors,°

Bells° in your parlors, wildcats in your kitchens,°

Saints° in your injuries, devils being offended,

Players° in your huswifery,° and huswives° in your beds.

Desdemona: O, fie upon thee, slanderer!   115

Iago: Nay, it is true, or else I am a Turk.°

You rise to play, and go to bed to work.

Emilia: You shall not write my praise.

Iago: No, let me not.

Desdemona: What wouldst thou write of me, if thou shouldst praise me?

Iago: O gentle lady, do not put me to 't,   120

For I am nothing if not critical.°

Desdemona: Come on, essay.°—There's one gone to the harbor?

Iago: Ay, madam.

---

100 *extend* give scope to. *breeding* training in the niceties of etiquette   105 *she has no speech*
i.e., she's not a chatterbox, as you allege   107 *still* always. *list* desire   110 *with thinking* i.e.,
in her thoughts only   111 *pictures out of doors* i.e., silent and well-behaved in public   112
Bells i.e., jangling, noisy, and brazen. *in your kitchens* i.e., in domestic affairs. (Ladies would
not do the cooking.)   113 *Saints* martyrs   114 *Players* idlers, triflers, or deceivers. *huswifery*
housekeeping. *huswives* hussies (i.e., women are "busy" in bed, or unduly thrifty in dispensing sexual favors)   116 *a Turk* an infidel, not to be believed   121 *critical* censorious   122
essay try

Desdemona: I am not merry, but I do beguile
    The thing I am° by seeming otherwise.   125
    Come, how wouldst thou praise me?
Iago: I am about it, but indeed my invention
    Comes from my pate as birdlime° does from frieze°—
    It plucks out brains and all. But my Muse labors,°
    And thus she is delivered: 130
    If she be fair and wise, fairness and wit,
    The one's for use, the other useth it.°
Desdemona: Well praised! How if she be black° and witty?
Iago: If she be black, and thereto have a wit,
    She'll find a white° that shall her blackness fit.°   135
Desdemona: Worse and worse.
Emilia: How if fair and foolish?
Iago: She never yet was foolish that was fair,
    For even her folly° helped her to an heir.°
Desdemona: These are old fond° paradoxes to make fools laugh i' th'
    alehouse. What miserable praise hast thou for her that's foul and   140
    foolish?
Iago: There's none so foul° and foolish thereunto,°
    But does foul° pranks which fair and wise ones do.
Desdemona: O heavy ignorance! Thou praisest the worst best. But what
    praise couldst thou bestow on a deserving woman indeed, one that,   145
    in the authority of her merit, did justly put on the vouch° of very
    malice itself?
Iago: She that was ever fair, and never proud,
    Had tongue at will, and yet was never loud,
    Never lacked gold and yet went never gay,°   150
    Fled from her wish, and yet said, "Now I may,"°
    She that being angered, her revenge being nigh,
    Bade her wrong stay° and her displeasure fly,
    She that in wisdom never was so frail
    To change the cod's head for the salmon's tail,°   155
    She that could think and ne'er disclose her mind,

---

125 *The thing I am* i.e., my anxious self   128 *birdlime* sticky substance used to catch small
birds. *frieze* coarse woolen cloth   129 *labors* (1) exerts herself (2) prepares to deliver a child
(with a following pun on *delivered* in line 130)   132 *The one's . . . it* i.e., her cleverness will
make use of her beauty   133 *black* dark-complexioned, brunette   135 *a white* a fair person
(with word-play on "wight," a person). *fit* (with sexual suggestion of mating)   138 *folly*
(with added meaning of "lechery, wantonness"). *to an heir* i.e., to bear a child   139 *fond*
foolish   142 *foul* ugly. *thereunto* in addition   143 *foul* sluttish   146 *put . . . vouch* compel
the approval   150 *gay* extravagantly clothed   151 *Fled . . . may* avoided temptation where
the choice was hers   153 *Bade . . . stay* i.e., resolved to put up with her injury patiently   155
To . . . tail i.e., to exchange a lackluster husband for a sexy lover (?) (*Cod's head* is slang for
"penis," and *tail*, for "pudendum.")

See suitors following and not look behind,
She was a wight, if ever such wight were—
Desdemona: To do what?
Iago: To suckle fools° and chronicle small beer.°   160
Desdemona: O most lame and impotent conclusion! Do not learn of him,
     Emilia, though he be thy husband. How say you, Cassio? Is he not a
     most profane° and liberal° counselor?
Cassio: He speaks home,° madam. You may relish° him more in° the
     soldier than in the scholar.   165

     [*Cassio and Desdemona stand together, conversing intimately.*]

Iago [*aside*]: He takes her by the palm. Ay, well said,° whisper. With as
     little a web as this will I ensnare as great a fly as Cassio. Ay, smile
     upon her, do; I will gyve° thee in thine own courtship.° You say true;°
     'tis so, indeed. If such tricks as these strip you out of your lieutenantry,
     it had been better you had not kissed your three fingers so oft, which   170
     now again you are most apt to play the sir° in. Very good; well kissed!
     An excellent courtesy! 'Tis so, indeed. Yet again your fingers to your
     lips? Would they were clyster pipes° for your sake! [*Trumpet within.*]
     The Moor! I know his trumpet.
Cassio: 'Tis truly so.   175
Desdemona: Let's meet him and receive him.
Cassio: Lo, where he comes!

     Enter Othello and attendants.

Othello: O my fair warrior!
Desdemona: My dear Othello!
Othello: It gives me wonder great as my content
     To see you here before me. O my soul's joy,   180
     If after every tempest come such calms,
     May the winds blow till they have wakened death,
     And let the laboring bark climb hills of seas
     Olympus-high, and duck again as low
     As hell's from heaven! If it were now to die,   185
     'Twere now to be most happy, for I fear
     My soul hath her content so absolute
     That not another comfort like to this
     Succeeds in unknown fate.°

160 *suckle fools* breastfeed babies. *chronicle small beer* i.e., keep petty household accounts,
keep track of trivial matters 163 *profane* irreverent, ribald. *liberal* licentious, free-
spoken 164 *home* right to the target. (A term from fencing.) *relish* appreciate. *in* in the
character of 166 *well said* well done 168 *gyve* fetter, shackle. *courtship* courtesy, show of
courtly manners. *You say true* i.e., that's right, go ahead 171 *the sir* i.e., the fine gentleman 173 *clyster pipes* tubes used for enemas and douches 189 *Succeeds . . . fate* i.e., can
follow in the unknown future

Desdemona: The heavens forbid
  But that our loves and comforts should increase   190
  Even as our days do grow!
Othello: Amen to that, sweet powers!
  I cannot speak enough of this content.
  It stops me here; it is too much of joy.
  And this, and this, the greatest discords be   195

  [*They kiss.*]°

  That e'er our hearts shall make!
Iago [*aside*]: O, you are well tuned now!
  But I'll set down° the pegs that make this music,
  As honest as I am.°
Othello: Come, let us to the castle.   200
  News, friends! Our wars are done, the Turks are drowned.
  How does my old acquaintance of this isle?—
  Honey, you shall be well desired° in Cyprus;
  I have found great love amongst them. O my sweet,
  I prattle out of fashion,° and I dote   205
  In mine own comforts.—I prithee, good Iago,
  Go to the bay and disembark my coffers.°
  Bring thou the master° to the citadel;
  He is a good one, and his worthiness
  Does challenge° much respect.—Come, Desdemona.—   210
  Once more, well met at Cyprus!

  Exeunt Othello and Desdemona [and all but Iago and Roderigo].

Iago [*to an attendant*]: Do thou meet me presently at the harbor. [*To
  Roderigo.*] Come hither. If thou be'st valiant—as, they say, base men°
  being in love have then a nobility in their natures more than is native to
  them—list° me. The Lieutenant tonight watches on the court of guard.° 215
  First, I must tell thee this: Desdemona is directly in love with him.
Roderigo: With him? Why, 'tis not possible.
Iago: Lay thy finger thus,° and let thy soul be instructed. Mark me with what
  violence she first loved the Moor, but° for bragging and telling her
  fantastical lies. To love him still for prating? Let not thy discreet heart 220
  think it. Her eye must be fed; and what delight shall she have to look on
  the devil? When the blood is made dull with the act of sport,° there

195 s.d. *They kiss* (The direction is from the Quarto.) 198 *set down* loosen (and hence
untune the instrument) 199 *As . . . I am* for all my supposed honesty 203 *desired* welcomed 205 *out of fashion* irrelevantly, incoherently (?) 207 *coffers* chests, baggage
208 *master* ship's captain 210 *challenge* lay claim to, deserve 213 *base men* even lowly
born men 215 *list* listen to *court of guard* guardhouse. (Cassio is in charge of the watch.)
218 *thus* i.e., on your lips 219 *but* only 222 *the act of sport* sex

should be, again to inflame it and to give satiety a fresh appetite,
loveliness in favor,° sympathy° in years, manners, and beauties—
all which the Moor is defective in. Now, for want of these required   225
conveniences,° her delicate tenderness will find itself abused,° begin
to heave the gorge,° disrelish and abhor the Moor. Very nature° will
instruct her in it and compel her to some second choice. Now, sir, this
granted—as it is a most pregnant° and unforced position—who stands
so eminent in the degree of° this fortune as Cassio does? A knave   230
very voluble,° no further conscionable° than in putting on the mere
form of civil and humane° seeming for the better compassing of
his salt° and most hidden loose affection.° Why, none, why, none.
A slipper° and subtle knave, a finder out of occasions, that has an
eye can stamp° and counterfeit advantages,° though true advantage   235
never present itself; a devilish knave. Besides, the knave is handsome,
young, and hath all those requisites in him that folly° and green°
minds look after. A pestilent complete knave, and the woman hath
found him° already.
Roderigo: I cannot believe that in her. She's full of most blessed condition.°   240
Iago: Blessed fig's end!° The wine she drinks is made of grapes. If she had
been blessed, she would never have loved the Moor. Blessed pudding!°
Didst thou not see her paddle with the palm of his hand? Didst not
mark that?
Roderigo: Yes, that I did; but that was but courtesy.   245
Iago: Lechery, by this hand. An index° and obscure° prologue to the history of lust and foul thoughts. They met so near with their lips that
their breaths embraced together. Villainous thoughts, Roderigo!
When these mutualities° so marshal the way, hard at hand° comes
the master and main exercise, th' incorporate° conclusion. Pish! But,   250
sir, be you ruled by me. I have brought you from Venice. Watch you°
tonight; for the command, I'll lay 't upon you.° Cassio knows you
not. I'll not be far from you. Do you find some occasion to anger Cassio,
either by speaking too loud, or tainting° his discipline, or from what
other course you please, which the time shall more favorably minister.°   255
Roderigo: Well.

---

224 *favor* appearance. *sympathy* correspondence, similarity   225–226 *required conveniences*
things conducive to sexual compatibility   226 *abused* cheated, revolted   227 *heave the gorge*
experience nausea. *Very nature* her very instincts   229 *pregnant* evident, cogent   230 *in the degree
of* as next in line for   231 *voluble* facile, glib.   *conscionable* conscientious, conscience-bound   232
humane polite, courteous.   233 *salt* licentious.   *affection* passion   234 *slipper* slippery   235 *an eye
can stamp* an eye that can coin, create.   *advantages* favorable opportunities   237 *folly* wantonness.   *green* immature   239 *found him* sized him up, perceived his intent   240 *condition* disposition   241 *fig's end* (See Act I, Scene iii, line 317, for the vulgar gesture of the fig.)   242 *pudding*
sausage   246 *index* table of contents.   *obscure* (i.e., the *lust and foul thoughts* in line 247 are secret,
hidden from view)   249 *mutualities* exchanges, intimacies.   *hard at hand* closely following   250
incorporate carnal   251 *Watch you* stand watch   252 *for the command . . . you* I'll arrange for you
to be appointed, given orders   254 *tainting* disparaging   255 *minister* provide

Iago: Sir, he's rash and very sudden in choler,° and haply° may strike
at you. Provoke him that he may, for even out of that will I cause
these of Cyprus to mutiny,° whose qualification° shall come into no
true taste° again but by the displanting of Cassio. So shall you have   260
a shorter journey to your desires by the means I shall then have to
prefer° them, and the impediment most profitably removed, without
the which there were no expectation of our prosperity.

Roderigo: I will do this, if you can bring it to any opportunity.

Iago: I warrant° thee. Meet me by and by° at the citadel. I must fetch his   265
necessaries ashore. Farewell.

Roderigo: Adieu.   *Exit.*

Iago: That Cassio loves her, I do well believe 't;
    That she loves him, 'tis apt° and of great credit.°
    The Moor, howbeit that I endure him not,   270
    Is of a constant, loving, noble nature,
    And I dare think he'll prove to Desdemona
    A most dear husband. Now, I do love her too,
    Not out of absolute lust—though peradventure
    I stand accountant° for as great a sin—   275
    But partly led to diet° my revenge
    For that I do suspect the lusty Moor
    Hath leaped into my seat, the thought whereof
    Doth, like a poisonous mineral, gnaw my innards;
    And nothing can or shall content my soul   280
    Till I am evened with him, wife for wife,
    Or failing so, yet that I put the Moor
    At least into a jealousy so strong
    That judgment cannot cure. Which thing to do,
    If this poor trash of Venice, whom I trace°   285
    For° his quick hunting, stand the putting on,°
    I'll have our Michael Cassio on the hip,°
    Abuse° him to the Moor in the rank garb°—
    For I fear Cassio with my nightcap° too—
    Make the Moor thank me, love me, and reward me   290
    For making him egregiously an ass

---

257 *choler* wrath. *haply* perhaps   259 *mutiny* riot. *qualification* appeasement.   260 *true taste*
i.e., acceptable state   262 *prefer* advance   265 *warrant* assure. *by and by* immediately   269
apt probable. *credit* credibility   275 *accountant* accountable   276 *diet* feed   285 *trace* i.e.,
train, or follow (?), or perhaps *trash*, a hunting term, meaning to put weights on a hunting
dog in order to slow him down   286 *For* to make more eager. *stand . . . on* respond properly when I incite him to quarrel   287 *on the hip* at my mercy, where I can throw him. (A
wrestling term.)   288 *Abuse* slander. *rank garb* coarse manner, gross fashion   289 *with my
nightcap* i.e., as a rival in my bed, as one who gives me cuckold's horns

And practicing upon° his peace and quiet
Even to madness. 'Tis here, but yet confused.
Knavery's plain face is never seen till used.   *Exit.*

SCENE II [CYPRUS. A STREET.]

Enter Othello's Herald with a proclamation.

Herald: It is Othello's pleasure, our noble and valiant general, that,
upon certain tidings now arrived, importing the mere perdition°
of the Turkish fleet, every man put himself into triumph:° some to
dance, some to make bonfires, each man to what sport and revels his
addiction° leads him. For, besides these beneficial news, it is the cele-   5
bration of his nuptial. So much was his pleasure should be proclaimed.
All offices° are open, and there is full liberty of feasting from this
present hour of five till the bell have told eleven. Heaven bless the
isle of Cyprus and our noble general Othello!

Exit.

SCENE III [CYPRUS. THE CITADEL.]

Enter Othello, Desdemona, Cassio, and attendants.

Othello: Good Michael, look you to the guard tonight.
Let's teach ourselves that honorable stop°
Not to outsport° discretion.
Cassio: Iago hath direction what to do,
But notwithstanding, with my personal eye   5
Will I look to 't.
Othello: Iago is most honest.
Michael, good night. Tomorrow with your earliest°
Let me have speech with you. [*To Desdemona.*]
                                 Come, my dear love,
The purchase made, the fruits are to ensue;
That profit's yet to come 'tween me and you.°—   10
Good night.

Exit [*Othello, with Desdemona and attendants*].

Enter Iago.

292 *practicing upon* plotting against   2 *mere perdition* complete destruction   3 *triumph* public
celebration   5 *addiction* inclination   7 *offices* rooms where food and drink are kept   2 *stop*
restraint   3 *outsport* celebrate beyond the bounds of   7 *with your earliest* at your earliest convenience   9–10 *The purchase . . . you* i.e., though married, we haven't yet consummated our love

Cassio: Welcome, Iago. We must to the watch.

Iago: Not this hour,° Lieutenant; 'tis not yet ten o' the clock. Our general cast° us thus early for the love of his Desdemona; who° let us not therefore blame. He hath not yet made wanton the night with her, and she is sport for Jove.   15

Cassio: She's a most exquisite lady.

Iago: And, I'll warrant her, full of game.

Cassio: Indeed, she's a most fresh and delicate creature.

Iago: What an eye she has! Methinks it sounds a parley° to provocation.   20

Cassio: An inviting eye, and yet methinks right modest.

Iago: And when she speaks, is it not an alarum° to love?

Cassio: She is indeed perfection.

Iago: Well, happiness to their sheets! Come, Lieutenant, I have a stoup° of wine, and here without° are a brace° of Cyprus gallants that would fain have a measure° to the health of black Othello.   25

Cassio: Not tonight, good Iago. I have very poor and unhappy brains for drinking. I could well wish courtesy would invent some other custom of entertainment.

Iago: O, they are our friends. But one cup! I'll drink for you.°   30

Cassio: I have drunk but one cup tonight, and that was craftily qualified° too, and behold what innovation° it makes here.° I am unfortunate in the infirmity and dare not task my weakness with any more.

Iago: What, man? 'Tis a night of revels. The gallants desire it.

Cassio: Where are they?   35

Iago: Here at the door. I pray you, call them in.

Cassio: I'll do 't, but it dislikes me.°   *Exit.*

Iago: If I can fasten but one cup upon him,
    With that which he hath drunk tonight already,
    He'll be as full of quarrel and offense°   40
    As my young mistress' dog. Now, my sick fool Roderigo,
    Whom love hath turned almost the wrong side out,
    To Desdemona hath tonight caroused°
    Potations pottle-deep;° and he's to watch.°
    Three lads of Cyprus—noble swelling° spirits,   45
    That hold their honors in a wary distance,°
    The very elements° of this warlike isle—

---

13 *Not this hour* not for an hour yet. *cast* dismissed 14 *who* i.e., Othello 20 *sounds a parley* calls for a conference, issues an invitation 22 *alarum* signal calling men to arms (continuing the military metaphor of *parley*, line 20) 24 *stoup* measure of liquor, two quarts 25 *without* outside. *brace* pair 26 *fain have a measure* gladly drink a toast 30 *for you* in your place. (Iago will do the steady drinking to keep the gallants company while Cassio has only one cup.) 31 *qualified* diluted 32 *innovation* disturbance, insurrection. *here* i.e., in my head 37 *it dislikes me* i.e., I'm reluctant 40 *offense* readiness to take offense 43 *caroused* drunk off 44 *pottle-deep* to the bottom of the tankard. *watch* stand watch 45 *swelling* proud 46 *hold . . . distance* i.e., are extremely sensitive of their honor 47 *very elements* typical sort

Have I tonight flustered with flowing cups,
And they watch° too. Now, 'mongst this flock of drunkards
Am I to put our Cassio in some action   50
That may offend the isle.—But here they come.

Enter Cassio, Montano, and gentlemen [servants following with wine].

If consequence do but approve my dream,°
My boat sails freely both with wind and stream.°
Cassio: 'Fore God, they have given me a rouse° already.
Montano: Good faith, a little one; not past a pint, as I am a soldier.   55
Iago: Some wine, ho! *[He sings.]*
　　　　　"And let me the cannikin° clink, clink,
　　　　　And let me the cannikin clink.
　　　　　A soldier's a man,
　　　　　O, man's life's but a span;°   60
　　　　　Why, then, let a soldier drink."
Some wine, boys!
Cassio: 'Fore God, an excellent song.
Iago: I learned it in England, where indeed they are most potent in potting.°
Your Dane, your German, and your swag-bellied Hollander—drink,   65
ho!—are nothing to your English.
Cassio: Is your Englishman so exquisite in his drinking?
Iago: Why, he drinks you,° with facility, your Dane° dead drunk; he sweats
not° to overthrow your Almain;° he gives your Hollander a vomit ere
the next pottle can be filled.   70
Cassio: To the health of our general!
Montano: I am for it, Lieutenant, and I'll do you justice.°
Iago: O sweet England! *[He sings.]*
　　　　　"King Stephen was a worthy peer,
　　　　　His breeches cost him but a crown;   75
　　　　　He held them sixpence all too dear,
　　　　　With that he called the tailor lown.

　　　　　He was a wight of high renown,
　　　　　And thou art but of low degree.
　　　　　'Tis pride that pulls the country down;   80
　　　　　Then take thy auld° cloak about thee."
Some wine, ho!

---

49 *watch* are members of the guard   52 *If . . . dream* if subsequent events will only substanti-
ate my scheme   53 *stream* current   54 *rouse* full draft of liquor   57 *cannikin* small drinking
vessel   60 *span* brief span of time. (Compare Psalm 39:6 as rendered in the 1928 Book of
Common Prayer: "Thou hast made my days as it were a span long.")   64 *potting* drinking   68 *drinks you* drinks.   *your Dane* your typical Dane   69 *sweats not* i.e., need not exert
himself.   *Almain* German   72 *I'll . . . justice* i.e., I'll drink as much as you.   *lown* lout, rascal.   *pride* i.e., extravagance in dress   81 *auld* old

Iago persuades Cassio to have a drink, "To the health of our general!" (II, iii, 71).

Cassio: 'Fore God, this is a more exquisite song than the other.

Iago: Will you hear 't again?

Cassio: No, for I hold him to be unworthy of his place that does those   85
    things. Well, God's above all; and there be souls must be saved, and
    there be souls must not be saved.

Iago: It's true, good Lieutenant.

Cassio: For mine own part—no offense to the General, nor any man of
    quality°—I hope to be saved.   90

Iago: And so do I too, Lieutenant.

Cassio: Ay, but, by your leave, not before me; the lieutenant is to be saved
    before the ancient. Let's have no more of this; let's to our affairs.—
    God forgive us our sins!—Gentlemen, let's look to our business. Do
    not think, gentlemen, I am drunk. This is my ancient; this is my   95
    right hand, and this is my left. I am not drunk now. I can stand well
    enough, and speak well enough.

Gentlemen: Excellent well.

Cassio: Why, very well then; you must not think then that I am
    drunk.   *Exit.*   100

90 *quality* rank

Montano: To th' platform, masters. Come, let's set the watch.°

    [*Exeunt Gentlemen.*]

Iago: You see this fellow that is gone before.
    He's a soldier fit to stand by Caesar
    And give direction; and do but see his vice.
    'Tis to his virtue a just equinox,°   105
    The one as long as th' other. 'Tis pity of him.
    I fear the trust Othello puts him in,
    On some odd time of his infirmity,
    Will shake this island.
Montano: But is he often thus?
Iago: 'Tis evermore the prologue to his sleep.   110
    He'll watch the horologe a double set,°
    If drink rock not his cradle.
Montano: It were well
    The General were put in mind of it.
    Perhaps he sees it not, or his good nature
    Prizes the virtue that appears in Cassio   115
    And looks not on his evils. Is not this true?

    Enter Roderigo.

Iago [*aside to him*]: How now, Roderigo?
    I pray you, after the Lieutenant; go.
    [*Exit Roderigo.*]
Montano: And 'tis great pity that the noble Moor
    Should hazard such a place as his own second   120
    With° one of an engraffed° infirmity.
    It were an honest action to say so
    To the Moor.
Iago: Not I, for this fair island.
    I do love Cassio well and would do much
    To cure him of this evil.   [*Cry within:* "Help! Help!"]
            But, hark! What noise?   125

    Enter Cassio, pursuing° Roderigo.

Cassio: Zounds, you rogue! You rascal!
Montano: What's the matter, Lieutenant?
Cassio: A knave teach me my duty?

---

101 *set the watch* mount the guard   105 *just equinox* exact counterpart. (*Equinox* is an equal length of days and nights.)   111 *watch . . . set* stay awake twice around the clock or *horologe*   120–121 *hazard . . . With* risk giving such an important position as his second in command to   121 *engraffed* engrafted, inveterate   s.d. *pursuing* (The Quarto text reads, "driving in.")

I'll beat the knave into a twiggen° bottle.
Roderigo: Beat me?
Cassio: Dost thou prate, rogue?   [*He strikes Roderigo.*]   130
Montano: Nay, good Lieutenant. [*Restraining him.*] I pray you, sir, hold
      your hand.
Cassio: Let me go, sir, or I'll knock you o'er the mazard.°
Montano: Come, come, you're drunk.
Cassio: Drunk?   [*They fight.*]   135
Iago [*aside to Roderigo*]: Away, I say. Go out and cry a mutiny.°

      [*Exit Roderigo.*]

      Nay, good Lieutenant—God's will, gentlemen—
      Help, ho!—Lieutenant—sir—Montano—sir—
      Help, masters!°—Here's a goodly watch indeed!

      [*A bell rings.*]°

      Who's that which rings the bell?—Diablo,° ho!   140
      The town will rise.° God's will, Lieutenant, hold!
      You'll be ashamed forever.

      Enter Othello and attendants [*with weapons*].

Othello: What is the matter here?
Montano: Zounds, I bleed still.
      I am hurt to th' death. He dies!   [*He thrusts at Cassio.*]
Othello: Hold, for your lives!
Iago: Hold, ho! Lieutenant—sir—Montano—gentlemen—   145
      Have you forgot all sense of place and duty?
      Hold! The General speaks to you. Hold, for shame!
Othello: Why, how now, ho! From whence ariseth this?
      Are we turned Turks, and to ourselves do that
      Which heaven hath forbid the Ottomites?°   150
      For Christian shame, put by this barbarous brawl!
      He that stirs next to carve for° his own rage
      Holds his soul light;° he dies upon his motion.°
      Silence that dreadful bell. It frights the isle
      From her propriety.° What is the matter, masters?   155

128 *twiggen* wicker-covered (Cassio vows to assail Roderigo until his skin resembles wickerwork
or until he has driven Roderigo through the holes in a wickerwork.)   133 *mazard* i.e., head.
(Literally, a drinking vessel.)   136 *mutiny* riot   139 *masters* sirs.   s.d. *A bell rings* (This direction is from the Quarto, as are *Exit Roderigo* at line 118, *They fight* at line 135, and *with weapons*
at line 142.)   140 *Diablo* the devil   141 *rise* grow riotous   149–150 *to ourselves . . . Ottomites*
inflict on ourselves the harm that heaven has prevented the Turks from doing (by destroying
their fleet)   152 *carve for* i.e., indulge, satisfy with his sword   153 *Holds . . . light* i.e., places
little value on his life.   *upon his motion* if he moves   155 *propriety* proper state or condition

Honest Iago, that looks dead with grieving,
Speak. Who began this? On thy love, I charge thee.
Iago: I do not know. Friends all but now, even now,
In quarter° and in terms° like bride and groom
Devesting them° for bed; and then, but now—
As if some planet had unwitted men—
Swords out, and tilting one at others' breasts
In opposition bloody. I cannot speak°
Any beginning to this peevish odds;°
And would in action glorious I had lost
Those legs that brought me to a part of it!
Othello: How comes it, Michael, you are thus forgot?°
Cassio: I pray you, pardon me. I cannot speak.
Othello: Worthy Montano, you were wont be° civil;
The gravity and stillness° of your youth
The world hath noted, and your name is great
In mouths of wisest censure.° What's the matter
That you unlace° your reputation thus
And spend your rich opinion° for the name
Of a night-brawler? Give me answer to it.
Montano: Worthy Othello, I am hurt to danger.
Your officer, Iago, can inform you—
While I spare speech, which something° now offends° me—
Of all that I do know; nor know I aught
By me that's said or done amiss this night,
Unless self-charity be sometimes a vice,
And to defend ourselves it be a sin
When violence assails us.
Othello: Now, by heaven,
My blood° begins my safer guides° to rule,
And passion, having my best judgment collied,°
Essays° to lead the way. Zounds, if I stir,
Or do but lift this arm, the best of you
Shall sink in my rebuke. Give me to know
How this foul rout° began, who set it on;
And he that is approved in° this offense,
Though he had twinned with me, both at a birth,
Shall lose me. What? In a town of° war

160

165

170

175

180

185

190

---

159 *In quarter* in friendly conduct, within bounds. *in terms* on good terms   160 *Devesting them* undressing themselves   163 *speak* explain   164 *peevish odds* childish quarrel   167 *are thus forgot* have forgotten yourself thus   169 *wont be* accustomed to be   170 *stillness* sobriety   172 *censure* judgment   173 *unlace* undo, lay open (as one might loose the strings of a purse containing reputation)   174 *opinion* reputation   178 *something* somewhat. *offends* pains   184 *blood* passion (of anger). *guides* i.e., reason   185 *collied* darkened   186 *Essays* undertakes   189 *rout* riot   190 *approved in* found guilty of   192 *town of* town garrisoned for

Yet wild, the people's hearts brim full of fear,
To manage° private and domestic quarrel?
In night, and on the court and guard of safety?°   195
'Tis monstrous. Iago, who began 't?
Montano [*to Iago*]: If partially affined,° or leagued in office,°
    Thou dost deliver more or less than truth,
    Thou art no soldier.
Iago: Touch me not so near.
    I had rather have this tongue cut from my mouth   200
    Than it should do offense to Michael Cassio;
    Yet, I persuade myself, to speak the truth
    Shall nothing wrong him. Thus it is, General.
    Montano and myself being in speech,
    There comes a fellow crying out for help,   205
    And Cassio following him with determined sword
    To execute° upon him. Sir, this gentleman

    [*indicating Montano*]

    Steps in to Cassio and entreats his pause.°
    Myself the crying fellow did pursue,
    Lest by his clamor—as it so fell out—   210
    The town might fall in fright. He, swift of foot,
    Outran my purpose, and I returned, the rather°
    For that I heard the clink and fall of swords
    And Cassio high in oath, which till tonight
    I ne'er might say before. When I came back—   215
    For this was brief—I found them close together
    At blow and thrust, even as again they were
    When you yourself did part them.
    More of this matter cannot I report.
    But men are men; the best sometimes forget.°   220
    Though Cassio did some little wrong to him,
    As men in rage strike those that wish them best,°
    Yet surely Cassio, I believe, received
    From him that fled some strange indignity,
    Which patience could not pass.°
Othello: I know, Iago,   225
    Thy honesty and love doth mince this matter,
    Making it light to Cassio. Cassio, I love thee,

---

194 *manage* undertake 195 *on . . . safety* at the main guardhouse or headquarters and on watch 197 *partially affined* made partial by some personal relationship. *leagued in office* in league as fellow officers 207 *execute* give effect to (his anger) 208 *his pause* him to stop 212 *rather* sooner 220 *forget* forget themselves 222 *those . . . best* i.e., even those who are well disposed 225 *pass* pass over, overlook

But nevermore be officer of mine.

Enter Desdemona, attended.

Look if my gentle love be not raised up.
I'll make thee an example.   230
Desdemona: What is the matter, dear?
Othello: All's well now, sweeting;
Come away to bed. [*To Montano.*] Sir, for your hurts,
Myself will be your surgeon.°—Lead him off.

[*Montano is led off.*]

Iago, look with care about the town
And silence those whom this vile brawl distracted.   235
Come, Desdemona. 'Tis the soldiers' life
To have their balmy slumbers waked with strife.

Exit [with all but Iago and Cassio].

Iago: What, are you hurt, Lieutenant?
Cassio: Ay, past all surgery.
Iago: Marry, God forbid!   240
Cassio: Reputation, reputation, reputation! O, I have lost my reputation!
I have lost the immortal part of myself, and what remains is bestial.
My reputation, Iago, my reputation!
Iago: As I am an honest man, I thought you had received some bodily wound; there is more sense in that than in reputation. Reputa-   245
tion is an idle and most false imposition,° oft got without merit and
lost without deserving. You have lost no reputation at all, unless
you repute yourself such a loser. What, man, there are more ways to
recover° the General again. You are but now cast in his mood°—a punishment more in policy° than in malice, even so as one would beat   250
his offenseless dog to affright an imperious lion.° Sue° to him again
and he's yours.
Cassio: I will rather sue to be despised than to deceive so good a
commander with so slight,° so drunken, and so indiscreet an officer.
Drunk? And speak parrot?° And squabble? Swagger? Swear? And   255
discourse fustian with one's own shadow? O thou invisible spirit of
wine, if thou hast no name to be known by, let us call thee devil!

---

233 *be your surgeon* i.e., make sure you receive medical attention   246 *false imposition*
thing artificially imposed and of no real value   249 *recover* regain favor with.   *cast in his mood*
dismissed in a moment of anger   250 *in policy* done for expediency's sake and as a public
gesture   250–251 *would . . . lion* i.e., would make an example of a minor offender in order
to deter more important and dangerous offenders   251 *Sue* petition   254 *slight* worthless
255 *speak parrot* talk nonsense, rant

Iago advises Cassio to ask Desdemona to plead his cause with Othello (II, iii, 238–297).

Iago: What was he that you followed with your sword? What had he done
    to you?

Cassio: I know not.   260

Iago: Is 't possible?

Cassio: I remember a mass of things, but nothing distinctly; a quarrel, but
    nothing wherefore.° O God, that men should put an enemy in
    their mouths to steal away their brains! That we should, with joy,
    pleasance, revel, and applause° transform ourselves into beasts!   265

Iago: Why, but you are now well enough. How came you thus recovered?

Cassio: It hath pleased the devil drunkenness to give place to the devil
    wrath. One unperfectness shows me another, to make me frankly de-
    spise myself.

Iago: Come, you are too severe a moraler.° As the time, the place, and   270
    the condition of this country stands, I could heartily wish this had
    not befallen; but since it is as it is, mend it for your own good.

263 *wherefore* why   265 *applause* desire for applause   270 *moraler* moralizer

Cassio: I will ask him for my place again; he shall tell me I am a drunkard.
Had I as many mouths as Hydra,° such an answer would stop them all.
To be now a sensible man, by and by a fool, and presently a beast! O,   275
strange! Every inordinate cup is unblessed, and the ingredient is a devil.
Iago: Come, come, good wine is a good familiar creature, if it be well used.
Exclaim no more against it. And, good Lieutenant, I think you think
I love you.
Cassio: I have well approved° it, sir. I drunk!   280
Iago: You or any man living may be drunk at a time,° man. I'll tell you
what you shall do. Our general's wife is now the general—I may say
so in this respect, for that° he hath devoted and given up himself to
the contemplation, mark, and denotement° of her parts° and graces.
Confess yourself freely to her; importune her help to put you in your   285
place again. She is of so free,° so kind, so apt, so blessed a disposition,
she holds it a vice in her goodness not to do more than she is
requested. This broken joint between you and her husband entreat
her to splinter;° and, my fortunes against any lay° worth naming, this
crack of your love shall grow stronger than it was before.   290
Cassio: You advise me well.
Iago: I protest,° in the sincerity of love and honest kindness.
Cassio: I think it freely;° and betimes in the morning I will beseech
the virtuous Desdemona to undertake for me. I am desperate of my
fortunes if they check° me here.   295
Iago: You are in the right. Good night, Lieutenant. I must to the watch.
Cassio: Good night, honest Iago.   *Exit Cassio.*
Iago: And what's he then that says I play the villain,
When this advice is free° I give, and honest,
Probal° to thinking, and indeed the course   300
To win the Moor again? For 'tis most easy
Th' inclining° Desdemona to subdue°
In any honest suit; she's framed as fruitful°
As the free elements.° And then for her
To win the Moor—were 't to renounce his baptism,   305
All seals and symbols of redeemèd sin—
His soul is so enfettered to her love
That she may make, unmake, do what she list,

---

274 *Hydra* the Lernaean Hydra, a monster with many heads and the ability to grow two
heads when one was cut off, slain by Hercules as the second of his twelve labors   280 *ap-*
proved proved   281 *at a time* at one time or another   283 *in . . . that* in view of this fact,
that   284 *mark, and denotement* (Both words mean "observation.")   *parts* qualities   286 *free*
generous   289 *splinter* bind with splints.   *lay* stake, wager   292 *protest* insist, declare   293
freely unreservedly   295 *check* repulse   299 *free* (1) free from guile (2) freely given   300
Probal probable, reasonable   302 *inclining* favorably disposed.   *subdue* persuade   303 *framed*
as fruitful created as generous   304 *free elements* i.e., earth, air, fire, and water, unrestrained
and spontaneous

Even as her appetite° shall play the god
With his weak function.° How am I then a villain,   310
To counsel Cassio to this parallel° course
Directly to his good? Divinity of hell!°
When devils will the blackest sins put on,°
They do suggest° at first with heavenly shows,
As I do now. For whiles this honest fool   315
Plies Desdemona to repair his fortune,
And she for him pleads strongly to the Moor,
I'll pour this pestilence into his ear,
That she repeals him° for her body's lust;
And by how much she strives to do him good,   320
She shall undo her credit with the Moor.
So will I turn her virtue into pitch,°
And out of her own goodness make the net
That shall enmesh them all.
    Enter Roderigo.   How now, Roderigo?

Roderigo: I do follow here in the chase, not like a hound that hunts,   325
but one that fills up the cry.° My money is almost spent; I have
been tonight exceedingly well cudgeled; and I think the issue will
be I shall have so much° experience for my pains, and so, with no
money at all and a little more wit, return again to Venice.

Iago: How poor are they that have not patience!   330
What wound did ever heal but by degrees?
Thou know'st we work by wit, and not by witchcraft,
And wit depends on dilatory time.
Does 't not go well? Cassio hath beaten thee,
And thou, by that small hurt, hast cashiered° Cassio.   335
Though other things grow fair against the sun,
Yet fruits that blossom first will first be ripe.°
Content thyself awhile. By the Mass, 'tis morning!
Pleasure and action make the hours seem short.
Retire thee; go where thou art billeted.   340
Away, I say! Thou shalt know more hereafter.
Nay, get thee gone.   *Exit Roderigo.*
          Two things are to be done.

---

309 *her appetite* her desire, or, perhaps, his desire for her   310 *function* exercise of faculties
(weakened by his fondness for her)   311 *parallel* corresponding to these facts and to his best
interests   312 *Divinity of hell* inverted theology of hell (which seduces the soul to its damnation)   313 *put on* further, instigate   314 *suggest* tempt   319 *repeals him* attempts to get
him restored   322 *pitch* i.e., (1) foul blackness (2) a snaring substance   326 *fills up the cry*
merely takes part as one of the pack   328 *so much* just so much and no more   335 *cashiered*
dismissed from service   336–337 *Though . . . ripe* i.e., plans that are well prepared and set
expeditiously in motion will soonest ripen into success

My wife must move° for Cassio to her mistress;
I'll set her on;
Myself the while to draw the Moor apart   345
And bring him jump° when he may Cassio find
Soliciting his wife. Ay, that's the way.
Dull not device° by coldness° and delay.   *Exit.*

ACT III

SCENE I [BEFORE THE CHAMBER OF OTHELLO AND DESDEMONA.]

Enter Cassio [and] Musicians.

Cassio: Masters, play here—I will content your pains°—
Something that's brief, and bid "Good morrow, General."[*They play.*]

[*Enter*] *Clown.*

Clown: Why, masters, have your instruments been in Naples, that they
speak i' the nose° thus?
A Musician: How, sir, how?   5
Clown: Are these, I pray you, wind instruments?
A Musician: Ay, marry, are they, sir.
Clown: O, thereby hangs a tail.
A Musician: Whereby hangs a tale, sir?
Clown: Marry, sir, by many a wind instrument° that I know. But, masters,   10
here's money for you. [*He gives money.*] And the General so likes your
music that he desires you, for love's sake,° to make no more noise with it.
A Musician: Well, sir, we will not.
Clown: If you have any music that may not° be heard, to 't again; but, as
they say, to hear music the General does not greatly care.   15
A Musician: We have none such, sir.
Clown: Then put up your pipes in your bag, for I'll away.° Go, vanish
into air, away!
                                                          Exeunt Musicians.
Cassio: Dost thou hear, mine honest friend?

---

343 *move* plead   342 *jump* precisely   344 *device* plot.   *coldness* lack of zeal   1 *content your
pains* reward your efforts   3–4 *speak i' the nose* (1) sound nasal (2) sound like one whose
nose has been attacked by syphilis. (Naples was popularly supposed to have a high incidence
of venereal disease.)   10 *wind instrument* (With a joke on flatulence. The *tail*, line 8, that
hangs nearby the *wind instrument* suggests the penis.)   12 *for love's sake* (1) out of friendship
and affection (2) for the sake of lovemaking in Othello's marriage   14 *may not* cannot   17
I'll away (Possibly a misprint, or a snatch of song?)

Cassio sends a message to Desdemona's gentle-woman (III, i, 21–24).

Clown: No, I hear not your honest friend; I hear you.   20
Cassio: Prithee, keep up° thy quillets.° There's a poor piece of gold for
thee. [*He gives money.*] If the gentle-woman that attends the General's wife be stirring, tell her there's one Cassio entreats her a little
favor of speech.° Wilt thou do this?
Clown: She is stirring, sir. If she will stir° hither, I shall seem° to notify   25
unto her.
Cassio: Do, good my friend.   *Exit Clown.*

    Enter Iago.

                In happy time,° Iago.
Iago: You have not been abed, then?
Cassio: Why, no. The day had broke

21 *keep up* do not bring out, do not use. *quillets* quibbles, puns 24 *a little . . . speech* the favor
of a brief talk 25 *stir* bestir herself (with a play on *stirring*, "rousing herself from rest"). *seem*
deem it good, think fit 27 *In happy time* i.e., well met

Before we parted. I have made bold, Iago,   30
To send in to your wife. My suit to her
Is that she will to virtuous Desdemona
Procure me some access.
Iago: I'll send her to you presently;
And I'll devise a means to draw the Moor   35
Out of the way, that your converse and business
May be more free.
Cassio: I humbly thank you for 't.   *Exit [Iago].*
                              I never knew
A Florentine° more kind and honest.

Enter Emilia.

Emilia: Good morrow, good Lieutenant. I am sorry   40
For your displeasure;° but all will sure be well.
The General and his wife are talking of it,
And she speaks for you stoutly.° The Moor replies
That he you hurt is of great fame° in Cyprus
And great affinity,° and that in wholesome wisdom   45
He might not but refuse you; but he protests° he loves you
And needs no other suitor but his likings
To take the safest occasion by the front°
To bring you in again.
Cassio: Yet I beseech you,
If you think fit, or that it may be done,   50
Give me advantage of some brief discourse
With Desdemona alone.
Emilia: Pray you, come in.
I will bestow you where you shall have time
To speak your bosom° freely.
Cassio: I am much bound to you.   *[Exeunt.]*   55

SCENE II [THE CITADEL.]

Enter Othello, Iago, and Gentlemen.

Othello [giving letters]: These letters give, Iago, to the pilot,
And by him do my duties° to the Senate.
That done, I will be walking on the works;°
Repair° there to me.

---

39 *Florentine* i.e., even a fellow Florentine. (Iago is a Venetian; Cassio is a Florentine.)   41
displeasure fall from favor   43 *stoutly* spiritedly   44 *fame* reputation, importance   45 *affinity* kindred, family connection   46 *protests* insists   48 *occasion . . . front* opportunity by the fore-
lock   54 *bosom* inmost thoughts   2 *do my duties* convey my respects   3 *works* breastworks,
fortifications   4 *Repair* return, come

Iago:	Well, my good lord, I'll do 't.	
Othello:	This fortification, gentlemen, shall we see 't?	5
Gentlemen:	We'll wait upon° your lordship.	*Exeunt.*

SCENE III [THE GARDEN OF THE CITADEL.]

Enter Desdemona, Cassio, and Emilia.

Desdemona: Be thou assured, good Cassio, I will do
    All my abilities in thy behalf.
Emilia: Good madam, do. I warrant it grieves my husband
    As if the cause were his.
Desdemona: O, that's an honest fellow. Do not doubt, Cassio,   5
    But I will have my lord and you again
    As friendly as you were.
Cassio: Bounteous madam,
    Whatever shall become of Michael Cassio,
    He's never anything but your true servant.
Desdemona: I know 't. I thank you. You do love my lord;   10
    You have known him long, and be you well assured
    He shall in strangeness° stand no farther off
    Than in a politic° distance.
Cassio: Ay, but, lady,
    That policy may either last so long,
    Or feed upon such nice and waterish diet,°   15
    Or breed itself so out of circumstance,°
    That, I being absent and my place supplied,°
    My general will forget my love and service.
Desdemona: Do not doubt° that. Before Emilia here
    I give thee warrant° of thy place. Assure thee,   20
    If I do vow a friendship I'll perform it
    To the last article. My lord shall never rest.
    I'll watch him tame° and talk him out of patience;°
    His bed shall seem a school, his board° a shrift;°
    I'll intermingle everything he does   25
    With Cassio's suit. Therefore be merry, Cassio,

---

6 *wait upon* attend   12 *strangeness* aloofness   13 *politic* required by wise policy   15 *Or . . .
diet* or sustain itself at length upon such trivial and meager technicalities   16 *breed . . .
circumstance* continually renew itself so out of chance events, or yield so few chances for
my being pardoned   17 *supplied* filled by another person   19 *doubt* fear   20 *warrant* guarantee   23 *watch him tame* tame him by keeping him from sleeping. (A term from falconry.)   *out
of patience* past his endurance   24 *board* dining table.   *shrift* confessional

For thy solicitor° shall rather die
Than give thy cause away.°

Enter Othello and Iago [at a distance].

Emilia: Madam, here comes my lord.
Cassio: Madam, I'll take my leave.   30
Desdemona: Why, stay, and hear me speak.
Cassio: Madam, not now. I am very ill at ease,
    Unfit for mine own purposes.
Desdemona: Well, do your discretion.°   *Exit Cassio.*
Iago: Ha? I like not that.   35
Othello: What dost thou say?
Iago: Nothing, my lord; or if—I know not what.
Othello: Was not that Cassio parted from my wife?
Iago: Cassio, my lord? No, sure, I cannot think it,
    That he would steal away so guiltylike,   40
    Seeing you coming.
Othello: I do believe 'twas he.
Desdemona: How now, my lord?
    I have been talking with a suitor here,
    A man that languishes in your displeasure.   45
Othello: Who is 't you mean?
Desdemona: Why, your lieutenant, Cassio. Good my lord,
    If I have any grace or power to move you,
    His present reconciliation take;°
    For if he be not one that truly loves you,   50
    That errs in ignorance and not in cunning,°
    I have no judgment in an honest face.
    I prithee, call him back.
Othello: Went he hence now?
Desdemona: Yes, faith, so humbled   55
    That he hath left part of his grief with me
    To suffer with him. Good love, call him back.
Othello: Not now, sweet Desdemon. Some other time.
Desdemona: But shall 't be shortly?
Othello: The sooner, sweet, for you.
Desdemona: Shall 't be tonight at supper?   60
Othello: No, not tonight.
Desdemona: Tomorrow dinner,° then?

---

27 *solicitor* advocate 28 *away* up 34 *do your discretion* act according to your own discretion 49 *His . . . take* let him be reconciled to you right away 51 *in cunning* wittingly 63
dinner (The noontime meal.)

Othello: I shall not dine at home.
 I meet the captains at the citadel.   65
Desdemona: Why, then, tomorrow night, or Tuesday morn,
 On Tuesday noon, or night, on Wednesday morn,
 I prithee, name the time, but let it not
 Exceed three days. In faith, he's penitent;
 And yet his trespass, in our common reason°—   70
 Save that, they say, the wars must make example
 Out of her best°—is not almost° a fault
 T' incur a private check.° When shall he come?
 Tell me, Othello. I wonder in my soul
 What you would ask me that I should deny,   75
 Or stand so mammering on.° What? Michael Cassio,
 That came a-wooing with you, and so many a time,
 When I have spoke of you dispraisingly,
 Hath ta'en your part—to have so much to do
 To bring him in!° By 'r Lady, I could do much—   80
Othello: Prithee, no more. Let him come when he will;
 I will deny thee nothing.
Desdemona: Why, this is not a boon.
 'Tis as I should entreat you wear your gloves,
 Or feed on nourishing dishes, or keep you warm,   85
 Or sue to you to do a peculiar° profit
 To your own person. Nay, when I have a suit
 Wherein I mean to touch° your love indeed,
 It shall be full of poise° and difficult weight,
 And fearful to be granted.   90
Othello: I will deny thee nothing.
 Whereon,° I do beseech thee, grant me this,
 To leave me but a little to myself.
Desdemona: Shall I deny you? No. Farewell, my lord.
Othello: Farewell, my Desdemona. I'll come to thee straight.° 95
Desdemona: Emilia, come.—Be as your fancies° teach you;
 Whate'er you be, I am obedient.   *Exit [with Emilia.]*
Othello: Excellent wretch!° Perdition catch my soul
 But I do love thee! And when I love thee not,

---

70 *common reason* everyday judgments   71–72 *Save . . . best* were it not that, as the saying
goes, military discipline requires making an example of the very best men. (He refers to *wars*
as a singular concept.)   72 *not almost* scarcely   73 *private check* even a private reprimand   76
mammering on wavering about   80 *bring him in* restore him to favor   86 *peculiar* particular,
personal   88 *touch* test   89 *poise* weight, heaviness; or equipoise, delicate balance involving hard choice   92 *Whereon* in return for which   95 *straight* straightway   96 *fancies* inclinations   98 *wretch* (A term of affectionate endearment.)

Chaos is come again.°   100
Iago: My noble lord—
Othello: What dost thou say, Iago?
Iago: Did Michael Cassio, when you wooed my lady,
    Know of your love?
Othello: He did, from first to last. Why dost thou ask?   105
Iago: But for a satisfaction of my thought;
    No further harm.
Othello: Why of thy thought, Iago?
Iago: I did not think he had been acquainted with her.
Othello: O, yes, and went between us very oft.
Iago: Indeed?   110
Othello: Indeed? Ay, indeed. Discern'st thou aught in that?
    Is he not honest?
Iago: Honest, my lord?
Othello: Honest. Ay, honest.
Iago: My lord, for aught I know.   115
Othello: What dost thou think?
Iago: Think, my lord?
Othello: "Think, my lord?" By heaven, thou echo'st me,
    As if there were some monster in thy thought
    Too hideous to be shown. Thou dost mean something. 120
    I heard thee say even now, thou lik'st not that,
    When Cassio left my wife. What didst not like?
    And when I told thee he was of my counsel°
    In my whole course of wooing, thou criedst "Indeed?"
    And didst contract and purse° thy brow together   125
    As if thou then hadst shut up in thy brain
    Some horrible conceit.° If thou dost love me,
    Show me thy thought.
Iago: My lord, you know I love you.
Othello: I think thou dost;   130
    And, for° I know thou'rt full of love and honesty,
    And weigh'st thy words before thou giv'st them breath,
    Therefore these stops° of thine fright me the more;
    For such things in a false disloyal knave
    Are tricks of custom,° but in a man that's just   135
    They're close dilations,° working from the heart

99–100 *And . . . again* i.e., my love for you will last forever, until the end of time when chaos will return. (But with an unconscious, ironic suggestion that, if anything should induce Othello to cease loving Desdemona, the result would be chaos.)   123 *of my counsel* in my confidence   125 *purse* knit   127 *conceit* fancy   131 *for* because   133 *stops* pauses   135 *of custom* customary   136 *close dilations* secret or involuntary expressions or delays

> That passion cannot rule.°
> *Iago:*   For° Michael Cassio,
> I dare be sworn I think that he is honest.
> *Othello:* I think so too.
> *Iago:*   Men should be what they seem;
> Or those that be not, would they might seem none!°   140
> *Othello:* Certain, men should be what they seem.
> *Iago:* Why, then, I think Cassio's an honest man.
> *Othello:* Nay, yet there's more in this.
> I prithee, speak to me as to thy thinkings,
> As thou dost ruminate, and give thy worst of thoughts   145
> The worst of words.
> *Iago:*   Good my lord, pardon me.
> Though I am bound to every act of duty,
> I am not bound to that° all slaves are free to.°
> Utter my thoughts? Why, say they are vile and false,
> As where's the palace whereinto foul things   150
> Sometimes intrude not? Who has that breast so pure
> But some uncleanly apprehensions
> Keep leets and law days,° and in sessions sit
> With° meditations lawful?°
> *Othello:* Thou dost conspire against thy friend,° Iago,   155
> If thou but think'st him wronged and mak'st his ear
> A stranger to thy thoughts.
> *Iago:*   I do beseech you,
> Though I perchance am vicious° in my guess—
> As I confess it is my nature's plague
> To spy into abuses, and oft my jealousy°   160
> Shapes faults that are not—that your wisdom then,°
> From one° that so imperfectly conceits,°
> Would take no notice, nor build yourself a trouble
> Out of his scattering° and unsure observance.
> It were not for your quiet nor your good,   165
> Nor for my manhood, honesty, and wisdom,
> To let you know my thoughts.
> *Othello:*   What dost thou mean?
> *Iago:* Good name in man and woman, dear my lord,

---

137 *That passion cannot rule* i.e., that are too passionately strong to be restrained (referring to the workings), or that cannot rule its own passions (referring to the heart). *For* as for 140 *none* i.e., not to be men, or not seem to be honest 148 *that* that which. *free to* free with respect to 153 *Keep leets and law days* i.e., hold court, set up their authority in one's heart. (*Leets* are a kind of manor court; *law days* are the days courts sit in session, or those sessions.) 154 *With* along with. *lawful* innocent 155 *thy friend* i.e., Othello 158 *vicious* wrong 160 *jealousy* suspicious nature 161 *then* on that account 162 *one* i.e., myself, Iago. *conceits* judges, conjectures 164 *scattering* random

Is the immediate° jewel of their souls.
Who steals my purse steals trash; 'tis something, nothing;   170
'Twas mine, 'tis his, and has been slave to thousands;
But he that filches from me my good name
Robs me of that which not enriches him
And makes me poor indeed.
Othello: By heaven, I'll know thy thoughts.   175
Iago: You cannot, if° my heart were in your hand,
Nor shall not, whilst 'tis in my custody.
Othello: Ha?
Iago: O, beware, my lord, of jealousy.
It is the green-eyed monster which doth mock
The meat it feeds on.° That cuckold lives in bliss   180
Who, certain of his fate, loves not his wronger;°
But O, what damnèd minutes tells° he o'er
Who dotes, yet doubts, suspects, yet fondly loves!
Othello: O misery!
Iago: Poor and content is rich, and rich enough,°   185
But riches fineless° is as poor as winter
To him that ever fears he shall be poor.
Good God, the souls of all my tribe defend
From jealousy!
Othello: Why, why is this?   190
Think'st thou I'd make a life of jealousy,
To follow still the changes of the moon
With fresh suspicions?° No! To be once in doubt
Is once° to be resolved.° Exchange me for a goat
When I shall turn the business of my soul   195
To such exsufflicate and blown° surmises
Matching thy inference.° 'Tis not to make me jealous
To say my wife is fair, feeds well, loves company,
Is free of speech, sings, plays, and dances well;
Where virtue is, these are more virtuous.   200
Nor from mine own weak merits will I draw
The smallest fear or doubt of her revolt,°
For she had eyes, and chose me. No, Iago,

---

169 *immediate* essential, most precious   176 *if* even if   179–180 *doth mock . . . on* mocks and torments the heart of its victim, the man who suffers jealousy   181 *his wronger* i.e., his faithless wife. (The unsuspecting cuckold is spared the misery of loving his wife only to discover she is cheating on him.)   182 *tells* counts   185 *Poor . . . enough* to be content with what little one has is the greatest wealth of all. (Proverbial.)   186 *fineless* boundless   192–193 *To follow . . . suspicions* to be constantly imagining new causes for suspicion, changing incessantly like the moon   194 *once* once and for all.   *resolved* free of doubt, having settled the matter   196 *exsufflicate and blown* inflated and blown up, rumored about, or, spat out and flyblown, hence, loathsome, disgusting   197 *inference* description or allegation   202 *doubt . . . revolt* fear of her unfaithfulness

I'll see before I doubt; when I doubt, prove;
And on the proof, there is no more but this—   205
Away at once with love or jealousy.
Iago: I am glad of this, for now I shall have reason
To show the love and duty that I bear you
With franker spirit. Therefore, as I am bound,
Receive it from me. I speak not yet of proof.   210
Look to your wife; observe her well with Cassio.
Wear your eyes thus, not° jealous nor secure.°
I would not have your free and noble nature,
Out of self-bounty,° be abused.° Look to 't.
I know our country disposition well;   215
In Venice they do let God see the pranks
They dare not show their husbands; their best conscience
Is not to leave 't undone, but keep 't unknown.
Othello: Dost thou say so?
Iago: She did deceive her father, marrying you;
And when she seemed to shake and fear your looks,   220
She loved them most.
Othello: And so she did.
Iago: Why, go to,° then!
She that, so young, could give out such a seeming,°
To seel° her father's eyes up close as oak,°
He thought 'twas witchcraft! But I am much to blame.   225
I humbly do beseech you of your pardon
For too much loving you.
Othello: I am bound° to thee forever.
Iago: I see this hath a little dashed your spirits.
Othello: Not a jot, not a jot.
Iago: I' faith, I fear it has.   230
I hope you will consider what is spoke
Comes from my love. But I do see you're moved.
I am to pray you not to strain my speech
To grosser issues° nor to larger reach°
Than to suspicion.   235
Othello: I will not.
Iago: Should you do so, my lord,
My speech should fall into such vile success°
Which my thoughts aimed not. Cassio's my worthy friend.

---

212 *not* neither.   *secure* free from uncertainty   214 *self-bounty* inherent or natural goodness
and generosity.   *abused* deceived   222 *go to* (An expression of impatience.)   223 *seeming*
false appearance   224 *seel* blind. (A term from falconry.)   *oak* (A close-grained wood.)   228
bound indebted (but perhaps with ironic sense of "tied")   234 *issues* significances.   *reach*
meaning, scope   238 *success* effect, result

My lord, I see you're moved.
Othello: No, not much moved.   240
  I do not think but Desdemona's honest.°
Iago: Long live she so! And long live you to think so!
Othello: And yet, how nature erring from itself—
Iago: Ay, there's the point! As—to be bold with you—
  Not to affect° many proposèd matches   245
  Of her own clime, complexion, and degree,°
  Whereto we see in all things nature tends—
  Foh! One may smell in such a will° most rank,
  Foul disproportion,° thoughts unnatural.
  But pardon me. I do not in position°   250
  Distinctly speak of her, though I may fear
  Her will, recoiling° to her better° judgment,
  May fall to match you with her country forms°
  And happily repent.°
Othello: Farewell, farewell!
  If more thou dost perceive, let me know more.   255
  Set on thy wife to observe. Leave me, Iago.
Iago [*going*]: My lord, I take my leave.
Othello: Why did I marry? This honest creature doubtless
  Sees and knows more, much more, than he unfolds.
Iago [*returning*]: My Lord, I would I might entreat your honor   260
  To scan° this thing no farther. Leave it to time.
  Although 'tis fit that Cassio have his place—
  For, sure, he fills it up with great ability—
  Yet, if you please to hold him off awhile,
  You shall by that perceive him and his means.°   265
  Note if your lady strain his entertainment°
  With any strong or vehement importunity;
  Much will be seen in that. In the meantime,
  Let me be thought too busy° in my fears—
  As worthy cause I have to fear I am—   270
  And hold her free,° I do beseech your honor.
Othello: Fear not my government.°
Iago: I once more take my leave.   *Exit.*
Othello: This fellow's of exceeding honesty,
  And knows all qualities,° with a learnèd spirit,   275

---

241 *honest* chaste 245 *affect* prefer, desire 246 *clime . . . degree* country, color, and social position 248 *will* sensuality, appetite 249 *disproportion* abnormality 250 *position* argument, proposition 252 *recoiling* reverting. *better* i.e., more natural and reconsidered 253 *fall . . . forms* undertake to compare you with Venetian norms of handsomeness 254 *happily repent* happily repent her marriage 261 *scan* scrutinize 265 *his means* the method he uses (to regain his post) 266 *strain his entertainment* urge his reinstatement 269 *busy* interfering 271 *hold her free* regard her as innocent 272 *government* self-control, conduct 275 *qualities* natures, types

Of human dealings. If I do prove her haggard,°
Though that her jesses° were my dear heartstrings,
I'd whistle her off and let her down the wind°
To prey at fortune.° Haply, for° I am black
And have not those soft parts of conversation°   280
That chamberers° have, or for I am declined
Into the vale of years—yet that's not much—
She's gone. I am abused,° and my relief
Must be to loathe her. O curse of marriage,
That we can call these delicate creatures ours   285
And not their appetites! I had rather be a toad
And live upon the vapor of a dungeon
Than keep a corner in the thing I love
For others' uses. Yet, 'tis the plague of great ones;
Prerogatived° are they less than the base.°   290
'Tis destiny unshunnable, like death.
Even then this forkèd° plague is fated to us
When we do quicken.° Look where she comes.

Enter Desdemona and Emilia.

If she be false, O, then heaven mocks itself!
I'll not believe 't.
Desdemona: How now, my dear Othello?   295
Your dinner, and the generous° islanders
By you invited, do attend° your presence.
Othello: I am to blame.
Desdemona: Why do you speak so faintly?
Are you not well?
Othello: I have a pain upon my forehead here.   300
Desdemona: Faith, that's with watching.° 'Twill away again.

[*She offers her handkerchief.*]

Let me but bind it hard, within this hour
It will be well.
Othello: Your napkin° is too little.

276 *haggard* wild (like a wild female hawk) 277 *jesses* straps fastened around the legs of a trained hawk 278 *I'd . . . wind* i.e., I'd let her go forever. (To release a hawk downwind was to invite it not to return.) 279 *prey at fortune* fend for herself in the wild. *Haply, for* perhaps because 280 *soft . . . conversation* pleasing graces of social behavior 281 *chamberers* gallants 283 *abused* deceived 290 *Prerogatived* privileged (to have honest wives). *the base* ordinary citizens. (Socially prominent men are especially prone to the unavoidable destiny of being cuckolded and to the public shame that goes with it.) 292 *forkèd* (An allusion to the horns of the cuckold.) 293 *quicken* receive life. (Quicken may also mean to swarm with maggots as the body festers, as in IV, ii, 69, in which case lines 292–293 suggest that *even then*, in death, we are cuckolded by *forkèd* worms.) 296 *generous* noble 297 *attend* await 301 *watching* too little sleep 303 *napkin* handkerchief

Let it alone.° Come, I'll go in with you.

[*He puts the handkerchief from him, and it drops.*]

Desdemona: I am very sorry that you are not well.   305

Exit [*with Othello*].

Emilia [*picking up the handkerchief*]: I am glad I have found this napkin.
This was her first remembrance from the Moor.
My wayward° husband hath a hundred times
Wooed me to steal it, but she so loves the token—
For he conjured her she should ever keep it—   310
That she reserves it evermore about her
To kiss and talk to. I'll have the work ta'en out,°
And give 't Iago. What he will do with it
Heaven knows, not I;
I nothing but to please his fantasy.°   315

Enter Iago.

Iago: How now? What do you here alone?
Emilia: Do not you chide. I have a thing for you.
Iago: You have a thing for me? It is a common thing°—
Emilia: Ha?
Iago: To have a foolish wife.   320
Emilia: O, is that all? What will you give me now
For that same handkerchief?
Iago: What handkerchief?
Emilia: What handkerchief?
Why, that the Moor first gave to Desdemona;   325
That which so often you did bid me steal.
Iago: Hast stolen it from her?
Emilia: No, faith. She let it drop by negligence,
And to th' advantage° I, being here, took 't up.
Look, here 'tis.
Iago: A good wench! Give it me.   330
Emilia: What will you do with 't, that you have been so earnest
To have me filch it?
Iago [*snatching it*]:   Why, what is that to you?
Emilia: If it be not for some purpose of import,
Give 't me again. Poor lady, she'll run mad
When she shall lack° it.

---

304 *Let it alone* i.e., never mind   308 *wayward* capricious   312 *work ta'en out* design of the
embroidery copied   315 *fantasy* whim   318 *common thing* (With bawdy suggestion; *com-*
mon suggests coarseness and availability to all comers, and *thing* is a slang term for the
pudendum.)   329 *to th' advantage* taking the opportunity   335 *lack* miss.

**Emilia gets the fateful handkerchief for
Iago (III, iii, 316–335).**

Iago: Be not acknown on 't.°   335
    I have use for it. Go, leave me.   *Exit Emilia.*
    I will in Cassio's lodging lose° this napkin
    And let him find it. Trifles light as air
    Are to the jealous confirmations strong
    As proofs of Holy Writ. This may do something.   340
    The Moor already changes with my poison.
    Dangerous conceits° are in their natures poisons,
    Which at the first are scarce found to distaste,°
    But with a little act° upon the blood
    Burn like the mines of sulfur.

    Enter Othello.

                                    I did say so.°   345
    Look where he comes! Not poppy nor mandragora°

---

335 *Be . . . on 't* do not confess knowledge of it   337 *lose* (The Folio spelling, *loose*, is a normal spelling for "lose," but it may also contain the idea of "let go," "release.")   342 *conceits* fancies, ideas   343 *distaste* be distasteful   344 *act* action, working   346 *mandragora* an opiate made of the mandrake root

Nor all the drowsy syrups of the world
Shall ever medicine thee to that sweet sleep
Which thou owedst° yesterday.
Othello: Ha, ha, false to me?
Iago: Why, how now, General? No more of that.   350
Othello: Avaunt! Begone! Thou hast set me on the rack.
   I swear 'tis better to be much abused
   Than but to know 't a little.
Iago: How now, my lord?
Othello: What sense had I of her stolen hours of lust?
   I saw 't not, thought it not, it harmed not me.   355
   I slept the next night well, fed well, was free° and merry;
   I found not Cassio's kisses on her lips.
   He that is robbed, not wanting° what is stolen,
   Let him not know 't and he's not robbed at all.
Iago: I am sorry to hear this.   360
Othello: I had been happy if the general camp,
   Pioners° and all, had tasted her sweet body,
   So° I had nothing known. O, now, forever
   Farewell the tranquil mind! Farewell content!
   Farewell the plumèd troops and the big° wars   365
   That makes ambition virtue! O, farewell!
   Farewell the neighing steed and the shrill trump,
   The spirit-stirring drum, th' ear-piercing fife,
   The royal banner, and all quality,°
   Pride,° pomp, and circumstance° of glorious war!   370
   And O, you mortal engines,° whose rude throats
   Th' immortal Jove's dread clamors° counterfeit,
   Farewell! Othello's occupation's gone.
Iago: Is 't possible, my lord?
Othello: Villain, be sure thou prove my love a whore!   375
   Be sure of it. Give me the ocular proof,
   Or, by the worth of mine eternal soul,
   Thou hadst been better have been born a dog
   Than answer my waked wrath!
Iago: Is 't come to this?
Othello: Make me to see 't, or at the least so prove it   380
   That the probation° bear no hinge nor loop
   To hang a doubt on, or woe upon thy life!

---

349 *thou owedst* you did own   356 *free* carefree   358 *wanting* missing   362 *Pioners* diggers of mines, the lowest grade of soldiers   363 *So* provided   365 *big* stately   369 *quality* character, essential nature   370 *Pride* rich display.   *circumstance* pageantry   371 *mortal engines* i.e., cannon. (*Mortal* means "deadly.")   372 *Jove's dread clamors* i.e., thunder   381 *probation* proof

Iago: My noble lord—
Othello: If thou dost slander her and torture me,
    Never pray more; abandon all remorse;°   385
    On horror's head horrors accumulate;°
    Do deeds to make heaven weep, all earth amazed;°
    For nothing canst thou to damnation add
    Greater than that.
Iago: O grace! O heaven forgive me!
    Are you a man? Have you a soul or sense?   390
    God b' wi' you; take mine office. O wretched fool,°
    That lov'st to make thine honesty a vice!°
    O monstrous world! Take note, take note, O world,
    To be direct and honest is not safe.
    I thank you for this profit,° and from hence°   395
    I'll love no friend, sith° love breeds such offense.°
Othello: Nay, stay. Thou shouldst be° honest.
Iago: I should be wise, for honesty's a fool
    And loses that° it works for.
Othello: By the world,
    I think my wife be honest and think she is not;   400
    I think that thou art just and think thou art not.
    I'll have some proof. My name, that was as fresh
    As Dian's° visage, is now begrimed and black
    As mine own face. If there be cords, or knives,
    Poison, or fire, or suffocating streams,   405
    I'll not endure it. Would I were satisfied!
Iago: I see, sir, you are eaten up with passion.
    I do repent me that I put it to you.
    You would be satisfied?
Othello: Would? Nay, and I will.
Iago: And may; but how? How satisfied, my lord?   410
    Would you, the supervisor,° grossly gape on?
    Behold her topped?
Othello: Death and damnation! O!
Iago: It were a tedious difficulty, I think,
    To bring them to that prospect. Damn them then,°
    If ever mortal eyes do see them bolster°   415
    More° than their own.° What then? How then?

---

385 *remorse* pity, penitent hope for salvation   386 *horrors accumulate* add still more horrors
387 *amazed* confounded with horror   391 *O wretched fool* (Iago addresses himself as a fool for
having carried honesty too far.)   392 *vice* failing, something overdone   395 *profit* profitable
instruction. *hence* henceforth   396 *sith* since. *offense* i.e., harm to the one who offers help
and friendship   397 *Thou shouldst be* it appears that you are. (But Iago replies in the sense
of "ought to be.")   399 *that* what   403 *Dian's* Diana, goddess of the moon and of chastity
411 *supervisor* onlooker   414 *Damn them then* i.e., they would have to be really incorrigible
415 *bolster* go to bed together, share a bolster   416 *More* other. *own* own eyes

What shall I say? Where's satisfaction?
It is impossible you should see this,
Were they as prime° as goats, as hot as monkeys,
As salt° as wolves in pride,° and fools as gross   420
As ignorance made drunk. But yet I say,
If imputation and strong circumstances°
Which lead directly to the door of truth
Will give you satisfaction, you might have 't.
Othello: Give me a living reason she's disloyal.   425
Iago: I do not like the office.
    But sith° I am entered in this cause so far,
    Pricked° to 't by foolish honesty and love,
    I will go on. I lay with Cassio lately,
    And being troubled with a raging tooth   430
    I could not sleep. There are a kind of men
    So loose of soul that in their sleeps will mutter
    Their affairs. One of this kind is Cassio.
    In sleep I heard him say, "Sweet Desdemona,
    Let us be wary, let us hide our loves!"   435
    And then, sir, would he grip and wring my hand,
    Cry "O sweet creature!" and then kiss me hard,
    As if he plucked up kisses by the roots
    That grew upon my lips; then laid his leg
    Over my thigh, and sighed, and kissed, and then   440
    Cried, "Cursèd fate that gave thee to the Moor!"
Othello: O monstrous! Monstrous!
Iago: Nay, this was but his dream.
Othello: But this denoted a foregone conclusion.°
    'Tis a shrewd doubt,° though it be but a dream.
Iago: And this may help to thicken other proofs   445
    That do demonstrate thinly.
Othello: I'll tear her all to pieces.
Iago: Nay, but be wise. Yet we see nothing done;
    She may be honest yet. Tell me but this:
    Have you not sometimes seen a handkerchief
    Spotted with strawberries° in your wife's hand?   450
Othello: I gave her such a one. 'Twas my first gift.
Iago: I know not that; but such a handkerchief—
    I am sure it was your wife's—did I today
    See Cassio wipe his beard with.

---

419 *prime* lustful   420 *salt* wanton, sensual. *pride* heat   422 *imputation . . . circumstances*
strong circumstantial evidence   427 *sith* since   428 *Pricked* spurred   443 *foregone con-*
clusion concluded experience or action   444 *shrewd doubt* suspicious circumstance   450
Spotted with strawberries embroidered with a strawberry pattern

Othello: If it be that—
Iago: If it be that, or any that was hers,   455
    It speaks against her with the other proofs.
Othello: O, that the slave° had forty thousand lives!
    One is too poor, too weak for my revenge.
    Now do I see 'tis true. Look here, Iago,
    All my fond° love thus do I blow to heaven.   460
    'Tis gone.
    Arise, black vengeance, from the hollow hell!
    Yield up, O love, thy crown and hearted° throne
    To tyrannous hate! Swell, bosom, with thy freight,°
    For 'tis of aspics'° tongues!   465
Iago: Yet be content.°
Othello: O, blood, blood, blood!
Iago: Patience, I say. Your mind perhaps may change.
Othello: Never, Iago. Like to the Pontic Sea,°
    Whose icy current and compulsive course   470
    Ne'er feels retiring ebb, but keeps due on
    To the Propontic° and the Hellespont,°
    Even so my bloody thoughts with violent pace
    Shall ne'er look back, ne'er ebb to humble love,
    Till that a capable° and wide revenge   475
    Swallow them up. Now, by yond marble° heaven,
    [*Kneeling*] In the due reverence of a sacred vow
    I here engage my words.
Iago: Do not rise yet.
    [*He kneels.°*] Witness, you ever-burning lights above,
    You elements that clip° us round about,   480
    Witness that here Iago doth give up
    The execution° of his wit,° hands, heart,
    To wronged Othello's service. Let him command,
    And to obey shall be in me remorse,°
    What bloody business ever.°   [*They rise.*]
Othello: I greet thy love,   485
    Not with vain thanks, but with acceptance bounteous,
    And will upon the instant put thee to 't.°

___

457 *the slave* i.e., Cassio   460 *fond* foolish (but also suggesting "affectionate")   463 *hearted*
fixed in the heart   464 *freight* burden   465 *aspics'* venomous serpents'   466 *content*
calm   469 *Pontic Sea* Black Sea   472 *Propontic* Sea of Marmara, between the Black Sea
and the Aegean.   *Hellespont* Dardanelles, straits where the Sea of Marmara joins with the
Aegean   475 *capable* ample, comprehensive   476 *marble* i.e., gleaming like marble and
unrelenting   479 s.d. *He kneels* (In the Quarto text, Iago kneels here after Othello has knelt
at line 477.)   480 *clip* encompass   482 *execution* exercise, action.   *wit* mind   484 *remorse*
pity (for Othello's wrongs)   485 *ever* soever   487 *to 't* to the proof

Within these three days let me hear thee say
That Cassio's not alive.

Iago: My friend is dead;
'Tis done at your request. But let her live.   490

Othello: Damn her, lewd minx!° O, damn her, damn her!
Come, go with me apart. I will withdraw
To furnish me with some swift means of death
For the fair devil. Now art thou my lieutenant.

Iago: I am your own forever.   *Exeunt.* 495

SCENE IV [BEFORE THE CITADEL.]

Enter Desdemona, Emilia, and Clown.

Desdemona: Do you know, sirrah,° where Lieutenant Cassio lies?°
Clown: I dare not say he lies anywhere.
Desdemona: Why, man?
Clown: He's a soldier, and for me to say a soldier lies, 'tis stabbing.
Desdemona: Go to. Where lodges he?   5
Clown: To tell you where he lodges is to tell you where I lie.
Desdemona: Can anything be made of this?
Clown: I know not where he lodges, and for me to devise a lodging and
    say he lies here, or he lies there, were to lie in mine own throat.°
Desdemona: Can you inquire him out, and be edified by report?   10
Clown: I will catechize the world for him; that is, make questions, and
    by them answer.
Desdemona: Seek him, bid him come hither. Tell him I have moved° my
    lord on his behalf and hope all will be well.
Clown: To do this is within the compass of man's wit, and therefore I 15
    will attempt the doing it.   *Exit Clown.*
Desdemona: Where should I lose that handkerchief, Emilia?
Emilia: I know not, madam.
Desdemona: Believe me, I had rather have lost my purse
    Full of crusadoes;° and but my noble Moor   20
    Is true of mind and made of no such baseness
    As jealous creatures are, it were enough
    To put him to ill thinking.
Emilia: Is he not jealous?
Desdemona: Who, he? I think the sun where he was born
    Drew all such humors° from him.

---

491 *minx* wanton   1 *sirrah* (A form of address to an inferior.)   *lies* lodges. (But the Clown
makes the obvious pun.)   9 *lie . . . throat* (1) lie egregiously and deliberately (2) use the wind-
pipe to speak a lie   13 *moved* petitioned   20 *crusadoes* Portuguese gold coins   25 *humors*
(Refers to the four bodily fluids thought to determine temperament.)

Othello's suspicions are building: "This hand of yours requires / A sequester from liberty . . ." (III, iv, 30–41).

| Emilia: | Look where he comes. | 25 |

    Enter Othello.

Desdemona: I will not leave him now till Cassio
    Be called to him.—How is 't with you, my lord?
Othello: Well, my good lady. [*Aside.*] O, hardness to dissemble!—
    How do you, Desdemona?
Desdemona: Well, my good lord.
Othello: Give me your hand. [*She gives her hand.*] This hand is moist, my lady.   30
Desdemona: It yet hath felt no age nor known no sorrow.
Othello: This argues° fruitfulness° and liberal° heart.
    Hot, hot, and moist. This hand of yours requires
    A sequester° from liberty, fasting and prayer,
    Much castigation,° exercise devout;°   35

---

32 *argues* gives evidence of. *fruitfulness* generosity, amorousness, and fecundity. *liberal* generous and sexually free   34 *sequester* separation, sequestration   35 *castigation* corrective discipline. *exercise devout* i.e., prayer, religious meditation, etc.

For here's a young and sweating devil here
That commonly rebels. 'Tis a good hand,
A frank° one.
Desdemona: You may indeed say so,
For 'twas that hand that gave away my heart.
Othello: A liberal hand. The hearts of old gave hands,°   40
But our new heraldry is hands, not hearts.°
Desdemona: I cannot speak of this. Come now, your promise.
Othello: What promise, chuck?°
Desdemona: I have sent to bid Cassio come speak with you.
Othello: I have a salt and sorry rheum° offends me;   45
Lend me thy handkerchief.
Desdemona: Here, my lord.   [*She offers a handkerchief.*]
Othello: That which I gave you.
Desdemona: I have it not about me.
Othello: Not?
Desdemona: No, faith, my lord.   50
Othello: That's a fault. That handkerchief
Did an Egyptian to my mother give.
She was a charmer,° and could almost read
The thoughts of people. She told her, while she kept it
'Twould make her amiable° and subdue my father   55
Entirely to her love, but if she lost it
Or made a gift of it, my father's eye
Should hold her loathèd and his spirits should hunt
After new fancies.° She, dying, gave it me,
And bid me, when my fate would have me wived,   60
To give it her.° I did so; and take heed on 't;
Make it a darling like your precious eye.
To lose 't or give 't away were such perdition°
As nothing else could match.
Desdemona: Is 't possible?
Othello: 'Tis true. There's magic in the web° of it.   65
A sibyl, that had numbered in the world
The sun to course two hundred compasses,°
In her prophetic fury° sewed the work;°
The worms were hallowed that did breed the silk,

---

38 *frank* generous, open (with sexual suggestion)   40 *The hearts . . . hands* i.e., in former
times, people would give their hearts when they gave their hands to something   41 *But . . .
hearts* i.e., in our decadent times, the joining of hands is no longer a badge to signify the
giving of hearts   43 *chuck* (A term of endearment.)   45 *salt . . . rheum* distressful head cold
or watering of the eyes   53 *charmer* sorceress   55 *amiable* desirable   59 *fancies* loves   61 *her*
i.e., to my wife   63 *perdition* loss   65 *web* fabric, weaving   67 *compasses* annual circlings.
(The *sibyl*, or prophetess, was two hundred years old.)   68 *prophetic fury* frenzy of prophetic
inspiration.   *work* embroidered pattern

And it was dyed in mummy° which the skillful   70
Conserved of° maidens' hearts.
Desdemona: I' faith! Is 't true?
Othello: Most veritable. Therefore look to 't well.
Desdemona: Then would to God that I had never seen 't!
Othello: Ha? Wherefore?
Desdemona: Why do you speak so startingly and rash?°   75
Othello: Is 't lost? Is 't gone? Speak, is 't out o' the way?°
Desdemona: Heaven bless us!
Othello: Say you?
Desdemona: It is not lost; but what an if° it were?
Othello: How?   80
Desdemona: I say it is not lost.
Othello: Fetch 't, let me see 't.
Desdemona: Why, so I can, sir, but I will not now.
This is a trick to put me from my suit.
Pray you, let Cassio be received again.
Othello: Fetch me the handkerchief! My mind misgives.   85
Desdemona: Come, come,
You'll never meet a more sufficient° man.
Othello: The handkerchief!
Desdemona: I pray, talk° me of Cassio.
Othello: The handkerchief!
Desdemona: A man that all his time°
Hath founded his good fortunes on your love,   90
Shared dangers with you—
Othello: The handkerchief!
Desdemona: I' faith, you are to blame.
Othello: Zounds!   *Exit Othello.*
Emilia: Is not this man jealous?   95
Desdemona: I ne'er saw this before.
Sure, there's some wonder in this handkerchief.
I am most unhappy in the loss of it.
Emilia: 'Tis not a year or two shows us a man.°
They are all but stomachs, and we all but° food;   100
They eat us hungerly,° and when they are full
They belch us.

Enter Iago and Cassio.

---

70 *mummy* medicinal or magical preparation drained from mummified bodies   71 *Conserved of* prepared or preserved out of   75 *startingly and rash* disjointedly and impetuously, excitedly   76 *out o' the way* lost, misplaced   79 *an if* if   87 *sufficient* able, complete   88 *talk* talk to   89 *all his time* throughout his career   99 *'Tis . . . man* i.e., you can't really know a man even in a year or two of experience (?), or, real men come along seldom (?)   100 *but* nothing but   101 *hungerly* hungrily

           Look you, Cassio and my husband.

Iago [*to Cassio*]: There is no other way; 'tis she must do 't.
    And, lo, the happiness!° Go and importune her.

Desdemona: How now, good Cassio? What's the news with you?   105

Cassio: Madam, my former suit. I do beseech you
    That by your virtuous° means I may again
    Exist and be a member of his love
    Whom I, with all the office° of my heart,
    Entirely honor. I would not be delayed.   110
    If my offense be of such mortal° kind
    That nor my service past, nor° present sorrows,
    Nor purposed merit in futurity
    Can ransom me into his love again,
    But to know so must be my benefit;°   115
    So shall I clothe me in a forced content,
    And shut myself up in° some other course,
    To fortune's alms.°

Desdemona: Alas, thrice-gentle Cassio,
    My advocation° is not now in tune.
    My lord is not my lord; nor should I know him,   120
    Were he in favor° as in humor° altered.
    So help me every spirit sanctified
    As I have spoken for you all my best
    And stood within the blank° of his displeasure
    For my free speech! You must awhile be patient.   125
    What I can do I will, and more I will
    Than for myself I dare. Let that suffice you.

Iago: Is my lord angry?

Emilia: He went hence but now,
    And certainly in strange unquietness.

Iago: Can he be angry? I have seen the cannon   130
    When it hath blown his ranks into the air,
    And like the devil from his very arm
    Puffed his own brother—and is he angry?
    Something of moment° then. I will go meet him.
    There's matter in 't indeed, if he be angry.   135

---

104 *the happiness* in happy time, fortunately met   107 *virtuous* efficacious   109 *office* loyal
service   111 *mortal* fatal   112 *nor . . . nor* neither . . . nor   115 *But . . . benefit* merely to
know that my case is hopeless will have to content me (and will be better than uncertainty)   117 *shut . . . in* confine myself to   118 *To fortune's alms* throwing myself on the mercy
of fortune   119 *advocation* advocacy   121 *favor* appearance. *humor* mood   124 *within the
blank* within point-blank range. (The *blank* is the center of the target.)   134 *of moment* of
immediate importance, momentous

Desdemona: I prithee, do so.   *Exit* [*Iago*].
                              Something, sure, of state,°
      Either from Venice, or some unhatched practice°
      Made demonstrable here in Cyprus to him,
      Hath puddled° his clear spirit; and in such cases
      Men's natures wrangle with inferior things,   140
      Though great ones are their object. 'Tis even so;
      For let our finger ache, and it indues°
      Our other, healthful members even to a sense
      Of pain. Nay, we must think men are not gods,
      Nor of them look for such observancy°   145
      As fits the bridal.° Beshrew me° much, Emilia,
      I was, unhandsome° warrior as I am,
      Arraigning his unkindness with° my soul;
      But now I find I had suborned the witness,°
      And he's indicted falsely.
Emilia: Pray heaven it be   150
      State matters, as you think, and no conception
      Nor no jealous toy° concerning you.
Desdemona: Alas the day! I never gave him cause.
Emilia: But jealous souls will not be answered so;
      They are not ever jealous for the cause,   155
      But jealous for° they're jealous. It is a monster
      Begot upon itself,° born on itself.
Desdemona: Heaven keep that monster from Othello's mind!
Emilia: Lady, amen.
Desdemona: I will go seek him. Cassio, walk hereabout.   160
      If I do find him fit, I'll move your suit
      And seek to effect it to my uttermost.
Cassio: I humbly thank your ladyship.

      Exit [*Desdemona with Emilia*].

      Enter Bianca.

Bianca: Save° you, friend Cassio!
Cassio: What make° you from home?
      How is 't with you, my most fair Bianca?   165
      I' faith, sweet love, I was coming to your house.

---

136 *of state* concerning state affairs   137 *unhatched practice* as yet unexecuted or undiscovered plot   139 *puddled* muddied   142 *indues* brings to the same condition   145 *observancy*
attentiveness   146 *bridal* wedding (when a bridegroom is newly attentive to his bride).
Beshrew me (A mild oath.)   147 *unhandsome* insufficient, unskillful   148 *with* before
the bar of   149 *suborned the witness* induced the witness to give false testimony   152 *toy*
fancy   156 *for* because   157 *Begot upon itself* generated solely from itself   164 *Save* God
save.   *make* do

Cassio explains to Bianca that he does not know how the handkerchief appeared in his room (III, iv, 171–186).

Bianca: And I was going to your lodging, Cassio.
    What, keep a week away? Seven days and nights?
    Eightscore-eight° hours? And lovers' absent hours
    More tedious than the dial° eightscore times?   170
    O weary reckoning!
Cassio: Pardon me, Bianca.
    I have this while with leaden thoughts been pressed;
    But I shall, in a more continuate° time,
    Strike off this score° of absence. Sweet Bianca,

    [*giving her Desdemona's handkerchief*]

    Take me this work out.°
Bianca: O Cassio, whence came this?   175
    This is some token from a newer friend.°
    To the felt absence now I feel a cause.
    Is 't come to this? Well, well.
Cassio: Go to, woman!
    Throw your vile guesses in the devil's teeth,
    From whence you have them. You are jealous now   180

169 *Eightscore-eight* one hundred sixty-eight, the number of hours in a week   170 *the dial* a complete revolution of the clock   173 *continuate* uninterrupted   174 *Strike . . . score* settle this account   175 *Take . . . . out* copy this embroidery for me   176 *friend* mistress

That this is from some mistress, some remembrance.
No, by my faith, Bianca.
Bianca: Why, whose is it?
Cassio: I know not, neither. I found it in my chamber.
I like the work well. Ere it be demanded°—
As like° enough it will—I would have it copied.   185
Take it and do 't, and leave me for this time.
Bianca: Leave you? Wherefore?
Cassio: I do attend here on the General,
And think it no addition,° nor my wish,
To have him see me womaned.   190
Bianca: Why, I pray you?
Cassio: Not that I love you not.
Bianca: But that you do not love me.
I pray you, bring° me on the way a little,
And say if I shall see you soon at night.   195
Cassio: 'Tis but a little way that I can bring you,
For I attend here; but I'll see you soon.
Bianca: 'Tis very good. I must be circumstanced.°

Exeunt omnes.

ACT IV

SCENE I [BEFORE THE CITADEL.]

Enter Othello and Iago.

Iago: Will you think so?
Othello: Think so, Iago?
Iago: What,
To kiss in private?
Othello: An unauthorized kiss!
Iago: Or to be naked with her friend in bed
An hour or more, not meaning any harm?
Othello: Naked in bed, Iago, and not mean harm?   5
It is hypocrisy against the devil.
They that mean virtuously and yet do so,
The devil their virtue tempts, and they tempt heaven.
Iago: If they do nothing, 'tis a venial° slip.
But if I give my wife a handkerchief—   10
Othello: What then?

184 *demanded* inquired for   185 *like* likely   189 *addition* i.e., addition to my reputation   194
bring accompany   198 *be circumstanced* be governed by circumstance, yield to your
conditions   9 *venial* pardonable

Iago: Why then, 'tis hers, my lord, and being hers,
    She may, I think, bestow 't on any man.
Othello: She is protectress of her honor too.
    May she give that?   15
Iago: Her honor is an essence that's not seen;
    They have it° very oft that have it not.
    But, for the handkerchief—
Othello: By heaven, I would most gladly have forgot it.
    Thou saidst—O, it comes o'er my memory   20
    As doth the raven o'er the infectious house,°
    Boding to all—he had my handkerchief.
Iago: Ay, what of that?
Othello: That's not so good now.
Iago: What
    If I had said I had seen him do you wrong?
    Or heard him say—as knaves be such abroad,°   25
    Who having, by their own importunate suit,
    Or voluntary dotage° of some mistress,
    Convincèd or supplied° them, cannot choose
    But they must blab—
Othello: Hath he said anything?
Iago: He hath, my lord; but, be you well assured,   30
    No more than he'll unswear.
Othello: What hath he said?
Iago: Faith, that he did—I know not what he did.
Othello: What? What?
Iago: Lie—
Othello: With her?
Iago: With her, on her; what you will.
Othello: Lie with her? Lie on her? We say "lie on her" when they belie°   35
    her. Lie with her? Zounds, that's fulsome.°—Handkerchief—
    confessions—handkerchief!—To confess and be hanged for his
    labor—first to be hanged and then to confess.°—I tremble at it.
    Nature would not invest herself in such shadowing passion without
    some instruction.° It is not words° that shakes me thus. Pish! Noses,   40
    ears, and lips.—Is't possible?—Confess—handkerchief!— O devil!

---

17 *They have it* i.e., they enjoy a reputation for it   21 *raven . . . house* (Allusion to the belief that the raven hovered over a house of sickness or infection, such as one visited by the plague.)   25 *abroad* around about   27 *voluntary dotage* willing infatuation   28 *Convincèd or supplied* seduced or sexually gratified   36 *belie* slander   36 *fulsome* foul   38 *first . . . to confess* (Othello reverses the proverbial *confess and be hanged;* Cassio is to be given no time to confess before he dies.)   39–40 *Nature . . . instruction* i.e., without some foundation in fact, nature would not have dressed herself in such an overwhelming passion that comes over me now and fills my mind with images, or in such a lifelike fantasy as Cassio had in his dream of lying with Desdemona   40 *words* mere words

Falls in a trance.

Iago: Work on,
My medicine, work! Thus credulous fools are caught,
And many worthy and chaste dames even thus,
All guiltless, meet reproach.—What, ho! My lord!   45
My lord, I say! Othello!

Enter Cassio.

How now, Cassio?
Cassio: What's the matter?
Iago: My lord is fall'n into an epilepsy.
This is his second fit. He had one yesterday.
Cassio: Rub him about the temples.
Iago: No, forbear.   50
The lethargy° must have his° quiet course.
If not, he foams at mouth, and by and by
Breaks out to savage madness. Look, he stirs.
Do you withdraw yourself a little while.
He will recover straight. When he is gone,   55
I would on great occasion° speak with you.

[*Exit Cassio.*]

How is it, General? Have you not hurt your head?
Othello: Dost thou mock me?°
Iago: I mock you not, by heaven.
Would you would bear your fortune like a man!
Othello: A hornèd man's a monster and a beast.   60
Iago: There's many a beast then in a populous city,
And many a civil° monster.
Othello: Did he confess it?
Iago: Good sir, be a man.
Think every bearded fellow that's but yoked°   65
May draw with you.° There's millions now alive
That nightly lie in those unproper° beds
Which they dare swear peculiar.° Your case is better.°
O, 'tis the spite of hell, the fiend's arch-mock,
To lip° a wanton in a secure° couch   70
And to suppose her chaste! No, let me know,

---

51 *lethargy* coma.   *his* its   56 *on great occasion* on a matter of great importance   58 *mock me* (Othello takes Iago's question about hurting his head to be a mocking reference to the cuckold's horns.)   62 *civil* i.e., dwelling in a city   65 *yoked* (1) married (2) put into the yoke of infamy and cuckoldry   66 *draw with you* pull as you do, like oxen who are yoked, i.e., share your fate as cuckold   67 *unproper* not exclusively their own   68 *peculiar* private, their own.   *better* i.e., because you know the truth   70 *lip* kiss.   *secure* free from suspicion

And knowing what I am,° I know what she shall be.°
Othello: O, thou art wise. 'Tis certain.
Iago: Stand you awhile apart;
    Confine yourself but in a patient list.°   75
    Whilst you were here o'erwhelmèd with your grief—
    A passion most unsuiting such a man—
    Cassio came hither. I shifted him away,°
    And laid good 'scuse upon your ecstasy,°
    Bade him anon return and here speak with me,   80
    The which he promised. Do but encave° yourself
    And mark the fleers,° the gibes, and notable° scorns
    That dwell in every region of his face;
    For I will make him tell the tale anew,
    Where, how, how oft, how long ago, and when   85
    He hath and is again to cope° your wife.
    I say, but mark his gesture. Marry, patience!
    Or I shall say you're all-in-all in spleen,°
    And nothing of a man.
Othello: Dost thou hear, Iago?
    I will be found most cunning in my patience;   90
    But—dost thou hear?—most bloody.
Iago: That's not amiss;
    But yet keep time° in all. Will you withdraw?

    [*Othello stands apart.*]

    Now will I question Cassio of Bianca,
    A huswife° that by selling her desires
    Buys herself bread and clothes. It is a creature   95
    That dotes on Cassio—as 'tis the strumpet's plague
    To beguile many and be beguiled by one.
    He, when he hears of her, cannot restrain°
    From the excess of laughter. Here he comes.

    Enter Cassio.

    As he shall smile, Othello shall go mad;   100
    And his unbookish° jealousy must conster°
    Poor Cassio's smiles, gestures, and light behaviors
    Quite in the wrong.—How do you now, Lieutenant?

---

72 *what I am* i.e., a cuckold. *she shall be* will happen to her 75 *in . . . list* within the bounds
of patience 78 *shifted him away* used a dodge to get rid of him 79 *ecstasy* trance 81 *encave*
conceal 82 *fleers* sneers. *notable* obvious 86 *cope* encounter with, have sex with 88 *all-
in-all in spleen* utterly governed by passionate impulses 92 *keep time* keep yourself steady
(as in music) 94 *huswife* hussy 98 *restrain* refrain 101 *unbookish* uninstructed. *conster*
construe

Cassio: The worser that you give me the addition°
   Whose want° even kills me.   105

Iago: Ply Desdemona well and you are sure on 't.
   [*Speaking lower.*] Now, if this suit lay in Bianca's power,
   How quickly should you speed!

Cassio [*laughing*]:   Alas, poor caitiff!°

Othello [*aside*]:   Look how he laughs already!   110

Iago: I never knew a woman love man so.

Cassio: Alas, poor rogue! I think, i' faith, she loves me.

Othello: Now he denies it faintly, and laughs it out.

Iago: Do you hear, Cassio?

Othello: Now he importunes him
   To tell it o'er. Go to!° Well said,° well said.   115

Iago: She gives it out that you shall marry her.
   Do you intend it?

Cassio: Ha, ha, ha!

Othello: Do you triumph, Roman?° Do you triumph?

Cassio: I marry her? What? A customer?° Prithee, bear some charity   120
   to my wit;° do not think it so unwholesome. Ha, ha, ha!

Othello: So, so, so, so! They laugh that win.°

Iago: Faith, the cry° goes that you shall marry her.

Cassio: Prithee, say true.

Iago: I am a very villain else.°   125

Othello: Have you scored me?° Well.

Cassio: This is the monkey's own giving out. She is persuaded I will marry
   her out of her own love and flattery,° not out of my promise.

Othello: Iago beckons° me. Now he begins the story.

Cassio: She was here even now; she haunts me in every place. I was the other   130
   day talking on the seabank° with certain Venetians, and thither comes
   the bauble,° and, by this hand,° she falls me thus about my neck—

   [*He embraces Iago.*]

Othello: Crying, "O dear Cassio!" as it were; his gesture imports it.

Cassio: So hangs and lolls and weeps upon me, so shakes and pulls me.
   Ha, ha, ha!   135

Othello: Now he tells how she plucked him to my chamber. O, I see that
   nose of yours, but not that dog I shall throw it to.°

---

104 *addition* title   105 *Whose want* the lack of which   109 *caitiff* wretch   115 *Go to* (An expression of remonstrance.)   *Well said* well done   119 *Roman* (The Romans were noted for their *triumphs* or triumphal processions.)   120 *customer* i.e., prostitute   120–121 *bear . . . wit* be more charitable to my judgment   122 *They . . . win* i.e., they that laugh last laugh best   123 *cry* rumor   125 *I . . . else* call me a complete rogue if I'm not telling the truth   126 *scored me* scored off me, beaten me, made up my reckoning, branded me   128 *flattery* self-flattery, self-deception   129 *beckons* signals   131 *seabank* seashore.   132 *bauble* plaything.   *by this hand* I make my vow   137 *not . . . to* (Othello imagines himself cutting off Cassio's nose and throwing it to a dog.)

Cassio: Well, I must leave her company.

Iago: Before me,° look where she comes.

Enter Bianca [with Othello's handkerchief].

Cassio: 'Tis such another fitchew!° Marry, a perfumed one.—What do   140
you mean by this haunting of me?

Bianca: Let the devil and his dam° haunt you! What did you mean by
that same handkerchief you gave me even now? I was a fine fool to
take it. I must take out the work? A likely piece of work,° that you
should find it in your chamber and know not who left it there! This is   145
some minx's token, and I must take out the work? There; give it your
hobbyhorse.° [*She gives him the handkerchief.*] Wheresoever you had it,
I'll take out no work on 't.

Cassio: How now, my sweet Bianca? How now? How now?

Othello: By heaven, that should be° my handkerchief!   150

Bianca: If you'll come to supper tonight, you may; if you will not, come
when you are next prepared for.°   *Exit.*

Iago: After her, after her.

Cassio: Faith, I must. She'll rail in the streets else.

Iago: Will you sup there?   155

Cassio: Faith, I intend so.

Iago: Well, I may chance to see you, for I would very fain speak with you.

Cassio: Prithee, come. Will you?

Iago: Go to.° Say no more.   [*Exit Cassio.*]

Othello [advancing]: How shall I murder him, Iago?   160

Iago: Did you perceive how he laughed at his vice?

Othello: O, Iago!

Iago: And did you see the handkerchief?

Othello: Was that mine?

Iago: Yours, by this hand. And to see how he prizes the foolish woman   165
your wife! She gave it him, and he hath given it his whore.

Othello: I would have him nine years a-killing. A fine woman! A fair
woman! A sweet woman!

Iago: Nay, you must forget that.

Othello: Ay, let her rot and perish, and be damned tonight, for she shall   170
not live. No, my heart is turned to stone; I strike it, and it hurts my
hand. O, the world hath not a sweeter creature! She might lie by an
emperor's side and command him tasks.

Iago: Nay, that's not your way.°

---

139 *Before me* i.e., on my soul   140 *'Tis . . . fitchew* what a polecat she is! Just like all the others.
(Polecats were often compared with prostitutes because of their rank smell and presumed lechery.)   142 *dam* mother   144 *A likely . . . work* a fine story   147 *hobbyhorse* harlot   150 *should
be* must be   152 *when . . . for* when I'm ready for you (i.e., never)   159 *Go to* (An expression
of remonstrance.)   174 *your way* i.e., the way you should think of her

Othello: Hang her! I do but say what she is. So delicate with her needle!   175
An admirable musician! O, she will sing the savageness out of a bear.
Of so high and plenteous wit and invention!°
Iago: She's the worse for all this.
Othello: O, a thousand, a thousand times! And then, of so gentle a condition!°
Iago: Ay, too gentle.°   180
Othello: Nay, that's certain. But yet the pity of it, Iago! O, Iago, the pity
of it, Iago!
Iago: If you are so fond° over her iniquity, give her patent° to offend, for
if it touch not you it comes near nobody.
Othello: I will chop her into messes.° Cuckold me?   185
Iago: O, 'tis foul in her.
Othello: With mine officer?
Iago: That's fouler.
Othello: Get me some poison, Iago, this night. I'll not expostulate with her,
lest her body and beauty unprovide° my mind again. This night, Iago.   190
Iago: Do it not with poison. Strangle her in her bed, even the bed she
hath contaminated.
Othello: Good, good! The justice of it pleases. Very good.
Iago: And for Cassio, let me be his undertaker.° You shall hear more by
midnight.   195
Othello: Excellent good. [*A trumpet within.*] What trumpet is that same?
Iago: I warrant, something from Venice.

Enter Lodovico, Desdemona, and attendants.

'Tis Lodovico. This comes from the Duke.
See, your wife's with him.
Lodovico: God save you, worthy General!
Othello: With all my heart,° sir.   200
Lodovico [*giving him a letter*]: The Duke and the senators of Venice greet you.
Othello: I kiss the instrument of their pleasures.

[*He opens the letter, and reads.*]

Desdemona: And what's the news, good cousin Lodovico?
Iago: I am very glad to see you, signor.
Welcome to Cyprus.   205
Lodovico: I thank you. How does Lieutenant Cassio?
Iago: Lives, sir.
Desdemona: Cousin, there's fall'n between him and my lord

---

177 *invention* imagination   179 *gentle a condition* wellborn and well-bred   180 *gentle* generous, yielding (to other men)   183 *fond* foolish. *patent* license   185 *messes* portions of meat,
i.e., bits   190 *unprovide* weaken, render unfit   194 *be his undertaker* undertake to dispatch
him   200 *With all my heart* i.e., I thank you most heartily

An unkind° breach; but you shall make all well.

Othello: Are you sure of that?   210

Desdemona: My lord?

Othello [reads]: "This fail you not to do, as you will—"

Lodovico: He did not call; he's busy in the paper.
    Is there division twixt my lord and Cassio?

Desdemona: A most unhappy one. I would do much   215
    T' atone° them, for the love I bear to Cassio.

Othello: Fire and brimstone!

Desdemona: My lord?

Othello: Are you wise?

Desdemona: What, is he angry?

Lodovico: Maybe the letter moved him;   220
    For, as I think, they do command him home,
    Deputing Cassio in his government.°

Desdemona: By my troth, I am glad on 't.°

Othello: Indeed?

Desdemona: My lord?   225

Othello: I am glad to see you mad.°

Desdemona: Why, sweet Othello—

Othello [striking her]: Devil!

Desdemona: I have not deserved this.

Lodovico: My lord, this would not be believed in Venice,   230
    Though I should swear I saw 't. 'Tis very much.°
    Make her amends; she weeps.

Othello: O devil, devil!
    If that the earth could teem° with woman's tears,
    Each drop she falls would prove a crocodile.°
    Out of my sight!

Desdemona: I will not stay to offend you. [*Going.*]   235

Lodovico: Truly, an obedient lady.
    I do beseech your lordship, call her back.

Othello: Mistress!

Desdemona [returning]: My lord?

Othello: What would you with her, sir?°   240

Lodovico: Who, I, my lord?

Othello: Ay, you did wish that I would make her turn.
    Sir, she can turn, and turn, and yet go on

---

209 *unkind* unnatural, contrary to their natures; hurtful 216 *atone* reconcile 222 *government* office 223 *on 't* of it 226 *I am . . . mad* i.e., I am glad to see that you are insane enough to rejoice in Cassio's promotion (?) (Othello bitterly plays on Desdemona's *I am glad.*) 231 *very much* too much, outrageous 233 *teem* breed, be impregnated 234 *falls . . . crocodile* (Crocodiles were supposed to weep hypocritical tears for their victims.) 240 *What . . . sir* (Othello implies that Desdemona is pliant and will do a *turn*, lines 242–244 for any man.)

And turn again; and she can weep, sir, weep;
And she's obedient,° as you say, obedient,   245
Very obedient.—Proceed you in your tears.—
Concerning this, sir—O well-painted passion!°—
I am commanded home.—Get you away;
I'll send for you anon.—Sir, I obey the mandate
And will return to Venice.—Hence, avaunt!   250

[*Exit Desdemona.*]

Cassio shall have my place. And, sir, tonight
I do entreat that we may sup together.
You are welcome, sir, to Cyprus.—Goats and monkeys!°   *Exit.*
Lodovico: Is this the noble Moor whom our full Senate
Call all in all sufficient? Is this the nature   255
Whom passion could not shake? Whose solid virtue
The shot of accident nor dart of chance
Could neither graze nor pierce?
Iago: He is much changed.
Lodovico: Are his wits safe? Is he not light of brain?
Iago: He's that he is. I may not breathe my censure   260
What he might be. If what he might he is not,
I would to heaven he were!°
Lodovico: What, strike his wife?
Iago: Faith, that was not so well; yet would I knew
That stroke would prove the worst!
Lodovico: Is it his use?°
Or did the letters work upon his blood°   265
And new-create his fault?
Iago: Alas, alas!
It is not honesty in me to speak
What I have seen and known. You shall observe him,
And his own courses will denote° him so
That I may save my speech. Do but go after,   270
And mark how he continues.
Lodovico: I am sorry that I am deceived in him.   *Exeunt.*

---

245 *obedient* (With much the same sexual connotation as *turn* in lines 242–244.)   247 *pas-sion* i.e., grief   253 *Goats and monkeys* (See III, iii, 419.)   260–262 *I may . . . were* i.e., I dare not venture an opinion as to whether he's of unsound mind, as you suggest, but, if he isn't, then it might be better to wish he were in fact insane, since only that could excuse his wild behavior   264 *use* custom   265 *blood* passions   269 *courses will denote* actions will reveal

SCENE II [THE CITADEL.]

Enter Othello and Emilia.

Othello: You have seen nothing then?
Emilia: Nor ever heard, nor ever did suspect.
Othello: Yes, you have seen Cassio and she together.
Emilia: But then I saw no harm, and then I heard
    Each syllable that breath made up between them.   5
Othello: What, did they never whisper?
Emilia: Never, my lord.
Othello: Nor send you out o' the way?
Emilia: Never.
Othello: To fetch her fan, her gloves, her mask, nor nothing?   10
Emilia: Never, my lord.
Othello: That's strange.
Emilia: I durst, my lord, to wager she is honest,
    Lay down my soul at stake.° If you think other,
    Remove your thought; it doth abuse your bosom.°   15
    If any wretch have put this in your head,
    Let heaven requite it with the serpent's curse!°
    For if she be not honest, chaste, and true,
    There's no man happy; the purest of their wives
    Is foul as slander.
Othello: Bid her come hither. Go.   20

Exit Emilia.

    She says enough; yet she's a simple bawd
    That cannot say as much.° This° is a subtle whore,
    A closet lock and key° of villainous secrets.
    And yet she'll kneel and pray; I have seen her do 't.

Enter Desdemona and Emilia.

Desdemona: My lord, what is your will?   25
Othello: Pray you, chuck, come hither.
Desdemona: What is your pleasure?
Othello: Let me see your eyes.
    Look in my face.
Desdemona: What horrible fancy's this?

---

14 *at stake* as the wager   15 *abuse your bosom* deceive you   17 *the serpent's curse* the curse pronounced by God on the serpent for deceiving Eve, just as some man has done to Othello and
Desdemona. (See Genesis 3:14.)   21–22 *she's . . . much* i.e., any procuress or go-between who
couldn't make up as plausible a story as Emilia's would have to be pretty stupid   22 *This* i.e.,
Desdemona   23 *closet lock and key* i.e., concealer

"Ah, Desdemon! Away, away, away!" (IV, ii, 43).

Othello [*to Emilia*]: Some of your function,° mistress.
 Leave procreants° alone and shut the door;   30
 Cough or cry "hem" if anybody come.
 Your mystery, your mystery!° Nay, dispatch.

 Exit Emilia.

Desdemona [*kneeling*]: Upon my knees, what doth your speech import?
 I understand a fury in your words,
 But not the words.   35
Othello: Why, what art thou?
Desdemona: Your wife, my lord, your true
 And loyal wife.
Othello: Come, swear it, damn thyself,
 Lest, being like one of heaven,° the devils themselves
 Should fear to seize thee. Therefore be double damned:
 Swear thou art honest.
Desdemona: Heaven doth truly know it.   40
Othello: Heaven truly knows that thou art false as hell.

---

29 *Some . . . function* i.e., practice your chosen profession, that of bawd (by guarding the
door) 30 *procreants* mating couples 32 *mystery* trade, occupation 38 *being . . . heaven*
looking like an angel

Desdemona: To whom, my lord? With whom? How am I false?
Othello [weeping]: Ah, Desdemon! Away, away, away!
Desdemona: Alas the heavy day! Why do you weep?
    Am I the motive° of these tears, my lord? 45
    If haply you my father do suspect
    An instrument of this your calling back,
    Lay not your blame on me. If you have lost him,
    I have lost him too.
Othello: Had it pleased heaven
    To try me with affliction, had they° rained 50
    All kinds of sores and shames on my bare head,
    Steeped me in poverty to the very lips,
    Given to captivity me and my utmost hopes,
    I should have found in some place of my soul
    A drop of patience. But, alas, to make me 55
    A fixèd figure for the time of scorn°
    To point his° slow and moving finger° at!
    Yet could I bear that too, well, very well.
    But there where I have garnered° up my heart,
    Where either I must live or bear no life, 60
    The fountain° from the which my current runs
    Or else dries up—to be discarded thence!
    Or keep it as a cistern° for foul toads
    To knot° and gender° in! Turn thy complexion there,°
    Patience, thou young and rose-lipped cherubin— 65
    Ay, there look grim as hell!°
Desdemona: I hope my noble lord esteems me honest.°
Othello: O, ay, as summer flies are in the shambles,°
    That quicken° even with blowing.° O thou weed,
    Who art so lovely fair and smell'st so sweet 70
    That the sense aches at thee, would thou hadst ne'er been born!
Desdemona: Alas, what ignorant sin° have I committed?
Othello: Was this fair paper, this most goodly book,
    Made to write "whore" upon? What committed?
    Committed? O thou public commoner!° 75

---

45 *motive* cause   50 *they* i.e., heavenly powers   56 *time of scorn* i.e., scornful world   57 *his* its.   *slow and moving finger* i.e., hour hand of the clock, moving so slowly it seems hardly to move at all. (Othello envisages himself as being eternally pointed at by the scornful world as the numbers on a clock are pointed at by the hour hand.)   59 *garnered* stored   61 *fountain* spring   63 *cistern* cesspool   64 *knot* couple.   *gender* engender.   *Turn . . . there* change your color, grow pale, at such a sight   65–66 *Patience . . . hell* (Even Patience, that rose-lipped cherub, will look grim and pale at this spectacle.)   67 *honest* chaste   68 *shambles* slaughter-house   69 *quicken* come to life.   *with blowing* i.e., with the puffing up of something rotten in which maggots are breeding   72 *ignorant sin* sin in ignorance   75 *commoner* prostitute

Othello berates Desdemona as a "strumpet" and "cunning whore" (IV, ii, 73–98).

I should make very forges of my cheeks,
That would to cinders burn up modesty,
Did I but speak thy deeds. What committed?
Heaven stops the nose at it and the moon winks;°
The bawdy° wind, that kisses all it meets,   80
Is hushed within the hollow mine° of earth
And will not hear 't. What committed?
    Impudent strumpet!
Desdemona: By heaven, you do me wrong.
Othello: Are not you a strumpet?
Desdemona: No, as I am a Christian.   85
    If to preserve this vessel° for my lord
    From any other foul unlawful touch
    Be not to be a strumpet, I am none.
Othello: What, not a whore?
Desdemona: No, as I shall be saved.   90
Othello: Is 't possible?
Desdemona: O, heaven forgive us!
Othello: I cry you mercy,° then.

79 *winks* closes her eyes. (The moon symbolizes chastity.) 80 *bawdy* kissing one and all 81 *mine* cave (where the winds were thought to dwell) 86 *vessel* body 92 *cry you mercy* beg your pardon

I took you for that cunning whore of Venice
That married with Othello. [*Calling out.*] You, mistress,
That have the office opposite to Saint Peter   95
And keep the gate of hell!

Enter Emilia.

                                You, you, ay, you!
We have done our course.° There's money for your pains.
                                          [*He gives money.*]
I pray you, turn the key and keep our counsel.
                                                      Exit.
Emilia: Alas, what does this gentleman conceive?°
      How do you, madam? How do you, my good lady?   100
Desdemona: Faith, half asleep.°
Emilia: Good madam, what's the matter with my lord?
Desdemona: With who?
Emilia: Why, with my lord, madam.
Desdemona: Who is thy lord?
Emilia: He that is yours, sweet lady.   105
Desdemona: I have none. Do not talk to me, Emilia.
      I cannot weep, nor answers have I none
      But what should go by water.° Prithee, tonight
      Lay on my bed my wedding sheets, remember;
      And call thy husband hither.   110
Emilia: Here's a change indeed!   *Exit.*
Desdemona: 'Tis meet I should be used so, very meet.°
      How have I been behaved, that he might stick°
      The small'st opinion° on my least misuse?°

      Enter Iago.

Iago: What is your pleasure, madam? How is 't with you?   115
Desdemona: I cannot tell. Those that do teach young babes
      Do it with gentle means and easy tasks.
      He might have chid me so, for, in good faith,
      I am a child to chiding.
Iago: What is the matter, lady?   120
Emilia: Alas, Iago, my lord hath so bewhored her,
      Thrown such despite and heavy terms upon her,
      That true hearts cannot bear it.

---

97 *course* business (with an indecent suggestion of "trick," turn at sex)   99 *conceive* suppose, think   101 *half asleep* i.e., dazed   108 *go by water* be expressed by tears   112 *meet* fitting   113 *stick* attach   114 *opinion* censure.   *least misuse* slightest misconduct

Desdemona: Am I that name, Iago?
Iago: What name, fair lady?   125
Desdemona: Such as she said my lord did say I was.
Emilia: He called her whore. A beggar in his drink
    Could not have laid such terms upon his callet.°
Iago: Why did he so?
Desdemona [*weeping*]: I do not know. I am sure I am none such.   130
Iago: Do not weep, do not weep. Alas the day!
Emilia: Hath she forsook so many noble matches,
    Her father and her country and her friends,
    To be called whore? Would it not make one weep?
Desdemona: It is my wretched fortune.
Iago: Beshrew° him for 't!   135
    How comes this trick° upon him?
Desdemona: Nay, heaven doth know.
Emilia: I will be hanged if some eternal° villain,
    Some busy and insinuating° rogue,
    Some cogging,° cozening° slave, to get some office,
    Have not devised this slander. I will be hanged else.   140
Iago: Fie, there is no such man. It is impossible.
Desdemona: If any such there be, heaven pardon him!
Emilia: A halter° pardon him! And hell gnaw his bones!
    Why should he call her whore? Who keeps her company?
    What place? What time? What form?° What likelihood?   145
    The Moor's abused by some most villainous knave,
    Some base notorious knave, some scurvy fellow.
    O heaven, that° such companions° thou'dst unfold,°
    And put in every honest hand a whip
    To lash the rascals naked through the world   150
    Even from the east to th' west!
Iago: Speak within door.°
Emilia: O, fie upon them! Some such squire° he was
    That turned your wit the seamy side without°
    And made you to suspect me with the Moor.
Iago: You are a fool. Go to.°
Desdemona: Alas, Iago,   155
    What shall I do to win my lord again?
    Good friend, go to him; for, by this light of heaven,

---

128 *callet* whore   135 *Beshrew* curse   136 *trick* strange behavior, delusion   137 *eternal* inveterate   138 *insinuating* ingratiating, fawning, wheedling   139 *cogging* cheating. *cozening*
defrauding   143 *halter* hangman's noose   145 *form* appearance, circumstance   148 *that*
would that. *companions* fellows. *unfold* expose   151 *within door* i.e., not so loud   152 *squire*
fellow   153 *seamy side without* wrong side out   155 *Go to* i.e., that's enough

I know not how I lost him. Here I kneel. [*She kneels.*]
If e'er my will did trespass 'gainst his love,
Either in discourse of thought° or actual deed,   160
Or that° mine eyes, mine ears, or any sense
Delighted them° in any other form;
Or that I do not yet,° and ever did,
And ever will—though he do shake me off
To beggarly divorcement—love him dearly,   165
Comfort forswear° me! Unkindness may do much,
And his unkindness may defeat° my life,
But never taint my love. I cannot say "whore."
It does abhor° me now I speak the word;
To do the act that might the addition° earn   170
Not the world's mass of vanity° could make me.

[*She rises.*]

Iago: I pray you, be content. 'Tis but his humor.°
    The business of the state does him offense,
    And he does chide with you.
Desdemona: If 'twere no other—   175
Iago: It is but so, I warrant.   [*Trumpets within.*]
    Hark, how these instruments summon you to supper!
    The messengers of Venice stays the meat.°
    Go in, and weep not. All things shall be well.

    Exeunt Desdemona and Emilia.

    Enter Roderigo.

    How now, Roderigo?   180
Roderigo: I do not find that thou deal'st justly with me.
Iago: What in the contrary?
Roderigo: Every day thou daff'st me° with some device,° Iago, and rather,
    as it seems to me now, keep'st from me all conveniency° than sup-
    pliest me with the least advantage° of hope. I will indeed no longer   185
    endure it, nor am I yet persuaded to put up° in peace what already I
    have foolishly suffered.
Iago: Will you hear me, Roderigo?

---

160 *discourse of thought* process of thinking   161 *that* if. (Also in line 163.)   162 *Delighted them*
took delight   163 *yet* still   166 *Comfort forswear* may heavenly comfort forsake   167 *defeat*
destroy   169 *abhor* (1) fill me with abhorrence (2) make me whorelike   170 *addition* title   171
vanity showy splendor   172 *humor* mood   178 *stays the meat* are waiting to dine   183 *thou
daff'st me* you put me off.   *device* excuse, trick   184 *conveniency* advantage, opportunity   185
advantage increase   186 *put up* submit to, tolerate

Roderigo starts to suspect Iago's duplicities.

Roderigo: Faith, I have heard too much, for your words and performances
are no kin together.

Iago: You charge me most unjustly.

Roderigo: With naught but truth. I have wasted myself out of my means.
The jewels you have had from me to deliver° Desdemona would half
have corrupted a votarist.° You have told me she hath received them
and returned me expectations and comforts of sudden respect° and
acquaintance, but I find none.

Iago: Well, go to, very well.

Roderigo: "Very well"! "Go to"! I cannot go to,° man, nor 'tis not very
well. By this hand, I think it is scurvy, and begin to find myself
fopped° in it.

Iago: Very well.

Roderigo: I tell you 'tis not very well.° I will make myself known to Desdemona. If she will return me my jewels, I will give over my suit and

190

195

200

---

193 *deliver* deliver to   194 *votarist* nun   195 *sudden respect* immediate consideration   198
I cannot go to (Roderigo changes Iago's *go to,* an expression urging patience, to I *cannot go
to,* "I have no opportunity for success in wooing.")   200 *fopped* fooled, duped   202 *not very
well* (Roderigo changes Iago's *very well,* "all right, then," to *not very well,* "not at all good.")

repent my unlawful solicitation; if not, assure yourself I will seek
satisfaction° of you.   205
Iago: You have said now?°
Roderigo: Ay, and said nothing but what I protest intendment° of doing.
Iago: Why, now I see there's mettle in thee, and even from this instant do
    build on thee a better opinion than ever before. Give me thy hand,
    Roderigo. Thou hast taken against me a most just exception; but yet   210
    I protest I have dealt most directly in thy affair.
Roderigo: It hath not appeared.
Iago: I grant indeed it hath not appeared, and your suspicion is not without
    wit and judgment. But, Roderigo, if thou hast that in thee indeed which
    I have greater reason to believe now than ever—I mean purpose, courage,   215
    and valor—this night show it. If thou the next night following enjoy
    not Desdemona, take me from this world with treachery and devise
    engines for° my life.
Roderigo: Well, what is it? Is it within reason and compass?
Iago: Sir, there is especial commission come from Venice to depute Cassio   220
    in Othello's place.
Roderigo: Is that true? Why, then Othello and Desdemona return again
    to Venice.
Iago: O, no; he goes into Mauritania and takes away with him the fair
    Desdemona, unless his abode be lingered here by some accident;   225
    wherein none can be so determinate° as the removing of Cassio.
Roderigo: How do you mean, removing of him?
Iago: Why, by making him uncapable of Othello's place—knocking
    out his brains.
Roderigo: And that you would have me to do?   230
Iago: Ay, if you dare do yourself a profit and a right. He sups tonight with
    a harlotry,° and thither will I go to him. He knows not yet of his
    honorable fortune. If you will watch his going thence, which I will
    fashion to fall out° between twelve and one, you may take him at
    your pleasure. I will be near to second your attempt, and he shall fall   235
    between us. Come, stand not amazed at it, but go along with me. I
    will show you such a necessity in his death that you shall think your-
    self bound to put it on him. It is now high° suppertime, and the night
    grows to waste.° About it.
Roderigo: I will hear further reason for this.   240
Iago: And you shall be satisfied.   *Exeunt.*

---

205 *satisfaction* repayment. (The term normally means settling of accounts in a
duel.) 206 *You . . . now* have you finished? 207 *intendment* intention 218 *engines for*
plots against 226 *determinate* conclusive 232 *harlotry* slut 234 *fall out* occur 238 *high*
fully. 239 *grows to waste* wastes away

SCENE III [THE CITADEL.]

Enter Othello, Lodovico, Desdemona, Emilia, and attendants.

Lodovico: I do beseech you, sir, trouble yourself no further.
Othello: O, pardon me; 'twill do me good to walk.
Lodovico: Madam, good night. I humbly thank your ladyship.
Desdemona: Your honor is most welcome.
Othello: Will you walk, sir?
O, Desdemona!   5
Desdemona: My lord?
Othello: Get you to bed on th' instant. I will be returned
    forthwith. Dismiss your attendant there.
    Look 't be done.
Desdemona: I will, my lord.   10

Exit [Othello, with Lodovico and attendants].

Emilia: How goes it now? He looks gentler than he did.
Desdemona: He says he will return incontinent,°
    And hath commanded me to go to bed,
    And bid me to dismiss you.
Emilia: Dismiss me?   15
Desdemona: It was his bidding. Therefore, good Emilia,
    Give me my nightly wearing, and adieu.
    We must not now displease him.
Emilia: I would you had never seen him!
Desdemona: So would not I. My love doth so approve him   20
    That even his stubbornness,° his checks,° his frowns—
    Prithee, unpin me—have grace and favor in them.

[Emilia prepares Desdemona for bed.]

Emilia: I have laid those sheets you bade me on the bed.
Desdemona: All's one.° Good faith, how foolish are our minds!
    If I do die before thee, prithee shroud me   25
    In one of these same sheets.
Emilia: Come, come, you talk.°
Desdemona: My mother had a maid called Barbary.
    She was in love, and he she loved proved mad°
    And did forsake her. She had a song of "Willow."
    An old thing 'twas, but it expressed her fortune,   30
    And she died singing it. That song tonight

12 *incontinent* immediately   21 *stubbornness* roughness. *checks* rebukes   24 *All's one* all
right. It doesn't really matter   26 *talk* i.e., prattle   28 *mad* wild, i.e., faithless

Will not go from my mind; I have much to do
But to go hang° my head all at one side
And sing it like poor Barbary. Prithee, dispatch.
Emilia: Shall I go fetch your nightgown?°   35
Desdemona: No, unpin me here.
    This Lodovico is a proper° man.
Emilia: A very handsome man.
Desdemona: He speaks well.
Emilia: I know a lady in Venice would have walked barefoot to Palestine   40
    for a touch of his nether lip.
Desdemona [singing]:
        "The poor soul sat sighing by a sycamore tree,
        Sing all a green willow;°
        Her hand on her bosom, her head on her knee,
        Sing willow, willow, willow.   45
        The fresh streams ran by her and murmured her moans;
        Sing willow, willow, willow;
        Her salt tears fell from her, and softened the stones—"
Lay by these.
    [*Singing.*] "Sing willow, willow, willow—"   50
Prithee, hie thee.° He'll come anon.°
    [*Singing.*] "Sing all a green willow must be my garland.
    Let nobody blame him; his scorn I approve—"
Nay, that's not next.—Hark! Who is 't that knocks?
Emilia: It's the wind.   55
Desdemona [singing]:
        "I called my love false love; but what said he then?
        Sing willow, willow, willow;
        If I court more women, you'll couch with more men."

So, get thee gone. Good night. Mine eyes do itch;
Doth that bode weeping?
Emilia: 'Tis neither here nor there.   60
Desdemona: I have heard it said so. O, these men, these men!
Dost thou in conscience think—tell me, Emilia—
That there be women do abuse° their husbands
In such gross kind?
Emilia: There be some such, no question.
Desdemona: Wouldst thou do such a deed for all the world?   65
Emilia: Why, would not you?
Desdemona: No, by this heavenly light!

32–33 *I . . . hang* I can scarcely keep myself from hanging   35 *nightgown* dressing gown   37 *proper* handsome   43 *willow* (A conventional emblem of disappointed love.)   51 *hie thee* hurry. *anon* right away   63 *abuse* deceive

Emilia prepares Desdemona for bed.

Emilia: Nor I neither by this heavenly light;
I might do 't as well i' the dark.
Desdemona: Wouldst thou do such a deed for all the world?
Emilia: The world's a huge thing. It is a great price   70
For a small vice.
Desdemona: Good troth, I think thou wouldst not.
Emilia: By my troth, I think I should, and undo 't when I had done. Marry,
I would not do such a thing for a joint ring,° nor for measures of
lawn,° nor for gowns, petticoats, nor caps, nor any petty exhibition.°   75
But for all the whole world! Uds° pity, who would not make her husband
a cuckold to make him a monarch? I should venture purgatory for 't.
Desdemona: Beshrew me if I would do such a wrong
For the whole world.
Emilia: Why, the wrong is but a wrong i' the world, and having the world   80
for your labor, 'tis a wrong in your own world, and you might quickly
make it right.
Desdemona: I do not think there is any such woman.
Emilia: Yes, a dozen, and as many
To th' vantage° as would store° the world they played° for.   85

---

74 *joint ring* a ring made in separate halves. 75 *lawn* fine linen. *exhibition* gift 76
Uds God's 85 *To th' vantage* in addition, to boot. *store* populate. *played* (1) gambled
(2) sported sexually

But I do think it is their husbands' faults
If wives do fall. Say that they slack their duties°
And pour our treasures into foreign laps,°
Or else break out in peevish jealousies,
Throwing restraint upon us?° Or say they strike us,   90
Or scant our former having in despite?°
Why, we have galls,° and though we have some grace,
Yet have we some revenge. Let husbands know
Their wives have sense° like them. They see, and smell,
And have their palates both for sweet and sour,   95
As husbands have. What is it that they do
When they change us for others? Is it sport?°
I think it is. And doth affection° breed it?
I think it doth. Is 't frailty that thus errs?
It is so, too. And have not we affections,   100
Desires for sport, and frailty, as men have?
Then let them use us well; else let them know,
The ills we do, their ills instruct us so.
Desdemona: Good night, good night. God me such uses° send
Not to pick bad from bad, but by bad mend!°   105

Exeunt.

ACT V

SCENE I [A STREET IN CYPRUS.]

Enter Iago and Roderigo.

Iago: Here stand behind this bulk.° Straight will he come.
Wear thy good rapier bare,° and put it home.
Quick, quick! Fear nothing. I'll be at thy elbow.
It makes us or it mars us. Think on that,
And fix most firm thy resolution.   5
Roderigo: Be near at hand. I may miscarry in 't.
Iago: Here, at thy hand. Be bold, and take thy stand.

---

87 *duties* marital duties 88 *pour . . . laps* i.e., are unfaithful, give what is rightfully ours
(semen) to other women 90 *Throwing . . . us* i.e., jealously restricting our freedom to see
other men 91 *scant . . . despite* reduce our allowance to spite us 92 *have galls* i.e., are capable
of resenting injury and insult 94 *sense* physical sense 97 *sport* sexual pastime 98 *affection*
passion 104 *uses* habit, practice 105 *Not . . . mend* i.e., not to learn bad conduct from
others' badness (as Emilia has suggested women learn from men), but to mend my ways by
perceiving what badness is, making spiritual benefit out of evil and adversity 1 *bulk* framework projecting from the front of a shop 2 *bare* unsheathed

[*Iago stands aside. Roderigo conceals himself.*]

Roderigo: I have no great devotion to the deed;
 And yet he hath given me satisfying reasons.
 'Tis but a man gone. Forth, my sword! He dies.   10

[*He draws.*]

Iago: I have rubbed this young quat° almost to the sense,°
 And he grows angry. Now, whether he kill Cassio
 Or Cassio him, or each do kill the other,
 Every way makes my gain. Live Roderigo,°
 He calls me to a restitution large   15
 Of gold and jewels that I bobbed° from him
 As gifts to Desdemona.
 It must not be. If Cassio do remain,
 He hath a daily beauty in his life
 That makes me ugly; and besides, the Moor   20
 May unfold° me to him; there stand I in much peril.
 No, he must die. Be 't so. I hear him coming.

 Enter Cassio.

Roderigo [*coming forth*]: I know his gait, 'tis he.—Villain, thou diest!

[*He attacks Cassio.*]

Cassio: That thrust had been mine enemy indeed,
 But that my coat° is better than thou know'st.   25
 I will make proof° of thine.

[*He draws, and wounds Roderigo.*]

Roderigo: O, I am slain!   [*He falls.*]

[*Iago, from behind, wounds Cassio in the leg, and exits.*]

Cassio: I am maimed forever. Help, ho! Murder! Murder!

 Enter Othello.

Othello: The voice of Cassio! Iago keeps his word.
Roderigo: O, villain that I am!
Othello: It is even so.   30
Cassio: O, help, ho! Light! A surgeon!
Othello: 'Tis he. O brave Iago, honest and just,

---

11 *quat* pimple, pustule. *to the sense* to the quick 14 *Live Roderigo* if Roderigo lives 16 *bobbed* swindled 21 *unfold* expose 25 *coat* (Possibly a garment of mail under the outer clothing, or simply a tougher coat than Roderigo expected.) 26 *proof* a test

That hast such noble sense of thy friend's wrong!
Thou teachest me. Minion,° your dear lies dead,
And your unblest fate hies.° Strumpet, I come.   35
Forth of° my heart those charms, thine eyes, are blotted;
Thy bed, lust-stained, shall with lust's blood be spotted.   *Exit Othello.*

Enter Lodovico and Gratiano.

Cassio: What ho! No watch? No passage?° Murder! Murder!
Gratiano: 'Tis some mischance. The voice is very direful.
Cassio: O, help!   40
Lodovico: Hark!
Roderigo: O wretched villain!
Lodovico: Two or three groan. 'Tis heavy° night;
    These may be counterfeits. Let's think 't unsafe
    To come in to° the cry without more help.   45

[*They remain near the entrance.*]

Roderigo: Nobody come? Then shall I bleed to death.

Enter Iago [in his shirtsleeves, with a light].

Lodovico: Hark!
Gratiano: Here's one comes in his shirt, with light and weapons.
Iago: Who's there? Whose noise is this that cries on° murder?
Lodovico: We do not know.
Iago: Did not you hear a cry?   50
Cassio: Here, here! For heaven's sake, help me!
Iago: What's the matter?

[*He moves toward Cassio.*]

Gratiano [*to Lodovico*]: This is Othello's ancient, as I take it.
Lodovico [*to Gratiano*]: The same indeed, a very valiant fellow.
Iago [*to Cassio*]: What° are you here that cry so grievously?
Cassio: Iago? O, I am spoiled,° undone by villains!   55
    Give me some help.
Iago: O me, Lieutenant! What villains have done this?
Cassio: I think that one of them is hereabout,
    And cannot make° away.
Iago: O treacherous villains!

[*To Lodovico and Gratiano.*]

    What are you there? Come in, and give some help.   60

34 *Minion* hussy (i.e., Desdemona)   35 *hies* hastens on   36 *Forth of* from out   38 *passage* people passing by   43 *heavy* thick, dark   45 *come in to* approach   49 *cries on* cries out   54 *What*
who (also at lines 60 and 66)   55 *spoiled* ruined, done for   59 *make* get

[They advance.]
Roderigo: O, help me there!
Cassio: That's one of them.
Iago: O murderous slave! O villain!

[He stabs Roderigo.]

Roderigo: O damned Iago! O inhuman dog!
Iago: Kill men i' the dark?—Where be these bloody thieves?—
        How silent is this town!—Ho! Murder, murder!—   65
        [To Lodovico and Gratiano.] What may you be? Are you of good or evil?
Lodovico: As you shall prove us, praise° us.
Iago: Signor Lodovico?
Lodovico: He, sir.
Iago: I cry you mercy.° Here's Cassio hurt by villains.   70
Gratiano: Cassio?
Iago: How is 't, brother?
Cassio: My leg is cut in two.
Iago: Marry, heaven forbid!
        Light, gentlemen! I'll bind it with my shirt.   75

[He hands them the light, and tends to Cassio's wound.]

Enter Bianca.

Bianca: What is the matter, ho? Who is 't that cried?
Iago: Who is 't that cried?
Bianca: O my dear Cassio!
        My sweet Cassio! O Cassio, Cassio, Cassio!
Iago: O notable strumpet! Cassio, may you suspect
        Who they should be that have thus mangled you?   80
Cassio: No.
Gratiano: I am sorry to find you thus. I have been to seek you.
Iago: Lend me a garter. *[He applies a tourniquet.]* So.—O, for a chair,°
        To bear him easily hence!
Bianca: Alas, he faints! O Cassio, Cassio, Cassio!   85
Iago: Gentlemen all, I do suspect this trash
        To be a party in this injury.—
        Patience awhile, good Cassio.—Come, come;
        Lend me a light.   *[He shines the light on Roderigo.]*
                    Know we this face or no?
        Alas, my friend and my dear countryman   90
        Roderigo! No.—Yes, sure.—O heaven! Roderigo!

---

67 *praise* appraise   70 *I cry you mercy* I beg your pardon   83 *chair* litter

Gratiano: What, of Venice?

Iago: Even he, sir. Did you know him?

Gratiano: Know him? Ay.

Iago: Signor Gratiano? I cry your gentle° pardon.   95
These bloody accidents° must excuse my manners
That so neglected you.

Gratiano: I am glad to see you.

Iago: How do you, Cassio? O, a chair, a chair!

Gratiano: Roderigo!

Iago: He, he, 'tis he. [*A litter is brought in.*] O, that's well said;° the chair.   100
Some good man bear him carefully from hence;
I'll fetch the General's surgeon. [*To Bianca.*] For you, mistress,
Save you your labor.°—He that lies slain here, Cassio,
Was my dear friend. What malice° was between you?

Cassio: None in the world, nor do I know the man.   105

Iago [*to Bianca*]: What, look you pale?—O, bear him out o' th' air.°

   [*Cassio and Roderigo are borne off.*]

Stay you,° good gentlemen.—Look you pale, mistress?—
Do you perceive the gastness° of her eye?—
Nay, if you stare,° we shall hear more anon.—
Behold her well; I pray you, look upon her.   110
Do you see, gentlemen? Nay, guiltiness
Will speak, though tongues were out of use.

   [*Enter Emilia.*]

Emilia: 'Las, what's the matter? What's the matter, husband?

Iago: Cassio hath here been set on in the dark
By Roderigo and fellows that are scaped.   115
He's almost slain, and Roderigo dead.

Emilia: Alas, good gentleman! Alas, good Cassio!

Iago: This is the fruits of whoring. Prithee, Emilia,
Go know° of Cassio where he supped tonight.
[*To Bianca.*] What, do you shake at that?   120

Bianca: He supped at my house, but I therefore shake not.

Iago: O, did he so? I charge you go with me.

Emilia: O, fie upon thee, strumpet!

Bianca: I am no strumpet, but of life as honest°
As you that thus abuse me.   125

---

95 *gentle* noble 96 *accidents* sudden events 100 *well said* well done 103 *Save . . . labor*
i.e., never you mind tending Cassio 104 *malice* enmity 106 *bear . . . air* (Fresh air was
thought to be dangerous for a wound.) 107 *Stay you* (Lodovico and Gratiano are evidently
about to leave.) 108 *gastness* terror 109 *stare* (Iago pretends to interpret Bianca's wild
looks as an involuntary confession of guilt.) 119 *know* learn 124 *honest* chaste

Emilia: As I? Faugh! Fie upon thee!
Iago: Kind gentlemen, let's go see poor Cassio dressed.°—
    Come, mistress, you must tell's another tale.
    Emilia, run you to the citadel
    And tell my lord and lady what hath happed.—   130
    Will you go on afore? [*Aside.*] This is the night
    That either makes me or fordoes° me quite.   *Exeunt.*

SCENE II [A BEDCHAMBER IN THE CITADEL.]

> *Enter Othello* [*with a light*], *and Desdemona in her bed.*°

Othello: It is the cause,° it is the cause, my soul.
    Let me not name it to you, you chaste stars!
    It is the cause. Yet I'll not shed her blood,
    Nor scar that whiter skin of hers than snow,
    And smooth as monumental° alabaster.   5
    Yet she must die, else she'll betray more men.
    Put out the light, and then put out the light.°
    If I quench thee, thou flaming minister,°
    I can again thy former light restore,
    Should I repent me;° but once put out thy light,   10
    Thou cunning'st pattern° of excelling nature,
    I know not where is that Promethean heat°
    That can thy light relume.° When I have plucked thy rose,
    I cannot give it vital growth again;
    It needs must wither. I'll smell thee on the tree.   15

    [*He kisses her.*]

    O balmy breath, that dost almost persuade
    Justice to break her sword! One more, one more.
    Be thus when thou art dead, and I will kill thee,
    And love thee after. One more, and that's the last.

    [*He kisses her.*]

    So sweet was ne'er so fatal. I must weep,   20
    But they are cruel° tears. This sorrow's heavenly;

---

127 *Cassio dressed* Cassio's wounds dressed   132 *fordoes* undoes, ruins.   s.d. *in her bed* (Either the curtains are drawn back to reveal the bed in a recessed area backstage, or the bed is "thrust out" onstage as the scene begins.)   1 *cause* i.e., cause of justice, the offense itself, which Othello must correct as an agent of justice   5 *monumental* i.e., used in making tombs and funeral monuments   7 *the light . . . light* the torch or lamp . . . Desdemona's life   8 *flaming minister* torch or lamp that serves me   10 *repent me* change my mind   11 *Thou . . . pattern* you skillfully wrought perfect example   12 *Promethean heat* divine fire. (Alluding to the theft of fire from heaven by Prometheus.)   13 *relume* rekindle   21 *cruel* unrelenting

Othello asks if Desdemona has confessed all her crimes (V, ii, 31–55).

It strikes where it doth love.° She wakes.
Desdemona: Who's there? Othello?
Othello: Ay, Desdemona.
Desdemona: Will you come to bed, my lord?   25
Othello: Have you prayed tonight, Desdemon?
Desdemona: Ay, my lord.
Othello: If you bethink yourself of any crime°
    Unreconciled as yet to heaven and grace,
    Solicit° for it straight.°   30
Desdemona: Alack, my lord, what may you mean by that?
Othello: Well, do it, and be brief. I will walk by.
    I would not kill thy unpreparèd spirit.
    No, heaven forfend!° I would not kill thy soul.
Desdemona: Talk you of killing?
Othello: Ay, I do.
Desdemona: Then heaven   35
    Have mercy on me!
Othello: Amen, with all my heart!
Desdemona: If you say so, I hope you will not kill me.

22 *It . . . love* (Compare Hebrews 12:6: "For whom the Lord loveth he chasteneth.")
28 *crime* sin   30 *Solicit* petition, pray.   *straight* immediately   34 *forfend* forbid

Othello: Humh!
Desdemona: And yet I fear you; for you're fatal then
    When your eyes roll so. Why I should fear I know not,   40
    Since guiltiness I know not; but yet I feel I fear.
Othello: Think on thy sins.
Desdemona: They are loves I bear to you.°
Othello: Ay, and for that thou diest.
Desdemona: That death's unnatural that kills for loving.
    Alas, why gnaw you so your nether lip?   45
    Some bloody passion shakes your very frame.
    These are portents; but yet I hope, I hope,
    They do not point on° me.
Othello: Peace, and be still!
Desdemona: I will so. What's the matter?   50
Othello: That handkerchief which I so loved and gave thee
    Thou gav'st to Cassio.
Desdemona: No, by my life and soul!
    Send for the man and ask him.
Othello: Sweet soul, take heed, take heed of perjury.
    Thou art on thy deathbed.   55
Desdemona: Ay, but not yet to die.
Othello: Yes, presently.°
    Therefore confess thee freely of thy sin;
    For to deny each article with oath
    Cannot remove nor choke the strong conception°
    That I do groan withal.° Thou art to die.   60
Desdemona: Then Lord have mercy on me!
Othello: I say, amen.
Desdemona: And have you mercy too! I never did
    Offend° you in my life; never loved Cassio
    But with such general warranty° of heaven
    As I might love. I never gave him token.   65
Othello: By heaven, I saw my handkerchief in 's hand.
    O perjured woman! Thou dost stone° my heart,
    And makes me call what I intend to do
    A murder, which I thought a sacrifice.
    I saw the handkerchief.
Desdemona: He found it, then.   70
    I never gave it him. Send for him hither;
    Let him confess a truth.

---

42 *They are . . . you* i.e., if I sinned, it was in loving you more than my father or more
than God   48 *point on* point at, predict what is to happen to   56 *presently* immediately   59
conception (1) belief in your guilt (2) plan in my mind   60 *groan withal* (1) groan at in sorrow (2) as in giving birth   63 *Offend* wrong   64 *warranty* sanction   67 *stone* turn to stone,
harden

Othello: He hath confessed.
Desdemona: What, my lord?
Othello: That he hath used thee.
Desdemona: How? Unlawfully?
Othello: Ay.
Desdemona: He will not say so.
Othello: No, his mouth is stopped;   75
   Honest Iago hath ta'en order° for 't.
Desdemona: O, my fear interprets. What, is he dead?
Othello: Had all his hairs been lives, my great revenge
   Had stomach for them all.
Desdemona: Alas, he is betrayed and I undone!   [*She weeps.*]   80
Othello: Out, strumpet! Weep'st thou for him to my face?
Desdemona: O, banish me, my lord, but kill me not!
Othello: Down, strumpet!
Desdemona: Kill me tomorrow; let me live tonight!
Othello: Nay, if you strive—   85
Desdemona: But half an hour!
Othello: Being done,° there is no pause.
Desdemona: But while I say one prayer!
Othello: It is too late.

   Smothers her.

Emilia [*at the door*]: My lord, my lord! What, ho! My lord, my lord!
Othello: What noise is this? Not dead? Not yet quite dead?
   I that am cruel am yet merciful;   90
   I would not have thee linger in thy pain.

   [*He dispatches her.*]

                                  So, so.
Emilia [*within*]: What, ho! My lord, my lord!
Othello: Who's there?
Emilia [*within*]: O, good my lord, I would speak a word with you!
Othello: Yes, 'tis Emilia.—By and by.—She's dead.
   'Tis like° she comes to speak of Cassio's death.—   95
   The noise was here.° Ha! No more moving?
   Still as the grave. Shall she come in? Were 't good?—
   I think she stirs again. No. What's best to do?
   If she come in, she'll sure speak to my wife.
   My wife! My wife! What wife? I have no wife.   100

---

76 *ta'en order* taken measures   86 *Being done* i.e., since justice has begun its relentless
course   95 *like* likely that   96 *here* (The Folio's *high* is possible, suggesting that the commotion of the attack on Cassio was loud.)

"It is too late" (V, ii, 87).

O, insupportable! O heavy hour!
Methinks it should be now a huge eclipse
Of sun and moon, and that th' affrighted globe
Should yawn° at alteration.°
Emilia [within]:   I do beseech you
That I may speak with you, O, good my lord!   105
Othello: I had forgot thee. O, come in, Emilia.—
Soft,° by and by. Let me the curtains draw.—

[*He closes the bed-curtains and opens the door.*]

Where art thou?

Enter Emilia.

                    What's the matter with thee now?
Emilia: O, my good lord, yonder's foul murders done!
Othello: What, now?   110
Emilia: But now, my lord.

---

104 *yawn* gape in amazement, i.e., move in an earthquake. (According to Pliny, earth-
quakes often happen during eclipses.) *at alteration* at these cataclysmic events in nature,
well suited to express the horror of Desdemona's death   107 *Soft* wait a minute   112 *error*
aberration, irregularity

Othello: It is the very error° of the moon;
    She comes more nearer earth than she was wont,
    And makes men mad.
Emilia: Cassio, my lord, hath killed a young Venetian   115
    Called Roderigo.
Othello: Roderigo killed?
    And Cassio killed?
Emilia: No, Cassio is not killed.
Othello: Not Cassio killed? Then murder's out of tune,
    And sweet revenge grows harsh.
Desdemona: O, falsely, falsely murdered!   120
Emilia: O Lord, what cry is that?
Othello: That? What?
Emilia: Out° and alas, that was my lady's voice.

    [*She opens the bed-curtains.*]

    Help, help, ho, help! O lady, speak again!
    Sweet Desdemona! O sweet mistress, speak!   125
Desdemona: A guiltless death I die.
Emilia: O, who hath done this deed?
Desdemona: Nobody; I myself. Farewell.
    Commend me to my kind lord. O, farewell!   [*She dies.*]
Othello: Why, how should she be murdered?
Emilia: Alas, who knows?   130
Othello: You heard her say herself it was not I.
Emilia: She said so. I must needs report the truth.
Othello: She's like a liar gone to burning hell!
    'Twas I that killed her.
Emilia: O, the more angel she,
    And you the blacker devil!   135
Othello: She turned to folly,° and she was a whore.
Emilia: Thou dost belie° her, and thou art a devil.
Othello: She was false as water.
Emilia: Thou art rash as fire to say
    That she was false. O, she was heavenly true!   140
Othello: Cassio did top her. Ask thy husband else.°
    O, I were damned beneath all depth in hell
    But that I did proceed upon just grounds
    To this extremity. Thy husband knew it all.
Emilia: My husband?   145

123 *Out* (A cry of dismay, intensifying *alas*.) 136 *folly* i.e., wantonness, fleshly sin 137 *belie*
slander 141 *else* i.e., if you don't believe me

Othello: Thy husband.
Emilia: That she was false to wedlock?
Othello: Ay, with Cassio. Nay, had she been true,
    If heaven would make me such another world
    Of one entire and perfect chrysolite,°   150
    I'd not have sold her for it.
Emilia: My husband?
Othello: Ay, 'twas he that told me on her first.
    An honest man he is, and hates the slime
    That sticks on filthy deeds.   155
Emilia: My husband?
Othello: What needs this iterance,° woman? I say thy husband.
Emilia: O mistress, villainy hath made mocks with° love!
    My husband say that she was false?
Othello: He, woman;
    I say thy husband. Dost understand the word?   160
    My friend, thy husband, honest, honest Iago.
Emilia: If he say so, may his pernicious soul
    Rot half a grain a day! He lies to th' heart.
    She was too fond of her most filthy bargain.
Othello: Ha?   [*He draws.*] 165
Emilia: Do thy worst!
    This deed of thine is no more worthy heaven
    Than thou wast worthy her.
Othello: Peace, you were best.°
Emilia: Thou hast not half that power to do me harm
    As I have to be hurt.° O gull!° O dolt!   170
    As ignorant as dirt! Thou hast done a deed—
    I care not for thy sword; I'll make thee known,
    Though I lost twenty lives.—Help! Help, ho, help!
    The Moor hath killed my mistress! Murder, murder!

    Enter Montano, Gratiano, and Iago.

Montano: What is the matter? How now, General?   175
Emilia: O, are you come, Iago? You have done well,
    That men must lay their murders on your neck.
Gratiano: What is the matter?
Emilia [*to Iago*]: Disprove this villain, if thou be'st a man.
    He says thou toldst him that his wife was false.   180
    I know thou didst not; thou'rt not such a villain.

---

150 *chrysolite* precious topaz 157 *iterance* iteration, repetition 158 *made mocks with* derided, made sport of 168 *you were best* it would be best for you 170 *to be hurt* i.e., to endure hurt. *gull* dupe

Speak, for my heart is full.
Iago: I told him what I thought, and told no more
 Than what he found himself was apt° and true.
Emilia: But did you ever tell him she was false?   185
Iago: I did.
Emilia: You told a lie, an odious, damnèd lie!
 Upon my soul, a lie, a wicked lie.
 She false with Cassio? Did you say with Cassio?
Iago: With Cassio, mistress. Go to, charm° your tongue.   190
Emilia: I will not charm my tongue; I am bound to speak.
 My mistress here lies murdered in her bed—
All: O heavens forfend!
Emilia: And your reports have set the murder on.
Othello: Nay, stare not, masters. It is true indeed.   195
Gratiano: 'Tis a strange truth.
Montano: O monstrous act!
Emilia: Villainy, villainy, villainy!
 I think upon 't—I think I smell 't! O villainy!
 I thought so then°—I'll kill myself for grief—
 O villainy, villainy!   200
Iago: What, are you mad? I charge you, get you home.
Emilia: Good gentlemen, let me have leave to speak.
 'Tis proper I obey him, but not now.
 Perchance, Iago, I will ne'er go home.
Othello: O! O! O!   [*Othello falls on the bed.°*]
Emilia: Nay, lay thee down and roar,   205
 For thou hast killed the sweetest innocent
 That e'er did lift up eye.°
Othello [*rising*]:   O, she was foul!
 I scarce did know you, uncle. There lies your niece,
 Whose breath indeed these hands have newly stopped.
 I know this act shows° horrible and grim.   210
Gratiano: Poor Desdemon! I am glad thy father's dead.
 Thy match was mortal to him, and pure grief
 Shore his old thread° in twain. Did he live now,
 This sight would make him do a desperate turn,°
 Yea, curse his better angel from his side,   215
 And fall to reprobance.°

---

184 *apt* plausible   190 *charm* keep silent (as though by a magic spell)   199 *then* (Perhaps at III, iii, 331–332, and IV, ii, 137–154.)   205 s.d. *Othello . . . bed* (This direction is from the Quarto, as also *He kisses her* at line 19 and *She dies* at line 129.)   207 *lift up eye* i.e., lift her eyes to heaven   210 *shows* looks   213 *Shore . . . thread* sheared the thread of his old age (as Atropos, one of the three Fates, was thought to do)   214 *turn* deed   216 *reprobance* damnation, i.e., suicide

Othello: 'Tis pitiful. But yet Iago knows
　　That she with Cassio hath the act of shame
　　A thousand times committed. Cassio confessed it;
　　And she did gratify° his amorous works   220
　　With that recognizance° and pledge of love
　　Which I first gave her. I saw it in his hand;
　　It was a handkerchief, an antique token
　　My father gave my mother.
Emilia: O God! O heavenly God!   225
Iago: Zounds, hold your peace.
Emilia: 'Twill out, 'twill out! I peace?
　　No, I will speak as liberal as the north.°
　　Let heaven and men and devils, let them all,
　　All, all, cry shame against me, yet I'll speak.
Iago: Be wise, and get you home.
Emilia: I will not.

　　　[*Iago threatens Emilia.*]

Gratiano: Fie!   230
　　Your sword upon a woman?
Emilia: O thou dull Moor! That handkerchief thou speak'st of
　　I found by fortune and did give my husband;
　　For often, with a solemn earnestness,
　　More than indeed belonged° to such a trifle,   235
　　He begged of me to steal 't.
Iago: Villainous whore!
Emilia: She give it Cassio? No, alas! I found it,
　　And I did give 't my husband.
Iago: Filth, thou liest!
Emilia: By heaven, I do not, I do not, gentlemen.
　　O murderous coxcomb!° What should such a fool   240
　　Do with so good a wife?
Othello: Are there no stones° in heaven
　　But what serves for the thunder?—Precious° villain!

　　　[*He runs at Iago; Montano disarms Othello. Iago, from behind, stabs Emilia.°*]

Gratiano: The woman falls! Sure he hath killed his wife.
Emilia: Ay, ay. O, lay me by my mistress' side.   245

---

220 *gratify* reward   221 *recognizance* token   227 *liberal as the north* freely as the north wind
(blows)   235 *belonged* was appropriate   240 *coxcomb* fool. (Addressed to Othello.)   242
stones bolts, such as those used for thunderbolts   243 *Precious* i.e., arrant, utter.   s.d. *He . . .
Emilia* (The Quarto text reads, "The Moor runs at Iago. Iago kills his wife." The Quarto also
specifies the exit of Iago at line 245 and the death of Emilia at line 260.)

Exit [Iago.]

Gratiano: He's gone, but his wife's killed.
Montano: 'Tis a notorious villain. Take you this weapon,
  Which I have here recovered from the Moor.
  Come, guard the door without. Let him not pass,
  But kill him rather. I'll after that same villain,   250
  For 'tis a damnèd slave.

Exit [with all but Othello and Emilia, who has been laid by Desdemona's side].

Othello: I am not valiant neither,
  But every puny whipster° gets my sword.
  But why should honor° outlive honesty?°
  Let it go all.
Emilia: What did thy song bode, lady?   255
  Hark, canst thou hear me? I will play the swan,
  And die in music. [*She sings.*] "Willow, willow, willow."
  Moor, she was chaste. She loved thee, cruel Moor.
  So come my soul to bliss as I speak true.
  So speaking as I think, alas, I die.   [*She dies.*] 260
Othello: I have another weapon in this chamber;
  It was a sword of Spain, the ice-brook's temper°—
  O, here it is. [*He finds a sword.*] Uncle, I must come forth.
Gratiano [within]: If thou attempt it, it will cost thee dear.
  Thou hast no weapon, and perforce must suffer.   265
Othello: Look in upon me then and speak with me,
  Or, naked° as I am, I will assault thee.

[*Enter Gratiano.*]

Gratiano: What is the matter?
Othello: Behold, I have a weapon;
  A better never did itself sustain
  Upon a soldier's thigh. I have seen the day   270
  That, with this little arm and this good sword,
  I have made my way through more impediments
  Than twenty times your stop.° But O, vain boast!
  Who can control his fate? 'Tis not so now.
  Be not afraid, though you do see me weaponed;   275
  Here is my journey's end, here is my butt°
  And very seamark° of my utmost sail.

---

253 *whipster* contemptible fellow (one who is always ready to whip out his sword)   254 *honor* i.e., the bravery for which one enjoys a soldier's reputation.   *honesty* true integrity   262 *the icebrook's temper* tempered in ice-cold water   267 *naked* unarmed   273 *stop* power (to stop)   276 *butt* goal, limit. (An archery term.)   277 *seamark* beacon (marking his destination or limit)

**"O Desdemon! Dead, Desdemon!
Dead! O! O!" (V, ii, 290).**

[*Gratiano steps back.*]

Do you go back dismayed? 'Tis a lost° fear;
Man but a rush° against Othello's breast
And he retires. Where should Othello go?   280

[*He turns to Desdemona.*]

Now, how dost thou look now? O ill-starred wench!
Pale as thy smock! When we shall meet at compt,°
This look of thine will hurl my soul from heaven,
And fiends will snatch at it. Cold, cold, my girl?
Even like thy chastity. O cursèd, cursèd slave!°   285
Whip me, ye devils,
From the possession of this heavenly sight!
Blow me about in winds! Roast me in sulfur!
Wash me in steep-down gulfs of liquid fire!
O Desdemon! Dead, Desdemon! Dead! O! O!   290

*Enter Lodovico, Cassio [carried in a litter°], Montano, and Iago [prisoner],
with officers.*

Lodovico: Where is this rash and most unfortunate man?

278 *lost* wasted, unneeded 279 *Man . . . rush* wield no more than a reed 282 *compt* account, judgment day 285 *slave* i.e., Othello himself 290 s.d. *in a litter* (The Quarto specifies that Cassio is "in a chair.")

Iago is taken prisoner and his plots are exposed (V, ii, 293–347).

Othello: That's he that was Othello. Here I am.
Lodovico: Where is that viper? Bring the villain forth.

[*Iago is led forward.*]

Othello: I look down towards his feet;° but that's a fable.
If that thou be'st a devil, I cannot kill thee.   295

[*He wounds Iago.*]

Lodovico: Wrench his sword from him.   [*Othello is disarmed.*]
Iago: I bleed, sir, but not killed.
Othello: I am not sorry neither. I'd have thee live,
For in my sense° 'tis happiness to die.
Lodovico: O thou Othello, that was once so good,
Fall'n in the practice° of a cursèd slave,°   300
What shall be said to thee?
Othello: Why, anything.

294 *towards his feet* i.e., to see if they are cloven, as the devil's are fabled to be   298 *in my sense* to one who feels as I do   300 *in the practice* through the plotting, into the snare.   *slave* villain

    An honorable murderer, if you will,
    For naught I did in hate, but all in honor.
Lodovico: This wretch hath part confessed his villainy.
    Did you and he consent° in Cassio's death?   305
Othello: Ay.
Cassio: Dear General, I never gave you cause.
Othello: I do believe it, and I ask your pardon.
    Will you, I pray, demand that demi-devil
    Why he hath thus ensnared my soul and body?   310
Iago: Demand me nothing. What you know, you know.
    From this time forth I never will speak word.
Lodovico: What, not to pray?
Gratiano: Torments° will ope your lips.
Othello: Well, thou dost best.   315
Lodovico: Sir, you shall understand what hath befall'n,
    Which, as I think, you know not. Here is a letter
    Found in the pocket of the slain Roderigo;
    And here another. [*He produces letters.*] The one of them imports
    The death of Cassio, to be undertook   320
    By Roderigo.
Othello: O villain!
Cassio: Most heathenish and most gross!°
Lodovico [*showing another paper*]: Now here's another discontented° paper
    Found in his pocket too. And this, it seems,
    Roderigo meant t' have sent this damnèd villain;   325
    But that belike° Iago in the interim
    Came in and satisfied him.°
Othello: O thou pernicious caitiff!—
    How came you, Cassio, by that handkerchief
    That was my wife's?
Cassio: I found it in my chamber;   330
    And he himself confessed but even now
    That there he dropped it for a special purpose
    Which wrought to his desire.°
Othello: O fool, fool, fool!
Cassio: There is besides in Roderigo's letter
    How he upbraids Iago, that he made him   335
    Brave° me upon the watch, whereon it came°
    That I was cast;° and even but now he spake,

---

305 *consent* agree   314 *Torments* torture   322 *gross* monstrous   323 *discontented* full of discontent   326 *belike* most likely   327 *Came . . . him* interposed and gave him satisfactory explanation   333 *wrought . . . desire* worked out as he wished, fitted in with his plan   336 *Brave* defy. *whereon it came* whereof it came about   337 *cast* dismissed

After long seeming dead, Iago hurt him,
Iago set him on.
Lodovico [to Othello]: You must forsake this room and go with us. 340
Your power and your command is taken off,°
And Cassio rules in Cyprus. For this slave,
If there be any cunning cruelty
That can torment him much and hold him long,°
It shall be his. You shall close prisoner rest° 345
Till that the nature of your fault be known
To the Venetian state.—Come, bring away.
Othello: Soft you;° a word or two before you go.
I have done the state some service, and they know 't.
No more of that. I pray you, in your letters, 350
When you shall these unlucky° deeds relate,
Speak of me as I am; nothing extenuate,
Nor set down aught in malice. Then must you speak
Of one that loved not wisely but too well;
Of one not easily jealous but, being wrought,° 355
Perplexed° in the extreme; of one whose hand,
Like the base Indian,° threw a pearl away
Richer than all his tribe; of one whose subdued° eyes,
Albeit unusèd to the melting mood,
Drop tears as fast as the Arabian trees 360
Their medicinable gum.° Set you down this;
And say besides that in Aleppo once,
Where a malignant and a turbaned Turk
Beat a Venetian and traduced the state,
I took by th' throat the circumcisèd dog 365
And smote him, thus.   [*He stabs himself.*°]
Lodovico: O bloody period!°
Gratiano: All that is spoke is marred.
Othello: I kissed thee ere I killed thee. No way but this,
Killing myself, to die upon a kiss. 370

[*He kisses Desdemona and dies.*]

Cassio: This did I fear, but thought he had no weapon;

---

341 *taken off* taken away   344 *hold him long* keep him alive a long time (during his torture)   345 *rest* remain   348 *Soft you* one moment   351 *unlucky* unfortunate   355 *wrought* worked upon, worked into a frenzy   356 *Perplexed* distraught   357 *Indian* (This reading from the Quarto pictures an ignorant savage who cannot recognize the value of a precious jewel. The Folio reading, *Iudean* or *Judean*, i.e., infidel or disbeliever, may refer to Herod, who slew Miriamne in a fit of jealousy, or to Judas Iscariot, the betrayer of Christ.)   358 *subdued* i.e., overcome by grief   361 *gum* i.e., myrr   366 s.d. *He stabs himself* (This direction is in the Quarto text.)   367 *period* termination, conclusion

For he was great of heart.
Lodovico [to Iago]:   O Spartan dog,°
More fell° than anguish, hunger, or the sea!
Look on the tragic loading of this bed.
This is thy work. The object poisons sight;   375
Let it be hid.° Gratiano, keep° the house,

[*The bed curtains are drawn.*]

And seize upon° the fortunes of the Moor,
For they succeed on° you. [*To Cassio.*] To you, Lord Governor,
Remains the censure° of this hellish villain,
The time, the place, the torture. O, enforce it!   380
Myself will straight aboard, and to the state
This heavy act with heavy heart relate.   *Exeunt.*

Questions

ACT I

1. What is Othello's position in society? How is he regarded by those who know him? By his own words, when we first meet him in Scene ii, what traits of character does he manifest?

2. How do you account for Brabantio's dismay on learning of his daughter's marriage, despite the fact that Desdemona has married a man so generally honored and admired?

3. What is Iago's view of human nature? In his fondness for likening men to animals (as in I, i, 49–50; I, i, 90–91; and I, iii, 385–386), what does he tell us about himself?

4. What reasons does Iago give for his hatred of Othello?

5. In Othello's defense before the senators (Scene iii), how does he explain Desdemona's gradual falling in love with him?

6. Is Brabantio's warning to Othello (I, iii, 293–294) an accurate or an inaccurate prophecy?

7. By what strategy does Iago enlist Roderigo in his plot against the Moor? In what lines do we learn Iago's true feelings toward Roderigo?

ACT II

1. What do the Cypriots think of Othello? Do their words (in Scene i) make him seem to us a lesser man or a larger one?

2. What cruelty does Iago display toward Emilia? How well founded is his distrust of his wife's fidelity?

3. In II, iii, 221, Othello speaks of Iago's "honesty and love." How do you account for Othello's being so totally deceived?

372 *Spartan dog* (Spartan dogs were noted for their savagery and silence.)
373 *fell* cruel   376 *Let it be hid* i.e., draw the bed curtains. (No stage direction specifies that the dead are to be carried offstage at the end of the play.)   *keep* remain in   377 *seize upon* take legal possession of   378 *succeed on* pass as though by inheritance to   379 *censure* sentencing

4. For what major events does the merrymaking (proclaimed in Scene ii) give opportunity?

ACT III

1. Trace the steps by which Iago rouses Othello to suspicion. Is there anything in Othello's character or circumstances that renders him particularly susceptible to Iago's wiles?
2. In III, iv, 49–98, Emilia knows of Desdemona's distress over the lost handkerchief. At this moment, how do you explain her failure to relieve Desdemona's mind? Is Emilia aware of her husband's villainy?

ACT IV

1. In this act, what circumstantial evidence is added to Othello's case against Desdemona?
2. How plausible do you find Bianca's flinging the handkerchief at Cassio just when Othello is looking on? How important is the handkerchief in this play? What does it represent? What suggestions or hints do you find in it?
3. What prevents Othello from being moved by Desdemona's appeal (IV, ii, 33–92)?
4. When Roderigo grows impatient with Iago (IV, ii, 181–205), how does Iago make use of his fellow plotter's discontent?
5. What does the conversation between Emilia and Desdemona (Scene iii) tell us about the nature of each?
6. In this act, what scenes (or speeches) contain memorable dramatic irony?

ACT V

1. Summarize the events that lead to Iago's unmasking.
2. How does Othello's mistaken belief that Cassio is slain (V, i, 27–34) affect the outcome of the play?
3. What is Iago's motive in stabbing Roderigo?
4. In your interpretation of the play, exactly what impels Othello to kill Desdemona? Jealousy? Desire for revenge? Excess idealism? A wish to be a public avenger who punishes, "else she'll betray more men"?
5. What do you understand by Othello's calling himself "one that loved not wisely but too well" (V, ii, 354)?
6. In your view, does Othello's long speech in V, ii, 348–366 succeed in restoring his original dignity and nobility? Do you agree with Cassio (V, ii, 372) that Othello was "great of heart"?

General Questions

1. What motivates Iago to carry out his schemes? Do you find him a devil incarnate, a madman, or a rational human being?
2. Whom besides Othello does Iago deceive? What is Desdemona's opinion of him? Emilia's? Cassio's (before Iago is found out)? To what do you attribute Iago's success as a deceiver?
3. How essential to the play is the fact that Othello is a black man, a Moor, and not a native of Venice?

4. In the introduction to his edition of the play in *The Complete Signet Classic Shakespeare*, Alvin Kernan remarks:

    > *Othello* is probably the most neatly, the most formally constructed of Shakespeare's plays. Every character is, for example, balanced by another similar or contrasting character. Desdemona is balanced by her opposite, Iago; love and concern for others at one end of the scale, hatred and concern for self at the other.

    Besides Desdemona and Iago, what other pairs of characters strike balances?

5. Consider any passage of the play in which there is a shift from verse to prose, or from prose to verse. What is the effect of this shift?

6. Indicate a passage that you consider memorable for its poetry. Does the passage seem introduced for its own sake? Does it in any way advance the action of the play, express theme, or demonstrate character?

7. Does the play contain any tragic *recognition*—as discussed in Chapter 25, a moment of terrible enlightenment, a "realization of the unthinkable"?

8. Does the downfall of Othello proceed from any flaw in his nature, or is his downfall entirely the work of Iago?

▪ WRITING *effectively*

UNDERSTANDING SHAKESPEARE

The basic problem a modern reader faces with Shakespeare is language. Shakespeare's English is now four hundred years old, and it differs in innumerable small ways from contemporary American English. Although Shakespeare's idiom may at first seem daunting, it is easily mastered if you make the effort. To grow comfortable with his language, you must immerse yourself in it. Fortunately, doing so isn't all that hard; you might even find it pleasurable.

▪ **Let your ears do the work.** There is no substitute for hearing Shakespeare's words in performance. After all, the plays were written to be seen, not to be read silently on the page. After reading the play, listen to or watch a recording of it. It sometimes helps to read along as you listen or watch, hitting the pause button as needed. If you can attend a live performance of any Shakespearean play, do so.

▪ **But read the text first.** Watching a production is never a full substitute for reading an assigned play. Many productions abridge the play, leaving passages out. Even more important, directors and actors choose a particular interpretation of a play, and their choices might skew your understanding of events and motivation if you are unfamiliar with the original itself.

■ **Before you write a paper, read the play again.** The first time through an Elizabethan-era text, you will almost certainly miss many things. As you grow more familiar with Shakespeare's language, you will be able to read it with greater comprehension. If you choose to write about a particular episode or character, carefully study the speeches and dialogue in question (and pay special attention to the footnotes) so that you understand each word.

■ **Enjoy yourself.** From Beijing to Berlin, Buenos Aires to Oslo, Shakespeare is almost universally acknowledged as the world's greatest playwright, a master entertainer as well as a consummate artist.

CHECKLIST: Writing About Shakespeare

☐ Read closely. Work through passages with difficult language.

☐ Pay special attention to footnotes.

☐ Read the play more than once if necessary.

☐ Watch a DVD or listen to an audio recording after reading a play. Immerse yourself in Shakespeare's language until it becomes familiar.

☐ As you view or listen to a play, read along, or revisit the text afterward.

☐ Carefully study any speeches and dialogue you choose to write about.

☐ Be sure you understand each word of any passage you decide to discuss or quote.

TOPICS FOR WRITING ON SHAKESPEARE

1. Write a defense of Iago.

2. "Never was any play fraught, like this of *Othello*, with improbabilities," wrote Thomas Rymer in a famous attack (*A Short View of Tragedy*, 1692). Consider Rymer's objection to the play, either answering it or finding evidence to back it up.

3. Suppose yourself a casting director assigned to a film version of *Othello*. What well-known actors would you cast in the principal roles? Write a report justifying your choices. Don't merely discuss the stars and their qualifications; discuss (with specific reference to the play) what Shakespeare appears to call for.

4. Emilia's long speech at the end of Act IV (iii, 84–103) has been called a Renaissance plea for women's rights. Do you agree? Write a brief, close analysis of this speech. How timely is it?

5. "The downfall of Oedipus is the work of the gods; the downfall of Othello is self-inflicted." Test this comment with reference to the two plays, and report your findings.

6. In what respects does *Hamlet* resemble a classical tragedy, such as *Oedipus the King*? In what ways is Shakespeare's play different? Is Hamlet, like Oedipus, driven to his death by some inexorable force (Fate, the gods, the nature of things)?

7. Write a defense of Hamlet's uncle, Claudius.

8. "Hamlet is a mentally unstable young man who is obsessed with his father's death. He is angry at his mother for remarrying so quickly. The Ghost is not real. It is only a projection of the Prince's deranged imagination." Write an essay to support or refute this argument. Use specific incidents in the play to back up your position.

27 THE MODERN THEATER

What You Will Learn in This Chapter

■ To identify and define *realism* as a dramatic mode

■ To describe the stagecraft developments of modern theater

■ To analyze classic works of modern theater

REALISM

The ancient art of the drama experienced a revival in the Renaissance and went through a number of changes over the next several centuries. The Elizabethan drama was marked by strong characterization, heightened and intense language, and crowded, sometimes sprawling plots. In the neoclassical period of the seventeenth and eighteenth centuries, greater emphasis was placed upon formality, decorum, and Aristotle's unities of time, place, and action. The early nineteenth century saw the rise of melodrama, with its florid dialogue, plots that relied heavily on often absurd coincidences, and crude stereotypes of good and evil characters. Through all these developments—from kings and generals to lords and ladies of high society to purehearted swashbucklers and craven villains—the one thing that seemed to remain constant was an absence of **realism**—the attempt to reproduce faithfully the surface appearance of life, especially that of ordinary people in everyday situations.

By the end of the nineteenth century, however, realism had become the drama's dominant mode. The writer most responsible for that shift was the Norwegian playwright Henrik Ibsen. From *Pillars of Society* (1877) to *Hedda Gabler* (1890), he wrote a series of prose dramas in which realistically portrayed middle-class characters face conflicts in their lives and relationships. They are often called "problem plays" because of their engagement of social issues, such as women's place in society (*A Doll's House*) and inherited venereal disease (*Ghosts*). In actuality, the social problems in these plays serve as a context for Ibsen's real concern, an examination of the complexities of human personality and psychology, especially those aspects of our natures that are hidden or repressed because of society's expectations.

Conventions of Realism

From Italian playhouses of the sixteenth century, the theater had inherited the **picture-frame stage**: a structure that holds the action within a **proscenium arch**, a gateway standing (as the word *proscenium* indicates) "in front of the scenery." This manner of constructing a playhouse in effect divided the actors from their audience; most commercial theaters even today are so constructed. But as the nineteenth century gave way to the twentieth, actors less often declaimed their passions in oratorical style in front of backdrops painted with waterfalls and volcanoes, while stationed exactly at the center of the stage as if to sing "duets meant to bring forth applause" (as Swedish playwright August Strindberg complained).

In the theater of Realism, a room was represented by a **box set**— three walls that joined in two corners and a ceiling that tilted as if seen in perspective—replacing drapery walls that had billowed and doors that had flapped, not slammed. Instead of posing at stage center and directly facing the audience to deliver key speeches, actors were instructed to speak from wherever the dramatic situation placed them, and now and then even to turn their backs upon the audience. They were to behave as if they were in a room with the fourth wall sliced away, unaware that they had an audience.

To encourage actors further to imitate reality, the influential director Constantin Stanislavsky of the Moscow Art Theater developed his famous system to help actors feel at home inside a playwright's characters. One of Stanislavsky's exercises was to have actors search their memories for personal experiences like those of the characters in the play; another was to have them act out things a character did *not* do in the play but might do in life. The system enabled Stanislavsky to bring authenticity to his productions of Chekhov's plays and of Maxim Gorky's *The Lower Depths* (1902), a play that showed the tenants of a sordid lodging house drinking themselves to death (and hanging themselves) in surroundings of realistic squalor. Stanislavsky's techniques are still used by stage and film actors today.

One of the pioneering works of Realism is Henrik Ibsen's *A Doll's House*. The play derives a good deal of its power from our ability to identify with its characters and the lives they live, an identification that Ibsen achieves in part by framing the action with the details of daily existence.

Henrik Ibsen

A Doll's House   1879

Translated by R. Farquharson Sharp
Revised by Viktoria Michelsen

Henrik Ibsen (1828–1906) was born in Skien, a seaport in Norway. When he was six, his father's business losses suddenly reduced his wealthy family to poverty. After a brief attempt to study medicine, young Ibsen worked as a stage manager in provincial Bergen; then, becoming known as a playwright, he moved to Oslo as artistic director of the National Theater—practical experiences that gained him firm grounding in his craft. Discouraged when his theater failed and the king turned down his plea for a grant to enable him to write, Ibsen left Norway and for twenty-seven years lived in Italy and Germany. There, in his middle years (1879–1891), he wrote most of his famed plays about small-town life, among them A Doll's House, Ghosts, An Enemy of the People, The Wild Duck, and Hedda Gabler. Introducing social problems to the stage, these plays aroused storms of controversy. Although best known as a Realist, Ibsen early in his career wrote poetic dramas based on Norwegian history and folklore: the tragedy Brand (1866) and the powerful, wildly fantastic Peer Gynt (1867). He ended as a Symbolist in John Gabriel Borkman (1896) and When We Dead Awaken (1899), both encompassing huge mountains that heaven-assaulting heroes try to climb. Late in life Ibsen returned to Oslo, honored at last both at home and abroad.

Henrik Ibsen

CHARACTERS

Torvald Helmer, a lawyer
Nora, his wife
Doctor Rank
Mrs. Kristine Linde
Nils Krogstad
The Helmers' three young children
Anne Marie, their nursemaid
Helene, the maid
A Porter

The action takes place in the Helmers' apartment.

ACT I

The scene is a room furnished comfortably and tastefully, but not extravagantly. At the back wall, a door to the right leads to the entrance hall. Another to the left leads to Helmer's study. Between the doors there is a piano. In the middle of the left-hand wall is a door, and beyond it a window. Near the window are a round table, armchairs, and a small sofa. In the right-hand wall, at the farther end, is another door, and on the same side, nearer the footlights, a stove, two easy chairs and a rocking chair. Between the stove and the door there is a small table. There are engravings on the walls, a cabinet with china and other small objects, and a small bookcase with expensively bound books. The floors are carpeted, and a fire burns in the stove. It is winter.

A bell rings in the hall. A moment later, we hear the door being opened. Enter Nora, humming a tune and in high spirits. She is wearing a hat and coat and carries a number of packages, which she puts down on the table to the right. She leaves

The 1896 production of *A Doll's House* at the Empire Theatre in New York.

the outer door open behind her. *Through the door we see a porter who is carrying a Christmas tree and a basket, which he gives to the maid, who has opened the door.*

Nora: Hide the Christmas tree carefully, Helene. Make sure the children don't see it till it's decorated this evening. (*To the Porter, taking out her purse.*) How much?
Porter: Fifty ore.
Nora: Here's a krone. No, keep the change.

(*The Porter thanks her and goes out. Nora shuts the door. She is laughing to herself as she takes off her hat and coat. She takes a bag of macaroons from her pocket and eats one or two, then goes cautiously to the door of her husband's study and listens.*)

Yes, he's there. (*Still humming, she goes to the table on the right.*)

Helmer (*calls out from his study*): Is that my little lark twittering out there?
Nora (*busy opening some of the packages*): Yes, it is!
Helmer: Is it my little squirrel bustling around?
Nora: Yes!
Helmer: When did my squirrel come home?

The 2009 adaptation of *A Doll's House* at the Donmar Warehouse in London, starring Gillian Anderson and Toby Stephens.

Nora: Just now. (*Puts the bag of macaroons into her pocket and wipes her mouth.*) Come in here, Torvald, and see what I bought.

Helmer: I'm very busy right now. (*A little later, he opens the door and looks into the room, pen in hand.*) Bought, did you say? All these things? Has my little spendthrift been wasting money again?

Nora: Yes, but, Torvald, this year we really can let ourselves go a little. This is the first Christmas that we don't have to watch every penny.

Helmer: Still, you know, we can't spend money recklessly.

Nora: Yes, Torvald, but we can be a little more reckless now, can't we? Just a tiny little bit! You're going to have a big salary and you'll be making lots and lots of money.

Helmer: Yes, after the New Year. But it'll still be a whole three months before the money starts coming in.

Nora: Pooh! We can borrow till then.

Helmer: Nora! (*Goes up to her and takes her playfully by the ear.*) The same little featherbrain! Just suppose that I borrowed a thousand kroner today, and you spent it all on Christmas, and then on New Year's Eve a roof tile fell on my head and killed me, and—

Nora (*putting her hand over his mouth*): Oh! Don't say such horrible things.

Helmer: Still, suppose that happened. What then?

Nora: If that happened, I don't suppose I'd care whether I owed anyone money or not.

Helmer: Yes, but what about the people who'd lent it to us?

Nora: Them? Who'd care about them? I wouldn't even know who they were.

Helmer: That's just like a woman! But seriously, Nora, you know how I feel about that. No debt, no borrowing. There can't be any freedom or beauty in a home life that depends on borrowing and debt. We two have managed to stay on the straight road so far, and we'll go on the same way for the short time that we still have to be careful.

Nora (moving towards the stove): As you wish, Torvald.

Helmer (following her): Now, now, my little skylark mustn't let her wings droop. What's the matter? Is my little squirrel sulking? (*Taking out his purse.*) Nora, what do you think I've got here?

Nora (turning round quickly): Money!

Helmer: There you are. (*Gives her some money.*) Do you think I don't know how much you need for the house at Christmastime?

Nora (counting): Ten, twenty, thirty, forty! Thank you, thank you, Torvald. That'll keep me going for a long time.

Helmer: It's going to have to.

Nora: Yes, yes, it will. But come here and let me show you what I bought. And all so cheap! Look, here's a new suit for Ivar, and a sword. And a horse and a trumpet for Bob. And a doll and doll's bed for Emmy. They're not the best, but she'll break them soon enough anyway. And here's dress material and handkerchiefs for the maids. Old Anne Marie really should have something nicer.

Helmer: And what's in this package?

Nora (crying out): No, no! You can't see that till this evening.

Helmer: If you say so. But now tell me, you extravagant little thing, what would you like for yourself?

Nora: For myself? Oh, I'm sure I don't want anything.

Helmer: But you must. Tell me something that you'd especially like to have— within reasonable limits.

Nora: No, I really can't think of anything. Unless, Torvald . . .

Helmer: Well?

Nora (playing with his coat buttons, and without raising her eyes to his): If you really want to give me something, you might . . . you might . . .

Helmer: Well, out with it!

Nora (speaking quickly): You might give me money, Torvald. Only just as much as you can afford. And then one of these days I'll buy something with it.

Helmer: But, Nora—

Nora: Oh, do! Dear Torvald, please, please do! Then I'll wrap it up in beautiful gold paper and hang it on the Christmas tree. Wouldn't that be fun?

Helmer: What do they call those little creatures that are always wasting money?

Nora: Spendthrifts. I know. Let's do as I suggest, Torvald, and then I'll have time to think about what I need most. That's a very sensible plan, isn't it?

Helmer (smiling): Yes, it is. That is, if you really did save some of the money I give you, and then really buy something for yourself. But if you spend it all on the housekeeping and all kinds of unnecessary things, then I just have to open my wallet all over again.

Nora: Oh, but, Torvald—

Helmer: You can't deny it, my dear little Nora. (*Puts his arm around her waist.*) She's a sweet little spendthrift, but she uses up a lot of money. One would hardly believe how expensive such little creatures are!

Nora: That's a terrible thing to say. I really do save all I can.

Helmer (laughing): That's true. All you can. But you can't save anything!

Nora (smiling quietly and happily): You have no idea how many bills skylarks and squirrels have, Torvald.

Helmer: You're an odd little soul. Just like your father. You always find some new way of wheedling money out of me, and, as soon as you've got it, it seems to melt in your hands. You never know where it's gone. Still, one has to take you as you are. It's in the blood. Because, you know, it's true that you can inherit these things, Nora.

Nora: Ah, I wish I'd inherited a lot of Papa's traits.

Helmer: And I wouldn't want you to be anything but just what you are, my sweet little skylark. But, you know, it seems to me that you look rather—how can I put it—rather uneasy today.

Nora: Do I?

Helmer: You do, really. Look straight at me.

Nora (looks at him): Well?

Helmer (wagging his finger at her): Has little Miss Sweet Tooth been breaking our rules in town today?

Nora: No, what makes you think that?

Helmer: Has she paid a visit to the bakery?

Nora: No, I assure you, Torvald—

Helmer: Not been nibbling pastries?

Nora: No, certainly not.

Helmer: Not even taken a bite of a macaroon or two?

Nora: No, Torvald, I assure you, really—

Helmer: Come on, you know I was only kidding.

Nora (going to the table on the right): I wouldn't dream of going against your wishes.

Helmer: No, I'm sure of that. Besides, you gave me your word. (*Going up to her.*) Keep your little Christmas secrets to yourself, my darling. They'll all be revealed tonight when the Christmas tree is lit, no doubt.

Nora: Did you remember to invite Doctor Rank?

Helmer: No. But there's no need. It goes without saying that he'll have dinner with us. All the same, I'll ask him when he comes over this morning. I've ordered some good wine. Nora, you have no idea how much I'm looking forward to this evening.

Nora: So am I! And how the children will enjoy themselves, Torvald!

Helmer: It's great to feel that you have a completely secure position and a big enough income. It's a delightful thought, isn't it?

Nora: It's wonderful!

Helmer: Do you remember last Christmas? For three whole weeks you hid yourself away every evening until long after midnight, making ornaments for the Christmas tree and all the other fine things that were going to be a surprise for us. It was the most boring three weeks I ever spent!

Nora: I wasn't bored.

Helmer (smiling): But there was precious little to show for it, Nora.

Nora: Oh, you're not going to tease me about that again. How could I help it that the cat went in and tore everything to pieces?

Helmer: Of course you couldn't, poor little girl. You had the best of intentions to make us all happy, and that's the main thing. But it's a good thing that our hard times are over.

Nora: Yes, it really is wonderful.

Helmer: This time I don't have to sit here and be bored all by myself, and you don't have to ruin your dear eyes and your pretty little hands—

Nora (clapping her hands): No, Torvald, I don't have to any more, do I! It's wonderfully lovely to hear you say so! *(Taking his arm.)* Now let me tell you how I've been thinking we should arrange things, Torvald. As soon as Christmas is over—*(A bell rings in the hall.)* There's the bell. *(She tidies the room a little.)* There's somebody at the door. What a nuisance!

Helmer: If someone's visiting, remember I'm not home.

Maid (in the doorway): A lady to see you, ma'am. A stranger.

Nora: Ask her to come in.

Maid (to Helmer): The doctor's here too, sir.

Helmer: Did he go straight into my study?

Maid: Yes, sir.

> *(Helmer goes into his study. The maid ushers in Mrs. Linde, who is in traveling clothes, and shuts the door.)*

Mrs. Linde (in a dejected and timid voice): Hello, Nora.

Nora (doubtfully): Hello.

Mrs. Linde: You don't recognize me, I suppose.

Nora: No, I don't know . . . Yes, of course, I think so—*(Suddenly.)* Yes! Kristine! Is it really you?

Mrs. Linde: Yes, it is.

Nora: Kristine! Imagine my not recognizing you! And yet how could I—*(In a gentle voice.)* You've changed, Kristine!

Mrs. Linde: Yes, I certainly have. In nine, ten long years—

Nora: Is it that long since we've seen each other? I suppose it is. The last eight years have been a happy time for me, you know. And so now you've come to town, and you've taken this long trip in the winter. That was brave of you.

Mrs. Linde: I arrived by steamer this morning.

Nora: To have some fun at Christmastime, of course. How delightful! We'll have such fun together! But take off your things. You're not cold, I hope.

(Helps her.) Now we'll sit down by the stove and be cozy. No, take this armchair. I'll sit here in the rocking chair. *(Takes her hands.)* Now you look like your old self again. It was only that first moment. You are a little paler, Kristine, and maybe a little thinner.

Mrs. Linde: And much, much older, Nora.

Nora: Maybe a little older. Very, very little. Surely not very much. *(Stops suddenly and speaks seriously.)* What a thoughtless thing I am, chattering away like this. My poor, dear Kristine, please forgive me.

Mrs. Linde: What do you mean, Nora?

Nora (gently): Poor Kristine, you're a widow.

Mrs. Linde: Yes. For three years now.

Nora: Yes, I knew. I saw it in the papers. I swear to you, Kristine, I kept meaning to write to you at the time, but I always put it off and something always came up.

Mrs. Linde: I understand completely, dear.

Nora: It was very bad of me, Kristine. Poor thing, how you must have suffered. And he left you nothing?

Mrs. Linde: No.

Nora: And no children?

Mrs. Linde: No.

Nora: Nothing at all, then?

Mrs. Linde: Not even any sorrow or grief to live on.

Nora (looking at her in disbelief): But, Kristine, is that possible?

Mrs. Linde (smiles sadly and strokes Nora's hair): It happens sometimes, Nora.

Nora: So you're completely alone. How terribly sad that must be. I have three beautiful children. You can't see them just now, because they're out with their nursemaid. But now you must tell me all about it.

Mrs. Linde: No, no, I want to hear about you.

Nora: No, you go first. I mustn't be selfish today. Today I should think only about you. But there is one thing I have to tell you. Do you know we've just had a fabulous piece of good luck?

Mrs. Linde: No, what is it?

Nora: Just imagine, my husband's been appointed manager of the bank!

Mrs. Linde: Your husband? That is good luck!

Nora: Yes, it's tremendous! A lawyer's life is so uncertain, especially if he won't take any cases that are the slightest bit shady, and of course Torvald has never been willing to do that, and I completely agree with him. You can imagine how delighted we are! He starts his job in the bank at New Year's, and then he'll have a big salary and lots of commissions. From now on we can live very differently. We can do just what we want. I feel so relieved and so happy, Kristine! It'll be wonderful to have heaps of money and not have to worry about anything, won't it?

Mrs. Linde: Yes. Anyway, I think it would be delightful to have what you need.

Nora: No, not only what you need, but heaps and heaps of money.

Mrs. Linde (smiling): Nora, Nora, haven't you learned any sense yet? Back in school you were a terrible spendthrift.

Nora (laughing): Yes, that's what Torvald says now. (*Wags her finger at her.*) But "Nora, Nora" isn't as silly as you think. We haven't been in a position for me to waste money. We've both had to work.

Mrs. Linde: You too?

Nora: Oh, yes, odds and ends, needlework, crocheting, embroidery, and that kind of thing. (*Dropping her voice.*) And other things too. You know Torvald left his government job when we got married? There was no chance of promotion, and he had to try to earn more money than he was making there. But in that first year he overworked himself terribly. You see, he had to make money any way he could, and he worked all hours, but he couldn't take it, and he got very sick, and the doctors said he had to go south, to a warmer climate.

Mrs. Linde: You spent a whole year in Italy, didn't you?

Nora: Yes. It wasn't easy to get away, I can tell you that. It was just after Ivar was born, but obviously we had to go. It was a wonderful, beautiful trip, and it saved Torvald's life. But it cost a tremendous amount of money, Kristine.

Mrs. Linde: I would imagine so.

Nora: It cost about four thousand, eight hundred kroner. That's a lot, isn't it?

Mrs. Linde: Yes, it is, and when you have an emergency like that it's lucky to have the money.

Nora: Well, the fact is, we got it from Papa.

Mrs. Linde: Oh, I see. It was just about that time that he died, wasn't it?

Nora: Yes, and, just think of it, I couldn't even go and take care of him. I was expecting little Ivar any day and I had my poor sick Torvald to look after. My dear, kind father. I never saw him again, Kristine. That was the worst experience I've gone through since we got married.

Mrs. Linde: I know how fond of him you were. And then you went off to Italy?

Nora: Yes. You see, we had money then, and the doctors insisted that we go, so we left a month later.

Mrs. Linde: And your husband came back completely recovered?

Nora: The picture of health!

Mrs. Linde: But . . . the doctor?

Nora: What doctor?

Mrs. Linde: Didn't your maid say that the gentleman who arrived here with me was the doctor?

Nora: Yes, that was Doctor Rank, but he doesn't come here professionally. He's our dearest friend, and he drops in at least once every day. No, Torvald hasn't been sick for an hour since then, and our children are strong and healthy, and so am I. (*Jumps up and claps her hands.*) Kristine! Kristine! It's good to be alive and happy! But how awful of me. I'm talking about nothing but myself. (*Sits on a nearby stool and rests her arms on her knees.*) Please don't be mad at me. Tell me, is it really true that you didn't love your husband? Why did you marry him?

Mrs. Linde: My mother was still alive then, and she was bedridden and helpless, and I had to provide for my two younger brothers, so I didn't think I had any right to turn him down.

Nora: No, maybe you did the right thing. So he was rich then?

Mrs. Linde: I believe he was quite well off. But his business wasn't very solid, and when he died, it all went to pieces and there was nothing left.

Nora: And then?

Mrs. Linde: Well, I had to turn my hand to anything I could find. First a small shop, then a small school, and so on. The last three years have seemed like one long workday, with no rest. Now it's over, Nora. My poor mother's gone and doesn't need me any more, and the boys don't need me, either. They've got jobs now and can manage for themselves.

Nora: What a relief it must be if—

Mrs. Linde: No, not at all. All I feel is an unbearable emptiness. No one to live for anymore. (*Gets up restlessly.*) That's why I couldn't stand it any longer in my little backwater. I hope it'll be easier to find something here that'll keep me busy and occupy my mind. If I could be lucky enough to find some regular work, office work of some kind—

Nora: But, Kristine, that's so awfully tiring, and you look tired out now. It'd be much better for you if you could get away to a resort.

Mrs. Linde (*walking to the window*): I don't have a father to give me money for a trip, Nora.

Nora (*rising*): Oh, don't be mad at me!

Mrs. Linde (*going up to her*): It's you who mustn't be mad at me, dear. The worst thing about a situation like mine is that it makes you so bitter. No one to work for, and yet you have to always be on the lookout for opportunities. You have to live, and so you grow selfish. When you told me about your good luck—you'll find this hard to believe—I was delighted less for you than for myself.

Nora: What do you mean? Oh, I understand. You mean that maybe Torvald could find you a job.

Mrs. Linde: Yes, that's what I was thinking.

Nora: He must, Kristine. Just leave it to me. I'll broach the subject very cleverly. I'll think of something that'll put him in a really good mood. It'll make me so happy to be of some use to you.

Mrs. Linde: How kind you are, Nora, to be so eager to help me! It's doubly kind of you, since you know so little of the burdens and troubles of life.

Nora: Me? I know so little of them?

Mrs. Linde (*smiling*): My dear! Small household cares and that sort of thing! You're a child, Nora.

Nora (*tosses her head and crosses the stage*): You shouldn't act so superior.

Mrs. Linde: No?

Nora: You're just like the others. They all think I'm incapable of anything really serious—

Mrs. Linde: Come on—

Nora: —that I haven't had to deal with any real problems in my life.

Mrs. Linde: But, my dear Nora, you've just told me all your troubles.

Nora: Pooh! That was nothing. (*Lowering her voice.*) I haven't told you the important thing.

Mrs. Linde: The important thing? What do you mean?

Nora: You really look down on me, Kristine, but you shouldn't. Aren't you proud of having worked so hard and so long for your mother?

Mrs. Linde: Believe me, I don't look down on anyone. But it's true, I'm proud and I'm glad that I had the privilege of making my mother's last days almost worry-free.

Nora: And you're proud of what you did for your brothers?

Mrs. Linde: I think I have the right to be.

Nora: I think so, too. But now, listen to this. I have something to be proud of and happy about too.

Mrs. Linde: I'm sure you do. But what do you mean?

Nora: Keep your voice down. If Torvald were to overhear! He can't find out, not under any circumstances. No one in the world must know, Kristine, except you.

Mrs. Linde: But what is it?

Nora: Come here. (*Pulls her down on the sofa beside her.*) Now I'll show you that I too have something to be proud and happy about. I'm the one who saved Torvald's life.

Mrs. Linde: Saved? How?

Nora: I told you about our trip to Italy. Torvald would never have recovered if he hadn't gone there—

Mrs. Linde: Yes, but your father gave you the money you needed.

Nora (smiling): Yes, that's what Torvald thinks, along with everybody else, but—

Mrs. Linde: But—

Nora: Papa didn't give us a penny. I was the one who raised the money.

Mrs. Linde: You? That huge amount?

Nora: That's right, four thousand, eight hundred kroner. What do you think of that?

Mrs. Linde: But, Nora, how could you possibly? Did you win the lottery?

Nora (disdainfully): The lottery? That wouldn't have been any accomplishment.

Mrs. Linde: But where did you get it from, then?

Nora (humming and smiling with an air of mystery): Hm, hm! Ha!

Mrs. Linde: Because you couldn't have borrowed it.

Nora: Couldn't I? Why not?

Mrs. Linde: No, a wife can't borrow money without her husband's consent.

Nora (tossing her head): Oh, if it's a wife with a head for business, a wife who has the brains to be a little clever—

Mrs. Linde: I don't understand this at all, Nora.

Nora: There's no reason why you should. I never said I'd borrowed the money. Maybe I got it some other way. *(Lies back on the sofa.)* Maybe I got it from an admirer. When a woman's as pretty as I am—

Mrs. Linde: You're crazy.

Nora: Now, you know you're dying of curiosity, Kristine.

Mrs. Linde: Listen to me, Nora dear. Have you done something rash?

Nora (sits up straight): Is it rash to save your husband's life?

Mrs. Linde: I think it's rash, without his knowledge, to—

Nora: But it was absolutely necessary that he not know! My goodness, can't you understand that? It was necessary he have no idea how sick he was. The doctors came to *me* and said his life was in danger and the only thing that could save him was to live in the south. Don't you think I tried first to get him to do it as if it was for me? I told him how much I would love to travel abroad like other young wives. I tried tears and pleading with him. I told him he should remember the condition I was in, and that he should be kind and indulgent to me. I even hinted that he might take out a loan. That almost made him mad, Kristine. He said I was thoughtless, and that it was his duty as my husband not to indulge me in my "whims and caprices," as I believe he called them. All right, I thought, you need to be saved. And that was how I came to think up a way out of the mess—

Mrs. Linde: And your husband never found out from your father that the money hadn't come from him?

Nora: No, never. Papa died just then. I'd meant to let him in on the secret and beg him never to reveal it. But he was so sick. Unfortunately, there never was any need to tell him.

Mrs. Linde: And since then you've never told your secret to your husband?

Nora: Good heavens, no! How could you think I would? A man with such strong opinions about these things! Besides, how painful and humiliating it would be for Torvald, with his masculine pride, to know that he owed me anything! It would completely upset the balance of our relationship. Our beautiful happy home would never be the same.

Mrs. Linde: Are you never going to tell him about it?

Nora (meditatively, and with a half smile): Yes, someday, maybe, in many years, when I'm not as pretty as I am now. Don't laugh at me! I mean, of course, when Torvald is no longer as devoted to me as he is now, when he's grown tired of my dancing and dressing up and reciting. Then it may be a good thing to have something in reserve—*(Breaking off.)* What nonsense! That time will never come. Now, what do you think of my great secret, Kristine? Do you still think I'm useless? And the fact is, this whole situation has caused me a lot of worry. It hasn't been easy for me to make my payments on time. I can tell you that there's something in business that's called quarterly interest, and something else called installment payments, and it's always so terribly difficult to keep up with them. I've had to save a little here and there, wherever I could, you understand. I haven't been able to put much aside from my housekeeping money, because Torvald has to live well. And I couldn't let my children be shabbily dressed. I feel I have to spend everything he gives me for them, the sweet little darlings!

Mrs. Linde: So it's all had to come out of your own allowance, poor Nora?

Nora: Of course. Besides, I was the one responsible for it. Whenever Torvald has given me money for new dresses and things like that, I've never spent more than half of it. I've always bought the simplest and cheapest things. Thank heaven, any clothes look good on me, and so Torvald's never noticed anything. But it was often very hard on me, Kristine, because it is delightful to be really well dressed, isn't it?

Mrs. Linde: I suppose so.

Nora: Well, then I've found other ways of earning money. Last winter I was lucky enough to get a lot of copying to do, so I locked myself up and sat writing every evening until late into the night. A lot of the time I was desperately tired, but all the same it was a tremendous pleasure to sit there working and earning money. It was like being a man.

Mrs. Linde: How much have you been able to pay off that way?

Nora: I can't tell you exactly. You see, it's very hard to keep a strict account of a business matter like that. I only know that I've paid out every penny I could scrape together. Many a time I was at my wits' end. *(Smiles.)* Then I used to sit here and imagine that a rich old gentleman had fallen in love with me—

Mrs. Linde: What! Who was it?

Nora: Oh, be quiet! That he had died, and that when his will was opened it said, in great big letters: "The lovely Mrs. Nora Helmer is to have everything I own paid over to her immediately in cash."

Mrs. Linde: But, my dear Nora, who could the man be?

Nora: Good gracious, can't you understand? There wasn't any old gentleman. It was only something that I used to sit here and imagine, when I couldn't think of any way of getting money. But it's all right now. The tiresome old gent can stay right where he is, as far as I'm concerned. I don't care about him or his will either, because now I'm worry-free. *(Jumps up.)* My goodness, it's delightful to think of, Kristine! Worry-free! To be able to have no worries, no worries at all! To be able to play and romp with the children! To be able to keep the house beautifully and have everything just the way Torvald likes it! And, just think of it, soon the spring will come and the big blue sky! Maybe we can take a little trip. Maybe I can see the sea again! Oh, it's a wonderful thing to be alive and happy.

(A bell rings in the hall.)

Mrs. Linde (rising): There's the bell. Perhaps I should be going.

Nora: No, don't go. No one will come in here. It's sure to be for Torvald.

Servant (at the hall door): Excuse me, ma'am. There's a gentleman to see the master, and as the doctor is still with him—

Nora: Who is it?

Krogstad (at the door): It's me, Mrs. Helmer.

(Mrs. Linde starts, trembles, and turns toward the window.)

Nora (takes a step toward him, and speaks in a strained, low voice): You? What is it? What do you want to see my husband for?

Krogstad: Bank business, in a way. I have a small position in the bank, and I hear your husband is going to be our boss now—

Nora: Then it's—

Krogstad: Nothing but dry business matters, Mrs. Helmer, that's all.

Nora: Then please go into the study.

(She bows indifferently to him and shuts the door into the hall, then comes back and makes up the fire in the stove.)

Mrs. Linde: Nora, who was that man?

Nora: A lawyer. His name is Krogstad.

Mrs. Linde: Then it really was him.

Nora: Do you know the man?

Mrs. Linde: I used to, many years ago. At one time he was a law clerk in our town.

Nora: That's right, he was.

Mrs. Linde: How much he's changed.

Nora: He had a very unhappy marriage.

Mrs. Linde: He's a widower now, isn't he?

Nora: With several children. There, now it's really caught. *(Shuts the door of the stove and moves the rocking chair aside.)*

Mrs. Linde: They say he's mixed up in a lot of questionable business.

Nora: Really? Maybe he is. I don't know anything about it. But let's not talk about business. It's so tiresome.

Doctor Rank (comes out of Helmer's study. Before he shuts the door he calls to Helmer): No, my dear fellow, I won't disturb you. I'd rather go in and talk to your wife for a little while.

(Shuts the door and sees Mrs. Linde.)

I beg your pardon. I'm afraid I'm in the way here too.

Nora: No, not at all. *(Introducing him:)* Doctor Rank, Mrs. Linde.

Rank: I've often heard that name in this house. I think I passed you on the stairs when I arrived, Mrs. Linde?

Mrs. Linde: Yes, I take stairs very slowly. I can't manage them very well.

Rank: Oh, some small internal problem?

Mrs. Linde: No, it's just that I've been overworking myself.

Rank: Is that all? Then I suppose you've come to town to get some rest by sampling our social life.

Mrs. Linde: I've come to look for work.

Rank: Is that a good cure for overwork?

Mrs. Linde: One has to live, Doctor Rank.

Rank: Yes, that seems to be the general opinion.

Nora: Now, now, Doctor Rank, you know you want to live.

Rank: Of course I do. However miserable I may feel, I want to prolong the agony for as long as possible. All my patients are the same way. And so are those who are morally sick. In fact, one of them, and a bad case too, is at this very moment inside with Helmer—

Mrs. Linde (sadly): Ah!

Nora: Who are you talking about?

Rank: A lawyer by the name of Krogstad, a fellow you don't know at all. He's a completely worthless creature, Mrs. Helmer. But even he started out by saying, as if it were a matter of the utmost importance, that he has to live.

Nora: Did he? What did he want to talk to Torvald about?

Rank: I have no idea. All I heard was that it was something about the bank.

Nora: I didn't know this—what's his name—Krogstad had anything to do with the bank.

Rank: Yes, he has some kind of a position there. *(To Mrs. Linde)* I don't know whether you find the same thing in your part of the world, that there are certain people who go around zealously looking to sniff out moral corruption, and, as soon as they find some, they put the person involved in some cushy job where they can keep an eye on him. Meanwhile, the morally healthy ones are left out in the cold.

Mrs. Linde: Still, I think it's the sick who are most in need of being taken care of.

Rank (shrugging his shoulders): Well, there you have it. That's the attitude that's turning society into a hospital.

(Nora, who has been absorbed in her thoughts, breaks out into smothered laughter and claps her hands.)

Rank: Why are you laughing at that? Do you have any idea what society really is?

Nora: What do I care about your boring society? I'm laughing at something else, something very funny. Tell me, Doctor Rank, are all the people who work in the bank dependent on Torvald now?

Rank: That's what's so funny?

Nora (smiling and humming): That's my business! *(Walking around the room.)* It's just wonderful to think that we have—that Torvald has—so much power over so many people. *(Takes the bag out of her pocket.)* Doctor Rank, what do you say to a macaroon?

Rank: Macaroons? I thought they were forbidden here.

Nora: Yes, but these are some Kristine gave me.

Mrs. Linde: What! Me?

Nora: Oh, well, don't be upset! How could you know that Torvald had forbidden them? I have to tell you, he's afraid they'll ruin my teeth. But so what? Once in a while, that's all right, isn't it, Doctor Rank? With your permission! *(Puts a macaroon into his mouth.)* You have to have one too, Kristine. And I'll have one, just a little one—or no more than two. *(Walking around.)* I am tremendously happy. There's just one thing in the world now that I would dearly love to do.

Rank: Well, what is it?

Nora: It's something I would dearly love to say, if Torvald could hear me.

Rank: Well, why can't you say it?

Nora: No, I don't dare. It's too shocking.

Mrs. Linde: Shocking?

Rank: Well then, I'd advise you not to say it. Still, in front of us you might risk it. What is it you'd so much like to say if Torvald could hear you?

Nora: I would just love to say—"Well, I'll be damned!"

Rank: Are you crazy?

Mrs. Linde: Nora, dear!

Rank: Here he is. Say it!

Nora (hiding the bag): Shh, shh, shh!

(Helmer comes out of his room, with his coat over his arm and his hat in his hand.)

Nora: Well, Torvald dear, did you get rid of him?

Helmer: Yes, he just left.

Nora: Let me introduce you. This is Kristine. She's just arrived in town.

Helmer: Kristine? I'm sorry, but I don't know any—

Nora: Mrs. Linde, dear, Kristine Linde.

Helmer: Oh, of course. A school friend of my wife's, I believe?

Mrs. Linde: Yes, we knew each other back then.

Nora: And just think, she's come all this way in order to see you.

Helmer: What do you mean?

Mrs. Linde: No, really, I—

Nora: Kristine is extremely good at bookkeeping, and she's very eager to work for some talented man, so she can perfect her skills—

Helmer: Very sensible, Mrs. Linde.

Nora: And when she heard that you'd been named manager of the bank— the news was sent by telegraph, you know—she traveled here as quickly as she could. Torvald, I'm sure you'll be able to do something for Kristine, for my sake, won't you?

Helmer: Well, it's not completely out of the question. I expect that you're a widow, Mrs. Linde?

Mrs. Linde: Yes.

Helmer: And you've had some bookkeeping experience?

Mrs. Linde: Yes, a fair amount.

Helmer: Ah! Well, there's a very good chance that I'll be able to find something for you—

Nora (clapping her hands): What did I tell you? What did I tell you?

Helmer: You've just come at a lucky moment, Mrs. Linde.

Mrs. Linde: How can I thank you?

Helmer: There's no need. *(Puts on his coat.)* But now you must excuse me—

Rank: Wait a minute. I'll come with you. *(Brings his fur coat from the hall and warms it at the fire.)*

Nora: Don't be long, Torvald dear.

Helmer: About an hour, that's all.

Nora: Are you leaving too, Kristine?

Mrs. Linde (putting on her cloak): Yes, I have to go and look for a place to stay.

Helmer: Oh, well then, we can walk down the street together.

Nora (helping her): It's too bad we're so short of space here. I'm afraid it's impossible for us—

Mrs. Linde: Please don't even think of it! Goodbye, Nora dear, and many thanks.

Nora: Goodbye for now. Of course you'll come back this evening. And you too, Dr. Rank. What do you say? If you're feeling up to it? Oh, you have to be! Wrap yourself up warmly.

(They go to the door all talking together. Children's voices are heard on the staircase.)

Nora: There they are! There they are!

(She runs to open the door. The nursemaid comes in with the children.)

Come in! Come in! *(Stoops and kisses them.)* Oh, you sweet blessings! Look at them, Kristine! Aren't they darlings?

Rank: Let's not stand here in the draft.

Helmer: Come along, Mrs. Linde. Only a mother will be able to stand it in here now!

(Rank, Helmer, and Mrs. Linde go downstairs. The Nursemaid comes forward with the children. Nora shuts the hall door.)

Nora: How fresh and healthy you look! Cheeks as red as apples and roses. *(The children all talk at once while she speaks to them.)* Did you have a lot of fun? That's wonderful! What, you pulled Emmy and Bob on the sled? Both at once? That was really something. You *are* a clever boy, Ivar. Let me take her for a little, Anne Marie. My sweet little baby doll! *(Takes the baby from the maid and dances her up and down.)* Yes, yes, mother will dance with Bob too. What! Have you been throwing snowballs? I wish I'd been there too! No, no, I'll take their things off, Anne Marie, please let me do it, it's such fun. Go inside now, you look half frozen. There's some hot coffee for you on the stove.

(*The Nursemaid goes into the room on the left. Nora takes off the children's things and throws them around, while they all talk to her at once.*)

Nora: Really! Did a big dog run after you? But it didn't bite you? No, dogs don't bite nice little dolly children. You mustn't look at the packages, Ivar. What are they? Oh, I'll bet you'd like to know. No, no, it's something boring! Come on, let's play a game! What should we play? Hide and seek? Yes, we'll play hide and seek. Bob will hide first. You want me to hide? All right, I'll hide first.

(*She and the children laugh and shout, and romp in and out of the room. At last Nora hides under the table. The children rush in and out looking for her, but they don't see her. They hear her smothered laughter, run to the table, lift up the cloth and find her. Shouts of laughter. She crawls forward and pretends to scare them. More laughter. Meanwhile there has been a knock at the hall door, but none of them has noticed it. The door is opened halfway and Krogstad appears. He waits for a little while. The game goes on.*)

Krogstad: Excuse me, Mrs. Helmer.

Nora (*with a stifled cry, turns round and gets up onto her knees*): Oh! What do you want?

Krogstad: Excuse me, the outside door was open. I suppose someone forgot to shut it.

Nora (*rising*): My husband is out, Mr. Krogstad.

Krogstad: I know that.

Nora: What do you want here, then?

Krogstad: A word with you.

Nora: With me? (*To the children, gently.*) Go inside to Anne Marie. What? No, the strange man won't hurt Mother. When he's gone we'll play another game. (*She takes the children into the room on the left, and shuts the door after them.*) You want to speak to me?

Krogstad: Yes, I do.

Nora: Today? It isn't the first of the month yet.

Krogstad: No, it's Christmas Eve, and it's up to you what kind of Christmas you're going to have.

Nora: What do you mean? Today it's absolutely impossible for me—

Krogstad: We won't talk about that until later on. This is something else. I presume you can spare me a moment?

Nora: Yes, yes, I can. Although . . .

Krogstad: Good. I was in Olsen's restaurant and I saw your husband going down the street—

Nora: Yes?

Krogstad: With a lady.

Nora: So?

Krogstad: May I be so bold as to ask if it was a Mrs. Linde?

Nora: It was.

Krogstad: Just arrived in town?

Nora: Yes, today.

Krogstad: She's a very good friend of yours, isn't she?

Nora: She is. But I don't see—

Krogstad: I knew her too, once upon a time.

Nora: I'm aware of that.

Krogstad: Are you? So you know all about it. I thought so. Then I can ask you, without beating around the bush. Is Mrs. Linde going to work in the bank?

Nora: What right do you have to question me, Mr. Krogstad? You're one of my husband's employees. But since you ask, I'll tell you. Yes, Mrs. Linde is going to work in the bank. And I'm the one who spoke up for her, Mr. Krogstad. So now you know.

Krogstad: So I was right, then.

Nora (walking up and down the stage): Sometimes one has a tiny little bit of influence, I should hope. Just because I'm a woman, it doesn't necessarily follow that—You know, when somebody's in a subordinate position, Mr. Krogstad, they should really be careful to avoid offending anyone who—who—

Krogstad: Who has influence?

Nora: Exactly.

Krogstad (changing his tone): Mrs. Helmer, may I ask you to use *your* influence on my behalf?

Nora: What? What do you mean?

Krogstad: Will you be kind enough to see to it that I'm allowed to keep my subordinate position in the bank?

Nora: What do you mean by that? Who's threatening to take your job away from you?

Krogstad: Oh, there's no need to keep up the pretence of ignorance. I can understand that your friend isn't very anxious to expose herself to the chance of rubbing shoulders with me. And now I realize exactly who I have to thank for pushing me out.

Nora: But I swear to you—

Krogstad: Yes, yes. But, to get right to the point, there's still time to prevent it, and I would advise you to use your influence to do so.

Nora: But, Mr. Krogstad, I have no influence.

Krogstad: Oh no? Didn't you yourself just say—

Nora: Well, obviously, I didn't mean for you to take it that way. Me? What would make you think I have that kind of influence with my husband?

Krogstad: Oh, I've known your husband since our school days. I don't suppose he's any more unpersuadable than other husbands.

Nora: If you're going to talk disrespectfully about my husband, I'll have to ask you to leave my house.

Krogstad: Bold talk, Mrs. Helmer.

Nora: I'm not afraid of you anymore. When the New Year comes, I'll soon be free of the whole thing.

Krogstad (controlling himself): Listen to me, Mrs. Helmer. If I have to, I'm ready to fight for my little job in the bank as if I were fighting for my life.

Nora: So it seems.

Krogstad: It's not just for the sake of the money. In fact, that matters the least to me. There's another reason. Well, I might as well tell you. Here's my situation. I suppose, like everybody else, you know that many years ago I did something pretty foolish.

Nora: I think I heard something about it.

Krogstad: It never got as far as the courtroom, but every door seemed closed to me after that. So I got involved in the business that you know about. I had to do something, and, honestly, I think there are many worse than me. But now I have to get myself free of all that. My sons are growing up. For their sake I have to try to win back as much respect as I can in this town. The job in the bank was like the first step up for me, and now your husband is going to kick me downstairs back into the mud.

Nora: But you have to believe me, Mr. Krogstad, it's not in my power to help you at all.

Krogstad: Then it's because you don't want to. But I have ways of making you.

Nora: You don't mean you'll tell my husband I owe you money?

Krogstad: Hm! And what if I did tell him?

Nora: That would be a terrible thing for you to do. *(Sobbing.)* To think he would learn my secret, which has been my pride and joy, in such an ugly, clumsy way—that he would learn it from you! And it would put me in a horribly uncomfortable position—

Krogstad: Just uncomfortable?

Nora (impetuously): Well, go ahead and do it, then! And it'll be so much the worse for you. My husband will see for himself how vile you are, and then you'll lose your job for sure.

Krogstad: I asked you if it's just an uncomfortable situation at home that you're afraid of.

Nora: If my husband does find out about it, of course he'll immediately pay you what I still owe, and then we'll be through with you once and for all.

Krogstad (coming a step closer): Listen to me, Mrs. Helmer. Either you have a very bad memory or you don't know much about business. I can see I'm going to have to remind you of a few details.

Nora: What do you mean?

Krogstad: When your husband was sick, you came to me to borrow four thousand, eight hundred kroner.

Nora: I didn't know anyone else to go to.

Krogstad: I promised to get you that amount—

Nora: Yes, and you did so.

Krogstad: I promised to get you that amount, on certain conditions. You were so preoccupied with your husband's illness, and you were so anxious to get the money for your trip, that you seem to have paid no attention to the conditions of our bargain. So it won't be out of place for me to remind you of them. Now, I promised to get the money on the security of a note which I drew up.

Nora: Yes, and which I signed.

Krogstad: Good. But underneath your signature there were a few lines naming your father as a co-signer who guaranteed the repayment of the loan. Your father was supposed to sign that part.

Nora: Supposed to? He did sign it.

Krogstad: I had left the date blank. That was because your father was supposed to fill in the date when he signed the paper. Do you remember that?

Nora: Yes, I think I remember. . . .

Krogstad: Then I gave you the note to mail to your father. Isn't that so?

Nora: Yes.

Krogstad: And obviously you mailed it right away, because five or six days later you brought me the note with your father's signature. And then I gave you the money.

Nora: Well, haven't I been paying it back regularly?

Krogstad: Fairly regularly, yes. But, to get back to the point, that must have been a very difficult time for you, Mrs. Helmer.

Nora: Yes, it was.

Krogstad: Your father was very sick, wasn't he?

Nora: He was very near the end.

Krogstad: And he died soon after?

Nora: Yes.

Krogstad: Tell me, Mrs. Helmer, can you by any chance remember what day your father died? On what day of the month, I mean.

Nora: Papa died on the 29th of September.

Krogstad: That's right. I looked it up myself. And, since that is the case, there's something extremely peculiar (*taking a piece of paper from his pocket*) that I can't account for.

Nora: Peculiar in what way? I don't know—

Krogstad: The peculiar thing, Mrs. Helmer, is the fact that your father signed this note three days after he died.

Nora: What do you mean? I don't understand—

Krogstad: Your father died on the 29th of September. But, look here. Your father dated his signature the 2nd of October. It is mighty peculiar, isn't it? (*Nora is silent.*) Can you explain it to me? (*Nora is still silent.*) And what's just as peculiar is that the words "October 2," as well as the year, are not in your father's handwriting, but in someone else's, which I think I recognize. Well, of course it can all be explained. Your father might have forgotten to date his signature, and someone else might have filled in the date before they knew that he had died. There's no harm in that. It all depends on the signature, and that's genuine, isn't it, Mrs. Helmer? It was your father himself who signed his name here?

Nora (after a short pause, lifts her head up and looks defiantly at him): No, it wasn't. I'm the one who wrote Papa's name.

Krogstad: Are you aware that you're making a very serious confession?

Nora: How so? You'll get your money soon.

Krogstad: Let me ask you something. Why didn't you send the paper to your father?

Nora: It was out of the question. Papa was too sick. If I had asked him to sign something, I'd have had to tell him what the money was for, and when he was so sick himself I couldn't tell him that my husband's life was in danger. It was out of the question.

Krogstad: It would have been better for you if you'd given up your trip abroad.

Nora: No, that was impossible. That trip was to save my husband's life. I couldn't give that up.

Krogstad: But didn't it ever occur to you that you were committing a fraud against me?

Nora: I couldn't take that into account. I didn't trouble myself about you at all. I couldn't stand you, because you put so many heartless difficulties in my way, even though you knew how seriously ill my husband was.

Krogstad: Mrs. Helmer, you evidently don't realize clearly what you're guilty of. But, believe me, my one mistake, which cost me my whole reputation, was nothing more and nothing worse than what you did.

Nora: You? You expect me to believe that you were brave enough to take a risk to save your wife's life?

Krogstad: The law doesn't care about motives.

Nora: Then the law must be very stupid.

Krogstad: Stupid or not, it's the law that's going to judge you, if I produce this paper in court.

Nora: I don't believe it. Isn't a daughter allowed to spare her dying father anxiety and concern? Isn't a wife allowed to save her husband's life? I don't know much about the law, but I'm sure there must be provisions for things like that. Don't you know anything about such provisions? You seem like a very poor excuse for a lawyer, Mr. Krogstad.

Krogstad: That's as may be. But business, the kind of business you and I have done together—do you think I don't know about that? Fine. Do what you want. But I can assure you of this. If I lose everything all over again, this time you're going down with me. *(He bows, and goes out through the hall.)*

Nora (appears buried in thought for a short time, then tosses her head): Nonsense! He's just trying to scare me! I'm not as naive as he thinks I am. *(Begins to busy herself putting the children's things in order.)* And yet . . . ? No, it's impossible! I did it for love.

Children (in the doorway on the left): Mother, the strange man is gone. He went out through the gate.

Nora: Yes, dears, I know. But don't tell anyone about the strange man. Do you
hear me? Not even Papa.

Children: No, Mother. But will you come and play with us again?

Nora: No, no, not just now.

Children: But, Mother, you promised us.

Nora: Yes, but I can't right now. Go inside. I have too much to do. Go inside,
my sweet little darlings.

> (*She gets them into the room bit by bit and shuts the door on them. Then she
> sits down on the sofa, takes up a piece of needlework and sews a few stitches,
> but soon stops.*)

> No! (*Throws down the work, gets up, goes to the hall door and calls out.*)
> Helene! Bring the tree in. (*Goes to the table on the left, opens a drawer, and
> stops again.*) No, no! It's completely impossible!

Maid (*coming in with the tree*): Where should I put it, ma'am?

Nora: Here, in the middle of the floor.

Maid: Do you need anything else?

Nora: No, thank you. I have everything I want.

> (*Exit Maid.*)

Nora (*begins decorating the tree*): A candle here, and flowers here. That horrible man! It's all nonsense, there's nothing wrong. The tree is going to be
magnificent! I'll do everything I can think of to make you happy, Torvald!
I'll sing for you, dance for you—

> (*Helmer comes in with some papers under his arm.*)

> Oh! You're back already?

Helmer: Yes. Has anyone been here?

Nora: Here? No.

Helmer: That's strange. I saw Krogstad going out the gate.

Nora: You did? Oh yes, I forgot, Krogstad was here for a moment.

Helmer: Nora, I can tell from the way you're acting that he was here begging
you to put in a good word for him.

Nora: Yes, he was.

Helmer: And you were supposed to pretend it was all your idea and not tell me
that he'd been here to see you. Didn't he beg you to do that too?

Nora: Yes, Torvald, but—

Helmer: Nora, Nora, to think that you'd be a party to that sort of thing! To
have any kind of conversation with a man like that, and promise him
anything at all? And to lie to me in the bargain?

Nora: Lie?

Helmer: Didn't you tell me no one had been here? (*Shakes his finger at her.*)
My little songbird must never do that again. A songbird must have a
clean beak to chirp with. No false notes! (*Puts his arm round her waist.*)

That's true, isn't it? Yes, I'm sure it is. (*Lets her go.*) We won't mention this again. (*Sits down by the stove.*) How warm and cozy it is here! (*Turns over his papers.*)

Nora (*after a short pause, during which she busies herself with the Christmas tree*): Torvald!

Helmer: Yes?

Nora: I'm really looking forward to the masquerade ball at the Stenborgs' the day after tomorrow.

Helmer: And I'm really curious to see what you're going to surprise me with.

Nora: Oh, it was very silly of me to want to do that.

Helmer: What do you mean?

Nora: I can't come up with anything good. Everything I think of seems so stupid and pointless.

Helmer: So my little Nora finally admits that?

Nora (*standing behind his chair with her arms on the back of it*): Are you very busy, Torvald?

Helmer: Well . . .

Nora: What are all those papers?

Helmer: Bank business.

Nora: Already?

Helmer: I've gotten the authority from the retiring manager to reorganize the work procedures and make the necessary personnel changes. I need to take care of it during Christmas week, so as to have everything in place for the new year.

Nora: Then that was why this poor Krogstad—

Helmer: Hm!

Nora (*leans against the back of his chair and strokes his hair*): If you weren't so busy, I would have asked you for a huge favor, Torvald.

Helmer: What favor? Tell me.

Nora: No one has such good taste as you. And I really want to look nice at the fancy-dress ball. Torvald, couldn't you take me in hand and decide what I should go as and what kind of costume I should wear?

Helmer: Aha! So my obstinate little woman has to get someone to come to her rescue?

Nora: Yes, Torvald, I can't get along at all without your help.

Helmer: All right, I'll think it over. I'm sure we'll come up with something.

Nora: That's so nice of you. (*Goes to the Christmas tree. A short pause.*) How pretty the red flowers look. But, tell me, was it really something very bad that this Krogstad was guilty of?

Helmer: He forged someone's name. Do you have any idea what that means?

Nora: Isn't it possible that he was forced to do it by necessity?

Helmer: Yes. Or, the way it is in so many cases, by foolishness. I'm not so heartless that I'd absolutely condemn a man because of one mistake like that.

Nora: No, you wouldn't, would you, Torvald?

Helmer: Many a man has been able to rehabilitate himself, if he's openly admitted his guilt and taken his punishment.

Nora: Punishment?

Helmer: But Krogstad didn't do that. He wriggled out of it with lies and trickery, and that's what completely undermined his moral character.

Nora: But do you think that that would—

Helmer: Just think how a guilty man like that has to lie and act like a hypocrite with everyone, how he has to wear a mask in front of the people closest to him, even with his own wife and children. And the children. That's the most terrible part of it all, Nora.

Nora: How so?

Helmer: Because an atmosphere of lies infects and poisons the whole life of a home. Every breath the children take in a house like that is full of the germs of moral corruption.

Nora (coming closer to him): Are you sure of that?

Helmer: My dear, I've seen it many times in my legal career. Almost everyone who's gone wrong at a young age had a dishonest mother.

Nora: Why only the mother?

Helmer: It usually seems to be the mother's influence, though naturally a bad father would have the same result. Every lawyer knows this. This Krogstad, now, has been systematically poisoning his own children with lies and deceit. That's why I say he's lost all moral character. *(Holds out his hands to her.)* And that's why my sweet little Nora must promise me not to plead his cause. Give me your hand on it. Come now, what's this? Give me your hand. There, that's settled. Believe me, it would be impossible for me to work with him. It literally makes me feel physically ill to be around people like that.

Nora (takes her hand out of his and goes to the opposite side of the Christmas tree): How hot it is in here! And I have so much to do.

Helmer (getting up and putting his papers in order): Yes, and I have to try to read through some of these before dinner. And I have to think about your costume, too. And it's just possible I'll have something wrapped in gold paper to hang up on the tree. *(Puts his hand on her head.)* My precious little songbird! *(He goes into his study and closes the door behind him.)*

Nora (after a pause, whispers): No, no, it's not true. It's impossible. It has to be impossible.

(The nursemaid opens the door on the left.)

Nursemaid: The little ones are begging so hard to be allowed to come in to see Mama.

Nora: No, no, no! Don't let them come in to me! You stay with them, Anne Marie.

Nursemaid: Very well, ma'am. *(Shuts the door.)*

Nora (pale with terror): Corrupt my little children? Poison my home? *(A short pause. Then she tosses her head.)* It's not true. It can't possibly be true.

ACT II

The same scene. The Christmas tree is in the corner by the piano, stripped of its ornaments and with burnt-down candle-ends on its disheveled branches. Nora's coat and hat are lying on the sofa. She is alone in the room, walking around uneasily. She stops by the sofa and picks up her coat.

Nora *(drops her coat)*: Someone's coming! *(Goes to the door and listens.)* No, there's no one there. Of course, no one will come today. It's Christmas Day. And not tomorrow either. But maybe . . . *(opens the door and looks out)* No, nothing in the mailbox. It's empty. *(Comes forward.)* What nonsense! Of course he can't be serious about it. A thing like that couldn't happen. It's impossible. I have three little children.

(Enter the nursemaid Anne Marie from the room on the left, carrying a big cardboard box.)

Nursemaid: I finally found the box with the costume.
Nora: Thank you. Put it on the table.
Nursemaid *(doing so)*: But it really needs to be mended.
Nora: I'd like to tear it into a hundred thousand pieces.
Nursemaid: What an idea! It can easily be fixed up. All you need is a little patience.
Nora: Yes, I'll go get Mrs. Linde to come and help me with it.
Nursemaid: What, going out again? In this horrible weather? You'll catch cold, Miss Nora, and make yourself sick.
Nora: Well, worse things than that might happen. How are the children?
Nursemaid: The poor little ones are playing with their Christmas presents, but—
Nora: Do they ask for me much?
Nursemaid: You see, they're so used to having their Mama with them.
Nora: Yes, but, Anne Marie, I won't be able to spend as much time with them now as I did before.
Nursemaid: Oh well, young children quickly get used to anything.
Nora: Do you think so? Do you think they'd forget their mother if she went away for good?
Nursemaid: Good heavens! Went away for good?
Nora: Anne Marie, I want you to tell me something I've often wondered about. How could you have the heart to let your own child be raised by strangers?
Nursemaid: I had to, if I wanted to be little Nora's nursemaid.
Nora: Yes, but how could you agree to it?
Nursemaid: What, when I was going to get such a good situation out of it? A poor girl who's gotten herself in trouble should be glad to. Besides, that worthless man didn't do a single thing for me.
Nora: But I suppose your daughter has completely forgotten you.

Nursemaid: No, she hasn't, not at all. She wrote to me when she was confirmed, and again when she got married.

Nora (putting her arms round her neck): Dear old Anne Marie, you were such a
good mother to me when I was little.

Nursemaid: Poor little Nora, you had no other mother but me.

Nora: And if my little ones had no other mother, I'm sure that you would—
What nonsense I'm talking! *(Opens the box.)* Go in and see to them. Now
I have to . . . You'll see how lovely I'll look tomorrow.

Nursemaid: I'm sure there'll be no one at the ball as lovely as you, Miss Nora.

(Goes into the room on the left.)

Nora (begins to unpack the box, but soon pushes it away from her): If only I dared
to go out. If only no one would come. If only I could be sure nothing
would happen here in the meantime. What nonsense! No one's going to
come. I just have to stop thinking about it. This muff needs to be brushed.
What beautiful, beautiful gloves! Stop thinking about it, stop thinking
about it! One, two, three, four, five, six—*(Screams.)* Aaah! Somebody
is coming—*(Makes a movement towards the door, but stands in hesitation.)*

(Enter Mrs. Linde from the hall, where she has taken off her coat and hat.)

Nora: Oh, it's you, Kristine. There's no one else out in the hall, is there? How
good of you to come!

Mrs. Linde: I heard you came by asking for me.

Nora: Yes, I was passing by. As a matter of fact, it's something you could help
me with. Let's sit down here on the sofa. Listen, tomorrow evening there's
going to be a fancy-dress ball at the Stenborgs'—they live upstairs from
us—and Torvald wants me to go as a Neapolitan fisher-girl and dance the
tarantella. I learned it when we were at Capri.

Mrs. Linde: I see. You're going to give them the whole show.

Nora: Yes, Torvald wants me to. Look, here's the dress. Torvald had it made
for me there, but now it's all so torn, and I don't have any idea—

Mrs. Linde: We can easily fix that. Some of the trim has just come loose here
and there. Do you have a needle and thread? That's all we need.

Nora: This is so nice of you.

Mrs. Linde (sewing): So you're going to be dressed up tomorrow, Nora. I'll
tell you what. I'll stop by for a moment so I can see you in your finery.
Oh, meanwhile I've completely forgotten to thank you for a delightful
evening last night.

Nora (gets up, and crosses the stage): Well, I didn't think last night was as
pleasant as usual. You should have come to town a little earlier, Kristine.
Torvald really knows how to make a home pleasant and attractive.

Mrs. Linde: And so do you, if you ask me. You're not your father's daughter
for nothing. But tell me, is Doctor Rank always as depressed as he was
yesterday?

Nora: No, yesterday it was especially noticeable. But you have to understand that he has a very serious disease. He has tuberculosis of the spine, poor creature. His father was a horrible man who always had mistresses, and that's why his son has been sickly since childhood, if you know what I mean.

Mrs. Linde (dropping her sewing): But, my dear Nora, how do you know anything about such things?

Nora (walking around the room): Pooh! When you have three children, you get visits now and then from—from married women, who know something about medical matters, and they talk about one thing and another.

Mrs. Linde (goes on sewing. A short silence): Does Doctor Rank come here every day?

Nora: Every day, like clockwork. He's Torvald's best friend, and a great friend of mine too. He's just like one of the family.

Mrs. Linde: But tell me, is he really sincere? I mean, isn't he the kind of man who tends to play up to people?

Nora: No, not at all. What makes you think that?

Mrs. Linde: When you introduced him to me yesterday, he told me he'd often heard my name mentioned in this house, but later I could see that your husband didn't have the slightest idea who I was. So how could Doctor Rank—?

Nora: That's true, Kristine. Torvald is so ridiculously fond of me that he wants me completely to himself, as he says. At first he used to seem almost jealous if I even mentioned any of my friends back home, so naturally I stopped talking about them to him. But I often talk about things like that with Doctor Rank, because he likes hearing about them.

Mrs. Linde: Listen to me, Nora. You're still like a child in a lot of ways, and I'm older than you and more experienced. So pay attention. You'd better stop all this with Doctor Rank.

Nora: Stop all what?

Mrs. Linde: Two things, I think. Yesterday you talked some nonsense about a rich admirer who was going to leave you his money—

Nora: An admirer who doesn't exist, unfortunately! But so what?

Mrs. Linde: Is Doctor Rank a wealthy man?

Nora: Yes, he is.

Mrs. Linde: And he has no dependents?

Nora: No, no one. But—

Mrs. Linde: And he comes here every day?

Nora: Yes, I told you he does.

Mrs. Linde: But how can such a well-bred man be so tactless?

Nora: I don't understand what you mean.

Mrs. Linde: Don't try to play dumb, Nora. Do you think I didn't guess who lent you the four thousand, eight hundred kroner?

Nora: Are you out of your mind? How can you even think that? A friend of ours, who comes here every day! Don't you realize what an incredibly awkward position that would put me in?

Mrs. Linde: Then he's really not the one?

Nora: Absolutely not. It would never have come into my head for one second. Besides, he had nothing to lend back then. He inherited his money later on.

Mrs. Linde: Well, I think that was lucky for you, my dear Nora.

Nora: No, it would never have crossed my mind to ask Doctor Rank. Although I'm sure that if I had asked him—

Mrs. Linde: But of course you won't.

Nora: Of course not. I have no reason to think I could possibly need to. But I'm absolutely certain that if I told Doctor Rank—

Mrs. Linde: Behind your husband's back?

Nora: I have to finish up with the other one, and that'll be behind his back too. I've got to wash my hands of him.

Mrs. Linde: Yes, that's what I told you yesterday, but—

Nora (walking up and down): A man can take care of these things so much more easily than a woman.

Mrs. Linde: If he's your husband, yes.

Nora: Nonsense! *(Standing still.)* When you pay off a debt you get your note back, don't you?

Mrs. Linde: Yes, of course.

Nora: And you can tear it into a hundred thousand pieces and burn up the filthy, nasty piece of paper!

Mrs. Linde (stares at her, puts down her sewing and gets up slowly): Nora, you're hiding something from me.

Nora: You can tell by looking at me?

Mrs. Linde: Something's happened to you since yesterday morning. Nora, what is it?

Nora (going nearer to her): Kristine! *(Listens.)* Shh! I hear Torvald. He's come home. Would you mind going in to the children's room for a little while? Torvald can't stand to see all this sewing going on. You can get Anne Marie to help you.

Mrs. Linde (gathering some of the things together): All right, but I'm not leaving this house until we've talked this thing through.

(She goes into the room on the left, as Helmer comes in from the hall.)

Nora (going up to Helmer): I've missed you so much, Torvald dear.

Helmer: Was that the seamstress?

Nora: No, it was Kristine. She's helping me fix up my dress. You'll see how nice I'm going to look.

Helmer: Wasn't that a good idea of mine, now?

Nora: Wonderful! But don't you think it's nice of me, too, to do what you said?

Helmer: Nice, because you do what your husband tells you to? Go on, you silly little thing, I am sure you didn't mean it like that. But I'll stay out of your way. I imagine you'll be trying on your dress.

Nora: I suppose you're going to do some work.

Helmer: Yes. (*Shows her a stack of papers.*) Look at that. I've just been at the bank. (*Turns to go into his room.*)

Nora: Torvald.

Helmer: Yes?

Nora: If your little squirrel were to ask you for something in a very, very charming way—

Helmer: Well?

Nora: Would you do it?

Helmer: I'd have to know what it is, first.

Nora: Your squirrel would run around and do all her tricks if you would be really nice and do what she wants.

Helmer: Speak plainly.

Nora: Your skylark would chirp her beautiful song in every room—

Helmer: Well, my skylark does that anyhow.

Nora: I'd be a little elf and dance in the moonlight for you, Torvald.

Helmer: Nora, you can't be referring to what you talked about this morning.

Nora (moving close to him): Yes, Torvald, I'm really begging you—

Helmer: You really have the nerve to bring that up again?

Nora: Yes, dear, you have to do this for me. You have to let Krogstad keep his job in the bank.

Helmer: My dear Nora, his job is the one that I'm giving to Mrs. Linde.

Nora: Yes, you've been awfully sweet about that. But you could just as easily get rid of somebody else instead of Krogstad.

Helmer: This is just unbelievable stubbornness! Because you decided to foolishly promise that you'd speak up for him, you expect me to—

Nora: That's not the reason, Torvald. It's for your own sake. This man writes for the trashiest newspapers, you've told me so yourself. He can do you an incredible amount of harm. I'm scared to death of him—

Helmer: Oh, I see, it's bad memories that are making you afraid.

Nora: What do you mean?

Helmer: Obviously you're thinking about your father.

Nora: Yes. Yes, of course. You remember what those hateful creatures wrote in the papers about Papa, and how horribly they slandered him. I believe they'd have gotten him fired if the department hadn't sent you over to look into it, and if you hadn't been so kind and helpful to him.

Helmer: My little Nora, there's an important difference between your father and me. His reputation as a public official was not above suspicion. Mine is, and I hope it will continue to be for as long as I hold my office.

Nora: You never can tell what trouble these men might cause. We could be so well off, so snug and happy here in our peaceful home, without a care in the world, you and I and the children, Torvald! That's why I'm begging you to—

Helmer: And the more you plead for him, the more you make it impossible for me to keep him. They already know at the bank that I'm going to fire

Krogstad. Do you think I'm going to let them all say that the new manager has changed his mind because his wife said to—

Nora: And what if they did?

Helmer: Right! What does it matter, as long as this stubborn little creature gets her own way! Do you think I'm going to make myself look ridiculous in front of my whole staff, and let people think that I can be pushed around by all sorts of outside influence? That would soon come back to haunt me, you can be sure! And besides, there's one thing that makes it totally impossible for me to have Krogstad working in the bank as long as I'm the manager.

Nora: What's that?

Helmer: I might have been able to overlook his moral failings, if need be—

Nora: Yes, you could do that, couldn't you?

Helmer: And I hear he's a good worker, too. But I knew him when we were boys. It was one of those rash friendships that so often turn out to be a millstone around the neck later on. I might as well tell you straight out, we were very close friends at one time. But he has no tact and no self-restraint, especially when other people are around. He thinks he has the right to still call me by my first name, and every minute it's Torvald this and Torvald that. I don't mind telling you, I find it extremely annoying. He would make my position at the bank intolerable.

Nora: Torvald, I can't believe you're serious.

Helmer: Oh no? Why not?

Nora: Because it's so petty.

Helmer: What do you mean, petty? You think I'm petty?

Nora: No, just the opposite, dear, and that's why I can't—

Helmer: It's the same thing. You say my attitude's petty, so I must be petty too! Petty! Fine! Well, I'll put a stop to this once and for all. (*Goes to the hall door and calls.*) Helene!

Nora: What are you going to do?

Helmer (*looking among his papers*): Settle it.

(*Enter Maid.*)

Here, take this letter downstairs right now. Find a messenger and tell him to deliver it, and to be quick about it. The address is on it, and here's the money.

Maid: Yes, sir. (*Exits with the letter.*)

Helmer (*putting his papers together*): There, Little Pigheaded Miss.

Nora (*breathlessly*): Torvald, what was that letter?

Helmer: Krogstad's notice.

Nora: Call her back, Torvald! There's still time. Oh, Torvald, call her back! Do it for my sake—for your own sake—for the children's sake! Do you hear me, Torvald? Call her back! You don't know what that letter can do to us.

Helmer: It's too late.

Nora: Yes, it's too late.

Helmer: My dear Nora, I can forgive this anxiety of yours, even though it's insulting to me. It really is. Don't you think it's insulting to suggest that I should be afraid of retaliation from a grubby pen-pusher? But I forgive you anyway, because it's such a beautiful demonstration of how much you love me. (*Takes her in his arms.*) And that is as it should be, my own darling Nora. Come what may, you can rest assured that I'll have both courage and strength if necessary. You'll see that I'm man enough to take everything on myself.

Nora (in a horror-stricken voice): What do you mean by that?

Helmer: Everything, I say.

Nora (recovering herself): You'll never have to do that.

Helmer: That's right, we'll take it on together, Nora, as man and wife. That's just how it should be. (*Caressing her.*) Are you satisfied now? There, there! Don't look at me that way, like a frightened dove! This whole thing is just your imagination running away with you. Now you should go and run through the tarantella and practice your tambourine. I'll go into my study and shut the door so I can't hear anything. You can make all the noise you want. (*Turns back at the door.*) And when Rank comes, tell him where I am.

(*Nods to her, takes his papers and goes into his room, and shuts the door behind him.*)

Nora (bewildered with anxiety, stands as if rooted to the spot and whispers): He's capable of doing it. He's going to do it. He'll do it in spite of everything. No, not that! Never, never! Anything but that! Oh, for somebody to help me find some way out of this! (*The doorbell rings.*) Doctor Rank! Anything but that—anything, whatever it is!

(*She puts her hands over her face, pulls herself together, goes to the door and opens it. Rank is standing in the hall, hanging up his coat. During the following dialogue it starts to grow dark.*)

Nora: Hello, Doctor Rank. I recognized your ring. But you'd better not go in and see Torvald just now. I think he's busy with something.

Rank: And you?

Nora (brings him in and shuts the door behind him): Oh, you know perfectly well I always have time for you.

Rank: Thank you. I'll make use of it for as long as I can.

Nora: What does that mean, for as long as you can?

Rank: Why, does that frighten you?

Nora: It was such a strange way of putting it. Is something going to happen?

Rank: Nothing but what I've been expecting for a long time. But I never thought it would happen so soon.

Nora (gripping him by the arm): What have you found out? Doctor Rank, you must tell me.

Rank (sitting down by the stove): I'm done for. And there's nothing I can do about it.

Nora (with a sigh of relief): Oh—you're talking about yourself?

Rank: Who else? And there's no use lying to myself. I'm the sickest patient I have, Mrs. Helmer. Lately I've been adding up my internal account. Bankrupt! In a month I'll probably be rotting in the ground.

Nora: What a horrible thing to say!

Rank: The thing itself is horrible, and the worst of it is all the horrible things I'll have to go through before it's over. I'm going to examine myself just once more. When that's done, I'll be pretty sure when I'm going to start breaking down. There's something I want to say to you. Helmer's sensitive nature makes him completely unable to deal with anything ugly. I don't want him in my sickroom.

Nora: Oh, but, Doctor Rank—

Rank: I won't have him there, period. I'll lock the door to keep him out. As soon as I'm quite sure that the worst has come, I'll send you my card with a black cross on it, and that way you'll know that the final stage of the horror has started.

Nora: You're being really absurd today. And I so much wanted you to be in a good mood.

Rank: With death stalking me? Having to pay this price for another man's sins? Where's the justice in that? In every single family, in one way or another, some such unavoidable retribution is being imposed.

Nora (putting her hands over her ears): Nonsense! Can't you talk about something cheerful?

Rank: Oh, this *is* something cheerful. In fact, it's hilarious. My poor innocent spine has to suffer for my father's youthful self-indulgence.

Nora (sitting at the table on the left): Yes, he did love asparagus and *pâté de foie gras*, didn't he?

Rank: Yes, and truffles.

Nora: Truffles, yes. And oysters too, I suppose?

Rank: Oysters, of course. That goes without saying.

Nora: And oceans of port and champagne. Isn't it sad that all those delightful things should take their revenge on our bones?

Rank: Especially that they should take their revenge on the unlucky bones of people who haven't even had the satisfaction of enjoying them.

Nora: Yes, that's the saddest part of all.

Rank (with a searching look at her): Hm!

Nora (after a short pause): Why did you smile?

Rank: No, it was you who laughed.

Nora: No, it was you who smiled, Doctor Rank!

Rank (rising): You're even more of a tease than I thought you were.

Nora: I am in a crazy mood today.

Rank: Apparently so.

Nora (putting her hands on his shoulders): Dear, dear Doctor Rank, we can't let death take you away from Torvald and me.

Rank: It's a loss that you'll easily recover from. Those who are gone are soon forgotten.

Nora (looking at him anxiously): Do you really believe that?

Rank: People make new friends, and then—

Nora: Who'll make new friends?

Rank: Both you and Helmer, when I'm gone. You yourself are already well on the way to it, I think. What was that Mrs. Linde doing here last night?

Nora: Oho! You're not telling me that you're jealous of poor Kristine, are you?

Rank: Yes, I am. She'll be my successor in this house. When I'm six feet under, this woman will—

Nora: Shh! Don't talk so loud. She's in that room.

Rank: Again today. There, you see.

Nora: She's just come to sew my dress for me. Goodness, how unreasonable you are! (*Sits down on the sofa.*) Be nice now, Doctor Rank, and tomorrow you'll see how beautifully I'll dance, and you can pretend that I'm doing it just for you—and for Torvald too, of course. (*Takes various things out of the box.*) Doctor Rank, come and sit down here, and I'll show you something.

Rank (sitting down): What is it?

Nora: Just look at these!

Rank: Silk stockings.

Nora: Flesh-colored. Aren't they lovely? It's so dark here now, but tomorrow—No, no, no! You're only supposed to look at the feet. Oh well, you have my permission to look at the legs too.

Rank: Hm!

Nora: Why do you look so critical? Don't you think they'll fit me?

Rank: I have no basis for forming an opinion on that subject.

Nora (looks at him for a moment): Shame on you! (*Hits him lightly on the ear with the stockings.*) That's your punishment. (*Folds them up again.*)

Rank: And what other pretty things do I have your permission to look at?

Nora: Not one single thing. That's what you get for being so naughty. (*She looks among the things, humming to herself.*)

Rank (after a short silence): When I'm sitting here, talking to you so intimately this way, I can't imagine for a moment what would have become of me if I'd never come into this house.

Nora (smiling): I believe you really do feel completely at home with us.

Rank (in a lower voice, looking straight in front of him): And to have to leave it all—

Nora: Nonsense, you're not going to leave it.

Rank (as before): And not to be able to leave behind the slightest token of my gratitude, hardly even a fleeting regret. Nothing but an empty place to be filled by the first person who comes along.

Nora: And if I were to ask you now for a—No, never mind!

Rank: For a what?

Nora: For a great proof of your friendship—

Rank: Yes, yes!

Nora: I mean a tremendously huge favor—

Rank: Would you really make me so happy, just this once?

Nora: But you don't know what it is yet.

Rank: No, but tell me.

Nora: I really can't, Doctor Rank. It's too much to ask. It involves advice, and help, and a favor—

Rank: So much the better. I can't imagine what you mean. Tell me what it is. You do trust me, don't you?

Nora: More than anyone. I know that you're my best and truest friend, so I'll tell you what it is. Well, Doctor Rank, it's something you have to help me prevent. You know how devoted Torvald is to me, how deeply he loves me. He wouldn't hesitate for a second to give his life for me.

Rank (leaning towards her): Nora, do you think that he's the only one—

Nora (with a slight start): The only one?

Rank: Who would gladly give his life for you.

Nora (sadly): Oh, is that it?

Rank: I'd made up my mind to tell you before I—I go away, and there'll never be a better opportunity than this. Now you know it, Nora. And now you know that you can trust me more than you can trust anyone else.

Nora (rises, deliberately and quietly): Let me by.

Rank (makes room for her to pass him, but sits still): Nora!

Nora (at the hall door): Helene, bring in the lamp. (*Goes over to the stove.*) Dear Doctor Rank, that was really horrible of you.

Rank: To love you just as much as somebody else does? Is that so horrible?

Nora: No, but to go and tell me like that. There was really no need—

Rank: What do you mean? Did you know—

(*Maid enters with lamp, puts it down on the table, and goes out.*)

Nora—Mrs. Helmer—tell me, did you have any idea I felt this way?

Nora: Oh, how do I know whether I did or I didn't? I really can't answer that. How could you be so clumsy, Doctor Rank? When we were getting along so nicely.

Rank: Well, at any rate, now you know that I'm yours to command, body and soul. So won't you tell me what it is?

Nora (looking at him): After what just happened?

Rank: I beg you to let me know what it is.

Nora: I can't tell you anything now.

Rank: Yes, yes. Please don't punish me that way. Give me permission to do anything for you that a man can do.

Nora: You can't do anything for me now. Besides, I really don't need any help at all. The whole thing is just my imagination. It really is. It has to be!

(Sits down in the rocking chair, and smiles at him.) You're a nice man, Doctor Rank. Don't you feel ashamed of yourself, now that the lamp is lit?

Rank: Not a bit. But maybe it would be better if I left—and never came back?

Nora: No, no, you can't do that. You must keep coming here just as you always did. You know very well Torvald can't do without you.

Rank: But what about you?

Nora: Oh, I'm always extremely pleased to see you.

Rank: And that's just what gave me the wrong idea. You're a puzzle to me. I've often felt that you'd almost just as soon be in my company as in Helmer's.

Nora: Yes, you see, there are the people you love the most, and then there are the people whose company you enjoy the most.

Rank: Yes, there's something to that.

Nora: When I lived at home, of course I loved Papa best. But I always thought it was great fun to sneak down to the maids' room, because they never preached at me, and I loved listening to the way they talked to each other.

Rank: I see. So I'm their replacement.

Nora (jumping up and going to him): Oh, dear, sweet Doctor Rank, I didn't mean it that way. But surely you can understand that being with Torvald is a little like being with Papa—

(Enter Maid from the hall.)

Maid: Excuse me, ma'am. *(Whispers and hands her a card.)*

Nora (glancing at the card): Oh! *(Puts it in her pocket.)*

Rank: Is something wrong?

Nora: No, no, not at all. It's just—it's my new dress—

Rank: What? Your dress is lying right there.

Nora: Oh, yes, that one. But this is another one, one that I ordered. I don't want Torvald to find out about it—

Rank: Oh! So that was the big secret.

Nora: Yes, that's it. Why don't you just go inside and see him? He's in his study. Stay with him for as long as—

Rank: Put your mind at ease. I won't let him escape. *(Goes into Helmer's study.)*

Nora (to the maid): And he's waiting in the kitchen?

Maid: Yes, ma'am. He came up the back stairs.

Nora: Didn't you tell him no one was home?

Maid: Yes, but it didn't do any good.

Nora: He won't go away?

Maid: No, he says he won't leave until he sees you, ma'am.

Nora: Well, show him in, but quietly. Helene, I don't want you to say anything about this to anyone. It's a surprise for my husband.

Maid: Yes, ma'am. I understand. *(Exit.)*

Nora: This horrible thing is really going to happen! It's going to happen in spite of me! No, no, no, it can't happen! I can't let it happen!

(She bolts the door of Helmer's study. The maid opens the hall door for Krogstad and closes it behind him. He is wearing a fur coat, high boots, and a fur cap.)

Nora (advancing towards him): Speak quietly. My husband's home.

Krogstad: What do I care about that?

Nora: What do you want from me?

Krogstad: An explanation of something.

Nora: Be quick, then. What is it?

Krogstad: I suppose you're aware that I've been let go.

Nora: I couldn't prevent it, Mr. Krogstad. I fought for you as hard as I could, but it was no use.

Krogstad: Does your husband love you so little, then? He knows what I can expose you to, and he still goes ahead and—

Nora: How can you think that he knows any such thing?

Krogstad: I didn't think so for a moment. It wouldn't be at all like dear old Torvald Helmer to show that kind of courage—

Nora: Mr. Krogstad, a little respect for my husband, please.

Krogstad: Certainly—all the respect he deserves. But since you've kept everything so carefully to yourself, may I be bold enough to assume that you see a little more clearly than you did yesterday just what it is that you've done?

Nora: More than you could ever teach me.

Krogstad: Yes, such a poor excuse for a lawyer as I am.

Nora: What is it you want from me?

Krogstad: Only to see how you're doing, Mrs. Helmer. I've been thinking about you all day. A mere bill collector, a pen-pusher, a—well, a man like me—even he has a little of what people call feelings, you know.

Nora: Why don't you show some, then? Think about my little children.

Krogstad: Have you and your husband thought about mine? But never mind about that. I just wanted to tell you not to take this business too seriously. I won't make any accusations against you. Not for now, anyway.

Nora: No, of course not. I was sure you wouldn't.

Krogstad: The whole thing can be settled amicably. There's no need for anyone to know anything about it. It'll be our little secret, just the three of us.

Nora: My husband must never know anything about it.

Krogstad: How are you going to keep him from finding out? Are you telling me that you can pay off the whole balance?

Nora: No, not just yet.

Krogstad: Or that you have some other way of raising the money soon?

Nora: No way that I plan to make use of.

Krogstad: Well, in any case, it wouldn't be any use to you now even if you did. If you stood in front of me with a stack of bills in each hand, I still wouldn't give you back your note.

Nora: What are you planning to do with it?

Krogstad: I just want to hold onto it, just keep it in my possession. No one who isn't involved in the matter will ever know anything about it. So, if you've been thinking about doing something desperate—

Nora: I have.

Krogstad: If you've been thinking about running away—

Nora: I have.

Krogstad: Or doing something even worse—

Nora: How could you know that?

Krogstad: Stop thinking about it.

Nora: How did you know I'd thought of that?

Krogstad: Most of us think about that at first. I did, too. But I didn't have the courage.

Nora (faintly): Neither do I.

Krogstad (in a tone of relief): No, that's true, isn't it? You don't have the courage either?

Nora: No, I don't. I don't.

Krogstad: Besides, it would have been an incredibly stupid thing to do. Once the first storm at home blows over . . . I have a letter for your husband in my pocket.

Nora: Telling him everything?

Krogstad: As gently as possible.

Nora (quickly): He can't see that letter. Tear it up. I'll find some way of getting money.

Krogstad: Excuse me, Mrs. Helmer, but didn't I just tell you—

Nora: I'm not talking about what I owe you. Tell me how much you want from my husband, and I'll get the money.

Krogstad: I don't want any money from your husband.

Nora: Then what do you want?

Krogstad: I'll tell you what I want. I want a fresh start, Mrs. Helmer, and I want to move up in the world. And your husband's going to help me do it. I've steered clear of anything questionable for the last year and a half. In all that time I've been struggling along, pinching every penny. I was content to work my way up step by step. But now I've been fired, and it's not going to be enough just to get my job back, as if you people were doing me some huge favor. I want to move up, I tell you. I want to get back into the bank again, but with a promotion. Your husband's going to have to find me a position—

Nora: He'll never do it!

Krogstad: Oh yes, he will. I know him. He won't dare object. And as soon as I'm back there with him, then you'll see! Inside of a year I'll be the manager's right-hand man. It'll be Nils Krogstad, not Torvald Helmer, who's running the bank.

Nora: That's never going to happen!

Krogstad: Do you mean that you'll—

Nora: I have enough courage for it now.

Krogstad: Oh, you can't scare me. An elegant, spoiled lady like you—

Nora: You'll see, you'll see.

Krogstad: Under the ice, maybe? Down in the cold, coal-black water? And then floating up to the surface in the spring, all horrible and unrecognizable, with your hair fallen out—

Nora: You can't scare me.

Krogstad: And you can't scare me. People don't do that kind of thing, Mrs. Helmer. Besides, what good would it do? I'd still have him completely in my power.

Nora: Even then? When I'm no longer—

Krogstad: Have you forgotten that your reputation is completely in my hands? (*Nora stands speechless, looking at him.*) Well, now I've warned you. Don't do anything foolish. I'll be expecting an answer from Helmer after he reads my letter. And remember, it's your husband himself who's forced me to act this way again. I'll never forgive him for that. Goodbye, Mrs. Helmer. (*Exits through the hall.*)

Nora (*goes to the hall door, opens it slightly and listens.*): He's leaving. He isn't putting the letter in the box. Oh no, no! He couldn't! (*Opens the door little by little.*) What? He's standing out there. He's not going downstairs. He's hesitating? Is he?

(*A letter drops into the box. Then Krogstad's footsteps are heard, until they die away as he goes downstairs. Nora utters a stifled cry, and runs across the room to the table by the sofa. A short pause.*)

Nora: In the mailbox. (*Steals across to the hall door.*) It's there! Torvald, Torvald, there's no hope for us now!

(*Mrs. Linde comes in from the room on the left, carrying the dress.*)

Mrs. Linde: There, I can't find anything more to mend. Would you like to try it on?

Nora (*in a hoarse whisper*): Kristine, come here.

Mrs. Linde (*throwing the dress down on the sofa*): What's the matter with you? You look so agitated!

Nora: Come here. Do you see that letter? There, look. You can see it through the glass in the mailbox.

Mrs. Linde: Yes, I see it.

Nora: That letter is from Krogstad.

Mrs. Linde: Nora! It was Krogstad who lent you the money!

Nora: Yes, and now Torvald will know all about it.

Mrs. Linde: Believe me, Nora, that's the best thing for both of you.

Nora: You don't know the whole story. I forged a name.

Mrs. Linde: My God!

Nora: There's something I want to say to you, Kristine. I need you to be my witness.

Mrs. Linde: Your witness? What do you mean? What am I supposed to—

Nora: If I should go out of my mind—and it could easily happen—

Mrs. Linde: Nora!

Nora: Or if anything else should happen to me—anything, for instance, that might keep me from being here—

Mrs. Linde: Nora! Nora! What's the matter with you?

Nora: And if it turned out that somebody wanted to take all the responsibility, all the blame, you understand what I mean—

Mrs. Linde: Yes, yes, but how can you imagine—

Nora: Then you must be my witness that it's not true, Kristine. I'm not out of my mind at all. I'm perfectly rational right now, and I'm telling you that no one else ever knew anything about it. I did the whole thing all by myself. Remember that.

Mrs. Linde: I will. But I don't understand all this.

Nora: How could you understand it? Or the miracle that's going to happen!

Mrs. Linde: A miracle?

Nora: Yes, a miracle! But it's so terrible, Kristine. I can't let it happen, not for the whole world.

Mrs. Linde: I'll go and see Krogstad right this minute.

Nora: No, don't. He'll do something to hurt you too.

Mrs. Linde: There was a time when he would have gladly done anything for my sake.

Nora: What?

Mrs. Linde: Where does he live?

Nora: How should I know? Yes (*feeling in her pocket*), here's his card. But the letter, the letter—

Helmer (calls from his room, knocking at the door): Nora!

Nora (cries out anxiously): What is it? What do you want?

Helmer: Don't be so afraid. We're not coming in. You've locked the door. Are you trying on your dress?

Nora: Yes, that's it. Oh, it's going to look so nice, Torvald.

Mrs. Linde (who has read the card): Look, he lives right around the corner.

Nora: But it's no use. It's all over. The letter's lying right there in the box.

Mrs. Linde: And your husband has the key?

Nora: Yes, always.

Mrs. Linde: Krogstad can ask for his letter back unread. He'll have to make up some reason—

Nora: But now is just about the time that Torvald usually—

Mrs. Linde: You have to prevent him. Go in and talk to him. I'll be back as soon as I can.

(*She hurries out through the hall door.*)

Nora (goes to Helmer's door, opens it and peeps in): Torvald!

Helmer (from the inner room): Well? May I finally come back into my own room? Come along, Rank, now you'll see—(*Stopping in the doorway.*) But what's this?

Nora: What's what, dear?

Helmer: Rank led me to expect an amazing transformation.

Rank (in the doorway): So I understood, but apparently I was mistaken.

Nora: Yes, nobody gets to admire me in my dress until tomorrow.

Helmer: But, my dear Nora, you look exhausted. Have you been practicing too much?

Nora: No, I haven't been practicing at all.

Helmer: But you'll have to—

Nora: Yes, of course I will, Torvald. But I can't get anywhere without you helping me. I've completely forgotten the whole thing.

Helmer: Oh, we'll soon get you back up to form again.

Nora: Yes, help me, Torvald. Promise that you will! I'm so nervous about it—all those people. I need you to devote yourself completely to me this evening. Not even the tiniest little bit of business. You can't even pick up a pen. Do you promise, Torvald dear?

Helmer: I promise. This evening I will be wholly and absolutely at your service, you helpless little creature. But first I'm just going to—(*Goes towards the hall door.*)

Nora: Just going to what?

Helmer: To see if there's any mail.

Nora: No, no! Don't do that, Torvald!

Helmer: Why not?

Nora: Torvald, please don't. There's nothing there.

Helmer: Well, let me look. (*Turns to go to the mailbox. Nora, at the piano, plays the first bars of the tarantella. Helmer stops in the doorway.*) Aha!

Nora: I can't dance tomorrow if I don't practice with you.

Helmer (going up to her): Are you really so worried about it, dear?

Nora: Yes, terribly worried about it. Let me practice right now. We have time before dinner. Sit down and play for me, Torvald dear. Criticize me and correct me, the way you always do.

Helmer: With great pleasure, if you want me to. (*Sits down at the piano.*)

Nora (takes a tambourine and a long multicolored shawl out of the box. She hastily drapes the shawl around her. Then she bounds to the front of the stage and calls out): Now play for me! I'm going to dance!

(*Helmer plays and Nora dances. Rank stands by the piano behind Helmer and watches.*)

Helmer (as he plays): Slower, slower!

Nora: I can't do it any other way.

Helmer: Not so violently, Nora!

Nora: This is the way.

Helmer (stops playing): No, no, that's not right at all.

Nora (laughing and swinging the tambourine): Didn't I tell you so?

Rank: Let me play for her.

Helmer (getting up): Good idea. I can correct her better that way.

(*Rank sits down at the piano and plays. Nora dances more and more wildly. Helmer has taken up a position beside the stove, and as she dances, he gives her frequent instructions. She doesn't seem to hear him. Her hair comes undone and falls over her shoulders. She pays no attention to it, but goes on dancing. Enter Mrs. Linde.*)

Mrs. Linde (standing as if spellbound in the doorway): Oh!

Nora (as she dances): What fun, Kristine!

Helmer: My dear darling Nora, you're dancing as if your life depended on it.

Nora: It does.

Helmer: Stop, Rank. This is insane! I said stop!

(*Rank stops playing, and Nora suddenly stands still. Helmer goes up to her.*)

I never would have believed it. You've forgotten everything I taught you.

Nora (throwing the tambourine aside): There, you see.

Helmer: You're going to need a lot of coaching.

Nora: Yes, you see how much I need it. You have to coach me right up to the last minute. Promise me you will, Torvald!

Helmer: You can depend on me.

Nora: You can't think about anything but me, today or tomorrow. Don't open a single letter. Don't even open the mailbox—

Helmer: You're still afraid of that man—

Nora: Yes, yes, I am.

Helmer: Nora, I can tell from your face that there's a letter from him in the box.

Nora: I don't know. I think there is. But you can't read anything like that now. Nothing nasty must come between us until this is all over.

Rank (whispers to Helmer): Don't contradict her.

Helmer (taking her in his arms): The child shall have her way. But tomorrow night, after you've danced—

Nora: Then you'll be free.

(*The Maid appears in the doorway to the right.*)

Maid: Dinner is served, ma'am.

Nora: We'll have champagne, Helene.

Maid: Yes, ma'am. (*Exit.*)

Helmer: Oh, are we having a banquet?

Nora: Yes, a banquet. Champagne till dawn! (*Calls out.*) And a few maca-roons, Helene. Lots of them, just this once!

Helmer: Come on, stop acting so wild and nervous. Be my own little skylark again.

Nora: Yes, dear, I will. But go inside now, and you too, Doctor Rank. Kristine, please help me do up my hair.

Rank (whispers to Helmer as they go out): There isn't anything—she's not expecting—?

Helmer: No, nothing like that. It's just this childish nervousness I was telling you about. *(They go into the right-hand room.)*

Nora: Well?

Mrs. Linde: Out of town.

Nora: I could tell from your face.

Mrs. Linde: He'll be back tomorrow evening. I wrote him a note.

Nora: You should have left it alone. Don't try to prevent anything. After all, it's exciting to be waiting for a miracle to happen.

Mrs. Linde: What is it that you're waiting for?

Nora: Oh, you wouldn't understand. Go inside with them, I'll be there in a moment.

> *(Mrs. Linde goes into the dining room. Nora stands still for a little while, as if to compose herself. Then she looks at her watch.)*

Five o'clock. Seven hours till midnight, and another twenty-four hours till the next midnight. And then the tarantella will be over. Twenty-four plus seven? Thirty-one hours to live.

Helmer (from the doorway on the right): Where's my little skylark?

Nora (going to him with her arms outstretched): Here she is!

ACT III

The same scene. The table has been placed in the middle of the stage, with chairs around it. A lamp is burning on the table. The door into the hall stands open. Dance music is heard in the room above. Mrs. Linde is sitting at the table idly turning over the pages of a book. She tries to read, but she seems unable to concentrate. Every now and then she listens intently for a sound at the outer door.

Mrs. Linde (looking at her watch): Not yet—and the time's nearly up. If only he doesn't—(Listens again.) Ah, there he is. (Goes into the hall and opens the outer door carefully. Light footsteps are heard on the stairs. She whispers.) Come in. There's no one else here.

Krogstad (in the doorway): I found a note from you at home. What does this mean?

Mrs. Linde: It's absolutely necessary that I have a talk with you.

Krogstad: Really? And is it absolutely necessary that we have it here?

Mrs. Linde: It's impossible where I live. There's no private entrance to my apartment. Come in. We're all alone. The maid's asleep, and the Helmers are upstairs at a dance.

Krogstad (coming into the room): Are the Helmers really at a dance tonight?

Mrs. Linde: Yes. Why shouldn't they be?

Krogstad: Certainly—why not?

Mrs. Linde: Now, Nils, let's have a talk.

Krogstad: What can we two have to talk about?

Mrs. Linde: Quite a lot.

Krogstad: I wouldn't have thought so.

Mrs. Linde: Of course not. You've never really understood me.

Krogstad: What was there to understand, except what the whole world could see—a heartless woman drops a man when a better catch comes along?

Mrs. Linde: Do you think I'm really that heartless? And that I broke it off with you so lightly?

Krogstad: Didn't you?

Mrs. Linde: Nils, did you really think that?

Krogstad: If not, why did you write what you did to me?

Mrs. Linde: What else could I do? Since I had to break it off with you, I had an obligation to stamp out your feelings for me.

Krogstad (wringing his hands): So that was it. And all this just for the sake of money!

Mrs. Linde: Don't forget that I had an invalid mother and two little brothers. We couldn't wait for you, Nils. Success seemed a long way off for you back then.

Krogstad: That may be so, but you had no right to cast me aside for anyone else's sake.

Mrs. Linde: I don't know if I did or not. Many times I've asked myself if I had the right.

Krogstad (more gently): When I lost you, it was as if the earth crumbled under my feet. Look at me now—a shipwrecked man clinging to a bit of wreckage.

Mrs. Linde: But help may be on the way.

Krogstad: It *was* on the way, till you came along and blocked it.

Mrs. Linde: Without knowing it, Nils. It wasn't till today that I found out I'd be taking your job.

Krogstad: I believe you, if you say so. But now that you know it, are you going to step aside?

Mrs. Linde: No, because it wouldn't do you any good.

Krogstad: Good? I would quit whether it did any good or not.

Mrs. Linde: I've learned to be practical. Life and hard, bitter necessity have taught me that.

Krogstad: And life has taught me not to believe in fine speeches.

Mrs. Linde: Then life has taught you something very sensible. But surely you believe in actions?

Krogstad: What do you mean by that?

Mrs. Linde: You said you were like a shipwrecked man clinging to a piece of wreckage.

Krogstad: I had good reason to say so.

Mrs. Linde: Well, I'm like a shipwrecked woman clinging to a piece of wreck-age, with no one to mourn for and no one to care for.

Krogstad: That was your own choice.

Mrs. Linde: I had no other choice—then.

Krogstad: Well, what about now?

Mrs. Linde: Nils, how would it be if we two shipwrecked people could reach out to each other?

Krogstad: What are you saying?

Mrs. Linde: Two people on the same piece of wreckage would stand a better chance than each one on their own.

Krogstad: Kristine, I . . .

Mrs. Linde: Why do you think I came to town?

Krogstad: You can't mean that you were thinking about me?

Mrs. Linde: Life is unendurable without work. I've worked all my life, for as long as I can remember, and it's been my greatest and my only pleasure. But now that I'm completely alone in the world, my life is so terribly empty and I feel so abandoned. There isn't the slightest pleasure in work-ing only for yourself. Nils, give me someone and something to work for.

Krogstad: I don't trust this. It's just some romantic female impulse, a high-minded urge for self-sacrifice.

Mrs. Linde: Have you ever known me to be like that?

Krogstad: Could you really do it? Tell me, do you know all about my past?

Mrs. Linde: Yes.

Krogstad: And you know what they think of me around here?

Mrs. Linde: Didn't you imply that with me you might have been a very dif-ferent person?

Krogstad: I'm sure I would have.

Mrs. Linde: Is it too late now?

Krogstad: Kristine, are you serious about all this? Yes, I'm sure you are. I can see it in your face. Do you really have the courage, then—

Mrs. Linde: I want to be a mother to someone, and your children need a mother. We two need each other. Nils, I have faith in your true nature. I can face anything together with you.

Krogstad (grasps her hands): Thank you, thank you, Kristine! Now I can find a way to clear myself in the eyes of the world. Ah, but I forgot—

Mrs. Linde (listening): Shh! The tarantella! You have to go!

Krogstad: Why? What's the matter?

Mrs. Linde: Do you hear them up there? They'll probably come home as soon as this dance is over.

Krogstad: Yes, yes, I'll go. But it won't make any difference. You don't know what I've done about my situation with the Helmers.

Mrs. Linde: Yes, I know all about that.

Krogstad: And in spite of that you still have the courage to—

Mrs. Linde: I understand completely what despair can drive a man like you to do.

Krogstad: If only I could undo it!

Mrs. Linde: You can't. Your letter's lying in the mailbox now.

Krogstad: Are you sure?

Mrs. Linde: Quite sure, but—

Krogstad (with a searching look at her): Is that what this is all about? That you want to save your friend, no matter what you have to do? Tell me the truth. Is that it?

Mrs. Linde: Nils, when a woman has sold herself for someone else's sake, she doesn't do it a second time.

Krogstad: I'll ask for my letter back.

Mrs. Linde: No, no.

Krogstad: Yes, of course I will. I'll wait here until Helmer comes home. I'll tell him he has to give me back my letter, that it's only about my being fired, that I don't want him to read it—

Mrs. Linde: No, Nils, don't ask for it back.

Krogstad: But wasn't that the reason why you asked me to meet you here?

Mrs. Linde: In my first moment of panic, it was. But twenty-four hours have gone by since then, and in the meantime I've seen some incredible things in this house. Helmer has to know all about it. This terrible secret has to come out. They have to have a complete understanding between them. It's time for all this lying and pretending to stop.

Krogstad: All right then, if you think it's worth the risk. But there's at least one thing I can do, and do right away—

Mrs. Linde (listening): You have to leave this instant! The dance is over. They could walk in here any minute.

Krogstad: I'll wait for you downstairs.

Mrs. Linde: Yes, please do. I want you to walk me home.

Krogstad: I've never been so happy in my entire life!

(Goes out through the outer door. The door between the room and the hall remains open.)

Mrs. Linde (straightening up the room and getting her hat and coat ready): How different things will be! Someone to work for and live for, a home to bring happiness into. I'm certainly going to try. I wish they'd hurry up and come home—(Listens.) Ah, here they are now. I'd better put on my things.

(Picks up her hat and coat. Helmer's and Nora's voices are heard outside. A key is turned, and Helmer brings Nora into the hall almost by force. She is in an Italian peasant costume with a large black shawl wrapped around her. He is in formal wear and a black domino—a hooded cloak with an eye-mask—which is open.)

Nora (hanging back in the doorway and struggling with him): No, no, no! Don't bring me inside. I want to go back upstairs. I don't want to leave so early.

Helmer: But, my dearest Nora—

Nora: Please, Torvald dear, please, please, only one more hour.

Helmer: Not one more minute, my sweet Nora. You know this is what we agreed on. Come inside. You'll catch cold standing out there.

(*He brings her gently into the room, in spite of her resistance.*)

Mrs. Linde: Good evening.

Nora: Kristine!

Helmer: What are you doing here so late, Mrs. Linde?

Mrs. Linde: You must excuse me. I was so anxious to see Nora in her dress.

Nora: Have you been sitting here waiting for me?

Mrs. Linde: Yes, unfortunately I came too late, you'd already gone upstairs. And I didn't want to go away again without seeing you.

Helmer (*taking off Nora's shawl*): Yes, take a good look at her. I think she's worth looking at. Isn't she charming, Mrs. Linde?

Mrs. Linde: Yes, indeed she is.

Helmer: Doesn't she look especially pretty? Everyone thought so at the dance. But this sweet little person is extremely stubborn. What are we going to do with her? Believe it or not, I almost had to drag her away by force.

Nora: Torvald, you'll be sorry you didn't let me stay, even if only for half an hour.

Helmer: Listen to her, Mrs. Linde! She danced her tarantella and it was a huge success, as it deserved to be, though maybe her performance was a tiny bit too realistic, a little more so than it might have been by strict artistic standards. But never mind about that! The main thing is, she was a success, a tremendous success. Do you think I was going to let her stay there after that, and spoil the effect? Not a chance! I took my charming little Capri girl—my capricious little Capri girl, I should say—I took her by the arm, one quick circle around the room, a curtsey to one and all, and, as they say in novels, the beautiful vision vanished. An exit should always make an effect, Mrs. Linde, but I can't make Nora understand that. Whew, this room is hot!

(*Throws his domino on a chair and opens the door to his study.*)

Why is it so dark in here? Oh, of course. Excuse me.

(*He goes in and lights some candles.*)

Nora (*in a hurried, breathless whisper*): Well?

Mrs. Linde (*in a low voice*): I talked to him.

Nora: And?

Mrs. Linde: Nora, you have to tell your husband the whole story.

Nora (*in an expressionless voice*): I knew it.

Mrs. Linde: You have nothing to fear from Krogstad, but you still have to tell him.

Nora: I'm not going to.

Mrs. Linde: Then the letter will.

Nora: Thank you, Kristine. Now I know what I have to do. Shh!

Helmer (coming in again): Well, Mrs. Linde, have you been admiring her?

Mrs. Linde: Yes, I have, and now I'll say goodnight.

Helmer: What, already? Is this your knitting?

Mrs. Linde (taking it): Yes, thank you, I'd almost forgotten it.

Helmer: So you knit?

Mrs. Linde: Yes, of course.

Helmer: You know, you ought to embroider.

Mrs. Linde: Really? Why?

Helmer: It's much more graceful-looking. Here, let me show you. You hold the
embroidery this way in your left hand, and use the needle with your right,
like this, with a long, easy sweep. Do you see?

Mrs. Linde: Yes, I suppose—

Helmer: But knitting, that can never be anything but awkward. Here, look.
The arms close together, the knitting needles going up and down. It's sort
of Chinese looking. That was really excellent champagne they gave us.

Mrs. Linde: Well, good night, Nora, and don't be stubborn anymore.

Helmer: That's right, Mrs. Linde.

Mrs. Linde: Good night, Mr. Helmer.

Helmer (seeing her to the door): Good night, good night. I hope you get home
safely. I'd be very happy to—but you only have a short way to go. Good
night, good night.

(She goes out. He closes the door behind her, and comes in again.)

Ah, rid of her at last! What a bore that woman is.

Nora: Aren't you tired, Torvald?

Helmer: No, not at all.

Nora: You're not sleepy?

Helmer: Not a bit. As a matter of fact, I feel very lively. And what about you?
You really look tired *and* sleepy.

Nora: Yes, I am very tired. I want to go to sleep right away.

Helmer: So, you see how right I was not to let you stay there any longer.

Nora: You're always right, Torvald.

Helmer (kissing her on the forehead): Now my little skylark is talking sense. Did
you notice what a good mood Rank was in this evening?

Nora: Really? Was he? I didn't talk to him at all.

Helmer: And I only talked to him for a little while, but it's a long time since
I've seen him so cheerful. *(Looks at her for a while and then moves closer to
her.)* It's delightful to be home again by ourselves, to be alone with you,
you fascinating, charming little darling!

Nora: Don't look at me like that, Torvald.

Helmer: Why shouldn't I look at my dearest treasure? At all the beauty that is mine, all my very own?

Nora (going to the other side of the table): I wish you wouldn't talk that way to me tonight.

Helmer (following her): You've still got the tarantella in your blood, I see. And it makes you more captivating than ever. Listen, the guests are starting to leave now. *(In a lower voice.)* Nora, soon the whole house will be quiet.

Nora: Yes, I hope so.

Helmer: Yes, my own darling Nora. Do you know why, when we're out at a party like this, why I hardly talk to you, and keep away from you, and only steal a glance at you now and then? Do you know why I do that? It's because I'm pretending to myself that we're secretly in love, and we're secretly engaged, and no one suspects that there's anything between us.

Nora: Yes, yes, I know you're thinking about me every moment.

Helmer: And when we're leaving, and I'm putting the shawl over your beautiful young shoulders, on your lovely neck, then I imagine that you're my young bride and that we've just come from our wedding and I'm bringing you home for the first time, to be alone with you for the first time, all alone with my shy little darling! This whole night I've been longing for you alone. My blood was on fire watching you move when you danced the tarantella. I couldn't stand it any longer, and that's why I brought you home so early—

Nora: Stop it, Torvald! Let me go. I won't—

Helmer: What? You're not serious, Nora! You won't? You won't? I'm your husband—

(There is a knock at the outer door.)

Nora (starting): Did you hear—

Helmer (going into the hall): Who is it?

Rank (outside): It's me. May I come in for a moment?

Helmer (in an irritated whisper): What does he want now? *(Aloud.)* Wait a minute! *(Unlocks the door.)* Come in. It's good of you not to pass by our door without saying hello.

Rank: I thought I heard your voice, and I felt like dropping by. *(With a quick look around.)* Ah, yes, these dear familiar rooms. You two are very happy and cozy in here.

Helmer: You seemed to be making yourself pretty happy upstairs too.

Rank: Very much so. Why shouldn't I? Why shouldn't we enjoy everything in this world? At least as much as we can, for as long as we can. The wine was first-rate—

Helmer: Especially the champagne.

Rank: So you noticed that too? It's almost unbelievable how much of it I managed to put away!

Nora: Torvald drank a lot of champagne tonight too.

Rank: Did he?

Nora: Yes, and it always makes him so merry.

Rank: Well, why shouldn't a person have a merry evening after a well-spent day?

Helmer: Well-spent? I'm afraid I can't take credit for that.

Rank (clapping him on the back): But I can, you know!

Nora: Doctor Rank, you must have been busy with some scientific investigation today.

Rank: Exactly.

Helmer: Listen to this! Little Nora talking about scientific investigations!

Nora: And may I congratulate you on the result?

Rank: Indeed you may.

Nora: Was it favorable, then?

Rank: The best possible result, for both doctor and patient—certainty.

Nora (quickly and searchingly): Certainty?

Rank: Absolute certainty. So wasn't I entitled to make a merry evening of it after that?

Nora: Yes, you certainly were, Doctor Rank.

Helmer: I think so too, as long as you don't have to pay for it in the morning.

Rank: Oh well, you can't have anything in this life without paying for it.

Nora: Doctor Rank, are you fond of fancy-dress balls?

Rank: Yes, if there are a lot of pretty costumes.

Nora: Tell me, what should the two of us wear to the next one?

Helmer: Little featherbrain! You're thinking of the next one already?

Rank: The two of us? Yes, I can tell you. You'll go as a good-luck charm—

Helmer: Yes, but what would be the costume for that?

Rank: She just needs to dress the way she always does.

Helmer: That was very nicely put. But aren't you going to tell us what you'll be?

Rank: Yes, my dear friend, I've already made up my mind about that.

Helmer: Well?

Rank: At the next fancy-dress ball I'm going to be invisible.

Helmer: That's a good one!

Rank: There's a big black cap . . . Haven't you ever heard of the cap that makes you invisible? Once you put it on, no one can see you anymore.

Helmer (suppressing a smile): Yes, that's right.

Rank: But I'm clean forgetting what I came for. Helmer, give me a cigar. One of the dark Havanas.

Helmer: With the greatest pleasure. *(Offers him his case.)*

Rank (takes a cigar and cuts off the end): Thanks.

Nora (striking a match): Let me give you a light.

Rank: Thank you. *(She holds the match for him to light his cigar.)* And now goodbye!

Helmer: Goodbye, goodbye, my dear old friend.

Nora: Sleep well, Doctor Rank.

Rank: Thank you for that wish.

Nora: Wish me the same.

Rank: You? Well, if you want me to. Sleep well! And thanks for the light.
(*He nods to them both and goes out.*)

Helmer (in a subdued voice): He's had too much to drink.

Nora (absently): Maybe.

(*Helmer takes a bunch of keys out of his pocket and goes into the hall.*)

Torvald! What are you going to do out there?

Helmer: Empty the mailbox. It's quite full. There won't be any room for the
newspaper in the morning.

Nora: Are you going to work tonight?

Helmer: You know I'm not. What's this? Someone's been at the lock.

Nora: At the lock?

Helmer: Yes, it's been tampered with. What does this mean? I never would
have thought the maid—Look, here's a broken hairpin. It's one of yours,
Nora.

Nora (quickly): Then it must have been the children—

Helmer: Then you'd better break them of those habits. There, I've finally got
it open.

(*Empties the mailbox and calls out to the kitchen.*)

Helene! Helene, put out the light over the front door.

(*Comes back into the room and shuts the door into the hall. He holds out his
hand full of letters.*)

Look at that. Look what a pile of them there are. (*Turning them over.*) What's
this?

Nora (at the window): The letter! No! Torvald, no!

Helmer: Two calling cards of Rank's.

Nora: Of Doctor Rank's?

Helmer (looking at them): Yes, Doctor Rank. They were on top. He must have
put them in there when he left just now.

Nora: Is there anything written on them?

Helmer: There's a black cross over the name. Look. What a morbid thing to
do! It looks as if he's announcing his own death.

Nora: That's exactly what he's doing.

Helmer: What? Do you know anything about it? Has he said anything to you?

Nora: Yes. He told me that when the cards came it would be his farewell to us.
He means to close himself off and die.

Helmer: My poor old friend! Of course I knew we wouldn't have him for very
long. But this soon! And he goes and hides himself away like a wounded
animal.

Nora: If it has to happen, it's better that it be done without a word. Don't you think so, Torvald?

Helmer (walking up and down): He's become so much a part of our lives, I can't imagine him not being with us anymore. With his poor health and his loneliness, he was like a cloudy background to our sunlit happiness. Well, maybe it's all for the best. For him, anyway. *(Standing still.)* And maybe for us too, Nora. Now we have only each other to rely on. *(Puts his arms around her.)* My darling wife, I feel as though I can't possibly hold you tight enough. You know, Nora, I've often wished you were in some kind of serious danger, so that I could risk everything, even my own life, to save you.

Nora (disengages herself from him, and says firmly and decidedly): Now you must go and read your letters, Torvald.

Helmer: No, no, not tonight. I want to be with you, my darling wife.

Nora: With the thought of your friend's death—

Helmer: You're right, it has affected us both. Something ugly has come between us, the thought of the horrors of death. We have to try to put it out of our minds. Until we do, we'll each go to our own room.

Nora (with her arms around his neck): Good night, Torvald. Good night!

Helmer (kissing her on the forehead): Good night, my little songbird. Sleep well, Nora. Now I'll go read all my mail. *(He takes his letters and goes into his room, shutting the door behind him.)*

Nora (gropes distractedly about, picks up Helmer's domino and wraps it around her, while she says in quick, hoarse, spasmodic whispers): Never to see him again. Never! Never! *(Puts her shawl over her head.)* Never to see my children again either, never again. Never! Never! Oh, the icy, black water, the bottomless depths! If only it were over! He's got it now, now he's reading it. Goodbye, Torvald . . . children!

(She is about to rush out through the hall when Helmer opens his door hurriedly and stands with an open letter in his hand.)

Helmer: Nora!

Nora: Ah!

Helmer: What is this? Do you know what's in this letter?

Nora: Yes, I know. Let me go! Let me get out!

Helmer (holding her back): Where are you going?

Nora (trying to get free): You're not going to save me, Torvald!

Helmer (reeling): It's true? Is this true, what it says here? This is horrible! No, no, it can't possibly be true.

Nora: It is true. I've loved you more than anything else in the world.

Helmer: Don't start with your ridiculous excuses.

Nora (taking a step towards him): Torvald!

Helmer: You little fool, do you know what you've done?

Nora: Let me go. I won't let you suffer for my sake. You're not going to take it
　　on yourself.

Helmer: Stop play-acting. (*Locks the hall door.*) You're going to stay right here
　　and give me an explanation. Do you understand what you've done? An-
　　swer me! Do you understand what you've done?

Nora (looks steadily at him and says with a growing look of coldness in her face): Yes,
　　I'm beginning to understand everything now.

Helmer (walking around the room): What a horrible awakening! The woman
　　who was my pride and joy for eight years, a hypocrite, a liar, worse than
　　that, much worse—a criminal! The unspeakable ugliness of it all! The
　　shame of it! The shame!

(Nora is silent and looks steadily at him. He stops in front of her.)

I should have realized that something like this was bound to happen. I
should have seen it coming. Your father's shifty nature—be quiet!—your
father's shifty nature has come out in you. No religion, no morality, no
sense of duty. This is my punishment for closing my eyes to what he did!
I did it for your sake, and this is how you pay me back.

Nora: Yes, that's right.

Helmer: Now you've destroyed all my happiness. You've ruined my whole fu-
　　ture. It's horrible to think about! I'm in the power of an unscrupulous
　　man. He can do what he wants with me, ask me for anything he wants,
　　give me any orders he wants, and I don't dare say no. And I have to sink
　　to such miserable depths, all because of a feather-brained woman!

Nora: When I'm out of the way, you'll be free.

Helmer: Spare me the speeches. Your father had always plenty of those on
　　hand, too. What good would it do me if you were out of the way, as you
　　say? Not the slightest. He can tell everybody the whole story. And if he
　　does, I could be wrongly suspected of having been in on it with you. Peo-
　　ple will probably think I was behind it all, that I put you up to it! And
　　I have you to thank for all this, after I've cherished you the whole time
　　we've been married. Do you understand what you've done to me?

Nora (coldly and quietly): Yes.

Helmer: It's so incredible that I can't take it all in. But we have to come to
　　some understanding. Take off that shawl. Take it off, I said. I have to try to
　　appease him some way or another. It has to be hushed up, no matter what
　　it costs. And as for you and me, we have to make it look as if everything
　　is just as it always was, but only for the sake of appearances, obviously.
　　You'll stay here in my house, of course. But I won't let you bring up the
　　children. I can't trust them to you. To think that I have to say these things
　　to someone I've loved so dearly, and that I still—No, that's all over. From
　　this moment on happiness is out of the question. All that matters now is
　　to save the bits and pieces, to keep up the appearance—

(The front doorbell rings.)

Helmer (with a start): What's that? At this hour! Can the worst—Can he— Go and hide yourself, Nora. Say you don't feel well. (*Nora stands motionless. Helmer goes and unlocks the hall door.*)

Maid (half-dressed, comes to the door): A letter for Mrs. Helmer.

Helmer: Give it to me. (*Takes the letter, and shuts the door.*) Yes, it's from him. I'm not giving it to you. I'll read it myself.

Nora: Go ahead, read it.

Helmer (standing by the lamp): I barely have the courage to. It could mean ruin for both of us. No, I have to know. (*Tears open the letter, runs his eye over a few lines, looks at a piece of paper enclosed with it, and gives a shout of joy.*) Nora! (*She looks at him questioningly.*) Nora! No, I'd better read it again. Yes, it's true! I'm saved! Nora, I'm saved!

Nora: And what about me?

Helmer: You too, of course. We're both saved, you and I. Look, he's returned your note. He says he's sorry and he apologizes—that a happy change in his life—what difference does it make what he says! We're saved, Nora! Nobody can hurt you. Oh, Nora, Nora! No, first I have to destroy these horrible things. Let me see. . . . (*Glances at the note.*) No, no, I don't want to look at it. This whole business will be nothing but a bad dream to me.

(*Tears up the note and both letters, throws them all into the stove, and watches them burn.*)

There, now it doesn't exist anymore. He says that you've known since Christmas Eve. These must have been a horrible three days for you, Nora.

Nora: I fought a hard fight these three days.

Helmer: And suffered agonies, and saw no way out but—No, we won't dwell on any of those horrors. We'll just shout for joy and keep saying, "It's all over! It's all over!" Listen to me, Nora. You don't seem to realize that it's all over. What's this? Such a cold, hard face! My poor little Nora, I understand. You find it hard to believe that I've really forgiven you. But I swear that it's true, Nora. I forgive you for everything. I know that you did it all out of love for me.

Nora: That's true.

Helmer: You've loved me the way a wife ought to love her husband. You just didn't have the awareness to see what was wrong with the means you used. But do you think I love you any less because you don't understand how to deal with these things? No, of course not. I want you to lean on me. I'll advise you and guide you. I wouldn't be a man if this womanly helplessness didn't make you twice as attractive to me. Don't think anymore about the hard things I said when I was so upset at first, when I thought everything was going to crush me. I forgive you, Nora. I swear to you that I forgive you.

Nora: Thank you for your forgiveness. (*She goes out through the door to the right.*)

Helmer: No, don't go—(*Looks in.*) What are you doing in there?

Nora (from within): Taking off my costume.

Helmer (standing at the open door): Yes, do. Try to calm yourself, and ease your
mind again, my frightened little songbird. I want you to rest and feel secure. I have wide wings for you to take shelter underneath. (*Walks up and
down by the door.*) What a warm and cozy home we have, Nora. Here's a
safe haven for you, and I'll protect you like a hunted dove that I've rescued
from a hawk's claws. I'll calm your poor pounding heart. It will happen,
little by little, Nora, believe me. In the morning you'll see it in a very different light. Soon everything will be exactly the way it was before. Before
you know it, you won't need my reassurances that I've forgiven you. You'll
know for certain that I have. You can't imagine that I'd ever consider re-
jecting you, or even blaming you? You have no idea what a man feels in his
heart, Nora. A man finds it indescribably sweet and satisfying to know that
he's forgiven his wife, freely and with all his heart. It's as if he's made her
his own all over again. He's given her a new life, in a way, and she's become
both wife and child to him. And from this moment on that's what you'll
be to me, my little scared, helpless darling. Don't worry about anything,
Nora. Just be honest and open with me, and I'll be your will and your
conscience. What's this? You haven't gone to bed yet? Have you changed?
Nora (in everyday dress): Yes, Torvald, I've changed.
Helmer: But why—It's so late.
Nora: I'm not going to sleep tonight.
Helmer: But, my dear Nora—
Nora (looking at her watch): It's not that late. Sit down here, Torvald. You and
I have a lot to talk about. (*She sits down at one side of the table.*)
Helmer: Nora, what is this? Why this cold, hard face?
Nora: Sit down. This is going to take a while. I have a lot to say to you.
Helmer (sits down at the opposite side of the table): You're making me nervous,
Nora. And I don't understand you.
Nora: No, that's it exactly. You don't understand me, and I've never under-
stood you either, until tonight. No, don't interrupt me. I want you to
listen to what I have to say. Torvald, I'm settling accounts with you.
Helmer: What do you mean by that?
Nora (after a short silence): Doesn't anything strike you as odd about the way
we're sitting here like this?
Helmer: No, what?
Nora: We've been married for eight years. Doesn't it occur to you that this is
the first time the two of us, you and I, husband and wife, have had a serious conversation?
Helmer: What do you mean by serious?
Nora: In the whole eight years—longer than that, for the whole time we've
known each other—we've never exchanged one word on any serious subject.
Helmer: Did you expect me to be constantly worrying you with problems that
you weren't capable of helping me deal with?
Nora: I'm not talking about business. I mean we've never sat down together
seriously to try to get to the bottom of anything.

Helmer: But, dearest Nora, what good would that have done you?

Nora: That's just it. You've never understood me. I've been treated badly, Torvald, first by Papa and then by you.

Helmer: What? The two people who've loved you more than anyone else?

Nora (shaking her head): You've never loved me. You just thought it was pleasant to be in love with me.

Helmer: Nora, what are you saying?

Nora: It's true, Torvald. When I lived at home with Papa, he gave me his opinion about everything, and so I had all the same opinions, and if I didn't, I kept my mouth shut, because he wouldn't have liked it. He used to call me his doll-child, and he played with me the way I played with my dolls. And when I came to live in your house—

Helmer: What kind of way is that to talk about our marriage?

Nora (undisturbed): I mean that I was just passed from Papa's hands to yours. You arranged everything according to your own taste, and so I had all the same tastes as you. Or else I pretended to, I'm not really sure which. Sometimes I think it's one way and sometimes the other. When I look back, it's as if I've been living here like a beggar, from hand to mouth. I've supported myself by performing tricks for you, Torvald. But that's the way you wanted it. You and Papa have committed a terrible sin against me. It's your fault that I've done nothing with my life.

Helmer: This is so unfair and ungrateful of you, Nora! Haven't you been happy here?

Nora: No, I've never really been happy. I thought I was, but it wasn't true.

Helmer: Not—not happy!

Nora: No, just cheerful. You've always been very kind to me. But our home's been nothing but a playroom. I've been your doll-wife, the same way that I was Papa's doll-child. And the children have been my dolls. I thought it was great fun when you played with me, the way they thought it was when I played with them. That's what our marriage has been, Torvald.

Helmer: There's some truth in what you're saying, even though your view of it is exaggerated and overwrought. But things will be different from now on. Playtime is over, and now it's lesson-time.

Nora: Whose lessons? Mine, or the children's?

Helmer: Both yours and the children's, my darling Nora.

Nora: I'm sorry, Torvald, but you're not the man to give me lessons on how to be a proper wife to you.

Helmer: How can you say that?

Nora: And as for me, who am I to be allowed to bring up the children?

Helmer: Nora!

Nora: Didn't you say so yourself a little while ago, that you don't dare trust them to me?

Helmer: That was in a moment of anger! Why can't you let it go?

Nora: Because you were absolutely right. I'm not fit for the job. There's another job I have to take on first. I have to try to educate myself. You're not the man to help me with that. I have to do that for myself. And that's why I'm going to leave you now.

Helmer (jumping up): What are you saying?

Nora: I have to stand completely on my own, if I'm going to understand myself and everything around me. That's why I can't stay here with you any longer.

Helmer: Nora, Nora!

Nora: I'm leaving right now. I'm sure Kristine will put me up for the night—

Helmer: You're out of your mind! I won't let you go! I forbid it!

Nora: It's no use forbidding me anything anymore. I'm taking only what belongs to me. I won't take anything from you, now or later.

Helmer: This is insanity!

Nora: Tomorrow I'm going home. Back to where I came from, I mean. It'll be easier for me to find something to do there.

Helmer: You're a blind, senseless woman!

Nora: Then I'd better try to get some sense, Torvald.

Helmer: But to desert your home, your husband, and your children! And aren't you concerned about what people will say?

Nora: I can't concern myself with that. I only know that this is what I have to do.

Helmer: This is outrageous! You're just going to walk away from your most sacred duties?

Nora: What do you consider to be my most sacred duties?

Helmer: Do you need me to tell you that? Aren't they your duties to your husband and your children?

Nora: I have other duties just as sacred.

Helmer: No, you do not. What could they be?

Nora: Duties to myself.

Helmer: First and foremost, you're a wife and a mother.

Nora: I don't believe that anymore. I believe that first and foremost I'm a human being, just as you are—or, at least, that I have to try to become one. I know very well, Torvald, that most people would agree with you, and that opinions like yours are in books, but I can't be satisfied anymore with what most people say, or with what's in books. I have to think things through for myself and come to understand them.

Helmer: Why can't you understand your place in your own home? Don't you have an infallible guide in matters like that? What about your religion?

Nora: Torvald, I'm afraid I'm not sure what religion is.

Helmer: What are you saying?

Nora: All I know is what Pastor Hansen said when I was confirmed. He told us that religion was this, that, and the other thing. When I'm away from all this and on my own, I'll look into that subject too. I'll see if what he said is true or not, or at least whether it's true for me.

Helmer: This is unheard of, coming from a young woman like you! But if religion doesn't guide you, let me appeal to your conscience. I assume you have some moral sense. Or do you have none? Answer me.

Nora: Torvald, that's not an easy question to answer. I really don't know. It's very confusing to me. I only know that you and I look at it in very different ways. I'm learning too that the law isn't at all what I thought it was, and I can't convince myself that the law is right. A woman has no right to spare her old dying father or to save her husband's life? I can't believe that.

Helmer: You talk like a child. You don't understand anything about the world you live in.

Nora: No, I don't. But I'm going to try. I'm going to see if I can figure out who's right, me or the world.

Helmer: You're sick, Nora. You're delirious. I'm half convinced that you're out of your mind.

Nora: I've never felt so clearheaded and sure of myself as I do tonight.

Helmer: Clearheaded and sure of yourself—and that's the spirit in which you forsake your husband and your children?

Nora: Yes, it is.

Helmer: Then there's only one possible explanation.

Nora: Which is?

Helmer: You don't love me anymore.

Nora: Exactly.

Helmer: Nora! How can you say that?

Nora: It's very painful for me to say it, Torvald, because you've always been so good to me, but I can't help it. I don't love you anymore.

Helmer (regaining his composure): Are you clearheaded and sure of yourself when you say that too?

Nora: Yes, totally clearheaded and sure of myself. That's why I can't stay here.

Helmer: Can you tell me what I did to make you stop loving me?

Nora: Yes, I can. It was tonight, when the miracle didn't happen. That's when I realized you're not the man I thought you were.

Helmer: Can you explain that more clearly? I don't understand you.

Nora: I've been waiting so patiently for the last eight years. Of course I knew that miracles don't happen every day. Then when I found myself in this horrible situation, I was sure that the miracle was about to happen at last. When Krogstad's letter was lying out there, never for a moment did I imagine that you would agree to his conditions. I was absolutely certain that you'd say to him: Go ahead, tell the whole world. And when he had—

Helmer: Yes, what then? After I'd exposed my wife to shame and disgrace?

Nora: When he had, I was absolutely certain you'd come forward and take the whole thing on yourself, and say: I'm the guilty one.

Helmer: Nora—!

Nora: You mean that I would never have let you make such a sacrifice for me? Of course I wouldn't. But who would have believed my word against yours? That was the miracle that I hoped for and dreaded. And it was to keep it from happening that made me want to kill myself.

Helmer: I'd gladly work night and day for you, Nora, and endure sorrow and poverty for your sake. But no man would sacrifice his honor for the one he loves.

Nora: Hundreds of thousands of women have done it.

Helmer: Oh, you think and talk like a thoughtless child.

Nora: Maybe so. But you don't think or talk like the man I want to be with for the rest of my life. As soon as your fear had passed—and it wasn't fear for what threatened me, but for what might happen to you—when the whole thing was past, as far as you were concerned it was just as if nothing at all had happened. I was still your little skylark, your doll, but now you'd handle me twice as gently and carefully as before, because I was so delicate and fragile. (*Getting up.*) Torvald, that's when it dawned on me that for eight years I'd been living here with a stranger and had borne him three children. Oh, I can't bear to think about it! I could tear myself into little pieces!

Helmer (*sadly*): I see, I see. An abyss has opened up between us. There's no denying it. But, Nora, can't we find some way to close it?

Nora: The way I am now, I'm no wife for you.

Helmer: I can find it in myself to become a different man.

Nora: Maybe so—if your doll is taken away from you.

Helmer: But to be apart!—to be apart from you! No, no, Nora, I can't conceive of it.

Nora (*going out to the right*): All the more reason why it has to be done.

(*She comes back with her coat and hat and a small suitcase which she puts on a chair by the table.*)

Helmer: Nora, Nora, not now! Wait till tomorrow.

Nora (*putting on her cloak*): I can't spend the night in a strange man's room.

Helmer: But couldn't we live here together like brother and sister?

Nora (*putting on her hat*): You know how long that would last. (*Puts the shawl around her.*) Goodbye, Torvald. I won't look in on the children. I know they're in better hands than mine. The way I am now, I'm no use to them.

Helmer: But someday, Nora, someday?

Nora: How can I tell? I have no idea what's going to become of me.

Helmer: But you're my wife, whatever becomes of you.

Nora: Listen, Torvald. I've heard that when a wife deserts her husband's house, the way I'm doing now, he's free of all legal obligations to her. In any event, I set you free from all your obligations. I don't want you to feel bound in the slightest, any more than I will. There has to be complete freedom on both sides. Look, here's your ring back. Give me mine.

Helmer: That too?

Nora: That too.

Helmer: Here it is.

Nora: Good. Now it's all over. I've left the keys here. The maids know all about how to run the house, much better than I do. Kristine will come by tomorrow after I leave her place and pack up my own things, the ones I brought with me from home. I'd like to have them sent to me.

Helmer: All over! All over! Nora, will you ever think about me again?

Nora: I know I'll often think about you, and the children, and this house.
Helmer: May I write to you, Nora?
Nora: No, never. You mustn't do that.
Helmer: But at least let me send you—
Nora: Nothing, nothing.
Helmer: Let me help you if you're in need.
Nora: No. I can't accept anything from a stranger.
Helmer: Nora . . . can't I ever be anything more than a stranger to you?
Nora (picking up her bag): Ah, Torvald, for that, the most wonderful miracle of all would have to happen.
Helmer: Tell me what that would be!
Nora: We'd both have to change so much that—Oh, Torvald, I've stopped believing in miracles.
Helmer: But I'll believe. Tell me! Change so much that . . . ?
Nora: That our life together would be a true marriage. Goodbye.

(*She goes out through the hall.*)

Helmer (*sinks down into a chair at the door and buries his face in his hands*): Nora! Nora! (*Looks around, and stands up.*) Empty. She's gone. (*A hope flashes across his mind.*) The most wonderful miracle of all . . . ?

(*The heavy sound of a closing door is heard from below.*)

Questions

ACT I

1. From the opening conversation between Helmer and Nora, what are your impressions of him? Of her? Of their marriage?
2. At what moment in the play do you understand why it is called *A Doll's House?*
3. In what ways does Mrs. Linde provide a contrast for Nora?
4. What in Krogstad's first appearance on stage, and in Dr. Rank's remarks about him, indicates that the bank clerk is a menace?
5. Of what illegal deed is Nora guilty? How does she justify it?
6. When the curtain falls on Act I, what problems now confront Nora?

ACT II

1. As Act II opens, what are your feelings on seeing the stripped, ragged Christmas tree? How is it suggestive?
2. What events that soon occur make Nora's situation even more difficult?
3. How does she try to save herself?
4. Why does Nora fling herself into the wild tarantella?

ACT III

1. For what possible reasons does Mrs. Linde pledge herself to Krogstad?
2. How does Dr. Rank's announcement of his impending death affect Nora and Helmer?

3. What is Helmer's reaction to learning the truth about Nora's misdeed? Why does he blame Nora's father? What is revealing (of Helmer's own character) in his remark, "From this moment on happiness is out of the question. All that matters now is to save the bits and pieces, to keep up the appearance—"?

4. When Helmer finds that Krogstad has sent back the note, what is his response? How do you feel toward him?

5. How does the character of Nora develop in this act?

6. How do you interpret her final slamming of the door?

General Questions

1. In what ways do you find Nora a victim? In what ways is she at fault?

2. Try to state the theme of the play. Does it involve women's rights? Self-fulfillment?

3. What dramatic question does the play embody? At what moment can this question first be stated?

4. What is the crisis? In what way is this moment or event a "turning point"? (In what new direction does the action turn?)

5. Eric Bentley, in an essay titled "Ibsen, Pro and Con" (*In Search of Theater* [New York: Knopf, 1953]), criticizes the character of Krogstad, calling him "a mere pawn of the plot." He then adds, "When convenient to Ibsen, he is a blackmailer. When inconvenient, he is converted." Do you agree or disagree?

6. Why is the play considered a work of Realism? Is there anything in it that does not seem realistic?

7. In what respects does *A Doll's House* seem to apply to life today? Is it in any way dated? Could there be a Nora in North America today?

Tennessee Williams

The Glass Menagerie   1945

Tennessee Williams (1911–1983) was born Thomas Lanier Williams in Columbus, Mississippi, went to high school in St. Louis, and graduated from the University of Iowa. As an undergraduate, he saw a performance of Ibsen's Ghosts and decided to become a playwright himself. His family bore a close resemblance to the Wingfields in The Glass Menagerie: his mother came from a line of Southern blue bloods (Tennessee pioneers); his sister Rose suffered from incapacitating shyness; and as a young man, Williams himself, like Tom, worked at a job he disliked (in a shoe factory where his father worked), wrote poetry, sought refuge in moviegoing, and finally left home to wander and hold odd jobs. He worked as a bellhop in a New

Tennessee Williams celebrating the 20th anniversary of *The Glass Menagerie*.

Orleans hotel; a teletype operator in Jacksonville, Florida; an usher and a waiter in New York. In 1945 The Glass Menagerie *scored a success on Broadway, winning a Drama Critics Circle award. Two years later Williams received a Pulitzer Prize for* A Streetcar Named Desire, *a grim, powerful study of a woman's illusions and frustrations, set in New Orleans. In 1955 Williams was awarded another Pulitzer Prize for* Cat on a Hot Tin Roof. *Besides other plays, including* Summer and Smoke *(1948),* Sweet Bird of Youth *(1959),* The Night of the Iguana *(1961),* Small Craft Warnings *(1973),* Clothes for a Summer Hotel *(1980), and* A House Not Meant to Stand *(1981), Williams wrote two novels, poetry, essays, short stories, and* Memoirs *(1975).*

> *Nobody, not even the rain, has such small hands.*
>
> —E. E. CUMMINGS

CHARACTERS

Amanda Wingfield, the mother. A little woman of great but confused vitality clinging frantically to another time and place. Her characterization must be carefully created, not copied from type. She is not paranoiac, but her life is paranoia. There is much to admire in Amanda, and as much to love and pity as there is to laugh at. Certainly she has endurance and a kind of heroism, and though her foolishness makes her unwittingly cruel at times, there is tenderness in her slight person.

Laura Wingfield, her daughter. Amanda, having failed to establish contact with reality, continues to live vitally in her illusions, but Laura's situation is even graver. A childhood illness has left her crippled, one leg slightly shorter than the other, and held in a brace. This defect need not be more than suggested on the stage. Stemming from this, Laura's separation increases till she is like a piece of her own glass collection, too exquisitely fragile to move from the shelf.

Tom Wingfield, her son. And the narrator of the play. A poet with a job in a warehouse. His nature is not remorseless, but to escape from a trap he has to act without pity.

Jim O'Connor, the gentleman caller. A nice, ordinary, young man.

SCENE. *An alley in St. Louis.*

PART I. *Preparation for a Gentleman Caller.*

PART II. *The Gentleman Calls.*

TIME. *Now and the Past.*

SCENE I

The Wingfield apartment is in the rear of the building, one of those vast hive-like conglomerations of cellular living-units that flower as warty growths in overcrowded urban centers of lower middle-class population and are symptomatic of the impulse of this largest and fundamentally enslaved section of American society to avoid fluidity and differentiation and to exist and function as one interfused mass of automatism.

The apartment faces an alley and is entered by a fire escape, a structure whose name is a touch of accidental poetic truth, for all of these huge buildings are always burning with the slow and implacable fires of human desperation. The fire escape is included in the set—that is, the landing of it and steps descending from it.

The scene is memory and is therefore unrealistic. Memory takes a lot of poetic license. It omits some details; others are exaggerated, according to the emotional value of the articles it touches, for memory is seated predominantly in the heart. The interior is therefore rather dim and poetic.

At the rise of the curtain, the audience is faced with the dark, grim rear wall of the Wingfield tenement. This building is flanked on both sides by dark, narrow alleys which run into murky canyons of tangled clotheslines, garbage cans, and the sinister latticework of neighboring fire escapes. It is up and down these side alleys that exterior entrances and exits are made during the play. At the end of

Five years after *The Glass Menagerie*'s Broadway debut, a movie version was filmed starring Kirk Douglas, Jane Wyman, Gertrude Lawrence, and Arthur Kennedy.

Tom's opening commentary, the dark tenement wall slowly becomes transparent and reveals the interior of the ground-floor Wingfield apartment.

Nearest the audience is the living room, which also serves as a sleeping room for Laura, the sofa unfolding to make her bed. Just beyond, separated by a wide arch or second proscenium with transparent faded portieres (or second curtain), is the dining room. In an old-fashioned what not in the living room are seen scores of transparent glass animals. A blown-up photograph of the father hangs on the wall of the living room, to the left of the archway. It is the face of a very handsome young man in a doughboy's First World War cap. He is gallantly smiling, ineluctably smiling, as if to say "I will be smiling forever."

Also hanging on the wall, near the photograph, are a typewriter keyboard chart and a Gregg shorthand diagram. An upright typewriter on a small table stands beneath the charts.

The audience hears and sees the opening scene in the dining room through both the transparent fourth wall of the building and the transparent gauze portieres of the dining-room arch. It is during this revealing scene that the fourth wall slowly ascends, out of sight. This transparent exterior wall is not brought down again until the very end of the play, during Tom's final speech.

The narrator is an undisguised convention of the play. He takes whatever license with dramatic convention is convenient to his purposes.

Tom enters, dressed as a merchant sailor, and strolls across to the fire escape. There he stops and lights a cigarette. He addresses the audience.

Karen Allen and John Malkovich in a 1987 film of *The Glass Menagerie*, directed by Paul Newman.

Tom: Yes, I have tricks in my pocket, I have things up my sleeve. But I am the opposite of a stage magician. He gives you illusion that has the appearance of truth. I give you truth in the pleasant disguise of illusion.

To begin with, I turn back time. I reverse it to that quaint period, the thirties, when the huge middle class of America was matriculating in a school for the blind. Their eyes had failed them, or they had failed their eyes, and so they were having their fingers pressed forcibly down on the fiery Braille alphabet of a dissolving economy.

In Spain there was revolution. Here there was only shouting and confusion. In Spain there was Guernica. Here there were disturbances of labor, sometimes pretty violent, in otherwise peaceful cities such as Chicago, Cleveland, St. Louis. . . . This is the social background of the play.

(Music Begins To Play.)

The play is memory. Being a memory play, it is dimly lighted, it is sentimental, it is not realistic. In memory everything seems to happen to music. That explains the fiddle in the wings.

I am the narrator of the play, and also a character in it. The other characters are my mother, Amanda, my sister, Laura, and a gentleman caller who appears in the final scenes. He is the most realistic character in the play, being an emissary from a world of reality that we were somehow set apart from. But since I have a poet's weakness for symbols, I am using this character also as a symbol; he is the long-delayed but always expected something that we live for.

There is a fifth character in the play who doesn't appear except in this larger-than-life-size photograph over the mantel. This is our father who left us a long time ago. He was a telephone man who fell in love with long distances; he gave up his job with the telephone company and skipped the light fantastic out of town. . . .

The last we heard of him was a picture postcard from Mazatlan, on the Pacific coast of Mexico, containing a message of two words: "Hello—Goodbye!" and an address. I think the rest of the play will explain itself. . . .

Amanda's voice becomes audible through the portieres.

(Legend On Screen: "Où Sont Les Neiges.")°

Tom divides the portieres and enters the dining room. Amanda and Laura are seated at a drop-leaf table. Eating is indicated by gestures without food or utensils. Amanda faces the audience. Tom and Laura are seated in profile. The

---

"Où Son Les Nieges": A slide bearing this line is to be projected on a stage wall. The phrase is part of a famous line from French poet François Villon's *Ballad of the Dead Ladies*. The full line *"Où Sont Les Neiges D'antan?,"* meaning "But, where are the snows of yester-year?," is projected on the wall later in this scene.

interior has lit up softly and through the scrim we see Amanda and Laura seated at the table.

Amanda *(calling):* Tom?

Tom: Yes, Mother.

Amanda: We can't say grace until you come to the table!

Tom: Coming, Mother. *(He bows slightly and withdraws, reappearing a few moments later in his place at the table.)*

Amanda *(to her son):* Honey, don't *push* with your *fingers.* If you have to push with something, the thing to push with is a crust of bread. And chew—chew! Animals have secretions in their stomachs which enable them to digest food without mastication, but human beings are supposed to chew their food before they swallow it down. Eat food leisurely, son, and really enjoy it. A well-cooked meal has lots of delicate flavors that have to be held in the mouth for appreciation. So chew your food and give your salivary glands a chance to function!

Tom deliberately lays his imaginary fork down and pushes his chair back from the table.

Tom: I haven't enjoyed one bite of this dinner because of your constant directions on how to eat it. It's you that make me rush through meals with your hawklike attention to every bite I take. Sickening—spoils my appetite—all this discussion of—animals' secretion—salivary glands—mastication!

Amanda *(lightly):* Temperament like a Metropolitan star!

Tom rises and walks toward the living room.

You're not excused from the table.

Tom: I am getting a cigarette.

Amanda: You smoke too much.

Laura rises.

Laura: I'll bring in the blanc mange.

Tom remains standing with his cigarette by the portieres.

Amanda *(rising):* No, sister, no, sister—you be the lady this time and I'll be the darky.

Laura: I'm already up.

Amanda: Resume your seat, little sister—I want you to stay fresh and pretty—for gentlemen callers!

Laura *(sitting down):* I'm not expecting any gentlemen callers.

Amanda *(crossing out to kitchenette, airily):* Sometimes they come when they are least expected! Why, I remember one Sunday afternoon in Blue Mountain—*(enters the kitchenette.)*

Tom: I know what's coming!

Laura: Yes. But let her tell it.
Tom: Again?
Laura: She loves to tell it.

Amanda returns with a bowl of dessert.

Amanda: One Sunday afternoon in Blue Mountain—your mother received—
seventeen!—gentlemen callers! Why, sometimes there weren't chairs
enough to accommodate them all. We had to send the nigger over to
bring in folding chairs from the parish house.
Tom (remaining at the portieres): How did you entertain those gentlemen callers?
Amanda: I understood the art of conversation!
Tom: I bet you could talk.
Amanda: Girls in those days *knew* how to talk, I can tell you.
Tom: Yes?

(Image On Screen: Amanda As A Girl On A Porch, Greeting Callers.)

Amanda: They knew how to entertain their gentlemen callers. It wasn't
enough for a girl to be possessed of a pretty face and a graceful figure—
although I wasn't slighted in either respect. She also needed to have a
nimble wit and a tongue to meet all occasions.
Tom: What did you talk about?
Amanda: Things of importance going on in the world! Never anything coarse
or common or vulgar. (*She addresses Tom as though he were seated in the
vacant chair at the table though he remains by the portieres. He plays this scene
as though reading from a script.*) My callers were gentlemen—all! Among
my callers were some of the most prominent young planters of the Mississippi Delta—planters and sons of planters!

*Tom motions for music and a spot of light on Amanda. Her eyes lift, her face
glows, her voice becomes rich and elegiac.*

(Screen Legend: "Où Sont Les Neiges D'antan?")

There was young Champ Laughlin who later became vice-president of the
Delta Planters Bank. Hadley Stevenson who was drowned in Moon Lake and
left his widow one hundred and fifty thousand in Government bonds. There
were the Cutrere brothers, Wesley and Bates. Bates was one of my bright particular beaux! He got in a quarrel with that wild Wainright boy. They shot it
out on the floor of Moon Lake Casino. Bates was shot through the stomach.
Died in the ambulance on his way to Memphis. His widow was also well
provided-for, came into eight or ten thousand acres, that's all. She married
him on the rebound—never loved her—carried my picture on him the night
he died! And there was that boy that every girl in the Delta had set her cap
for! That beautiful, brilliant young Fitzhugh boy from Greene County!
Tom: What did he leave his widow?

Amanda: He never married! Gracious, you talk as though all of my old admirers had turned up their toes to the daisies!

Tom: Isn't this the first you've mentioned that still survives?

Amanda: That Fitzhugh boy went North and made a fortune—came to be known as the Wolf of Wall Street! He had the Midas touch, whatever he touched turned to gold! And I could have been Mrs. Duncan J. Fitzhugh, mind you! But—I picked your *father!*

Laura (rising): Mother, let me clear the table.

Amanda: No, dear, you go in front and study your typewriter chart. Or practice your shorthand a little. Stay fresh and pretty!—It's almost time for our gentlemen callers to start arriving. (*She flounces girlishly toward the kitchenette.*) How many do you suppose we're going to entertain this afternoon?

Tom throws down the paper and jumps up with a groan.

Laura (alone in the dining room): I don't believe we're going to receive any, Mother.

Amanda (reappearing, airily): What? No one—not one? You must be joking! (*Laura nervously echoes her laugh. She slips in a fugitive manner through the half-open portieres and draws them gently behind her. A shaft of very clear light is thrown on her face against the faded tapestry of the curtains. Faintly the music of "The Glass Menagerie" is heard as she continues, lightly.*) Not one gentleman caller? It can't be true! There must be a flood, there must have been a tornado!

Laura: It isn't a flood, it's not a tornado, Mother. I'm just not popular like you were in Blue Mountain. . . . (*Tom utters another groan. Laura glances at him with a faint, apologetic smile. Her voice catches a little.*) Mother's afraid I'm going to be an old maid.

(The Scene Dims Out With The "Glass Menagerie" Music.)

SCENE II

On the dark stage the screen is lighted with the image of blue roses. Gradually Laura's figure becomes apparent and the screen goes out. The music subsides.

Laura is seated in the delicate ivory chair at the small clawfoot table. She wears a dress of soft violet material for a kimono—her hair is tied back from her forehead with a ribbon. She is washing and polishing her collection of glass. Amanda appears on the fire escape steps. At the sound of her ascent, Laura catches her breath, thrusts the bowl of ornaments away, and seats herself stiffly before the diagram of the typewriter keyboard as though it held her spellbound. Something has happened to Amanda. It is written in her face as she climbs to the landing: a look that is grim and hopeless and a little absurd. She has on one of those cheap or imitation velvety-looking cloth coats with imitation fur collar. Her hat is five or six years old, one of those dreadful cloche hats that were worn in the late

Twenties, and she is clutching an enormous black patent-leather pocketbook with nickel clasps and initials. This is her full-dress outfit, the one she usually wears to the D.A.R. Before entering she looks through the door. She purses her lips, opens her eyes wide, rolls them upward and shakes her head. Then she slowly lets herself in the door. Seeing her mother's expression Laura touches her lips with a nervous gesture.

Laura: Hello, Mother, I was—(*She makes a nervous gesture toward the chart on the wall. Amanda leans against the shut door and stares at Laura with a martyred look.*)

Amanda: Deception? Deception? (*She slowly removes her hat and gloves, continuing the sweet suffering stare. She lets the hat and gloves fall on the floor—a bit of acting.*)

Laura (*shakily*): How was the D.A.R. meeting? (*Amanda slowly opens her purse and removes a dainty white handkerchief which she shakes out delicately and delicately touches to her lips and nostrils.*) Didn't you go to the D.A.R. meeting, Mother?

Amanda (*faintly, almost inaudibly*): —No.—No. (*Then more forcibly.*) I did not have the strength—to go to the D.A.R. In fact, I did not have the courage! I wanted to find a hole in the ground and hide myself in it forever! (*She crosses slowly to the wall and removes the diagram of the typewriter keyboard. She holds it in front of her for a second, staring at it sweetly and sorrowfully—then bites her lips and tears it in two pieces.*)

Laura (*faintly*): Why did you do that, Mother? (*Amanda repeats the same procedure with the chart of the Gregg Alphabet.*) Why are you—

Amanda: Why? Why? How old are you, Laura?

Laura: Mother, you know my age.

Amanda: I thought that you were an adult; it seems that I was mistaken. (*She crosses slowly to the sofa and sinks down and stares at Laura.*)

Laura: Please don't stare at me, Mother.

Amanda closes her eyes and lowers her head. There is a ten-second pause.

Amanda: What are we going to do, what is going to become of us, what is the future?

There is another pause.

Laura: Has something happened, Mother? (*Amanda draws a long breath, takes out the handkerchief again, goes through the dabbing process.*) Mother, has—something happened?

Amanda: I'll be all right in a minute, I'm just bewildered—(*She hesitates.*)—by life . . .

Laura: Mother, I wish that you would tell me what's happened.

Amanda: As you know, I was supposed to be inducted into my office at the D.A.R. this afternoon. (**Screen Image: A Swarm of Typewriters.**) But I stopped off at Rubicam's Business College to speak to your teachers about your having a cold and ask them what progress they thought you were making down there.

Laura: Oh . . .

Amanda: I went to the typing instructor and introduced myself as your mother. She didn't know who you were. "Wingfield," she said, "We don't have any such student enrolled at the school!"

I assured her she did, that you had been going to classes since early in January.

"I wonder," she said, "if you could be talking about that terribly shy little girl who dropped out of school after only a few days' attendance?"

"No," I said, "Laura, my daughter, has been going to school every day for the past six weeks!"

"Excuse me," she said. She took the attendance book out and there was your name, unmistakably printed, and all the dates you were absent until they decided that you had dropped out of school.

I still said, "No, there must have been some mistake! There must have been some mix-up in the records!"

And she said, "No—I remember her perfectly now. Her hands shook so that she couldn't hit the right keys! The first time we gave a speed test, she broke down completely—was sick at the stomach and almost had to be carried into the wash room! After that morning she never showed up any more. We phoned the house but never got any answer"—While I was working at Famous-Barr, I suppose, demonstrating those—(*She indicates a brassiere with her hands.*) Oh! I felt so weak I could barely keep on my feet! I had to sit down while they got me a glass of water! Fifty dollars' tuition, all of our plans—my hopes and ambitions for you—just gone up the spout, just gone up the spout like that. (*Laura draws a long breath and gets awkwardly to her feet. She crosses to the Victrola and winds it up.*) What are you doing?

Laura: Oh! (*She releases the handle and returns to her seat.*)

Amanda: Laura, where have you been going when you've gone out pretending that you were going to business college?

Laura: I've just been going out walking.

Amanda: That's not true.

Laura: It is. I just went walking.

Amanda: Walking? Walking? In winter? Deliberately courting pneumonia in that light coat? Where did you walk to, Laura?

Laura: All sorts of places—mostly in the park.

Amanda: Even after you'd started catching that cold?

Laura: It was the lesser of two evils, Mother. (**Screen Image: Winter Scene In Park.**) I couldn't go back there. I—threw up—on the floor!

Amanda: From half past seven till after five every day you mean to tell me you walked around in the park, because you wanted to make me think that you were still going to Rubicam's Business College?

Laura: It wasn't as bad as it sounds. I went inside places to get warmed up.

Amanda: Inside where?

Laura: I went in the art museum and the bird houses at the Zoo. I visited the penguins every day! Sometimes I did without lunch and went to the movies. Lately I've been spending most of my afternoons in the Jewel box, that big glass house where they raise the tropical flowers.

Amanda: You did all this to deceive me, just for deception? *(Laura looks down.)* Why?

Laura: Mother, when you're disappointed, you get that awful suffering look on your face, like the picture of Jesus' mother in the museum!

Amanda: Hush!

Laura: I couldn't face it.

There is a pause. A whisper of strings is heard.

(Legend On Screen: "The Crust Of Humility.")

Amanda (hopelessly fingering the huge pocketbook): So what are we going to do the rest of our lives? Stay home and watch the parades go by? Amuse ourselves with the glass menagerie, darling? Eternally play those worn-out phonograph records your father left as a painful reminder of him? We won't have a business career—we've given that up because it gave us nervous indigestion! *(She laughs wearily.)* What is there left but dependency all our lives? I know so well what becomes of unmarried women who aren't prepared to occupy a position. I've seen such pitiful cases in the South—barely tolerated spinsters living upon the grudging patronage of sisterhusband or brother's wife!—stuck away in some little mousetrap of a room—encouraged by one in-law to visit another—little birdlike women without any nest—eating the crust of humility all their life!

Is that the future that we've mapped out for ourselves? I swear it's the only alternative I can think of! *(She pauses.)* It isn't a very pleasant alternative, is it? *(She pauses again.)* Of course—some girls *do marry.* *(Laura twists her hands nervously.)* Haven't you ever liked some boy?

Laura: Yes. I liked one once. *(She rises.)* I came across his picture a while ago.

Amanda (with some interest): He gave you his picture?

Laura: No, it's in the yearbook.

Amanda (disappointed): Oh—a high school boy.

(Screen Image: Jim As A High-School Hero Bearing A Silver Cup.)

Laura: Yes. His name was Jim. *(Laura lifts the heavy annual from the claw-foot table.)* Here he is in *The Pirates of Penzance.*

Amanda (absently): The what?

Laura: The operetta the senior class put on. He had a wonderful voice and we sat across the aisle from each other Mondays, Wednesdays, and Fridays in the Aud. Here he is with the silver cup for debating! See his grin?

Amanda (absently): He must have had a jolly disposition.

Laura: He used to call me—Blue Roses.

(Image: Blue Roses.)

Amanda: Why did he call you such a name as that?

Laura: When I had that attack of pleurosis—he asked me what was the matter when I came back. I said pleurosis—he thought that I said Blue Roses! So that's what he always called me after that. Whenever he saw me, he'd holler, "Hello, Blue Roses!" I didn't care for the girl he went out with. Emily Meisenbach. Emily was the best-dressed girl at Soldan. She never struck me, though, as being sincere . . . It says in the Personal Section—they're engaged. That's—six years ago! They must be married by now.

Amanda: Girls that aren't cut out for business careers usually wind up married to some nice man. *(Gets up with a spark of revival.)* Sister, that's what you'll do!

Laura utters a startled, doubtful laugh. She reaches quickly for a piece of glass.

Laura: But, Mother—

Amanda: Yes? *(She goes over to the photograph.)*

Laura (in a tone of frightened apology): I'm—crippled!

Amanda: Nonsense! Laura, I've told you never, never to use that word. Why, you're not crippled, you just have a little defect—hardly noticeable, even! When people have some slight disadvantage like that, they cultivate other things to make up for it—develop charm—and vivacity—and—charm! That's all you have to do! *(She turns again to the photograph.)* One thing your father had *plenty of*—was *charm!*

(The Scene Fades Out With Music.)

SCENE III

(Legend On The Screen: "After The Fiasco—")

Tom speaks from the fire escape landing.

Tom: After the fiasco at Rubicam's Business College, the idea of getting a gentleman caller for Laura began to play a more and more important part in Mother's calculations. It became an obsession. Like some archetype of the universal unconscious, the image of the gentleman caller haunted our small apartment. . . . **(Screen Image: Young Man At The Door Of A**

House With Flowers.) An evening at home rarely passed without some
allusion to this image, this specter, this hope. . . . Even when he wasn't
mentioned, his presence hung in Mother's preoccupied look and in my
sister's frightened, apologetic manner—hung like a sentence passed upon
the Wingfields!

Mother was a woman of action as well as words. She began to take
logical steps in the planned direction. Late that winter and in the early
spring—realizing that extra money would be needed to properly feather
the nest and plume the bird—she conducted a vigorous campaign on the
telephone, roping in subscribers to one of those magazines for matrons
called *The Homemaker's Companion*, the type of journal that features the
serialized sublimations of ladies of letters who think in terms of delicate
cuplike breasts, slim, tapering waists, rich, creamy thighs, eyes like wood
smoke in autumn, fingers that soothe and caress like strains of music, bodies as powerful as Etruscan sculpture.

(Screen Image: The Cover of a Glamor Magazine.)

*Amanda enters with the telephone on a long extension cord. She is spotlighted
in the dim stage.*

Amanda: Ida Scott? This is Amanda Wingfield! We *missed* you at the D.A.R.
last Monday! I said to myself: She's probably suffering with that sinus
condition! How is that sinus condition?

Horrors! Heaven have mercy!—You're a Christian martyr, yes, that's
what you are, a Christian martyr!

Well, I just now happened to notice that your subscription to the *Companion's* about to expire! Yes, it expires with the next issue, honey!—just
when that wonderful new serial by Bessie Mae Hopper is getting off to
such an exciting start. Oh, honey, it's something that you can't miss! You
remember how *Gone With the Wind* took everybody by storm? You simply
couldn't go out if you hadn't read it. All everybody *talked* was Scarlett
O'Hara. Well, this is a book that critics already compare to *Gone With the
Wind*. It's the *Gone With the Wind* of the post-World-War generation!—
What?—Burning?—Oh, honey, don't let them burn, go take a look in the
oven and I'll hold the wire! Heavens—I think she's hung up!

(The Scene Dims Out.)

**(Legend On Screen: "You Think I'm In Love With Continental Shoe-
makers?")**

*Before the lights come up again, the violent voices of Tom and Amanda are
heard. They are quarreling behind the portieres. In front of them stands Laura
with clenched hands and panicky expression. A clear pool of light is on her
figure throughout this scene.*

Tom: What in Christ's name am I—

Amanda (shrilly): Don't you use that—

Tom: —supposed to do!

Amanda: —expression! Not in my—

Tom: Ohhh!

Amanda: —presence! Have you gone out of your senses?

Tom: I have, that's true, *driven* out!

Amanda: What is the matter with you, you—big—big—IDIOT!

Tom: Look—I've got *no thing*, no single thing—

Amanda: Lower your voice!

Tom: —in my life here that I can call my OWN! Everything is—

Amanda: Stop that shouting!

Tom: Yesterday you confiscated my books! You had the nerve to—

Amanda: I took that horrible novel back to the library—yes! That hideous book by that insane Mr. Lawrence. (*Tom laughs wildly.*) I cannot control the output of diseased minds or people who cater to them—(*Tom laughs still more wildly.*) BUT I WON'T ALLOW SUCH FILTH BROUGHT INTO MY HOUSE! No, no, no, no, no!

Tom: House, house! Who pays rent on it, who makes a slave of himself to—

Amanda (fairly screeching): Don't you DARE to—

Tom: No, no, I mustn't say things! *I've* got to just—

Amanda: Let me tell you—

Tom: I don't want to hear any more!

> *He tears the portieres open. The dining-room area is lit with a turgid smoky red glow. Now we see Amanda; her hair is in metal curlers and she is wearing a very old bathrobe, much too large for her slight figure, a relic of the faithless Mr. Wingfield. The upright typewriter now stands on the drop-leaf table, along with a wild disarray of manuscripts. The quarrel was probably precipitated by Amanda's interruption of Tom's creative labor. A chair lies overthrown on the floor. Their gesticulating shadows are cast on the ceiling by the fiery glow.*

Amanda: You *will* hear more, you—

Tom: No, I won't hear more, I'm going out!

Amanda: You come right back in—

Tom: Out, out, out! Because I'm—

Amanda: Come back here, Tom Wingfield! I'm not through talking to you!

Tom: Oh, go—

Laura (desperately): —Tom!

Amanda: You're going to listen, and no more insolence from you! I'm at the end of my patience! (*He comes back toward her.*)

Tom: What do you think I'm at? Aren't I supposed to have any patience to reach the end of, Mother? I know, I know. It seems unimportant to you,

what I'm *doing*—what *I want* to do—having a little *difference* between
them! You don't think that—

Amanda: I think you've been doing things that you're ashamed of. That's why
you act like this. I don't believe that you go every night to the movies.
Nobody goes to the movies night after night. Nobody in their right minds
goes to the movies as often as you pretend to. People don't go to the
movies at nearly midnight, and movies don't let out at two A.M. Come in
stumbling. Muttering to yourself like a maniac! You get three hours' sleep
and then go to work. Oh, I can picture the way you're doing down there.
Moping, doping, because you're in no condition.

Tom (wildly): No, I'm in no condition!

Amanda: What right have you got to jeopardize your job? Jeopardize the security of us all? How do you think we'd manage if you were—

Tom: Listen! You think I'm crazy about the *warehouse? (He bends fiercely
toward her slight figure.)* You think I'm in love with the Continental
Shoemakers? You think I want to spend fifty-five *years* down there in
that—*celotex interior!* with—*fluorescent—tubes!* Look! I'd rather somebody picked up a crowbar and battered out my brains—than go back
mornings! I *go!* Every time you come in yelling that God-damn *"Rise and
Shine!" "Rise and Shine!"* I say to myself *"How lucky dead people are!"* But
I get up. I *go!* For sixty-five dollars a month I give up all that I dream of
doing and being *ever!* And you say self—*self's* all I ever think of. Why,
listen, if self is what I thought of, Mother, I'd be where he is—GONE!
(He points to his father's picture.) As far as the system of transportation
reaches! *(He starts past her. She grabs his arm.)* Don't grab at me, Mother!

Amanda: Where are you going?

Tom: I'm going to the *movies!*

Amanda: I don't believe that lie!

*Tom (Tom crouches toward her, overtowering her tiny figure. She backs away, gasp-
ing):* I'm going to opium dens! Yes, opium dens, dens of vice and criminals' hangouts, Mother. I've joined the Hogan gang, I'm a hired assassin,
I carry a tommy-gun in a violin case! I run a string of cat houses in the
Valley! They call me Killer, Killer Wingfield, I'm leading a double-life,
a simple, honest warehouse worker by day, by night a dynamic *czar* of
the *underworld,* Mother. I go to gambling casinos, I spin away fortunes
on the roulette table! I wear a patch over one eye and a false mustache,
sometimes I put on green whiskers. On those occasions they call me—*El
Diablo!* Oh, I could tell you many things to make you sleepless! My enemies plan to dynamite this place. They're going to blow us all sky-high
some night! I'll be glad, very happy, and so will you! You'll go up, up on a
broomstick, over Blue Mountain with seventeen gentlemen callers! You
ugly—babbling old—*witch. . . . (He goes through a series of violent, clumsy
movements, seizing his overcoat, lunging to the door, pulling it fiercely open.*

The women watch him, aghast. His arm catches in the sleeve of the coat as he struggles to pull it on. For a moment he is pinioned by the bulky garment. With an outraged groan he tears the coat off again, splitting the shoulder of it, and hurls it across the room. It strikes against the shelf of Laura's glass collection, and there is a tinkle of shattering glass. Laura cries out as if wounded.)

(Music Legend: "The Glass Menagerie.")

Laura (shrilly): My glass!—menagerie. . . . *(She covers her face and turns away.)*

But Amanda is still stunned and stupefied by the "ugly witch" so that she barely notices this occurrence. Now she recovers her speech.

Amanda (in an awful voice): I won't speak to you—until you apologize! *(She crosses through the portieres and draws them together behind her. Tom is left with Laura. Laura clings weakly to the mantel with her face averted. Tom stares at her stupidly for a moment. Then he crosses to the shelf. He drops awkwardly on his knees to collect the fallen glass, glancing at Laura as if he would speak but couldn't.)*

("The Glass Menagerie" Music Steals In As The Scene Dims Out.)

SCENE IV

The interior of the apartment is dark. There is a faint light in the alley. A deep-voiced bell in a church is tolling the hour of five.

Tom appears at the top of the alley. After each solemn boom of the bell in the tower, he shakes a little noisemaker or rattle as if to express the tiny spasm of man in contrast to the sustained power and dignity of the Almighty. This and the unsteadiness of his advance make it evident that he has been drinking.

As he climbs the few steps to the fire escape landing light steals up inside. Laura appears in the front room in a nightdress. She notices that Tom's bed is empty.

Tom fishes in his pockets for his door key, removing a motley assortment of articles in the search, including a shower of movie ticket stubs and an empty bottle. At last he finds the key, but just as he is about to insert it, it slips from his fingers. He strikes a match and crouches below the door.

Tom (bitterly): One crack—and it falls through!

Laura opens the door.

Laura: Tom! Tom, what are you doing?
Tom: Looking for a door key.
Laura: Where have you been all this time?
Tom: I have been to the movies.
Laura: All this time at the movies?

Tom: There was a very long program. There was a Garbo picture and a Mickey Mouse and a travelogue and a newsreel and a preview of coming attractions. And there was an organ solo and a collection for the Milk Fund—simultaneously—which ended up in a terrible fight between a fat lady and an usher!

Laura (innocently): Did you have to stay through everything?

Tom: Of course! And, oh, I forgot! There was a big stage show! The head-liner on this stage show was Malvolio the Magician. He performed wonderful tricks, many of them, such as pouring water back and forth between pitchers. First it turned to wine and then it turned to beer and then it turned to whiskey. I know it was whiskey it finally turned into because he needed somebody to come up out of the audience to help him, and I came up—both shows! It was Kentucky Straight Bourbon. A very generous fellow, he gave souvenirs. (He pulls from his back pocket a shimmering rainbow-colored scarf.) He gave me this. This is his magic scarf. You can have it, Laura. You wave it over a canary cage and you get a bowl of goldfish. You wave it over the goldfish bowl and they fly away canaries. . . . But the wonderfullest trick of all was the coffin trick. We nailed him into a coffin and he got out of the coffin without removing one nail. (He has come inside.) There is a trick that would come in handy for me—get me out of this two-by-four situation! (He flops onto the bed and starts removing his shoes.)

Laura: Tom—shhh!

Tom: What're you shushing me for?

Laura: You'll wake up Mother.

Tom: Goody, goody! Pay 'er back for all those "Rise an' Shines." (He lies down, groaning.) You know it don't take much intelligence to get yourself into a nailed-up coffin, Laura. But who in hell ever got himself out of one without removing one nail?

As if in answer, the father's grinning photograph lights up.

(**The Scene Dims Out.**)

Immediately following, the church bell is heard striking six. At the sixth stroke the alarm clock goes off in Amanda's room, and after a few moments we hear her calling: "Rise and Shine! Rise and Shine! Laura, go tell your brother to rise and shine!"

Tom (sitting up slowly): I'll rise—but I won't shine.

The light increases.

Amanda: Laura, tell your brother his coffee is ready.

Laura slips into the front room.

Laura: Tom!—It's nearly seven. Don't make Mother nervous. (*He stares at her stupidly.*) (*Beseechingly*) Tom, speak to Mother this morning. Make up with her, apologize, speak to her!

Tom: She won't to me. It's her that started not speaking.

Laura: If you just say you're sorry she'll start speaking.

Tom: Her not speaking—is that such a tragedy?

Laura: Please—please!

Amanda (*calling from the kitchenette*): Laura, are you going to do what I asked you to do, or do I have to get dressed and go out myself?

Laura: Going, going—soon as I get on my coat! (*She pulls on a shapeless felt hat with a nervous, jerky movement, pleadingly glancing at Tom. She rushes awkwardly for her coat. The coat is one of Amanda's, inaccurately made-over, the sleeves too short for Laura.*) Butter and what else?

Amanda (*entering from the kitchenette*): Just butter. Tell them to charge it.

Laura: Mother, they make such faces when I do that.

Amanda: Sticks and stones can break our bones, but the expression on Mr. Garfinkel's face won't harm us! Tell your brother his coffee is getting cold.

Laura (*at the door*): Do what I asked you, will you, will you, Tom?

He looks sullenly away.

Amanda: Laura, go now or just don't go at all!

Laura (*rushing out*): Going—going! (*A second later she cries out. Tom springs up and crosses to the door. Tom opens the door.*)

Tom: Laura?

Laura: I'm all right. I slipped, but I'm all right.

Amanda (*peering anxiously after her*): If anyone breaks a leg on those fire escape steps, the landlord ought to be sued for every cent he possesses! (*She shuts the door. Now she remembers she isn't speaking to Tom and returns to the other room.*)

As Tom comes listlessly for his coffee, she turns her back to him and stands rigidly facing the window on the gloomy gray vault of the areaway. Its light on her face with its aged but childish features is cruelly sharp, satirical as a Daumier print. The music of "Ave Maria," is heard softly.

Tom glances sheepishly but sullenly at her averted figure and slumps at the table. The coffee is scalding hot; he sips it and gasps and spits it back in the cup. At his gasp, Amanda catches her breath and half turns. Then she catches herself and turns back to the window. Tom blows on his coffee, glancing sidewise at his mother. She clears her throat. Tom clears his. He starts to rise, sinks back down again, scratches his head, clears his throat again. Amanda coughs. Tom raises his cup in both hands to blow on it, his eyes staring over the rim of it at his mother for several moments. Then he slowly sets the cup down and awkwardly and hesitantly rises from the chair.

Tom (hoarsely): Mother. I—I apologize. Mother. (*Amanda draws a quick, shuddering breath. Her face works grotesquely. She breaks into childlike tears.*) I'm sorry for what I said, for everything that I said, I didn't mean it.

Amanda (sobbingly): My devotion has made me a witch and so I make myself hateful to my children!

Tom: No, you *don't*.

Amanda: I worry so much, don't sleep, it makes me nervous!

Tom (gently): I understand that.

Amanda: I've had to put up a solitary battle all these years. But you're my right-hand bower! Don't fall down, don't fail!

Tom (gently): I try, Mother.

Amanda (with great enthusiasm): Try and you will *succeed*! (*The notion makes her breathless.*) Why, you—you're just *full* of natural endowments! Both of my children—they're *unusual* children! Don't you think I know it? I'm so—*proud*! Happy and—feel I've—so much to be thankful for but—promise me one thing, son!

Tom: What, Mother?

Amanda: Promise, son, you'll—never be a drunkard!

Tom (turns to her grinning): I will never be a drunkard, Mother.

Amanda: That's what frightened me so, that you'd be drinking! Eat a bowl of Purina!

Tom: Just coffee, Mother.

Amanda: Shredded wheat biscuit?

Tom: No. No, Mother, just coffee.

Amanda: You can't put in a day's work on an empty stomach. You've got ten minutes—don't gulp! Drinking too-hot liquids makes cancer of the stomach. . . . Put cream in.

Tom: No, thank you.

Amanda: To cool it.

Tom: No! No, thank you, I want it black.

Amanda: I know, but it's not good for you. We have to do all that we can to build ourselves up. In these trying times we live in, all that we have to cling to is—each other. . . . That's why it's so important to—Tom, I—I sent out your sister so I could discuss something with you. If you hadn't spoken I would have spoken to you. (*She sits down.*)

Tom (gently): What is it, Mother, that you want to discuss?

Amanda: Laura!

Tom puts his cup down slowly.

(Legend On Screen: "Laura.")

(Music: "The Glass Menagerie.")

Tom: —Oh.—Laura . . .

Amanda (touching his sleeve): You know how Laura is. So quiet but—still water runs deep! She notices things and I think she—broods about them.
(Tom looks up.) A few days ago I came in and she was crying.

Tom: What about?

Amanda: You.

Tom: Me?

Amanda: She has an idea that you're not happy here.

Tom: What gave her that idea?

Amanda: What gives her any idea? However, you do act strangely. I—I'm not
criticizing, understand *that*! I know your ambitions do not lie in the warehouse, that like everybody in the whole wide world—you've had to—
make sacrifices, but—Tom—Tom—life's not easy, it calls for—Spartan
endurance! There's so many things in my heart that I cannot describe to
you! I've never told you but I—*loved* your father. . . .

Tom (gently): I know that, Mother.

Amanda: And you—when I see you taking after his ways! Staying out late—
and—well, you *had* been drinking the night you were in that—terrifying
condition! Laura says that you hate the apartment and that you go out
nights to get away from it! Is that true, Tom?

Tom: No. You say there's so much in your heart that you can't describe to me.
That's true of me, too. There's so much in my heart that I can't describe
to *you*! So let's respect each other's—

Amanda: But, why—*why*, Tom—are you always so *restless*? Where do you *go*
to, nights?

Tom: I—go to the movies.

Amanda: Why do you go to the movies so much, Tom?

Tom: I go to the movies because—I like adventure. Adventure is something I
don't have much of at work, so I go to the movies.

Amanda: But, Tom, you go to the movies *entirely* too *much*!

Tom: I like a lot of adventure.

*Amanda looks baffled, then hurt. As the familiar inquisition resumes, Tom
becomes hard and impatient again. Amanda slips back into her querulous attitude
toward him.*

(Image On Screen: Sailing Vessel With Jolly Roger.)

Amanda: Most young men find adventure in their careers.

Tom: Then most young men are not employed in a warehouse.

Amanda: The world is full of young men employed in warehouses and offices
and factories.

Tom: Do all of them find adventure in their careers?

Amanda: They do or they do without it! Not everybody has a craze for adventure.

Tom: Man is by instinct a lover, a hunter, a fighter, and none of those instincts are given much play at the warehouse!

Amanda: Man is by instinct! Don't quote instinct to me! Instinct is something that people have got away from! It belongs to animals! Christian adults don't want it!

Tom: What do Christian adults want, then, Mother?

Amanda: Superior things! Things of the mind and the spirit! Only animals have to satisfy instincts! Surely your aims are somewhat higher than theirs! Than monkeys—pigs—

Tom: I reckon they're not.

Amanda: You're joking. However, that isn't what I wanted to discuss.

Tom (rising): I haven't much time.

Amanda (pushing his shoulder): Sit down.

Tom: You want me to punch in red at the warehouse, Mother?

Amanda: You have five minutes. I want to talk about Laura.

(Screen Legend: "Plans And Provisions.")

Tom: All right! What about Laura?

Amanda: We have to be making some plans and provisions for her. She's older than you, two years, and nothing has happened. She just drifts along doing nothing. It frightens me terribly how she just drifts along.

Tom: I guess she's the type that people call home girls.

Amanda: There's no such type, and if there is, it's a pity! That is unless the home is hers, with a husband!

Tom: What?

Amanda: Oh, I can see the handwriting on the wall as plain as I see the nose in front of my face! It's terrifying! More and more you remind me of your father! He was out all hours without explanation—Then *left! Goodbye!* And me with the bag to hold. I saw that letter you got from the Merchant Marine. I know what you're dreaming of. I'm not standing here blindfolded. *(She pauses.)* Very well, then. Then *do* it! But not till there's somebody to take your place.

Tom: What do you mean?

Amanda: I mean that as soon as Laura has got somebody to take care of her, married, a home of her own, independent—why, then you'll be free to go wherever you please, on land, on sea, whichever way the wind blows! But until that time you've got to look out for your sister. I don't say me because I'm old and don't matter! I say for your sister because she's young and dependent.

  I put her in business college—a dismal failure! Frightened her so it made her sick at her stomach. I took her over to the Young People's

League at the church. Another fiasco. She spoke to nobody, nobody spoke to her. Now all she does is fool with those pieces of glass and play those worn-out records. What kind of a life is that for a girl to lead!

Tom: What can I do about it?

Amanda: Overcome selfishness! Self, self, self is all that you ever think of! (*Tom springs up and crosses to get his coat. It is ugly and bulky. He pulls on a cap with earmuffs.*) Where is your muffler? Put your wool muffler on! (*He snatches it angrily from the closet, tosses it around his neck and pulls both ends tight.*) Tom! I haven't said what I had in mind to ask you.

Tom: I'm too late to—

Amanda (*catching his arm—very importunately; then shyly*): Down at the warehouse, aren't there some—nice young men?

Tom: No!

Amanda: There *must* be—some . . .

Tom: Mother—

He gestures.

Amanda: Find out one that's clean-living—doesn't drink and ask him out for sister!

Tom: What?

Amanda: For *sister!* To *meet!* Get *acquainted!*

Tom (*stamping to the door*): Oh, my go-osh!

Amanda: Will you? (*He opens the door, imploringly.*) Will you? (*He starts down the fire escape.*) Will you? *Will* you? Will you, dear?

Tom (*calling back*): Yes!

Amanda closes the door hesitantly and with a troubled but faintly hopeful expression.

(Screen Image: The Cover Of A Glamor Magazine.)

The spotlight picks up Amanda at the phone.

Amanda: Ella Cartwright? This is Amanda Wingfield! How are you, honey? How is that kidney condition? (*There is a five-second pause.*) Horrors! (*There is another pause.*) You're a Christian martyr, yes, honey, that's what you are, a Christian martyr! Well, I just now happened to notice in my little red book that your subscription to the *Companion* has just run out! I knew that you wouldn't want to miss out on the wonderful serial starting in this new issue. It's by Bessie Mae Hopper, the first thing she's written since *Honeymoon for Three.* Wasn't that a strange and interesting story? Well, this one is even lovelier, I believe. It has a sophisticated, society background. It's all about the horsey set on Long Island!

(The Light Fades Out.)

SCENE V

(Legend On The Screen: "Annunciation.")

Music is heard as the light slowly comes on.

It is early dusk of a spring evening. Supper has just been finished in the Wingfield apartment. Amanda and Laura in light-colored dresses are removing dishes from the table in the dining room, which is shadowy, their movements formalized almost as a dance or ritual, their moving forms as pale and silent as moths. Tom, in white shirt and trousers, rises from the table and crosses toward the fire escape.

Amanda (as he passes her): Son, will you do me a favor?
Tom: What?
Amanda: Comb your hair! You look so pretty when your hair is combed! *(Tom slouches on the sofa with the evening paper. Its enormous headline reads: "Franco Triumphs.")* There is only one respect in which I would like you to emulate your father.
Tom: What respect is that?
Amanda: The care he always took of his appearance. He never allowed himself to look untidy. *(He throws down the paper and crosses to fire escape.)* Where are you going?
Tom: I'm going out to smoke.
Amanda: You smoke too much. A pack a day at fifteen cents a pack. How much would that amount to in a month? Thirty times fifteen is how much, Tom? Figure it out and you will be astounded at what you could save. Enough to give you a night-school course in accounting at Washington U.! Just think what a wonderful thing that would be for you, son!

Tom is unmoved by the thought.

Tom: I'd rather smoke. *(He steps out on the landing, letting the screen door slam.)*
Amanda (sharply): I know! That's the tragedy of it. . . . *(Alone, she turns to look at her husband's picture.)*

(Dance Music: "The World Is Waiting For The Sunrise.")

Tom (to the audience): Across the alley from us was the Paradise Dance Hall. On evenings in spring the windows and doors were open and the music came outdoors. Sometimes the lights were turned out except for a large glass sphere that hung from the ceiling. It would turn slowly about and filter the dusk with delicate rainbow colors. Then the orchestra played a waltz or a tango, something that had a slow and sensuous rhythm. Couples would come outside, to the relative privacy of the alley. You could see them kissing behind ash pits and telephone poles. This was the compensation for lives that passed like mine, without any change or adventure. Adventure and change were imminent in this year. They were waiting around the corner for all these kids. Suspended in the mist over Berchtesgaden, caught in the folds of Chamberlain's umbrella. In Spain there was Guernica! But here there was only hot swing music and liquor, dance halls, bars, and movies, and sex that hung in the gloom like a chandelier and flooded the world with brief, deceptive rainbows. . . . All the world was waiting for bombardments!

Amanda turns from the picture and comes outside.

Amanda (*sighing*): A fire escape landing's a poor excuse for a porch. (*She spreads a newspaper on a step and sits down, gracefully and demurely as if she were settling into a swing on a Mississippi veranda.*) What are you looking at?

Tom: The moon.

Amanda: Is there a moon this evening?

Tom: It's rising over Garfinkel's Delicatessen.

Amanda: So it is! A little silver slipper of a moon. Have you made a wish on it yet?

Tom: Um-hum.

Amanda: What did you wish for?

Tom: That's a secret.

Amanda: A secret, huh? Well, I won't tell mine either. I will be just as mysterious as you.

Tom: I bet I can guess what yours is.

Amanda: Is my head so transparent?

Tom: You're not a sphinx.

Amanda: No, I don't have secrets. I'll tell you what I wished for on the moon. Success and happiness for my precious children! I wish for that whenever there's a moon, and when there isn't a moon, I wish for it, too.

Tom: I thought perhaps you wished for a gentleman caller.

Amanda: Why do you say that?

Tom: Don't you remember asking me to fetch one?

Amanda: I remember suggesting that it would be nice for your sister if you brought home some nice young man from the warehouse. I think I've made that suggestion more than once.

Tom: Yes, you have made it repeatedly.

Amanda: Well?

Tom: We are going to have one.

Amanda: What?

Tom: A gentleman caller!

(The Annunciation Is Celebrated With Music.)

Amanda rises.

(Image On Screen: A Caller With A Bouquet.)

Amanda: You mean you have asked some nice young man to come over?
Tom: Yep. I've asked him to dinner.
Amanda: You really did?
Tom: I did!
Amanda: You did, and did he—*accept?*
Tom: He did!
Amanda: Well, well—well, well! That's—lovely!
Tom: I thought that you would be pleased.
Amanda: It's definite, then?
Tom: Very definite.
Amanda: Soon?
Tom: Very soon.
Amanda: For heaven's sake, stop putting on and tell me some things, will you?
Tom: What things do you want me to tell you?
Amanda: *Naturally* I would like to know when he's *coming!*
Tom: He's coming tomorrow.
Amanda: *Tomorrow?*
Tom: Yep. Tomorrow.
Amanda: But, Tom!
Tom: Yes, Mother?
Amanda: Tomorrow gives me no time!
Tom: Time for what?
Amanda: Preparations! Why didn't you phone me at once, as soon as you
  asked him, the minute that he accepted? Then, don't you see, I could
  have been getting ready!
Tom: You don't have to make any fuss.
Amanda: Oh, Tom, Tom, Tom, of course I have to make a fuss! I want things
  nice, not sloppy! Not thrown together. I'll certainly have to do some fast
  thinking, won't I?
Tom: I don't see why you have to think at all.
Amanda: You just don't know. We can't have a gentleman caller in a pigsty!
  All my wedding silver has to be polished, the monogrammed table linen
  ought to be laundered! The windows have to be washed and fresh curtains
  put up. And how about clothes? We have to *wear* something, don't we?
Tom: Mother, this boy is no one to make a fuss over!
Amanda: Do you realize he's the first young man we've introduced to your
  sister? It's terrible, dreadful, disgraceful that poor little sister has never received a single gentleman caller! Tom, come inside! (*She opens the screen
  door.*)
Tom: What for?
Amanda: I want to ask you some things.
Tom: If you're going to make such a fuss, I'll call it off, I'll tell him not to
  come.

Amanda: You certainly won't do anything of the kind. Nothing offends people worse than broken engagements. It simply means I'll have to work like a Turk! We won't be brilliant, but we will pass inspection. Come on inside. (*Tom follows her inside, groaning.*) Sit down.

Tom: Any particular place you would like me to sit?

Amanda: Thank heavens I've got that new sofa! I'm also making payments on a floor lamp I'll have sent out! And put the chintz covers on, they'll brighten things up! Of course I'd hoped to have these walls re-papered. . . . What is the young man's name?

Tom: His name is O'Connor.

Amanda: That, of course, means fish—tomorrow is Friday! I'll have that salmon loaf—with Durkee's dressing! What does he do? He works at the warehouse?

Tom: Of course! How else would I—

Amanda: Tom, he—doesn't drink?

Tom: Why do you ask me that?

Amanda: Your father *did*!

Tom: Don't get started on that!

Amanda: He *does* drink, then?

Tom: Not that I know of!

Amanda: Make sure, be certain! The last thing I want for my daughter's a boy who drinks!

Tom: Aren't you being a little premature? Mr. O'Connor has not yet appeared on the scene!

Amanda: But will tomorrow. To meet your sister, and what do I know about his character? Nothing! Old maids are better off than wives of drunkards!

Tom: Oh, my God!

Amanda: Be still!

Tom (*leaning forward to whisper*): Lots of fellows meet girls whom they don't marry!

Amanda: Oh, talk sensibly, Tom—and don't be sarcastic! (*She has gotten a hairbrush.*)

Tom: What are you doing?

Amanda: I'm brushing that cowlick down! (*She attacks his hair with the brush.*) What is this young man's position at the warehouse?

Tom (*submitting grimly to the brush and the interrogation*): This young man's position is that of a shipping clerk, Mother.

Amanda: Sounds to me like a fairly responsible job, the sort of a job *you* would be in if you just had more *get-up*. What is his salary? Have you any idea?

Tom: I would judge it to be approximately eighty-five dollars a month.

Amanda: Well—not princely, but—

Tom: Twenty more than I make.

Amanda: Yes, how well I know! But for a family man, eighty-five dollars a month is not much more than you can just get by on. . . .

Tom: Yes, but Mr. O'Connor is not a family man.

Amanda: He might be, mightn't he? Some time in the future?

Tom: I see. Plans and provisions.

Amanda: You are the only young man that I know of who ignores the fact that the future becomes the present, the present the past, and the past turns into everlasting regret if you don't plan for it!

Tom: I will think that over and see what I can make of it!

Amanda: Don't be supercilious with your mother! Tell me some more about this—what do you call him?

Tom: James D. O'Connor. The D. is for Delaney.

Amanda: Irish on *both* sides! *Gracious!* And doesn't drink?

Tom: Shall I call him up and ask him right this minute?

Amanda: The only way to find out about those things is to make discreet inquiries at the proper moment. When I was a girl in Blue Mountain and it was suspected that a young man drank, the girl whose attentions he had been receiving, if any girl *was*, would sometimes speak to the minister of his church, or rather her father would if her father was living, and sort of feel him out on the young man's character. That is the way such things are discreetly handled to keep a young woman from making a tragic mistake!

Tom: Then how did you happen to make a tragic mistake?

Amanda: That innocent look of your father's had everyone fooled! He *smiled*—the world was *enchanted!* No girl can do worse than put herself at the mercy of a handsome appearance! I hope that Mr. O'Connor is not too good-looking.

Tom: No, he's not too good-looking. He's covered with freckles and hasn't too much of a nose.

Amanda: He's not right-down homely, though?

Tom: Not right-down homely. Just medium homely, I'd say.

Amanda: Character's what to look for in a man.

Tom: That's what I've always said, Mother.

Amanda: You've never said anything of the kind and I suspect you would never give it a thought.

Tom: Don't be suspicious of me.

Amanda: At least I hope he's the type that's up and coming.

Tom: I think he really goes in for self-improvement.

Amanda: What reason have you to think so?

Tom: He goes to night school.

Amanda (beaming): Splendid! What does he do, I mean study?

Tom: Radio engineering and public speaking!

Amanda: Then he has visions of being advanced in the world! Any young man who studies public speaking is aiming to have an executive job some day!

And radio engineering? A thing for the future! Both of these facts are very illuminating. Those are the sort of things that a mother should know concerning any young man who comes to call on her daughter. Seriously or—not.

Tom: One little warning. He doesn't know about Laura. I didn't let on that we had dark ulterior motives. I just said, why don't you come and have dinner with us? He said okay and that was the whole conversation.

Amanda: I bet it was! You're eloquent as an oyster. However, he'll know about Laura when he gets here. When he sees how lovely and sweet and pretty she is, he'll thank his lucky stars he was asked to dinner.

Tom: Mother, you mustn't expect too much of Laura.

Amanda: What do you mean?

Tom: Laura seems all those things to you and me because she's ours and we love her. We don't even notice she's crippled any more.

Amanda: Don't say crippled! You know that I never allow that word to be used!

Tom: But face facts, Mother. She is and—that's not all—

Amanda: What do you mean "not all"?

Tom: Laura is very different from other girls.

Amanda: I think the difference is all to her advantage.

Tom: Not quite all—in the eyes of others—strangers—she's terribly shy and lives in a world of her own and those things make her seem a little peculiar to people outside the house.

Amanda: Don't say peculiar.

Tom: Face the facts. She is.

(The Dance Hall Music Changes To A Tango That Has A Minor And Somewhat Ominous Tone.)

Amanda: In what way is she peculiar—may I ask?

Tom *(gently)*: She lives in a world of her own—a world of little glass ornaments, Mother. . . . *(He gets up. Amanda remains holding the brush, looking at him, troubled.)* She plays old phonograph records and—that's about all—*(He glances at himself in the mirror and crosses to the door.)*

Amanda *(sharply)*: Where are you going?

Tom: I'm going to the movies. *(He goes out the screen door.)*

Amanda: Not to the movies, every night to the movies! *(She follows quickly to the screen door.)* I don't believe you always go to the movies! *(He is gone. Amanda looks worriedly after him for a moment. Then vitality and optimism return and she turns from the door, crossing to the portieres.)* Laura! Laura! *(Laura answers from the kitchenette.)*

Laura: Yes, Mother.

Amanda: Let those dishes go and come in front! *(Laura appears with a dish towel. Amanda speaks to her gaily.)* Laura, come here and make a wish on the moon!

(Screen Image: The Moon)

Laura (entering): Moon—moon?
Amanda: A little silver slipper of a moon. Look over your left shoulder, Laura, and make a wish! (*Laura looks faintly puzzled as if called out of sleep. Amanda seizes her shoulders and turns her at an angle by the door.*) Now! Now, darling, *wish*!
Laura: What shall I wish for, Mother?
Amanda (her voice trembling and her eyes suddenly filling with tears): Happiness! Good fortune!

The sound of the violin rises and the stage dims out.

SCENE VI

The light comes up on the fire escape landing. Tom is leaning against the grill, smoking.

(Screen Image: The High School Hero.)

Tom: And so the following evening I brought Jim home to dinner. I had known Jim slightly in high school. In high school Jim was a hero. He had tremendous Irish good nature and vitality with the scrubbed and polished look of white chinaware. He seemed to move in a continual spotlight. He was a star in basketball, captain of the debating club, president of the senior class and the glee club and he sang the male lead in the annual light operas. He was always running or bounding, never just walking. He seemed always at the point of defeating the law of gravity. He was shooting with such velocity through his adolescence that you would logically expect him to arrive at nothing short of the White House by the time he was thirty. But Jim apparently ran into more interference after his graduation from Soldan. His speed had definitely slowed. Six years after he left high school he was holding a job that wasn't much better than mine.

(Screen Image: The Clerk.)

He was the only one at the warehouse with whom I was on friendly terms. I was valuable to him as someone who could remember his former glory, who had seen him win basketball games and the silver cup in debating. He knew of my secret practice of retiring to a cabinet of the washroom to work on my poems when business was slack in the warehouse. He called me Shakespeare. And while the other boys in the warehouse regarded me with suspicious hostility, Jim took a humorous attitude toward me. Gradually his attitude affected the others, their hostility wore off and they also began to smile at me as people smile at an oddly fashioned dog who trots across their path at some distance.

I knew that Jim and Laura had known each other at Soldan, and I had heard Laura speak admiringly of his voice. I didn't know if Jim remembered her or not. In high school Laura had been as unobtrusive as Jim had been astonishing. If he did remember Laura, it was not as my sister, for when I asked him to dinner, he grinned and said, "You know, Shakespeare, I never thought of you as having folks!"

He was about to discover that I did. . . .

(Legend On Screen: "The Accent Of A Coming Foot.")

The light dims out on Tom and comes up in the Wingfield living room—a delicate, lemony light. It is about five on a Friday evening of late spring which comes "scattering poems in the sky."

Amanda has worked like a Turk in preparation for the gentleman caller. The results are astonishing. The new floor lamp with its rose silk shade is in place, a colored paper lantern conceals the broken light fixture in the ceiling, new billowing white curtains are at the windows, chintz covers are on chairs and sofa, a pair of new sofa pillows make their initial appearance. Open boxes and tissue paper are scattered on the floor.

Laura stands in the middle of the room with lifted arms while Amanda crouches before her, adjusting the hem of a new dress, devout and ritualistic. The dress is colored and designed by memory. The arrangement of Laura's hair is changed; it is softer and more becoming. A fragile, unearthly prettiness has come out in Laura: she is like a piece of translucent glass touched by light, given a momentary radiance, not actual, not lasting.

Amanda (impatiently): Why are you trembling?
Laura: Mother, you've made me so nervous!
Amanda: How have I made you nervous?
Laura: By all this fuss! You make it seem so important!
Amanda: I don't understand you, Laura. You couldn't be satisfied with just sitting home, and yet whenever I try to arrange something for you, you seem to resist it. (*She gets up.*) Now take a look at yourself. No, wait! Wait just a moment—I have an idea!
Laura: What is it now?

Amanda produces two powder puffs which she wraps in handkerchiefs and stuffs in Laura's bosom.

Laura: Mother, what are you doing?
Amanda: They call them "Gay Deceivers"!
Laura: I won't wear them!
Amanda: You will!
Laura: Why should I?
Amanda: Because, to be painfully honest, your chest is flat.

Laura: You make it seem like we were setting a trap.

Amanda: All pretty girls are a trap, a pretty trap, and men expect them to be. **(Legend On Screen: "A Pretty Trap.")** Now look at yourself, young lady. This is the prettiest you will ever be! (*She stands back to admire Laura.*) I've got to fix myself now! You're going to be surprised by your mother's appearance!

Amanda crosses through the portieres, humming gaily. Laura moves slowly to the long mirror and stares solemnly at herself. A wind blows the white curtains inward in a slow, graceful motion and with a faint, sorrowful sighing.

Amanda (from somewhere behind the portieres): It isn't dark enough yet. (*Laura turns slowly before the mirror with a troubled look.*)

(Legend On Screen: "This Is My Sister: Celebrate Her With Strings!" Music Plays.)

Amanda (laughing, still not visible): I'm going to show you something. I'm going to make a spectacular appearance!

Laura: What is it, Mother?

Amanda: Possess your soul in patience—you will see! Something I've resurrected from that old trunk! Styles haven't changed so terribly much after all. . . . (*She parts the portieres.*) Now just look at your mother! (*She wears a girlish frock of yellowed voile with a blue silk sash. She carries a bunch of jonquils—the legend of her youth is nearly revived. Now she speaks feverishly.*) This is the dress in which I led the cotillion. Won the cakewalk twice at Sunset Hill, wore one Spring to the Governor's Ball in Jackson! See how I sashayed around the ballroom, Laura? (*She raises her skirt and does a mincing step around the room.*) I wore it on Sundays for my gentlemen callers! I had it on the day I met your father . . . I had malaria fever all that Spring. The change of climate from East Tennessee to the Delta—weakened resistance—I had a little temperature all the time—not enough to be serious—just enough to make me restless and giddy! Invitations poured in—parties all over the Delta!—"Stay in bed," said Mother, "you have fever!"—but I just wouldn't. I took quinine but kept on going, going! Evenings, dances! Afternoons, long, long rides! Picnics—lovely! So lovely, that country in May—all lacy with dogwood, literally flooded with jonquils! That was the spring I had the craze for jonquils. Jonquils became an absolute obsession. Mother said, "Honey, there's no more room for jonquils." And still I kept on bringing in more jonquils. Whenever, wherever I saw them, I'd say, "Stop! Stop! I see jonquils!" I made the young men help me gather the jonquils! It was a joke, Amanda and her jonquils! Finally there were no more vases to hold them, every available space was filled with jonquils. No vases to hold them? All right, I'll hold them myself! And then I—(*She stops in front of the picture.*) **(Music Plays.)** met your father! Malaria fever and jonquils and then—this—boy. . . . (*She switches on the rose-colored lamp.*) I hope they get here before it starts to rain. (*She crosses the room and places the jonquils in a bowl on the table.*) I gave your brother a little extra change so he and Mr. O'Connor could take the service car home.

Laura (*with an altered look*): What did you say his name was?

Amanda: O'Connor.

Laura: What is his first name?

Amanda: I don't remember. Oh, yes, I do. It was—Jim!

Laura sways slightly and catches hold of a chair.

(Legend On Screen. "Not Jim!")

Laura (*faintly*): Not—Jim!

Amanda: Yes, that was it, it was Jim! I've never known a Jim that wasn't nice!

(Music: The Music Becomes Ominous.)

Laura: Are you sure his name is Jim O'Connor?

Amanda: Yes. Why?

Laura: Is he the one that Tom used to know in high school?

Amanda: He didn't say so. I think he just got to know him at the warehouse.

Laura: There was a Jim O'Connor we both knew in high school—(*Then, with effort.*) If that is the one that Tom is bringing to dinner—you'll have to excuse me, I won't come to the table.

Amanda: What sort of nonsense is this?

Laura: You asked me once if I'd ever liked a boy. Don't you remember I showed you this boy's picture?

Amanda: You mean the boy you showed me in the yearbook?

Laura: Yes, that boy.

Amanda: Laura, Laura, were you in love with that boy?

Laura: I don't know, Mother. All I know is I couldn't sit at the table if it was him!

Amanda: It won't be him! It isn't the least bit likely. But whether it is or not, you will come to the table. You will not be excused.

Laura: I'll have to be, Mother.

Amanda: I don't intend to humor your silliness, Laura. I've had too much from you and your brother, both! So just sit down and compose yourself till they come. Tom has forgotten his key so you'll have to let them in, when they arrive.

Laura (*panicky*): Oh, Mother—*you* answer the door!

Amanda (*lightly*): I'll be in the kitchen—busy!

Laura: Oh, Mother, please answer the door, don't make me do it!

Amanda (*crossing into the kitchenette*): I've got to fix the dressing for the salmon. Fuss, fuss—silliness!—over a gentleman caller!

The door swings shut. Laura is left alone.

(Legend On Screen: "Terror!")

She utters a low moan and turns off the lamp—sits stiffly on the edge of the sofa, knotting her fingers together.

(Legend On Screen: "The Opening Of A Door!")

Tom and Jim appear on the fire escape steps and climb to the landing. Hearing their approach, Laura rises with a panicky gesture. She retreats to the portieres. The doorbell rings. Laura catches her breath and touches her throat. Low drums sound.

Amanda (calling): Laura, sweetheart! The door!

Laura stares at it without moving.

Jim: I think we just beat the rain.
Tom: Uh-huh. (*He rings again, nervously. Jim whistles and fishes for a cigarette.*)
Amanda (very, very gaily): Laura, that is your brother and Mr. O'Connor! Will you let them in, darling?

Laura crosses toward the kitchenette door.

Laura (breathlessly): Mother—you go to the door!

Amanda steps out of the kitchenette and stares furiously at Laura. She points imperiously at the door.

Laura: Please, please!
Amanda (in a fierce whisper): What is the matter with you, you silly thing?
Laura (desperately): Please, you answer it, *please!*
Amanda: I told you I wasn't going to humor you, Laura. Why have you chosen this moment to lose your mind?
Laura: Please, please, please, you go!
Amanda: You'll have to go to the door because I can't!
Laura (despairingly): I can't either!
Amanda: Why?
Laura: I'm *sick!*
Amanda: I'm sick, too—of your nonsense! Why can't you and your brother be normal people? Fantastic whims and behavior! (*Tom gives a long ring.*) Preposterous goings on! Can you give me one reason—(*She calls out lyrically.*) Coming! Just one second!—why should you be afraid to open a door? Now you answer it, Laura!
Laura: Oh, oh, oh . . . (*She returns through the portieres, darts to the Victrola, winds it frantically and turns it on.*)
Amanda: Laura Wingfield, you march right to that door!

Laura: Yes—yes, Mother!

> *A faraway, scratchy rendition of "Dardanella" softens the air and gives her strength to move through it. She slips to the door and draws it cautiously open. Tom enters with the caller, Jim O'Connor.*

Tom: Laura, this is Jim. Jim, this is my sister, Laura.

Jim (stepping inside): I didn't know that Shakespeare had a sister!

Laura (retreating, stiff and trembling, from the door): How—how do you do?

Jim (heartily, extending his hand): Okay!

> *Laura touches it hesitantly with hers.*

Jim: Your hand's *cold*, Laura!

Laura: Yes, well—I've been playing the Victrola. . . .

Jim: Must have been playing classical music on it! You ought to play a little hot swing music to warm you up!

Laura: Excuse me—I haven't finished playing the Victrola. . . .

> *She turns awkwardly and hurries into the front room. She pauses a second by the Victrola. Then she catches her breath and darts through the portieres like a frightened deer.*

Jim (grinning): What was the matter?

Tom: Oh—with Laura? Laura is—terribly shy.

Jim: Shy, huh? It's unusual to meet a shy girl nowadays. I don't believe you ever mentioned you had a sister.

Tom: Well, now you know. I have one. Here is the *Post Dispatch.* You want a piece of it?

Jim: Uh-huh.

Tom: What piece? The comics?

Jim: Sports! *(He glances at it.)* Ole Dizzy Dean is on his bad behavior.

Tom (uninterest): Yeah? *(He lights a cigarette and goes over to the fire escape door.)*

Jim: Where are *you* going?

Tom: I'm going out on the terrace.

Jim (going after him): You know, Shakespeare—I'm going to sell you a bill of goods!

Tom: What goods?

Jim: A course I'm taking.

Tom: Huh?

Jim: In public speaking! You and me, we're not the warehouse type.

Tom: Thanks—that's good news. But what has public speaking got to do with it?

Jim: It fits you for—executive positions!

Tom: Awww.

Jim: I tell you it's done a helluva lot for me.

(Image On Screen: Executive At His Desk.)

Tom: In what respect?

Jim: In every! Ask yourself what is the difference between you an' me and men in the office down front? Brains?—No!—Ability?—No! Then what? Just one little thing—

Tom: What is that one little thing?

Jim: Primarily it amounts to—social poise! Being able to square up to people and hold your own on any social level!

Amanda (from the kitchenette): Tom?

Tom: Yes, Mother?

Amanda: Is that you and Mr. O'Connor?

Tom: Yes, Mother.

Amanda: Well, you just make yourselves comfortable in there.

Tom: Yes, Mother.

Amanda: Ask Mr. O'Connor if he would like to wash his hands.

Jim: Aw, no—no—thank you—I took care of that at the warehouse. Tom—

Tom: Yes?

Jim: Mr. Mendoza was speaking to me about you.

Tom: Favorably?

Jim: What do you think?

Tom: Well—

Jim: You're going to be out of a job if you don't wake up.

Tom: I am waking up—

Jim: You show no signs.

Tom: The signs are interior.

(Image On Screen: The Sailing Vessel With Jolly Roger Again.)

Tom: I'm planning to change. (*He leans over the fire escape rail, speaking with quiet exhilaration. The incandescent marquees and signs of the first-run movie houses light his face from across the alley. He looks like a voyager.*) I'm right at the point of committing myself to a future that doesn't include the warehouse and Mr. Mendoza or even a night-school course in public speaking.

Jim: What are you gassing about?

Tom: I'm tired of the movies.

Jim: Movies!

Tom: Yes, movies! Look at them—(*A wave toward the marvels of Grand Avenue.*) All of those glamorous people—having adventures—hogging it all, gobbling the whole thing up! You know what happens? People go to the *movies* instead of *moving*! Hollywood characters are supposed to have all the adventures for everybody in America, while everybody in America sits in a dark room and watches them have them! Yes, until there's a war. That's when adventure becomes available to the masses! *Everyone's* dish, not only Gable's! Then the people in the dark room come out of the dark room to have some adventures themselves—goody, goody! It's our turn now, to go to the South Sea Island—to make a safari—to be exotic, far-off—But I'm not patient. I don't want to wait till then. I'm tired of the *movies* and I am *about* to move!

Jim (incredulously): Move?

Tom: Yes!

Jim: When?

Tom: Soon!

Jim: Where? Where?

The music seems to answer the question, while Tom thinks it over. He searches in his pockets.

Tom: I'm starting to boil inside. I know I seem dreamy, but inside—well, I'm boiling! Whenever I pick up a shoe, I shudder a little thinking how short life is and what I am doing! Whatever that means. I know it doesn't mean shoes—except as something to wear on a traveler's feet! *(He finds what he has been searching for in his pockets and holds out a paper to Jim.)* Look—

Jim: What?

Tom: I'm a member.

Jim (reading): The Union of Merchant Seamen.

Tom: I paid my dues this month, instead of the light bill.

Jim: You will regret it when they turn the lights off.

Tom: I won't be here.

Jim: How about your mother?

Tom: I'm like my father. The bastard son of a bastard! Did you notice how he's grinning in his picture in there? And he's been absent going on sixteen years!

Jim: You're just talking, you drip. How does your mother feel about it?

Tom: Shhh! Here comes Mother! Mother is not acquainted with my plans!

Amanda (coming through the portieres): Where are you all?

Tom: On the terrace, Mother.

They start inside. She advances to them. Tom is distinctly shocked at her appearance. Even Jim blinks a little. He is making his first contact with girlish Southern vivacity and in spite of the night-school course in public speaking is somewhat thrown off the beam by the unexpected outlay of social charm. Certain responses are attempted by Jim but are swept aside by Amanda's gay laughter and chatter. Tom is embarrassed but after the first shock Jim reacts very warmly. He grins and chuckles, is altogether won over.

(Image On Screen: Amanda As A Girl.)

Amanda (coyly smiling, shaking her girlish ringlets): Well, well, well, so this is
   Mr. O'Connor. Introductions entirely unnecessary. I've heard so much
   about you from my boy. I finally said to him, Tom—good gracious!—why
   don't you bring this paragon to supper? I'd like to meet this nice young
   man at the warehouse!—Instead of just hearing him sing your praises so
   much! I don't know why my son is so stand-offish—that's not Southern
   behavior!

   Let's sit down and—I think we could stand a little more air in here!
   Tom, leave the door open. I felt a nice fresh breeze a moment ago. Where
   has it gone to? Mmm, so warm already! And not quite summer, even.
   We're going to burn up when summer really gets started. However, we're
   having—we're having a very light supper. I think light things are better
   fo' this time of year. The same as light clothes are. Light clothes an' light
   food are what warm weather calls fo'. You know our blood gets so thick
   during th' winter—it takes a while fo' us to *adjust* ou'selves!—when the
   season changes . . . It's come so quick this year. I wasn't prepared. All of a
   sudden—heavens! Already summer! I ran to the trunk an' pulled out this
   light dress—Terribly old! Historical almost! But feels so good—so good
   an' co-ol, y' know. . . .
Tom: Mother—
Amanda: Yes, honey?
Tom: How about—supper?
Amanda: Honey, you go ask Sister if supper is ready! You know that Sister is
   in full charge of supper! Tell her you hungry boys are waiting for it. (*To
   Jim*) Have you met Laura?
Jim: She—
Amanda: Let you in? Oh, good, you've met already! It's rare for a girl as sweet
   an' pretty as Laura to be domestic! But Laura is, thank heavens, not only
   pretty but also very domestic. I'm not at all. I never was a bit. I never
   could make a thing but angel-food cake. Well, in the South we had so
   many servants. Gone, gone, gone. All vestige of gracious living! Gone
   completely! I wasn't prepared for what the future brought me. All of
   my gentlemen callers were sons of planters and so of course I assumed
   that I would be married to one and raise my family on a large piece of
   land with plenty of servants. But man proposes—and woman accepts the
   proposal! To vary that old, old saying a little bit—I married no planter!
   I married a man who worked for the telephone company! That gallantly
   smiling gentleman over there! (*She points to the picture.*) A telephone
   man who—fell in love with long-distance! Now he travels and I don't
   even know where! But what am I going on for about my—tribulations?
   Tell me yours—I hope you don't have any! Tom?
Tom (returning): Yes, Mother?
Amanda: Is supper nearly ready?

Tom: It looks to me like supper is on the table.

Amanda: Let me look—(*She rises prettily and looks through portieres.*) Oh, lovely! But where is Sister?

Tom: Laura is not feeling well and she says that she thinks she'd better not come to the table.

Amanda: What? Nonsense! Laura? Oh, Laura!

Laura (from the kitchenette, faintly): Yes, Mother.

Amanda: You really must come to the table. We won't be seated until you come to the table! Come in, Mr. O'Connor. You sit over there, and I'll . . . Laura? Laura Wingfield! You're keeping us waiting, honey! We can't say grace until you come to the table!

The kitchenette door is pushed weakly open and Laura comes in. She is obviously quite faint, her lips trembling, her eyes wide and staring. She moves unsteadily toward the table.

(Screen Legend: "Terror!")

Outside a summer storm is coming on abruptly. The white curtains billow inward at the windows and there is a sorrowful murmur and deep blue dusk.

Laura suddenly stumbles; she catches at a chair with a faint moan.

Tom: Laura!

Amanda: Laura! (*There is a clap of thunder.*) **(Screen Legend: "Ah!")** (*Despairingly.*) Why, Laura, you *are* ill, darling! Tom, help your sister into the living room, dear! Sit in the living room, Laura—rest on the sofa. Well! (*To Jim as Tom helps his sister to the sofa in the living room*) Standing over the hot stove made her ill! I told her that it was just too warm this evening, but—(*Tom comes back to the table.*) Is Laura all right now?

Tom: Yes.

Amanda: What *is* that? Rain? A nice cool rain has come up! (*She gives Jim a frightened look.*) I think we may—have grace—now . . . (*Tom looks at her stupidly.*) Tom, honey—you say grace!

Tom: Oh . . . "For these and all thy mercies—" (*They bow their heads, Amanda stealing a nervous glance at Jim. In the living room Laura, stretched on the sofa, clenches her hand to her lips, to hold back a shuddering sob.*) God's Holy Name be praised—

(The Scene Dims Out.)

SCENE VII

It is half an hour later. Dinner is just being finished in the dining room. Laura is still huddled upon the sofa, her feet drawn under her, her head resting on a pale blue pillow, her eyes wide and mysteriously watchful. The new floor lamp with its shade

of rose-colored silk gives a soft, becoming light to her face, bringing out the fragile,
unearthly prettiness which usually escapes attention. From outside there is a steady
murmur of rain, but it is slackening and soon the air outside becomes pale and lumi-
nous as the moon breaks through the clouds. A moment after the curtain rises, the
lights in both rooms flicker and go out.

Jim: Hey, there, Mr. Light Bulb!

Amanda laughs nervously.

(Legend On Screen: "Suspension Of A Public Service.")

Amanda: Where was Moses when the lights went out? Ha-ha. Do you know
the answer to that one, Mr. O'Connor?

Jim: No, Ma'am, what's the answer?

Amanda: In the dark! (*Jim laughs appreciatively.*) Everybody sit still. I'll light
the candles. Isn't it lucky we have them on the table? Where's a match?
Which of you gentlemen can provide a match?

Jim: Here.

Amanda: Thank you, sir.

Jim: Not at all, Ma'am!

Amanda (*as she lights the candles*): I guess the fuse has burnt out. Mr. O'Connor,
can you tell a burnt-out fuse? I know I can't and Tom is a total loss when
it comes to mechanics. (*They rise from the table and go into the kitchen-*
ette, from where their voices are heard.) Oh, be careful you don't bump into
something. We don't want our gentleman caller to break his neck. Now
wouldn't that be a fine howdy-do?

Jim: Ha-ha! Where is the fuse-box?

Amanda: Right here next to the stove. Can you see anything?

Jim: Just a minute.

Amanda: Isn't electricity a mysterious thing? Wasn't it Benjamin Franklin
who tied a key to a kite? We live in such a mysterious universe, don't
we? Some people say that science clears up all the mysteries for us. In my
opinion it only creates more! Have you found it yet?

Jim: No, Ma'am. All these fuses look okay to me.

Amanda: Tom!

Tom: Yes, Mother?

Amanda: That light bill I gave you several days ago. The one I told you we
got the notices about?

(Legend: "Ha!")

Tom: Oh—yeah.

Amanda: You didn't neglect to pay it by any chance?

Tom: Why, I—

Amanda: Didn't! I might have known it!

Jim: Shakespeare probably wrote a poem on that light bill, Mrs. Wingfield.

Amanda: I might have known better than to trust him with it! There's such a high price for negligence in this world!

Jim: Maybe the poem will win a ten-dollar prize.

Amanda: We'll just have to spend the remainder of the evening in the nine-teenth century, before Mr. Edison made the Mazda lamp!

Jim: Candlelight is my favorite kind of light.

Amanda: That shows you're romantic! But that's no excuse for Tom. Well, we got through dinner. Very considerate of them to let us get through dinner before they plunged us into everlasting darkness, wasn't it, Mr. O'Connor?

Jim: Ha-ha!

Amanda: Tom, as a penalty for your carelessness you can help me with the dishes.

Jim: Let me give you a hand.

Amanda: Indeed you will not!

Jim: I ought to be good for something.

Amanda: Good for something? (*Her tone is rhapsodic.*) You? Why, Mr. O'Connor, nobody, *nobody's* given me this much entertainment in years—as you have!

Jim: Aw, now, Mrs. Wingfield!

Amanda: I'm not exaggerating, not one bit! But Sister is all by her lonesome. You go keep her company in the parlor! I'll give you this lovely old cande-labrum that used to be on the altar at the church of the Heavenly Rest. It was melted a little out of shape when the church burnt down. Lightning struck it one spring. Gypsy Jones was holding a revival at the time and he intimated that the church was destroyed because the Episcopalians gave card parties.

Jim: Ha-ha.

Amanda: And how about you coaxing Sister to drink a little wine? I think it would be good for her! Can you carry both at once?

Jim: Sure. I'm Superman!

Amanda: Now, Thomas, get into this apron!

Jim comes into the dining room, carrying the candelabrum, its candles lighted, in one hand and a glass of wine in the other. The door of the kitchenette swings closed on Amanda's gay laughter; the flickering light approaches the portieres. Laura sits up nervously as Jim enters. She can hardly speak from the almost intolerable strain of being alone with a stranger.

(Screen Legend: "I Don't Suppose You Remember Me At All!")

At first, before Jim's warmth overcomes her paralyzing shyness, Laura's voice is thin and breathless, as though she had just run up a steep flight of stairs. Jim's attitude is gently humorous. While the incident is apparently unimportant, it is to Laura the climax of her secret life.

Jim: Hello there, Laura.

Laura (faintly): Hello. *(She clears her throat.)*

Jim: How are you feeling now? Better?

Laura: Yes. Yes, thank you.

Jim: This is for you. A little dandelion wine. *(He extends the glass toward her with extravagant gallantry.)*

Laura: Thank you.

Jim: Drink it—but don't get drunk! *(He laughs heartily. Laura takes the glass uncertainly; laughs shyly.)* Where shall I set the candles?

Laura: Oh—oh, anywhere . . .

Jim: How about here on the floor? Any objections?

Laura: No.

Jim: I'll spread a newspaper under to catch the drippings. I like to sit on the floor. Mind if I do?

Laura: Oh, no.

Jim: Give me a pillow?

Laura: What?

Jim: A pillow!

Laura: Oh . . . *(She hands him one quickly.)*

Jim: How about you? Don't you like to sit on the floor?

Laura: Oh—yes.

Jim: Why don't you, then?

Laura: I—will.

Jim: Take a pillow! *(Laura does. She sits on the floor on the other side of the candelabrum. Jim crosses his legs and smiles engagingly at her.)* I can't hardly see you sitting way over there.

Laura: I can—see you.

Jim: I know, but that's not fair, I'm in the limelight. *(Laura moves her pillow closer.)* Good! Now I can see you! Comfortable?

Laura: Yes.

Jim: So am I. Comfortable as a cow. Will you have some gum?

Laura: No, thank you.

Jim: I think that I will indulge, with your permission. *(He musingly unwraps it and holds it up.)* Think of the fortune made by the guy that invented the first piece of chewing gum. Amazing, huh? The Wrigley Building is one of the sights of Chicago—I saw it when I went up to the Century of Progress. Did you take in the Century of Progress?

Laura: No, I didn't.

Jim: Well, it was quite a wonderful exposition. What impressed me most was the Hall of Science. Gives you an idea of what the future will be in America, even more wonderful than the present time is! *(There is a pause. Jim smiles at her.)* Your brother tells me you're shy. Is that right, Laura?

Laura: I—don't know.

Jim: I judge you to be an old-fashioned type of girl. Well, I think that's a pretty good type to be. Hope you don't think I'm being too personal—do you?

Laura (hastily, out of embarrassment): I believe I *will* take a piece of gum, if you—don't mind. (*Clearing her throat.*) Mr. O'Connor, have you—kept up with your singing?

Jim: Singing? Me?

Laura: Yes. I remember what a beautiful voice you had.

Jim: When did you hear me sing?

Laura does not answer, and in the long pause which follows a man's voice is heard singing offstage.

Voice:

> O blow, ye winds, heigh-ho,
> A-roving I will go!
> I'm off to my love
> With a boxing glove—
> Ten thousand miles away!

Jim: You say you've heard me sing?

Laura: Oh, yes! Yes, very often . . . I—don't suppose—you remember me—at all?

Jim (smiling doubtfully): You know I have an idea I've seen you before. I had that idea soon as you opened the door. It seemed almost like I was about to remember your name. But the name that I started to call you—wasn't a name! And so I stopped myself before I said it.

Laura: Wasn't it—Blue Roses?

Jim (springing up, grinning): Blue Roses! My gosh, yes—Blue Roses! That's what I had on my tongue when you opened the door! Isn't it funny what tricks your memory plays? I didn't connect you with high school somehow or other. But that's where it was; it was high school. I didn't even know you were Shakespeare's sister! Gosh, I'm sorry.

Laura: I didn't expect you to. You—barely knew me!

Jim: But we did have a speaking acquaintance, huh?

Laura: Yes, we—spoke to each other.

Jim: When did you recognize me?

Laura: Oh, right away!

Jim: Soon as I came in the door?

Laura: When I heard your name I thought it was probably you. I knew that Tom used to know you a little in high school. So when you came in the door—well, then I was—sure.

Jim: Why didn't you *say* something, then?

Laura (breathlessly): I didn't know what to say, I was—too surprised!

Jim: For goodness' sakes! You know, this sure is funny!

Laura: Yes! Yes, isn't it, though . . .

Jim: Didn't we have a class in something together?

Laura: Yes, we did.

Jim: What class was that?

Laura: It was—singing—chorus!

Jim: Aw!

Laura: I sat across the aisle from you in the Aud.

Jim: Aw.

Laura: Mondays, Wednesdays, and Fridays.

Jim: Now I remember—you always came in late.

Laura: Yes, it was so hard for me, getting upstairs. I had that brace on my leg—it clumped so loud!

Jim: I never heard any clumping.

Laura (wincing at the recollection): To me it sounded like—thunder!

Jim: Well, well, well, I never even noticed.

Laura: And everybody was seated before I came in. I had to walk in front of all those people. My seat was in the back row. I had to go clumping all the way up the aisle with everyone watching!

Jim: You shouldn't have been self-conscious.

Laura: I know, but I was. It was always such a relief when the singing started.

Jim: Aw, yes, I've placed you now! I used to call you Blue Roses. How was it that I got started calling you that?

Laura: I was out of school a little while with pleurosis. When I came back you asked me what was the matter. I said I had pleurosis—you thought I said *Blue Roses.* That's what you called me after that!

Jim: I hope you didn't mind.

Laura: Oh, no—I liked it. You see, I wasn't acquainted with many—people. . . .

Jim: As I remember you sort of stuck by yourself.

Laura: I—I—never had much luck at—making friends.

Jim: I don't see why you wouldn't.

Laura: Well, I—started out badly.

Jim: You mean being—

Laura: Yes, it sort of—stood between me—

Jim: You shouldn't have let it!

Laura: I know, but it did, and—

Jim: You were shy with people!

Laura: I tried not to be but never could—

Jim: Overcome it?

Laura: No, I—I never could!

Jim: I guess being shy is something you have to work out of kind of gradually.

Laura (sorrowfully): Yes—I guess it—

Jim: Takes time!

Laura: Yes—

Jim: People are not so dreadful when you know them. That's what you have to remember! And everybody has problems, not just you, but practically everybody has got some problems. You think of yourself as having the only problems, as being the only one who is disappointed. But just look around you and you will see lots of people as disappointed as you are. For instance, I hoped when I was going to high school that I would be further along at this time, six years later, than I am now. You remember that wonderful write-up I had in *The Torch?*

Laura: Yes! *(She rises and crosses to the table.)*

Jim: It said I was bound to succeed in anything I went into! *(Laura returns with the high school yearbook.)* Holy Jeez! *The Torch!* *(He accepts it reverently. They smile across the book with mutual wonder. Laura crouches beside him and they begin to turn the pages. Laura's shyness is dissolving in his warmth.)*

Laura: Here you are in *The Pirates of Penzance!*

Jim (wistfully): I sang the baritone lead in that operetta.

Laura (raptly): So—*beautifully!*

Jim (protesting): Aw—

Laura: Yes, yes—beautifully—beautifully!

Jim: You heard me?

Laura: All three times!

Jim: No!

Laura: Yes!

Jim: All three performances?

Laura (looking down): Yes.

Jim: Why?

Laura: I—wanted to ask you to—autograph my program.

Jim: Why didn't you ask me to?

Laura: You were always surrounded by your own friends so much that I never had a chance to.

Jim: You should have just—

Laura: Well, I—thought you might think I was—

Jim: Thought I might think you was—what?

Laura: Oh—

Jim (with reflective relish): I was beleaguered by females in those days.

Laura: You were terribly popular!

Jim: Yeah—

Laura: You had such a—friendly way—

Jim: I was spoiled in high school.

Laura: Everybody—liked you!

Jim: Including you?

Laura: I—yes, I—did, too—(*She gently closes the book in her lap.*)

Jim: Well, well, well!—Give me that program, Laura. (*She hands it to him. He signs it with a flourish.*) There you are—better late than never!

Laura: Oh, I—what a—surprise!

Jim: My signature isn't worth very much right now. But some day—maybe—it will increase in value! Being disappointed is one thing and being discouraged is something else. I am disappointed but I'm not discouraged. I'm twenty-three years old. How old are you?

Laura: I'll be twenty-four in June.

Jim: That's not old age!

Laura: No, but—

Jim: You finished high school?

Laura (with difficulty): I didn't go back.

Jim: You mean you dropped out?

Laura: I made bad grades in my final examinations. (*She rises and replaces the book and the program on the table. Her voice is strained.*) How is—Emily Meisenbach getting along?

Jim: Oh, that kraut-head!

Laura: Why do you call her that?

Jim: That's what she was.

Laura: You're not still—going with her?

Jim: I never see her.

Laura: It said in the "Personal" section that you were—engaged!

Jim: I know, but I wasn't impressed by that—propaganda!

Laura: It wasn't—the truth?

Jim: Only in Emily's optimistic opinion!

Laura: Oh—

(Legend: "What Have You Done Since High School?")

Jim lights a cigarette and leans indolently back on his elbows smiling at Laura with a warmth and charm which lights her inwardly with altar candles. She remains by the table, picks up a piece from the glass menagerie collection, and turns it in her hands to cover her tumult.

Jim (after several reflective puffs on his cigarette): What have you done since high school? (*She seems not to hear him.*) Huh? (*Laura looks up.*) I said what have you done since high school, Laura?

Laura: Nothing much.

Jim: You must have been doing something these six long years.

Laura: Yes.

Jim: Well, then, such as what?

Laura: I took a business course at business college—

Jim: How did that work out?

Laura: Well, not very—well—I had to drop out, it gave me—indigestion—

Jim laughs gently.

Jim: What are you doing now?

Laura: I don't do anything—much. Oh, please don't think I sit around doing nothing! My glass collection takes up a good deal of time. Glass is something you have to take good care of.

Jim: What did you say—about glass?

Laura: Collection I said—I have one—(*She clears her throat and turns away again, acutely shy.*)

Jim (abruptly): You know what I judge to be the trouble with you? Inferiority complex! Know what that is? That's what they call it when someone low-rates himself! I understand it because I had it, too. Although my case was not so aggravated as yours seems to be. I had it until I took up public speaking, developed my voice, and learned that I had an aptitude for science. Before that time I never thought of myself as being outstanding in any way whatsoever! Now I've never made a regular study of it, but I have a friend who says I can analyze people better than doctors that make a profession of it. I don't claim that to be necessarily true, but I can sure guess a person's psychology, Laura! (*He takes out his gum.*) Excuse me, Laura. I always take it out when the flavor is gone. I'll use this scrap of paper to wrap it in. I know how it is to get it stuck on a shoe. (*He wraps the gum in paper and puts it in his pocket.*) Yep—that's what I judge to be your principal trouble. A lack of confidence in yourself as a person. You don't have the proper amount of faith in yourself. I'm basing that fact on a number of your remarks and also on certain observations I've made. For instance that clumping you thought was so awful in high school. You say that you even dreaded to walk into class. You see what you did? You dropped out of school, you gave up an education because of a clump, which as far as I know was practically non-existent! A little physical defect is what you have. Hardly noticeable even! Magnified thousands of times by imagination! You know what my strong advice to you is? Think of yourself as *superior* in some way!

Laura: In what way would I think?

Jim: Why, man alive, Laura! Just look about you a little. What do you see? A world full of common people! All of 'em born and all of 'em going to die! Which of them has one-tenth of your good points! Or mine! Or anyone else's, as far as that goes—gosh! Everybody excels in some one thing. Some in many! (*He unconsciously glances at himself in the mirror.*) All you've got to do is discover in *what*! Take me, for instance. (*He adjusts his tie at the mirror.*) My interest happens to lie in electro-dynamics. I'm taking a course in radio engineering at night school, Laura, on top of a fairly responsible job at the warehouse. I'm taking that course and studying public speaking.

Laura: Ohhhh.

Jim: Because I believe in the future of television! (*Turning his back to her.*) I wish to be ready to go up right along with it. Therefore I'm planning to get in on the ground floor. In fact I've already made the right connections and all that remains is for the industry itself to get under way! Full steam—(*His eyes are starry.*) Knowledge—Zzzzzp! Money—Zzzzzp!— Power! That's the cycle democracy is built on! (*His attitude is convincingly dynamic. Laura stares at him, even her shyness eclipsed in her absolute wonder. He suddenly grins.*) I guess you think I think a lot of myself!

Laura: No—o-o-o, I—

Jim: Now how about you? Isn't there something you take more interest in than anything else?

Laura: Well, I do—as I said—have my—glass collection—

A peal of girlish laughter rings from the kitchenette.

Jim: I'm not right sure I know what you're talking about. What kind of glass is it?

Laura: Little articles of it, they're ornaments mostly! Most of them are little animals made out of glass, the tiniest little animals in the world. Mother calls them a glass menagerie! Here's an example of one, if you'd like to see it! This one is one of the oldest. It's nearly thirteen. (*He stretches out his hand.*) (**Music: "The Glass Menagerie."**) Oh, be careful—if you breathe, it breaks!

Jim: I'd better not take it. I'm pretty clumsy with things.

Laura: Go on, I trust you with him! (*She places the piece in his palm.*) There now—you're holding him gently! Hold him over the light, he loves the light! You see how the light shines through him?

Jim: It sure does shine!

Laura: I shouldn't be partial, but he is my favorite one.

Jim: What kind of a thing is this one supposed to be?

Laura: Haven't you noticed the single horn on his forehead?

Jim: A unicorn, huh?

Laura: Mmm-hmmm!

Jim: Unicorns—aren't they extinct in the modern world?

Laura: I know!

Jim: Poor little fellow, he must feel sort of lonesome.

Laura (smiling): Well, if he does, he doesn't complain about it. He stays on a shelf with some horses that don't have horns and all of them seem to get along nicely together.

Jim: How do you know?

Laura (lightly): I haven't heard any arguments among them!

Jim (grinning): No arguments, huh? Well, that's a pretty good sign! Where shall I set him?

Laura: Put him on the table. They all like a change of scenery once in a while!

Jim: Well, well, well, well—(*He places the glass piece on the table, then raises his arms and stretches.*) Look how big my shadow is when I stretch!

Laura: Oh, oh, yes—it stretches across the ceiling!

Jim (crossing to the door): I think it's stopped raining. (*He opens the fire escape door and the background music changes to a dance tune.*) Where does the music come from?

Laura: From the Paradise Dance Hall across the alley.

Jim: How about cutting the rug a little, Miss Wingfield?

Laura: Oh, I—

Jim: Or is your program filled up? Let me have a look at it. (*He grasps an imaginary card.*) Why, every dance is taken! I'll just have to scratch some out. (**Waltz Music: "La Golondrina."**) Ahhh, a waltz! (*He executes some sweeping turns by himself, then holds his arms toward Laura.*)

Laura (breathlessly): I—can't dance!

Jim: There you go, that inferiority stuff!

Laura: I've never danced in my life!

Jim: Come on, try!

Laura: Oh, but I'd step on you!

Jim: I'm not made out of glass.

Laura: How—how—how do we start?

Jim: Just leave it to me. You hold your arms out a little.

Laura: Like this?

Jim (taking her in his arms): A little bit higher. Right. Now don't tighten up, that's the main thing about it—relax.

Laura (laughing breathlessly): It's hard not to.

Jim: Okay.

Laura: I'm afraid you can't budge me.

Jim: What do you bet I can't? (*He swings her into motion.*)

Laura: Goodness, yes, you can!

Jim: Let yourself go, now, Laura, just let yourself go.

Laura: I'm—

Jim: Come on!

Laura: —trying!

Jim: Not so stiff—easy does it!

Laura: I know but I'm—

Jim: Loosen th' backbone! There now, that's a lot better.

Laura: Am I?

Jim: Lots, lots better! (*He moves her about the room in a clumsy waltz.*)

Laura: Oh, my!

Jim: Ha-ha!

Laura: Oh, my goodness!

Jim: Ha-ha-ha! (*They suddenly bump into the table, and the glass piece on it falls to the floor. Jim stops the dance.*) What did we hit on?

Laura: Table.

Jim: Did something fall off it? I think—

Laura: Yes.

Jim: I hope that it wasn't the little glass horse with the horn!

Laura: Yes. (*She stoops to pick it up.*)

Jim: Aw, aw, aw. Is it broken?

Laura: Now it is just like all the other horses.

Jim: It's lost its—

Laura: Horn! It doesn't matter. Maybe it's a blessing in disguise.

Jim: You'll never forgive me. I bet that that was your favorite piece of glass.

Laura: I don't have favorites much. It's no tragedy, Freckles. Glass breaks so easily. No matter how careful you are. The traffic jars the shelves and things fall off them.

Jim: Still I'm awfully sorry that I was the cause.

Laura (smiling): I'll just imagine he had an operation. The horn was removed to make him feel less—freakish! (*They both laugh.*) Now he will feel more at home with the other horses, the ones that don't have horns . . .

Jim: Ha-ha, that's very funny! (*Suddenly he is serious.*) I'm glad to see that you have a sense of humor. You know—you're—well—very different! Surprisingly different from anyone else I know! (*His voice becomes soft and hesitant with a genuine feeling.*) Do you mind me telling you that? (*Laura is abashed beyond speech.*) I mean it in a nice way—(*Laura nods shyly, looking away.*) You make me feel sort of—I don't know how to put it! I'm usually pretty good at expressing things, but—this is something that I don't know how to say! (*Laura touches her throat and clears it—turns the broken unicorn in her hands. His voice becomes softer.*) Has anyone ever told you that you were pretty? (*There is a pause, and the music rises slightly. Laura looks up slowly, with wonder, and shakes her head.*) Well, you are! In a very different way from anyone else. And all the nicer because of the difference, too. (*His voice becomes low and husky. Laura turns away, nearly faint with the novelty of her emotions.*) I wish that you were my sister. I'd teach you to have some confidence in yourself. The different people are not like other people, but being different is nothing to be ashamed of. Because other people are not such wonderful people. They're one hundred times one thousand. You're one times one! They walk all over the earth. You just stay here. They're common as—weeds, but—you—well, you're—*Blue Roses!*

(Image On Screen: Blue Roses.)

(The Music Changes.)

Laura: But blue is wrong for—roses . . .

Jim: It's right for you! You're—pretty!

Laura: In what respect am I pretty?

Jim: In all respects—believe me! Your eyes—your hair—are pretty! Your hands are pretty! (*He catches hold of her hand.*) You think I'm making this up because I'm invited to dinner and have to be nice. Oh, I could do that! I could put on an act for you, Laura, and say lots of things without being very sincere. But this time I am. I'm talking to you sincerely. I happened to notice you had this inferiority complex that keeps you from feeling comfortable with people. Somebody needs to build your confidence up and make you proud instead of shy and turning away and—blushing. Somebody—ought to—*kiss* you, Laura! (*His hand slips slowly up her arm to her shoulder as the music swells tumultuously. He suddenly turns her about and kisses her on the lips. When he releases her, Laura sinks on the sofa with a bright, dazed look. Jim backs away and fishes in his pocket for a cigarette.*) **(Legend On Screen: "A Souvenir.")** Stumblejohn! (*He lights the cigarette, avoiding her look. There is a peal of girlish laughter from Amanda in the kitchenette. Laura slowly raises and opens her hand. It still contains the little broken glass animal. She looks at it with a tender, bewildered expression.*) Stumblejohn! I shouldn't have done that—That was way off the beam. You don't smoke, do you? (*She looks up, smiling, not hearing the question. He sits beside her rather gingerly. She looks at him speechlessly—waiting. He coughs decorously and moves a little farther aside as he considers the situation and senses her feelings, dimly, with perturbation. He speaks gently.*) Would you—care for a—mint? (*She doesn't seem to hear him but her look grows brighter even.*) Peppermint? Life Saver? My pocket's a regular drug store— wherever I go . . . (*He pops a mint in his mouth. Then he gulps and decides to make a clean breast of it. He speaks slowly and gingerly.*) Laura, you know, if I had a sister like you, I'd do the same thing as Tom. I'd bring out fellows and—introduce her to them. The right type of boys—of a type to—appreciate her. Only—well—he made a mistake about me. Maybe I've got no call to be saying this. That may not have been the idea in having me over. But what if it was? There's nothing wrong about that. The only trouble is that in my case—I'm not in a situation to—do the right thing. I can't take down your number and say I'll phone. I can't call up next week and—ask for a date. I thought I had better explain the situation in case you—misunderstood it and—I hurt your feelings. . . . (*There is a pause. Slowly, very slowly, Laura's look changes, her eyes returning slowly from his to the glass figure in her palm. Amanda utters another gay laugh in the kitchenette.*)

Laura (faintly): You—won't—call again?

Jim: No, Laura, I can't. *(He rises from the sofa.)* As I was just explaining, I've—got strings on me. Laura, I've—been going steady! I go out all the time with a girl named Betty. She's a home-girl like you, and Catholic, and Irish, and in a great many ways we—get along fine. I met her last summer on a moonlight boat trip up the river to Alton, on the *Majestic.* Well—right away from the start it was—love! **(Legend On Screen: Love!)** *(Laura sways slightly forward and grips the arm of the sofa. He fails to notice, now enrapt in his own comfortable being.)* Being in love has made a new man of me! *(Leaning stiffly forward, clutching the arm of the sofa, Laura struggles visibly with her storm. But Jim is oblivious; she is a long way off.)* The power of love is really pretty tremendous! Love is something that—changes the whole world, Laura! *(The storm abates a little and Laura leans back. He notices her again.)* It happened that Betty's aunt took sick, she got a wire and had to go to Centralia. So Tom—when he asked me to dinner—I naturally just accepted the invitation, not knowing that you— that he—that I—*(He stops awkwardly.)* Huh—I'm a stumblejohn *(He flops back on the sofa. The holy candles on the altar of Laura's face have been snuffed out. There is a look of almost infinite desolation. Jim glances at her uneasily.)* I wish that you would—say something. *(She bites her lip which was trembling and then bravely smiles. She opens her hand again on the broken glass figure. Then she gently takes his hand and raises it level with her own. She carefully places the unicorn in the palm of his hand, then pushes his fingers closed upon it.)* What are you—doing that for? You want me to have him? Laura? *(She nods.)* What for?

Laura: A—souvenir . . .

She rises unsteadily and crouches beside the Victrola to wind it up.

(Legend On Screen: "Things Have A Way Of Turning Out So Badly.")

(Or Image: "Gentleman Caller Waving Goodbye! Gaily.")

At this moment Amanda rushes brightly back into the living room. She bears a pitcher of fruit punch in an old-fashioned cut-glass pitcher, and a plate of macaroons. The plate has a gold border and poppies painted on it.

Amanda: Well, well, well! Isn't the air delightful after the shower? I've made you children a little liquid refreshment. *(She turns gaily to Jim.)* Jim, do you know that song about lemonade?

> "Lemonade, lemonade
> Made in the shade and stirred with a spade—
> Good enough for any old maid!"

Jim (uneasily): Ha-ha! No—I never heard it.

Amanda: Why, Laura! You look so serious!

Jim: We were having a serious conversation.

Amanda: Good! Now you're better acquainted!

Jim (uncertainly): Ha-ha! Yes.

Amanda: You modern young people are much more serious-minded than my generation. I was so gay as a girl!

Jim: You haven't changed, Mrs. Wingfield.

Amanda: Tonight I'm rejuvenated! The gaiety of the occasion, Mr. O'Connor! *(She tosses her head with a peal of laughter, spilling some lemonade.)* Oooo! I'm baptizing myself!

Jim: Here—let me—

Amanda (setting the pitcher down): There now. I discovered we had some maraschino cherries. I dumped them in, juice and all!

Jim: You shouldn't have gone to that trouble, Mrs. Wingfield.

Amanda: Trouble, trouble? Why, it was loads of fun! Didn't you hear me cutting up in the kitchen? I bet your ears were burning! I told Tom how outdone with him I was for keeping you to himself so long a time! He should have brought you over much, much sooner! Well, now that you've found your way, I want you to be a very frequent caller! Not just occasional but all the time. Oh, we're going to have a lot of gay times together! I see them coming! Mmm, just breathe that air! So fresh, and the moon's so pretty! I'll skip back out—I know where my place is when young folks are having a—serious conversation!

Jim: Oh, don't go out, Mrs. Wingfield. The fact of the matter is I've got to be going.

Amanda: Going, now? You're joking! Why, it's only the shank of the evening, Mr. O'Connor!

Jim: Well, you know how it is.

Amanda: You mean you're a young workingman and have to keep workingmen's hours. We'll let you off early tonight. But only on the condition that next time you stay later. What's the best night for you? Isn't Saturday night the best night for you workingmen?

Jim: I have a couple of time-clocks to punch, Mrs. Wingfield. One at morning, another one at night!

Amanda: My, but you *are* ambitious! You work at night, too?

Jim: No, Ma'am, not work but—Betty! *(He crosses deliberately to pick up his hat. The band at the Paradise Dance Hall goes into a tender waltz.)*

Amanda: Betty? Betty? Who's—Betty? *(There is an ominous cracking sound in the sky.)*

Jim: Oh, just a girl. The girl I go steady with! *(He smiles charmingly. The sky falls.)*

(Legend On Screen: "The Sky Falls.")

Amanda (a long-drawn exhalation): Ohhhh . . . Is it a serious romance, Mr. O'Connor?

Jim: We're going to be married the second Sunday in June.

Amanda: Ohhhh—how nice! Tom didn't mention that you were engaged to be married.

Jim: The cat's not out of the bag at the warehouse yet. You know how they are. They call you Romeo and stuff like that. (*He stops at the oval mirror to put on his hat. He carefully shapes the brim and the crown to give a discreetly dashing effect.*) It's been a wonderful evening, Mrs. Wingfield. I guess this is what they mean by Southern hospitality.

Amanda: It really wasn't anything at all.

Jim: I hope it don't seem like I'm rushing off. But I promised Betty I'd pick her up at the Wabash depot, an' by the time I get my jalopy down there her train'll be in. Some women are pretty upset if you keep 'em waiting.

Amanda: Yes, I know—The tyranny of women! (*Extends her hand.*) Goodbye, Mr. O'Connor. I wish you luck—and happiness—and success! All three of them, and so does Laura!—Don't you, Laura?

Laura: Yes!

Jim (taking Laura's hand): Goodbye, Laura. I'm certainly going to treasure that souvenir. And don't you forget the good advice I gave you. (*He raises his voice to a cheery shout.*) So long, Shakespeare! Thanks again, ladies. Good night!

He grins and ducks jauntily out. Still bravely grimacing, Amanda closes the door on the gentleman caller. Then she turns back to the room with a puzzled expression. She and Laura don't dare to face each other. Laura crouches beside the Victrola to wind it.

Amanda (faintly): Things have a way of turning out so badly. I don't believe that I would play the Victrola. Well, well—well—Our gentleman caller was engaged to be married! (*She raises her voice.*) Tom!

Tom (from the kitchenette): Yes, Mother?

Amanda: Come in here a minute. I want to tell you something awfully funny.

Tom (entering with a macaroon and a glass of the lemonade): Has the gentleman caller gotten away already?

Amanda: The gentleman caller has made an early departure. What a wonderful joke you played on us!

Tom: How do you mean?

Amanda: You didn't mention that he was engaged to be married.

Tom: Jim? Engaged?

Amanda: That's what he just informed us.

Tom: I'll be jiggered! I didn't know about that.

Amanda: That seems very peculiar.

Tom: What's peculiar about it?

Amanda: Didn't you call him your best friend down at the warehouse?

Tom: He is, but how did I know?

Amanda: It seems extremely peculiar that you wouldn't know your best friend was going to be married!

Tom: The warehouse is where I work, not where I know things about people!

Amanda: You don't know things anywhere! You live in a dream; you manufacture illusions! (*He crosses to the door.*) Where are you going?

Tom: I'm going to the movies.

Amanda: That's right, now that you've had us make such fools of ourselves. The effort, the preparations, all the expense! The new floor lamp, the rug, the clothes for Laura! All for what? To entertain some other girl's fiancé! Go to the movies, go! Don't think about us, a mother deserted, an unmarried sister who's crippled and has no job! Don't let anything interfere with your selfish pleasure! Just go, go, go—to the movies!

Tom: All right, I will! The more you shout about my selfishness to me the quicker I'll go, and I won't go to the movies!

Amanda: Go, then! Go to the moon—you selfish dreamer!

Tom smashes his glass on the floor. He plunges out on the fire escape, slamming the door. Laura screams in fright. The dance-hall music becomes louder. Tom stands on the fire escape, gripping the rail. The moon breaks through the storm clouds, illuminating his face.

(Legend On Screen: "And So Goodbye . . .")

Tom's closing speech is timed with what is happening inside the house. We see, as though through soundproof glass, that Amanda appears to be making a comforting speech to Laura, who is huddled upon the sofa. Now that we cannot hear the mother's speech, her silliness is gone and she has dignity and tragic beauty. Laura's hair hides her face until, at the end of the speech, she lifts her head to smile at her mother. Amanda's gestures are slow and graceful, almost dancelike, as she comforts her daughter. At the end of her speech she glances a moment at the father's picture—then withdraws through the portieres. At the close of Tom's speech, Laura blows out the candles, ending the play.

Tom: I didn't go to the moon, I went much further—for time is the longest distance between two places. Not long after that I was fired for writing a poem on the lid of a shoe-box. I left Saint Louis. I descended the steps of this fire escape for a last time and followed, from then on, in my father's footsteps, attempting to find in motion what was lost in space. I traveled around a great deal. The cities swept about me like dead leaves, leaves that were brightly colored but torn away from the branches. I would have stopped, but I was pursued by something. It always came upon me unawares, taking me altogether by surprise. Perhaps it was a familiar bit of music. Perhaps it was only a piece of transparent glass. Perhaps I am walking along a street at night, in some strange city, before

I have found companions. I pass the lighted window of a shop where perfume is sold. The window is filled with pieces of colored glass, tiny transparent bottles in delicate colors, like bits of a shattered rainbow. Then all at once my sister touches my shoulder. I turn around and look into her eyes. Oh, Laura, Laura, I tried to leave you behind me, but I am more faithful than I intended to be! I reach for a cigarette, I cross the street, I run into the movies or a bar, I buy a drink, I speak to the nearest stranger—anything that can blow your candles out! *Laura bends over the candles.* For nowadays the world is lit by lightning! Blow out your candles, Laura—and so Goodbye. . . .

She blows the candles out.

Questions

1. How do Amanda's dreams for her daughter contrast with the realities of the Wingfields' day-to-day existence?
2. What suggestions do you find in Laura's glass menagerie? In the glass unicorn?
3. In the cast of characters, Jim O'Connor is listed as "a nice, ordinary, young man." Why does his coming to dinner have such earthshaking implications for Amanda? For Laura?
4. Try to describe Jim's feelings toward Laura during their long conversation in Scene VII. After he kisses her, how do his feelings seem to change?
5. Near the end of the play, Amanda tells Tom, "You live in a dream; you manufacture illusions!" What is ironic about her speech? Is there any truth in it?
6. Who is the main character in *The Glass Menagerie?* Tom? Laura? Amanda? (It may be helpful to review the definition of a protagonist.)
7. Has Tom, at the conclusion of the play, successfully made his escape from home? Does he appear to have fulfilled his dream?
8. How effective is the device of accompanying the action by projecting slides on a screen, bearing titles and images? Do you think most producers of the play are wise to leave it out?

EXPERIMENTAL DRAMA

In the latter part of the twentieth century, experimental drama, greatly influenced by the traditions of earlier Symbolist, Expressionist, and absurdist theater, flourished. For example, David Henry Hwang's work combines realistic elements with ritualistic and symbolic devices drawn from Asian theater (see his one-act play, *The Sound of a Voice,* in "Plays for Further Reading"). Caryl Churchill's *Top Girls* (1982) presents a dinner party in which a contemporary woman invites legendary women from history to a dinner party in a restaurant. Tony Kushner's *Angels in America* (1992) also mixes realism and fantasy to dramatize the plight of AIDS. Shel Silverstein, popular author of children's poetry, wrote a raucous one-man play, *The Devil and Billy Markham* (1991), entirely in rime, about a series of fantastic adventures in hell featuring a hard-drinking gambler and the Prince of Darkness. Silverstein's play is simultaneously experimental in form but traditional in content with its homage to American ballads and tall tales.

Experimental theater continues to exert a strong influence on contemporary drama. The following play, Milcha Sanchez-Scott's *The Cuban Swimmer*, deftly assimilates several dramatic styles—symbolism, new naturalism, ethnic drama, theater of the absurd—to create a brilliant original work. The play is simultaneously a family drama, a Latin comedy, a religious parable, and a critique of a media-obsessed American culture.

Milcha Sanchez-Scott

The Cuban Swimmer

1984

Milcha Sanchez-Scott was born in 1955 on the island of Bali. Her father was Colombian. Her mother was Chinese, Indonesian, and Dutch. Her father's work as an agronomist required constant travel, so when the young Sanchez-Scott reached school age, she was sent to a convent boarding school near London where she first learned English. Colombia, however, remained the family's one permanent home. Every Christmas and summer vacation was spent on a ranch in San Marta, Colombia, where four generations of family lived together. When Sanchez-Scott was fourteen, her

Milcha Sanchez-Scott

family moved to California. After attending the University of San Diego, where she majored in literature and philosophy, she worked at the San Diego Zoo and later at an employment agency in Los Angeles. Her first play, Latina, *premiered in 1980 and won seven Drama-Logue awards.* Dog Lady *and* The Cuban Swimmer *followed in 1984. Sanchez-Scott then went to New York for a year to work with playwright Irene Fornes, in whose theater workshop she developed* Roosters *(1988). A feature-film version of* Roosters, *starring Edward James Olmos, was released in 1995. Her other plays include* Evening Star *(1989),* El Dorado *(1990), and* The Old Matador *(1995). Sanchez-Scott lives in Los Angeles.*

CHARACTERS

Margarita Suárez, the swimmer
Eduardo Suárez, her father, the coach
Simón Suárez, her brother
Aída Suárez, her mother
Abuela, her grandmother
Voice of Mel Munson
Voice of Mary Beth White

Voice of Radio Operator

SETTING. *The Pacific Ocean between San Pedro and Catalina Island.*

TIME. *Summer.*

Live conga drums can be used to punctuate the action of the play.

SCENE I

Pacific Ocean. Midday. On the horizon, in perspective, a small boat enters upstage left, crosses to upstage right, and exits. Pause. Lower on the horizon, the same boat, in larger perspective, enters upstage right, crosses and exits upstage left. Blackout.

SCENE II

Pacific Ocean. Midday. The swimmer, Margarita Suárez, is swimming. On the boat following behind her are her father, Eduardo Suárez, holding a megaphone, and Simón, her brother, sitting on top of the cabin with his shirt off, punk sunglasses on, binoculars hanging on his chest.

Eduardo (*leaning forward, shouting in time to Margarita's swimming*): Uno, dos, uno, dos. Y uno, dos°. . . keep your shoulders parallel to the water.
Simón: I'm gonna take these glasses off and look straight into the sun.
Eduardo (*through megaphone*): Muy bien, muy bien° . . . but punch those arms in, baby.
Simón (*looking directly at the sun through binoculars*): Come on, come on, zap me. Show me something. (*He looks behind at the shoreline and ahead at the sea.*) Stop! Stop, Papi! Stop!

(*Aída Suárez and Abuela, the swimmer's mother and grandmother, enter running from the back of the boat.*)

Aída and Abuela: Qué? Qué es?°
Aída: Es un shark?°
Eduardo: Eh?
Abuela: Que es un shark dicen?°

(*Eduardo blows whistle. Margarita looks up at the boat.*)

Simón: No, Papi, no shark, no shark. We've reached the halfway mark.

Uno, dos, uno, dos. Y uno, dos: One, two, one, two. And one, two.   *Muy bien, muy bien:* Very good, very good.   *Qué? Qué es?:* What? What is it?   *Es un shark?:* Is it a shark?   *Que es un shark dicen?:* Did they say a shark?

A 2005 production of *The Cuban Swimmer* at the People's Light and Theatre, Malvern, Pennsylvania.

Abuela (looking into the water): A dónde está?°
Aída: It's not in the water.
Abuela: Oh, no? Oh, no?
Aída: No! A poco do you think they're gonna have signs in the water to say you are halfway to Santa Catalina? No. It's done very scientific. A ver, hijo,° explain it to your grandma.
Simón: Well, you see, Abuela—*(He points behind.)* There's San Pedro. *(He points ahead.)* And there's Santa Catalina. Looks halfway to me.

(Abuela shakes her head and is looking back and forth, trying to make the decision, when suddenly the sound of a helicopter is heard.)

Abuela (looking up): Virgencita de la Caridad del Cobre. Qué es eso?°

(Sound of helicopter gets closer. Margarita looks up.)

Margarita: Papi, Papi!

(A small commotion on the boat, with everybody pointing at the helicopter above. Shadows of the helicopter fall on the boat. Simón looks up at it through binoculars.)

A dónde está?: Where is it?   *A ver, hijo:* Look here, son.   *Virgencita de la Caridad del Cobre. Qué es eso?:* Virgin of Charity. What is that?

Papi—qué es? What is it?

Eduardo (through megaphone): Uh . . . uh . . . uh, *un momentico . . . mi hija.°* . . .
Your *papi's* got everything under control, understand? Uh . . . you just keep
stroking. And stay . . . uh . . . close to the boat.

Simón: Wow, *Papi!* We're on TV, man! Holy Christ, we're all over the fucking
U.S.A.! It's Mel Munson and Mary Beth White!

Aída: *Por Dios!°* Simón, don't swear. And put on your shirt.

(*Aída fluffs her hair, puts on her sunglasses and waves to the helicopter. Simón
leans over the side of the boat and yells to Margarita.*)

Simón: Yo, Margo! You're on TV, man.

Eduardo: Leave your sister alone. Turn on the radio.

Margarita: *Papi! Qué está pasando?°*

Abuela: *Que es la televisión dicen?* (*She shakes her head.*) *Porque como yo no
puedo ver nada sin mis espejuelos.°*

(*Abuela rummages through the boat, looking for her glasses. Voices of Mel
Munson and Mary Beth White are heard over the boat's radio.*)

Mel's Voice: As we take a closer look at the gallant crew of *La Havana* . . . and
there . . . yes, there she is . . . the little Cuban swimmer from Long Beach,
California, nineteen-year-old Margarita Suárez. The unknown swimmer is
our Cinderella entry . . . a bundle of tenacity, battling her way through the
choppy, murky waters of the cold Pacific to reach the Island of Romance . . .
Santa Catalina . . . where should she be the first to arrive, two thousand dollars and a gold cup will be waiting for her.

Aída: Doesn't even cover our expenses.

Abuela: *Qué dice?*

Eduardo: Shhhh!

Mary Beth's Voice: This is really a family effort, Mel, and—

Mel's Voice: Indeed it is. Her trainer, her coach, her mentor, is her father,
Eduardo Suárez. Not a swimmer himself, it says here, Mr. Suárez is
head usher of the Holy Name Society and the owner-operator of
Suárez Treasures of the Sea and Salvage Yard. I guess it's one of those
places—

Mary Beth's Voice: If I might interject a fact here, Mel, assisting in this swim
is Mrs. Suárez, who is a former Miss Cuba.

Mel's Voice: And a beautiful woman in her own right. Let's try and get a
closer look.

---

un momentico . . . mi hija: just a second, my daughter.   *Por Dios!:* For God's Sake!   *Papi! Qué está
pasando?:* Dad! What's happening?   *Que es la televisión dicen? Porque como yo no puedo ver nada sin
mis espejuelos:* Did they say television? Because I can't see without my glasses.

(Helicopter sound gets louder. Margarita, frightened, looks up again.)

Margarita: Papi!

Eduardo (through megaphone): Mi hija, don't get nervous . . . it's the press. I'm handling it.

Aída: I see how you're handling it.

Eduardo (through megaphone): Do you hear? Everything is under control. Get back into your rhythm. Keep your elbows high and kick and kick and kick and kick . . .

Abuela (finds her glasses and puts them on): Ay sí, es la televisión° . . . *(She points to helicopter.)* Qué lindo mira° . . . *(She fluffs her hair, gives a big wave.)* Aló América! Viva mi Margarita, viva todo los Cubanos en los Estados Unidos!°

Aída: Ay por Dios, Cecilia, the man didn't come all this way in his helicopter to look at you jumping up and down, making a fool of yourself.

Abuela: I don't care. I'm proud.

Aída: He can't understand you anyway.

Abuela: Viva . . . *(She stops.)* Simón, cómo se dice viva?°

Simón: Hurray.

Abuela: Hurray for mi Margarita y for all the Cubans living en the United States, y un abrazo . . . Simón, abrazo . . .

Simón: A big hug.

Abuela: Sí, a big hug to all my friends in Miami, Long Beach, Union City, except for my son Carlos, who lives in New York in sin! He lives . . . *(She crosses herself.)* in Brooklyn with a Puerto Rican woman in sin! No decente . . .

Simón: Decent.

Abuela: Carlos, no decente. This family, decente.

Aída: Cecilia, por Dios.

Mel's Voice: Look at that enthusiasm. The whole family has turned out to cheer little Margarita on to victory! I hope they won't be too disappointed.

Mary Beth's Voice: She seems to be making good time, Mel.

Mel's Voice: Yes, it takes all kinds to make a race. And it's a testimonial to the all-encompassing fairness . . . the greatness of this, the Wrigley Invitational Women's Swim to Catalina, where among all the professionals there is still room for the amateurs . . . like these, the simple people we see below us on the ragtag La Havana, taking their long-shot chance to victory. Vaya con Dios!°

Ay sí, es la televisión: Oh yes, it is the television.   *Qué lindo mira:* Look how pretty.   *Aló América! Viva mi Margarita, viva todo los Cubanos en los Estados Unidos!:* Hello America! Hurray for my Margarita, hurray for all the Cubans in the United States!   *cómo se dice viva?:* how do you say "viva" [in English]?   *Vaya con Dios!:* Go with God! [God bless you.]

(Helicopter sound fading as family, including Margarita, watch silently. Static as Simón turns radio off. Eduardo walks to bow of boat, looks out on the horizon.)

Eduardo *(to himself):* Amateurs.

Aída: Eduardo, that person insulted us. Did you hear, Eduardo? That he called us a simple people in a ragtag boat? Did you hear . . . ?

Abuela *(clenching her fist at departing helicopter):* Mal-Rayo los parta!°

Simón *(same gesture):* Asshole!

(Aída follows Eduardo as he goes to side of boat and stares at Margarita.)

Aída: This person comes in his helicopter to insult your wife, your family, your daughter . . .

Margarita *(pops her head out of the water):* Papi?

Aída: Do you hear me, Eduardo? I am not simple.

Abuela: Sí.

Aída: I am complicated.

Abuela: Sí, demasiada complicada.

Aída: Me and my family are not so simple.

Simón: Mom, the guy's an asshole.

Abuela *(shaking her fist at helicopter):* Asshole!

Aída: If my daughter was simple, she would not be in that water swimming.

Margarita: Simple? Papi . . . ?

Aída: Ahora, Eduardo, this is what I want you to do. When we get to Santa Catalina, I want you to call the TV station and demand an apology.

Eduardo: Cállete mujer! Aquí mando yo.° I will decide what is to be done.

Margarita: Papi, tell me what's going on.

Eduardo: Do you understand what I am saying to you, Aída?

Simón *(leaning over side of boat, to Margarita):* Yo Margo! You know that Mel Munson guy on TV? He called you a simple amateur and said you didn't have a chance.

Abuela *(leaning directly behind Simón):* Mi hija, insultó a la familia. Desgraciado!

Aída *(leaning in behind Abuela):* He called us peasants! And your father is not doing anything about it. He just knows how to yell at me.

Eduardo *(through megaphone):* Shut up! All of you! Do you want to break her concentration? Is that what you are after? Eh?

(Abuela, Aída and Simón shrink back. Eduardo paces before them.)

Swimming is rhythm and concentration. You win a race aquí. *(Pointing to his head.)* Now . . . *(To Simón.)* you, take care of the boat, Aída y Mama . . . do something. Anything. Something practical.

Mal-Rayo los parta!: To hell with you!   Cállete mujer! Aquí mando yo: Quiet woman! I'm in charge here.

(Abuela and Aída get on knees and pray in Spanish.)

Hija, give it everything, eh? . . . *por la familia. Uno . . . dos . . . .* You must win.

(Simón goes into cabin. The prayers continue as lights change to indicate bright sunlight, later in the afternoon.)

SCENE III

Tableau for a couple of beats. Eduardo on bow with timer in one hand as he counts strokes per minute. Simón is in the cabin steering, wearing his sunglasses, baseball cap on backward. Abuela and Aída are at the side of the boat, heads down, hands folded, still muttering prayers in Spanish.

Aída and Abuela *(crossing themselves)*: En el nombre del Padre, del Hijo y del Espíritu Santo amén.°
Eduardo *(through megaphone)*: You're stroking seventy-two!
Simón *(singing)*: Mama's stroking, Mama's stroking seventy-two. . . .
Eduardo *(through megaphone)*: You comfortable with it?
Simón *(singing)*: Seventy-two, seventy-two, seventy-two for you.
Aída *(looking at the heavens)*: Ay, Eduardo, *ven acá,*° we should be grateful that *Nuestro Señor*° gave us such a beautiful day.
Abuela *(crosses herself)*: *Sí, gracias a Dios.*°
Eduardo: She's stroking seventy-two, with no problem. *(He throws a kiss to the sky.)* It's a beautiful day to win.
Aída: *Qué hermoso!*° So clear and bright. Not a cloud in the sky. *Mira! Mira!*° Even rainbows on the water . . . a sign from God.
Simón *(singing)*: Rainbows on the water . . . you in my arms . . .
Abuela and Eduardo *(looking the wrong way)*: Dónde?
Aída *(pointing toward Margarita)*: There, dancing in front of Margarita, leading her on . . .
Eduardo: Rainbows on . . . Ay coño! It's an oil slick! You . . . you . . . *(To Simón.)* Stop the boat. *(Runs to bow, yelling.)* Margarita! Margarita!

(On the next stroke, Margarita comes up all covered in black oil.)

Margarita: Papi! Papi . . . !

(Everybody goes to the side and stares at Margarita, who stares back. Eduardo freezes.)

En el nombre del Padre, del Hijo y del Espíritu Santo amén: In the name of the Father, the Son, and the Holy Ghost, Amen.   *ven acá:* look here.   *Nuestro Señor:* Our Father [God].   *Sí, gracias a Dios:* Yes, thanks be to God.   *Qué hermoso!:* How beautiful!   *Mira!:* Look!

Aída: Apúrate, Eduardo, move . . . what's wrong with you . . . *no me oíste,*° get my daughter out of the water.

Eduardo (softly): We can't touch her. If we touch her, she's disqualified.

Aída: But I'm her mother.

Eduardo: Not even by her own mother. Especially by her own mother. . . . You always want the rules to be different for you, you always want to be the exception. (*To Simón.*) And you . . . you didn't see it, eh? You were playing again?

Simón: Papi, I was watching . . .

Aída (interrupting): Pues, do something Eduardo. You are the big coach, the monitor.

Simón: Mentor! Mentor!

Eduardo: How can a person think around you? (*He walks off to bow, puts head in hands.*)

Abuela (looking over side): Mira como todos los little birds are dead. (*She crosses herself*)

Aída: Their little wings are glued to their sides.

Simón: Christ, this is like the La Brea tar pits.

Aída: They can't move their little wings.

Abuela: Esa niña tiene que moverse.°

Simón: Yeah, Margo, you gotta move, man.

   (*Abuela and Simón gesture for Margarita to move. Aída gestures for her to swim.*)

Abuela: Anda niña, muévete.°

Aída: Swim, hija, swim or the *aceite*° will stick to your wings.

Margarita: Papi?

Abuela (taking megaphone): Your papi say "move it!"

   (*Margarita with difficulty starts moving.*)

Abuela, Aída and Simón (laboriously counting): Uno, dos . . . uno, dos . . . anda . . . uno, dos.

Eduardo (running to take megaphone from Abuela): Uno, dos . . .

   (*Simón races into cabin and starts the engine. Abuela, Aída and Eduardo count together.*)

Simón (looking ahead): Papi, it's over there!

Eduardo: Eh?

Simón (pointing ahead and to the right): It's getting clearer over there.

Eduardo (through megaphone): Now pay attention to me. Go to the right.

Apúrate . . . no me oíste: Finish this . . . didn't you hear me?   *Esa niña tiene que moverse:* That girl has to move.   *Anda niña, muévete:* Come on, girl, move.   *aceite:* oil.

(Simón, Abuela, Aída and Eduardo all lean over side. They point ahead and to the right, except Abuela, who points to the left.)

Family *(shouting together):* Para yá!° Para yá!

(Lights go down on boat. A special light on Margarita, swimming through the oil, and on Abuela, watching her.)

Abuela: Sangre de mi sangre,° you will be another to save us. En Bolondron, where your great-grandmother Luz Suárez was born, they say one day it rained blood. All the people, they run into their houses. They cry, they pray, *pero* your great-grandmother Luz she had *cojones* like a man. She run outside. She look straight at the sky. She shake her fist. And she say to the evil one, "Mira . . . *(Beating her chest.) coño, Diablo, aquí estoy si me quieres.*"° And she open her mouth, and she drunk the blood.

BLACKOUT

SCENE IV

Lights up on boat. Aída and Eduardo are on deck watching Margarita swim. We hear the gentle, rhythmic lap, lap, lap of the water, then the sound of inhaling and exhaling as Margarita's breathing becomes louder. Then Margarita's heartbeat is heard, with the lapping of the water and the breathing under it. These sounds continue beneath the dialogue to the end of the scene.

Aída: Dios mío. Look how she moves through the water. . . .
Eduardo: You see, it's very simple. It is a matter of concentration.
Aída: The first time I put her in water she came to life, she grew before my eyes. She moved, she smiled, she loved it more than me. She didn't want my breast any longer. She wanted the water.
Eduardo: And of course, the rhythm. The rhythm takes away the pain and helps the concentration.

(Pause. Aída and Eduardo watch Margarita.)

Aída: Is that my child or a seal. . . .
Eduardo: Ah, a seal, the reason for that is that she's keeping her arms very close to her body. She cups her hands, and then she reaches and digs, reaches and digs.
Aída: To think that a daughter of mine. . . .
Eduardo: It's the training, the hours in the water. I used to tie weights around her little wrists and ankles.

Para yá: Over there.   *Sangre de mi sangre:* Blood of my blood.   *Mira . . . coño, Diablo, aquí estoy si me quieres:* Look . . . damn it, Devil, here I am if you want me.

Aída: A spirit, an ocean spirit, must have entered my body when I was carrying her.

Eduardo (to Margarita): Your stroke is slowing down.

> *(Pause. We hear Margarita's heartbeat with the breathing under, faster now.)*

Aída: Eduardo, that night, the night on the boat . . .

Eduardo: Ah, the night on the boat again . . . the moon was . . .

Aída: The moon was full. We were coming to America. . . . *Qué romantico.*

> *(Heartbeat and breathing continue.)*

Eduardo: We were cold, afraid, with no money, and on top of everything, you were hysterical, yelling at me, tearing at me with your nails. *(Opens his shirt, points to the base of his neck.)* Look, I still bear the scars . . . telling me that I didn't know what I was doing . . . saying that we were going to die. . . .

Aída: You took me, you stole me from my home . . . you didn't give me a chance to prepare. You just said we have to go now, now! Now, you said. You didn't let me take anything. I left everything behind. . . . I left everything behind.

Eduardo: Saying that I wasn't good enough, that your father didn't raise you so that I could drown you in the sea.

Aída: You didn't let me say even a good-bye. You took me, you stole me, you tore me from my home.

Eduardo: I took you so we could be married.

Aída: That was in Miami. But that night on the boat, Eduardo. . . . We were not married, that night on the boat.

Eduardo: *No pasó nada!°* Once and for all get it out of your head, it was cold, you hated me, and we were afraid. . . .

Aída: *Mentiroso!°*

Eduardo: A man can't do it when he is afraid.

Aída: Liar! You did it very well.

Eduardo: I did?

Aída: Sí. Gentle. You were so gentle and then strong . . . my passion for you so deep. Standing next to you . . . I would ache . . . looking at your hands I would forget to breathe, you were irresistible.

Eduardo: I was?

Aída: You took me into your arms, you touched my face with your fingertips . . . you kissed my eyes . . . *la esquina de la boca y°* . . .

Eduardo: *Sí, Sí*, and then . . .

No pasó nada!: Nothing happened!   *Mentiroso!:* Liar!   *la esquina de la boca y . . . :* the corner of the mouth and . . .

Aída: I look at your face on top of mine, and I see the lights of Havana in your eyes. That's when you seduced me.

Eduardo: Shhh, they're gonna hear you.

(*Lights go down. Special on Aída.*)

Aída: That was the night. A woman doesn't forget those things . . . and later that night was the dream . . . the dream of a big country with fields of fertile land and big, giant things growing. And there by a green, slimy pond I found a giant pea pod and when I opened it, it was full of little, tiny baby frogs.

(*Aída crosses herself as she watches Margarita. We hear louder breathing and heartbeat.*)

Margarita: Santa Teresa. Little Flower of God, pray for me. San Martín de Porres, pray for me. Santa Rosa de Lima, *Virgencita de la Caridad del Cobre,* pray for me. . . . Mother pray for me.

SCENE V

Loud howling of wind is heard, as lights change to indicate unstable weather, fog and mist. Family on deck, braced and huddled against the wind. Simón is at the helm.

Aída: Ay Dios mío, qué viento.°

Eduardo (through megaphone): Don't drift out . . . that wind is pushing you out. (*To Simón.*) You! Slow down. Can't you see your sister is drifting out?

Simón: It's the wind, *Papi.*

Aída: Baby, don't go so far. . . .

Abuela (to heaven): Ay Gran Poder de Dios, quita este maldito viento.°

Simón: Margo! Margo! Stay close to the boat.

Eduardo: Dig in. Dig in hard. . . . Reach down from your guts and dig in.

Abuela (to heaven): Ay Virgen de la Caridad del Cobre, por lo más tú quieres a pararla.

Aída (putting her hand out, reaching for Margarita): Baby, don't go far.

(*Abuela crosses herself. Action freezes. Lights get dimmer, special on Margarita. She keeps swimming, stops, starts again, stops, then, finally exhausted, stops altogether. The boat stops moving.*)

Eduardo: What's going on here? Why are we stopping?

Simón: *Papi,* she's not moving! Yo Margo!

(*The family all run to the side.*)

Ay Dios mío, qué viento: Oh my God, what wind.   Ay Gran Poder de Dios, quita este maldito viento: By the great power of God, keep the cursed winds away.

Eduardo: Hija! . . . Hijita! You're tired, eh?

Aída: *Por supuesto* she's tired. I like to see you get in the water, waving your arms and legs from San Pedro to Santa Catalina. A person isn't a machine, a person has to rest.

Simón: Yo, Mama! Cool out, it ain't fucking brain surgery.

Eduardo (to Simón): Shut up, you. *(Louder to Margarita.)* I guess your mother's right for once, huh? . . . I guess you had to stop, eh? . . . Give your brother, the idiot . . . a chance to catch up with you.

Simón (clowning like Mortimer Snerd): Dum dee dum dee dum ooops, ah shucks . . .

Eduardo: I don't think he's Cuban.

Simón (like Ricky Ricardo): Oye, Lucy! I'm home! Ba ba lu!

Eduardo (joins in clowning, grabbing Simón in a headlock): What am I gonna do with this idiot, eh? I don't understand this idiot. He's not like us, Margarita. *(Laughing.)* You think if we put him into your bathing suit with a cap on his head . . . *(He laughs hysterically.)* You think anyone would know . . . huh? Do you think anyone would know? *(Laughs.)*

Simón (vamping): Ay, *mi amor.* Anybody looking for tits would know.

(Eduardo slaps Simón across the face, knocking him down. Aída runs to Simón's aid. Abuela holds Eduardo back.)

Margarita: Mía culpa!° Mía culpa!

Abuela: Qué dices hija?

Margarita: Papi, it's my fault, it's all my fault. . . . I'm so cold, I can't move. . . . I put my face in the water . . . and I hear them whispering . . . laughing at me. . . .

Aída: Who is laughing at you?

Margarita: The fish are all biting me . . . they hate me . . . they whisper about me. She can't swim, they say. She can't glide. She has no grace. . . . Yellowtails, bonita, tuna, man-o'-war, snub-nose sharks, *los baracudas* . . . they all hate me . . . only the dolphins care . . . and sometimes I hear the whales crying . . . she is lost, she is dead. I'm so numb, I can't feel. *Papi!* Papi! Am I dead?

Eduardo: Vamos, baby, punch those arms in. Come on . . . do you hear me?

Margarita: Papi . . . Papi . . . forgive me. . . .

(All is silent on the boat. Eduardo drops his megaphone, his head bent down in dejection. Abuela, Aída, Simón, all leaning over the side of the boat. Simón slowly walks away.)

Mía culpa!: It's my fault!

Aída: Mi hija, qué tienes?

Simón: Oh, Christ, don't make her say it. Please don't make her say it.

Abuela: Say what? Qué cosa?

Simón: She wants to quit, can't you see she's had enough?

Abuela: Mira, para eso. Esta niña is turning blue.

Aída: Oyeme, mi hija. Do you want to come out of the water?

Margarita: Papi?

Simón (to Eduardo): She won't come out until you tell her.

Aída: Eduardo . . . answer your daughter.

Eduardo: Le dije to concentrate . . . concentrate on your rhythm. Then the rhythm would carry her . . . ay, it's a beautiful thing, Aída. It's like yoga, like meditation, the mind over matter . . . the mind controlling the body . . . that's how the great things in the world have been done. I wish you . . . I wish my wife could understand.

Margarita: Papi?

Simón (to Margarita): Forget him.

Aída (imploring): Eduardo, por favor.

Eduardo (walking in circles): Why didn't you let her concentrate? Don't you understand, the concentration, the rhythm is everything. But no, you wouldn't listen. (Screaming to the ocean.) Goddamn Cubans, why, God, why do you make us go everywhere with our families? (He goes to back of boat.)

Aída (opening her arms): Mi hija, ven, come to Mami. (Rocking.) Your mami knows.

(Abuela has taken the training bottle, puts it in a net. She and Simón lower it to Margarita.)

Simón: Take this. Drink it. (As Margarita drinks, Abuela crosses herself.)

Abuela: Sangre de mi sangre.

(Music comes up softly. Margarita drinks, gives the bottle back, stretches out her arms, as if on a cross. Floats on her back. She begins a graceful backstroke. Lights fade on boat as special lights come up on Margarita. She stops. Slowly turns over and starts to swim, gradually picking up speed. Suddenly as if in pain she stops, tries again, then stops in pain again. She becomes disoriented and falls to the bottom of the sea. Special on Margarita at the bottom of the sea.)

Margarita: Ya no puedo . . . I can't. . . . A person isn't a machine . . . es mi culpa . . . Father forgive me . . . Papi! Papi! One, two. Uno, dos. (Pause.) Papi! A dónde estás? (Pause.) One, two, one, two. Papi! Ay, Papi! Where are you . . . ? Don't leave me. . . . Why don't you answer me? (Pause. She starts to swim, slowly.) Uno, dos, uno, dos. Dig in, dig in. (Stops swimming.) Por favor, Papi! (Starts to swim again.) One, two, one, two. Kick from your hip,

kick from your hip. (*Stops swimming. Starts to cry.*) Oh God, please. . . .
(*Pause.*) Hail Mary, full of grace . . . dig in, dig in . . . the Lord is with thee.
. . . (*She swims to the rhythm of her Hail Mary.*) Hail Mary, full of grace
. . . dig in, dig in . . . the Lord is with thee . . . dig in, dig in. . . . Blessed art
thou among women. . . . *Mami*, it hurts. You let go of my hand. I'm lost.
. . . And blessed is the fruit of thy womb, now and at the hour of our
death. Amen. I don't want to die, I don't want to die.

(*Margarita is still swimming. Blackout. She is gone.*)

SCENE VI

*Lights up on boat, we hear radio static. There is a heavy mist. On deck we see only
black outline of Abuela with shawl over her head. We hear the voices of Eduardo,
Aída, and Radio Operator.*

Eduardo's Voice: La Havana! Coming from San Pedro. Over.
Radio Operator's Voice: Right, DT6-6, you say you've lost a swimmer.
Aída's Voice: Our child, our only daughter . . . listen to me. Her name is
    Margarita Inez Suárez, she is wearing a black one-piece bathing suit cut
    high in the legs with a white racing stripe down the sides, a white bathing
    cap with goggles and her whole body covered with a . . . with a . . .
Eduardo's Voice: With lanolin and paraffin.
Aída's Voice: Sí . . . *con lanolin and paraffin.*

(*More radio static. Special on Simón, on the edge of the boat.*)

Simón: Margo! Yo Margo! (*Pause.*) Man don't do this. (*Pause.*) Come on.
    . . . Come on. . . . (*Pause.*) God, why does everything have to be so hard?
    (*Pause.*) Stupid. You know you're not supposed to die for this. Stupid. It's
    his dream and he can't even swim. (*Pause.*) Punch those arms in. Come
    home. Come home. I'm your little brother. Don't forget what Mama
    said. You're not supposed to leave me behind. *Vamos*, Margarita, take
    your little brother, hold his hand tight when you cross the street. He's so
    little. (*Pause.*) Oh Christ, give us a sign. . . . I know! I know! Margo, I'll
    send you a message . . . like mental telepathy. I'll hold my breath, close
    my eyes, and I'll bring you home. (*He takes a deep breath; a few beats.*)
    This time I'll beep . . . I'll send out sonar signals like a dolphin. (*He
    imitates dolphin sounds.*)

(*The sound of real dolphins takes over from Simón, then fades into sound of
Abuela saying the Hail Mary in Spanish, as full lights come up slowly.*)

SCENE VII

Eduardo coming out of cabin, sobbing, Aída holding him. Simón anxiously scanning the horizon. Abuela looking calmly ahead.

Eduardo: Es mi culpa, sí, es mi culpa.° *(He hits his chest.)*
Aída: Ya, ya viejo.° . . . it was my sin . . . I left my home.
Eduardo: Forgive me, forgive me. I've lost our daughter, our sister, our grand-daughter, *mi carne, mi sangre, mis ilusiones.° (To heaven.) Dios mío,* take me . . . take me, I say . . . Goddammit, take me!
Simón: I'm going in.
Aída and Eduardo: No!
Eduardo (grabbing and holding Simón, speaking to heaven): God, take me, not my children. They are my dreams, my illusions . . . and not this one, this one is my mystery . . . he has my secret dreams. In him are the parts of me I cannot see.

(Eduardo embraces Simón. Radio static becomes louder.)

Aída: I . . . I think I see her.
Simón: No, it's just a seal.
Abuela (looking out with binoculars): Mi nietacita, dónde estás? *(She feels her heart.)* I don't feel the knife in my heart . . . my little fish is not lost.

(Radio crackles with static. As lights dim on boat, Voices of Mel and Mary Beth are heard over the radio.)

Mel's Voice: Tragedy has marred the face of the Wrigley Invitational Women's Race to Catalina. The Cuban swimmer, little Margarita Suárez, has reportedly been lost at sea. Coast Guard and divers are looking for her as we speak. Yet in spite of this tragedy the race must go on because . . .
Mary Beth's Voice (interrupting loudly): Mel!
Mel's Voice (startled): What!
Mary Beth's Voice: Ah . . . excuse me, Mel . . . we have a winner. We've just received word from Catalina that one of the swimmers is just fifty yards from the breakers . . . it's, oh, it's . . . Margarita Suárez!

(Special on family in cabin listening to radio.)

Mel's Voice: What? I thought she died!

(Special on Margarita, taking off bathing cap, trophy in hand, walking on the water.)

Es mi culpa, sí, es mi culpa: It's my fault, yes, it's my fault.   Ya, ya viejo: Yes, yes, old man.   mi carne, mi sangre, mis ilusiones: my flesh, my blood, my dreams.

Mary Beth's Voice: Ahh . . . unless . . . unless this is a tragic . . . No . . . there she is, Mel. Margarita Suárez! The only one in the race wearing a black bathing suit cut high in the legs with a racing stripe down the side.

(Family cheering, embracing.)

Simón (screaming): Way to go, Margo!

Mel's Voice: This is indeed a miracle! It's a resurrection! Margarita Suárez, with a flotilla of boats to meet her, is now walking on the waters, through the breakers . . . onto the beach, with crowds of people cheering her on. What a jubilation! This is a miracle!

(Sound of crowds cheering. Lights and cheering sounds fade.)

BLACKOUT

DOCUMENTARY DRAMA

Some playwrights combine experimental and naturalistic elements, creating documentary works that dramatize actual events. British dramatist Michael Frayn presented the European physicists who did the work preceding the atom bomb in *Copenhagen* (1998) and explored the career of director Max Reinhardt in Nazi-era Austria in *Afterlife* (2008). Actress-playwright Anna Deavere Smith created an extremely innovative version of documentary drama in which she performed *all* of the roles herself in bravura one-woman shows. Using the actual words of real people, she constructed performance pieces to explore complex social events such as the race riots in Crown Heights, Brooklyn, in 1991 and in Los Angeles in 1992.

Anna Deavere Smith

Scenes from Twilight: Los Angeles, 1992   1994

Anna Deavere Smith was born in Baltimore, Maryland, in 1950, the daughter of a businessman and an elementary school principal. She graduated from Beaver College in 1971 and earned a Master of Fine Arts degree from the American Conservatory Theater in 1977. She taught drama at Stanford University from 1990 to 2000 and is presently a professor at both the Tisch School of the Arts at New York University and the NYU School of Law. Over many years Smith has conducted more than two thousand interviews; from them she has fashioned a number of works of "documentary theater,"

Anna Deavere Smith

each of which is a stage presentation in which a single performer speaks a series of monologues using the actual words of her interview subjects. The best-known of these are Fires in the Mirror *(1993), drawn from the 1991 race riots in Crown Heights, Brooklyn,* Twilight: Los Angeles, 1992 *(1994), derived from the 1992 riot in that city, and* Let Me Down Easy *(2009), which examines health care issues. Smith has frequently performed these pieces herself, winning rave reviews both for the works and for her extraordinary ability to bring to life characters of both sexes and many ages and races. In its review of* Twilight: Los Angeles, 1992, *the* New York Times *said: "Anna Deavere Smith is the ultimate impressionist: she does people's souls." As an actress, she has also made many appearances on stage and in films, including* Philadelphia *and* The American President, *and has been seen on television in* The West Wing *and* Nurse Jackie. *Included here are three scenes from the more than fifty monologues in* Twilight: Los Angeles, 1992.

CHARACTERS

Angela King, Rodney King's aunt, African American
Mrs. Young-Soon Han, former liquor store owner, Korean American, 40s, heavy accent
Twilight Bey, gang truce organizer, African American, early 30s/late 20s, Crips gang.

GENERAL PRODUCTION NOTE

A slide with the following language should begin the show, just after lights down and before any other visual image:

This play is based on interviews conducted by Anna Deavere Smith soon after the race riots in Los Angeles of 1992. All words were spoken by real people and are verbatim from those interviews.

ANGELA KING
Rodney King's Aunt

Here's a Nobody

Returning from white iron-gated doorway. To her stool. Heavy pounding rain outside. Day. On her stool, in her studio. Crying, has been crying, prior to the speech for ten minutes straight.

We weren't raised like this.
We weren't raised with no black and white thing.
We were raised with all kinds of friends.
Mexicans, Indians, blacks, whites, Chinese
Most of our friends were Spanish.
Who'd have thought this would happen to us?
Well, I guess there's a first time for everything you know.

(Blowing her nose, she stops crying. A sense in the rest of the speech that she is recovering from a long cry.)

I guess you want me to tell the story
I don't know if you understand sometimes I'm just not in the mood, you know just not in the mood.

(Slight pause.)

His brother Galen called to say "Cops done beat Glen up!"
Talkin' about Rodney.
I said "What?"
"Police. They got it on tape."
And when I was just turning the channels
I saw this white car.
I heard him holler,
I recognized him layin' there on the ground
that's what got me.
And he looked just like his father too.
Galen was the one used to favor his father.
Now Rodney looks just like him, identical.
I don't know if it's when you lose a life
it comes back in somebody else.
Oh you should have seen him.
It's a hell of a look.
went through three plastic surgeons just to get Rodney to look like
Rodney again.
I tell him he's got a lot
to be thankful for.
A hell of a lot.
He couldn't talk, just der der der
I said, "Goddamn!"

(Angry.)

My brother's son out there was lookin' like hell
that I saw in that bed and I was gonna fight for every bit of
our justice and fairness.
That (Officer) Koon
that's the one in the whole trial,
that man showed no-kind-of-remorse-at-all,
you know that?
He sit there like "it ain't
no big thing
and I
will do it it *again*."

And he smile at you.
The nerve,
the audacity!
But I didn't give a damn if it was the President's
whatever it was.

   (Slight pause, responding to a question.)

You see how everybody rave when something happens with the
President of the United States?
You know, 'cause he's a higher sort?
Okay, here's a nobody.
But the way they beat him.
This is the way I felt towards him.
You understand what I'm sayin' now?
You do? Alright.

   (She lights a "More" cigarette, or long brown cigarette.)

MRS. YOUNG-SOON HAN
Former Liquor Store Owner

Swallowing the Bitterness

   At a low coffee table. Deep voice.

When I was in Korea,
I used to watch many luxurious Hollywood lifestyle movies.
I never saw any poor man,
any black
maybe one housemaid?
Until last year
I believed America is the best.
I still believe it.
I don't deny that now.
Because I'm victim.
But
as
the year ends in ninety-two,
and we were still in turmoil,
and having all the financial problems,
and mental problems,
then a couple months ago,
I really realized that
Korean immigrants were left out
from this

Anna Deavere Smith as Mrs. Young-Soon Han.

society and we were nothing.
What is our right?
Is it because we are Korean?
Is it because we have no politicians?
Is it because we don't
speak good English?
Why?
Why do we have to be left out?

> *(She is hitting her hand on the coffee table.)*

We are not qualified to have medical treatment!
We are not qualified to get, uh,
food stamps!

> *(She hits the table once.)*

No GR!

> *(Hits the table once.)*

No welfare!

> *(Hits the table once.)*

Anything!
Many Afro-Americans

> (*Two quick hits.*)

who never worked

> (*One hit.*)

they get
at least minimum amount

> (*One hit.*)

of money

> (*One hit.*)

to survive!

> (*One hit.*)

We don't get any!

> (*Large hit with full hand spread.*)

Because we have a *car*!

> (*One hit.*)

and we have a *house*!

> (*Pause six seconds.*)

And we are *high tax payers*!

> (*One hit.*)

> (*Pause fourteen seconds.*)

Where do I finda [sic] justice?
Okay, black people
Probably,
believe they won
by the trial?
Even some complains only half, right
justice was there?
But I watched the television
that Sunday morning
Early morning as they started
I started watch it all day.
They were having party, and then they celebrated (*Pronounced
ceLEbreted.*)

all of South Central,
all the churches,
they finally found that justice exists
in this society.
Then where is the victims' rights?
They got their rights
by destroying *innocent Korean merchants (Louder.)*
They have a lot of respect, *(Softer.)*
as I do
for Dr. Martin King?
He is the only model for black community.
I don't care Jesse Jackson.
But,
he was the model
of non-violence
Non-violence?
They like to have hiseh [sic] spirits.
What about last year?
They destroyed innocent people!

    (Five second pause.)

And I wonder if that is really justice, *(And a very soft "uh" after "justice"*
    like "justicah," but very quick.)
to get their rights
in this way.

    (Thirteen second pause.)

I waseh swallowing the bitternesseh.
Sitting here alone, and watching them.
They became all hilarious.

    (Three second pause.)

And uh,
in a way I was happy for them,
and I felt glad for them,
at least they got something back, you know.
Just lets forget Korean victims or other victims
who are destroyed by them.
They have fought
for their rights

    (One hit simultaneous with the word "rights.")

over two centuries

    (One hit simultaneous with "centuries.")

and I have a lot of sympathy and understanding for them.
Because of their effort, and sacrificing,
other minorities, like Hispanic
or Asians
maybe we have to suffer more
by mainstream,
you know?
That's why I understand.
And then
I like to be part of their
'joyment.
But.
That's why I had mixed feeling
as soon as I heard the verdict.
I wish I could
live together
with eh [sic] blacks
but after the riots
there were too much differences
The fire is still there
how do you call it

(*She says a Korean word asking for translation. In Korean, she says "igniting fire."*)

igni
igniting fire
It canuh
burst out any time.

TWILIGHT BEY
Organizer, Gang Truce
Limbo

Walking the full stage and around the table from the dinner party.

So a lot of times when I've brought up ideas to my homeboys,
They say
"Twilight
that's before your time
that's something you can't do now."
When I talked about the truce back in 1988,
that was something they considered before its time.
Yet

Anna Deavere Smith as Twilight Bey.

in 1992,
we made it
realistic.
So to me, it's like I'm stuck in limbo,
like the sun is stuck between night and day,
in the twilight hours,
You know?
I'm in an area not many people exist.
Night time to me
is like a lack of sun.
And I don't affiliate
darkness with anything negative.
I affiliate
darkness of what was first
because it *was first*
and then relative to my complexion,
I am a *dark* individual,

and with me stuck in limbo
I see the darkness as myself
I see the light *(he lights a candle)* as knowledge and the wisdom
of the world and understanding others.
And in order for me to be, a to be, a true human being.
I can't forever dwell in darkness.
I can't forever dwell in the idea,
just identifying with people like me, and understanding me and
mine.
So twilight
is
that time
between day and night
limbo
I call it limbo.

> *(He blows out the candle and walks off the stage.)*

Questions

1. Angela King says of her nephew, Rodney, "I tell him he's got a lot / to be thankful for." Is she being deliberately ironic? Is there a larger irony in her comment?
2. Do you find Mrs. Young-Soon Han to be a sympathetic character? Why or why not?
3. Does the speech by Twilight Bey, which concludes the play, seem conciliatory? Does it explain why the play is called *Twilight*?
4. Taking these monologues together, what do you see as the mood that emerges from the text—despair? hopefulness? resignation? Explain.

■ WRITING *effectively*

THINKING ABOUT DRAMATIC REALISM

When critics use the word *realism* in relation to a play, are they claiming it is true to life? Not necessarily. Realism generally refers to certain dramatic conventions that emerged during the nineteenth century. A realistic play is not necessarily any truer to life than an experimental one, although the conventions of Realist drama have become so familiar to us that other kinds of drama—though no more artificial—can seem mannered and even bizarre to the casual viewer. Remember, though, that all drama—even the theater of Realism—is artifice.

- ▪ **Notice the conventions of Realist drama.** Compare, for example, a play by Henrik Ibsen with one by Sophocles. Ibsen's characters speak in prose, not verse. His settings are drawn from contemporary life, not a legendary past. His characters are ordinary middle-class citizens, not kings, queens, and aristocrats.

- ▪ **Be aware that the inner lives, memories, and motivations of the characters play a crucial role in the dramatic action.** Ibsen, like other Realist playwrights, seeks to portray the complexity of human psychology—especially motivation—in detailed, subtle ways. In contrast, Shakespeare appears less interested in the reason for Iago's villainy than its consequences. Did Iago have an unhappy childhood or a troubled adolescence? These questions do not greatly matter in Renaissance drama, but to Ibsen they become central. In *A Doll's House*, for example, we can infer that Nora's self-absorption and naiveté result from her father's overprotection.

- ▪ **Remember though, Realist drama does not necessarily come any closer than other dramatic styles to getting at the truths of human existence.** *A Doll's House*, for example, does not provide a more profound picture of psychological struggle than *Oedipus the King*. But Ibsen does offer a more detailed view of his protagonist's inner life and her daily routine.

CHECKLIST: Writing About a Realist Play

- ☐ List every detail the play gives about the protagonist's past. How does each detail affect the character's current behavior?
- ☐ What is the protagonist's primary motivation? What are the origins of that motivation?
- ☐ Do the other characters understand the protagonist's deeper motivations?
- ☐ How much of the plot arises from misunderstandings among characters?
- ☐ Do major plot events grow from characters' interactions? Or, do they occur at random?
- ☐ How does the protagonist's psychology determine his or her reactions to events?

TOPICS FOR WRITING ON REALISM

1. How relevant is *A Doll's House* today? Do women like Nora still exist? How about men like Torvald? Build an argument, either that the concerns of *A Doll's House* are timeless and universal or that the issues addressed by the play are historical, not contemporary.

2. Placing yourself in the character of Ibsen's Torvald Helmer, write a defense of him and his attitudes as he himself might write it.

3. Who is the protagonist of *The Glass Menagerie*? Give the reasons for your choice. Is there an antagonist? If so, who is it, and why?

4. At the end of *The Glass Menagerie*, Amanda says to Tom, "You live in a dream; you manufacture illusions." Discuss the degree to which this is true of each of the characters in the play.

5. Choose a character from Milcha Sanchez-Scott's *The Cuban Swimmer* and examine his or her motivations. What makes your character act as he or she does? Present evidence from the play to back up your argument.

6. Describe some of the difficulties of staging *The Cuban Swimmer* as a play. What would be lost or gained by remaking it as a movie?

7. How effective is the technique of *Twilight: Los Angeles, 1992*? Does the lack of interplay between characters make it less dramatic, or is there sufficient drama in what the speakers say and the ways in which they present themselves?

8. Write a paper that compares and contrasts the different points of view of two characters in *Twilight: Los Angeles, 1992*.

9. Imagine you're a casting director. Choose a play from this chapter and cast it with well-known television and movie stars. Explain, in depth, what qualities in the characters you hope to emphasize by your casting choices.

10. Al Capovilla of Folsom Lake Center College has developed an ingenious assignment based on Ibsen's *A Doll's House* that asks students to combine the skills of a literary critic with those of a lawyer. Here is Professor Capovilla's assignment:

> You are the family lawyer for Torvald and Nora Helmer. The couple comes to you with a request. They want you to listen to an account of their domestic problems and recommend whether they should pursue a divorce or try to reconcile.
>
> You listen to both sides of the argument. (You also know everything that is said by every character.)
>
> Now, it is your task to write a short decision. In stating your opinion, provide a clear and organized explanation of your reasoning. Show both sides of the argument. You may employ as evidence anything said or done in the play.
>
> Conclude your paper with your recommendation. What do you advise under the circumstances—divorce or an attempt at reconciliation?

▶ TERMS FOR *review*

Realism ▶ An attempt to reproduce faithfully on the stage the surface appearance of life, especially that of ordinary people in everyday situations. In a historical sense, Realism (usually capitalized) refers to a movement in nineteenth-century European theater. Realist drama customarily focused on the middle class (and occasionally the working class) rather than the aristocracy.

Naturalism ▶ A type of drama in which the characters are presented as products or victims of environment and heredity. Naturalism, considered an extreme form of Realism, customarily depicts the social, psychological, and economic milieu of the primary characters.

Proscenium arch ▶ An architectural picture frame or gateway "standing in front of the scenery" (as the name *proscenium* indicates) that separates the auditorium from the raised stage and the world of the play.

Picture-frame stage ▶ A stage that holds the action within a proscenium arch, with painted scene panels (receding into the middle distance) designed to give the illusion of three-dimensional perspective. Picture-frame stages became the norm throughout Europe and England into the twentieth century.

Box set ▶ A stage set consisting of three walls joined in two corners and a ceiling that tilts, as if seen in perspective, to provide the illusion of scenic realism for interior rooms.

28 PLAYS FOR FURTHER READING

David Henry Hwang

The Sound of a Voice   1983

David Henry Hwang (b. 1957) grew up in San
Gabriel, California, the son of first-generation Chinese
immigrants. He was born into a family of musicians: his
mother was a concert pianist, his sister plays cello in a
string quartet, and he studied the violin. In 1979, as a
senior at Stanford University, he directed his first play,
F.O.B. (an acronym for "fresh off the boat"), in a dor-
mitory lounge. F.O.B. was later staged at the New York
Shakespeare Festival Public Theater and won a 1981
Obie Award. The Sound of a Voice was also produced
at the Public Theater as part of a double bill with another
one-act play by Hwang, The House of Sleeping Beau-

David Henry Hwang

ties. Hwang enjoyed his greatest commercial and critical success with M. Butterfly
(1988), which won the Tony Award for best play. His other plays include Face Value
(1993), Golden Child (1997), and Yellowface (2007). While some of his plays are
realistic in their approach, Hwang has always been fascinated by the possibilities of symbolic drama. In The Sound of a Voice, he creates a timeless, placeless scene in which
two characters named Man and Woman act out a story reminiscent of a folk legend or
a traditional Japanese Nō drama (a type of symbolic aristocratic drama developed in the
fourteenth century in which a ghost recounts the struggles of his or her life for a traveler). Hwang's interest in nonrealistic and experimental drama has also led him to explore
opera. He has collaborated with composer Philip Glass on three works: 1000 Airplanes
on the Roof (1988), a science-fiction music drama; The Voyage (1992), an allegorical
grand opera commissioned by New York's Metropolitan Opera for the 500th anniversary
of Christopher Columbus's arrival in America; and The Sound of a Voice (2003), a
combined staging of the following play with The House of Sleeping Beauties. He has
also written the books for the shows Aida (2000), with music by Elton John and lyrics
by Tim Rice, and Tarzan (2006), with music and lyrics by Phil Collins. Hwang lives in
New York City.

CHARACTERS

Man, fifties, Japanese
Woman, fifties, Japanese

SETTING. Woman's house, in a remote corner of the forest.

American Repertory Theater's 2003 production of *The Sound of a Voice* in Cambridge, Massachusetts.

SCENE I

Woman pours tea for Man. Man rubs himself, trying to get warm.

Man: You're very kind to take me in.

Woman: This is a remote corner of the world. Guests are rare.

Man: The tea—you pour it well.

Woman: No.

Man: The sound it makes—in the cup—very soothing.

Woman: That is the tea's skill, not mine. (*She hands the cup to him.*) May I get you something else? Rice, perhaps?

Man: No.

Woman: And some vegetables?

Man: No, thank you.

Woman: Fish? (*Pause.*) It is at least two days' walk to the nearest village. I saw no horse. You must be very hungry. You would do a great honor to dine with me. Guests are rare.

Man: Thank you.

Woman (*Woman gets up, leaves. Man holds the cup in his hands, using it to warm himself. He gets up, walks around the room. It is sparsely furnished, drab, except for one shelf on which stands a vase of brightly colored flowers. The flowers stand out in sharp contrast to the starkness of the room. Slowly, he* *reaches out towards them. He touches them. Quickly, he takes one of the flowers from the vase, hides it in his clothes. He returns to where he had sat previously. He waits. Woman re-enters. She carries a tray with food.):* Please. Eat. It will give me great pleasure.

Man: This—this is magnificent.

Woman: Eat.

Man: Thank you. *(He motions for Woman to join him.)*

Woman: No, thank you.

Man: This is wonderful. The best I've tasted.

Woman: You are reckless in your flattery. But anything you say, I will enjoy hearing. It's not even the words. It's the sound of a voice, the way it moves through the air.

Man: How long has it been since you last had a visitor? *(Pause.)*

Woman: I don't know.

Man: Oh?

Woman: I lose track. Perhaps five months ago, perhaps ten years, perhaps yesterday. I don't consider time when there is no voice in the air. It's pointless. Time begins with the entrance of a visitor, and ends with his exit.

Man: And in between? You don't keep track of the days? You can't help but notice—

Woman: Of course I notice.

Man: Oh.

Woman: I notice, but I don't keep track. *(Pause.)* May I bring out more?

Man: More? No. No. This was wonderful.

Woman: I have more.

Man: Really—the best I've had.

Woman: You must be tired. Did you sleep in the forest last night?

Man: Yes.

Woman: Or did you not sleep at all?

Man: I slept.

Woman: Where?

Man: By a waterfall. The sound of the water put me to sleep. It rumbled like the sounds of a city. You see, I can't sleep in too much silence. It scares me. It makes me feel that I have no control over what is about to happen.

Woman: I feel the same way.

Man: But you live here—alone?

Woman: Yes.

Man: It's so quiet here. How can you sleep?

Woman: Tonight, I'll sleep. I'll lie down in the next room, and hear your breathing through the wall, and fall asleep shamelessly. There will be no silence.

Man: You're very kind to let me stay here.

Woman: This is yours. (*She unrolls a mat; there is a beautiful design of a flower on the mat. The flower looks exactly like the flowers in the vase.*)
Man: Did you make it yourself?
Woman: Yes. There is a place to wash outside.
Man: Thank you.
Woman: Goodnight.
Man: Goodnight. (*Man starts to leave.*)
Woman: May I know your name?
Man: No. I mean, I would rather not say. If I gave you a name, it would only be made-up. Why should I deceive you? You are too kind for that.
Woman: Then what should I call you? Perhaps—"Man Who Fears Silence"?
Man: How about, "Man Who Fears Women"?
Woman: That name is much too common.
Man: And you?
Woman: Yokiko.
Man: That's your name?
Woman: It's what you may call me.
Man: Goodnight, Yokiko. You are very kind.
Woman: You are very smart. Goodnight.

(*Man exits. Hanako° goes to the mat. She tidies it, brushes it off. She goes to the vase. She picks up the flowers, studies them. She carries them out of the room with her. Man re-enters. He takes off his outer clothing. He glimpses the spot where the vase used to sit. He reaches into his clothing, pulls out the stolen flower. He studies it. He puts it underneath his head as he lies down to sleep, like a pillow. He starts to fall asleep. Suddenly, a start. He picks up his head. He listens.*)

SCENE II

Dawn. Man is getting dressed. Woman enters with food.

Woman: Good morning.
Man: Good morning, Yokiko.
Woman: You weren't planning to leave?
Man: I have quite a distance to travel today.
Woman: Please. (*She offers him food.*)
Man: Thank you.
Woman: May I ask where you're travelling to?
Man: It's far.
Woman: I know this region well.

Hanako: The woman.

Man: Oh? Do you leave the house often?

Woman: I used to. I used to travel a great deal. I know the region from those days.

Man: You probably wouldn't know the place I'm headed.

Woman: Why not?

Man: It's new. A new village. It didn't exist in "those days." (*Pause.*)

Woman: I thought you said you wouldn't deceive me.

Man: I didn't. You don't believe me, do you?

Woman: No.

Man: Then I didn't deceive you. I'm travelling. That much is true.

Woman: Are you in such a hurry?

Man: Travelling is a matter of timing. Catching the light. (*Woman exits; Man finishes eating, puts down his bowl. Woman re-enters with the vase of flowers.*) Where did you find those? They don't grow native around these parts, do they?

Woman: No; they've all been brought in. They were brought in by visitors. Such as yourself. They were left here. In my custody.

Man: But—they look so fresh, so alive.

Woman: I take care of them. They remind me of the people and places outside this house.

Man: May I touch them?

Woman: Certainly.

Man: These have just blossomed.

Woman: No; they were in bloom yesterday. If you'd noticed them before, you would know that.

Man: You must have received these very recently. I would guess—within five days.

Woman: I don't know. But I wouldn't trust your estimate. It's all in the amount of care you show to them. I create a world which is outside the realm of what you know.

Man: What do you do?

Woman: I can't explain. Words are too inefficient. It takes hundreds of words to describe a single act of caring. With hundreds of acts, words become irrelevant. (*Pause.*) But perhaps you can stay.

Man: How long?

Woman: As long as you'd like.

Man: Why?

Woman: To see how I care for them.

Man: I *am* tired.

Woman: Rest.

Man: The light?

Woman: It will return.

SCENE III

Man is carrying chopped wood. He is stripped to the waist. Woman enters.

Woman: You're very kind to do that for me.

Man: I enjoy it, you know. Chopping wood. It's clean. No questions. You take your axe, you stand up the log, you aim—pow!—you either hit it or you don't. Success or failure.

Woman: You seem to have been very successful today.

Man: Why shouldn't I be? It's a beautiful day. I can see to those hills. The trees are cool. The sun is gentle. Ideal. If a man can't be successful on a day like this, he might as well kick the dust up into his own face. (*Man notices Woman staring at him. Man pats his belly, looks at her.*) Protection from falls.

Woman: What? (*Man pinches his belly, showing some fat.*) Oh. Don't be silly. (*Man begins slapping the fat on his belly to a rhythm.*)

Man: Listen—I can make music—see?—that wasn't always possible. But now—that I've developed this—whenever I need entertainment.

Woman: You shouldn't make fun of your body.

Man: Why not? I saw you. You were staring.

Woman: I wasn't making fun. (*Man inflates his cheeks.*) I was just—stop that!

Man: Then why were you staring?

Woman: I was—

Man: Laughing?

Woman: No.

Man: Well?

Woman: I was—Your body. It's . . . strong. (*Pause.*)

Man: People say that. But they don't know. I've heard that age brings wisdom. That's a laugh. The years don't accumulate here. They accumulate here. (*Pause; he pinches his belly.*) But today is a day to be happy, right? The woods. The sun. Blue. It's a happy day. I'm going to chop wood.

Woman: There's nothing left to chop. Look.

Man: Oh. I guess . . . that's it.

Woman: Sit. Here.

Man: But—

Woman: There's nothing left. (*Man sits; Woman stares at his belly.*) Learn to love it.

Man: Don't be ridiculous.

Woman: Touch it.

Man: It's flabby.

Woman: It's strong.

Man: It's weak.

Woman: And smooth.

Man: Do you mind if I put on my shirt?

Woman: Of course not. Shall I get it for you?

Man: No. No. Just sit there. (*Man starts to put on his shirt. He pauses, studies his body.*) You think it's cute, huh?

Woman: I think you should learn to love it. (*Man pats his belly, talks to it.*)

Man (*to belly*): You're okay, sir. You hang onto my body like a great horseman.

Woman: Not like that.

Man (*ibid.°*): You're also faithful. You'll never leave me for another man.

Woman: No.

Man: What do you want me to say? (*Woman walks over to Man. She touches his belly with her hand. They look at each other.*)

SCENE IV

Night. Man is alone. Flowers are gone from stand. Mat is unrolled. Man lies on it, sleeping. Suddenly, he starts. He lifts up his head. He listens. Silence. He goes back to sleep. Another start. He lifts up his head, strains to hear. Slowly, we begin to make out the strains of a single shakuhachi° playing a haunting line. It is very soft. He strains to hear it. The instrument slowly fades out. He waits for it to return, but it does not. He takes out the stolen flower. He stares into it.

SCENE V

Day. Woman is cleaning, while Man relaxes. She is on her hands and knees, scrubbing. She is dressed in a simple outfit, for working. Her hair is tied back. Man is sweating. He has not, however, removed his shirt.

Man: I heard your playing last night.

Woman: My playing?

Man: *Shakuhachi.*

Woman: Oh.

Man: You played very softly. I had to strain to hear it. Next time, don't be afraid. Play out. Fully. Clear. It must've been very beautiful, if only I could've heard it clearly. Why don't you play for me sometime?

Woman: I'm very shy about it.

Man: Why?

Woman: I play for my own satisfaction. That's all. It's something I developed on my own. I don't know if it's at all acceptable by outside standards.

Man: Play for me. I'll tell you.

Woman: No; I'm sure you're too knowledgeable in the arts.

Man: Who? Me?

Woman: You being from the city and all.

Man: I'm ignorant, believe me.

---

ibid.: an abbreviation of the Latin word *ibidem*, meaning "in the same place." *shakuhachi*: a Japanese bamboo flute.

Woman: I'd play, and you'd probably bite your cheek.

Man: Ask me a question about music. Any question. I'll answer incorrectly. I guarantee it.

Woman: Look at this.

Man: What?

Woman: A stain.

Man: Where?

Woman: Here? See? I can't get it out.

Man: Oh. I hadn't noticed it before.

Woman: I notice it every time I clean.

Man: Here. Let me try.

Woman: Thank you.

Man: Ugh. It's tough.

Woman: I know.

Man: How did it get here?

Woman: It's been there as long as I've lived here.

Man: I hardly stand a chance. (*Pause.*) But I'll try. Uh—one—two—three—four! One—two—three—four! See, you set up . . . gotta set up . . . a rhythm—two—three—four. Like fighting! Like battle! One—two—three—four! Used to practice with a rhythm . . . beat . . . battle! Yes! (*The stain starts to fade away.*) Look—it's—yes!—whoo!—there it goes—got the sides—the edges—yes!—fading quick—fading away—ooo—here we come—towards the center—to the heart—two—three—four—slow—slow death—tough—dead! (*Man rolls over in triumphant laughter.*)

Woman: Dead.

Man: I got it! I got it! Whoo! A little rhythm! All it took! Four! Four!

Woman: Thank you.

Man: I didn't think I could do it—but there—it's gone—I did it!

Woman: Yes. You did.

Man: And you—you were great!

Woman: No—I was carried away.

Man: We were a team! You and me!

Woman: I only provided encouragement.

Man: You were great! You were! (*Man grabs Woman. Pause.*)

Woman: It's gone. Thank you. Would you like to hear me play *shakuhachi*?

Man: Yes I would.

Woman: I don't usually play for visitors. It's so . . . I'm not sure. I developed it—all by myself—in times when I was alone. I heard nothing—no human voice. So I learned to play *shakuhachi*. I tried to make these sounds resemble the human voice. The *shakuhachi* became my weapon. To ward off the air. It kept me from choking on many a silent evening.

Man: I'm here. You can hear my voice.

Woman: Speak again.

Man: I will.

SCENE VI

Night. Man is sleeping. Suddenly, a start. He lifts his head up. He listens. Silence. He strains to hear. The shakuhachi melody rises up once more. This time, however, it becomes louder and more clear than before. He gets up. He cannot tell from what direction the music is coming. He walks around the room, putting his ear to different places in the wall, but he cannot locate the sound. It seems to come from all directions at once, as omnipresent as the air. Slowly, he moves towards the wall with the sliding panel through which the Woman enters and exits. He puts his ear against it, thinking the music may be coming from there. Slowly, he slides the door open just a crack, ever so carefully. He peeks through the crack. As he peeks through, the Upstage wall of the set becomes transparent, and through the scrim, we are able to see what he sees. Woman is Upstage of the scrim. She is tending a room filled with potted and vased flowers of all variety. The lushness and beauty of the room Upstage of the scrim stands out in stark contrast to the barrenness of the main set. She is also transformed. She is a young woman. She is beautiful. She wears a brightly colored kimono. Man observes this scene for a long time. He then slides the door shut. The scrim returns to opaque. The music continues. He returns to his mat. He picks up the stolen flower. It is brown and wilted, dead. He looks at it. The music slowly fades out.

SCENE VII

Morning. Man is half-dressed. He is practicing sword maneuvers. He practices with the feel of a man whose spirit is willing, but the flesh is inept. He tries to execute deft movements, but is dissatisfied with his efforts. He curses himself, and returns to basic exercises. Suddenly, he feels something buzzing around his neck—a mosquito. He slaps his neck, but misses it. He sees it flying near him. He swipes at it with his sword. He keeps missing. Finally, he thinks he's hit it. He runs over, kneels down to recover the fallen insect. He picks up two halves of a mosquito on two different fingers. Woman enters the room. She looks as she normally does. She is carrying a vase of flowers, which she places on its shelf.

Man: Look.
Woman: I'm sorry?
Man: Look.
Woman: What? *(He brings over the two halves of mosquito to show her.)*
Man: See?
Woman: Oh.
Man: I hit it—chop!
Woman: These are new forms of target practice?
Man: Huh? Well—yes—in a way.
Woman: You seem to do well at it.
Man: Thank you. For last night. I heard your *shakuhachi.* It was very loud, strong—good tone.

Woman: Did you enjoy it? I wanted you to enjoy it. If you wish, I'll play it for you every night.

Man: Every night!

Woman: If you wish.

Man: No—I don't—I don't want you to treat me like a baby.

Woman: What? I'm not.

Man: Oh, yes. Like a baby. Who you must feed in the middle of the night or he cries. Waaah! Waaah!

Woman: Stop that!

Man: You need your sleep.

Woman: I don't mind getting up for you. (*Pause.*) I would enjoy playing for you. Every night. While you sleep. It will make me feel—like I'm shaping your dreams. I go through long stretches when there is no one in my dreams. It's terrible. During those times, I avoid my bed as much as possible. I paint. I weave. I play *shakuhachi*. I sit on mats and rub powder into my face. Anything to keep from facing a bed with no dreams. It is like sleeping on ice.

Man: What do you dream of now?

Woman: Last night—I dreamt of you. I don't remember what happened. But you were very funny. Not in a mocking way. I wasn't laughing at you. But you made me laugh. And you were very warm. I remember that. (*Pause.*) What do you remember about last night?

Man: Just your playing. That's all. I got up, listened to it, and went back to sleep. (*Man gets up, resumes practicing with his sword.*)

Woman: Another mosquito bothering you?

Man: Just practicing. Ah! Weak! Too weak! I tell you, it wasn't always like this. I'm telling you, there were days when I could chop the fruit from a tree without ever taking my eyes off the ground. (*He continues practicing.*) You ever use one of these?

Woman: I've had to pick one up, yes.

Man: Oh?

Woman: You forget—I live alone—out here—there is . . . not much to sustain me but what I manage to learn myself. It wasn't really a matter of choice.

Man: I used to be very good, you know. Perhaps I can give you some pointers.

Woman: I'd really rather not.

Man: C'mon—a woman like you—you're absolutely right. You need to know how to defend yourself.

Woman: As you wish.

Man: Do you have something to practice with?

Woman: Yes. Excuse me. (*She exits. He practices more. She re-enters with two wooden sticks. He takes one of them.*) Will these do?

Man: Nice. Now, show me what you can do.

Woman: I'm sorry?

Man: Run up and hit me.

Woman: Please.

Man: Go on—I'll block it.

Woman: I feel so . . . undignified.

Man: Go on. (*She hits him playfully with stick.*) Not like that!

Woman: I'll try to be gentle.

Man: What?

Woman: I don't want to hurt you.

Man: You won't—Hit me! (*Woman charges at Man, quickly, deftly. She scores a hit.*) Oh!

Woman: Did I hurt you?

Man: No—you were—let's try that again. (*They square off again. Woman rushes forward. She appears to attempt a strike. He blocks that apparent strike, which turns out to be a feint. She scores.*) Huh?

Woman: Did I hurt you? I'm sorry.

Man: No.

Woman: I hurt you.

Man: No.

Woman: Do you wish to hit me?

Man: No.

Woman: Do you want me to try again?

Man: No.

Woman: Thank you.

Man: Just practice there—by yourself—let me see you run through some maneuvers.

Woman: Must I?

Man: Yes! Go! (*She goes to an open area.*) My greatest strength was always as a teacher. (*Woman executes a series of deft movements. Her whole manner is transformed. Man watches with increasing amazement. Her movements end. She regains her submissive manner.*)

Woman: I'm so embarrassed. My skills—they're so—inappropriate. I look like a man.

Man: Where did you learn that?

Woman: There is much time to practice here.

Man: But you—the techniques.

Woman: I don't know what's fashionable in the outside world. (*Pause.*) Are you unhappy?

Man: No.

Woman: Really?

Man: I'm just . . . surprised.

Woman: You think it's unbecoming for a woman.

Man: No, no. Not at all.

Woman: You want to leave.

Man: No!

Woman: All visitors do. I know. I've met many. They say they'll stay. And they do. For a while. Until they see too much. Or they learn something new. There are boundaries outside of which visitors do not want to see me step. Only who knows what those boundaries are? Not I. They change with every visitor. You have to be careful not to cross them, but you never know where they are. And one day, inevitably, you step outside the lines. The visitor knows. You don't. You didn't know that you'd done anything different. You thought it was just another part of you. The visitor sneaks away. The next day, you learn that you had stepped outside his heart. I'm afraid you've seen too much.

Man: There are stories.

Woman: What?

Man: People talk.

Woman: Where? We're two days from the nearest village.

Man: Word travels.

Woman: What are you talking about?

Man: There are stories about you. I heard them. They say that your visitors never leave this house.

Woman: That's what you heard?

Man: They say you imprison them.

Woman: Then you were a fool to come here.

Man: Listen.

Woman: Me? Listen? You. Look! Where are these prisoners? Have you seen any?

Man: They told me you were very beautiful.

Woman: Then they are blind as well as ignorant.

Man: You are.

Woman: What?

Man: Beautiful.

Woman: Stop that! My skin feels like seaweed.

Man: I didn't realize it at first. I must confess—I didn't. But over these few days—your face has changed for me. The shape of it. The feel of it. The color. All changed. I look at you now, and I'm no longer sure you are the same woman who had poured tea for me just a week ago. And because of that I remembered—how little I know about a face that changes in the night. (*Pause.*) Have you heard those stories?

Woman: I don't listen to old wives' tales.

Man: But have you heard them?

Woman: Yes. I've heard them. From other visitors—young—hotblooded—or old—who came here because they were told great glory was to be had by killing the witch in the woods.

Man: I was told that no man could spend time in this house without falling in love.

Woman: Oh? So why did you come? Did you wager gold that you could come out untouched? The outside world is so flattering to me. And you—are you like the rest? Passion passing through your heart so powerfully that you can't hold onto it?

Man: No! I'm afraid!

Woman: Of what?

Man: Sometimes—when I look into the flowers, I think I hear a voice—from inside—a voice beneath the petals. A human voice.

Woman: What does it say? "Let me out"?

Man: No. Listen. It hums. It hums with the peacefulness of one who is completely imprisoned.

Woman: I understand that if you listen closely enough, you can hear the ocean.

Man: No. Wait. Look at it. See the layers? Each petal—hiding the next. Try and see where they end. You can't. Follow them down, further down, around—and as you come down—faster and faster—the breeze picks up. The breeze becomes a wail. And in that rush of air—in the silent midst of it—you can hear a voice.

Woman (grabs flower from Man): So, you believe I water and prune my lovers? How can you be so foolish? (*She snaps the flower in half, at the stem. She throws it to the ground.*) Do you come only to leave again? To take a chunk of my heart, then leave with your booty on your belt, like a prize? You say that I imprison hearts in these flowers? Well, bits of my heart are trapped with travellers across this land. I can't even keep track. So kill me. If you came here to destroy a witch, kill me now. I can't stand to have it happen again.

Man: I won't leave you.

Woman: I believe you. (*She looks at the flower that she has broken, bends to pick it up. He touches her. They embrace.*)

SCENE VIII

Day. Woman wears a simple undergarment, over which she is donning a brightly colored kimono, the same one we saw her wearing Upstage of the scrim. Man stands apart.

Woman: I can't cry. I don't have the capacity. Right from birth, I didn't cry. My mother and father were shocked. They thought they'd given birth to a ghost, a demon. Sometimes I've thought myself that. When great sadness has welled up inside me, I've prayed for a means to release the pain from my body. But my prayers went unanswered. The grief remained inside me. It would sit like water, still. (*Pause; she models her kimono.*) Do you like it?

Man: Yes, it's beautiful.

Woman: I wanted to wear something special today.

Man: It's beautiful. Excuse me. I must practice.

Woman: Shall I get you something?

Man: No.

Woman: Some tea, maybe?

Man: No. (*Man resumes swordplay.*)

Woman: Perhaps later today—perhaps we can go out—just around here. We can look for flowers.

Man: Alright.

Woman: We don't have to.

Man: No. Let's.

Woman: I just thought if—

Man: Fine. Where do you want to go?

Woman: There are very few recreational activities around here, I know.

Man: Alright. We'll go this afternoon. (*Pause.*)

Woman: Can I get you something?

Man (*turning around*): What?

Woman: You might be—

Man: I'm not hungry or thirsty or cold or hot.

Woman: Then what are you?

Man: Practicing. (*Man resumes practicing; Woman exits. As soon as she exits, he rests. He sits down. He examines his sword. He runs his finger along the edge of it. He takes the tip, runs it against the soft skin under his chin. He places the sword on the ground with the tip pointed directly upwards. He keeps it from falling by placing the tip under his chin. He experiments with different degrees of pressure. Woman re-enters. She sees him in this precarious position. She jerks his head upward; the sword falls.*)

Woman: Don't do that!

Man: What?

Woman: You can hurt yourself!

Man: I was practicing!

Woman: You were playing!

Man: I was practicing!

Woman: It's dangerous.

Man: What do you take me for—a child?

Woman: Sometimes wise men do childish things.

Man: I knew what I was doing!

Woman: It scares me.

Man: Don't be ridiculous. (*He reaches for the sword again.*)

Woman: Don't! Don't do that!

Man: Get back! (*He places the sword back in its previous position, suspended between the floor and his chin, upright.*)

Woman: But—

Man: Sssssh!

Woman: I wish—

Man: Listen to me! The slightest shock, you know—the slightest shock— surprise—it might make me jerk or—something—and then . . . so you must be perfectly still and quiet.

Woman: But I—

Man: Sssssh! (*Silence.*) I learned this exercise from a friend—I can't even remember his name—good swordsman—many years ago. He called it his meditation position. He said, like this, he could feel the line between this world and the others because he rested on it. If he saw something in another world that he liked better, all he would have to do is let his head drop, and he'd be there. Simple. No fuss. One day, they found him with the tip of his sword run clean out the back of his neck. He was smiling. I guess he saw something he liked. Or else he'd fallen asleep.

Woman: Stop that.

Man: Stop what?

Woman: Tormenting me.

Man: I'm not.

Woman: Take it away!

Man: You don't have to watch, you know.

Woman: Do you want to die that way—an accident?

Man: I was doing this before you came in.

Woman: If you do, all you need to do is tell me.

Man: What?

Woman: I can walk right over. Lean on the back of your head.

Man: Don't try to threaten—

Woman: Or jerk your sword up.

Man: Or scare me. You can't threaten—

Woman: I'm not. But if that's what you want.

Man: You can't threaten me. You wouldn't do it.

Woman: Oh?

Man: Then I'd be gone. You wouldn't let me leave that easily.

Woman: Yes, I would.

Man: You'd be alone.

Woman: No. I'd follow you. Forever. (*Pause.*) Now, let's stop this nonsense.

Man: No! I can do what I want! Don't come any closer!

Woman: Then release your sword.

Man: Come any closer and I'll drop my head.

Woman (Woman slowly approaches Man. She grabs the hilt of the sword. She looks into his eyes. She pulls it out from under his chin.): There will be no more of this. (*She exits with the sword. He starts to follow her, then stops. He touches under his chin. On his finger, he finds a drop of blood.*)

SCENE IX

Night. Man is leaving the house. He is just about out, when he hears a shakuhachi *playing. He looks around, trying to locate the sound. Woman appears in the doorway to the outside.* Shakuhachi *slowly fades out.*

Woman: It's time for you to go?

Man: Yes. I'm sorry.

Woman: You're just going to sneak out? A thief in the night? A frightened child?

Man: I care about you.

Woman: You express it strangely.

Man: I leave in shame because it is proper. (*Pause.*) I came seeking glory.

Woman: To kill me? You can say it. You'll be surprised at how little I blanch. As if you'd said, "I came for a bowl of rice," or "I came seeking love" or "I came to kill you."

Man: Weakness. All weakness. Too weak to kill you. Too weak to kill myself. Too weak to do anything but sneak away in shame. (*Woman brings out Man's sword.*)

Woman: Were you even planning to leave without this? (*He takes sword.*) Why not stay here?

Man: I can't live with someone who's defeated me.

Woman: I never thought of defeating you. I only wanted to take care of you. To make you happy. Because that made me happy and I was no longer alone.

Man: You defeated me.

Woman: Why do you think that way?

Man: I came here with a purpose. The world was clear. You changed the shape of your face, the shape of my heart—rearranged everything—created a world where I could do nothing.

Woman: I only tried to care for you.

Man: I guess that was all it took. (*Pause.*)

Woman: You still think I'm a witch. Just because old women gossip. You are so cruel. Once you arrived, there were only two possibilities: I would die or you would leave. (*Pause.*) If you believe I'm a witch, then kill me. Rid the province of one more evil.

Man: I can't—

Woman: Why not? If you believe that about me, then it's the right thing to do.

Man: You know I can't.

Woman: Then stay.

Man: Don't try and force me.

Woman: I won't force you to do anything. (*Pause.*) All I wanted was an escape—for both of us. The sound of a human voice—the simplest thing to find, and the hardest to hold onto. This house—my loneliness is etched into the walls. Kill me, but don't leave. Even in death, my spirit would rest here and be comforted by your presence.

Man: Force me to stay.

Woman: I won't. (*Man starts to leave.*) Beware.

Man: What?

Woman: The ground on which you walk is weak. It could give way at any moment. The crevice beneath is dark.

Man: Are you talking about death? I'm ready to die.

Woman: Fear for what is worse than death.

Man: What?

Woman: Falling. Falling through the darkness. Waiting to hit the ground. Picking up speed. Waiting for the ground. Falling faster. Falling alone. Waiting. Falling. Waiting. Falling.

(Woman wails and runs out through the door to her room. Man stands, confused, not knowing what to do. He starts to follow her, then hesitates, and rushes out the door to the outside. Silence. Slowly, he re-enters from the outside. He looks for her in the main room. He goes slowly towards the panel to her room. He throws down his sword. He opens the panel. He goes inside. He comes out. He unrolls his mat. He sits on it, cross-legged. He looks out into space. He notices near him a shakuhachi. He picks it up. He begins to blow into it. He tries to make sounds. He continues trying through the end of the play. The Upstage scrim lights up. Upstage, we see the Woman. She is young. She is hanging from a rope suspended from the roof. She has hung herself. Around her are scores of vases with flowers in them whose blossoms have been blown off. Only the stems remain in the vases. Around her swirl the thousands of petals from the flowers. They fill the Upstage scrim area like a blizzard of color. Man continues to attempt to play. Lights fade to black.)

Edward Bok Lee

El Santo Americano   2001

Edward Bok Lee was born in Fargo, North Dakota, the son of Korean immigrants. He attended kindergarten in Seoul, South Korea, but grew up mostly in North Dakota and Minnesota. He received a B.A. in comparative literature from the University of Minnesota and an M.F.A. from Brown University. While enrolled in a graduate program in comparative literature at the University of California, Berkeley, he wrote his first full-length play, St. Petersburg: An Exodus (2000). Lee writes plays, poetry, fiction, and memoir. A former bartender, custodian, journalist, and translator, Lee has performed his work in the United States, Europe, and Asia, as well as on public radio and on television, including MTV. His prose and poetry collection Real Karaoke People (2005)

Edward Bok Lee

won the Asian American Literary Award and the PEN/Open Book Award. Lee currently teaches at Metropolitan State University. El Santo Americano (2001) was originally developed as part of a "ten-minute-play" project at the Guthrie Theater in Minneapolis. His other plays include Athens County (1997) and History K (2003). "Art can show you," Lee has observed, "the interior of another person's life and soul, if only just for a few minutes."

CHARACTERS

Clay, a man
Evalana, his wife

TIME. *Present*
PLACE. *The desert at night.*

Clay (*driving at night, 80 mph*): that's because in Mexico it's normal to wear a mask. almost everybody does. silk and satin and form-fitting lycra. it makes the whole body more aerodynamic. you ought see them flying around, doing triple flips in mid-air. they got these long flowing capes like colorful wings sprouting from their shoulders. they don't talk much, though. not the great ones. the silence is mysterious. it adds a kind of weight to them when they climb into the ring. get a guy with that much gold and glitter on him here and you know he'd have to talk shit. in Mexico they just wrestle. the masks come from thousands and thousands of years ago. fiestas. ancient rituals. slip one over your head and you could become a tiger or donkey, a bat or giant lizard. a corn spirit dancing under the clouds for rain. those were your gods if you lived back then. you'll like it there in Mexico. don't you think you'll like it there? Jesse?

(*Evalana, brooding, eventually looks in the backseat then faces front again.*)

Clay: he asleep back there?
    a growing boy needs his sleep.
    yes he does.
    you hungry?
Evalana: don't talk to me.
Clay: hard to fall asleep on an empty stomach.
Evalana: i can't sleep.
Clay: you ain't tried to.

(*She checks her outburst, then looks in the backseat again, perhaps adjusting their son's blanket, then faces front. they drive on for a time.*)

Clay (*looking in rearview mirror*): hey there Jesse.
    you have a nice nap?
    we'll be there come morning, so you just sit back.

how you like that comic book i got you?
Jesse?
what's the matter, boy? you not feeling well?
Jesse?
Evalana: sometimes he sleeps with his eyes open.
Clay: like you.
Evalana: i do not sleep with my eyes open.
Clay: how do you know?
Evalana: i know.
Clay: how?
Evalana: 'cause someone would have said something. including you.
Clay: people do all kinds of things they're not aware of.
my daddy used to wander through the house all night, buck naked,
up and down the stairs. opening and closing windows.
carrying only his briefcase chockfull of all the vending machine products
he sold.
combs. candy. chicken bouillon.
my momma warned if we woke him up he'd have a heart attack.
so we just let him sleepwalk.
he didn't know.
Evalana: maybe somebody should have told him.
Clay: he didn't want to know.

(*They drive on.*)

Evalana: you talk in your sleep.
you snore.
you drool.
and you fart. all night.

(*They drive on awhile.*)

Clay: i love you, Ev.
Evalana: jesus, Clay. listen to yourself.
your whole life you been faking it.
fake husband. fake father.
fake man. that's what they ought to call you:
Fake Man.

(*Clay drives on for a little while longer through the night, then pulls the car to a stop on the side of the road and gets out. he walks a good ways away from the car, holding a flashlight in one hand and a gun in the other—not aimed at her, but clearly present, under the starlight. Evalana hesitates, then gets out, the flashlight's beam now on her.*)

Clay (*directs flashlight beam to a place in the brush*): there's a bush over there.

(Evalana, hesitant at first, then grabs her purse and crosses past Clay.)

Evalana *(off)*: i won't run!
i promise!

(Clay thinks, then lowers flashlight beam and switches it off. dim moonlight. sounds of desert at night.)

Clay: you should have seen me last week, Ev!

Darton, he cut me a break! he didn't have to, but he did 'cause i been loyal to him all these years! you remember when we used to work at the turkey plant together! the smell on my hands when i'd come home and try to kiss you . . .

the match was against the eleventh-ranked contender! brand new guy, from Montreal! Kid Canuck they call him! long blonde hair, tan, all bulked up in white trunks with a red maple leaf you know where! some rich producer's nephew or something! he was scheduled to wrestle the Sheik in the opening match, but the old guy had a hernia while they was warming up, so Darton, he give me a break and put me on the bill against Kid Canuck at the last minute!

we didn't have time to choreograph much action! i think he was kind of nervous! two minutes in he starts grabbing my hair! hard! for real! trying to get the audience more into it! he wasn't telegraphing his head butts neither! soon enough my nose was a cherry caught under a dump-truck! the blood all over sure got the crowd into it boy! up till then they was pretty quiet, waiting for the main headliners to come out!

raking my eyes, slapping my face. i told him to ease up, it don't work like that here, but he wasn't listening. dancing around. cursing at me in French. winding his right arm up, then smacking me hard with the left until both my ears are firebells going off.

now i can take just about anything. you know me. i've been pile-drived, figure-foured, and suplexed into losses by the best of them. but on this particular night, something happened. and one pop i took in the mouth shot my adrenaline way up, my blood running all over hell now like carbolic acid, and him twisting my arm for real, not giving a flying fuck about my bad elbow, my bad back, or my five-year-old son, who don't even like to watch wrestling no more 'cause he's ashamed, 'cause his friends call his daddy a loser, and he don't know what to say or believe in, and the next thing i knew i had that pretty boy son of a bitch Kid Canuck down hard on the mat in a scorpion leg lock!!

they had to haul him off on a stretcher!

i was a little dazed yet, and the crowd, they didn't know what to think!

then the referee threw my arm up under the hot lights and before i knew it all the noise in the arena was more like cheering! it was a chemical thing! at first some people in the upper bleachers stood up! and then all of them did! everywhere! stomping, and starting to chant my name! and not 'cause they hated the other guy! they didn't! they was cheering 'cause i beat the guy fair and square! he gave up out of pain, right there in the middle of the ring! i had him wrenched in that scorpion leg lock a good two minutes screaming like a baby, like a cut pig, like a man in real pain! and they knew it!

you can't fake that! they'd seen so much phony bullshit through the years, and they could tell this match was different! and they appreciated that! they appreciated being shown the truth, just once in their sorry-ass lives!

Darton threw a wet towel at my face in the locker room.

i went out on a limb for you! he says. six months of planning and promotion! tens of thousands of dollars! t-shirts! coffee mugs! now who the hell's gonna believe Kid Canuck is a contender for the federation championship when he lost his debut match to you!!

i told him i was sorry, and after a while he put his hand on my shoulder. asked me what i'd been thinking there in the ring. tell me the truth, he says. so i can go home and feel at least a little bad about firing your dumb ass.

and i wanted to say that i did it for you.

for my wife, Evalana, who i never gave nothing to believe in.

and i did it for my boy, Jesse, who only ever got to see his daddy get beat time and again. i wanted to tell him i did it 'cause my wife and child was out there in the audience. not living in some other town. i wanted to say you was both out there watching over me. 'cause where else would you be?

Ev? Evalana!

(*Clay switches on flashlight and directs its beam onto the "bush" in the desert. Evalana has run off. he directs the flashlight all around, searching in vain.*)

shit.

(*Clay turns off the flashlight and sits down on a stone. in the moonlight, he pulls out from his pocket a colorful Mexican wrestler's mask and slips it over his head. he sits there in the darkness alone for a moment. he then, as a little boy might, twirls the gun on his finger, and pretends what it'd be like to shoot himself in the head. he tries it from a couple different angles, in strange fun. eventually he places the gun in his mouth, holds it there for a second or two with his hand, then lets go. it remains stuck there in his mouth from here on out. eventually, out of the darkness of the desert, Evalana reappears.*)

Evalana: once, when i was about Jesse's age, we took a trip to California. Disneyland. we drove all the way cross country in Daddy's Ford Falcon. Ma said it was the honeymoon she never got. a lot of the highway had just been tarred, and you could feel it. i thought we was gonna sail on forever into the future. it was somewhere in Arizona that Daddy woke us all up so we could see this great big dam at night. we stood there looking down at the bright lights and roaring darkness. Ma moved off to one side and stared down, a thousand feet.

i knew she wanted to jump.

then suddenly, she pointed at something. look, Ev, she said. a rainbow!

Shane and Darlene came running over, climbing up on the guard-rail but they couldn't see nothing. neither could Daddy.

a few hours later, somewhere outside of Flagstaff i told them i saw that rainbow too. it wasn't just Ma who saw it. i saw it too. Shane and Darlene were asleep now. Ma didn't say nothing. we drove on deeper into the night. then Daddy looked at me. i could see his eyes in the rear view mirror. hovering there in the blackness. "there's no such thing as a rainbow at night," he said. "not a real rainbow anyway."

the next day at dusk we camped on high ground. from where i stood looking down, you could see all the layers of sediment carved in the side of the mountains they cleared away for the highways a long time ago. red, black, brown, white, and sometimes almost blue, like a human vein in the side of a mountain, running parallel to the horizon. i stood there a long time, watching all the layers of earthen rainbows darkening all around me. then slowly, i noticed something. in the far distance, a cluster of fallen stars. only, it wasn't a cluster of stars, but a town. far off the highway, down there in the middle of nowhere. you wouldn't even notice it by day. but at night you could see something. twinkling. i imagined i'd been born in that town, and that that was where we was all heading back to. not Disneyland. but that town shining with tiny stars that weren't really stars, surrounded by rainbows that weren't really rainbows. but erosion. as far as the eye could see. for thousands and thousands of years. both real and imaginary. like that town down there in the valley at night. just barely shimmering. like . . . Eden.

(*We hear the sound of their car start and drive off into the night. Clay in mask with gun still in mouth and Evalana slowly turn to watch the vehicle go, converging closer together as they walk and watch. "Jesse" has driven off into the night. once the sound of the car has faded into the distance, Clay in mask with gun in mouth and Evalana slowly turn to one another. after a moment, Evalana reaches up and removes the gun from Clay's mouth and slowly points it at him.*

Fade to black.)

END OF PLAY

Jane Martin

Pomp and Circumstance 1995

The identity of Jane Martin is a closely guarded secret. No biographical details, public statements, or photographs of this Kentucky-based playwright have been published, nor has she given any interviews or made any public appearances. Often called "America's best known, unknown playwright," Martin first came to public notice in 1981 for Talking With, *a collection of monologues that received a number of productions worldwide and won a Best Foreign Play of the Year award in Germany. Of Martin's many plays, others include* What Mama Don't Know *(1988),* Cementville *(1991),* Keely and Du *(which was a finalist for the 1993 Pulitzer Prize),* Middle-Aged White Guys *(1995),* Jack and Jill *(1996),* Mr. Bundy *(1998),* Anton in Show Business *(2000),* Flaming Guns of the Purple Sage *(2001),* Beauty *(2001), and* Good Boys *(2002). Her most recent work is* Sez She *(2005), a monologue play for five actresses.*

THE CAST

King
Composer

TIME

18th Century, perhaps

PLACE

A throne room

> *A king. He waits. He does accounts. A musician enters. He kneels. The king looks up.*

King: Ah. Didn't see you come in. You're a . . .
Composer: Bachweist, your Majesty.
King: Ah. You wouldn't know anything about ships' keels, would you?
Composer: Keels, your Majesty?
King: Keels. What it costs to build one, more specifically?
Composer: I know nothing of keels, your majesty.
King: Nor do I. Nor does any generalist. Do you know what a millwright does or how many a country ought to have?
Composer: It is beyond me, your Majesty.
King: Of course it is, and you are doubtless an intelligent man. (*A pause.*) You are an intelligent man?
Composer: Of a sort, your Majesty.
King: Exactly. Of a sort. As am I. My intelligence has to do with power, and yours has to do with . . . ?

Composer: Harmonics, your Majesty.

King: Really? Oh, yes, you're Bachweist. Well, Bachweist, power in the end has to do with the treasury. I'm the King, you see, I dispense. And if I'm cagey about it, the key people stay indebted, and the monarchy thrives. Dispensing, however, isn't easy because it's all value judgments. Millwrights, Bachweist, who are they and what should I put down for them? I could find out, of course, I have advisors, but advisors, Bachweist, have agendas . . . agendas. There is no such thing, Bachweist, as objective advice, and there is never enough money . . . I'm sure you understand?

Composer: Yes, your Majesty.

King: I see I've left you groveling. Please rise if you'd be more comfortable.

Composer: If you don't mind.

King: They say you're a genius, Bachweist. Are you?

Composer: Yes, your Majesty.

King: Ah. What is that?

Composer: A genius?

King: How does one know? That you are, I mean?

Composer: One's work surpasses all expectations. It is nonpareil. Logic cannot explain it. It is beyond definition.

King: Like a millwright. I'm quite hostile toward anything I can't define, Bachweist. It's one of the problems I've always had with music. Plus, it never fits in with my mood, whereas everything else, certainly every*one* else, does if he/she has any sense. Anything that doesn't accommodate me, opposes me. You catch my drift? Well, this is all bullshit isn't it, Bachweist? The point is I need a court composer. Austria has one. Lichtenstein has one. Budapest has one. I mustn't be caught short. People feel more comfortable with power if it has taste. You're available, I take it?

Composer: I would be . . . honored.

King: Of course you would. Go ahead, sell yourself.

Composer: Your Majesty?

King: Sell yourself. Sell yourself, man. We've only got ten minutes here before the millwrights.

Composer (A set piece): At two, my father put down his French horn and I, picking it up, played by ear the exercises he had struggled with by the fire. At four, I composed my "30 Etudes for Piano and Violin." At five, my first symphony. At seven, I was presented on violin with the Imperial orchestra. At nine, I toured Europe giving concerts of my own work before nine heads of state, three kings, two queens, and a parliamentary democracy. At fourteen, I completed an opera that brought a convention of musicologists screaming to their feet and, in my maturity, am a recognized master of sixteen instruments, have thirty-one published symphonies, have performed in twenty-three nations, and have been offered astonishing fees at stud. To put it briefly.

King (Applauding lightly): Well done, Bachweist. And what can you do for me?

Composer: I can make you immortal.

King: Already been taken care of.

Composer: I can delight you.

King: Kings don't delight, Bachweist, children delight.

Composer: I can carry you away on gossamer wings of melody.

King: Bachweist, you better kneel down again. *(He does.)* I'm not interested in your talent, man, it's peripheral to the real business of governing, or even living for that matter. Oh, it's useful with women, but my position is a stronger aphrodisiac than that. Only other musicians could possibly be interested in music in any meaningful way. And critics, of course, as a way of making a reputation. No, Bachweist, what I want from you is the following: a few ceremonial pieces on demand, hummable, naturally. A printable paragraph on my respect for and understanding of art. Some good groveling to make clear my position, and a resolute and articulated belief that you haven't been censored in anyway. Satire might sometime be a problem, Bachweist, but that's beyond the province of serious music, in any case. But this is trifling. You're eccentric, I hope? I hear you're eccentric?

Composer: I have been so described, your Majesty.

King: Really kinky?

Composer: Pit bulls, your Majesty.

King (Impressed): First rate, by God! You're well dressed, Bachweist, that's a drawback.

Composer: I compose wearing only a codpiece made from the hearts of salamanders.

King: Now, we're getting somewhere. Food?

Composer: The skin of cucumbers.

King: Sleep?

Composer: Never, your Majesty.

King: Living arrangement?

Composer: I prefer to pass the evening inside a freshly killed horse.

King: Are these inclinations, Bachweist?

Composer: They are necessary to a career in the arts.

King: Quite so. A nation needs distraction, Bachweist. If the populace seriously thought about the situation we find ourselves in they would go mad. This is the role of the artist. A bourgeois artist would be as useless as the ox coccyges. You don't mind dying young?

Composer: It's expected.

King: The suicide of a great artist is the creme de la creme of distraction. How would you do it?

Composer: I would publicly eat, over the period of one month, a large civic statue of no distinction.

King: Very distracting.

Composer: I hope so, your Majesty.

King: Compensation?

Composer: Beyond my wildest dreams.

King: That won't be much. You won't be wanting me to appreciate you, will you?

Composer: I do without.

King (Holding out his hand): Good choice. *(Bachweist takes it.)* We'll have a proclamation out presently.

Composer: Do you find power satisfactory, your Majesty?

King: Only when I consider the alternatives. And art?

Composer: It's a fraud, Majesty, but someone has to do it.

King: I know exactly what you mean. Well, time for the wheelwrights. I suppose for form's sake I ought to hear you play something. Something short.

Composer: I would be honored.

King: Of course you would. You won't mind if I work?

Composer: Pay no attention.

King: You're a useful luxury, Bachweist. Play away.

(Bachweist raises his violin and begins to play superbly. The king eyes him icily.)

King: Thrilling.

(Bachweist plays on dramatically. The king opens his account book and works. A moment. Lights out.)

END OF PLAY

Brighde Mullins

Click

2001

Brighde Mullins (b. 1963) was born into a military family at Camp Lejeune, North Carolina, and was raised in Las Vegas, Nevada. Her plays have been developed and produced in New York, Dallas, Salt Lake City, London, Los Angeles, and San Francisco. Her full-length plays include The Bourgeois Pig; Rare Bird; Those Who Can, Do; Monkey in the Middle; Teach; Fire Eater; Topographical Eden; *and* Increase. Click, *her darkly comic one-act play, was commissioned by the Actors Theatre of Louisville for the 2001 Humana Festival. Her awards include a Guggenheim Fellowship in Playwriting, a United States Artists Fellowship in Literature, a Whiting Foundation*

Brighde Mullins

Award, a Gold Medal from the Pinter Review, and an NEA Fellowship, and her book of poems, Water Stories (2003), was nominated for a Pushcart Prize. She has taught at Brown University and was the Director of Creative Writing at Harvard (where she was also a Briggs-Copeland Lecturer in Playwriting). Presently Mullins teaches at the University of Southern California, where she directs the Master of Professional Writing Program. She also teaches in the Theatre Department at the University of California, Santa Barbara. Mullins lives in Los Angeles.

CHARACTERS

Man
Woman

SCENE. *Dark stage. The low hum of a bad phone connection over thousands of miles. The voices of a Man and a Woman are heard; they are in the middle of a conversation.*

Man: —what are you doing?
Woman: Doing?
Man: While you're talking to me. I hear something. What are you doing?
Woman: What does it sound like?
Man: Click—click—click
Woman (*in a rush, in one breath*): Oh—that click?—it's the window blind in a breeze, a slight breeze, it's me unsnapping my tortoise shell barrette, I clipped and unclipped it, it's my Italian lighter lighting up my last blonde gauloise, it's some cheap Christmas trash racketing its way down the street, it's my birthstone ring hitting the floor, it's a bird's beak tapping, it's Morse code, it's an urgent message we can't decipher but need to know, it's the deadbolt on the back-door, it's the heater clacking into action, it's the clock stuck on One, One, One, it's a glitch on the wires, it's the loose jawbone that clicks in my head from where I took a fall on the ice last winter. It's my nailclipper.
Man: I'm really sick of your metaphors.
Woman: You used to like my turns of phrase.
Man: That was before I started re-hab.
Woman: Recovery takes the Poetry out of Things, huh?
Man: At a nickel a minute from a payphone in a drafty corridor, yeah. I'd say so.

(*slight beat*)

Yeah. It's all just words.
Woman: That's all we have right now, isn't it? You're two thousand miles away and we're reduced to Words, Right?

Man: Yeah. I guess so.

Woman: So the corridor is drafty.

Man: Yeah.

Woman: What color are the walls?

Man: Green.

Woman: Make me see the green.

Man: Greenish.

Woman: A brown green or a yellow green?

Man: Cocktail olive green. Drab green. Military green.

Woman: Windows?

Man: One up high. Too small for a body to crawl through.

Woman: Describe it.

Man: High. And sideways. And there are tables, and old mouldy arm-chairs, they give off a smell like sweat and urine—or maybe it's like old cheese—

Woman: Brie?

Man: Cracker Barrel—sharp and sickly—and there are magazines, lots of them. Piles of old *National Geographics*. And God all of this and talking to you and "this is like" and "this is like." "Nothing" is "Like Anything" except that I could use something like a drink.

(sound in: CLICK)

Man: There's that click again. Are you opening a beer?

Woman (momentary pause): I'm opening a SODA.

Man: You're drinking beer! You're drinking beer while I'm calling you from rehab?

Woman: I understand how very difficult this is for you, and I'm talking to you and I'm trying to be supportive. I would never drink a beer while talking to you.

(pause)

It's a lite beer. It's practically a soda.

Man: A *lite* beer? I have to go.

Woman: Wait. That was a Metaphor—

(SOUND IN: Click. Dead Wire)

Hullo? Hey? Hey.

END PLAY

August Wilson

Fences 1985

August Wilson (1945–2005) was born in Pittsburgh,
one of six children of a German American father and an
African American mother. His parents separated early,
and the young Wilson was raised on the Hill, a Pittsburgh ghetto neighborhood. Although he quit school in
the ninth grade when a teacher wrongly accused him of
submitting a ghost-written paper, Wilson continued his
education in local libraries, supporting himself by working as a cook and stock clerk. In 1968 he co-founded
a community troupe, the Black Horizons Theater,
staging plays by LeRoi Jones and other militants; later
he moved from Pittsburgh to Saint Paul, Minnesota,

August Wilson

where at last he saw a play of his own performed. Jitney, his first important work, won
him entry to a 1982 playwrights' conference at the Eugene O'Neill Theater Center.
There, Lloyd Richards, dean of Yale University School of Drama, took an interest in
Wilson's work and offered to produce his plays at Yale. Ma Rainey's Black Bottom
was the first to reach Broadway (in 1985), where it ran for ten months and received an
award from the New York Drama Critics Circle. In 1987 Fences, starring Mary Alice
and James Earl Jones, won another Critics Circle Award, as well as a Tony Award
and the Pulitzer Prize for best American play of its year. It set a box office record for
a Broadway nonmusical. Joe Turner's Come and Gone (1988) also received high
acclaim, and The Piano Lesson (1990) won Wilson a second Pulitzer Prize. His
subsequent plays were Two Trains Running (1992), Seven Guitars (1995), King
Hedley II (2000), Gem of the Ocean (2003), and Radio Golf (2005).

    Wilson's ten plays, each one set in a different decade of the 1900s, constitute his
"Century Cycle" that traces the black experience in America throughout the twentieth
century. Seamlessly interweaving realistic and mythic approaches, filled with vivid characters, pungent dialogue, and strong dramatic scenes, it is one of the most ambitious
projects in the history of the American theater and an epic achievement in our literature.
Wilson died of liver cancer in October 2005, a few months after completing the final
play in his cycle. Two weeks after his death the Virginia Theater on Broadway was re-
named the August Wilson Theater in his honor. A published poet as well as a dramatist,
Wilson once told an interviewer, "After writing poetry for twenty-one years, I approach
a play the same way. The mental process is poetic: you use metaphor and condense."

For Lloyd Richards, Who Adds to Whatever He Touches

> When the sins of our fathers visit us
> We do not have to play host.
> We can banish them with forgiveness
> As God, in His Largeness and Laws.

—AUGUST WILSON

LIST OF CHARACTERS

Troy Maxson
Jim Bono, Troy's friend
Rose, Troy's wife
Lyons, Troy's oldest son by previous marriage
Gabriel, Troy's brother
Cory, Troy and Rose's son
Raynell, Troy's daughter

SETTING. *The setting is the yard which fronts the only entrance to the Maxson household, an ancient two-story brick house set back off a small alley in a big-city neighborhood. The entrance to the house is gained by two or three steps leading to a wooden porch badly in need of paint.*

A relatively recent addition to the house and running its full width, the porch lacks congruence. It is a sturdy porch with a flat roof. One or two chairs of dubious value sit at one end where the kitchen window opens onto the porch. An old-fashioned icebox stands silent guard at the opposite end.

The yard is a small dirt yard, partially fenced, except for the last scene, with a wooden saw horse, a pile of lumber, and other fence-building equipment set off to the side. Opposite is a tree from which hangs a ball made of rags. A baseball bat leans against the tree. Two oil drums serve as garbage receptacles and sit near the house at right to complete the setting.

THE PLAY. *Near the turn of the century, the destitute of Europe sprang on the city with tenacious claws and an honest and solid dream. The city devoured them. They swelled its belly until it burst into a thousand furnaces and sewing machines, a thousand butcher shops and bakers' ovens, a thousand churches and hospitals and funeral parlors and money-lenders. The city grew. It nourished itself and offered each man a partnership limited only by his talent, his guile, and his willingness and capacity for hard work. For the immigrants of Europe, a dream dared and won true.*

The descendants of African slaves were offered no such welcome or participation. They came from places called the Carolinas and the Virginias, Georgia, Alabama, Mississippi, and Tennessee. They came strong, eager, searching. The city rejected them and they fled and settled along the riverbanks and under bridges in shallow, ramshackle houses made of sticks and tarpaper. They collected rags and wood. They sold the use of their muscles and their bodies. They cleaned houses and washed clothes, they shined shoes, and in quiet desperation and vengeful pride, they stole, and lived in pursuit of their own dream. That they could breathe free, finally, and stand to meet life with the force of dignity and whatever eloquence the heart could call upon.

By 1957, the hard-won victories of the European immigrants had solidified the industrial might of America. War had been confronted and won with new energies that used loyalty and patriotism as its fuel. Life was rich, full, and flourishing. The Milwaukee Braves won the World Series, and the hot winds of change that would make the sixties a turbulent, racing, dangerous, and provocative decade had not yet begun to blow full.

ACT I

SCENE I

It is 1957. Troy and Bono enter the yard, engaged in conversation. Troy is fifty-three years old, a large man with thick, heavy hands; it is this largeness that he strives to fill out and make an accommodation with. Together with his blackness, his largeness informs his sensibilities and the choices he has made in his life.

Of the two men, Bono is obviously the follower. His commitment to their friendship of thirty-odd years is rooted in his admiration of Troy's honesty, capacity for hard work, and his strength, which Bono seeks to emulate.

It is Friday night, payday, and the one night of the week the two men engage in a ritual of talk and drink. Troy is usually the most talkative and at times he can be crude and almost vulgar, though he is capable of rising to profound heights of expression. The men carry lunch buckets and wear or carry burlap aprons and are dressed in clothes suitable to their jobs as garbage collectors.

Bono: Troy, you ought to stop that lying!

Troy: I ain't lying! The nigger had a watermelon this big. (*He indicates with his hands.*) Talking about . . . "What watermelon, Mr. Rand?" I liked to fell out! "What watermelon, Mr. Rand?" . . . And it sitting there big as life.

Bono: What did Mr. Rand say?

Troy: Ain't said nothing. Figure if the nigger too dumb to know he carrying a watermelon, he wasn't gonna get much sense out of him. Trying to hide that great big old watermelon under his coat. Afraid to let the white man see him carry it home.

Bono: I'm like you . . . I ain't got no time for them kind of people.

Troy: Now what he look like getting mad cause he see the man from the union talking to Mr. Rand?

Bono: He come to me talking about . . . "Maxson gonna get us fired." I told him to get away from me with that. He walked away from me calling you a troublemaker. What Mr. Rand say?

Troy: Ain't said nothing. He told me to go down the Commissioner's office next Friday. They called me down there to see them.

Bono: Well, as long as you got your complaint filed, they can't fire you. That's what one of them white fellows tell me.

Mary Alice, Ray Aranha, and James Earl Jones in Yale Repertory Theatre's 1985 world premiere of *Fences*.

Troy: I ain't worried about them firing me. They gonna fire me cause I asked a question? That's all I did. I went to Mr. Rand and asked him, "Why? Why you got the white mens driving and the colored lifting?" Told him, "what's the matter, don't I count? You think only white fellows got sense enough to drive a truck. That ain't no paper job! Hell, anybody can drive a truck. How come you got all whites driving and the colored lifting?" He told me "take it to the union." Well, hell, that's what I done! Now they wanna come up with this pack of lies.

Bono: I told Brownie if the man come and ask him any questions . . . just tell the truth! It ain't nothing but something they done trumped up on you cause you filed a complaint on them.

Troy: Brownie don't understand nothing. All I want them to do is change the job description. Give everybody a chance to drive the truck. Brownie can't see that. He ain't got that much sense.

Bono: How you figure he be making out with that gal be up at Taylors' all the time . . . that Alberta gal?

Troy: Same as you and me. Getting just as much as we is. Which is to say nothing.

Bono: It is, huh? I figure you doing a little better than me . . . and I ain't saying what I'm doing.

Troy: Aw, nigger, look here . . . I know you. If you had got anywhere near that gal, twenty minutes later you be looking to tell somebody. And the first one you gonna tell . . . that you gonna want to brag to . . . is gonna be me.

Viola Davis and Denzel Washington in the 2010 Broadway production of *Fences*.

Bono: I ain't saying that. I see where you be eyeing her.

Troy: I eye all the women. I don't miss nothing. Don't never let nobody tell you Troy Maxson don't eye the women.

Bono: You been doing more than eyeing her. You done bought her a drink or two.

Troy: Hell yeah, I bought her a drink! What that mean? I bought you one, too. What that mean cause I buy her a drink? I'm just being polite.

Bono: It's alright to buy her one drink. That's what you call being polite. But when you wanna be buying two or three . . . . that's what you call eyeing her.

Troy: Look here, as long as you known me . . . you ever known me to chase after women?

Bono: Hell yeah! Long as I done known you. You forgetting I knew you when.

Troy: Naw, I'm talking about since I been married to Rose?

Bono: Oh, not since you been married to Rose. Now, that's the truth, there. I can say that.

Troy: Alright then! Case closed.

Bono: I see you be walking up around Alberta's house. You supposed to be at Taylors' and you be walking up around there.

Troy: What you watching where I'm walking for? I ain't watching after you.

Bono: I seen you walking around there more than once.

Troy: Hell, you liable to see me walking anywhere! That don't mean nothing cause you see me walking around there.

Bono: Where she come from anyway? She just kinda showed up one day.

Troy: Tallahassee. You can look at her and tell she one of them Florida gals. They got some big healthy women down there. Grow them right up out the ground. Got a little bit of Indian in her. Most of them niggers down in Florida got some Indian in them.

Bono: I don't know about that Indian part. But she damn sure big and healthy. Woman wear some big stockings. Got them great big old legs and hips as wide as the Mississippi River.

Troy: Legs don't mean nothing. You don't do nothing but push them out of the way. But them hips cushion the ride!

Bono: Troy, you ain't got no sense.

Troy: It's the truth! Like you riding on Goodyears!

(*Rose enters from the house. She is ten years younger than Troy, her devotion to him stems from her recognition of the possibilities of her life without him: a succession of abusive men and their babies, a life of partying and running the streets, the Church, or aloneness with its attendant pain and frustration. She recognizes Troy's spirit as a fine and illuminating one and she either ignores or forgives his faults, only some of which she recognizes. Though she doesn't drink, her presence is an integral part of the Friday night rituals. She alternates between the porch and the kitchen, where supper preparations are under way.*)

Rose: What you all out here getting into?

Troy: What you worried about what we getting into for? This is men talk, woman.

Rose: What I care what you all talking about? Bono, you gonna stay for supper?

Bono: No, I thank you, Rose. But Lucille say she cooking up a pot of pigfeet.

Troy: Pigfeet! Hell, I'm going home with you! Might even stay the night if you got some pigfeet. You got something in there to top them pigfeet, Rose?

Rose: I'm cooking up some chicken. I got some chicken and collard greens.

Troy: Well, go on back in the house and let me and Bono finish what we was talking about. This is men talk. I got some talk for you later. You know what kind of talk I mean. You go on and powder it up.

Rose: Troy Maxson, don't you start that now!

Troy (puts his arm around her): Aw, woman . . . come here. Look here, Bono . . . when I met this woman . . . I got out that place, say, "Hitch up my pony, saddle up my mare . . . there's a woman out there for me somewhere. I looked here. Looked there. Saw Rose and latched on to her." I latched on to her and told her—I'm gonna tell you the truth—I told her, "Baby,

I don't wanna marry, I just wanna be your man." Rose told me . . . tell him what you told me, Rose.

Rose: I told him if he wasn't the marrying kind, then move out the way so the marrying kind could find me.

Troy: That's what she told me. "Nigger, you in my way. You blocking the view! Move out the way so I can find me a husband." I thought it over two or three days. Come back—

Rose: Ain't no two or three days nothing. You was back the same night.

Troy: Come back, told her . . . "Okay, baby . . . but I'm gonna buy me a banty rooster and put him out there in the backyard . . . and when he see a stranger come, he'll flap his wings and crow . . ." Look here, Bono, I could watch the front door by myself . . . it was that back door I was worried about.

Rose: Troy, you ought not talk like that. Troy ain't doing nothing but telling a lie.

Troy: Only thing is . . . when we first got married . . . forget the rooster . . . we ain't had no yard!

Bono: I hear you tell it. Me and Lucille was staying down there on Logan Street. Had two rooms with the outhouse in the back. I ain't mind the outhouse none. But when that goddamn wind blow through there in the winter . . . that's what I'm talking about! To this day I wonder why in the hell I ever stayed down there for six long years. But see, I didn't know I could do no better. I thought only white folks had inside toilets and things.

Rose: There's a lot of people don't know they can do no better than they doing now. That's just something you got to learn. A lot of folks still shop at Bella's.

Troy: Ain't nothing wrong with shopping at Bella's. She got fresh food.

Rose: I ain't said nothing about if she got fresh food. I'm talking about what she charge. She charge ten cents more than the A&P.

Troy: The A&P ain't never done nothing for me. I spends my money where I'm treated right. I go down to Bella, say, "I need a loaf of bread, I'll pay you Friday." She give it to me. What sense that make when I got money to go and spend it somewhere else and ignore the person who done right by me? That ain't in the Bible.

Rose: We ain't talking about what's in the Bible. What sense it make to shop there when she overcharge?

Troy: You shop where you want to. I'll do my shopping where the people been good to me.

Rose: Well, I don't think it's right for her to overcharge. That's all I was saying.

Bono: Look here . . . I got to get on. Lucille going be raising all kind of hell.

Troy: Where you going, nigger? We ain't finished this pint. Come here, finish this pint.

Bono: Well, hell, I am . . . if you ever turn the bottle loose.

Troy (hands him the bottle): The only thing I say about the A&P is I'm glad Cory got that job down there. Help him take care of his school clothes and things. Gabe done moved out and things getting tight around here. He got that job . . . He can start to look out for himself.

Rose: Cory done went and got recruited by a college football team.

Troy: I told that boy about that football stuff. The white man ain't gonna let him get nowhere with that football. I told him when he first come to me with it. Now you come telling me he done went and got more tied up in it. He ought to go and get recruited in how to fix cars or something where he can make a living.

Rose: He ain't talking about making no living playing football. It's just something the boys in school do. They gonna send a recruiter by to talk to you. He'll tell you he ain't talking about making no living playing football. It's a honor to be recruited.

Troy: It ain't gonna get him nowhere. Bono'll tell you that.

Bono: If he be like you in the sports . . . he's gonna be alright. Ain't but two men ever played baseball as good as you. That's Babe Ruth and Josh Gibson.° Them's the only two men ever hit more home runs than you.

Troy: What it ever get me? Ain't got a pot to piss in or a window to throw it out of.

Rose: Times have changed since you was playing baseball, Troy. That was before the war. Times have changed a lot since then.

Troy: How in hell they done changed?

Rose: They got lots of colored boys playing ball now. Baseball and football.

Bono: You right about that, Rose. Times have changed, Troy. You just come along too early.

Troy: There ought not never have been no time called too early! Now you take that fellow . . . what's that fellow they had playing right field for the Yankees back then? You know who I'm talking about, Bono. Used to play right field for the Yankees.

Rose: Selkirk?°

Troy: Selkirk! That's it! Man batting .269, understand? .269. What kind of sense that make? I was hitting .432 with thirty-seven home runs! Man batting .269 and playing right field for the Yankees! I saw Josh Gibson's daughter yesterday. She walking around with raggedy shoes on her feet. Now I bet you Selkirk's daughter ain't walking around with raggedy shoes on her feet! I bet you that!

Josh Gibson: legendary catcher in the Negro Leagues whose batting average and home-run totals far outstripped Major League records; he died of a stroke at age 35 in January 1947, three months before Jackie Robinson's debut with the Brooklyn Dodgers.   *Selkirk:* Andy Selkirk, Yankee outfielder who hit .269 in 118 games in 1940.

Rose: They got a lot of colored baseball players now. Jackie Robinson° was the first. Folks had to wait for Jackie Robinson.

Troy: I done seen a hundred niggers play baseball better than Jackie Robinson. Hell, I know some teams Jackie Robinson couldn't even make! What you talking about Jackie Robinson. Jackie Robinson wasn't nobody. I'm talking about if you could play ball then they ought to have let you play. Don't care what color you were. Come telling me I come along too early. If you could play . . . then they ought to have let you play.

(Troy takes a long drink from the bottle.)

Rose: You gonna drink yourself to death. You don't need to be drinking like that.

Troy: Death ain't nothing. I done seen him. Done wrassled with him. You can't tell me nothing about death. Death ain't nothing but a fastball on the outside corner. And you know what I'll do to that! Lookee here, Bono . . . am I lying? You get one of them fastballs, about waist high, over the outside corner of the plate where you can get the meat of the bat on it . . . and good god! You can kiss it goodbye. Now, am I lying?

Bono: Naw, you telling the truth there. I seen you do it.

Troy: If I'm lying . . . that 450 feet worth of lying! *(Pause.)* That's all death is to me. A fastball on the outside corner.

Rose: I don't know why you want to get on talking about death.

Troy: Ain't nothing wrong with talking about death. That's part of life. Everybody gonna die. You gonna die, I'm gonna die. Bono's gonna die. Hell, we all gonna die.

Rose: But you ain't got to talk about it. I don't like to talk about it.

Troy: You the one brought it up. Me and Bono was talking about baseball . . . you tell me I'm gonna drink myself to death. Ain't that right, Bono? You know I don't drink this but one night out of the week. That's Friday night. I'm gonna drink just enough to where I can handle it. Then I cuts it loose. I leave it alone. So don't you worry about me drinking myself to death. 'Cause I ain't worried about Death. I done seen him. I done wrestled with him.

Look here, Bono . . . I looked up one day and Death was marching straight at me. Like Soldiers on Parade! The Army of Death was marching straight at me. The middle of July, 1941. It got real cold just like it be winter. It seem like Death himself reached out and touched me on the shoulder. He touch me just like I touch you. I got cold as ice and Death standing there grinning at me.

Rose: Troy, why don't you hush that talk.

Jackie Robinson: the first African American to play in Major League Baseball, joined the Brooklyn Dodgers in 1947.

Troy: I say . . . what you want, Mr. Death? You be wanting me? You done brought your army to be getting me? I looked him dead in the eye. I wasn't fearing nothing. I was ready to tangle. Just like I'm ready to tangle now. The Bible say be ever vigilant. That's why I don't get but so drunk. I got to keep watch.

Rose: Troy was right down there in Mercy Hospital. You remember he had pneumonia? Laying there with a fever talking plumb out of his head.

Troy: Death standing there staring at me . . . carrying that sickle in his hand. Finally he say, "You want bound over for another year?" See, just like that . . . "You want bound over for another year?" I told him, "Bound over hell! Let's settle this now!"

It seem like he kinda fell back when I said that, and all the cold went out of me. I reached down and grabbed that sickle and threw it just as far as I could throw it . . . and me and him commenced to wrestling.

We wrestled for three days and three nights. I can't say where I found the strength from. Everytime it seemed like he was gonna get the best of me, I'd reach way down deep inside myself and find the strength to do him one better.

Rose: Every time Troy tell that story he find different ways to tell it. Different things to make up about it.

Troy: I ain't making up nothing. I'm telling you the facts of what happened. I wrestled with Death for three days and three nights and I'm standing here to tell you about it. *(Pause.)* Alright. At the end of the third night we done weakened each other to where we can't hardly move. Death stood up, throwed on his robe . . . had him a white robe with a hood on it. He throwed on that robe and went off to look for his sickle. Say, "I'll be back." Just like that. "I'll be back." I told him, say, "Yeah, but . . . you gonna have to find me!" I wasn't no fool. I wasn't going looking for him. Death ain't nothing to play with. And I know he's gonna get me. I know I got to join his army . . . his camp followers. But as long as I keep my strength and see him coming . . . as long as I keep up my vigilance . . . he's gonna have to fight to get me. I ain't going easy.

Bono: Well, look here, since you got to keep up your vigilance . . . let me have the bottle.

Troy: Aw hell, I shouldn't have told you that part. I should have left out that part.

Rose: Troy be talking that stuff and half the time don't even know what he be talking about.

Troy: Bono know me better than that.

Bono: That's right. I know you. I know you got some Uncle Remus in your blood. You got more stories than the devil got sinners.

Troy: Aw hell, I done seen him too! Done talked with the devil.

Rose: Troy, don't nobody wanna be hearing all that stuff.

(Lyons enters the yard from the street. Thirty-four years old, Troy's son by a previous marriage, he sports a neatly trimmed goatee, sport coat, white shirt, tieless and buttoned at the collar. Though he fancies himself a musician, he is more caught up in the rituals and "idea" of being a musician than in the actual practice of the music. He has come to borrow money from Troy, and while he knows he will be successful, he is uncertain as to what extent his lifestyle will be held up to scrutiny and ridicule.)

Lyons: Hey, Pop.

Troy: What you come "Hey, Popping" me for?

Lyons: How you doing, Rose? *(He kisses her.)* Mr. Bono. How you doing?

Bono: Hey, Lyons . . . how you been?

Troy: He must have been doing alright. I ain't seen him around here last week.

Rose: Troy, leave your boy alone. He come by to see you and you wanna start all that nonsense.

Troy: I ain't bothering Lyons. *(Offers him the bottle.)* Here . . . get you a drink. We got an understanding. I know why he come by to see me and he know I know.

Lyons: Come on, Pop . . . I just stopped by to say hi . . . see how you was doing.

Troy: You ain't stopped by yesterday.

Rose: You gonna stay for supper, Lyons? I got some chicken cooking in the oven.

Lyons: No, Rose . . . thanks. I was just in the neighborhood and thought I'd stop by for a minute.

Troy: You was in the neighborhood alright, nigger. You telling the truth there. You was in the neighborhood cause it's my payday.

Lyons: Well, hell, since you mentioned it . . . let me have ten dollars.

Troy: I'll be damned! I'll die and go to hell and play blackjack with the devil before I give you ten dollars.

Bono: That's what I wanna know about . . . that devil you done seen.

Lyons: What . . . Pop done seen the devil? You too much, Pops.

Troy: Yeah, I done seen him. Talked to him too!

Rose: You ain't seen no devil. I done told you that man ain't had nothing to do with the devil. Anything you can't understand, you want to call it the devil.

Troy: Look here, Bono . . . I went down to see Hertzberger about some furniture. Got three rooms for two-ninety-eight. That what it say on the radio. "Three rooms . . . two-ninety-eight." Even made up a little song about it. Go down there . . . man tell me I can't get no credit. I'm working every day and can't get no credit. What to do? I got an empty house with some raggedy furniture in it. Cory ain't got no bed. He's sleeping on a pile of rags on the floor. Working every day and can't get no credit. Come back here—Rose'll tell you—madder than hell. Sit down . . . try to figure what I'm gonna do. Come a knock on the door. Ain't been living here but three days. Who know I'm here? Open the door . . . devil standing there bigger than life. White fellow . . . got on good clothes and everything. Standing there with a clipboard in his hand. I ain't had to say nothing. First words come out of his mouth was . . . "I understand you need some furniture and can't get no credit." I liked to fell over. He say "I'll give you all the credit you want, but you got to pay the interest on it." I told him, "Give me three rooms worth and charge whatever you want." Next day a truck pulled up here and two men unloaded them three rooms. Man what drove the truck give me a book. Say send ten dollars, first of every month to the address in the book and every thing will be alright. Say if I miss a payment the devil was coming back and it'll be hell to pay. That was fifteen years ago. To this day . . . the first of the month I send my ten dollars, Rose'll tell you.

Rose: Troy lying.

Troy: I ain't never seen that man since. Now you tell me who else that could have been but the devil? I ain't sold my soul or nothing like that, you understand. Naw, I wouldn't have truck with the devil about nothing like that. I got my furniture and pays my ten dollars the first of the month just like clockwork.

Bono: How long you say you been paying this ten dollars a month?

Troy: Fifteen years!

Bono: Hell, ain't you finished paying for it yet? How much the man done charged you?

Troy: Aw hell, I done paid for it. I done paid for it ten times over! The fact is I'm scared to stop paying it.

Rose: Troy lying. We got that furniture from Mr. Glickman. He ain't paying no ten dollars a month to nobody.

Troy: Aw hell, woman. Bono know I ain't that big a fool.

Lyons: I was just getting ready to say . . . I know where there's a bridge for sale.

Troy: Look here, I'll tell you this . . . it don't matter to me if he was the devil. It don't matter if the devil give credit. Somebody has got to give it.

Rose: It ought to matter. You going around talking about having truck with the devil . . . God's the one you gonna have to answer to. He's the one gonna be at the Judgment.

Lyons: Yeah, well, look here, Pop . . . Let me have that ten dollars. I'll give it back to you. Bonnie got a job working at the hospital.

Troy: What I tell you, Bono? The only time I see this nigger is when he wants something. That's the only time I see him.

Lyons: Come on, Pop, Mr. Bono don't want to hear all that. Let me have the ten dollars. I told you Bonnie working.

Troy: What that mean to me? "Bonnie working." I don't care if she working. Go ask her for the ten dollars if she working. Talking about "Bonnie working." Why ain't you working?

Lyons: Aw, Pop, you know I can't find no decent job. Where am I gonna get a job at? You know I can't get no job.

Troy: I told you I know some people down there. I can get you on the rubbish if you want to work. I told you that the last time you came by here asking me for something.

Lyons: Naw, Pop . . . thanks. That ain't for me. I don't wanna be carrying nobody's rubbish. I don't wanna be punching nobody's time clock.

Troy: What's the matter, you too good to carry people's rubbish? Where you think that ten dollars you talking about come from? I'm just supposed to haul people's rubbish and give my money to you cause you too lazy to work. You too lazy to work and wanna know why you ain't got what I got.

Rose: What hospital Bonnie working at? Mercy?

Lyons: She's down at Passavant working in the laundry.

Troy: I ain't got nothing as it is. I give you that ten dollars and I got to eat beans the rest of the week. Naw . . . you ain't getting no ten dollars here.

Lyons: You ain't got to be eating no beans. I don't know why you wanna say that.

Troy: I ain't got no extra money. Gabe done moved over to Miss Pearl's paying her the rent and things done got tight around here. I can't afford to be giving you every payday.

Lyons: I ain't asked you to give me nothing. I asked you to loan me ten dollars. I know you got ten dollars.

Troy: Yeah, I got it. You know why I got it? Cause I don't throw my money away out there in the streets. You living the fast life . . . wanna be a musician . . . running around in them clubs and things . . . then, you learn to take care of yourself. You ain't gonna find me going and asking nobody for nothing. I done spent too many years without.

Lyons: You and me is two different people, Pop.

Troy: I done learned my mistake and learned to do what's right by it. You still trying to get something for nothing. Life don't owe you nothing. You owe it to yourself. Ask Bono. He'll tell you I'm right.

Lyons: You got your way of dealing with the world . . . I got mine. The only thing that matters to me is the music.

Troy: Yeah, I can see that! It don't matter how you gonna eat . . . where your next dollar is coming from. You telling the truth there.

Lyons: I know I got to eat. But I got to live too. I need something that gonna help me to get out of the bed in the morning. Make me feel like I belong in the world. I don't bother nobody. I just stay with my music cause that's the only way I can find to live in the world. Otherwise there ain't no telling what I might do. Now I don't come criticizing you and how you live. I just come by to ask you for ten dollars. I don't wanna hear all that about how I live.

Troy: Boy, your mama did a hell of a job raising you.

Lyons: You can't change me, Pop. I'm thirty-four years old. If you wanted to change me, you should have been there when I was growing up. I come by to see you . . . ask for ten dollars and you want to talk about how I was raised. You don't know nothing about how I was raised.

Rose: Let the boy have ten dollars, Troy.

Troy (to Lyons): What the hell you looking at me for? I ain't got no ten dollars. You know what I do with my money. *(To Rose.)* Give him ten dollars if you want him to have it.

Rose: I will. Just as soon as you turn it loose.

Troy (handing Rose the money): There it is. Seventy-six dollars and forty-two cents. You see this, Bono? Now, I ain't gonna get but six of that back.

Rose: You ought to stop telling that lie. Here, Lyons. *(She hands him the money.)*

Lyons: Thanks, Rose. Look . . . I got to run . . . I'll see you later.

Troy: Wait a minute. You gonna say, "thanks, Rose" and ain't gonna look to see where she got that ten dollars from? See how they do me, Bono?

Lyons: I know she got it from you, Pop. Thanks. I'll give it back to you.

Troy: There he go telling another lie. Time I see that ten dollars . . . he'll be owing me thirty more.

Lyons: See you, Mr. Bono.

Bono: Take care, Lyons!

Lyons: Thanks, Pop. I'll see you again.

(Lyons exits the yard.)

Troy: I don't know why he don't go and get him a decent job and take care of that woman he got.

Bono: He'll be alright, Troy. The boy is still young.

Troy: The *boy* is thirty-four years old.

Rose: Let's not get off into all that.

Bono: Look here . . . I got to be going. I got to be getting on. Lucille gonna be waiting.

Troy (puts his arm around Rose): See this woman, Bono? I love this woman. I love this woman so much it hurts. I love her so much . . . I done run out of ways of loving her. So I got to go back to basics. Don't you come by my house Monday morning talking about time to go to work . . . 'cause I'm still gonna be stroking!

Rose: Troy! Stop it now!

Bono: I ain't paying him no mind, Rose. That ain't nothing but gin-talk. Go on, Troy. I'll see you Monday.

Troy: Don't you come by my house, nigger! I done told you what I'm gonna be doing.

(The lights go down to black.)

SCENE II

The lights come up on Rose hanging up clothes. She hums and sings softly to herself. It is the following morning.

Rose *(sings)*:

> Jesus, be a fence all around me every day
> Jesus, I want you to protect me as I travel on my way
> Jesus, be a fence all around me every day

(Troy enters from the house.)

> Jesus, I want you to protect me
> As I travel on my way

(To Troy.) 'Morning. You ready for breakfast? I can fix it soon as I finish hanging up these clothes.

Troy: I got the coffee on. That'll be alright. I'll just drink some of that this morning.

Rose: That 651 hit yesterday. That's the second time this month. Miss Pearl hit for a dollar . . . seem like those that need the least always get lucky. Poor folks can't get nothing.

Troy: Them numbers don't know nobody. I don't know why you fool with them. You and Lyons both.

Rose: It's something to do.

Troy: You ain't doing nothing but throwing your money away.

Rose: Troy, you know I don't play foolishly. I just play a nickel here and a nickel there.

Troy: That's two nickels you done thrown away.

Rose: Now I hit sometimes . . . that makes up for it. It always comes in handy when I do hit. I don't hear you complaining then.

Troy: I ain't complaining now. I just say it's foolish. Trying to guess out of six hundred ways which way the number gonna come. If I had all the money niggers, these Negroes, throw away on numbers for one week— just one week—I'd be a rich man.

Rose: Well, you wishing and calling it foolish ain't gonna stop folks from playing numbers. That's one thing for sure. Besides . . . some good things come from playing numbers. Look where Pope done bought him that restaurant off of numbers.

Troy: I can't stand niggers like that. Man ain't had two dimes to rub together. He walking around with his shoes all run over bumming money for ciga- rettes. Alright. Got lucky there and hit the numbers . . .

Rose: Troy, I know all about it.

Troy: Had good sense, I'll say that for him. He ain't throwed his money away. I seen niggers hit the numbers and go through two thousand dollars in four days. Man bought him that restaurant down there . . . fixed it up real nice . . . and then didn't want nobody to come in it! A Negro go in there and can't get no kind of service. I seen a white fellow come in there and order a bowl of stew. Pope picked all the meat out of the pot for him. Man ain't had nothing but a bowl of meat! Negro come behind him and ain't got nothing but the potatoes and carrots. Talking about what numbers do for people, you picked a wrong example. Ain't done nothing but make a worser fool out of him than he was before.

Rose: Troy, you ought to stop worrying about what happened at work yesterday.

Troy: I ain't worried. Just told me to be down there at the Commissioner's office on Friday. Everybody think they gonna fire me. I ain't worried about them firing me. You ain't got to worry about that. (*Pause.*) Where's Cory? Cory in the house? (*Calls.*) Cory?

Rose: He gone out.

Troy: Out, huh? He gone out 'cause he know I want him to help me with this fence. I know how he is. That boy scared of work.

(*Gabriel enters. He comes halfway down the alley and, hearing Troy's voice, stops.*)

Troy (continues): He ain't done a lick of work in his life.

Rose: He had to go to football practice. Coach wanted them to get in a little extra practice before the season start.

Troy: I got his practice . . . running out of here before he get his chores done.

Rose: Troy, what is wrong with you this morning? Don't nothing set right with you. Go on back in there and go to bed . . . get up on the other side.

Troy: Why something got to be wrong with me? I ain't said nothing wrong with me.

Rose: You got something to say about everything. First it's the numbers . . . then it's the way the man runs his restaurant . . . then you done got on Cory. What's it gonna be next? Take a look up there and see if the weather suits you . . . or is it gonna be how you gonna put up the fence with the clothes hanging in the yard?

Troy: You hit the nail on the head then.

Rose: I know you like I know the back of my hand. Go on in there and get you some coffee . . . see if that straighten you up. 'Cause you ain't right this morning.

(*Troy starts into the house and sees Gabriel. Gabriel starts singing. Troy's brother, he is seven years younger than Troy. Injured in World War II, he has a metal plate in his head. He carries an old trumpet tied around his waist and believes with every fiber of his being that he is the Archangel Gabriel. He carries a chipped basket with an assortment of discarded fruits and vegetables he has picked up in the Strip District and which he attempts to sell.*)

Gabriel (singing):
>> Yes, ma'am, I got plums
>> You ask me how I sell them
>> Oh ten cents apiece
>> Three for a quarter
>> Come and buy now
>> 'Cause I'm here today
>> And tomorrow I'll be gone

> *(Gabriel enters.)*

Hey, Rose!

Rose: How you doing, Gabe?

Gabriel: There's Troy . . . Hey, Troy!

Troy: Hey, Gabe.

> *(Exit into kitchen.)*

Rose (to Gabriel): What you got there?

Gabriel: You know what I got, Rose. I got fruits and vegetables.

Rose (looking in basket): Where's all these plums you talking about?

Gabriel: I ain't got no plums today, Rose. I was just singing that. Have some tomorrow. Put me in a big order for plums. Have enough plums tomorrow for St. Peter and everybody.

> *(Troy reenters from kitchen, crosses to steps.)*

> *(To Rose.)* Troy's mad at me.

Troy: I ain't mad at you. What I got to be mad at you about? You ain't done nothing to me.

Gabriel: I just moved over to Miss Pearl's to keep out from in your way. I ain't mean no harm by it.

Troy: Who said anything about that? I ain't said anything about that.

Gabriel: You ain't mad at me, is you?

Troy: Naw . . . I ain't mad at you, Gabe. If I was mad at you I'd tell you about it.

Gabriel: Got me two rooms. In the basement. Got my own door too. Wanna see my key? *(He holds up a key.)* That's my own key! Ain't nobody else got a key like that. That's my key! My two rooms!

Troy: Well, that's good, Gabe. You got your own key . . . that's good.

Rose: You hungry, Gabe? I was just fixing to cook Troy his breakfast.

Gabriel: I'll take some biscuits. You got some biscuits? Did you know when I was in heaven . . . every morning me and St. Peter would sit down by the gate and eat some big fat biscuits? Oh, yeah! We had us a good time. We'd sit there and eat us them biscuits and then St. Peter would go off to sleep and tell me to wake him up when it's time to open the gates for the judgment.

Rose: Well, come on . . . I'll make up a batch of biscuits.

(*Rose exits into the house.*)

Gabriel: Troy . . . St. Peter got your name in the book. I seen it. It say . . . Troy Maxson. I say . . . I know him! He got the same name like what I got. That's my brother!

Troy: How many times you gonna tell me that, Gabe?

Gabriel: Ain't got my name in the book. Don't have to have my name. I done died and went to heaven. He got your name though. One morning St. Peter was looking at his book . . . marking it up for the judgment . . . and he let me see your name. Got it in there under M. Got Rose's name . . . I ain't seen it like I seen yours . . . but I know it's in there. He got a great big book. Got everybody's name what was ever been born. That's what he told me. But I seen your name. Seen it with my own eyes.

Troy: Go on in the house there. Rose going to fix you something to eat.

Gabriel: Oh, I ain't hungry. I done had breakfast with Aunt Jemimah. She come by and cooked me up a whole mess of flapjacks. Remember how we used to eat them flapjacks?

Troy: Go on in the house and get you something to eat now.

Gabriel: I got to sell my plums. I done sold some tomatoes. Got me two quarters. Wanna see? (*He shows Troy his quarters.*) I'm gonna save them and buy me a new horn so St. Peter can hear me when it's time to open the gates. (*Gabriel stops suddenly. Listens.*) Hear that? That's the hell-hounds. I got to chase them out of here. Go on get out of here! Get out!

(*Gabriel exits singing.*)

> Better get ready for the judgment
> Better get ready for the judgment
> My Lord is coming down

(*Rose enters from the house.*)

Troy: He gone off somewhere.

Gabriel (*offstage*):

> Better get ready for the judgment
> Better get ready for the judgment morning
> Better get ready for the judgment
> My God is coming down

Rose: He ain't eating right. Miss Pearl say she can't get him to eat nothing.

Troy: What you want me to do about it, Rose? I done did everything I can for the man. I can't make him get well. Man got half his head blown away . . . what you expect?

Rose: Seem like something ought to be done to help him.

Troy: Man don't bother nobody. He just mixed up from that metal plate he got in his head. Ain't no sense for him to go back into the hospital.

Rose: Least he be eating right. They can help him take care of himself.

Troy: Don't nobody wanna be locked up, Rose. What you wanna lock him up for? Man go over there and fight the war . . . messin' around with them Japs, get half his head blown off . . . and they give him a lousy three thousand dollars. And I had to swoop down on that.

Rose: Is you fixing to go into that again?

Troy: That's the only way I got a roof over my head . . . cause of that metal plate.

Rose: Ain't no sense you blaming yourself for nothing. Gabe wasn't in no condition to manage that money. You done what was right by him. Can't nobody say you ain't done what was right by him. Look how long you took care of him . . . till he wanted to have his own place and moved over there with Miss Pearl.

Troy: That ain't what I'm saying, woman! I'm just stating the facts. If my brother didn't have that metal plate in his head . . . I wouldn't have a pot to piss in or a window to throw it out of. And I'm fifty-three years old. Now see if you can understand that!

(*Troy gets up from the porch and starts to exit the yard.*)

Rose: Where you going off to? You been running out of here every Saturday for weeks. I thought you was gonna work on this fence?

Troy: I'm gonna walk down to Taylors'. Listen to the ball game. I'll be back in a bit. I'll work on it when I get back.

(*He exits the yard. The lights go to black.*)

SCENE III

The lights come up on the yard. It is four hours later. Rose is taking down the clothes from the line. Cory enters carrying his football equipment.

Rose: Your daddy like to had a fit with you running out of here this morning without doing your chores.

Cory: I told you I had to go to practice.

Rose: He say you were supposed to help him with this fence.

Cory: He been saying that the last four or five Saturdays, and then he don't never do nothing, but go down to Taylors'. Did you tell him about the recruiter?

Rose: Yeah, I told him.

Cory: What he say?

Rose: He ain't said nothing too much. You get in there and get started on your chores before he gets back. Go on and scrub down them steps before he gets back here hollering and carrying on.

Cory: I'm hungry. What you got to eat, Mama?

Rose: Go on and get started on your chores. I got some meat loaf in there. Go on and make you a sandwich . . . and don't leave no mess in there.

(*Cory exits into the house. Rose continues to take down the clothes. Troy enters the yard and sneaks up and grabs her from behind.*)

Troy! Go on, now. You liked to scared me to death. What was the score of the game? Lucille had me on the phone and I couldn't keep up with it.

Troy: What I care about the game? Come here, woman. (*He tries to kiss her.*)

Rose: I thought you went down Taylors' to listen to the game. Go on, Troy! You supposed to be putting up this fence.

Troy (attempting to kiss her again): I'll put it up when I finish with what is at hand.

Rose: Go on, Troy. I ain't studying you.

Troy (chasing after her): I'm studying you . . . fixing to do my homework!

Rose: Troy, you better leave me alone.

Troy: Where's Cory? That boy brought his butt home yet?

Rose: He's in the house doing his chores.

Troy (calling): Cory! Get your butt out here, boy!

(*Rose exits into the house with the laundry. Troy goes over to the pile of wood, picks up a board, and starts sawing. Cory enters from the house.*)

Troy: You just now coming in here from leaving this morning?

Cory: Yeah, I had to go to football practice.

Troy: Yeah, what?

Cory: Yessir.

Troy: I ain't but two seconds off you noway. The garbage sitting in there overflowing . . . you ain't done none of your chores . . . and you come in here talking about "Yeah."

Cory: I was just getting ready to do my chores now, Pop . . .

Troy: Your first chore is to help me with this fence on Saturday. Everything else come after that. Now get that saw and cut them boards.

(*Cory takes the saw and begins cutting the boards. Troy continues working. There is a long pause.*)

Cory: Hey, Pop . . . why don't you buy a TV?

Troy: What I want with a TV? What I want one of them for?

Cory: Everybody got one. Earl, Ba Bra . . . Jesse!

Troy: I ain't asked you who had one. I say what I want with one?

Cory: So you can watch it. They got lots of things on TV. Baseball games and everything. We could watch the World Series.

Troy: Yeah . . . and how much this TV cost?

Cory: I don't know. They got them on sale for around two hundred dollars.

Troy: Two hundred dollars, huh?

Cory: That ain't that much, Pop.

Troy: Naw, it's just two hundred dollars. See that roof you got over your head at night? Let me tell you something about that roof. It's been over ten years since that roof was last tarred. See now . . . the snow come this winter and sit up there on that roof like it is . . . and it's gonna seep inside. It's just gonna be a little bit . . . ain't gonna hardly notice it. Then the next thing you know, it's gonna be leaking all over the house. Then the wood rot from all that water and you gonna need a whole new roof. Now, how much you think it cost to get that roof tarred?

Cory: I don't know.

Troy: Two hundred and sixty-four dollars . . . cash money. While you thinking about a TV, I got to be thinking about the roof . . . and whatever else go wrong here. Now if you had two hundred dollars, what would you do . . . fix the roof or buy a TV?

Cory: I'd buy a TV. Then when the roof started to leak . . . when it needed fixing . . . I'd fix it.

Troy: Where you gonna get the money from? You done spent it for a TV. You gonna sit up and watch the water run all over your brand new TV.

Cory: Aw, Pop. You got money. I know you do.

Troy: Where I got it at, huh?

Cory: You got it in the bank.

Troy: You wanna see my bankbook? You wanna see that seventy-three dollars and twenty-two cents I got sitting up in there?

Cory: You ain't got to pay for it all at one time. You can put a down payment on it and carry it on home with you.

Troy: Not me. I ain't gonna owe nobody nothing if I can help it. Miss a payment and they come and snatch it right out of your house. Then what you got? Now, soon as I get two hundred dollars clear, then I'll buy a TV. Right now, as soon as I get two hundred and sixty-four dollars, I'm gonna have this roof tarred.

Cory: Aw . . . Pop!

Troy: You go on and get you two hundred dollars and buy one if ya want it. I got better things to do with my money.

Cory: I can't get no two hundred dollars. I ain't never seen two hundred dollars.

Troy: I'll tell you what . . . you get you a hundred dollars and I'll put the other hundred with it.

Cory: Alright, I'm gonna show you.

Troy: You gonna show me how you can cut them boards right now.

(Cory begins to cut the boards. There is a long pause.)

Cory: The Pirates won today. That makes five in a row.

Troy: I ain't thinking about the Pirates. Got an all-white team. Got that boy
. . . that Puerto Rican boy . . . Clemente.° Don't even half-play him. That
boy could be something if they give him a chance. Play him one day and
sit him on the bench the next.

Cory: He gets a lot of chances to play.

Troy: I'm talking about playing regular. Playing every day so you can get your
timing. That's what I'm talking about.

Cory: They got some white guys on the team that don't play every day. You
can't play everybody at the same time.

Troy: If they got a white fellow sitting on the bench . . . you can bet your last
dollar he can't play! The colored guy got to be twice as good before he get
on the team. That's why I don't want you to get all tied up in them sports.
Man on the team and what it get him? They got colored on the team and
don't use them. Same as not having them. All them teams the same.

Cory: The Braves got Hank Aaron and Wes Covington. Hank Aaron hit two
home runs today. That makes forty-three.

Troy: Hank Aaron ain't nobody. That's what you supposed to do. That's how
you supposed to play the game. Ain't nothing to it. It's just a matter of
timing . . . getting the right follow-through. Hell, I can hit forty-three
home runs right now!

Cory: Not off no major-league pitching, you couldn't.

Troy: We had better pitching in the Negro leagues. I hit seven home runs off
of Satchel Paige.° You can't get no better than that!

Cory: Sandy Koufax.° He's leading the league in strikeouts.

Troy: I ain't thinking of no Sandy Koufax.

Cory: You got Warren Spahn° and Lew Burdette.° I bet you couldn't hit no
home runs off of Warren Spahn.

Troy: I'm through with it now. You go on and cut them boards. *(Pause.)* Your
mama tell me you done got recruited by a college football team? Is that right?

Cory: Yeah. Coach Zellman say the recruiter gonna be coming by to talk to
you. Get you to sign the permission papers.

Clemente: Hall of Fame outfielder Roberto Clemente, a dark-skinned Puerto Rican, played 17
seasons with the Pittsburgh Pirates.   *Satchel Paige . . . Sandy Koufax . . . Warren Spahn . . . Lew
Burdette:* The great Satchel Paige pitched many years in the Negro Leagues; beginning in 1948,
when he was in his forties and long past his prime, he appeared in nearly 200 games in the American League. Star pitchers Sandy Koufax of the Dodgers and Warren Spahn and Lew Burdette of
the Braves were all white.

Troy: I thought you supposed to be working down there at the A&P. Ain't you suppose to be working down there after school?

Cory: Mr. Stawicki say he gonna hold my job for me until after the football season. Say starting next week I can work weekends.

Troy: I thought we had an understanding about this football stuff? You suppose to keep up with your chores and hold that job down at the A&P. Ain't been around here all day on a Saturday. Ain't none of your chores done . . . and now you telling me you done quit your job.

Cory: I'm going to be working weekends.

Troy: You damn right you are! And ain't no need for nobody coming around here to talk to me about signing nothing.

Cory: Hey, Pop . . . you can't do that. He's coming all the way from North Carolina.

Troy: I don't care where he coming from. The white man ain't gonna let you get nowhere with that football noway. You go on and get your book-learning so you can work yourself up in that A&P or learn how to fix cars or build houses or something, get you a trade. That way you have something can't nobody take away from you. You go on and learn how to put your hands to some good use. Besides hauling people's garbage.

Cory: I get good grades, Pop. That's why the recruiter wants to talk with you. You got to keep up your grades to get recruited. This way I'll be going to college. I'll get a chance . . .

Troy: First you gonna get your butt down there to the A&P and get your job back.

Cory: Mr. Stawicki done already hired somebody else 'cause I told him I was playing football.

Troy: You a bigger fool than I thought . . . to let somebody take away your job so you can play some football. Where you gonna get your money to take out your girlfriend and whatnot? What kind of foolishness is that to let somebody take away your job?

Cory: I'm still gonna be working weekends.

Troy: Naw . . . naw. You getting your butt out of here and finding you another job.

Cory: Come on, Pop! I got to practice. I can't work after school and play football too. The team needs me. That's what Coach Zellman say . . .

Troy: I don't care what nobody else say. I'm the boss . . . you understand? I'm the boss around here. I do the only saying what counts.

Cory: Come on, Pop!

Troy: I asked you . . . did you understand?

Cory: Yeah . . .

Troy: What?!

Cory: Yessir.

Troy: You go on down there to that A&P and see if you can get your job back. If you can't do both . . . then you quit the football team. You've got to take the crookeds with the straights.

Cory: Yessir. *(Pause.)* Can I ask you a question?

Troy: What the hell you wanna ask me? Mr. Stawicki the one you got the questions for.

Cory: How come you ain't never liked me?

Troy: Liked you? Who the hell say I got to like you? What law is there say I got to like you? Wanna stand up in my face and ask a damn fool-ass question like that. Talking about liking somebody. Come here, boy, when I talk to you.

(Cory comes over to where Troy is working. He stands slouched over and Troy shoves him on his shoulder.)

Straighten up, goddammit! I asked you a question . . . what law is there say I got to like you?

Cory: None.

Troy: Well, alright then! Don't you eat every day? *(Pause.)* Answer me when I talk to you! Don't you eat every day?

Cory: Yeah.

Troy: Nigger, as long as you in my house, you put that sir on the end of it when you talk to me.

Cory: Yes . . . sir.

Troy: You eat every day.

Cory: Yessir!

Troy: Got a roof over your head.

Cory: Yessir!

Troy: Got clothes on your back.

Cory: Yessir.

Troy: Why you think that is?

Cory: Cause of you.

Troy: Aw, hell I know it's cause of me . . . but why do you think that is?

Cory (hesitant): 'Cause you like me.

Troy: Like you? I go out of here every morning . . . bust my butt . . . putting up with them crackers every day . . . cause I like you? You about the biggest fool I ever saw. *(Pause.)* It's my job. It's my responsibility! You understand that? A man got to take care of his family. You live in my house . . . sleep you behind on my bedclothes . . . fill you belly up with my food . . . cause you my son. You my flesh and blood. Not cause I like you! Cause it's my duty to take care of you. I owe a responsibility to you!

Let's get this straight right here . . . before it go along any further . . . I ain't got to like you. Mr. Rand don't give me my money come payday cause he likes me. He gives me cause he owe me. I done give you everything I had to give you. I gave you your life! Me and your mama worked that out between us. And liking your black ass wasn't part of the bargain. Don't you try and go through life worrying about if somebody like you or not. You best be making sure they doing right by you. You understand what I'm saying, boy?

Cory: Yessir.

Troy: Then get the hell out of my face, and get on down to that A&P.

(*Rose has been standing behind the screen door for much of the scene. She enters as Cory exits.*)

Rose: Why don't you let the boy go ahead and play football, Troy? Ain't no harm in that. He's just trying to be like you with the sports.

Troy: I don't want him to be like me! I want him to move as far away from my life as he can get. You the only decent thing that ever happened to me. I wish him that. But I don't wish him a thing else from my life. I decided seventeen years ago that boy wasn't getting involved in no sports. Not after what they did to me in the sports.

Rose: Troy, why don't you admit you was too old to play in the major leagues? For once . . . why don't you admit that?

Troy: What do you mean too old? Don't come telling me I was too old. I just wasn't the right color. Hell, I'm fifty-three years old and can do better than Selkirk's .269 right now!

Rose: How's was you gonna play ball when you were over forty? Sometimes I can't get no sense out of you.

Troy: I got good sense, woman. I got sense enough not to let my boy get hurt over playing no sports. You been mothering that boy too much. Worried about if people like him.

Rose: Everything that boy do . . . he do for you. He wants you to say "Good job, son." That's all.

Troy: Rose, I ain't got time for that. He's alive. He's healthy. He's got to make his own way. I made mine. Ain't nobody gonna hold his hand when he get out there in that world.

Rose: Times have changed from when you was young, Troy. People change. The world's changing around you and you can't even see it.

Troy (*slow, methodical*): Woman . . . I do the best I can do. I come in here every Friday. I carry a sack of potatoes and a bucket of lard. You all line up at the door with your hands out. I give you the lint from my pockets. I give you my sweat and my blood. I ain't got no tears. I done spent them. We go upstairs in that room at night . . . and I fall down on you and try to blast a hole into forever. I get up Monday morning . . . find my lunch on the table. I go out. Make my way. Find my strength to carry me through to the next Friday. (*Pause.*) That's all I got, Rose. That's all I got to give. I can't give nothing else.

(*Troy exits into the house. The lights go down to black.*)

SCENE IV

It is Friday. Two weeks later. Cory starts out of the house with his football equipment. The phone rings.

Cory *(calling):* I got it! *(He answers the phone and stands in the screen door talking.)* Hello? Hey, Jesse. Naw . . . I was just getting ready to leave now.

Rose *(calling):* Cory!

Cory: I told you, man, them spikes is all tore up. You can use them if you want, but they ain't no good. Earl got some spikes.

Rose *(calling):* Cory!

Cory *(calling to Rose):* Mam? I'm talking to Jesse. *(Into phone.)* When she say that? *(Pause.)* Aw, you lying, man. I'm gonna tell her you said that.

Rose *(calling):* Cory, don't you go nowhere!

Cory: I got to go to the game, Ma! *(Into the phone.)* Yeah, hey, look, I'll talk to you later. Yeah, I'll meet you over Earl's house. Later. Bye, Ma.

(Cory exits the house and starts out the yard.)

Rose: Cory, where you going off to? You got that stuff all pulled out and thrown all over your room.

Cory *(in the yard):* I was looking for my spikes. Jesse wanted to borrow my spikes.

Rose: Get up there and get that cleaned up before your daddy get back in here.

Cory: I got to go to the game! I'll clean it up when I get back.

(Cory exits.)

Rose: That's all he need to do is see that room all messed up.

(Rose exits into the house. Troy and Bono enter the yard. Troy is dressed in clothes other than his work clothes.)

Bono: He told him the same thing he told you. Take it to the union.

Troy: Brownie ain't got that much sense. Man wasn't thinking about nothing. He wait until I confront them on it . . . then he wanna come crying seniority. *(Calls.)* Hey, Rose!

Bono: I wish I could have seen Mr. Rand's face when he told you.

Troy: He couldn't get it out of his mouth! Liked to bit his tongue! When they called me down there to the Commissioner's office . . . he thought they was gonna fire me. Like everybody else.

Bono: I didn't think they was gonna fire you. I thought they was gonna put you on the warning paper.

Troy: Hey, Rose! *(To Bono.)* Yeah, Mr. Rand like to bit his tongue.

(Troy breaks the seal on the bottle, takes a drink, and hands it to Bono.)

Bono: I see you run right down to Taylors' and told that Alberta gal.

Troy (calling): Hey, Rose! *(To Bono.)* I told everybody. Hey, Rose! I went down there to cash my check.

Rose (entering from the house): Hush all that hollering, man! I know you out here. What they say down there at the Commissioner's office?

Troy: You supposed to come when I call you, woman. Bono'll tell you that. *(To Bono.)* Don't Lucille come when you call her?

Rose: Man, hush your mouth. I ain't no dog . . . talk about "come when you call me."

Troy (puts his arm around Rose): You hear this, Bono? I had me an old dog used to get uppity like that. You say, "C'mere, Blue!" . . . and he just lay there and look at you. End up getting a stick and chasing him away trying to make him come.

Rose: I ain't studying you and your dog. I remember you used to sing that old song.

Troy (he sings):

> Hear it ring! Hear it ring!
> I had a dog his name was Blue.

Rose: Don't nobody wanna hear you sing that old song.

Troy (sings):

> You know Blue was mighty true.

Rose: Used to have Cory running around here singing that song.

Bono: Hell, I remember that song myself.

Troy (sings):

> You know Blue was a good old dog.
> Blue treed a possum in a hollow log.

That was my daddy's song. My daddy made up that song.

Rose: I don't care who made it up. Don't nobody wanna hear you sing it.

Troy (makes a song like calling a dog): Come here, woman.

Rose: You come in here carrying on, I reckon they ain't fired you. What they say down there at the Commissioner's office?

Troy: Look here, Rose . . . Mr. Rand called me into his office today when I got back from talking to them people down there . . . it come from up top . . . he called me in and told me they was making me a driver.

Rose: Troy, you kidding!

Troy: No I ain't. Ask Bono.

Rose: Well, that's great, Troy. Now you don't have to hassle them people no more.

(Lyons enters from the street.)

Troy: Aw hell, I wasn't looking to see you today. I thought you was in jail. Got it all over the front page of the *Courier* about them raiding Sefus's place . . . where you be hanging out with all them thugs.

Lyons: Hey, Pop . . . that ain't got nothing to do with me. I don't go down
there gambling. I go down there to sit in with the band. I ain't got nothing
to do with the gambling part. They got some good music down there.

Troy: They got some rogues . . . is what they got.

Lyons: How you been, Mr. Bono? Hi, Rose.

Bono: I see where you playing down at the Crawford Grill tonight.

Rose: How come you ain't brought Bonnie like I told you? You should have
brought Bonnie with you, she ain't been over in a month of Sundays.

Lyons: I was just in the neighborhood . . . thought I'd stop by.

Troy: Here he come . . .

Bono: Your daddy got a promotion on the rubbish. He's gonna be the first
colored driver. Ain't got to do nothing but sit up there and read the paper
like them white fellows.

Lyons: Hey, Pop . . . if you knew how to read you'd be alright.

Bono: Naw . . . naw . . . you mean if the nigger knew how to *drive* he'd be
alright. Been fighting with them people about driving and ain't even got
a license. Mr. Rand know you ain't got no driver's license?

Troy: Driving ain't nothing. All you do is point the truck where you want it
to go. Driving ain't nothing.

Bono: Do Mr. Rand know you ain't got no driver's license? That's what I'm
talking about. I ain't asked if driving was easy. I asked if Mr. Rand know
you ain't got no driver's license.

Troy: He ain't got to know. The man ain't got to know my business. Time he
find out, I have two or three driver's licenses.

Lyons (going into his pocket): Say, look here, Pop . . .

Troy: I knew it was coming. Didn't I tell you, Bono? I know what kind of
"Look here, Pop" that was. The nigger fixing to ask me for some money.
It's Friday night. It's my payday. All them rogues down there on the
avenue . . . the ones that ain't in jail . . . and Lyons is hopping in his shoes
to get down there with them.

Lyons: See, Pop . . . if you give somebody else a chance to talk sometime,
you'd see that I was fixing to pay you back your ten dollars like I told you.
Here . . . I told you I'd pay you when Bonnie got paid.

Troy: Naw . . . you go ahead and keep that ten dollars. Put it in the bank. The
next time you feel like you wanna come by here and ask me for something
. . . you go on down there and get that.

Lyons: Here's your ten dollars, Pop. I told you I don't want you to give me
nothing. I just wanted to borrow ten dollars.

Troy: Naw . . . you go on and keep that for the next time you want to ask me.

Lyons: Come on, Pop . . . here go your ten dollars.

Rose: Why don't you go on and let the boy pay you back, Troy?

Lyons: Here you go, Rose. If you don't take it I'm gonna have to hear about it
for the next six months. (*He hands her the money.*)

Rose: You can hand yours over here too, Troy.

Troy: You see this, Bono. You see how they do me.

Bono: Yeah, Lucille do me the same way.

(*Gabriel is heard singing offstage. He enters.*)

Gabriel: Better get ready for the Judgment! Better get ready for . . . Hey! . . . Hey! . . . There's Troy's boy!

Lyons: How are you doing, Uncle Gabe?

Gabriel: Lyons . . . The King of the Jungle! Rose . . . hey, Rose. Got a flower for you. (*He takes a rose from his pocket.*) Picked it myself. That's the same rose like you is!

Rose: That's right nice of you, Gabe.

Lyons: What you been doing, Uncle Gabe?

Gabriel: Oh, I been chasing hellhounds and waiting on the time to tell St. Peter to open the gates.

Lyons: You been chasing hellhounds, huh? Well . . . you doing the right thing, Uncle Gabe. Somebody got to chase them.

Gabriel: Oh, yeah . . . I know it. The devil's strong. The devil ain't no push-over. Hellhounds snipping at everybody's heels. But I got my trumpet waiting on the judgment time.

Lyons: Waiting on the Battle of Armageddon, huh?

Gabriel: Ain't gonna be too much of a battle when God get to waving that Judgment sword. But the people's gonna have a hell of a time trying to get into heaven if them gates ain't open.

Lyons (*putting his arm around Gabriel*): You hear this, Pop. Uncle Gabe, you alright!

Gabriel (*laughing with Lyons*): Lyons! King of the Jungle.

Rose: You gonna stay for supper, Gabe? Want me to fix you a plate?

Gabriel: I'll take a sandwich, Rose. Don't want no plate. Just wanna eat with my hands. I'll take a sandwich.

Rose: How about you, Lyons? You staying? Got some short ribs cooking.

Lyons: Naw, I won't eat nothing till after we finished playing. (*Pause.*) You ought to come down and listen to me play, Pop.

Troy: I don't like that Chinese music. All that noise.

Rose: Go on in the house and wash up, Gabe . . . I'll fix you a sandwich.

Gabriel (*to Lyons, as he exits*): Troy's mad at me.

Lyons: What you mad at Uncle Gabe for, Pop?

Rose: He thinks Troy's mad at him cause he moved over to Miss Pearl's.

Troy: I ain't mad at the man. He can live where he want to live at.

Lyons: What he move over there for? Miss Pearl don't like nobody.

Rose: She don't mind him none. She treats him real nice. She just don't allow all that singing.

Troy: She don't mind that rent he be paying . . . that's what she don't mind.

Rose: Troy, I ain't going through that with you no more. He's over there cause he want to have his own place. He can come and go as he please.

Troy: Hell, he could come and go as he please here. I wasn't stopping him. I ain't put no rules on him.

Rose: It ain't the same thing, Troy. And you know it.

(Gabriel comes to the door.)

Now, that's the last I wanna hear about that. I don't wanna hear nothing else about Gabe and Miss Pearl. And next week . . .

Gabriel: I'm ready for my sandwich, Rose.

Rose: And next week . . . when that recruiter come from that school . . . I want you to sign that paper and go on and let Cory play football. Then that'll be the last I have to hear about that.

Troy (to Rose as she exits into the house): I ain't thinking about Cory nothing.

Lyons: What . . . Cory got recruited? What school he going to?

Troy: That boy walking around here smelling his piss . . . thinking he's grown. Thinking he's gonna do what he want, irrespective of what I say. Look here, Bono . . . I left the Commissioner's office and went down to the A&P . . . that boy ain't working down there. He lying to me. Telling me he got his job back . . .telling me he working weekends . . . telling me he working after school . . . Mr. Stawicki tell me he ain't working down there at all!

Lyons: Cory just growing up. He's just busting at the seams trying to fill out your shoes.

Troy: I don't care what he's doing. When he get to the point where he wanna disobey me . . . then it's time for him to move on. Bono'll tell you that. I bet he ain't never disobeyed his daddy without paying the consequences.

Bono: I ain't never had a chance. My daddy came on through . . . but I ain't never knew him to see him . . . or what he had on his mind or where he went. Just moving on through. Searching out the New Land. That's what the old folks used to call it. See a fellow moving around from place to place . . . woman to woman . . . called it searching out the New Land. I can't say if he ever found it. I come along, didn't want no kids. Didn't know if I was gonna be in one place long enough to fix on them right as their daddy. I figured I was going searching too. As it turned out I been hooked up with Lucille near about as long as your daddy been with Rose. Going on sixteen years.

Troy: Sometimes I wish I hadn't known my daddy. He ain't cared nothing about no kids. A kid to him wasn't nothing. All he wanted was for you to learn how to walk so he could start you to working. When it come time for eating . . . he ate first. If there was anything left over, that's what you got. Man would sit down and eat two chickens and give you the wing.

Lyons: You ought to stop that, Pop. Everybody feed their kids. No matter how hard times is . . . everybody care about their kids. Make sure they have something to eat.

Troy: The only thing my daddy cared about was getting them bales of cotton in to Mr. Lubin. That's the only thing that mattered to him. Sometimes I used to wonder why he was living. Wonder why the devil hadn't come and got him. "Get them bales of cotton in to Mr. Lubin" and find out he owe him money . . .

Lyons: He should have just went on and left when he saw he couldn't get nowhere. That's what I would have done.

Troy: How he gonna leave with eleven kids? And where he gonna go? He ain't knew how to do nothing but farm. No, he was trapped and I think he knew it. But I'll say this for him . . . he felt a responsibility toward us. Maybe he ain't treated us the way I felt he should have . . . but without that responsibility he could have walked off and left us . . . made his own way.

Bono: A lot of them did. Back in those days what you talking about . . . they walk out their front door and just take on down one road or another and keep on walking.

Lyons: There you go! That's what I'm talking about.

Bono: Just keep on walking till you come to something else. Ain't you never heard of nobody having the walking blues? Well, that's what you call it when you just take off like that.

Troy: My daddy ain't had them walking blues! What you talking about? He stayed right there with his family. But he was just as evil as he could be. My mama couldn't stand him. Couldn't stand that evilness. She run off when I was about eight. She sneaked off one night after he had gone to sleep. Told me she was coming back for me. I ain't never seen her no more. All his women run off and left him. He wasn't good for nobody.

When my turn come to head out, I was fourteen and got to sniffing around Joe Canewell's daughter. Had us an old mule we called Greyboy. My daddy sent me out to do some plowing and I tied up Greyboy and went to fooling around with Joe Canewell's daughter. We done found us a nice little spot, got real cozy with each other. She about thirteen and we done figured we was grown anyway . . . so we down there enjoying ourselves . . . ain't thinking about nothing. We didn't know Greyboy had got loose and wandered back to the house and my daddy was looking for me. We down there by the creek enjoying ourselves when my daddy come up on us. Surprised us. He had them leather straps off the mule and commenced to whupping me like there was no tomorrow. I jumped up, mad and embarrassed. I was scared of my daddy. When he commenced to whupping on me . . . quite naturally I run to get out of the way. (*Pause.*) Now I thought he was mad cause I ain't done my work. But I see where he was chasing me off so he could have the gal for himself. When I see what the matter of it was, I lost all fear of my daddy. Right there is where I become a man . . . at fourteen years of age. (*Pause.*) Now it was my turn to run him off. I picked up them same reins that he had used on me. I picked up them reins and commenced to whupping on him. The gal jumped up and run off . . . and when my daddy turned to face me, I could see why the devil had never come to get him . . . cause he was the devil himself. I don't know what happened. When I woke up, I was laying right there by the creek, and Blue . . . this old dog we had . . . was licking my face. I thought I was blind. I couldn't see nothing. Both my eyes were swollen shut. I layed there and cried. I didn't know what I was gonna do. The only thing I knew was the time had come for me to leave my daddy's house. And right there the world suddenly got big. And it was a long time before I could cut it down to where I could handle it.

Part of that cutting down was when I got to the place where I could feel him kicking in my blood and knew that the only thing that separated us was the matter of a few years.

(Gabriel enters from the house with a sandwich.)

Lyons: What you got there, Uncle Gabe?

Gabriel: Got me a ham sandwich. Rose gave me a ham sandwich.

Troy: I don't know what happened to him. I done lost touch with everybody except Gabriel. But I hope he's dead. I hope he found some peace.

Lyons: That's a heavy story, Pop. I didn't know you left home when you was fourteen.

Troy: And didn't know nothing. The only part of the world I knew was the forty-two acres of Mr. Lubin's land. That's all I knew about life.

Lyons: Fourteen's kinda young to be out on your own. *(Phone rings.)* I don't even think I was ready to be out on my own at fourteen. I don't know what I would have done.

Troy: I got up from the creek and walked on down to Mobile. I was through with farming. Figured I could do better in the city. So I walked the two hundred miles to Mobile.

Lyons: Wait a minute . . . you ain't walked no two hundred miles, Pop. Ain't nobody gonna walk no two hundred miles. You talking about some walking there.

Bono: That's the only way you got anywhere back in them days.

Lyons: Shhh. Damn if I wouldn't have hitched a ride with somebody!

Troy: Who you gonna hitch it with? They ain't had no cars and things like they got now. We talking about 1918.

Rose (entering): What you all out here getting into?

Troy (to Rose): I'm telling Lyons how good he got it. He don't know nothing about this I'm talking.

Rose: Lyons, that was Bonnie on the phone. She say you supposed to pick her up.

Lyons: Yeah, okay, Rose.

Troy: I walked on down to Mobile and hitched up with some of them fellows that was heading this way. Got up here and found out . . . not only couldn't you get a job . . . you couldn't find no place to live. I thought I was in freedom. Shhh. Colored folks living down there on the riverbanks in whatever kind of shelter they could find for themselves. Right down there under the Brady Street Bridge. Living in shacks made of sticks and tarpaper. Messed around there and went from bad to worse. Started stealing. First it was food. Then I figured, hell, if I steal money I can buy me some food. Buy me some shoes too! One thing led to another. Met your mama. I was young and anxious to be a man. Met your mama and had you. What I do that for? Now I got to worry about feeding you and her. Got to steal three times as much. Went out one day looking for somebody to rob . . . that's what I was, a robber. I'll tell you the truth. I'm ashamed of it today. But it's the truth. Went to rob this fellow . . . pulled out my knife . . . and he pulled out a gun. Shot me in the chest. It felt just like somebody had taken a hot branding iron and laid it on me. When he shot me I jumped at him with my knife. They told me I killed him and they put me in the penitentiary and locked me up for fifteen years. That's where I met Bono. That's where I learned how to play baseball. Got out that place and your mama had taken you and went on to make life without me. Fifteen years was a long time for her to wait. But that fifteen years cured me of that robbing stuff. Rose'll tell you. She asked me when I met her if I had gotten all that foolishness out of my system. And I told her, "Baby, it's you and baseball all what count with me." You hear me, Bono? I meant it too. She say, "Which one comes first?" I told her, "Baby, ain't no doubt it's baseball . . . but you stick and get old with me and we'll both outlive this baseball." Am I right, Rose? And it's true.

Rose: Man, hush your mouth. You ain't said no such thing. Talking about, "Baby you know you'll always be number one with me." That's what you was talking.

Troy: You hear that, Bono. That's why I love her.

Bono: Rose'll keep you straight. You get off the track, she'll straighten you up.

Rose: Lyons, you better get on up and get Bonnie. She waiting on you.

Lyons (gets up to go): Hey, Pop, why don't you come on down to the Grill and hear me play?

Troy: I ain't going down there. I'm too old to be sitting around in them clubs.

Bono: You got to be good to play down at the Grill.

Lyons: Come on, Pop . . .

Troy: I got to get up in the morning.

Lyons: You ain't got to stay long.

Troy: Naw, I'm gonna get my supper and go on to bed.

Lyons: Well, I got to go. I'll see you again.

Troy: Don't you come around my house on my payday.

Rose: Pick up the phone and let somebody know you coming. And bring Bonnie with you. You know I'm always glad to see her.

Lyons: Yeah, I'll do that, Rose. You take care now. See you, Pop. See you, Mr. Bono. See you, Uncle Gabe.

Gabriel: Lyons! King of the Jungle!

(*Lyons exits.*)

Troy: Is supper ready, woman? Me and you got some business to take care of. I'm gonna tear it up too.

Rose: Troy, I done told you now!

Troy (*puts his arm around Bono*): Aw hell, woman . . . this is Bono. Bono like family. I done known this nigger since . . . how long I done know you?

Bono: It's been a long time.

Troy: I done know this nigger since Skippy was a pup. Me and him done been through some times.

Bono: You sure right about that.

Troy: Hell, I done know him longer than I known you. And we still standing shoulder to shoulder. Hey, look here, Bono . . . a man can't ask for no more than that. (*Drinks to him.*) I love you, nigger.

Bono: Hell, I love you too . . . but I got to get home see my woman. You got yours in hand. I got to go get mine.

(*Bono starts to exit as Cory enters the yard, dressed in his football uniform. He gives Troy a hard, uncompromising look.*)

Cory: What you do that for, Pop?

(*He throws his helmet down in the direction of Troy.*)

Rose: What's the matter? Cory . . . what's the matter?

Cory: Papa done went up to the school and told Coach Zellman I can't play football no more. Wouldn't even let me play the game. Told him to tell the recruiter not to come.

Rose: Troy . . .

Troy: What you Troying me for. Yeah, I did it. And the boy know why I did it.

Cory: Why you wanna do that to me? That was the one chance I had.

Rose: Ain't nothing wrong with Cory playing football, Troy.

Troy: The boy lied to me. I told the nigger if he wanna play football . . . to keep up his chores and hold down that job at the A&P. That was the conditions. Stopped down there to see Mr. Stawicki . . .

Cory: I can't work after school during the football season, Pop! I tried to tell you that Mr. Stawicki's holding my job for me. You don't never want to listen to nobody. And then you wanna go and do this to me!

Troy: I ain't done nothing to you. You done it to yourself.

Cory: Just cause you didn't have a chance! You just scared I'm gonna be better than you, that's all.

Troy: Come here.

Rose: Troy . . .

(*Cory reluctantly crosses over to Troy.*)

Troy: Alright! See. You done made a mistake.

Cory: I didn't even do nothing!

Troy: I'm gonna tell you what your mistake was. See . . . you swung at the ball and didn't hit it. That's strike one. See, you in the batter's box now. You swung and you missed. That's strike one. Don't you strike out!

(*Lights fade to black.*)

ACT II

SCENE I

The following morning. Cory is at the tree hitting the ball with the bat. He tries to mimic Troy, but his swing is awkward, less sure. Rose enters from the house.

Rose: Cory, I want you to help me with this cupboard.

Cory: I ain't quitting the team. I don't care what Poppa say.

Rose: I'll talk to him when he gets back. He had to go see about your Uncle Gabe. The police done arrested him. Say he was disturbing the peace. He'll be back directly. Come on in here and help me clean out the top of this cupboard.

(*Cory exits into the house. Rose sees Troy and Bono coming down the alley.*)

Troy . . . what they say down there?

Troy: Ain't said nothing. I give them fifty dollars and they let him go. I'll talk to you about it. Where's Cory?

Rose: He's in there helping me clean out these cupboards.

Troy: Tell him to get his butt out here.

(*Troy and Bono go over to the pile of wood. Bono picks up the saw and begins sawing.*)

Troy (to Bono): All they want is the money. That makes six or seven times I done went down there and got him. See me coming they stick out their *hands.*

Bono: Yeah. I know what you mean. That's all they care about . . . that money. They don't care about what's right. (*Pause.*) Nigger, why you got to go and get some hard wood? You ain't doing nothing but building a little old fence. Get you some soft pine wood. That's all you need.

Troy: I know what I'm doing. This is outside wood. You put pine wood inside
the house. Pine wood is inside wood. This here is outside wood. Now you
tell me where the fence is gonna be?

Bono: You don't need this wood. You can put it up with pine wood and it'll
stand as long as you gonna be here looking at it.

Troy: How you know how long I'm gonna be here, nigger? Hell, I might just
live forever. Live longer than old man Horsely.

Bono: That's what Magee used to say.

Troy: Magee's a damn fool. Now you tell me who you ever heard of gonna pull
their own teeth with a pair of rusty pliers.

Bono: The old folks . . . my granddaddy used to pull his teeth with pliers. They
ain't had no dentists for the colored folks back then.

Troy: Get clean pliers! You understand? Clean pliers! Sterilize them! Besides
we ain't living back then. All Magee had to do was walk over to Doc
Goldblum's.

Bono: I see where you and that Tallahassee gal . . . that Alberta . . . I see where
you all done got tight.

Troy: What you mean "got tight"?

Bono: I see where you be laughing and joking with her all the time.

Troy: I laughs and jokes with all of them, Bono. You know me.

Bono: That ain't the kind of laughing and joking I'm talking about.

(Cory enters from the house.)

Cory: How you doing, Mr. Bono?

Troy: Cory? Get that saw from Bono and cut some wood. He talking about
the wood's too hard to cut. Stand back there, Jim, and let that young boy
show you how it's done.

Bono: He's sure welcome to it.

(Cory takes the saw and begins to cut the wood.)

Whew-e-e! Look at that. Big old strong boy. Look like Joe Louis. Hell,
must be getting old the way I'm watching that boy whip through that
wood.

Cory: I don't see why Mama want a fence around the yard noways.

Troy: Damn if I know either. What the hell she keeping out with it? She ain't
got nothing nobody want.

Bono: Some people build fences to keep people out . . . and other people build
fences to keep people in. Rose wants to hold on to you all. She loves you.

Troy: Hell, nigger, I don't need nobody to tell me my wife loves me. Cory . . .
go on in the house and see if you can find that other saw.

Cory: Where's it at?

Troy: I said find it! Look for it till you find it!

(*Cory exits into the house.*)

What's that supposed to mean? Wanna keep us in?

Bono: Troy . . . I done known you seem like damn near my whole life. You and Rose both. I done know both of you all for a long time. I remember when you met Rose. When you was hitting them baseball out the park. A lot of them old gals was after you then. You had the pick of the litter. When you picked Rose, I was happy for you. That was the first time I knew you had any sense. I said . . . My man Troy knows what he's doing . . . I'm gonna follow this nigger . . . he might take me somewhere. I been following you too. I done learned a whole heap of things about life watching you. I done learned how to tell where the shit lies. How to tell it from the alfalfa. You done learned me a lot of things. You showed me how to not make the same mistakes . . . to take life as it comes along and keep putting one foot in front of the other. (*Pause.*) Rose a good woman, Troy.

Troy: Hell, nigger, I know she a good woman. I been married to her for eighteen years. What you got on your mind, Bono?

Bono: I just say she a good woman. Just like I say anything. I ain't got to have nothing on my mind.

Troy: You just gonna say she a good woman and leave it hanging out there like that? Why you telling me she a good woman?

Bono: She loves you, Troy. Rose loves you.

Troy: You saying I don't measure up. That's what you trying to say. I don't measure up cause I'm seeing this other gal. I know what you trying to say.

Bono: I know what Rose means to you, Troy. I'm just trying to say I don't want to see you mess up.

Troy: Yeah, I appreciate that, Bono. If you was messing around on Lucille I'd be telling you the same thing.

Bono: Well, that's all I got to say. I just say that because I love you both.

Troy: Hell, you know me . . . I wasn't out there looking for nothing. You can't find a better woman than Rose. I know that. But seems like this woman just stuck onto me where I can't shake her loose. I done wrestled with it, tried to throw her off me . . . but she just stuck on tighter. Now she's stuck on for good.

Bono: You's in control . . . that's what you tell me all the time. You responsible for what you do.

Troy: I ain't ducking the responsibility of it. As long as it sets right in my heart . . . then I'm okay. Cause that's all I listen to. It'll tell me right from wrong every time. And I ain't talking about doing Rose no bad turn. I love Rose. She done carried me a long ways and I love and respect her for that.

Bono: I know you do. That's why I don't want to see you hurt her. But what you gonna do when she find out? What you got then? If you try and juggle

both of them . . . sooner or later you gonna drop one of them. That's
common sense.

Troy: Yeah, I hear what you saying, Bono. I been trying to figure a way to
work it out.

Bono: Work it out right, Troy. I don't want to be getting all up between you
and Rose's business . . . but work it so it come out right.

Troy: Aw hell, I get all up between you and Lucille's business. When you
gonna get that woman that refrigerator she been wanting? Don't tell me
you ain't got no money now. I know who your banker is. Mellon° don't
need that money bad as Lucille want that refrigerator. I'll tell you that.

Bono: Tell you what I'll do . . . when you finish building this fence for Rose . . .
I'll buy Lucille that refrigerator.

Troy: You done stuck your foot in your mouth now!

(*Troy grabs up a board and begins to saw. Bono starts to walk out the yard.*)

Hey, nigger . . . where you going?

Bono: I'm going home. I know you don't expect me to help you now. I'm
protecting my money. I wanna see you put that fence up by yourself.
That's what I want to see. You'll be here another six months without me.

Troy: Nigger, you ain't right.

Bono: When it comes to my money . . . I'm right as fireworks on the Fourth
of July.

Troy: Alright, we gonna see now. You better get out your bankbook.

(*Bono exits, and Troy continues to work. Rose enters from the house.*)

Rose: What they say down there? What's happening with Gabe?

Troy: I went down there and got him out. Cost me fifty dollars. Say he was
disturbing the peace. Judge set up a hearing for him in three weeks. Say to
show cause why he shouldn't be re-committed.

Rose: What was he doing that cause them to arrest him?

Troy: Some kids was teasing him and he run them off home. Say he was
howling and carrying on. Some folks seen him and called the police.
That's all it was.

Rose: Well, what's you say? What'd you tell the judge?

Troy: Told him I'd look after him. It didn't make no sense to recommit the
man. He stuck out his big greasy palm and told me to give him fifty dollars
and take him on home.

Rose: Where's he at now? Where'd he go off to?

Troy: He's gone on about his business. He don't need nobody to hold his
hand.

Mellon: banker and industrialist Andrew Mellon (1855–1937), U.S. Treasury Secretary 1921–32,
was active in philanthropic enterprises, especially in his native Pittsburgh.

Rose: Well, I don't know. Seem like that would be the best place for him if they did put him into the hospital. I know what you're gonna say. But that's what I think would be best.

Troy: The man done had his life ruined fighting for what? And they wanna take and lock him up. Let him be free. He don't bother nobody.

Rose: Well, everybody got their own way of looking at it I guess. Come on and get your lunch. I got a bowl of lima beans and some cornbread in the oven. Come on get something to eat. Ain't no sense you fretting over Gabe.

(Rose turns to go into the house.)

Troy: Rose . . . got something to tell you.

Rose: Well, come on . . . wait till I get this food on the table.

Troy: Rose!

(She stops and turns around.)

I don't know how to say this. *(Pause.)* I can't explain it none. It just sort of grows on you till it gets out of hand. It starts out like a little bush . . . and the next thing you know it's a whole forest.

Rose: Troy . . . what is you talking about?

Troy: I'm talking, woman, let me talk. I'm trying to find a way to tell you . . . I'm gonna be a daddy. I'm gonna be somebody's daddy.

Rose: Troy . . . you're not telling me this? You're gonna be . . . what?

Troy: Rose . . . now . . . see . . .

Rose: You telling me you gonna be somebody's daddy? You telling your *wife* this?

(Gabriel enters from the street. He carries a rose in his hand.)

Gabriel: Hey, Troy! Hey, Rose!

Rose: I have to wait eighteen years to hear something like this.

Gabriel: Hey, Rose . . . I got a flower for you. *(He hands it to her.)* That's a rose. Same rose like you is.

Rose: Thanks, Gabe.

Gabriel: Troy, you ain't mad at me is you? Them bad mens come and put me away. You ain't mad at me is you?

Troy: Naw, Gabe, I ain't mad at you.

Rose: Eighteen years and you wanna come with this.

Gabriel (takes a quarter out of his pocket): See what I got? Got a brand new quarter.

Troy: Rose . . . it's just . . .

Rose: Ain't nothing you can say, Troy. Ain't no way of explaining that.

Gabriel: Fellow that give me this quarter had a whole mess of them. I'm gonna keep this quarter till it stop shining.

Rose: Gabe, go on in the house there. I got some watermelon in the Frigidaire. Go on and get you a piece.

Gabriel: Say, Rose . . . you know I was chasing hellhounds and them bad mens come and get me and take me away. Troy helped me. He come down there and told them they better let me go before he beat them up. Yeah, he did!

Rose: You go on and get you a piece of watermelon, Gabe. Them bad mens is gone now.

Gabriel: Okay, Rose . . . gonna get me some watermelon. The kind with the stripes on it.

(*Gabriel exits into the house.*)

Rose: Why, Troy? Why? After all these years to come dragging this in to me now. It don't make no sense at your age. I could have expected this ten or fifteen years ago, but not now.

Troy: Age ain't got nothing to do with it, Rose.

Rose: I done tried to be everything a wife should be. Everything a wife could be. Been married eighteen years and I got to live to see the day you tell me you been seeing another woman and done fathered a child by her. And you know I ain't never wanted no half nothing in my family. My whole family is half. Everybody got different fathers and mothers . . . my two sisters and my brother. Can't hardly tell who's who. Can't never sit down and talk about Papa and Mama. It's your papa and your mama and my papa and my mama . . .

Troy: Rose . . . stop it now.

Rose: I ain't never wanted that for none of my children. And now you wanna drag your behind in here and tell me something like this.

Troy: You ought to know. It's time for you to know.

Rose: Well, I don't want to know, goddamn it!

Troy: I can't just make it go away. It's done now. I can't wish the circumstance of the thing away.

Rose: And you don't want to either. Maybe you want to wish me and my boy away. Maybe that's what you want? Well, you can't wish us away. I've got eighteen years of my life invested in you. You ought to have stayed upstairs in my bed where you belong.

Troy: Rose . . . now listen to me . . . we can get a handle on this thing. We can talk this out . . . come to an understanding.

Rose: All of a sudden it's "we." Where was "we" at when you was down there rolling around with some godforsaken woman? "We" should have come to an understanding before you started making a damn fool of yourself. You're a day late and a dollar short when it comes to an understanding with me.

Troy: It's just . . . She gives me a different idea . . . a different understanding about myself. I can step out of this house and get away from the pressures and problems . . . be a different man. I ain't got to wonder how I'm gonna pay the bills or get the roof fixed. I can just be a part of myself that I ain't never been.

Rose: What I want to know . . . is do you plan to continue seeing her. That's all you can say to me.

Troy: I can sit up in her house and laugh. Do you understand what I'm saying. I can laugh out loud . . . and it feels good. It reaches all the way down to the bottom of my shoes. (*Pause.*) Rose, I can't give that up.

Rose: Maybe you ought to go on and stay down there with her . . . if she's a better woman than me.

Troy: It ain't about nobody being a better woman or nothing. Rose, you ain't the blame. A man couldn't ask for no woman to be a better wife than you've been. I'm responsible for it. I done locked myself into a pattern trying to take care of you all that I forgot about myself.

Rose: What the hell was I there for? That was my job, not somebody else's.

Troy: Rose, I done tried all my life to live decent . . . to live a clean . . . hard . . . useful life. I tried to be a good husband to you. In every way I knew how. Maybe I come into the world backwards, I don't know. But . . . you born with two strikes on you before you come to the plate. You got to guard it closely . . . always looking for the curve-ball on the inside corner. You can't afford to let none get past you. You can't afford a call strike. If you going down . . . you going down swinging. Everything lined up against you. What you gonna do. I fooled them, Rose. I bunted. When I found you and Cory and a halfway decent job . . . I was safe. Couldn't nothing touch me. I wasn't gonna strike out no more. I wasn't going back to the penitentiary. I wasn't gonna lay in the streets with a bottle of wine. I was safe. I had me a family. A job. I wasn't gonna get that last strike. I was on first looking for one of them boys to knock me in. To get me home.

Rose: You should have stayed in my bed, Troy.

Troy: Then when I saw that gal . . . she firmed up my backbone. And I got to thinking that if I tried . . . I just might be able to steal second. Do you understand after eighteen years I wanted to steal second.

Rose: You should have held me tight. You should have grabbed me and held on.

Troy: I stood on first base for eighteen years and I thought . . . well, goddamn it . . . go on for it!

Rose: We're not talking about baseball! We're talking about you going off to lay in bed with another woman . . . and then bring it home to me. That's what we're talking about. We ain't talking about no baseball.

Troy: Rose, you're not listening to me. I'm trying the best I can to explain it to you. It's not easy for me to admit that I been standing in the same place for eighteen years.

Rose: I been standing with you! I been right here with you, Troy. I got a life too. I gave eighteen years of my life to stand in the same spot with you.

Don't you think I ever wanted other things? Don't you think I had dreams and hopes? What about my life? What about me. Don't you think it ever crossed my mind to want to know other men? That I wanted to lay up somewhere and forget about my responsibilities? That I wanted someone to make me laugh so I could feel good? You not the only one who's got wants and needs. But I held on to you, Troy. I took all my feelings, my wants and needs, my dreams . . . and I buried them inside you. I planted a seed and watched and prayed over it. I planted myself inside you and waited to bloom. And it didn't take me no eighteen years to find out the soil was hard and rocky and it wasn't never gonna bloom.

But I held on to you, Troy. I held you tighter. You was my husband. I owed you everything I had. Every part of me I could find to give you. And upstairs in that room . . . with the darkness falling in on me . . . I gave everything I had to try and erase the doubt that you wasn't the finest man in the world. And wherever you was going . . . I wanted to be there with you. Cause you was my husband. Cause that's the only way I was gonna survive as your wife. You always talking about what you give . . . and what you don't have to give. But you take too. You take . . . and don't even know nobody's giving!

(*Rose turns to exit into the house; Troy grabs her arm.*)

Troy: You say I take and don't give!
Rose: Troy! You're hurting me!
Troy: You say I take and don't give.
Rose: Troy . . . you're hurting my arm! Let go!
Troy: I done give you everything I got. Don't you tell that lie on me.
Rose: Troy!
Troy: Don't you tell that lie on me!

(*Cory enters from the house.*)

Cory: Mama!
Rose: Troy. You're hurting me.
Troy: Don't you tell me about no taking and giving.

(*Cory comes up behind Troy and grabs him. Troy, surprised, is thrown off balance just as Cory throws a glancing blow that catches him on the chest and knocks him down. Troy is stunned, as is Cory.*)

Rose: Troy. Troy. No!

(*Troy gets to his feet and starts at Cory.*)

Troy . . . no. Please! Troy!

(*Rose pulls on Troy to hold him back. Troy stops himself.*)

Troy (*to Cory*): Alright. That's strike two. You stay away from around me, boy. Don't you strike out. You living with a full count. Don't you strike out.

(*Troy exits out the yard as the lights go down.*)

SCENE II

It is six months later, early afternoon. Troy enters from the house and starts to exit the yard. Rose enters from the house.

Rose: Troy, I want to talk to you.

Troy: All of a sudden, after all this time, you want to talk to me, huh? You ain't wanted to talk to me for months. You ain't wanted to talk to me last night. You ain't wanted no part of me then. What you wanna talk to me about now?

Rose: Tomorrow's Friday.

Troy: I know what day tomorrow is. You think I don't know tomorrow's Friday? My whole life I ain't done nothing but look to see Friday coming and you got to tell me it's Friday.

Rose: I want to know if you're coming home.

Troy: I always come home, Rose. You know that. There ain't never been a night I ain't come home.

Rose: That ain't what I mean . . . and you know it. I want to know if you're coming straight home after work.

Troy: I figure I'd cash my check . . . hang out at Taylors' with the boys . . . maybe play a game of checkers . . .

Rose: Troy, I can't live like this. I won't live like this. You livin' on borrowed time with me. It's been going on six months now you ain't been coming home.

Troy: I be here every night. Every night of the year. That's 365 days.

Rose: I want you to come home tomorrow after work.

Troy: Rose . . . I don't mess up my pay. You know that now. I take my pay and I give it to you. I don't have no money but what you give me back. I just want to have a little time to myself . . . a little time to enjoy life.

Rose: What about me? When's my time to enjoy life?

Troy: I don't know what to tell you, Rose. I'm doing the best I can.

Rose: You ain't been home from work but time enough to change your clothes and run out . . . and you wanna call that the best you can do?

Troy: I'm going over to the hospital to see Alberta. She went into the hospital this afternoon. Look like she might have the baby early. I won't be gone long.

Rose: Well, you ought to know. They went over to Miss Pearl's and got Gabe today. She said you told them to go ahead and lock him up.

Troy: I ain't said no such thing. Whoever told you that is telling a lie. Pearl ain't doing nothing but telling a big fat lie.

Rose: She ain't had to tell me. I read it on the papers.

Troy: I ain't told them nothing of the kind.

Rose: I saw it right there on the papers.

Troy: What it say, huh?

Rose: It said you told them to take him.

Troy: Then they screwed that up, just the way they screw up everything. I ain't worried about what they got on the paper.

Rose: Say the government send part of his check to the hospital and the other part to you.

Troy: I ain't got nothing to do with that if that's the way it works. I ain't made up the rules about how it work.

Rose: You did Gabe just like you did Cory. You wouldn't sign the paper for Cory . . . but you signed for Gabe. You signed that paper.

(The telephone is heard ringing inside the house.)

Troy: I told you I ain't signed nothing, woman! The only thing I signed was the release form. Hell, I can't read, I don't know what they had on that paper! I ain't signed nothing about sending Gabe away.

Rose: I said send him to the hospital . . . you said let him be free . . . now you done went down there and signed him to the hospital for half his money. You went back on yourself, Troy. You gonna have to answer for that.

Troy: See now . . . you been over there talking to Miss Pearl. She done got mad cause she ain't getting Gabe's rent money. That's all it is. She's liable to say anything.

Rose: Troy, I seen where you signed the paper.

Troy: You ain't seen nothing I signed. What she doing got papers on my brother anyway? Miss Pearl telling a big fat lie. And I'm gonna tell her about it too! You ain't seen nothing I signed. Say . . . you ain't seen nothing I signed.

(Rose exits into the house to answer the telephone. Presently she returns.)

Rose: Troy . . . that was the hospital. Alberta had the baby.

Troy: What she have? What is it?

Rose: It's a girl.

Troy: I better get on down to the hospital to see her.

Rose: Troy . . .

Troy: Rose . . . I got to go see her now. That's only right . . . what's the matter . . . the baby's alright, ain't it?

Rose: Alberta died having the baby.

Troy: Died . . . you say she's dead? Alberta's dead?

Rose: They said they done all they could. They couldn't do nothing for her.

Troy: The baby? How's the baby?

Rose: They say it's healthy. I wonder who's gonna bury her.

Troy: She had family, Rose. She wasn't living in the world by herself.

Rose: I know she wasn't living in the world by herself.

Troy: Next thing you gonna want to know if she had any insurance.

Rose: Troy, you ain't got to talk like that.

Troy: That's the first thing that jumped out your mouth. "Who's gonna bury her?" Like I'm fixing to take on that task for myself.

Rose: I am your wife. Don't push me away.

Troy: I ain't pushing nobody away. Just give me some space. That's all. Just give me some room to breathe.

(Rose exits into the house. Troy walks about the yard.)

Troy (with a quiet rage that threatens to consume him): Alright . . . Mr. Death. See now . . . I'm gonna tell you what I'm gonna do. I'm gonna take and build me a fence around this yard. See? I'm gonna build me a fence around what belongs to me. And then I want you to stay on the other side. See? You stay over there until you're ready for me. Then you come on. Bring your army. Bring your sickle. Bring your wrestling clothes. I ain't gonna fall down on my vigilance this time. You ain't gonna sneak up on me no more. When you ready for me . . . when the top of your list say Troy Maxson . . . that's when you come around here. You come up and knock on the front door. Ain't nobody else got nothing to do with this. This is between you and me. Man to man. You stay on the other side of that fence until you ready for me. Then you come up and knock on the front door. Anytime you want. I'll be ready for you.

(The lights go down to black.)

SCENE III

The lights come up on the porch. It is late evening three days later. Rose sits listening to the ball game waiting for Troy. The final out of the game is made and Rose switches off the radio. Troy enters the yard carrying an infant wrapped in blankets. He stands back from the house and calls.

Rose enters and stands on the porch. There is a long, awkward silence, the weight of which grows heavier with each passing second.

Troy: Rose . . . I'm standing here with my daughter in my arms. She ain't but a wee bittie little old thing. She don't know nothing about grownups' business. She innocent . . . and she ain't got no mama.

Rose: What you telling me for, Troy?

(She turns and exits into the house.)

Troy: Well . . . I guess we'll just sit out here on the porch.

(He sits down on the porch. There is an awkward indelicateness about the way he handles the baby. His largeness engulfs and seems to swallow it. He speaks loud enough for Rose to hear.)

A man's got to do what's right for him. I ain't sorry for nothing I done. It felt right in my heart. *(To the baby.)* What you smiling at? Your daddy's a big man. Got these great big old hands. But sometimes he's scared. And right now your daddy's scared cause we sitting out here and ain't got no home. Oh, I been homeless before. I ain't had no little baby with me. But I been homeless. You just be out on the road by your lonesome and you see one of them trains coming and you just kinda go like this . . .

(He sings as a lullaby.)

> Please, Mr. Engineer let a man ride the line
> Please, Mr. Engineer let a man ride the line
> I ain't got no ticket please let me ride the blinds

(Rose enters from the house. Troy, hearing her steps behind him, stands and faces her.)

She's my daughter, Rose. My own flesh and blood. I can't deny her no more than I can deny them boys. *(Pause.)* You and them boys is my family. You and them and this child is all I got in the world. So I guess what I'm saying is . . . I'd appreciate it if you'd help me take care of her.

Rose: Okay, Troy . . . you're right. I'll take care of your baby for you . . . cause . . . like you say . . . she's innocent . . . and you can't visit the sins of the father upon the child. A motherless child has got a hard time. *(She takes the baby from him.)* From right now . . . this child got a mother. But you a womanless man.

(Rose turns and exits into the house with the baby. Lights go down to black.)

SCENE IV

It is two months later. Lyons enters the street. He knocks on the door and calls.

Lyons: Hey, Rose! *(Pause.)* Rose!

Rose (from inside the house): Stop that yelling. You gonna wake up Raynell. I just got her to sleep.

Lyons: I just stopped by to pay Papa this twenty dollars I owe him. Where's Papa at?

Rose: He should be here in a minute. I'm getting ready to go down to the church. Sit down and wait on him.

Lyons: I got to go pick up Bonnie over her mother's house.

Rose: Well, sit it down there on the table. He'll get it.

Lyons (enters the house and sets the money on the table): Tell Papa I said thanks. I'll see you again.

Rose: Alright, Lyons. We'll see you.

(Lyons starts to exit as Cory enters.)

Cory: Hey, Lyons.

Lyons: What's happening, Cory? Say man, I'm sorry I missed your graduation. You know I had a gig and couldn't get away. Otherwise, I would have been there, man. So what you doing?

Cory: I'm trying to find a job.

Lyons: Yeah I know how that go, man. It's rough out here. Jobs are scarce.

Cory: Yeah, I know.

Lyons: Look here, I got to run. Talk to Papa . . . he know some people. He'll be able to help get you a job. Talk to him . . . see what he say.

Cory: Yeah . . . alright, Lyons.

Lyons: You take care. I'll talk to you soon. We'll find some time to talk.

(Lyons exits the yard. Cory wanders over to the tree, picks up the bat, and assumes a batting stance. He studies an imaginary pitcher and swings. Dissatisfied with the result, he tries again. Troy enters. They eye each other for a beat. Cory puts the bat down and exits the yard. Troy starts into the house as Rose exits with Raynell. She is carrying a cake.)

Troy: I'm coming in and everybody's going out.

Rose: I'm taking this cake down to the church for the bake sale. Lyons was by to see you. He stopped by to pay you your twenty dollars. It's laying in there on the table.

Troy (going into his pocket): Well . . . here go this money.

Rose: Put it in there on the table, Troy. I'll get it.

Troy: What time you coming back?

Rose: Ain't no use in you studying me. It don't matter what time I come back.

Troy: I just asked you a question, woman. What's the matter . . . can't I ask you a question?

Rose: Troy, I don't want to go into it. Your dinner's in there on the stove. All you got to do is heat it up. And don't you be eating the rest of them cakes in there. I'm coming back for them. We having a bake sale at the church tomorrow.

(Rose exits the yard. Troy sits down on the steps, takes a pint bottle from his pocket, opens it and drinks. He begins to sing.)

Troy:

      Hear it ring! Hear it ring!

Had an old dog his name was Blue
You know Blue was mighty true
You know Blue was a good old dog
Blue treed a possum in a hollow log
You know from that he was a good old dog

(*Bono enters the yard.*)

Bono: Hey, Troy.

Troy: Hey, what's happening, Bono?

Bono: I just thought I'd stop by to see you.

Troy: What you stop by and see me for? You ain't stopped by in a month of Sundays. Hell, I must owe you money or something.

Bono: Since you got your promotion I can't keep up with you. Used to see you every day. Now I don't even know what route you working.

Troy: They keep switching me around. Got me out in Greentree now . . . hauling white folks' garbage.

Bono: Greentree, huh? You lucky, at least you ain't got to be lifting them barrels. Damn if they ain't getting heavier. I'm gonna put in my two years and call it quits.

Troy: I'm thinking about retiring myself.

Bono: You got it easy. You can *drive* for another five years.

Troy: It ain't the same, Bono. It ain't like working the back of the truck. Ain't got nobody to talk to . . . feel like you working by yourself. Naw, I'm thinking about retiring. How's Lucille?

Bono: She alright. Her arthritis get to acting up on her sometime. Saw Rose on my way in. She going down to the church, huh?

Troy: Yeah, she took up going down there. All them preachers looking for somebody to fatten their pockets. (*Pause.*) Got some gin here.

Bono: Naw, thanks. I just stopped by to say hello.

Troy: Hell, nigger . . . you can take a drink. I ain't never known you to say no to a drink. You ain't got to work tomorrow.

Bono: I just stopped by. I'm fixing to go over to Skinner's. We got us a domino game going over his house every Friday.

Troy: Nigger, you can't play no dominoes. I used to whup you four games out of five.

Bono: Well, that learned me. I'm getting better.

Troy: Yeah? Well, that's alright.

Bono: Look here . . . I got to be getting on. Stop by sometime, huh?

Troy: Yeah, I'll do that, Bono. Lucille told Rose you bought her a new refrigerator.

Bono: Yeah, Rose told Lucille you had finally built your fence . . . so I figured we'd call it even.

Troy: I knew you would.

Bono: Yeah . . . okay. I'll be talking to you.

Troy: Yeah, take care, Bono. Good to see you. I'm gonna stop over.

Bono: Yeah. Okay, Troy.

(*Bono exits. Troy drinks from the bottle.*)

Troy:

> Old Blue died and I dug his grave
> Let him down with a golden chain
> Every night when I hear old Blue bark
> I know Blue treed a possum in Noah's Ark.
> Hear it ring! Hear it ring!

(*Cory enters the yard. They eye each other for a beat. Troy is sitting in the middle of the steps. Cory walks over.*)

Cory: I got to get by.

Troy: Say what? What's you say?

Cory: You in my way. I got to get by.

Troy: You got to get by where? This is my house. Bought and paid for. In full. Took me fifteen years. And if you wanna go in my house and I'm sitting on the steps . . . you say excuse me. Like your mama taught you.

Cory: Come on, Pop . . . I got to get by.

(*Cory starts to maneuver his way past Troy. Troy grabs his leg and shoves him back.*)

Troy: You just gonna walk over top of me?

Cory: I live here too!

Troy (*advancing toward him*): You just gonna walk over top of me in my own house?

Cory: I ain't scared of you.

Troy: I ain't asked if you was scared of me. I asked you if you was fixing to walk over top of me in my own house? That's the question. You ain't gonna say excuse me? You just gonna walk over top of me?

Cory: If you wanna put it like that.

Troy: How else am I gonna put it?

Cory: I was walking by you to go into the house cause you sitting on the steps drunk, singing to yourself. You can put it like that.

Troy: Without saying excuse me???

(*Cory doesn't respond.*)

I asked you a question. Without saying excuse me???

Cory: I ain't got to say excuse me to you. You don't count around here no more.

Troy: Oh, I see . . . I don't count around here no more. You ain't got to say excuse me to your daddy. All of a sudden you done got so grown that your daddy don't count around here no more . . . Around here in his own house and yard that he done paid for with the sweat of his brow. You done got so grown to where you gonna take over. You gonna take over my house. Is that right? You gonna wear my pants. You gonna go in there and stretch out on my bed. You ain't got to say excuse me cause I don't count around here no more. Is that right?

Cory: That's right. You always talking this dumb stuff. Now, why don't you just get out my way?

Troy: I guess you got someplace to sleep and something to put in your belly. You got that, huh? You got that? That's what you need. You got that, huh?

Cory: You don't know what I got. You ain't got to worry about what I got.

Troy: You right! You one hundred percent right! I done spent the last seventeen years worrying about what you got. Now it's your turn, see? I'll tell you what to do. You grown . . . we done established that. You a man. Now, let's see you act like one. Turn your behind around and walk out this yard. And when you get out there in the alley . . . you can forget about this house. See? Cause this is my house. You go on and be a man and get your own house. You can forget about this. Cause this is mine. You go on and get yours cause I'm through with doing for you.

Cory: You talking about what you did for me . . . what'd you ever give me?

Troy: Them feet and bones! That pumping heart, nigger! I give you more than anybody else is ever gonna give you.

Cory: You ain't never gave me nothing! You ain't never done nothing but hold me back. Afraid I was gonna be better than you. All you ever did was try and make me scared of you. I used to tremble every time you called my name. Every time I heard your footsteps in the house. Wondering all the time . . . what's Papa gonna say if I do this? . . . What's he gonna say if I do that? . . . What's Papa gonna say if I turn on the radio? And Mama, too . . . she tries . . . but she's scared of you.

Troy: You leave your mama out of this. She ain't got nothing to do with this.

Cory: I don't know how she stand you . . . after what you did to her.

Troy: I told you to leave your mama out of this!

(He advances toward Cory.)

Cory: What you gonna do . . . give me a whupping? You can't whup me no more. You're too old. You just an old man.

Troy (shoves him on his shoulder): Nigger! That's what you are. You just another nigger on the street to me!

Cory: You crazy! You know that?

Troy: Go on now! You got the devil in you. Get on away from me!

Cory: You just a crazy old man . . . talking about I got the devil in me.

Troy: Yeah, I'm crazy! If you don't get on the other side of that yard . . . I'm gonna show you how crazy I am! Go on . . . get the hell out of my yard.

Cory: It ain't your yard. You took Uncle Gabe's money he got from the army to buy this house and then you put him out.

Troy (advances on Cory): Get your black ass out of my yard!

(Troy's advance backs Cory up against the tree. Cory grabs up the bat.)

Cory: I ain't going nowhere! Come on . . . put me out! I ain't scared of you.

Troy: That's my bat!

Cory: Come on!

Troy: Put my bat down!

Cory: Come on, put me out.

(Cory swings at Troy, who backs across the yard.)

What's the matter? You so bad . . . put me out!

(Troy advances toward Cory.)

Cory (backing up): Come on! Come on!

Troy: You're gonna have to use it! You wanna draw that bat back on me . . . you're gonna have to use it.

Cory: Come on! . . . Come on!

(Cory swings the bat at Troy a second time. He misses. Troy continues to advance toward him.)

Troy: You're gonna have to kill me! You wanna draw that bat back on me. You're gonna have to kill me.

(Cory, backed up against the tree, can go no farther. Troy taunts him. He sticks out his head and offers him a target.)

Come on! Come on!

(Cory is unable to swing the bat. Troy grabs it.)

Troy: Then I'll show you.

(Cory and Troy struggle over the bat. The struggle is fierce and fully engaged. Troy ultimately is the stronger, and takes the bat from Cory and stands over him ready to swing. He stops himself.)

Go on and get away from around my house.

(Cory, stung by his defeat, picks himself up, walks slowly out of the yard and up the alley.)

Cory: Tell Mama I'll be back for my things.

Troy: They'll be on the other side of that fence.

    (*Cory exits.*)

Troy: I can't taste nothing. Helluljah! I can't taste nothing no more. (*Troy assumes a batting posture and begins to taunt Death, the fastball on the outside corner.*) Come on! It's between you and me now! Come on! Anytime you want! Come on! I be ready for you . . . but I ain't gonna be easy.

    (*The lights go down on the scene.*)

SCENE V

The time is 1965. The lights come up in the yard. It is the morning of Troy's funeral. A funeral plaque with a light hangs beside the door. There is a small garden plot off to the side. There is noise and activity in the house as Rose, Lyons, and Bono have gathered. The door opens and Raynell, seven years old, enters dressed in a flannel nightgown. She crosses to the garden and pokes around with a stick. Rose calls from the house.

Rose: Raynell!
Raynell: Mam?
Rose: What you doing out there?
Raynell: Nothing.

    (*Rose comes to the door.*)

Rose: Girl, get in here and get dressed. What you doing?
Raynell: Seeing if my garden growed.
Rose: I told you it ain't gonna grow overnight. You got to wait.
Raynell: It don't look like it never gonna grow. Dag!
Rose: I told you a watched pot never boils. Get in here and get dressed.
Raynell: This ain't even no pot, Mama.
Rose: You just have to give it a chance. It'll grow. Now you come on and do what I told you. We got to be getting ready. This ain't no morning to be playing around. You hear me?
Raynell: Yes, Mam.

    (*Rose exits into the house. Raynell continues to poke at her garden with a stick. Cory enters. He is dressed in a Marine corporal's uniform, and carries a duffel-bag. His posture is that of a military man, and his speech has a clipped sternness.*)

Cory (to Raynell): Hi. (*Pause.*) I bet your name is Raynell.
Raynell: Uh huh.
Cory: Is your mama home?

    (*Raynell runs up on the porch and calls through the screen door.*)

Raynell: Mama . . . there's some man out here. Mama?

(*Rose comes to the door.*)

Rose: Cory? Lord have mercy! Look here, you all!

(*Rose and Cory embrace in a tearful reunion as Bono and Lyons enter from the house dressed in funeral clothes.*)

Bono: Aw, looka here . . .

Rose: Done got all grown up!

Cory: Don't cry, Mama. What you crying about?

Rose: I'm just so glad you made it.

Cory: Hey Lyons. How you doing, Mr. Bono.

(*Lyons goes to embrace Cory.*)

Lyons: Look at you, man. Look at you. Don't he look good, Rose. Got them Corporal stripes.

Rose: What took you so long?

Cory: You know how the Marines are, Mama. They got to get all their paperwork straight before they let you do anything.

Rose: Well, I'm sure glad you made it. They let Lyons come. Your Uncle Gabe's still in the hospital. They don't know if they gonna let him out or not. I just talked to them a little while ago.

Lyons: A Corporal in the United States Marines.

Bono: Your daddy knew you had it in you. He used to tell me all the time.

Lyons: Don't he look good, Mr. Bono?

Bono: Yeah, he remind me of Troy when I first met him. (*Pause.*) Say, Rose, Lucille's down at the church with the choir. I'm gonna go down and get the pallbearers lined up. I'll be back to get you all.

Rose: Thanks, Jim.

Cory: See you, Mr. Bono.

Lyons (with his arm around Raynell): Cory . . . look at Raynell. Ain't she precious? She gonna break a whole lot of hearts.

Rose: Raynell, come and say hello to your brother. This is your brother, Cory. You remember Cory.

Raynell: No, Mam.

Cory: She don't remember me, Mama.

Rose: Well, we talk about you. She heard us talk about you. (*To Raynell.*) This is your brother, Cory. Come on and say hello.

Raynell: Hi.

Cory: Hi. So you're Raynell. Mama told me a lot about you.

Rose: You all come on into the house and let me fix you some breakfast. Keep up your strength.

Cory: I ain't hungry, Mama.

Lyons: You can fix me something, Rose. I'll be in there in a minute.

Rose: Cory, you sure you don't want nothing? I know they ain't feeding you right.

Cory: No, Mama . . . thanks. I don't feel like eating. I'll get something later.

Rose: Raynell . . . get on upstairs and get that dress on like I told you.

(Rose and Raynell exit into the house.)

Lyons: So . . . I hear you thinking about getting married.

Cory: Yeah, I done found the right one, Lyons. It's about time.

Lyons: Me and Bonnie been split up about four years now. About the time Papa retired. I guess she just got tired of all them changes I was putting her through. *(Pause.)* I always knew you was gonna make something out your-self. Your head was always in the right direction. So . . . you gonna stay in . . . make it a career . . . put in your twenty years?

Cory: I don't know. I got six already, I think that's enough.

Lyons: Stick with Uncle Sam and retire early. Ain't nothing out here. I guess Rose told you what happened with me. They got me down the workhouse. I thought I was being slick cashing other people's checks.

Cory: How much time you doing?

Lyons: They give me three years. I got that beat now. I ain't got but nine more months. It ain't so bad. You learn to deal with it like anything else. You got to take the crookeds with the straights. That's what Papa used to say. He used to say that when he struck out. I seen him strike out three times in a row . . . and the next time up he hit the ball over the grand-stand. Right out there in Homestead Field. He wasn't satisfied hitting in the seats . . . he want to hit it over everything! After the game he had two hundred people standing around waiting to shake his hand. You got to take the crookeds with the straights. Yeah, Papa was something else.

Cory: You still playing?

Lyons: Cory . . . you know I'm gonna do that. There's some fellows down there we got us a band . . . we gonna try and stay together when we get out . . . but yeah, I'm still playing. It still helps me to get out of bed in the morn-ing. As long as it do that I'm gonna be right there playing and trying to make some sense out of it.

Rose (calling): Lyons, I got these eggs in the pan.

Lyons: Let me go on and get these eggs, man. Get ready to go bury Papa. *(Pause.)* How you doing? You doing alright?

(Cory nods. Lyons touches him on the shoulder and they share a moment of silent grief. Lyons exits into the house. Cory wanders about the yard. Raynell enters.)

Raynell: Hi.

Cory: Hi.

Raynell: Did you used to sleep in my room?

Cory: Yeah . . . that used to be my room.

Raynell: That's what Papa call it. "Cory's room." It got your football in the closet.

(*Rose comes to the door.*)

Rose: Raynell, get in there and get them good shoes on.

Raynell: Mama, can't I wear these? Them other one hurt my feet.

Rose: Well, they just gonna have to hurt your feet for a while. You ain't said they hurt your feet when you went down to the store and got them.

Raynell: They didn't hurt then. My feet done got bigger.

Rose: Don't you give me no backtalk now. You get in there and get them shoes on.

(*Raynell exits into the house.*)

Ain't too much changed. He still got that piece of rag tied to that tree. He was out here swinging that bat. I was just ready to go back in the house. He swung that bat and then he just fell over. Seem like he swung it and stood there with this grin on his face . . . and then he just fell over. They carried him on down to the hospital, but I knew there wasn't no need . . . why don't you come on in the house?

Cory: Mama . . . I got something to tell you. I don't know how to tell you this . . . but I've got to tell you . . . I'm not going to Papa's funeral.

Rose: Boy, hush your mouth. That's your daddy you talking about. I don't want hear that kind of talk this morning. I done raised you to come to this? You standing there all healthy and grown talking about you ain't going to your daddy's funeral?

Cory: Mama . . . listen . . .

Rose: I don't want to hear it, Cory. You just get that thought out of your head.

Cory: I can't drag Papa with me everywhere I go. I've got to say no to him. One time in my life I've got to say no.

Rose: Don't nobody have to listen to nothing like that. I know you and your daddy ain't seen eye to eye, but I ain't got to listen to that kind of talk this morning. Whatever was between you and your daddy . . . the time has come to put it aside. Just take it and set it over there on the shelf and forget about it. Disrespecting your daddy ain't gonna make you a man, Cory. You got to find a way to come to that on your own. Not going to your daddy's funeral ain't gonna make you a man.

Cory: The whole time I was growing up . . . living in his house . . . Papa was like a shadow that followed you everywhere. It weighed on you and sunk into your flesh. It would wrap around you and lay there until you couldn't tell which one was you anymore. That shadow digging in your flesh. Trying to crawl in. Trying to live through you. Everywhere I looked, Troy

Maxson was staring back at me . . . hiding under the bed . . . in the closet. I'm just saying I've got to find a way to get rid of that shadow, Mama.

Rose: You just like him. You got him in you good.

Cory: Don't tell me that, Mama.

Rose: You Troy Maxson all over again.

Cory: I don't want to be Troy Maxson. I want to be me.

Rose: You can't be nobody but who you are, Cory. That shadow wasn't nothing but you growing into yourself. You either got to grow into it or cut it down to fit you. But that's all you got to make life with. That's all you got to measure yourself against that world out there. Your daddy wanted you to be everything he wasn't . . . and at the same time he tried to make you into everything he was. I don't know if he was right or wrong . . . but I do know he meant to do more good than he meant to do harm. He wasn't always right. Sometimes when he touched he bruised. And sometimes when he took me in his arms he cut.

When I first met your daddy I thought . . . Here is a man I can lay down with and make a baby. That's the first thing I thought when I seen him. I was thirty years old and had done seen my share of men. But when he walked up to me and said, "I can dance a waltz that'll make you dizzy," I thought, Rose Lee, here is a man that you can open yourself up to and be filled to bursting. Here is a man that can fill all them empty spaces you been tipping around the edges of. One of them empty spaces was being somebody's mother.

I married your daddy and settled down to cooking his supper and keeping clean sheets on the bed. When your daddy walked through the house he was so big he filled it up. That was my first mistake. Not to make him leave some room for me. For my part in the matter. But at that time I wanted that. I wanted a house that I could sing in. And that's what your daddy gave me. I didn't know to keep up his strength I had to give up little pieces of mine. I did that. I took on his life as mine and mixed up the pieces so that you couldn't hardly tell which was which anymore. It was my choice. It was my life and I didn't have to live it like that. But that's what life offered me in the way of being a woman and I took it. I grabbed hold of it with both hands.

By the time Raynell came into the house, me and your daddy had done lost touch with one another. I didn't want to make my blessing off of nobody's misfortune . . . but I took on to Raynell like she was all them babies I had wanted and never had.

(The phone rings.)

Like I'd been blessed to relive a part of my life. And if the Lord see fit to keep up my strength . . . I'm gonna do her just like your daddy did you . . . I'm gonna give her the best of what's in me.

Raynell (entering, still with her old shoes): Mama . . . Reverend Tolliver on the phone.

(Rose exits into the house.)

Raynell: Hi.

Cory: Hi.

Raynell: You in the Army or the Marines?

Cory: Marines.

Raynell: Papa said it was the Army. Did you know Blue?

Cory: Blue? Who's Blue?

Raynell: Papa's dog what he sing about all the time.

Cory (singing):

> Hear it ring! Hear it ring!
> I had a dog his name was Blue
> You know Blue was mighty true
> You know Blue was a good old dog
> Blue treed a possum in a hollow log
> You know from that he was a good old dog.
> Hear it ring! Hear it ring!

(Raynell joins in singing.)

Cory and Raynell:

> Blue treed a possum out on a limb
> Blue looked at me and I looked at him
> Grabbed that possum and put him in a sack
> Blue stayed there till I came back
> Old Blue's feets was big and round
> Never allowed a possum to touch the ground.

> Old Blue died and I dug his grave
> I dug his grave with a silver spade
> Let him down with a golden chain
> And every night I call his name
> Go on Blue, you good dog you
> Go on Blue, you good dog you.

Raynell:

> Blue laid down and died like a man
> Blue laid down and died . . .

Both:

> Blue laid down and died like a man
> Now he's treeing possums in the Promised Land
> I'm gonna tell you this to let you know
> Blue's gone where the good dogs go
> When I hear old Blue bark
> When I hear old Blue bark
> Blue treed a possum in Noah's Ark
> Blue treed a possum in Noah's Ark.

(Rose comes to the screen door.)

Rose: Cory, we gonna be ready to go in a minute.

Cory *(to Raynell):* You go on in the house and change them shoes like Mama told you so we can go to Papa's funeral.

Raynell: Okay, I'll be back.

(Raynell exits into the house. Cory gets up and crosses over to the tree. Rose stands in the screen door watching him. Gabriel enters from the alley.)

Gabriel *(calling):* Hey, Rose!

Rose: Gabe?

Gabriel: I'm here, Rose. Hey, Rose, I'm here!

(Rose enters from the house.)

Rose: Lord . . . Look here, Lyons!

Lyons: See, I told you, Rose . . . I told you they'd let him come.

Cory: How you doing, Uncle Gabe?

Lyons: How you doing, Uncle Gabe?

Gabriel: Hey, Rose. It's time. It's time to tell St. Peter to open the gates. Troy, you ready? You ready, Troy. I'm gonna tell St. Peter to open the gates. You get ready now.

(Gabriel, with great fanfare, braces himself to blow. The trumpet is without a mouthpiece. He puts the end of it into his mouth and blows with great force, like a man who has been waiting some twenty-odd years for this single moment. No sound comes out of the trumpet. He braces himself and blows again with the same result. A third time he blows. There is a weight of impossible description that falls away and leaves him bare and exposed to a frightful realization. It is a trauma that a sane and normal mind would be unable to withstand. He begins to dance. A slow, strange dance, eerie and life-giving. A dance of atavistic signature and ritual. Lyons attempts to embrace him. Gabriel pushes Lyons away. He begins to howl in what is an attempt at song, or perhaps a song turning back into itself in an attempt at speech. He finishes his dance and the gates of heaven stand open as wide as God's closet.)

That's the way that go!

BLACKOUT

Susan Glaspell at work, around 1913.

WRITING

WRITING

29 WRITING ABOUT LITERATURE

Assigned to write an essay on *Hamlet*, a student might well wonder, "What can I say that hasn't been said a thousand times before?" Often the most difficult aspect of writing about a story, poem, or play is the feeling that we have nothing unique to say.

Remember though that in the study of literature common sense is never out of place. For most of a class hour, a professor once rhapsodized about the arrangement of the contents of W. H. Auden's *Collected Poems*. Auden, he claimed, was a master of thematic continuity, who had brilliantly placed the poems in the order that they ingeniously complemented each other. Near the end of the hour, his theories were punctured—with a great inaudible pop—when a student, timidly raising a hand, pointed out that Auden had arranged the poems in the book not by theme but in alphabetical order according to the first word of each poem. The professor's jaw dropped: "Why didn't you say that sooner?" The student was apologetic: "I—I was afraid I'd sound too *ordinary*."

Don't be afraid to state a conviction, though it seems obvious. Does it matter that you may be repeating something that has been said before? What matters more is that you are actively engaged in thinking about literature. There are excellent old ideas as well as new ones. You have something to say.

READ ACTIVELY

Most people read in a relaxed, almost passive way. They let the story or poem carry them along without asking too many questions. To write about literature well, however, you need to *read actively*, paying special attention to various aspects of the text. Here are some steps to get you started:

- **Preview the text.** To get acquainted with a work of literature before you settle in for a closer reading, skim it for an overview of its content and organization. Pay attention to the title. Take a quick look at all parts of the work. Even a book's cover, preface, introduction, footnotes, and biographical notes about the author can provide you with some context for reading the work itself.

▪ **Read closely. Look up any unfamiliar words, allusions, or references.** Often the very words you may be tempted to skim over will provide the key to a work's meaning. Thomas Hardy's poem "The Ruined Maid" will remain elusive to a reader unfamiliar with the archaic meaning of the word "ruin"—a woman's loss of virginity to a man other than her husband.

▪ **Take notes. Annotate the text.** Read with a highlighter and pencil at hand, making appropriate annotations to the text. Later, you'll easily be able to review these highlights, and, when you write your paper, quickly refer to supporting evidence.

• Underline words, phrases, or sentences that seem interesting or important, or that raise questions.
• Jot down brief notes in the margin ("*key symbol—this foreshadows the ending,*" for example, or "*dramatic irony*").
• Use lines or arrows to indicate passages that seem to speak to each other—for instance, all the places in which you find the same theme or related symbols.

Robert Frost
Nothing Gold Can Stay

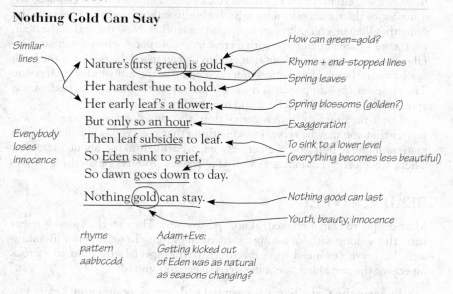

Similar lines

Nature's first green is gold,
Her hardest hue to hold.
Her early leaf's a flower;
But only so an hour.
Then leaf subsides to leaf.
So Eden sank to grief,
So dawn goes down to day.

Nothing gold can stay.

How can green=gold?
Rhyme + end-stopped lines
Spring leaves
Spring blossoms (golden?)
Exaggeration
To sink to a lower level
(everything becomes less beautiful)

Everybody loses innocence

Nothing good can last
Youth, beauty, innocence

rhyme pattern aabbccdd

Adam+Eve:
Getting kicked out of Eden was as natural as seasons changing?

- **Reread as needed.** If a piece is short, read it several times. Often, knowing the ending of a poem or short story will allow you to extract new meaning from its beginning and middle. If the piece is longer, reread the passages you thought important enough to highlight.

- **Read poetry aloud.** There is no better way to understand a poem than to effectively read it aloud. Read slowly, paying attention to punctuation cues. Listen for the audio effects.

- **Read the whole play—not just the dialogue, but also everything in italics, including stage directions and descriptions of settings.** The meaning of a scene, or even of an entire play, may depend on the tone of voice in which an actor is supposed to deliver a significant line or upon the actions described in the stage directions, as in this passage from Susan Glaspell's *Trifles.*

Mrs. Peters (to the other woman): Oh, her fruit; it did freeze. *(To the County Attorney)* She worried about that when it turned so cold. She said the fire'd go out and her jars would break.

Sheriff: Well, can you beat the women! Held for murder and worryin' about her preserves.

> Both men are insulting toward Mrs. Wright.

County Attorney: I guess before we're through she may have something more serious than preserves to worry about.

Hale: Well, women are used to worrying over trifles.

> He _thinks_ he's being kind.

(The two women move a little closer together.)

> The women side with each other.

County Attorney (with the gallantry of a young politician): And yet, for all their worries, what would we do without the ladies? *(The women do not unbend.* He goes to the sink, takes a dipperful of water from the pail and pouring it into a basin, washes his hands. Starts to wipe them on the roller towel, turns it for a cleaner place.) Dirty towels! *(Kicks his foot against the pans under the sink.)* Not much of a housekeeper, would you say, ladies?

> Courtesy toward women, but condescending

> The two women aren't buying it.

Mrs. Hale (stiffly): There's a great deal of work to be done on a farm.

> She holds back, but she's mad.

> Small, insignificant things or not? Play's title. Significant word? The men miss the "clues"—too trifling.

> I don't like this guy!

THINK ABOUT THE READING

Once you have reread the work, you can begin to process your ideas about it. To get started thinking about fiction or drama, try the following steps:

- **Identify the protagonist and the conflict.** Whose story is being told? What does that character desire more than anything else? What stands in the way of that character's achievement of his or her goal? The answers to these questions can give you a better handle on the plot.

- **Consider the point of view.** What does it contribute to the work? How might the tale change if told from another point of view?

- **Think about the setting.** Does it play a significant role in the plot? How does setting affect the tone?

- **Notice key symbols.** If any symbols catch your attention as you go, be sure to highlight each place in which they appear in the text. What do these symbols contribute to the work's meaning? (Remember, not every image is a symbol—only those important recurrent persons, places, or things that seem to suggest more than their literal meaning.)

- **Look for the theme.** Is the work's central meaning stated directly? If not, how does it reveal itself?

- **Think about tone and style.** How would you characterize the style in which the story or play is written? Consider elements such as diction, sentence structure, tone, and organization. How does the work's style contribute to its tone?

You might consider some different approaches when thinking about a poem.

- **Let your emotions guide you into the poem.** Do any images or phrases call up a strong emotional response? If so, try to puzzle out why those passages seem so emotionally loaded. In a word or two, describe the poem's tone.

- **Determine what's literally happening in the poem.** Separating literal language from figurative or symbolic language can be one of the trickiest— and most essential—tasks in poetic interpretation. Begin by working out the literal. Who is speaking the poem? To whom? Under what circumstances? What happens in the poem?

- **Ask what it all adds up to.** Once you've pinned down the literal action of the poem, it's time to take a leap into the figurative. What is the significance of the poem? Address symbolism, any figures of speech, and any language that means one thing literally but suggests something else. In "My Papa's Waltz," for example, Theodore Roethke tells a simple story of a father dancing his small son around a kitchen. The language of the poem suggests much more, however, implying that while the father is rough to the point of violence, the young boy hungers for his attention.

- **Consider the poem's shape on the page, and the way it sounds.** What patterns of sound do you notice? Are the lines long, short, or a mixture of both? How do these elements contribute to the poem's effect?

- **Pay attention to form.** If a poem makes use of rime or regular meter, ask yourself how those elements contribute to its meaning. If it is in a fixed form, such as a sonnet or villanelle, how do the demands of that form serve to set its tone? If the form calls for repetition—of sounds, words, or entire lines—how does that repetition underscore the poem's message? If, on the other hand, the poem is in free verse—without a consistent pattern of rime or regular meter—how does this choice affect the poem's feel?

- **Take note of line breaks.** If the poem is written in free verse, pay special attention to its line breaks. Poets break their lines with care, conscious that readers pause momentarily over the last word in any line, giving that word special emphasis. Notice whether the lines tend to be broken at the ends of whole phrases and sentences or in the middle of phrases. Then ask yourself what effect is created by the poet's choice of line breaks. How does that effect contribute to the poem's meaning?

PLAN YOUR ESSAY

If you have actively reread the work you plan to write about and have made notes or annotations, you are already well on your way to writing your paper. Your mind has already begun to work through some initial impressions and ideas. Now you need to arrange those early notions into an organized and logical essay. Here is some advice on how to manage the writing process:

- **Leave yourself time.** Good writing involves thought and revision. Anyone who has ever been a student knows what it's like to pull an all-nighter, churning out a term paper hours before it is due. Still, the best writing takes time. Your ideas need to marinate. For the sake of your writing—not to mention your sanity—it's far better to get the job started well before your deadline.

- **Choose a subject you care about.** If you have been given a choice of literary works to write about, always choose the play, story, or poem that evokes the strongest emotional response. Your writing will be liveliest if you feel engaged by your subject.

- **Know your purpose.** As you write, keep the assignment in mind. You may have been asked to write a response, in which you describe your reactions to a literary work. Perhaps your purpose is to interpret a work, analyzing how one or more of its elements contribute to its meaning. You may have been instructed to write an evaluation, in which you judge a work's merits. Whatever the assignment, how you approach your essay will depend in large part on your purpose.

▪ **Define your topic narrowly.** Worried about having enough to say, students sometimes frame their topic so broadly that they can't do justice to it in the allotted number of pages. Your paper will be stronger if you go more deeply into a well-focused subject than if you choose a gigantic subject and touch on most aspects of it only superficially. A thorough explication of a short story is hardly possible in a 250-word paper, but an explication of a paragraph or two could work in that space. A profound topic ("The Character of Hamlet") might overflow a book, but a more focused one ("Hamlet's View of Acting" or "Hamlet's Puns") could result in a manageable paper.

PREWRITING: GENERATE IDEAS AND ISSUES

Topic in hand, you can begin to get your ideas on the page. To generate new ideas and clarify the thoughts you already have, try one or more of the following useful prewriting techniques as one student did preparing a paper on Robert Frost's poem "Nothing Gold Can Stay."

▪ **Brainstorm.** Writing quickly, list everything that comes into your mind about your subject. Set a time limit—ten or fifteen minutes—and force yourself to keep adding items to the list, even when you think you have run out of things to say. Sometimes, if you press onward past the point where you feel you are finished, you will surprise yourself with new and fresh ideas.

> gold = early leaves/blossoms
> Or gold = something precious (both?)
> early leaf = flower (yellow blossoms)
> spring (lasts an hour)
> Leaves subside (sink to lower level)
> Eden = paradise = perfection = beauty
> Loss of innocence?
> What about original sin?
> Dawn becomes day (dawn is more precious?)
> Adam and Eve had to fall? Part of natural order.
> seasons/days/people's lives
> Title = last line: perfection can't last
> spring/summer/autumn
> dawn/day
> Innocence can't last

▢ **Cluster.** This prewriting technique works especially well for visual thinkers. In clustering, you build a diagram to help you explore the relationships among your ideas. To get started, write your subject at the center of a sheet of paper. Circle it. Then jot down ideas, linking each to the central circle with lines. As you write down each new idea, draw lines to link it to related old ideas. The result will look something like the following web.

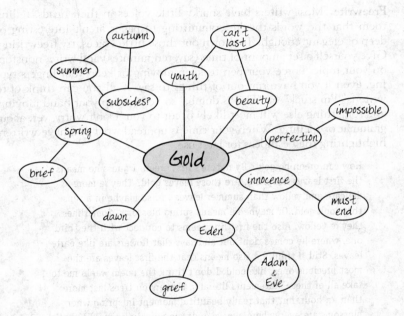

■ **List.** Look over the notes and annotations that you made in your active reading of the work. You have probably already underlined or noted more information than you can possibly use. One way to sort through your material to find the most useful information is to make a list of the important items. It helps to make several short lists under different headings. Here are some lists you might make after rereading Frost's "Nothing Gold Can Stay." Don't be afraid to add more comments or questions on the lists to help your thought process.

Images	Colors
leaf ("early leaf")	green
flower	gold ("hardest hue to hold")
dawn	
day	
Eden	
gold	

<u>Key Actions</u>
gold is hard to hold
early leaf lasts only an hour
leaf subsides to leaf (what does this mean???)
Eden sinks to grief (paradise is lost)
dawn goes down to day
gold can't stay (perfection is impossible?)

■ **Freewrite.** Most writers have snarky little voices in their heads, telling them that the words they're committing to paper aren't interesting or deep or elegant enough. To drown out those little voices, try freewriting. Give yourself a set amount of time (say, ten minutes) and write, nonstop, on your topic. Force your pen to keep moving or keep your fingers typing, even if you have run out of things to say. If all you can think of to write is "I'm stuck" or "This is dumb," so be it. Keep your hand moving, and something else will most likely occur to you. Don't worry, yet, about grammar or spelling. When your time is up, read what you have written, highlighting the best ideas for later use.

> How can green be gold? By nature's first green, I guess he means
> the first leaves in spring. Are those leaves gold? They're more
> delicate and yellow than summer leaves . . . so maybe in a sense
> they look gold. Or maybe he means spring blossoms. Sometimes
> they're yellow. Also the first line seems to connect with the third
> one, where he comes right out and says that flowers are like early
> leaves. Still, I think he also means that the first leaves are the
> most precious ones, like gold. I don't think the poem wants me to
> take all of these statements literally. Flowers on trees last more
> than an hour, but that really beautiful moment in spring when
> blossoms are everywhere always ends too quickly, so maybe that's
> what he means by "only so an hour." I had to look up "subsides."
> It means to sink to a lower level . . . as if the later leaves will be
> less perfect than the first ones. I don't know if I agree. Aren't fall
> leaves precious? Then he says, "So Eden sank to grief" which
> seems to be saying that Adam and Eve's fall would have happened
> no matter what they did, because everything that seems perfect
> falls apart . . . . nothing gold can stay. Is he saying Adam and Eve
> didn't really have a choice? No matter what, everything gets
> older, less beautiful, less innocent . . . even people.

■ **Journal.** Your instructor might ask you to keep a journal in which you jot down your ideas, feelings, and impressions before they are fully formulated. Sometimes a journal is meant for your eyes only; in other instances your instructor might read it. Either way, it is meant to be informal and immediate, and to provide raw material that you may later choose to refine into a formal essay. Here are some tips for keeping a useful journal:

- Get your ideas down as soon as they occur to you.
- Write quickly.
- Jot down your feelings about and first impressions of the story, poem, or play you are reading.
- Don't worry about grammar, spelling, or punctuation.
- Don't worry about sounding academic.
- Don't worry about whether your ideas are good or bad ones; you can sort that out later.
- Try out invention strategies, such as freewriting, clustering, and outlining.
- Keep writing, even after you think you have run out of things to say. You might surprise yourself.
- Write about what interests you most.
- Write in your journal on a regular basis.

■ **Outline.** Some topics by their very nature suggest obvious ways to organize a paper. "An Explication of a Sonnet by Wordsworth" might mean simply working through the poem line by line. If this isn't the case, some kind of outline will probably prove helpful. Your outline needn't be elaborate to be useful. While a long research paper on several literary works might call for a detailed outline, a 500-word analysis of a short story's figures of speech might call for just a simple list of points in the order that makes the most logical sense—not necessarily, of course, the order in which those thoughts first came to mind.

1. Passage of time = fall from innocence
   blossoms
   gold
   dawn
   grief

2. Innocence = perfection
   Adam and Eve
   loss of innocence = inevitable
   real original sin = passing of time
   paradise sinks to grief

3. Grief = knowledge
   experience of sin & suffering
   unavoidable as grow older

DEVELOP YOUR ARGUMENT

Once you have finished a rough outline of your ideas, you need to refine it into a clear and logical shape. You need to state your thesis—your paper's main claim—clearly and then support it with logical and accurate evidence. Here is a practical approach to this crucial stage of the writing process:

▪ **Consider your purpose.** As you develop your argument, be sure to refer back to the specific assignment; let it guide you. Your instructor might request one of the following kinds of papers:

- *Response*, in which you explore your reaction to a work of literature.
- *Evaluation*, in which you assess the literary merits of a work.
- *Interpretation*, in which you discuss a work's meaning. If your instructor has assigned an interpretation, he or she may have more specifically asked for an *analysis*, *explication*, or *comparison/contrast* essay, among other possibilities.

▪ **Remember your audience.** Practically speaking, your professor (and sometimes your classmates) will be your paper's primary audience. Some assignments, however, specify a particular audience beyond your professor and classmates. Keep your readers in mind. Be sure to adapt your writing to meet their needs and interests. If, for example, the audience has presumably already read a story under discussion, you won't need to relate the plot in its entirety. Instead, you will be free to bring up only those plot points that serve as evidence for your thesis.

▪ **Narrow your topic to fit the assignment.** Though you may be tempted to choose a broad topic so that you will have no shortage of things to say, remember that a good paper needs focus. Your choice should be narrow enough for you to do it justice in the space and time allotted.

▪ **Decide on a thesis.** Just as you need to know your destination before you set out on a trip, you need to decide what point you're traveling toward before you begin your first draft. Start by writing a provisional thesis sentence: a summing up of the main idea or argument your paper will explore. While your thesis doesn't need to be outrageous or deliberately provocative, it does need to take a stand. A clear, decisive statement gives you something to prove and lends vigor to your essay.

> **WORKING THESIS**
>
> The poem argues that like Adam and Eve we all lose our innocence and the passage of time is inevitable.

This first stab at a thesis sentence gave its author a sense of purpose and direction that allowed him to finish his first draft. Later, as he revised his essay, he found he needed to refine his thesis to make more specific and focused assertions.

STRENGTHEN YOUR ARGUMENT: RHETORICAL APPEALS

An argumentative essay states its thesis—its main claim—and tries to influence the reader's opinion. Argumentative essays have something in common with opinion pieces and editorials, as well as with most political speeches. All of these forms are used to try to convince people of something.

After you've formulated a thesis, your task is clear: you need to convince your audience that your thesis is correct. It will help to have an understanding of some key elements of argument as you write to persuade your reader. Effective argumentation requires you to combine logical reasoning with emotional appeals. Remember that you need to speak to both the reader's heart and mind. Additionally, you need to recognize that in any piece you write, your own credibility will be on display through your tone and manner.

Common approaches to effective argumentation—also called **rhetorical appeals**—are traditionally divided into three basic types:

- *Logos* (**logical argumentation**). This approach persuades an audience through logic or reason. *Logos* is the part of an argument that appeals to the head, not the heart. Is the claim of your essay clear? Is the argumentation logical? Is the evidence you offer reasonable? *Logos* is the aspect of the argument a reader can most easily define and analyze. It is essential to get your logical argumentation right in order to convince a reader of your thesis.

- *Pathos* (**emotional persuasion**). This approach evokes emotion or empathy. *Pathos* is the aspect of an argument that appeals to the heart. An argument that uses *pathos* creates an emotional response rather than an intellectual one. Logic alone is often not enough to convince a reader. If you can also make the reader respond with emotion, he or she is more likely to be convinced by your argument.

- *Ethos* (**credibility**). This approach establishes the credibility or character of the writer or speaker. Obviously, readers are more likely to believe the argument of someone who is an established expert on the topic being discussed or someone they believe to be honorable and trustworthy. Credibility can be established through the tone and style of the essay itself, or independently, through the known reputation of the writer.

Logical Argumentation: Evidence and Organization

Logos or logical argumentation requires clear and compelling evidence in support of claims. Here are some pointers on building the logical structure of your argument:

- **State your claims.** Your essay's main claim is your thesis—the central point of your paper. It should be clear, focused, and convincing. Your paper will be more interesting, though, if its main claim is not something entirely obvious. What is a claim? Any time you make a statement you intend to be taken as true, you have made a claim. Some claims are unlikely to be contradicted ("the sky is blue" or "today is Tuesday"), but others are debatable ("every college sophomore dreams of running off to see the world"). The process of supporting your claims will help you clarify and refine your ideas.

▪ **Offer evidence.** When you offer a debatable claim, you should support it with evidence. When you write about a work of literature, the most convincing evidence generally comes from the text itself. Direct quotations from the poem, play, or story under discussion can provide particularly convincing support for your claims. Be sure to introduce any quotation by putting it in the context of the larger work. It is even more important to follow up each quotation with your own analysis of what it shows about the work.

▪ **Evaluate how well your evidence supports your claim.** If you were to make the claim that today's weather is absolutely perfect and offer as your evidence the blue sky, your logic would include an unspoken **assumption**, or **warrant**: sunny weather is perfect weather. Not everyone will agree with your example, though. Some folks (perhaps farmers) might prefer rain. In making any argument, including one about literature, you may find that you sometimes need to explain why your evidence is sound. This is especially true when the evidence you provide can lead to conclusions other than the one you are hoping to prove.

▪ **Refine your thesis as necessary.** If you find the evidence doesn't support certain aspects of your thesis, then refine the thesis. Remember: until you turn in your essay, it is a work in progress. Anything can and should be changed if it doesn't further the development of your paper's main idea.

▪ **Organize your argument.** Unless you are writing an explication that works its way line by line through an entire literary work, you will need to make crucial decisions about how to shape your essay. Its order should be driven by the logic of your argument, not by the structure of the story, play, or poem you're discussing. In other words, you need not work your way mechanically from start to finish through your source material, touching on every point. Instead, choose only the major points needed to prove your thesis, and present them in whatever order best supports your claim. A rough outline can help you to determine the best order.

Emotional Argumentation

Pathos, or emotional argumentation, requires you to go beyond simply presenting the logical elements of your argument. You also need to create an emotional connection and response in the reader that will lead him or her to support your point of view. Here are some pointers on building the emotional framework for your argument.

▪ **Create a human connection.** Don't let your entire essay consist of abstract argumentation and support. What emotions can you describe or invoke that will earn the reader's attention and endorsement? How do you use that emotion to support your point of view? Always remember that you are writing for your fellow human beings, not for a computer.

- **Observe and describe emotion.** When you write about a short story, poem, or play, there is almost always emotional content in the text. (Sometimes the emotions are explicit; sometimes they are mostly implied.) Observe how the author evokes and uses that *pathos* to express his or her meaning. Find an emotional element in the work you are discussing and describe it in a way that invites the reader to respond in a manner appropriate to your argument. Don't hesitate to communicate your own emotions, if they are relevant to your argument. Give an example or anecdote that conveys that emotion.

- **Review the role of emotion in your argumentation.** Once you have drafted your essay, review its emotional content. Do you use *pathos* to support any of your points? If so, do you use it effectively? (Unfocused emotion may actually undermine your logical arguments and credibility.) Revise your essay accordingly to strengthen its emotional connection to the reader. Find those points in your essay where you can make an emotional connection to support your reasoning. Find the right example to create emotional support for your argument.

Credibility: Tone and Balance

Ethos, or credibility, is the reader's sense of the author's character and reliability—how trustworthy does the author seem? When weighing the merits of any claim, you probably take into account the credibility of the person making the case. Often this happens almost automatically. An expert on any given topic has a certain brand of authority not available to most of us. Fortunately, there are other ways to establish your own credibility. To strengthen the credibility of your argument, you should also consider the following principles:

- **Keep your tone thoughtful.** Your reader will develop a sense of who you are through your words. If you come across as belligerent, flippant, or disrespectful to those inclined to disagree with your views, you may lose your reader's goodwill. If you seem to exaggerate your evidence, the reader will discount your credibility. Therefore, express your ideas calmly and thoughtfully. A level tone demonstrates that you are interested in thinking through an issue or idea, not in bullying your reader into submission.

- **Take opposing arguments into account.** To make an argument more convincing, demonstrate familiarity with other possible points of view. Doing so indicates that you have taken other claims into account before arriving at your thesis; it reveals your fairness as well as your understanding of your subject matter. In laying out other points of view, though, be sure to represent them fairly but also to respectfully make clear why your thesis is the soundest claim; you don't want your reader to doubt where you stand.

▪ **Demonstrate your knowledge.** To gain your reader's trust, it helps to demonstrate a solid understanding of your subject matter. Always check your facts; factual errors can call your knowledge into doubt. It also helps to have a command of the conventions of writing. Errors in punctuation, spelling, or grammar can undermine your credibility.

CHECKLIST: Developing an Argument

- ☐ What is your essay's purpose?
- ☐ Who is your audience?
- ☐ Is your topic narrow enough?
- ☐ Is your thesis interesting and thought-provoking?
- ☐ Is your thesis reasonable? Can you support it with logical evidence?
- ☐ Are there emotional elements or examples you can use to support your thesis?
- ☐ Does everything in your essay support your thesis?
- ☐ Have you considered and refuted alternative views?
- ☐ Is your tone thoughtful?
- ☐ Is your argument sensibly organized? Are similar ideas grouped together? Does one point lead logically to the next?

DRAFT YOUR ARGUMENT

Seated at last, you prepare to write, only to find yourself besieged with petty distractions. All of a sudden you remember a friend you had promised to call, some double-A batteries you were supposed to pick up, a neglected cup of coffee (in another room) growing colder by the minute. If your paper is to be written, you have only one course of action: collar these thoughts and for the moment banish them. Here are a few tips for writing your rough draft:

▪ **Review your argument.** The shape of your argument, its support, and the evidence you have collected will form the basis of your rough draft.

▪ **Get your thoughts down.** The best way to draft a paper is to get your ideas down quickly. At this stage, don't fuss over details. The critical, analytical side of your mind can worry about spelling, grammar, and punctuation later. For now, let your creative mind take charge. This part of yourself has the good ideas, insight, and confidence. Forge ahead. Believe in yourself and in your ideas.

▪ **Write the part you feel most comfortable with first.** There's no need to start at the paper's beginning and work your way methodically through to the end. Instead, plunge right into the parts of the paper you feel most prepared to write. You can always go back later and fill in the blanks.

- **Leave yourself plenty of space.** As you compose, leave plenty of space between lines and set wide margins. When later thoughts come to you, you will easily be able to go back and squeeze them in.

- **Focus on the argument.** Whenever you bring up a new point, it's good to tie it back to your thesis. If you can't find a way to connect a point to your thesis, it's probably better to leave it out of your paper and come up with a point that advances your central claim.

- **Does your thesis hold up?** If, as you write, you find that most of the evidence you uncover is not helping you prove your paper's thesis, it may be that the thesis needs honing. Adjust it as needed.

- **Be open to new ideas.** Writing rarely proceeds in a straight line. Even after you outline your paper and begin to write and revise, expect to discover new thoughts—perhaps the best thoughts of all. If you do, be sure to invite them in.

SAMPLE STUDENT ROUGH DRAFT: ARGUMENT PAPER

Here is a student's rough draft for an argument essay on "Nothing Gold Can Stay."

On Robert Frost's "Nothing Gold Can Stay"

Most of the lines in the poem "Nothing Gold Can Stay" by Robert Frost focus on the changing of the seasons. The poem's first line says that the first leaves of spring are actually blossoms, and the actual leaves that follow are less precious. Those first blossoms only last a little while. The reader realizes that nature is a metaphor for a person's state of mind. People start off perfectly innocent, but as time passes, they can't help but lose that innocence. The poem argues that like Adam and Eve we all lose our innocence and the passage of time is inevitable.

The poem's first image is of the color found in nature. The early gold of spring blossoms is nature's "hardest hue to hold." The color gold is associated with the mineral gold, a precious commodity. There's a hint that early spring is nature in its perfect state, and perfection is impossible to hold on to. To the poem's speaker, the colors of early spring seem to last only an hour. If you blink, they are gone. Like early spring, innocence can't last.

The line "leaf subsides to leaf" brings us from early spring through summer and fall. The golden blossoms and delicate leaves of spring subside, or sink to a lower level, meaning they become less special and beautiful. There's nothing more special and beautiful than a baby, so people are the same way. In literature, summer often means the prime of your life, and autumn often means the declining years. These times are less beautiful ones. "So dawn goes down to day" is a similar kind of image. Dawns are unbelievably colorful and beautiful but they don't last very long. Day is nice, but not as special as dawn.

The most surprising line in the poem is the one that isn't about nature. Instead it's about human beings. Eden may have been a garden (a part of nature), but it also represents a state of mind. The traditional religious view is that Adam and Eve chose to disobey God and eat from the tree of knowledge. They could have stayed in paradise forever if they had followed God's orders. So it's surprising that Frost writes "So Eden sank to grief" in a poem that is all about how inevitable change is. It seems like he's saying that no matter what Adam and Eve had done, the Garden of Eden wouldn't stay the paradise it started out being. When Adam and Eve ate the apple, they lost their innocence. The apple is supposed to represent knowledge, so they became wiser but less perfect. But the poem implies that no matter what Adam and Eve had done, they would have grown sadder and wiser. That's true for all people. We can't stay young and innocent.

It's almost as if Frost is defying the Bible, suggesting that there is no such thing as sin. We can't help getting older and wiser. It's a natural process. Suffering happens not because we choose to do bad things but because passing time takes our innocence. The real original sin is that time has to pass and we all have to grow wiser and less innocent.

The poem "Nothing Gold Can Stay" makes the point that people can't stay innocent forever. Suffering is the inevitable result of the aging process. Like the first leaves of spring, we are at the best at the very beginning, and it's all downhill from there.

REVISE YOUR ARGUMENT

A writer rarely—if ever—achieves perfection on the first try. For most of us, good writing is largely a matter of revision. Once your first draft is done, you can—and should—turn on your analytical mind. Painstaking revision is more than just tidying up grammar and spelling. It might mean expanding your ideas or sharpening the focus by cutting out any unnecessary thoughts. To achieve effective writing, you must have the courage to be merciless. Tear your rough drafts apart and reassemble their pieces into a stronger order. As you revise, consider the following:

■ **Be sure your thesis is clear, decisive, and thought-provoking.** The most basic ingredient in a good essay is a strong thesis—the sentence in which you summarize the claim you are making. Your thesis should say something more than just the obvious; it should be clear and decisive and make a point that requires evidence to persuade your reader to agree. A sharp, bold thesis lends energy to your argument. A revision of the working thesis used in the rough draft above provides a good example.

WORKING THESIS

The poem argues that like Adam and Eve we all lose our innocence and the passage of time is inevitable.

This thesis may not be bold or specific enough to make for an interesting argument. A careful reader would be hard pressed to disagree with the observation that Frost's poem depicts the passage of time or the loss of innocence. In a revision of his thesis, however, the essay's author pushes the claim further, going beyond the obvious to its implications.

REVISED THESIS

In "Nothing Gold Can Stay," Frost makes a bold claim: sin, suffering, and loss are inevitable because the passage of time causes everyone to fall from grace.

Instead of simply asserting that the poem looks with sorrow on the passage of time, the revised thesis raises the issue of why this is so. It makes a more thought-provoking claim about the poem. An arguable thesis can result in a more energetic, purposeful essay. A thesis that is obvious to everyone, on the other hand, leads to a static, dull paper.

■ **Ascertain whether the evidence you provide supports your argument.** Does everything within your paper work to support its thesis sentence? While a solid paper might be written about the poetic form of "Nothing Gold Can Stay," the student paper above would not be well served by bringing the subject up unless the author could show how the poem's form contributes to its message that time causes everyone to lose his or her innocence. If you find yourself including information that doesn't serve your argument, consider going back into the poem, story, or play for more useful evidence. On the other hand, if you're beginning to have a sneaking feeling that your thesis itself is shaky, consider reworking *it* so that it more accurately reflects the evidence in the text.

■ **Check whether your argument is logical.** Does one point lead naturally to the next? Reread the paper, looking for logical fallacies, moments in which the claims you make are not sufficiently supported by evidence, or the connection between one thought and the next seems less than rational. Classic logical fallacies include making hasty generalizations, confusing cause and effect, or using a non sequitur, a statement that doesn't follow from the statement that precedes it. An example of two seemingly unconnected thoughts may be found in the second paragraph of the draft above:

> To the poem's speaker, the colors of early spring seem to last only an hour. If you blink, they are gone. Like early spring, innocence can't last.

Though there may well be a logical connection between the first two sentences and the third one, the paper doesn't spell that connection out. Asked to clarify the warrant, or assumption, that makes possible the leap from the subject of spring to the subject of innocence, the author revised the passage this way:

> To the poem's speaker, the colors of early spring seem to last only an hour. When poets write of seasons, they often also are commenting on the life cycle. To make a statement that spring can't last more than an hour implies that a person's youth (often symbolically associated with spring) is all too short. Therefore, the poem implies that innocent youth, like spring, lasts for only the briefest time.

The revised version spells out the author's thought process, helping the reader to follow the argument.

■ **Supply transitional words and phrases.** To ensure that your reader's journey from one idea to the next is a smooth one, insert transitional words and phrases at the start of new paragraphs or sentences. Phrases such as "in contrast" and "however" signal a U-turn in logic, while those such as "in addition" and "similarly" alert the reader that you are continuing in the same direction you have been traveling. Seemingly inconsequential words and phrases such as "also" and "as well" or "as mentioned above" can smooth the reader's path from one thought to the next, as in the following example:

DRAFT

Though Frost is writing about nature, his real subject is humanity. In literature, spring often represents youth. Summer symbolizes young adulthood, autumn stands for middle age, and winter represents old age. The adult stages of life are, for Frost, less precious than childhood, which passes very quickly. The innocence of childhood is, like those spring leaves, precious as gold.

ADDING TRANSITIONAL WORDS AND PHRASES

Though Frost is writing about nature, his real subject is humanity. As mentioned above, in literature, spring often represents youth. Similarly, summer symbolizes young adulthood, autumn stands for middle age, and winter represents old age. The adult stages of life are, for Frost, less precious than childhood, which passes very quickly. Also, the innocence of childhood is, like those spring leaves, precious as gold.

- **Make sure each paragraph contains a topic sentence.** Each paragraph in your essay should develop a single idea; this idea should be conveyed in a topic sentence. As astute readers often expect to get a sense of a paragraph's purpose from its first few sentences, a topic sentence is often well placed at or near a paragraph's start.

- **Make a good first impression.** Your introductory paragraph may have seemed just fine as you began the writing process. Be sure to reconsider it in light of the entire paper. Does the introduction draw readers in and prepare them for what follows? If not, be sure to rework it, as the author of the rough draft above did. Look at his first paragraph again:

DRAFT OF OPENING PARAGRAPH

Most of the lines in the poem "Nothing Gold Can Stay" by Robert Frost focus on the changing of the seasons. The poem's first line says that the first leaves of spring are actually blossoms, and the actual leaves that follow are less precious. Those first blossoms only last a little while. The reader realizes that nature is a metaphor for a person's state of mind. People start off perfectly innocent, but as time passes, they can't help but lose that happy innocence. The poem argues that like Adam and Eve we all lose our innocence and the passage of time is inevitable.

While serviceable, this paragraph could be more compelling. Its author improved it by adding specifics to bring his ideas to more vivid life. For example, the rather pedestrian sentence "People start off perfectly innocent, but as time passes, they can't help but lose that innocence," became this livelier one: "As babies we are all perfectly innocent, but as time passes, we can't help but lose that innocence." By adding a specific image—the baby—the author gives the reader a visual picture to illustrate the abstract idea of innocence. He also sharpened his thesis sentence, making it less general and more thought-provoking. By varying the length of his sentences, he made the paragraph less monotonous.

REVISED OPENING PARAGRAPH

Most of the lines in Robert Frost's brief poem "Nothing Gold Can Stay" focus on nature: the changing of the seasons and the fading of dawn into day. The poem's opening line asserts that the first blossoms of spring are more precious than the leaves that follow. Likewise, dawn is more special than day. Though Frost's subject seems to be nature, the reader soon realizes that his real subject is human nature. As babies we are all perfectly innocent, but as time passes, we can't help but lose that happy innocence. In "Nothing Gold Can Stay," Frost makes a bold claim: sin, suffering, and loss are inevitable because the passage of time causes everyone to fall from grace.

■ **Remember that last impressions count too.** Your paper's conclusion should give the reader some closure, tying up the paper's loose ends without simply (and boringly) restating all that has come before. The author of the rough draft above initially ended his paper with a paragraph that repeated the paper's main ideas without pushing those ideas any further:

DRAFT OF CONCLUSION

The poem "Nothing Gold Can Stay" makes the point that people can't stay innocent forever. Grief is the inevitable result of the aging process. Like the first leaves of spring, we are at the best at the very beginning, and it's all downhill from there.

While revising his paper, the author realized that the ideas in his next-to-last paragraph would serve to sum up the paper. The new final paragraph doesn't simply restate the thesis; it pushes the idea further, in its last two sentences, by exploring the poem's implications.

REVISED CONCLUSION

Some people might view Frost's poem as sacrilegious, because it seems to say that Adam and Eve had no choice; everything in life is doomed to fall. Growing less innocent and more knowing seems less a choice in Frost's view than a natural process like the changing of golden blossoms to green leaves. "Eden sank to grief"

not because we choose to do evil things but because time takes
away our innocence as we encounter the suffering and loss of
human existence. Frost suggests that the real original sin is that
time has to pass and we all must grow wiser and less innocent.

- **Give your paper a compelling title.** Like the introduction, a title should
be inviting to readers, giving them a sense of what's coming. Provide
enough specifics to pique your reader's interest. "On Robert Frost's 'Nothing Gold Can Stay'" is a duller, less informative title than "Lost Innocence in Robert Frost's 'Nothing Gold Can Stay,'" which may spark the
reader's interest and prepare him or her for what is to come.

CHECKLIST: Revising Your Argument

- ☐ Is your thesis clear? Can it be sharpened?
- ☐ Does all your evidence serve to advance the argument put forth in
your thesis?
- ☐ Is your argument logical?
- ☐ Have you made an emotional connection with the reader?
- ☐ Does your presentation seem credible?
- ☐ Do transitional words and phrases signal movement from one idea to
the next?
- ☐ Does each paragraph contain a topic sentence?
- ☐ Does your introduction draw the reader in? Does it prepare the reader
for what follows?
- ☐ Does your conclusion tie up the paper's loose ends? Does it avoid
merely restating what has come before?
- ☐ Is your title compelling?

SOME FINAL ADVICE ON REWRITING

- **Whenever possible, get feedback from a trusted reader.** In every
project, there comes a time when the writer has gotten so close to the
work that he or she can't see it clearly. A talented roommate or a tutor in
the campus writing center can tell you what isn't yet clear on the page,
what questions still need answering, or what line of argument isn't yet as
persuasive as it could be.
- **Be willing to refine your thesis.** Once you have fleshed out your whole
paper, you may find that your original thesis is not borne out by the rest of
your argument. If so, you will need to rewrite your thesis so that it more
precisely fits the evidence at hand.

▪ **Be prepared to question your whole approach to a work of literature.** On occasion, you may even need to entertain the notion of throwing everything you have written into the wastebasket and starting over again. Occasionally having to start from scratch is the lot of any writer.

▪ **Rework troublesome passages.** Look for skimpy paragraphs of one or two sentences—evidence that your ideas might need more fleshing out. Can you supply more evidence, more explanation, more examples or illustrations?

▪ **Cut out any unnecessary information.** Everything in your paper should serve to further its thesis. Delete any sentences or paragraphs that detract from your focus.

▪ **Aim for intelligent clarity when you use literary terminology.** Critical terms can help sharpen your thoughts and make them easier to handle. Nothing is less sophisticated or more opaque, however, than too many technical terms thrown together for grandiose effect: "The mythic *symbolism* of this *archetype* is the *antithesis* of the *dramatic situation*." Choose plain words you're already at ease with. When you use specialized terms, do so to smooth the way for your reader—to make your meaning more precise. It is less cumbersome, for example, to refer to the *tone* of a story than to say, "the way the author makes you feel what she is talking about."

▪ **Set your paper aside for a while.** Even an hour or two away from your essay can help you return to it with fresh eyes. Remember that the literal meaning of "revision" is "seeing again."

▪ **Finally, carefully read your paper one last time to edit it.** Now it's time to sweat the small stuff. Check any uncertain spellings, scan for run-on sentences and fragments, pull out a weak word and send in a stronger one. Like soup stains on a job interviewee's tie, finicky errors distract from the overall impression and prejudice your reader against your essay.

Here is the revised version of the student paper we have been examining.

Noah Gabriel

Professor James

English 2171

7 October 2015

Lost Innocence in

Robert Frost's "Nothing Gold Can Stay"

Most of the lines in Robert Frost's brief poem "Nothing Gold Can Stay" focus on nature: the changing of the seasons and the fading of dawn into day. The poem's opening line asserts that the first blossoms of spring are more precious than the leaves that follow. Likewise, dawn is more special than day. Though Frost's subject seems to be nature, the reader soon realizes that his real subject is human nature. As babies we are all perfectly innocent, but as time passes, we can't help but lose that happy innocence. In "Nothing Gold Can Stay," Frost makes a bold claim: sin, suffering, and loss are inevitable because the passage of time causes everyone to fall from grace.

Thesis sentence states the main claim

The poem begins with a deceptively simple sentence: "Nature's first green is gold." The subject seems to be the first, delicate leaves of spring which are less green and more golden than summer leaves. However, the poem goes on to say, "Her early leaf's a flower" (line 3), indicating that Frost is describing the first blossoms of spring. In fact, he's describing both the new leaves and blossoms. Both are as rare and precious as the mineral gold. They are precious because they don't last long; the early gold of spring blossoms is nature's "hardest hue to hold" (2). Early spring is an example of nature in its perfect state, and perfection is impossible to hold on to. To the poem's speaker, in fact, the colors of early spring seem to last only an hour. When poets write of seasons, they often also are commenting on the life cycle. To make a statement that spring can't last more than an hour implies that a person's youth (often symbolically associated with spring) is all too short. Therefore, the poem implies that innocent youth, like spring, lasts for only the briefest time.

Logos: textual evidence backs up thesis

Assumption (or warrant) is spelled out

Claim

Gabriel 2

While Frost takes four lines to describe the decline of the spring blossoms, he picks up the pace when he describes what happens next. The line, "Then leaf subsides to leaf" (5) brings us from early spring through summer and fall, compressing three seasons into a single line. Just as time seems to pass slowly when we are children, and then much more quickly when we grow up, the poem moves quickly once the first golden moment is past. The word "subsides" feels important. The golden blossoms and delicate leaves of spring subside, or sink to a lower level, meaning they become less special and beautiful.

Significant word is looked at closely

Though Frost is writing about nature, his real subject is humanity. As mentioned above, in literature, spring often represents youth. Similarly, summer symbolizes young adulthood, autumn stands for middle age, and winter represents old age. The adult stages of life are, for Frost, less precious than childhood, which passes very quickly, as we later realize. Also, the innocence of childhood is, like those spring leaves, precious as gold.

Claim

Ethos: credibility of writer enhanced by intelligent generalizations about literature

Frost shifts his view from the cycle of the seasons to the cycle of a single day to make a similar point. Just as spring turns to summer, "So dawn goes down to day" (7). Like spring, dawn is unbelievably colorful and beautiful but doesn't last very long. Like "subsides," the phrase "goes down" implies that full daylight is actually a falling off from dawn. As beautiful as daylight is, it's ordinary, while dawn is special because it is more fleeting.

Key phrase is analyzed closely

Among these natural images, one line stands out: "So Eden sank to grief" (6). This line is the only one in the poem that deals directly with human beings. Eden may have been a garden (a part of nature) but it represents a state of mind—perfect innocence. In the traditional religious view, Adam and Eve chose to disobey God by eating an apple from the tree of knowledge. They were presented with a choice: to be obedient and remain in paradise forever, or to disobey God's order. People often speak of that first choice as "original sin." In this religious view, "Eden sank to grief" because the first humans chose to sin.

Claim

Gabriel 3

Frost, however, takes a different view. He compares the Fall of Man to the changing of spring to summer, as though it was as inevitable as the passage of time. The poem implies that no matter what Adam and Eve did, they couldn't remain in paradise. Original sin in Frost's view seems less a voluntary moral action than a natural, if unhappy sort of maturation. The innocent perfection of the garden of Eden couldn't possibly last. The apple represents knowledge, so in a symbolic sense God wanted Adam and Eve to stay unknowing, or innocent. But the poem implies that it was inevitable that Adam and Eve would gain knowledge and lose their innocence, becoming wiser but less perfect. They lost Eden and encountered "grief," the knowledge of suffering and loss associated with the human condition. This is certainly true for the rest of us human beings. As much as we might like to, we can't stay young or innocent forever.

Some people might view Frost's poem as sacrilegious, because it seems to say that Adam and Eve had no choice; everything in life is doomed to fall. Growing less innocent and more knowing seems less a choice in Frost's view than a natural process like the changing of golden blossoms to green leaves. "Eden sank to grief" not because we choose to do evil things but because time takes away our innocence as we encounter the suffering and loss of human existence. Frost suggests that the real original sin is that time has to pass and we all must grow wiser and less innocent.

Claim

Pathos: appeal to common emotional response

Ethos: credibility built through recognition and reconciliation of different viewpoint

Restatement of thesis

Gabriel 4

Work Cited

Frost, Robert. "Nothing Gold Can Stay." *Backpack Literature: An Introduction to Fiction, Poetry, Drama, and Writing*, edited by X. J. Kennedy and Dana Gioia, 5th ed., Pearson, 2016, p. 541.

WHAT'S YOUR PURPOSE? COMMON APPROACHES TO WRITING ABOUT LITERATURE

It is crucial to keep your paper's purpose in mind. When you write an academic paper, you are likely to have been given a specific set of marching orders. Maybe you have been asked to write for a particular audience besides the obvious one (your professor, that is). Perhaps you have been asked to describe your personal reaction to a literary work. Maybe your purpose is to interpret a work, analyzing how one or more of its elements contribute to its meaning. You may have been instructed to write an evaluation in which you judge a work's merits. Let the assignment dictate your paper's tone and content. Below are several commonly used approaches to writing about literature.

Explication

Explication is the patient unfolding of meanings in a work of literature. An explication proceeds carefully through a story, passage, or poem, usually interpreting it line by line—perhaps even word by word, dwelling on details a casual reader might miss and illustrating how a work's smaller parts contribute to the whole. Alert and willing to take pains, the writer of such an essay notices anything meaningful that isn't obvious, whether it is a colossal theme suggested by a symbol or a little hint contained in a single word.

To write an honest explication of an entire story takes time and space, and is a better assignment for a long term paper, an honors thesis, or a dissertation than a short essay. A thorough explication of Nathaniel Hawthorne's "Young Goodman Brown," for example, would likely run much longer than the rich and intriguing short story itself. Ordinarily, explication is best suited to a short passage or section of a story: a key scene, a critical conversation, a statement of theme, or an opening or closing paragraph.

In drama, explication is best suited to brief passages—a key soliloquy, for example, or a moment of dialogue that lays bare the play's theme. Closely examining a critical moment in a play can shed light on the play in its entirety. To be successful, an explication needs to concentrate on a brief passage, probably not much more than 20 lines long.

Storytellers who are especially fond of language invite closer attention to their words than others might. Edgar Allan Poe, for one, is a poet sensitive to the rhythms of his sentences and a symbolist whose stories abound in potent suggestions. Here is a student's explication of a short but essential passage in "The Tell-Tale Heart." The passage occurs in the third paragraph of the story, and to help us follow the explication, the student quotes the passage in full at the paper's beginning.

An unusually well-written essay, "By Lantern Light" cost its author two or three careful revisions. Rather than attempting to say something about *everything* in the passage from Poe, she selects only the details that strike her as most meaningful. In her very first sentence, she briefly shows us how the passage functions in the context of Poe's story: how it clinches our suspicions that the narrator is mad. Notice too that the student who wrote the essay doesn't inch through the passage sentence by sentence, but freely takes up its details in an order that seems appropriate to her argument.

Susan Kim

Professor A. M. Lundy

English 100

20 May 2015

By Lantern Light: An Explication of

a Passage in Poe's "The Tell-Tale Heart"

And every night, about midnight, I turned the latch of his door

and opened it—oh, so gently! And then, when I had made

an opening sufficient for my head, I put in a dark lantern, all

closed, closed, so that no light shone out, and then I thrust in

my head. Oh, you would have laughed to see how cunningly I

thrust it in! I moved it slowly—very, very slowly, so that I might

not disturb the old man's sleep. It took me an hour to place my

whole head within the opening so far that I could see him as he

lay upon his bed. Ha!—would a madman have been so wise as

this? And then, when my head was well in the room, I undid the

lantern cautiously—oh, so cautiously—cautiously (for the hinges

creaked)—I undid it just so much that a single thin ray fell upon

the vulture eye. And this I did for seven long nights—every night

just at midnight—but I found the eye always closed; and so it was

impossible to do the work; for it was not the old man who vexed

me, but his Evil Eye. (par. 3)

Quotes passage to be explicated

Although Edgar Allan Poe has suggested in the first lines of his story "The Tell-Tale Heart" that the person who addresses us is insane, it is only when we come to the speaker's account of his preparations for murdering the old man that we find his madness fully revealed. Even more convincingly

Thesis sentence —statement of paper's main claim

than his earlier words (for we might possibly think that someone who claims to hear things in heaven and hell is a religious mystic), these preparations reveal him to be mad. What strikes us is that they are so elaborate and meticulous. A significant detail is the exactness of his schedule for spying: "every night just at midnight." The words with which he describes his motions also convey the most extreme care (and I will indicate them by italics): "how wisely I proceeded—with *what caution*," "I turned the latch of his door and opened it—oh, so *gently*!" "how *cunningly* I thrust it [my head] in! I moved it slowly—*very, very slowly*," "I undid the lantern *cautiously*—oh, *so cautiously—cautiously*." Taking a whole hour to intrude his head into the room, he asks, "Ha!—would a madman have been so wise as this?" But of course the word *wise* is unconsciously ironic, for clearly it is not wisdom the speaker displays, but an absurd degree of care, an almost fiendish ingenuity. Such behavior, I understand, is typical of certain mental illnesses. All his careful preparations that he thinks prove him sane only convince us instead that he is mad.

Obviously his behavior is self-defeating. He wants to catch the "vulture eye" open, and yet he takes all these pains not to disturb the old man's sleep. If he behaved logically, he might go barging into the bedroom with his lantern ablaze, shouting at the top of his voice. And yet, if we can see things his way, there *is* a strange logic to his reasoning. He regards the eye as a creature in itself, quite apart from its possessor. "It was not," he says, "the old man who vexed me, but his Evil Eye." Apparently, to be inspired to do his deed, the madman needs to behold the eye—at least, this is my understanding of his remark, "I found the eye always closed; and so it was impossible to do the work." Poe's choice of the word *work*, by the way, is also revealing. Murder is made to seem a duty or a job; and anyone who so regards murder is either extremely cold-blooded, like a hired killer for a gangland assassination, or else deranged. Besides, the word suggests again the curious sense of detachment that the speaker feels toward the owner of the eye.

Textual evidence supports claim

Topic sentence on narrator's mad logic

Kim 3

In still another of his assumptions, the speaker shows that he is madly logical, or operating on the logic of a dream. There seems to be a dreamlike relationship between his dark lantern "all closed, closed, so that no light shone out," and the sleeping victim. When the madman opens his lantern so that it emits a single ray, he is hoping that the eye in the old man's head will be open too, letting out its corresponding gleam. The latch that he turns so gently, too, seems like the eye, whose lid needs to be opened in order for the murderer to go ahead. It is as though the speaker is *trying* to get the eyelid to lift. By taking such great pains and by going through all this nightly ritual, he is practicing some kind of magic, whose rules are laid down not by our logic, but by the logic of dreams.

Conclusion pushes thesis further, making it more specific.

Kim 4

Work Cited

Poe, Edgar Allan. "The Tell-Tale Heart." *Backpack Literature: An Introduction to Fiction, Poetry, Drama, and Writing*, edited by X. J. Kennedy and Dana Gioia, 5th ed., Pearson, 2016, pp. 40–45.

Explication is a particularly useful way to help unravel a poem's complexities. An explication, however, should not be confused with a paraphrase, which puts the poem's literal meaning into plain prose. While an explication might include some paraphrasing, it does more than simply restate. It explains a poem, in great detail, showing how each part contributes to the whole. In writing an explication of a poem, keep the following tips in mind:

- **Start with the poem's first line, and keep working straight through to the end.** As needed, though, you can take up points out of order.
- **Read closely, addressing the poem's details.** You may choose to include allusions, the denotations or connotations of words, the possible meanings

of symbols, the effects of certain sounds and rhythms and formal elements (rime schemes, for instance), the sense of any statements that contain irony, and other particulars.

■ **Show how each part of the poem contributes to the meaning of the whole.** Your explication should go beyond dissecting the pieces of a poem; it should also integrate them to cast light on the poem in its entirety.

Here is a successful student-authored explication of Robert Frost's "Design." The assignment was to explain whatever in the poem seemed most essential, in not more than 750 words. This excellent paper finds something worth unfolding in every line of Frost's poem, without seeming mechanical. Although the student proceeds sequentially through the poem from the title to the last line, he takes up some points out of order, when it serves his purpose. In paragraph two, for example, he looks ahead to the poem's ending and briefly states its main theme in order to relate it to the poem's title. In the third paragraph, he explicates the poem's later image of the heal-all, relating it to the first image. He also comments on the poem's form ("Like many other sonnets"), on its similes and puns, and on its denotations and connotations.

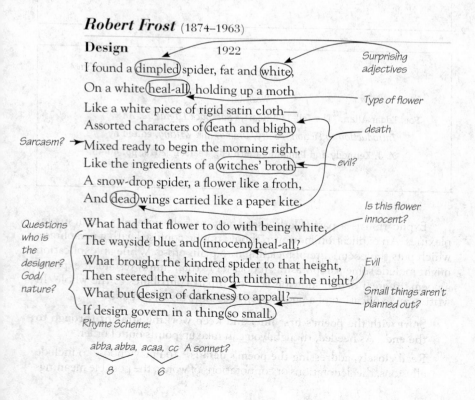

Robert Frost (1874–1963)

Design   1922

Surprising adjectives

I found a (dimpled) spider, fat and (white),
On a white (heal-all), holding up a moth — *Type of flower*
Like a white piece of rigid satin cloth—
Assorted characters of (death and blight) — *death*
Sarcasm? → Mixed ready to begin the morning right,
Like the ingredients of a (witches' broth) ← *evil?*
A snow-drop spider, a flower like a froth,
And (dead) wings carried like a paper kite.

Is this flower innocent?

Questions who is the designer? God/ nature?
What had that flower to do with being white,
The wayside blue and (innocent) heal-all?
What brought the kindred spider to that height,   *Evil*
Then steered the white moth thither in the night?
What but (design of darkness) to appall?—   *Small things aren't planned out?*
If design govern in a thing (so small.)

Rhyme Scheme:

abba, abba, acaa, cc   *A sonnet?*

    8   6

Ted Jasper

Professor Koss

English 130

21 November 2014

An Unfolding of Robert Frost's "Design"

"I always wanted to be very observing," Robert Frost once told an
audience, after reading aloud his poem "Design." Then he added, "But I
have always been afraid of my own observations" (qtd. in Cook 126–27).
What could Frost have observed that could scare him? Let's examine the
poem in question and see what we discover.

Starting with the title, "Design," any reader of this poem will find
it full of meaning. As the *Merriam-Webster Dictionary* defines *design*,
the word can denote among other things a plan, purpose, or intention
("Design"). Some arguments for the existence of God (I remember from
Sunday School) are based on the "argument from design": that because
the world shows a systematic order, there must be a Designer who made
it. But the word *design* can also mean "a deliberate undercover project
or scheme" such as we attribute to a "designing person" ("Design"). As
we shall see, Frost's poem incorporates all of these meanings. His poem
raises the old philosophic question of whether there is a Designer, an evil
Designer, or no Designer at all.

Like many other sonnets, "Design" is divided into two parts. The
first eight lines draw a picture centering on the spider, who at first seems
almost jolly. It is *dimpled* and *fat* like a baby, or Santa Claus. The spider
stands on a wildflower whose name, *heal-all*, seems ironic: a heal-all is
supposed to cure any disease, but this flower has no power to restore life
to the dead moth. (Later, in line ten, we learn that the heal-all used to
be blue. Presumably, it has died and become bleached-looking.) In the
second line we discover, too, that the spider has hold of another creature,
a dead moth. We then see the moth described with an odd simile in line
three: "Like a white piece of rigid satin cloth." Suddenly, the moth
becomes not a creature but a piece of fabric—lifeless and dead—and

Explores language

yet *satin* has connotations of beauty. Satin is a luxurious material used in rich formal clothing, such as coronation gowns and brides' dresses. Additionally, there is great accuracy in the word: the smooth and slightly plush surface of satin is like the powder-smooth surface of moths' wings. But this "cloth," rigid and white, could be the lining to Dracula's coffin.

In the fifth line an invisible hand enters. The characters are "mixed" like ingredients in an evil potion. Some force doing the mixing is behind the scene. The characters in themselves are innocent enough, but when brought together, their whiteness and look of *rigor mortis* are overwhelming. There

Refers to sound

is something diabolical in the spider's feast. The "morning right" echoes the word *rite*, a ritual—in this case apparently a Black Mass or a Witches' Sabbath. The simile in line seven ("a flower like a froth") is more ambiguous and harder to describe. Froth is white, foamy, and delicate—something found on a brook in the woods or on a beach after a wave recedes. However, in the natural world, froth also can be ugly: the foam on a polluted stream or a rabid dog's mouth. The dualism in nature—its beauty and its horror—is there in that one simile.

Transition words

So far, the poem has portrayed a small, frozen scene, with the dimpled killer holding its victim as innocently as a boy holds a kite.

Quotes secondary source

Already, Frost has hinted that Nature may be, as Radcliffe Squires suggests, "Nothing but an ash-white plain without love or faith or hope, where ignorant appetites cross by chance" (87). Now, in the last six

Discusses theme

lines of the sonnet, Frost comes out and directly states his theme. What else could bring these deathly pale, stiff things together "but design of darkness to appall"? The question is clearly rhetorical; we are meant to answer, "Yes, there does seem to be an evil design at work here!" I take the next-to-last line to mean, "What except a design so dark and sinister that we're appalled by it?" "Appall," by the way, is the second pun in the

Defines key word

poem: it sounds like *a pall* or shroud. (The derivation of *appall*, according to *Merriam-Webster*, is ultimately from a Latin word meaning "to be pale"—an interesting word choice for a poem full of pale white

Jasper 3

images ["Appall"].) *Steered* carries the suggestion of a steering-wheel or rudder that some pilot had to control. Like the word *brought*, it implies that some invisible force charted the paths of spider, heal-all, and moth, so that they arrived together.

Having suggested that the universe is in the hands of that sinister force (an indifferent God? Fate? the Devil?), Frost adds a note of doubt. The Bible tells us that "His eye is on the sparrow," but at the moment the poet doesn't seem sure. Maybe, he hints, when things in the universe drop below a certain size, they pass completely out of the Designer's notice. When creatures are this little, maybe God doesn't bother to govern them but just lets them run wild. And possibly the same mindless chance is all that governs human lives. And because this is even more senseless than having an angry God intent on punishing us, it is, Frost suggests, the worst suspicion of all.

Answers question raised in introduction

Conclusion

Jasper 4

Works Cited

"Appall." *Merriam-Webster.com*, 2015, www.merriam-webster.com/
    dictionary/appall.

Cook, Reginald. *Robert Frost: A Living Voice.* U of Massachusetts
    P, 1974.

"Design." *Merriam-Webster.com*, 2015, www.merriam-webster.com/
    dictionary/design.

Frost, Robert. "Design." *Collected Poems, Prose and Plays,* Library of
    America, 1995, p. 275.

Squires, Radcliffe. *The Major Themes of Robert Frost.* U of Michigan
    P, 1963.

Analysis

Examining a single component of a piece of literature can afford us a better understanding of the entire work. This is perhaps why in most literature classes students are asked to write at least one **analysis** (from the Greek: "breaking up"), an essay that breaks a work into its elements and, usually, studies one part closely. A topic for an analysis might be "The Character of Alice Walker's Dee," in which the writer would concentrate on showing us Dee's highly individual features and traits of personality, or perhaps "The Theme of Fragility in *The Glass Menagerie*" or "Imagery of Light and Darkness in Frost's 'Design.'"

In this book, you probably already have encountered a few brief analyses: the discussion of connotations in William Blake's "London" (pages 423–24), for instance, or the examination of symbols in T. S. Eliot's "The *Boston Evening Transcript*" (pages 527–28). To write an analysis, remember three key points:

▪ **Focus on a single, manageable element.** Some possible choices are tone, irony, literal meaning, imagery, theme, and symbolism. If you are writing about poetry, you could also consider sound, rhythm, rime, or form.

▪ **Show how this element contributes to the meaning of the whole.** While no element of a work exists apart from all the others, by taking a closer look at one particular aspect of the work, you can see the whole more clearly.

▪ **Support your contentions with specific references to the work you are analyzing.** Quotations can be particularly convincing.

The student papers that follow are examples of brief analyses. The first paper analyzes the imagery of Elizabeth Bishop's poem "The Fish." The second paper analyzes Shakespeare's play *Othello* in light of Aristotle's famous definition of tragedy (discussed on page 686).

Woods 1

Becki Woods

Professor Bernier

English 220

23 February 2015

Faded Beauty: Bishop's Use of Imagery in "The Fish"

First sentence gives name of author and work

Upon first reading, Elizabeth Bishop's "The Fish" appears to be a simple fishing tale. A close investigation of the imagery in Bishop's highly detailed description, however, reveals a different sort of poem. The real theme of Bishop's poem is a compassion and respect for the fish's lifelong struggle to

survive. By carefully and effectively describing the captured fish, his
reaction to being caught, and the symbols of his past struggles to stay
alive, Bishop creates, through her images of beauty, victory, and survival,
something more than a simple tale.

    The first four lines of the poem are quite ordinary and factual:

    I caught a tremendous fish

    and held him beside the boat

    half out of water, with my hook

    fast in a corner of his mouth. (lines 1-4)

Except for *tremendous*, Bishop's persona uses no exaggerations—unlike
most fishing stories—to set up the situation of catching the fish. The
detailed description begins as the speaker recounts the event further,
noticing something signally important about the captive fish: "He didn't
fight" (5). At this point the poem begins to seem unusual: most fish stories
are about how ferociously the prey resists being captured. The speaker
also notes that the "battered and venerable / and homely" fish offered no
resistance to being caught (8–9). The image of the submissive attitude of
the fish is essential to the theme of the poem. It is his "utter passivity
[that] makes [the persona's] detailed scrutiny possible" (McNally 192).

    Once the image of the passive fish has been established, the speaker
begins an examination of the fish itself, noting that "Here and there / his
brown skin hung in strips / like ancient wallpaper" (9–11). By comparing
the fish's skin to wallpaper, the persona creates, as Sybil Estess argues,
"implicit suggestions of both artistry and decay" (713). Images of peeling
wallpaper are instantly brought to mind. The comparison of the fish's
skin and wallpaper, though "helpful in conveying an accurate notion of
the fish's color to anyone with memories of Victorian parlors and their
yellowed wallpaper . . . is," according to Nancy McNally, "even more useful
in evoking the associations of deterioration which usually surround
such memories" (192). The fish's faded beauty has been hinted at in the
comparison, thereby setting up the detailed imagery that soon follows:

Thesis sentence

Topic sentence

Quotation from secondary source

Topic sentence

Essay moves systematically through poem, from start to finish

He was speckled with barnacles,
fine rosettes of lime,
and infested
with tiny white sea-lice,
and underneath two or three
rags of green weed hung down. (16–21)

Textual evidence, mix of long and short quotations

The persona sees the fish as he is; the infestations and faults are not left out of the description. Yet, at the same time, the fisher "express[es] what [he/she] has sensed of the character of the fish" (Estess 714).

Bishop's persona notices "shapes like full-blown roses / stained and lost through age" on the fish's skin (14–15). The persona's perception of the fish's beauty is revealed along with a recognition of its faded beauty, which is best shown in the description of the fish's being speckled with barnacles and spotted with lime. However, the fisher observes these spots and sees them as rosettes—as objects of beauty, not just ugly brown spots. These images contribute to the persona's recognition of beauty's having become faded beauty.

Transitional phrase begins topic sentence

The poem next turns to a description of the fish's gills. The imagery in "While his gills were breathing in / the terrible oxygen" (22–23) leads "to the very structure of the creature" that is now dying (Hopkins 201).

Textual evidence, mix of long and short quotations

The descriptions of the fish's interior beauty—"the coarse white flesh / packed in like feathers," the colors "of his shiny entrails," and his "pink swim-bladder / like a big peony"—are reminders of the life that seems about to end (27–28, 31–33).

Topic sentence

The composite image of the fish's essential beauty—his being alive— is developed further in the description of the five fish hooks that the captive, living fish carries in his lip:

grim, wet, and weaponlike,
hung five old pieces of fish-line,
. . . .
with all their five big hooks
grown firmly in his mouth. (50–51, 54–55)

As if fascinated by them, the persona, observing how the lines must have been broken during struggles to escape, sees the hooks as "medals with their ribbons / frayed and wavering, / a five-haired beard of wisdom / trailing from his aching jaw" (61–64), and the fisher becomes enthralled by re-created images of the fish's fighting desperately for his life on at least five separate occasions—and winning. Crale Hopkins suggests that "[i]n its capability not only for mere existence, but for action, escaping from previous anglers, the fish shares the speaker's humanity" (202), thus revealing the fisher's deepening understanding of how he or she must now act. The persona has "all along," notes Estess, "describe[d] the fish not just with great detail but with an imaginative empathy for the aquatic creature. In her more-than-objective description, [the fisher] relates what [he/she] has seen to be both the pride and poverty of the fish" (715). It is at this point that the narrator of this fishing tale has a moment of clarity. Realizing the fish's history and the glory the fish has achieved in escaping previous hookings, the speaker sees everything become "rain-bow, rainbow, rainbow!" (75)—and then unexpectedly lets the fish go.

Quotations from secondary sources

Bishop's "The Fish" begins by describing an event that might easily be a conventional story's climax: "I caught a tremendous fish" (1). The poem, however, develops into a highly detailed account of a fisher noticing both the age and the faded beauty of the captive and his present beauty and past glory as well. The fishing tale is not simply a recounting of a capture; it is a gradually unfolding epiphany in which the speaker sees the fish in an entirely new light. The intensity of this encounter between an apparently experienced fisher in a rented boat and a battle-hardened fish is delivered through the poet's skillful use of imagery. It is through the description of the capture of an aged fish that Bishop offers her audience her theme of compassion derived from a respect for the struggle for survival.

Conclusion

Restatement of thesis, in light of all that comes before it.

Works Cited

Bishop, Elizabeth. "The Fish." *Backpack Literature: An Introduction to Fiction, Poetry, Drama, and Writing*, edited by X. J. Kennedy and Dana Gioia, 5th ed., Pearson, 2016, pp. 434-36.

Estess, Sybil P. "Elizabeth Bishop: The Delicate Art of Map Making." *Southern Review*, vol. 13, no. 4, Autumn 1977, pp. 705–27.

Hopkins, Crale D. "Inspiration as Theme: Art and Nature in the Poetry of Elizabeth Bishop." *Arizona Quarterly*, vol. 32, 1976, pp. 200–02.

McNally, Nancy L. "Elizabeth Bishop: The Discipline of Description." *Twentieth Century Literature*, vol. 11, 1966, pp. 192-94.

Janet Housden

Professor Barth

English 201

3 November 2015

Othello: Tragedy or Soap Opera?

When we hear the word "tragedy," we usually think of either a terrible real-life disaster, or a dark and serious drama filled with pain, suffering, and loss that involves the downfall of a powerful person due to some character flaw or error in judgment. William Shakespeare's *Othello* is such a drama. Set in Venice and Cyprus during the Renaissance, the play tells the story of Othello, a Moorish general in the Venetian army, who has just married Desdemona, the daughter of a Venetian nobleman. Through the plotting of a jealous villain, Iago, Othello is deceived into believing that Desdemona has been unfaithful to him. He murders her in revenge, only to discover too late how he has been tricked. Overcome by shame and grief, Othello kills himself.

First paragraph gives name of author and work

Key plot information avoids excessive retelling

Housden 2

Dealing as it does with jealousy, murder, and suicide, the play is certainly dark, but is *Othello* a true tragedy? In the fourth century BC, the Greek philosopher Aristotle proposed a formal definition of tragedy (Kennedy and Gioia 686), which only partially fits *Othello*.

The first characteristic of tragedy identified by Aristotle is that the protagonist is a person of outstanding quality and high social position. While Othello is not of royal birth as are many tragic heroes and heroines, he does occupy a sufficiently high position to satisfy this part of Aristotle's definition. Although Othello is a foreigner and a soldier by trade, he has risen to the rank of general and has married into a noble family, which is quite an accomplishment for an outsider. Furthermore, Othello is generally liked and respected by those around him. He is often described by others as being "noble," "brave," and "valiant." By virtue of his high rank and the respect he commands from others, Othello would appear to possess the high stature commonly given to the tragic hero in order to make his eventual fall seem all the more tragic.

While Othello displays the nobility and high status commonly associated with the tragic hero, he also possesses another, less admirable characteristic, the flaw or character defect shared by all heroes of classical tragedy. In Othello's case, it is a stunning gullibility, combined with a violent temper that once awakened overcomes all reason. These flaws permit Othello to be easily deceived and manipulated by the villainous Iago and make him easy prey for the "green-eyed monster" (3.3.179).

It is because of this tragic flaw, according to Aristotle, that the hero is at least partially to blame for his own downfall. While Othello's "free and open nature, / That thinks men honest that but seem to be so" (1.3.383–84) is not a fault in itself, it does allow Iago to convince the Moor of his wife's infidelity without one shred of concrete evidence. Furthermore, once Othello has been convinced of Desdemona's guilt, he makes up his mind to take vengeance, and says that his "bloody thoughts with violent pace / Shall ne'er look back, ne'er ebb to humble love" (3.3.473–74). He thereby

Central question is raised

Thesis statement provides response

Topic sentence on Othello's social position

Essay systematically applies Aristotle's definition of tragedy to Othello

Topic sentence on Othello's tragic flaw

Quotes from play as evidence to support point

renders himself deaf to the voice of reason, and ignoring Desdemona's protestations of innocence, brutally murders her, only to discover too late that he has made a terrible mistake. Although he is goaded into his crime by Iago, who is a master at manipulating people, it is Othello's own character flaws that lead to his horrible misjudgment.

Topic sentence elaborates on idea raised in previous paragraphs

Aristotle's definition also states that the hero's misfortune is not wholly deserved, that the punishment he receives exceeds his crime. Although it is hard to sympathize with a man as cruel as Othello is to the innocent Desdemona, Othello pays an extremely high price for his sin of gullibility. Othello loses everything—his wife, his position, even his life. Even though it's partially his fault, Othello is not entirely to blame, for without Iago's interference it's highly unlikely that things would turn out as they do. Though it seems incredibly stupid on Othello's part, that a man who has travelled the world and commanded armies should be so easily deceived, there is little evidence that Othello has had much experience with civilian society, and although he is "declined / Into the vale of years" (3.3.281–82) Othello has apparently never been married before. By his own admission, "little of this great world can I speak / More than pertains to feats of broils and battle" (1.3.88–89). Furthermore, Othello has no reason to suspect that "honest Iago" is anything but his loyal friend and supporter.

Topic sentence on Othello's misfortune

Transitional words signal argument's direction

While it is understandable that Othello could be fooled into believing Desdemona unfaithful, the question remains whether his fate is deserved. In addition to his mistake of believing Iago's lies, Othello commits a more serious error: he lets himself be blinded by anger. Worse yet, in deciding to take vengeance, he also makes up his mind not be swayed from his course, even by his love for Desdemona. In fact, he refuses to listen to her at all, "lest her body and beauty unprovide my mind again" (4.1.190), therefore denying her the right to defend herself. Because of his rage and unfairness, perhaps Othello deserves his fate more than Aristotle's ideal tragic hero. Othello's punishment does exceed his crime, but just barely.

Topic sentence elaborates on Othello's misfortune

According to Aristotle, the tragic hero's fall gives the protagonist deeper understanding and self-awareness. Othello departs from Aristotle's model in that Othello apparently learns nothing from his mistakes. He never realizes that he is partly at fault. He sees himself only as an innocent victim and blames his misfortune on fate rather than accepting responsibility for his actions. To be sure, he realizes he has been tricked and deeply regrets his mistake, but he seems to feel that he was justified under the circumstances, "For naught I did in hate, but all in honor" (5.2.303). Othello sees himself not as someone whose bad judgment and worse temper have resulted in the death of an innocent party, but as one who has "loved not wisely but too well" (5.2.354). This failure to grasp the true nature of his error indicates that Othello hasn't learned his lesson.

Topic sentence on whether Othello learns from his mistakes

Neither accepting responsibility nor learning from his mistakes, Othello fails to fulfill yet another of Aristotle's requirements. Since the protagonist usually gains some understanding along with his defeat, classical tragedy conveys a sense of human greatness and of life's unrealized potentialities—a quality totally absent from *Othello*. Not only does Othello fail to learn from his mistakes, but he never really realizes what those mistakes are, and it apparently never crosses his mind that things could have turned out any differently. "Who can control his fate?" Othello asks (5.2.274), and this defeatist attitude, combined with his failure to salvage any wisdom from his defeat, separates *Othello* from the tragedy as defined by Aristotle.

Topic sentence elaborating further on whether Othello learns from his errors

The last part of Aristotle's definition states that viewing the conclusion of a tragedy should result in catharsis for the audience, and that the audience should be left with a feeling of exaltation rather than depression. Unfortunately, the feeling we are left with after viewing *Othello* is neither catharsis nor exaltation but rather a feeling of horror, pity, and disgust at the senseless waste of human lives. The deaths of Desdemona and Othello, as well as those of Emilia and Roderigo, serve no purpose whatsoever. They die not in the service of a great cause but because of lies, treachery, jealousy,

Topic sentence on catharsis

Housden 5

and spite. Their deaths don't even benefit Iago, who is directly or indirectly responsible for all of them. No lesson is learned, no epiphany is reached, and the audience, instead of experiencing catharsis, is left with its negative feeling unresolved.

Restatement of thesis

Since *Othello* only partially fits Aristotle's definition of tragedy, it is questionable whether or not it should be classified as one. Though it does involve a great man undone by a defect in his own character, the hero gains neither insight nor understanding from his defeat, and so there can be no inspiration or catharsis for the audience, as there would be in a "true" tragedy. *Othello* is tragic only in the everyday sense of the word, the way a

Conclusion

plane crash or fire is tragic. At least in terms of Aristotle's classic definition, *Othello* ultimately comes across as more of a melodrama or soap opera than a tragedy.

Housden 6

Works Cited

Kennedy, X. J., and Dana Gioia, editors. *Backpack Literature: An Introduction to Fiction, Poetry, Drama, and Writing.* 5th ed., Pearson, 2016, pp. 686-88.

Shakespeare, William. *Othello: The Moor of Venice. Backpack Literature: An Introduction to Fiction, Poetry, Drama, and Writing,* edited by X. J. Kennedy and Dana Gioia, 5th ed., Pearson, 2016, pp. 742-852.

Comparison and Contrast

If you were to write on "The Humor of Alice Walker's 'Everyday Use' and John Updike's 'A & P,'" you would probably employ one or two methods. You might use **comparison**, placing the two stories side by side and pointing out their similarities, or **contrast**, pointing out their differences. Most of the time, in dealing with two pieces of literature, you will find them similar in some ways and different in others, and you'll use both methods. Keep the following points in mind when writing a comparison-contrast paper:

- **Choose works with something significant in common.** This will simplify your task, and also help ensure that your paper hangs together. Before you start writing, ask yourself if the two pieces you've selected throw some light on each other. If the answer is no, rethink your selection.

- **Choose a focus.** Simply ticking off every similarity and difference between two poems or stories would make for a slack and rambling essay. More compelling writing would result from better-focused topics such as "The Experience of Coming of Age in James Joyce's 'Araby' and William Faulkner's 'Barn Burning.'"

- **Don't feel you need to spend equal amounts of time on comparing and contrasting.** If your chosen works are more similar than different, you naturally will spend more space on comparison, and vice versa.

- **Don't devote the first half of your paper to one work and the second half to the other.** This simple structure may weaken your essay if it leads you to keep the two works in total isolation from each other. After all, the point is to see what can be learned by comparison. There is nothing wrong in discussing all of poem A first, then discussing poem B—if in discussing B you keep referring back to A. Another strategy is to do a point-by-point comparison of the two works all the way through your paper—dealing first, perhaps, with their themes, then with their central metaphors, and finally, with their respective merits.

- **Before you start writing, draw up a brief list of points you would like to touch on.** Then address each point, first in one work and then in the other. A sample outline follows for a paper on William Faulkner's "A Rose for Emily" and Katherine Mansfield's "Miss Brill." The essay's topic is "Adapting to Change: The Characters of Emily Grierson and Miss Brill."

1. Adapting to change (both women)
   Miss Brill more successful
2. Portrait of women
   Miss Emily—unflattering
   Miss Brill—empathetic
3. Imagery
   Miss Emily—morbid
   Miss Brill—cheerful

4. Plot

    Miss Emily

       - loses sanity

       - refuses to adapt

    Miss Brill

       - finds place in society

       - adapts

5. Summary: Miss Brill is more successful

■ **Emphasize the points that interest you the most.** This strategy will help keep you from following your outline in a plodding fashion ("Well, now it's time to whip over to Miss Brill again . . .").

■ **If the assignment allows, consider applying comparison and contrast in an essay on a single story or play.** You might, for example, analyze the attitudes of the younger and older waiters in Hemingway's "A Clean, Well-Lighted Place."

The following student-written paper compares and contrasts the main characters in "A Rose for Emily" and "Miss Brill." Notice how the author focuses the discussion on a single aspect of each woman's personality—the ability to adapt to change and the passage of time. By looking through the lens of three different elements of the short story—diction, imagery, and plot—this clear and systematic essay convincingly argues its thesis.

Ortiz 1

Michelle Ortiz

Professor Gregg

English 200

25 May 2015

Successful Adaptation in

"A Rose for Emily" and "Miss Brill"

In William Faulkner's "A Rose for Emily" and Katherine Mansfield's "Miss Brill," the reader is given a glimpse into the lives of two old women living in different worlds but sharing many similar characteristics. Both Miss Emily and Miss Brill attempt to adapt to a changing environment as they grow older. Through the authors' use of language, imagery, and plot, it becomes clear to the reader that Miss Brill is more successful at adapting to the world around her and finding happiness.

Clear statement of thesis

Ortiz 2

In "A Rose for Emily," Faulkner's use of language paints an unflattering picture of Miss Emily. His tone evokes pity and disgust rather than sympathy. The reader identifies with the narrator of the story and shares the townspeople's opinion that Miss Emily is somehow "perverse." In "Miss Brill," however, the reader can identify with the title character. Mansfield's attitude toward the young couple at the end makes the reader hate them for ruining the happiness that Miss Brill has found, however small it may be.

Textual evidence on language supports thesis

The imagery in "A Rose for Emily" keeps the reader from further identifying with Miss Emily by creating several morbid images of her. For example, there are several images of decay throughout the story. The house she lived in is falling apart and described as "filled with dust and shades . . . an eyesore among eyesores." Emily herself is described as being "bloated like a body long submerged in motionless water." Faulkner also uses words like "skeleton," "dank," "decay," and "cold" to reinforce these morbid, deathly images.

Imagery in Faulkner's story supports argument

In "Miss Brill," however, Mansfield uses more cheerful imagery. The music and the lively action in the park make Miss Brill feel alive inside. She notices the other old people that are in the park are "still as statues," "odd," and "silent." She says they "looked like they'd just come from dark little rooms or even—even cupboards." Her own room is later described as a "cupboard," but during the action of the story she does not include herself among those other old people. She still feels alive.

Contrasting imagery in Mansfield's story supports argument

Through the plots of both stories the reader can also see that Miss Brill is more successful in adapting to her environment. Miss Emily loses her sanity and ends up committing a crime in order to control her environment. Throughout the story, she refuses to adapt to any of the changes going on in the town, such as the taxes or the mailboxes. Miss Brill is able to find her own special place in society where she can be happy and remain sane.

Characters contrasted with examples drawn from plots

Ortiz 3

The final conclusion is stated and the thesis is restated

In "A Rose for Emily" and "Miss Brill" the authors' use of language and the plots of the stories illustrate that Miss Brill is more successful in her story. Instead of hiding herself away she emerges from the "cupboard" to participate in life. She adapts to the world that is changing as she grows older, without losing her sanity or committing crimes, as Miss Emily does. The language of "Miss Brill" allows the reader to sympathize with the main character. The imagery in the story is lighter and less morbid than in "A Rose for Emily." The resulting portrait is of an aging woman who has found creative ways to adjust to her lonely life.

Response Paper

One popular form of writing assignment is the **response paper**, a short essay that expresses your personal reaction to a work of literature. Both instructors and students often find the response paper an ideal introductory writing assignment. It provides you with an opportunity to craft a focused essay about a literary work, but it does not usually require any outside research. What it does require is careful reading, clear thinking, and honest writing.

The purpose of a response paper is to convey your thoughts and feelings about an aspect of a particular literary work. It isn't a book report (summarizing the work's content) or a book review (evaluating the quality of a work). A response paper expresses what you experienced in reading and thinking about the assigned text. Your reaction should reflect your background, values, and attitudes in response to the work, not what the instructor thinks about it. You might consider your response paper a conversation with the work you have just read. What questions does it seem to ask you? What reactions does it elicit? You might also regard your paper as a personal message to your instructor telling him or her what you really think about one of the reading assignments.

Of course, you can't say everything you thought and felt about your reading in a short paper. Focus on an important aspect (such as a main character, setting, or theme) and discuss your reaction to it. Don't gush or meander. Personal writing doesn't mean disorganized writing. Identify your main ideas and present your point of view in a clear and organized way. Once you get started you might surprise yourself by discovering that it's fun to explore your own responses. Stranger things have happened.

Here are some tips for writing a successful response paper of your own:

- **Make quick notes as you read or reread the work.** Don't worry about writing anything organized at this point. Just write a word or two in the margin noting your reactions as you read (e.g., "how unpleasant!" or "very interesting"). These little notes will jog your memory when you go back to write your paper.

- **Consider which aspect of the work affected you the most.** That aspect will probably be a good starting point for your response.

- **Be candid in your writing.** Remember that the literary work is only half of the subject matter of your paper. The other half is your reaction.

- **Try to understand and explain why you have reacted the way you did.** It's not enough just to state your responses. You also want to justify or explain them.

- **Refer to the text in your paper.** Demonstrate to the reader that your response is based on the text. Provide specific textual details and quotations wherever relevant.

The following paper is one student's response to Tim O'Brien's story "The Things They Carried" (Chapter 8).

Martin 1

Ethan Martin

English 99

Professor Merrill

31 March 2015

"Perfect Balance and Perfect Posture": Reflecting on

"The Things They Carried"

Reading Tim O'Brien's short story "The Things They Carried" became a very personal experience. It reminded me of my father, who is a Vietnam veteran, and the stories he used to tell me. Growing up, I regularly asked my dad to share stories from his past—especially about his service in the United States Marine Corps. He would rarely talk about his tour during the Vietnam War for more than a few minutes, and what he shared was usually the same: the monsoon rain could chill to the bone, the mosquitoes would never stop biting, and the M-16 rifles often jammed in a moment of crisis. He dug a new foxhole where he slept every night, he traded the cigarettes from his C-rations for food, and—since he was the radio man of his platoon—the combination of his backpack and radio was very heavy during the long, daily walks through rice paddies and jungles. For these reasons, "The Things They Carried" powerfully affected me.

While reading the story, I felt as if I was "humping" (par. 4) through Vietnam with Lieutenant Jimmy Cross, Rat Kiley, Ted Lavender, and especially Mitchell Sanders—who carries the 26-pound radio and battery. Every day, we carry our backpacks to school. Inside are some objects that we need to use in class: books, paper, and pens. But most of us probably include "unnecessary" items that reveal something about who we are or what we value—photographs, perfume, or good-luck charms. O'Brien uses this device to tell his story. At times he lists the things that the soldiers literally carried, such as weapons, medicine, and flak jackets. These military items weigh between 30 and 70 pounds, depending on one's rank or function in the platoon. The narrator says, "They carried all they could bear, and then some, including a silent awe for the terrible power of the things they carried" (par. 12).

Some of this "terrible power" comes from the sentimental objects the men keep. Although these are relatively light, they weigh down the hearts of the soldiers. Lt. Jimmy Cross carries 10-ounce letters and a pebble from Martha, a girl in his hometown who doesn't love him back. Rat Kiley carries comic books, and Norman Bowker carried a diary. I now own the small, water-logged Bible that my father carried through his tour in Vietnam, which was a gift from his mother. When I open its pages, I can almost hear his voice praying to survive the war.

The price of such survival is costly. O'Brien's platoon carries ghosts, memories, and "the land itself" (par. 39). Their intangible burdens are heavier than what they carry in their backpacks. My father has always said

Martin 3

that, while he was in Vietnam, an inexpressible feeling of death hung
heavy in the air, which he could not escape. O'Brien notes that an
emotional weight of fear and cowardice "could never be put down, it
required perfect balance and perfect posture" (par. 77), and I wonder if
this may be part of what my father meant.

Both Tim O'Brien and my father were wounded by shrapnel, and now
they both carry a Purple Heart. They carry the weight of survival. They
carry memories that I will never know. "The Things They Carried" is not
a war story about glory and honor. It is a portrait of the psychological
damage that war can bring. It is a story about storytelling and how hard
it can be to find the truth. And it is a beautiful account of what the
human heart can endure.

Martin 4

Work Cited

O'Brien, Tim. "The Things They Carried." *Backpack Literature: An
Introduction to Fiction, Poetry, Drama, and Writing,* edited by
X. J. Kennedy and Dana Gioia, 5th ed., Pearson, 2016, pp. 321-36.

THE FORM OF YOUR FINISHED PAPER

If your instructor has not specified the form of your finished paper, follow these
commonly accepted guidelines:

- Choose standard letter-size (8 1/2 × 11) white paper.
- Use standard, easy-to-read type fonts, such as Times New Roman. Be sure
  the italic type style contrasts with the regular style.

- Give your name, your instructor's name, the course number, and the date at the top left-hand corner of your first page, starting one inch from the top.

- On all pages, insert a header—your last name and the page number—in the upper right-hand corner, one-half inch from the top.

- Remember to give your paper a title that reflects your thesis.

- Leave an inch or two of margin on all four sides of each page.

- If you include a works-cited section, begin it on a new page.

- Double-space your text, including quotations and notes. Don't forget to double-space the works-cited page also.

- Italicize the titles of longer works—books, full-length plays, periodicals, and book-length poems such as *The Odyssey*. The titles of shorter works— poems, articles, or short stories—should appear in quotation marks.

What's left to do but hand in your paper? By now, you may be glad to see it go. But a good paper is not only worth submitting; it is also worth keeping. If you return to it after a while, you may find to your surprise that it will preserve and even renew what you have learned.

Topics for Writing About Fiction

Topics for Brief Papers (250–500 Words)

1. Explicate the opening paragraph or first few lines of a story. Show how the opening prepares the reader for what will follow. In an essay of this length, you will need to limit your discussion to the most important elements of the passage you explicate; there won't be room to deal with everything. Or, as thoroughly as the word count allows, explicate the final paragraph of a story. What does the ending imply about the fates of the story's characters, and about the story's take on its central theme?

2. Select a story that features a first-person narrator. Write a concise yet thorough analysis of how that character's point of view colors the story.

3. Consider a short story in which the central character has to make a decision or must take some decisive step that will alter the rest of his or her life. Faulkner's "Barn Burning" is one such story; another is Updike's "A & P." As concisely and as thoroughly as you can, explain the nature of the character's decision, the reasons for it, and its probable consequences (as suggested by what the author tells us).

4. Choose two stories that might be interesting to compare and contrast. Write a brief defense of your choice. How might these two stories illuminate each other?

5. Choose a key passage from a story you admire. As closely as the word count allows, explicate that passage and explain why it strikes you as an important moment in the story. Concentrate on the aspects of the passage that seem most essential.

Topics for More Extended Papers (600–1,000 Words)

1. Write an analysis of a short story, focusing on a single element, such as point of view, theme, symbolism, character, or the author's voice (tone, style, irony).

2. Compare and contrast two stories with protagonists who share an important personality trait. Make character the focus of your essay.

3. Write a thorough explication of a short passage (preferably not more than four sentences) in a story you admire. Pick a crucial moment in the plot, or a passage that reveals the story's theme. You might look to the paper "By Lantern Light" (page 1115) as a model.

4. Write an analysis of a story in which the protagonist experiences an epiphany or revelation of some sort. Describe the nature of this change of heart. How is the reader prepared for it? What are its repercussions in the character's life? Some possible story choices are Alice Walker's "Everyday Use," William Faulkner's "Barn Burning," or Raymond Carver's "Cathedral."

5. Imagine a reluctant reader, one who would rather play video games than crack a book. Which story in this book would you recommend to him or her? Write an essay to that imagined reader, describing the story's merits.

Topics for Long Papers (1,500 Words or More)

1. Write an analysis of a longer work of fiction. Concentrate on a single element of the story, quoting as necessary to make your point.

2. Read three or four short stories by an author whose work you admire. Concentrating on a single element treated similarly in all of the stories, write an analysis of the author's work as exemplified by your chosen stories.

3. Choose two stories that treat a similar theme. Compare and contrast the stance each story takes toward that theme, marshalling quotations and specifics as necessary to back up your argument.

4. Browse through newspapers and magazines for a story with the elements of good fiction. Now rewrite the story *as* fiction. Then write a one-page accompanying essay explaining the challenges of the task. What did it teach you about the relative natures of journalism and fiction?

Topics for Writing About Poetry

Topics for Brief Papers (250–500 Words)

1. Write a concise *explication* of a short poem of your choice. Concentrate on those facets of the poem that you think most need explaining. (For a sample explication, see page 1119.)

2. Write an *analysis* of a short poem, focusing on how a single key element shapes its meaning. (A sample analysis appears on page 1122.) Some possible topics are:

   - Tone in Edna St. Vincent Millay's "Recuerdo"
   - Imagery in Wallace Stevens's "The Emperor of Ice-Cream"
   - Kinds of irony in Thomas Hardy's "The Workbox"

- Theme in W. H. Auden's "Musée des Beaux Arts"
- Extended metaphor in Langston Hughes's "The Negro Speaks of Rivers" (Explain the one main comparison that the poem makes and show how the whole poem makes it. Other poems that would lend themselves to a paper on extended metaphor include Emily Dickinson's "Because I could not stop for Death," and Adrienne Rich's "Aunt Jennifer's Tigers.")

(To locate any of these poems, see the Index of Authors and Titles.)

3. Select a poem in which the main speaker is a character who for any reason interests you. You might consider, for instance, Robert Browning's "Soliloquy of the Spanish Cloister," T. S. Eliot's "The Love Song of J. Alfred Prufrock," or Rhina Espaillat's "Bilingual/Bilingüe." Then write a brief profile of this character, drawing only on what the poem tells you (or reveals). What is the character's age? Situation in life? Attitude toward self? Attitude toward others? General personality? Do you find this character admirable?

4. Although both of these poems tell a story, what happens in the poem isn't necessarily obvious: T. S. Eliot's "The Love Song of J. Alfred Prufrock" and Edwin Arlington Robinson's "Luke Havergal." Choose one of these poems, and in a paragraph sum up what you think happens in it. Then in a second paragraph, ask yourself: what, *besides* the element of story, did you consider in order to understand the poem?

Topics for More Extended Papers (600–1,000 Words)

1. Perform a line-by-line explication of a brief poem of your choice. Imagine that your audience is unfamiliar with the poem and needs your assistance in interpreting it.

2. Compare and contrast any two poems that treat a similar theme. Let your comparison bring you to an evaluation of the poems. Which is the stronger, more satisfying one?

3. Write a comparison-contrast essay on any two or more poems by a single poet. Look for two poems that share a characteristic thematic concern. Here are some possible topics:
   - Mortality in the work of John Keats
   - Nature in the poems of William Wordsworth
   - How Emily Dickinson's lyric poems resemble hymns
   - E. E. Cummings's approach to the free-verse line
   - Gerard Manley Hopkins's sonic effects

Topics for Long Papers (1,500 Words or More)

1. Review an entire poetry collection by a poet featured in this book. You will need to communicate to your reader a sense of the work's style and thematic preoccupations. Finally, make a value judgment about the work's quality.

2. Read five or six poems by a single author. Start with a poet featured in this book, and then find additional poems at the library or on the Internet. Write an analysis of a single element of that poet's work—for example, theme, imagery, diction, or form.

3. Write a line-by-line explication of a poem rich in matters to explain or of a longer poem that offers ample difficulty. While relatively short, Gerard Manley

Hopkins's "The Windhover" is a poem that will take a good bit of time to explicate. Even a short, apparently simple poem such as Robert Frost's "Stopping by Woods on a Snowy Evening" can provide more than enough material to explicate thoughtfully in a longer paper.

4. Write an analysis of a certain theme (or other element) that you find in the work of two or more poets. It is probable that in your conclusion you will want to set the poets' works side by side, comparing or contrasting them, and perhaps making some evaluation. Here are some sample topics to consider:
   - Langston Hughes, Gwendolyn Brooks, and Dudley Randall as Prophets of Social Change
   - What It Is to Be a Woman: The Special Knowledge of Sylvia Plath, Anne Sexton, and Adrienne Rich
   - The Complex Relations Between Fathers and Children in the Poetry of Robert Hayden, Rhina Espaillat, and Theodore Roethke
   - Making Up New Words for New Meanings: Neologisms in Lewis Carroll and Kay Ryan

Topics for Writing About Drama

Topics for Brief Papers (250–500 words)

1. Analyze a key character from any of the plays in this book. Two choices might be Tom Wingfield in *The Glass Menagerie* and Torvald Helmer in *A Doll's House*. What motivates that character? Point to specific moments in the play to make your case.

2. When the curtain comes down on the conclusion of some plays, the audience is left to decide exactly what finally happened. In a short informal essay, state your interpretation of the conclusion of *El Santo Americano* or *The Glass Menagerie*. Don't just give a plot summary; tell what you think the conclusion means.

3. Sum up the main suggestions you find in one of these meaningful objects (or actions): the handkerchief in *Othello*; the Christmas tree in *A Doll's House* (or Nora's doing a wild tarantella); Laura's collection of figurines in *The Glass Menagerie*.

4. Attend a play and write a review. In an assignment this brief, you will need to concentrate your remarks on either the performance or the script itself. Be sure to back up your opinions with specific observations.

Topics for More Extended Papers (600–1,000 Words)

1. From a play you have enjoyed, choose a passage that strikes you as difficult, worth reading closely. Try to pick a passage not longer than about 20 lines. Explicate it—give it a close, sentence-by-sentence reading—and explain how this small part of the play relates to the whole. For instance, any of the following passages might be considered memorable (and essential to their plays):
   - Othello's soliloquy beginning "It is the cause, it is the cause, my soul" (*Othello*, 5.2.1–22).

- Oedipus to Teiresias, speech beginning "Wealth, sovereignty and skill" (*Oedipus the King*, l. 418–76).
- Nora to Mrs. Linde, speech beginning "Yes, someday, maybe, in many years when I am not as pretty as I am now . . ." (*A Doll's House*, page 869).

2. Analyze the complexities and contradictions to be found in a well-rounded character from a play of your choice. Some good subjects might be Othello, Nora Helmer (in *A Doll's House*), or Tom Wingfield (in *The Glass Menagerie*).

3. Take just a single line or sentence from a play, one that stands out for some reason as greatly important. Perhaps it states a theme, reveals a character, or serves as a crisis (or turning point). Write an essay demonstrating its importance—how it functions, why it is necessary. Some possible lines include:

- Iago to Roderigo: "I am not what I am" (*Othello*, 1.1.67).
- Amanda to Tom: "You live in a dream; you manufacture illusions!" (*The Glass Menagerie*, Scene vii).

4. Write an analysis essay in which you single out an element of a play for examination—character, plot, setting, theme, dramatic irony, tone, language, symbolism, conventions, or any other element. Try to relate this element to the play as a whole. Sample topics: "The Function of Teiresias in *Oedipus the King*," "Imagery of Poison in *Othello*," "Williams's Use of Magic-Lantern Slides in *The Glass Menagerie*."

5. How would you stage an updated production of a play by Shakespeare, Sophocles, or Ibsen, transplanting it to our time? Choose a play, and describe the challenges and difficulties of this endeavor. How would you overcome them—or, if they cannot be overcome, why not?

Topics for Long Papers (1,500 Words or More)

1. Choose a play you have read and admire from this book, and read a second play by the same author. Compare and contrast the two plays with attention to a single element—a theme they have in common, or a particular kind of imagery, for example.

2. Read *Othello* and view a movie version of the play. You might choose Oliver Parker's 1995 take on the play with Laurence Fishburne and Kenneth Branagh, or even *O* (2001), an updated version that takes a prep school as its setting and a basketball star as its protagonist. Review the movie. What does it manage to convey of the original? What gets lost in the translation?

3. Choosing any of the works in "Plays for Further Reading" or taking some other modern or contemporary play your instructor suggests, report any difficulties you encountered in reading and responding to it. Explicate any troublesome passages for the benefit of other readers.

4. Attend a play and write an in-depth review, taking into account many elements of the drama: acting, direction, staging, costumes, lighting, and—if the work is relatively new and not a classic—the play itself.

30 WRITING A RESEARCH PAPER

> ## What You Will Learn in This Chapter
>
> - To choose a topic for your research paper
> - To find and evaluate sources
> - To organize, write, and revise your research paper
> - To cite and document your sources using MLA style

Why is it worthwhile to write a research paper? (Apart from the fact that you want a passing grade in the class, that is.) While you can learn much by exploring your own responses to a literary work, there is no substitute for entering into a conversation with others who have studied and thought about your topic. Literary criticism is that conversation. Your reading will expose you to the ideas of others who can shed light on a story, poem, or play. It will introduce you to the wide range of informed opinions that exist about literature, as about almost any subject. Sometimes, too, your research will uncover information about an author's life that leads you to new insights into a literary work. Undertaking a research paper gives you a chance to test your ideas against those of others, and in doing so to clarify your own opinions.

BROWSE THE RESEARCH

The most daunting aspect of the research paper may well be the mountains of information available on almost any literary subject. It can be hard to know where to begin. Sifting through books and articles is part of the research process. Unfortunately, the first material you uncover in the library or on the Internet is rarely the evidence you need to develop or support your thesis. Keep looking until you uncover helpful sources.

Another common pitfall in the process is the creeping feeling that your idea has already been examined a dozen times over. But take heart: like Odysseus, tie yourself to the mast so that when you hear the siren voices of published professors, you can listen without abandoning your own point of view. Your idea may have been treated, but not yet by you. Your particular take on a topic is bound to be different from someone else's. After all, thousands of books have been written on Shakespeare's plays, but people still find new things to say about them.

CHOOSE A TOPIC: FORMULATE YOUR ARGUMENT

▪ **Find a topic that interests you.** A crucial first step in writing a research paper is coming up with a topic that interests you. If you start with a topic that bores you, the process will be a chore and yield dull results. But if you begin with a topic that intrigues you, developing a compelling research question becomes easier, and seeking its answer will prove to be a more engaging process. The paper that results will inevitably be stronger and more interesting.

▪ **Find a way to get started.** Browsing through online journal articles and blogs, or skimming through books of literary criticism in the library, can help to spark an idea or two. Prewriting techniques such as brainstorming, freewriting, listing, and clustering can also help you to generate ideas on a specific work of literature. If you take notes and jot down ideas as they occur to you, when you start the formal writing process you will discover you have already begun.

▪ **Keep your purpose and audience in mind.** Refer often to the assignment, and approach your essay accordingly. Think of your audience as well—is it your professor, your classmates, or some hypothetical reader? As you plan your essay, keep your audience's expectations and needs in mind.

▪ **Identify an argument—your thesis—that you hope to support with research, and look for material that will help you demonstrate its plausibility.** Your thesis is a work in progress. Do not be afraid to let it evolve as you research your topic and reflect on your findings. Remember: the ideal research paper is based on your own observations and interpretations of a literary text.

BEGIN YOUR RESEARCH

Writing a research paper on literature calls for two kinds of sources. First, there are your primary sources—the literary works that are the central subject of your paper. Then there are your secondary sources—the critical or biographical books, articles, web and database resources that discuss the author or work you are examining. In writing a research paper, your task is to use both kinds of sources to develop a sustained and logical discussion of a specific topic.

Reliable Web Sources

As you begin your research, your first impulse may be to search online for websites and blogs that discuss your topic. If so, proceed with care. Websites may be written and published by anybody for any purpose, with no oversight. Even the online reference site *Wikipedia*, for example, is an amalgamation of voluntary contributors and is rife with small factual errors and contributor biases. Carefully analyze any material you gather from a general online search and compare it with other reputable sources of information. To garner the best sources possible, take these steps:

■ **Begin your search at a reliable website.** To avoid sloppy and inaccurate sites, begin your search with one of the following excellent guides through cyberspace:

- *Library of Congress's Alcove 9.* Fortunately, you don't have to trek to Washington to visit this venerable institution's annotated collection of reference websites in the humanities and social sciences. For your purpose—writing a literary research paper—access the Subject Index, click on "Literatures in English," and then click "Literary Criticism." This will take you to a list of metapages and websites with collections of reliable critical and biographical materials on authors and their works. (A metapage provides links to other websites.)

- *ipl2.* The aggregation of two popular research websites, *Internet Public Library* and *Librarians' Internet Index*, *ipl2* is hosted and maintained by Drexel University's College of Science and Technology and a consortium of other universities. This site lets you search for literary criticism by author, work, country of origin, or literary period.

- *Library Spot.* This is a portal to more than 5,000 libraries around the world, and to periodicals, online texts, reference works, and links to metapages and websites on any topic including literary criticism. This carefully maintained site is published by StartSpot Mediaworks, Inc., in the Northwestern University/Evanston Research Park in Evanston, Illinois.

- *Voice of the Shuttle.* Research links in more than twenty-five categories in the humanities and social sciences, including online texts, libraries, academic websites, and metapages, may be found at this site. It was developed and is maintained by Dr. Alan Liu in the English Department of the University of California, Santa Barbara.

■ **Learn to use Internet search engines effectively.** If you do decide to start with a general search of the web, try using the "advanced" search option, entering keywords to get results that contain those words ("LITERARY CRITICISM" "A DOLL'S HOUSE" or SYMBOLISM "THE LOTTERY"). Many Internet search engines provide a link to an advanced search form that offers ways for you to refine or restrict the scope of your search by date, website source, or country.

Print Resources

Don't overlook books and print journals. Until quite recently, most literary material existed solely in print—and only some of these resources have been transferred into digital formats. When you are hunting down secondary sources, a good place to begin is your campus library. Plan to spend some time thumbing through scholarly books and journals, looking for passages that you find particularly interesting or that pertain to your topic. Begin your search with the online catalog to get a sense of where you might find the books and journals you need.

To choose from the many books available on your library's shelves and through interlibrary loan, you might turn to book reviews for a sense of which volumes would best suit your purpose. *Book Review Digest* contains the full texts of many book reviews and excerpts of others. The *Digest* may be found in printed form in the reference section of your campus library, which may also provide access to the online version. Whether you are using the online or print version, you will need the author's name, title, and date of first publication of any book for which you hope to find a review.

Also helpful is the multivolume *Dictionary of Literary Biography*. This useful series of more than 360 volumes has entries on most well-known authors and presents excerpts of the best scholarship with complete citations. You may be able to research your entire paper from this comprehensive source alone. Many schools have either a print version of this reference work or subscribe to its online database.

Scholarly journals are another excellent resource for articles on your topic. Indexes to magazines and journals may be found in your library's reference section or on your library's website.

Online Databases

Most college libraries subscribe to specialized online database services covering all academic subjects—treasure troves of reliable sources. If you find yourself unsure of how to use your library's database system, ask the reference librarian to help you get started. Or explore the section on databases or research tools on your library's website to see what your school has available on literature. Many college library home pages provide students with access to subscription databases, which means that if you really can't bear to leave your comfy desk at home, you can still pay a virtual visit. The following databases are particularly useful for literary research:

- *Literature Resource Center* (Thomson Gale) provides biographies, bibliographies, and critical analyses of more than 120,000 authors and their work. This information is culled from journal articles and reference works.

- *MLA International Bibliography*, the Modern Language Association's database, is an excellent way to search for books and full-text articles on literary topics.

- *Google Scholar* provides one of the simplest ways to broadly search for a topic across a vast array of publicly available scholarly articles, theses, books, and other research documents. Some documents may require a university login to access.

- *JSTOR*, a nonprofit organization, indexes articles or abstracts from an archive of journals in more than fifty disciplines.

- *Literature Online (LION)* provides a vast searchable database of critical articles and reference works as well as full texts of more than 300,000 works of prose, poetry, and drama.

- *Project Muse*, a collaboration between publishers and libraries, offers access to more than 400 journals in the humanities, arts, and social sciences.
- *EBSCO*, a multisubject resource, covers literature and the humanities, as well as the social sciences, the medical sciences, linguistics, and other fields.

CHECKLIST: Finding Reliable Sources

☐ Locate reputable websites by starting at a reputable website designed for that purpose.

☐ Visit your campus library. Ask the reference librarian for advice.

☐ Check the library catalog for books and journals on your topic.

☐ Look into the online databases subscribed to by your library.

Visual Images

The web is an excellent source of visual images. If a picture, chart, or graph will enhance your argument, you may find the perfect one via an image search on Google, PicSearch, or other search engines. The digital collections at the Library of Congress website offer a wealth of images documenting American political, social, and cultural history—including portraits, prints, photographs, letters, and original manuscripts. Remember, though, that not all images are available for use by the general public. If there is an image you want to use, check for a copyright notice to see if its originator allows it to be reproduced. If so, you may include the photograph, provided you credit your source as you would if you were quoting text.

One note on images: use them carefully. Choose visuals that provide supporting evidence for the point you are trying to make or that enhance your reader's understanding of the work. Label your images with captions. Your goal should be to make your argument more convincing. In the example included here, a reproduction of Brueghel's painting helps to advance the author's argument and provide insight into Auden's poem.

Fig. 1. *Landscape with the Fall of Icarus* by Pieter Brueghel the Elder (c. 1558, Musées Royaux des Beaux-Arts de Belgique, Brussels)

W. H. Auden's poem "Musée des Beaux Arts" refers to a specific painting to prove its point that the most honest depictions of death take into account the way life simply goes on even after the most tragic of events. In line 14, Auden turns specifically to Pieter Brueghel the Elder's masterwork *The Fall of Icarus* (see Fig. 1), pointing to the painting's understated depiction of tragedy. In this painting, the death of Icarus does not take place on center stage. A plowman and his horse take up the painting's foreground, while the leg of Icarus falling into the sea takes up a tiny portion of the painting's lower-right corner. A viewer who fails to take the painting's title into account might not even notice Icarus at all.

CHECKLIST: Using Visual Images

☐ Use images as evidence to support your argument.
☐ Use images to enhance communication and understanding.
☐ Refer to the images in your text.
☐ Label each image with a figure number—"Fig. 1" in the example above—and provide a title or caption.
☐ Check copyrights.
☐ Include sources in a works-cited list.

EVALUATE YOUR SOURCES

Trustworthy Resources Build Your Paper's Credibility

It's an old saying, but a useful one: don't believe everything you read. The fact that a book or an article is printed and published doesn't necessarily mean it is accurate or unbiased. Likewise, the highest-ranking results of your web search may not be the most reliable or credible. Resources fall into two categories: scholarly and popular. Scholarly articles and books are written by and for faculty, scholars, and researchers and they feature original research, scholarly or academic language, and full citations for sources. Popular articles and books are written by journalists or professional writers for a general audience. These articles tend to be shorter, use simpler language, and rarely provide full citations of their sources. How can you ensure that the resource you are considering is a scholarly one?

Begin your search in a place that has taken some of the work out of quality control—your school library. Books and articles you find there are regarded by librarians as having some obvious merit. If your search takes you beyond the library and online, though, you will need to be discerning when choosing resources. As you weigh the value of each document, take the following into account:

- **Look closely at information provided about the author.** Is he or she known for expertise in the field? What are the author's academic or association credentials? Is there any reason to believe that the author is biased in any way? For example, a biography of an author written by that author's son or daughter might not be as unbiased as one written by a scholar with no personal connections. If the document appears online, is the web entry unsigned and anonymous? If the website is sponsored by an organization, is it a reputable one?

- **Determine the publisher's reliability.** Books, articles, and blogs published by an advocacy group might be expected to take a particular—possibly biased—slant on an issue. Be aware also that some books are published by vanity presses, companies that are paid by an author to publish his or her books. As a result, vanity press-published books generally aren't subject to the same rigorous quality control as those put out by more reputable publishing houses.

  A word of warning: individual student pages posted on university sites have not necessarily been reviewed by that university and are not reliable sources of information. Also, postings on *Wikipedia* are not subject to a scholarly review process and have been found to contain inaccuracies. It's safer to use a published encyclopedia.

- **Always check for a publication date.** If a document lists an edition number, check to see whether you are using the latest edition of the material. If the article appears on a website or blog, when was it last updated? In some cases you may want to base your essay on the most current information or theories, so you will want to steer toward the most recently published material.

▪ **For periodicals, decide whether a publication is an academic journal or a popular magazine.** What type of reputation does it have? Obviously, you do not want to use a magazine that periodically reports on Elvis sightings and alien births. And even articles on writers in magazines such as *Time* and *People* are likely to be too brief and superficial for purposes of serious research. Instead, choose scholarly journals designed to enhance the study of literature.

▪ **Consult experts.** Cornell University Library has two good online documents with guidance for analyzing sources, titled "Critically Analyzing Information Sources" and "Distinguishing Scholarly from Non-Scholarly Periodicals." Your school's research librarian or library website may have similar resources.

CHECKLIST: Evaluating Your Sources

☐ Who wrote it? What are the author's credentials?

☐ Is he or she an expert in the field?

☐ Does he or she appear to be unbiased toward the subject matter?

☐ Does the content seem consistent with demonstrated scholarship?

☐ Is the publisher reputable? Is it an advocacy group or a vanity press?

☐ Is the source an online journal or magazine? Is it scholarly or popular?

☐ When was the source published? Do later editions exist? If so, would a later edition be more useful?

ORGANIZE YOUR RESEARCH

▪ **Get your thoughts down on note cards or the equivalent on your laptop.** Once you have amassed your secondary sources, it will be time to begin reading in earnest. As you do so, be sure to take notes on any passage that pertains to your topic. A convenient way to organize your many thoughts is to write them down on index cards, which are easy to shuffle and rearrange. If you prefer to use your computer to take notes, you might consider using digital note-card software like *SimpleNote* or *EverNote*. For longer papers, it may be worthwhile to look into more sophisticated programs like *Scrivener*, which give you additional tools for planning and structuring your research and writing. Whatever approach you use, keep to a single fact or opinion on each card. This will make it easier for you to shuffle the deck and re-envision the order in which you deliver information to your reader.

▪ **Keep careful track of the sources of quotations and paraphrases.** As you take notes, make it unmistakably clear which thoughts and phrases are yours and which derive from others. (Remember, *quotation* means using the exact words of your source and placing the entire passage in quotation marks and citing the author. *Paraphrase* means expressing the ideas of your source in your own words, again citing the author.) Bear in mind the cautionary tale of a well-known historian, Doris Kearns Goodwin. She was charged with plagiarizing sections of two of her famous books when her words were found to be jarringly similar to those published in other books. Because she had not clearly indicated on her note cards which ideas and passages were hers and which came from other sources, Goodwin was forced to admit to plagiarism. Her enormous reputation suffered from these charges, but you can learn from her mistakes and save your own reputation—and your grades.

- **Keep track of the sources of ideas and concepts.** When an idea is inspired by or directly taken from someone else's writing, be sure to jot down the source on that same card or in your computer file. Your deck of cards or computer list will function as a working bibliography, which later will help you put together a works-cited list. To save yourself work, keep a separate list of the sources you're using. Then, as you make the note, you need write only the material's author or title and page reference on the card in order to identify your source. It's also useful to classify the note in a way that will help you to organize your material, making it easy, for example, to separate cards that deal with a story's theme from cards that deal with point of view or symbolism. Another helpful tip is to use an online bibliography manager like *EasyBib*, *Mendeley*, *RefWorks*, or *Zotero*. Many of these services will let you create an account to store your list of sources online and will also generate correctly formatted bibliographies for free.

- **Make notes of your own thoughts and reactions to your research.** When a critical article sparks your own original idea, be sure to capture that thought in your notes and mark it as your own. As you plan your paper, these notes may form the outline for your arguments.

- **Make photocopies or printouts to simplify the process and ensure accuracy.** Scholars once had to spend long hours copying out prose passages by hand. Luckily, for a small investment you can simply photocopy or print your sources to ensure accuracy in quoting and citing your sources. If you do photocopy material from a source, you should make it a habit to also copy the publication page from the front of the book. This will ensure you always have the full title and citation information for your bibliography. Some instructors will require you to hand in photocopies of your original sources with the final paper, along with printouts of articles downloaded from an Internet database. Even if this is not the case, photocopying your sources and holding onto your printouts can help you to reproduce quotations accurately in your essay—and accuracy is crucial.

ORGANIZE YOUR PAPER

With your thesis in mind and your notes spread before you, draw up an outline—a rough map of how best to argue your thesis and present your material. Determine what main points you need to make, and look for quotations that support those points. Even if you generally prefer to navigate the paper-writing process without a map, you will find that an outline makes the research-paper writing process considerably smoother. When organizing information from many different sources, it pays to plan ahead.

MAINTAIN ACADEMIC INTEGRITY

What Is Plagiarism?

Simply put, plagiarism is the use of another person's words, ideas, research, or arguments without giving proper credit to their source. In Western academic settings, plagiarism is viewed as a serious type of theft or forgery. By claiming someone else's ideas and language as your own, you rob them of the rightful recognition of their intellectual labor. On the other hand, if you responsibly recognize and respond to the scholarly work of others with proper citations, your own writing will convey more authority and competence.

Papers for Sale Are Papers That "F"ail

Do not be seduced by the apparent ease of cheating by computer. Your Internet searches may turn up several sites that offer term papers to download (just as you can find pornography, political propaganda, and questionable get-rich-quick schemes!). Most of these sites charge money for what they offer, but a few do not, happy to strike a blow against the "oppressive" insistence of English teachers that students learn to think and write.

Plagiarized term papers are an old game: the fraternity file and the "research assistance" service have been around far longer than the computer. It may seem easy enough to download a paper, put your name at the head of it, and turn it in for an easy grade. As any writing instructor can tell you, though, such papers usually stick out like a sore thumb. The style will be wrong, the work will not be consistent with other work by the same student in any number of ways, and the teacher will sometimes even have seen the same phony paper before. The ease with which electronic texts are reproduced makes this last possibility increasingly likely.

The odds of being caught and facing the unpleasant consequences are reasonably high. It is far better to take the grade you have earned for your own effort, no matter how mediocre, than to try to pass off someone else's work as your own. Even if, somehow, your instructor does not recognize your submission as a plagiarized paper, you have diminished your character through dishonesty and lost an opportunity to learn something on your own.

A Warning Against Internet Plagiarism

Plagiarism detection services are often a professor's ally in the battle against academic dishonesty. Questionable research papers can be sent to these services (such as Turnitin.com and EVE2), which perform complex searches of the Internet and of a growing database of purchased term papers. The research paper will be returned to the professor with plagiarized sections annotated and the sources documented. The end result will certainly be a failing grade on the essay, possibly a failing grade for the course, and, depending on the policies of your university, the very real possibility of expulsion.

ACKNOWLEDGE ALL SOURCES

The brand of straight-out dishonesty described above is one type of plagiarism. There is, however, another, subtler kind: when students incorporate somebody else's words *or* ideas into their papers without giving proper credit. To avoid this second—sometimes quite accidental—variety of plagiarism, familiarize yourself with the conventions for acknowledging sources. First and foremost, remember to give credit to any writer who supplies you with ideas, information, or specific words and phrases.

Using Quotations

- **Acknowledge your source when you quote a writer's words or phrases.** When you use someone else's words or phrases, you should reproduce his or her exact words in quotation marks, and be sure to properly credit the source.

  > Already, Frost has hinted that Nature may be, as Radcliffe Squires suggests, "Nothing but an ash-white plain without love or faith or hope, where ignorant appetites cross by chance" (87).

- **If you quote more than four lines, set your quotation off from the body of the paper.** Start a new line; indent half an inch and type the quotation, double-spaced. (You do not need to use quotation marks, as the format tells the reader the passage is a quotation.)

  > Samuel Maio made an astute observation about the nature of Weldon Kees's distinctive tone:
  >
  > > Kees has therefore combined a personal subject matter with an impersonal voice—that is, one that is consistent in its tone evenly recording the speaker's thoughts without showing any emotional intensity which might lie behind those thoughts. (136)

Citing Ideas

■ **Acknowledge your source when you mention a critic's ideas.** Even if you are not quoting exact words or phrases, be sure to acknowledge the source of any original ideas or concepts you have used.

> Another explanation is suggested by Daniel Hoffman, a critic who has discussed the story: the killer hears the sound of his *own* heart (227).

■ **Acknowledge your source when you paraphrase a writer's words.** To paraphrase a critic, you should do more than just rearrange his or her words: you should translate them into your own original sentences—again, always being sure to credit the original source. As an example, suppose you wish to refer to an insight of Randall Jarrell, who commented as follows on the images of spider, flower, and moth in Robert Frost's poem "Design":

RANDALL JARRELL'S ORIGINAL TEXT

Notice how the *heal-all*, because of its name, is the one flower in all the world picked to be the altar for this Devil's Mass; notice how *holding up* the moth brings something ritual and hieratic, a ghostly, ghastly formality, to this priest and its sacrificial victim.[1]

It would be too close to the original to write, without quotation marks, these sentences:

PLAGIARIZED REWORDING

Frost picks the *heal-all* as the one flower in all the world to be the altar for this Devil's Mass. There is a ghostly, ghastly formality to the spider *holding up* the moth, like a priest holding a sacrificial victim.

This rewording, although not exactly in Jarrell's language, manages to steal his memorable phrases without giving him credit. Nor is it sufficient just to include Jarrell's essay in the works-cited list at the end of your paper. If you do, you are still a crook; you merely point to the scene of the crime. Instead, think through Jarrell's words to the point he is making, so that it can be restated in your own original way. If you want to keep any of his striking phrases (and why not?), put them exactly as he wrote them in quotation marks:

---

[1] *Poetry and the Age* (Alfred A. Knopf, 1953) p. 42.

APPROPRIATE PARAPHRASE, ACKNOWLEDGES SOURCE

As Randall Jarrell points out, Frost portrays the spider as a kind of priest in a Mass, or Black Mass, elevating the moth like an object for sacrifice, with "a ghostly, ghastly formality" (42).

Note also that this improved passage gives Jarrell the credit not just for his words but for his insight into the poem. Both the idea and the words in which it was originally expressed are the properties of their originator. Finally, notice the page reference that follows the quotation (this system of documenting your sources is detailed in the next section).

DOCUMENT SOURCES USING MLA STYLE

You must document everything you take from a source. When you quote from other writers, when you borrow their information, when you summarize or paraphrase their ideas, make sure you give them proper credit. Identify the writer by name and cite the book, magazine, newspaper, pamphlet, website, or other source you have used.

The conventions that govern the proper way to document sources are available in the *MLA Handbook*, Eighth Edition (2016). The following brief list of pointers is not meant to take the place of the *MLA Handbook* itself, but to give you a basic sense of the rules for documentation.

Keep a List of Sources

Keep a working list of your research sources—all the references from which you might quote, summarize, paraphrase, or take information. When your paper is in finished form, it will end with a neat copy of the works you actually used (once called a "Bibliography," now titled "Works Cited").

Use Parenthetical References

In the body of your paper, every time you refer to a source, you need to provide information to help a reader locate it in your works-cited list. You can usually give just the author's name and a page citation in parentheses. For example, if you are writing a paper on Weldon Kees's sonnet "For My Daughter" and want to include an observation you found on page 136 of Samuel Maio's book *Creating Another Self*, write:

One critic has observed that the distinctive tone of "For My Daughter" depends on Kees's combination of "personal subject matter with an impersonal voice" (Maio 136).

If you mention the author's name in your sentence, you need give only the page number in your reference:

> As Samuel Maio has observed, Kees creates a distinctive tone in
> this sonnet by combining a "personal subject with an impersonal
> voice" (136).

If you have two books or magazine articles by Samuel Maio in your works-cited list, how will the reader tell them apart? In your text, refer to the title of each book or article by condensing it into a word or two. Condensed book titles are italicized, and condensed article titles are still placed within quotation marks.

> One critic has observed that the distinctive tone of "For My Daughter"
> depends on Kees's combination of "personal subject matter with an
> impersonal voice" (Maio, *Creating* 136).

Create a Works-Cited List

- **Provide a full citation for each source on your works-cited page.** At the end of your paper, in your list of works cited, your reader will find a full description of your source—for the above examples, a critical book:

> Maio, Samuel. *Creating Another Self: Voices in Modern American
> Personal Poetry*. 2nd ed., Thomas Jefferson UP, 2005.

- **Put your works-cited list in proper form.** The *MLA Handbook* provides detailed instructions for citing a myriad of different types of sources, from books to *YouTube* videos. To format your list:

1. Start a new page for the works-cited list, and continue the page numbering from the body of your paper.
2. Center the title, "Works Cited," one inch from the top of the page.
3. Double-space between all lines (including after title and between entries).
4. Type each entry beginning at the left-hand margin. If an entry runs longer than a single line, indent the following lines one-half inch from the left-hand margin.
5. Alphabetize each entry according to the author's last name.

Cite Sources in MLA Style

Each entry in your list should contain all relevant information, as available, that helps your reader locate your source.

Core Elements of Each Entry

1. **Author's full name** as it appears on the title page or section of the work, last name first, followed by a period.

   (a) If the author has a different role than writing the work, identify that role (e.g. "editor" or "translator").

   (b) If the work is published without the author's name, skip this element.

2. **Title of source** (include the subtitle, if there is one, separated from the title by a colon), followed by a period.

   (a) Italicize titles of major works such as books, plays, websites, paintings, photographs, television shows, albums, etc.

   (b) Use quotation marks for titles of shorter works such as poems, short stories, newspaper or journal articles, episodes in television series, song titles, etc.

3. **Title of container,** italicized, and followed by comma. The MLA has coined the term "container" as a descriptor for the place where your source is "held," some examples being the:

   - magazine or newspaper that published source article
   - website that published source article
   - television series of which source episode is part
   - dictionary that contains source definition
   - anthology that printed source poem
   - website that published source blog or comment

4. **Other contributors,** followed by a comma. These are individuals involved in creating the source or its container, if relevant. Precede the names of contributors with a description of their role, e.g.:

   - translated by
   - performance by
   - edited by

5. **Version,** followed by a comma. Oftentimes works are updated or published in different forms. Be sure to identify the specific version you used. Some examples:

   - Book editions are cited as: 2nd ed, rev. ed., updated ed., or expanded ed.
   - Film versions might be cited as: uncut version or director's cut version.

6. **Number**, followed by comma. If your source's container uses a numbering system, be sure to cite the numbers. Some examples:

   ▪ Academic journals often use volumes and numbers, i.e. vol. 7, no. 2.

   ▪ Television series often number episodes, i.e. season 4, episode 7.

   ▪ Books can be issued in multi-volume sets, i.e. vol. 3.

7. **Publisher**, followed by comma. Publishers are generally found on the copyright section of your book or website, but there are circumstances in which publisher information is unavailable.

   (a) **Use the full name of the publisher.** Eliminate articles (*A, An, The*) and business abbreviations (*Co., Corp., Inc., Ltd.*). Abbreviate the names of university presses, by using the letters *U* (for University) and *P* (for Press).

Publisher's Name	Proper Citation
Harvard University Press	Harvard UP
University of Chicago Press	U of Chicago P
Alfred A. Knopf, Inc.	Alfred A. Knopf

   (b) **You can omit the publisher's name in circumstances where it does not add additional information), e.g.:**

   ▪ periodical or newspaper

   ▪ work published by the author

   ▪ website whose name is the same as the publisher

8. **Publication date**, followed by comma. Many sources have more than one publication date, particularly when works are published in multiple media. The *MLA Handbook* suggests citing the date that is most relevant to your use of the source.

9. **Location**, followed by period. MLA uses the word "location" to designate whatever specific information will help your reader pinpoint your source most easily, e.g.:

   ▪ page numbers (abbreviated as *p.* for a single page or *pp.* for a range of pages)

   ▪ web addresses such as URLs, DOIs (digital object identifiers), or permalinks

   ▪ disc numbers

   ▪ physical locations—the name of the museum where you viewed a piece of art, or the location where you heard an author give a speech, etc.

Each of your entries should end with a period, no matter what element it concludes with. Remember, if the information is not available, you can safely leave it out of your citation. You should focus on providing all the relevant information in a clear manner. Don't worry if you are unsure exactly how properly to cite your source: the 8th edition of the *MLA Handbook* reassures us "there is often more than one way to document a source" (4).

Example Citations

Using the practice template created by the MLA, let's consider how the citation for a standard book entry is developed:

> Maio, Samuel. *Creating Another Self: Voice in Modern American Personal Poetry*. 2nd ed., Thomas Jefferson UP, 2005.

AUTHOR / TITLE

1. Author.	Maio, Samuel.
2. Title of source.	*Creating Another Self: Voice in Modern American Personal Poetry.*

CONTAINER 1

3. Title of container,	
4. Other contributors,	
5. Version,	2nd ed.,
6. Number,	
7. Publisher,	Thomas Jefferson UP,
8. Publication date,	2005,
9. Location.	

Here is the development of a citation for an article found on the web:

> "The Poet at Work." *Emily Dickinson Museum*, Trustees of Amherst College, www.emilydickinsonmuseum.org/poet_at_work.

AUTHOR / TITLE

1. Author.	(No author cited)
2. Title of source.	"The Poet at Work."

CONTAINER 1

3. Title of container,	*Emily Dickinson Museum,*
4. Other contributors,	
5. Version,	
6. Number,	
7. Publisher,	Trustees of Amherst College,
8. Publication date,	
9. Location.	www.emilydickinsonmuseum.org/poet_at_work.

Two "Containers"

Sometimes you will find a source (e.g. a journal article) that is included in a "container" (the journal), which you accessed from a second, larger "container" (e.g. an online database). As another example, your source might be a TV episode, which is part of a TV series (the first container), which you streamed from *Netflix* (the second, larger container). When you have multiple containers, use the same procedures to provide complete information for each one. Study the MLA's template below to work through the citation for a print article that was accessed in an online database.

Nelson, Raymond. "The Fitful Life of Weldon Kees." *American Literary History,* vol. 1, no. 4, Winter 1989, pp. 816–52. *JSTOR,* www.jstor.org/stable/489775.

AUTHOR / TITLE

1. Author.	Nelson, Raymond.
2. Title of source.	"The Fitful Life of Weldon Kees."

CONTAINER 1

3. Title of container,	*American Literary History,*
4. Other contributors,	
5. Version,	
6. Number,	vol. 1, no. 4,
7. Publisher,	
8. Publication date,	Winter 1989,
9. Location.	pp. 816–52.

CONTAINER 2

3. Title of container,	*JSTOR,*
4. Other contributors,	
5. Version,	
6. Number,	
7. Publisher,	
8. Publication date,	
9. Location.	www.jstor.org/stable/489775.

Optional Elements

You may include any additional elements in your entry that you think are relevant to your use of the source. Place them with the core elements they relate to so the inclusion makes sense for the reader. Some optional elements commonly added include:

- **Date of original publication,** or prior publication dates
- **City of publication,** particularly if the book was published in many countries
- **Other facts about the source,** e.g. it is part of a unique series
- **Added descriptor for an unexpected type of source** (e.g. a personal meeting with an author or an unpublished letter)
- **Date you accessed online resource** will be relevant in some cases

Additional Resources on MLA Style

Refer as necessary to the *MLA Handbook* or to the "Reference Guide for Citations" examples in this book. The MLA also has a website with tips and advice—*style.mla.org*—or you may find it helpful to use an online citation manager such as *EasyBib* or *Zotero* to generate the citation for a source automatically.

CONCLUDING THOUGHTS

A well-crafted research essay is a wondrous thing—as delightful, in its own way, as a well-crafted poem or short story or play. Good essays prompt thought and add to knowledge. Writing a research paper sharpens your own mind and exposes you to the honed insights of other thinkers. Think of anything you write as a piece that could be published for the benefit of other people interested in your topic. After all, such a goal is not as far-fetched as it seems: this textbook, for example, features a number of papers written by students. Why shouldn't yours number among them? Aim high.

REFERENCE GUIDE FOR MLA CITATIONS

Here are examples of the types of citations you are likely to need for most student papers. The formats follow current MLA style for works-cited lists.

PRINT PUBLICATIONS

Books

No Author Listed

The Chicago Manual of Style. 16th ed., U of Chicago P, 2010.

One Author or Editor

Middlebrook, Diane Wood. *Anne Sexton: A Biography.* Houghton
   Mifflin, 1991.

Monteiro, George, editor. *Conversations with Elizabeth Bishop.* UP of
   Mississippi, 1996.

Two Authors or Editors

Jarman, Mark, and Robert McDowell. *The Reaper: Essays.* Story Line
   Press, 1996.

Craig, David, and Janet McCann, editors. *Odd Angles of Heaven:
   Contemporary Poetry by People of Faith.* Harold Shaw Publishing,
   1994.

Three or More Authors

Phillips, Rodney, et al. *The Hand of the Poet.* Rizzoli International
   Publications, 1997.

Multiple Works by the Same Author

Bawer, Bruce. *The Aspect of Eternity.* Graywolf Press, 1993.

---. "Civilized Pleasures." *The Hudson Review,* vol. 59, no. 1, Spring 2006.
   JSTOR, www.jstor.org/stable/i20464510.

---. *Diminishing Fictions: Essays on the Modern American Novel and Its
   Critics.* Graywolf Press, 1988.

Corporate Author and Publisher

Reading at Risk: A Survey of Literary Reading in America. National
Endowment for the Arts, June 2004.

Author and Editor

Shakespeare, William. *The Sonnets.* Edited by G. Blakemore Evans,
Cambridge UP, 1996.

Translator

Dante Alighieri. *Inferno: A New Verse Translation.* Translated by Michael
Palma, W. W. Norton, 2002.

Introduction, Preface, Foreword, or Afterword

Lapham, Lewis. Introduction. *Understanding Media: The Extensions of
Man,* by Marshall McLuhan, MIT P, 1994, pp. vi–x.

Thwaite, Anthony. Preface. *Contemporary Poets,* edited by Thomas Riggs,
6th ed., St. James Press, 1996, pp. vii–viii.

Work in an Anthology

Rodriguez, Richard. "Aria: A Memoir of a Bilingual Childhood." *The Best
American Essays of the Century,* edited by Robert Atwan and Joyce
Carol Oates, Houghton Mifflin, 2001, pp. 447–66. Best American
Series.

Translation in an Anthology

Neruda, Pablo. "We Are Many." Translated by Alastair Reid. *Literature:
An Introduction to Fiction, Poetry, Drama, and Writing,* edited by
X. J. Kennedy and Dana Gioia, 13th ed., Pearson, 2016,
pp. 916-17.

Revised or Subsequent Edition

Janouch, Gustav. *Conversations with Kafka.* Translated by Goronwy Rees,
rev. ed., New Directions Publishing, 1971.

Republished Book

Ellison, Ralph. *Invisible Man*. 1952. Vintage Books, 1995.

Multivolume Work

Wellek, René. *A History of Modern Criticism, 1750–1950*. 8 vols., Yale UP, 1955–92.

One Volume of a Multivolume Work

Wellek, René. *A History of Modern Criticism, 1750–1950*. Vol. 7, Yale UP, 1991. 8 vols.

Book in a Series

Ross, William T. *Weldon Kees*. Twayne Publishing, 1985. Twayne's United States Authors Series, 484.

Signed Article in a Reference Book

Cavoto, Janice E. "Harper Lee's *To Kill a Mockingbird*." *The Oxford Encyclopedia of American Literature*, edited by Jay Parini, vol. 2, Oxford UP, 2004, pp. 418–21.

Unsigned Encyclopedia Article—Standard Reference Book

"James Dickey." *The New Encyclopaedia Britannica: Micropaedia*. 15th ed., 1987.

Dictionary Entry

"Design." *Merriam-Webster's Collegiate Dictionary*. 11th ed., 2003.

Periodicals

Journal

Salter, Mary Jo. "The Heart Is Slow to Learn." *The New Criterion*, vol. 10, no. 8, Apr. 1992, pp. 23–29.

Signed Magazine Article

Gioia, Dana. "Studying with Miss Bishop." *The New Yorker*, 5 Sept. 1986, pp. 90–101.

Unsigned Magazine Article

"The Real Test." *New Republic*, 5 Feb. 2001, p. 7.

Newspaper Article

Lyall, Sarah. "In Poetry, Ted Hughes Breaks His Silence on Sylvia Plath." *The New York Times*, 19 Jan. 1998, natl. ed., pp. A1+.

Signed Book Review

Fugard, Lisa. "Divided We Love," Review of *Unaccustomed Earth*, by Jhumpa Lahiri. *The Los Angeles Times*, 30 Mar. 2008, p. R1.

Unsigned, Untitled Book Review

Review of *Otherwise: New and Selected Poems*, by Jane Kenyon. *Virginia Quarterly Review*, vol. 72, no. 1, Winter 1996, p. 136.

WEB RESOURCES

Website

Liu, Alan, director. *Voice of the Shuttle*. English Dept., U of California Santa Barbara, vos.ucsb.edu.

Document on a Website

"A Hughes Timeline." *PBS*, Public Broadcasting Service, www.pbs.org. wgbh/masterpiece/americancollection/cora/hughes_timeline.html.

"Wallace Stevens." *Poets.org.*, Academy of American Poets, www.poets. org/poetsorg/poet/wallace-stevens.

Online Reference Database

"Brooks, Gwendolyn." *Encyclopaedia Britannica,* www.britannica.com/
biography/Gwendolyn-Brooks.

Entire Online Book, Previously Appeared in Print

Jewett, Sarah Orne. *The Country of the Pointed Firs.* 1896. *Project
Gutenberg,* 11 July 2008, www.gutenberg.org/files/367/
367-h/367-h.htm. Ebook 367.

Article in an Online Newspaper

Atwood, Margaret. "The Writer: A New Canadian Life-Form." *The
New York Times on the Web,* 18 May 1997, www.nytimes.com/
books/97/05/18/bookend/bookend.html.

Article in an Online Magazine

Garner, Dwight. "Jamaica Kincaid." *Salon,* 13 Jan. 1996, www.salon.
com/1996/01/13/kincaid_2/.

Article in an Online Scholarly Journal

Carter, Sarah. "From the Ridiculous to the Sublime: Ovidian and Neo-
platonic Registers in *A Midsummer Night's Dream.*" *Early Modern
Literary Studies,* vol 12, no. 1, May 2006, pp. 1–31, purl.oclc.org/
emls/12-1/cartmnd.htm.

Article from a Scholarly Journal, Part of an Archival Online Database

Finch, Annie. "My Father Dickinson: On Poetic Influence." *The Emily
Dickinson Journal,* vol. 17, no. 2, 2008, pp. 24–38. *Project
Muse,* www.muse.jhu.edu/journals/emily_dickinson_journal/
v017/17.2.finch.html.

Article Accessed via a Library Subscription Service

Seitler, Dana. "Unnatural Selection: Mothers, Eugenic Feminism, and Charlotte Perkins Gilman's Regeneration Narratives." *American Quarterly*, vol. 55, no. 1, Mar. 2003, pp. 61–87. *ProQuest*, search.proquest.com.libproxy1.usc.edu/docview/223310934/5B0B8A7854AE4085PQ/1?accountid=14789

Online Blog

Gioia, Ted. "*White Teeth* by Zadie Smith." *The New Canon: The Best in Fiction Since 1985*, www.thenewcanon.com/white_teeth.html.

Vellala, Rob. "Gilman: No Trouble to Anyone." *The American Literary Blog*, 17 Aug. 2010, americanliteraryblog.blogspot.com/search/label/Charlotte%20Perkins%20Gilman.

Twitter

Tan, Amy (AmyTan). "#TenThingsNotToSayToAWriter My life would make a great story. If you write it, we can split royalties 50–50." *Twitter*, 30 July 2015, 9:19 p.m., twitter.com/AmyTan/status/626970316087132161.

Photograph or Painting Accessed Online

Langston Hughes in 1936. *Wikimedia Commons*, Wikimedia Foundation, commons.wikimedia.org/wiki/Langston_Hughes#/media/File:Langston_Hughes_1936.jpg.

Bruegel, Pieter, *Landscape with the Fall of Icarus*. c.1558. Musées Royaux des Beaux-Arts de Belgique, Brussels. *Ibiblio*, U of North Carolina-Chapel Hill/Center for the Public Domain, www.ibiblio.org/wm/paint/auth/bruegel.

Video Accessed Online

"Ozymandias: Percy Bysshe Shelley." *YouTube*, E-Verse Radio, 13 Mar. 2007, www.youtube.com/watch?v=6xGa-fNSHaM.

Podcast

Writer's Almanac. Narrated by Garrison Keillor, 23 Feb. 2016, www.writersalmanac.org/episodes/20160223.

OTHER MEDIA
Compact Disc (CD)

Shakespeare, William. *The Complete Arkangel Shakespeare: 38 Fully-Dramatized Plays*. Narrated by Eileen Atkins and John Gielgud, read by Imogen Stubbs, Joseph Fiennes, et al., Audio Partners, 2003.

DVD

Hamlet. By William Shakespeare, performance by Laurence Olivier, Eileen Herlie, and Basil Sydney, 1948. Criterion Collection, 2010.

Film

Hamlet. By William Shakespeare, directed by Franco Zeffirelli, performances by Mel Gibson, Glenn Close, Helena Bonham Carter, Alan Bates, and Paul Scofield, Warner Bros., 1991.

Television or Radio Program

Moby Dick. By Herman Melville, directed by Franc Roddam, performances by Patrick Stewart and Gregory Peck, 2 episodes, USA Network, 16-17 Mar. 1998.

Television Series

The Wire. By David Simon, Blown Deadline/HBO, 2002-2008.

Episode of a Television Series

"Old Cases." *The Wire*, by David Simon, season 1, episode 4, Blown Deadline/HBO, 23 June 2002.

Episode of a Television Series Seen on DVD

"Old Cases." *The Wire: The Complete First Season*, by David Simon,
 episode 4, HBO Video, 2004.

Episode of a Television Series Streamed Online

"Old Cases." *The Wire: The Complete First Season*, by David Simon,
 episode 4. *Amazon Prime*, www.amazon.com/
 The-Detail/dp/B00BSEJR9C/ref=sr_1_1?s=instant-
 video&ie=UTF8&qid=1459816276&sr=1-1&keywords=the+wire.

Live Performance

Heartbreak House. By George Bernard Shaw, directed by Robin
 Lefevre, performances by Philip Bosco and Swoosie Kurtz,
 Roundabout Theater Company, 1 Oct. 2006, New York.

LITERARY CREDITS

FICTION

Achebe, Chinua: "Dead Men's Path," copyright © 1972, 1973 by Chinua Achebe; from GIRLS AT WAR: AND OTHER STORIES by Chinua Achebe. Used by permission of Doubleday, an imprint of the Knopf Doubleday Publishing Group, a division of Random House LLC. All rights reserved.

Alexie, Sherman: "This Is What It Means to Say Phoenix, Arizona" from THE LONE RANGER AND TONTO FISTFIGHT IN HEAVEN, copyright 1993, 2005 by Sherman Alexie. Used by permission of Grove/Atlantic, Inc. Any third party use of this material, outside of this publication, is prohibited.

Atwood, Margaret: "Happy Endings" from GOOD BONES AND SIMPLE MURDERS by Margaret Atwood, copyright © 1983, 1992, 1994, by O.W. Toad Ltd. Used by permission of Nan A. Talese, an imprint of the Knopf Doubleday Publishing Group, a division of Random House LLC. All rights reserved.

Borges, Jorge Luis: "The Gospel According to Mark" from COLLECTED FICTIONS by Jorge Luis Borges, translated by Andrew Hurley, copyright © 1998 by Maria Kodama. Translation copyright © 1998 by Penguin Putnam Inc. Used by permission of Viking Penguin, a division of Penguin Group (USA) LLC.

Carver, Raymond: "Cathedral" from CATHEDRAL by Raymond Carver, copyright © 1981, 1982, 1983 by Raymond Carver. Used by permission of Alfred A. Knopf, an imprint of the Knopf Doubleday Publishing Group, a division of Random House LLC. All rights reserved.

Chopin, Kate: "The Storm" by Kate Chopin from THE COMPLETE WORKS OF KATE CHOPIN. Copyright © 1969, Louisiana State University Press. Used by permission of Louisiana State University Press.

Cisneros, Sandra: "The House on Mango Street" from THE HOUSE ON MANGO STREET. Copyright © 1984 by Sandra Cisneros. Published by Vintage Books, a division of Random House, Inc., and in hardcover by Alfred A. Knopf in 1994. By permission of Susan Bergholz Literary Services, New York, NY, and Lamy, NM. All rights reserved.

Faulkner, William: "A Rose for Emily," copyright © 1930 and renewed 1958 by William Faulkner; from COLLECTED STORIES OF WILLIAM FAULKNER by William Faulkner. Used by permission of Random House, an imprint and division of Random House LLC. All rights reserved.

Faulkner, William: "Barn Burning," copyright © 1950 by Random House, Inc. Copyright renewed 1977 by Jill Faulkner Summers; from COLLECTED STORIES OF WILLIAM FAULKNER by William Faulkner. Used by permission of Random House, an imprint and division of Random House LLC. All rights reserved.

Gioia, Dana; Tan, Amy: "Talking with Amy Tan," excerpted from an interview with Amy Tan conducted by NEA for "The Big Read," August 7, 2006.

Hemingway, Ernest: "A Clean Well-Lighted Place," reprinted with the permission of Scribner Publishing Group, a division of Simon & Schuster, Inc., from THE SHORT STORIES OF ERNEST HEMINGWAY by Ernest Hemingway. Copyright 1933 by Charles Scribner's Sons. Copyright renewed 1961 by Mary Hemingway. All rights reserved.

Jackson, Shirley: "The Lottery" from THE LOTTERY by Shirley Jackson. Copyright © 1948, 1949 by Shirley Jackson. Copyright renewed 1976, 1977 by

POETRY

POEMS OF ROBERT CREELEY, 1945–1975; permission conveyed through Copyright Clearance Center, Inc.

Cummings, E.E. "anyone lived in a pretty how town". Copyright 1940, © 1968, 1991 by the Trustees for the E.E. Cummings Trust. Used by permission of Liveright Publishing Corporation.

Cummings, E.E.: "Buffalo Bill 's". Copyright 1923, 1951, © 1991 by the Trustees for the E.E. Cummings Trust. Copyright © 1976 by George James Firmage, from COMPLETE POEMS: 1904–1962 by E.E. Cummings, edited by George J. Firmage. Used by permission of Liveright Publishing Corporation.

Cummings, E.E.: "in Just-". Copyright 1923, 1951, © 1991 by the Trustees for the E.E. Cummings Trust. Copyright © 1976 by George James Firmage. Used by permission of Liveright Publishing Corporation.

Cunningham, J.V.: "Friend, on this scaffold Thomas More lies dead." Reprinted with permission.

Deutsch, Babette: "The Falling Flower" by Arakida Moritake, translated by Babette Deutsch. Copyright 1957. Reprinted by permission of Benjamin Yarmolinsky and the Estate of Babette Deutsch.

Dickinson, Emily: "because I could not stop for Death," "The Lightening is a yellow Fork," reprinted by permission of the publishers and the Trustees of Amherst College from THE POEMS OF EMILY DICKINSON: The Belknap Press of Harvard University Press, Copyright © 1998 by the President and Fellows of Harvard College, Copyright © 1951, 1955, 1979, 1983 by the President and Fellows of Harvard College.

Dickinson, Emily: "My Life had stood – a Loaded Gun" reprinted by permission of the publishers and the Trustees fo Amherst College from THE POEMS OF EMILY DICKINSON: VARIORUM EDITION, The Belknap Press of Harvard University Press, Copyright © 1998 by the President and Fellows of Harvard College, Copyright © 1951, 1955, 1979, 1983 by the President and Fellows of Harvard College.

Dinesen, Isak: Excerpt from OUT OF AFRICA by Isak Dinesen. New York: Random, 1972.

Doolittle, H.: "Helen" by H.D. (Hilda Doolittle), from COLLECTED POEMS, 1912–1944, copyright © 1982 by The Estate of Hilda Doolittle. Reprinted by permission of New Directions Publishing Corp.

Espaillat, Rhina P.: "Bilingual/Bilingüe" by Rhina P. Espaillat. Reprinted by permission of the author.

Foley, Adelle: "Learning to Shave (Father teaching son)" by Adelle Foley. Reprinted with permission from Adelle Foley.

Frost, Robert: "Desert Places" from the book THE POETRY OF ROBERT FROST edited by Edward Connery Lathem. Copyright © 1923, 1928, 1969 by Henry Holt and Company, copyright © 1936, 1942, 1951, 1956 by Robert Frost, copyright © 1964, 1970 by Lesley Frost Ballantine. Reprinted by permission of Henry Holt and Company, LLC.

Frost, Robert: "Acquainted with the Night" from the book THE POETRY OF ROBERT FROST edited by Edward Connery Lathem. Copyright © 1923, 1928, 1969 by Henry Holt and Company, LLC, copyright © 1936 1942, 1951, 1956 by Robert Frost, copyright © 1964, 1970 by Lesley Frost Ballantine. Reprinted by permission of Henry Holt and Company, LLC.

Frost, Robert: "Nothing Gold Can Stay" from the book THE POETRY OF ROBERT FROST edited by Edward Connery Lathem. Copyright © 1923, 1928, 1969 by Henry Holt and Company, LLC, copyright © 1936 1942, 1951, 1956 by Robert Frost, copyright © 1964, 1970 by Lesley Frost Ballantine. Reprinted by permission of Henry Holt and Company, LLC.

Frost, Robert: "Stopping by Woods on a Snowy Evening" from the book THE POETRY OF ROBERT FROST edited by Edward Connery Lathem. Copyright © 1923, 1928, 1969 by Henry Holt and Company, LLC, copyright © 1936 1942, 1951, 1956 by Robert Frost, copyright © 1964, 1970 by Lesley Frost Ballantine. Reprinted by permission of Henry Holt and Company, LLC.

Frost, Robert: "The Secret Sits" from the book THE POETRY OF ROBERT FROST edited by Edward Connery Lathem. Copyright © 1969 by Henry Holt and Company, copyright © 1942 by Robert Frost, copyright © 1970 by Lesley Frost Ballantine. Reprinted by permission of Henry Holt and Company, LLC.

Ginsberg, Allen: All lines from "A Supermarket in California" from COLLECTED POEMS 1947–1980 by Allen Ginsberg. Copyrights © in 1955 by Allen Ginsberg.

DRAMA

PHOTO CREDITS

Fiction

1: Jim McHugh/Los Angeles; 2: Jim McHugh; 9: E. Boyd Smith; 12: SuperStock/SuperStock; 18: Bettmann/Corbis; 32: Library of Congress, Prints & Photographs Division, [LC-USZC2-6403]; 40: Library of Congress, Prints & Photographs Division, [LC-USZ62-10610]; 45: file/AP Photo; 56: New York Times Co./Getty Images; 64: © Everett Collection; 72: BALTEL/SIPA/Newscom; 77: © Bettmann/Corbis; 85: Pearson Education; 104: J.A. Scholten/Missouri History Museum; 123: Bettmann/Corbis; 127: Zuma Press/Newscom; 128: imago stock&people/Newscom; 151: Bettmann/Corbis; 172: Alamy; 187: Zuma Press/Newscom; 190: Alicia Wagner Calzada/Newscom; 193: Image Asset Management Ltd./Alamy; 194: Oliver Morris/Getty Images; 206: Pearson Education; 207: Lebrecht Music and Arts Photo Library/Alamy; 215: Library of Congress, Prints & Photographs Division, [LC-USZ62-49035]; 229: Marion Wood Kolisch/Newscom; 235: AP Photo; 246: © Christopher Felver/Corbis; 256: © Sophie Bassouls/Sygma/Corbis; 260: Library of Congress, Prints & Photographs Division, [LC-DIG-cwpbh-01082]; 271: Bettmann/Corbis; 276: Library of Congress, Prints & Photographs Division, [LC-DIG-van-5a52142]; 287: © Marc Brasz/Corbis; 296: Lebrecht Music and Arts Photo Library/Alamy; 301: Mary Evans Picture Library/Alamy; 303: Lebrecht Music and Arts Photo Library/Alamy; 307: Everett Collection Inc/Alamy; 321: Harry Ransom Center; The University of Texas at Austin; 336: Apic/Hulton Archive/Getty Images; 349: AP Photo; 355: © Hulton-Deutsch Collection/Corbis.

Poetry

359: © Christopher Felver/Corbis; 360: Steve Yeater/AP Photo; 417: Oleg Golovnev/Shutterstock; 449: Thomas W. Roster; 516: Erich Lessing/Art Resource, NY; 562: © Christopher Felver/CORBIS; 565: Scala/Art Resource, NY; 566: © Everett Collection; 567: © The British Library/HIP/The Image Works; 568: © Bettmann/Corbis; 571: Album/Newscom; 575: © Christopher Felver/Corbis; 576: The Emily Dickinson Collection, Amherst College Archives & Special Collections; 578: © Bettmann/Corbis; 579: AP Photo; 583: Everett Collection; 588: Archive Pics/Alamy; 592: Popperfoto/Getty Images; 594: MPI/Getty Images; 595: Hulton Archive/Getty Images; 597: GL Archive/Alamy; 600: Copyright Shirley Geok-Lin Lim; 602: Everett Collection Inc/Alamy;

603: © Underwood & Underwood/Corbis; 606: © Bettmann/Corbis; 609: Scott Foresman; 613: Georgios Kollidas/Alamy; 615: © Bettmann/Corbis; 619: Library of Congress, Prints & Photographs Division, [LC-USZ62-89948]; 619: Library of Congress, Prints & Photographs Division, [LC-USZ62-82784]; 620: AKG Images; 625: Lebrecht Music and Arts Photo Library/Alamy.

Drama

627: JM11 WENN Photos/Newscom; 628: Frank Franklin II/AP Photo; 629: Timothy Hiatt/Getty Images; 633: AP Photo; 643: Ellen Locy, Echo Theatre; 657: Utah Shakespeare Festival; 663: The Granger Collection, NYC — All rights reserved; 666: © Geraint Lewis/Alamy; 669: Janette Pellegrini/Getty Images; 673: Mark Garvin; 685: Bettmann/Corbis Images; 688: Bettmann/Corbis Images; 689: Merlyn Severn/Getty Images; 737: Andrea Pistolesi/Getty Images; 738: © Georgios Kollidas/Alamy; 740, 741, 745, 758, 761, 768, 778, 784, 788, 800, 806, 811, 822, 824, 828, 832, 839, 842, 848, 849 photos by Karl Hugh. Copyright Utah Shakespeare Festival 2008; 859: © Hulton-Deutsch Collection/Corbis; 860: TCS Photos 29 (A Doll's House), Harvard Theatre Collection, Houghton Library, Harvard University; 861: Geraint Lewis/Alamy; 918: Library of Congress, Prints & Photographs Division, [LC-USZ62-128957]; 920: © Everett Collection; 921: Everett Collection; 973: Courtesy of Milcha Sanchez-Scott; 975: Mark Garvin; 988: Jay Thompson Archives/Center Theatre Group; 992: Jay Thompson Archives/Center Theatre Group; 996: Jay Thompson Archives/Center Theatre Group; 1001: Adam Rountree/Getty Images; 1002: Suzan Hanson and Herbert Perry in the American Repertory Theater's 2003 world premiere production of the The Sound of a Voice in Cambridge, Massachusetts. Photo by Richard Feldman; 1017: Jeff Wheeler/Newscom; 1026: Cam Sanders; 1029: RICH SUGG/KRT/Newscom; 1032: © 1987 Ron Scherl/StageImage/The Image Works; 1033: JM11 WENN Photos/Newscom.

Writing

1087: The New York Public Library/Art Resource.

INDEX OF AUTHORS
AND TITLES

A number in **bold** refers you to the page on which you will find the author's biography.

INDEX OF
LITERARY TERMS

Page numbers indicate discussion of terms in anthology. A page number in **bold** indicates entry in a **Terms for Review** section. *n* following a page number indicates entry in a note.